CAMPBELL ARMSTRONG

Jig
Mazurka
Mambo

CHANCELLOR
PRESS

Jig first published in Great Britain in 1987 by Hodder and Stoughton Limited

Mazurka first published in Great Britain in 1988 by Hodder and Stoughton Limited

Mambo first published in Great Britain in 1990 by Hodder and Stoughton Limited

This collected edition first published in Great Britain in 1993
by Chancellor Press
an imprint of Reed International Books Limited
Michelin House, 81 Fulham Road, London SW3 6RB
and Auckland, Melbourne, Singapore and Toronto

A CIP catalogue record for this book is available from the British Library

ISBN 1 85152 486 X

Printed and bound in Great Britain by The Bath Press, Avon

Contents

CAMPBELL ARMSTRONG

Jig

Acknowledgements
My gratitude is due to Tom Congdon, whose editorial wizardry approaches that magical condition – alchemy. And to Richard Pine, who encouraged and helped and offered all kinds of wonderful assistance from the start of the Irish dance. And to Arthur Pine, whose staunch, supportive feeling about this novel made a world of difference. I would also like to thank Dave Post of Computer Services, Sedona, Arizona, and Chief Engineer Mike Wilson for their kindness, as well as my English editor, Nick Sayers, for all his help and thoughtful co-operation.

Rebecca Armstrong co-piloted this book
with me. Her splendid insight and her
fine judgement made her, in every sense,
a full partner in this novel.

I am of Ireland
And of the holy land
    Of Ireland.
Good sir, pray I thee,
For of saint charity,
Come and dance with me
    In Ireland.

The Irish Dancer
ANONYMOUS

1 Latitude 40 N, Longitude 60 W

Captain Liam O'Reilly didn't enjoy the crossing whenever the Courier was on board. A funereal man who spoke in monosyllables, the Courier rarely moved from his tiny cabin all the way from the coast of Maine to the disembarkation point in the west of Ireland. He had no fewer than *three* briefcases this trip, each locked and chained to a single bracelet on his wrist. Usually he carried only one, which he clutched throughout the entire voyage. Three briefcases threw the men off balance. When he'd come aboard by launch eleven miles off the coast of Maine, he'd looked very clumsy, his skinny body listing to one side.

Why did he carry three this time? Liam O'Reilly turned the question over in his mind as he stood on the bridge and listened to the rattle of the ship's engines. He wondered how many more Atlantic crossings the two-thousand-ton *Connie O'Mara* was going to see unless she was completely stripped and refurbished. A rotting old tub, she'd begun her career in 1926, hauling various ores round the Cape of Good Hope.

When O'Reilly had won the old biddy in a drunken game of cut-throat poker with some dubious shipbrokers in Panama City in 1963, his first thought was to offer the ship to the Cause. Initially the Cause had been reluctant to accept O'Reilly's generosity because of the costs involved in maintaining the vessel. But a ship was a ship, even if it did look like a great floating turd and leak like a colander. In twenty crossings she had carried automatic weapons, explosives and – when the Courier was on board – considerable sums of operating cash for the Cause. She'd done all this without mishap and O'Reilly was proud of the fact.

He smoked a small black cheroot. A moon appeared briefly, then the night was black again. O'Reilly wondered about going amidships to look in on the Courier, but it was an unwritten rule that the man was to be left alone, except when he needed cups of the weak Darjeeling he habitually drank.

The bloody man! O'Reilly thought. He had a detrimental influence on the small crew of the *Connie*. He carried doom around with him the way some people always have a supply of cigarettes. Or maybe it was just the way the Courier put people in mind of their own mortality. Somehow you just knew that a man who looked exactly like the Courier was the same fellow who'd greasepaint your face when you were dead and comb down your hair before you were suitable for boxed presentation at your wake.

O'Reilly strolled on the deck. The March night was very cold. He sucked icy sea air into his lungs. He looked at the black Atlantic. Friend, enemy. Wife, mistress. Life, death. Its dark, amorphous nature had a symmetry that only a man like Liam O'Reilly could understand. He tossed his dead cheroot overboard. There were footsteps along the deck.

O'Reilly recognised the young seaman Houlihan. This was Houlihan's second crossing on the *Connie*. Liam O'Reilly preferred age and experience, but there were times when you had to make do with what you got.

'The man just asked for some tea,' Houlihan said.

O'Reilly placed the young seaman's accent as that of a Galway man. 'Make it weak. It's the only way he'll have it. The closer it looks like piss, the better he likes it.'

'Aye, Captain.'

Houlihan vanished quietly along the deck. O'Reilly picked flakes of tobacco from his teeth and listened to the steady throb of the engines. He might have been listening to his own heartbeat, so well did he know the noises of his vessel. He walked a few paces, the engines seemed to throb inside his head, and then he understood there was something not quite right, something amiss in the great darkness around him.

The second engineer was a small, sharp-faced man called Waddell. He wore an oil-stained pair of very old coveralls and a woollen hat pulled down over his ears. Although it was hot in the engine room, Waddell didn't feel it. He checked his watch. It was two minutes before nine o'clock, United States Eastern Time.

At nine o'clock exactly, Waddell was going to cut the *Connie's* engines.

He ran one dirty hand across his oily face. He listened to the chug of the engines. He made a pretence of checking various valves and pressure gauges. Brannigan, the chief engineer, was drinking coffee out of a tin mug and flicking through the pages of an old copy of *The Irish Times*. From the pocket of his coveralls Waddell took a large wrench, which he weighed in the palm of one hand.

Brannigan, his back turned to the other man, slurped his coffee and remarked on something he was reading in his newspaper. Waddell wasn't listening to him. He was thinking about piracy, which was a word he didn't much care for. He had spent much of his life in the engine rooms of ships and, like a physician who must kill his own patient, so Waddell disliked the task of shutting down the very system he was paid to keep running. He looked at the back of the chief engineer's head, thinking that he'd always got along well with Brannigan. It was a terrible pity.

Waddell stared at his wrench.

He lowered his head, ducked under an overhanging pipe, and hit Ollie Brannigan once right behind the ear. The chief engineer moaned but didn't go down. Instead, he twisted his face round in shock to look at Waddell.

Waddell grunted and struck Brannigan again, this time hammering the wrench down on the man's nose. Brannigan's face suddenly spurted blood. He dropped his tin mug and the newspaper and went down on his knees, groaning, covering his face with his hands.

Jesus God! Waddell had to hit him a *third* time.

He heard metal crush Brannigan's skull, then the chief engineer was silent, stretched back across the oily floor. Waddell, sweating now, dropped the wrench.

It was one minute past nine o'clock.

To pass time during a crossing, the man known as the Courier often sang quietly to himself. He had a decent baritone voice, though this wasn't a fact known to many people since the Courier maintained a façade of strict anonymity. He came from a long line of men who could carry a decent tune. Hadn't his grandfather, Daniel Riordan, toured the music halls at the turn of the century, thrilling all Ireland with his voice? The Courier, who knew he'd never be in the same class as the Great Riordan, was proud of his voice all the same.

Just as there was a knock on the door of his cabin, the Courier was halfway through one of his personal favourites, *She Moved Through The Fair.*

> 'Then she went her way homeward with one star awake
> 'As the swan in the evening moves over the lake.'

The door opened. 'Your tea, sir,' the young seaman said.

'I don't recall asking for tea,' the Courier answered. He wondered if the young man had heard him singing. The possibility embarrassed him a little. He watched the seaman place a tray on the bunk-side table.

'Captain's orders, sir. Will there be anything else?'

The Courier didn't reply. With a nod of his head he indicated that he wanted to be left alone. He noticed how the seaman – Houlihan, wasn't it? – let his eyes drift across the three briefcases just before he went out of the cabin. The chains tethered to the Courier's wrist jingled as he reached for the tea mug. Those bloody briefcases made him nervous. He was never happier than when he was rid of them. He didn't feel good until Finn took the briefcases from him in Ireland.

The Courier sipped his tea. He thought it was a little strange that O'Reilly had seen fit to send the tea in, because O'Reilly wasn't exactly Captain Congeniality.

It tasted odd. Was there too much sugar in it?

He took a second sip and he felt blood rush to his head and his eyeballs filled with moisture and his heart was squeezed in a painfully tight vice and his balance went all wrong. He felt he was going to explode. He couldn't breathe and there was something hard and very hot rising in his throat. He tried to stand up but his legs were a thousand miles away from him. He slithered from the edge of the bunk to the floor, hearing the teatray clatter past him.

He lay gasping for air, trying to undo the knot of his dark tie even as he realised two things.

One, he was dying.

And two, the ship had become deathly quiet all around him and the sound of the churning engines had stilled.

This same sudden absence of noise chilled Captain O'Reilly. His first response was automatic. The fucking engines had broken down, which he'd been expecting to happen for a long time now. But then he realised something else.

Out there, a hundred yards or so from the *Connie* the ghostly shape of a white yacht had materialised. It showed no lights and O'Reilly had the weird impression there was nobody on board the strange vessel, that it had come up out of the black like some kind of spirit ship bearing the bones of dead sailors. It lay in the darkness in a menacing way, seeming barely to move on the swell. O'Reilly could see no flag, no identifying marks, no name on the bow, no sign of life anywhere. It had appeared out of nowhere, hushed and anonymous. O'Reilly peered into the dark. The vessel looked to him like a sixty-foot diesel yacht, but he couldn't be sure unless the moon broke the cloud cover and gave him enough light so he wouldn't feel like a blind man. There was a knot of tension at the back of his throat.

Be careful, O'Reilly. Be cautious.

He went inside the bridge and opened the gun cabinet, which contained ten pistols and six semi-automatic rifles. He took out one of the semis. He saw the yacht drifting closer, as if whoever manned the damn thing wanted a collision and wouldn't be satisfied with anything else.

He rang the alarm. Within moments he heard the sound of his crewmen scurrying along the deck. Some of them, just wakened from sleep, wore only long thermal underwear. O'Reilly passed out his supply of weapons to the crewmen, urging them to hold their fire unless he gave them a signal. Then he went on watching the movement of the white yacht.

Seventy yards.

Sixty.

The appearance of the yacht might simply be accidental, some hapless nautical tourist veering too close to the *Connie*, a fancy Dan with a white cap and a double-breasted blazer and a fat wife in a bikini, except this wasn't the weather for casual seagoing. You couldn't be certain. O'Reilly had lived a long time with the fear that one of these crossings would end badly, terminated by either British or American authorities or some godless mixture of the two.

It was floating closer.

Fifty yards –

Forty –

O'Reilly narrowed his eyes. Momentarily he thought about the *Mary Celeste*. Maybe this yacht was something like that. An empty vessel. All signs of life inexplicably gone. One of the mysteries of an ocean that already had so many and all of them impenetrable.

Twenty-five yards.

Twenty.

He raised a hand in the air. There was no option now but to open fire. What else could he do, given the importance of the Courier's briefcases and the fear he suddenly felt, which made him so cold to his bones? And what had happened to the bloody engines?

Even before he could lower his hand to order his crew to fire, there was a white blaze of searchlights from the yacht. Blinded, O'Reilly turned his face away from the glare.

As he did so, the gunfire began.

It lit up the Atlantic night with the brilliance of a thousand flares, slicing obscenely through the body of the *Connie*, smashing the glass of the bridge, battering the hull – and it went on and on, an indiscriminate kind of firing that seemed to have no end to it, as if whoever fired the guns did so with utter abandon. O'Reilly lay face down on the floor of the bridge, listening to the air whine above his head. All around him he could hear the moans of those of his crewmen who were still alive. As for the rest, they had been cut down brutally and were in that place where only God or a good undertaker could help them.

O'Reilly, whose only wound was a glass cut in his forehead, lay very still. He was thinking of the Courier now. There was only one reason to attack the *Connie* like this – to steal what the Courier had in his possession. What else was worth taking on this big tub of rust? Madness, bloody madness.

Christ in heaven, how could he help the Courier when he couldn't even help himself? What was he supposed to do? Crawl down from the bridge and smuggle the Courier away in a lifeboat?

The gunfire stopped.

The silence filling the night was deep and complete.

O'Reilly blinked into the harsh white searchlights. He could hardly see the vessel because of the intensity of the lights. But he knew what it was – *a ringer, a viper in swan's feathers, a gunboat disguised as a very expensive pleasure craft*.

He rose to his knees. Here and there, blitzed where they'd come on deck, crewmen lay dead. One or two, wounded beyond medical assistance, crawled like rats across the deck. O'Reilly felt a great sadness for them. He thought about the widows and orphans this fucking yacht had suddenly created, and his sorrow became rage. *The hell with it! The hell with it all!*

He levelled his rifle and was about to spray the white boat with gunfire when he heard a voice from behind and something hard was pushed against the side of his skull.

'I'd be putting the gun away, sir.'

O'Reilly turned, saw the young seaman standing behind him.

'Well, now,' O'Reilly said. The young man's pistol was pressed directly at his head.

The seaman smiled. 'It's all over.'

'Houlihan. You double-crossing bastard.'

Houlihan said nothing.

O'Reilly put his rifle down. 'Do I have time to pray?' His mouth was very dry. Somewhere nearby, one of his crew members screamed out in agony. The awful sound of a man dying. Dear God.

'Of course you do, if you're a praying man,' Houlihan answered, and he shot Liam O'Reilly twice in the skull.

Houlihan stepped inside the Courier's cabin. The dead man lay beside his bunk. His eyes wide open and his mouth contorted in an expression of pain. One hand was at his neck and his face was a bright blood-red. His legs had been drawn into a foetal position and Darjeeling tea stained his white shirt.

Houlihan bent over the body. He examined the briefcases. Each had a combination lock. He fingered the chain that was shackled to the dead man's wrist. Then, from a pouch on his hip, Houlihan drew out a long, serrated knife.

He went to work.

2 London

Frank Pagan stepped out of his 1982 Camaro and surveyed the dark street of terraced houses. Televisions flickered in windows, throwing out pale blue lights. Now and again he could see a shadow pass in front of a curtain. It was a grubby street on the fringes of the Hammersmith district of London, and it reminded Pagan of his origins. He'd been born and raised on a street almost exactly like this one, except that in his memory the house where he'd been brought up didn't seem so small and grim as the houses facing him now. Terraces of narrow dwellings. A triumph of working-class architecture.

He closed the door of the car quietly and walked in the direction of number 43 Eagleton Street. He paused once and stared towards the end of the street, where an unmarked car of Scotland Yard's Special Branch was parked. Ostentatious bugger, Pagan thought. Nothing looks so much like a police car as one trying to appear inconspicuous. It was in the vicinity officially to provide what was called 'back-up', as if its occupants were gunslingers and Pagan an agent of the Wells Fargo Company.

Pagan found 43, a two-storeyed terraced house that had been built in the late 1930s. He walked up the driveway and rapped on the door. There was a shuffling from inside and the door opened about two inches. A red face, which had the raw look of a badly peeled potato, appeared in the space.

Pagan stepped forward, shoving the door back briskly. The potato face scowled.

Pagan wandered inside a small living-room that smelled of damp. A TV was playing. He switched it off at once, and the room was suddenly black.

'Find a light, Charlie,' he said.

Charlie Locklin, in shirtsleeves and grey flannel pants, turned on a lamp. Its base was of yellow ceramic in the form of a mermaid. Pagan sat down, crossing his legs.

Charlie Locklin remained standing. With his TV dead, he looked uncertain about everything, a man who had lost his only map to reality. He shoved his hands inside the pockets of his flannel pants which were held up by a frayed leather belt.

'We need to talk, Charlie,' Pagan said.

'What would I have to say to you?' Charlie Locklin asked in a sullen way. He had a hybrid accent, part Dublin, suffused with some Cockney variations.

'This and that.' Pagan gazed round the room. It was crowded with plastic furniture. 'Class place, Charlie.'

Charlie Locklin appeared wary, as well he might. There were half a dozen hand grenades under the floorboards, and an old Luger, in good working order, concealed beneath some boxes in the attic. Locklin was a stout man with a variety of tattoos on his bare arms. Hearts and flowers and serpents. They had a gangrenous tint, as if they'd been done by a half-blind tattoo artist at some decrepit seaside resort. Pagan had decided long ago that there was something essentially squalid about the Charlie Locklins of this world. They needed squalor to hatch out their violent little schemes the way a fly needs decay for its larvae.

'I don't like you coming here,' Locklin said.

'I don't like *being* here, Charlie.' Pagan rose, went to the window, parted the drapes. The mean little street with its blue windows winked back at him. About four miles away was Her Majesty's Prison at Wormwood Scrubs, a formidable place. 'Blown anything up recently, Charlie? Been playing with any explosives?'

'I don't know what you're talking about, Pagan.'

'Last night somebody blew up a car in Mayfair. Nice car. A Jaguar. Unfortunately, there was a person in it at the time.'

Charlie Locklin looked puzzled. 'I'm not responsible for that.'

There was a silence. Pagan looked at a clock on the mantelpiece. It was of imitation marble, and it had stopped at ten minutes past four. He had the impression that it had ceased working years ago, so that it was always four ten in this miserable little house.

'What I want, Charlie, is a little information. I want to pick your brain. Such as it is.' A microscope might have been useful, Pagan thought.

Charlie Locklin took a cigarette from a battered pack and lit it, letting Pagan's insult float over his head. 'I don't have anything to say to you, Pagan.'

'Not very far from where we sit right now there's a jail called the Scrubs. It isn't pleasant, it isn't nice, it isn't even a *safe* place, especially for somebody with your particular political affiliations. The Scrubs wouldn't be beneficial to your health, Charlie boy.'

'I know all about your Scrubs,' Charlie Locklin said.

'I could throw away the key. Get you off the streets, Charlie. One less arsehole for me to worry about. I'm an inventive kind of man. I could come up with a decent reason. For example, if I was to search your house, Charlie, who knows what I might find? Our judicial system isn't charitable to men like you these days. The British don't think it's sociable for the Irish to be blowing up shops and hotels and planting bombs in cars.'

'I've never blown up anything!'

'Come on, Charlie. What about Torquay?'

'What the fuck! All I had was some gelignite. I never used it. I was holding it for a friend.'

'Charlie, when a known sympathiser of the IRA is found skulking down a basement in

Torquay with nineteen pounds of gelignite on his person, it's a pretty fair deduction that he's not planning some simple weekend gardening. And when you add the fact that our beloved Prime Minister was in Torquay at the same time, well, it doesn't look like you're going in for a little sunbathing, does it?' Pagan took his hands out of his raincoat pockets and looked at them. They were big and blunt, like a couple of hammers. He had inherited his father's hands, a bricklayer's hands.

Charlie Locklin sat down on the arm of a sofa and peered at Frank Pagan through cigarette smoke. 'I was holding the jelly for a friend.'

'Sure you were.'

'I could get a knee job for talking to you,' Locklin said.

'Nobody's going to shoot your knees off, Charlie. We talk. I leave. It's dark outside. Who's going to know I've ever been here?' Pagan found himself wishing that Charlie Locklin *would* get his knees shot off because it would be one less scum to deal with, and that's what Locklin was as far as Pagan was concerned. *Scum.*

Charlie Locklin tossed his cigarette into the fireplace and watched it smoulder. Then he looked at the useless clock on the mantelpiece. Pagan stirred in his seat. Whenever he plunged into the maze of Irish terrorism, he had the sensation of being locked within a labyrinth of mirrors. Images came at you, then receded. Truths were distorted, lies enlarged. And what you were left with at the end was a handful of broken glass, like something out of a child's ruined kaleidoscope.

'Let me throw you a name, Charlie.'

'I'm listening.'

'Jig.' Pagan pronounced the word slowly.

Charlie Locklin smiled. 'If you've come here to talk about Jig, you'd be a damn sight better off talking about the bloody wind. Jig! He's a fucking mystery.'

'I know he's a mystery, Charlie. Point is, what do you know?'

'Nothing. Not a thing.' Locklin laughed, as if the very idea of anyone knowing the *real* identity of Jig was too much of a joke to bear. Jig had all the reality of an Irish mist or one of those mythical figures of Celtic prehistory, like Cuchulain.

Pagan rose. 'Give me a name, Charlie. Tell me the name of somebody who might know something.'

'You're daft, Pagan. You know that? You come in here and you ask daft questions.'

'Who's likely to know, Charlie? *Give me a name.*' Pagan leaned forward, pressing his face close to that of the Irishman. He had a way of making his jaw jut and the small veins in his temples bulge that changed his entire appearance. He could look dangerous and rough-edged, and when he rubbed his big hands together as he was doing now they appeared to Charlie Locklin like two flesh-coloured mallets.

Charlie Locklin stepped away. 'It's a closed shop.'

'A closed shop, Charlie? Are you telling me that the Irish are capable of keeping secrets? You don't expect me to believe that, do you?'

'It's the gospel. I swear it –'

'Don't give me saints and your dead mother. I can't stand all that Irish sentimentality shit. I want Jig. And somebody must know where I can find him. Jesus Christ, he can't operate the way he does without some kind of support system. There's got to be *somebody,* Charlie.' Did Pagan hear a tiny note of despair in his own voice just then? Or was it merely fatigue? He hadn't slept in twenty-four hours.

Charlie Locklin shook his head. 'I'm not your man, Mr. Pagan.'

Mister, Pagan thought. When Charlie Locklin called him Mister, it was almost certain he was being sincere. Pagan shoved his hands back into his pockets. He stared a moment at the mermaid table lamp. It struck him that it would be more plausible to locate a live mermaid in Hammersmith than a mysterious Irish terrorist who was known only as Jig, a shadowy figure forever on the farthest edges of his vision. Pagan sighed.

Last night in Mayfair, Jig had blown up a Jaguar driven by Walter Whiteford, the British ambassador to Ireland. Pagan recalled the debris, the broken glass, the shards of metal that had been scattered halfway down South Audley Street. But mainly it was Whiteford's head he remembered. It had been found lying twenty-five feet from the rest of his torso. How would you describe that look on the decapitated face? Surprise? Astonishment? Maybe it was disappointment for a career that had ended abruptly. Whiteford was going to be the new ambassador to the Republic of Ireland. He hadn't even started the job although he'd given press conferences during which he expressed his desire to see the death penalty brought back for Irish hoodlums who committed acts of terrorism. This had clearly endeared him to Jig. Pagan thought. Foolhardy man with a big mouth. Well, Walter wasn't shooting his mouth off any more.

Pagan moved towards the door. The weariness he felt had a cutting edge to it. He wanted to get out of this dreary little house and into the cold street, where the wind might blow away all the cobwebs in his brain.

Charlie Locklin followed him to the door. 'I swear to God, it's a closed shop,' he said.

'I heard you the first time, Charlie.' Pagan raised one finger in the air, a menacing little gesture. He flicked it beneath Charlie Locklin's nose. 'If I ever find you've been lying to me, I'll have your Irish arse inside the Scrubs in quicker time than it takes you to fart. You understand me, Charlie?'

Locklin moved back from the wagging finger. 'I swear, Mr. Pagan. None of the boys have ever known anything like it. I mean, usually you hear something. Some little thing, at least. But you don't even hear a *whisper* about this Jig. And that's the truth.'

Pagan nodded. He was out in the darkened driveway now.

'Just remember,' he said. 'You hear anything, you call me. If you don't . . .'

He let the threat dangle in the night air. Threats were always more pointed when you didn't spell them out. He walked in the direction of his Camaro. The American car, parked among small British Fords and Minis, looked totally out of place in this narrow street. American cars were one of Pagan's weaknesses. He liked their style, their flash.

He turned back once when he reached the car, seeing the TV already flickering in the window of Charlie Locklin's living room. He had the intense urge to stride back to the house and put his fist through something. The TV, maybe. Or Charlie Locklin's skull.

He opened the door of the car and climbed in behind the wheel. He gunned the Camaro through the streets, aware of the car from Scotland Yard following him at a distance. He reached the M4 motorway and slammed his foot down on the gas pedal, watching the speed rise. When he had the Camaro up to ninety he took a cassette tape from the glove compartment and punched it into the deck. Then he rolled the window down and cold air blasted his face. He was cutting across the lanes, leaving gutless British saloon cars trailing behind him, honking their horns at the madman in the Yankee gas guzzler.

It was the only way to travel. He looked in the rearview mirror. He couldn't see the car from Scotland Yard but he knew it had to be somewhere at his back. The signs that said HEATHROW flashed past in a blur. Office building became streaks of dying light. A hundred. A hundred and five. The Camaro vibrated. The music filled the car at maximum volume.

Come on over, baby, whole lotta shakin' goin' on . . .

They didn't make rock and roll like this any more. Now it was all pretension and posturing boys in make-up. It was a yawn these days.

Pagan beat his hands on the steering-wheel.

> *I said now come on over, baby, we really got*
> *the bull by the horn.*

'I ain't fakin,' Pagan sang at the top of his voice. One hundred and ten. The reality of speed. Everything was focused. Everything was crystal and hard. Speed and loud music and the wind making your face smart. *'There's a whole lotta shakin' goin' on!'*

He saw the flashing lights behind him. He smiled, drove the pedal as far to the floor as it would go, took the Camaro up to one hundred and fifteen, teased the Special Branch car a few miles more. This is it. This is the way to squash old pains. Let the poison drain out of your system at one hundred and twenty miles an hour with the Killer drowning all your thoughts.

He released the pedal. He pulled the car onto the shoulder and waited. The Rover from Scotland Yard drew in behind him. Pagan shut the music off, closed his eyes. The man from Special Branch was called Downey. He wore a soft felt hat, the brim of which he pulled down over his forehead. He had a waxed moustache and his breath smelt of spearmint. He stuck his head in the window of the Camaro and said, 'Frank, for Christ's sake, why do you keep doing this?'

Pagan looked at the policeman, grinned. 'Therapy, my old dear.'

Downey shook his old head. 'You been drinking, Frank?'

Pagan blew into the man's face. 'What do you think?'

'This is the third time in the last ten days,' Downey said. 'One day, you'll kill yourself. Bound to happen. Is that what you want, Frank?'

'Can I count on you, Downey?'

'Count on me for what?'

'To be a pallbearer. To bear my pall. You'd look good in black.'

Downey stepped away from the Camaro. He said. 'Funerals depress me. Yours might be different. Might be uplifting.'

'Wall to wall merriment,' Pagan said. 'Would be quite a ceremony. Everybody from Scotland Yard would turn out and cheer.'

'Right,' Downey said.

Pagan smiled. He slid the Camaro forward a couple of yards, then stuck his head out of the window and looked back at Downey. 'You been eating scrambled eggs, Downey?'

'Scrambled eggs?'

'You got some stuck to your wax there.'

Downey's hand shot to his upper lip. He felt nothing. 'Fuck off, Frank,' he said.

But Pagan was already gone.

Frank Pagan's office overlooked Golden Square on the edge of Soho. It was an impersonal place, filled with chrome and leather furniture. At night – and it was ten o'clock by the time he got there – you could catch a thin glimpse of the lights of Piccadilly, that garish heart of London.

Pagan had visited countless houses similar to Charlie Locklin's during the past twenty-four hours. He had talked with scores of people exactly like Charlie in Irish enclaves throughout London, such as Kilburn and Cricklewood and Chalk Farm, known IRA sympathisers and those with affiliations to that nebulous terrorist network. He'd talked with criminals who'd done time for bombings and other acts of what Pagan considered thuggery. He hadn't turned up anything on Jig. He hadn't expected to. What he'd encountered was a solid wall of silence and ignorance. Everybody had *heard* of Jig, of course, because the bloody man was notorious and his name was in all the tabloids, but nobody *knew* anything about him.

Even those journalists who had written with sneaking respect for Jig's bravado, and who had sometimes seemed even to *glorify* the man in bold headlines, had never been able to uncover anything. It was as if Jig existed in a place far beyond the scope of all their investigative techniques, a place beyond probing, a fact that made him even more of a hero in certain quarters of Fleet Street. His name was mentioned often, in a tone that was almost reverential, in the wine bars and pubs of the newspaper district. Jig had become more than a terrorist. He was a star, the brightest entity in the whole constellation of terrorists. There were even some who thought the assassination of Walter Whiteford – an unpopular man with unpopular right-wing views – a justifiable act on a level with mercy-killing. This prominence Jig enjoyed reflected badly on Pagan's section. That Jig could vanish after his killings without so much as a trace made Pagan feel useless – and yet at the same time all the more determined to catch the man.

Pagan had moments when he wondered if Jig actually existed. Then he'd think it all through again and he'd be struck by the fact that the acts of terrorism perpetrated by Jig were different in sheer quality from random bombings of hotels and busy stores and crowded streets – and he realised there was something about this character Jig he actually *admired*, albeit in the most grudging way. The man *never* did anything that would harm an innocent bystander. The man was *always* careful to select his victim and the proper circumstances, when there was nobody else around to be harmed by an explosive device or a badly aimed shot. It was a kind of tact, Pagan thought, a strange form of charity at the heart of violence.

Pagan peered down towards Piccadilly Circus now. Jig was almost an artist. It was as if he were signing his violent portraits, as if he were saying how unlike the regular IRA rabble he was, underlining a difference between himself and all the rest, those butchers who gave no thought to children and women and anybody else who just happened to get caught accidentally in the crossfire. It was a crude war, but Jig gave it his own civilised flourish.

For a second, Pagan thought about his boyhood, when he'd spent a couple of summers with his grandparents in County Cork. He'd developed a great fondness for the Irish and a sympathy for their plight as inhabitants of one of the most troubled countries in Europe, but he'd never seen a solution to their problems in the violence of the Irish Republican Army. He couldn't even imagine a situation in which the South, free of British sovereignty since 1921, would be reunited with the North. The Irish were a fractured people, polarised by religions, distanced by bigotries, and hammered to the cross of their history, which had given up more martyrs than there were holy saints in Rome.

Pagan moved away from the window. He turned his thoughts again to Jig and the sight of what was left of Walter Whiteford on South Audley Street. When Jig had first entered Pagan's lexicon of terrorism, it had been with the murder in 1982 of Lord Drumcannon, an old judge with a known hatred of the IRA and a propensity to sentence its members to long prison terms. Drumcannon had been shot once through the head by a sniper while walking his beagles on his country estate at Chiddingly in Sussex. The body, surrounded by yapping dogs, had been found by a gamekeeper. There was a solitary bullet hole in the centre of the skull. One shot, which was all Jig ever seemed to need.

The next victim had been George Connaught, Member of Parliament for a district in Northern Ireland. Connaught was a hardline Protestant, the kind who thrived on the conflict between religious parties. he had been gunned down – and this was an example of Jig's talent, his daring, Pagan thought – in broad daylight in Westminster in the spring of 1983. The MP, who revered Queen and Country as if they were twin mistresses he kept in the same apartment, had been walking back to the House of Commons after lunch at his club. One shot had been fired from a passing car, piercing Connaught's heart.

And then Sir Edward Shackleton, chief of the Royal Ulster Constabulary, a man of known paranoia concerning his personal safety, had been blown up in his bed in suburban Belfast one night by means of a high-tech explosive device triggered long distance, a sophisticated piece of equipment which, according to Pagan's analysts, had been manufactured in East Germany.

The list was growing long and it was going to grow longer still.

Frank Pagan shut his eyes. He thought about the phone calls after the killings. The taped voice. The accent seemed almost impossible to place, even though some of the best experts in dialects had analysed it over and over.

This is Jig. I have just killed Walter Whiteford in
the name of freedom for the people of Ireland.
I am not finished yet. I have a long way to go . . .

It was always that simple, always that deadly, the same dry, terrifying delivery. Pagan had listened to the tapes a hundred times. He had listened to the words and the silences between them, the quick intakes of breath, the pauses, as if he might one day be capable of imagining the man's face on the basis of his voice alone. The voice had sometimes even intruded on his dreams, where it echoed and reverberated like the sound of a man whispering in a large empty cathedral.

The door of his office opened and he looked up to see Foxworth there.

Robbie Foxworth – Foxie – was Pagan's assistant, a young man with a scalp of bright red hair, which gave some substance to his nickname. Foxie had been to Eton and Cambridge, and he talked with ball bearings in his mouth. What Pagan didn't know about Foxie was that the young man did a wicked impersonation of him at parties, right down to the South London accent and the way Pagan walked – his back straight and his long legs taking great strides. Foxie called this the Pagan Strut.

'Burning the old midnight oil?' Pagan asked.

Foxie smiled. He had one of those sly little smiles you can never quite recall later with any certainty. He sat down in the chair that faced Pagan. He had been with Pagan's section, which dealt exclusively with terrorism (Irish, or related thereto), for about eighteen months. On paper this section was supposed to work with Scotland Yard's Special Branch, but Pagan had eased his own people out from under the men at the Yard, whom he publicly called 'good civil servants' and privately 'all-round arseholes'.

Consequently, the section operated with considerable freedom, answerable only to the secretary whose office was responsible for Irish affairs. Foxie was related to the secretary in a minor way – a fifteenth cousin three times removed, or something equally farfetched that Pagan had trouble remembering. (The English were obsessed with bloodlines, to a point that lay somewhere off the coast of reason.)

Foxie said, 'I have an item of some interest, Frank.'

Pagan saw a slip of telex paper come across the desk towards him. He picked it up, scanned it, then read it a second time more slowly. He put the telex down and tipped his chair back. 'Well, well,' he said quietly.

Foxie gazed at his superior. There were moments when he thought Frank Pagan represented a triumph of incongruity. Pagan didn't *talk* the way anyone else in the section did because he hadn't been to an expensive public school. Pagan didn't *dress* like his colleagues either. He dispensed with three-piece pinstripe suits in favour of trendy loose-fitting clothes that seemed to have been purchased off the rack in secondhand stores, where they might have been hanging since the middle of the 1950s. Now and then Pagan even wore Hawaiian shirts that lit up a room like a light bulb. An odd bird, Foxie thought, with his tennis shoes and blue jeans and his jazzy American car.

Foxie sat back in his chair. He remembered there had been that awful business about Pagan's wife a few years ago. Foxie had no way of knowing how *that* might have affected his superior, but colleagues who had been with the section since its formation in 1979 whispered that Pagan had gone through a period of heavy drinking, which was understandable in the terrible circumstances.

'Somebody's been very busy,' Pagan said.

'Do you think the Americans were behind it?'

'Does it sound like an American operation to you, Foxie?'

Foxie shrugged. 'Who else could have done it?' He saw Pagan get up and walk to the window. In a certain light Frank Pagan looked younger than thirty-nine. It was only when you get up close you noticed the thin lines around his eyes and mouth. There were glints of grey in his short hair, which he wore brushed back across his head.

'I can't see them doing this kind of barbarism,' Pagan said. 'I can see the Yanks seizing the ship, but I can't see them getting this carried away.'

'They sometimes get a little . . . overzealous,' Foxie said. 'Our cousins *are* fond of a little bloodletting, Frank. They think it's good for the soul.'

Pagan stared at the telex. The *Connie O'Mara* had been found drifting in the North Atlantic by a Norwegian freighter, the *Trondheim*. Thirteen bodies had been discovered on board, eleven of them dead from gunshot wounds, one with a crushed skull, the other killed by means that hadn't yet been established. The *Connie* had been towed to New York City were US Coast Guard officials and cops from the New York City Police Department had examined the carnage before calling in the FBI.

The telex, which was a duplicate, had been sent by the FBI to the Special Branch at Scotland Yard because the vessel was suspected of having had a longtime connection with the IRA. The FBI rather cheerfully considered Irish terrorism strictly a British problem. The *Connie* had been in Pagan's own computerised records for the last year or so and presumably in FBI records for at least that long because computers, which Pagan imbued with a malice of their own, had an uncanny way of tapping into one another's data banks. A lack of manpower for surveillance, and the vastness of the Atlantic Ocean, had contributed to the fact that the *Connie* hadn't been high on Pagan's list of priorities.

'I thought pirates had gone out of fashion,' Pagan said. 'We've got somebody out there doing a Long John Silver routine.'

'If it wasn't us and it wasn't the Americans, Frank, who was it?'

Pagan touched his eyelids with his fingertips. The violent fate of one small boat, which might or might not have been ferrying arms to Ireland, didn't excite him. What he kept coming back to was the idea of catching Jig, and he couldn't see any kind of connection between the *Connie O'Mara* and the elusive killer. At some other time, maybe, the piracy might have intrigued him more than it did, but not now. Besides, whoever had hijacked the *Connie* had done Pagan's section a favour. It was one less problem, in the whole morass of Irish affairs, to worry about. He was under pressure from the press, the secretary, and the public to put Jig out of business. So what did one small ship matter when you were working like hell to keep from buckling beneath the weight of clamorous demands?

He tossed the telex down. 'Let Special Branch worry about it, Foxie. Let them have this one. The commissioner used to be in the navy. He'd relish a mystery with a nautical flavour.'

Foxie looked a little disappointed. He had expected a more enthusiastic reaction to the telex. He picked the piece of paper from Pagan's desk and said, 'I adore that gruesome touch at the end, don't you?'

'Appeals to your darker side, does it, Foxie?'

'It does,' Foxie said, grinning. 'I mean, what's the point in hacking off a fellow's hand?'

Pagan was quiet for a moment. He was thinking of going home. He was thinking of sleep. The empty apartment. The hollows of his life.

'Presumably because something was attached to his wrist,' Pagan answered, pressing a hand to his mouth to cover a yawn.

English-Welsh Border

On the rare occasions when he drank, the man known as Jig preferred Jameson's Irish Whiskey. In the empty buffet car of the train that carried him from London to Holyhead in Wales – where he would take the ferry across the Irish Sea to Dublin – he sipped the whiskey slowly, occasionally swirling it around on the surface of his tongue. He looked the length of the car, conscious of his solitude.

He set his glass down on the table and the liquid shivered to the rhythms of the locomotive. He stared from the window at the darkness of the English countryside. The platforms of small stations whisked past as the train hammered through the night. Some of them, he noticed, were no longer in operation. They'd been closed down and boarded up, economy measures taken by an English government that nevertheless always seemed to have the means of funding a standing army in Northern Ireland.

He shut his eyes. He realised he wanted a cigarette, but he'd given up smoking several weeks ago although the desire was always there. It was a matter of will to deny yourself. And he had become accustomed to a life of such denials, a life lived in doorways and the dank rooms of cheap hotels, a life of watching and waiting, surrounded by shadows. It was an existence lived at one remove from yourself, as though you were nothing more than a transient in your own body.

He looked from the window again. He wouldn't sleep until he was safely back in Dublin, even though he understood he wasn't ever safe anywhere these days. From his canvas bag he took out a copy of *The Daily Express* and saw the headline:

JIG'S DANCE OF DEATH

He turned to the inside pages. There was a shrill editorial about the inadequacy of British security forces. The writer posed the question: *Are we utterly incapable of catching this monster? Are we always to be victims of vicious Irish terrorism?*

A monster, Jig thought. He never thought of himself as either monster or terrorist. These were threadbare labels applied by the enemy, terms intended to elicit revulsion and horror from the British public and to obscure the real issue which, in Jig's mind at least, was that of a people fighting for the right of national unity, without British intervention.

There was a terse comment from an official called Frank Pagan, who was apparently in charge of the office conducting the investigation into the murder of Walter Whiteford. It said: *Every possible line of inquiry is being pursued*. Nothing else.

Jig tossed the paper aside. Every possible line of inquiry, he thought. It was the standard comment of any bewildered official. What did it actually mean? He wondered about this Pagan a moment. He imagined a tight-lipped humourless man, a sombre bureaucrat who wore dark suits and overcoats. A man of plodding technique. Maybe he wasn't that way at all. Maybe he had moments of inspiration, little hunches he played now and again. It was interesting to know your adversary's name. It was like being one small point ahead in the game.

He tossed the newspaper aside and rose from his seat, stepping out into the corridor of the car. Through open windows a cold night wind rushed against him and he shivered, drawing the collar on his unremarkable grey coat up against his face. He thought of Finn sitting inside the house in Dun Laoghaire, and he had a mental image of the gaunt old man smiling as he read about the death of Ambassador Whiteford in *The Irish Times*. Finn never showed any excitement when a mission was successfully accomplished. *You're a professional, boy,* he'd once said. *And professionals don't expect praise for success. Only criticism for failure.* Finn had other ways, quiet ways, of expressing his pleasure. A quick soldierly hug, a couple of glasses of the wretched peppermint schnapps he seemed to adore – often to his detriment – and a bright youthful light in his blue eyes which belied his age and the exhausting years he'd given to a struggle that at times seemed endless.

Jig removed a thin thread from the lapel of his coat and let it drift out of the window into the darkness. Then he turned to look along the corridor, past the doorways of compartments lit by thin yellow-bright light bulbs. Three policemen, two in uniform and one dressed in a bulky gaberdine raincoat, appeared at the end of the corridor. Jig watched them peer inside empty compartments as they approached him. The plainclothes man was enormous, his head almost reaching the ceiling. He had the smallest mouth Jig had ever seen on another human being. The two uniformed cops were ridiculously young, their bland faces covered with adolescent fuzz. Jig looked out through the open window just as the train plunged into a tunnel and the wheels roared in a deafening way and the carriages clacked and echoed. He had known that sooner or later cops would board the train, just as they would be swarming airports and seaports in the wake of Walter Whiteford's death.

The plainclothes policeman was clumsily polite and spoke with a Welsh accent, a kind of dull singsong. 'Do you have any papers, sir?' he asked.

'Papers?' Jig asked.

'Passport. Identification. Anything like that.'

The train came out of the tunnel and there was a slender crescent of moon in the black sky. 'Are you looking for somebody in particular?' Jig asked. He opened his canvas bag and rummaged around inside. He felt no tension, no sense of danger. Whatever anxiety he might have experienced at the fear of discovery he kept under control. Any such feeling would have been irrational. The cops didn't know what he looked like, they had no description of him. They were operating in total darkness.

The plainclothesman looked into Jig's face. 'You read the newspapers, sir?'

'Now and again.'

'Then you'll have read about Whiteford, I expect.'

Jig, who enjoyed this part of the game, who liked the sport of coming close to his pursuers, feigned a look of surprise. 'You're looking for Jig?' he asked.

The cop nodded. He uttered a weary sigh. The two uniformed officers, who might have been hatched out of the same pod, were staring at Jig's bag as if they expected it to contain bombs or grenades. Young and nervous and raw.

'I hope you find him,' Jig said, removing a passport from his bag and handing it to the plainclothes cop.

The cop took the passport, which had been issued by the Republic of Ireland, and leafed through it. He glanced at the photograph, then at Jig's face before handing the document back. 'You live in Dublin?'

Jig nodded.

'What kind of work do you do, Mr Doyle?' he asked.

Jig took a small wooden toy out of his bag. It was a miniature rocking horse, immaculately carved, finely detailed. He watched the policeman take it and examine it.

'I sell toys,' Jig said.

'Very pretty,' the cop said.

'Danish. Sturdy. Won't break easily.'

The policeman returned the miniature to Jig, who placed it back inside the bag.

'Thanks for your time,' the policeman said.

'No problem, Officer.'

Jig watched the three cops continue along the corridor. He wanted to call out to them. He wanted to tell them that he wished them luck in their hunt and that Jig was the kind of bastard who gave decent Irishmen a bad name and deserved the hangman's rope, but he restrained himself. Playing the game with them was one thing, but drawing attention to yourself was another. If they remembered anything about him later they'd mainly remember the small wooden horse, not his face nor how he was dressed nor the way he spoke. He saw them disappear through the door at the end of the corridor, and then he was alone again.

He caught a faint reflection of himself in glass and he had the thought that if he were to die now of some sudden ailment the only identification in his possession would be that of a certain John Doyle, commercial traveller in wooden toys imported from Scandinavia. His bag would yield up nothing more sinister than samples of his line – a small toy drummer, the miniature horse, a puppet tangled up in its own strings.

Of anyone called Jig, there would be absolutely no trace at all.

3 Roscommon, New York

Former United States Senator Harry Cairney stood at the window of his second-floor library, a room lined with books and filled with dark antique furniture that reflected everything with the accuracy of mirrors. He watched the helicopter come in view over the slate-coloured waters of Roscommon Lake. There were four men in the chopper, three who had come to Roscommon to meet with Cairney, and a pilot who would unload his human cargo and fly promptly away, counting his improbably high fee and forgetting anything he ever knew about his passengers and their destination. Amnesia, Cairney thought, did not come cheaply.

The senator stared past the chopper now, out beyond the far shores of the lake where the trees were deep and secretive in the snow. When he had purchased this estate in 1958, it had been nine hundred acres of jungle and a rundown Victorian mansion owned by a senile German brewer who, in his madness, travelled the world collecting broken nude statues, most of them missing limbs and noses and, in extreme cases, their entire heads. The old German had been proud of his huge collection. *They remind me, Senator Cairney,* the brewer had said at the time of escrow, *of human infirmity.*

Cairney, forty-eight at the time, lacked any desire to be reminded of anything so undignified as human infirmity. He had removed the statues, renovated the big house, redesigned the gardens, and stocked the lake – known then as Lake Arthur – with rainbow trout and bass. Then he had renamed the property Roscommon, after the castle built in 1280 in Ireland by Robert de Ufford, although there were still old-timers in the nearby town of Rhinebeck who referred to the estate as Old Franz's place, Brewmeister Palace. Nine hundred acres of prime Dutchess County real estate – a mere ninety minutes up the leafy Taconic Parkway from Manhattan – surrounded by dense trees and rectangles of meadowland. A safe retreat from the problems of the world, except that the world had a tiresome tendency to intrude on the senator's sense of security.

He watched the chopper land slowly on the vast front lawn. Bare rosebushes shook from the power of the big whirring blades. Clouds, weighted with more snow, floated away over the lake. The senator watched three men get out of the chopper and saw them scurry beneath the beating blades in the direction of the house. He thought for a second of the telephone call he had received only some eight hours before from Ireland. He was going to have to convey the message to his visitors, an unpleasant prospect. But the whole thing was unpleasant, a calamity of enormous proportions. He caught his breath and heard a wheezing sound in the depths of his chest. Lately, he'd begun to experience human frailty for himself – waking in the night, struggling for oxygen, feeling himself skirt the edges of a panic, like a man who looks down from a great height to see below him the abyss of death.

He was reluctant to move from the window. The stereo, which he had built into the study walls, was playing one of his favourite records, John McCormack singing *The Rose of Tralee*. He never tired of listening to it because it reminded him of his first wife, Kathleen, who had died some seventeen years before.

She was lovely and fair as the rose of the summer.
Yet 'twas not her beauty alone that won me . . .

Harry Cairney closed his eyes a moment. It seemed to him that McCormack's voice on this old recording came from a place beyond the grave. He sighed, turning from the window, crossing the floor to the landing. Voices drifted up from below. He could hear Mulhaney over everyone else, because that was the big man's style, loud and blustery and forever dying to be heard. A little dizzy, Cairney looked down the long staircase. He was filled with dread. The meeting was necessary: no, more than that – it was urgent. But he didn't have the heart for it anymore. It was odd how age sucked the guts out of you, strange the way it eroded your fighting spirit. Age took away and, like some terrible miser, seemed to give nothing back. Not even wisdom. Not even that small consolation. Membership in the Fund-raisers, he reflected, was definitely a young man's game.

He moved to the stairs.

'Darling?'

Celestine stood in the door of the bedroom. Her beauty affected him as it always did. It made his heart roar inside his chest and chased his blood pressure up a ladder, and he wasn't old Harry Cairney any more, he wasn't the retired senator from New York, he was a giddy young man enchanted by love, blinded by his own desires. *Celestine, his wife*. She had her yellow hair pulled back tight the way she sometimes wore it and it gave her beauty a rather gaunt quality, almost stark, as if her soul were laid bare. Her blue eyes were filled with all the electricity that might ever have been issued by lightening and trapped in conductors. Harry Cairney thanked the God in whom he'd lately come to believe for sending Celestine to him at this stage of his life.

And – wonder of wonders! – it was no classic case of a young woman marrying an old man for his money and esteem, no thirty-five-year-old fortune hunter, a power groupie, marrying a former United States senator for whatever cachet this might bestow upon her. She had married Harry Cairney the *man*, not the politician who had been part of the Kennedy inner circle and who'd known every major figure that had moved across the stage of the times and who'd had his picture taken with Jack and Lyndon and de Gaulle and Willy Brandt and Harold Macmillan and Eamon de Valera. It was, Harry Cairney thought, a miracle in a time when miracles were rare as unicorns. And this miracle was that Celestine, who might have been nothing more than a paid companion in the winter of his life, a mercenary, actually loved him. She *loved* him even in his age and frailty, and she drove him to moments of desire that would have been indecent in a much younger man.

'Do you have to meet these people?' she asked, and there was concern in the blue eyes that subtly altered their colour, darkening the shade of cobalt to something no rainbow could ever register.

'Yes,' the senator said. 'I have to.'

'Who are they anyhow?'

'Business associates.' He smiled at his wife.

Celestine wore nothing more fancy than blue jeans and a plaid shirt, but she would have looked astonishingly lovely in an A & P grocery bag. She came across the hallway and laid her hand on his arm. 'I don't want you to overdo it,' she said. She pressed her mouth against the side of his face. Harry Cairney, who came alive whenever his wife touched him, patted her carefully on the cheek.

'I won't overdo anything, I promise,' he said.

'Be sure,' she said. 'I love you.'

Cairney moved away from his young wife reluctantly and began to go down the stairs where, around the long oval table in the dining-room, the three men who had come to Roscommon by helicopter were already drinking shots of brandy poured from a crystal decanter.

Mulhaney, his face the colour of a radish, was already on his second brandy when Harry Cairney stepped into the dining-room. Mulhaney, who was a big man with enormous hands, crowded a room somehow, filling more space and sucking in more air than an individual had a right to. Harry Cairney moved to his place at the end of the oval table and sat down, smiling briefly at Mulhaney and then looking at the faces of the other men. Only young Kevin Dawson stood up at Cairney's entrance as a gesture of respect. God bless you, Kevin, the senator thought.

At the age of thirty-seven, Kevin Dawson had a sense of what Cairney considered decency. He was a conciliatory person, someone who seemed forever anxious not to give offence. *Nice* was a word that came to Cairney's mind. Kevin's brother Thomas, known to his political enemies as Grinning Tommy, was the President of the United States. Cairney often wondered if Kevin Dawson's membership in the Fund-raisers was the young man's way of compensating for the fact that his brother occupied the White House, as if Kevin were carving out his own special territory where his imposing brother couldn't and wouldn't go.

The other man in the room, Nicholas Linney, barely glanced at Cairney as he sat down. Linney was a man of the New Age, happy with spreadsheets and computerised data and satisfied, in a way that was almost sexual, with vast networks of interconnected intelligence. Linney's face had a peculiar hue, something like the colour of an unroasted coffee bean. Maybe, the senator reflected, it came from staring at small green letters on screens all day long. But there was a sense of controlled violence about Linney, hidden pressures. Harry Cairney always had the feeling that Linney would gladly have blown up his computers and torched his spreadsheets for a chance to go out into the direct line of battle. He could imagine Nick Linney skulking the alleys of Belfast with a rifle stuck underneath his overcoat and hatred for British soldiers in his heart. He was, in fact, a gun freak, and it was rumoured that he took himself off to isolated beaches with his firearms and shot round after round into watermelons or pumpkins or any kind of fruit or vegetable that suggested, however remotely, a human skull.

'Gentlemen,' Cairney said when he was seated. There was a breathless quality to his voice, the result of the simple act of coming down a flight of stairs. He felt as if his lungs were dried out and useless, withered inside his chest like two prunes.

The three men watched him now, each seemingly wary of what he might have to say. He clasped his hands on the table. 'Big Jock' Mulhaney, as the press always called the man who led and allegedly mismanaged a branch of the most powerful trade union in the United States, puffed his lips out like a bloated goldfish and remarked, 'Let's get down to it, Senator. Let's get down to the brass tacks. Let's just cut the fucking gentlemen shit.'

The former senator winced. Mulhaney had been born with a talent for gracelessness, the way some people are cursed with muscular dystrophy.

Harry Cairney looked down at the polished surface of the table. He was aware of the sound of his young wife moving in the room immediately above.

'We've been ripped off,' Mulhaney said. 'Why don't we boil it down to that?' We've been shafted.'

'As you say,' Harry Cairney agreed. 'We've been shafted.'

'So the only question is who the fuck did it,' Mulhaney said.

There was a quietness in the room now, as if all sound had seeped out from a crack in the wall. Harry Cairney recognised what lay under the silence – there was mistrust, a sense of treachery, a certain lopsided tension that went back and forth between the four men in the room. This animus was sharp and cutting and fearful. The Fund-raisers had been contaminated. The suspicion in the room was as tangible as the presence of an uninvited guest.

Linney opened a folder and said, 'The total loss is ten point two million dollars in used currency and negotiable bonds.'

'I don't think figures are in dispute,' Cairney said, and his voice was feeble.

'Damned right they're not in dispute,' Mulhaney said. For a second he grinned his most charming grin, the one he always used when he walked in the vanguard of the St Patrick's Day Parade on Fifth Avenue, his green sash across his big broad chest and his lips faintly green from the dye neighbourhood bars introduced into their beers. 'What we've got to consider here, friends, is a matter of betrayal.'

Harry Cairney rubbed his eyes. 'You don't imagine that somebody in this room is responsible for the piracy?' This idea shook him, but it was a reality he knew he had to face even if the notion of a traitor in the ranks was a blasphemy. But if it hadn't been one of the Fund-raisers, then who the hell *had* taken the money? His eyes moved from one man to the next around the table, but what could he possibly tell from their faces? Mulhaney's accusative look, Dawson's tentative expression, Nick Linney's tightly drawn lips – appearances could hide almost anything.

Mulhaney ran a fingertip round the rim of his brandy glass. 'There are four of us in this goddam room, and each one of us knew the destination of the ship as well as the route and the cargo she carried.' The big man paused. 'The conclusion's goddam obvious.'

'We can't assume that one of us is responsible,' Kevin Dawson said in his high-pitched voice. It was a voice that would keep Dawson out of public politics because it didn't fill a room and it couldn't be used to project anything solemn. Whenever he grew excited, he could sound like a man on helium gas. 'I don't see any justification for that.'

'Don't you now?' Mulhaney, who had always disliked anything to do with the Dawsons and resented what he thought of as Kevin Dawson's privileged world – old Connecticut money, the fucking landed gentry with all its feudal powers, big brother in the White House – was adopting one of his characteristic attitudes, a certain snide belligerence. 'Do you have a better suggestion, Dawson?'

Kevin Dawson answered in a patient way. 'I don't see any merit in leaping to conclusions, Jock. That's all.'

'Conclusions,' Mulhaney snorted. He had a habit of forcing words out through his nasal passages. 'You're a fence-sitter, Dawson. You're never happy unless you're politely perched on some fucking fence.'

Dawson tilted his chair back, said nothing.

Again silence, Cairney stared through the window at the waters of Roscommon Lake. He thought of a small dark ship gunned on the high seas. Blood on the waters. For too many years now, back as far as the old days at the Clan-na-Gael in Philadelphia and the Irish Republican Brotherhood, back as far as the times when the Cause had been glad to receive a few Thompson submachine-guns and several thousand cartridges in the 1930s from their American sympathisers, he'd been promoting the Cause and raising funds secretively and nothing was more demanding, more exhausting, than secrecy, a darkly brooding mistress. Even Celestine, and Kathleen before her, had no idea about Cairney's activities.

He had first come to this country as a bright young man of eighteen in the spring of 1928 from Dublin, yet he'd never really left his homeland entirely, nor had he ever forgotten the Troubles that divided and ruptured his country. He might talk with an American accent and have served as a public figure during several administrations in Washington, but his heart was still through and through Irish. Now, as he looked at the faces of the men in the room and imagined the small dark ship machine-gunned, he realised that all he truly wanted was peace and privacy and a chance to spend his last years uninterrupted by the demands of the Cause. He wanted to spend this precious time with Celestine and nobody else. If the Fund-raisers were to continue, they would have to go on without him. But this wasn't the time to announce his retirement.

'Can the money be replaced?' he asked. He was trying to steer the meeting into less troubled areas. A little diplomatic sleight of hand, which he knew would be futile.

'Not through my sources,' Linney said. 'They're not going to be happy to invest again in the present circumstances. Besides, they're tightening the purse-strings these days.'

Cairney knew that the millions of dollars that flowed through Linney's hands came mainly from Arab countries, especially from Libya, whose leadership was keen to promote revolution wherever it might be found. Linney also had access to funds from the Soviet bloc, from dour men who perceived the creation of a kind of Cuba off the coast of Great Britain, a socialist thorn in the pale white English thigh.

'And *my* people have given too much already,' Mulhaney said. 'Hell, you all know that. I can't go back and dip into the funds. It's not like the old days when a union boss could treat union funds like his own private bank. I've got lawyers and shit-headed accountants to explain things to. I can't even get twenty bucks out of petty cash without signing in triplicate. As it stands, the membership of my union wouldn't be completely happy to know where their contributions go. Except the fellows from the old country.' Mulhaney drew on a cigar and looked bleakly convincing.

Cairney stared across the table at young Kevin Dawson.

Dawson shook his head. 'I don't think I would have very much luck either. The families are all tired of giving. And they're all getting weary of the bloodshed. It gets more difficult all the time.'

Cairney stood up and walked to the window. The families Dawson had referred to were mainly New English Irish – third or fourth or even fifth generation – great clans of wealthy American-Irish who were happy to contribute money so long as they weren't involved by name. Most of them had returned once in their lifetimes to the old country to look at ancient parish records in obscure villages and come home clutching Irish lace or Waterford glass or Donegal tweed. And for most of them one sentimental journey to the motherland, the mythical Erin, was enough to last forever.

Cairney turned away from the window now. He was aware of the intricate complexities of financing the IRA, the networks that were made, the delicate interconnections of disparate elements, the secret cells and the chains invisibly linked. He was aware of how frail, how tenuous, everything was, and he knew that the lost money could not be replaced for many months, perhaps even years.

He moved slowly back to the table. He sat down. He poured himself one small shot of brandy. One beneficial little snifter he held in a hand noticeably shaking. The currents in this room upset him. Was there anything more destructive than unfocused paranoia?

'Let's get back to the biggie,' Mulhaney said. 'Let's get back to the missing money. Let's imagine that somebody in this room, somebody with total knowledge of the *Connie* and her cargo, decided to line his own pockets. Let's play with that notion.'

Nicholas Linney looked up from an open folder that lay in front of him. 'Which one of us do you have in mind, Jock?'

Mulhaney looked mysterious. 'I have my own ideas,' he said quietly.

'You want to share them with us?' Linney asked. An aggressive vein appeared in his forehead, a mauve cord. 'You want to let us know the name of the person you suspect? Is it me? Do you think I had something to do with it? Say what you're thinking. Don't keep us in the fucking dark, Jock.'

Harry Cairney cleared his throat and said, 'It doesn't have to be one of us, Jock. The British could have seized the *Connie*.'

'Which poses another question, Senator,' Mulhaney replied. 'If the British took the money, how the hell did they *know* what was aboard the *Connie*? Unless somebody in this goddam room told them. It keeps coming back to the same fucking thing. Somebody in this room.' And Mulhaney turned his face slowly, gazing at each man in turn, as if he were privy to information he wasn't about to share with anyone else.

Kevin Dawson said, 'The ship might have been taken by agents of our own federal government.'

'And they'd slaughter the crew, would they?' Mulhaney made a scornful little noise. He didn't believe the feds capable of such carnage. He had a curiously naive faith, common among self-made men, in the inherent fairness of law-and-order agencies.

'All I'm saying,' Kevin Dawson answered, 'is that the British aren't the only candidates. And it doesn't follow that somebody in this room betrayed us. We might have been under surveillance for a long time. The British, the feds – they have their own sources of intelligence. They wouldn't necessarily need the help of anybody here.'

Harry Cairney held up one hand. 'I really don't think it much matters who took the money, gentlemen. I really don't think that's the issue here.'

'Of course it fucking matters,' Mulhaney said.

Cairney shook his head. Mulhaney could be very tiresome. Cairney said nothing for a moment. He raised his finger to his dry lips and glanced around the faces in the room. They were all watching him and he felt exposed beneath their eyes.

'The point is, Ireland believes that *we're* responsible for the loss,' he said, pronouncing his words very slowly. 'Our Irish connection believes – rightly or wrongly – that one of us, perhaps even more than one, was behind the piracy.'

Harry Cairney heard the sound of Celestine playing her piano overhead. It was very soft, distant, oddly moving. She was playing something baroque and intricate and it suggested tranquillity.

'And I have the very strong impression,' he added, pausing, raising his eyes to the ceiling, 'that they will send somebody to find the missing money because they're not going to sit back and shrug their shoulders over the loss. It's not their style.'

'Did they say they were sending somebody?' Mulhaney wanted to know.

'I was led to believe so,' Cairney answered, remembering the angry Irish over the transatlantic phone connection that had said *We need that bloody money and we need it badly. And I have just the person to get it.* It had been an unpleasant conversation, one in which Cairney had been obliged to listen to a tirade that was no more palatable for being uttered in a lilting, musical accent.

Mulhaney asked, 'And how is this *somebody* supposed to get the money back, for Christ's sake? If one of us in this room took the goddam stuff, how would this *somebody* even know where to *find* any one of us? How would he even know where to start looking?'

Cairney felt a little flutter in an eyelid, as if a moth had landed there. The sound of Celestine's piano had stopped. 'I have no idea, Jock.'

'Ireland doesn't even know our names. Our identities. So what do they think they'll accomplish by sending some asshole over here? What's he going to do? Huh? We've always operated in secrecy, Harry. Is this messenger boy going to unmask us?'

'I can't answer your questions, Jock. I don't have the answers. But my best guess is that they're not going to send any messenger boy. They'll send a man who knows his business. And whoever he is, he's going to be goddam determined to find out what happened to the entire operating budget of the Irish Republican Army for one whole year.

Nicholas Linney closed his buff-coloured folder. He blinked his narrow eyes. 'Let me get this straight. Are we meant to understand that this guy represents a *threat* to our personal safety? Is he going to come here armed?'

There was an unmistakable relish in Linney's voice. He sounded like a man who had been confined too long to the drudgery of paperwork and whose blood quickened at the possibility of physical menace. For a moment Cairney wondered if Linney had played a role in the murderous hijacking, but he dismissed the speculation as fruitless. Linney, Mulhaney, Dawson – any one of this trio might have had his own reasons for arranging the piracy. Cairney, who disliked the track of his own suspicions, pushed the thought out of his mind.

He said, 'I can only assume this man would carry a weapon, Nick. But if you have nothing to hide, you have nothing to worry about.'

Linney smiled. It was a humourless little movement of his mouth. 'Believe me, Senator, I'm not remotely worried. I can take care of myself.'

'I'm sure you can,' Cairney said. 'What really concerns me is the fact that we can't predict how this person will behave. We don't know how he operates, if he's rational, if he's given to violence. We're in the dark as much as he is. And since that's the case, it would be wise for each of us to take whatever precautions we think necessary. At least until the situation is resolved.'

Kevin Dawson smiled uncertainly. 'You don't really imagine we're in danger, do you?'

Cairney shrugged. 'I don't know. Ireland sends a man who doesn't know our names, doesn't know if one of us is responsible for this terrible situation, a man whose only mission is the recovery of the money by whatever means. Put yourself in his shoes. How would you act if you had been entrusted with a task like this one? How would you behave?'

Cairney listened to the silence that followed his questions. He thought now of the faceless figure who would come from Ireland. He imagined somebody stalking the Fund-raisers, a shadowy man driven by his sense of justice, of setting right a terrible wrong. He tried to envisage such a man, and even as he did so he experienced an unsettling chill. People who betrayed the Cause always paid an awful price because it was the one crime that was neither forgiven nor forgotten – and if somebody in this room *had* played a part in the seizure of the *Connie's* cargo, then Cairney could almost feel sorry for the culprit. Almost.

As he turned away from the window and the cold sight of the frozen trees around the lake, he wondered how this Irishman was going to proceed with his efforts. What if he did find out the identities of the Fund-raisers? What then? Was he going to come and knock on the front door and ask polite questions? Cairney severly doubted that approach. The Irishman would have other ways, quite possibly unpleasant ones, of getting the truth. Cairney shivered slightly. He was too old to face the prospect of physical threats, even violence. But he understood one thing – that whoever came from Ireland was sure to be a man who was determined to get results, no matter what lengths he might have to go to achieve them.

'The whole thing's academic anyway,' Mulhaney said, blowing smoke rings. 'The guy has absolutely no way of finding us.'

'I wish I could be as certain as you, Jock,' Cairney said unhappily, staring down into the polished wood surface of the oval table where the reflected faces of the Fund-raisers, like men drowning in clear water, looked back at him.

4 Dublin

The girl told Patrick Cairney he had the eyes of a devil, which he found amusing. She was called Rhiannon Canavan and she was a tall red-haired girl with wide hips and small sculpted breasts, and she lay in Cairney's bed in his tiny flat near the Fitzgibbon Street Garda Station, which was close to the main road between Swords and Dublin and not the quietest place in which to live. Cairney stretched out alongside her, feeling himself slip into that dreamy place at the end of intense lovemaking. He placed the flat of his hand against her belly, and she purred as a cat might, rolling her long body towards him and circling his legs with her own.

'The eyes of a devil,' she said again, and she bit Cairney lightly on the side of his neck.

'And you're a vampire,' he answered.

'A hussy is what I am. Or it's what you've made me anyhow. For the love of God, what am I doing here? Did you put something in my drink, Patrick Cairney?'

'I didn't think you noticed.'

'I remember seeing this funny little envelope in your hand.'

'Himalayan Fucking Powder,' he said. 'Ancient Tibetan secret recipe. Guaranteed.'

'You say wicked things.' She sat upright, straddling him. Her breasts swung lightly in the half light of the room. In the distance, the sound of a police car could be heard whining in the night.

'I don't think I'd personally like to live with the police on my doorstep,' she said.

'Why? What have you got to hide?'

'Obviously nothing,' and she arched her back, tilting her face away from him. She was, so she had told him in the pub, a nurse in the Richmond Hospital, and he wasn't to think that just because nurses had poor reputations she was going to hop into the sack with him straight off the bloody bat, even if he did have the eyes of the devil and his charming American manners into the bargain.

'Nurse Canavan,' he said in a fraudulent Irish accent. 'I am having this Jaysus of a pain between my legs. Can you do anything about it, out of daycent Christian kindness?'

'I think I have the prescription for you,' and she swung her body around, lowering her face to his groin and taking him softly into her mouth. And then she moved away from him, rolling on her back, and he entered her even as he continued to hear the sirens of police cars outside in the night. There were depths here, Cairney thought, and he was afraid of them. In the half light of the room Rhiannon Canavan had her eyes closed and her mouth open, and she was holding on to Cairney as if he were a carnival ride that scared her. Spent, Cairney fell away from her, but she still held onto him.

'Are all Americans that loud?' she asked.

'I'm an average screamer,' he told her.

Nurse Canavan reached for a cigarette and lit it, and her face was briefly illuminated by the flare of her Bic. She had a wonderfully straight Irish jaw, a fine generous mouth, and high cheekbones which gave her face a certain delicate strength.

'So tell me,' she said. 'You're at Trinity, did you say?'

'Trinity,' Cairney answered.

'And you're one of them wealthy Americans that comes over here to study at Daddy's expense, is that it?'

Cairney shook his head 'Daddy's money can't buy happiness. Besides, he doesn't support me. I have a small income from teaching undergraduate classes at Trinity. He's never really approved of my studies. He doesn't see the point to them.'

'I must say he has a case, Patrick Cairney. It seems to me a young man like yourself shouldn't be poking around so much in the past.'

'And where should I be poking?'

'You know something? You're disgusting.' She laughed again. She had one of those rich sincere laughs that change the temperature of rooms, like fine resonant music.

'Seriously now,' she said. 'Is archaeology a field for a young man?'

'We study the past to understand the future,' Cairney intoned solemnly.

'You,' and she nudged him with an elbow. 'Are you never serious?'

'I have my moments.'

Rhiannon crushed out her cigarette and lay back. 'Does it really matter how much a loaf of bread cost in ancient Egypt?'

'I like to think it helps us understand inflation.'

Cairney peered at the cinder of light that lay against the window, thrown on the glass by a faraway streetlamp. He felt both comfortable and secure with this lovely girl at his side. She offset something of the lonely edge he frequently experienced – a stranger in a strange country. And yet it wasn't alien at all because there was a sense in which he'd been familiar with it all his life, courtesy of his father, who had instilled in him the wonders of Irish culture and history. Harry Cairney, who for most of the year had been an absentee father in Washington, returned each summer to Roscommon to indoctrinate his son in the melancholic songs and stories that were part of the Irish tradition, tales of defeats and victories, old loves, poems about the Old Lammas Fair in Ballycastle and the headlands of Kerry and the braes of Strasala. When other kids were out in hot sandlots tossing baseballs at their fathers, Patrick Cairney would sit with a fishing pole on the bank of a river and listen to his father recite the last words of the patriot Robert Emmet on the eve of his execution. Even now the young man could remember Emmet's speech. *When my country takes her place among the nations of the earth, then and not till then, let my epitaph be written. I have done.* Harry Cairney had been less a father than a kind of history instructor whose view of the past was coloured by the romanticism of the Irish exile. All through his childhood the boy had wished for a father like the one other kids had, those young vigorous men who'd throw a baseball at you or take you one-on-one on a basketball court to get down with you in a scrimmage. But Harry, who was fifty years older than his son, had seemed remote even then, removed from Patrick both by years and memories of a faraway island. As if he felt guilty about his absences, Harry forced himself on his son during the summer, but never quite in the way Patrick Cairney wanted. He was too old and too dignified, too *detached*, to get down in a sandlot and dirty his hands. He was too *sophisticated* to go inside a sporting-goods store and discuss the merits of this or that baseball bat. Consequently, when Patrick thought of his father now he felt a curious combination of admiration and pity, the former because Harry had occupied an exalted position in politics and was highly regarded by everyone – and the latter because the world Cairney had tried to foist on his son was an old man's dead reality and therefore pathetic.

Patrick Cairney got out of bed and went into the small kitchen, where he filled a glass with water. He carried it back to the bedroom and slipped under the sheets beside the girl. Once more through the night came the quick whine of a Garda car.

'You've gone very quiet all of a sudden,' Rhiannon said.

'*I am Ireland: I am older than the Old Woman of Beare*,' he recited. '*Great my glory: I that bore Cuchulain the valiant*.'

'*Great my shame*,' the girl replied. '*My own children that sold their mother*.' She paused a second. 'Patrick Pearse. Sure, I've known that since I was no higher than a blade of grass. Where did you learn it?'

'From my father,' Cairney answered. 'Didn't I mention he was born right here in Dublin? Above a shop at number 29 Patrick Street, to be exact.'

'And overseas he went to make his fortune,' Rhiannon said.

Cairney nodded. 'I don't think he ever really left this country.'

The girl pressed her face into Cairney's shoulder, her damp lips against his skin. Something had changed in the room in the space of a few minutes. Somebody had left the door open, and that old Celtic wraith Melancholy had gatecrashed.

'The funny thing, as Irish as he still is, he's never been back here to visit,' Cairney said. And he envisaged Harry Cairney as he'd last seem him two years ago, some months before the old man had unexpectedly married Celestine Cunningham of Boston in a private ceremony. Cairney had never met the woman but apparently the old man was overjoyed with the match. He'd written a couple of times to say so. When his letters weren't extolling the virtues of Celestine, they were arguing Cairney to visit this place or that, as if the son might vicariously undertake a pilgrimage that the father had always meant to make for himself. *Take a walk through St Anne's Park near the Dollymount Strand and smell the roses* or *Don't forget to have a jar in the Stag's Head at Dame Court*. In these letters Cairney could still hear the strident voice of the man who had turned all his short boyhood summers, which should have been treasured times, into diatribes against the sheer perfidy of the English and the atrocities they had committed in Ireland.

Cairney said, 'He wants to keep a memory of Ireland the way it was, not the way it is now. He romanticises things that were never romantic to begin with.'

'And I see nothing wrong in such a thing,' Rhiannon said. 'Why shouldn't old men have their illusions?'

Cairney nodded. Why not indeed? he wondered. Memories preserved in amber were inured to change. Harry Cairney's Ireland was the Dear Green Place, the *Sean-Bhean Bhock*, the Old Woman of Sorrow. His was an Ireland of martyrs, a place of ghosts. It was the doomed Easter Rising of 1916, when Harry Cairney's heroes – Patrick Pearse and Eamon de Valera and James Connolly – had seized the General Post Office on O'Connell Street and Boland's Mills in the south of Dublin and the English had crushed the insurgency with field guns and a gunboat on the River Liffey, consequently creating a new generation of martyrs.

It was an Ireland where Harry Cairney's heroes were executed by the English. John McBride, Pearse himself, James Connolly (wounded, carried by stretcher to the firing squad), Thomas MacDonagh, names that had echoed like bells through Patrick Cairney's formative years. And all the others – the glamorous Countess Markievicz who had stalked the streets of Dublin with a great plumed hat and a revolver, the beautiful Maude Gonne, who had captivated the heart of Yeats, running firearms into Ireland in defiance of the English, bold Rory O'Connor and his men who had dramatically seized the Four Courts Building in Dublin.

An old man's illusions . . .

What did they all come down to now, those clichés of glories lost and won? Patrick Cairney wondered. In what did all this romance and glamour and bravery distil itself?

The answer was simple. Squalor in Ulster, where courage had yielded to indiscriminate acts of terrorism and where, behind the walls of Her Majesty's Maze Prison – formerly Long Kesh Prison or, in convict terminology, the Lazy K – so-called political prisoners, members of the militant Provisional IRA, smeared their excrement on the walls of their cells and women did the same with their menstrual blood.

Patrick Cairney wondered if his father ever thought about that, the way courage had become eroded by sheer human indignity. He doubted the older man ever did: *memories preserved in amber . . .*

He propped himself up on one elbow. He stroked the side of the girl's face.

'For a student, Patrick Cairney, you've got a pretty fine physique,' Rhiannon said. 'What is it you do? Lift weights? Pump iron, as they say? Or is it just those old books you plough through are so heavy they build your muscles up?'

'I dig,' he answered.

'Dig? With a shovel?'

He nodded. 'I dig holes in the ground.'

'Like a navvy.'

'That's all I am, Nurse. A navvy with a purpose. When a labourer digs, he isn't looking for anything. But when I dig, I'm searching.'

'And what have you ever found?'

'I once found a Coca-Cola bottle circa 1930.'

'What treasure.' *Traysure* was how she pronounced the word.

'You don't expect to find such a thing buried in the Egyptian desert,' he said. It was best this way, he thought, best to keep everything at a level of flippancy he could handle. He stared at the darkened window. The silence of the night beyond the window was dense, impenetrable, as if it were the quiet left behind by all the lost causes of the world. He moved his body closer to the girl, holding her. For some reason the last stanza of Patrick Pearse's *Renunciation* went through his mind.

> I have turned my face
> To this road before me
> To the deed that I see
> And the death I shall die.

Cheerful little ditty, he thought.

When he heard the sound of the telephone ringing from the kitchen, he wanted to freeze it out of his brain.

'It could be important,' the girl said. 'Why don't you answer it?'

Cairney said nothing. The telephone went on ringing.

'Good news. You can never tell.'

'At midnight on a Saturday?' he asked.

After ten, twelve rings, the sound stopped.

Cairney's relief lasted only a moment, because the telephone started up again, and this time it seemed louder that before.

'Maybe it's a girlfriend,' Rhiannon said.

'I don't have one.'

'And you expect me to believe that, do you?'

Cairney tossed the bedsheets aside. The room was cold around him. He went inside the kitchen and picked up the telephone and stood there shivering as he listened to the voice on the other end of the line. When he hung up he returned to the bedroom. He sat down on the mattress.

'Well?' the girl asked.

'You should never answer a telephone that rings after twelve o'clock.'

Rhiannon crushed out her cigarette. 'That bad?'

Cairney sighed. He looked slightly flustered. 'A sickness in the family.'

'I'm sorry.'

Cairney reached out for the girl's hand, touching it softly. 'My father,' he said. 'A mild heart attack.'

5 Dun Laoghaire, Republic of Ireland

It was an old whitewashed house on the outskirts of the resort town of Dun Laoghaire on the south shore of Dublin Bay and in the grey dawn it appeared translucent. The house was surrounded by walls and thick trees. The only means of entrance was through a set of large iron gates, behind which a small gatehouse stood. Usually the gatehouse was occupied by a man who kept a nine-millimetre Brazilian Taurus semi-automatic pistol in his waistband and an FN assault rifle propped against the wall. On this morning, however, the gatehouse was empty and the iron gates were unlocked.

A beige VW came to a halt outside the whitewashed house. As it did so, a man appeared in the doorway. He was called Finn. Although he was in his late fifties, he carried himself in the erect manner of one who has been a soldier in his time. He was imposing – even in the pale dawn one could see the long white hair that fell over his shoulder and the suggestion of strength in his eyes. He came down the steps to greet the driver of the Volkswagen and together both men went inside the house. The driver, the young man known as Jig, noticed the empty gatehouse. It was never occupied whenever he came to this house because Finn required that his visits here take place with the utmost confidentiality. The guard was always sent away at such times. Even within the Association of the Wolfe secrets were stratified. No one person, other than Finn, knew everything that was going on. It was his way of maintaining control.

The sitting-room was filled with harps. Finn collected them assiduously. He never played because he was tone deaf, but there were strange little moments when, with all the windows open and the wind coming in off the Irish Sea, he could hear a random music created by nature as the air stirred the strings and made them vibrate. Many of the thirty or so harps were gorgeous gilt creations, inlaid with mother-of-pearl carved with extraordinary care. Sometimes, Finn would reach out and pluck a string, setting up tiny quivering cacophonies as he crossed the room.

Finn sat down. He wore a simple fisherman's sweater and baggy cord pants and sneakers that looked as if they'd been chewed by a neurotic dog. He ran his fingers nervously through his long white hair, and for a moment Jig perceived Finn as a kind of aged hippie, an eccentric guru who'd been to the mountain and come back bearing a message – which, in one sense, was true enough. Today, though, Finn looked gaunt, almost hungry, his huge cheekbones prominent in the lean face.

He pulled a strand of hair from his head and held it up to the light at the window, examining it. 'My bloody hair is beginning to fall out,' he said. He had an actor's voice. It came booming out of his chest.

He stood up, moving towards one of the harps. He angrily ran his fingers over all the strings and the room rippled with sound.

'This bloody country!' Finn shouted suddenly, as if the climate of Ireland were responsible for his hair loss. 'This godforsaken island of good intentions, dried-up old nuns, and bloody gossips! I tell you, there are times when I want nothing more than to just turn my back on the whole bloody place and let it sink into the ocean and see if I care!' Finn paused. 'You know what the ocean would do? Eh? It would spit the bloody island back *up* again! And you know why, boy? Because it's too much fucking trouble, that's why! Besides, what ocean would want the taste of a man like Ivor McInnes in it?'

Ivor McInnes, a Protestant minister who until recently had had a parish in Belfast, was Finn's bête noire. McInnes, who specialised in sermons that were critical of Catholicism in general and the IRA in particular, was symptomatic, in Finn's mind, of the wrongs that plagued the island today. There were just too many hard-core Protestants, with views that were sometimes to the far right of bigotry, wandering the land. Finn thought all extremists should be incarcerated and the key thrown away. He brought up the name of McInnes at every opportunity, rather in the way a man with congested lungs might bring up phlegm.

The young man watched as Finn wandered around the room, plucking the strings until the whole room was humming and singing.

Over the endless vibrations, Finn was talking rapidly. He moved backwards and forwards, waving his arms in an erratic fashion. He was ranting about how he'd struggled for supreme control of the finances of the Irish Republican Army, how he'd formed the ultra-secret innermost cell called the Association of the Wolfe precisely for the purpose of handling income. How, since 1981, he'd taken great pains to make sure that the money that came from 'the friends overseas' was spread carefully and discreetly around, because he wanted to keep it out of the hands of the extremists. He wanted an end to the *atrocious* image the IRA had made for itself. What bloody good did it do to blow up a London bus, say? Wasn't that a waste of explosives and *terrible* PR into the bargain? If there was to be killing, it had to be selective. If there were to be assassinations, only hostile political targets were to be picked. Nothing else could ever be justified.

Finn shook his head from side to side. 'Aside from the almighty dent that buying arms puts in our budget, do you know where our money goes, Jig?'

Jig shook his head. Finn had never talked about the particulars of finance before.

'I'll tell you. It goes to the Catholic families in the North when the man of the house is stuck in some bloody British jail because he was stupid enough to try and set off a bomb in the Tower of London and get himself caught. Do you know what this maintenance money costs us every year? Have you any idea? What will those women and children do if we can't get money to them?'

Santa Claus, Jig thought, dispensing banknotes from a sack.

'I'll tell you something else you didn't know,' Finn continued. 'Money gets ploughed into keeping the Gaelic alive. It goes to finance teachers and students and the publication of works in Irish. How can we sit around and talk English if we're supposed to be an independent country? English is a barbaric tongue, Jig, a mishmash. It doesn't have the sweetness of the Gaelic. Have you ever imagined what it would have sounded like if Bill Shakespeare had written in the Gaelic? Imagine *Hamlet* in Irish.'

Finn smiled. The harps trembled and rattled. Jig stood very still. He'd never heard this kind of desperate note in Finn's voice before. The news of the *Connie O'Mara* had clearly wounded the old man in a deep place.

Finn stood at the window now, his hands folded behind his back. 'She was a fine ship run by fine men,' he said, his voice a whisper suddenly. 'Liam O'Reilly grew up with me down in Bantry. A good man. And now he's dead and they're all dead and the bloody money's gone. Our money, boy. Our purse.'

Jig said nothing.

Finn rubbed him lightly on the shoulder. 'You're going to get it back for me, boy. Aren't you?'

The young man looked into Finn's eyes. What he saw there was a kind of madness, a needle-sharp single-mindedness. He imagined that the ancient saints who went out into the wilderness for months at a time had looked exactly like this. A manic light.

'If there's a way,' Jig answered.

'No ifs, Jig. There's always a way,' Finn moved back to the window. He stood looking out as if he anticipated enemies in the shrubbery. 'The bloody Americans,' he muttered.

'You think they're responsible?'

'For many years now, we've had sympathetic songbirds inside the New York City Police Department because that place is still basically an Irish colony. And the information that reached me last night is that the *Connie's* crew was slaughtered by American weapons.'

'American weapons are widely available,' the young man said.

Finn spread his hands out. 'There's more. I'm not quite finished. The same source was kind enough to mention the contents of a ballistics report conducted by the gentlemen of the Federal Bureau of Investigation.'

'And?'

'The ammunition used was something called SS109, which is manufactured by an American company called the Olin Corporation. This kind of ammunition, they tell me, is used in the Colt M–16A2 automatic rifle, also American.'

Jig licked his lips, which were dry. 'All right. Suppose the pirates were American. How do you narrow that down to specific individuals, Finn? The last time I heard, there were more than two hundred million people in the United States.'

'Simple, simple,' Finn answered. 'Consider this. A group of men collects a large sum of money for the Cause. Imagine one of this group says to himself that the poor old *Connie O'Mara* is a sitting duck just waiting to be shot and plucked. This treacherous bastard sees gold in front of his eyes. He can taste it. He decides he's going to make his own arrangements and to hell with the Cause! He's going to make himself rich at our expense!'

There were little spots of saliva at the corners of Finn's mouth. 'Only this group of men knew the cargo and destination of the *Connie*. Only *this* group, boy. Nobody else. And one of them is our fucking Judas. One of them *has* to be. It could only have been an inside job. I'll swear by that.'

Jig absorbed all this for a second. 'Who are the members of this group?' he asked. He knew what Finn's answer would be.

'Now right there you encounter your first obstacle,' Finn said. 'The lines of communication were established in such a way that the money always came from what we might call sources unknown. Even the telephone number I call in America is never the same one twice. All this was done in the sainted name of secrecy, of course, which we all know is a two-faced bastard that can easily work against you.'

The young man spread his hands in a perplexed manner. 'Where do you expect me to start?'

Finn narrowed his eyes. 'I'll give you a name and that's all I can give you.'

'Who?'

'A certain Father Tumulty in New York.'

'What can a priest tell me?'

'I never said the man was a priest, did I now?' Finn looked faintly mischievous.

'How do you want me to handle all this?' Jig asked.

Finn studied the young man's face. It was a good face, handsome and strong, with eyes that suggested layers of inner conviction. *You chose this one well, Finn.* There was steel in this boy, there was backbone and guts and, best of all, a chill dedication to the Cause. He placed one hand on Jig's shoulder. 'I'd be the happiest man in God's earth if I could tell you the names of the men who call themselves the Fund-raisers, because if I knew that we would sit down the way we usually do and devise a blueprint of action for you. I can tell you the *kind* of men they are. I can tell you they're the sort of men who've always been drawn to the Cause because it brings a small sense of danger into their otherwise drab lives. It gives them the illusion of *purpose*, boy. They send large sums of money over here then they sit back on their fat Yankee arses and feel very Irish. They've paid their dues. They think they belong. They think they *understand*. They think they're part of the whole bloody struggle. But they're not. They're money men, and *they* don't have any blood on their lovely white hands. They have silly little dreams in their head, but the only dream worth a damn is the one you're prepared to die for. And these men aren't ready to die for anything just yet, thank you very much. They're not Irish. They're Americans. They beat their chests and call themselves *Irish*-Americans, and they put on a big green production every St Patrick's Day, but they're about as Irish as the Queen of England. Personally I long for the day when we won't need such men . . .' Finn, who had a moment of uneasiness, a sense of uncertainty, a sudden nagging doubt, glanced at the boy. 'I know the kind of men they are, but I don't know their names, and I don't know how many of them are in the group. Three, four, six, I just don't know. Consequently . . .' and here he took a deep breath, 'we don't have a blueprint, boy. Only a burning bloody need for *that money*.'

The young man knew the kind of American Finn was talking about. He didn't care for them any more than Finn did, but his private feelings were irrelevant to him right then. He said, 'You still haven't answered my question, Finn. How do you want me to handle this?'

Finn rubbed the tip of his long straight nose. 'You have to keep several things in mind. One, the members of this group are going to be more than a little paranoid right now. The money's gone. They're going to be accusing one another and suspecting one another. They're going to be nervous, boy. And a nervous man isn't altogether a predictable one. Remember that. Two, when you find out who is involved in the Fund-raisers, you've got to proceed on the possibility that each and every one of them is the traitor. None of them is going to be happy to see you, because they're going to think that you *suspect* each of them of this awful crime. None of them will want to be your friend.' Finn looked suddenly exasperated. 'Ah, Jesus, it's a tricky situation.'

The young man blinked at the morning light climbing against the window. *None of them will want to be your friend*. He had no friends other than Finn, nor did he imagine ever needing any. He could have made friends if he'd wanted to, because he had an easy charm he was able to turn on and off and he had the kind of looks that others found attractive. But friendships were for other people. They were part of ordinary lives.

Finn put his hands in the pockets of his pants. 'Approach them carefully. Try to take them off guard if you can. But expect them to lie to you. Expect them to shift suspicions onto other members. Expect them to deny they have anything to do with sending money to Ireland. And don't be surprised if some of them treat you with outright animosity. As I said, these are nervous men. Push them a little if you feel you have to, but bear in mind this sorry fact – we'll probably need the services of some of these men in the future.'

The young man said nothing. He hadn't anticipated making a trip to America, and he found the prospect just a little unsettling. When he operated on the British mainland or in Northern Ireland, he always did so with a specific plan in mind, a detailed map of what he was supposed to do and how it was going to be achieved. Now, though, it seemed as if Finn expected him to go into America blind, which was an idea he didn't like. When you didn't have a plan, it was difficult to maintain control. He didn't want to go to America, but if Finn commanded him, then he'd obey. It would never have occurred to him to question Finn's orders.

The harp strings in the big room had all stilled now, and there was only a pale lingering echo of any noise.

Finn sat down, crossing his long legs and adjusting his baggy cord pants as if they had a razor-sharp crease that needed to be preserved. He was a man of small, endearing vanities. 'You'll need a gun, although I hope with all my heart you don't have to use it. But it would be downright foolish to go into this without one. Tumulty can help you there. I don't want you going into one of those bloody Irish bars in Queens and picking up what our American friends call a Saturday Night Special, Jig. I don't want you making any kind of contact with the Irish rabble that collects money in tin cans and sends cheap handguns to post-office boxes in Belfast or Derry. They mean well, no doubt, but they drink too much and they talk too bloody much, and we don't need any kind of gossip about you.'

Jig nodded. What he suddenly wished was that Finn was going to the United States with him. For a moment he felt a twinge of loneliness, but he put the sensation out of his mind. He had chosen this life. Nobody had selected it for him. Finn, certainly, had nudged him in the direction of this existence, but finally the choice had been entirely his own.

'One other thing,' Finn said, regretting his anger when he'd talked on the telephone with his anonymous American contact. He'd blurted out some threat about sending a man over, and now he was sorry about it. Quick to rage and say things he wished he hadn't – would he never change? 'They'll be expecting you over there.'

'Somebody's always expecting me, Finn.'

The old man didn't speak for a time. He reached for the bottle of peppermint schnapps that sat on a table against the wall, then changed his mind about drinking. He wanted to be cold sober. 'You did a fine job with Whiteford,' he said in a low voice.

Jig shrugged. The compliment was unexpected and quite uncharacteristic of Finn. He wasn't sure how to take it. 'It went off as we planned.' It was all he could think of to say.

'And you'll do a fine job in America too, because I want you *and* our money back here in one piece. That money means a lot, boy. Without it . . .'

'I understand,' Jig said.

Finn clapped the palm of his hand against the young man's shoulder. 'Remember this. If it becomes unpleasant at any time in America – and you know what I mean by that – your life is more important to me than any one of the Fund-raisers.' And then, as if this confession were something he regretted, he turned away from Jig.

'Let's talk about the cash you'll need for this trip,' he said, and once again set the harp strings dancing with flourishes of his hands.

Finn slept for thirty minutes after Jig had gone. It was troubled sleep and he woke with the feeling of having dreamed something disastrous that he couldn't recall on waking. Something to do with Jig.

When he got up, he went into the bathroom to shave. He studied his face in the mirror awhile. It was a lean, chiselled face, criss-crossed by lines and filled with small hollows under the cheekbones. What Finn saw looking back at him from the mirror was a man who had a special sense of history at a special time.

The idea of founding the Association of the Wolfe had come to him when he perceived the general disunity of the Cause, when he had seen the need for strong hands on the financial reins. Secretive centralised planning was the answer to the outrages of the *eedjit* rabble. If you didn't give the hotheads money, how could they buy weapons and explosives for their little sorties in Belfast and on the English mainland, when all they ever got was a damned bad press?

The ultimate goal of the Association was that old dream – to get the British out of the North and unite Ireland once and for all. Two separate Irelands was as much a travesty of history as two separate Germanies. An artificial border, created by the English and maintained by its soldiers, was a farce, a rupture inflicted by the politics of hatred. The Association was named after Wolfe Tone who in 1796 had attempted to land 12,000 French soldiers on Bantry Bay to help overthrow English supremacy. When the mission failed and Tone was captured, he asked for death before a firing squad, cutting his own throat when his request was denied.

Finn believed in selective assassination. He had a list of intended victims, which was composed mainly of British politicians who were against the prospect of a united Ireland. The list also included several Northern Irish diehards, those iron-skulled morons, like Ivor McInnes, who swore on their own lives that the Union Jack would always fly over Belfast, that Ulster would always belong to the Queen. If you systematically assassinated enough of these jackasses, sooner or later the cost in blood was going to prove too expensive to the English. They'd be happy to leave Ulster, which was something they should have done years ago if they'd had any decency – which they clearly did not have.

Finn turned away from the mirror. He had a sense of things slipping away from him. Without control of the purse, how could he control the extremists? But now the purse was gone, and the thought brought a bitter taste into his mouth. Liam O'Reilly was dead. So was the Courier. Finn closed his eyes and observed a quiet moment of mourning for old comrades, both members of the Association.

He went down the stairs. In his small office, a spartan room with a desk and a chair and bare white walls, he picked up the telephone. He began to dial a number but stopped halfway through and set the phone back. What was he going to say? What was he going to tell the Saint? He stood at the window, stroking his jaw. What in God's name was he supposed to say? The Saint didn't believe in credit. He was always in a hurry to deliver his goods and get paid.

Finn picked up the telephone a second time. He dialled nervously. It was a number in the port city of Rostock in East Germany. It rang only once before it was picked up. Finn spoke his name.

The voice at the other end was guttural New York City. 'I got tired waiting, Finn.'

Finn said nothing a moment. The connection was poor. 'There's been a problem. A cash problem.'

'Maybe for you, Finn. I ain't got problems.'

Finn saw a blackbird fly past his window. *Pack up all my cares and woe,* he thought. 'Listen to me. I need some time.'

'Time's run out, fella. You know how much it costs when you got a Greek boat to rent? When you got an Arab crew that sits round on its duff all day and they still gotta get paid? Then you add the fact I got harbour personnel to grease here. You know how much that runs, Finn?'

Finn's throat was dry. 'I need a week. Maybe more than a week.'

'Tough titty,' the guy said. 'I'm trying to tell ya, Finn. You're shit outta luck, man.'

'What do you mean? What do you mean I'm out of luck?'

'I got tired of waiting. I already sold the cargo, Finn.'

'*You did what*?' Finn shouted. '*You did what?*'

'Guy came up with a good offer. I said sure thing. What the hell. I wanna sit round in Rostock for the rest of my life, Finn? Wait for you?'

'This is a joke,' Finn said. His voice was very low, even. A nerve had begun to work at the side of his head.

'No joke. I don't joke about my cargo – '

'You sold it! How could you *do* such a thing like that, in the name of Jesus!'

'Hey, it ain't like you and me had a written contract, pal. You wanna sue? Be my guest.'

Finn shut his eyes tightly. First the money. Now a whole boatload of arms and explosives. The very air he breathed seemed poisoned with treacheries.

'You're trying to tell me a buyer just came along? Out of the bloody blue?'

'Right,' the Saint said. 'I'm a businessman, Finn. This is a business. I gotta sell. I gotta eat.'

'Who was this buyer?'

'I can't answer a dumb question like that.'

'Who was he?' Finn trembled with rage.

'Hey, Finn. I don't ask questions. Guy paid, I delivered. Simple and clean. Now I just wanna get my ass outta this town, which I intend to do in the next few hours. This ain't exactly a day at the beach, Finn. You ever been in Rostock?'

'I'd like to know the name of this person.'

There was a crackling sound over the line. The Saint said, 'Listen, Finn. I keep confidences. Understand? The guy who took over delivery of the cargo, he was a South American. A Venezuelan or something. He waved cold cash and I took it. That's all I'm saying.'

Finn said, 'I'll go elsewhere. I'll find another supplier! Damn you – '

The line was already dead. Finn slammed down the receiver. He sat, dismayed, spreading his arms on his desk and laying his face against them.

The shipment was gone.

He raised his face. A bloody Venezuelan! A bloody Venezuelan had purchased the whole boatload of arms and high-tech explosives, for Christ's sake! Probably to waste them in some fucking futile border skirmish that didn't matter a damn in the scheme of things. An arms shipment like that took *months* to put together. If Jig recovered the missing money, Finn thought he could set up another deal, but not through the Saint, who, like most of his mercenary kind, didn't have much in the way of honour and loyalty. But it would take time to make another deal, and Finn wasn't very patient. God in heaven, he'd lived all his life with his dream of a free Ireland, from the time he was a small boy in Bantry and all through his years of service with the IRA, when he'd done everything a man could do. He'd planted bombs in England. He'd robbed mail trains. During the Second World War he'd gone into Northern Ireland to sabotage a British troop ship that was carrying soldiers to fight in Europe. A lot of blood had been spilled in pursuit of the dream. A lot of fine men had died.

But without weapons and explosives, you might as well hang a CLOSED sign on your door. If Jig didn't recover the money, it was back to homemade hand grenades and other dubious devices that were absolutely undependable. Which meant he couldn't keep up the pressure on the English to get out of Ulster. If Finn was truly afraid of anything, it was the idea of dying before he saw his dream come true.

He turned his thoughts to Jig.

There was a lot riding on that young man's shoulders. Jig had never let him down in the past, no matter how difficult or complicated the task. But this was something altogether different. Apart from Tumulty, Jig would have no support in America. There was no network in place to assist him if he needed help over there. And there was no network for the simple reason that Finn had never imagined the need for Jig to operate in the USA. Scoundrels, he thought. All of them, from the Fund-raisers to the Saint, a scurvy black-hearted bunch.

It was more than the lack of a network, though, that troubled Finn now. And it was more than the treachery of men. It was the fact that Jig, who had been highly trained to kill men, was going into a situation where his particular form of expertise wasn't going to be of any damned use to him. He wasn't going to be called upon to plant explosive devices or track some potential victim through the scope of a sniper's rifle. He was being asked to do something in which he had utterly no experience. He was being asked to *investigate* a crime. To solve a specific problem. *To sleuth.*

Finn had a strange lurching sensation around his heart. *You're sending an assassin into a situation that calls for a detective's talents.* In the name of God, Finn, what have you done? Have you asked the impossible of that boy? Have you packed him off to be devoured by bloody Yankee vultures?

But there was nobody else to send. There was no other man Finn could trust. It was really that simple. He could have enlisted some young hothead who would have gone blundering into America, but what good would that have done? If anybody could get that money back, it was Jig. From the very start of their association Finn had seen a dark streak in the boy, an unrelenting determination in his heart. He was the stuff of an assassin. He had nerves of marble and a hawk's fastidious eye for detail. He had required careful shaping, of course. He had needed the rough edges smoothed away. Some of his political notions had been naive and idealistic back when the young man had first been brought to Finn's attention. Finn remembered now how Jig had hung around the fringes of political action groups in Dublin, acquiring a certain notoriety for his habit of espousing extremism and advocating grand gestures – such as the bombing of Buckingham Palace or the Houses of Parliament. For security reasons, Finn never attended such meetings himself. They were too easily infiltrated by plainclothes Garda and other enemies of the Cause, but the old man had a network of people who brought him reports – who was saying what, the kinds of schemes being plotted, anything that might intrigue Finn. In enthusiasms and energy, in the stark apocalyptic suggestions he carelessly made, Jig had put Finn in mind of his own younger self – the raw boy from Bantry who wanted to change the world with one grand stroke. Ah, the innocence of it all! The sheer unfettered naïvety! But the possibilities inherent in the young man – these were the things that had interested Finn most.

His first private meeting with the boy took place in an isolated bird sanctuary at Booterstown on Dublin Bay where, surrounded by squalls of gulls and anxiously watchful wading birds Finn had talked of the need for patience and careful judgement when it came to the problem of getting the British out. He had deliberately circled his real purpose in interviewing the young man, which was his own need for a person who could become the kind of assassin required by the Association of the Wolfe. Was this boy the one? Or was his impulsive streak unharnessable? These were the early days of the Association and Finn, disgusted by the outbreak of IRA bombings and killings on the British mainland, spoke of the importance of selective assassination. There, at Booterstown, knocked by a harsh wind and the cuffs of his pants caked with soft mud, Finn made his distinction between an ordinary IRA gunman, a hothead, and the kind of dedicated assassin the Cause really needed.

The young man had listened, his mind seemingly elsewhere, his eyes distant and unresponsive. Each of Finn's questions had been answered in short, unrevealing sentences. The boy's background, his interests – these were dismissed, as if they had absolutely no relevance and Finn was impertinent to ask so many questions. Finn had the feeling that the young man thought his time was being unforgivably wasted. Dragged out in the first light of dawn to some bloody bird sanctuary and for what? So that a nosy old man could pose silly questions?

What's the point of all this? the boy asked.

Finn, a little irritated by the young man's abrasive edge, had answered this question with one of his own. *Why do you hate the English so much*?

Does it matter? Jig asked.

Finn had watched a flock of seagulls rise up and go screaming towards the sea, which was barely visible in the muffled fog of the early morning. *Answer my question*, he'd said.

The young man had replied tersely, almost as if he were editing his own material in his head. He had been in the North about two years ago, he said, and in Belfast, that ruined city, he had come across the bagged bodies of two infant children on the sidewalk outside a house that had been ravaged by British soldiers because they suspected the place was filled with arms. Armoured cars and tanks and soldiers milled around in confusion. It transpired that the two children had been alone in the house when the British assault took place. But what Jig remembered most were the two bundles on the sidewalk and the way blood soaked through the material of the bags and the sounds of old women sobbing, like the sombre women of Greek tragedies, in the doorways of the street.

Finn had thought there was something unconvincing about this story. He didn't doubt that it was true, but atrocities were alas commonplace in Belfast. Everybody and his uncle had at least one horror story to tell. By itself, it wasn't enough to produce the kind of venom that was present in Jig whenever he spoke of the English. Was the young man simply trying to say that he was a humanitarian outraged by the casual and utterly useless deaths of small children? Finn didn't buy that. It was too easy, facile. He had the strong feeling that Jig, for whatever reasons, was going through his memory on a highly selective basis. That something was being left out of the narrative. He flirted briefly with the notion that perhaps Jig was one of those psychopathic types that were unfortunately drawn to the Cause because it offered a justification for their violent tendencies, but he dismissed this because there was a certain authenticity in the way the boy had delivered his story. Just the same, Finn still felt dissatisfied. If he was going to find a use for this young man, he needed to be absolutely certain of him.

It's not enough, boy, Finn said.

What more to you want? Jig asked.

Hatred doesn't spring from one isolated incident.

Doesn't it?

Finn shook his head. *There's got to be more.*

The young man had smiled then, which was something he apparently didn't do very often. His normal expression was one of grimness, an unrelaxed look that suggested a life of forever being tense. *Wary,* maybe that was the word Finn had wanted. It was a good quality in a killer. An assassin had to have an edge. But Finn needed more than what this young man had told him before he could recruit him.

Do you want a history lesson, Finn? Is that it? Do you want me to tell you how the British presence in this country sickens me?

You can't tell me anything about bloody history, boy.

I didn't think so.

Together, they had walked silently through the sanctuary, scaring birds out of the rushes and puddles and mudbanks. When they paused beneath some trees. Finn asked, *Do you know your way around a gun?*

Jig said he did.

Finn paused for a second. *We'll talk again,* was what he had finally said, drifting under the trees and away from the boy, who watched sullenly.

When Finn had gone several yards the young man had called out. *I'm tired of talk. Is that all anybody ever does in this country?*

Finn had smiled to himself but hadn't looked back.

Now, staring at the telephone on his desk, Finn felt despair. All the work, all the planning – and the Saint turns around and sells to the first fucking buyer that comes along with a stuffed wallet!

Dear God. He needed to get out of this house for a time. He wanted the sharp morning air on his face and the sea breezes blowing at him and the chance to get his thoughts straight. Maybe he'd go into Dublin. He always had a relaxing time there. Maybe he'd go and see Molly, who had a flat in the suburb of Palmerstown. Molly had ways of unwinding him and God! he needed that now.

He dressed himself slowly in his best suit, a three-piece black worsted with squared shoulders. It was an old-fashioned suit and it looked peculiarly Irish. He dabbed his underarms with deodorant. Then he piled his long hair up on top of his head and covered it with an old black felt hat. He put on a pair of sunglasses. Without these small precautions, his long hair would have drawn attention, and he believed in a low profile when he had to go out in public. He didn't want to look eccentric on the streets, not even in these times when there were punk rockers on Grafton Street with their hair dyed pink and safety pins hanging from their nostrils.

He picked up the telephone and called a number. It was that of the man who usually sat armed out in the gatehouse and who lived nearby.

'George,' Finn said. 'Will you bring the car around now?'

George said, 'Certainly. Where are we headed?'

Finn hesitated a second. 'Into town. I think a trip into town would be very nice.'

He stepped out of the house and walked down the driveway towards the gatehouse. The March morning was unusually sunny and the only clouds in the sky lay somewhere out in the middle of the Irish Sea – drifting, he hoped, over to England. He sat inside the gatehouse for five minutes, then he saw the old Daimler approach. He hoped America would be kind to Jig. If Jig couldn't get that money back . . . Finn didn't want to think the worst.

The tyres of the Daimler crunched on gravel. Finn opened the rear door, climbed inside.

'Palmerstown,' Finn said.

The driver nodded. He had driven the Old Man to Palmerstown many times before.

Dublin

'No goodbyes,' Patrick Cairney told the girl.

'I want to drive you to the airport. What's wrong with that?'

'I hate airports. I hate farewells. I get a lump in my throat. My eyes water. I fall to pieces.'

Rhiannon Canavan was dressed in her nurse's uniform, over which she wore a green coat with the sleeves dangling empty. Cairney thought she looked particularly lovely.

'Didn't I slip away from the hospital just so I could take you to the airport?'

'I'll call you from the States,' he said.

'Oh, sure you will.'

'Why do you doubt that?'

She shrugged. 'Maybe there's something just a wee bit thrust-and-run about you, Cairney. I don't see you calling me at all.'

'Cross my heart.'

'I'll drop you off. I won't even come with you *inside* the blasted place!'

Cairney relented. 'Promise?'

'I give you my word.'

Cairney reached out to touch her face.

'Will you come back to me when your father's better?'

'Or worse.'

Rhiannon put a fingertip against his mouth. 'Don't say that. I'm sure he's going to be just fine.'

Cairney looked at the sky from the window. There was somewhere a weak suggestion of the sun that had been in the heavens earlier but that now lay behind a clutch of miserly clouds. He took Rhiannon Canavan in his arms and held her tightly.

She said, 'Some people make complete recoveries from mild heart attacks, you know. I've seen it happen hundreds of times.'

Cairney didn't speak.

There was a dry weakness at the back of his throat. He played with the idea that it would be perfect to stay right here where he was. Just him and this lovely girl in this small apartment. Their own uninterrupted love nest. Silence and exhaustion and the sweetness of flesh. They could lie here and make love and die of malnutrition.

'I've never been in America,' the girl said. 'Sure, I have millions of aunts and uncles and cousins I've never seen. I think most of them live in Union City, New Jersey. Is it pretty there?'

'In New Jersey?'

'Yeh. Is it pretty?'

'It has its moments. I don't think Union City is one of them, though.'

Rhiannon Canavan looked at her small wristwatch. 'Are you packed?' she asked, all at once practical. 'You don't have a lot of time, Patrick.'

'I'm packed.'

'We don't even have time for a quickie, do we?'

'How quick's a quickie?' he asked.

'Now that depends entirely on you, doesn't it?'

Patrick Cairney smiled. He wondered if he could lose himself a moment in sheer blind passion, if there was an oxygen bubble inside the vacuum he felt.

Rhiannon kissed him on the lips. It was a warm kiss and he was drawn down into it where he found himself in a well-lit place where there existed neither airplanes nor schedules nor long journeys to make. It was like drowning in tepid, scented water, peacefully and without panic, watching yourself circle and go down and circle and go down again, until there was no further place left to sink to and you were blissfully on the bottom. He slid his hands between the buttons of her uniform, feeling the small breasts under his palms. Her nipples were hard. He worked the uniform open, pushing it back from her shoulders. Her green coat fell to the floor. He traced a line with his fingertips from her breasts to her navel and then down across her smooth stomach, which had a lustrous silken texture.

Afterwards, Rhiannon said, 'I hate heart attacks.'

George Scully, the driver of the Daimler that dropped Finn off in Palmerstown, parked the car on St Stephen's Green and walked until he came to the large covered marketplace known as the Powerscourt Townhouse, which he entered from South William Street. He passed stalls selling earrings and lace items and Celtic crosses carved in stone and recordings of the Clancy Brothers, and he rose to the upper tier where he entered a coffee shop. He bought a milky coffee, took it to a table, sat down, drummed his fingers impatiently. he knew he didn't have much time before he would have to get back to the car and pick up the Old Man.

Presently, he heard the sound of somebody whistling tunelessly and a shadow fell across the table. The driver looked up and smiled. The newcomer wore a navy-blue seaman's coat and a woollen hat drawn down over his ears.

'I'll be quick,' George Scully said.

The other man nodded. He sat down, looking around the coffee shop.

The driver leaned across the table. 'It's just like we thought it would be. He's sending Jig.'

'Is he now?'

George Scully said, 'I couldn't hear this very well because the Old Man takes precautions like nobody's business, but he's definitely sending Jig.' Scully paused and ran the tip of a finger round the rim of his cup. 'Sometimes Jig uses a passport in the name of John Doyle. Sometimes not. I happened to be the one who picked up the passport for him, so what I'm telling you is reliable.'

The man in the seaman's jacket nodded. 'Jig,' he said quietly. 'Well now. Isn't that something?'

Scully said, 'The New York connection is a certain Father Tumulty. Your friends in Belfast will want to know that, I'm sure.' Scully was silent a second. He bit uncertainly on his lower lip. 'Come to Dun Laoghaire around ten. The Old Man's with his fancy woman right now, and he's going to be drunk when he gets home.'

'We'll be there.'

'The gates will be unlocked. I won't be in the gatehouse.'

'Fine,' the man in the seaman's jacket said.

George Scully stared into his coffee. He said, 'Ten years I've been with the Old Man. Ten years of guarding him, running his bloody errands. Long before he started getting all his grand ideas. He wasn't always the way he is now, a bloody big shot. And what have I got to show for it? Sweet fuck all.'

The man in the seaman's jacket took a brown envelope from inside his shirt and pressed it down on the table and George Scully picked it up quickly, hiding it under his coat.

'It's all there, Scully. Twenty-five thousand English pounds.'

George Scully looked unhappy. 'I never thought I'd see this day,' he remarked.

'You've earned the cash,' the other man said.

'There's a bad name for what I'm doing,' Scully said solemnly.

'Aye. But you could think of it another way. You're making your own little contribution to ending the Troubles, aren't you?'

Scully placed a hand around his coffee cup. 'We'll see, won't we?'

The other man went back out through the Powerscourt Townhouse to the streets. He walked rapidly, pausing only at the Market Arcade to place a coin in the can of a blind penny-whistle player.

The blind man was playing *The Minstrel Boy.*

The Minstrel Boy to the war is gone,
In the ranks of death you'll find him.

The ranks of death.

Jesus, there was going to be a lot of dying.

The man, whose name was Seamus Houlihan and who four nights ago had been employed as an ordinary seaman on the *Connie O'Mara,* found a taxi to take him to Connolly Station, where he'd be in time to meet Waddell coming off the train from Belfast.

6 London

'Vile,' said Sir John Foulkes, who had a flamboyant handlebar moustache and Edwardian sideburns. 'This business with Walter Whiteford. Utterly vile, Frank.'

Frank Pagan looked from the window of the Under-secretary's office. A barge was making its way up the River Thames, leaving a wake like a water beetle.

'Why are these assassinations always so vile?' the Under-secretary asked. It was not so much a question as a reflection on the lack of common decency in the world. The Under-secretary defined decency in terms of the right breeding, the right schools, and ultimately something that was called 'good form', itself a consequence of being expensively raised and educated. It was a vicious circle of privilege, and Pagan sometimes resented it.

Pagan was surrounded every day of his working life with members of the Old School Tie Network, characters who talked casually about going up to Scotland where they had property reserved entirely for grouse shooting or salmon fishing. It was hard at times for Pagan to believe that this was the late twentieth century. He had moments when he leaned towards a form of primitive socialism in which there wouldn't be an aristocracy and the land would belong to everybody. Dream on.

The Under-secretary fidgeted with the cuffs of his white shirt. Pagan turned away from the view of the Thames. Today, because he knew he was meeting the Under-secretary, Pagan had made a few concessions. He'd left his blue jeans and sneakers at home. He wore an olive-coloured suit and brown slip-on shoes and his slim silk necktie was pale green. All good earth tones, he thought, and by his own standards subdued.

'I am certain to figure somewhere in a future assassination plan,' the Under-secretary said. He swept a hand through the air. 'It's not a prospect I relish.'

Pagan moved his head slightly. The Under-secretary was new to Irish affairs. Previously, he had been considered an expert on trade unions. Pagan wondered about his credentials. A knowledge of wage negotiations and how to talk with mining or railway leaders – tasks at which he hadn't been very successful, a fact that perhaps explained his present posting (which was more of a punishment than a job) – wouldn't help him in the quicksands of Irish matters. Pagan understood how these unsuitable appointments happened. It was pal helping pal, one Old Boy to another, and to hell with credentials. Only your school background mattered, Incompetence in the higher echelons of power, Pagan thought, could always be traced back to the fact that unqualified men had gone to the right public schools. It was a good way to run a country.

Sir John had his cuffs to his liking now. 'Ireland is a nightmare to me, Frank. I have times when I *think* I've penetrated its various complexities. But then it seems to slip away from me.' He stroked his enormous moustache. The satirical magazine *Private Eye* had christened him Furry Jake.

'It does that,' Pagan agreed.

'Why in the name of God are we still in Northern Ireland?'

Pagan smiled. He wondered if the Under-secretary really wanted an answer or whether he'd just asked another of those rhetorical questions in which, like all politicians, he specialised. Pagan decided he'd answer anyway. 'Because it's what the Protestant majority wants, Sir John.'

'We should just get the hell out of Ulster and say, "There, chaps, go work out your own differences with the South".'

Pagan laid a hand on the Under-secretary's huge desk. There wasn't a piece of paper anywhere. He glanced at the bookshelves. Several histories of Ireland were stacked there. They looked as if they hadn't been opened. 'We can't let them settle their own differences so long as the Protestant majority in the North wants to remain a part of the United Kingdom,' he said. 'If the day comes when the North wants to be a part of a unified Ireland, fine. Personally I don't see that happening. There's too much hatred between Catholic and Protestant.

The Under-secretary leaned back in his padded leather chair.

'And there are too many suspicions on both sides,' Pagan continued, wondering if it was easier for Furry Jake to get his history in small doses like this instead of having to crack open the tomes on the bookshelf. Sometimes Pagan encountered an almost wilful simple-mindedness in the higher reaches of power that appalled him. People like the Under-secretary, in defiance of the tenets of Darwinism, hadn't evolved since the days when the British Empire could put down a Zulu uprising with a handful of rifles and some good men.

Pagan said, 'The Protestants in the North are scared shitless by the predominance of the Catholic Church in the South. They think that in a unified Ireland they'd be discriminated against because then they'd be in a minority. They don't like giving up their present status. Right now they're the lords of all they survey, but there's a tide rising against them.'

The Under-secretary didn't look very interested. He had the expression of an unwilling participant in a crammer course. There was also the fact that he wasn't absolutely sure of Frank Pagan's loyalties. Some said Pagan was just a little too *soft* on the South.

Pagan went on regardless. There was a certain wicked enjoyment in the idea of instructing the Under-secretary in his job and knowing that you were causing him a minor irritation. 'The Catholics in the Republic don't trust the Protestants in the North because of their allegiance with England. And there's been too much English misbehaviour in the past.' *Misbehaviour,* he thought. There was a neat little euphemism. 'People don't forget quickly. They can't forget how the English have treated Ireland over the centuries. They can't put aside the fact that the English have gone periodically into Ireland and filled the streets with Irish blood.'

'That's ancient history, Frank.' Sir John made a small gesture of impatience.

'To you maybe. But England has a dirty name over there. It stands for Oliver Cromwell slaughtering the inhabitants of Wexford in 1649 and then as a gesture of *real* goodwill, committing atrocities on priests of the Roman Catholic Church. It's a potato famine and starvation, which was exploited by English landowners who didn't exactly shed tears when they saw Irishman either starve to death or being packed into emigrant ships – coffin ships – because it meant they didn't have to rent their land to the bloody peasants. It's the fact that in six miserable years in the late 1840s, one million people died as a result of famine, while the English landlords didn't suffer a bit. Quite the opposite; the buggers prospered.'

The Under-secretary frowned. Pagan leaned against the bookshelves. Instant history, he thought.

'And the Irish can't forget that in our own century the English crushed the Easter Rising of 1916 with more enthusiasm than the event merited. Somehow we managed to kill about five hundred men of the Irish Volunteers, a militant group of *really* dangerous men who were poorly armed and badly trained and were never any match for English field guns. And then we went on to execute the leaders of the Rising in front of firing squads. We did a wonderful job all around, didn't we?'

Sir John stood up. A joint cracked in his leg. He didn't say anything for a time. With his back to Pagan he looked down at the river. 'You sound rather sympathetic to the Irish, Frank.'

'I've tried to understand them, that's all. You might give it a shot yourself, Sir John. Open a book or two. Do yourself a favour.'

The Under-secretary stared at him curiously. He wasn't happy with Pagan's tone, but then he wasn't sure if Pagan was really the right man for the job anyway. His search for Jig, for example , hadn't exactly been a resounding success. 'IRA gunmen wander the streets of Belfast,' he said after a while. 'They shoot British soldiers. Protestants arm themselves in basements to fight against Catholics and the IRA. And we've got this lunatic fellow Jig doing all kinds of damage.' The Under-secretary fingered his moustache and quietly suppressed a belch, pulling his chin down into his neck. It was all very polite, Pagan thought.

The Under-secretary went on, 'Damned troublesome island, Frank. Hardly worth the bother. it's not as if we actually *get* anything out of it save for a great deal of grief, is it? It's not as if they're one of the OPEC nations sitting on millions of barrels of oil or something like that. Sooner we're out of it, the better.'

Pagan said nothing. Furry Jake's ignorance and insensitivity were really quite impressive.

'How do you propose to catch Jig, Frank?'

This question echoed inside Pagan like a minor chord struck on piano keys. 'I wish I had the answer to that,' he said, a bleak little response to the problem that dogged him constantly.

The Under-secretary turned. 'It has to be given top priority, Frank.'

'It has,' Pagan replied.

'I mean *top*, Frank.'

Pagan nodded. The Under-secretary annoyed him the way all his kind did. They issued their orders and then went out to lunch at their clubs. Fine old sherry and quail eggs and men dozing in leather armchairs behind copies of *The Daily Telegraph*. The death of the British Empire in microcosm in the fancy clubs of Pall Mall, where you needed a pedigree from Debrett's *Peerage* before you could actually breathe the air.

'What about the business with the ship?' the Under-secretary asked.

Only that morning Foxie had brought him another telex on the matter, this time one sent from the FBI to Scotland Yard. Pagan had read the thing quickly.

'Special Branch is handling that,' he said. 'My whole section is busy with Jig. Exclusively.'

'Mmmmm,' the Under-secretary said. 'Just the same, Frank, I wish you had paid it some attention yourself. It does come under your domain, after all.'

The little arsehole was scolding him. Pagan studied his fingernails a moment. 'My latest information is that we've had a positive ID of the individual whose hand was severed at the wrist. One Sean Riordan, aka the Courier, a resident of Philadelphia. His function was the delivery of capital to his sources in Ireland from sources unknown in the United States. So it's fair to assume the *Connie* was carrying an amount of cash.'

'Why do the Americans insist on sending money to those brutes?'

Pagan shrugged. He could have made an easy answer: historic ties. But it went deeper that that, down into the mists of darker emotions and old sentiments and an idealised conception of Ireland that was aroused in many Irish-Americans whenever they heard the first few bars of *Danny Boy*. This sedimentary yearning had a way of opening wallets.

The Under-secretary asked, 'Do you have any opinion who seized this money?'

'No, I don't. But you can bet that the IRA will be more than unhappy about the whole thing. What I wonder is how they're going to react.'

Furry Jake smiled. The idea of the IRA suffering a setback pleased him hugely. 'One other thing, Frank. I don't much care for the press we've been getting. I don't think you should say anything to reporters. Let the commissioner do any talking that has to be done. He likes to see his name in print.'

'All I ever said was "no comment".'

'I know that, but some of our journalists take that as an admission of defeat. The commissioner has more . . . experience in handling the press that you, Frank.' The Under-secretary looked at his watch. 'Well, Frank. Keep me posted , will you?'

'I will, Sir John.'

'And you will make sure Special Branch keeps its vigilance?'

'I've already requested that security at your home be doubled,' Pagan said.

'My wife worries,' said the Under-secretary, smiling thinly.

And you don't, of course. Pagan went to the door. He heard Sir John clear his throat.

'Catch him, Frank, Catch Jig.'

Pagan stopped at the door.'

The Under-secretary said, 'No matter what it takes, you must catch this fellow.'

'Exactly how do you want him?' Pagan asked. There was a faint hint of sarcasm in his voice, which the Under-secretary didn't notice. *Catch Jig*. Just like that. What the hell did the Under-secretary think Frank Pagan had been *trying* to do?

The Under-secretary looked a little puzzled. 'What do you mean how do I want him?'

'Dead or alive?' Pagan asked. Poached? Toasted? Pickled? Take your pick, Sir John.'

'Ah.' The Under-secretary was quiet a moment. 'I don't think it matters one way or another with scum like that, do you?'

'Quite,' Pagan said and stepped out into a carpeted corridor. *Catch Jig*.

The Under-secretary called out to him, 'Been meaning to ask. Who's your tailor, Frank?'

Pagan stopped. He looked back into the office. 'Nobody in particular. Sometimes Harry's Nostalgia Boutique on the Portobello Road. Sometimes Crolla on Dover Street. Why? You want the addresses?'

'Not really,' said the Under-secretary.

Dublin

The man known as Jig did not leave the Republic of Ireland from Dublin Airport, although he went there initially. He was accustomed to creating a maze of his own movements. At the terminal he went inside the men's room and locked himself in a cubicle where he changed his clothes.

He did this as an ordinary, everyday precaution, something that had become second nature to him. He removed his suit and shoes, stuffed them inside his canvas bag, then put on an old pair of faded cord pants and a heavy sweater. He placed a cap firmly on his head and pulled it down over his brow. On his feet he wore the kind of sturdy boots a casual labourer might have worn. Anyone who saw him emerge from the men's room would have seen a man on his way to look for work somewhere – a man who shuffled a little, like somebody defeated by the prospects of ever finding employment. He wore a money belt concealed beneath his sweater. It contained ten thousand American dollars, one thousand pounds in sterling and five hundred Irish punts.

He walked out of the terminal and into the parking lot. The car he chose was a drab brown Hillman Minx. In the old days, a car might have been left there for him on purpose but now, with all Finn's mania for secrecy, cars were stolen, not supplied. A supplied car had the distinct disadvantage of being arranged in *advance*, which afforded one's enemies the chance and the time to find out about it. Stealing, Finn always reasoned, was less risky because it was random.

The Minx spluttered and hacked like an old man in a terminal ward. Jig drove it as far as the Connolly Station in Dublin, where he bought a train ticket for Belfast. Once there, he would fly to Glasgow and take a bus to Prestwick Airport on the Ayrshire coast, where he'd catch a flight to New York City.

It was a circuitous and time-consuming route, but it was one of Finn's maxims that you saved time by spending some, that when you were in a hurry you were always prone to that evil demon Carelessness. Survival, Finn always said, is a matter of attention to the mundane. A matter, boyo, of *detail*.

Jig opened a newspaper on the train and red an editorial that referred to Walter Whiteford's decapitation. It was funny, though. He couldn't make a mental picture of a headless man, couldn't see the head tearing away from the body and rolling down a cobblestoned street. He had a gift for abstraction. He didn't think in particulars when it came to violence. He always tried to make his acts of violence swift and clean and painless. Finn had drummed this into him. Even now Jig could hear the old man's melodic voice in his head. *You only need to kill. You don't need to make your victims suffer. In and out with precision, boy, never needless cruelty. This is a war, not a torture chamber.* Walter Whiteford wouldn't have had the time to feel anything. Gone. Like that. Like a candle blown out on an empty Mayfair street. *You don't kill the meek, and you don't kill the innocent. You only kill the harmful, and even then you do it with economy and speed and grace.*

Economy, speed, grace. Jig remembered how Finn, at the point of farewell, had foregone his usual firm handshake in favour of an embrace which had been tight and almost painful as if the old man were reluctant at the last to send Jig on such an unmapped errand. There had been none of the usual last-minute instructions, no quiet encouragement, just an odd imploring look in Finn's eyes which had put Jig in mind of a man facing the impossibilities of ever seeing his ambitions realised. It wasn't a look Jig liked to see. For a second it hadn't been Finn's face at all, it had lost buoyancy and strength and resilience, like a mask cast suddenly aside by its wearer. It was more than the loss of money. Jig knew that. It was the loss of all the schemes and plans and uses that the money was good for.

Jig had a sense of sleep coming in on a dark cloud, so he rose and stood in the corridor with the window open and the rainy air blowing against his face. The fresh smell of the nearby sea came rushing towards him.

He had left Dublin before on other missions. But this time, with the wind blowing at his face and the rain on his skin, this time was different for reasons he didn't altogether understand.

He stood at the window and he thought about the great love he had for this country. He thought of the valleys of Glendalough and Immaal and Clara. The bewitching landscape of Kerry and the great peninsulas of Iveragh and Dingle. The towns of Tralee and Inch and Kenmare and that strange uninhabited group of islands called the Blaskets, which sat lonely in the Atlantic tide. Once, the largest of the Blaskets had been called the next parish to America.

America. And goodbye, Mr Pagan.

He watched the rails slide past under the March sky, and he wondered when he'd see Ireland and Finn again.

London

Frank Pagan lived alone in a flat at the top of a Victorian house in Holland Park. There had been a time in his life when he had enjoyed the place, when he'd found himself hurrying home from the office and taking the steps two at a time in his haste. Now when the street door closed behind him, he went up through the dark slowly.

He took out his key when he reached the apartment.

Inside, the air was trapped and stale. He turned on the living-room lamp and poured himself a glass of scotch, which he carried inside the bedroom. The bed was unmade, the room cold. He sat on the edge of the bed without taking off his raincoat. Bleak House, he thought.

His usual method of cutting back the edge of bleakness was to play rock music loudly. He liked it full blast and raucous enough for dainty Miss Gabler in the flat below to rush upstairs complaining about that 'dreadful Negro music' and Pagan would say, Now, now, Hedda (even though her name was Cynthia), we mustn't criticise music on racial grounds, must we? A dose of Little Richard or some early Jerry Lee Lewis usually worked for him, but tonight he didn't want to play the stereo.

His condition was paralysis of the heart.

He reached out across the clutter of the bedside table and touched a framed photograph of his wife, Roxanne, then drew his hand away as if it had been scalded. There was still too much pain here. Sometimes he wondered if it would ever go away entirely. It had been more than two years now and there was still the same old nightmare, there were still times when he'd sit up in the darkened bedroom and smoke cigarettes and imagine he heard the sounds of Roxanne moving in the other rooms.

Once, when he'd drunk too much Chivas Regal, he stumbled through the apartment calling out her name. Banging doors open, slamming them shut, saying his wife's name over and over like some incantation, he stalked her. The rooms were all empty, all dark. He'd never encountered anything like that kind of emptiness before. It was worse than any pain he could ever have imagined.

Dreams, Pagan thought. Roxanne was gone. He glanced at the photograph. It was a fine face with wide bright eyes that were filled with an amused intelligence. The mouth suggested great depths of humour. It was the kind of mouth that had been built for smiling. Sweet Christ, how he had loved her! Even now, he loved her. *But Roxanne was gone*. Then why in the name of God did he keep sensing her presence in this bloody flat?

He got up from the bed and wandered inside the kitchen. There were eggshells in the sink and coffee stains on the surface of the stove. He sat on the kitchen table and finished his drink and his eyes brimmed with moisture. He wiped them with the sleeve of his coat. Maudlin behaviour. He was being drawn down into the morbid centre of himself. He poured a second drink.

'Roxanne,' Pagan whispered. 'Dear Roxanne.'

Outside, a March wind came rushing out of the night, springing through the shrubbery. He heard the branch of a tree knock against the side of the house.

Pagan sat down, fidgeted with his glass. He liked to think of himself as a practical man living in a practical world, one without psychic interference. He liked to think his personal radio was tuned only to what was broadcast in reality, not to ghosts, not to dreams. But what was this presence of Roxanne he kept feeling? Why did he keep talking aloud to a woman who was no longer alive?

Pagan closed his eyes tightly. He didn't need to remember any of this.

Roxanne Pagan, twenty-seven years of age, had died at Christmas, 1984, killed on a Kensington Street. She had been doing some last-minute Christmas shopping. She didn't know that a man called Eddie Rattigan had planted a bomb inside a wastebasket beside a bus stop. She didn't know that her own life was destined to collide with the violent longing of Eddie Rattigan, who later told the police he wanted to make a political statement on behalf of all IRA soldiers held in Northern Irish jails.

Roxanne Pagan had been passing the wastebasket when the explosion took place. Eddie Rattigan's bomb killed seven people and injured a dozen others. Eddie Rattigan's 'political statement' killed Roxanne and tore the heart out of Frank Pagan's life, shattering his world in a matter of a second.

Pagan blinked at the window. He remembered Eddie Rattigan's trial. He recalled the small man's interminable smirk during the whole proceedings. Rattigan was *pleased* with himself. *Pleased* that his bomb had actually worked! After Rattigan was sentenced to life imprisonment Pagan had worked for months on a wild plan to get inside Wormwood Scrubs and kill the man. But the notion of vengeance passed, and he was left with an emptiness that had been with him ever since.

Pagan went into the bedroom. He wanted to sleep but he didn't want to close his eyes because he knew the nightmare would rush in at him again. In this awful dream he was running down that Kensington street towards Roxanne and he was always too late to warn her. He shouted her name until his throat ached but she never heard him, never turned in his direction. Turn! For God's sake, turn! Pagan would scream. Screaming, running. And then the explosion came. Which was when Pagan always woke, shivering and afraid and racked by unspeakable grief.

He removed his coat and tossed it across a chair. Then he kicked off his shoes and sat with his back to a pillow, his glass in his hand. He understood that he was a lonely man, but he'd come to terms with that. Once or twice since Roxanne's death he'd gone out, hitting a couple of bars where single people stared morosely at one another and casual sexual assignations were made with all the passion of people selecting lamb chops out of a butcher's window. The whole scene depressed Pagan. If he didn't belong there, where did he belong? Here in this apartment with a phantom? Was that his future?

He smoked a cigarette. He had a third drink. Halfway through it his front doorbell rang. He glanced at the bedside clock: 9:45. He went inside the living-room, where he switched on the intercom button.

'Who is it?' he said.

'Drummond, Mr Pagan. It's Jerry Drummond.' The voice crackled up from the street.

'What do you want?'

'I have a message for you.'

'I'm listening, Jerry.'

'Not like this. Let me come up, Mr Pagan.'

Pagan sighed. He pressed the buzzer that opened the street door. He heard the sound of footsteps on the stairs. Then Drummond's soft knock at the door.

A small man with pointed ears, Jerry Drummond wore long sidewhiskers and invariably had a green silk scarf knotted at his throat. His nickname, perhaps predictably, was the Leprechaun.

'I'm not meaning to disturb you, Mr Pagan,' Drummond said as he came into the room.

'It's late, Jerry.'

'So it is, so it is.' Jerry Drummond sat down, taking a flat tin from his overcoat. There would be, Pagan knew, the usual elaborate performance of rolling a cigarette, which Drummond did with all the intensity of an architect designing a cathedral.

'And how is yerself today?' the Leprechaun asked.

Pagan nodded. 'I've known better days, Jerry.'

The little man lit his cigarette and his cheeks subsided into huge hollows as he puffed. 'Haven't we all known better days?'

'What do you have for me, Jerry?' Pagan asked.

'Oh,' said the Leprechaun mysteriously, twinkling like a Christmas tree light.

'I haven't got all night. You said you had a message, Jerry.'

The little man smoked furiously. At one time, he'd been a promising apprentice jockey at a stable in Newmarket, but a fondness for alcohol and a lack of discipline had finished his career quickly. Now, he was an odd-job man who was also one of Pagan's many connections to the puzzle known as Ireland.

'It's from some of the boys,' the Leprechaun said.

'Which boys?'

'I'm not at liberty to say, Mr Pagan.'

'Then I don't want to hear, Jerry. You know what I think about anonymous messages.'

Jerry Drummond was using his open left hand as an ashtray. 'I do, I do,' he said. 'But

I'm just a simple messenger. I can't tell you everything you think you want to know, can I? A messenger has only limited information, after all. He's like a walk-on part in a play, when you think about it – '

Sighing, Pagan interrupted. He knew the little man could gab all night long, going off at tangents. 'Who sent you, Jerry?'

Drummond was quiet for a time. 'Shall we just say it's a certain party interested in bringing Jig to justice?'

'Jig?'

'Right.'

'What about Jig?' A tiny flutter went through Pagan's heart.

Drummond leaned forward, looking conspiratorial. 'I'm to tell you that Jig is on his way to the United States of America, Mr Pagan.'

'And why would Jig be going to the United States, Jerry?'

'I understand there's a small matter of some missing money to be settled, Mr Pagan.'

Pagan finished his scotch and set the glass down. 'How do you know this, Jerry?'

'Tut-tut,' Drummond said, his eyes wide.

Pagan said, 'If you expect me to believe your story, Jerry, you'd better tell me its source. Otherwise, I'm going to throw you out of here. Bodily.'

'Ah, the English don't know the meaning of hospitality, do they now?' the Leprechaun smiled. He tilted his tiny pear-shaped face back and stared at the ceiling. 'Let me say this much, seeing as how you threatened me with physical violence just then and me being a peaceable sort of fellow and all. Let me just say the message comes from members of the Free Ulster Volunteers, Mr Pagan.'

'That bunch of scum?'

'They're fine men, Mr Pagan. They believe in keeping Northern Ireland for Britain. Could anybody have a finer goal than that, eh?'

The Free Ulster Volunteers. In recent years Frank Pagan had become bewildered by the proliferation of groups and sects that had arisen in Ireland. There was a thicket of them, each with its own initials. And they spawned themselves on almost a daily basis. Even with the help of computers, it was impossible to keep track. On the Protestant side, Pagan had heard such names as the Tartan Hand, Tara (an allegedly homosexual group of anti-Catholics), the Ulster Defence Association, the Ulster Freedom Fighters, the New Apprentice Boys, the Free Ulster Liberation Army. The Catholic IRA had split into cells and groups, some of them of a religious nature, some with Marxist objectives, others with ties to terrorist groups in Germany and Italy. Disenchanted IRA members had formed their own outfits. The Irish Liberation Army. The New Sinn Fein. The Catholic Brotherhood. More recently Pagan had heard whispers concerning something called the Association of the Wolfe, supposedly run by a man named Finn, who appeared nowhere in Pagan's data banks. Some of these organisations were chimerical. Others exaggerated their membership. A few had power. Finn was said to have his hands on the bankbooks, but whoever Finn was – and Pagan suspected the name was a pseudonym – he obviously led a secluded life, far removed from the conflicts of Belfast and Derry. Certainly, none of Pagan's sources knew the man.

Pagan sighed. Irish goulash. Rich, impenetrable, inedible, filled as it was with alphabet macaroni.

The Free Ulster Volunteers was a Belfast-based clandestine group of Protestant thugs who specialised in torturing and killing anybody with a connection to the IRA. When they couldn't find a bona fide IRA member, any passing Catholic would do. Now and then, they slipped over the border into the Republic to make a hit.

The FUV was allegedly connected, in tenuous ways, with a Belfast zealot called the Reverend Ivor McInnes, a pastor without a church. He'd been ejected from the official Presbyterian Church for preaching sermons designed to encourage his congregation in the belief that Catholicism, like cigarettes, was bad for your health and should therefore be abolished. McInnes still wore his dog collar and drew huge crowds of Ulster Loyalists to hear him speak in public places. He was one of those fire and brimstone shouters who could raise the temperature of a mob to boiling point. He was a man of many gifts – charm, eloquence, and that nebulous quality called charisma – but Pagan considered them wasted ones. Ivor was utterly committed, some would say blindly so, to a Northern Ireland free of any Catholic influence. He didn't want his own little domain, all five thousand square miles of it, all one million and a half souls, tainted by popery, dogged by priests and nuns. Pagan had never been able to prove conclusively that Ivor was the power behind the FUV. If he was, he somehow contrived cunningly to keep himself removed from the organisation.

'Exactly who in the Free Ulster Volunteers sent you here? Ivor McInnes?'

'Now, Mr Pagan. We all know the Reverend isn't associated with the FUV, don't we?'

'Don't make me laugh, Jerry.'

The Leprechaun smoothed out the folds in his coat. 'Can't we just say the FUV sent me here and leave it at that?'

'It's not precise enough, Jerry. Give me a name. Give me something authentic.'

The Leprechaun sighed. It was a long-drawn-out sound. 'One name, that's all.'

'One's enough,' Pagan said.

'John Waddell.'

'Waddell?' Frank Pagan brought an image of Waddell to mind. He was a short man with a sharp face that was practically all snout. Eight months ago Pagan had interviewed John Waddell in connection with the killing of an IRA man in the London suburb of Chalk Farm. At the time, Pagan hadn't been impressed by Waddell, who struck him as strangely timid and not at all the kind of material the FUV would use in an assassination. He'd released Waddell for lack of evidence, convinced that the man hadn't had anything to do with the murder. Too scared. Too gun-shy. Now he wasn't so certain. The FUV absorbed all types, especially the meek and the cowardly, who found the courage to act only when they were concealed under the umbrella of a movement. 'Your information came *directly* from John Waddell?'

'I'm not saying,' Drummond answered.

'But he's involved.'

'Mr Pagan, you asked for a name, I gave you one. Don't be pressing me for more than I can give you.'

Pagan thought for a second. 'Why would the Free Ulster Volunteers want me to have this message, Jerry?'

'You're looking for Jig, are you not?'

Pagan nodded. His mouth was dry. He filled two glasses with scotch and gave one to Drummond.

Drummond smacked his lips and said, 'You've got the resources to find him. You and the Yanks between you. You can find him before he kills anybody else.' The word 'kills' came out of the Leprechaun's mouth as *culls*. Pagan disliked the hard accent of Belfast. The Dublin lilt, by contrast, could be musical and hypnotic.

'How does the FUV come by this information?' Pagan asked.

'That's something I wouldn't know,' Drummond answered. 'I'm only told so much, Mr Pagan, and it would be fruitless for me to speculate, wouldn't it now? But the members of the FUV would like for you to get your hands on Jig and hang the bastard. They don't like seeing somebody going around killing politicians who are sympathetic to the free Protestants of the North.'

Pagan sipped his drink. 'We don't hang people in this country, Jerry.'

'More's the pity.'

'I almost agree with you,' Pagan said.

There was a silence in the room. The missing money the Leprechaun had mentioned was presumably the same that had been on the *Connie O'Mara*. Attached, Pagan guessed, to the Courier's wrist. But there was something here that didn't quite fit, and he felt faintly uneasy. How the hell did the Free Ulster Volunteers get this information? How did they get so close to Jig that they knew his movements? Or had Jerry Drummond been sent here to convey false information? But that made absolutely no sense. Why would the little man come here with a pack of lies?

He looked at the Leprechaun. 'What else can you tell me, Jerry?'

'I've already told you a wee bit more than I intended, Mr Pagan. What else is there?'

'America's a big place.'

Drummond finished his drink and stood up. He was twinkling again and there was a certain mischief in his eyes. 'Oh, didn't I mention New York, Mr Pagan?'

'No, you didn't mention New York.'

'And Father Tumulty? Did I mention him?'

Pagan shook his head. This was so typical of Drummond. He'd dole his message out in fragments, getting as much mileage out of it as he possibly could. He was like a comedian taking a tortuous, suspenseful route to his punch line.

'Who's Father Tumulty?' Pagan asked.

'Sounds like a priest to me,' and Drummond smiled.

Pagan heard the night wind spring up again. 'Is that the complete message now, Jerry?'

'Aye,' Drummond seemed hesitant. 'Wait. There's one other thing. Jig sometimes uses a passport made out in the name of John Doyle.'

Pagan took the empty glass out of Drummond's hand. 'Why don't your friends in the FUV go after Jig themselves?'

'All the way to New York, Mr Pagan? They couldn't afford that kind of expense. You, on the other hand, you travel all expenses paid, don't you? Besides, they don't have your resources, Mr Pagan. Nor your expertise. And you'd have the Americans to help you out, with their computers and all. The only computer I ever saw belonging to a member of the FUV was a small Japanese thing he used for playing Pac-Man. Then it went on the blink.'

Pagan watched the little man a moment. 'You really expect me to drop everything and transport myself to New York on your say-so, Jerry?'

The Leprechaun looked hurt. 'Mr Pagan, have I ever given you false information? Have I ever done that?'

'No.'

'Didn't I tell you about that shipment of rifles in Ostend? The ones in cool boxes marked butter that were destined for Dublin? Didn't I do that for you? And wasn't that true?'

Pagan nodded his head.

'Didn't I tell you about a small IRA bomb factory right here in Fulham? Right here on your own doorstep? Was that a lie?'

'Jerry, your information has always been high quality. But this is something quite different.'

'I don't see why you would disbelieve me now.'

'Maybe because I don't exactly trust your FUV friends, Jerry.'

The Leprechaun got out of his chair. 'Cross my heart, Mr Pagan. This is all on the level. Jig is on his way to New York City. And you'd be a fool to ignore that fact.' 'Fool' pronounced *fule*.

Pagan watched the little man go out. Alone again, he found the apartment smaller than before. The walls pressed in on him. It made sense, he thought, that Jig would be the one to track down the missing capital. The man was a hunter. He had predatory instincts and the capability of vanishing on the wind. But how did the FUV get hold of this information?

The question turned over in his mind again, and he had the feeling he was missing something, something important. Puzzled, he went back inside the bedroom and sat down. For a moment he tried to imagine Jig's face. A young man, an unremarkable face you wouldn't look twice at in the street, drab unassuming clothes. Perhaps a nervous mannerism. A tic in the jaw. A fingernail biter. A way of smoking cigarettes right down to the filter. Nicotine stains. Slightly discoloured teeth. And maybe there was a light in his eye, something that suggested intensity. He had to be intense, committed to his purpose. Highly trained too. The kind of training that wasn't available in Ireland. The kind you went abroad to get in places like Libya and Cuba.

Pagan lay back across the bed. Had the American suppliers of the money somehow turned their thinking around and seized their capital back on the high seas?

Pagan sat up now. The sense of being perplexed wouldn't leave him. There was something a little askew, out of joint. He couldn't think what except that there were small threads he couldn't quite stitch together. They kept unravelling in his mind.

He reached for the photograph of Roxanne and held it tilted under the bedside lamp so that the glass caught the yellow glow of electricity.

'New York City,' Pagan said to his ghost. 'It's been a long time.'

7 Dun Laoghaire, Republic of Ireland

Finn woke in his dark bedroom, his throat dry. He pushed himself into an upright position, and there was a pain at the back of his head. It was the whiskey he'd drunk at Molly's. Now he had one hell of a hangover. He should have known better – his old body couldn't take the drink the way it used to. Sweet Jesus! He could remember times when he'd wake with a big black dog of a hangover and start drinking right away and go on for three or four days at a time.

He left the room and stepped out onto the landing.

Halfway down the stairs he stopped. He listened to the darkness. He had a fine instinct for the night. He thought sometimes he had a personal angel who whispered nocturnal warnings in his ear. In the distance he heard the cry of an owl. But there was some other thing too, something he couldn't altogether place, like the soft sound of an animal moving in the undergrowth.

He reached the bottom step and looked across the room filled with harps. There was thin crystal moonlight falling through the window. He stood motionless, listening. The owl had gone. But there was still something else, an undercurrent.

Finn padded inside the kitchen, bare feet slapping floorboards. He drew a glass of water from the tap and devoured it quickly. He rinsed the glass, because he was a tidy man and had always been fastidious in his way, perhaps because he'd lived a solitary life without a wife to help him. He was married to the Cause like a bloody nun married to Christ. If he could turn back the clocks of his life, what he'd do was marry Molly Newbigging and get a decent job and settle down with a big brood of kids. He thought of Molly's white thighs and her large rounded breasts and that way she had of seeing straight through to the bones of him.

He left the kitchen, moving along a narrow hallway in the direction of his small study. There was a loaded pistol in his desk. It was a Mauser that dated from the 1920s and it had once belonged to old Dan Breen, commandant of the Third Tipperary Brigade of the IRA. The pistol was of great sentimental value to Finn because it had been given to him personally by Breen shortly before the old fellow died in 1969.

Finn stepped inside his study. He stared at the gun, then reached down for it and picked it up, holding it loosely in his right hand. The feel of the weapon made him think of the first time he'd ever entrusted Jig with a task. It had happened during their third or fourth meeting, which had taken place on a cold morning at Glasnevin Cemetery.

Finn, who was invariably spooked by places of death because he resented anything as disruptive as the act of dying, had stared for a long time into the boy's eyes. What the hell did he really know about this young man anyway? After a few clandestine encounters, what could he really say he'd learned about the young man's history? The boy constantly dismissed his past as irrelevant. He was as much a mystery as he'd been in the beginning, and the only thing Finn didn't doubt was his commitment to justice and his yearning for action. These were real enough. But there were walls around him still, and Finn was uneasy with men who erected barricades. If he was ever to know this young man, if he was ever to cross the wall, he was going to have to take the first step himself. A big step – because its only basis was Finn's own hunch, his instinct that the boy could prove valuable to the Association of the Wolfe and the Cause in general. There were times in one's life when intuition overrode the dictates of sweet reason, and this was going to be one of them. And Finn, who had an almost arrogant pride in his ability to judge character, had an instinct about the boy that was almost as clear as a melody in his head.

A certain man has to be eliminated.

Who and where? Jig asked.

Don't you want to know the why of it, boy?

Jig shook his head and looked between rows of tombstones. *I know what you stand for. If you consider this man your enemy, what else do I need to know?*

I'm flattered by your trust in me, Finn had answered. *But you've got a lot to learn. You trust too easily. You react too quickly. You're too bloody impatient.*

Maybe I need a teacher, Finn.

Finn had strolled among ancient graves, noticing broken crosses and moss climbing over stone and a bedraggled cat asleep on a fallen marker. He'd studied the names of the dead. O'Hara. Ryan. Corcoran. Fine Irish names. Brendan Behan, whom Finn remembered as a hotblooded young IRA recruit, was buried somewhere at Glasnevin, dead and wasted by drink.

Teach me, Finn, the boy said.

Finn had turned to look at the young man again. He'd seen it then in the boy's face, almost as if a guard had slipped and fallen away. It was the face of a kid anxious to please an elder, a vulnerable look that Finn wouldn't have thought belonged in the boy's repertoire of expressions. It was uncharacteristic and eager, without a hint of toughness, and it was

Finn's first real encounter with what he thought of as the young man's inner self. For the first time, too, Finn felt a strong affection for the boy, a sensation that took him by surprise. It was this moment, in which he perceived Jig's naked enthusiasm, that made Finn take the revolver from the pocket of his overcoat and pass it slowly to the young man.

There's no pleasure in killing, boy, if you're after thrills, I don't need you. Let's get that straight from the start. I don't need a vandal or a hooligan. I want somebody who understands the reasons behind his actions.

I'm not looking for thrills, Finn.

And when you work for me there's no money in it. You'll get enough to keep yourself in food and shelter, but nobody ever got rich from the Cause.

I don't remember ever asking for money, Finn.

It was the answer Finn had expected. *You'd have to go to Belfast*, he said. *A man called Cassidy is doing some damage to us.*

That was all. Cassidy's offence, which the boy hadn't asked about, hadn't even seemed to *care* about, was that he had been talking too freely with the British Army about IRA operations. Jig had gone to Belfast before the end of that same week and shot Cassidy as he was stepping out of a public house called the Butcher's Arms at closing time. One shot, delivered with accuracy. One shot, then Jig was gone. He had the eye of a natural marksman and the affinity of a night creature for the crevices of darkness in which to hide. Later, when the young man had returned to the Republic, Finn had told him that in future he'd need a nom de guerre. *We'll call you Jig*, he'd said. *If you're the dancer I think you might be, it's a damn good name.* I moulded you, Jig, he thought. You gave me the basic edifice and I improved it. And somewhere along the way we came to understand and maybe even love one another a little bit too. And where are you now, Jig? Where the hell have I sent you?

He wished Jig were beside him in this house. He needed the young man's nerve, because his own wasn't what it had been in the old days when he'd been as sharp as a razor and as daring as anything that ever cavorted on a trapeze. The old days! Jesus, the old days had been fine, but they were gone, and what faced him now was the stark reality of danger. With his pistol in front of him, he stepped back into the hallway and moved towards the room with the harps. He went to the window and looked in the direction of the gatehouse.

George Scully, reliable George, was on guard tonight.

Finn breathed on the window-pane. The guardhouse was in darkness, which meant nothing in itself because Scully might have turned out the light simply to enjoy the quiet of the night. George, who had been with Finn for years, had been known to turn the light off and lean against the wall and prop up his feet and breathe the sea air into his lungs while he recited the poems of W. B. Yeats quietly to himself.

A shiver went through Finn. The hairs on the back of his neck bristled. Something was going on out there. Something that pressed upon the whitewashed house and set up a vibration audible only to his ears. He shut his eyes, listened. He thought suddenly of that poor boat hijacked on the high seas, he thought of the dead men and the missing money, and the shipload of arms that had slipped away from him. He was sick to his heart.

Eyes open now, pistol forward. *Beware, Finn.* It was the voice of his angel. He could hear it clearly.

He moved among the harps, his pistol trained on the doorway.

He held his breath and stood very still. It was always possible, he supposed, that someone had overpowered Scully down there in the gatehouse. But there would have been shooting, wouldn't there? Scully would have fired off one of his weapons, wouldn't he? Unless he'd been taken out suddenly, with no warning and no time to defend himself.

Finn moved very slightly.

His heart, his bloody heart, thumped upon his ribs like a rabbit stuck in a snare. He moved an inch, two inches, edging between harps, going in the direction of the doorway. Dan Breen's Mauser was heavy in his hand.

Out in the hallway now. Facing the front door. Waiting.

Was that the wind that rattled the shrubbery and set it shaking?

He moved slowly down the narrow hallway.

He placed one hand on the door handle.

Then he drew the door open and peered out into the night, his Mauser raised for action.

There were two men outside, both holding automatic weapons. Finn barely had time to register this fact before he heard the first few rounds. He thought it strange that he felt nothing although he knew he'd been hit.

He staggered backwards down the corridor into the room of harps, aware of blood seeping out of his body, conscious of the hushed voice that said *I told you, Finn. Beware. I told you that*. Finn skidded across the floor of the big room, his legs abruptly cut out from beneath his body, his feet slithering over pools of his own lost blood, and he stumbled against a harp, his head tipping forward between the strings of the instrument so that he was stuck there like some beast cruelly trapped, aware of death coming in on wings. Finn gazed at the window where the halfhearted moon floated in the terrible night sky. There were footsteps behind him. There were other voices in the room. They made sounds he was beyond understanding because he was listening to something else.

He was listening to his angel, whom he had come to recognise as Death.

Come to me, Finn.

He blinked his eyes.

Then the room was filled with more gunfire, which he heard as a deaf man might hear thunder. Vibrations, not sounds. His face slid between harp strings, and the pistol dropped from his hand, and he went down slowly into his own blood where he lay very still.

Waddell placed the Stoeger Max II rifle on the floor. He was shaking violently, and when he looked down at Finn's body, the long white hair covered with great scarlet slashes, he wanted to be sick. He put one hand up to his mouth. Houlihan came into the room and stared at the wasted body and there was no expression at all on his face.

'I thought he'd never die,' Houlihan said. 'Did you see the way he was bouncing like a rubber ball about this fucking room? I thought he'd never go down! Tough old shit.'

Waddell nodded his head. There was excitement in Houlihan's voice.

'He had a lot of heart,' Houlihan remarked.

Waddell wanted to be elsewhere. Another city. Another galaxy. He needed a drink, something to settle him down. Something to calm him. He looked around the room, found a bottle of schnapps and drank from it quickly.

'Ah, John, you need to develop an attitude,' Houlihan said. 'You need to be as hard as a nail.'

Waddell said nothing.

'Finn's a casualty of war. That's all,' Houlihan said. He took the bottle from Waddell. He didn't drink. Instead, he turned the cap over in the palm of his hand so that Waddell could see several perforations in the metal.

'Tricky,' Houlihan said. 'But we won't be needing this any more.'

'Is that what I think it is?' Waddell asked.

'A small microchip listening device. The blessings of Yankee technology. But our man Scully won't be listening to Finn any more, will he?' Houlihan stuck the cap in his pocket. 'For one thing, Scully's probably a thousand miles away by this time. And God knows, *nobody* will be listening to Finn any more.' Houlihan laughed. It was an empty, mirthless sound, like a cough.

Waddell felt the schnapps heat his chest. He looked into his companion's eyes, which were hard and cold.

Houlihan said, 'Call Belfast, John. Tell them we succeeded. They're waiting to hear. Take your share of the credit.'

Waddell went out of the room. Credit, he thought. He didn't need credit like this. He found a telephone in Finn's office. Houlihan came into the room behind him.

'What are you waiting for, John? We don't have all night.'

Waddell put his hand on the receiver. He felt weak all of a sudden.

'Go on,' Houlihan said. 'I know they'll be anxious to hear Finn's out of the way. It means the green light for America.'

America, Waddell thought.

He picked up the telephone.

'It's a strange thing about blood,' Houlihan was saying. 'It's all the same, John. Black man or white man. Protestant or Catholic. It's the same taste. No difference. English blood or American. It all looks and tastes the same.'

American blood, Waddell thought. He wondered how Houlihan knew about the taste of the stuff.

He dialled the number in Belfast, and after a few moments it was answered by the Reverend Ivor McInnes, who spoke with a pronounced English mainland accent that Waddell knew was Liverpool.

'It's done,' Waddell said.

'On the contrary,' the voice answered. 'It's only just beginning.'

8 New York City

Joseph X. Tumulty couldn't quite believe that he had received the call after all this time. He had lived with the knowledge that there was always some slight possibility of such a thing, a shadow that lay over the life he had built for himself here, but he'd never actually believed it. But there it was. *The call from Ireland*. Now he was nervous and tense and possessed with the uneasy feeling that threads were being pulled in the night, that his destiny was being woven by hands he couldn't see. It wasn't a good feeling at all. He was a man who liked to be in charge of his own affairs.

He stood in the doorway of St Finbar's Mission on Canal Street in the grubby southern part of Manhattan, his black coat drawn up at the collar, his fighter's nose made red by a chill river wind. From the kitchen behind him came the smell of food and the sounds of hungry men, quite beyond the dictates of good manners, attacking their plates of stew. To many people it might have been an unpleasant noise, but to Joe Tumulty it had a gladdening effect.

He looked along the sidewalk. He'd been thinking about the call ever since he'd received it twenty-four hours ago. He was listening still to the voice of Finn on the telephone – that mellifluous singing voice that could seduce and flatter and cajole and make any man believe that there were indeed fairies at the bottom of his garden. But this time there had been something else in Finn's voice, and Joe Tumulty had been trying to pin the quality down for almost a day now. What was it? Sometimes Tumulty thought it was weariness, at other times fear. He wasn't sure. All he knew was that Finn's call had disturbed the equilibrium of his life and that he didn't want any conflict between the work he was doing on Canal Street and the demands of the Cause.

A drunk lay about fifteen feet down the sidewalk. Tumulty had been watching him for the last couple of minutes. The man lay face down, arms outstretched. He wore a pair of pants at least three sizes too large for him. His threadbare overcoat was pulled up around his waist, revealing a thin cotton shirt that was no protection from the bitter wind. The man could die there and nobody would care. He could die among the plastic bags of trash and the roaches. But Joseph Tumulty wasn't about to let any man die within shouting distance of St Finbar's, which was named after the sixth-century founder of the City of Cork.

'Are you going to help him, Father Joe?'

Tumulty turned. The man who'd asked the question was known only as Scissors which was said to be a reference to the trade of barber he'd once carried out. Now, five nights out of seven, Scissors was drunk. Tonight he happened to be sober. He had a ravaged face and the kind of luminescent eyes you sometimes see on street people – a result of nutritional deficiency, a lack of vitamins, and a totally depleted body. It was a look Joe Tumulty had come to know very well on Canal Street.

'Of course I am,' Tumulty said.

He put out one hand and squeezed Scissors' frail shoulder. There was misfortune everywhere, Tumulty thought. And most of it seemed to congregate here at the southern tip of Manhattan. Tumulty attacked human misery wherever he found it. Father Joe, crusader. The point was, if he didn't do it, then people like the man who lay there right now would probably perish.

The former barber blinked at the body on the sidewalk. 'He's a young one,' Scissors said.

Tumulty moved down the steps. He knew that alcohol was no great respecter of age. All kinds of people found their way to St Finbar's Mission, young and old, skilled and unskilled – and what they had in common was a descent from society, from lives that might have been useful. Tumulty liked to think he could give them back some form of hope. He fed them, often clothed them, prayed for them, counselled them. He entered their broken lives and applied the only salve he knew, which was to care for them even when they had forgotten how to care for themselves.

As he crossed the sidewalk he was conscious of a tan-coloured car parked about half a block away. It had been parked there for the past two hours. The man who sat behind the wheel appeared to be engrossed in a book. The whole thing made Tumulty nervous. It wasn't exactly the kind of place where a man would station his car to do a quiet spot of reading. His first response was that the car contained an agent of the bloody Internal Revenue Service. The IRS was always on his back these days, ever since he had split from the official Catholic Church to create his own mission on Canal Street. The tax-exempt status of charities and religious orders had been coming under a lot of scrutiny lately. It wasn't that the government was after Tumulty's income, because that was laughably small. But they could cause all kinds of nuisances by examining his accounts and asking to see cancelled cheques, just to make sure St Finbar's was what it claimed to be – a non-profit venture. Besides – and this was something he didn't like to think about, something he'd chosen to ignore – there was a certain bank account, held in his own name, that contained money Finn had given him and that he had absolutely no way of explaining.

Maybe he was being paranoid. Maybe Finn's phone call had made him that way. He suddenly felt that the night was filled with things he couldn't trust.

He crossed the sidewalk. He bent down beside the young man and very lightly placed a hand on the man's arm. The young man didn't move. Joe Tumulty moved his hand to touch the side of the man's face. The smell of booze was strong, as if it had been stitched into the threads of the man's coat. Tumulty turned his face to one side a moment. His eyes watered.

'Get up,' Tumulty said.

The man was still.

Tumulty slipped his hand under the man's face and raised it slowly up from the hard sidewalk. He was about thirty and appeared to be in good health. His face was pale but showed none of the usual signs of decay Tumulty had come to expect on people like this. The lips were open a little way, and the teeth were good. Whoever this drunk was, he hadn't been on the streets for very long. Tumulty stared a moment in the direction of the parked car. The shadowy figure inside had his head tilted back and appeared now to be asleep.

'Can you get up?' Tumulty asked. 'I'll help you.'

The young man's eyes opened.

'Put your arm round my shoulder,' Tumulty said. 'We'll get you indoors.'

'Who are you?' the young man asked.

'Joseph Tumulty. They sometimes call me Father Joe.'

The young man closed his eyes again. There was a faint smile on his lips.

'Is it safe?' he asked.

'Safe?'

'Is it safe to come inside?'

'Of course it is. What do you – ' Tumulty didn't finish his question because the young man's eyes opened again, and they were clear, bright, with no bleariness, no bloodshot quality. Joseph Tumulty was remembering Finn's phone call again. He was remembering Finn saying *Take good care of him, Joe. He's a fine lad*. This is the one, Tumulty thought, and he felt a strange little sensation around his heart. He had a slight difficulty in catching his breath.

'You can never be too sure,' the young man said. He slung his arm around Joe Tumulty's shoulder and raised himself to a standing position.

'You're from Finn,' Tumulty said, and his voice had become a whisper.

The young man nodded.

Tumulty stared at the light falling from the doorway of St Finbar's and the outline of the man known as Scissors who stood at the top of the steps, then he glanced once in the direction of the parked car.

Take good care of him, Joe.

'You're Jig,' Tumulty said.

'The very same.'

The wind that blew off the Hudson brought ice with it, hardening dead branches and imparting a spare look to the skyscrapers. Frank Pagan thought the city resembled a large ice palace. He had a room at the Parker Meridien on West 57th Street, a costly hotel that his per diem expenses didn't cover. When he'd last been in New York he'd stayed with

Roxanne at the Gotham, which was now a hollow locked shell with boarded-up windows on the corner of 55th and 5th. A deserted hotel was fitting somehow. A black epitaph.

Four years ago. The first year of their marriage. An anniversary trip. What he recalled now was Roxanne's flushed excitement in Manhattan, how like a small child she'd been, going on Fifth Avenue and strolling through Tiffany's and Cartier's and Harry Winston's, asking endless questions of patient sales clerks. Pagan had bought her a silver locket at Fortunoff's, which she'd been wearing the day she died. Pagan wore the locket now. City of Memories. How could he feel anything but uneasy in this town?

On his first night at the Parker, when he was still groggy from jet-lag, Pagan had a meeting with an FBI agent called Arthur Zuboric in the piano bar. Zuboric, a squat man with a Zapata moustache and a suntan achieved under the lamps of a health spa, had the look of a mournful bandit. He wasn't exactly happy with the notion of helping Frank Pagan, since he had a caseload up to here, but the order had come down from Bureau headquarters in Washington, so what could he do? Reciprocity was the catchword here. I'll scratch your back, sometime in the future you'll scratch mine. So here he was scratching Frank Pagan and listening to Broadway show tunes on a piano and wondering about the limey's clothes.

Baggy tweed jacket, bright shirt, blue jeans, no tie. The casual look. Zuboric had the feeling, though, that there wasn't anything casual about Frank Pagan himself. The face was too intense. The mouth reminded Zuboric of a tight rubber band, and the grey eyes had a fierce quality. The word Zuboric had heard about Frank Pagan was *determined*.

The guy had built himself a solid reputation in the Special Branch at Scotland Yard, where he'd specialised in anti-terrorist tactics. Once, Pagan had been involved in a shoot-out with Libyan terrorists in a London street. He killed three that day. On another occasion, he'd captured some Italian anarchists after a chase through London Airport. Somewhere along the way he'd been given his own section, practically independent of the Yard, thus causing some resentment among the older hands, who didn't like Frank Pagan's style or the way he dressed or the fact he wasn't quite forty yet. They envied his autonomy. The term for Frank Pagan, Zuboric decided, was *maverick*. All this stuff was in the file Washington had hurriedly put together for Zuboric. It was impressive material, but he wished the English wouldn't go dragging their Irish problem into the United States. Who the fuck needed that? Bunch of micks with guns, spouting shit about freedom.

He stuffed some peanuts in his mouth. The piano was giving him a royal headache. 'We ran your Father Tumulty through the computer, Frank. Mind if I call you Frank? Call me Artie. Arthur's an old man's name, I always think.'

Pagan didn't mind what the agent called him. He was only interested in Tumulty.

'Clean as a whistle,' Zuboric went on. 'So I put a field agent on it who tells me there's only one priest in the whole of New York City called Tumulty. Joseph X.'

Zuboric tasted his rum and Coke and made a face. 'Uncommon name,' he said. 'The thing is, this Joseph X. Tumulty isn't a priest any more. Seems he either left the RC Church or got himself thrown out for some reason. Whatever, Tumulty runs a mission called St Finbar's down on Canal Street.'

Pagan looked at the pianist absently, then turned his thoughts to the idea of a lapsed priest having a connection with Jig. Irish labyrinths, little connections between this person and that, this furtive group with some other, on and on into the maze. Pagan thought a moment about the Leprechaun and the Free Ulster Volunteers and their alleged leader, the Reverend Ivor McInnes. Now there was a strange link, a failed jockey and a Presbyterian minister. And here was another, a lapsed priest and an assassin. Only in the murky world of Irish terrorism, Pagan thought. Only there could you find these weird bonds.

Zuboric said, 'The Immigration and Naturalisation Service records say that Father Tumulty entered the United States in October 1978 from Ireland. He came complete with permanent residence status as a priest. His church was Our Lady of the Sorrows on Staten Island, where he stayed two years. Since then he's been caring for broken souls on Canal Street.'

Zuboric drained his glass. 'According to INS records, Joseph Tumulty came fresh out of a seminary in Bantry to the United States. The INS always runs a police check on potential immigrants in their country of origin. Tumulty was clean in Ireland too, Frank.'

'Clean or very clandestine,' Pagan said. 'I've known priests sympathetic to the IRA. They get involved in a little gunrunning on the side. Or they skim the collection plate to make contributions. A little adventure compensates for the stress of celibacy.'

'No doubt,' Zuboric remarked. 'Maybe this Tumulty is a sympathiser. But if he is, he's playing his cards pretty close to his chest.'

Pagan sat back in his chair. 'If he's Jig's contact in the United States, then he can't be Mr Clean altogether.'

Zuboric fidgeted with his empty glass. 'I guess,' he said. 'I put a man on Canal Street. But what am I supposed to tell him, Frank? Keep your eyes open for a guy you don't know what he looks like?

'Has your man talked to Tumulty?'

Zuboric shook his head. 'I didn't want to take that step before I talked to you.'

'Good,' Pagan said. He didn't like the idea of some FBI field agent trudging over territory he thought of as his own.

Zuboric said, 'So far as somebody using a passport in the name of John Doyle, Immigration has no record of anyone by that name. It doesn't mean much. Your man could have entered illegally through Canada, or he could have come into the US under another name.' Zuboric paused. 'What's your next move?'

'Canal Street. Talk to Tumulty.'

Zuboric sighed. He wondered what kind of metal Frank Pagan was made of. Guy gets off a plane after a five-hour flight through time zones and wants to start work right away. Zuboric played with the word *obsessed* for a moment. He'd seen obsessed law enforcement officers before. He'd seen how something unsolved just nibbled away at them until they were completely devoured and more than somewhat insane. Maybe Frank Pagan was wandering towards the abyss.

Zuboric said nothing for a moment. His present caseload involved a kidnapping in White Plains, a group of Communist dissidents suspected of illegal arms purchases in the Bronx, and a Lebanese diplomat who was smuggling dope in the diplomatic pouch. He didn't need Frank Pagan's problems. He didn't need a priest who might be an IRA sleeper. He didn't need some Irish assassin wandering around his turf. There were times in Artie Zuboric's life when he wondered what it was that he did *need*, periods of uncertainty when he played with such notions as 'career moves' and 'upward mobility', neither of which seemed appropriate within the structure of the Bureau, where promotion depended on the incomprehensible whim of the Director. Zuboric often longed for a life where the pressures were less weighty and the rewards somewhat more tangible. What had the goddam Bureau ever done for him anyhow? He had one broken marriage behind him and now he was in love with a girl called Charity who danced in a topless bar, a girl whom he wanted to marry but who had continually spurned him because she wanted no part of any man gung ho enough to be associated with the feds. Zuboric spent a lot of time thinking about ways of getting Charity to accept him. Money and good prospects might have helped. It galled

Zuboric to think of his beloved Charity flashing her tits in front of drooling strangers. He wanted to take her away from all that.

'I don't understand why you can't settle this Irish crap once and for all, Frank. Why don't you just pull your soldiers out of Ulster and tell the Irish to go fuck themselves? What is it? Some colonial hangover?

Frank Pagan smiled. 'Why don't *you* do something about stopping the flow of American money into IRA coffers?' he asked.

Zuboric said, 'Tell me how I can dictate what private citizens do with their money, Frank. Then maybe I can help you. Besides, we have a President who's a stage Irishman, and he's got an enormous Irish-American vote around here, which he isn't going to throw away by legislating against mick fund-raisers. And if they choose to send bucks to some rebels, what's he gonna do? Anyhow, I'm not absolutely convinced there's much more than chump change flowing from here to Ireland.'

Chump change, Pagan thought. Colourful Americanism. But Zuboric was quite wrong. There was far more than chump change leaving the United States. Both men went outside. The wind off the East River blew scraps of paper along the sidewalks. Zuboric shivered. He thought Pagan looked immune to the cold.

'You got a weapon, Frank?'

'I brought a Bernadelli in my luggage,' Pagan replied.

Zuboric shivered again. 'Don't go waving it in public. The local cops frown on that kind of ostentation. They don't like foreigners with guns, even if your business here is lawful.'

'It's a precaution,' Pagan said. 'I don't like guns.'

'Yeah,' Zuboric said. He whistled for a cab. A dirty yellow vehicle slid towards the sidewalk. Zuboric told the driver Canal Street.

'You're coming with me?' Pagan asked.

'I'm instructed to extend to you every courtesy, et cetera et cetera. But my orders don't stop there, Frank. I go where you go.'

'It isn't necessary,' Pagan replied. 'I work better alone.'

'Yeah, I bet you do.' Zuboric settled down in the back of the cab. 'But as long as this character Jig is on US territory, your problem is my problem. I wish it was otherwise, believe me. I don't care about the Bog People, Frank. They can blow one another up every hour on the hour, so long as they don't do it in the United States of America. And if Jig has it in mind to track down some missing money, there's probably a good chance of bloodshed. In which case, I want to be around.'

Pagan watched the lights of Broadway flicker past. He didn't like the notion of being dogged by an FBI agent. He liked to work on his own. He had never been a team player, which was why he hadn't fitted in at Special Branch. Too many team players. Too much paperwork. He supposed the FBI was exactly the same. Compartments. People in boxes. Rivalries and grudges and tiny jealousies.

Zuboric said, 'You think this Tumulty guy is going to talk to you, Frank?'

Pagan looked at the agent a moment. Zuboric's suntanned face was incongruous in a wintry city. 'I'm an optimist, Artie.'

'Priests take vows of silence. They're pretty good at keeping secrets.'

'We'll see,' Pagan said.

There were fifty or sixty men inside St Finbar's Mission. They sat at tables or wandered aimlessly around trying to scrounge cigarettes from one another. The kitchen was a large room with an enormous stove located at one side. Stacked against one wall was a large pile of thin mattresses enveloped in sheets of clear plastic. Smoke and cooking smells and the sweaty aroma of despair mingled in the air. A crucifix hung to the wall. Here and there were slogans from Alcoholics Anonymous. THE TWELVE STEPS OF AA. EASY DOES IT. ONE DAY AT A TIME.

Frank Pagan stood on the threshold of the room, gazing in the direction of the counter that surrounded the stove. Faces turned towards him, then away again. They had the nervously furtive expressions of men who have reached the bottom and can't find their way up from the pits.

Pagan moved to the cooking area. Soups and stews were simmering in big aluminium urns. He raised a lid and peered at carrots and onions floating on a greasy brown surface. He realised he hadn't eaten anything since the alleged Beef Wellington on the flight, but his hunger was at one remove from himself, like somebody else's sensation.

He looked round the room. What he felt in the air was mainly a sense of hopelessness that came in waves towards him. Casualties of the system. The unemployed. The alcoholic. The mentally defective. He glanced at Zuboric, who was clearly uneasy here. Pagan leaned against the wall, folding his arms. All those faces: he wondered if any one of them could be Jig.

'Can I be of assistance?'

Pagan turned. The man who asked the question was probably in his early thirties, unshaven, his dark blue coat covered with scuff marks, his dark curly hair uncombed. There was a smell of liquor on his breath and dark circles under his eyes.

'I'm looking for Father Tumulty,' Pagan said.

The man looked quickly in Zuboric's direction, then back at Pagan. 'Who shall I say is asking for him?'

Pagan hesitated. 'He wouldn't know my name.'

Zuboric stepped forward and said, 'Just point us in Tumulty's direction.'

The man rubbed his hands together. 'Father Joe's pretty busy right now.'

'Look,' Zuboric said. 'Either you go get him or we'll go looking for him. It's all the same to me.'

The big-stick approach, Pagan thought. It wasn't always the most fruitful. He watched the man go across the room and out through a door into a hallway. The door closed behind him. Without hesitation, Pagan headed after the man. Zuboric, sighing, followed. The corridor was narrow, badly lit, the air even more stale than inside the kitchen.

There was a flight of stairs at the end of the hallway. Pagan saw the man disappear into the gloom at the top. He went after him. Zuboric, his overcoat flapping, came up behind. When they reached the landing, which was lit by a solitary bare light bulb, they saw a halfway open door in front of them. Through the crack Pagan observed a desk and a lamp. There was no sign of the man they had followed. Instead, another figure appeared in the doorway, a squat man with crewcut hair and powerful arms that hung from rolled-up shirt sleeves.

'Is it taxes?' the man asked.

'Taxes?' Pagan said. He shook his head.

'Only I'm having trouble with the IRS, you see. They questioned my non-profit status. They're always sending people around to see me. People that look a lot like you,' and the man gestured towards Zuboric. 'All I do is feed those poor folk downstairs. I don't see why the IRS would bother me. Are you sure you're not with them?'

'Positive,' Zuboric said.

'I'm Joe Tumulty,' the man said. He looked at Zuboric warily. 'What can I do for you?'

'Let's go in your office,' Zuboric said.

'Certainly, certainly.'

It was a small room. The walls were covered with religious portraits, the desk strewn with papers. Mostly bills, Pagan noticed. He had the impression that St Finbar's Mission wasn't exactly a solvent concern. Many of the invoices had demands stamped on them in red ink. There were several envelopes from the Internal Revenue Service, pale brown and unopened. If Father Joe was a conduit for American money going to Ireland, he certainly wasn't skimming any off the top for himself.

'Please sit,' Tumulty said. He had short blunt fingers. His face was not the kind you'd automatically associate with anything so ethereal as the priesthood. He reminded Frank Pagan of the kind of priest who liked to get down in the dirt with his parishioners or instruct street urchins in the arts of pugilism. There was a quiet toughness about the man, a quality of having been seasoned on the streets. He'd need that kind of quality working in a place like this. 'I don't know your names, gentlemen.' His accent was irish, but it had become refined. There were small American inflections.

'Zuboric. Arthur Zuboric. Federal Bureau of Investigation.' The agent flipped a wallet open, showing his ID.

'Tumulty said, 'Impressive.' Then he looked at Pagan. 'And you?'

'Frank Pagan.'

'London. Am I right?'

'Right.'

'I have an ear for accents,' Tumulty said. He took the IRS envelopes and stacked them in a small pile.

Pagan said, 'You're doing good work downstairs.'

'God's work,' Tumulty said. 'Which you can't always do within the confines of the established Church, alas. It isn't easy either. I locked heads with my church to create this place. And ever since then I believe the bishop has been pulling all kinds of delicate little threads behind the scenes to make life more difficult for me. Sometimes there are inexplicable shortages of food from the city's food banks. Delays in delivery that don't make sense. I often think the bloody bishop is behind this business with the IRS. Spiteful little man.'

'Is that why you left the Church? To do God's work?'

Tumulty nodded. 'I grew dissatisfied. Bishops play golf with realtors. They belong to country clubs. I didn't join the Church to develop a taste for sherry and a knack for parish politics.' He smiled. When he did so the face, which had a slightly battered look, resembled a baseball glove that has seen one season too many. Pagan guessed Tumulty was somewhere in his late forties.

'So you know I left the Church, do you? It doesn't surprise me. I heard somebody had been asking questions on the street. I thought it was a tax snoop. The FBI indeed! Should I be flattered or afraid?'

Zuboric tapped a foot impatiently. 'You don't have anything to be afraid of, do you?'

'Now that depends.' Tumulty leaned forward into the direct light of the desk lamp and said, 'Since you gentlemen know a little something about me, isn't it fair that you tell me something of yourselves? What brings you to St Finbar's? It can't be the cuisine, I'm sure.'

'Your name cropped up in connection with an investigation – '

'My name?' Tumulty laughed. 'I can't imagine my name coming up in the context of any investigation unless it's something to do with the bloody IRS. What are you investigating anyway?'

'Murder,' Zuboric said.

'Ahhh.' Tumulty sat back in his chair. 'And who's been killed?'

Frank Pagan stood up. Instead of answering Tumulty's question, he asked one of his own. 'What connections do you have in Ireland, Joe?'

'By connections, d'you mean family? Friends? I have a great many –'

Pagan shook his head. 'I'm talking about political contacts.'

'I'm not a political animal.'

Zuboric hunched over his chair and said, 'That's not what we hear, Joe.'

'You've got poor information then.'

Pagan walked around the room. He paused under a garish portrait of the Virgin Mary, who regarded him with technicolour sorrow.

'The taste in art isn't very sophisticated, is it?' Tumulty said. 'I'd especially throw that one out except some of my patrons here are devout men in a simplistic way. Icons console them.'

Zuboric asked, 'What does the name Jig mean to you?'

Pagan was annoyed. He wanted to play this more slowly, wanted to wander around the subject of Jig in an indirect way before deciding whether to spring the name on Tumulty, but Artie Zuboric, an apparent graduate from the bulldozer school of questioning, was off and running in his own direction. Pagan could see that it was going to be difficult to work with the FBI agent.

'It's a dance, of course,' Tumulty said.

'Can it,' Zuboric said. His tone was one of irritation. Pagan thought Zuboric looked like a heavy in some low-budget Spanish western with his Mexican-style moustache and drooping eyelids. All he needed was a toothpick, something to dangle from his lips.

'Should it mean anything else?' Tumulty blinked.

Frank Pagan went back across the room and sat on the priest's desk. 'Not a dance exactly. Not this time, Joe.'

'Tell me then. If it isn't a dance, then what are you talking about?'

'A killer,' Pagan said.

'Preposterous,' Tumulty said. 'A killer! What would I be doing with a killer, for God's sake?'

'We understand he has plans to visit you. Maybe he's already done so. Has he? Has Jig been here *already,* Joe?' Zuboric asked.

Pagan rubbed his eyes. He was feeling fuzzy, fatigued. He had one of those waking moments when the lack of sleep causes a slight hallucination. Joseph Tumulty's desk lamp seemed to shimmer in front of his eyes and the walls of the room become darker beyond the reaches of electricity.

'Why should this killer come to see me?' Tumulty asked.

'Suppose you tell me, Joe.'

Tumulty stood up. 'I think this has gone far enough, gentlemen. I've got hungry people waiting. If you don't mind.' He took a step towards the door, and Zuboric reached out, fastening his hand round the Irishman's wrist.

'Stick around,' Zuboric said.

Pagan looked at the FBI man's hand clamped on the priest's wrist. Tumulty didn't look unduly concerned about being grabbed and held. The expression on the Irishman's face was one of pity. It might have been the look of a priest listening to something especially pathetic in the confessional.

'Is it a nightstick next?' Tumulty asked. 'Or have nightsticks gone out of fashion? Do you use the butt of your pistols these days?'

'No nightsticks. No guns.' Pagan shrugged. 'All we want is a little information.'

Tumulty said, 'Which I don't have. Sorry and all that. How often do I have to say it, Mr Pagan?' Zuboric let his hand fall back to his side.

'Now can I go and feed my people?' Tumulty asked. 'They expect that of me downstairs.'

Pagan nodded wearily. 'We'll talk again, Joe.'

'I don't doubt that. But you'll keep getting the same answers.'

Pagan watched him a moment, thinking about the small things that gave a man away. A little sweat. The nervous motion of an eyelid. A flutter of hands. The human body as a lie detector. He moved towards the door. 'What would your people have to eat if you weren't around to care for them? If, for example, you were to find yourself lodging in Attica?'

Tumulty said, 'They might starve. They might end up sleeping on the streets. God knows, the kind of people I take in here aren't always welcome at some of the more genteel missions. But then I don't have any plans to abandon them, Pagan. And I most certainly don't plan on Attica.'

Frank Pagan smiled. 'The best-laid plans, and so forth,' he said. 'You know how it goes, don't you?' He pushed the door open and stepped out onto the landing. He turned back to Tumulty and added, 'Be seeing you.'

It was very cold in the attic. Jig huddled deep inside his overcoat. For a time he'd been listening to the sounds of voices that floated up through an air-conditioning vent, but then there had been silence, followed by footsteps. When the attic door opened a little way he found himself looking into the yellow beam of a flashlight. Tumulty stood there.

'You live dangerously,' Tumulty said.

Jig stared into the light. He smelled food. Tumulty was carrying a plate in one hand. Jig took the plate and the plastic fork and started to eat. He hadn't eaten in a long time. With his mouth full, he said. 'All I did was go downstairs for food. When I saw those characters, I couldn't resist the impulse.'

Tumulty sat cross-legged on the floor. He produced a pack of cigarettes and lit one.

'Suppose they'd somehow gotten hold of a picture of you?' Tumulty said. 'Suppose they had a description from somewhere?'

'But they didn't.'

Tumulty sighed. 'How did they know you were coming here anyhow?'

Jig set the plate aside. 'Good stew,' he said.

'I asked a question.'

'I don't have the answer,' Jig said.

'It doesn't worry you?'

'I came to America to do a job. Nothing else.'

Tumulty sighed again. 'How did they find out about me? Only myself and Finn knew you were coming here. Since I didn't tell anybody, there's only one conclusion. Something went wrong at Finn's end.'

Jig thought a moment about Finn. He couldn't afford to worry about the old man. The money had to be found. Nothing changed that. The only thing of any importance was the task he'd been sent to do. Despite himself, he felt a small chord of concern echo in his head, but he rejected it. Finn would have been the first to tell him that worry only weakened a man's concentration, disrupted his single-mindedness. Worry was a peripheral pastime and an unworthy one.

He adjusted his grubby overcoat, which smelled of alcohol. He had soaked the material of the coat with a half pint of very cheap rum, and now the pungent aroma was irritating him.

'They'll come back,' Tumulty said.

'And you'll tell them nothing.'

'I've never been tested,' Tumulty said. 'I don't know my limits.'

'You'll tell them nothing,' Jig said again.

Tumulty rubbed his leg. He had a cramp suddenly. 'I think they've got a man outside on the street.'

Jig nodded. 'I saw him before. He was a cinch to spot. Looks like a boy in the Marines, all short hair and jaw. He's sitting inside a tan Chrysler. He looks very conspicuous and very bored, Joe. Anyway, what did he see? Another bum staggering along the pavement, that's all. Another drunk falling down.'

Tumulty said, 'You look like a derelict, I'll grant you that.' He stood up, still clawing at his leg. 'But this whole situation worries me. What happened at Finn's end? And how much does this Pagan know?'

'Worry about something else, Joe. Worry about how you're going to help me.'

Tumulty was quiet. From the kitchen far below came the noise of a drunk singing. 'The Irish members of the flock think they're the Mormon Tabernacle Choir sometimes. I better get back down there. It's a bloody zoo.'

Jig reached out and touched Tumulty's arm. 'I'll need a decent pistol.'

Tumulty nodded but said nothing.

'And if it can be done, I'll feel better if I have a collapsible rifle as well. Just in case.'

'It's going to take a little time.'

'I don't have much time.'

'I can't hurry a thing like this,' Tumulty said. 'Especially now, when I've got those two characters breathing down my neck.'

Tumulty turned towards the attic door. The singing from below was growing louder.

My feet are here on Broadway this blessed
harvest morn
But O the ache that's in them for the spot
where I was born . . .

Jig said, 'I'll also need names, Joe. Names of anyone connected with the Fund-raisers.'

'Of course you will. Otherwise, how will you know who to shoot?'

'Do I detect disapproval in your voice?'

Tumulty said nothing.

'I never shoot anybody unless I have to,' Jig said. 'Does that ease your conscience?'

'Sometimes the Cause overrides conscience,' Tumulty said. 'If it didn't, I'd still be a priest.' He waved the flashlight. The beam illuminated the attic, picking out various objects. A dressmaker's dummy. A heap of old hatboxes. Piles of newspapers. 'I suggest you vanish from here and come back in two days. I also suggest you don't use the telephone to get in contact with me.'

'Two days,' Jig said.

'I can't do anything in less,' Tumulty said.

Jig watched Tumulty move towards the door.

Tumulty said, 'I still think you took an unnecessary risk.'

Jig replied, 'At least I know what my enemy looks like, Joe. Which is more than Frank Pagan knows about me.'

Jig saw the door shut. Tumulty had taken the flashlight with him and the attic was once again completely dark. Jig sat with his back to the wall. Frank Pagan, he thought. A tall straight-backed man with a strong jaw and a face that might have been handsome if it hadn't looked like it was cast in cement. Frank Pagan. Here in America. Well, well.

Jig listened to the song rising up from the kitchen.

When I was young and restless, my mind was
ill at ease
Through dreaming of America and gold beyond
the seas . . .

He closed his eyes. What difference did it make to him if the Englishman was here in the United States? Since Frank Pagan hadn't identified him, it meant that the Englishman was operating in the dark. Which in turn meant that Finn, no matter what might have happened to him in Ireland, no matter how any information had leaked to Pagan, hadn't revealed Jig's identity. It was the one thing that Finn, whom Jig had come to perceive as being somehow immune to harm and danger, an indestructible embodiment of the Cause, would never do. He'd cut out his tongue before he revealed any of the secrets he kept. Anyway, the old man knew how to look after himself.

Jig got up and wandered around the attic, trying to keep warm. He dismissed Frank Pagan from his mind and instead turned his thoughts to the business of passing the next couple of days. He was impatient to do what he'd come to America for, but he was at the mercy of Joseph Tumulty, and he didn't like the feeling of having to rely on anyone but himself.

He stopped moving.

The maudlin song continued to float up towards him and, even though he disliked the sensation, he felt a pricking of homesickness, a faint longing for the things he'd left behind.

In the back of the cab that headed in the direction of the Parker Meridien, Zuboric said, 'I think the fucker knows.'

'Of course he knows. But what would you do, Artie? Beat information out of him? Take him down into a dungeon and kick the shit out of him until he talks?' Pagan asked.

'Yeah.' Zuboric spread his hands, gazed at his fingernails. 'It's your ball game, Frank. You want to play it softly, that's your business. You want to be Mr Nice, fine by me.'

Pagan thought: Mr Nice. He could have threatened Tumulty directly. He could have menaced him with a variety of pressures, including physical violence. But what would that have achieved? If Tumulty was IRA, then he'd embrace martyrdom happily. Broken ribs and bruises would be like badges of merit to Father Joe. No, it was better to leave threats hanging in the air, unspoken, veiled, and let Tumulty's imagination go to work on them. He was still a little unhappy with Zuboric's blunderbuss attitude and the way the whole interview had been conducted, but he decided not to criticise directly for the moment. He didn't want to alienate Zuboric, and with him the whole FBI, unless it was completely unavoidable.

Zuboric said, 'I'll keep my man in place. Maybe get a tap on the guy's phone. Maybe.'

'Which he'll expect,' Pagan remarked. He watched the streets. Times Square. He'd photographed Roxanne here, right outside a HoJo's. She wanted her picture taken there, because the place looked wonderfully sleazy. He had overworked the camera that summer. Roxanne outside the CBS building. Roxanne eating a huge pretzel at the Statue of Liberty. That's what this place suggested to Pagan. A series of old snapshots. Pictures of another life lived by another man. He remembered suddenly a detail of Roxanne: the way her lips felt when they touched his own. The taste of her. The warmth.

It was details like this that killed him. He felt empty. Restless.

He leaned forward and told the cab driver to pull over.

Zuboric said, 'Where you going, Frank?'

Pagan stepped out on to the sidewalk. 'I need a little exorcism,' he said.

Arthur Zuboric frowned in puzzlement. 'Whatever,' he said.

9 Roscommon, New York

Former United States Senator Harry Cairney rose very slowly from his bed and looked from the window at Roscommon Lake, which was sullen and utterly still in the windless morning. Cairney found himself longing for spring, true spring, which sometimes at nights he smelled on the cold air. When each spring came he wondered if it might be his last. Morbid speculations.

He pressed his forehead against the window-pane and saw Celestine riding her black mare, Jasmine, along the shore. Celestine's yellow hair floated out behind her, and her body rose and fell with the rhythms of the animal. Cairney watched this fluent amalgam of woman and horse until Celestine had galloped out of sight. Then a black four-wheel-drive vehicle appeared between the trees. The jeep had the words DUTCHESS SECURITY painted on it. Cairney had hired them immediately after the emergency meeting with Kevin Dawson and the others a few days ago. Now the black vehicle was always out there, occupied by two men who carried automatic pistols and rifles.

Celestine hadn't questioned him about the presence of the security men. If she thought about them at all, she presumably attributed them to an old man's groundless fears for his home and property. He watched a pall of exhaust hang in the wintry air, then he turned from the window.

The light in the bedroom was poor. Misshapen clouds, leaden and dreadful, filled the sky. Sighing, Cairney reflected on the fact that he'd recently fallen into the habit of reminiscing, ransacking his memory and speaking his recollections aloud, even though he knew he was sometimes repeating himself. He'd say *I remember the time when Lyndon decided he didn't want the presidency. I remember he told me he didn't give a rat's fuck for the job any more, even though he'd lusted after it all his life, and now here he was with his ambition realised except it was goddam empty,* and Celestine would nod her head sweetly and smile, as if she'd never heard Harry's stories before. Softening of the brain, Cairney thought. A shiver of senility. Old age and death terrified him. He thought nothing could be lonelier than death.

The door of the bedroom opened. Celestine, in blue jeans and a heavy plaid jacket, stepped inside. Her pale skin had been buffed by the cold air. Her cheeks were faintly red and her eyes bright, and she looked to Cairney like something that winter, at its most artful, had created especially for him. Young. So goddam young. He touched her face with his palm. All his morose thoughts dissolved. Celestine was life and vitality – a light that pierced his gloom.

She spread her hands in front of the fire. 'Why are you out of bed, Harry?'

Cairney coughed loudly, then popped a Kleenex from the box on the bedside table and raised it to the tip of his nose. 'God, I hate lying in bed, Cel,' he complained.

'How the devil are you going to get well if you don't rest?'

Scolding him. Smiling as she did so. Cairney sometimes felt like a small boy caught raiding the cookie jar. He liked the feeling. 'Nag, nag,' he said. His voice sounded strange to him. Thick, coming from a distance. He wondered about the condition of his lungs. It had to be a swamp in there.

'For your own good, old man,' Celestine said. She sat on the bed and removed the riding boots from her long legs. She tossed her hair back. Cairney watched her. He had loved his first wife, Kathleen, but not with this kind of intensity. He absorbed every little detail of Celestine, as if he were afraid of her somehow slipping away from him. He made orbits around her sun, like some satellite planet. With Kathleen, the relationship had evolved through the years into one of comfortable friendship, lacking passion but filled just the same with mutual understanding. With Kathleen, Cairney had always been in control. He had no control at all when it came to Celestine. He'd relinquished it cheerfully.

'Lie down,' she said, and she patted the bed.

Cairney did as he was told. He made a great show of moaning about her commands. She propped herself up on an elbow and looked at him, tracing a line down his cheek with her fingernail.

'Are we going to work at getting better, Harry?' she asked.

'Yes,' he answered.

'Doctor's orders, Harry. Listen to your physician.'

'Tully's a broken-down old Irish sawbones.'

'Stop being irascible. It doesn't become you.'

Cairney smiled. The nearness of his wife was like a cocoon, a place to shelter. 'Well, he is.'

'He's highly experienced – '

'That's a euphemism for over the hill.'

'Harry, Harry, Harry.' Celestine tapped a fingernail on his lip. 'I think you like playing the role of an old codger, don't you?'

'An old codger is what I am, sweetheart.'

Celestine pressed her face against Harry Cairney's cheek. 'You're not so bad, Harry. You're not so bad.' She rolled away from him, staring up at the ceiling.

He glanced at her. She was wearing what he thought of as her secretive expression. It was the look she always had when she was about to surprise him with a birthday present or something unexpected at Christmas. He always saw through it because Celestine, no matter how damn hard she tried, didn't have the knack for guile.

'Out with it,' he said.

'Out with what?'

'Whatever it is that's making you look so smug.'

'Smug? Me?'

'Yeah. You.'

She sat up, clutching her knees and smiling.

'I don't know if you're well enough for surprises, Harry. Tully said you needed peace and rest.'

'Jesus Christ,' Cairney grumbled. 'Are you going to tell me what it is that makes you look like a cat that's swallowed the bloody canary whole?'

'Patrick called early this morning.'

'Patrick? My Patrick?'

'The very same.'

Cairney reached for another Kleenex and sneezed into it, causing a tiny pain in the centre of his chest. 'Why didn't you wake me, for God's sake?'

'Tully said you needed your sleep.'

Cairney dismissed Tully with a gesture of his hand. 'I haven't spoken with Patrick since God knows when.'

Celestine ran her fingers through her hair. 'You'll get the chance soon enough, Harry.'

'What do you mean?'

'He called from Albany. From the airport. He's on his way to Roscommon, even as we sit here.'

Cairney laid a hand against his chest. 'Patrick!' he said. 'Why the hell didn't he let me know he was coming?'

'Don't get excited, Harry.'

'He could've called. I'd have made arrangements to have him picked up, Cel.'

Celestine massaged Cairney's shoulders. 'He said he was going to rent a car in Albany and drive here.'

Cairney sat up, swinging his feet to the floor.

'Lie down, Harry.'

'And have my son come here and see me like an invalid?'

'Which is what you are.'

Cairney wandered to the fireplace. Patrick. His only child. The boy who left Boston University to go to Dublin and study archaeology. When he wasn't off digging in some ridiculous desert, he was deep inside books and old documents and God knows what. He was thirty years old, and Harry Cairney thought it was time his son stopped being the eternal student and did something useful with his life. He wasn't going to say so to Patrick because all the arguments were old and had been used up years ago and Patrick was an independent soul who'd go his own way anyhow. What Cairney couldn't understand was the boy's infatuation with ancient things. He loved his son fiercely. Differences of opinion didn't inhibit that feeling. Just the same, he wished Patrick would come back to America permanently and take up something less . . . esoteric than digging in the graves of long-dead men. But Patrick had never expressed the desire to leave Dublin nor any interest in anything other than useless archaeology. Now he was coming home to a sick father and security men crawling over the estate. Terrific.

Celestine stood behind him, blowing warm breath on the back of his neck. 'Shouldn't we be killing the fatted calf or something?' she asked.

Cairney turned to her with a smile. 'You'll like him. I know you will.'

'I hope he likes me,' Celestine said. She was quiet a moment. 'I'll make you a deal. I'll let you get dressed and come downstairs on the condition you don't do anything strenuous and you limit your intake to one glass of brandy. A small one.'

Cairney coughed again. 'You drive a hard bargain, woman.'

Celestine said, 'I want a husband who's healthy, Harry.'

'Okay,' Cairney said. 'It's a deal.'

Celestine removed her plaid jacket and tossed it over a chair. 'I'm going to take a shower and dress in something suitable for my stepson.' She paused, laughed quietly. 'He's only five years younger than me, Harry! How can I possibly be somebody's stepmother?'

She moved towards the bathroom, pausing in the doorway.

'You really ought to tell your guarddogs out there that we're expecting company, Harry. You wouldn't want them shooting at your own son, would you?'

Cairney nodded. He watched his wife discard her shirt, saw how it slipped from her body as she stepped inside the bathroom. The door shut and then there was the rattle of water falling inside the shower stall and after a moment the sound of Celestine singing.

Patrick Cairney parked his rented Dodge Colt at the side of the road and stepped out, leaving the engine running. He'd come off the Taconic Parkway near Rhinebeck where a minor road branched in the direction of Roscommon. Out here, miles from any major city, the air smelled good and he took it into his lungs deeply. The landscape was covered with crusted snow. He stared across the frozen fields and the stark clumps of woodland. It was the landscape of his childhood and he knew it thoroughly, all the tracks, the hiding places, the best trees to climb. When he considered his boyhood now, the recollection was touched by a strange little sense of emptiness, as if his only memories were forlorn ones – which wasn't entirely true. Harry had provided a few good things to look back on – a camping trip one summer to the deep woods of Maine, or the time one humid August when they'd gone together up into the Adirondacks and fished Sacandaga Lake. Even there, though, Harry had never strayed too far from civilisation and the nearest phone booth because he always wanted to keep in touch, which to Senator Cairney meant placing one call every day to his Washington office.

Patrick Cairney stepped back inside his car. He drove carefully on slippery pavement. When he reached the gates of the estate he got out and pushed them open. A black jeep came out of the trees towards him. There were two men inside. One carried a rifle across his knees, the other climbed out and approached Cairney. He was a stocky man with a pistol strapped to his belt and he came over the snow cautiously. Across the side panel of the vehicle were the words DUTCHESS SECURITY.

'You Patrick?' the man asked.

Cairney nodded.

The man hitched up his belt. 'Okay. You're expected.'

Cairney studied the man a second. He had the look of security guards everywhere. His face had become pinched from years of scrutinising people. Around his eyes was a dense mass of wrinkles. 'What's with all the security?' Cairney asked.

The man shrugged. He didn't answer Cairney's question. He turned and went back to the jeep, where he climbed in beside his partner. Cairney returned to the Dodge Colt and watched the black jeep reverse. It vanished behind a clump of trees. Security guards. What was Harry worried about? His collection of old Celtic manuscripts he'd gathered over the years? Or was it those mouldy manuscripts of Yeats and George Bernard Shaw and Joyce that bothered him? Cairney wondered if there were burglars of a literary persuasion in the area, masked men planning to heist the precious scrap of beer-stained paper on which Brendan Behan had written: *To my pal Harry Cairney, may he colonise Amerika*. The old man had that one framed and prominently displayed on the desk in his office.

The house came in view. Patrick Cairney had always thought of it as a monstrosity, sprawling cross the landscape like an immense mausoleum. Given a smokestack, it might have passed as a crematorium. It wasn't a house that invited you inside. It lacked any welcoming warmth. Cairney pulled up at the foot of the steps, glancing a moment at Roscommon Lake, then he got out of the car. He marvelled at it all – the mansion, the estate, everything that one poor but overwhelmingly ambitious Irish immigrant had pulled together in his lifetime. There was something to be said, after all, for making your career one of public service in America.

The door at the top of the steps opened. Celestine Cunningham Cairney stood there, looking down at him. She wore tailored tan slacks, a chocolate-brown sweater, a peach-coloured chiffon scarf. Her soft blond hair hung at her shoulders. Patrick Cairney, who had always thought his father must exaggerate Celestine's beauty in his letters because he was blinded by love, felt astonishment. The woman had the kind of loveliness that stopped men dead in their tracks, that made all heads turn in crowded rooms and silenced cocktail-party conversations. She moved down the steps without any of the self-consciousness of beautiful women, as if she were quite unaware of the way she looked.

She reached the bottom step and she laid one hand on her stepson's arm. 'Welcome,' she said. 'Harry's told me a lot about you.'

She leaned forward and kissed Cairney on the cheek. A stepmother's kiss, tentative and quick and just a little awkward. Cairney wasn't sure what to say. He was still trying to recover from his surprise. What had he expected anyhow? A good-looking matronly woman, maybe, somebody with the face and body of a sympathetic head nurse. Somebody, at best, handsome. But not this. This vision. And, although he didn't like the question, it entered his mind anyway: *What did she see in an old man like Harry Cairney*?

'Harry's waiting for you.'

Patrick Cairney looked over Celestine's shoulder. His father appeared in the doorway, smaller than Cairney remembered him, shrunken, his silver hair thinner than before and his eyes, under the great overhanging forehead, set in deep shadow.

'Let me hear it, Pat,' Harry Cairney called out in a voice that was curiously cracked.

Patrick Cairney hesitated before he sang. *'You haven't an arm and you haven't a leg,/You're an eyeless, noseless, chickenless egg –'*

His father sang the next two lines hoarsely. *'You'll have to be put with a bowl to beg,/O Johnny, we hardly knew ye!'*

'With drums and guns, and guns and drums,/The enemy nearly slew ye –'

'My darling dear, you look so queer,/O Johnny, I hardly knew ye!'

Then the old man was laughing, and Patrick Cairney climbed the steps quickly, thinking how the way they greeted each other never changed. It was a ritual as well preserved as his father's mythical vision of Ireland. And Patrick found it empty and meaningless, a routine first developed in his childhood. It had been embarrassing even back then. Now it was worse because it was forced and ridiculous. Both men embraced, then Harry Cairney stepped back and said, 'Let me look at you, Pat. Let me take a good long look at you. You've put on some muscles since I last saw you. It must be all those Irish potatoes you've been eating.'

Patrick Cairney glanced at Celestine, who was coming up the steps. She said, 'Did somebody give you permission to come out here into the cold, Harry?'

Cairney winked at his son. 'She never lets up,' he said. 'She keeps an old man in check.'

'Somebody has to,' Celestine said. She slipped her arm through Harry's and she smiled at her stepson. It was a good smile, the kind Patrick Cairney thought you could bask in on a chilly winter's day. Like having your own private sun.

'Now let's all go indoors,' Celestine said. She shivered as she ushered Harry inside the house.

'I'll fetch my luggage,' Patrick Cairney said.

He went back down the steps to the Dodge Colt. He reached inside and lifted his bag from the rear seat. He closed the door. He saw the black security jeep appear on the shore of Roscommon Lake, idling between bare trees.

John F. Kennedy Airport, New York

The man from the State Department was called J. W. Sweeting. He wore a three-piece suit and his hair was immaculately brushed over his broad skull. He had a brown leather briefcase with his initials embossed on it. He sat in the arrivals lounge at John F. Kennedy Airport and studied the man he'd just met from the London flight. The Reverend Ivor McInnes was big, weighed somewhere in the region of two hundred and twenty pounds, none of it flab. He had a large, craggy face that was handsome in a fleshy way. He was about fifty, Sweeting reckoned. The eyes were green and lively and burned into you whenever you looked at them. The British press called him Ivor the Terrible, which

Sweeting thought he understood. There was the scent of brimstone hanging all around the Reverend McInnes. Sweeting knew he wouldn't like to sit through one of McInnes's sermons, which would be all thunder and spit. And yet like many people before him J. W. Sweeting realised that there was something attractive about McInnes, a certain quality of roguish charm which, as a political tool, could be extremely useful. It was easy to imagine Ivor swaying large crowds, shaping them any way he wanted.

Sweeting tapped his briefcase. 'I'll go over the conditions of entry for you,' he said.

McInnes smiled. 'No need, no need,' he said in an accent that reminded Sweeting of a Liverpool rock singer. 'I know them all. Your embassy people in London, the gargoyles of Grosvenor Square, already put me through their wire-mesh procedures.'

Sweeting rubbed his embossed initials with a fingertip. 'In case there's any misunderstanding, Reverend, you were granted an entry visa on the condition that you refrain from speaking in public places or giving inflammatory interviews to the press. State is adamant about that.'

McInnes swivelled his green eyes up to the high ceiling and looked very impatient. 'I know all this, young man.'

Sweeting sighed. It was the sigh of a man carrying out his duty regardless. 'You are to refrain from all and any public assemblies. You are also ordered to refrain from addressing any private assemblies, clubs, and associations, organisations, and the like, which are considered partisan in nature. You are prohibited from activities designed to raise funds for any partisan organisations with which you might be associated in Northern Ireland.'

'Can I actually breathe?' McInnes asked. 'Or am I forbidden the use of your air as well?'

Sweeting ignored this. 'You are also deterred from making political statements concerning British or American policy in Ireland, the Irish Republican Army, the conditions of Irish political prisoners in British jails, and any remarks, ambiguous or otherwise, about the Roman Catholic Church.'

'Did somebody tear up your Constitution? Did somebody just decide to disregard that wonderful document in my case?' McInnes was looking amused rather than annoyed.

Sweeting went on, 'Your stay is limited to ten days and restricted to New York City and its environs. Any other movements must be cleared in advance with a representative of the State Department. To wit, me. And I'll turn down any and all requests you might make. Is all this clear?'

McInnes nodded. 'Loud and clear.'

'Any violation of these conditions will result in your expulsion from the United States. Between you and me, I think you're lucky to get this visa. The fact is, State pursues a policy of fairness towards both sides in the Irish question. If we let in, say, a priest from Tipperary, then we can't keep out a minister from Belfast. Even one whose own church has rejected him.'

'Are you a Catholic?' McInnes asked.

'Is that relevant?'

McInnes grinned. He had strong white teeth. He brought his face very close to Sweeting's. It was a characteristic of his, this closing of the distance between himself and his listener, and it forced an uneasy intimacy on whoever Ivor was talking to. 'I have this reputation, Mr Sweeting. They say I hate Roman Catholics. I admit I have my differences with the Church of Rome, friend, but as far as individual Catholics are concerned, I don't hate them. They're misguided people, that's all.' McInnes paused. His grin created little squares of puckered flesh all across the expanse of his face. 'My own church failed to understand that, Mr Sweeting. They interpreted my objections to Rome as attacks on individual Catholics. Which wasn't what I intended. Far from it.'

Sweeting stepped back a pace. McInnes had been talking very loudly and several people were staring at him.

'You're misunderstood, is that what you're saying?' Sweeting asked.

'I'm damned in certain quarters whenever I open my mouth.'

'Maybe you should keep it shut more often,' J. W. Sweeting said.

Ivor McInnes smiled. He placed one of his big hands on Sweeting's shoulder and rocked the man from the State Department very slightly back and forth. Sweeting once more stepped away. McInnes reminded him of one of those TV salesmen who pitched Herbalife or urged you to send your dollars to some church beamed into your living-room from a satellite in the sky. He made you feel you were the most important thing in his life when he talked to you. It was the way the green eyes concentrated on your face and the easy manner, the quiet little touches, the familiarity. He was convincing, Sweeting thought, but so were all the blow-dried evangelists of the airwaves. Where McInnes had the edge over his electronic rivals was in the way he looked – he was rumpled instead of embalmed in polyester, and his silver hair had never been styled beneath a dryer but was umkempt and grew down over his collar.

'You're not a stuffy little man, are you, Mr Sweeting?' McInnes said. 'I thought everybody in the State Department had had their sense of humour expunged at birth. I thought they had their wit circumcised along with their foreskins.'

J. W. Sweeting passed the palm of one hand over his forehead. He was inexplicably nervous all at once. In theory, he should have loathed a man like McInnes. In practice, he was finding it difficult. The green eyes suggested amusement and a benign tolerance for the sorrows of the human condition, and the smile, that big wide-mouthed expression, was magnetic. What Sweeting had expected to encounter was a hateful bigot, which would have been easy to handle. McInnes didn't come across that way at all. Indeed, he appeared reasonable and easygoing, a man given to instant friendships, huge handshakes, intimate gestures. A man who played on your sympathies by insisting, with a downturned mouth, that he was misunderstood by his enemies, which was a terrible cross he had to carry. He was goddam *likeable*.

McInnes rubbed his chin. 'You're not a bad fellow, Sweeting. And because I like you I'll make life easy for you. I'll go along with all your restrictions. I'll whistle any tune you care to hear whether I like it or not, because I'm not here on any political mission. I'll tell you something else. I smell the White House behind all these conditions of yours. I smell Tommy Dawson at work.'

'Like the State Department, the President is neutral in the Irish question,' Sweeting said.

McInnes laughed. It was a curious sound, a throaty wheeze. 'Neutral? Tommy Dawson's a black-hearted Catholic Irishman who makes pilgrimages to the dear little town of Ardare in the Republic of Ireland where his grandparents were born. He's about as neutral as the Pope, Mr Sweeting. And he hates anybody from the North. He hates Ulster.'

Sweeting wasn't going to be drawn into the question of Thomas Dawson's Irish heritage or the matter of his sympathies. He returned to the only subject he was interested in. 'If you restrict yourself to the research you say you want to do here, then we'll get along just famously.'

McInnes nodded his head. 'What could be more peaceful and worthy than writing the saga of Ulster labourers in the history of the American railroad? All that sweat and toil. All the sadness of the immigrant worker. The longings. The hopes. The dreams. By God, it's a rich tale. And a complicated one. Besides, I'm a minister without a congregation, and a man has to make a living somehow.'

'Indeed,' Sweeting said. He thought of how, in support of his visa application, McInnes had submitted a copy of a contract with a small university press for his projected history. It was one book Sweeting would manage not to read, if indeed it was ever likely to see the light of publication.

McInnes picked up his suitcase from the floor. 'I'm booked into the Essex House on Central Park, Mr Sweeting.'

'I know,' Sweeting said.

McInnes winked at the man. 'I thought you might.'

Wildwood, Long Island

Big Jock Mulhaney drove his four-wheel-drive vehicle slowly over damp sands. He had a view of Long Island Sound, which looked dismal and abandoned in the sullen light of afternoon. He wore a thick flannel jacket and waterproof pants, and he had a baseball cap pulled down squarely on his head. It wasn't the kind of clothing he usually favoured. His tastes ran to rather bright three-piece suits, large checks and flashy herringbones, accompanied by wide-knotted neckties. But today he wasn't travelling in his usual environment either, which was bounded by his penthouse over union headquarters in Brooklyn and the midtown Manhattan clubs he patronised, where his fellow members regarded him with all the suspicion Old Money has for the nouveau riche. He was viewed, he knew, as an upstart, a man who didn't belong in the more rarefied heights of society. He was a brawler, a climber, a loudmouth, and he suffered from the most heinous condition of all – which was naked ambition – but there was a certain shrewdness to him that nobody disrespected.

Now, as the four-wheel-drive vehicle slithered into ruts and a vicious wind stirred the waters of the sound, Mulhaney wondered if it was bad judgement to be out here at all. For one thing, expanses of nature made him nervous. He couldn't take too many trees. He couldn't stand silences and great spaces. For another, he wasn't sure he should be meeting with Nicholas Linney anyhow, but who else was he going to confide in? He couldn't go to Harry Cairney with his theory unless he had some backing. So he needed Linney's approval and support.

Besides, there was another reason for his uneasiness, one he didn't want to think about. It was the simple fact that he had recently been obliged to cover some very bad investments with money that had been earmarked for Ireland. It wasn't any great sum, a mere $450,000 skimmed from his total contribution of $1.9 million, and he was going to return it next time funds were raised, and nobody was going to find out about it anyway – but just the same the mere prospect of discovery made him feel apprehensive. What if one of the other Fund-raisers found out about the shortage? Hell, that would make Big Jock the prime suspect in the hijacking of the *Connie*. How could it not? A man who could 'borrow' from Irish funds for his own private purposes wasn't a man who could be trusted. It had been a stupid thing to do, admittedly, but he'd been pressured by creditors, and he hadn't been thinking clearly, and he didn't want any kind of public scandal attached to his name. Thomas Dawson had recently announced a committee of inquiry into the financial practices of unions, and Mulhaney didn't like the idea of coming under the scrutiny of a bunch of congressional jerk-offs who were bound to ask tough questions. He'd covered his shortage this time, and so had spared himself some potential embarrassment, but he'd done it only at the expense of the Irish. But it wasn't something he intended to continue doing. *Fuck Tommy Dawson*, he thought. Always pointing a mighty finger at the unions, slinging accusations, digging for dirt.

Mulhaney's vehicle became bogged down in the soft wet sands. He switched off the engine and stared the length of the beach. *What if this Irishman they were all so goddam afraid of found out about the shortage*? He shook his head. The Irishman wasn't going to get within a hundred miles of him, so he wasn't going to worry about that notion.

He got out of the vehicle and turned the collar of his jacket up against the whining wind. In the distance there was the sound of gunfire, a constant rapid knocking that was muted by the churning waters. He walked a little way. He moved awkwardly because the heavy sands inhibited his progress, and every now and again spray splashed up and blinded him. Christ, he hated this place. He stopped and removed a small silver flask from his pocket. He opened it, sipped some cognac, then stuck the flask away again. Ahead, a hundred or so yards along the seafront, he could see Linney's Land-Rover, which had been painted in camouflage colours. The trouble with Nick Linney, Mulhaney thought, was the guy was some kind of nut. He read *Soldier of Fortune* and believed every word of it. He was into weaponry and combat and guerilla techniques, and he went through the pages of *Soldier of Fortune* with a big yellow marker in his fist, circling stories and advertisements that interested him.

Mulhaney kept walking. Now he could see Linney lying flat on the sand. The sound of gunfire was constant. Blap-blap-blap. As he got closer, Mulhaney noticed the targets Linney was using. Close to the shoreline, the guy had set up row after row of cantaloupes, and he was currently blasting away at them. Every now and then one of them would explode and rise up in the air in pulpy smithereens. Linney was from outer space, Mulhaney thought.

'Nick!' he called out.

Linney stood up, raised one arm in greeting. He was dressed in combat clothing. He even had a beret, which he wore at a precarious angle. Mulhaney noticed the heavy army boots. Grenades lay on the sands alongside an assortment of weapons. Jesus, the guy was a one-man militia.

Linney stared in the direction of the cantaloupes. Then he held out the weapon he'd been using as if he wanted Mulhaney to inspect it and give it some seal of approval. Mulhaney wasn't happy around firearms.

'The M–16A2,' Linney said proudly.

Jock Mulhaney nodded. The melons, most of them shattered, were being sucked at by the tide.

'Feel it, Jock,' Linney thrust the weapon out in the manner used by gun freaks the world over when they're in apprehensive company. Cavalier. A little too casual.

Mulhaney held the gun for a moment before returning it. He wondered how Linney got hold of weapons that private citizens weren't supposed to have. 'Yeah. Feels solid,' was all he could say.

'Excellent piece,' Linney said. He pointed out some features, such as the new muzzle brake/compensator and the integral brass deflector, and Mulhaney made humming sounds, as if he might be remotely interested. Mulhaney hoped that if any one of the Fund-raisers ever found out about the 'borrowed' cash it wouldn't be Nick Linney.

Linney swung the weapon back towards the rows of cantaloupes and fired off a couple of shots. Mulhaney watched one of the melons explode and then hit the water, carried away like a mutant jellyfish.

'Very nice, Nick,' Mulhaney said.

Linney smiled, then put the gun inside his Land-Rover and lit a cigarette. There were oilstains on the backs of his fingers. He smoked in silence for a time, his face turned out towards the waters, before he tossed the cigarette away and looked at Mulhaney.

'What's on your mind, Jock?' he asked.

'You have to ask?'

Nicholas Linney beat the palm of one hand upon the panel of his vehicle. 'I get the impression you suspect me, Jock. I got that feeling when we were at Roscommon.'

Mulhaney shook his head. 'I considered it, I admit.'

'And you changed your mind?'

Mulhaney took his flask out again. He wished he'd brought a cigar with him to complement the flavour of the cognac, but he'd left his case behind. He swallowed, offered the flask to Linney, who declined.

Mulhaney said, 'Yeah. I changed my mind. Which is why I drove all the fucking way out here to see you.'

Linney pulled a pair of sunglasses over his eyes even though the sky was gloomy and overcast. 'I'm listening, Jock.'

'Okay. First, I ruled out Cairney. He's been in this business for nearly fifty goddam years and I can't see him screwing the Irish at this stage of the game. He's been on the Cause's side since I was in fucking diapers and you weren't even born, so why would he dump on it now?'

Linney said, 'I'll go along with that. It wasn't Cairney.'

'Okay. I ruled out myself because I *know* I didn't have anything to do with the *Connie*.'

Linney smiled. 'I'm supposed to take your word for this, Jock?'

'Hear me out,' Mulhaney said. 'Okay. I eliminated Cairney and myself. Leaving you and Kev Dawson.'

'Don't keep me in suspense, Jock.'

'First, I figured it might be you. You wanna know why? Because you're the guy that *physically* takes the money to the Courier – '

'I never saw the Courier in my life,' Linney said.

'Okay. Let me put it another way. You give the money to a guy who gives the money to the Courier. Right?'

Linney adjusted his dark glasses. 'Something like that.'

'Fine,' Mulhaney said. He glanced at the demolished melons, understanding now why Nick Linney had an effect on him. It was more than just the gun thing, it was something in Linney's physical qualities that unsettled him. That strangely coloured face, which reminded Mulhaney of a lime. The guy's general air of self-confidence and the feeling you got that when a nuclear holocaust came, Linney was going to be among the survivors, bottled up in some fucking concrete cellar with his guns and dried fruits and astronaut foods. Linney always looked as if he knew something the rest of the human race had either ignored or forgotten.

Mulhaney played with the surface of his flask. 'I ruled you out, Nick, because I couldn't see you turning against the Cause. I couldn't quite get a fix on that. I mean, you bring in more money than the rest of us put together, and if you wanted to steal it you'd find an easier way than going to the trouble of hijacking a fucking ship. You could have stolen the money at the source, for Christ's sake! You could have pocketed the money you raised and then told us that your donors just couldn't come through and who the hell would have been any the wiser?'

Nicholas Linney crossed his arms on his chest. He looked like some tinpot general in a South American jungle army. 'And that leaves Kevin Dawson,' he said.

'Kevin Dawson.' Mulhaney gouged out a pattern with the heel of his shoe in the damp sands.

'He's got money coming out his ears. Why would he want more?'

Mulhaney smiled. 'It wasn't the cash he was after, Nick. His family owns about half of fucking Connecticut, so he wasn't looking for financial gain. You wanna know what I think?'

Linney took off his sunglasses. 'Tell me, Jock.'

'Okay. I see it happening like this. Let's say he gets a call from Tom Dawson in the White House. Big Brother's unhappy. He doesn't like money flowing out of America and into Ireland. He's in a flap because all that money coming from the States makes him look bad with his bosom buddies in London, who are about the only fucking allies he's got in the world, and they've been bitching about American aid to Irish terrorists. He says to Kev that it's got to stop. And Kev, who's never been a man to deny Big Brother anything, tells him about a certain shipment aboard a certain small vessel. Wonderful, Tommy thinks. We'll put a stop to that one. He gets on the phone, talks to some of his cronies, and these cronies put together a bunch of fucking killers. Vets. Former marines who've been twiddling their thumbs since the Bay of Pigs. Whatever. The money's taken. Tommy is happy, Kev hasn't let Big Brother down, the crew isn't around to point the finger at anyone, and there's no awkward publicity.'

Nicholas Linney reached for the M–16A2 and held it against his side. He fired off two shots, missing the cantaloupes both times. Mulhaney's ears rang from the noise of the gunfire. Linney studied the barrel of the weapon for a moment, then turned to look at Mulhaney.

'What kind of proof do you have that Kev Dawson went running off to the White House, Jock?'

Mulhaney shrugged. He had been so convinced by his own theory that the matter of proof hadn't occurred to him. To him it was blatantly obvious that Kevin Dawson was the turncoat, and even if he had constructed a scenario that might or might not have been correct, that alone didn't detract from the basic feeling of rightness he had. And he wasn't accustomed, in the world of ass-kissers and yes-men in which he insulated himself, to having his judgements questioned because proof was lacking. Kevin Dawson was the one. The only candidate. Everyone *knew* that the Dawsons weren't a trustworthy bunch.

Linney said, 'For all I know you could have come out here to tell me this story because you wanted to avert suspicion from yourself.'

Mulhaney was quiet. *Does this bastard suspect me of something?* he wondered. The speculation filled him with a cold fear. He said, 'I could have. But I didn't.'

'I've only got your word for that, Jock. Which leaves us right back where we started.' Linney looked out towards Long Island Sound. 'What makes you so sure that *I* didn't arrange the whole thing anyhow?'

Mulhaney felt spray rise up against his face as the wind forced itself over the tide. 'Because I know it was Kev Dawson, for Christ's sake,' he said. 'A process of simple elimination, Nick.'

'It's not so simple, Jock. Show me proof. I need to see proof before I can go along with your story. From where I stand, Kev Dawson's always been reliable when it comes to raising funds. I need something that might convince me otherwise. I need a smoking gun, friend. Right now, I'm thinking that you dislike Kevin Dawson so intensely you'd hang anything on him. Jesus, you hate that whole goddam family.'

'There's nothing personal in any of this,' Mulhaney said. He sipped from his flask again. Coming out here to talk to Linney – a waste of time. He had hoped that Linney would become an ally and together they'd go see Cairney and lay the story in front of the old man and let him decide how to deal with Dawson. Now Linney was asking for proof, for God's sake. What did he want? Taped conversations? Transcripts?

'It's not exactly the kind of thing where proof's easy to come by,' he said, a little deflated.

He had revealed himself to Linney and now, having been rebuffed by the man, he felt very defensive. 'Okay. So maybe my theory isn't correct. Maybe it happened some other way and Kev Dawson had motives I haven't even thought about. Maybe the family empire is strapped for cash, I don't know. But I *know* he's the one.'

Linney said, 'Let me tell you what I think. The money's gone and that's a mystery. I've never been happy with mysteries, Jock. Detective stories, bodies inside locked rooms, that kind of thing never appealed to me. I like facts. The harder the better. This gun, for instance. It's a hard fact. Right?'

Mulhaney nodded in a sullen way.

Linney ran the palm of one hand over the weapon. It was almost a lover's caress. The gun might have been the leg of a mistress. 'I don't give a shit right now about who took the money because the only hard fact I can see is that some guy is coming here from Ireland. And that makes me very unhappy. Do you think he's going to sit down and discuss the missing money over a friendly cup of tea?'

Mulhaney said nothing. He hadn't given a lot of thought to this shadowy Irishman who seemed to terrify everybody but himself.

'The fuck he is,' Linney went on. 'If I was that guy I'd have a bad attitude. I wouldn't be disposed towards kindness. I wouldn't make polite inquiries. I wouldn't trust a fucking soul. If I was him, I'd be ready to do violence.' Linney paused, gazing at Mulhaney's florid face. 'Suppose this character runs you down, Jock. What would you tell him?'

'I'd give him Kevin Dawson,' Mulhaney said quickly.

'What if he doesn't believe you? Who would you give him next? Cairney? Me?'

Mulhaney shuffled his feet in the sand. He was always out of his depth when it came to hypothetical matters. Ifs played no role in Mulhaney's world. He didn't answer Linney's question.

'This guy isn't going to be your friend, Jock. You better understand that.'

Mulhaney smiled now. He was uncomfortable with the way Linney was talking. 'How would you behave if he came to you?' he asked.

Linney made a gesture with the weapon. 'I'm ready for anything,' he answered.

'Jesus,' Mulhaney said. 'You talk as if this guy's going to find us. I think you're paranoid.'

'Is there another way to be?' Nicholas Linney asked.

10 New York City

Frank Pagan was very cold on the rooftop. He wore a heavy overcoat and a plaid scarf and thick gloves, but even so the wind squeezed through his clothing. He sometimes walked in circles, stamping his feet for warmth, but he never strayed far from the view overlooking the entrance to St Finbar's Mission. It was just after 8:30 a.m. and the frozen wind, which had been blowing all night, hadn't died with daylight.

He could see Zuboric's field agent parked down the block a little way, a young man called Orson Cone, a graduate of Brigham Young University in Utah. He was keen, bright-eyed. He'd been with the agency for only eighteen months and he was still fresh enough to think stakeouts were a big deal. Earlier, when Pagan had talked with Orson Cone, he'd noticed a copy of *The Book of Mormon* lying face down on the backseat of the car. With his straight white teeth and closely cropped fair hair, Cone reminded Pagan of a surfer, one who'd had an encounter with Jesus out on the waves.

Cone had nothing to report. He'd been sitting inside his car for about ten hours and, apart from the clientele that drifted in and out of St Finbar's, he'd seen nothing of interest. Since there was only one exit, and Cone hadn't seen Tumulty leave the place, it was a safe assumption the Irishman was still inside. Pagan, still dislocated by the change of clocks, went into a rundown building that housed two import-export companies, a shabby PR outfit called Images, and a telephone answering service, and climbed the unlit stairs to the roof. There, surrounded by scrawny city pigeons, he watched the street.

Frank Pagan yawned. Last night, when he left Zuboric, he'd walked several blocks back to the Parker Meridien. He'd stood for a while in the bar, nursing a scotch and soda and studying one of the waitresses, an attractive young girl with a certain airheaded approach to things, a giggler who was forever making the wrong change or dropping glasses. Her name, she told him, was Mandi with an *i*. He'd wondered about introducing himself, just to see where it might lead. But he couldn't imagine performing an act of sexual exorcism with somebody called Mandi with an *i*, so he'd gone up to his room. Sleep hadn't exactly come in like an angel. He tossed around restlessly for hours; then, tired of being tired, he dressed and returned to Canal Street, walking all the way down Broadway to the edge of Chinatown.

Now he beat his gloved hands together and watched his breath mist on the frigid air and concentrated on St Finbar's Mission, wondering about Joseph X. Tumulty. Sooner or later, the man would step outside. Eventually, he'd have to go somewhere. And Frank Pagan wanted to know where.

His eyes stung as the wind scoured the rooftops, making TV antennae tremble. He huddled deeper inside his coat, trying to shrink himself down into a place where the wind wouldn't hurt him. Hopeless. He blinked at the street. Inside his car Orson Cone sat motionless, no doubt drawing his patience from *The Book of Mormon*. A simple faith. Frank Pagan had always envied simple faiths. His own God was a different kind of joker altogether – complicated and brooding, seated masked at the inaccessible centre of some intricate labyrinth. A totally whimsical character with more than a touch of cruelty. He never returned your calls.

Pagan looked along the sidewalk, where the wind skirted across plastic trash bags, making them ripple. He propped his elbows on the top of the wall, leaned forward a little way.

'If you fall, don't expect me to catch you,' Zuboric said.

Pagan turned around. Artie Zuboric was coming across the roof, his coat flapping behind him. His nose was red from the cold. There was an angry expression on his face.

'I know,' Pagan said. 'I didn't call you.'

'Damn right you didn't call me,' Zuboric said. 'Next time you move, I want to know about it.'

'Cone told you I was here.'

'Cone called me as soon as he saw you.'

Pagan shrugged. 'I couldn't sleep. I came back here.'

'I'm mildly pissed off, Frank. I don't care what time it is; when you have the urge to hit the streets, you let me know.'

Pagan said, 'I assumed you'd need your beauty sleep, Artie.'

Zuboric grunted and glanced towards St Finbar's Mission. He checked the FBI car, then turned back to Pagan, his anger subsided. 'By the way, I couldn't get authorisation for a phone tap.'

'No?' Pagan thought he detected a tiny note of pleasure in Artie Zuboric's voice.

'Insufficient reason,' Zuboric said. 'Happens.'

Pagan said nothing for a moment. He had the feeling that a telephone tap wouldn't have yielded anything anyway. Not if Joe Tumulty was a careful man. Besides, if Joe *thought* there was a tap on his phone, then that suspicion was as good as any eavesdropping device might have been.

'Something bothers me.' Zuboric cupped his hands and lit a cigarette. 'You're betting on Jig getting in touch with Tumulty. But I keep coming back to the possibility that your man's been and gone, Frank. In which event, you're freezing your ass off on this godforsaken roof for nothing.'

Pagan had already considered this. 'I'm betting on another possibility altogether, Artie. I'm betting Jig needs something only Tumulty can get for him.'

'Like what?'

'The tools of his trade,' Pagan said. 'I don't see Jig trying to score an ordinary gun somewhere, Artie. And the chances are he didn't arrive in this country carrying anything. He's too careful. If Joe's been an IRA connection here all along, he's bound to have contacts in the kind of speciality weapon Jig might need. When you boil it right down, I think Joe's the only chance we've got.'

'And what makes you think he hasn't already supplied Jig?'

'Unless Tumulty keeps weapons on his premises, which I doubt, they'd have to be specially ordered. That takes time.'

Pagan looked at the grimy windows of St Finbar's. They were impossible to see through. Whoever said cleanliness was next to godliness hadn't tried to peer inside Tumulty's soup kitchen.

Zuboric said, 'Tumulty's going to have his eyes open, Frank. He isn't going to walk through the street without looking over his shoulder a whole lot. He won't be an easy tail.'

Pagan smiled. He said, 'Tailing's one of my good points. If I do it alone.'

'Christ, you keep trying, don't you?' Zuboric said.

'He'll spot a pair, Artie. You know that. If we work this together, he's going to spot us as quickly as I spotted you last night.'

Zuboric looked pained. He didn't say anything. He stared down into the traffic going along Canal Street. Last night, when Pagan had stepped abruptly out of the cab, Zuboric had taken the taxi one block farther before getting out; then he'd followed Pagan back to his hotel. His orders were specific. Washington was going to be very unhappy if Frank Pagan was turned loose in the city. The possibility of bloodshed had them worried. What it meant for Zuboric was a terrific pain in the ass. He had to keep a lid on Frank Pagan and make sure the Englishman didn't do anything drastic to attract attention. Especially violence.

It was a can of fucking worms, and Zuboric was very unhappy.

'I can't do it, Frank. I can't let you out of my sight.'

'Suppose I just slipped away when you weren't looking?'

'No can do.'

Pagan put his gloves back on. 'Fuck it, Artie. If I choose to go out on my own, what the hell are you going to do to stop me?'

Zuboric looked at the Englishman. 'Tell you the truth, Frank, I don't know what I'd do if you were just to take a hike,' he said. 'I know Washington would have my balls for paperweights, though.'

Pagan went to the edge of the roof and leaned against the wall. There was a movement in the doorway of St Finbar's Mission. Joseph X. Tumulty appeared, the collar of his priestly black coat drawn up to his face.

'There he is, Artie,' Pagan said.

Zuboric peered into the street.

'Now what?' Frank Pagan asked. 'Do I go alone?'

'No way.'

Joseph Tumulty didn't feel the cold. He walked in the direction of Lafayette Street. He passed the FBI car, the tan Chrysler with the fair-haired young man inside. The agent had his face in a book, trying to appear inconspicuous. Tumulty barely noted him. He was concentrating on reaching Lafayette. He knew there were others, that the solitary agent in the Chrysler wasn't alone. When he reached the corner of Lafayette, he looked back. There were several people on the sidewalk, but he saw neither Frank Pagan nor the FBI agent with the Slavic name.

Tumulty, who had been recruited by Padraic Finn while still at the seminary in Bantry, tried to remain calm. Years ago, before he'd come to the United States, membership in an IRA cell had seemed gloriously romantic to him. The adventurer-priest. The swashbuckler behind the dog collar. He'd been swept away by Finn's persuasive tongue, carried along on old glories. Finn's Ireland was going to be a paradise, a land of unity where the old hatreds were demolished forever.

The idea of being an IRA connection in New York City was, quite simply, a thrill. It was also a part of his heritage, his background. Tumulty men had been associated with one or other of the Free Ireland movements ever since the nineteenth century. But, as it turned out, it had seemed an abstraction to him, like having membership in a club he never attended. Even the annual chore he was instructed to perform had never felt remotely dangerous. Once a year he received a telephone call from an anonymous person instructing him to travel to Augusta, Maine, and check into a motel, which was always a different one each time.

There, he'd wait in his room until he was contacted by the same individual informing him to proceed to a certain place, sometimes an abandoned gasoline station, sometimes a deserted factory, and once even the football field of a local high school. Tumulty would do as he was told. It was always at night when the encounters took place. The man would appear, seemingly out of nowhere, and give Tumulty a briefcase, which Tumulty would then deliver to another man known as the Courier in one of the small towns along the Maine coast. Cutler, Vinalhaven, and on the last occasion – when there had been three briefcases – Jonesport. After the Courier took possession of the cases, Tumulty's job was finished. He never asked questions. He knew what the cases contained, and he understood the Courier transported them to Ireland, but that was the extent of it.

It was only by accident that he'd discovered the identity of the man who supplied him with the briefcases.

He went north on Lafayette, heading in the direction of Little Italy. Outside a small produce store he stopped to examine a basket of apples. He looked back the way he'd come. There was still no sign of either the Englishman or the FBI character. Tumulty paid for an apple and crunched into it as he moved towards Mulberry Street. He passed an Italian social club, then a flashy new trattoria, and the smells of espresso and pastries drifted out to him. Beneath his heavy overcoat he was perspiring and his heart was hammering at his ribs. Somebody *had* to be following him.

He crossed Mulberry Street. His throat was very dry and he had difficulty swallowing. There was a quiet sense of panic inside him. It wasn't so much the idea of being followed that troubled him, rather it was the realisation that he was uncertain of how much he could stand if he was caught. He didn't know his own limits or the extent of his endurance if it came down to threats like the one he'd heard last about Attica. The idea of incarceration wasn't so terrible in itself – after all, many good men had been jailed for their work in the Cause – it was the prospect of being removed from St Finbar's Mission that clawed at him. Who would run the place if he was gone? Who would care for those men? Who would be as interested in saving their lives as he was? They were the lowest characters in the whole social hierarchy. Many of them were of the kind that other missions didn't like to accept – the obviously deranged, the potentially violent, men who were beyond the reaches of polite social agencies. It was a vanity, he knew, to think of himself as indispensable, but when it came to St Finbar's he sidestepped his own humility. Why shouldn't he be proud of himself?

He tossed the apple away and went inside a delicatessen where he pretended to examine the salami that hung in the window. There was a fine layer of sweat on his forehead. St Finbar's Mission would fall apart without him, he was convinced of that. Hadn't he carved the place out of practically nothing anyhow? Hadn't he begged and borrowed money to renovate the building and buy bedding and cooking equipment and then gone out into the drab streets looking for clients, sometimes having to drag them to the kitchen when they appeared reluctant? He'd given all his energies to the project. But more than that, more than time and effort and sweat, he'd brought to the place his own form of love and charity – which the established Church hadn't needed. Shaping St Finbar's had seemed to Tumulty a holy thing to do, and a practical expression of Christian love. Christ's love wasn't to be found in the chicanery of parish politics or out on golf courses where bishops rode their little fringed carts and discussed stock options. God didn't thrive in upper-class social settings. If He was anywhere, He was down there on the streets with the poor and needy, and Tumulty was nothing more than an instrument for God's work. God's world wasn't stained glass and velvet cushions and hypocrisy. He existed wherever hearts were breaking and men cried out in terrible need. St Finbar's Mission had become Joseph Tumulty's personal cathedral, the place where he felt spiritually closest to his deity.

From his coat pocket Tumulty removed a small black notebook Finn had given him the day he left Ireland. It was a cheap little book, perhaps thirty pages in all, and it contained only one name and address, written in Finn's flamboyant hand. The pages fell open at the centre because Tumulty had studied the name many times, wondering if and when he might have to use it. He'd tried on several occasions to commit it to memory, but somehow he hadn't trusted himself to do so. He stared at the writing, then shut the book and returned it to his coat pocket.

Go to this man, Finn had said. *Only when you need something badly, something you don't know how to get on your own.*

Tumulty went back on to the street. He reached the corner of Mulberry and Kenmare, and there he paused. He remembered now the last trip to Maine and the man who'd given him the briefcases in the snowbound parking lot of an old filling station. The man who never gave his name, who kept his conversation to an absolute minimum and who was always in a hurry to leave. The man with the peculiar unhealthy colour to his face. The man whose photograph Tumulty had accidentally come across in the pages of *The New York Times*, in an article concerning those mysterious brokers whose speciality was that of arranging mergers between corporations who didn't want the values of their stocks affected by advance publicity of their plans. A middleman, someone who operated in the fiscal shadows. His name was Nicholas Linney and he operated a company called Urrisbeg International.

Tumulty understood he wasn't meant to know Nicholas Linney's identity. But the fact was he *did* know it. There was no way of forgetting he knew it. And he was going to give it to Jig because Jig needed a name.

He turned into Kenmare. Halfway along the block he stopped, turning to check the sidewalk behind him. Even though he saw nobody who looked as if he might be following him, his instincts told him otherwise. People like Frank Pagan were smarter at this kind of thing than he could ever be. People like Pagan knew the tricks of this trade. Tumulty, rubbing a hand over his clammy forehead, looked across the street. He found himself gazing at the window of a small shop that sold religious artifacts. It had to be wrong. He took out his book and checked the address again. How could this possibly be the right place?

Plaster virgins looked mournfully out at him from behind the dirt-streaked window. Gaudy prints depicted the crucifixion. There were crosses and rosaries draped all over the place. There were Shroud of Turin souvenirs. It was a joyless window display. Tumulty went in the direction of the shop, walked a few paces beyond it to the corner, then stopped. This was the critical part. This was the moment.

He had a sudden inspiration. He'd call the shop, tell his contact to meet him somewhere. He went inside a phone booth and flipped through the pages of a ragged directory, looking for an entry under Santacroce, which was the name Finn had written in the notebook. He didn't find any name that corresponded with the address. Damn. Tumulty pressed his face wearily against the cold glass of the phone booth. He looked back the way he'd come. Cars. Pedestrians. How could he possibly tell if *anyone* was following him?

He stepped out of the phone booth. He took a handkerchief from his coat pocket and blew his nose. He examined the front of the shop again. It had no name. Inside the window, everything was covered in dust. The place looked as if it hadn't had customers in years. There were even framed paintings of the old Pope, Pius XII.

Dear God, Tumulty said to himself. He'd go in. He had to. What did it matter if anyone saw him? He wanted to buy a religious picture for St Finbar's Mission. There. It was as simple as that, if anybody asked. He had the perfect excuse for being in a shop like this, didn't he?'

He pushed the door open. A small bell rang over his head. It was gloomy inside and the air smelled stale, a mixture of sandalwood and dampness. He approached the counter and a curtain was parted at the back of the room. A man appeared.

'Santacroce?' Tumulty asked. There was a crack in his voice.

The old guy said to Frank Pagan, 'This is kinda exciting. This kinda thing don't happen to me every day.'

Pagan and Zuboric sat hunched in the narrow backseat of the old man's 1973 Opel. It was a shabby car with great chunks torn out of the upholstery. The floor was covered with discarded fast-food wrappers and mouldy french fries that looked like blunt pencils. Bumper stickers were plastered all over the back of the car, attesting to the man's extensive travels.

'I'd never a done this if it hadn't been for that FBI badge,' the man said. His name was Fogarty, and he'd been parked on Canal Street when Pagan had suggested that he might like to help in a 'confidential government investigation'. Fogarty was scouring missions and soup kitchens all across the East Coast in the quest for some long-lost alcoholic brother. Pagan was sure it was a sad tale, but he didn't encourage Fogarty to tell it.

The old man was delighted by the diversion. It was odd, Pagan reflected, how quickly the average citizen could slip into an undercover role. Fogarty narrowed his eyes and watched the street, and when he spoke his voice was hushed. It was the way he'd seen it in the movies. It was something to tell the folks back in Sunbury, Pennsylvania.

'What's this guy done anyhow?' Fogarty asked.

Zuboric said nothing. Commandeering a car and involving a private citizen hadn't been his idea. But he had to admit that this battered old jalopy was perfect because nobody would ever expect the FBI to travel with such a marked absence of style.

'Can't tell me, right?' Fogarty asked.

'Right,' Pagan said. Up the block a way Tumulty had disappeared inside a shop.

'Confidential stuff, right?'

Pagan nodded. The old man chuckled. 'I'll be damned,' he said.

Pagan told him to drive forward slowly and park at the end of the block. The only available space was alongside a fire hydrant. Fogarty took it, even though it was illegal.

Pagan turned round in his seat. The store into which Tumulty had gone was the kind that sold tawdry religious items.

Zuboric took out a notebook and scribbled down the address of the store, then tucked the book away. The smell of ancient fried foods was getting to him. Under his feet Big Mac wrappers made crinkling noises.

'He's taking his time,' Zuboric said.

Fogarty twisted around to look at the FBI man. 'Whyn't you just bust into that joint and go for broke?'

Zuboric smiled politely, said nothing.

'I get it,' Fogarty remarked. 'You want the whole syndicate, don't you? It ain't just one guy. Right?'

'Right,' Pagan said, wondering which particular movie was playing in the old man's head.

'I'll be damned,' Fogarty said.

Tumulty stepped out into the street now. He was carrying a large crucifix, unwrapped. He held it clutched against his side. He looked this way and that, then he began moving along the sidewalk.

'An ostentatious display of holiness,' Pagan said.

Zuboric nodded. 'He wants to be seen looking innocent.'

'You think he's afraid of vampires, Artie?'

'I think he's afraid period.'

St André des Monts, Quebec

The old DC–4 landed awkwardly on an airstrip located several miles from the village of St André des Monts, east of St Hyacinthe in south-east Quebec. The airfield had been used by the Royal Canadian Air Force during World War II, and then abandoned. The hangars had rotted and become overgrown with weeds, and the landing strip had subsided here and there, cracked by severe winters. The plane bounced a couple of times before it slid to a halt in front of a hangar. A man in a ski mask and goggles came out of a hangar and, leaning his face away from the sharp wind that blew across the field, walked towards the DC–4.

The door of the plane opened. Including pilot and co-pilot, there were six men on board. The man in the ski mask watched them disembark, scurrying down a rope ladder. They had been airborne for a little more than thirteen hours, and they moved wearily. But before any of them could rest there was cargo to be unloaded.

The man, who was called Fitzjohn, took his goggles off and rubbed his eyes. It had been his responsibility to find a suitable airfield as close as possible to the Canadian border with New York State. Posing as a businessman interested in opening a flying school, he'd searched for a location for months. This field was the best he'd found. Its present owner lived in Montreal and rarely visited the place, so Fitzjohn had considered it safe for his purpose.

Fitzjohn greeted Seamus Houlihan, who was the first man off the plane.

'You could've laid on better weather, Fitz,' Houlihan said, covering his face with the collar of his seaman's jacket.

'You're lucky it isn't snowing,' Fitzjohn replied.

Houlihan looked across the bleak airfield. In the distance there was ragged barbed wire and a couple of bleached signs that at one time had read NO ADMITTANCE. Bare trees grew beyond the fence. A Ryder rental truck sat alongside a hangar.

'Some place,' Houlihan said, shivering. 'The arsehole of the world.'

'It's everything you asked for.' Fitzjohn wanted to say something about how long it had taken him to locate this spot, he wanted to mention how many weeks he'd spent away from his home in Camden, New Jersey, but Houlihan was never interested in that kind of detail.

Houlihan stepped towards the nearest hangar and looked beyond the broken door at the dark interior. Fitzjohn had forgotten how suspicious Houlihan was. Every dark place contained the possibility of menace for Seamus Houlihan. The inside of the young man's mind had to be like the interconnected tunnels of a gloomy sewer. Fitzjohn was glad that his own role was coming to an end. After the border crossing he'd go back to New Jersey and sink into his own anonymous life and hope he'd never hear from the Free Ulster Volunteers again. He wasn't cut out for this kind of life. He had an American wife and two small kids and Armagh Jail, in Northern Ireland, where he'd spent two years for possession of hand grenades, was just an unpleasant memory now. Aside from the deprivation of liberty, what he resented most about Armagh was the fact that it was a British jail, and he was a British subject who'd armed himself against possible attacks from the IRA. A man protecting himself, that was all. He had always been loyal to Queen and country. The trouble was, Britain wasn't winning the struggle against the IRA. British policy in Northern Ireland was chicken-hearted. The army didn't crush the IRA with enough force.

John Waddell and the other men stood close to the plane. Fitzjohn smiled at them. He knew Waddell from the old days in Belfast, but the other characters were unfamiliar to him. He thought John Waddell looked like a dying rat, pale and shuddering in the cold air.

Houlihan made introductions. One of the men, a stocky figure with a scar running from the corner of his ear to his upper lip, was called Rorke. Another was named McGrath, a tense individual with the nervous eyes of a street fighter and a mouth that had very few teeth. They looked, Fitzjohn thought, seasoned in violence. Houlihan then introduced the pilot and the co-pilot, both of whom appeared anxious to be back inside the plane and out of this forsaken place. They'd delivered their cargo, which was the extent of their commitment, and they wanted to go home. The pilot was called Braxton and the co-pilot Lessingham. They were both English, both former air force pilots. Their last employment had been to airlift Libyan troops into Chad.

Braxton smiled in a pale way, then turned his face upwards, checking the sky. 'I'd like to be on my way, Seamus.' He pronounced the name correctly. *Shaymus*. Englishmen sometimes couldn't get their tongues around Irish names.

'And so you will, Braxton,' Houlihan said. 'Just as soon as we get this beast unloaded.'

Houlihan scanned the inside of the hangar again, as if his first examination of the place hadn't satisfied him. 'Have you found us a crossing?'

Fitzjohn said, 'I have.'

'Good, good,' Houlihan remarked.

There was a silence. In the distance wind rattled the rusted barbed wire and shook the ancient signs. Fitzjohn looked at Houlihan. There was an odd expression on the young man's face. He appeared to be staring inward, into his own black mind. He licked his lips, shifted his weight from one foot to the other. Fitzjohn had a premonitory moment, a sense of something unpleasant about to happen. He glanced at the pilot, Braxton, then looked back at Houlihan, who had one hand inside the deep pocket of his navy-blue jacket.

Fitzjohn *knew*.

He watched Houlihan take a pistol out of the pocket and turn very slowly towards the pilot, who stepped back a pace, his mouth open, a hand extended in front of his face.

The explosion of the gun roared in Fitzjohn's ears. He saw Braxton's face blown apart, the impact of the bullet throwing the body back several feet. Braxton lay face down under the fuselage of the DC–4, his arms pressed beneath his body. From the opening in his skull there was blood and grey fluid creating a puddle under his cheek. The co-pilot, Lessingham, stared at Houlihan in utter disbelief and then turned away, hurrying towards the rope ladder that hung from the door of the plane. He began to scramble upwards and the ladder swayed back and forth with the movements of his body.

Houlihan shot him in the back of the skull. Lessingham, caught in the strands of rope, twisted round, his face turning towards the hangar. One of his eyes was gone.

'Jesus God,' Fitzjohn whispered.

Houlihan smiled. He went over to Braxton's body and kicked it gently. 'Mercenary bastards,' he said. 'You can't trust people who do things only for the money.'

New York City

In his hotel room Frank Pagan had found a radio station that played nothing but old rock and roll. He was lying on the bed and listening to the late Gene Vincent hiccuping through *Be-Bop-a-Lula*, when the telephone rang. It was Foxworth calling from London.

'How are things in the land where people say Hi and Have a Nice Day?' Foxie asked.

Pagan turned Gene Vincent down. The connection with London was bad and Foxie's voice echoed.

'Cold,' Pagan said. 'Brass-monkey weather.'

'I have a tiny snippet of info for you, Frank. It may interest you.'

Pagan massaged a bare foot. He stared at the window where the midday light, filtered by a drape, was pallid.

Foxie said, 'Our old chum Ivor the Terrible is practically your next-door neighbour. Did you know that?'

'McInnes is here? In New York?'

'I am reliably informed by a young gal who works at the American fortress in Grosvenor Square that the Reverend Ivor McInnes obtained a temporary visa for research purposes.'

'What's he researching? New ways to boil Catholics?'

'Would you believe a book? A work of history?'

'Didn't know he could read,' Pagan said.

'He's staying at the Essex House,' Foxie said. 'Thought you might like to know.'

Later, when he'd replaced the telephone and turned up the volume of the radio to catch Buddy Holly's *Rock Around the Ollie Vee*, he sat cross-legged on the bed and closed his eyes and turned Foxie's news around in his mind. It was the familiar old labyrinth again. It was the Irish version of Join the Dots. Why was McInnes in New York at this particular time? Pagan didn't buy the idea of Ivor writing a book unless it was a polemic concerning the satanic ideology of the Roman Catholic Church and nobody was going to issue him a visa for that kind of lunacy. So why was he here? Coincidence? Pagan never trusted coincidence.

He opened his eyes. There was a knock on his door. He went across the room, undid the lock. Zuboric came inside, rubbing his cold hands together. He sat down in an armchair and made a face at the music that filled the room.

'Does it have to be that loud?' the agent asked.

'Is there any other way, Artie? Great rock was intended to be deafening.' Pagan made no move to adjust the volume. Quite the contrary. He wished he could make it even louder, but the tiny radio was already at maximum.

'What is with you and this music, Frank? You caught in a time warp?' Zuboric took a notebook out of his coat.

'They don't make music like this any more. It's all so bloody humourless these days. People with pink and green hair taking themselves seriously, spouting messages I don't want to hear.' Pagan sat on the edge of the bed. The music had changed to Chuck Berry. *Maybelline*.

Zuboric had to raise his voice to be heard over the noise. 'The shop in Little Italy belongs to a certain Michelangelo "The Saint" Santacroce.'

'The Saint?'

'That's what they call him. He doesn't exactly live up to it, though. Two terms in Attica. One for tampering with a jury. The other for illegal possession of automatic weapons.' Zuboric paused, looking over the top of his notebook. 'Here's the kicker, Frank. The weapons were all nicely crated when Santacroce was busted. Crated *and* labelled. Guess where they were going?'

'Ireland,' Pagan said.

'You got it.'

'What did the crates say? Butter?'

'Holy Bibles.'

Frank Pagan lay back across the bed and inspected the ceiling. 'What will they think of next?' he asked.

11 Roscommon, New York

It was seven o'clock before Celestine persuaded Harry Cairney he should retire. She escorted him upstairs, helped him undress. He was already sound asleep when she left the bedroom and went back down to the library, where Patrick Cairney sat in front of the log fire with a brandy glass in his hand. There was music playing on the stereo, Harry's music, the old Irish stuff he loved. Celestine turned the record player off. She sat down in the chair facing her stepson and picked up her own brandy from the coffee table. She looked at Patrick, as if she were trying to see some resemblance to his father in the young man's face.

'Don't tell your father,' she said. 'But I can only take Irish music in small doses. He's been playing it all afternoon. Too much.'

Patrick Cairney smiled. He'd been pleased to see his father leave the room because Harry had been headed in the direction of garrulous reminiscence, induced no doubt by the music. The entire afternoon had been filled with Irish tunes, ranging from *If You Ever Go Across the Sea to Ireland* to the inevitable rebel song *Kevin Barry.* Too much indeed, Patrick Cairney thought. An onslaught that dulled the senses after a while. Only Harry himself had been animated by the music, tapping his feet, rapping his fingertips on his knees, sitting sometimes with eyes closed and mouth half open, an old man travelling in old realms.

Once or twice, Patrick Cairney had felt so irritated that he'd wanted to turn the music off and go grab his father and shake him, as if to impress upon the old man the fact that all the songs in the world couldn't bring his private Ireland back to him. The same damn music, the same damn memories, and Patrick Cairney had heard them all a hundred times before. The brainwashed childhood, he thought. The childhood riddled through and rotted by Harry Cairney's nostalgia, his fake dreams. If Harry loved Ireland the way he claimed, then why had he never done anything about the Troubles there? Why had he never – not *once* in all his years in Washington – gone on record as condemning sectarian violence and supporting some kind of acceptable solution? The answer was simple – it was enough for Harry to sit with his eyes shut and his foot tapping and listen to the same old goddam songs. His dreams were safe things, retreats from a world where men and women and children died needlessly, and torture and terror were a part of every child's vocabulary.

In the glow from the fire, which was the only source of light in the large panelled room, Celestine's face was half ridden by rippling shadows. Cairney thought the firelight gave her beauty a mysterious quality. She sipped some brandy, then set the glass down and extended her long fingers in front of the flames. She continued to look at Cairney, her stare disarming.

'You don't understand this marriage, do you? You see a relatively young woman married to a man much older, and you wonder why.'

Cairney made a small sound of protest, but the truth was otherwise. He *had* been wondering.

'Maybe you're even thinking I married Harry for money and security,' she said.

Again Cairney protested. 'It never crossed my mind.'

'I love him,' she said. 'It's really that simple.'

Cairney finished his drink. 'And he dotes on you.'

Celestine settled back in her armchair, crossing her legs. 'I met your father quite by chance. I was doing PR work for one of those companies he lends his name to, a textile concern in Boston. They like to have Senator Harry Cairney on their stationery. He came to visit the company, and there was a luncheon in his honour, and we talked, and we met again the next day. He proposed to me within the week. I accepted.'

A whirlwind, Cairney thought. All during the afternoon he'd watched Celestine and Harry's mutual adoration society, the little touches between them, the long looks of affection they shared. And still, somehow, it didn't sit right with him except he wasn't sure why. The age difference, that was all. The curious contrast between this obviously healthy young woman and Harry Cairney's frailty. The other question that had gone through his mind was why a woman as vivacious as Celestine would want to lock herself away in the isolation of Roscommon. He had underestimated love, nothing more. It was an emotion he always underestimated.

Celestine stood up. 'I wasn't looking for anybody, Patrick. Marriage was the very last thing on my mind. I'd already been through one, and I wasn't enchanted by the experience. And I'm not interested in Harry's money. I want you to know that.'

Celestine's shadow was large on the wall behind her. She stretched her arms, then ran her fingers through hair that settled back in place immediately, as if it hadn't been disturbed at all.

'He charmed the heart out of me, Patrick. He's capable of that. He paid so much attention to me – he still does – that I felt like the centre of his universe. I was never in awe of him or his position. I didn't even *notice* the difference in our ages. It was all perfectly natural. I don't think anything in my entire life has ever been so natural.' She was quiet a moment, staring at Cairney with a frank look on her face. 'Why do I feel I have to explain myself to you?'

'You don't,' Cairney said.

'Maybe I want you to like me. Maybe I don't want you to have any doubts about me. Maybe all I really need is for you to understand that I love your father and that I'll take care of him. He's a wonderful man, Patrick, and I want him to be really healthy again. It's just such a heartache to see him sick.' She smiled now and the expression of concern that had appeared on her lovely face dissolved. 'Do you like to walk?'

'Sure.'

'I always take a stroll about this time,' she said. 'Want to keep me company?'

Cairney got up. He turned to look from the window. Roscommon was in darkness. The moon lay under thick clouds.

They went downstairs. Cairney put on his overcoat, and Celestine dressed in a fur jacket. Outside, they crossed the expanse of front lawn in silence until they reached the shore of Roscommon Lake, a dark disc stretching in front of them.

They walked the shoreline to a stand of bare trees. There, Celestine paused and looked out across the water. The lake made a soft knocking sound, a whisper of reeds. Cairney glanced back the way they'd come, seeing the black outline of the house. He had a brief image of his mother, Kathleen, a tall, round-faced woman with the kindest eyes he'd ever seen on any human being. Kathleen, who had never really been at home in Roscommon because she disliked its size and location, had presided over the big house like some unwilling empress whose emperor was constantly elsewhere. Cairney smiled to himself because the memory was warm and good. It had about it the tranquillity of recollected love.

The sound of a vehicle broke the stillness. Headlights appeared through the trees. It was the security jeep, which parked some yards away. A man came towards them, carrying a flashlight. He was the same man Cairney had seen that afternoon.

'Cold enough for you, Mrs Cairney?' the man asked.

Celestine didn't answer. In the beam of the flashlight she looked unhappy. The man stood very still, shining the beam towards the shore of the lake.

'Just the routine check,' the guard said.

Celestine turned away. When the man had returned to the jeep and the vehicle had moved off in a southerly direction, she said, 'I hate them. They're always nearby. Even when I can't see them, I feel them.'

'Why are they here?' Cairney asked.

'Harry's idea. He mumbled something about protecting his valuables. He thinks somebody is going to rob this place. I pretend the security goons don't bother me. But they're a nuisance.'

She moved along the shore. Cairney followed. The moon broke free from clouds and showered the lake with silver. Celestine stopped, turned to him, laid a hand on his arm.

'The trouble with your father is he thinks he's a young man all over again,' she said. 'He thinks he can do all the things he used to do when he was in his twenties. I can't get him to stay in bed. He won't follow his physician's orders.' She sighed. She dropped her hand to her side. 'I'm tired of telling him things for his own good.'

'He's a stubborn man,' Cairney said.

'Maybe he'd listen to you,' she said.

'I doubt it. The Senator's never been much of a listener.'

'Why do you call him that?' she asked.

'The Senator?' Cairney shrugged. 'I'm not absolutely sure. I guess I've always thought of him that way. The Senator from New York.'

'It's just the way you say it. It's almost as if you resent the sound of the word. Or the man behind it.'

'I don't resent him,' Cairney replied. 'And I don't mean to sound that way either.' He paused now, listening to the rustle of some night creature foraging nearby. If you listened closely, as he always did, even the most superficially placid nights were alive with undercurrents of noise. Resentment, he thought. That was only a part of it. It was more, the sense of being locked constantly in a relationship that was composed of conflicting emotions. Pity and love. Annoyance and admiration. It was a deep conflict and there were times – especially in Ireland, where he felt as if he were stalked by the ghost of Harry Cairney's younger self, a spectre who had the knowledgeable persistence of a tourist guide – when it twisted inside him with the certainty of a knife.

Celestine turned her face around to him just as the moon poked through cloud again. Staring at her, looking at the moonlight in her hair and the shadows under her cheekbones and the silvery flecks in her eyes, Cairney felt a little flicker of attraction that he pushed away almost as soon as it touched him. He moved back from Celestine. Your stepmother, for God's sake. Your father's wife. He wondered if she'd noticed, if his expression had betrayed anything. He was annoyed with himself. He didn't like unwanted feelings coming up out of nowhere and startling him. They suggested hidden places inside himself that he didn't know about, unmapped territory within his own psyche.

She went on talking about Harry's health. How his bronchial condition had recently worsened. How sometimes in the night she'd sit listening to his breathing, actually *waiting* in dread for the sound to stop. Cairney was hardly listening. Her words swept past him. He wanted to go back indoors. Get out of this moonlight, which was affecting him in uncomfortable ways. He shivered and looked towards the house. He thought of his father asleep in the upstairs bedroom.

'I don't want anything to happen to him,' she said.

'He's made of old shoe leather,' Cairney said. 'As a kid, I used to think he was indestructible.'

'That's the trouble, Patrick. He isn't.'

Cairney was silent. He put his hands into the pockets of his coat. A wind rose off Roscommon Lake. Cairney started to move in the direction of the house. Celestine followed.

'You're tired,' she said.

'A little.'

They walked back. Celestine paused on the steps of the house. Cairney, who had reached the door, looked back down at her.

She said, 'I don't want to lose him, Patrick. But Tully says his lungs are badly congested. This last bronchial attack really hit him where it hurts.'

Cairney didn't say anything. He gazed at the expression of concern on Celestine's face. He wanted to reach out and comfort her. Instead, he ushered her inside the entrance room, where it was warm.

Celestine removed her fur jacket. 'At least there's one consolation, Patrick. His doctor says he has a heart like an ox. That's something.'

Cairney smiled. 'What do you expect? It's a good Irish heart. They don't make them that way anymore.'

Celestine laughed. She pushed open the door that led to the sitting-room. She hesitated in the doorway a moment, watching Cairney's face. Then she said, 'Let's have a nightcap.'

The White House, Washington DC

Thomas Dawson, President of the United States, former senator from Connecticut, ate only yoghurt and raisins for his evening meal. He had a phobia about putting on weight, and he monitored his caloric intake carefully, using a small calculator he carried with him everywhere. He stuck his plastic spoon inside his yoghurt carton and sat back in his chair, punching the buttons of his calculator.

When he was through he looked up at his brother Kevin, who was standing on the other side of the desk. Kevin was pale and nervous and his voice a little higher than usual on this particular evening. With damn good reason, the President thought.

Thomas Dawson stood up. He fixed Kevin with the Dawson Grin, which had been patented years before during the first Senate campaign. It was a bright expression suggesting honesty and easy confidence. It appealed to women and it didn't threaten men, and it was perhaps the most important expression any politician could be blessed with, attractive and unmenacing. It was the smile of a man from whom you would buy a used car and go home feeling good about it, and you'd never think to complain when it started to leak oil on the second day.

'Kevin,' he said, using the tone of one brother to another, reassuring and almost conspiratorial.

Kevin Dawson shifted his feet. Whenever he visited his brother in the Oval Office, he felt the weight of history pressing down on him, and he was overawed like a schoolboy. Jesus, this was his own brother! They'd been brought up together, played together, shared a bedroom – and he could hardly talk to the man! Even now, when he'd come here to speak about his fears and look for a little support, words hadn't come easily. This meekness, which often took the form of a rather elaborate politeness, had long been the fatal flaw in his character. He was a man who found it easy to be overcome, whose arguments were always the first to be swept aside in any debate. Sometimes he wished he had the heart for confronting the world face on.

'The Irish question's a delicate one for me,' Thomas Dawson said. 'My general policy, at least in public, has been to ignore it. Leave it to the British. We pump in a few bucks to Belfast every now and then, and we do considerable trade with Dublin. But we don't play favourites. Don't take sides. Keep everybody happy. It's a balancing act and it's goddam tricky.'

Kevin Dawson watched his brother come around the large desk. He reflected on the fact that the politics of the presidency changed a man. Thomas Dawson had become sombre, more serious, and at the same time somewhat devious. Even the Dawson Grin seemed jaded, little more than reflex.

'Privately, it's another matter. You know that as well as anyone, Kevin. God, it's only been a hundred years since old Noel Dawson sailed from Killarney. How could I not feel some kind of attachment to the old country? How could I not take sides?' The President smiled sadly. 'The trouble is, I'm not a private person any more. It's one of the first things you find out in this job. Every damn thing you do is public. Even my diet, Kevin. I had a publisher offer me a ridiculous sum of money for my goddam diet! Can you imagine that? Wanted to call it the White House Diet or some such thing.'

He spread his hands on the desk. Finely manicured nails glinted under the green lampshade. 'Consider this, Kevin. There's a large Irish vote out there. Right now, I have it in my pocket the way no American president outside of Kennedy ever had it. I can count on it and that's a nice feeling in politics because usually the only thing you can take for granted is the electorate being fickle.' The President sat up on the edge of his desk and played with the empty yoghurt carton. 'I'd be pretty damn stupid to screw around with this support. It would be suicidal to alienate it.'

Kevin Dawson bit the inside of his cheek. What was his brother trying to tell him? He remembered Thomas Dawson when he'd been plain old Tommy, eighteen years of age and a halfway decent quarterback at Princeton. Simple unadulterated Tommy, without a devious bone in his body. He failed to make the connection between the President and that young man who had loved nothing more than football, beer, and cheerleaders, in any order you liked. Now Thomas Dawson watched his weight, didn't drink beer, paid no attention to football, and – instead of dallying with cheerleaders – was married to a glacial woman called Eleanor, who was always travelling the country in her relentless and entirely manic crusade against the indiscriminate dumping of radioactive wastes. Mrs Radioactivity, Kevin thought. Eleanor Dawson was an ice princess, a woman with all the sexual charm of cake frosting. Kevin could never imagine his brother in bed with her. With her high cheekbones and her fashionable demeanour and the calm way she handled herself with press and public, she was an absolutely perfect wife for a president.

Thomas Dawson examined his fingernails. 'I've always turned a blind eye to your little gang of fund-raisers, Kevin. I've always considered that side of you your own private business. Despite the potential embarrassment you represent, I've never told you what to do. Have I?'

Kevin Dawson shook his head.

'I've let you run as you please,' the President said. He reached out and clapped his brother on the shoulder and all at once Kevin Dawson was sixteen years old again, confiding to his big brother that he'd gotten a girl into trouble and what the hell should he do about it. He felt small.

The President sat down behind his desk. He had a red-covered folder in front of him. He flipped it open. 'Maybe I should have kept a firmer hand on you,' he said. He shrugged, stared at the several sheets of paper inside the folder. 'And now you come here and tell me that some Irishman might be a menace to your life. Which wouldn't have been the case if you'd quit hanging around with those Irish fanatics.' The President was careful enough not to name them, even if he knew who they were. His was a life of sometimes pretending ignorance of things he knew. It was a way of thinking in which he became two distinct people, and then two more, splitting and multiplying his personalities like some primitive cell.

'Yes,' Kevin Dawson said quietly. His face assumed an expression of regret. His cheeks sagged and his lips turned down and his eyes seemed to shrink into his head.

The President said, 'The problem is, he's not just *some* Irishman, Kevin. The man who's got you steamed up is none other than Jig. Ring a bell?'

'Jig?' Kevin's throat constricted. '*They sent Jig?*'

The President nodded his head. 'I'm told he entered the United States within the last forty-eight hours, give or take a few. He's suspected to be in the New York City area. We're not sure.'

Kevin Dawson sat down, something he didn't usually do in this particular office. He felt something very cold settle on his heart. He stared at his brother, as if he were expecting the President to tell him that he'd been joking about Jig, but Thomas Dawson's expression didn't change and the seriousness in his eyes didn't go away. Kevin realised that a small nerve had begun to beat in his throat and his hands were suddenly trembling. In a million years he could never have imagined Jig's orbit touching his own. What the hell did *his* life have to do with that of the famous Irish assassin? They were worlds apart. But here was Thomas Dawson telling him otherwise. Kevin closed his eyes. 'You're not *sure?*' he asked. 'What the hell does that mean?'

The President was quiet for a long time. 'I've been trying to explain something to you Kevin. I've been trying to instruct you in the realities of my position.'

Realities, Kevin Dawson thought. The only reality that concerned him right then was the notion of Jig lurking out there in the shadows of his life. It had been bad enough to imagine a faceless Irishman, but now that this figure had been identified, it was much worse. For the first time since he'd become associated with the Fund-raisers he felt a sense of fear. He tried to remember Jock Mulhaney's reassurances about how this Irishman would never find them in any case, but how could the big man's bluster console him now? Even Harry Cairney hadn't seemed very convinced that the group's anonymity was inviolate. Cairney had given the opposite impression, that the secrecy in which the group had always operated was goddam *fragile*. Kevin Dawson leaned forward in his chair, clenching his hands between his knees. 'You must be doing *something* to catch this guy, Tom.'

Thomas Dawson closed the red-covered file. 'You're not listening to me. You're not paying attention. Jig's become something of a folk hero in every Irish bar from Boston to Philadelphia and back again. They sing songs about him. They adulate him. He's the Irish Pimpernel, Kevin. And you know how the Irish love their heroes. The daring of the man. The mystery. He kills English politicians and disappears as if he doesn't exist! They just adore all that. He's been written up in *Newsweek* and *Time*. The guy's a goddam saviour as far as the Irish are concerned.'

Kevin Dawson watched his brother stroll round the office. It dawned on him now. 'You're not going out of your way to catch him, is that it? You're going to give this killer a free rein. Are you telling me that?'

'Not exactly.'

'I'm lost, Tommy. Enlighten me.'

'The votes,' Thomas Dawson said. 'If I place myself firmly behind a massive effort to catch this man, how are the votes going to go? How are the Irish going to mark their ballots next time around? Are they going to pull their little levers for the man who approved of a massive manhunt to catch their hero?' He looked at his younger brother seriously. 'I have a number of promises to keep while I occupy this office. And the only currency a president has is the vote of the people. In my case, Kevin, the Irish-American community constitutes a sizeable proportion of that vote. It's like having money in the bank. And I don't want to squander it. I don't want to take the risk of tossing it all away. Have you seen the opinion polls lately, Kevin? It seems like I'm having what the pros call an image problem. Some people out there perceive their President as a man who doesn't make decisions quickly enough. I don't like that.'

Kevin Dawson didn't speak. He heard the sound of a door closing at the back of his brain.

'I'm not going to give them a martyr, Kevin. I'm not going to be the one to take their folk hero away from them.' Thomas Dawson looked up at the ceiling. When he spoke again his voice was low. 'Besides, it's my understanding he's only looking for the men in your little group, Kevin. It's not as if he's a threat to the population at large, who don't even know the man's in the country. And I intend to keep it that way.'

Kevin Dawson shook his head. 'I can't believe I'm hearing this.'

'Try,' the President said. 'Try a little harder.'

'You'll sit here and do absolutely nothing about him?'

'I didn't say that, Kevin. At this moment there's an English agent called Frank Pagan in New York City who's getting some assistance from the FBI.'

'How much is "some"?' Kevin asked.

The President shrugged. 'Just enough.'

Kevin Dawson tried to see inside his brother's head. There was a cynical balance sheet in that skull. The President was weighing four men, one of whom was his own brother, against his previous Irish-American vote. 'Doesn't it matter to you that *my* life might be in danger? Jig kills people, for Christ's sake! It's his profession. And they aren't sending a professional assassin from Ireland for the good of his goddam health. If he doesn't recover the money . . .' He didn't finish this sentence.

'I don't think for one moment that Jig is going to find you. I know how your little gang covers its tracks.'

'Yeah, I keep hearing how good we are at secrecy,' Kevin Dawson said. 'Pardon me if I'm not convinced.'

Thomas Dawson laid a hand on his brother's arm. 'I'm prepared to put a couple of Secret Service agents at your disposal.'

Kevin Dawson looked at his brother. For a moment the touch of the President's hand on his arm reminded him of the man he used to have as a brother, when life had been carefree and political ambition hadn't taken total control of Tommy's personality. 'I've got a Secret Service agent already,' he said.

'One man who does nothing but escort your daughters to school,' the President said. 'You need your protection beefed up, Kevin. And you'll have it before the end of the night.'

Kevin Dawson looked suitably grateful. 'Suppose this Frank Pagan character gets lucky? Suppose he captures Jig? What will you do with the guy if you catch him?'

'I don't think I can answer that.'

'A Jimmy Hoffa style disappearance? The Irish hero simply vanishes off the face of the earth and nobody knows where or why?'

The President didn't answer his brother's questions. He sat back down behind his desk and put the red file inside a drawer. 'Let me ask *you* something, Kev. Who really took the money from that ship?'

'I haven't got a clue.'

'No ideas?'

Kevin Dawson shrugged. It was a question he'd asked himself frequently. His immediate impulse was to suspect Mulhaney, but this was totally unfair, a suspicion motivated by a personal dislike for the man. It could have been Mulhaney. It could have been Linney. Even Harry Cairney. The problem was that all four men, himself included, would come under Jig's suspicion. What if Jig somehow reached the conclusion that he, Kevin Dawson, was responsible for the affair? What if Jig got to Mulhaney, say, and Big Jock, to divert suspicion from himself, managed to convince the Irishman that the guilty party was

Dawson? Kevin Dawson's fear intensified. Suspicions created other suspicions. Possibilities led to other possibilities. He had the feeling of a man locked within a complex hall of mirrors, images reflecting themselves to an inscrutable infinity so that you could never find the true source of them. *And there was no way out*. He didn't like thinking this way, didn't like the panic rising in him.

The President placed his feet up on the desk and crumbled his empty yoghurt carton, flipping it towards a wastebasket. 'If there's a next time, Kevin, you ought to be a tad more careful.'

'I don't think there will be a next time,' Kevin Dawson said.

He went towards the door. He thought of going out into the darkness of the city and the prospect didn't appeal to him. Despite its floodlights, its illuminated tourist attractions, Washington was a city of too many dark places.

'What about the others?' he asked, turning in the doorway.

'Others?'

'My associates. I don't imagine they can count on your protection as well.'

'They're not exactly my blood relations, are they?'

There was a small indifferent light in Thomas Dawson's eyes. Callous, Kevin thought. Maybe that came with the territory. With the subterfuges of the office. The great numbers game the President played. The numbers justified anything. Everything.

Kevin Dawson opened the door.

The President said, 'Two things, Kevin. The first, you don't mention Jig to any of your . . . associates. So far as I'm concerned, Jig isn't in this country. I don't want anybody saying otherwise.'

'What's the second?' Kevin Dawson asked.

'We never had this conversation.'

St Bernard des Bois, Quebec

The Ryder truck was parked in the forecourt of a gas station. Fitzjohn sat behind the wheel. The other men in the cab were Houlihan and Waddell. Rorke and McGrath travelled in the back with the cargo that had been unloaded from the DC–4. Houlihan squinted through the windshield at the unlit gasoline sign that hung like a small deflated moon over the pumps, then he glanced at his watch.

'Am I right, Fitz? Is it seven-thirty in New York City?'

Fitzjohn looked at his Rolex and nodded.

'All these bloody time zones confuse the hell out of a man,' Houlihan said. He slumped back in his seat and closed his eyes. 'Let's hear about the route, Fitz.'

Fitzjohn stared at the sign in the gas-station window, which read FERMÉ/CLOSED. He was still thinking about what had happened at the airfield, and no matter how hard he tried he couldn't get rid of the images. The weird look on Houlihan's face. The dead bodies of the pilots. In fucking cold blood, without even so much as a blink of an eye. Houlihan hadn't mentioned the incident since they'd left the airstrip. It was over and done with. Already ancient history. Two dead airmen whose only crime, so far as Fitzjohn could tell, was that Houlihan hadn't trusted them. Seamus Houlihan, judge and jury and executioner, all rolled into one.

'There's an old road twelve miles from here,' he said without turning to Houlihan. He couldn't look at the man. 'It's a dirt road that leads to a fishery. The fishery's closed this time of the year because of the weather, which suits us fine. Nobody travels that way.'

'And where does your road lead?' Houlihan asked.

'Beyond the fishery, it turns into a narrow path that goes between some trees, then it passes an abandoned farmhouse. There are fields after that.'

'Open fields?'

Fitzjohn nodded. 'We cross the fields for about two miles. On the other side there's a track that comes out just north of Highway Twenty-seven.'

'Highway Twenty-seven?' Houlihan opened his eyes. 'That doesn't mean a thing to me, Fitz.'

'It's in the State of Maine.'

'What about the Border Patrol?' Waddell spoke for the first time since they'd left the airfield. He'd become pale and totally withdrawn, gazing speechlessly out of the window for mile after mile. He moved only when he lit cigarettes, chainsmoking them in silence. His brown-stained fingers trembled in his lap.

'The nearest port of entry is at a place called Coburn-Gore. It's about two miles away from the spot where we join Highway Twenty-seven. I don't think we're likely to encounter any Border Patrol.' Fitzjohn paused. 'It's not as if we're coming in from Mexico, after all. The Border Patrol down there are fanatics. Anyway, this truck has New Jersey plates, and that helps.'

Houlihan asked, 'Can we get across the fields without getting stuck?'

Fitzjohn said, 'I don't see why not. The snow's hard and there haven't been any fresh falls in more than a week.'

'And this Highway Twenty-seven, where does it lead us?'

'All the way to Interstate Nine-five.'

Nobody spoke for a time. Fitzjohn could hardly wait to get inside the US, because it meant he would leave the truck to Houlihan and the others, then make his way back to New Jersey. Relief. An end to this damned business as far as he was concerned. He didn't want to know what Houlihan planned to do in America. He didn't need to have that kind of knowledge.

'I've got a phone call to make,' Houlihan said.

Houlihan climbed out of the cab. He moved across the forecourt of the gas station, then went inside the phone booth and picked up the receiver.

Fitzjohn watched him from the cab. He was about to say to Waddell that he thought Seamus Houlihan might benefit from being locked up in a padded room, but why bother? For one thing, Waddell might take it into his head to pass such a remark on to Houlihan, which wasn't a marvellous prospect. For another, everybody involved in this escapade had to be a little mad, himself included. Except Houlihan was more than that. He was lethal.

12 New York City

Joseph X. Tumulty looked from the window of his office down into the darkened street. Earlier, a navy-blue Ford had parked halfway along the block, and the tan Chrysler that had been stationed there drove off. It was the changing of the guard. He peered across the way. There was a light in the office building opposite St Finbar's Mission. Tumulty could see a fat man sitting behind a desk. He was counting papers, flicking them back and licking his thumb every so often.

Tumulty turned from the window and went to his desk. He sat down, adjusting the lamp so that the light didn't shine directly into his face. He unlocked the middle drawer and took out a leather pouch, which he unzipped. There was seven thousand five hundred dollars inside. This money had been given to him by Padraic Finn more than three years ago. A contingency fund, which Finn, with the canniness of a man who understood that money *worked* for you, had placed in an interest-bearing account under Tumulty's name. When Tumulty had gone just before closing-time to make the withdrawal – a tense moment, standing in a line that never seemed to move – he had the feeling he'd been followed to the bank. He'd withdrawn all the money and closed the account. Santacroce wanted six thousand dollars. Six thousand would have fed the clientele of St Finbar's for about four months.

Tumulty absently regarded the religious artifacts on the walls. The Mexican cross he'd bought that day in Santacroce's store lay propped against the wall near the window. The Christ figure nailed to the wood was gory in the way Latin Americans loved. Blood filled up the eyes and dripped from the most unlikely places in the wooden body. Tumulty thought Jesus looked more perplexed than sorrowful. It was a distasteful piece but he hadn't wanted to leave Santacroce's store empty-handed. For appearance's sake.

Santacroce had said the merchandise might take some time to get together. Arrangements had to be made. He estimated twenty-four hours maximum, maybe a whole lot sooner. It depended on a variety of factors, none of which the gun merchant volunteered to explain. Tumulty hadn't asked either. He'd been very anxious to get out of that stifling little shop with its smell of old sandalwood and lacquer and dust. And away from Santacroce too, whose white puffy face and slitlike eyes seemed to suggest he was in the business, plain and simple, of death.

Twenty-four hours. Tumulty wondered a moment about Jig. When was he coming back? He couldn't remember if he'd told Jig two days or three. And then there was the unpleasant prospect of picking up a package from Santacroce and getting it back to this place. He knew it was crazy to bring weapons inside St Finbar's, but what was his alternative? He couldn't think of a place where he might safely stash guns.

He hated the feeling of St Finbar's being under siege like this. The idea scared him. And if it came down to a choice between the Cause and his own little mission here on Canal Street, the desperate souls he cared for, which way would he go? That was the Big One. Would he go to jail before giving up Jig? Or would he quietly surrender the assassin to Frank Pagan so that he might get on with his life's work in peace – if indeed peace was attainable after an act of treachery?

From the kitchen below there came the sound of voices. Babble. The smell of cooking floated inside his office. It was time, he thought, for prayer, the quest for guidance. He folded his hands together and closed his eyes, inclining his forehead to the tips of his fingers. For most of his life this act had been invigorating for him, although at times God's responses were difficult to catch. Sometimes Tumulty felt he was pursuing a sweet, silvery thread through empty reaches of the ether, fumbling towards a divine light. But there were other moments when he achieved the light, and then a great calm would come over him and he would glimpse a way through the mysteries of the divinity.

He sat very still. He tried to concentrate on the inner voice that was for him his means of communication when it came to prayer. A secretive little voice, which sometimes sounded like a tiny whisper in the vastness of the cosmos. He opened his eyes, frustrated. It wasn't happening today. There were crossed wires in his brain, and other thoughts kept intruding. Guns and politics, secular matters. He made fists of his thick hands and clenched them on the surface of the desk. *Guidance, dear God. Show me.* He stood up and wandered to the window, looked down into the street, saw that the navy-blue Ford was still in place there. *Guidance,* he thought again. Instead of God's voice, what he heard was Finn saying *The Cause is a holy one, Joe. And God knows that. There's no conflict, none at all, between serving God and the Cause. You wouldn't be the first man of the cloth to embrace them both.*

Tumulty wanted to believe this. The problem lay in violence and murder, neither of which he could possibly condone. It seemed to him that the Cause and God were diametrically opposed to each other. The former promoted death, the latter life. It was the difference between a total eclipse and the warming light of the sun. Dear Christ, how had he ever stumbled into this dilemma? More to the point, was there any way to resolve it? To square his religious beliefs with the demands of the Cause?

A sound in the doorway of his office made him turn around. The tall, skinny figure who stood there was a man called McCune, who blinked into the room with watery blue eyes. McCune wore a flannel shirt, open at the neck so that his large Adam's apple was visible, like some kind of growth, in his scrawny throat.

'We're wondering when you're coming down, Father Joe,' the man said.

Tumulty stared at the man. McCune had been one of his earliest successes. When he'd first encountered him, McCune had been a suicidal drunk with violent tendencies, a former railway engineer canned by the railroad for hauling eight hundred tons of coal through Pennsylvania while extremely intoxicated. McCune had lost his wife and kids, home, and any sense of his own dignity. It had taken time and patience, but Tumulty had given him back the dignity at least. McCune had been sober for almost a year and worked as a night clerk in a hotel on Eleventh Avenue. It wasn't much – but self-worth, Tumulty knew, was a quality you retrieved only in small stages.

'I almost forgot,' Tumulty said.

McCune looked a little surprised. 'You've never forgotten before.'

Tumulty nodded, smiling at McCune. *This man trusts me,* he thought. *This man thinks he owes his life to me.*

'I'll be down in a minute,' Tumulty said. Every night at the same time he conducted an Alcoholics Anonymous meeting in the kitchen. It was an event for which he was always punctual because he believed that one of the basic ingredients for sobriety was commitment to responsibility. And he had to show the men at the meeting that he took his own responsibilities in earnest. He had to set examples. You could show how much you cared only by your actions.

'I'll tell the others,' McCune said, then hesitated. 'Is something troubling you?'

Tumulty was about to answer when the telephone on his desk rang.

He stared at the sound. Two rings, then silence. Followed by two more rings. It was Santacroce's signal.

So soon.

Too soon. He hadn't expected to hear from Santacroce until next morning at the earliest. He felt panicked. He stared at McCune, then at the Christ on the Mexican cross, but all he found in the eyes was an impossible blankness.

'I'm fine,' he said to McCune. It was the first time he'd ever lied to any of his clients at St Finbar's.

Frank Pagan sat behind the wheel of a rented 1974 Eldorado convertible. He'd found a place in the Village that specialised in renting old convertibles and, since he'd always wanted to drive a Cadillac, he'd hired this big dark-green monster with battered upholstery and a cracked dash and a rusted-out body. The radio worked. Pagan had it tuned to an FM rock station that was playing the entire cycle of Fats Domino's hits.

Zuboric, who felt in the Eldorado like a pimp fallen on hard times, said, 'I grew out of that music. When the sixties came to an end, I was into more jazz. Modern jazz. Dizzie Gillespie, like that.'

Pagan looked at the FBI man. The tone in Zuboric's voice was admonitory, as if he were really advising Frank Pagan to grow up. Rock and roll was for kids. Pagan had come to think of Artie Zuboric as an appendage he couldn't shake, a hump on his back, a growth attached to his body. He might not have minded so much if Zuboric had simply been a tail, someone who followed his movements unobtrusively, but the FBI man was a constant physical presence.

Pagan rubbed his gloved hands together. The chill inside the car was pervasive, bleeding through his bulky leather jacket. Along Canal Street, where he was parked, was a navy-blue Ford occupied by Orson Cone's relief, an older man called Tyson Bruno. Tyson Bruno was taciturn and morose. He had one of those wooden faces upon which expressions have a very hard time. He sat inside his Ford like a block of cement, defined by his duty, which was simply that of observing the comings and goings at St Finbar's. Like Orson Cone, Tyson Bruno was also a kind of decoy, somebody in place for Tumulty to spot. Orson Cone and Tyson Bruno. Americans had the most peculiar names. When he'd been in New York before with Roxanne, they'd drunk too much champagne one night and in a hilarious mood they'd gone through the pages of the Manhattan phonebook, discovering such oddities as Neddy Bummer and Bobbi Plapp, which Roxanne had laughed over, saying it sounded like a baby farting into a diaper. Harmless times, he thought now. Laughter before dying.

'We should've put somebody outside Santacroce's,' Pagan said. It wasn't the first time he'd made the suggestion. He recalled what he'd said that afternoon when they'd tracked Tumulty to a bank. *Nobody is watching Santacroce*. Artie Zuboric hadn't seemed very interested.

'I told you. Lack of manpower, Frank.' Zuboric shrugged. Pagan had still to learn that his problems got low priority here.

'Lack of manpower. No phone tap. One agent in the street. This is a shoestring operation. If you and I split up, one of us could watch Tumulty, the other Santacroce. Manpower problem solved in one swoop. Maybe that's a little too logical for you, though.'

Zuboric wasn't going to respond to this. He wasn't going to be drawn into another argument with Pagan over human resources. He lit a cigarette and coughed a couple of times. The trouble with Frank Pagan was his sheer fucking persistence. He wouldn't let something go once he'd taken a bite out of it. He kept digging, kept trying to operate on his own. He was the same goddam way with Jig. He was consumed by Jig. Probably he dreamed Jig at nights. Had Jig for breakfast.

Zuboric sighed. What he really wanted to do was bust Tumulty and Santacroce both, because that was one way of putting Jig out of circulation. Deprive the guy of his connections. Isolate him. He'd mentioned this briefly to Pagan but good old Frank dismissed it. It was clear Frank Pagan wanted to run this show his own way, which was something Zuboric couldn't allow. He shut his eyes, let his cigarette dangle from his lip, and thought about Charity, and wondered where she was right this moment and whether she'd ever consent to marry him. The last time he'd asked, Charity told him she'd think about it when he wasn't married to the goddam Bureau and his prospects had improved. Prospects, he thought now. Sitting in a draughty Eldorado with a cop who was manic and argumentative – his prospects didn't seem entirely *rosy*. Maybe he should never have fallen quite this heavily for a gorgeous girl in a topless bar, but that was the way the cards had been dealt and what could you do but pick them up, see if you could play them? The trouble was, Charity was used to high rollers, and Artie Zuboric couldn't compete on that level.

Pagan stuck the key in the ignition. He played with the power switches. He made his seat go backwards and forwards, then he had the windows going up and down. There was a certain kind of limey, Zuboric reflected, who was enchanted by American flash. Big cars and loud music and Hawaiian shirts. Pagan was one of them. Zuboric attributed it to a kind of insecurity, cultural inferiority, as if the Tower of London and Shakespeare and Stonehenge weren't enough to be going on with. They had to immerse themselves in things American. Pagan was like a kid in a whole new playground. Zuboric suddenly wondered if Frank Pagan was afraid of the threshold of forty, if the way he dressed and behaved had something to do with his reluctance to face the big four-oh.

Pagan leaned forward against the steering wheel.

'Ah-hah,' he said. 'There goes our boy.'

Zuboric looked along the street at the sight of Joe Tumulty coming out of St Finbar's. Here we go again, he thought, as Frank Pagan slid the huge car slowly forward.

Ivor McInnes stepped out of the Essex House and walked along Central Park South. It was eight o'clock and he'd just eaten a satisfying dinner in the hotel. He turned onto Fifth Avenue, looking at the lights along the thoroughfare. He had in mind a specific destination, but first he intended to walk as far as 49th Street. He looked at his wristwatch and checked the time; then he thought a moment about J. W. Sweeting, the lackey from the State Department. McInnes had fought a great many battles with bureaucracy in his life, most recently with the asinine leaders of his own Presbyterian Church, who were dismayed by the controversy that had always surrounded him and had stripped him of his parish. They were men of limited imagination. What the hell did it matter? McInnes had never been a truly *religious* man. All along he'd seen the Presbyterian pulpit as a convenient place from which to influence the politics of Northern Ireland, an attitude that had embarrassed Presbyterian churchmen, who failed to notice a very obvious fact of life in the country – that churches weren't just places where people went to sing hymns and hear sermons, they were instruments of social and political usefulness. The Catholic Church, cunning as ever, had always known that. Priests hid IRA members in their chapels or carried weapons back and forth. The Protestant clergy, on the other hand, had been slow on the uptake, immersed in the drudgery of committees and do-good schemes. For Ivor McInnes, that simply wasn't enough. And now the time for talking, the time for conciliation, had passed.

He stopped outside St Patrick's Cathedral. A priest appeared on the steps, said something to a tourist with a camera, then agreed to have his picture taken with the cathedral in the background. McInnes saw a flashbulb pop. St Patrick's made him uneasy. It was a vast stronghold of Catholicism, and in McInnes's world anything remotely connected to the Vatican was distasteful. He thought that any church that took ordinary tap water and did some abracadabra over it and called it holy was still locked into the superstitions of the Dark Ages. Therefore backward. Therefore a breeding ground for ignorance. There were times when he felt sorry for people who had been indoctrinated by the Roman Catholic Church, which he placed at the level of a cult, with its brainwashing tactics and Latinate mumbo jumbo and the highly curious notion of confession. It wasn't that he detested individual Catholics as such – he considered them merely misguided, suckers swayed by a holy carnival of stained-glass mysteries and enthralled by the stigmata and prone to the hysteria of seeing wooden effigies shed salt tears. No, it was more the fact that he completely resented the enormous power and riches and influence of the Vatican, from whence all Catholic conspiracies emanated – including the one that threatened to engulf Northern Ireland.

He reached 49th Street. He was in love with New York. It was a city with a delightfully sinful face. Every human weakness was pandered to somehow here. There was a sense of freedom that didn't exist in Belfast. Poor dear Belfast, a broken-hearted city with its military checkpoints and burned-out buildings. A city of fear. McInnes mainly blamed the Catholics for the atmosphere. They bred like flies in such RC ghettos as Ballymurphy and Turf Lodge and Andersonstown, which were nothing more than nurseries for future IRA gunmen. A time would come, McInnes had warned his congregation in his parting sermon, when Catholics would outnumber Protestants in Northern Ireland – and then what? It would be like bloody South Africa, a minority straining to hold on to power in the face of a hostile majority. A prescription for doom. A prescription Ivor McInnes wasn't going to see filled.

He left Fifth Avenue and walked until he came to a phone booth located outside a bar called Lonnigan's, one of those Irish pubs scattered around Manhattan. Posters in the window advertised *ceilidhs*, nights of folk singing and dancing. McInnes went inside the booth. He checked his watch again. He felt apprehensive now. A taste of the duck he'd eaten came back into his mouth, a film of scum on the surface of his tongue. What if something had gone very wrong? What then? He laid his hand on the receiver and inclined his forehead on the glass. By nature he was a relentless optimist, and like others of this persuasion he was sometimes prey to a certain brief dread of failure.

He drummed his fingers on the receiver.

The telephone rang. He picked it up immediately.

He heard Seamus Houlihan's voice.

'We're crossing tonight,' Houlihan said. He sounded as if he were trapped inside a tunnel.

'Fine,' McInnes said. He was flooded with relief that Houlihan had at least arrived. At the same time, the idea that the border crossing was yet to take place pricked his capacity for dread again. Tension made a nerve move in his eyelid. 'Has Fitzjohn found a place to cross?'

'He says so.'

McInnes looked into the street. A high-stepping girl went past, and he tracked her with his eyes. 'The flight was uneventful?'

'It was,' Houlihan said.

McInnes paused. He wasn't exactly happy about Seamus Houlihan having any responsibility. Seamus was the kind of man who'd kill somebody if they happened to look at him with any trace of hostility. He didn't have much going on in the brain department. People like Houlihan were useful, but only up to a point. When they'd outlived their functions, they could become utterly embarrassing.

'Same time tomorrow night, Seamus. And good luck.'

McInnes put the receiver back. He moved out of the phone booth and went along the sidewalk. The girl was just ahead of him, her hips swaying beneath her overcoat. On other trips to this city, at a time when he hadn't been banned by his own church and harassed by the State Department, he'd been struck by the number of beautiful women here. It seemed to him they came dropping out of the sky like bright pennies.

He reached the Hotel Strasbourg, stopping only a moment outside the dimly lit lobby. He looked up and down the sidewalk, then he went inside the hotel and moved towards the stairway, passing the night clerk who didn't even glance up at him. The carpet under his feet was threadbare and elaborately stained. On the second floor McInnes looked for Room 220. When he found it he knocked quietly on the door. He heard the girl's voice call out to him. He stepped into the room, which was lit only by a weak bulb in a lamp on the bedside table.

'Am I on time?' he asked. He felt only the smallest misgiving. He had needs, and they had to be satisfied, and this was nothing more than a transaction of skin – although he knew he would change it, by an act of his imagination, into something more than that.

The girl, who wore only the underwear McInnes had requested by telephone, smiled at him. 'You're the one talks like John Lennon,' she said. 'It's cute. You're kinda cute yourself.'

McInnes moved to the bed. He looked down at the girl. In a moment he was going to take the shortcut out of his tension, but right then he just wanted to look. She was skinny and her breasts were very small, and she must have been just sixteen. McInnes took off his coat and laid a hand on the girl's thin thigh. The girl didn't move. She stared at him coolly. Then she slid languidly down the pillow and stretched her long legs, parting them a little as she moved. He brought his hand up to the edge of her red panties. He continued up to the cups of her red bra, which fastened in the front. He undid the clip, pushed the bra aside.

'Tell me your name,' he said.

'Elva.'

'Elva.' McInnes moved her long fair hair between his fingers. It was a moment that took his breath away. Here, in this shabby room, touching this delightful yellow-haired girl, he could pretend. Pretend he was elsewhere in another room at another time and that he held somebody else in his arms, and then there wouldn't be any sense of shame or treachery.

'Elva,' he said again. It was the wrong name and it had the wrong number of syllables, but he could still pretend anyhow. He closed his eyes and lowered his mouth to her nipples, lost in the pungent scent of her perfume and her supple young flesh.

The girl held on to the big man tightly. She couldn't know that this same man who whimpered in her ear and pretended that she was another woman altogether had set in motion a sequence of events she'd read about in the newspapers in the days ahead. She thought he was just another weirdo who liked to fuck with a dog collar around his neck.

If Joseph Tumulty knew there was a big green car tracking him a block away, he gave no indication of it. He walked slowly, calmly, pausing every now and then to study menus in the windows of Chinese restaurants along Mott Street. Frank Pagan, who had to concentrate on a variety of driving problems – stop lights, impatient drivers behind him, kamikaze pedestrians in front, and the fact he was driving on the wrong side of the road – found the Cadillac as unresponsive as a broken-down horse. Something clanked under the hood and the vehicle had a tendency to stray to the left. There was also an ominous smell of burning oil.

Zuboric said, 'You should've let me drive.'

'Why should you get all the fun, Artie?'

'Fun?'

Zuboric leaned out of the window and flipped his middle finger at the honking car immediately behind. It was a standard sign of the road in New York City. Pagan hunched over the wheel and tried to keep an eye on Tumulty, who was lingering too long this time outside a place called Yang. Was he going inside to eat? Was this outing nothing more than an innocent Chinese dinner? Frank Pagan braked as a couple of teenage Chinese boys walked directly in front of the Cadillac. Ahead, almost a block away, Tumulty was moving again. Pagan let the car roll slowly forward, knowing it was only a matter of time before Tumulty would become aware of the vehicle, if he hadn't done so already.

Tumulty kept walking. He had begun to move a little faster. Then, quite suddenly, he disappeared. It was almost as if he'd vaporised right there on the street. Pagan pressed his foot down hard on the gas and drove to the place where the Irishman had vanished. It was a narrow alley, a crevice between two buildings. Even if he'd wanted to, he couldn't have taken the Cadillac into that tiny space. There was only one thing to do.

Bye-bye, Arthur.

He pushed his door open and stepped out into the street. He said to Zuboric, 'You wanted to drive, Artie. She's all yours,' and he headed towards the alley, ignoring Zuboric, who was shouting at him to get back in the car. Behind the Cadillac there was a knot of cars occupied by impatient drivers, every one of them hammering on horns. Pagan smiled and felt a pleasant sense of liberation as he went into the alley and saw Joe Tumulty turning a corner at the far end.

Pagan made his way past piles of garbage in plastic bags, trash cans, old cardboard boxes jettisoned by restaurants and stores. He reached the corner where Tumulty had turned, and he saw Joe moving along the street about a block ahead, his black coat flapping around his ankles. Tumulty hesitated, looked back. Pagan stepped into the doorway of a store that sold electronic gadgets. Fuzz-busters. Listening devices. There was, as yet, no gadgetry that could render you invisible. Tumulty, on the move again, went around a corner. Pagan followed. If he had his geography correct, the Irishman was heading towards Mulberry Street.

On Mulberry, Tumulty didn't head for Kenmare Street and Santacroce's store as Pagan had expected. Instead, he went inside a tenement whose ground floor was occupied by an Italian restaurant and whose upper floors appeared to be apartments. The restaurant called Il Tevere, was one of those chintzy places with red-checked tablecloths and candles stuck in Chianti bottles, a whole style Pagan thought had gone out of fashion. A smell of garlic and tomato sauce poured out into the cold air. Pagan gazed up at the windows over the restaurant, wondering how many apartments were in the building and which one Joe Tumulty might have entered.

He moved towards the door through which Tumulty had gone. It wasn't locked. It opened into a long very narrow hallway covered with faded black-and-white lino, like some ancient, cracked chessboard. There was a flight of stairs at the end. They faded up into gloom at the top. Pagan went quietly along the corridor. At the foot of the stairs he stopped, tilting his head and listening, but the building was quiet save for music coming through the wall from the next-door restaurant. *O Sole Mio*. Accordion music yet. There was something intrinsically absurd about any instrument you had to squeeze. He climbed the stairs, pausing only when he reached a landing.

A single closed door faced him. At the end of the landing there was a second flight of stairs. Pagan ignored the door for the moment and climbed upwards. He reached another landing, another door. This one was halfway open, revealing an unlit apartment beyond. Removing his gun from the holster he wore in the small of his back, he went inside cautiously. He saw total disarray – bags of cement, bricks, stacks of wood, stepladders, all kinds of building materials. He noticed that the walls of the apartment had been ripped out, exposing old beams. Somebody was renovating this place. Room after room had been torn apart. Windows were covered with sheets of thick plastic, and there was the smell of fresh paint in the air.

He turned, went back to the stairs, descended slowly. When he reached the first landing again he looked at the closed door. There were only two apartments in the building, and if one of them was empty, then Tumulty had to be in the other.

He waited. He had no way of knowing how many people were inside the place. He glanced down the stairway into the hall. The music from the Italian restaurant was louder now. *Funiculi, Funicula.* It was a song he particularly disliked. If that kind of music continued to assail him, he wasn't sure how long he could stand it before he took a chance and kicked the door down. Screw waiting. Screw the torture of Italian opera. The only thing worse than Italian opera was probably Vic Damone or Al Martino. It was a toss-up.

He heard a sound from behind the door. The creak of a floorboard, it was hard to say. Then there was silence again. What the hell was Tumulty doing in there? What if he was simply visiting a friend? Pagan frowned. He wished Tumulty had gone back to Santacroce's little shop, because then at least he'd have guessed that a gun transaction was under way. Here, it could be anything.

He wasn't very good at waiting. His concentration slackened. He moved a little, back to the stairs going upwards. He had the protection of shadows there. If somebody were to open the door quite suddenly, he wouldn't see Frank Pagan. There was another sound now from the apartment, and he brought his gun up again. He tensed, filled with a sense of expectancy. He saw the door open a little way. A bar of pale light from the room caused him to blink.

A figure appeared. Pagan made out the shape of a fat man in a navy-blue three-piece suit. A jewelled tiepin glinted against the man's white shirt, and his cuff links sparkled. He went to the edge of the landing and looked down into the hallway. Then he turned and stood on the threshold of the apartment. He made a curious grinding noise with his teeth, and he wheezed as he moved, as if his bulk were a little too much for his lungs. His eyes were tiny, surrounded by mounds of pallid flesh. Pagan, hidden by shadow, watched him.

The fat man called back into the apartment, 'Thought I heard something.' Whoever he'd spoken to inside didn't answer. The fat man waddled back to the top of the stairs again.

Pagan felt perspiration form between his skin and the surface of his pistol. Fattie took a handkerchief out of his pocket and pressed it between his plump hands as he peered down into the hallway. There was an expression of doubt on his face. He turned towards the apartment.

'Say, did you lock that door down there when you came in?'

Again there was no answer from inside. The fat man shook his head.

Irritated by the lack of response from inside, the fat man pushed the door wide open. Pagan had a glimpse of the interior. A lamp, a coffee table, and an armchair occupied by Joseph X. Tumulty, who looked white and rather unhappy.

The fat man turned to shut the door behind him. Pagan moved. In four quick steps he was across the landing before Fattie had a chance to react. The fat man swore in surprise and tried to slam the door but Pagan kicked it back and heard the wood strike the man's head. It was a satisfying noise, like the whack of a cricket bat on a ball. The fat man slumped against the wall, holding a hand to his forehead. Joe Tumulty, whose astonishment had frozen him into the armchair, made a small moaning sound. He stared at Pagan blankly.

The fat man, bleeding from his brow, managed a mirthless smile. 'You the law?'

'Joe knows who I am. Don't you, Joe?' Pagan said.

Tumulty nodded. There was no colour in his face.

The fat man looked at Tumulty with disgust. 'Fucking Irish,' he said. 'I always get problems when it comes to the fucking Irish. Goddam.'

'Welcome to the club,' Pagan said. 'Are you Santacroce?'

The fat man nodded and wiped his brow with his handkerchief. 'You let this fucker follow you, Joey? Not smart. Not at all smart.'

Pagan moved towards Tumulty's armchair. There was a leather attaché case on the floor. 'Open it,' he said to Tumulty, jerking the hand that held the gun.

Trembling, Tumulty set the case on his lap and flipped it open. It contained a pistol, a rifle with a collapsible stock and three sets of sights. Everything had been neatly packed inside the case, fitted into compartments that had been specially made to hold the weapons. They were handcrafted weapons, tailored for the needs of a professional killer.

'Very nice, Joe,' Pagan said. 'Jig would love them.'

'What happens to me now?' Tumulty asked in a hoarse voice.

'You oughta have your fucking head blown off,' Santacroce said.

'It's a consideration,' Pagan said. He looked across the room at Santacroce. The man was calm, unreasonably so in the circumstances. But he knew the score. He knew the jeopardies of his trade. He'd been here before. Even so, he was too acquiescent, and Pagan didn't like it.

'So, Santacroce said. 'They sending the English in these days to help out?'

'Something like that,' Pagan said.

Tumulty asked his question again. 'What happens to me?'

'You're going to fucking jail,' Santacroce said.

'Is that right?' Tumulty asked Pagan.

Pagan said, 'It doesn't look too good, Joe.'

Santacroce laughed. 'Amateurs. Jesus. I shoulda known better. I gotta call my fucking lawyer. Awright with you?'

The fat man walked calmly across the room to the telephone, which was located on a small desk beneath the window. Pagan, suddenly uncertain about the legality of criminals making phone calls in this country, saw him apply the handkerchief to his forehead as he moved. Santacroce picked up the receiver and started to punch in numbers. Without really thinking, Pagan was mentally counting the digits the fat man pressed on the push buttons. The count wasn't right. It came only to six. On a level of awareness that was instinctive more than anything else, Pagan realised the Saint was talking into a dead phone.

Santacroce said, 'Sam? I got a problem.'

Pagan saw the fat man turn away so that he was facing the window with his back to the room.

'Yeah,' Santacroce mumbled. 'I'll hold.'

Pagan tightened his grip on his pistol. What the hell was the fat man doing? Did he take Pagan for a complete fool?

'Yeah, I'm still holding,' Santacroce said. 'Don't leave me hanging too long, Sam.'

'Put the phone down,' Pagan said. 'Put the fucking phone down.'

Santacroce turned with a cold smile on his face.

Pagan didn't know where it came from, but there was a gun in the fat man's hand, a weapon that must have been concealed somewhere in his clothing. It caught the light, flared as Santacroce started to go into a defensive crouch, his big body bending at the hips, the gun hand held out in front of him, his other arm raised in the air for balance. For a fat man he seemed almost dainty right then, his whole body coordinated delicately as if in some dance.

Frank Pagan fired one shot.

Santacroce clutched his arm and cried out in pain, dropping his gun and falling backwards, the drapes at the window coming loose from their clips in a series of harsh little *clicks* and folding all around him like a collapsed tent. And then he was gone in a confusion of shattered glass and buckled frames. Pagan rushed to the window and looked down. The fat man lay on the sidewalk, the curtains still covering his body in the fashion of a shroud. People were emerging from the restaurant, crowding around the corpse, then staring up and pointing at the broken window.

Joe Tumulty asked, 'Is he dead?'

Pagan said nothing. He backed away from the window.

'Oh, God.' Tumulty got up from the armchair.

Pagan wondered what Artie Zuboric was going to say about all this. He speculated on the depths of Artie's wrath. What was he supposed to have done anyway? Let Santacroce shoot him?

Tumulty said, 'I can't go to jail, Pagan.'

Frank Pagan stared a moment at the broken glass, feeling the cold wind blow in off Mulberry Street. The curtain rings rattled on the brass rod. The idea of Santacroce lying down there on the concrete depressed him. He turned his gun over in his hand. The death-maker. The eliminator. He had no rapport with guns the way some cops had, cleaning them endlessly, refining them, always reading gun literature, even naming their guns as if they were pets. He put the weapon back inside his holster and looked at Tumulty.

'There may be a way out for you, Joe.'

'How?'

'I can't promise anything,' Pagan said. 'But a little cooperation on your part could be beneficial.'

Tumulty straightened his back and looked for all the world like a prizefighter coming out for a round in which he knew he was going to be demolished. 'I'm listening.'

Roscommon, New York

Patrick Cairney wasn't able to sleep. He lay in the second-floor bedroom, staring at the darkened window and listening to the old house. He recognised familiar little noises. The way a stair creaked. The sound made by the wind thrusting an elm against a downstairs window. They were echoes of the childhood he'd spent here when he'd convinced himself that a house as large and as solid as Roscommon had to be haunted. Back then, his imagination fired, he'd seen all kinds of apparitions – ghostly hands upon the windows, odd monsters slinking through shrubbery. Harry had conspired with him in this creation of a netherworld. *Of course there's ghosts, boy. Don't let anybody tell you otherwise. What would the Irish be without their banshees?*

He hated this house now as he'd hated it then. It was big and cold and furtive, and he always had the very odd impression that it contained undiscovered rooms, hidden chambers he could never quite locate. He remembered Harry's answer when, around the age of nine, he'd mentioned this suspicion to his father. *Sure there are secret passages, Paddy. Where else would I hide fine Irish gunmen on the run from the bloody British?*

Fine Irish gunmen, Patrick Cairney thought. Why could he find so few memories of his own goddam father that weren't related in one way or another to Ireland? When he ransacked his own past, when he rummaged his recollections, all he ever heard was the same monotonous drumbeat that was Harry's voice.

Patrick turned on the bedside lamp. Along the hallway was the bedroom his father shared with Celestine. He'd watched Celestine drift along the landing about thirty minutes ago. At the door of her bedroom she'd looked back and smiled and said goodnight to him and then, disappearing with a languid wave of her hand, she'd left him feeling suddenly lonely there, as if he were the only occupant of the house.

He stepped out of bed. This room was the one he'd had as a kid. All his old books were still stacked on the shelves. He ran a fingertip over the spines. *The Call of the Wild. A Treasury of Irish Legends. Kidnapped*. Relics of a lost boy. In another mood, he might have yielded to the brief comfort of nostalgia. He might have wallowed in that place where a young man sees the child he used to be and wonders about the direction his life has taken since, the crossroads missed, the paths ignored, the fragmented geography of his movements. He was sure that if the boy could talk to the man he'd say how surprised he was that things had turned out like they had. And yet – was it so surprising when you considered the father who had raised the child!

He sat on the edge of the mattress. He looked at his overnight bag, situated on the top of the dressing-table. He hadn't even unpacked. Restless, he thought about Rhiannon Canavan, but that kind of image, lascivious as it was, didn't cut into his loneliness. It only underlined it. He remembered the way he'd last seen Rhiannon Canavan at Dublin Airport and how she'd watched him across the terminal building. He'd looked around at her once and for a moment wanted to go back and hold her one final time. Weaknesses, he thought. All his longings were faults.

He shut his eyes, clenched his hands, pictured the way Celestine had raised her fingers in the air at the moment of her departure, and thought he'd never seen any gesture so innocently sexual in all his life. Innocence, he reflected, was the keyword. Sexuality was in the beholder's eye, and he'd done just a little too much beholding, that was all. You didn't go around being attracted to your own stepmother.

He lay back across the bed. The nightcap with Celestine had been two generous brandies, the second of which he'd left unfinished. She'd talked about herself, her first marriage to an architect called Webster. It was closed kind of talk, not very revealing, nothing about her family, her background. Polite chat. A stepmother eager to befriend the son she'd suddenly inherited. Now and then he'd seen a kind of glaze go over her eyes like blinds drawn down on windows, as if she were afraid of getting too close to revealing her own personality. Was that coyness? If so, it was a rare quality and endearing.

He heard the sound of someone knocking at his door, and at first he thought it was just the elm tree rattling again on the downstairs window. But when he realised it wasn't he rose from the bed and quickly took a robe out of his bag, tying the cord and stepping towards the door in one hurried movement.

'I couldn't sleep,' she said.

Cairney felt awkward. He made a meaningless gesture with one hand. Celestine entered the room. She wore a pink satin robe, floor-length, and her yellow hair was tied up at the back of her head.

'Am I disturbing you, Pat?'

'No,' and Cairney closed the door, glancing along the hallway as he did so.

Celestine looked around the room. 'I've often wondered about the boy whose room this used to be.'

'Now you know.'

'I don't really know,' she answered him. She fiddled with the cord of her robe, working the knot with her finger. Cairney didn't move. He had the uneasy feeling that any movement on his part could be misconstrued. He didn't want this woman in his bedroom. He didn't want any of the odd little responses she caused him to have.

'I see a boy's books, but that's all,' she said. Her blue eyes seemed stark and glassy in the light from the lamp. 'You needn't look so pale, Patrick.'

'Pale?'

'When I was a child I had this fish that died by jumping out of the bowl. When I found it, it was exactly the colour you are right now. Does my presence in this room upset you?'

Cairney watched Celestine wander around the room, touching things as she moved. The edge of the drapes. The spines of books. She stopped at the dressing-table. Lamplight made small delicate shadows in the folds of her robe, which clung to her flat stomach. She was lean, and Cairney knew that the body beneath the robe was hard and taut and yet that it would yield in the right places. *Harry's wife*, he thought. *The Senator's wife*. He tried to absent himself from his responses to her, to step away from his own reactions. God, it was difficult. It was just so damned hard to shut your eyes and ignore this woman's compelling beauty and her nearness and the faint notion he had that he could go to her now and slip the robe from her body and draw her down to the bed with him. Was her presence here telling him that? Was she saying she was available?

She was standing very close to his canvas bag. 'The truth is, Harry's been snoring worse than usual since this recent attack. I know he can't help it but it drives me up the wall.' She put the palm of her hand on top of his bag, which was lying open. He felt a tension in his throat.

'So here I am,' she said. 'I thought we might go down and have one last nightcap. It might help me sleep. And I don't like to drink alone. There's something a little pathetic about it.'

He couldn't take his eyes away from her hand. He realised he should have closed the bag after moving his robe, but he'd been hurried. It was a mistake. He saw that now. He should have taken the time.

'I like this room,' Celestine said. 'It gets a lot of light in summer. It must have been a pleasant room for you, Patrick.'

'I have some good memories,' Cairney said, and turned towards the door. 'Shall we go downstairs?'

'Are you rushing me, Patrick? It just so happens that this is one of my favourite rooms in the entire house. Sometimes I come here and I sit. I just sit in the chair by the window. There's a good view of the lake. Sixteen rooms in this big house and this is the one I like best.'

Cairney realised something then. The two brandies Celestine had drunk before had affected her more than he'd realised. Her speech was just a little slurred. Not much, just enough to notice. There were red flushes on her cheeks.

He reached out, turned the door-handle. 'A nightcap sounds like a great idea,' he said.

'You're in such a hurry,' Celestine said. She looked at him, her mouth open a little way, the top of one finger pressed to her lower lip. There was something mischievous in the gesture.

Then Cairney saw her palm slide along the top of the bag. He started towards her, thinking he'd slip the bag away from her, perhaps pretend there was something in it he needed, but before he could make his move she was lifting an object out and turning it over in her hand, her expression one of interest.

He could feel his blood turn cold.

'Where did you get this?' she asked.

'It's just a souvenir I picked up at the airport.'

Celestine fingered the object, stroking it with the tips of her fingers. 'It's very pretty,' she said.

Cairney shivered. A draught came up the staircase and moved along the hallway through the open door of the bedroom. He stepped towards Celestine, took the object from her hand, then dropped it back inside the bag, where it lay on top of his passport.

It was a miniature wooden horse, a Scandinavian import.

'Let's have that drink,' he said, and he was conscious of an awkward tone in his own voice. He clasped her arm and led her gently out of the room. On the landing, the relief he felt was intense. She had come within a mere half inch of the passport made out in the name of John Doyle.

13 New York City

Arthur Zuboric's office was located in Lower Manhattan in a building that had absolutely no distinguishing features. Frank Pagan thought he'd never been inside a place with less personality. It was a testimonial to bureaucratic blandness, erected in the sky by architects who lacked any kind of taste. Zuboric, looking very pale beneath his sun-lamp tan, stared across the room at a wall where there was a college diploma with his name on it. Pagan imagined he heard Artie ticking like an overwound watch.

Zuboric sighed, then said, 'First you split, leaving me stranded in that goddam pimp-mobile you rented. Then you shoot a guy. You actually *shoot* a guy, which is a mess I had to clean up with local cops, which I needed like a haemorrhoid. Jesus Christ. I mean, Jesus *Christ*, Pagan.'

Pagan tilted his chair back at the wall. There wasn't a great deal to say in the circumstances. He folded his arms against his chest. It was best to let Zuboric continue to tick until his clockwork had run down.

'Don't get me wrong, Pagan. Santacroce's death is no loss to the civilised world. There's not going to be a great weeping and gnashing of teeth. And his criminal connections aren't going to cause a run on Kleenex – but holy shit, there was a fucking corpse on the goddam sidewalk and a whole *gang* of diners with napkins tucked in their shirts, and they *saw* him lying there.'

'It probably put them off their osso bucco,' Pagan remarked. Bad timing. A look of pain crossed Zuboric's face.

The FBI man got up from behind his desk and strolled around the small room. There was a window looking down over the towers of Manhattan, and Artie Zuboric paused there a moment, surveying the night with a miserable expression. Not more than an hour ago he'd had the Director on the telephone from DC. The Director never raised his voice, had never been heard to shout, but he had a way with anger like nobody else Zuboric knew. He spoke quietly, clipping his words. Leonard M. Korn terrified Arthur Zuboric. Sometimes Artie had nightmares in which he was alone in an interrogation room with the man and he felt so paralysed, so over-awed, he couldn't answer any of his superior's questions, including the one concerning his own name. *Is there no way, Zuboric, of keeping this Englishman under lock and key? Is he to be allowed to run through the streets as he pleases*? There had been a very long pause after which the Director had spoken the most ominous sentence Zuboric had ever heard in his life. *For your sake, Zuboric, let us hope that not one word of this unfortunate incident ever reaches a newspaper.* This chilled Zuboric to his bones. Suddenly whatever meagre prospects he'd had before appeared to dwindle and then finally disappear in front of his eyes.

Now Zuboric said, 'You landed me in the shit.'

'Santacroce drew a gun,' Pagan answered. 'It was either him or me.'

Zuboric touched his moustache in a thoughtful way. It was obvious to Pagan whom Zuboric would have preferred between those alternatives.

Artie sat down. There were papers littered across his desk and a computer terminal attached to a printer. Every now and then the printer would hiccup into action and paper would roll out of the device, but Zuboric paid it no attention. He buried his face in his hands a second, then sighed again, looking across the room at the Englishman.

'And now you tell me you've got some cockeyed plan for that mick.'

In the time that had passed since the shooting of Santacroce, Pagan had gone over the scheme a couple of times, approaching it from all the angles he could think of, testing it and weighing it and then giving it his private seal of approval. It wasn't watertight and he wouldn't trust it in a storm, but it was the best he could do.

'Joe Tumulty doesn't want to go to jail, Artie. It's a powerful incentive.'

'What did you do, Pagan? Offer him immunity? Huh? Just take the law into your own hands and tell him he's walking away scot-free if he plays a little game for you?'

Frank Pagan gazed at the window. Out there in the night sky there were the lights of a passing plane. He felt a small homesick longing. Wintry London. Somehow it seemed farther away than a six-hour plane ride, like an impossible city of his own imagination.

Zuboric said, 'You can't just fuck around with the laws of this country, Frank. I don't know what it's like where you come from, but here you can't promise a guy something that's not in your power to give him.'

Pagan stood up. He studied the college diploma on the wall. It had been issued by the University of Michigan at Ann Arbor. He wondered a moment about the pathways of a man's life that led from a degree in business administration to the Federal Bureau of Investigation, then he thought of Joe Tumulty, who sat along the corridor in a locked room, presumably staring at the blank walls and worrying about his sorry predicament. With a man like Tumulty, whose political affiliation threatened the ruin of his charity work, his shot at sainthood, you couldn't ever really be sure of anything.

'He'll give us Jig,' Pagan said. Was that a small lack of conviction in his own voice? Confidence, Frank.

'What makes you think he won't call Jig and warn him?'

Pagan put his hands in his pockets. 'He doesn't know how to get in touch with him. He doesn't have a phone number. He doesn't have an address. He doesn't know where Jig is.'

'He isn't exactly a mine of information, is he?'

'Do you expect him to know more? Do you think Jig goes around giving out personal information, Artie? You think he passes out a nice little business card embossed with his name and number? Occupation, assassin?'

'Did Tumulty at least give you a description?'

'Nothing that's going to help. Thirtyish. Five eleven. A hundred and sixty pounds. Dark curly hair.'

'That's terrific,' Zuboric said. 'You know what I really think, Frank? Father Joe is jerking you off.'

Pagan smiled now. 'I think Father Joe and myself have come to an understanding.'

Zuboric lit a cigarette and narrowed his eyes against the smoke. 'When's Jig supposed to show?'

'Tomorrow, the next day. Tumulty isn't certain.'

'Tumulty's a fucking mine of uncertainty.'

Zuboric shook his head. Frank Pagan had given up that one thing any cop should have considered his greatest asset: objectivity. His peripheral vision was severely damaged. Zuboric, for his part, wouldn't trust the mick as far as he could throw a crucifix, and as a reasonably good Catholic he'd never have thrown one anyhow. He sighed again, unhappy with the condition of his life. Was he really supposed to let this character Tumulty walk away from here with a loaded attaché case? What was he going to say to the Director? These questions hung bleakly in his mind.

Frank Pagan was still studying Zuboric's diploma. He was very tired all at once. He covered a yawn with the palm of his hand. 'I'm going back to my hotel,' he said.

'I'll ride with you.'

'Of course.' Pagan turned away from the diploma. 'We should keep Joe here overnight and release him in the morning. A small taste of imprisonment might be a useful reminder to him.'

Zuboric agreed half-heartedly.

Frank Pagan moved to the centre of the room and stood directly under a strip of fluorescent light. 'Before we release Joe, there's a couple of things we ought to do. First, there's a certain Englishman I'd like to talk to. And second, we ought to pay a visit to a tailor.'

An Englishman and a tailor. Zuboric felt he had just been asked to solve an impossible riddle. 'What Englishman? What tailor?'

Frank Pagan smiled in the knowing way that so infuriated Zuboric. 'It can wait until morning,' he replied.

Quebec-Maine Border

A freezing rain had begun to fall all along the border country from Lake Champlain to Edmundston. It pounded on the roof of the Ryder truck with such ferocity that the two men who sat silently in the back with the cargo – McGrath and Rorke – felt they were trapped inside a very large yellow drum.

The headlights of the vehicle faintly picked out trees obscured by the torrent. Behind the wheel, Fitzjohn could see hardly a thing save for great drops of moisture illuminated by the lights. He was nearly blinded. Every now and then the wheels of the truck would spin on old snow that was turning to slush. Waddell slept with his head tilted against the window, his mouth hanging open. Houlihan, who sat in the centre, was truly alert, turning his pistol around every so often in his hands, like a man anxious to keep checking reality.

'How much farther is it?' Houlihan wanted to know.

Fitzjohn wasn't sure but he lied because it was best to appease Houlihan whenever he could. 'Five, six miles.'

The Ryder truck rattled and shook. Fitzjohn was a proficient driver who'd made scores of nocturnal runs from Northern Ireland over the border into the Republic, driving through some hostile terrain to do so, but he'd had no experience of anything quite like this. The wipers worked furiously backwards and forwards but they couldn't keep up with the deluge. How in the name of God could John Waddell sleep through all this?

Trees and more trees and nothing beyond the feeble reach of the lights except a darkness the like of which Fitzjohn had never known. If there was a God, he'd forsaken this stretch of country for sure.

Houlihan whistled quietly for a time. Fitzjohn recognised the tune as that Protestant anthem, *The Battle of the Boyne*, which celebrated the defeat of Catholic forces by King William of Orange in July 1690. Old hatreds. Very old hatreds.

In a tuneless voice Houlihan sang a couple of lines. '*With blow and shout put our foes to the rout/The day we crossed the water.*' And then he was silent, which made Fitzjohn nervous. He understood something he'd known all along but had refused to acknowledge – that

Seamus Houlihan could quite casually blow off the top of his head and dump him by the side of the road, if such a whim ever moved him. It was a numbing insight.

'Are you sure you know where you're going, Fitz?' Houlihan asked.

Fitzjohn nodded and said, 'I didn't expect this kind of weather. It's a bad time of year for country like this.'

'Aye,' Houlihan said. Something in the way he used simple words, little negatives and affirmatives, suggested that Seamus Houlihan was a man to whom language had all the firmness of quicksand. It was as if everything he uttered could be construed in different ways on different levels. Treacherous and shifting, Fitzjohn thought.

Ahead, quite suddenly, there were lights.

Houlihan leaned forward, straining to see through the rain. 'What's that?' he asked, and the gun was back out in his hand, the barrel propped against the dash.

Fitzjohn braked. The big yellow truck slowed. The lights disappeared, then returned a second later. In a nervous voice Fitzjohn said it was the highway, that the lights were those of passing cars.

'America,' Houlihan said. He nudged Waddell, who woke suddenly and peered out into the dark.

'Here we are, John. Here we are in America.'

Waddell mumbled something. Ever since the airfield he'd been either asleep or ashen and withdrawn, and Fitzjohn suspected that the man had no stomach for any of this business. But John Waddell had always gone along with Houlihan, no matter what. It was almost as if Houlihan had cast a spell over the man. Or was it some form of hero worship, with Waddell always tagging along behind?

'Well?' Houlihan asked Fitzjohn. 'Are we going to sit here and wait for the bloody weather to change?'

Fitzjohn took his foot from the brake and the truck, its hood steaming with rain, rolled in the direction of the highway. This was the worst part, Fitzjohn knew that. Although he understood that an illicit border crossing at this godforsaken point was simpler, say, than crossing from Mexico, just the same his nerves were abruptly shrill. The concept had seemed easier than the reality, which was cold and wet, dreamlike and menacing.

The disaster happened about fifty yards from the pavement. The faint track along which the truck had been moving suddenly ended and the land dipped into a basin before rising up a slope to the highway. The hollow was muddy and impossible, and the truck, straining as hard as it might, didn't make it up the incline. It slithered, then slid back down through slush, wheels spinning noisily and dense exhaust rising into the icy rain. Dear Christ, Fitzjohn thought. This was the last thing he'd anticipated. He'd imagined only a clear run onto the highway, not this, not anything like this bloody great ditch.

Seamus Houlihan angrily slapped his pistol on the dash. Fitzjohn swore, shoved his foot down hard on the gas pedal, and tried to ram the truck back up the slope again but failed a second time as the Ryder slipped down into the hollow, where it sat with its big wheels uselessly turning.

'Try it again!' Houlihan shouted.

Fitzjohn plunged the truck into first gear, thrust the gas pedal to the floor, and tried a third time to force the heavy vehicle up the incline to the highway, which was suddenly lit by the lights of a passing car. He turned off his own headlights and prayed for invisibility even as he felt the truck lose traction about halfway up the slope. It rolled down again with a terrible inevitability. Fitzjohn shut his eyes and wanted to weep out of sheer bloody frustration. Beside him in the cab, Seamus Houlihan was very quiet all of a sudden. It was the kind of brooding silence in which Fitzjohn could sense the man's capacity for danger.

'I'll give it another shot,' Fitzjohn said.

'No. We'll push. We'll push this bastard up on to the road. Waddell, get behind the wheel. Fitz, get McGrath and Rorke out of the back,' and Houlihan shoved the door open quickly, thrusting Fitzjohn out into the freezing rain then following him around to the back of the truck. Fitzjohn opened the rear door.

'Is it a breakdown or what?' McGrath asked from the dark interior.

'Push! Get your shoulder behind this fucker and push!' Houlihan, who seemed immune to the cold and the relentless rain, was already pressing his body against the back of the truck. All four men strained in the numbing rain, inching the truck up the slope. Fitzjohn, his skull like a block of ice, felt utterly hopeless. How could four of them get this truck up a slushy slope? Maybe on a dry day with no mind-splitting rain to blind you and ruin your footing, maybe you could do it then, maybe. He felt his lungs turn to crystal. There was absolutely no feeling in his ungloved hands. Push! Houlihan was screaming. *Push! Fucking push!* The truck edged upwards, then Houlihan was screaming again, like some creature who wasn't flesh and blood at all but a creation of the harsh elements. *Push! Push! Push! Waddell, give it some bloody petrol, man!*

John Waddell, dragged out of sleep and unhappy at the controls of an unfamiliar vehicle, eased his foot down on the gas pedal. He brought the clutch halfway up from the floor. The rough grinding of the gears sent a series of little shock waves through his body. There was a cramp in his foot, and he wasn't sure if he could handle this strange vehicle.

For fuck's sake, Waddy! Give it more petrol!

Waddell's foot slipped on the clutch. He heard the engine stall and die. He turned the key in the ignition quickly, heard the motor come back to life, then he let out the clutch, but the truck didn't move. The wheels churned and dense exhaust spumed out into the freezing rain, but the bloody truck *wasn't going anywhere*! Pray, Waddell thought. Pray it gets up this damned slope.

Then he was suddenly dazzled, suddenly terrified, by headlights that came lancing down through the rain. He blinked his eyes furiously against the constant glare of the lights. As he did so, the truck died under him again and he had to shove his foot down hard on the brake to stop the thing from rolling back down the incline.

Outside, Fitzjohn wiped water from his eyes and peered into the same bright lights that had startled Waddell. He thought, Jesus, not now, not now. There was the brief glow of the car's interior light, then a door slammed and a figure moved in front of the beams with a flashlight that he shone towards the Ryder truck. 'Don't move!' the man from the car shouted in an authoritative voice.

'Don't any one of you move or I'll blow your fucking heads off!'

Houlihan did the strangest thing then. He tossed his head back and laughed, and it was a weird noise that managed to override the pounding rain. The figure started down the incline towards the truck, his flashlight making the rainy air sparkle. Houlihan laughed a second time and shouted, 'We're stuck! We ran straight off the bloody road!'

Fitzjohn shut his eyes and pressed his face against the metal panel of the truck. God, if the figure from the car was an agent of the Border Patrol he was going to find Seamus Houlihan's thick accent very strange indeed. And if he was a cop it was going to be just as bad, because he was surely going to insist on a search of the vehicle, and then what? Fitzjohn stared at the movement of the flashlight. The figure was approaching the truck, and Fitzjohn saw for the first time that the man held a shotgun pressed against his side.

When he was almost level with the Ryder the man said, 'Let's see some identification.'

It was the wrong request to make of Seamus Houlihan, who knew only one way to identify himself. Fitzjohn opened his mouth and was about to speak – anything, a lie, anything at all to fill the horrible void – when he noticed Seamus Houlihan's hand going towards the pocket of his jacket. The man with the shotgun made a gesture with his flashlight.

'You move that hand too fast and you can kiss it goodbye,' he said.

'I was only going to show you my papers,' Houlihan responded.

'Reach for them slowly. Very slowly. Slow as you know how. The rest of you characters back off from the truck. The guy behind the wheel – put your brake on and step outside.'

Waddell climbed down from the cab. In his anxiety, he hadn't checked to make certain that the emergency brake was firmly in place and so the truck, swaying slightly from side to side in the slicing rain, began to drift slowly back down the incline.

The man with the shotgun shouted at Waddell. 'Get back in there and put the fucking brake on, asshole!'

Waddell moved towards the cab and was reaching up to the door handle when Houlihan – always the opportunist, always seizing the unguarded moment and twisting it to his own advantage – took out his pistol and fired off two shots. The flashlight fell, and the man cried out in pain before going down into the slush, where he lay with his face pressed into the ground. Houlihan walked to the place where the flashlight was located. He picked it up, turning the beam on the man's face.

Fitzjohn stared at the scene.

A glare of rainy light.

Houlihan standing over the man.

The echo of gunfire.

The runaway truck slithering to a halt in the mud.

John Waddell was the first to speak, and his voice trembled. 'Who was he?'

Seamus Houlihan turned away from the body. 'According to his pretty uniform, he was a gentleman of the United States Border Patrol.'

Fitzjohn had a sour taste in his mouth. Even after they had laboured to push the truck onto the highway, after they had shoved the agent's car down into the hollow and hastily covered the corpse with frozen slush, the taste was still with him, mile after rainy mile.

Roscommon, New York

It was early morning and the sky over Roscommon was the colour of salmon flesh, a pale pink sun slatting through the cloud cover. An unusual day, neither winter nor spring but some uncharted hiatus between the two. Even the snow that covered the landscape was a curious rose tint. Harry Cairney, walking with the help of a cane, stopped at the edge of the lake. He said nothing for a time, then turned to his son, and there was a small look of expectation in his eyes.

'What do you make of her, Patrick?'

Patrick Cairney tossed a flat stone out across the water, watching it skip three times before sinking. 'She's a beautiful woman,' he answered.

The old man smiled. 'After your mother died, I thought that was it. End of the ball game. Well, that didn't happen.' The Senator poked the tip of his stick into the snow. 'You think God figured he owed me a favour? You think he said there's one old Paddy needs a good turn?'

Patrick Cairney gazed across the lake. He had spent a restless night after the final brandy with Celestine. What he saw when he lay in bed later and shut his eyes was Celestine's robe clinging to her body by firelight and the way she sat with her legs spread in front of her, so that there were shadows deepening the length of her thighs. What he couldn't decide was whether it was the unconscious physical gesture of a woman who'd had too much brandy or something else – and when he reached that borderline, a place of sheer discomfort, he stopped speculating.

'I was surprised by joy,' Harry Cairney said. 'It crept up on me.'

'I can understand that,' Patrick Cairney wasn't sure that he could, though. Joy wasn't a feeling with which he had any regular acquaintance.

The old man clapped his son on the shoulder. 'Dear God, it does me good to see you again, Pat. You should come back more often. You shouldn't be traipsing all over the goddam world digging in tombs or whatever it is you do. What's the point to all that anyhow? You think it matters to an Appalachian dirt farmer or some Boston longshoreman if King Tut was left-handed or had rotten teeth? It's not going to change any lives, is it? And what do we live for if it isn't to try and *change* a few things?'

This was an old argument. Whenever he heard it, Patrick was always beset by the feeling that he'd somehow disappointed Harry, let him down in some unforgivable way. That he was to be blamed for failing to meet Harry's expectations for him. What the hell did the old man want anyhow? A younger copy of himself? A nice buttoned-down young man happy to go into politics, which Harry had made the family business? Patrick Cairney had given law a try once some years back simply to please the old man, and he'd been utterly miserable. It was the last time he'd ever even attempted to gratify his father. If Harry still entertained ambitions on his son's behalf, they were well and truly doomed to failure. And if this fact disappointed him, then that was a burden the old man had to carry. Patrick couldn't be responsible for his father's feelings about him.

Patrick Cairney tossed another stone out on the lake. A wintry bird rose up out of the trees. Both men moved a little way along the shore. For a moment Patrick wanted to tell the old man that he *was* trying to change a few things but in his *own* way.

Harry Cairney caught his son's arm. 'Tell me about Dublin. I want to hear about Ireland.'

Patrick Cairney knew what the old man wanted to hear and it wasn't the hard brutal world of northern cities like Belfast and Derry with their burned-out buildings and bloody casualties. He wanted to hear only the same unchanging litany of heroes and martyrs. Patrick Cairney said nothing. It was cowardly of Harry to dream his time away in the comfort and security of Roscommon, to hide behind his record collection and his Celtic documents, and ignore the real troubles in his homeland. Patrick – who had gone to Ireland expecting to find the glowing island of song and poetry that Harry had always pictured for him, only to discover something relentlessly terrible behind the romance and the myth – felt contempt for the old man and everything he represented.

'I used to meet a pretty young girl under Waterhouse's clock on Dame Street in Dublin,' the old man remarked. 'I sometimes wonder if that clock's still there. She was very fond of a shop called Butler's by O'Connell Bridge. It sold musical instruments. Polly liked to browse in that place for hours. Sweet girl.'

Patrick Cairney smiled thinly. He wanted to say that it was gone, it was all gone, that another world had taken the place of everything the old man remembered. He glanced across the lawn at the house, which had a pink tint in the hallucinogenic morning light. He was thinking of Celestine moving through the rooms of that big house. He was thinking of the lithe way she moved, the slight forward thrust of hips and the fair hair bouncing against her shoulders and that strange little electric light in her eyes, which he found indefinable and puzzling. He didn't need these thoughts, for God's sake. He didn't need to wander in this direction. He had come to the United States for one reason only and nothing, not a goddam thing in the world, was going to interfere with his purpose.

Harry Cairney let his hand fall from his son's arm. He drew a sinewy line in the snow with the tip of his cane. 'When are you going to this symposium of yours?'

'Tomorrow,' Patrick Cairney replied.

'And after that – will you come back here?'

'I hadn't planned on it.'

'You don't need the excuse of a symposium to visit me. This is still your home, Patrick.'

'I know,' Patrick said. He thought how remarkable it was that he had developed a knack of believing in his own fictions. It was the simplest thing in the world to believe that there really *was* a symposium of archaeologists in New York City he was going to attend. He could picture the room in which the event would take place. He could invent faces, and he could give those faces names. Afterwards he could describe, if anyone asked, how the room smelled and the kind of cigarettes Professor So-and-So smoked and what the lecturer from Oxford had to say about Etruscan pottery. When you lived a life grounded in lies and deception, all the lines of reality became blurred.

He remembered the simple lie he'd told Rhiannon Canavan about his father's heart attack the night Padraic Finn had telephoned with the news of the *Connie*. Had he known that his father was really unwell, he might have chosen a different fabrication, but in the end it made no difference at all. Even his identities were lies. He was no longer Patrick Cairney. Neither was he John Doyle, traveller in Scandinavian trinkets.

He was Jig and all his experiences were Jig's.

The months spent training in the savage wasteland of the Libyan desert with Qaddafi's mad guerillas, who valued human life as much as a match flame. The endless days crawling over burning sand when you had nothing to drink and your throat had the texture of sandpaper and the gun and backpack you carried became the heaviest burden in all your experience. Freezing nights when you slept naked under a moon of relentless ice and shivered so badly you felt your skin was coming loose from your skeleton. These were Jig's experiences. And it was Jig who had become the hardened professional under Padraic Finn's guidance, who had sworn allegiance to the Association of the Wolfe and the goal of Irish unity, achieved through a programme of political assassination. A programme carried out by professionals who had no desire for the old ways of martyrdom and considered self-destruction beneath contempt. It wasn't a dreamer's Ireland. It was a hard place, and there were hard goals to accomplish, and these couldn't be left to the amateurs, the homemade grenade groups, the desperate little losers who tossed bottles of fiery gasoline at British soldiers and thought they were brave for doing so. Sad, misguided men who dreamed the dreams of hooligans. Finn's programme would eventually change everything. Jig had a complete belief that in the end, weary of death and the assassinations of its political figures, the British would have no choice but to withdraw.

It was Padraic Finn who had smoothed the abrasive surface of Patrick Cairney. It was Finn, surrogate father, mentor, who had insisted on Libyan training and then, in a further process of refinement, six months at the Patrice Lumumba University in Moscow where Cairney had learned the uses of high-tech explosives. If Harry had provided the early, relentless indoctrination, then it was Finn who had carried this out of the realm of vague impracticality and vapid rhetoric into the real world. He thought of Finn now, and the remote possibility that something might have happened to the old man in Ireland caused him fleeting concern – but what he came back to was Finn's own maxim. *I'm expendable. You're expendable. Only the Cause has permanence.* Cairney lifted his face and looked up at the sky. He could still picture Finn, in baggy cord pants and fisherman's sweater, standing at the window in the room of harps. He could still hear Finn say *The Cause is a killing mistress. It seeks your total devotion and never excuses your weaknesses. It demands your complete commitment and it rewards your infidelity, not with forgiveness and understanding, but with death . . .*

'Let's walk back,' Harry Cairney said. 'It's damn cold out here. Besides, we shouldn't neglect Celestine. You ought to get to know her a little better.'

A harmless suggestion, Patrick Cairney thought. But there was no such thing in his life anymore. He couldn't make the ordinary connections other people made. He lived in the shadows he'd created for himself.

They moved across the lawn in the direction of the house. The young man clutched his father's elbow when they reached the steps, which were slick underfoot. He noticed how his father puffed as he climbed. Inside the house Celestine appeared at the foot of the stairs.

'Did you walk far?' she asked.

'Just to the lake,' the old man said. He started to take off his coat. Celestine helped, fussing around him.

Patrick Cairney watched her. She had her yellow hair pulled back tightly, making her sky-blue eyes prominent in her face. She wore faded blue jeans and a red silk shirt and she was barefoot. She looked impossibly young. She might have been a young girl strolling through the grass at an open-air rock concert, someone you followed with your eyes and wondered who was lucky enough to be screwing her. And then you might track her through the crowd and lose her, knowing you'd never see her again.

She moved towards him now. There was a scent of perfume in the air around her. She laid her fingertips on his wrist and said, 'I'll make breakfast. I expect you're both hungry.'

Patrick Cairney hung his coat on the rack, turning his face away from Celestine. He had developed a sense of danger that was like having some kind of internal compass whose needle would vibrate whenever danger was near, and he had the awareness now of that needle swinging madly inside his brain – and it had nothing to do with the idea that a man called Frank Pagan was in New York City looking for him, it had nothing to do with whatever calamity might have happened to Finn in Ireland, it had nothing to do with his reason for being in the United States. It was connected entirely to the touch of this woman's fingertips on his bare skin, which provoked a warm and unsettling physical response inside him. Sometimes there was an inexplicable chemistry between two people, instant, like a small Polaroid of emotion. If that was the thing happening between himself and Celestine, he had no room for it in his world.

He said, 'I could eat.'

But he still didn't look at her because he knew he had absolutely no mastery right then over his own expression. He didn't like that. He didn't like yielding up any of his control over himself. Without control he was a dead man. Finn had told him once that Jig was an instrument, a very fine instrument of destruction. But what Patrick Cairney felt as he avoided Celestine's eyes was a distressing knowledge of flaws in the structure of this instrument – a damaged reed, a faulty valve, something he'd have to repair in such a way that it would never fail him again.

New Rockford, Connecticut

The two Secret Service agents were of Hispanic descent. One was called Lopez, the other Garcina. They sat motionless and squat in a blue car parked in the driveway beneath Kevin Dawson's study. Now and again Dawson would walk to the window and look out at them. They never seemed to move. What did they do down there in the car? he wondered.

Dawson went towards his desk. It was strewn with papers. Many of them were invitations of the kind routinely extended to a brother of the President of the United States. The opening of a new office block in Manhattan. A fund-raising banquet on behalf of scientific research in Antarctica. Kevin Dawson attended as many of these functions as he could because he considered it his duty to wave the Dawson flag in public whenever possible. Duty was an important word in the Dawson lexicon. Sometimes Kevin thought that the entire Dawson clan had been selectively bred with public service in mind.

He sat and pushed his chair back against the wall. From another part of this large Victorian house, which had been in the Dawson family for more than eighty years, he could hear the sounds of his daughters, Louise and Kitty, getting ready for school. Running water. The rattle of a spoon in a bowl. Kitty's high-pitched laughter. Martha, Kevin's wife, drove the girls every morning to the stop where they boarded the big yellow bus that took them to a grade school in New Rockford. At one time Martha had argued that the girls ought to attend a private school, but Kevin, pressured somewhat by his own brother who saw the chance to score some points for democracy and egalitarianism, insisted they go to a public school like normal kids. Thomas Dawson, locked into a marriage that seemed destined to be childless, was always bringing such minor pressures to bear on the family, the kids especially. He saw them, Kevin Dawson thought at times, as the children he didn't have himself.

There was the sound of footsteps on the stairs and then Louise and Kitty came running into his office to say goodbye to him. Kevin Dawson embraced his daughters, hugging them hard. A small ritual of family. Sometimes, when he stood in the doorway of their bedroom and watched them sleep, he was filled with an awesome love.

Louise, grown-up at eleven and graceful in the way of a ballet dancer with her long skinny body, wanted to know about the men parked in the driveway. Dawson stepped back from his daughters. They had a way of scrutinising him that made him feel as though he were made of glass. The eyes of innocence, he thought.

'The President ordered those men to be here,' he said slowly. 'For our protection.'

'Protection from what?' Kitty asked. She was balanced on one foot like a stork. At the age of nine, Kitty resembled her mother in a manner that could take Kevin's breath away.

'Well, the President has enemies. And because we're part of the President's family, we have the same enemies.' He let this casual lie hang in the air, wondering if the girls were really buying it the way Martha had done. He had muttered vaguely about a rash of Dawson hate mail when he'd explained the presence of the Secret Service agents to his wife. Apart from Martyns, the agent who accompanied the kids to school and remained there all day long, Kevin had always refused Secret Service protection in the past even if, as the President's brother, he was entitled to it.

'It isn't anything that should worry you guys, though. It's a precaution, that's all.'

Louise said to her sister, 'It's politics as usual.'

Kitty looked thoughtful. 'Politics is a dirty game.' Her small oval face was earnest.

'Where did you hear that?' he asked.

'*Everybody* knows *that*, Daddy,' Kitty said.

'Everybody,' Louise agreed. 'Didn't you know that about politics, Daddy?'

There were moments when Dawson understood that his daughters liked to bait him in tiny ways. Affectionate little jibes, jokes, verbal conspiracies.

Martha appeared in the doorway. She was a small woman whose looks had deteriorated since the birth of Kitty. Kevin, who adored his wife beyond any means of measurement, didn't notice changes in her. He didn't see the wrinkles edging the eyes. He didn't see the thin lines that stretched from the corners of her mouth, nor did he notice the streaks of silver that had appeared in her black hair. All he ever saw was the girl he'd proposed to one wet afternoon in Bayville when a summer storm had raked the waters of Long Island Sound and Martha had pressed her lips against the back of his hand and whispered *Yes*. Kevin had built his whole life around that whisper of acceptance.

'Let's go, girls,' she said. 'We don't want to miss the bus, do we?'

'I don't think you want an honest answer to that question, Mom,' Louise said.

Martha kissed Kevin. 'I'll be right back,' she said, herding the girls out of the room. She blew another kiss at her husband as she drew the door shut.

From the window Kevin watched his family get inside the station wagon. Martyns followed in the blue sedan. Kevin gazed until both cars had gone out of sight down the long curve of the driveway and the stand of ancient elms. He went back to his desk and began to sift through the papers.

He was searching for the file that contained a monthly computerised printout detailing the ebb and flow of the Dawson family fortune, which came from such diverse sources as condominiums in Dallas and Houston, dairy farms in Wisconsin, New York, and Ohio, a chain of small-town newspapers that extended from Oregon to Florida, and a pineapple plantation in Hawaii. The whole thing was a maze of corporations, and it was Kevin Dawson's function to manage this labyrinth, which grew more complex every month.

He found the file and flipped it open. He stared at the columns of figures, prepared by a centralised computer bank in Jersey City, which recorded every business transaction in the Dawson empire from the purchase of paper clips to the financial lubrication of some local politician. It was difficult to concentrate. His mind kept drifting to Jig and to the crazy idea that he was in danger. He tried to persuade himself he was safe – after all, there were Secret Service agents stationed outside – but he couldn't still the anxiety he felt.

He closed the file and stood up, stretching his arms. He disliked being vulnerable. All Kevin Dawson had ever really craved was a peaceful life, the life of a family man. Wife and kids. Dogs and roses. But destiny, that crooked schemer, had arranged for him to be born into the Dawson clan with all its political ambitions, its history of ruthless business intrigues. His grandfather had been impeached by the House of Representatives in 1929 for 'immoral and unacceptable' trading in the stock market. His father, the one-time United States ambassador to Italy, had been maligned in the late 1930s for his uncritical attitude towards Mussolini and criticised even more strongly in the fifties for having a tumultuous affair with a Greek opera singer, a histrionic woman the press called 'Dawson's Diva'. It was as if the Dawson clan went out of its way to court turbulence and self-destruction. What chance did he have for a peaceful life with a background like that?

His telephone rang. He picked up the receiver and heard the voice of Nicholas Linney.

'Mulhaney thinks he's got it all figured out,' Linney said.

Dawson pinched the bridge of his nose. 'Figured what, Nick?'

'Who took the money.' Linney had a flat nasal accent, like that of a man with stuffed sinuses.' He figures you.'

'Me? Why me?'

'He's got some cockeyed reasons of his own.'

'I'm sure he has,' Kevin Dawson said. 'Do I want to hear them?'

Linney was quiet a moment. 'I didn't find them convincing. He's full of shit. I think he's laying down smokescreens, if you want my opinion.'

'Smokescreens?'

'Yeah. He makes an accusation like that, it takes the heat off him.'

'Why would *he* feel any heat, Nick?'

'If he had a hand in the hijacking he would,' Linney answered.

'You think he did?'

'I hear rumours. I hear things about Mulhaney privately investing union funds and losing some hefty change on Wall Street. I hear things about auditors moving in on his union, wanting to check the books. I think maybe he's been skimming. Chipping away at the Irish money. Mending fences.'

There was a long silence. Dawson thought about the wholesale paranoia that the hijacking of the *Connie O'Mara* had brought, and he doubted that the Fund-raisers could ever function as a unit again. He realised he welcomed this prospect. It was a step in the direction of the untroubled life he sought. His ambitions for Ireland belonged to another time in his life, to his youth when he'd been less prudent than he was now. Dawson turned his thoughts briefly to Mulhaney. If Jig ever got to Big Jock, then it was a pretty sure bet that Mulhaney *would* send the killer here to Connecticut. *Kev Dawson's the one*, Mulhaney would say. *Kev Dawson took the money*. Mulhaney hated the Dawson family, and Thomas especially, ever since the President had created a commission to look into union funds. Big Jock would love to create problems for the Dawsons. Kevin Dawson understood that he feared Mulhaney almost as much as Jig. Mulhaney, dictated to by blind hatreds and prejudice and the fear of seeing his power eroded by a presidential commission, would go out of his way to make life difficult for anyone connected to the Dawson family. If he couldn't get Tommy directly, then Kevin would do.

'You really believe any of this, Nick?'

'It's a possibility, that's all. Guy's got a cash-flow problem.'

'Here's something else to consider, Nick. Maybe you're the one setting up a smokescreen.'

'I like that,' Linney said.

'My point is, Nick, when this kind of suspicion starts, where the hell does it stop? Where do we draw the line, for God's sake? None of this mutual accusation shit is going to get the money back. It's sick to go around blaming somebody when there isn't a goddam shred of evidence.'

'I'm not accusing anybody,' Linney answered calmly. 'I'm examining options, that's all.'

'Examining options,' Dawson said. He had always found Nick Linney to be a cold character, somebody whose personality seemed indefinable at bottom. A human enigma. His encounters with Linney invariably left him feeling faintly depressed, as if he'd run into somebody hovering on the sociopathic margin of things. For a second Dawson had the urge to mention Jig, but he'd promised his brother – and Kevin, no matter what, always tried to keep his word.

'You come up with any bright ideas, you call me,' Linney said.

'Immediately,' Dawson replied.

'And if you see any strange-looking Irishmen hanging around, you be careful.'

'Is that supposed to be funny?'

'Take it any way you like,' Nicholas Linney said.

When Dawson had hung up he opened the bottom drawer of his desk and took out a bottle of Dewar's White Label. He poured himself a small shot and sipped it. Drinking just after breakfast. A bad sign, he thought.

Carrying his shot glass, he got up and wandered to the window. The hills on the other side of the road appeared secretive and barren. He looked across the lawn at the wrought-iron fence that faced the narrow road. It seemed oddly flimsy to Kevin Dawson just then, as if even the slightest breeze might flatten it.

He finished his drink.

He saw the station wagon come up the driveway. Martha stepped out. She looked tiny to Dawson. Vulnerably pale beneath the monochrome of the sky. He raised one hand and waved, but she didn't see him. When she'd passed out of his sight in the direction of the house, a wave of cold fear ran through him. It wasn't just the wrought-iron fence that was fragile. It was his whole life.

14 New York City

In his room at the Essex House Ivor McInnes woke at seven thirty a.m. as he usually did. He shaved and showered and had breakfast sent up by room service. He ate at the window, chewing on streaky pieces of what passed for bacon in America, pausing every now and then to look in the direction of Central Park. He perused *The New York Times* casually, then set it aside and continued to gaze out into the park. He drank several cups of coffee, then left his room and rode the elevator down into the lobby where he wandered towards the telephones.

Today, he thought, would have to be spent in the New York Public Library. Taking notes, reading, satisfying those morons at the State Department on the chance that he was being observed. He glanced across the crowded lobby before he dialled the number in White Plains. He punched in a handful of change at the operator's request and after a moment he heard a voice saying, 'Memorial Presbyterian Church. This is the Reverend Duncanson speaking.'

'I would like to know the times of your Sunday services,' McInnes said.

'Seven a.m. and ten,' Duncanson answered. He had a firm oratorial voice, a voice made for pulpits. 'I can tell from your accent you're a long way from home. Do you want to attend one of our services?'

'I'd like to,' McInnes answered.

'We always welcome guests at Memorial. Especially those from overseas.'

A nice man, McInnes thought. A decent man. 'Which is the more popular service?' he asked.

Duncanson laughed quietly. 'Oddly enough, my congregation prefers the sunrise service. They tell me my sermon is more mellow at that time of day. Can we expect you?'

'You can.'

'Introduce yourself to me after,' Duncanson said. 'I know your lovely country well.' He paused a moment. 'My text this coming sunday is John, chapter one, verse nine.'

'Ah,' McInnes said. ' "If we confess our sins, he is faithful and just to forgive us our sins and to cleanse us from all unrighteousness." '

'You know your Bible,' Duncanson said.

'Some of it,' Ivor McInnes answered.

When he'd hung up he stood in the lobby for a time and rattled coins in the pockets of his pants. The Memorial Presbyterian Church, which he had visited during his last trip to the USA in 1983, was one of those picture-postcard American churches, white framed and steepled and looking as if it were a Norman Rockwell construct. Its congregation was rich and influential, consisting mainly of well-heeled commuters who held executive positions in New York City. It was a hive of the American WASP. Unlike his own church in the Shankill district of Belfast, Memorial Presbyterian would never have any difficulty raising funds for new pews or a stained-glass window or an elaborate organ.

He rode the elevator back up to the seventeenth floor, still caressing the coins in his pockets. He strolled along the corridor to his room. When he saw the two men framed against the window at the end of the corridor he didn't break his stride. Instead, he took out his room key and inserted it into the lock of the door as the pair approached him. He turned to look at them. He had met Frank Pagan briefly once before, during an Irish peace conference in Westminster in the winter of 1984. Pagan had talked that day about the need for cooperation between the law-enforcement agencies of both Irelands, if terrorism was ever to be destroyed. A touching little speech, McInnes had thought at the time. Liberal, fair-minded and totally impractical. He remembered now how the conference had broken down into a shambles, a slanging match between himself and the bishop of Dublin, who'd droned on for hours about the violation of Catholic civil rights in Ulster. McInnes had always regarded the bishop as a cousin of the Prince of Darkness anyway.

'Frank Pagan! This *is* a surprise,' McInnes said, suppressing the terrible temptation to ask Pagan if he'd had any luck in catching up with Jig. There were moments in McInnes's life when he had to struggle fiercely with his sense of mischief, and this was one of them. He wondered if he looked suitably surprised by Pagan's appearance.

Frank Pagan had the kind of face that was difficult to read. He'd be a hell of a man to play cards against, McInnes thought. He stared into Pagan's grey eyes, which reminded him of cinders.

'This is Arthur Zuboric,' Pagan said. 'FBI.'

The suntanned man with the drooping moustache nodded his head. McInnes looked at him a second, then back to Pagan.

'What brings you to New York City?' McInnes asked. He stepped into his room and the two men followed him.

'Funny,' Pagan said. 'You took the words right out of my mouth, Ivor.'

McInnes sat in the armchair by the window. 'You must know why *I'm* here,' he said. 'Your bloody people in London know just about everything.'

'I understand you're writing a book,' Pagan said.

'Correct.' McInnes noticed a muscle working in the Englishman's jaw.

Pagan smiled. 'What's the title?'

'I haven't made up my mind yet.' McInnes saw the FBI man move to the window where he slid the curtain back and looked out, as if he suspected all manner of nefarious events to be taking place in Central Park.

Pagan picked up a Gideon Bible and flipped the pages for a time. McInnes drummed the tips of his fingers against the table. He was ready for anything Frank Pagan might ask.

'You know, of course, that I'm looking for Jig.'

'Now how would *I* know something like that?' McInnes, like any good actor, had all kinds of facial expressions at his command. The one he chose to assume right then was innocence. His large eyelids rose and his eyes widened.

'Because my information came from *you*, courtesy of that merry band of yours, the Free Ulster Volunteers.'

'Because members of the FUV belonged to my former congregation, Frank, doesn't mean I'm a card-carrying member myself,' McInnes said. 'I categorically deny any association with that organisation, and I challenge you to prove otherwise. I don't deny *knowing* members of the FUV, Frank. It would be difficult not to. But as for myself, I've always steered clear of involvement.'

'Ivor, Ivor.' Pagan sighed. 'I didn't just come up the Thames on a water biscuit. I wasn't exactly born yesterday. You, or a representative of yours called John Waddell, sent the Leprechaun to see me in London with the information that Jig had come to the USA.'

'The Leprechaun?' McInnes stood up. He looked at Zuboric and said, 'Your English friend here has a fanciful imagination. Next thing he'll be telling me he converses with gnomes and counts elves among his dearest chums.'

'You're a droll fellow, Ivor,' Pagan said.

McInnes laughed again, a big throaty sound. It was as if he had an untuned accordion lodged in his larynx. 'As for John Waddell, well, you've lost me.'

'How did you find out Jig was coming to America, Ivor?'

'You're barking up the wrong tree.'

'I don't really think so,' Pagan said. 'Every time the Free Ulster Volunteers move, it's because you're sitting backstage pulling their strings.'

'You're on shaky ground, Frank.'

McInnes gazed at the blank TV. For a moment he considered the complicated mosaic of this whole operation, and it filled him with a dizzy sense of achievement. It had taken three years to get this far, three years planning and scheming and infiltrating and carefully sliding each delicate part into its correct place. And now, even with Pagan and his American sidekick in his hotel room, he could almost taste the triumph in everything that had been assembled. In a life filled with strife and dissension and disappointment, victory was a new flavour for him and he enjoyed it. What he also enjoyed was playing a little game with Frank Pagan, who was labouring in a blind place indeed.

'Did you come to my hotel just to harangue me, Frank?' he asked. 'Did you come here to make false accusations?'

Pagan rose from the bed. 'I've got a problem, Ivor. Let me see if I can explain it to you. First, I get this snippet of information about Jig. No matter how hard you deny it, I know it comes from you. The horse's mouth. I get on a plane. *Voilà*. New York. Second, as coincidence would have it, I find my old pal Ivor in the same city, researching a book. I don't put a lot of faith in coincidence, Ivor, and since I've had the miserable fortune to actually struggle through some of your writing in pamphlet form, I don't put much faith in your literary talents either. Do you see where I'm going?'

McInnes shook his head. 'You're still barking, Frank.'

'Something's going on. Something's happening.' Pagan's eyes, which McInnes had thought cindery before, appeared to have caught fire.

Ivor McInnes looked out at Central Park. A watery sun, the colour of sulphur, hung over bare trees. He had a sudden image of the girl in the Hotel Strasbourg, and he felt a weird little outbreak of guilt at the memory. It was one of the drawbacks of Presbyterianism, this smothering guilt that sometimes attacked you unawares.

'Check with my publisher if you want to know about my book, Frank,' he said. 'I'm sure he'd tell you the book's no sham.'

Pagan glanced at his wristwatch, then looked in the direction of the FBI man, whose silence had been faintly disturbing to McInnes. After a lifetime of speechmaking and pulpit thumping, McInnes abhorred silences.

McInnes said, 'I hope you find your man, Frank. Jig's a bloody menace to peaceful people everywhere. Especially to the Loyalists in Ireland. If he keeps killing, the British are going to think very carefully about the cost of maintaining a presence in the province. And what would happen to the Loyalists then?'

'What exactly are you loyal to?' Pagan asked. 'Enlighten me.'

'Queen and country of course,' McInnes replied.

'Your patriotism's touching. But you left something out, Ivor.'

'What?'

'You forgot your *overriding* loyalty, didn't you? The only one in your life. To yourself. To Ivor McInnes. That's the only true allegiance *you* understand.'

'Frank, Frank,' McInnes said, his voice filled with the weariness of a man who is tired of being vilified unjustly. 'You're beginning to believe all the things you read about me in the newspapers. I credited you with more sense than that, my friend. Aren't you being just a trifle hasty in your character assassination? Besides, you forget something. Something important.'

'What's that?'

'We're on the *same* side. We both want to see Jig behind bars, don't we? We both want to see an end to IRA terrorism, don't we? You forget, Frank, that I'm an ardent supporter of the government you work for. You shouldn't let something that bloody important slip your mind. Whether you like it or not, we're *allies*.' And here McInnes placed one of his large hands on Pagan's shoulder and squeezed it in a confidential way.

Frank Pagan stared at McInnes. His face was hard and cold again, and there was a distance in his eyes. McInnes wondered about the reservoirs of anger inside the man. He let his hand drop to his side.

'You overlook a major difference,' Pagan said, his voice flat, words clipped. 'I don't play on bigotry and fear, McInnes. I don't incite people to meaningless acts of violence. And I don't use scum like the Free Ulster Volunteers to do my dirty work for me.'

McInnes, who realised he'd struck a vibrant chord here, simply shrugged. 'I've been accused of bigotry before, Frank, and I daresay I'll be accused again. I challenge you to find anything in my speeches or my writing to support that charge. You'll find that *nowhere* have I ever uttered or written a single word that could justifiably be construed as bigotry. What I have done, and what I'll continue to do' – and here McInnes flashed his widest smile – 'is to criticise the policies of the Roman Catholic Church, which I consider an impediment to any kind of progress. You look at any poor country, you'll find the Catholic Church somewhere in the picture. You look at any poor country racked by a runaway birthrate and you'll find priests and nuns holding total dominion over the peasants. The Vatican doesn't want adherents and converts, it wants prisoners. It wants people who are scared to ask questions. It wants numbers, and it dangles the threat of excommunication over anybody who has the guts to ask straightforward questions. Take something dead simple, Frank. Take your average parish priest. What in the name of God does he know about women and marriage and raising children? Nothing! He leads a celibate life, with his head stuck up his arse. And yet he's the man who's supposed to give *guidance* to people whose marriages are falling apart or husbands who are impotent? It's this same church that has kept the Republic of Ireland in bondage for centuries, with its censorship and its damned laws of contraception and its attitude to divorce.'

McInnes paused now. His voice, which had been kept at a constant, restrained pitch, had filled the small hotel room like air blown into a balloon. 'It's the same church that has been behind the Troubles in Ulster. Do you think Ulster would be in its present pitiful condition if the Catholic Church weren't there? We're an impoverished, backward society, Frank. We should be in the vanguard of European life, but instead what do we get? Bloody handouts from British politicians. A little charity from Westminster. And you can say what you like about the FUV, Frank, but it's people like them that keep the Catholic IRA from turning Northern Ireland into a complete bloodbath.'

Pagan shook his head. There was something just a little mesmerising about McInnes when he was in full flight. He could make even the most irrational arguments sound forcibly convincing. What you had to do when you confronted Ivor was to keep in mind that his arguments appealed only to unanalytical audiences already predisposed to his point of view. If you didn't, you ran the risk of having your head addled. He was annoyed with himself for having allowed Ivor to launch into a speech. He was also annoyed that his own composure was slipping. 'You make the FUV sound like a peace-keeping force. What's your big dream, McInnes? A Nobel Peace Prize?'

McInnes was determined not to be drawn by insults. He found it remarkable how blind Frank Pagan could be. Why didn't the man accept the fact that they were both on the same side when you got right down to it? What was so difficult about that notion?

'My aim's simple,' McInnes said. 'I've said it many times before and I'll say it again. I want an end to the IRA. Can you deny you want the same thing?'

'The problem with talking to somebody like you is the feeling I get of hammering my head against a bloody brick wall,' Pagan said. 'You have a bad habit, Ivor, of twisting things around so that they'll fit your thesis.'

'You didn't answer my question, Frank.'

'Okay. I don't deny it. I want to see terrorism finished. But are you sure that's what *you* really want?'

'What is that supposed to mean?'

'It's simple. Without having the Catholics and the IRA to rant about, what would you do with your time, Ivor? Just think how bloody bored you'd be.'

McInnes smiled. 'Bored but at peace, Frank.'

Pagan looked at his wristwatch. 'It's been fun talking to you and I'm sorry we have to run. In the meantime, Ivor, keep out of trouble and try to have a nice day.'

'I always have nice days,' McInnes said.

He watched Pagan close the door quietly. Alone, he moved to the window and saw two brightly dressed joggers pounding through Central Park. He placed the palm of his hand upon the glass, leaving a print. Pagan, of course, was mistaken. Without the IRA, the Catholics in the North would have no real protection, which meant they would migrate to the South – that medieval, Church-choked country where they belonged – leaving Ulster in the hands of Protestants. And McInnes, whose vision encompassed an Ulster free of sectarian violence, would have a major role to play in the formation of this shining new society. It was really very simple. There would be a great many things to keep him occupied in the future.

He put on his overcoat. He'd spend the afternoon in the public library, leafing through old records and documents and making sure he took notes conscientiously. It would be difficult, though. He knew his mind would keep drifting to the Memorial Presbyterian Church in White Plains.

Sunday at seven. Two days from now. The first step. He felt suddenly excited and anxious. It had been a long road, and it had been filled with deprivation for him. But now at least, he could read the signs along the way. He put his hand on the telephone but then drew it away again quickly. This urge to speak, to make contact, to utter aloud the excitement he felt – he had to let it subside. To make any kind of contact now would be to break rules. And the rules had been observed stringently ever since the beginning. Even in times of the utmost difficulty.

He stepped out into the corridor just in time to see Frank Pagan and Zuboric get into the elevator. Pagan looked briefly in his direction, raised a hand in the air, then the elevator doors slid shut behind him.

Frank Pagan was depressed in the thrift shop. Old clothing had its own peculiar smell, reminiscent of locked attics and damp chests filled with mouldering papers. It wasn't the sleazy ambience of the store that brought him down, though. It was the encounter with McInnes. To be drawn into an argument with Ivor was like trying to do a butterfly stroke in a small bathtub. You never got anywhere.

Pagan picked out a very old black overcoat and tried it on. He turned to Artie Zuboric. 'How do I look?'

'Sensational,' Zuboric said. He found an enormous Hawaiian shirt, which might have housed the entire Barnum and Bailey Circus. He examined the pattern, a nightmare of pineapples and Venus flytraps.

Pagan took off the overcoat. It wasn't grubby enough for St Finbar's. He found a more likely garment on the next rack, an old raincoat with tattered epaulettes and faded stains tattooing the sleeves.

Frank Pagan tried on the raincoat. He wandered towards a cracked wall mirror at the far end of the store and stared at his own reflection. 'The trouble with Ivor is he shapes the world to suit himself. It's a common trait among megalomaniacs.'

Zuboric lifted a red and black checked suit from a rack and held it up. He'd seen another side of Frank Pagan in the room at the Essex House. He'd caught the distinct vibrations of the man's capacity for anger. It was enjoyable to see the fault lines in Pagan's surface. '*Are* you on the same side, Frank?'

Frank Pagan turned away from his reflection and looked at Zuboric, wondering if the agent was trying to goad him. 'The Irish problem turns up some strange companions,' he said. 'Maybe McInnes and I have a common enemy. And maybe our goals overlap. But what McInnes loves is strife. He feeds on it. If there wasn't any trouble, he'd go out and manufacture some.'

'He says he's writing a book – '

Pagan snorted. 'McInnes spews out pamphlets that make *The Protocols of the Elders of Zion* seem positively charitable. If you've ever got a few minutes to waste and you want some insight into Ivor's mind, I suggest you read the one entitled *The Roman Catholic Conspiracy in Northern Ireland*. In that priceless work he actually advocates sterilisation for the Roman Catholic women of Ulster after they've had two babies. So the idea of him writing a book is fucking laughable. Unless he's found a publisher who specialises in madness. Which isn't *altogether* an impossibility.'

Zuboric said, 'So what's he doing here then?'

Pagan shrugged. 'I wish I knew. The only thing I know for certain is I don't trust him. And I don't trust the coincidence of him being here. What you have to keep remembering about Ivor is that he's clever and he's cunning. You might disagree with the things he says, but you don't underestimate him. And there are thousands of people in Ulster who agree with his every word. That kind of support shouldn't be overlooked either.'

'You said he was involved with the Free Ulster Volunteers. He denied that. What's the score there?'

'We've had him watched and we've had him followed, and we've never been able to pin that connection on him directly. The chances are that he's behind the FUV, but he's very careful. If he ever makes contact with them, we don't know about it. I've got sources that say he meets with FUV members secretly, but when it comes down to documented proof, I can never get my hands on any. I work on the assumption that he's the leader, but I can't guarantee it.' Pagan paused a second, casting an eye round the store. 'Ulster's filled with secrets. And Ivor knows a whole lot of them, but he isn't telling.'

Zuboric watched Pagan plunge into a mountain of old shoes now. There was footwear of every variety. Sandals, battered slippers, two-tone horrors, beat-up climbing boots. A sweaty odour arose from the heap. There was no way in the world he'd try on any of the shoes himself, but Pagan, who'd already removed his own casual leather jobs, was plucking a dilapidated pair of brown brogues from the heap. He sat on the floor and placed one of the shoes on his left foot. He suddenly reminded Zuboric of a kid getting dressed up for Halloween. He had this quality of enthusiasm.

'Fine, don't you think?' Pagan asked.

'Yeah. Terrific.'

'Now I need a shirt and a pair of trousers.' Pagan wandered off to another pile of clothing and Zuboric followed. Pagan chose an antique flannel shirt that was missing several buttons. The cuffs were frayed. Pants next, a pair of crumpled old flannels with enormous fly buttons and broken belt loops. When he had his wardrobe assembled Pagan said, 'It's a pity about that suntan of yours.'

Zuboric was unhappy with the notion of Pagan infiltrating St Finbar's. At first, Artie had wanted to dress up the way Pagan was planning to do, and position himself inside the soup kitchen dressed as one of its clientele. But this notion had disintegrated as soon as he'd tried on an old tweed coat and looked at himself in the mirror. There was absolutely *no way* he could pass himself off as a derelict with a complexion as healthy as his. He looked too good to carry off a charade like the one Pagan was going to play. Instead, Zuboric planned to conceal himself in Tumulty's office while Pagan mingled with the deadbeats downstairs. There was a certain ironic symbolism in this arrangement that Zuboric enjoyed.

'You should stay out of spas,' Pagan said. 'And avoid suntan lamps in future. They're unnatural.'

'And look as white as you? No thanks.'

'Didn't I tell you, Artie? The way I look is all the rage in London this winter. Everybody's trying it.'

Pagan took his purchases to the desk where a frail old man with a face that resembled a spider's web operated an ancient cash register.

When they were outside on the street, Pagan said, 'It's time to release Father Joe.'

Zuboric looked across the street at Pagan's big green Cadillac. There was a tiny knot in his stomach, a vague tension. He wanted a tidy conclusion to this whole murky business. He wanted to escort Frank Pagan to Kennedy Airport and watch him step aboard a flight to London, which would thankfully be the last of the guy. But first there was the uncertainty of Jig.

They crossed the street to the car. Pagan took the key out of his pocket, and as he was about to insert it into the door of the vehicle he saw a girl come out of a delicatessen half a block away, and his heart jumped as if electricity had coursed through his body.

Roxanne.

He dropped the bag of secondhand clothes. His lungs were tight in his chest and his hands trembled.

'Something wrong?' Zuboric asked.

Pagan said nothing. He watched the girl move along the sidewalk, her thick black hair floating behind her. The way she walked. The way her hair flew up from her neck and shoulders. He shut his eyes a moment, and when he opened them again the girl was already turning the corner at the end of the block. *Fool.* Deceived by resemblances. Misled by impressions. He felt weak. He had to lean against the side of the car.

'Frank?' Zuboric asked.

'It's nothing. I thought I saw somebody I used to know. That's all.'

Zuboric picked up the bag of clothing from the pavement and gave it to Pagan, who clutched it in an absentminded way against his chest. Pagan looked along the empty sidewalk. He had the depressing realisation that if he lived a million years, if he lived long enough to see the sun shrivel in the sky and the earth freeze and wither and the planets plunge into eternal darkness, he'd never see Roxanne again. He'd see resemblances in a hundred places, but never again the real person. It was quite a thought.

He opened the car door, his hand still trembling. He got in behind the wheel. What he needed was something desperately simple. He needed to fuck the spectre of Roxanne out of existence. It came down to that. But what were you supposed to do if that particular appetite had died? If all the women you ever saw didn't match the memory of a dead woman? If your heart was empty?

'You're sure you're okay?' Zuboric asked.

Pagan smiled. 'I'm in great shape.'

Roscommon, New York

Celestine Cairney listened to Harry's Irish music float out through the open door of his study. She paused on the threshold of the room, watching Harry and his son sit close together near the fire. A flask of brandy and two glasses stood on the coffee table. It was late afternoon and the sun had gone behind the trees, and the only light in the study was the glow of the log fire. Harry leaned towards his son and said something, and the young man laughed, perhaps a little too politely. It was the laughter of somebody who hadn't quite learned the language of mirth. An artificial sound.

Celestine leaned against the door jamb. The Irish music made her uneasy at times because it was the music of ghosts, the music of Harry's first marriage, with all its comfortable intimacies. She had mental pictures of Harry and his first wife sitting by the fire while this music wove through the air around them.

She moved very slightly. Neither man was aware of her presence. She liked the idea of observing people when they didn't know she was watching. She studied Patrick. He was a good-looking man in an intense way. He had serious eyes and a certain strength about him, but there was an aura of privacy, almost a force field, that one couldn't get through easily. She had the impression of somebody who lived in his own secret fortress. He wasn't like Harry at all, outgoing and gregarious with that facile Irish charm he could trot out whenever it suited him. These were the gifts of a politician. The necessary equipment.

Come back, Paddy Reilly, to Ballyjamesduff,
Come home, Paddy Reilly, to me.

All Harry's music was like this. It was all drenched with yearning. Now there was a break in the song and the thin notes of a fiddle filled the room.

Patrick Cairney had seen her. He rose from his chair. Harry smiled and stretched out a hand in her direction.

'She's been spying on us,' he said.

Celestine moved into the room. 'Why would I do that, Harry? You don't have any secrets from me, love.'

Harry stood up now too. 'Want a brandy?' he asked.

'I don't want to interrupt this reunion,' she said. 'Besides, I was on my way to take a shower before dinner.'

She gazed at Patrick Cairney. She found his awkwardness in her presence a little touching. The way he'd reacted last night when she'd gone to his bedroom was amusing. He'd been like a kid who'd smuggled a girl inside his dormitory against all the school rules. He seemed now like a man who wished he were someplace else. She knew exactly what kind of effect she had on him. In her lifetime, she'd come to understand that her beauty often devastated people. Certain men didn't know how to react to her. She had had her share of flowers and lovers' poems and men who stuttered and fumbled around her. She considered her appearance a genetic accident, useful but finally transient. She never saw in the mirror what other people saw when they beheld her, almost as if her appearance were something apart from what she thought of as her inner self, her reality. Extreme good looks, such as her own, were often interpreted wrongly. Men looked at her and they couldn't get beyond her appearance and down into the place where she really lived. They couldn't begin to think their way beyond her surfaces.

Most men anyway.

'You could never interrupt anything, my dear,' Harry said.

He had that look on his face. Total devotion. Utter bliss. There were moments when her husband's love made her feel uncomfortable. Harry gave it so wholeheartedly and without qualification that it was like a light he was forever shining into her eyes. Sometimes she felt blinded by it.

She warmed her hands in front of the fire. Patrick Cairney moved out of her way, but there was a second of contact between them, a tiny friction as her body touched his. She liked the connection. She liked the expression on Patrick's face, the effort he made to conceal his discomfort.

'I was riding and I'm grubby,' she said. She spread her legs in front of the fire. 'I can't sit down to dinner in this condition.'

Harry reached for her hand. His skin had the feel of rice paper. She took his fingers in her palm. They were cold with that unfathomable coldness of age. She took her hand away and walked back across the room to the door. What she frequently longed for was warmth – another climate altogether, where she wouldn't be confronted by the chills of a long winter. What was she doing in this big house located on this huge frozen estate? Why in the name of God had she ever agreed to come here to this place of isolation and snow and security guards who watched her lasciviously through their binoculars whenever she went outside?

She reached the doorway. She shivered slightly. 'Dinner will be ready in about thirty minutes,' she said. 'I'll meet you in the dining-room.'

'What are we having?' Harry asked.

'The speciality of the house. Corned beef and cabbage. What else?' If there had been such a thing as Irish wine, a Cabernet Killarney or a Château Galway, say, she would have served that as well. She disliked the stodge of Irish food.

'Ah,' Harry said, delighted. He was showing off his wife for the benefit of his son. 'Didn't I tell you, Pat? Didn't I tell you she knows how to warm an old man's heart?'

Patrick nodded. He fiddled with the stopper of the crystal brandy flask. He wasn't looking at Celestine. She left the room and moved along the landing. She paused outside the door of Patrick's bedroom. What she remembered was how furtive he'd been last night about his canvas bag and the small wooden horse, which he'd practically seized from her hand and stuffed back inside the bag as if it were a souvenir too precious for anyone else to sully. Curious. She was tempted to sneak inside the room and explore it in his absence. Instead, she continued towards her own bedroom.

She went inside the bathroom and removed her clothes, catching glimpses of herself in the mirror. She had small breasts and a flat stomach. She thought her hips were probably a little too narrow, but otherwise it was a good body, firm and smooth and untouched as yet by age. She let her hair fall over her shoulders as she turned to the shower stall. The water was very hot, the way she liked it. Steam rose against her flesh, glistened in her hair, filled her nostrils. She took soap from the dish and made lather all over her body, smoothing the soap slowly over her breasts and across the surface of her stomach. She titled her head back against the tiled wall, closing her eyes.

She slid the soap between her inner thighs to her pubic hair, as though it were a lover's hand she was directing. She moved it back and forward slowly between her legs and then the bar slipped from her hand and now there was nothing between herself and her body. With the tips of her fingers she stroked herself gently, very gently, anticipating the pleasure. Her fantasies were always tropical. There were always exotic flowers and a suffocating humidity and a hint of danger, like an indistinct presence just beyond her field of vision. Her imaginary lover's face kept changing, first one of the men she'd known in her life, then another and another coming at her in quick succession until she settled on the one who could please her fantasies best. But this time the face that finally came before her was that of a man who'd never been her lover, and this realisation excited her, this new perspective made her nerves tingle.

He remained stubbornly fixed in her mind.

Faster now. Faster. She had a sense of something warm flowing through her body, something molten that was located deep inside her. She heard herself moan. She bit the knuckles of her left hand and she gasped, and for a second her whole body was rigid before she fell apart inside, as if she were destroyed by the astonishing ferocity of pleasure. She slid down slowly against the tiled wall to a sitting position, her eyes still shut against the pounding water, her hand limp between her thighs.

She didn't move for a long time.

She thought it weird she'd allowed Patrick Cairney to participate in her fantasy. Out of all the men she'd known in her life, she'd selected one who was off limits, who was forbidden by the fact of her marriage. She stood up, reached for a towel, started to dry herself carefully.

Patrick Cairney, she thought. My fantasy lover.

She rubbed condensation from the mirror, making a small space in which she could see her face. Her smile was enigmatic, even to herself.

New York City

Dressed in the clothes he'd purchased at the thrift shop, Frank Pagan put down the half-empty bowl and said, 'It's pretty bland, Joe. It needs a dash of something. Tarragon, Paprika. Something to spice it up. Some Worcester sauce would do it.'

Joseph X. Tumulty wore a crucifix about his neck, a small flash of gold against his black shirt. Every now and then his hand went to it, his ungainly fingers fumbling with the miniature Jesus. 'The men here are better served by nutrition that haute cuisine, Mr Pagan.'

'You may have a point.' Pagan stared into the bowl, which sat on Tumulty's desk. 'Have you got everything straight in your mind, Joe?'

Tumulty nodded. These men were playing with him, and he resented them for it. He laid his hands in front of him and saw how the skin glistened with sweat. He was beginning to discover that fear had various strata of intensity. The fear he'd felt before when Frank Pagan had burst into the room on Mulberry Street and shot Santacroce was nothing to what he was going through now at the prospect of facing Jig again.

Lying to him. Entrapping him. Setting him up. He felt very small and very weak. But a promise had been held out to him like a carrot to a donkey. If he did what was asked of him, he wouldn't go to jail. It was that simple. Who would run this place if he was incarcerated? He couldn't depend on volunteers to keep the whole thing going, and he couldn't stand the idea of St Finbar's being shut down, his people having to go hungry. God knows, they had little enough in their lives as it was. They *relied* on him and how could he deprive them of that? And what would happen to people like McCune, people he had saved, if their mentor went to prison? Tumulty saw only sheer disaster. His night of solitude in a cell had convinced him that he could stand the strain of being locked up, but he couldn't take the notion of being removed from Canal Street. He had prayed in the small cell. He had gone down on his knees and searched his mind for God. God, the great problem solver, the unlocker of puzzles, had responded only with a roaring silence, as if he had abdicated his place in the firmament. And Tumulty understood what the absences were saying to him. *He was on his own in this situation.*

'When Jig comes into the kitchen,' he told Pagan in a monotone, 'I'll say a specific blessing when we sit down to eat. "*The Lord hath done great things for us, whereof we are glad.*' After we've eaten, I'll signal for Jig to follow me up to my office. You'll come up behind to block his retreat. Jig and I will come in here. Mr Zuboric will be waiting.'

Pagan thought there was something incongruous about Psalm 126, verse 3 when you spoke it aloud inside a soup kitchen, but the choice of phrase had come from Arthur Zuboric who didn't believe Tumulty could be trusted to devise his own code. Pagan suspected there was some spiteful part of Artie that wanted to see this whole scheme fall to pieces so he could quietly gloat. A gloating discontent was apparently built into Artie's circuitry.

Tumulty asked, 'Do you enjoy this, Mr Pagan? Do you enjoy seeing me squirm?'

Pagan didn't answer. He hardly heard the question. He was wondering about fear. He was wondering whether Joe Tumulty's fear was going to be strong enough to lead him into betraying Jig. Or whether at the last moment the priest might experience some spasm of courage. He was sure that Tumulty had courage inside him – otherwise he wouldn't have gone to the meeting with Santacroce in the first place. Pagan glanced at the attaché case that sat on the floor beside the desk. It contained the two customised weapons, but as a precaution all the ammunition had been removed.

Tumulty looked at Frank Pagan. 'It's a hell of a thing you're asking me to do. You know that?'

'You got yourself into it in the first place, Joe. I didn't enroll you in the IRA, did I?' Pagan asked. 'Just remember this. Don't fuck around with me when it comes to Jig. Don't even think about it.'

Tumulty wandered in the direction of a painting of the Virgin Mary that hung at the back of the room. He looked up at it for a moment, drawn into the eyes. He was being asked to betray more than an individual called Jig. He was being asked to betray the Cause and himself along with it. He found a little consolation in the fact he hadn't exactly told his captors very much. He hadn't said anything about the deliveries in Maine, and he hadn't mentioned Nicholas Linney, and his description of Jig had been vague at best. Small consolations. He turned away from the Virgin.

Something else occurred to him for the first time. The notion of reprisals. If he gave these men Jig, he might just as well be signing his own execution order, because a day would come when another gunman would be sent from Ireland to even the score. There was nothing more terrible than a traitor so far as the Cause was concerned. No crime was greater than treason.

A rock, Tumulty thought. And a very hard place. Somewhere, if only he could find it, there had to be a solution, a compromise. *Guidance*, he thought. But he knew that God wasn't about to show him the way. Prayer, this time, was a dead connection.

He said, 'I'll do it. You don't need to worry.' Even as he committed himself, he was still frantically searching. How could he even *think* of betraying the Cause? He'd been raised with a belief in the sanctity of the Cause, just as he'd been brought up in the seminary to believe that God's authority was the only one. Little divisions of the heart. Pangs. If he couldn't get the weapons to Jig – and he was certain that was out of the question now –

then what small thing could he do to help the man? Think, Joseph. Think hard. There has to be a way.

'I'm not worried,' Pagan said. He managed to keep the tension out of his voice. But he *was* concerned. When you backed a man into a corner, any man, there were sometimes reserves of surprising defiance. Was Joe going to find that nerve of resistance?

Tumulty sat down. He experienced a moment of calm. What he realised was that Jig, who had seen Frank Pagan before, was going to recognise the man, no matter Pagan's ridiculous old clothes and his unkempt hair. Jig was going to know.

Then what?

15 Albany, New York

It was a cheap joint at the edge of the Interstate – unpainted cinderblock, a flamingo-coloured neon sign with the words CAPITOL CITY MOTEL, a cracked swimming pool, drained for the winter. Fitzjohn walked round the pool, Waddell in tow. He paused when they reached the diving board. On the other side of the pool was the motel bar, where Rorke and McGrath had gone for a drink. Seamus Houlihan was up in his room – resting, he'd said. Seamus always looked as if he was carrying the bloody world on his shoulders and enjoying its weight regardless.

The five merry men, Fitzjohn thought. He heard Rorke's weird laughter float out of the bar. It had the staccato quality of a pneumatic drill. Fitzjohn put his hands in the pockets of his pants and shivered in the night wind. The lights that hung around the entrance to the bar gave the place all the cheer of a pauper's Christmas.

Waddell said, 'I suppose you'll be leaving tomorrow, Fitz.'

Fitzjohn nodded. 'After I drive you to Tarrytown, I'm going home to New Jersey. That's my arrangement.'

Waddell raised his sharp little face and smiled. 'Back to the family, eh?'

'Back to the family,' Fitzjohn said.

'You'll be looking forward to it, I expect.'

'You don't know how much.'

Waddell moved to the rim of the pool. He made a funny little plunging gesture with his hands, then stepped back. 'I had a wife and a kid once,' he said. 'About ten years ago. We had a small house in Ballysillen. I was second engineer on a ship at that time. The day they died I was on board a Liberian vessel called the *Masurado*, somewhere in the Gulf of Oman. I'm working in the engine room when the captain himself comes down to see me. He says to me he just received a message. My wife and kid are dead.' Waddell's voice was very flat, unemotional.

'What happened was they got burned to death,' he went on. 'They were trapped inside the house when some soldiers and the local IRA started a gun battle. Snipers everywhere. Explosions. Somehow the house started to burn. Nobody ever told me who was responsible for that. I don't suppose it matters much.'

'I'm sorry,' Fitzjohn said. Another waste, another tragedy in the ongoing horror that was Ulster. He wondered how Waddell coped with the pain.

'It's a fucking long time ago.' Waddell looked very sad as he turned his face to Fitzjohn. 'It's best to bury it.'

'Yes,' Fitzjohn said.

Waddell ran the back of his hand over his lips. 'About a month after it happened, I ran into Seamus Houlihan. I'd known him for years. I told him about the wife and kid. You know what Seamus did?'

Fitzjohn shook his head.

'Seamus went out that same night and killed two men. One was a high-up in the IRA, a man called Costello. The other was a British soldier. Seamus said it was retribution.'

'Retribution?' Fitzjohn asked.

'It was to help even the score, you see.' Waddell reached out to touch the diving board. 'I never asked him to do anything like that, you understand.' He took a cigarette out of his coat pocket, a Woodbine. He lit it in a furtive way, cupping both hands against the wind. 'I always owed him something for that.'

Fitzjohn thought it was a strange kind of debt, a murderous obligation. 'You didn't ask him to do anything for you, so how can you owe him?'

Waddell shrugged. 'It's the way I see it.' He sucked the Woodbine deeply in the manner of a man who has spent time deprived of tobacco. 'I know Seamus and I know what his faults are, you see. But he's been a bloody good friend to me.'

The emphasis was on 'bloody', Fitzjohn thought. He wondered how many victims Houlihan had left strewn behind him. He had the sudden desire to leave Albany tonight and get away from the madman and whatever atrocities he was planning, because he was afraid. Maybe, after the work he'd done finding the airfield and the long hours spent driving the Ryder, Houlihan would be understanding. Jesus, that was a contradiction in terms! Houlihan would probably shoot him if he mentioned anything about leaving. On the other hand, he didn't exactly relish the idea of driving this gang to Tarrytown and discovering there that he'd outlived his usefulness, that he was destined to stare down the barrel of Seamus's gun. He had no intention of being pressed into premature retirement.

'What are the plans after Tarrytown?' he asked Waddell.

Waddell said, 'That's not for me to say.'

Fitzjohn thought about the crates inside the rental truck. In a hesitant way he asked, 'Don't you get sick of it all, John? Don't you want an end to all the killing?' As soon as he'd phrased the questions, he wondered if Waddell would report them to his bloody good friend. Houlihan, a product of Protestant Belfast street gangs and Armagh Jail, which was where Fitzjohn had first encountered him, would regard such questions as a sign of unacceptable weakness. In Houlihan's world, chaos and violence were moral constants, necessities.

Waddell didn't answer immediately. He tossed his Woodbine away and turned up the collar of his coat. 'Sometimes I think a peaceful life would be very pleasant,' he said. 'I suppose that's what you've got for yourself in New Jersey?'

Fitzjohn said that it was.

'Then why did you agree to be a part of all this if your life's so bloody wonderful?' Waddell asked.

Fitzjohn answered quietly. 'You know what they say, John. Once you're in the FUV, you're always in.'

A slight despair touched Fitzjohn just then. Here he was in the United States of America, a new life, and when he'd been asked to do a job for the FUV he'd jumped at it without consideration, like a man programmed into the ruts of old hatreds. He hadn't known the nature of the job, nor had he ever stopped to ask. It was only now that he truly realised the FUV was the culmination of feelings he should have left behind in Northern Ireland, otherwise he was doing nothing more than hauling used baggage into his new life.

He wondered if he could sneak away in the night, if he could wait until the others were asleep and then vanish swiftly. Maybe he could hitch a ride to Albany County Airport and fly back to New Jersey. Home. He'd forget he ever participated in any of this insanity. He didn't belong with people like Seamus Houlihan these days, or with thugs like Rorke and McGrath. They stood for the old world and the senselessness of a war whose roots were buried in a history that should have been forgotten long ago. He turned the prospect of departure around in his mind. A risky business. Maybe. But waiting might prove fatal.

A movement on the balcony caught his eye and he looked up. Houlihan was standing there, legs apart, hands on the rail.

'Waddell, Fitz,' Houlihan called down. 'I'd like to see you and the others in my room right away.'

'Right, Seamus,' Waddell replied.

Fitzjohn started towards the stairway, looking back once at the empty swimming pool. He wondered how long Houlihan had been standing on the balcony and whether he'd heard any of the conversation with Waddell.

Roscommon, New York

Patrick Cairney had drunk just a little more of his father's brandy than he intended. When he went inside his bedroom and lay down, his head was spinning. He didn't close his eyes because that way the spinning was worse. He had to sit up and concentrate on something inside the room, an object he could focus on until the nausea had passed. He stared hard at his canvas bag, which sat locked on the dresser. After dinner there had been several toasts proposed by Harry. Sentimental toasts, tributes to the composers of the Proclamation of the Irish Republic written at Easter 1916 at the time of the Rising.

All Harry's heroes had been signatories of the Proclamation, and he could recite the entire document by heart. Certain words came back to Cairney. *Supported by her exiled children in America . . . Ireland strikes in full confidence of victory . . . We pledge our lives and the lives of our comrades-in-arms to the cause of Irish freedom . . .* We pledge our lives, Cairney thought, though not necessarily our brains or our skills. During the toasts he'd fought with the urge to silence Harry and stuff the empty words down his throat and tell him how little significance they had, how meaningless they really were. This streak of cruelty inside himself wasn't surprising, but what astounded him was the forceful way it had suddenly risen. Harry's beatific expression, the way he sniffed as he recited the sacrosanct old sentiments – Patrick Cairney despised it all, the facile nature of Harry's words, the easy emotions. He despised a life given over to talk, endless talk, and no action.

The Cause needed action. Not the empty rattling of old men.

He let his thoughts drift back to the beginning, the very beginning, when he had first come to Finn's attention. In those days he'd gone around the fringes of clandestine political groups in Dublin as if his head were going to explode. Here he was in a divided country where injustice was a commonplace event and, if you excluded the mad bombers and the angry snipers, nothing much was being done to correct the situation and get the English out. Here he was on an island whose northern section was constantly on the edge of apocalypse. When he'd visited Ulster he'd been sickened by the flames and the raddled buildings and the rubber bullets fired by British soldiers and the checkpoints and the Saracen cars and tanks and the kids who mindlessly parroted a hatred they had inherited, a whole desolate world galaxies removed from Harry's green dreams that had been spoon-fed to him throughout childhood. And he'd been impatient back then, insanely so, driven by an urge to transform his emotions into direct physical action. People were suspicious of him because he was American. Because he hadn't been born and raised in Ireland. He wanted to tell them he knew more about Ireland and its history than any of them.

But it wasn't until he'd gravitated into Finn's orbit that the opportunity came up to serve the Cause. He remembered now the precise moment in Glasnevin Cemetery when Finn had given him a gun and a mission to accomplish. It was the most perfect moment in his life. He'd stepped through a door into a different world where justice was something you pursued outside courts of law, where you moved beyond the realms of the Queen's laws and her lawyers and judges, those bewigged fools whose only interest lay in the maintenance of a status quo that had always protected them and their privileges. You created your own justice. And it was fair, the way it was supposed to be.

Finn said once, *It's a monastic life this. There's no glamour and no comfort. You can't have a family and kids. You can't hold down some regular job. You're always going to be standing outside of things, and every bloody shadow you see will make you wonder if there's a gun concealed in it. You want that, Jig?*

Yes. Yes he wanted that. He wanted that the way he had never wanted anything else. He had given up his life for the Cause. *But where would the Cause be if he didn't get that missing money back?*

Now he pushed the window open, hoping the cold air would clear his brain. Four brandies had brought him to this condition, but then he wasn't accustomed to alcohol. He looked out at the shadowy waters of Roscommon Lake. The night was intensely cold, moonless. He drew the window shut. He was suddenly anxious to get away from Roscommon, anxious for action, anxious to locate Finn's money.

He was thirsty. He opened the door and gazed down the flight of stairs to the first floor. The house was silent and dark, save for a thin light that burned dimly somewhere below. He moved towards the stairs and went down. He stepped inside the large kitchen – stainless steel surfaces and high-tech appliances, he noticed, which meant Celestine had redecorated the room since Kathleen's time, when the kitchen had been chintzy and floral. He found a glass and pressed it against the ice dispenser, then he filled it with water from the faucet. He drained the glass quickly, and stood with his back pressed against the sink. Once, this kitchen had been the warm heart of the house. Now it seemed more like a transplant, a triumph of the new technology. What did it tell him about the difference between Kathleen and Celestine? he wondered.

He became conscious of a voice drifting very faintly towards him through the open door. It was Celestine's. For a moment he wondered if she and Harry had come back downstairs for a nightcap, but as he strained to listen he realised he heard only one voice. He set his glass down inside the sink and went out of the kitchen. There was a thin light that burned through the crack of a doorway at the end of the hall. He moved towards it, even as he realised that he should have gone the other way to the stairs and back up to his bedroom. This was none of his business. Nothing that happened at Roscommon had anything to do with him.

He stopped outside the sitting-room. Celestine was standing with her back to the door, a telephone receiver held in place between shoulder and jaw. She wore a blue silk robe that shimmered in the light from a nearby lamp and in one hand she held a glass of whiskey. Cairney heard her say, 'I'm not making it up,' and then she turned around and saw him in the doorway, and her expression was one of restrained surprise, almost as though she'd expected to find him standing there. She put the receiver down, perhaps a little too quickly, and the first thing Cairney thought was that she had a lover somewhere, somebody she talked to when Harry was fast asleep upstairs. He didn't like the idea, but it made some kind of sense. How could Harry satisfy her at his age and in his health? Why *wouldn't* she look elsewhere for consolation? *I'm not making it up*. He wondered what she was referring to.

'I spy,' she said lightly, like a child involved in a game of hide-and-seek.

He pushed the door open. 'I didn't mean to creep up on you.'

'Enter.' She gestured with her glass. It was an expansive motion, a little careless. She was slightly drunk. Cairney had a small insight into her life. A beautiful young woman married to a man forty years older than she was, probably lonely in the isolation of Roscommon – what was there to do at times but blur her life with liquor? And perhaps a lover she met now and again.

'Harry's physician,' she said, pointing to the phone. 'I make my daily progress report. Dutifully.'

Patrick Cairney wondered if that was a lie. He'd become so good at telling them himself, he should have been expert at detecting them in others, but he wasn't. She had hung up so quickly, though, without any farewell, and it was so late in the evening for a routine medical report, that he assumed it wasn't Harry's physician on the other end of the line. He watched her go to an armchair and sit, crossing her legs. Between the folds of the robe a stretch of pale thigh was visible briefly before she rearranged the garment.

'Want a drink?' she asked.

'I've had too much already.'

'People talk about the Irish Problem, but they miss the point,' she said. She indicated her drink. '*This* is the Irish Problem. Jameson's elixir of life.'

Cairney smiled. Maybe he was mistaken. Maybe there wasn't any man in Celestine's life other than Harry. He was so accustomed to paranoid thinking, to looking for levels of meaning beneath the superficial, that it was difficult to regard things in any normal fashion. An assassin's habit. You came to think that every situation was fraught with hidden significances. Nothing was ever ordinary, nothing innocent.

Celestine put her glass down on the coffee table. She let her hands fall into her lap. 'Why don't you sit down, Patrick?'

He didn't move. 'I was thinking of going back upstairs. I need some sleep.'

She turned her face slowly towards him. At a certain angle, her beauty seemed to have been sculpted in delicate, fragile detail. The fine mouth, the perfectly straight nose, the strong jaw that suggested a streak of determination. 'Harry told me he wanted you to go into politics.'

'He had some notion I'd follow him into the Senate, I guess.'

'Why didn't you?'

'I'm not a committee man,' he answered. 'I don't work well in collaboration with others.'

'A loner. Or was it rebellion against Daddy?'

Cairney shrugged. 'Maybe both.'

Celestine reached out for her glass. She raised it to her lips but didn't drink. 'Why archaeology?' She said this last word in a manner that might almost have been mocking, as if she couldn't bring herself to believe that he was really what he said he was.

'Why not?'

'It just seems so quaint, that's all. I have this image of you in khaki shorts and a pith helmet, directing a bunch of Arabs to dig holes in the sand. You never wanted to be famous like Harry? You never wanted your name to become a household word?'

'Never.' Cairney moved towards the door. The security of the unlit hallway. *I never wanted to be anything like my father.*

'Why is it I always get the impression you're running away from me? What is it? Don't you care for my company?' she asked.

'I'm just tired.'

She stood up. She drained her glass, set it down. 'Don't go. Stay a little longer.'

Her hands were stretched out towards him, and the expression on her face was one he couldn't quite read. A look of anxiety? He wasn't certain. But he recognised one thing beyond any doubt – his compass was going crazy again. He couldn't cross the space between himself and Celestine, couldn't possibly move towards her and clasp those hands in his own. Couldn't touch her. And then he thought: *I could, I could go to her so goddam easily.* He felt like a man flirting with the notion of his own ruin. Yet it appealed, the whole idea caught his fancy. *There, Harry. I had your wonderful wife. How does that affect your gorgeous dreams? Your infallibly beautiful wife and your cosy little world at Roscommon where you live your life falsely?*

He stared at her. He imagined how readily his father must have fallen in love with this woman. He could see the old man losing his heart like a bird deliriously set free.

'Please stay,' she said.

He looked at the paleness of her shoulders and the way the silk robe hung loosely against her body.

'You're leaving in the morning, I understand,' she said.

Cairney nodded his head. Why was he still here in this room, this danger zone? He had no business in this place.

Her hands were still held out to him. 'I have the feeling you won't be coming back.'

'Maybe,' he said.

She lowered her hands slowly to her side. 'You're afraid of me,' she said.

He wanted to say he was more afraid of himself than anything else. But he didn't speak.

'You don't have to be,' she said. 'Why are you always so twitchy around me?'

'I didn't notice.'

'I come near you, you jump. I ought to get one of those little bells lepers used to carry. I'd ring it whenever I moved within ten feet of you.'

Cairney pressed his fingertips to his eyelids to ease his headache. Harry's wife, he thought. Keep remembering that.

'I make you tense,' she said.

'No –'

'Look at yourself, Patrick. You can't wait to get away from me, can you? Can't wait to hurry upstairs to your little bedroom.' She picked up her empty glass and sighed. She looked very fragile just then. 'I'm sorry. I shouldn't be talking to you like this. Forget I ever said anything. I drink too much sometimes and say things I don't mean, that's all. My mouth has a mind of its own. Change the subject.'

He leaned against the wall. 'I think you're unhappy,' he said. Jesus, it was the wrong thing to say. It was provocative, which meant it needed explanation. He should have simply said goodnight and gone upstairs, but now, in a sense, he'd committed himself.

Celestine poured herself another shot of Jameson's. 'Is that how you see me?'

'I think so.'

'And I thought I kept it hidden.'

'Not very well.'

She passed her glass from one hand to the other. 'Certain days. Certain moods. I'm not unhappy all the time. You catch me on a bad day, that's all.'

'Maybe it's Roscommon at winter. I remember how it used to drive me stir-crazy as a kid.'

'Maybe.' She sipped the whiskey. 'I try to be cheerful for your father's sake, but it isn't easy. Sometimes I feel I've buried myself here in a large grey tomb and my whole life's come to a dead stop. But this is his home. How can I tell him I can't stand it here at times? How can I say that to him? It's not his fault I get into these moods. He tries very hard to make me happy.' She paused. 'I didn't use to drink this way.'

Cairney said, 'When Harry's better, why don't you get him to take you on a trip? Maybe you could talk him into a Caribbean cruise on that boat of his.'

'I get seasick and I don't like ocean cruises,' she said. She raised the glass to her mouth and then, changing her mind, stuck it down on the table. 'The last time we went anywhere I kept throwing up all the way from Maine to St Barthélmy. I don't *want* to be unhappy. It seems so goddam ungrateful somehow.'

'Harry wouldn't think so. You only have to tell him you'd like a change of scenery, that's all.'

She was quiet for a very long time before she said, 'I took a trip to Boston last fall. Alone. The whole New England in fall bit. I drove through Maine and Vermont and Connecticut. Harry understood I needed to get away. I missed him, so I came home after a couple of days. But I need more than just getting away, Patrick. I don't think a change of scenery's going to cut it.'

She came very close to him now, looking at him in a searching way. He felt the air around him change. It was suddenly charged with electricity. He thought, *No, it's wrong, it doesn't happen like this*, but he didn't move out of her way.

'There,' she said. 'You're doing it again.'

'Doing what again?'

'Looking tense.'

She placed one hand against the side of his face. Her flesh was surprisingly cool. There was a fragrance from her skin suggestive of lime. Cairney didn't move. He shut his eyes. He felt the silk of her robe against his arms, the pressure of her small breasts against his chest, her hair upon the side of his face. He expected it, he knew it was coming, and he knew he ought to resist it, but the kiss took him by surprise anyhow, the movement of her lips against his and the way her fingers touched the back of his neck and the contact of her tongue against his. Dear God, it was easy to drift out into a dream, into an unreal world where there were no rules to govern this kind of situation, a place where Celestine was a perfect stranger to him.

Suddenly she stepped back from him. 'Forgive me,' she said. 'I didn't mean that to happen. I'm more drunk than I thought.'

He opened his eyes. The yearning he felt was intolerable.

'I'm sorry,' was all he could think to say, cursing himself for his own weakness. He heard one of Finn's old warnings. *If you lose concentration, you're history.* He remembered the day Finn had said this. They'd been walking together close to the Martello Tower in Sandycove, where James Joyce had once lived. He remembered the seriousness in Finn's voice. *Concentration will save your life one day.*

He turned away from her and went quickly out into the hallway. What the hell was he *doing*? What was he playing at? He climbed the stairs and when he reached the landing he stopped, listening to the silences of the big house all around him. He had a driving urge to go back down again. Instead he went inside his bedroom and closed the door.

He checked his wristwatch. It was almost midnight. In a few hours he'd be gone from Roscommon. He'd be out of Celestine Cairney's life.

He took off his clothes and lay down with his hands tucked behind his head and just before he drifted into sleep it all came back to him, the touch of silk, her scent, the feel of her hair and the intimate warmth of her mouth. He realised, with an awareness that was painfully sharp and very depressing, that he desired the woman as much as he'd ever desired anyone.

He wanted his father's wife.

New York City

Joseph X. Tumulty stepped inside his office. He saw Zuboric dozing in an armchair. The FBI man opened his eyes as soon as Tumulty came in and squinted into the light from the desk lamp.

'What time is it?' Zuboric asked.

'Twenty past midnight.' Tumulty moved to his desk and sat down. He was glad to notice that his hands didn't tremble, that he'd somehow managed to control his nervousness. The idea that had come to him was inspired less by God than his own desperation. But he was in a position where the question *Why not*? didn't merit an answer. He simply had to do *something*.

'Is Pagan downstairs?' Zuboric asked.

'Yes.' Tumulty thought of Frank Pagan, dressed like a hobo and propped against the kitchen wall downstairs. When Tumulty had been shelling eggs to scramble for the morning breakfast, he'd been aware of Pagan watching him intently, his eyes two keen scanning instruments that constantly measured and analysed, studying the other men in the big room as they spread mattresses on the floor and started settling down for the night.

Tumulty leafed through a variety of invoices. He was conscious of the FBI agent observing him.

He said to Zuboric, 'Paperwork. I used to imagine God's work would have nothing to do with bureaucracy.'

Zuboric grunted. He wasn't very interested.

Tumulty picked up a pen and began to make calculations on a scratch pad. When he'd written a column of figures that were utterly meaningless, he glanced at Zuboric again. The agent was looking at him blankly.

'I'm hopeless at maths,' Tumulty said, in what he assumed was a lighthearted kind of voice. 'I need a calculator. But all I could probably afford is an abacus, and I don't know how to work those things.'

The agent looked glum and uncomfortable in the armchair. Tumulty scribbled again. He hoped he looked like a man struggling over figures that would never add up no matter how hard he worked. He tore off the top sheet and began to write on the one underneath, conscious all the time of Zuboric watching him.

'I don't know how the Chinese manage,' the priest said, smiling. Was this silly banter convincing the agent? It was hard to tell anything from Zuboric's face, except that the man was vigilant.

Tumulty pressed the pen down on the new sheet of paper. He would have to do this quickly. He muttered in the manner of somebody calculating as he wrote, but what he set down on the paper had nothing to do with sums of money. He ripped the sheet from the pad and crumpled it, setting it to one side. Then he tossed his pencil down and stood up, scooping up the crumpled paper and smuggling it into the pocket of his pants. He felt pretty damn good, but was he going to get away with it?

'Ah, well,' he said. 'I'm too tired to go on.'

He was sure Zuboric hadn't noticed anything, hadn't seen the writing on the piece of paper, hadn't caught him slipping the sheet into his pocket. The real problem would come later when he tried to pass the paper to Jig. But at least he'd committed himself to a course of action, a move designed to appease his conscience. Perhaps it was possible, after all, to serve both God and the Cause provided you fudged round some delicate ethical questions. And if God disapproved, Joseph Tumulty trusted that he could win forgiveness somehow.

At best, the piece of paper would be helpful to Jig. At worst, like an atheist on his deathbed turning to prayer, Tumulty felt he had covered all his bets.

Albany, New York

Houlihan's allocation of rooms at the Capital City Motel meant that Fitzjohn shared with Waddell, while Rorke and McGrath were together in the next room. Only Houlihan had a place to himself. Fitzjohn wished it had been otherwise. It was going to be difficult to leave because he wasn't sure that Waddell was sound asleep yet. Fitzjohn turned over on his narrow bed and looked across the room at his companion. Waddell's mouth was open and his eyes were closed, but every now and then he'd mumble and change the position of his body.

Earlier, Houlihan had convened a brief meeting in which he talked about an early morning departure. The destination was White Plains, New York. He wanted everybody to be up and ready to leave by six a.m., which caused Rorke to grumble briefly. Houlihan had pointed out that this was no bloody vacation they were on and when he said six a.m. sharp he meant *sharp*. After that, Rorke had been very quiet.

'What's in White Plains?' Fitzjohn had asked.

'What does it matter to you, Fitz? You get off in Tarrytown, don't you?' Houlihan had pronounced the word Tarrytown as though it were a bad taste in his mouth. 'You're going to be out of it. You've done your work. And we're all grateful.'

Houlihan hadn't looked remotely grateful, Fitzjohn thought. There was something just a little guarded in the man's eyes. The expression had struck a chord of concern inside Fitzjohn, and now he was glad he'd committed himself to leaving. If he didn't go now, he knew he wouldn't get another chance. The prospect of dying in Tarrytown, or anywhere else for that matter, didn't enthrall him. And he didn't trust Houlihan to let him go with a cheery farewell. Cheery farewells were not exactly Houlihan's style. The best you could find to say about Seamus was that he wasn't big on the social graces.

Fitzjohn sat upright. He stared at Waddell, whose hands were limp on his chest. Waddell's breathing was regular and deep, but he still made occasional sounds suggestive of a man deprived of oxygen on the ocean floor. Fitzjohn moved from the bed. He went to the closet and very quietly took out his holdall. Waddell chose that moment to kick his legs so abruptly that the blanket flew from his bed.

Fitzjohn saw Waddell sit up, grope for the blanket like a blind man, then draw it over his body once more. For a long time Fitzjohn didn't move. He listened to the sound of Waddell's shallow breathing. When he was absolutely certain the man was asleep, Fitzjohn reached for the door handle and turned it gently, then he stepped out onto the balcony. He noticed that the window of Houlihan's room was dark as he moved cautiously towards the stairs.

The motel bar was still open below. He turned up the collar of his coat against the biting chill of the night air, then he started to descend slowly. He looked towards the swimming pool. A cat slunk around the rim, then was gone with a rattle of leaves into the shrubbery. The whole night around him seemed like some large dark satellite dish that caught every noise, every movement, and amplified them.

At the bottom of the stairs he shifted his bag from one hand to the other. Now he had only to cross the pool area and he was gone.

He moved away from the stairs, passed the door of the bar, walked around the edge of the empty pool. He could see the road beyond the pink neon sign. The highway to freedom. New Jersey and home. He'd be safe there. Nobody would bother them again. Nobody would come looking for him.

He slid between a couple of parked cars and reached the spot where earlier he'd parked the Ryder truck. It looked luminously yellow under the pale lamps of the motel. Grinding his teeth nervously, he started to pick up his pace, walking away from the truck and heading for the road.

'What's your hurry, Fitz?'

Fitzjohn froze. He heard the noise of something inside him slipping and crumbling.

Houlihan climbed down from the cab of the Ryder. Fitzjohn, filled with bottomless dread, watched him. It had never occurred to him that Houlihan would be in the truck. Such a possibility hadn't crossed his mind. But then he hadn't thought *any* of this through. He'd been impetuous instead of careful. Fool.

'I just came down to fetch a map,' Houlihan said. 'Wasn't that a stroke of good fortune?'

Fitzjohn's tongue was cold lead in his mouth. He wanted to speak, couldn't think of anything to say. The dread was worse now. It was a sensation into which he sank like a man swallowed by swamp. As he looked at Houlihan he was conscious of the highway at his back. He could run. He could just drop the bloody bag and turn and run because the darkness out there would cover him.

'I thought you seemed a wee bit uncomfortable with all this.' Houlihan, smiling, made a gesture with his hand. 'Marriage does that to some people. Makes them forget where they started out from. Puts soft ideas into their heads. You're not the man you used to be, Fitz. I've been thinking that ever since Quebec. You're soft. It's amazing you lasted this long.'

Fitzjohn had never felt this paralysed in his life. Why the hell couldn't he *run*? 'This isn't what you think, Seamus.'

'No? I see my man leaving in the middle of the night with his bag packed and all – what am I supposed to think?'

Fitzjohn put the bag down. It occurred to him that a swift movement might take Houlihan off guard, a sudden kick, a punch. It might buy him a little extra time. The problem was how to get within striking range of Houlihan without making him suspicious. If it came down to a fair test of strength, Fitzjohn knew it wouldn't take Seamus long to overpower him. The key lay in speed and accuracy and surprise.

'Are you going to tell me you didn't like this fine motel, Fitz? Are you going to tell me you decided to find yourself something more comfortable?'

Fitzjohn moved nearer to Houlihan. One swing, he thought. One almighty swing. 'Let me explain,' he heard himself say.

Houlihan laughed. 'Save your fucking breath.'

Fitzjohn lunged. It was a sad effort. Houlihan sidestepped and tripped him and Fitzjohn went sprawling, colliding with the side of the truck. Dizzy, he slid to the ground and lay there looking up at the other man. Somehow his mouth had filled with blood. He must have split his gum when he hit the truck.

'You don't cross me,' Houlihan said. 'Nobody crosses me, Fitz.'

Houlihan bent down. He had his gun in his hand now. With the other hand he took a length of wire from the pocket of his seaman's jacket.

'Get inside the truck, Fitz. I think we ought to discuss your future in private.'

Fitzjohn pushed himself to a standing position. He couldn't take his eyes away from the wire in Seamus's hand. 'I don't want to go into the truck,' he said.

'The way I see it, you don't have a fucking choice, Fitz.'

Roscommon, New York

Celestine stepped inside the bedroom, which was dark and cold, and she stood motionless until her eyes had become accustomed to the absence of light. Now she could make out the window and the moonless sky beyond and the branches of black trees. Her body was chill under the silk robe and her nipples hard and there were goose bumps all over her flesh. She went towards the bed, where she hesitated again. Then, reaching out, she caught the sheet and drew it back quietly. He didn't move. She could make out the dim shape of his naked body. He lay fast sleep in a foetal position.

She sat on the edge of the mattress. With the tips of her fingers she traced a line on his thigh and then moved her hand, light as air, to the flat surface of his belly. It had become too long a time since she'd touched flesh as firm as her own, and it took her breath away. She shut her eyes and remembered the kiss, wondering if her drunken act had really fooled him. She'd been drinking, but not enough to make her do anything she hadn't wanted to. She ran her fingers up his side, then pressed them softly on his lips, feeling the warmth of his breath. She lowered her face and brushed her lips against the curve of his hip and the desire she felt was unbearable, as if all her self-awareness had crystallised in this one thing, a beautiful naked young man stretched out before her.

'Wake,' she whispered. She leaned close to his face and ran her tongue in the folds of his ear, whispering over and over, 'Wake, wake.'

He stirred and moaned quietly and she drew her hand down to his cock, which was hard almost as soon as she began to stroke it. She could feel the veins beneath the skin. She touched the tip, the opening, which was moist under her finger.

'There's nothing wrong,' she said. 'There's nothing wrong in any of this. It's right, Patrick. It's very right. You know that, don't you?'

He turned his body, lying now on the flat of his back. She felt his hands press down on her shoulders, as if he wanted to force her head into his groin and take him in her mouth, but he didn't need to force because she was more than willing. She licked the pubic hair that grew up around the navel and then she started to move her face down slowly, feeling his cock stiff against her cheek. She took strands of her hair and made a web round the penis, stroking it slowly, feeling it grow harder and harder as she touched it. She parted her lips and sucked him for a moment, then she drew her body up over his so that she was straddling him climbing him, struggling out of her robe at the same time. She wanted all of him, wanted everything he could possibly give of his strength and his youth, she wanted to feel his mouth upon her cunt, and then she'd take him deep inside her, far into the privacy of herself where it was warm and black and nothing that lived in the outside world mattered.

She said his name over and over. It came to have a mystical sound the more she repeated it, the syllables of some magical ritual. She felt his lips against her navel, and she squeezed her eyes tightly shut because she was no longer interested in anything she might see in this dim bedroom. This was the world, here and now, this blind place where she burrowed and where her blood rushed.

And then he was limp and motionless and she thought he must have come prematurely in his excitement, but that wasn't it because she didn't feel any wetness on her.

'What's wrong?'

He moved out from under her without saying anything. She reached over him and turned on the bedside lamp and watched him rub his eyes as he rolled away from her.

'What is it?' she asked.

He looked round for his robe, found it, put it on.

'Get dressed,' he said. He picked up her blue silk robe from the floor and tossed it at her.

'Just like that?'

'Just like that, Celestine.'

'What is it, Patrick? An attack of conscience?'

He turned his back on her, walked to the window, looked out. He was shaking his head.

'Look at me,' she said.

She went to him, laid her face against his spine. He shivered.

'You think it's wrong, don't you?' she asked.

'I don't think it. I *know,*' he replied. His voice was cold and lifeless. 'Why the hell did you marry him? That's what I don't understand.

'Because I love him.'

'You'll pardon me if suddenly I find that hard to believe,' Cairney said.

'I don't care what you believe! I love him as well as I can. Which is how he loves me, Patrick. *As well as he can*. And in certain departments that unfortunately isn't enough.'

'You didn't think about that before, did you?'

She had a sense of her life pressing in on her, the barren trees of this huge estate, the unattractive waters of the lake, the forlornness of it all. 'I didn't have choices, Patrick.' She hadn't meant to utter this sentence. It was bound to puzzle him and she couldn't begin to explain. She drew her robe around her.

'You could have chosen *not* to marry him.'

She shook her head. 'It wasn't like that. You don't know what you're saying.'

'Enlighten me then.'

Celestine went towards the door, leaving Cairney's question unanswered. She turned and smiled at him. 'It's in your eyes. It's in all your behaviour since you came here. You want me. I want you. It's undeniable. So what happens next?'

'Nothing,' Cairney said. 'Nothing can happen.'

'We'll see.'

She went out of the room, closing the door quietly.

It was one a.m. and bitterly cold when Patrick Cairney left the house and walked along the shore. He picked up stones and tossed them out across the water, listening to them hit out there in the darkness. He was angry with himself. He could make petty, unconvincing excuses – he was half asleep when he first felt Celestine touch him. He hadn't fully understood what she was doing and how he was responding because at first the experience had had the texture of a dream in which he had absolutely no control over events. Excuses, excuses. He couldn't brush aside the hard animal thing that possessed him or the amazing desire that had almost consumed him. He could wrestle it, certainly, but he couldn't pin it.

It was only a small consolation that he'd pulled himself back at the last possible moment when he'd encountered the weak phantom of his own conscience. His private policeman, the one that stopped the flow of traffic inside his head. But that was no consolation to him at all the more he thought about it. The desire was still there. The longing was still strong. His own sense of shame was intact. He picked up a heavy stone, turning it around in his hand, and he remembered her smell, the touch of her fingers on his body, her mouth. The clarity of the recollection shook him. What he suddenly wished for was another world, an alternative reality, in which Celestine wasn't his father's wife and Jig didn't exist. Wishing was a game for fools. It wasn't going to change the world. And he hadn't come to America to be embroiled in the sexual dissatisfaction of Celestine Cairney.

He took a deep breath of the cold air. There was a certain madness in the night, an insanity of the heart. He drew his arm back as far as it would go and released the stone and he heard it strike out in the middle of the lake. He wished sensations could be released as easily.

He turned from the lake and went back through the trees. He'd leave Roscommon tonight. He'd drive away now. It was the simplest solution he could think of. Distance was a benefactor. A salve.

Halfway back across the frozen lawn he stopped, looking up at the black house. Upstairs, a light was burning in one of the windows. It was the window of his own room. It could only mean that Celestine had gone back in there. Suddenly he wasn't thinking about her any more. He was thinking instead of the canvas bag with the cheap lock and Celestine's curiosity about the small wooden horse.

He hurried inside the house and climbed the stairs quickly. When he reached his own room he pushed the door open and stepped inside. The place was in blackness but he had an intuition that she'd been there only moments before. He switched on the bedside lamp. The room felt different to him, violated in some fashion, and yet nothing had been moved, nothing changed. the bag still sat on the dresser where he'd left it. He stepped closer to look at it. He took out the key from his pocket and turned it in the lock.

Nothing had been touched inside the bag. Nothing had been moved. The wooden horse, the passports, the clothing, everything was the same as it had been. He closed the bag, locked it, wondering about the fear he'd suddenly felt. What possible reason could Celestine have for going through his belongings anyway?

He turned to the bed, where a sheet of violet notepaper was propped against his pillow. This was the reason she'd come back to his room. To leave a message. He picked up the paper and read:

Next time

There wasn't going to be a next time, he thought.

He picked up his bag, stuffed the note inside his pocket, gazed at the rumpled bedsheets, which suggested a consummation rather than an interruption, then switched off the lamp. He made his way quietly down the stairs. Once outside, he walked in the direction of his rented Dodge.

He wouldn't be so careless in New York as he had been here at Roscommon. He wouldn't be so careless, in both heart and action, ever again.

16 New York City

Dressed in thrift-store garments, Frank Pagan woke in a cramped position, every muscle in his body locked. He opened his eyes and checked his watch. It was five-fifty a.m. and still dark, and he was propped against the wall of the dining room in St Finbar's Mission, where he had spent the most uncomfortable night of his life. He stared at the outlines of sleeping men who lay on mattresses all across the floor and he thought of how the entire night had been filled with the strangest sounds – men coughing, wheezing, snoring, wandering blindly around in a manner Pagan found vaguely menacing (he had an image at one point of somebody trying to cut this throat), men stumbling, cursing, spitting, striking matches for surreptitious cigarettes, men hacking their larynxes to shreds, men rattling while they slept as if marbles rolled back and forth in their rib cages, men crying out, sobbing, uttering incomprehensible phrases in the language of sleep. Once, Pagan had been startled into wakefulness by the cry *Don't leave me, Ma*! Now the air inside St Finbar's was filled with the odour of tooth decay, gum disease, old booze, greasy clothing, yesterday's smoke, and the incongruous and almost shocking antiseptic scent of air deodorant that Joseph X. Tumulty, awake before anyone else, had sprayed through the room.

Pagan stood up and cautiously stretched. His first conscious thought was always of coffee.

He moved carefully around the mattresses and into the kitchen where he found a jar of instant Maxwell House. He boiled some water in a saucepan, poured it into a large mug, dumped in a tablespoon of the crystals, and sipped. The brew was as subtle as crank oil, but it had the effect of starting his heart.

Joseph Tumulty appeared in the doorway. He looked brisk and freshly showered, hair wet and eyes shining. The priest nodded to Pagan, then went to the refrigerator, where he removed a huge bowl of eggs ready for scrambling. Pagan, anxious about Joe's mood, his frame of mind, and the depth of his commitment when it came to fingering Jig, watched the priest carefully. He thought that Tumulty looked a little too composed, and he wondered why.

'Sleep well?' Pagan asked.

'Very.' Tumulty set the bowl of eggs on the table. Then he laid out rashers of bacon, enough to feed an army. He struck a match and lit the burners on the huge stove. After he'd done this he took six loaves of bread from a bin and peeled the cellophane wrapping away.

'I couldn't get used to sharing my bedroom,' Pagan said. Joe Tumulty had spent the night on a mattress by the door. 'Especially with noisy strangers.'

'I don't notice it any more,' Tumulty replied. 'Besides, a lot of these men have become my best friends. They're a mixed crew, but you'll find that even the worst of them have some small redeeming quality that's worth exploring.'

My best friends, Pagan thought. There was something about Joe Tumulty to admire. His dedication. His selflessness. He felt sorry that Joe had become ensnared in this whole affair. He could see how it happened – growing up in Ireland, listening to the legends, drifting into a cause almost before he had time to understand what he was doing.

'How many people do you get for breakfast?' Pagan asked.

'Fifty. Sixty. I've had as many as a hundred in here and as few as twenty-five.'

'What time do you serve?'

'Seven.'

Pagan drained his mug of coffee. 'You haven't changed your mind?'

'About Jig?' Tumulty was pulling skillets and broiling pans out of a cupboard. 'I gave you my word, didn't I?'

Pagan wondered about Tumulty's word. There had been a change, some small and almost indefinable alteration in the man, and it perplexed him. He watched the priest go about the business of preparing breakfast. There were undercurrents here that Pagan caught, only he couldn't understand them, couldn't arrange them into a meaningful alignment. Was Joe planning something? Had he come up with something devious?

'I'd be very unhappy if you backed out now,' Pagan said. Which was to phrase it mildly. 'We understand one another, don't we?'

'I think we do,' Tumulty answered.

'There's no going back, Joe.'

'I haven't changed my mind, Mr Pagan. I'll do *exactly* as you asked.'

There. A very tiny tone of irritation in Tumulty's voice. A quick little flash of light in the eyes that was almost a defiance. What are you up to? Pagan wondered. Maybe nothing. Maybe the expectation of Jig had simply raised Pagan's own anxieties and now he saw shadows were he should have seen only light.

Tumulty was laying out slices of bread in a tray. Pagan wandered round the kitchen.

'Jig might not come today,' Tumulty said. 'Nothing's certain. He might not even choose to come at mealtime, in which case my saying the grace you want me to say is going to sound very strange.'

'He's going to think mealtime is the safest time. In Jig's trade, crowds mean security.'

Tumulty looked up from the tray of bread. 'Shouldn't you be out there at a table, Mr Pagan? I don't allow my customers inside the kitchen. You'll stand out like a sore thumb.'

Pagan walked into the dining-room. Men were waking, sitting on their beds or struggling to their feet, folding the mattresses away, stashing pillows inside the cupboards that lined the walls. There was a great deal of throat clearing and hawking and already the air was thick with cigarette smoke. Pagan sat down at an empty table and took a very crumpled cigarette out of his coat pocket, lighting it and coughing in what he hoped was an authentic way. He looked around the room, watching men stagger into the emptiness of a new day that was going to be exactly like the one before. The debris of the Great Society. It was odd that in the richest country on the planet, and not very far from Wall Street, where the great money machine cranked daily, men were forced to eat and sleep in a slough like St Finbar's. Pagan's old socialism found such a contrast inhuman. What democracy and capitalism really needed, he thought, was a conscience. In a world like that, though, pigs could fly.

He put out his cigarette and thought about Artie Zuboric sitting upstairs in Tumulty's office, then about the two agents on Canal Street. Orson Cone was located on the roof across the street. Tyson Bruno sat inside an all-night coffee hangout on the corner. Everything was in place, everything was set. It only needed Jig to step into this room for the picture to be complete. Pagan took a deep breath. Something troubled him, something he couldn't quite define. A sensation of unease. He felt enmeshed by two different strands of spider-webbing. One, sticky and mysterious, led back to Ivor the Terrible and his enigmatic purpose in New York. The other was directly linked to Jospeh X. Tumulty and that quietly upbeat mood of his.

Pagan shook his head. He couldn't allow himself any kind of misgiving. He had no room in his head for anything else except Jig. He stared in the direction of the kitchen. Tumulty turned to look at him.

The priest smiled and winked, then went back to work.

The smile was one thing, Pagan thought. The wink was quite another. How the fuck could Joe Tumulty, who was on the point of betraying a man, look so bloody secretive and confident?

Patrick Cairney left his rented Dodge in an underground parking lot at Broadway and Grand. Every mile he'd travelled from Roscommon had taken him farther from Celestine and closer to his own purpose, and so he'd driven at speeds far in excess of the limit, a curious adrenalin rushing through him. He realised he could put Celestine out of his mind, and all the turmoil she caused, only if he didn't forget – even for a fraction of time – that he was Jig and Jig had only one reason for being in America.

What Celestine had accomplished was the arousal of an appetite he couldn't afford to have. She'd succeeded in breaking his concentration, diffusing his energies. It was beyond the consideration of any morality now, beyond the ugly idea that what had almost happened between him and Celestine was akin to some kind of incest. It came down to something more practical, the unsettling realisation of a weakness inside himself, an odd awareness like something left over from another life. He needed strength, singularity of purpose, total focus. He had no use for the distraction of a beautiful young woman locked in a frustrating marriage to an unhealthy old man. What he really sought was that ideal state for a man who had purposely chosen a lonely life – immunity against feelings and the confusion they produced.

When you had that kind of immunity, you had control. Over your urges, your flaws, your limitations. Over yourself.

He'd stopped briefly near Peekskill, changing his clothes in a public rest room. Now he wore the shabby coat and shapeless flannels he'd worn on his first visit to St Finbar's and, as he emerged from the parking lot, he had the appearance of a deadbeat, even to the fashion in which he walked – unsteadily, like a drunk whose whole mind is consumed by the idea of the next drink. He felt comfortable in disguise. He liked the idea of melting into any background he chose. Only at Roscommon had his disguise felt awkward. It was increasingly difficult to be Patrick Cairney, Harry's boy, the kid who lived in the sad shadows of the Senator.

When he turned on to Canal Street it was barely daylight, a sombre morning with a scavenging wind pushing itself through the gulleys of Manhattan. He shuffled along, a pitiful figure to anyone who observed him. But this was New York and nobody who passed paid him any attention other than the cursory one of steering away from his path. He paused to look at himself in the window of a store. Almost perfect. The oversized coat concealed the muscularity of his body and the grey flannel shirt, worn outside the pants, hid the money belt. Only the face and hands bothered him. Too clean. He stepped into an alley and plunged his hands inside a trashcan, bringing out an assortment of garbage. Damp newspapers were best for what he wanted because the ink came off on his fingers and he could rub it lightly over his face. When he came out of the alley back into Canal Street his face was smudged and his hands black.

It was about six blocks to St Finbar's. He crossed Center Street, then he stopped. He bent to tie his lace. It was more than a matter of being vigilant now. He had to listen to his own keen instincts and keep his eye on the internal compass. There were factors involved he didn't like. For one thing, he was uncertain of Tumulty. Had the priest obtained the weapons yet? Or had he collapsed under pressure? For another, there was the distinct possibility that Frank Pagan was still around. Cairney felt he was weighing intangibles, like a man placing feathers on scales that didn't register.

He continued to the next corner. Carefully, his eyes swept along Canal Street. Among the parked vehicles there was none that immediately suggested the presence of the FBI. This meant nothing, though. It might indicate only that agents had taken the trouble to conceal themselves more thoroughly in the neighbourhood. He had the feeling he was walking through a minefield. A man with few choices. He needed the weapons. Even more, he needed information from Tumulty. A name, an address, anything at all that would lead him in the direction of the stolen money. If Tumulty let him down on that score, where else could he possibly turn? He'd go back to Ireland with nothing achieved. He'd be letting Padraic Finn down, which was something he hadn't ever done. Something he intended never to do.

He kept moving.

Outside the entrance to St Finbar's there were half a dozen or so derelicts standing on the steps. A faint aroma of fried food drifted towards Cairney, and he stopped again. He had an inherent suspicion of anything that looked normal, the way St Finbar's did right now. He might have been staring at a painting whose detail seemed bland and absolutely right, but at the same time this very banality suggested a sinister occurrence just under the surface.

He scanned the parked cars again, then the windows of the street, rooftops, doorways, but he saw nothing out of the ordinary. Swaying like a man who had just stepped out of a wrecked train, he kept walking. When he reached the steps he paused. He stuffed his hands in the pockets of his coat and glanced quickly at the faces around him. They were stunned, glazed by defeat. One or two had the desperate hardened look of men who have had a lifetime of crime imposed upon them. Cairney felt a kind of affinity for them.

'What time's breakfast here?' he asked.

One of the men, a gnarled character with a silvery beard, said, 'Seven. If you turn up at seven-oh-five, you miss grace. Don't matter none. You eat anyways.'

Cairney peered inside the dining-room. He saw groups of men at tables, but no sign of Tumulty.

'Religion and breakfast, they don't mix so good for me,' the man with the beard said.

Cairney nodded. He guessed it was probably close to seven by now.

'You new around here?' the man asked.

'Yeah.'

'Seems I seen you one time before.'

Cairney said nothing. Inside the dining-room men were shuffling in the direction of the serving area. Still no Tumulty. It crossed Cairney's mind that if he could somehow catch the priest's eye Tumulty might give him a sign, a gesture to reassure him that it was safe to enter.

'Last week maybe,' the man was saying. 'Was you here last week?'

'Could be.'

The little group was silent now, as if they were weighing information of a vital nature. One of them, a short man with a face mottled by alcohol, eventually said, 'I had a Rolex one time. Good timepiece.'

Somebody laughed at this, and Cairney smiled. There was a certain incoherence about these men, conversational leaps difficult to follow. The death of synapses, he thought. He moved closer to the threshold of the dining-room. The smell of bacon was strong, nauseating. He experienced a familiar tingling in his nervous system. It was what he'd come to think of as the Moment, that point in time when either he committed himself or he stepped back. It was that place where he could choose to pull the trigger or press the detonating device or else abort his plans entirely. He listened to himself, the sound of his blood, the way his heart thumped. His body, in that peculiar vocabulary it had developed, was talking to him.

He quickly scanned the street again. He saw nothing unusual. It occurred to him that if anything *had* gone wrong, Joe Tumulty would have managed to give him a sign of some kind. In the absence of any warning, what else could he assume except that everything was fine? Like a swimmer cautiously testing water, he put one foot inside the dining-room. And then he had momentum going and was moving towards the serving area, picking up a tray, a plate, cutlery, shuffling in line behind the other men. He faced Joe Tumulty, who stood behind trays of simmering food with a large spatula in his hand. There was nothing on the priest's face, no recognition, no surprise, nothing. Cairney watched two strips of bacon, a slab of toast and a spoonful of scrambled eggs fall on his plate, and then he turned away, carrying his tray in the direction of a table.

When he sat down he saw Frank Pagan on the other side of the room.

Calmly, Cairney cut one of the bacon strips in half. He didn't let his eyes linger long on Pagan. He stared at his food as he chewed on the rasher. He tasted absolutely nothing. In one sense, now, he seemed to stand in a place outside himself, figuring, assessing possibilities like a meteorologist studying a cloud formation. Objectively. Coolly. If Frank Pagan had infiltrated the place, there was the chance that he wasn't alone. Perhaps others, dressed as Pagan was, sat in the dining-room at this very moment. This was the first consideration. The second was even more bleak. Tumulty must have known that Pagan was here. Why then hadn't the priest warned Cairney? Had Tumulty sold out? Had Tumulty *betrayed* him? Be still, he told himself. Be very still. To run now would bring Frank Pagan chasing after him. Besides, there was always another possibility, that Tumulty was simply playing along with Pagan's game and had no intention of betraying Jig.

Cairney sought the quiet centre of himself. The place of supreme calm, detachment. It had always been easy to locate in the past but now, as if Celestine had tampered with it and damaged it, he couldn't quite find the correct frame of mind. He came close, but there was an uneasiness that made clear thinking difficult. He worked at suppressing his nerves, his heartbeat, the way his thoughts were beginning to race.

Tumulty had come to the middle of the room. He was calling for prayer. He held his hands up in the air but he didn't turn his face in Jig's direction.

'You all know the rules,' Tumulty was saying over the clacking of forks and knives. 'You all know we say grace at St Finbar's before we eat.' Nobody was paying much attention to him. 'Silence, please,' Tumulty said.

When he had some semblance of quiet, which was broken by coughing and the occasional belch, Joseph X. Tumulty closed his eyes and inclined his head.

He said, 'We thank Thee, Heavenly Father, for what we are about to receive.'

A long silence. Tumulty looked as if he were locked in some internal struggle. Then he added, 'The Lord hath done great things for us, whereof we are glad. Amen.'

Cairney glanced at Frank Pagan, who was digging heartily into his breakfast. Tumulty, after his quick little prayer, was threading his way between tables, finally approaching the one where Cairney sat. Cairney looked up at the priest. Tumulty made a small gesture with his head, indicating that Cairney should follow him. The younger man rose just as Tumulty disappeared through the doorway in the direction of the stairs. Cairney walked very slowly, turning to glance at Frank Pagan again. The Englishman had stopped eating. He was staring bleakly at his empty plate.

Cairney stood very still on the threshold of the dark hallway. He'd caught something just then. A vibration. Something in the way Frank Pagan gazed at his plate. It was the look of a person *pretending* to study, when his mind was elsewhere. The sideways movement of the eyes. The apparent absentmindedness of expression that was an attempt to conceal a highly focused brain. Cairney knew that look. Suppressed excitement. Hidden tension. He understood that Frank Pagan was going to get up from the table at any moment and follow him out into the hallway.

Tumulty, balanced on the bottom step, had a finger to his mouth for silence.

'You've sold me,' Cairney whispered.

'Will you please shut up?' Tumulty said.

'You bastard, you sold me.'

Tumulty shook his head. 'They forced me. It's not what you think.'

Cairney said nothing. He wondered how much force it had taken to turn Joe Tumulty around.

'Is Pagan alone?' he asked.

Tumulty said, 'There's another one in my office upstairs.'

'I'm in a hell of a spot then,' Cairney said. He looked up the stairway. He was thinking wildly now, which wasn't the way Jig had been trained to react. But all the truisms his instructors had drummed into him about turning adversity to your own advantage meant absolutely nothing right then. He had walked straight into this.

'There's one way out,' Tumulty said.

'How?'

Tumulty was moving quietly up the stairs. Cairney, who felt he had little to lose, followed. They reached the landing. The door of Tumulty's office stood open. On the other side of the landing was a second door.

'In there,' Tumulty whispered. 'The bathroom window.'

As Cairney moved towards the door, Tumulty pressed a piece of paper into his hand like an uncle surreptitiously passing a five-dollar bill to a favourite nephew.

'They took the weapons,' Tumulty said, his quiet voice filled with apprehension. 'This is the best I can do. Now go. For God's sake, go.'

Before Cairney could open the bathroom door he heard Frank Pagan coming up the stairs. At the same time he was conscious of a man standing in the door of Tumulty's office. He had a pistol in his hand. It was clear from the expression on the man's face that he'd use the gun without weighing ethical questions beforehand. Indeed, he had his arm extended now and was going into the kind of crouch universally favoured by law enforcement officers. Only Joe Tumulty stood between Cairney and the weapon.

'Stand very still,' the man said. 'Don't even breathe.'

Cairney, shielded by the priest, saw Frank Pagan rushing upwards. From the folds of his clothing Pagan had produced a weapon. There was a curious little smile on Pagan's face that wasn't quite triumph. It contained fatigue.

Pagan reached the landing. With the gun held out in front of him, he approached cautiously. 'I want a damn good look at what we've caught.'

Cairney turned his face away. There was one slender chance left to him. It would take a quick smooth movement, a moment of sudden imbalance in the group of people around him, temporary confusion. He concentrated hard, reaching down into the depths of himself for the answer. One perfect motion. That was all. He felt elated all at once, anticipating the moment of action, his entire being consumed by the notion of movement. He was alert now, and sharp, and his senses had the efficiency of surgical instruments. Tumulty's frightened face, Pagan's smile, the other man's hard little eyes – all these things made a heightened impression on him. And then he was out in a place where there was no thinking, no rationalising, nothing but pure movement and the overwhelming instinct to survive, a place that was quicksilver, where he ceased to exist except as an embodiment of action.

He did two things at once in a movement so fluid, so swift, that it was a blur to the other people around him. He pushed Tumulty forward, thrusting him forcefully across the landing in the direction of the man with the Mexican moustache, and he simultaneously swung his leg upwards at a right angle to his body, his foot connecting with Frank Pagan's hand. Pagan didn't drop the gun and the blow barely affected him, but it was the opening Cairney knew he had to achieve, the fraction in time when the concentration all around him was punctured, the only time he'd ever have.

He lunged towards the bathroom door, which swung away from him, and then he was inside, kicking the door shut at his back and sliding the bolt in place hurriedly before he ran towards the window at the far end. He heard two gunshots, wood tearing, the rattle of a bullet on the lock, all sounds from another world. He lashed at the window with his foot. Glass shattered and the rotted wood frame collapsed, creating a jagged opening out on to the roofs above Canal Street. He squeezed through to the roof. He heard, distantly, the bathroom door being kicked open, and then Frank Pagan was shouting, but Cairney wasn't about to stop and listen. He scampered gracelessly along the roof, struggling to maintain his balance on a surface made slick by morning frost.

The sound of a gunshot split the air around his head. He heard the bullet burst into the concrete casing of a chimney just beyond him. The shot had come from across Canal Street, not from behind as he'd expected. He glanced at the other side of the street, seeing a figure on the roof opposite. Crouching low, he crossed the roof. The firing continued, kicking up fragments of asphalt and brick. He kept his head down as he moved in the direction of the next building. How many men had Pagan planted in the vicinity? When he leaped the narrow space from one rooftop to the next, he heard Pagan call out again and he turned to look. The Englishman was two buildings behind and running, and his breath left small clouds on the chill air.

'Jig!' Pagan shouted.

Cairney smiled and slithered down the incline of the roof that faced away from Canal Street so that at least he was out of the line of fire from across the way. He heard Pagan grunting, and then there was the sound of gunfire coming from Pagan's direction. The first shot was erratic, whining several feet from Cairney's head and crashing uselessly into brickwork. The second, closer and more urgent, cleaved the air about three feet from his shoulder. Either Frank Pagan wasn't a very good shot or else he wasn't shooting to kill.

Why would he want to kill Jig anyhow? Cairney wondered. Like the curator of a zoo who has coveted a certain exotic animal for years, Pagan wanted to *capture* the creature that had tantalised him for so long – he didn't want a corpse. He couldn't put a dead man on display. Where was the satisfaction in that? Pagan wasn't going to shoot his own prize.

Cairney found something amusing in this perception. He took a deep breath, listened to Pagan calling out his name, then he ran. He reached the roof of the next building, a flat expanse of concrete with a couple of wooden tubs in which the brown wreckage of dead plants wilted in hard soil. Two deck chairs and a plastic table. Somebody's summer eyrie dead in the grip of winter. At the centre of the roof there was a door. He dashed towards it. A season of moisture had swollen the wood, jamming the door tightly. Cairney kicked at the handle, then thrust his shoulder against the wood and the door flew backwards, revealing a flight of steps. He plunged down into the darkness below. It was an empty office building, a shabby place that seemed to house a variety of small companies.

On the first landing Cairney stopped. He looked back up the way he'd come. He heard the sound of Frank Pagan on the rooftop. Then he moved to the next flight of steps and went down quickly. Now, free from the exposure of the roof, he thought about his predicament. Unless there was a rear exit to this building he'd have to leave by the front door, which would lead him straight back on to Canal Street. A sorry prospect. Another alternative, which he rejected immediately, was to conceal himself somewhere inside the building and wait the whole thing out – but that was a trap he wasn't going to encourage. The building would be sealed off and thoroughly ransacked, and he'd be discovered sooner or later. There was one other possibility, also rejected, and that was to confront Frank Pagan, somehow overpower him and get the gun away, but he knew that the Englishman, taken by surprise once, wasn't going to allow himself to be caught off balance a second time.

He heard Pagan on the floor above. He took the next flight of stairs and found himself on the first floor, a hallway with a glass door to Canal Street. He turned in the opposite direction, back along the hall. Pagan was directly overhead and coming down loudly, his feet clattering on the wooden steps. Cairney ran to the end of the corridor. There, the only possible route he could take was down to the basement. If there were no rear exit from the basement, then his chance of escape was screwed. He shoved the basement door open and found himself going down into the dark heart of the building. It was a large room of angular steam-pipes and the kind of dampness no boiler could ever dispel, and the air, like that inside a box locked for years, was still and rancid and unbreathable. He could see nothing save for a slot of pale light in the distance. It had to come from a window, and if there were a window then there might also be a door if the original architect, in his infinite wisdom, had included both in his plans. Moving, hands outstretched in the dark like a blind man, he crossed the basement floor, which was strewn with objects – boxes, rags, bundles of papers, tools.

He heard Pagan call out to him again. The man's voice sounded muffled down here in this stifling space.

'You can't get away, Jig. There's no place for you to go. Even if you got out of here, there are twenty or thirty men outside. Think about it.'

Cairney said nothing in reply. He went towards the source of light. He heard Pagan come after him. The man was moving with great caution, measuring his steps.

'In your situation, Jig, I'd call it a day,' Pagan said.

Cairney put his ear towards the origin of the sound. How far, how near, was Frank Pagan? He cursed this abominable darkness that prevented him from estimating distances. Pagan could be thirty feet away, or a lot closer. He just couldn't tell.

He ducked his head beneath an overhanging pipe and saw, just ahead of him, the rectangle of a window, light filtering in from outside. It was perhaps fifteen feet from where he stood. The problem with light was the fact that, as soon as he reached the window, he'd create a silhouette for Frank Pagan to see. A cobweb brushed his forehead and he wiped it aside. Still keeping his head low and his shoulders hunched, he approached the source of the light.

There was no goddam door, only the window, ridiculously small and streaked with dirt, impossible for him to squeeze through.

'Jig,' Pagan called out, 'You don't have a chance, man.'

Cairney wanted to tell Pagan that he could talk all day and it would make no difference because Jig hadn't been programmed to surrender, but he said nothing. He went down on the floor now, crawling towards the light. Tilting his head up, he stared at the pane of glass. He'd have to be a midget to get out through that space. He pressed his face into the dirt of the floor, thinking, thinking. Finn had once told him that there was no box a man couldn't get out of except despair, and it was despair, like a cold-gloved hand, that touched the fringes of his mind now.

Twenty or thirty men. Was Frank Pagan lying? Cairney had only seen three, Pagan included.

He went forward on his hands and knees.

Out of the dark he heard Pagan's voice again. 'Jig? Why don't you talk to me?'

Cairney, flat against the wall under the window, moved his head slightly. Pagan was very close now. He could hear the man breathing.

Cairney stretched his hand along the wall. His finger encountered a hollow rectangle of metal, an opening that puzzled him only a moment before he understood what it was.

A coal-chute.

Unused probably for forty, fifty years, filled with dirt and stuffed with garbage, it was a goddam coal-chute, a way out! He gripped the inside of the metal opening and drew himself slowly up into the black funnel, which ran at a sloping angle towards the street. There would be a lid, of course, but beyond that cover there would be air and daylight and opportunity. He climbed, shoving aside the assorted detritus of whoever had used this basement over the years, through the dank narrow tube where the trapped air was even worse than in the basement itself. Beer bottles and cans and ancient newspapers and the pervasive stench of urine. Straining, he reached the cover and thumped it desperately with the heel of his hand, and it yielded in a shower of rusted flakes that fell into his eyes, but at the same time there was daylight, streaming against his face from the alley behind the building.

A few more feet. That was all. A few more feet and he'd be clear.

He felt Frank Pagan's hand clutch his ankle. It was a ferocious grip, powerful, and it threatened to bring him down out of his precarious position inside the chute and back into the basement. He freed one of his legs in the cramped space and kicked out as hard as he could, bringing his foot down on Pagan's fingers. He heard Pagan say *Bastard*, then felt his fingers slacken. He was free. With one last thrust, he shoved his face up beyond the lid of the chute and hauled himself out into the alley. It was empty. No men. No cars. Nothing. He reached down and slammed the cover shut before he turned and ran.

Washington, DC

The Director of the FBI was a small man called Leonard M. Korn. He wore rimless glasses to correct his notorious short-sightedness, and he shaved his head so that it resembled a blunt little bullet. He spoke always quietly, never raising his voice, not even when angry. To his subordinates, he was perhaps the most frightening man on the face of the planet. His sense of control, both of himself and the Bureau, was awesome. His taste for punishment, when an agent had disappointed him, was absolutely merciless. Many good agents, with otherwise meticulous records, had found themselves posted to places like Nebraska and South Dakota because they had made a single slip. With more bitterness than affection, some said the middle initial of his name stood for Magoo, the cartoon character Korn resembled in appearance though not in action.

About an hour after Jig had vanished in an alley behind Canal Street, Leonard M. Korn was seated behind his desk at Bureau Headquarters staring at his Special Deputy, a man named Walter Bull. Bull had been with the Bureau all through the Hoover years and was known to be a big-league survivor around whom administrations came and went. A plump man with a face that resembled a used khaki handkerchief, Bull perspired regularly and copiously, no matter the temperature of the day. He was sweating as he stood in front of Korn's desk right then. His associates called him B. O. Bull.

Korn folded his small white hands on his blotting-pad. He had been listening very carefully to his Special Deputy, and now Bull was quiet, waiting for a response. Korn manipulated silences, an old ploy in the power game. He knew how to use them, how long to let them last. He let this particular silence linger for almost a minute before he said, 'I think it's a hoax, frankly.'

Bull didn't say anything in reply. He was staring at Korn's bald head, where an enormous vein pulsed just under the skin.

Korn unfolded his little hands. They looked like baby albino rodents to Walter Bull. 'A man can pick up a telephone and say anything he likes under the cover of anonymity, Walter. He can lay the blame for a certain event on anyone or any party he chooses because he knows he can hang up the phone and disappear without a trace. And nobody is any the wiser.'

Walter Bull nodded. His penchant for longevity within the Bureau came from his natural gift for servility. He had spent many years agreeing with the different men who occupied the chair in which Leonard M. Korn now sat. Like a good call-girl, he knew how to give pleasing service.

Korn continued. 'There are certain people in our society, Walter, who have nothing better to do than send the Bureau off on wild-goose chases. This caller in Albany seems to fit that particular category.'

Bull said, 'I wondered if it might be connected with Jig.'

Korn narrowed his eyes. The whole subject of Jig was supposed to be secret, the way the White House wanted it. But Korn knew that in the grapevine of the Bureau nothing remained concealed very long, especially from a man like Bull, who had access to almost everything.

'Jig is persona non grata, Walter,' Korn said. 'We ought to keep that clearly in mind. Officially, Jig doesn't exist.'

'Of course, sir,' Bull turned towards the door, stopped. 'What'll I tell Albany?'

'I'll take care of that,' Korn replied.

Walter Bull went out, leaving his trademark aroma behind, thick cologne and sweat.

Alone, Leonard Korn realised he would have to place two telephone calls. The first would be to the field office in Albany, giving strict instructions that the crime was to be handled discreetly and that no information was to be given either to the Albany PD or to the newspapers. The second and more important call would be to the White House.

Korn wasn't altogether sure that it *was* Jig who had committed this crime in provincial Albany and then called the local FBI office to claim responsibility on behalf of the Irish Republican Army. But why take any chances? President Thomas Dawson, deeply concerned as he was with the Irish assassin, would want to be informed anyway. Korn didn't plan to place this call at once, though. He wanted to wait until he had heard from Agent Arthur J. Zuboric that the Englishman's scheme in New York City had worked. It would be very gratifying to tell Thomas Dawson that Jig was safely in custody and that the Bureau, somewhat maligned in recent years, could be counted on to come through in the end. If there was one obsession in Leonard Korn's life, it was the reputation of the Bureau. He had neither wife nor mistress. Nor had he any intimate friends. The Bureau was all things to him, and he loved it with more passion than he was ever capable of showing to a human being. He loved its computers, its chicanery, its internecine power struggles. But more than anything else, he adored the possibility of its omniscience. He liked to think that a day would come when a sneeze in the Oval Office would register on the Bureau's data banks before it even tickled the President's nostrils. Leonard M. Korn's ideal of the FBI was a huge cyclopean entity made of stainless steel, unblemished, all-seeing, its bloodstream composed of infinite corpuscles of information, its heart one enormous muscle forever pumping data, its brain an insomniac scanning device classifying all this data day and night.

If the plan in New York City worked, excellent. And if it didn't – well, the blame could always be laid on Frank Pagan, a perfect scapegoat, thus sparing the Bureau any Presidential wrath.

Leonard M. Korn smiled. He liked having things both ways.

17 New York City

Artie Zuboric said, 'It was a brilliant plan, Frank. It was probably the most brilliant plan I've ever been associated with. When I'm an old man looking back I'll remember it with total fucking admiration. I'll gather my grandchildren up on my lap and tell them about the day Frank Pagan tried to catch an Irish gunman.'

Pagan flexed his bruised fingers. He didn't like sarcasm at the best of times and he found Zuboric's brand particularly juvenile. His hand stung. He rubbed it gently, then stared from the window of Zuboric's office.

'You had a clear shot at him,' Zuboric said. 'When he was standing there on that landing, Frank, you could have taken him out. You had all the time in the world.'

And on the rooftop too, Pagan thought. But he hadn't narrated the chase to Zuboric in any detail. He'd fogged the pursuit through the basement, not because he thought it embarrassing but because he wasn't about to throw more fuel on Artie's little bonfire of sarcasm.

'Granted he moved like lightning,' Zuboric said. 'Granted it was unexpected. But that doesn't excuse you, Frank. If I'd had the same opportunity, I'd have pulled my trigger. But I was knocked on my ass when Tumulty crashed into me. So I didn't have a shot. You bombed, Frank. You screwed up.'

Pagan watched the street, where a shaft of gloomy March sunlight penetrated the greyness of things. What he kept coming back to was Jig's smile on the rooftop, the moment when the man had turned and glanced back and the smile on his lips was somehow knowing, as if Jig understood that Frank Pagan wasn't going to shoot him in the back. But that wasn't it either, it wasn't anything so sentimental, so *nice*, as an unwillingness to shoot a defenceless human being. It was something else. It had nothing to do with any concept of fair play.

He had never *dreamed* of taking Jig dead, that's what it came down to. Even if he had never entirely admitted it to himself before now, he had always imagined Jig alive, intact. He had always envisaged himself looking Jig straight in the eye and taking the measure of the man, talking to him, questioning him, as if there were some revelation to be found in the mystery of Jig's soul. He wanted an *understanding* of the assassin, something you couldn't get from a dead man. He wanted to *know* Jig, who played the game of terrorism according to his own meticulous rules. It was his appreciation of Jig's calculated acts of violence, so economic and accurate, that made it difficult to gun the man down in cold blood. And if there was irony in this, in his unwillingness to meet Jig's violence with violence of his own, Pagan wasn't going to recognise it. He wanted Jig badly, but not dead. Not shipped back to England in a bloody box, which would have been an empty triumph.

There was even something admirable, Pagan thought, in the fact that Jig, during that first visit to St Finbar's, had actually *approached* Pagan to ask if he could help. There was gall in the man, and bravado, and surely an overwhelming sense of confidence. To come straight up to Pagan and look him in the eye the way he'd done – it was quite an act.

Pagan rubbed his aching hand again. He wondered if he was simply trying to rationalise his own failure, trying to explain it away in manageable sentiments. He thought suddenly of Eddie Rattigan's bomb and how it had destroyed Roxanne, and he realised that what he felt towards Jig was almost a kind of gratitude for the fact that the assassin had introduced *dignity* into the whole Irish conflict, that he had transcended the brutal behaviour of the Eddie Rattigans of this world. He thought of the enormous gulf that separated somebody like Rattigan from Jig. Rattigan killed the innocent, the blameless, the harmless bystander. Jig would never have casually detonated a bomb at a public bus-stop. He would never have indulged in such mindless destruction. He would never have taken Roxanne away. You didn't shoot a man like Jig in the back. 'I want him alive. That's all.'

'You could've shot to wound,' Zuboric snapped. 'You ever think about that?'

Pagan didn't respond. He considered the two shots he'd fired at Jig on the rooftops. The first had been a warning, fired in the vague chance that Jig would stop running. Vague indeed. The second had gone close to Jig, but Pagan wasn't sure now if that bullet had been intended to wound the man. In the heat of the moment, in the confusion of the chase, he hadn't had time to take careful aim.

Zuboric said, 'I get this sneaky feeling you've been after Jig too long. I think you've actually begun to admire the sonofabitch. You want him alive because you can't understand what makes you admire him, so you'd like to sit down with him over tea and crumpets and tell him what a jolly good fight he's fought. It wouldn't be the first time that's happened to a cop.'

'Call me unpatriotic, but I don't eat crumpets,' Pagan said. He was remembering the basement, the moment of contact when Jig, finding the means of escape in a coal-chute, had finally lunged out at him with his foot. He'd almost had Jig then. Almost. A coal-chute! It was extraordinary how people who wanted desperately to survive somehow always managed to find the means of survival in the basic material around them. Somebody other than Jig, somebody with less of a sharp instinct to escape, might never have found that opening in the basement. Chalk up another point for the man, Pagan thought. Did that wonderment at Jig's ability, his slipperiness, constitute admiration?

Zuboric stared at Pagan. He was beginning to perceive his life in terms of how much the Englishman irritated him. The prospect of calling the Director with news of the Canal Street Fuck-Up, which was like a newspaper headline in his mind, made him very unhappy. He had been putting it off ever since they'd come back to his office. Why had he ever listened to Pagan anyway? He was suddenly very weary. Of his office, his job, the Bureau, the whole ball of wax. And last night, when he'd been in bed with Charity, who always made the act of sex seem like an enormous favour on her part, she'd once again reiterated her determination never to marry anyone who didn't have two cents to rub together. Especially a man connected with any law enforcement outfit. She'd had her share, she said, of deadbeats in the past. Zuboric hadn't wanted to hear about her past particularly. It was the future he was interested in, and it was going to be a wintry future if Charity wasn't in it. She had driven him last night to the limits of sexual bliss. He didn't like to wonder how she'd learned some of the tricks she knew.

He picked up a pen and rapped it on his desk, still staring at the Englishman. 'As for Tumulty, I knew that cocksucker couldn't be trusted,' Zuboric said. 'I knew it all along.'

'You told me that,' Pagan answered. 'You were very *happy* to tell me that, Arthur.'

'Jesus, Frank. I saw the guy slip something into Jig's hand. I don't know what exactly. A piece of paper. Something. I was standing in the goddam doorway watching.'

Pagan closed his eyes. His entire body hurt from the exertion of rooftop acrobatics. He was thinking of Tumulty now, whom they had brought back to Zuboric's office from Canal Street. Father Joe was locked inside a cell along the corridor. He claimed that Zuboric was imagining things, there was no piece of paper, nothing. Maybe it was time to turn the screws on Joe a little tighter.

'I'll talk to him again,' Pagan said.

Zuboric shrugged and tossed a key into Pagan's hand. 'Be my guest. In the meantime, I've got the unpleasant task of reporting this failure, Frank. If you don't see me again, it's because I've been abruptly transferred to Carlsbad, New Mexico.'

'I'll come and visit you,' Pagan said in the doorway. 'I've always wanted to see the bat caves.'

'I bet,' Zuboric replied, thinking that the caves of Carlsbad would be a perfectly fitting place for Frank Pagan to die and be buried in, under a million tons of bat shit. 'After you've talked to Tumulty, do me a favour and make sure you lock the door behind you, huh? We wouldn't want to lose two Irishmen in one day, would we?'

Frank Pagan slid the key in the lock and stepped inside the room where Joe Tumulty sat propped up in the corner. Zuboric's last remark niggled him. He suddenly wished he'd shot Jig on the roof when he'd had the chance. Who the hell would have cared anyway in the long run other than himself? He'd have been a hero. The Man Who Killed Jig. So what the fuck was he doing, dickering with this appreciation of his prey? What was this bullshit about wanting Jig alive? If he'd gunned the Irishman down he wouldn't have had to put up with Zuboric's snide comments.

'You really let me down, Joe.' He spoke between clenched teeth. He felt confined inside a triangle whose sides consisted of Zuboric's criticism, Tumulty's pig-headedness, and his own failure to apprehend Jig. He wasn't in the mood to fart around with Tumulty.

Tumulty didn't speak. Pagan squatted alongside him. The priest blinked, then closed his eyes slowly.

'What was written on the paper, Joe?'

'There was no bloody paper.'

'My arse. Zuboric saw you.'

'Look. I said the grace you wanted. I put the finger on your man. Don't blame me if he slipped out of your hands. I did everything you expected, so why the hell am I locked up like this?'

Pagan placed his hand on Tumulty's shoulder. 'You're locked up because you're a fucking criminal, Joe. You impeded the investigation of a Federal agency. I bet you just loved it when Jig pushed you into Zuboric, didn't you? I bet you loved making that little contribution to Jig's escape.'

'I made no contribution,' Tumulty said.

'What was on the paper?'

'I'd like to call a lawyer.'

'No lawyer,' Pagan said.

'It's my constitutional right.'

'What right? What constitution? You don't have any rights, Joe. You signed them all away when you helped Jig.'

'There's something to the effect that a man's innocent until he's proven guilty – '

'Where did you hear a fairy-tale like that?'

Tumulty sighed. 'Thank God this is a country of litigation and hungry lawyers. I'll sue. You'll see.'

Pagan smiled. 'What was on the paper, Joe?'

Tumulty shut his eyes again. He tipped his face to one side, away from Pagan. Pagan reached out and deftly took Joe's cheek between thumb and forefinger and pinched very hard. Tumulty's eyes watered before Pagan released his grip.

Pagan stood up. 'I'll tell you what really bothers me about all this, Joe. It isn't the fact that you'll probably go to jail. It's the end of the road for all that good work you've been doing down on Canal Street. It's curtain time, folks. No more good works. No more charity. You've lost your little bid for sainthood, Joe. Pity.'

'There isn't a court in the country that would send me to jail,' Tumulty said, rubbing his cheek and looking annoyed.

Pagan shrugged. 'Even if you don't go to jail, your life's going to be sheer hell, Joe. You know what Zuboric is planning?'

Tumulty shook his head.

'First, he's contacting some friends in the IRS who owe him a favour. You know how that works. Zuboric reckons his tax pals can hassle you so much you'll *wish* you'd been sent to prison. That's for starters. Second, he's going to arrange for the local health department to go through your establishment hunting for sanitary violations. They also owe Zuboric favours. In other words, they're going to be hard on you.' Pagan paused. He wasn't absolutely sure if Tumulty was absorbing this. 'I'm not finished yet. He's also making arrangements to bring the local cops down on you.'

'He can't do that.'

'He can do anything he likes. The Director of the FBI is God, which makes Artie Zuboric a minor kind of deity by association. He asks for something in this town, everybody is ready to just bloody jump for him. You'll see. As far as the cops coming in, it seems they're going to suspect some of your clients of carrying narcotic contraband and using your place as the source, as it were, of their deals. Suddenly, no more St Finbar's. Big headlines. Lapsed Priest Runs Drug Ring. Tabloids love anything to do with lapsed priests, don't they?'

Tumulty said, 'This is blackmail.'

'Hardly, Joe. All I'm doing is painting you a picture of your dilemma. Bleak days lie ahead. Unless, of course, you decide that cooperation is the best way to go.'

The priest stood up. He studied Frank Pagan a moment. Then, very deliberately, he said, 'There was no paper. I gave Jig absolutely nothing.'

'I admire a man who sticks to his story,' Pagan said. He turned to the door. 'Don't let anybody convince you to change it.'

He went out. He drew a cup of water from the cooler in the corridor and drank it, leaning against the wall and staring at a portrait of Thomas Dawson. He thought Dawson looked vapid, homogenised. But these were the very qualities the American electorate found endearing in its Presidents.

He crumpled his little wax cup. He wondered if Joseph X. Tumulty was pondering the exaggerated portrait of doom Pagan had painted for him. Maybe. God knows, he had to do something to shake Tumulty loose from his posture of innocence.

Pagan moved back in the direction of Zuboric's office just as the agent, looking as if the heavens had parted and God had roared angrily at him, stepped out into the corridor.

'I thought you'd be in Carlsbad by now,' Pagan said.

Zuboric had a sheet of paper in his hand. 'I just talked with the Director.'

'And?'

'He's angry. He's angry and goddam impatient. He doesn't think a whole lot of you, Frank. Quote. If the limey doesn't shape up, I'll have him shipped back to England so fast his feet won't touch the ground. Unquote.'

'Harsh words,' Pagan said. He didn't remotely care what Leonard M. Korn had to say about him.

Zuboric waved the sheet of paper. 'Which brings me to this tidbit of information he gave me. It seems that a man was murdered early this morning in Albany. He'd been garrotted by a length of wire and dumped in a culvert. A very nasty death.'

'Garrotting can be unpleasant,' Pagan agreed.

'The killer called the local FBI office at two a.m. and claimed that the killing had been carried out by the Irish Republican Army.'

'In Albany? *New York*?'

Zuboric nodded. 'My precise reaction, Frank.'

'It's a hoax. It has to be.'

'Also my first reaction. But it becomes more plausible when you hear about the victim.' Zuboric read from the paper. *'Alexander Fitzjohn, aged thirty-eight, resident of Camden, New Jersey. Entered the United States legally from Belfast in August 1984.'*.

'Belfast?' Pagan said. He wondered where this was leading.

'According to what I've got here, Frank, Fitzjohn had once been a member of the Free Ulster Volunteers.'

Pagan reached quickly for the paper. It was covered in Zuboric's scrawl. He must have taken it all down very quickly over the telephone. 'It doesn't add up. It doesn't make any sense at all. Even if it was some old score being settled, since when has the IRA started to make hits overseas? The Libyans, yes. The Bulgarians, sometimes. But I've never heard of the IRA playing that kind of long-distance game.'

'Maybe there's a local cell,' Zuboric said.

'Maybe.'

Pagan handed the paper back. Zuboric said, 'There's another possibility.'

'Which is?'

'It could have been Jig.'

Pagan opened his mouth to reply when he heard the sound of Joseph Tumulty banging on the locked door of his room.

Patrick Cairney drove his rented Dodge through the streets of Lower Manhattan. Dressed still in the clothes he'd worn at St Finbar's, he realised he'd have to change into something more in keeping with the brand-new vehicle he was driving. When he came to Battery Park he found a secluded place where he could change without being seen. Even when he'd discarded the dirty old clothes and dumped them in a trash container, he felt unclean.

He took out the piece of paper Joe Tumulty had given him. He read it quickly, memorised it, tore the sheet into thin ribbons and tossed them into the wind which ferried them carelessly down towards the river. *The name,* he thought. It was all he had. No guns. Nothing but the name. What was he supposed to do without a weapon?

As he looked out over Battery Park, he was conscious of the great expanse of the Atlantic beyond Gowanus Bay and The Narrows, and it occurred to him that the tide that rimmed the shores of Staten Island was the same that eventually found its way back to Dingle and Castletown, Galway and Donegal. He listened a moment to the squealing of gulls in the distance, and he wondered about this upsurge of longing that filled him. He'd been in Ireland too long, he thought. It had rubbed off on him, the sentimentality, the emigrant's yearning.

He didn't move for a time. His body still shook from the recent effort on the rooftops of Canal Street. It was the first time in his life he'd ever come close to capture, and he didn't like the feeling. He'd evaded Frank Pagan in the end, but it was a situation he should never have encountered in the first place. He blamed Tumulty. It should have been possible for Tumulty to warn him *not* to come inside that bloody soup kitchen. It ought to have been possible for the priest to get some kind of sign to him before he'd taken that first fateful step into the place. But Joe Tumulty, who must have been playing both ends against the middle, had behaved like the deplorable amateur he really was. Why the fuck had Finn put a man like Tumulty in America anyway? Bad judgement on Finn's part? Or was Tumulty just rusted from inactivity? Cairney, who couldn't believe that Finn would ever show careless judgement, had no answers to these questions. But he knew one thing for sure – the worst outcome of the whole thing was that Frank Pagan now knew what Jig looked like and the exposure worried Cairney. Suddenly Jig had a face. He had features. Characteristics. He was no longer just a name. His anonymity was gone.

Goddam. Patrick Cairney shut his eyes and let the breeze blow against his skin. For a second he considered aborting the whole thing right then and going back to Ireland and Finn. He thought about telling Finn that his cover, so laboriously assembled and protected, had been shattered. The game could no longer be played by the same rules. What would Finn say? Would Finn simply retire Jig? Put him out to pasture? Patrick Cairney loathed that prospect. He couldn't stand the idea of Finn patting him on the shoulder and saying that he'd had a good innings but now it was time to close up shop. He'd *get* the goddam money back! He'd get it back and to hell with the fact that he'd been seen and was now neatly stored in Frank Pagan's memory. He opened his eyes and took several deep breaths. He realised then that he needed control over his thoughts as much as his actions. What had he been thinking about, for Christ's sake? Defeat? Retirement? He smiled these notions away. He'd complete the task he'd been sent all this way to do, and nothing, *nothing* was going to stop him.

He walked back to his car, jammed the key in the ignition and drove away from the park. He went back down through the streets of Lower Manhattan, heading for the Brooklyn Battery Tunnel. He was acutely aware of time pressing down on him now. What if Joe Tumulty had given the name to Frank Pagan as well? Inside the tunnel, as if enclosed spaces troubled him, he felt apprehensive. It was the lack of a blueprint that unnerved him, the absence of a concrete plan that concerned him. It was also the realisation that he had no way of knowing what this Nicholas Linney was like and how he was going to receive a caller who had some hard questions to ask and who wanted quick truthful answers.

He was going in blind.

And he didn't like that idea at all, because every success he'd had in the past had come about as a result of good planning, the kind of planning you did with your eyes wide open and your vision uncluttered.

Bridgehampton, Long Island

Nicholas Linney lobbed the tennis ball over the net to where the plump East German, absurd in white shorts and Nike sneakers and a baggy white shirt, lunged with his racket and missed. It was the East German's habit to stamp his feet petulantly on the concrete court every time he missed an easy return. Linney, playing at half-throttle, was bored. But it was necessary every so often, for purely commercial purposes, to entertain these yahoos from behind the Iron Curtain.

'I think I call quits,' the East German said.

'Fine,' Linney answered.

He walked off the court back towards the house. The East German, Gustav Rasch, came flopping alongside him, his mammaries bouncing up and down.

'I am perhaps too old a little,' Rasch said, breathing very hard.

'You're not old,' Linney lied. 'A little out of shape, maybe.'

Linney stepped on to the terrace. The house he owned in Bridgehampton had cost him 2.7 million dollars three years ago. It was a sprawling structure, the result of various owners adding whimsies of their own to the original dwelling – a greenhouse, a glass-walled breakfast room, servant quarters at the rear. Linney sprawled in a deckchair. The East German, who had heard that Nicholas Linney's hospitality was always exciting, plopped into a chaise-longue.

Linney offered him a drink. Grapefruit juice and Tanqueray gin spiked with chopped mint leaves. The breakfast speciality of the house. For quite some time neither man spoke. Linney lit a cigarette and looked across the tennis court. Dead leaves, scraps from last fall, blew in little pockets of air stirred up by the wind.

'Is a nice house,' Rasch said.

'Thank you.' Linney filled two glasses from a flask, passing one to the East German, who drank as if his life were running out.

Linney put his glass down. Rasch had already finished his drink and was helping himself to another.

'Now,' Rasch said, and licked his thick lips. 'Is important we talk money.'

Linney wanted to talk money, but only on his own terms, and only after Rasch had sampled the pleasures of the house. 'Later,' he said. 'If you're agreeable, that is.'

Rasch crossed his arms on his large chest. He was still smiling. 'Perhaps we touch on subject briefly now. Then later more?'

'Very well,' Linney said.

'My people are unhappy,' Rasch remarked.

'So are mine.'

'Of course. We are all unhappy. My people see their money go on board a ship and then *zoom*, no more money. Swallowed up by the sea, no?'

Linney sipped his drink. He had invited Rasch out here to Bridgehampton for the sole purpose of exploring further fund-raising opportunities. It looked, as he'd told Harry Cairney at Roscommon, very bleak. The East Germans and their Soviet overlords could be very tight when it came to disbursing money.

'There are some of us who do not like this kind of investment,' Rasch went on. 'Is money wasted, they say. Bad policy to throw money into Ireland. What is Ireland, they ask, but a wart in the Irish Sea? Now, these people are very very happy because they can . . .' Rasch faltered.

'Gloat?' Linney suggested.

'Indeed.' Rasch put his empty glass down. 'They gloat. They say security is bad and Ireland is unworthy of money anyway and why spend more?'

Linney made a little gesture with his hand. This business about the missing money nagged at him. He'd always enjoyed a good working relationship with his contributors but now, because one of the Fund-raisers had committed an act of treachery, all that was threatened. So far as Linney was concerned, the most likely candidate was Mulhaney. But in the absence of any hard evidence, what could he do about his suspicions? Big Jock was devious and greedy and he'd been plundering Teamster funds in the North-East for years. Linney would have liked to get Big Jock in some white-tiled, soundproofed cellar and hammer the fucking truth out of him.

Something else crossed his mind now. It was the two M–16A2s he had inside the house. It was no *major* deal, but about six months ago he'd come into possession of the two automatic rifles as well as a half-dozen Fabrique Nationale assault rifles, those lovely Belgian babies, from a gun-dealer he'd met at a survivalist training-camp in the Poconos. The dealer, who was the kind of man Linney ran into at these camps, where quiet machismo and boastful innuendo were the common currency of conversation, claimed he had a shipment of a hundred guns he was interested in selling to any interested party, if such a thing could be arranged. Linney, with more bravado than prudence, had allowed – with a small show of self-importance – that he was at least in the position of *exploring* the possibility of sending the guns to a buyer he knew in Ireland. He offered to transport the two automatic rifles and the six FN weapons as samples and if there was interest he'd get back to the dealer. All this was discussed discreetly, and it had intrigued Linney enormously to be involved in the clandestine business of running guns.

He'd taken the weapons, and sent the FN rifles to the address of an acquaintance in Cork, but he'd kept the M–16A2s for himself because they were prized weapons and difficult to acquire. Linney had paid cash for all the guns and hadn't heard from the gun merchant again. Nor had he been surprised, because those kinds of deals fell through more frequently than they ever came to fruition. But the thing that worried him slightly now was the possibility of this business coming to light. He hadn't done anything dishonest. He'd simply kept the guns he wanted for himself and sent the rest. And he hadn't screwed the Irish out of any money to do so, which was something he'd never dream of doing. But they were a sensitive, touchy crew in the old country, and if they heard that two precious samples of the M–16A2 had been diverted, they could quite possibly be upset. When it came to the Cause, the people in Ireland hated the idea of anybody fucking with it. And Linney's decision to keep the two guns could be interpreted as interference. It wasn't much – but it bothered Linney. What if they'd heard over in Ireland about the two samples they never received? What if, in the murky world of gun-dealing, information had come up? What if the gun-dealer asked some Irish acquaintance *By the way, what did you think of the M–16A2s?*

It wasn't likely. But Nicholas Linney's mind had a twist that often exaggerated possibilities. He had the thought that if they found out about the two guns, they could leap to the conclusion that Linney wasn't altogether loyal – and that could perhaps lead to more stinging accusations. Such as the hijacking of a small ship. The idea of being falsely accused filled him with a certain little jolt of excitement. It wasn't going to happen that way, of course, but the possibility was enough to increase the voltage of his adrenalin.

'More contributions are conditional,' Rasch was saying. He beamed as if he were pleased with his mastery of English. 'One, your security measures in the future we must approve.'

'In triplicate?' Linney asked.

Rasch didn't know the word so he ignored it. 'And two, no more money will be donated until you have catched the criminals and they are very punished.'

Nicholas Linney pulled a sliver of mint leaf from his glass and rolled it between his hands. How could security plans be submitted to some fucking committee in East Berlin? Apart from the fact that such a process would take forever, Linney realised that with so many people involved agreements could never be reached. The whole business of raising money would become bogged down in forms, those fucking forms of which the East Europeans were so fond and which seemed to Linney the paper foundation on which all Communism was built. If the Arab patrons were going to be as difficult as the East Europeans, you could practically kiss everything off. Linney sniffed mint on the palms of his hands. He was suddenly very impatient and restless and more than a little annoyed by the way things were turning out.

Rasch settled back in the chaise-longue. 'I must know if you are soon catching the pirates. Is expected of me.'

'That's a police matter, Gustav.' Even as he said this Linney knew that no American agency, neither the FBI nor the cops nor the Coast Guard, gave a flying fuck about a ship with Liberian registry and an Irish crew that had been attacked in international waters.

'No,' Rasch said. 'Is a matter of your house being in order, Nicholas.'

Linney said nothing. He was thinking of the two M–16A2s he had in his study.

Your own house in order, he thought.

He looked down over the tennis-court at the willow trees that marked his property line. There was an iron fence beyond the trees. It wasn't going to keep anyone out who was determined to get in, such as this Irishman old Harry had mentioned. Let him show his face around here, Linney thought. *Let him try.* He had enough weapons stashed inside the house to keep a goddam army at bay for days. And for quite some time now, in fact ever since he'd been rejected by the draft board for Vietnam because of fallen arches, he'd been frustrated by the fact that all he ever got to shoot were watermelons and cantaloupes and plastic bottles filled with water. It was time to ponder a different kind of target.

The Irishman. Linney had spent some time trying to imagine the guy's state of mind. He'd reached the conclusion that the Irishman was going to treat each one of the Fund-raisers as a suspect. He wasn't going to come off like some tightly-wrapped detective with a few penetrating questions to ask and leave it at that. No, this fucker was going to be hard and menacing, which was a prospect Nicholas Linney enjoyed. Besides, Linney didn't put a whole lot of faith in the value of the Fund-raisers' anonymity. Secrecy always had a weakness in it somewhere. And the weakness here was the priest, Joseph Tumulty, who was the liaison between the Americans and the IRA. Sometimes Linney got the impression that Tumulty knew a little more than he ever said. He'd always meant to get rid of Tumulty and strengthen that weak link in the chain, but he'd never quite done it – and he knew why. It was simply that he *liked* the vulnerability in the chain because it gave everything a delicious edge, a little tinge of danger in the otherwise mundane chore of delivering large sums of cash. He enjoyed that. It provided spice during the cold nights when you were skulking around Maine with briefcases stuffed with dough.

Nicholas Linney finished his drink. *This Irishman is going to suspect everybody,* he thought. *Including me.* Let him come here. Let him show his face.

He turned to Rasch and smiled. 'Let's go indoors,' he said. 'We can talk about all this later.'

Rasch stood up hastily. 'I have been waiting.'

Linney draped an arm loosely around Rasch's shoulder as they moved across the terrace. Sliding glass doors opened into a lounge the length of the house. It was furnished in pastels, the minimalist look, lean chairs and low-slung coffee tables and a couple of sparse paintings of the Anaemic School. Linney liked understatement. He had no taste for the brash. He liked clean lines and crisp angles. Even in his politics he favoured simple alignments and economy. His activities on behalf of the Fund-raisers, for example, served two purposes at once. They satisfied his Irishness, handed down to him from his father, Brigadier Mad Jack Linney of the IRA, a dashing figure with a black eyepatch who had been shot to death in Belfast in October 1955, and they created useful bonds with the Arabs and the East Europeans which helped in his other commercial enterprises. He often steered foreign capital into foundering Western businesses threatened by either bankruptcy or takeover. It was amazing sometimes to Linney how much Eastern European money had been used to help pump new blood into the arteries of capitalism.

Passing a large salt-water fishtank in which a variety of exotic species flickered back and forth, Linney walked across the floor to a door on the other side of the room. It opened into a very large bedroom. Two girls, neither of whom was more than fifteen, sat listening to rock music. They were easily corrupted, Linney thought. When he first brought them to this country, they had been shy and retiring, delicate little things who understood nothing about Western ways. Now Linney wondered how long he could keep them before they wanted their freedom, a Western concept that, like rock music and whirlpool baths and TV, they'd grasped all too quickly.

Linney indicated for them to come out into the lounge. They wore simple pastel dresses, so that they were coordinated with the room they entered. Their hair, shiny and black and long, lay in an uncluttered way over their shoulders, exactly as Linney liked it. Each girl was long-legged and lithe and small-breasted. When they smiled they did so in a shy manner, turning their dark brown eyes down. They were beautiful and still acquiescent in a way one rarely found among Western girls these days.

'Ah,' Rasch said. 'Supreme.'

'I'm glad you approve,' Linney said.

'Will they undress?' Rasch asked.

The girls took off their dresses and stood in white underwear that made their skin seem starkly ochre.

'They have names?' Rasch asked.

Linney shrugged. 'I call them Dancer and Prancer.'

'Pardon?' Rasch said.

'Not their real names. I bought them in Phnom Penh.'

'A fine purchase,' Rasch said. 'Very fine. Is no problem to bring them to United States?'

'There were visa considerations,' Linney answered.

'Paperwork.' Rasch looked as if he understood the labyrinthine requirements of bureaucracy.

'Which one do you favour?' Linney asked.

The East German strolled around the girls, nodding his head. This was precisely what he had come to Nicholas Linney's home for, the satisfaction of appetites that went undernourished in East Berlin, where he had a wife who resembled a Sumo wrestler. He weighed a delicate breast in his hand, fingered a fine hip, patted a lean buttock. The girls didn't move. They were accustomed to being assessed by Linney's associates, men of Western culture who regarded them like oxen.

Rasch turned to Linney with a grin on his face. 'Such pretty little birds,' he said. 'I like them both.'

Patchogue, Long Island

'It's not Jig's style,' Frank Pagan said. 'For one thing, he *never* claims he's made a kill on behalf of the Irish Republican Army. He never says *anything* like that. If he had reason to kill somebody in Albany, why would he change his usual message?'

Zuboric, sitting in the passenger seat of Pagan's Cadillac, had his hands clenched tensely in his lap because he didn't like Pagan's idea of driving, which was to occupy the fast lane at around ninety-five miles an hour and keep a leaden foot on the gas pedal, ignoring anything in his way. Pagan was a fast man on the horn, thrusting his palm down and holding it there until the driver in front switched lanes.

'If it wasn't Jig, who was it?' Zuboric asked.

Pagan shrugged. He had the alarming habit of not looking where he was going. He forced the Cadillac up to a shaky eighty-five and turned his face to Zuboric. 'I don't have an answer to that. None of it makes sense. I can't imagine some local IRA cell in Albany doing anything like this. I can't even imagine the *existence* of a cell in Albany. Christ, what would they do anyway in the middle of New York State? Hold jumble sales to raise funds for weapons? Coconut shies? Sell little flags you can stick in your lapel?'

'Watch the road, Frank,' Zuboric said.

Pagan banged his horn again, and the car in front, a canary-yellow Corvette, moved into the slow lane. 'Another thing that bothers me is the connection. An old FUV man turns up dead in Albany at the same time as Ivor McInnes is here in New York.'

'They don't have to be connected,' Zuboric said. He favoured the Jig hypothesis plain and simple. It was the only logical one and besides he was tired of bird-dogging Pagan. How sweet it would be to have a quick wrap on this whole business and be rid of Frank fucking Pagan once and for all. Then he could go back to the tangled affair that was his own life. *A topless bar, for Chrissakes. Shaking her wonderful tits for all and sundry to see. Drooling men with hard-ons under their overcoats*. Zuboric couldn't take any of this. He had to get Charity away from that life.

'Maybe not,' Pagan answered.

'Jig had time to kill a man in Albany and then get to New York.'

'He had time, certainly,' Pagan said. 'I don't know why he'd want to kill Fitzjohn, though.'

'Consider this,' Zuboric opened his eyes. 'Jig finds out this character Fitzjohn had something to do with the missing money. Fitzjohn won't tell him anything. Jig kills him.'

Pagan was unconvinced. 'Why kill somebody who might have information you want? What sense does that make? If Fitzjohn knew something, Jig wouldn't kill him. He'd try everything he could to get the information out of the man, but he wouldn't kill him. That would be a sheer waste of resources.' Pagan rubbed his eyes, taking both hands off the wheel to do so. Zuboric sat straight forward in his seat like a drowning man looking for something to clutch.

'Frank, for Chrissakes.'

Pagan returned his hands to the wheel. 'It just doesn't add up. Jig came back to St Finbar's for two reasons. One was guns. The other was a name. And Tumulty only knew one name. Nicholas Linney. He said he'd never heard of Fitzjohn, so he couldn't tell Jig that one.'

'Maybe Jig brought the name with him from Ireland,' Zuboric said. He felt weary. It seemed to him that the whole Irish situation, at least so far as it had been imported into the United States, was too complex to contemplate. Complicated allegiances, obscure motivations. He understood it was best to keep it all simple in his mind. It was the Catholic against Protestant, basically. Any side issues, any sudden tributaries, were not worth exploring if you wanted to retain your sanity, a possession Frank Pagan had almost relinquished.

'If he knew of Fitzjohn before he left Ireland, why would he go to all the trouble of getting a name from Tumulty? He understood the risks involved in going to Canal Street. Why take those risks if he already had a lead to the missing money? And if he did have a lead, why kill it?' Pagan peered into the rearview mirror. He changed lanes abruptly, overtook a large Mayflower van, then swung back out into the fast lane and gave the big Caddie more gas.

Zuboric had an image of the Cadillac, and all who sailed in her, crashing off the highway and plummeting down an embankment. A fiery death. This whole trip across Long Island wouldn't have been necessary if Pagan had used his gun on Jig the first time round, a perception that made Zuboric resentful.

'Maybe we're going to Bridgehampton for nothing.'

Pagan didn't think so. He had the feeling that poor Joe Tumulty, faced with premature eviction from St Finbar's and the end of all his humanitarian labours, had finally been truthful. And if it hadn't been for Artie Zuboric blurting out Jig's name at that first meeting with Tumulty, if Pagan had been given the chance to take slower steps, more circumspect ones, the chance to run things his own way, then Tumulty would have been less defensive and more easily caught unawares. And perhaps Jig would have been simpler to snare. Hindsight, blessed hindsight, Pagan thought. It was an overrated quality.

'We'll find out soon enough,' he said.

'What if Jig's already been there?' Zuboric asked.

'That's something else we'll find out,' Pagan replied.

He pressed the gas pedal to the floor, rolled his window down, turned on the radio just as the town of Patchogue slipped past on the edge of Highway 27, and heard the sound of Freddie Common singing *Palisades Park*, an anthem from an innocent time.

Roscommon, New York

Celestine Cairney listened to her husband's music drift out through the open door of his library. It seemed more melancholy than usual this morning. It fitted Harry's mood, certainly. Ever since he'd learned that his son had gone abruptly in the middle of the night he'd retreated behind the wall of his music, his silence chilly and his face pale and haunted. Patrick's manner of departure had disappointed him. No farewell. No final hug. No promises to keep in touch.

She stood on the threshold of the room, looking across the floor at her husband. He sat in a large wing-back chair beside the fireplace, unaware of her. He appeared very frail, his skinny white hands clasped in his lap, his eyes closed under white lids, his head moving very slightly in time to the music. She didn't have the heart to talk with him. She had no way of explaining Patrick's departure to him, even if she wanted to.

She went down the long flight of stairs to the hallway below. Inside the sitting-room she stood at the window and looked out over the expanse of land that sloped down to the shore of the lake. She twisted her fingers together. When she tried to remember her visit to Patrick Cairney's bedroom her memories were evasive. The taste of the man, the way he felt – these things came back to her with a clarity. But there was something else that eluded her. What did she want to call it? His essence? His private self? Perhaps it was the simple mystery of the unattainable, longing for the thing you can never have.

No. It had nothing to do with the ache of remembered desire or the way it clawed at her heart or the fact that Patrick Cairney was her husband's son.

It was another kind of mystery altogether, concrete and tangible.

She pressed her cheek against the cold glass. Outside, the early morning sun had a faint mist hanging around it. A veil. Like the veil Patrick Cairney drew over himself.

She turned away from the window. Her hand went out to the telephone and lingered over it. The obvious place to begin was with the archaeological departments of universities, but today was Saturday and those offices would be shut. It would have to wait, she thought. She sat down, struggling with her impatience and the sense of excitement she suddenly felt. She knew she was on to something, but precisely what she couldn't quite say. It was almost as if Patrick Cairney were a book she had somehow opened in the middle at a suspenseful part, a tease that would compel her to read to the end where everything enigmatic would be clarified in one stunning revelation.

Harry came inside the room, moving slowly. Celestine took his hand and held it against her breasts.

'I can't understand it,' he said. 'Why did he leave like that?'

Celestine didn't speak.

Cairney inclined his head so that it touched his wife's shoulder. 'Did he strike you as being unhappy about something? Did I say something to upset him?'

She shook her head and said no, he hadn't.

'There's something restless about that boy,' Cairney said. 'There's always been this restless centre to him. It's like he's never fully at ease anywhere.'

'I can't imagine why,' Celestine replied.

Harry Cairney, who felt very old this morning, closed his eyes. His sense of unhappiness was strong, like a blade in his chest. He'd been looking forward to spending the morning with his son, talking of his favourite subject, Ireland, reminiscing, reliving a past that was going to die when he did. He'd awakened that morning with old memories vitally refreshed, things he wanted to tell Patrick, sights and sounds he wanted to convey to the boy – the clattering old trams that used to run all over the city with their Amstel Lager Beer and Bovril and Neaves Food signs, along the North Circular Road and Rathmines Road and Sackville Street out to Phoenix Park (although he couldn't remember the exact routes now, as if the geography of his beloved Dublin had collapsed in his memory), the smells of loose tea in Sheridan's on North Earl Street, how he'd bought his first real pair of shoes at the Popular Boot Emporium on South Great George's Street, and Croke Park where on March 14, 1921, the British had surrounded a crowd of ten thousand at a football game and opened fire, volley after volley, wounding and killing the blameless. Fourteen dead. Fifty-seven injured. His memory had become all at once a crowded place, but what goddam good were memories when you didn't have your boy to share them with? Patrick would have been interested in hearing these things. He was always interested in his father's recollections. He loved Ireland just as the old man did.

Celestine put her arms around Harry and drew him against her body. 'I'm sure he'll call,' she said.

She stroked the side of his face very deliberately, almost as if she were seeking resemblances between the old man to whom she was married and the young man who had left her, in the dead of night, with enigmas.

'Love me,' Harry Cairney said.

'Here? Now?'

'Here and now.'

She put her hand between the folds of his robe, cupping his testicles in her palm. His skin was cold. She worked her fingers over the shaft of his penis, which was infirm and soft until she began to stroke it energetically. She listened to the low sound he made as he grew excited – a quiet moaning, a whispering of words she could never quite catch. His breath quickened and there was rasping from his tired lungs.

She parted his robe and went down on her knees. Looking upwards once at the whiteness of his body, the sagging pectoral muscles, the folds of his neck, she shut her eyes and transported herself to an imagined place and time, where she knelt, exactly as she was doing now, at the feet of another man, whose body was Patrick Cairney's.

18 Bridgehampton, Long Island

Patrick Cairney parked his car on Ocean Road at the edge of Bridgehampton. Like the other small resorts in the area known as The Hamptons, Bridgehampton had the feel of a place abandoned for the winter. Empty cafés, closed bars, gulls squabbling in a forlornly quarrelsome way in the cloudy sky over the beach. The man known as Nicholas Linney lived in this village. Earlier, in Southampton, Cairney had consulted a local telephone directory and learned that Linney lived at a number 19 Wood Lane. When he'd been inside the phone booth, he'd experienced an urge to call Finn, just to pick up the telephone and make the transatlantic connection and hear Finn's voice. He'd let his fingertips linger on the black receiver. He had nothing to report to Finn yet.

Wood Lane, a private estate of the kind that suggested wealthy inhabitants and the likelihood of a private security patrol, was a narrow thoroughfare running at a right angle from Ocean Road. In summer, the lane would have been leafy and dense and green, but now the trees were barren, affording him absolutely no cover. He left his car on Ocean Road, the canvas bag locked inside the trunk.

He began to walk. He felt conspicuous even though he understood that many of the houses on the lane, hidden behind shrubbery and walls, had been vacated for the winter. Once, he heard the sound of a child shouting, followed by the noise of a ball bouncing against stone. After that, nothing.

He had no idea of what he was going to do when he found number 19. A great deal depended on the attitude of Nicholas Linney, which was an unpredictable factor. In an ideal world, Linney would be a reasonable man who would discuss the problem of the money calmly, rationally. In this same world Nicholas Linney would know precisely what had happened to the *Connie*'s cargo and he'd tell Cairney at once. But Finn had talked of the need for caution. *Expect them to lie to you. Expect outright animosity towards you.*

Take them off guard, if you can.

When he reached number 19 he kept moving, noticing a wrought-iron fence and, some distance beyond, a one-storey house surrounded by sycamores. There were three vehicles parked in the driveway. A Mercedes, a BMW, and a Land Rover painted in camouflage. He came to the place where the iron fence ended, and he stopped. A house built on one level was good because it meant he didn't have to worry about anybody concealed in upstairs rooms. A small bonus. The cars suggested two things. Either Nicholas Linney collected foreign autos or else he had a visitor.

What Cairney wished for right then was the obscurity of night, darkness. His best plan was to wait for nightfall and hope that Nicholas Linney would emerge alone from the house at some point. But he couldn't afford to wait. It was really that simple. He couldn't afford the luxury of time because he had absolutely no way of knowing what Joe Tumulty might have told Pagan. If the priest had pointed Pagan in this direction, then time was truly of the essence. He might be trapped inside an hourglass and slipping with the sands.

He studied the fence. He considered a direct approach, straight up to the front door like a Jehovah's Witness or a man from the Fuller Brush Company, but he decided against that. It came back again to the fact he couldn't *predict* anything in this situation. Linney might be reasonable. Or he might not be. Stealth was the most prudent approach to the house. And if he was going to climb this fence he'd have to do it at the corner where a small stand of pine trees would conceal him from the windows of the place.

The fence was easy. He hauled himself up, dropped quickly down on the other side. As he stood under the pines he was conscious of music issuing from the house. There was a harsh sound of a man laughing. The music stopped. The house was silent again.

It was perhaps fifty feet from the pines to the side of the house where an empty terrace overlooked a concrete tennis-court. For that distance he would have no cover. A man stepped out of the house and moved on to the terrace, where he sat down at a table and propped his feet up and poured himself a drink. Cairney, seeking invisibility, pressed himself against the trunk of a tree. He had the thought that if this were some other situation, the kind he was used to, the kind where it was a matter of bringing down a particular target you fixed through the scope of a rifle, then he wouldn't feel this uncertain. The man on the terrace, for example. How simple it would have been, in other circumstances, to shoot him. But even if he *had* been armed, Finn hadn't given him a mandate for violence.

Now there was more laughter from the house. A girl's laugh this time, high-pitched. False and polite. Cairney stood very still. Then, tensing his body, he moved out from under his cover and headed in the direction of the front door, passing the parked cars quickly.

He reached out and turned the door handle. The door wasn't locked. He opened it an inch, two inches, seeing a square of hallway beyond. He stepped into the house, closed the door softly, then stood very still in the centre of the hall, listening, concentrating, wondering about the next step. Other doors, each of them closed, faced him. Which one to try?

Then, suddenly, one of the doors opened and a beautiful oriental girl stood there wrapped in a large white towel, her black hair hanging on her shoulders and her dark eyes wide with surprise.

Cairney stared at her. The girl must have assumed he was a guest in the house because she did something that amazed him then. She let the towel slip from her body, stepped over it and, with her arms held out, came towards him. Cairney reached for her wrist, twisted it, swung her around so that she had her back to him, then held her tightly against him like a shield. The girl's reaction surprised him. She giggled, almost as if force were a regular occurrence in her life. She *expected* men to treat her this way. He clamped his hand across her lips.

'Linney,' he said. 'Show me where Linney is.'

The girl made a small sound into Cairney's palm. He could feel her wet lips, her teeth, the tiny tip of her tongue. She moved forward. Cairney kept his hold on her, following her towards the doorway from which she'd emerged. There was a large bedroom beyond.

A plump man, who wasn't the one Cairney had seen on the terrace, lay naked on the bed while another girl, remarkably similar to the one Cairney grasped, attended to his needs. She had her face buried deep in the man's groin. The man sat upright quickly, staring at Cairney with an expression of stunned vulnerability. He shoved the girl away from himself and he grabbed the bedsheet, hauling it quickly up over his body.

'Who are you?' the man asked. He had a foreign accent, European of some kind.

Cairney still held the girl tightly. 'Linney?' he asked.

The plump man shook his head and looked angry. The girl who'd been shoved so rudely aside gazed at Cairney as if she didn't know quite what to make of him. There was a dull defensive quality in her face.

'Who are you?' the plump man asked again and then started to rise from the bed, his expression now one of alarm. He began to make for the door, the bedsheet hanging loosely from his body. Cairney hesitated only a moment over his options. He could let this man leave the bedroom – but then what? The look on the man's face suggested that of some outraged burgher searching for the nearest telephone to call the police. And that was a complication Patrick Cairney didn't need.

'Don't go any further,' Cairney said. 'Stop right where you are.'

The plump man paid no attention. He was about six feet from the door and still hurrying when Cairney said, 'Don't take another step.'

The man ignored him.

Cairney clenched his fist and struck the man on the side of the head. It wasn't the fiercest of blows but it had an immediate effect. The plump man's eyes rolled and he gasped and then appeared to implode as he staggered back across the floor onto the bed. The bedsheet, like some outsized shroud, collapsed around him. It was crude and Cairney regretted having to do it, but there was no way he could have let the man stroll out of here. He looked down at the unconscious figure, feeling curiously depressed by the sight of the open mouth and the broken skin on the side of the scalp. It shouldn't have been necessary, it should have been simple and smooth and uneventful. Instead, he'd been drawn into an act of violence that seemed all the more upsetting to him because of its very intimacy, the connection of his flesh with that of another, the moment of harsh contact, bone on bone. It wasn't violence from a distance, the kind he was accustomed to. It was close up and personal, and it made him unhappy. He was still holding the girl, still staring at the inert figure on the bed, when he heard a man's voice from beyond the bedroom door.

Rasch? Are you finished in there?

And then the door opened and the man from the terrace stood on the threshhold. He appeared only slightly surprised by Cairney's presence. There was a momentary widening in the eyes, and then he was smiling, as if the unexpected appearance of a total stranger were an everyday event.

'You can let the girl go,' he said. 'I don't like having my property mistreated.'

Cairney didn't release the girl. He ran his eye over the man, but he didn't notice the presence of any weapon. Besides, since the man was dressed only in shorts and sweatshirt, there were no obvious hiding-places for a gun.

'Linney,' Cairney said.

Nicholas Linney nodded. He gazed a moment at Gustav Rasch on the bed. Then he turned his face back to Cairney.

'You're the one they sent from Ireland,' Linney said. *This was the one everybody was so worried about. This was the man Harry Cairney had said was going to be so fucking good at his business.* Nicholas Linney felt a rush of pleasure to his head, a keen anticipation, an awareness of combat. He'd find out how good this guy was supposed to be. This guy was about to discover that Nick Linney wasn't some overweight German clerk. All at once Linney's chest was tight and his heartbeat had the persistence of a funeral drum.

Cairney let the girl go. She sat on the edge of the bed, pushing her glossy black hair out of her eyes. The other girl reached for her friend's hand and held it.

'I'm the one,' Cairney said.

Nicholas Linney took a step back out of the bedroom. Cairney moved after him. Linney glanced at the man's overcoat, seeing how one hand was thrust inside a pocket now. *He has a gun in there*. And he wouldn't carry one unless he intended to use it somewhere down the line. Linney thought of all the weapons he had inside his office. He'd play along, he'd wait for the moment, the opening. It was bound to come. There was a wonderful irony in the idea of killing this hotshot with one of the M–16A2s that had been intended for Ireland. Linney was enormously pleased by it.

Both men stood inside a large living-room. There was a massive fishtank where small electric colours darted back and forth.

Cairney said, 'We need to talk. You know what I've come for.'

Linney smiled. His goddam heart wouldn't stop hammering. Here was a situation he'd wanted all along, his own private little war. Right here in his own living-room. He could already feel the stark warmth of the automatic rifle between his hands.

'Suppose I tell you what I know. What guarantees can you give me you won't shoot me when you've heard everything I have to say?'

'I don't give guarantees,' Cairney said. He wondered why Linney had talked about shooting, and then it dawned on him that the man imagined there was a gun in his pocket. Fine. Let him think so.

'You pump me dry of information, what fucking good am I to you after that?' Linney asked. 'I need something. I gotta have a guarantee. Something.'

Cairney, who saw on Linney's face a desperation that lay beneath the intensity, felt suddenly relaxed. With barely any effort he'd established control here. He'd taken command. The game was his and he could play it however he liked. Whatever uncertainty he'd felt before fell away from him. He felt the way he had when he'd assassinated Lord Drumcannon, that elation when the man had appeared in the sight of his rifle, that moment when you knew the game was over and the result already sealed beyond doubt and all that was left was the mere bloody formality of the victim falling. *You've got this one*, he told himself. *You've cornered this one. And all because he thinks you've got a gun concealed in your pocket*.

'Somebody broke a contract,' he said. 'Somebody screwed the Cause. It's not the kind of situation where I can offer you immunity, Linney. For all I know, you might be the man I'm looking for.'

Linney shook his head. It was just as he'd expected. This fucker suspected *him*. 'Not me, friend.'

Cairney moved forward. He was very close to Linney now.

'Who gave you my name anyway?' Linney asked. He glanced a second at the half-open door of his office. He could turn quickly, he could make it inside, slam the door hard behind him. He could do it. He could get to a weapon. It all depended on letting this fucker think everything was going his way. 'It was that scumbag priest, wasn't it? He sent you here.'

Cairney said nothing. He had a tremor, a fleeting doubt, that Nicholas Linney was preoccupied with something, that his mind was feverishly working in some other direction. Cairney bunched his hand in his coat pocket and moved it very slightly to emphasise the phantom gun.

Linney saw the gesture. He'd never been faced with a gunman before, and he felt the vibrancy of the challenge. His mind was astonishingly clear and sharp. He had a sense of a steel spring coiled deep inside him. Play along with the guy, he thought. Lull him. Then *move*.

'What is it you want? Names? Addresses?'

'I want everything you can give me, Linney.'

Nicholas Linney had his back flush to the wall now. He looked at the man a moment, then said, 'In my office. I got all the information there.' Linney indicated a door to his right.

'After you,' Cairney said.

Linney took a step towards his office. He sucked air deeply into his lungs and felt that spring inside him suddenly unwind.

Now!

He shoved the door open and slammed it hard behind him and before Cairney could get a foot in he heard Nicholas Linney bolting the door. And then there was another sound from within the locked room, one that Cairney recognised only too well. It was the click of a magazine being shoved hurriedly into a rifle. And then Nicholas Linney roared aloud, the strange cry of a man exalted by the prospect of battle.

Cairney reacted immediately.

He threw himself to one side, rolling over and over in the direction of the sliding glass-doors, so that he was out of the line of fire. When the sound of automatic gunfire started, he heard it split the silence of the house like a hammer smashing glass, and then the two girls were screaming and grabbing one another for protection against the random, blind assault of bullets that traversed the living-room and buried themselves in plaster.

Cairney blinked involuntarily. Linney was shooting wildly through the door of his office, his bullets tearing huge holes in the wood and spraying the air with splinters. It was desperate stuff and Cairney, cursing himself for having been misled by his own sense of supremacy, closed his eyes and pressed his face down into the floor. Linney kept firing madly, the door shook and vibrated, the splinters flew, the girls screamed. It was insane, a world that had only a moment ago been regulated and under control turned totally upside-down and gone berserk.

One of the oriental girls was struck by the spray inside the bedroom and was screaming because there was an enormous hole in her stomach. The other girl, covered by her blood, lay flat on the floor and cried for a time until she became quiet. The gunfire pierced woodwork and mirrors and windows, creating chaos and debris. A stereo blew up in a violent plume of smoke and sparks, and the chandelier threw out tiny shards of crystal that created a glassy rain. The fishtank exploded like a dynamited kaleidoscope, showering the room with yellow and blue and red fish.

Cairney saw the plump man on the bed slither to the floor in a tangle of bedsheets and a snowstorm of feathers released from a punctured pillow. He lay beside the two girls, both of whom had been hit.

And then abruptly the firing stopped and the silence was the most profoundly unsettling Cairney had ever heard. He raised his face and looked at the door, which was buckled and split and hanging precariously from its hinges. What was Linney doing now? Reloading?

Listening, Cairney heard the sound of dying fish flapping desperately in puddles of shallow water. He crawled through the sliding glass-doors to the terrace where a rough wind rising up off the ocean scoured his face. The carnage, so sudden, so unexpected, had shaken him. It wasn't supposed to be like this, he thought. It wasn't supposed to get away from him like this. He had had *goddam* Linney right where he wanted him – and now, Christ, it had fallen apart.

He heard the noise of the broken door being kicked down, then the sound of Linney moving in the room, feet squelching through the water from the fishtank.

Cairney peered through the glass doors. Linney, his back to Cairney, was holding a pistol out in front of himself as he moved. He walked hesitantly towards the bedroom, trying to keep his balance on the slippery floor. Cairney watched. He knew Linney could turn around at any second and see him framed in the glass doors, a perfect target.

There was twenty feet, twenty-five at most, separating Cairney from Linney, who was standing now in the threshhold of the bedroom. It might be the only chance Cairney would ever have. He would have to move now or not at all.

He stepped through the glass doors back inside the room, moving with all the stealth he'd learned in the desert, moving as the Libyans always said 'like a man whose feet are the wind', watching Linney who was regarding the girls inside the bedroom. Fifteen feet, ten. How far could he travel across this watery floor before Linney heard him and turned around and fired his pistol? Ten feet. Nine. Eight.

When Cairney was a mere six feet away, some instinct made Linney swing quickly round, firing one shot that was unfocused and wild and went flying past Cairney's cheek into the glass panel of the door. Cairney bent low, shoulders hunched, every muscle in his body relaxed and ready now for the move he'd have to make before Linney found his range and fired again. He threw himself across the room with neither grace nor elegance, an anxious linebacker, his shoulder crunching into the man's face. There was the sound of bone breaking as the man slithered on the watery floor and tumbled back against the wall. The blow confused and pained Linney but didn't render him unconscious. The pistol clattered across the ceramic tile of the floor and Cairney, turning away from the other man, picked it up.

Linney watched him grimly. Then, using the wall for support, he made it to his feet. 'I gave it a good fucking shot, didn't I?' He seemed very pleased with himself. 'You're not bad. You know that?'

Cairney shook his head. None of this should ever have happened. *This chaos and destruction. None of it.* He could think of nothing to say. He felt brutalised. This was so far removed from any sequence of events he could possibly have anticipated. He couldn't have dreamed this even if he'd dreamed a hundred years. *There's no thrill in killing,* Finn had said once. But there was, if you were a man like Nicholas Linney. What did Linney resemble anyhow but the kind of random killer that Finn had always loathed? A lover of easy death and casual destruction?

'Mulhaney took the money,' Linney said. His jaw must have been broken because he spoke as if he had a mouth filled with old socks.

'Mulhaney?' Cairney asked.

Linney grimaced in pain. He raised one hand to his lips and probed the inside of his mouth and removed a filling, a small gold nugget that lay in his palm. Cairney glanced a second inside the bedroom. The plump man, whose nakedness in death seemed oddly childlike, like that of an unnaturally huge baby, was surrounded by feathers from the wrecked pillow. The girls, who lay beneath him, looked only mildly surprised.

Nicholas Linney's face had already begun to swell. 'Mulhaney runs the North-Eastern branch of the Teamsters. Big Bad Jock.'

Cairney knew the name now. It was one he always associated with questionable labour practices, slush funds, Las Vegas intrigues.

'What makes you think Mulhaney has the money?'

Nicholas Linney said, 'Take my word for it. I thought at first it had to be Dawson, but what would he want money for? He's got it coming out of his ass.'

Dawson. Another name now. 'Who's Dawson?'

Linney smiled. The expression caused him obvious pain. His face contorted. 'You don't know anything, do you? They really sent you here blind, didn't they?'

'I asked about Dawson.' Cairney made a gesture with the pistol.

'Kevin Dawson,' Linney said. 'Big brother Tommy occupies the White House.'

Kevin Dawson, the quiet member of the Dawson clan, the background figure whose family was sometimes trotted out for the edification of wholesome America. They just adored Kevin and his wife and kids in the heartland. Cairney was surprised by the names Linney tossed out. But how could he trust a man like Linney, who was capable of doing and saying anything?

Linney said, 'You got my word. You want Mulhaney.'

Your word. 'Where do I find him?'

Linney shuffled towards the broken door, beyond which was a room whose walls were stacked with gunracks. There were all kinds of weapons, competition rifles, shotguns, black powder muskets, handguns. On the floor lay the automatic rifle that had been used to blast through the door. Linney, who was thinking about the pistol he kept in the centre drawer of his desk, slumped into a chair and punched some buttons on a computer console. A small amber screen lit up and a disc-drive whirred.

'There,' Linney said.

A name, and address. Cairney studied them. He committed them to memory. He felt strangely removed from himself now, like somebody going through the motions. He concentrated on pulling himself together. It didn't matter what had happened here, he still had his work to do. He still had Finn's task to carry out. He couldn't afford to dwell on the outrage perpetrated by Nicholas Linney. He stared at the shimmering little letters. His eyes began to hurt. He looked at Linney, who had his hands in his lap.

Linney said, 'You're thinking I'll call Mulhaney, right? If you let me live, I'll call him. Isn't that what's on your mind? Hey, I give you my word, I won't warn him. Why should I? If he stole the goddam money, he deserves to die.'

'What do you deserve?' Cairney asked with contempt. 'You think *you* deserve to live?'

Linney forced a little smile. He moved one hand towards the centre drawer of his desk. *Nobody beats Nicholas Linney,* he thought. *Nobody leaves my house thinking I'm some fucking loser. I trained myself for exactly this kind of situation*. 'I gave you what you wanted, guy. That merits some consideration.'

'The price was high, Linney.'

Linney shrugged. He drummed his fingertips on the handle of the drawer. This guy was fast, but Linney believed he could be even quicker. 'Sometimes you have to pay it.'

Cairney felt the weight of the pistol in his hand. It would be the simplest thing in the world to turn the gun on Linney. If he left Linney alive, who could predict what the man would do then? He couldn't afford to step out of this house and walk away from Linney, who could start making frantic little calls. It was a strange moment for Cairney. He could see a vein throb in Linney's head. He had an unsettling sense of Linney's life, the blood coursing through the man's body. This was a living presence, not a distant figure fixed in the heart of a scope. There were only a couple of inches between Cairney and the man, and he found himself longing for space, longing for the lens of a scope, longing for *distance*. If he had that kind of separation from this monster, he'd kill him without blinking an eye.

Linney stared at the gun. He curled one finger around the handle of the drawer. *Go for it, Nick. Just go for it. You got nothing to lose because this fucker is going to kill you anyway.* 'Mulhaney's in bad shape financially. He needed money more than the rest of us.'

The rest of us. 'How many are there, Linney?'

'Come on, guy. I gave you what you wanted. Don't get greedy.'

'How many, Linney?'

Linney did something desperate then. He swivelled his chair around, a gesture that was meant to be casual, easygoing, just a man turning his chair in preparation for getting up out of it – but it was a feint, a sorry kind of deception, because all at once there was a pistol in the centre of his hand, a weapon he'd slipped from the desk in a very smooth motion, and he was bringing it round very quickly in Cairney's direction –

Cairney shot him once through the side of his face. Linney was knocked backwards and out of the chair, one hand uplifted to his cheek as if death were a sudden facial blemish, and then the hand dropped like a stone and Linney followed its downward path to the floor. He lay looking up at the ceiling of his gun-room, seeing nothing.

Cairney stared at the body. *Jesus Christ*. There was a terrible slippage going on here, a downhill slope into destruction. His hand shook. He couldn't find his own private centre. He couldn't find the place of calm retreat. It was as if a storm had broken out inside himself. Four people had died in this goddam house and all because he'd come here looking for information. Looking for Finn's money. He shut his eyes a moment. The death of Linney shouldn't have touched him. He was accustomed to killing. But he'd never shot anyone at such close range before. Okay, Linney had sought death, Linney had manufactured that destiny for himself, but what about the two girls? What was their role in this? Had they ever even *heard* about the Cause?

He opened his eyes. He heard a car crunch into the driveway. He stepped to the window, saw a dark green Cadillac. Quickly, he moved into the living-room and went to the sliding doors, then out on to the terrace where he saw Frank Pagan climb from the big green car. Nimble and silent, unseen by Pagan, Cairney vaulted the terrace wall and skipped across the tennis-court to the fence, which he climbed swiftly. And then he was back in the lane, hurrying away.

New York City

Ivor McInnes left the Essex House and walked south on Fifth Avenue. He went along Fifty-Seventh Street, checking his watch, looking in shop windows. The whole array of American consumer goods dazzled him as it always did, the flash and the glitter and the sheer availability of such things. He spotted a thrift-shop that sold only furs, and he thought that only in America could such a place exist. Did the rich dames on Central Park toss their used lynx coats this way? Did those blue-rinsed old biddies you saw walking their poodles, manicured little dogs that seemed to shit politely on sidewalks, bring their weary minks to the fur thrift-shop? Amazing America!

When he reached Broadway he headed south. Broadway disappointed. He always expected the Great White Way, showgirls stepping out of limos and maybe the sight of some great actress hurrying inside a theatre, last-minute rehearsals. But it was all sleazy little restaurants and an atmosphere of congealed grease. At Times Square he found the public telephone he needed, then he went inside the booth and checked his watch again. The phone rang almost immediately. Seamus Houlihan was nothing if not punctual.

McInnes picked up the receiver.

'We're in place,' Houlihan said.

'Good man.' McInnes ran the tip of a finger between his dog-collar and his neck.

'I had to take out Fitz,' Houlihan said. 'He was trying to skip.'

The disposal of Fitzjohn was of no real concern to McInnes, who had long ago understood that human life, a tenuous business at best, was nothing when you weighed it against ultimate victory. Fitzjohn had been a mere foot soldier, and they were always the first casualties. 'What did you do with the body?'

Houlihan told him.

McInnes listened closely. He couldn't believe what Houlihan was telling him. When Houlihan was through with his story, McInnes was quiet for a while, drumming his fingertips on a filthy pane of glass. If he hated anything, if anything in the world aroused his ire beyond the dangerous philosophies of the Catholic Church, it was when a meticulous plan was interrupted by needless variations, such as the variation Houlihan had introduced in Albany.

'What the hell did you expect to *achieve* by calling the bloody FBI?' McInnes asked. 'Jesus in heaven, Seamus, what the hell were you *thinking* about?'

'It seemed like a good idea to set the ball rolling,' Houlihan said in a curt voice.

'The ball, Seamus, was not supposed to be set rolling until tomorrow. Sunday, Seamus. White Plains. Remember?'

Houlihan was quiet on the other end of the line. McInnes, who experienced a stricture around his heart, had the feeling of a man who has completed an elaborate jigsaw only to find a piece removed during his absence by a wilful hand.

'Don't you see it, Seamus? It's too bloody soon.'

Houlihan still didn't speak. What McInnes felt down the line was the young man's hostility. The killing of Fitzjohn had presumably been necessary in Houlihan's questionable judgement, but the next step – which Seamus had taken without consultation – was not very bright. But then you couldn't expect anything bright out of Seamus. He was great when it came to demolition work. Beyond that he was useless. McInnes thought about Houlihan's unhappy background. Perhaps allowances could be made for a man who was the offspring of an absentee Catholic father and a Protestant mother who had become a drunken bigot of the worst kind. Houlihan must have spent years hating the man who had fathered and abandoned him.

McInnes said, 'It removes the element of surprise, Seamus. Don't you see that? It's like sending them a bloody telegram. You were instructed to wait until you'd done your work in White Plains before calling.'

Sweet Jesus Christ, McInnes thought. It had long been one of the problems of the Free Ulster Volunteers, this lack of good responsible men and the need to draft street scum who killed for the joy of killing and who were misled, by their own acts of violence, into thinking they were actually *smart*. McInnes had always been troubled by this. For every good man he brought into the FUV, there was always a psychopath with a terrible need for blood. What McInnes longed for was a figure like Jig, somebody who killed but who always obeyed instructions. Somebody who didn't step outside the limits of his authority. Jig, he thought. Even somebody like Jig was running out of time. And luck. And sometimes luck, that erratic barometer, swung away from you in the direction of your enemies. Jig's time was coming.

'Now they're going to be out beating the fields with sticks,' McInnes said. 'And all because you took it into your thick head to make a bloody phone call, Seamus. God in heaven, I didn't want them to have an inkling until the work in White Plains is done with.'

Houlihan was heard to clear his throat. 'They can beat the fields with sticks all they want. They're not going to find us, are they?'

McInnes stared across the street at a movie-house marquee. There was a double feature, PUSSIES IN BOOTS AND G-STRING FOLLIES. Somewhat incongruously, two nuns went past the theatre, hobbling in their black boots. McInnes watched them, two middle-aged brides of Christ, their juices all dried up. A lifetime of celibacy was likely to drive you mad, he thought. It was no wonder they believed in such unlikely things as holy water and the infallibility of the Pope and that philosophical absurdity The Holy Ghost. And these women ran schools and influenced the minds of small children, venting all their accumulated frustrations on the souls of infants. Dear God! McInnes turned his thoughts to what he perceived as the final solution for Ulster, and it had nothing to do with the persecution of Catholics or denial of their rights to their own schools and churches. The answer was so bloody simple nobody had ever thought it could work. You repatriated the Catholics, that's what you did. You sent them to the Republic of Ireland. There they could pursue their religious beliefs until doomsday in a society already priest-soaked and dominated by His Holiness, the Gaffer of The Vatican. There would be no more civil strife, no more violence. Ulster would be free, and the Catholics happy. *So damned simple.*

'No, they're probably not going to find you, Seamus. All I'm saying is you didn't follow my instructions. I didn't just sit down and make everything up on the spur of the moment. I worked bloody hard and I planned a long bloody time, Seamus. And I won't have it bollocksed by somebody who takes it into his head to change my plans.'

McInnes fell silent. What good did it do to scream at Houlihan, whose temperament was unpredictable at best? If you didn't butter up people like Seamus, they were likely to fold their tents. And then where would you be? McInnes controlled himself. When the time was ripe, he'd find a way to dispose of Houlihan and the others. In the future he perceived for himself, there was no room for thugs.

'We'll forget it this time,' he said. 'But next time follow the blueprint, Seamus.'

Houlihan said nothing.

'Good luck tomorrow,' McInnes said.

He stepped out of the stale phone booth and wandered through Times Square. He had a slippery sense of his own fate lying in the clumsy hands of a man like Seamus Houlihan. By calling the FBI, what Seamus had done was to set that whole federal machine in motion too soon. McInnes thought he could already hear the wheels grinding away, the cogs clicking. If they ran a check on Fitz, they'd discover his affiliation with the Free Ulster Volunteers, which might in turn lead them directly to himself. Naturally, he'd deny everything, but just the same he saw little connecting threads here he didn't remotely like. The whole point of the exercise had been to keep the FUV name out of everything. But now it was likely to come up, and there was nothing he could do about it except look totally innocent if anyone asked about Fitzjohn. There was Frank Pagan to consider as well. When Pagan learned about the death of Fitzjohn, if he hadn't already done so, he'd be back sniffing around like some big bloodhound. Pagan was desperate to pin something, *anything*, on the Reverend Ivor McInnes.

There was another possibility, of course, that the FBI might automatically associate Jig with the slaying of Fitzjohn, which would fit McInnes's scheme of things very nicely indeed. Jig was a pain in the arse, but he wasn't the whole IRA by any stretch of the imagination.

Bloody Houlihan. What a nuisance.

McInnes stopped in front of a movie poster. The star of PUSSIES IN BOOTS was a girl with the unlikely name of Mysterioso McCall. She had breasts that suggested two of God's more inspired miracles. Either that or silicone. For a second McInnes experienced a terrible pang of longing.

He took a last look at the poster and turned north on Broadway, stepping back in the general direction of his hotel. On the corner of Fifty-Second Street he stopped, looked back the way he'd come, saw no sign of anyone following him, then he made a right turn.

Inside a darkened cocktail bar on Fifty-Second he ordered a ginger ale which he took to a corner table by the telephone.

He checked his watch again. Almost noon. He sipped his drink, waited, staring now and again at the phone. He was in the right place at the right time, but when the phone hadn't rung by twenty past twelve he finished his ginger ale and went back out on to the street again, a little lonely suddenly, a little forlorn, thinking of warm flesh and the consolations of love and how a silent telephone could bring a very special dismay all its own.

Bridgehampton, Long Island

Frank Pagan stared at a gorgeous angelfish that expired in the middle of the floor, slowly flapping its body and looking for all the world like the wing of an exotic bird. The fish hypnotised him, held him captive. If he didn't take his eyes away from the sight of the pathetic thing shuddering down into its own doom, then he wouldn't have to look again at the wreckage of this house. Having gone once from room to room, he had no desire to do so again. It was best left to somebody like Artie Zuboric, who seemingly had the stomach for this kind of wholesale destruction. Businesslike, brisk, Zuboric was flitting here and there and his Italian shoes squelched on the sodden floor.

'Two men, two girls,' Zuboric said, bending to look at the dying fish.

Two men, two girls. Zuboric could make this tally of death sound like a football result. Pagan took his eyes from the fish and moved towards the room that was filled with guns. In there lay one of the dead men, minus a major portion of his face. There was something depressing in the sight of so much death. It ate at your spirit, filled your mind with darkness, numbed you. There was an automatic rifle on the floor.

Zuboric came into the gun-room. He was holding an imitation leather wallet, flicking it open and checking the various cards inside.

'I guess this belonged to the guy in the bedroom,' Zuboric said. 'A certain Gustav Rasch. There's a bunch of stuff here in German. Can you read kraut?'

Pagan, who had an elementary knowledge of German, took the wallet. He scanned the cards, each sealed inside a plastic window. There was a Carte Blanche, a Communist Party membership card issued in East Berlin, a Visa – a mixture of gritty socialism and suave capitalism. At the back of the wallet was a small plastic card identifying Gustav Rasch as a member of the East Berlin Trades and Cultural Mission, which was one of those meaningless societies they were forever inventing to send men into the West. Trade and culture, Pagan thought. Tractors and Tolstoy. Plutonium and Prokofiev. Pagan closed the wallet. The smell of death was overwhelming to him. He shoved a window open and caught a scent of the sea, good cleansing ozone with a dash of salt. There was blood on his fingertips, which he wiped clean against the curtains.

Zuboric took the wallet back. 'What was Gustav Rasch doing here?' he asked. 'What's the connection between an East German and Nicholas Linney?'

Pagan shook his head. The bizarre bedfellows of terrorism again, odd couples coming together in the night like hungry lovers, consuming each other before parting as total strangers. He didn't feel up to discussing the nebulous terrorist connections that were made in all the dark corners of the planet.

'If the guy in the bedroom's Rasch, this character lying here must be Nicholas Linney,' Zuboric said.

Pagan said nothing.

'Our friend Jig,' Zuboric said. 'He had a field day here.'

Pagan stepped around the body on the floor. He tried to imagine Jig coming here and going through this house and leaving such wreckage behind him. Pagan's imagination wasn't functioning well. All the pictures he received were shadowy transmissions. If Jig had been responsible for all this, then the man's style had undergone drastic changes. Whoever had shot this place up had done so indiscriminately. Jig's violence had never been like this in the past. Why would he change now? What kind of circumstances would force him to perpetrate these horrors? There was nowhere in all of this a trace of Jig's signature. There was no elegance here.

Pagan watched Zuboric go out across the living-room to the bedroom, saw him bend over the body of one of the dead girls whose stomach had been ripped open. A wave of pain coursed through Pagan's head. He thought, perhaps inevitably, of Roxanne, whose body they had not allowed him to see after her death. He had yearned for a sight of her back then, driven by a sickness to look one last time at what was left of the woman he'd loved. That desire struck him now as mad and morbid, but grief derailed you, leaving you empty and haunted and bewildered.

Pagan gazed at the racks of guns. He tried to reconstruct the events that had taken place here, but it was a maze with an impossible centre. He looked at the door, which was riddled and splintered and lay off its hinges. This damage had obviously been done by the M–16, but who the hell had been firing the thing? Had Jig somehow been trapped inside this room and forced to shoot his way out?

Pagan could hear Zuboric sloshing around in the living-room. The aquatic sleuth. What the hell did he think he was going to find amidst puddles of salt water and slivers of broken glass and the demolished innards of an expensive stereo system?

Pagan turned his attention to the surface of the desk. A variety of papers lay around in disarray, most of them computer printouts with references to ostmarks, roubles and zlotys. If Linney dabbled in Communist currencies, what Pagan wondered was just how much of this funny money found its way, via the United States, into Ireland. Nicholas Linney gathered roubles here, coaxed ostmarks there, and sent them, suitably converted into US currency, to the IRA, using Joseph X. Tumulty as a link in the chain. But how long was that chain? And where did it reach?

Pagan looked at the illuminated screen of a computer console. There was a name and address in amber letters. Pagan stared at it in wonderment. Jock Mulhaney. Mulhaney was known even in Britain for his good-will publicity tour of Ireland, both North and South, when he'd made a tour of what the press called 'the trouble spots', giving impressive speeches in small border towns about how the real tragedy of Ireland was unemployment. At the time, carried away by his own rhetoric, Big Jock had pledged to do what he could about steering US industry into Ireland, which was a promise he could never deliver upon. Ignoring the fact that he had a vested interest in keeping jobs in America, the Irish considered Big Jock something of a proletarian hero. And here he was on Linney's little screen. Well, well.

Connections.

Pagan stared at the keyboard. There was a scroll key, which he touched rather gingerly, because he didn't have an easy rapport with the new technology. The screen whisked Big Jock's name away, replacing it suddenly with two others.

Pagan gazed at the letters with astonishment. The amber treasure trove of information. He felt a sudden quickening of his nerves as he recognised the names that glimmered in front of him. More connections. Lovely connections. He scribbled them down on a piece of paper torn from Linney's printer, then put the paper inside his pocket. He heard the sound of Zuboric coming back across the living-room. He quickly scanned the keyboard, looking for an off key, anything to kill the screen before Zuboric came inside the room.

There was no way he was going to share this stuff with the FBI agent. He couldn't find an appropriate key so he yanked the plug out of the wall and the screen went wonderfully blank, carrying the names of Kevin Dawson and Harry Cairney off into some electronic limbo. With a look of innocence, Frank Pagan turned to see Zuboric enter.

'Here's the way I see it,' Zuboric said. 'Jig comes in. He gets inside the gun-room somehow. Something goes wrong. Maybe Linney says he doesn't know anything about the money. Who knows? Jig becomes more than a little upset and decides to vent some spleen, the results of which are obvious,' and Zuboric made a loose gesture with his hand. 'Put it another way, Frank. Your cunning, clever assassin, the guy you seem to admire so much, is no better than a fucking fruitcake going berserk inside a crowded tenement on a hot summer evening in Harlem with a cheap twenty-two in his hand.'

'It's one scenario,' Pagan answered, still thinking about the names on Linney's computer. Connections, threads linking one powerful name with another. 'It's not the only one, Artie. Even if you're half in love with it.'

'Frank Pagan, attorney for the defence,' Zuboric said.

Pagan clenched his large hands. There was this terrible urge to hit Zuboric. Nothing damaging, nothing that would leave an ungodly bruise or break a bone, just a straight solid punch that would silence the guy for a time. Zuboric's attitudes, his way of doing business, were beginning to pall.

Zuboric, who didn't like the expression on Pagan's face, turned away. 'You can also assume Jig's armed by now,' he said. 'He sure as hell wouldn't leave without helping himself to a gun or two. Don't you wish you'd shot the fucker when you had the chance?'

Pagan understood the process going on here. Jig was going to be blamed for this massacre, and he, Pagan, was standing nicely in line to take some of the heat as well. That was the Bureau's tactic. When things go wrong, blame Frank Pagan. And all the blue-eyed boys in Leonard Korn's Army stayed Kleenex-fresh.

'Jig didn't do this,' he said.

Zuboric had a thin smile on his face. 'You say. How do you know what Jig did or didn't do?'

It was a fair question and one Frank Pagan had no specific answer for.

'And that killing in Albany,' Zuboric said. 'How can you say it wasn't Jig?' The agent shook his head. 'I'll tell you. He's on a goddam rampage, Frank. He's got the taste of blood in his mouth.'

'And that's what you'll tell Washington?'

'I'll give them my considered opinion,' Zuboric said.

Pagan saw Zuboric step out of the room, heard him move inside the kitchen. There was the sound of the telephone being lifted. Then Zuboric was talking in a low voice.

Pagan looked at the body of Nicholas Linney. He wished somebody in this house could come back, even on a temporary basis, from death, and tell him the exact truth about what had happened here. But there were only stilled pulses and hearts that no longer beat and voices forever silenced.

Camp David, Maryland

It was five o'clock in the afternoon before Thomas Dawson finally met with Leonard M. Korn. The President didn't like to conduct business on a Saturday, which was the day he habitually set aside for reading, catching up on the voluminous amount of material his aides and cabinet members prepared for him. It was a bleak afternoon, already dark, and there was a nasty rain slicing through the trees around the Presidential compound at Camp David. Leonard M. Korn, who arrived in a black limousine, had the kind of presence that made a dark day darker still. What was it about him? Dawson wondered. He somehow seemed to absorb all the light around him and never release it, like a black mirror.

When Korn stepped inside the Presidential quarters, Dawson was lounging on a sofa wearing blue jeans and boots and a plaid flannel shirt, all purchased from L. L. Bean. He sat upright, shuffled some papers, smiled coldly at Korn. Korn was a leftover from the previous administration, an appointee made by Dawson's predecessor who'd been a Republican in the cowboy tradition, an old man who dreamed nights of a world policed by US gunboats.

'Take a pew,' the President said.

Korn sat stiffly in his black gaberdine overcoat. He removed several sheets of paper from his briefcase.

'Here is the information we've gathered on the casualties,' he said, thrusting the sheets towards Thomas Dawson, who waved them aside.

'Suppose you give me the details briefly, Len,' Dawson said. His eyes were tired from reading reports on such arcane matters as the butter glut in the Midwest, farm foreclosures on the Great Plains, proposals to alter corporate tax structures.

'Nicholas Linney ran a company called Urrisbeg International,' Korn said. 'Linney had fingers in a great many pies, Mr President.'

Korn paused. Dawson had grown immune to the clichés of language that surrounded him on a daily basis. A great many pies. Too many cooks. People in glass houses. Imaginative language was the first casualty of any bureaucracy.

'He had been investigated by Treasury two years ago. There was some suspicion of illegal dealing in foreign currencies,' Korn said. 'East European mainly. He was cleared.'

Thomas Dawson nodded. He remembered Nicholas Linney well, and the recollection troubled him. He stood up. Once or twice, in the years before he had become President, he had played tennis with Nick Linney at fund-raising tournaments that were described under the general umbrella of Celebrity Invitationals. The celebrities were always ambitious politicians, game-show hosts, bargain-basement actors and tired comedians who had bought real estate in Palm Springs when that place was just a stopover in the desert. He squeezed his eyes shut very tightly. He was thinking of his brother now. He wished he'd never heard of the Fund-raisers. He wished even more that Kevin had stuck to running the family empire, keeping his nose out of Irish matters, and staying away from people like Linney.

'The second male victim was Gustav Rasch,' Korn said. 'An East Berlin party hack. He came to the US periodically. General gopher. Sometimes he wanted to buy a piece of US technology. Sometimes he wanted to tout a touring ballet company.'

Leonard M. Korn placed the sheets flat on the briefcase that lay on his lap. The expression on the Presidential face struck him as a little queasy, sea-sick.

'Linney was involved in raising funds to be sent to Ireland,' Korn continued. 'This much we've learned. As for Rasch, perhaps he was an investor, perhaps not. It doesn't matter very much at this stage, especially to Gustav Rasch. The two dead girls were probably Linney's personal harlots. He imported them from Cambodia as housemaids. They simply got in Jig's way.'

Harlots, Dawson thought. Quaint puritanical word. He remembered Nick Linney's fondness for oriental girls. He coughed quietly into his hand then asked, 'Can we assume Jig retrieved the stolen money and has returned to Ireland?' It was the kind of question a man asked with his fingers crossed.

Leonard M. Korn shook his head, as if the question were too naïve to contemplate. 'We can't assume anything, Mr President. If Linney didn't have the money, Jig would go looking elsewhere for it. It's that simple. Until we have evidence to the contrary we have to work on the understanding that he's still in the country, still actively searching. And the killing isn't going to stop. One man in Albany isn't very significant. But four people in Bridgehampton – well, that's a different kettle of fish.'

Dawson walked to the window. He'd never seen fish in a kettle in his whole life. Outside, under the rainy trees, Secret Servicemen stood around like drenched though vigilant birds. He thought of the two men he had supplied to brother Kevin. He wondered if, in the circumstances, two was enough.

'Do you have any suggestions?' Dawson turned to look at Korn.

Leonard M. Korn stood up. In his platform shoes, which were made specially for him by a discreet shoemaker on Atlantic Avenue in Virginia Beach, he stood five foot nine inches tall. It wasn't imposing but the shaved head added a quality of menace to his appearance.

Korn took a deep breath. 'Thus far, my agency has had only minimal involvement. As per your own instructions, sir. And thus far the show has been run, so to speak, by the Englishman Pagan. With marked lack of success.' He lowered his voice on this last sentence, a tone he hoped would not presume to question the President's judgement. 'I'd advise a fullscale manhunt,' he went on. 'I could activate every available agent in and around New York. That way, I firmly believe we could see conclusive results, which is something we haven't been getting from Frank Pagan.'

Thomas Dawson returned to the sofa and sat down. He understood Korn's need to blame this character Pagan, but the idea of a fullscale manhunt was totally unacceptable. Given the Bureau's heavy-handedness, there would inevitably be publicity. And where you had publicity you also had public reaction, which was a scandalously fickle barometer.

He was certain of only one thing. He was not about to alienate his precious, dependable Irish-American Catholic vote. So slender was the margin between further residency in the White House and the unseemly role of useless ex-President, fitted out in pathetic plaid knickerbockers and paraded on the golf circuit, that Dawson needed all the support he could muster. Publicity would be fine for Korn and his Bureau, especially if Jig were landed in the FBI net. But it could well be another matter for Thomas Dawson. Things were getting out of hand, admittedly, but he was going to turn down Korn's gung-ho suggestion.

'I'll think about it,' he finally said.

An objection formed on Korn's lips, but he said nothing. He understood the meeting was over. He was waiting only for the President to dismiss him.

'In the meantime,' Dawson said, 'we continue to play it all very quietly. *Sotto voce.*'

Korn nodded. Although he wondered how long it could continue to be played *sotto voce*, he wasn't going to voice this aloud. Presidents, like sticks of dynamite, had to be handled with care. They needed flattery, reassurance, agreement.

'Thanks for coming, Len,' Dawson said. 'Remember. Quietly. Very quietly. And keep me informed.'

When Korn had gone, Thomas Dawson lay down on the sofa and stared at the rain sweeping the window. He thought again of Kevin. If Jig had found his way to Linney, how long before he reached Kevin?

He pondered the prospect of calling Kevin. He had given his brother two seasoned Secret Servicemen – what else could he possibly do? If he stepped up the Secret Service detachment at his brother's house, for example, sooner or later somebody was going to notice. There was always somebody, deep in a Washington cellar, who kept tabs on such things. There were always gossip columnists as well, who were drawn like doomed little moths to the Dawson flame and who were never very far from the centre of Kevin's life.

Dawson-Watchers who reported each and every Dawson social engagement with a shrill passion and who knew, courtesy of their sensitive antennae and inside informers, the things that went on around Kevin's household. And if these snoops observed a goddam battalion of Secret Servicemen lingering in New Rockford, they'd be pecking away at their portable Olivettis like a crowd of clucking birds.

The trouble with being President of the United States, he thought, was the sheer weight of the secrets you felt you had to keep. Jig's presence in the country, the murder of Nicholas Linney, Kevin's fund-raising activities. It was all just a little too much.

There was one simple solution to the immediate problem of Kevin's safety, and when it occurred to him he picked up the telephone and dialled his brother's number in Connecticut. It was answered by the woman who ran the Dawson household in New Rockford, an old family retainer named Agatha Bates. Agatha, ageless and humourless, was one of those stiffbacked examples of New England spinster who were bred less frequently these days. She had been connected with the Dawson family one way or another for most of her life.

'Kevin's gone,' she said. She wasn't impressed by young Tommy being President. He'd always been the least of the Dawsons in her mind. Too ambitious. Too sneaky. Character flaws.

'Gone?'

'Took the family,' she said.

'Where?'

'Up to the cabin.'

The cabin was a primitive wooden shack located thirty miles from Lake Candlewood. It was a place without electricity. No telephone. No amenities. It was where Kevin took his wife and kids when he wanted privacy, when he felt the need to retreat. Kevin had this notion, which Thomas Dawson found quaint and yet politically useful at times, about family unity, togetherness. He was always dragging Martha and the girls out into the wilderness. Backpacking, camping, fishing, communing with nature.

'Did he say when he was coming back, Agatha?'

'Sunday night,' she answered.

'What time?'

'Didn't say. And I didn't ask. Just threw some stuff into the station wagon and left. The two men from Washington went up there with him.'

'Fine,' Dawson said. 'I'll call him Sunday night.'

He put the receiver down. At least Kevin would be safe up at Lake Candlewood with the Secret Servicemen protecting him. At least he'd be safe until he returned to New Rockford, which was when Thomas Dawson was going to suggest that Hawaii or the Virgin Islands would be a pleasant change of pace this time of year.

19 New York City

Frank Pagan did not get the chance to think about the information he'd taken from Nicholas Linney's computer until nine o'clock in the evening. There had been delays in Bridgehampton while Zuboric, looking extremely secretive, hung around waiting for the telephone to ring with instructions from God in Washington. There had also been a visit from two men who drove a rather anonymous van and who carted the corpses away in plastic bags. When the phone finally rang at approximately seven-thirty, hours after they'd first arrived in Bridgehampton, Zuboric spoke into it briefly then hung up. It was apparent that no new instructions were forthcoming from Washington, at least for the time being.

They drove back into the city in the green Cadillac, Zuboric subdued and thoughtful. He escorted Pagan inside the Parker Meridien, his manner that of a male nurse attending a certifiable lunatic.

'Stay home, Frank. I'll be in touch.'

Pagan stepped inside an elevator and was glad when the doors slid shut. He locked himself inside his room and lay for a while on the bed. He took the piece of paper out of his coat and stared at it, smiling at the idea of slipping something past the vigilant Arthur. As his eyes scanned his scrawled handwriting, he couldn't help thinking of the dead girls again. The direction of his thoughts irked him. You could see everything through a prism of grief if you wanted to, you could dwell on morbid associations, but it was a hell of a way to live a life.

He called room service and had them send up a bottle of Vat 69, a scotch sometimes referred to as the Pope's phone number. He half-hoped that Mandi with an 'i' would appear in the doorway, but the scotch was finally delivered by a young Greek whose English was riddled with fault-lines.

Pagan poured himself a generous glass, dropped in some ice. Harry Cairney. Kevin Dawson. Jock Mulhaney. All good Irish lads and perfect candidates for raising and dispersing IRA funds. Who else could they be but Nicholas Linney's comrades? Harry Cairney, the retired Senator from New York, had been part of that Irish Mafia in Washington which included Congressman Tip O'Neill and Senator Moynihan. He had served on various committees that had pumped funds into the Republic of Ireland. It seemed perfectly natural that the retired Senator, under the surface of his public persona, would be involved in something a little darker than political gestures of good-will. And Kevin Dawson, the President's baby brother, had made several trips to Ireland to pay homage to the Dawson ancestry. The visits were always surrounded by tight security and excessive publicity. The Irish loved Kevin and his family and adored Kevin's loyalty to the country of his heritage. He was shown such adulation in Ireland that it must have gone straight to his brain and perhaps compensated somewhat for any sense of inferiority he might have felt about his brother's prominence. Sigmund Pagan.

Pagan closed his eyes. The next step was the question of what to do with the knowledge. He wasn't going to enlist the help of Zuboric, he was sure of that. Their reluctant marriage of convenience was heading down the slipway to divorce. Artie's problem was obvious – he accepted as gospel the first solution he thought of, and nothing could make a dent. For example, his unshakable conviction that Jig was responsible for the slaughter in Bridgehampton – there was just no way in the world to make Artie consider alternatives. He didn't have the imagination for them. Besides, it was easier to lay the blame on Jig than go to the trouble of exploring other possibilities. There was something of lazy discontent in Artie's makeup, the death of natural curiosity, a dangerous thing for a man licensed to carry a gun and use it.

Pagan thought of the zigzagging geographical patterns involved here. New Rockford. Brooklyn. Rhinebeck. Why couldn't it have been convenient – Cairney and Dawson and Mulhaney all under one roof right here next door to The Russian Tea Room? Sure. But what then? Would he have gone to them and sat them all down nicely and talked to them of Jig? *If you happen to run into Jig, be a sport and let me know?* They would deny any association with the act of collecting funds for Ireland. They were secretive men accustomed to operating furtively, and each was a public figure. They weren't going to want their Irish activities made common knowledge. If you ever broached the subject with them, they were bound to look as if they'd never heard of Ireland, let alone the Irish Republican Army.

What the fuck had really happened in that Bridgehampton house anyway? He wondered now if Jig had discovered the same names from the same source, Linney's wonderful computer. If he had, there was no way of knowing which of the three men he would visit next. Besides, there was also no way of knowing if Nicholas Linney had been able to point Jig in the direction of the missing money. *It's buried under a tree in my back yard, Jig. It's banked in Zurich and here's the account number.* You had to work on the assumption that Jig was out there still hunting and that sooner or later he would pay a visit to the names on Linney's list. But when? To guess Jig's movements was close to impossible, even for Frank Pagan who had made a study of his prey like a meteorologist examining shifts in the wind. Finally, there was just no certainty.

He stood up, moved absently around the room. Problems had a habit of multiplying. Now he thought of the man called Fitzjohn garrotted in Albany. And Ivor the Terrible sitting cosily over in the Essex House. You could play with these threads all the goddam day. You could ruin your health. The link he especially didn't like was the one that seemingly connected Fitzjohn with Ivor. That whole FUV thing troubled him. Ivor McInnes's presence bugged him. Why the *hell* was he here at the same time as Jig? And why had the FUV informed Pagan that Jig was in the US anyway? He kept returning to this particular conundrum, although now it had become more complicated with the murder of Fitzjohn. He was irritable and jumpy and filled with the urge to cut through all the mystifying shit at one stroke, as if all the various questions in his mind were in reality one huge question, something that could be resolved with one equally huge answer. *Give me the simple life.*

What was Fitzjohn doing in Albany? Why had he been murdered? What came back to Pagan again and again was the notion that Ivor McInnes was the key to these questions. That if you could get inside Ivor's head the mysteries would begin to dissolve. The idea of the descent into Ivor's mind wasn't an exactly pleasant prospect, but then nothing about this whole business was what you might call delightful. Pagan picked up the telephone, called Foxworth's home number in Fulham, rousing the young man from inebriated sleep. Foxworth loved to dig into the data banks, which he did with all the enthusiasm of a fanatical mechanic getting inside the engine of a car.

'Get your arse over to the office,' Pagan said. 'I need some information. The name is Alex Fitzjohn. Got it?'

'My arse is hungover,' Foxie complained, his voice made small by distance and drink.

'Move it, sonnie. I'll call you back in a couple of hours.'

'Yes, master.'

Pagan hung up. He was tired but the inside of his head had come to resemble a pinball machine in which balls ricochetted maddeningly back and forth. He looked at his precious piece of paper again. Mulhaney wasn't far away. Brooklyn was nearer than either Rhinebeck or New Rockford, Connecticut. Would it do any good to go and talk to Mulhaney? Or simply to stake out the place where Mulhaney lived? Pagan was undecided. If Jig decided not to go to Brooklyn but went instead to either Rhinebeck or New Rockford, you would be wasting a great deal of time. This whole dilemma needed a small army of men, and Pagan knew he wasn't going to get them from Zuboric. Nor did he want them, not if they were afflicted by Zuboric's lack of insight. It wasn't the first time in Frank Pagan's career that he wished he were more than one individual. Three or four Pagans, clones, would have been useful.

Where now? he wondered. What next? He couldn't just *sit* here in his room. And it made no sense to visit Ivor until he had some word on Fitzjohn.

He wondered what Brooklyn looked like at night.

He put his overcoat on and stepped out into the corridor. He rode the elevator to the third floor, got out, took the stairs. He knew Zuboric would have a man nearby, maybe Orson Cone or good old Tyson Bruno, probably seated right now in the piano bar, chewing peanuts and nursing a Virgin Mary and watching for a sight of the tricky Pagan. Crossing the lobby, Pagan found himself surrounded by a jabbering party of fashionable French tourists who were seemingly agitated about the non-arrival of their luggage from Air France and were talking litigation, in the intensely shrill way of excited Parisians. Pagan merged smoothly with the French party. It was good cover – though not absolutely good enough. He saw Tyson Bruno come hurrying across the lobby towards him, coat flapping, face anxious. Pagan smiled and gave Bruno a victory sign even as Tyson, looking altogether unhappy with the course of events, collided with one of the Parisians, a woman who might have stepped from the pages of *Elle*.

Pagan hurried past the front desk and out on to Fifty-Seventh Street and then he was lost in the inscrutable Manhattan night as he headed, with a bright feeling of truancy, towards the place where he'd parked his Cadillac.

White Plains, New York

The Memorial Presbyterian Church dated from the early years of the twentieth century. A large white frame construction with a steeple and a cast-iron bell that hadn't yet been replaced by an electronic sound system, it occupied a huge corner lot of prime White Plains real estate. Its congregation had dwindled steadily over the years and now numbered about three hundred and fifty members, of which two hundred or so were active churchgoers. Adorned by stained-glass windows, an enormous organ, and polished mahogany pews, it was a rich church, a highly profitable enterprise which received generous endowments from the estates of past members. During the hours of darkness, a solitary floodlight shone upwards at the steeple, bathing the front of the church in a white light that suggested purity and cleanliness. One might imagine God himself perched up there in a place beyond the light, a materialisation of spirit just out of the range of the human eye.

John Waddell, who had always been a religious man despite the violent deaths of his wife and child – which might have damaged any man's faith – thought that Memorial Presbyterian was like no other church he'd ever seen. He was accustomed to grubby little halls, joylessly dark places of worship in Belfast, where the hymnbooks fell apart in your hands and the congregation sang in a dirgelike way and everything smelled of gloomy dampness. Memorial, on the other hand, might have passed as God's private residence. Waddell was awed by the artful floodlight and the shadows up there in the belfry. Inside, after McGrath had forced a rear door open, Waddell was overwhelmed by the beauty of stained-glass and the rich reflective wood of pews and pulpit and the way the pipes of the vast organ rose up into vaulted shadows. He felt humbled. He had an urge to sit in one of the pews and pray. Only Houlihan's impatient glance prevented him.

All day long Seamus had been in a grim mood. It was connected, Waddell guessed, with the disappearance of Fitzjohn. Suddenly, in the night, Fitzjohn had gone. Nobody asked questions, though. Nobody went up to Houlihan to inquire about Fitz, because Seamus had that look on his face which meant *don't fuck with me*. Now, as he ran a hand over the smooth surface of a pew, Waddell watched Houlihan move towards the pulpit. McGrath was standing and staring at the reaches of the organ pipes. Rorke, fingering the scar on his face, looked bewildered by the whole display of Presbyterian opulence. Wasn't Presbyterianism meant to be a grim little religion with no display of ostentation? Not here in America. Nobody in the Land of Plenty wanted to buy the original Scottish package, which was spare and hard and gritty and had been exported intact to Northern Ireland by the fervent followers of John Knox and Calvin. But Americans preferred a little comfort with their God. There were even pillows lining the pews!

'It's like a chapel,' Rorke said, referring to Roman Catholic churches. 'It's like a fucking Fenian chapel.'

Houlihan stood in the pulpit. Waddell thought he looked satanic up there.

'Get over to the organ,' Houlihan said to Rorke, who moved immediately, stopping only when he reached the keyboard.

Waddell, raised in a tradition where the authority of the Protestant Church was unquestionable, sacrosanct, thought it odd to hear voices raised beyond a whisper. And Rorke's earlier profanity was wildly out of place. But there was a whole uncharted area here that confused John Waddell. On the one hand, there was the Ulster cause. On the other, the authority of the Protestant Church. Normally, these went hand in hand without causing him any kind of dilemma. But now, now that he knew what Houlihan was planning to do in this place, he felt a curious sense of division. In the end he knew he'd go along with Seamus, because that was what he always did, but the doubts he entertained were not easily cast off. The work Seamus planned to do here was something unusual for the FUV, something that ran at a right angle to Waddell's understanding of the Volunteers. If Memorial were a Catholic church – no problem. But it wasn't. It wasn't a Roman church.

Houlihan came down from the pulpit. 'We don't have all fucking night,' he said. 'I'd like to get this done and get the hell out of here.'

Waddell listened to the vague echo made by the sound of Houlihan's sneakers. Every small sound was amplified inside this place. As a kid he'd imagined that if you swore in church God's long finger – a huge talon in the boy's mind – would come down out of the sky and pierce you. He wasn't so very far removed from this kind of image now. He felt dread. The thing they were doing here was wrong, no matter how you looked at it. And God was still up there, sinister and birdlike, His claw ready to strike.

Houlihan approached. He seemed very tall in the dim interior of the church. 'What's *your* problem?' he asked.

Waddell said, 'I just don't like being here, that's all.'

Houlihan smiled. 'You're a superstitious wee fart, Waddy. Because I like you as much as I do, I'm going to let you in on a secret.' Houlihan brought his face very close. 'There's no such thing as God. Or if there is, he fell asleep a long time ago.'

Waddell returned the young man's smile although rather nervously. He would have followed Houlihan to the gates of hell and back, but this was the first time Seamus had ever spoken so openly about his religious attitudes. Waddell traced the line of the organ pipes up into the ceiling. You could imagine Something stirring up there in the darkness, no matter what Seamus thought.

'God's for nuns, John,' Houlihan said. 'God's for priests and nuns and RCs. And if he exists he's become so bloody addicted to incense fumes by this time his mind's addled. So lets get this fucking show on the road. Okay?'

John Waddell nodded. Across the vast stretches of the pews he saw Rorke bent under the keyboard of the organ. McGrath, standing close to Rorke, wore a backpack from which he took an object that he passed down to Rorke. The scarfaced man grunted and took it.

'Are we ready?' Houlihan asked.

'Aye. Just about,' McGrath called back.

John Waddell held his breath. He had never wanted to be out of a place so badly in all his life. There was the sudden sound of air escaping from the organ pipes. It was a single musical note that echoed briefly.

'Jesus Christ,' Houlihan said.

'Sorry,' Rorke mumbled. 'Accident.'

'Clumsy bastard,' Houlihan said.

Waddell could hear the echo of that single note, so deep, so profound, long after it was inaudible to anyone else inside the church. He had the distinct feeling that Somebody was trying to tell him something.

Brooklyn, New York

Big Jock Mulhaney had spent his professional life pumping flesh and slapping backs and eating chicken dinners at fund-raisers. He was a gregarious animal, at home in the company of men, sharing a confidence here, eliciting a favour there, joking, smoking, and yet always scanning the company for the important faces the way a bat will use radar to seek out prey.

Mulhaney, who sipped a glass of wine and chomped on his cigar, was presently seated at the head table in his own banquet hall, a very large room inside his union's headquarters in Brooklyn. Teamster Tower had been constructed in 1975 to Jock's specifications. Apart from the banquet hall, it contained a dancehall, five reception rooms, six floors of offices and, perched at the very top, Jock's private quarters, a two-storey penthouse decorated in what Jock's fag designer called 'oatmeal', but which Mulhaney referred to as porridge. He adjusted his cummerbund and stared across the diners at the other tables.

The event taking place was the annual March bash, a stag affair Jock threw for the prominent Irish members of the union the week before St Patrick's Day. In the course of the year, the Italians, Poles, Scandies and Latinos would all have dinners of their own, but the Irish one was closest to Mulhaney's heart. The diners, some three hundred of them, had eaten their way through a menu of Dublin coddle, imported Dublin prawn, french fries and mint-green gelato, and now they were embarking on the important course of the meal, Irish coffee.

The Irish-Americans in the banquet hall belonged to scores of different organisations. The Loyal Order of Hibernia, The Sons of Killarney, The Ancient Order of St Patrick, The Society of Galwaymen, The Loyal Boys of Wexford, The Clans of Kilkenny. Some of them wore green sashes with gold lettering attesting to their particular affiliation. There were even a couple of local priests, men made red-facedly benign by brandy. Mulhaney, who was a member of every society, who joined clubs and fraternities like a man with no tomorrows, had a simple green shamrock in the lapel of his tux.

The waiters moved swiftly around dispensing Irish coffee when it was time for Jock's speech. Six brandies and a bottle of fine claret inside him, he stood up and acknowledged the round of applause from the tables. His people were blindly loyal to him. He gazed cheerfully across the faces, cleared his throat, held up his hands for silence. He had a standard speech he made every year at the same time with only minor variations.

He rambled on a while about union solidarity, made a token reference to the state of unionism in the Soviet countries, spoke with embarrassing nostalgia about his mother and the way she had with Irish stew back in the old days in Boston, and then asked for a moment of prayer for peace in the Old Country. After that, he suggested everyone adjourn to the bar and listen to the live music, which was provided every year by three middle-aged men from Cork who called themselves The Paul Street Brothers, after a famous thoroughfare in their native city. The room cleared out. The corridors become clogged with men seeking fresh drinks in the commodious bar established in one of the reception rooms, where the musicians were already singing *If You Ever Go Across The Sea to Oireland* . . .

Patrick Cairney, who sat at the back of the room alongside the contingent from Union City, New Jersey, considered the speech the tiresome kind of thing Harry might have loved. He went out into the corridor, pressed on all sides by men wearing green sashes. The cigar smoke and brandy fumes created an altogether dizzying perfume that suggested the complacency of affluence. They were all affluent men here with soft hands. There was nobody in this assembly who laid bricks or carried hods or dug ditches these days. Cairney, who had a plastic shamrock fixed to the lapel of his dark blue suit, watched Mulhaney work the crowd.

Big Jock pumped flesh vigorously, traded jokes, heard secrets whispered in his ear, promised a favour here, a favour there. He was like some pontiff strolling through a herd of lowly cardinals. It wouldn't have been surprising to see somebody's mouth pressed against his ring.

Now Jock shoved his way towards the bar where a waiter immediately served him a double brandy on a silver tray. Unlike the lesser prelates, the minor bishops and the insignificant abbots, Mulhaney didn't have to stand in line. He had a confidential conversation with a member from Buffalo, he made expansive promises to a man from Schuylerville, and he swore on his mother's grave he'd hammer certain fuckers to the wall when it came time to negotiate a new contract on behalf of his members in Wilmington, Delaware. He was basking in warmth, smoke, adulation, and the glow of good drink in his body. There was a narcotic effect here he couldn't get anywhere else. It was the life of Riley, and he'd worked damn hard to get here, and what he felt now was that he deserved every second of it. This was his world, and he dominated it like a large red sun.

'How did my speech go?' Mulhaney asked one of the priests, knowing the answer in advance.

'It was *choost* delightful. Delightful,' the priest answered, happy to fawn on Mulhaney, who provided the best free cuisine in the whole diocese.

Patrick Cairney stood against the wall. The music was deafening. The hubbub of voices droned in his head relentlessly. He lightly touched the gun he carried inside the waistband of his pants. The problem here was to get Mulhaney alone. It would come. Even if he had to conceal himself inside the building until the party was finally over, the moment would come. He continued to observe Mulhaney, who was now standing face to face with a priest. Both men had clearly drunk too much.

Cairney closed his eyes a moment. He was thinking about Nicholas Linney and trying not to. And those two dead girls. That whole thing in Bridgehampton had been a disaster. No, it was more, disaster was too feeble, too mild for the carnage that had gone on in that house. He remembered Linney's face at the moment when he'd blown half the head off, the torrent of blood, the abrupt searing of the man's scalp, the splinters of bone and gristle that hurled themselves against the wall.

He couldn't let these images plague him now. He couldn't afford to. He wanted to salvage something here in Brooklyn, provided Mulhaney didn't go in for amateur heroics. He didn't look as if he had the kind of *edge* Linney had had. Just the same, Cairney was thankful he was armed. He opened his eyes, remembering Frank Pagan arriving in Bridgehampton and wondering if the Englishman were somewhere nearby now. If so, he'd have to work fast. He'd have to get information out of Mulhaney quickly if he could, which was where the gun would be useful to him.

There was a tension inside him, when what he needed most was cool. *Don't be your own worst enemy,* Finn said once. *A man like Jig has so many real enemies, he doesn't need to make himself one.*

Jock Mulhaney drained his brandy glass and, still shaking outstretched hands, rubbing shoulders, exchanging pleasantries, made his way out along the hallway. His bladder ached from all the drink he'd consumed. He walked quickly in the direction of the toilets. The first one he came to was jammed. Standing room only and an atmosphere heady with urine and cigars. He backed out of it. He went towards the reception area, passing silent desks and covered typewriters and unlit lamps. There was a bathroom here the receptionists used. He liked the notion of skipping inside a woman's john.

Cairney saw the big man slip along the corridor and followed quietly. The band was playing *Kitty of Coleraine*. Mulhaney had paused outside a door marked LADIES. He appeared uncertain about whether to go inside or not. Cairney was conscious of the vast expanse of the reception area and the black street beyond the plate-glass windows and the limousines parked out there. *Go inside, Mulhaney. Open the door, go in. Let's be alone a moment, you and I.* The moment he wanted was coming sooner than he'd expected.

Mulhaney stepped into the toilet, noticing a tampon machine and a dispenser of packaged colognes and the fact that all the cubicles were empty, their doors lying open. He moved inside one of the cubicles. He unzipped, emptied his bladder, flushed his cigar butt away. He rinsed his hands, dried them under a hot-air machine which roared inside the empty toilet, and hummed the tune the band was playing.

He was leaning towards the mirror and fluffing his thick hairpiece with a comb when the door swung open behind him. He saw a young man come in. Dark hair, blue suit, well built, unknown to Mulhaney. But with three hundred guests here, how could he know everybody?

'Good speech,' the young man said.

Mulhaney smiled. He slapped the young man on the back.

'We've met before,' Mulhaney said. He had a practised way of pretending to remember everyone, as if names were forever on the tip of his tongue. 'Aren't you with the Syracuse contingent?'

The young man shook his head. 'I don't think we've ever met.'

'I never forget a face.' Mulhaney farted very quietly just then, and looked cheerful. 'Better an empty house than a bad tenant, huh?'

'Right.' Cairney turned on the cold water faucet full blast but made no move to dip his hand in the stream.

Mulhaney gazed into the fast-running stream of water a second. He was conscious of the way the young man stared at him in the mirror. What was it about the intensity in those hard brown eyes that disturbed Mulhaney just then? He turned away from the young man, which was when he felt a circle of pressure against the base of his spine and the warmth of the man's breath upon the back of his neck. Glancing into the mirror, Mulhaney saw the gleam of the pistol pressed into his back. Horrified, he heard himself gasp, felt his body slacken. In his entire lifetime it was the first time anyone had ever pulled a gun on him. How did some fucking mugger find his way inside this place?

'My inside pocket,' he said. 'The wallet. Take the whole fucking wallet. There's probably a couple hundred bucks in it.'

The young man jammed the gun hard against the backbone. 'I'm looking for more than that, Jock,' he said.

Pain brought moisture into Mulhaney's eyes. There was an awful moment here when he felt himself slip into cracks of darkness, saw his own hearse roll through the streets of Brooklyn, heard Father Donovan of All Saints deliver the graveside eulogy in that hollow voice of his – *He was a flawed man, but a good one*. Even imagined the *wake*, for Chrissakes, boiled ham and stale sandwiches curling and flat Guinness and drunks babbling over his open coffin.

'Jesus Christ,' Mulhaney said. Darkness had become realisation. And realisation brought him a sense of horror. *This young man was The One*.

'Linney said you took the cash.'

'Linney?'

'Don't bluff it out with me, Jock. Just point me to the money.'

'I don't have it, Linney's a fucking liar.'

The gun went deeper this time. Mulhaney, catching a glimpse of his face in the mirror, barely recognised himself. His big red face had turned pale like a skinless beet boiled in angry water.

'Where is it?' the young man asked.

'I told you, I don't know,' and Mulhaney wondered why nobody was looking for him, why his goons weren't stalking the goddam corridors for him right now. God knows, they were paid enough to take care of him.

The pressure of the gun was enormous. Mulhaney thought it would bore a hole in his spine. The young man sighed. 'I'm tired, Jock. And I don't have a whole lot of time.'

'I don't know where the money is, I swear it.'

Cairney thought about bringing the gun up, smacking it against Mulhaney's head. Something to underline his seriousness. Some token violence. It was tempting, and he felt pressured, but he didn't do it, didn't like the idea of it. He just kept the pistol riveted to Mulhaney's spine and hoped he wouldn't have to use force.

'Linney said you took it. Talk to me, Jock. Talk fast. Don't make me hurt you.'

Mulhaney twisted his head around, looked at the young man. It occurred to him that he could play for time here. Sooner or later somebody was going to come looking for him. He could stall, though the hard light in the man's eyes suggested that stalling was a precarious business. But he didn't like the position he was in and he didn't care for being at someone else's mercy, and his pride, that cavernous place where he lived his life, was hurt. And he hadn't scratched his way to the top of the union without having more than his share of sheer Irish pig-headedness.

'You're not going to walk out of here,' he said and his voice was stronger now. 'You're not going to walk away from this, friend. I've got a small army out there. I've got people who take care of me.'

Cairney rammed the pistol deeper into Mulhaney's flesh and the big man moaned. 'I don't have time for this, Jock. Tell me what I need to know and I'm gone.'

'Look, Linney's a liar. Linney wouldn't know the truth if it hit him in the goddam eyes. He makes shit up all the goddam time. If he sent you here it was to make a fucking idiot out of you.'

Cairney felt the intensity of fluorescent light against the top of his head. *'Where's the money?'* There was a note of desperation in the sound of his question. He didn't like it, didn't like the way he had begun to sound and feel. He knew that at any moment somebody was bound to come inside the room, that his time alone with Mulhaney was very limited.

'I won't ask you again, Jock.'

Mulhaney thought he had seen something in the young man's eyes. A certain indecision. The signs of some inner turmoil. He said, 'Even if I knew anything, do you honestly think I'd fucking tell *you*?

Cairney brought the gun up and smacked it against Mulhaney's mouth. Blood flowed out of Big Jock's lips and over the small shamrock he wore in his lapel. The pain Mulhaney felt was more humiliating than insufferable. He lost his balance and went down on his knees. His expensive bridgework, three thousand dollars worth of dental artistry, slid from his mouth and lay cracked on the tiled floor. He reached for it, but Cairney kicked it away, and the pink plate and the gold inlays and the plastic teeth went slithering towards one of the cubicles where it struck the pedestal of a toilet and broke completely apart.

'Jesus Christ,' Mulhaney muttered.

Cairney was trembling slightly. He felt sweat under his collar. He shoved the gun against Mulhaney's forehead and pressed it hard upon the bone. 'Talk, Mulhaney. And make it fast.'

Mulhaney, whose vanity was as enormous as his pride, covered his empty mouth with his hand. There were streaks of blood between his fingers. He blurted out his words from behind his hand. 'Kev Dawson. You're looking for Kevin Dawson. He's the only one who could have taken it. It couldn't have been the Old Man.'

'The Old Man?'

'He's been at this game too long to start thieving now,' Mulhaney said. He was conscious of the pistol on his brow. It was a terrible feeling.

'Tell me about the Old Man, Jock.'

Mulhaney looked down at his blood on the white-tiled floor. 'The Old Man had nothing to do with this,' he said, and his voice sounded funny to him when he spoke. Without his teeth, the inside of his mouth felt like a stranger's mouth. He'd give this bastard Dawson, but he wasn't about to give him the Old Man immediately. He'd do it in the end, he'd be a damn fool not to, but meantime he'd hand Dawson over gladly. 'My bet is Kev took some heat from his big brother. There was pressure. Something like that. It had to be politically too tricky for Tommy. The Old Man couldn't have had a goddam thing to do with it.'

As Mulhaney spoke, the toilet door swung open and a middle-aged man in a black tuxedo stepped inside from the hallway. He wore a frilly pink shirt and matching cummerbund, into which was tucked a pistol. The man was called Keefe and he was one of Mulhaney's bodyguards, a Union heavy who was paid a hefty fee to protect his boss.

'Keefe,' Mulhaney cried out.

Keefe, formerly a bouncer in a Las Vegas nightclub, was a tough man but slow. He reached inside his cummerbund for his gun and even as he did so Cairney, possessed with a feeling of inevitability, with a sense of things sliding away from him in a manner he couldn't stop, shot Keefe once through the centre of his chest. The sound of the gun roared in the white-tiled, windowless room. Keefe staggered across the slippery floor, his legs buckling and his hands stretched out in front of him. He collided with a cubicle door and he fell forward against the john. His gun dropped to the floor and slipped across the slick tiles to Mulhaney's feet. Cairney watched Big Jock's hand hover above the gun a moment.

'Don't,' Cairney said. *'Don't even think about it.'*

Jock Mulhaney pulled his hand back to his side. It wasn't worth it. The young guy would shoot him if he even moved an inch towards Keefe's weapon. And Jock had no appetite for violent death.

Cairney kicked the gun away. The music had stopped. The whole building had become quiet. The only sound he registered was Mulhaney's heavy breathing.

Mulhaney said, 'You got a problem, kid. In about ten seconds three hundred guys are gonna descend on this room.'

Cairney looked at the door. Three hundred guys. The suddenness of silence was unsettling to him. He glanced at Mulhaney, who was still on his knees. Blood ran down from the big man's mouth.

Cairney opened the toilet door a little way. He stared across the reception room. Drawn by the sound of gunfire, men in tuxedoes were emerging slowly from the banquet room. Cairney bit his lower lip. If he acted now, if he moved promptly, he could get out of this toilet and through the reception area to the street before any of the men could reach him. *Provided none of them were armed.* He glanced back at Mulhaney, who was staring at him open-mouthed.

'Get up on your feet, Jock.'

Mulhaney gripped the rim of the washbasin and hauled himself to a standing position.

'Now move over here,' Cairney said.

Mulhaney came across the floor.

'In front of me, Jock. You're about to be useful.'

Cairney pressed his gun into the small of Mulhaney's back and pushed the big man through the door, out into the reception area. Men were still coming down the corridor that opened into the reception room.

'Tell them, Jock. They move and you're dead. They call the cops and you're history.'

Mulhaney, whose vanity caused him to hold a hand up against his toothless mouth, mumbled. 'You hear that, you guys?'

Cairney, moving sideways towards the front doors with Mulhaney as a shield, stared at the faces that watched him. Each one had the slightly imbalanced look of a man wrenched suddenly out of inebriation into sobriety. Their eyes bored into him, and Cairney realised he'd never felt quite this exposed before. It didn't matter now. It didn't matter because his anonymity had already been shattered by Frank Pagan. The only important thing was to get out of here in one piece. He felt fragmented, though, as if the whole reason for coming to America had broken and, like smashed glass, lay in shards all about him. He was halfway across the reception room now and none of the watchers had moved and Mulhaney, he knew, wasn't brave enough to try and break away. He was going to get out of here, but he was leaving empty-handed, and the perception depressed him. Finn had entrusted him with a task and he wasn't even *close* to achieving it. Maybe it was luck. Maybe that was it. Maybe he'd been lucky in the past and now that vein had run completely dry. And maybe he wasn't the man Finn thought he was, that all his achievements in the past had been purely fortunate. Jig, the dancer. *Why am I not dancing now?* he wondered. He didn't feel like the man who had assassinated Lord Drumcannon and had blown up Walter Whiteford on a Mayfair street. He didn't feel daring and carefree and composed and cold-blooded. His past actions seemed like those of some other man.

'Keep moving, Jock.' Six feet to the plate-glass doors. The street.

He pressed the gun into Jock's spine and heard the big man grunt quietly.

'Only a few more feet, Jock,' he said.

'Fuck you,' Mulhaney said. He was playing to his audience. He was showing that he was still a brave man who could talk back even when the pressure was on. And if he could talk to some fucking hoodlum like this, think how he could ram it home to builders and contractors when he didn't have a goddam gun in his back!

Cairney reached the doors and knocked them open with his foot. The air in the street was cold and sharp. He wondered how much time he had before the cops arrived. He knew it was inevitable that somebody inside the building had sneaked away into an office to place a quiet call, that pretty soon the street would be filled with patrol cars.

'Okay,' Mulhaney said. 'You've made it out of the building. What now?'

Cairney said, 'We've got unfinished business. You were going to tell me about the Old Man, Jock.'

'I gave you Kev Dawson.'

Cairney shoved the gun into the nape of Mulhaney's neck. 'Don't stall, Jock.' He looked the length of the dark street in both directions. It was silent now, but it wasn't going to stay that way for very long. Through the glass doors he was conscious of the men inside. They stood around indecisively, but that was a situation that could change at any moment. They were Irish and they'd been drinking, and they might decide to move into boisterous action, regardless of the fact that Mulhaney had a gun at his head.

'*Hurry,*' Cairney said. And even as he said this he heard footsteps along the sidewalk and turned his face quickly, seeing somebody move in the soft shadows between the parked limousines and the wall of the building. The figure stopped suddenly and dropped to the sidewalk. There was the sound of a gun going off and a flash of light from the place where the man lay and the plate-glass doors shattered, showering the air with bright splinters.

Surprised, Cairney moved back, pressing himself against the wall. He was aware of Mulhaney lunging away from him, the glass doors swinging, Big Jock thrusting himself inside the safety of the building. Cairney fired his weapon at the man along the sidewalk and heard the sound of the bullet knock upon the hood of a limousine. He backed away, sliding against the wall and out of the light that fell from the building. He sought darkness, places where he couldn't be seen. He fired his gun again. This time the shot slashed concrete. The man returned the fire, and the air around Cairney's head screamed.

Cairney kept moving away. He was about ten feet from the corner of the building and conscious of the need to get the hell out of this place. He saw the figure move now, scampering behind one of the parked limousines. The man's face passed momentarily under the light that fell from the reception room.

It was Frank Pagan.

Cairney reached the corner of the buildings, where there was a badly lit side street and rows of shuttered little shops. He was seized by the impulse to stay exactly where he was and fight it out with Frank Pagan, as if what he wanted to prove to the Englishman was that he didn't have to run away as he had done on Canal Street, but how would that have taken him any closer to the money? Priorities, he thought. And Frank Pagan – despite the fact that the man was always just behind him like some kind of dogged spectre – wasn't top of his list.

He stared a moment at the car behind which Pagan was crouched. Then he turned and sprinted into the darkness of the side street, weaving between parked cars and trashcans, zigzagging under weak streetlamps, like a man following a maze of his own creation. He could hear Pagan coming after him, but the Englishman wasn't fast enough to close the gap that Cairney was widening with every stride. The echoes of Pagan's movements grew quieter and quieter until there was no sound at all. When he was absolutely certain he'd lost Pagan, he lay down beneath a railroad bridge and closed his eyes, listening to his own heart rage against his ribs.

Pagan had known about Linney. Then about Mulhaney.

Cairney opened his eyes, staring up into the black underside of the bridge. *Was it safe to assume that Pagan also knew about Kevin Dawson?*

Cairney sat with his back to the brickwork now. He felt the most curious emptiness he had ever experienced. It drained his heart and created vacuums throughout his mind. He knew he had to get up and make his way back to the place where he'd left his car, but he sat numb and motionless. There was an uncharacteristic need inside him to make contact, a connection with somebody *somewhere*. He thought he'd call Finn, but he couldn't see any point in relating failure to the man. He didn't want Finn to be disappointed in him. And he didn't want Finn to think he'd sent the wrong man from Ireland. That he'd sent a man who wasn't equipped for this task. He couldn't bear the idea of Finn thinking badly of him.

He shut his eyes again. The face that floated up through his mind, and a warped, pellucid image like something refracted in shallow water, was Celestine's.

Frank Pagan went back in the direction of the union building. He was breathless, and his whole body, jarred by the effort of running, was a mass of disconnected pulses. Jig's speed hadn't surprised him. He'd seen Jig in action before. But this time it was the manner of the man's disappearance that impressed him. It was almost as if Jig had vaporised down one of the narrow streets. Stepped out of this dimension and into another one. For a time, Pagan had managed to keep the man in his sight, but with every corner Jig turned Pagan realised that his hope of catching up was dwindling. Then, finally, somewhere between a canal and weedy old railroad track, Jig had disappeared in the blackness, with the deftness of a rodent.

Goddam. Pagan resented the idea that Jig was swifter than he, more agile, more attuned to the hiding-places offered by the night. He envied Jig's affinity for invisibility. Now he had the feeling that even if he were to seal off the surrounding twenty blocks, he still wouldn't find the man. *Goddam again.* These close encounters only frustrated him. What also bothered him, even if he didn't like to admit it, was the insurmountable fact that Jig must have at least ten years on him, that his own youth had long ago begun to recede, and time – the dreaded erosion of clocks – was making impatient claims on his body.

He walked slowly, like a man skirting the blades of open razors. When he reached the broken glass doors he paused, making one huge, concentrated effort to catch his breath. He stepped inside the reception room and saw Mulhaney sitting on one of the huge black leather sofas, surrounded by anxious men in evening wear and green sashes. Mulhaney had a bloodied handkerchief up to his mouth.

Pagan pushed his way towards the sofa, elbowing men out of the way. Mulhaney, enjoying the attention he was getting, peered over the top of the handkerchief at him. Pagan showed his ID in a swift way, sweeping it in front of Mulhaney's eyes before the union boss had time to register it.

'I've got a few questions,' Pagan said.

Mulhaney dabbed at his lip. His bare gums were pink and bloody. 'What kind of ID was that?'

Pagan ignored the question. 'You have a private office somewhere? I'd like to talk to you alone.'

Mulhaney looked puzzled. 'I'm perfectly happy where I am,' he said.

'Okay.' Pagan shrugged and lowered himself on to the arm of the sofa. 'What did the guy want with you, Jock?'

'He was a mugger, for Christ's sake. What the fuck you think he wanted?'

Pagan shook his head. 'He was sent here from Ireland. You know that. I know that.'

'Ireland?' Mulhaney looked blank. He appealed to the other men around him. 'Who is this guy? Who let him in here?'

'What did you tell him?' Pagan asked.

'Hey,' Mulhaney said. 'Let's see that ID again, fellah.'

'Did you tell him where he could find the money? Or did you send him somewhere else?'

Mulhaney stood up. His eyes had a bruised, angry look. 'I don't know what the hell you're talking about. Somebody toss this knucklehead outta here. Ireland, for Christ's sake! My man Keefe's been shot dead and you're babbling about fucking Ireland!'

'Keefe?'

'My bodyguard. Mugger shot him.'

Another corpse. One way or another, Jig was leaving bodies strewn behind him. What had happened to the fastidious assassin? Pagan hesitated a second before reaching out to grip Mulhaney's wrist tightly. 'What did you tell him, Jock? Did you send him to Dawson? Did you tell him Cairney was the man to see? Or did you tell him something else altogether? What did you say to him?'

Mulhaney made a gesture of exasperation. 'Out,' he said.

Pagan felt various hands grab him. It hadn't been terrific strategy to come in here and confront Jock, but on the other hand there was always the chance that Mulhaney might be taken off guard and give Pagan the answers he was looking for. Big Jock, though, was set on a course of complete denial, which wasn't entirely surprising. Pagan wished he could have had time alone with the man. It might have made a difference in Mulhaney's attitude. Surrounded by his sycophants, Big Jock was forceful and stubborn.

Pagan pulled himself free of his assailants. He stepped to one side. 'It's important, Jock. I need to know.'

'I've had it with you,' Mulhaney said. He looked at the faces of the men. 'Toss this nut out.'

Pagan was still struggling to catch his breath. 'If I leave here, I walk. Under my own steam.'

'Walk then,' Mulhaney said.

Pagan pushed his way back through the crowd towards the glass doors. He moved out on to the street, where he turned and glanced back through broken glass at the sight of Mulhaney holding forth for his audience. *I hit the guy a couple of times*, he was saying. *Then he pulls this piece on me, which is when poor Keefe walks in.*

I bet you hit him, Pagan thought.

He moved away from the building, just as two patrol cars turned the corner into the street, their lamps slashing holes in the darkness and their sirens screaming like voices in purgatory.

New York City

'It's raining in Piccadilly Circus,' Foxie said, his voice unusually crisp and clear, given the great distances of the Atlantic. 'Doesn't that make you homesick?'

'Why? I'm having a ball here,' Pagan replied. The muscles in his legs throbbed from running. He lay on the bed and stared up at the ceiling of his room in the Parker Meridien. 'What have you got for me?'

'Straight to the point, eh?' Foxie's voice faded a second. 'According to my little screen, Alex Fitzjohn did time in Armagh Jail in 1977 for possession of grenades. Six months. Somewhere in this period he must have thrown in his lot with the FUV. They recruit in jails, of course.' Foxie paused. 'My head hurts and my throat's dry. There are gremlins inside my brain doing things with dental drills.'

'Don't drink until you're grown up,' Pagan said.

'Whenever. Back to Fitz. Suspected of participation in at least three border incidents. One the bombing of a pub. Two, the attempted assassination of a priest. A failure, that one. Three, a brief shoot-out with the Garda. And inconclusive affair, it would seem.'

Pagan was suddenly impatient. 'Is there anything that ties him directly with McInnes?'

'Ivor's a careful sort of chap,' Foxie said. 'You know how damned hard it is to get reliable documentation on whether he's running the FUV or not. However . . .' and here Foxworth paused.

'I'm all ears,' Pagan said.

'There is one very grubby photograph in our possession. It's about seven years old. Somebody stored it in Fitzjohn's file, which is on the inactive list. It really ought to have been put in Ivor's. There's a lot of clerical idiocy around here, Frank.'

'Foxie, please,' Pagan said.

'One description coming right up. The picture shows Ivor stepping out of his church. He's robed up to sermonise, so we can assume he's just delivered himself of one of his brimstone jobs. Around Ivor are a few people. There's a lot of smiling going on. Somebody is reaching out to shake Ivor's hand. Maybe to congratulate him on his words of wisdom? Whatever. In the midst of the people gathered on the steps of the church is one Alex Fitzjohn. He's about five feet away from Ivor, and he's smiling. But Ivor isn't looking at him. Ivor's staring at the man offering the handshake.' Foxie paused. 'That's it, Frank.'

Pagan massaged the side of his head, which had begun to ache. It had been a long day, and he was exhausted now. A peculiar kind of exhaustion too, as if a rainy mist were crawling through his brain. He was thinking of Jig and how the man had managed to slide away from him once again on the streets of Brooklyn. *What had Mulhaney told Jig?*

'It's not a hell of a lot, is it?' Pagan said. 'I'm looking for a connection and all we've got is a photograph that doesn't even show Ivor and Alex making *eye*-contact.'

'It doesn't exactly confirm that they're bosom buddies,' Foxworth agreed. 'The best case you could make is that they probably knew each other. Probably.'

Pagan sat down on the edge of his bed. He'd hoped for something more substantial than an old inconclusive photograph. Something definitive. Something Ivor couldn't possibly deny. But all he really had was a weak hand that was useful for a couple of bluffs, nothing more.

'By the way, Frank. The Secretary popped into the office.'

'That's a first,' Pagan said. 'Did you call the *Guinness Book of Records*?'

'He came in the day after you left. Quite the grand tour. He expressed some – shall we say misgivings – about your sojourn in the Americas? Doesn't think you should be gallivanting about over there. Thinks your information from the FUV about Jig is spotty and doesn't justify your trip. People don't say *spotty* much these days, do they?'

'Tell him to stuff it,' Pagan said.

'I think I hear the quiet sharpening of the axe, Frank. Furry Jake is no friend of yours. And you've got all those delicious enemies at the Yard who love the idea of you being away because, heaven forbid, they can make waves. Get the Sec's ear and whisper anti-Pagan slogans into it. It's not a glowing horoscope, is it?'

'In other words, if I don't get Jig, don't come home.'

'It's what I'm hearing, Frank. Apropos of Jig, how goes it?'

'I haven't quite booked my return flight, Foxie.'

'When you do, I very much hope you won't be travelling unaccompanied.'

'Take aspirins for your hangover,' Pagan said. 'And go back to bed.'

Pagan put the receiver down. The sharpening of the axe, he thought. You leave your desk and the vultures start to circle. You step away and suddenly it's The Night of the Long Knives. What else could you expect? People were unhappy with him. People didn't like the way he ran his section. People like Furry Jake thought little of Pagan's tailor and, by extension, little of Pagan too. Scotland Yard wanted control over him. They didn't like an upstart having power. And they revelled, *God did they ever,* in the idea of Jig's eluding Pagan's grasp.

Pagan poured another scotch. Jesus Christ, was this job *that* important to him? He could run security in the private sector and earn twice as much as he was paid now. But what he hated was the idea of scumbags waiting for him to fall, waiting for him to come home empty-handed because then they could pounce on him and denigrate him with that particularly wicked smugness certain pencil-pushers have for those who work out in the field, the real world.

He was agitated by the confinement of his room. He wanted to get out of the narrow little rectangle in which he was trapped. He put on a jacket and went down in the elevator to the piano bar.

Silence. The pianist had gone. The bar was almost empty. Pagan sat up on a stool and ordered a Drambuie. Mandi with an 'i' was cleaning the surface of a table in the corner. When she saw Pagan she smiled and drifted over to him. She was small and she moved with economy, like a dancer. It was all an illusion of coordination. Halfway towards him she dropped her order-pad and pencil and giggled as she bent to pick them up because loose change tumbled out of her pocket and went off in a series of little wheels across the floor.

He wondered what she'd be like in bed. It was the first time he'd entertained this notion quite so clearly in years and it took him by surprise. There was something else too – a small shiver of ridiculous guilt, almost as if the thought of having sex with this girl were somehow a betrayal of Roxanne. And he wondered at the tenacious hold the dead could sometimes have over the living. Could he ever shake himself free?

'I drop things,' she said.

'I never noticed.'

The giggle was high-pitched and, although he wasn't a man enamoured of giggling, he did find something endearing in it.

'Palsy,' she said. 'Or is it dropsy?'

Pagan sipped his Drambuie. He studied her over the rim of his glass. She had dark hair naturally curled, creating an overall effect of a head covered with bubbles. She had a small heart-shaped mouth and straight teeth. There was humour in the face. Mandi was a woman who liked to laugh at herself. Going to bed with her would be some kind of romp through innocence, with no serious attachments, no kinks, no entanglements. Quick rapture and a fond goodbye.

'Enjoying your stay?' she asked.

Pagan shrugged. 'It's a bewildering city.'

The girl placed her hands on the surface of the bar. She had chubby, cherubic hands, dimpled. Straightforward, good-natured Mandi. An uncomplicated girl. It was all there in the hands and the brightness of the eyes. Simplicity. The uncluttered life.

'You need a guide,' she said. 'If you want to see the place properly.'

There was an opening here, but Pagan was slow to move towards it. He was out of touch, rusty.

'I'm Mandi, by the way.'

He nodded. He was going to say he knew that already but why bother? 'Frank Pagan.'

'Good to know you, Frank. You're from London, right?'

'Does it show?'

'It's the way you talk. It's like Michael Caine in that picture. God, what was it called?' She pursed her small lips and concentrated. 'I'm hopeless when it comes to remembering names.'

No memory. Forever dropping things. Why did he find her clumsiness sweet? She must go through her life in a sweet-natured daze. She wouldn't need drugs or alcohol because reality made her dizzy enough.

'*Alfie*!' she said. 'That's the one.'

'I remember it vaguely.'

'Are you on your own?' she asked. Another opening.

Pagan was about to say that he was, he was about to say that he was weary of his own company, that he needed a bout of companionship and would she be interested, when he noticed Tyson Bruno sitting in a dark corner of the bar. Whatever nascent appetite he'd begun to feel abruptly shrivelled inside him. The mood was spoiled, sullied. He pushed his glass away and got down from the stool, glancing at Bruno's hardened wooden face.

'I'd like to be,' he said. The waitress looked puzzled.

Pagan moved across the thick carpet of the bar and out into the lobby towards the banks of elevators. For a moment there he'd felt an old mood returning, a need rising inside him, a desire to do something simple and natural, like touching a woman, like bringing quickness back into his circulation, yesterday's heats, yesterday's passions, something that would slash away at his ghost. But Tyson Bruno's face had risen out of the darkness to spoil things, reminding Pagan of the contrast between his own sorry little world where men and women died painfully and treachery was a viable currency, and the world of a cocktail waitress in a 57th Street hotel who dropped things and laughed at herself and lived an uncomplicated life. Two planets, different orbits.

He travelled up in the elevator, thinking of himself as perhaps the first man in history to suffer from a case of premature exorcism. When the car reached his floor, the doors slid open and he looked down the long corridor towards his room. Fuck it, he thought. He needed life and liveliness. And the real trick to that was to say no to self-analysis and no to your history. If you wanted to live, you just went out and did it.

He stepped back into the elevator and returned to the bar.

Mandi was gone.

But Tyson Bruno was still there, coming across the floor with an ape's grace.

'Don't run out on me again, Pagan,' Bruno said. 'I don't like being made stupid.'

'That takes no great effort, Tyson.' Pagan felt weary.

'I hate smartasses,' Bruno said. 'Where did you go anyhow?'

'I always wanted to see Brooklyn by moonlight.'

'Sure.' Tyson Bruno folded his thick arms across his chest. He had a mean, dangerous look all at once, that of a man who lives with violent solutions to tough questions. Pagan stared at the tiny eyes, which resembled the pits of a cherry.

'See it doesn't happen again,' Tyson Bruno said.

'I never promise the impossible, Tyson.'

Pagan turned away and headed back towards the elevators.

White Plains, New York

It was eight minutes past seven a.m. when the Reverend Duncanson began his Sunday morning sermon in Memorial Presbyterian Church. The congregation numbered about two hundred people, and Duncanson was pleased to see so many young people in attendance. He wondered if the Englishman who had telephoned was among the worshippers. His sermon, perhaps a little too heavy for the spring weather that had suddenly surfaced this day, concerned the confession of sins and God's ability to refresh and cleanse the sinner. It was a dark, wintry speech, and it tended, like most of Duncanson's sermons, to ramble through thickets of personal anecdote, non-sequiturs, and erudite attempts at word-play.

His eyes scanned the congregation as he spoke. A bright March sun fell upon the stained glass, creating a nice dappled effect along the central pews. He spoke of confessional needs, carefully making a distinction between the *inner* need of man to ask forgiveness, and the *outer* compulsion, a Catholic notion that would bring momentary uneasiness to some of his members. The very word *confession* was loaded.

The Reverend Duncanson glanced at his watch, which he always took from his wrist and laid alongside his notes. He had been speaking now for thirteen minutes. He needed to pick up the pace and bring everything to a conclusion within the next two minutes. After years of sermonising he had the ability to edit his own material in his head. He sometimes thought he was like a stand-up comic who intuited his audience's mood and shuffled his material accordingly.

Seven-fifteen.

The second hand of Duncanson's watch swept forward.

He closed his sermon after he'd talked for fifteen minutes. He nodded in the direction of the organist, a middle-aged woman who raised her hands above the keyboard, ready to strike. The congregation rose, hymnbooks open.

'We will now sing the Twenty-Third Psalm,' Duncanson announced. 'The Lord is My Shepherd.'

The organist rippled off the introductory chords.

The great pipes took the sound, transformed it, scattered it through the uppermost parts of the church. It swelled, died, then came back again, a vast flood of music. As Duncanson opened his mouth to sing, he saw a sudden ball of flame rise up from the keyboard and engulf the organist, surrounding her with a wall of fire that spread upwards with a horrific crackling. The force of released heat was so intense he felt it burn the skin at the side of his face. Then there was an explosion from the dead centre of the church, a blast that shook the entire building and blew out the stained-glass windows.

Duncanson rushed down from the pulpit, unaware in all the smoke and screaming and confusion that his robe had caught fire. Another blast rocked the area around the pulpit, a violent outburst of flame and dark smoke that suggested something released from the fissures of hell. By this time, the ceiling was ablaze, wooden beams consumed by flame. The hymnbooks were burning. The pews were burning. People were burning too, screaming as they tried to rush through the suffocating smoke towards doorways they couldn't find. Babies. Young men and women. The fire attacked everything.

And then there was still another explosion, the last one Duncanson heard. It brought the organ pipes down out of the walls, a tumble of plaster and bolts and woodwork and electrical wires which conveyed flame down into the basement of the church where the oil-fuelled central heating system was located. When the oil caught fire the air became dead air, unbreathable, filling lungs with a searing poison.

Some people made it out through the madness and the panic to the lawn in front of the church where they saw that the steeple was one ragged mass of blue flame whipped by breeze and spreading in a series of fiery licks across the entire roof. Others, trapped and suffocated inside, barely heard the final explosion as the oil-tank went up because the world of fire had become a silent place for them, all noise sucked out by a vacuum of intense heat, a scorched epicentre where no sound penetrated, no air stirred, the vast parched heart of destruction.

Stamford, Connecticut

Seamus Houlihan dialled a telephone number in New York City from a phone booth beside an industrial park in Stamford. It was eight-thirty on a sunlit Sunday morning. As he listened to the sound of the phone ringing, he looked across the street at John Waddell, who sat in the driver's seat of the yellow rental truck. The truck had begun to bother Houlihan. It was too big, too conspicuous. They'd have to ditch it soon. McInnes had said he wanted them to dump the truck after Connecticut, but Houlihan thought it might be a damn good thing to be rid of it right now, before the next stage. Maybe he'd steal a smaller vehicle, though it would need to have a large trunk to keep the weapons in.

He winked at Waddell, who looked white. A stolen vehicle was a fucking risk, that was the snag. People actively looked for them. Their numbers and descriptions were put on lists. Cops, who wouldn't blink at a rented truck, would be on your arse quick enough if they spotted you in a stolen car.

It was all right for McInnes, Houlihan thought. He sat in his fancy hotel and called all the shots. He wasn't out here getting himself grubby, doing the deeds, *working*. McInnes was terrific at organisation. Houlihan had to admit that much, but the man was always at one remove from the centre of it all, the place where things really happened. And he was always getting his name in the papers, always basking in publicity, another thing Houlihan resented.

Over the phone, Houlihan listened to the ringing tones and wondered if anybody was ever going to answer. Thinking of McInnes irritated him. He hadn't felt good about McInnes ever since the man had scolded him for the action in Albany. *Stick to the blueprint, Seamus. Be a good boy, Seamus. Keep your nose clean, Seamus.*

Yessir and up yours.

What McInnes resembled at times was one of those figures of authority from Houlihan's past. A judge. A cop. A screw. A counsellor. All the fuckers who either sent you to jail or spoke softly to you about taking your place in society. They had you coming and going, those characters did. McInnes couldn't stand the idea of anyone else showing some initiative, some imagination. That's what it all boiled down to. McInnes didn't like the idea of Seamus Houlihan doing something on his own.

Fuck him, Houlihan thought. McInnes thinks he knows it all.

The phone was finally answered.

A man said, 'Federal Bureau of Investigation. Please hold.'

'I won't hold,' Houlihan said.

'Sorry, sir. I have to ask you to wait.'

'I've waited long enough, shithead.'

'Sir –'

'Listen close. You'll hear this only once.' And here Seamus paused, enjoying himself. He winked at wee Waddy again and smiled.

20 New York City

Patrick Cairney woke in a hotel on Eighth Avenue. It was called The Hotel Glasgow, a peeling old crone of a place with murky hallways and dampness. When he checked his watch he saw that it was almost eight-thirty in the morning, and a frigid New York spring sun was streaming through the brown window blind. He'd come to this place very late last night, after Brooklyn, and fallen asleep immediately on the narrow bed, a long sleep filled towards its end with a dream.

He'd dreamed he was back in the Libyan desert where he was trying to dismantle and clean an automatic rifle. An odd weapon Cairney had never seen before. It was composed of parts that didn't fit. Once you had the gun stripped down, you couldn't put it back together again no matter how much you pushed and manoeuvred and tried to force things. The damn gun, a trick weapon, wouldn't be reassembled. It was a distressing dream, panicky, inexact, one of those insanely catered affairs of the unconscious when streams of incongruous people gatecrash.

Celestine had been in there somewhere towards the end. She'd picked up the befuddling gun, and with three or four quick movements of her hands she had the whole thing snapped back together again. *There*, she kept saying to him. *There, there, there*. What the hell was she doing in his dream anyhow?

Cairney got out of the hard little bed. He dismissed dreams as messages from nowhere, sediment stirred by the uncontrolled brain. He didn't see in dreams the things soothsayers did, prophecies and portents, future disasters. He went inside the small showerstall and drummed tepid water all over his body. When he was finished he dressed quickly. He packed his canvas bag, locked it, left the room. But the dream, as if it were a narrative in a seductive tongue, still whispered in his mind.

He travelled down to the lobby by the stairs because elevators were always too claustrophobic for him. Outside, where the sun was cold, he crossed the street and walked in the direction of the garage where he'd parked the Dodge. It was a sleazy stretch of Eighth Avenue, pawnshops and fast-food places and porno stores. He entered the dimly lit garage cautiously, distrustful of dark places. He found the car on the second level exactly as he'd left it. Unmolested, unvandalised. He unlocked it, drove it past the ticket booth, paid his fee, and then he was out into harsh white sunshine, heading north. By the time he reached Columbus Circle he was hungry but he didn't want to stop until he was clear of the city.

Finally, when he was close to Yonkers, he pulled into a twenty-four-hour place that served the whole staggering array of American roadside cuisine. He took a table near a window and chewed on a strange red hot-dog, which he left half-eaten. He drank two cups of coffee, and for the first time that day his brain which had been numb and unresponsive, kicked into gear. Low gear.

You'll have times when you can do nothing but abort, boy. You'll have times when circumstances are stacked up against you. The trick then is to step away without despair.

Without despair, Cairney thought. But he could feel a certain sickness in his heart. Ever since he'd entered the United States, he'd encountered one set of circumstances after another that provoked nothing but despair in him. But he wouldn't abort. Not now. Not ever. Was it his fault that Tumulty had been playing both ends against the middle? Was it his fault that Linney had turned out to be some kind of frantic madman? Was it his fault that Mulhaney's bodyguard had chosen to come through the door of the restroom when he did and then draw his goddam gun? You were sometimes faced with extremely limited choices. And sometimes you had no choices at all, because events narrowed all around you and went off at their own uncontrollable speed, and the only thing you could do was follow the track of chaos and make the best of what you had.

Finn's money, the Cause's money, had taken on a grail-like quality in his mind. It shimmered and tantalised and then, as though it were a mirage, vanished even as you thought you were close to it. He had moments now when he wondered if it ever existed or, if it did, whether it was buried forever in some inaccessible place beyond human reach. All he knew was that the money was surrounded by accusations and treacheries and suspicions. People told lies. They made up stories. Linney had been sure that Mulhaney was responsible for the theft. Mulhaney had pointed to Kevin Dawson. And he'd also mentioned somebody enigmatically known as the Old Man, who appeared to occupy a position of authority that put him in a place beyond suspicion.

What Cairney suddenly wondered was how a man like Frank Pagan would have gone about the task of searching for the money. Pagan, presumably, had been trained in investigative skills, quietly gathering data, knowing the questions to ask, knowing how to assess the answers. Frank Pagan, perhaps, had insights that were denied Jig, a deeper human understanding, an ability to cut through lies and deceptions and misleading statements. Frank Pagan *understood* people because he lived in their midsts. Jig didn't. Jig didn't know people. Jig had cut himself off from ordinary society by his own choice. Cairney could imagine Pagan operating on some intuitive level, knowing when he was hearing bullshit and when he was hearing the truth. Cairney, trained to assassinate, trained to track, to plant explosive devices, to use rifles, to survive in extreme conditions, in arctic cold and desert heat – Cairney had never learned a goddam thing, in all his training, about the puzzlingly intricate clockwork of the human heart. And it was hurting him now.

He picked up the half-eaten hot-dog and shredded it surgically into fragments between his fingers. It was useless to speculate on what gifts he had and didn't have. It was the wrong time. It was the wrong time to entertain even the smallest kind of doubt. To think that Finn – in his anger and frustration – had sent the wrong kind of man to America.

Cairney pushed the dissected hot-dog aside.

I'll get the money, he thought.

I'll get it and take it back to Finn and say There, there's your money.

And Finn would receive it with a small smile of pleasure, the smile Cairney liked, the one that made him feel as if he were basking in his own private sunlight. The kind of smile he'd never seen on his own father's face. *I knew you'd do it, boy. I never had any doubt. And the Cause is forever grateful to you.*

Kevin Dawson. He had to concentrate on Kevin Dawson. Given the amount of documentation on the private lives of the Dawson clan, given all the reams of publicity so loved by the tabloids, it wasn't going to be very difficult to locate the Dawson home. But Cairney knew that Dawson was going to be surrounded by the kind of protection afforded brothers of the President. Which meant extreme caution. And then there was always Frank Pagan to consider.

Cairney stared through the window at a stream of traffic sliding north. Hundreds of Sunday afternoon travellers, whole families complete with dogs, hurrying to dinners with in-laws or visits to the zoo or places of worship. He watched them with solemn detachment for a time.

He stood up, paid for his food, then moved in the direction of the door. There was a payphone in the lobby. He stopped. Glancing through the glass door at his small red Dodge, he was seized by an impulse to pick up the receiver. He dialled a number, punched in coins.

Celestine's voice was thin when she answered. 'Hello?'

Cairney listened. Didn't speak. Why the hell had he made this call? It wasn't as if he needed to hear his father's voice, was it? It was something else, something he didn't want to think abut.

'Hello?'

Cairney opened his mouth, but he remained silent.

'Is anyone there?' she asked.

He took the receiver away from his ear. He pictured her standing with the telephone pressed to the side of her face, perhaps a lock of fair hair hanging falling across a cheekbone, her slim legs set slightly apart. The image was strong in his mind, and teasing, and desirable. The sound of her voice brought back to him the night she'd come to his bedroom, and he trembled very slightly.

'Patrick? Is that you?'

Now why would she think that? Why would she think of *his* name? He replaced the receiver and went outside to the parking-lot. He unlocked his car, stepped in behind the wheel. He drove away from the restaurant, the sun laying a white film over his rear window.

The White House, Washington

Shortly after Seamus Houlihan's anonymous phone call had been logged by the FBI in New York City, Leonard M. Korn stepped inside the Oval Office like a man with a mission in life. Thomas Dawson saw this at once. Magoo had fire in his myopic eyes. If it were any hotter there, his contact lenses would melt. The President understood Korn's manner. The man had come here looking for a free hand. He wanted to hear Dawson say that the wolves could be released now, the pack liberated, the time was ripe. The FBI could tear apart the whole goddam Eastern seaboard, if that's what it took to catch one Irish terrorist.

Korn saw indecision in Thomas Dawson. Indecision and subterfuge. But how could Dawson explain away the bombing of a church in White Plains to the soothed satisfaction of the public? A faulty boiler? Or would he go with some natural phenomenon, like spontaneous combustion? Korn's Bureau, his agency, his love, was like a caged leopard clawing bars, ready to pounce. This time it wasn't four casualties in a house in Bridgehampton. This one couldn't be kept under wraps.

Dawson ran a fingertip over his lower lip and said, 'It doesn't make any sense to me, Len. Why come to the United States and blow up a goddam church, for Christ's sake?'

Korn enjoyed Dawson's discomfort. The changing currents of international terrorist policy meant nothing to the Director. He was interested only in apprehending the culprit. More specifically, he was interested in being *seen* to do it.

'I can understand the death of Linney,' Dawson continued. 'He was involved in these clandestine Irish affairs. But a whole churchload of people? Come on. Why the hell this escalation?'

'Jig may have been after just one person in that church,' Korn suggested. 'It's possible.'

Dawson sighed. 'If it was Jig,' he said. 'Do we have any really *hard* evidence that he's responsible?'

Korn considered this a naïve question. 'He's our only candidate, Mr President.'

Thomas Dawson stood up. He could hear Korn panting at the leash.

'Jig only came here to recover money,' the President said. 'I don't see where bombing churches fits on his agenda.'

'Terrorists aren't like you and me,' Korn said. 'They don't function with normal motives. They aren't driven by normal impulses. We know absolutely nothing about Jig, so how can we say what he is or isn't capable of doing?'

Dawson poked his blotting-pad with the tip of a silver letter-knife. 'The latest count is seventy-eight,' he said. 'Seventy-eight, for Christ's sake!'

'It may rise,' Korn said.

Dawson ignored what he felt was a rather distasteful eagerness in Korn's voice. Seventy-eight people was a hell of a tally. What was he going to tell America? What would he announce into that great ear out there? So far, the only information it had received was of an explosion inside a church. No explanation given, a simple headline on news programmes. But by this time the journalists would be scavenging the disaster-site like vultures. Sometimes Dawson thought that freedom of the press was the enemy of democracy. Why couldn't it be muzzled?

All at once he felt a real need to draw people around him, cabinet members, image-makers, advisers, counsellors, poll-takers, speechwriters, he wanted every possible scenario thoroughly analysed before he did anything. Would this act of Jig's alienate the Irish from their hero when – and if – they learned about it? Would there be outrage? Or would it somehow draw the clans tighter together? Imponderable questions.

He stared at Korn who gazed back at him with expectation.

The American public could wait, the journalists could dig, the rumours could fly and multiply with the speed of maggots in a rancid stew, Korn could pop some bloodcells. But Thomas Dawson wasn't going to drop the starter's flag for the FBI until he'd consulted with his own policy-makers.

He saw he had savaged his blotter with the letter-opener. 'It's not my decision alone, Len. I can't tell you to go ahead with this manhunt of yours until I've talked with my Cabinet.'

Korn was annoyed, but not absolutely surprised. He'd always thought Tom Dawson the wrong man for number 1600. He was in too many people's pockets, for one thing. This whole love affair he conducted with the Irish-Americans was way out of whack. There was one group that had him by the balls. And the Irish-Americans weren't the only ones. He was in deep with the Italians, the Puerto-Ricans, the farmers. If it moved in sufficient numbers, if it had the capability to organise itself and knew how to pull a voting-lever, then Tommy Dawson was probably obligated to it.

'While you *consult*, Mr President, an Irish terrorist is out there, planning God knows what next move, and we have a total of four men on the case – *four*, count them – one of whom is an Englishman that two of the remaining three spend most of their time watching, for God's sake.'

Dawson held a hand in the air. 'You'll have a decision soon.'

'How soon is soon?' Korn asked. 'And will it be soon enough?'

Korn moved to the door. He had a flair at times for melodramatic exit lines. He enjoyed the one he left hanging on the air as he reached for the door handle.

Dawson was damned if he was going to give Korn the satisfaction of the last word. Angered by Korn's manner, he said, 'If your goddam Bureau wasn't like some goddam elephant that hollers because it fears extinction, if it knew how to conduct an investigation with any kind of tact and discretion, if it wasn't manned by so many fuck-ups and psychopaths, I'd say go ahead. I'd give you my blessing. But we know what it would really be like, don't we, Len? There would be inexplicable leaks to the press. There would be interviews with Len Korn, master of counter-terrorist tactics. It would become a full-blown media circus for the glorification of King Korn and his personal adversary, Jig. Black and white! Good guys and bad guys! All the lines of conflict nicely drawn for the masses to understand! God bless the FBI and goodnight!'

Leonard Korn had the black sensation that he'd overstepped the mark. He turned to the President with a small insincere smile on his face. 'I spoke out of turn,' he said.

'Damn right you did.'

'Sorry.'

Dawson smiled back with an equal lack of warmth. 'Too much tension, Len. Too much stress. And stress kills.'

'So they say, Mr President.'

When Korn had gone, Thomas Dawson did something he never did in public. He lit a cigarette, a Winston, and sucked the smoke deeply inside his lungs. It was the most satisfying thing he'd done in a long time. He put the cigarette out carefully, dropped the butt in a wastebasket, then sprayed the air with a small can of Ozium he kept in his desk. He sat back and shut his eyes. It wasn't just the violence done against the Memorial Presbyterian Church in White Plains that troubled him. It was also the old Irish thread, that dark green bloodsoaked thread, linking the late Nicholas Linney to brother Kevin.

He tried to get Kevin on the telephone again, only to learn from Agatha Bates that the family hadn't returned yet from their cabin at Lake Candlewood. And no, she wasn't precisely sure when to expect them either. What was this goddam urge Kevin felt every now and again to take his family into inaccessible places? This fondness for the rough outdoors and kerosene lights and dried foods?

Thomas Dawson hung up, frustrated, tense and, for the first time in his entire Presidency, truly afraid. Kevin, he felt, was going to be okay because he had the Secret Servicemen around him. But as for himself and his Presidency – that could be quite another matter.

New York City

It was the pounding on the door of his room that woke Frank Pagan at five past nine. He hadn't meant to sleep this late. Last night, when he'd walked away from Tyson Bruno, he had intended to sleep four hours, maybe even less, but he still hadn't quite recovered from the ravages of jet-lag. He pulled on a robe, opened the door, saw Artie Zuboric outside. Zuboric swept inside the room immediately. Pagan saw at once that something was up. Artie looked both driven and yet rather pleased with himself. The agent drifted to the window, pulled back the drape, let the room fill with wintry sunlight. Pagan wondered if he was about to be lectured for slipping the leash last night and leaving Tyson Bruno stranded. But it wasn't that.

'A church has been bombed,' Artie said at once. 'A Presbyterian church in White Plains, New York.'

'Bombed? With a b?'

'With a big b,' Zuboric said. 'Somebody planted explosives in the place. Seventy-eight people are dead. The explosives went off in the middle of the sunrise service. Nice timing, huh?'

Pagan absorbed this information, feeling tense as he did so. Zuboric wasn't telling him this for nothing. There was something else coming. Pagan waited, seeing how Zuboric enjoyed dispensing this information.

'The bombing happened around seven-twenty this morning. At approximately eight-thirty a man called my office in New York City and claimed responsibility on behalf of the Irish Republican Army.'

Pagan licked his lips, suddenly dry. 'Which you attributed to Jig, of course.'

Zuboric eased into sarcasm. 'I don't see a whole bus-load of Irish terrorists running around New York State, do you?'

'It's damned convenient to blame Jig,' Pagan replied. 'It's so nicely packaged and wrapped for you. It's so fucking American. If you can wrap it, you can also buy it. And I don't buy it any more than I buy the incident at Bridgehampton.'

'Why? Because you think you've got Jig pegged as a Boy Scout? The honourable terrorist? Helps old ladies cross streets before he blows them up? Grow up, Pagan. He doesn't have any scruples. He doesn't give a shit who he hurts.'

Pagan sat on the bed. He could tell Zuboric that Jig operated differently, that Jig was a new refinement in a very old conflict, that there was no way in the world, given Jig's past acts of terrorism, he was going to blow up a whole church and the people in it. He could tell Zuboric that Jig wasn't in the habit of murdering the innocent. But he saw no point in saying such things because he could smell the lust for blood, Jig's blood, coming from Zuboric. He could smell the sweat of the lynch-mob eager to hang a victim in a public place for the intense gratification of the masses. Hang first, ask questions later. People in Zuboric's frame of mind were notoriously narrow in their vision, and decidedly uncharitable.

'Face it, Frank,' Zuboric said. 'Your man's an animal. And the sooner you realise this, the sooner we can catch him. You've been playing it as if this cocksucker was civilised, which he isn't. He's a fucking *beast*. He ought to be shot on sight.'

Pagan looked for a calm controlled corner of himself, and found it. He had the thought that if only he'd captured Jig last night in Brooklyn, if only that chase through mean streets had ended differently, then Jig would be in custody now and beyond suspicion of any terrorism in White Plains. If. Pagan had a very bad relationship with conditionals. He considered them the lepers of English grammar. He hadn't caught Jig, and it was pointless now to have regrets.

'What exactly did the caller say?'

'You can hear the tape.'

'I'd like that,' Pagan said. He remembered all the hours he'd spent in London listening to Jig's voice, that strange flat drone which announced each new assassination in a cold detached way. He'd even brought in two professors of dialect to analyse the accent. One said it was British West Country, the other that Jig had obviously spent time in America but was working to disguise the fact. Academic dispute, and totally useless.

'I'll come down to your office,' Pagan said.

'Be my guest.' Zuboric had gloves on his hands and he rubbed them together. He watched Pagan step towards the bathroom and he said, 'I also hear you split last night.'

Pagan nodded.

'Like to tell me where you went?'

'No,' Pagan said.

Zuboric raised one of his fingers in the air, shaking it from side to side. 'I'm fucking sick of you, Frank. I'm fucking sick and tired of the way you want to do things.'

'It's mutual,' Pagan replied.

'You think you can go after this Irish moron on your own. You think your way's the only way. Let me remind you, Pagan. This isn't your country. You don't have any jurisdiction here except what we choose to give you. If we withdrew our support, you'd be nothing. And if we want to kick you out unceremoniously and go after this Jig ourselves, what the hell can you do about it?'

Pagan stood in the bathroom doorway, flicking a towel idly against the wall. He wondered if there was any sense in getting angry. At whom would it be directed anyway? Artie and the FBI? Furry Jake and the butchers of Scotland Yard? Or at the barbaric nature of those who set off explosives in a church? He decided to say nothing. Zuboric's head was a Ziploc bag, deeply refrigerated and impossible to open and colder than hell once you managed to tear it apart. He went inside the bathroom, closing the door quietly.

He looked at his pale face in the mirror. Eyes slightly bloodshot. Small dark circles. *The IRA blows up a church in White Plains, New York. The IRA kills a man called Fitzjohn in Albany. Fitzjohn almost certainly had a connection with Ivor McInnes, though not one that would stand up in a court of law.* What was going on? He brushed his teeth and made a horrible face at himself, mouth open and jaw thrust forward and tongue sticking out. You look your age, Frankie, he thought. This morning, finally, you can see the effect of Old Father Time's facial. Even inside the body, in the places you couldn't see, his organs felt ancient and sluggish and all used-up.

Roscommon, New York

Harry Cairney answered the telephone on the second ring. He heard the familiar voice of Jock Mulhaney.

'He was here, Harry. Last night,' Mulhaney said.

Cairney didn't ask who. He knew. He gazed silently out of the window, seeing the security jeep move between stands of bare trees. He felt a small tic under his eye and he put a hand to the place.

'He came right here, Harry,' Mulhaney was saying. 'Are you listening?'

'Yes,' Cairney said. 'I'm listening.' If the man sent from Ireland could get inside Mulhaney's headquarters, how could one small jeep keep him at bay if he found his way here? It was an appalling thought.

'He killed one of my people,' Big Jock said. 'He threatened me.'

'What did you tell him?'

'Harry, what the fuck you think I told him? Nothing, for Christ's sake.'

Nothing, the old man thought. He wondered about that. 'And he left? He just left after you said you had nothing to tell him?'

'That was when he shot Keefe.'

'Keefe?'

'A bodyguard.'

Cairney watched the jeep along the shore of Roscommon Lake, then it was gone.

'Then another guy showed up. An English guy. He was looking for our crazy Irish friend.'

An Englishman. Harry Cairney looked at his wife, who was sitting cross-legged before the fire. By firelight she seemed frail, composed of porcelain. He hated the idea of anyone coming here and putting her in a situation of menace because of something that he himself was responsible for. He couldn't stand the notion of that. He watched Celestine stretch her legs, reach for her toes, absent-minded exercise. Cairney observed this fluid gesture with the expression of a connoisseur absorbing a particularly lovely painting, then opened the centre drawer of his desk. He looked inside at the handgun, an old Browning. He might not be a young man any more, but by God he hadn't forgotten how to fight. And he would, if it came to that.

Mulhaney was still talking. 'This English character asked some questions, Harry. He mentioned your name.'

'My name?' Harry Cairney's heart skipped one small telling beat. 'Who was this man?'

'I don't know.'

'Have you any idea where he is now?'

'Uh-huh.'

Cairney was silent. 'Do you think he might be coming this way?'

Mulhaney didn't answer at once.

'I don't know if he knows about you, Harry. I really don't.'

'Does he know Linney?'

'He mentioned Nick's name.'

'Dawson?'

'He knows about Dawson too.'

Cairney closed the drawer. Celestine was watching him. Cairney turned his back to her and quietly said, 'Then I imagine there's a damn good chance he knows about me.'

Mulhaney said, 'I don't know what he knows, Harry. All I can say is he's young and he's quick and he's ruthless.'

'It's a ruthless business.' Cairney turned once more to his wife and smiled. 'Thanks for calling, Jock.'

He put the receiver down. It was over, then. The secrecy had been more fragile than he'd ever realised. He went towards his wife, laid his hand on her scalp.

'What was all that about?' Celestine asked. 'What's a ruthless business?'

Cairney didn't answer. He didn't want her involved. He couldn't bring himself to make up a lie either.

'I'd like a drink,' he said. 'Am I allowed one?'

'Very tiny.'

She kissed his cheek as she went out of the room. Downstairs in the kitchen she poured a small shot of brandy and mixed a vodka martini for herself. She glanced at the kitchen clock. It was just after noon. She sampled her drink, arranged the glasses on a tray, then headed back upstairs. She didn't go inside the study at once. Instead she entered Patrick's room, set the tray on the bedside table, and looked at the various photographs of Cairney as a boy. There was one that depicted him at thirteen, maybe fourteen, sitting cross-legged among other members of a school football team. He had a helmet in his lap. Another showed him in shorts and sweatshirt, poised to release a discus. He was well-muscled and taught even then, but it was the face she stared at. She saw only that eager open quality of youth, the smile of innocence, nothing of the secret darkness in the eyes he had as a man. What do you know? she asked the face. What do you really know?

Old pictures yielded nothing. They were interesting only as history, mileposts on the road to somewhere else. She touched the surface of a photograph with her fingertips, imagining she felt Cairney's skin under glass. Some hours ago, when the telephone had rung and nobody talked, she was convinced that the person on the other end of the line was Patrick. Now she wasn't so sure. Some instinct had suggested it at the time, but now she wondered if it were just the blindly hopeful reaction of a woman intrigued. Intrigued, she thought. There was a word belonging to the cheap romances. Intrigue was for lady librarians vacationing in Corsica or swanning about the Taj Mahal by moonlight. Intrigue wasn't a good word when it came to serious business. And what else was all this but serious?

She heard Harry coughing along the landing. She switched off the bedside lamp, picked up the tray, left Patrick's room quickly. Harry was standing in the door of the study, watching her.

'Wrong room,' he said.

She laughed his remark away. She kissed him and together they went inside the study. She sat in front of the fire and sipped her drink and listened to a log slip in the flames. Harry sat down beside her eventually, and she laid her head in his lap, closing her eyes.

'He was quite a sportsman,' she said lazily.

He looked at her in a puzzled way. His mind was elsewhere.

She opened her eyes, looking up at him. 'Your son.'

'Oh.' Cairney, held captive in his wife's blue eyes, made a small mental adjustment. The curse of age, this difficulty in focusing. 'He had one year, I remember, when sports became an obsession. He slept and dreamed sports. He had the makings of a fair quarterback. You were looking at the old photographs?'

She nodded. Firelight made her hair very gold.

Cairney stared at the window. 'He was always like that, always picking up on something. Then he'd become obsessed with it for a while, before he moved along to something else. He wouldn't stick with a thing. He'd overdose on it when he was interested, but when the interest went flat he'd just move on. Compulsive behaviour. Always searching.'

'Archaeology must have been different for him then,' she said. 'He's been doing it for years now, hasn't he?'

'It's the damnedest thing,' the old man said. 'I sent him to Yale. He was going to do law, he said. He spent a year at Yale, then suddenly I received a postcard from him. He's in Ireland, for God's sake!'

'Just like that?'

'Dropped law. Dropped Yale. Wanted to learn more about the past, he said. Wanted to enroll in Trinity College. I didn't mind that. After all, I suppose I'm the one that gave him a taste of the past in the first place – but archaeology!'

Harry gazed into firelight. There was an ache inside him. He realised he was hurting from the way Patrick had so abruptly left. When you were old, even small emotional slights became exaggerated inside you. You wanted to look towards death without that kind of pain.

'He went overseas a lot,' he continued. 'This desert. That desert. He was always sending me postcards from strange places.'

Celestine was very quiet for a time. She was trying to imagine Patrick Cairney turning brown under a desert sun. It was a fine image and it was exact. Where else would he have gone but to the deserts of the Middle East?

'For long periods, I'd hear absolutely nothing from him. Then there'd be a flurry of postcards from places with Arab names. I worried at first, but then I had to let go of that. He was grown up. It was his life. I couldn't influence him any more.'

'Did you ever influence him?'

Harry laughed quietly. 'He's the only one who could answer that.'

Celestine raised her head, sipped some of her drink. She wanted to know more about Patrick Cairney. Tomorrow morning, first thing. That's when she'd know something Harry couldn't possibly tell her. Maybe. Or maybe she was simply tracking a mystery that didn't exist, a construct of her own mind, something to pass the time with the way people whittled on sticks or took up water-colours. *No. She was sure. Damned sure.*

'Are you proud of him?' she asked.

'Proud?' Harry Cairney smiled. 'I never asked myself that.'

Celestine pressed the palms of her hands against her thighs. The loose-fitting cotton robe she wore slipped up to her knees and she could feel the heat from the fire lay a band of warmth against her calves.

'Why all these questions?' the old man asked.

'He's my stepson, don't forget. You don't have a monopoly on him. I want to know him better, that's all.'

Cairney looked suddenly rather solemn. 'Be warned,' he said. 'He's not so easy to know.'

Celestine closed her eyes again. 'I don't believe he's as difficult as you suggest,' she answered.

Cairney patted the back of her hand. It was all right to talk about Patrick, it was fine, but finally it only produced in him an illusion of normality. Sitting here by firelight, his wife's head in his lap. The surfaces of the very ordinary. The taste of brandy. Family chatter. He turned his face back towards the window. Out there the world was quite a different place. But he would maintain a front of calm because he was good at that. He had a lifetime of self-control in public office behind him, a decent support-system. He wasn't given to easy panic or impulsive acts. Everything would go on as it had done before the *Connie* was stricken at sea. Life, marriage, love.

'We need music,' he said, starting to rise.

She shook her head. 'Let's enjoy the peace, Harry.'

He rose anyhow. He walked to his desk and looked at the Browning once more. It was years since he'd fired the gun.

Celestine, propped up on her elbows, was watching him. 'What's the big attraction there, Harry?'

He closed the drawer slowly.

He came back across the room and sat down beside her. 'Nothing will ever happen to you,' he said. 'I want you to know that.'

Celestine looked surprised. 'Why would anything happen to me, Harry? This is Roscommon. And nothing ever happens here.'

Harry Cairney closed his eyes. He thought he felt it in the very air around him, a shiver, as if the atmosphere of this house had changed with Mulhaney's phone call. It was a sinister feeling, and he didn't like it. It resembled those disquieting moments when you felt that somebody, somewhere, was walking on your grave.

New Rockford, Connecticut

It was two o'clock in the afternoon when Kevin Dawson received a telephone call from his brother in the White House. Thomas Dawson sounded very weary when he spoke.

'How was Candlewood?'

'Candlewood was terrific,' Kevin Dawson replied. 'You ought to try it some time. That place never lets me down. I always come back feeling refreshed.'

'My idea of roughing it is to watch black and white TV,' the President said. 'One Boy Scout to a family is okay. Two would be a travesty of genetic theory.'

Kevin Dawson heard the sounds of his daughters from the foot of the stairs. They were involved in a game of what they'd described as 'cut-throat poker', which they played to rules of their own random making. It was altogether incomprehensible.

Thomas Dawson said, 'It's been a long winter.'

Puzzled, Kevin reached out and closed the door of his office with his knee. 'You didn't call to discuss the length of the seasons,' he said.

'True.'

Another pause.

Kevin sat down, tilting his chair back against the wall. With one hand he managed to pour himself a scotch. He heard the door of the Secret Service vehicle open and close in the driveway below. Both agents, whom the kids had christened Cisco and Pancho, had spent the weekend in obvious discomfort, sleeping in a two-man tent because there was no extra room in the small cabin. They took their meals alone, laboriously burning things over a Coleman stove and filling the cold, sharp air with a dark brown pollution that smelled Kitty said, like a skunk on a spit.

'It's been a long winter, and you're about ready for a vacation,' Thomas Dawson said.

'It's that bad, huh?'

'It's that bad. Nicholas Linney has been murdered.'

'Linney?' Kevin felt an odd tightness in his throat. His voice sounded very high, even to himself.

'I don't have to spell out the implications.'

'Was it Jig?' Kevin asked.

'Almost certainly. By the way, I don't want this news bruited about, Kev. You understand me?'

Kevin Dawson drained his glass. He reached for the bottle, poured himself a second shot. All the invigoration he'd brought back with him from Candlewood was draining away. He had the very strange feeling he'd just been kicked in the stomach and couldn't breathe properly. How in God's name had Jig managed to track Linney down? Kevin curled the telephone cord tightly around his wrist.

He heard Martha and the kids coming up the stairs. Their voices echoed in this great sprawling house.

'I don't think you're seriously in danger, Kevin. You've got protection there. But why take any needless chances?'

Protection, Kevin thought. What it came down to was the fact that all the security in the world couldn't prevent somebody getting to you, if he was determined enough, and crazy enough, to find a way.

'What do you suggest?' Kevin asked.

'Hawaii. Make it a business trip with a little R & R on the side. Check into the family interests out there, but take Martha and the kids as well. Stay until Jig's been caught. How soon can you get out of there?'

Kevin Dawson wasn't sure. There were business meetings of one kind or another on Monday morning and Martha was the guest of honour at a breakfast in Stamford sponsored by the Make-A-Wish Foundation, which was her favourite charity. It would take more than a terrorist threat to make her cancel. 'Tomorrow afternoon,' he said. 'I can't see getting away from here before that.'

'I'd like it if you left earlier, Kevin.'

'I don't see how.'

Kevin heard his brother light up one of his infrequent cigarettes.

'I've just been talking with what the press always calls "my closest advisers", Kevin. Terrorists are the new bogeymen. They've replaced Communists in the American nightmare. If I lose some of the Irish vote by sticking the full fury of the FBI on somebody as famous as Jig, I'm advised I'll pick it up again with the rednecks who have orgasms when they know there's a firm Presidential hand on the old helm of state. The Law and Order Ticket. The Jerry Falwell Brigade. Imagine a Catholic climbing into bed beside those polyester gangsters!'

Kevin Dawson couldn't imagine anything like that. But his brother had gone so far into cynicism that nothing was surprising these days. Thomas Dawson, human being, was almost a lost cause. Not quite gone, but fading fast. Tom would climb into bed with any group that could deliver votes. He was less a President than a calculating machine. If the Irish couldn't be counted on, you dumped them and looked around for substitutes. The politics of expediency, of numbers. Tommy would have sat down to supper with a consortium of the KKK, the John Birchers, the Posse Comitatus and The Unification Church, if he thought this crew could deliver.

'We were weak on law and order during the campaign,' Thomas Dawson said. 'I know it lost us the Midwest and the South. Maybe my advisers are smarter than I think.'

'Maybe,' Kevin said.

'Call me from Hawaii.'

'I'll do that.'

'Goodnight, Kevin.'

Kevin Dawson put the telephone down. The door of his office swung open and Martha stood there. She was dressed in faded blue jeans and an old red parka. There were streaks of mud on her hiking boots. Her Candlewood Collection. Kevin loved it.

'The girls and I are going to watch some Disney thing on TV,' she said. 'Wanna join us?'

Kevin Dawson nodded. He reached for his wife, held her wrists in his hands. 'Later,' he said.

Martha smiled. 'I want you to know I had a wonderful weekend. I didn't even mind Pancho and Cisco and their awful cooking. I just had a terrific time.'

'Me too.'

Kevin wondered how to approach the subject of a trip to Hawaii. Martha hated to travel very far from her home. A day trip to Stamford was as far as she liked to go.

'Why don't you watch your movie, then we'll put the kids to bed as early as possible. You can slip, as they say, into something more comfortable, and I'll open a bottle of wine.' Kevin thought that a couple of glasses of burgundy would make the notion of Hawaii palatable to her. She might not cancel her luncheon in Stamford, but she might be persuaded that Waikiki was a good idea. Sometimes you had to coax Martha along, seduce her into acceptance. Besides, nothing was more pleasurable in Kevin Dawson's world than the act of making love to his own wife.

'You've got a funny look in your eyes,' she said.

'Don't I.'

'I know that look, Kevin Dawson.'

'You should. You're the one that put it there.'

She raised her face up and kissed him, standing on tip-toes. 'I look like somebody from the combat zone,' she said. She went to the door, turned back to him. 'Next time you see me I'll be gorgeous.'

'You always are,' Kevin Dawson said, but his wife had already gone.

He sat alone in his room, staring absently at a pile of business papers. He couldn't keep Nicholas Linney out of his mind. He kept seeing Nick as he'd seen him last at Roscommon, kept hearing Linney say he could take care of himself. Well, he hadn't. He hadn't taken care of himself at all. He thought now of Harry Cairney and Mulhaney and he considered calling them. But what was there to say? And neither of them had troubled to call him, which meant they had nothing to say either.

Kevin Dawson walked to the window. He looked down at the Secret Servicemen. One of them – Cisco, Pancho, Kevin wasn't sure – stared up at him and smiled. A fleeting expression, then it was gone. Kevin stared across the meadowlands that stretched all the way from his house to the road. Beyond the ribbon of concrete the hills rose up, pocked with mysterious shadows and dark trees. It was a landscape he had been familiar with all his life, except that now it appeared strange to him, and threatening, as if it might conceal the Irishman somewhere in its crevices.

New York City

The voice on the tape said: *I'm claiming responsibility on behalf of the Irish Republican Army for the explosions in the Memorial Church at White Plains. Have you got that, shithead? I don't intend to repeat it.* And then the tape went silent, the line dead. Frank Pagan pressed the rewind button on the Grundig and listened for the third time. Zuboric drummed a lead pencil on the surface of his desk, watching Pagan carefully. You couldn't tell, from the surfaces of the Englishman's face, what he might be thinking.

The voice filled the room again. Pagan pushed the stop button. He looked at Zuboric.

'It's Irish. There's no mistaking that,' Pagan said.

Zuboric stroked his moustache. There was something in Pagan's eyes he didn't like. He wasn't quite sure what it was, but a strange little film had appeared in the ashen greyness. A sneaky quality. It was as if Pagan's eyes were being bleached of what colour they possessed. Zuboric wished he had a passport valid for entry into the Englishman's mind.

'Is it Jig?' the FBI agent asked.

Pagan stared down at the reels of the Grundig. 'It could be,' he said.

'You're not convinced, naturally.'

'I'm just not sure. There's distortion. And maybe he's disguising the voice. It could be Jig.'

Zuboric appeared satisfied with this. Frank Pagan walked up and down the office and then returned to the Grundig, as if he needed to hear the voice one last time to be absolutely sure. He pushed the play button, listened, killed the machine.

'I'm still not one hundred per cent certain,' Pagan said.

'We don't *need* one hundred per cent certainty, Frank.'

No, Pagan thought. You don't. He looked at Zuboric's college diploma which hung just over his head and wondered what institution of Higher Learning had been so foolish as to bestow any kind of degree on Zuboric. Obviously it was one that didn't specialise in imaginative pursuits.

'I'd like to have the original Jig tapes relayed from England,' Pagan said. 'A comparison would erase any doubt.'

Zuboric was about to make an answer to this when the telephone rang. Pagan watched the agent pick up the receiver. Zuboric's body was suddenly tense, at attention, which meant only one thing. Leonard M. Korn was on the other end of the line. Pagan listened to the occasional 'Yes sir' which Zuboric dropped into a conversation that was otherwise one-sided. Yessir, yessir, three bags full, sir.

Zuboric put the receiver down. 'Well well.' He was positively beaming. Pagan thought ships could guide themselves by the beacon that was Zuboric's face right then.

'As of eight o'clock tonight,' Zuboric said, glancing at his wristwatch, 'the Director is placing himself in charge of the Jig operation.'

'Ah,' Pagan said. 'Divine intervention.'

Zuboric rubbed his hands together. 'Tomorrow morning, one hundred agents will be working fulltime on Jig. *One hundred*.' Zuboric laughed in an excited way. He was like a lottery winner, Pagan thought. Blue-collar, worked hard all his days, liked the occasional sixer of Schlitz, a game of bowling Fridays – and lo and behold! His number has just come up and he doesn't know what to say. I'm happy for you, Artie, Pagan thought. Spend it wisely.

'The Director estimates we'll have Jig in a matter of days.'

Pagan said nothing. He mistrusted the optimism of law-enforcement officers, especially those who dwelt on Olympian heights the way Korn did. Probably the guy in charge of the Jack the Ripper investigation had said much the same kind of thing a hundred years ago, and *he* was still searching.

'I'm going back to my hotel,' Pagan said. 'I'm tired.'

'I'll keep you company, Frank.'

'Of course you will.'

Pagan did up the buttons of his overcoat. He glanced once at the Grundig machine. He thought again of repeating his proposal to have the original tapes of Jig relayed from London, but suddenly it was redundant, suddenly those tapes wouldn't make a damn bit of difference. The hunt was on and the night was filled with baying hounds. And there was going to be noise, so much noise that nobody was going to stop and listen to tapes of the real Jig. Even if they did, they wouldn't hear them anyway because blood had a way of singing into your ears, making you deaf. The hunt mentality, whether it was Federal agents thrashing around for Jig or plum-rumped English squires intent on diminishing the evil fox population, was akin to insanity. It was blinded and restricted, and obsessive.

Whoever had called the FBI about White Plains wasn't Jig. He didn't sound *remotely* like Jig. There was no way in the world Jig had made that phone call. Pagan had hoped to use his apparent uncertainty as a ploy, a way of winning a little time and getting the real tapes played. But he saw further manoeuvres as totally useless now. There was no future in arguing, in trying to convince Zuboric. For his own part, he knew what he was going to do. It wasn't the smartest move he'd ever contemplated, but at the same time he couldn't see any alternatives. He had tried to play this whole thing by FBI rules and regulations, but that time was long past. He hadn't come all this way to America to have his quarry trapped in some bloody corner by morons like Zuboric. He hadn't made this trip to see that kind of travesty happen. He wanted Jig, but not on the sort of terms dictated by the hangmen of the Federal Bureau of Investigation.

Pagan locked the door of his room at the Parker Meridien. He sat for a time on the edge of the bed. He was motionless, like a man in the still centre of meditation. Then, when he moved, he did so with the economy of somebody driven by a solitary purpose. He checked his gun, stuck it in the waistband of his pants at the back. He left the room. It was all movement now. Down in the elevator. Out into the lobby. Heading for the street.

Tyson Bruno came across the lobby towards him.

Pagan swept past the agent into the street, but Bruno came after him swiftly. It was interesting, Pagan thought. There was no effort on Bruno's part to conceal himself, no shadow-work going on. It was out in the open. Maybe Bruno had been surprised by Pagan's sudden appearance and the quickness of his stride and hadn't had time to hide himself. What the hell, it was completely academic now.

Pagan stopped, turned around, waited until Bruno was level with him. Tyson Bruno, who was built like an outhouse, looked very solid in the dusk of Fifty-Seventh Street.

'Before you even ask me one question, Bruno old boy, the answer is dead simple. I'm going for a walk and I don't want you on my arse. Is that clear enough for you?'

Tyson Bruno grinned. He was a man who enjoyed adversity. If he hadn't stepped inside the labyrinthine clasp of the FBI, he would have been a happy bouncer in a sleazy strip-joint. 'I go where you go, Pagan. This time, you don't take a hike on me.'

Pagan turned, continued to walk. Bruno was still coming up behind him. On Fifth Avenue, Pagan made a right. Bruno was still behind him.

'Your last warning, Ty,' Pagan said, looking back at the man.

'You shouldn't be doing this,' Bruno said.

Pagan moved away. He was tired of boxes. Tired of restrictions. Tired by fools who, left to their own devices, courted lunacy. He paused at a stoplight. Bruno was right behind him, still grinning. Pagan glanced at him.

'I just keep coming,' Bruno said.

Pagan made as if to step off the sidewalk and cross the street. He moved an inch or two then stopped abruptly, bunching his hands together and swinging them as if he held a hammer. The connection with Bruno's jaw made a delicious crunching sound. Reverberations created ripples, like tiny springs, all the way up Pagan's arms to his shoulders. Tyson, off balance, hopeless, sat down on the edge of the kerb and said, 'Hey!' He was bleeding from the lip, and his eyes looked like two glazed pinballs under the bleak glow of the streetlamps.

Pagan didn't stop. He ran to the other side of the street and began to move along Fifty-Sixth, past the windows of closed restaurants and travel agencies, past the plastic sacks of garbage and a solitary sleeping wino, a failed candidate for St Finbar's Mission. Pagan stopped running only when he reached Fifty-Fifth and Broadway and was certain that Tyson Bruno was nowhere near him. Winded, he paused in the doorway of a closed Greek sandwich shop, where the scent of yesterday's fried lamb filled his nostrils.

It occurred to him that he had done more than burn his bridges. He had exploded them in such a way that the whole bloody river was on fire.

21 New York City

With a newspaper rolled up under his arm Ivor McInnes stepped into Central Park. It was barely dawn and the sky above Manhattan was the colour of milk. McInnes followed a narrow pathway between the trees until he came to an unoccupied bench. He wiped a layer of thin frost from the wooden slats, then sat down and unfolded his newspaper.

Photographs, headlines. They leaped out at him. For a moment he couldn't read because his eyes watered and his hand trembled. But there it was! McInnes had the feeling, given to very few men, that something he'd long dreamed was finally taking form in reality.

He stared at the newspaper again. He didn't see what other men might see there, a story of outrageous vandalism. He saw glory instead. He looked at the pictures of the smoking church, the tight little crowds of people gathered on the sidewalk, the shots of firemen aiming their hoses into the carnage. He felt for the victims, of course. It was only natural. A man without feelings was a dead man. But these feelings were small considerations compared with the balance of history. And it was history, or rather his personal piece of it, that enthralled Ivor McInnes.

He folded the newspaper over. For a while he stared into the trees. There was a breath of spring in the chill early morning around him. A sense of fresh breakthroughs, newness. He spread the newspaper flat on the bench and read the story through, unable to control the excitement that overcame him.

There was of course no mention yet of the IRA. Nobody was going to release that information to the public so soon. There hadn't been time to analyse Houlihan's call, there hadn't been time in Washington to prepare a public face or concoct a feasible story to cover this incident. A church had blown up. Why? What had caused it? The paper didn't say. The reporter didn't know. There wasn't even speculation. McInnes smiled and rubbed his face with the palm of a hand. The powers of law and order could sit on this one, he realised. They could stall and prevaricate, if they didn't want to alarm the public with the news that IRA terrorists were suddenly operating within the continental United States. But they couldn't stall forever.

After today, they couldn't even stall for a moment.

McInnes folded the newspaper again and was about to rise when he became conscious of somebody sitting down on the bench beside him.

Frank Pagan said, 'Interesting reading.'

'A damn tragedy,' McInnes said and glanced at Pagan's big hands, which were bone-white and tense on the man's knees. There was a sense of power about Pagan, a force held narrowly in check as if by some enormous inner effort. What had he come for at this time of the bloody morning? McInnes wondered.

'What do you think caused it, Ivor? A whole church gone in a flash. I mean, what do you think really caused such a thing to happen?'

'The paper doesn't say,' McInnes answered. Was Frank Pagan baiting him? McInnes dismissed the suspicion. Pagan was groping in the dark.

'Your opinion, Ivor. You must have one. You usually do.'

McInnes shrugged.

'God works in mysterious ways,' Pagan remarked.

'Isn't that the truth?'

A jogger went past. A pot-bellied middle-aged man with a scarlet headband and expensive sneakers. There was total desperation in his eyes.

Pagan said, 'Somebody told me the IRA claimed the job in White Plains.'

'The IRA?'

'Strikes me as farfetched,' Pagan said. 'How does it strike you?'

'Hard to believe,' McInnes answered. 'They'd be operating pretty far from home, wouldn't they?'

Pagan smiled. He stared at McInnes for a while. 'It's not their style, is it?' he asked.

'Styles change. Anything's possible.'

'Anything's possible. But why bring their war into the United States?'

'You're asking me? I've always found the Catholic mind unfathomable, Frank. I know this much, though. If it's the IRA, it's not going to end with some church. Once those fellows get a taste of blood, they don't know when to stop.'

Pagan was quiet now. McInnes was conscious of the man's cold stare, which made him uncomfortable. Frank Pagan, with his inside track, would of course know about the IRA story. But why would he casually mention this? McInnes wondered. Pagan was like a bloody submarine, operating way below the surface in a place where the waters were murky. You could never tell where the man was headed or what torpedoes he might fire.

Pagan draped an arm across the back of the bench. 'It's funny,' he said quietly. 'Now it's the church. Before that it was Alex Fitzjohn.'

'Fitzjohn?' So here it was at last. Fitzjohn's name, as McInnes had expected, had finally cropped up. He tried not to appear defensive.

Pagan nodded. 'Alex Fitzjohn was murdered in Albany, New York. The IRA claimed responsibility for that one too.'

'I didn't hear anything about that,' McInnes said.

'It wasn't in the papers, Ivor.'

McInnes, who had the gift of supreme detachment when he needed it, stared blankly into Pagan's face. 'Well,' was all he said. He tapped the bench with his newspaper.

'You ever hear of Alex Fitzjohn, Ivor?'

McInnes shook his head.

Pagan said, 'He was a member of the Free Ulster Volunteers. I thought you might have run into him along the way somewhere.'

'We're back at that again, are we?' McInnes said. 'We're back at the FUV again?'

'Why not,' Pagan said. 'Do you deny knowing Alex Fitzjohn?'

'I know a lot of people in Ulster, Frank. I know a lot of Fitzes. Fitzthis, Fitzthat. I told you before, I have absolutely no connection with the Volunteers. To suggest otherwise is a falsehood. I can't remember anyone by the name of Alex Fitzjohn.' McInnes smiled and stared across the park. In the milky light of dawn the trees appeared to have been brushed lightly with an off-white enamel paint. 'I have enemies, Frank. You know that. Certain people in Ulster have always tried to discredit me. Certain Catholics.' McInnes crossed his legs and leaned closer to Frank Pagan. 'For years the Catholic Church has been putting out stories about me. Incredible lies. They say I'm the leader of the FUV, among other things. The reason's very simple. They don't like what I have to say, Frank. They don't like my criticisms. They've been in a cave of superstition for centuries. And they don't like what I do. *I shine some light into that cave. I attack their idolatry.* They fight back the only way they know how, which is dirty.'

McInnes paused. His large handsome face was intense now. The light in his eyes, like some laser, could have bored two neat holes in a plank of wood.

'What I really object to, Frank, isn't just the Roman Catholic attitude to social issues. It's bad enough when they tell some unemployed labourer with nine kids that he can't get his wife on the pill. Keep on breeding, they say, and to hell with the misery. You'll get your rewards in the afterlife, sonny. It's bad enough when they tell people they can erase their sins by mumbojumboing over some set of bloody beads, Frank. But what I truly find deplorable is the damned backwardness of it all. It's late in the twentieth century and we're in the throes of a vast technological revolution and the Catholic Church belongs to another time. It doesn't like progress because it means that people have more information. And more information, as we well know, leads to freedoms. And that's what the Catholic Church doesn't like. People who are free to think, Frank. *They want men and women in bondage.*' McInnes shut his eyes for a moment. He moved one hand through the air, inscribing a pattern of some kind. 'It keeps Ulster in the Dark Ages, Frank. It keeps my country from going forward. It hates the new technology. It doesn't know what to do with it. It wants its adherents to live in blind obedience to the dictates of the Vatican. Consider this Frank. *In Dublin priests actually bless the fleet of Aer Lingus!* Can you believe that? Priests bless the planes! What does that tell you about the Catholic Church? It's trying to impose superstition upon high technology! It makes me uneasy and it makes me angry because, with the present Catholic birthrate, it won't be long before Ulster is dominated by the Vatican the way the Republic is. Then we kiss the whole of Ireland goodbye. And back to the Dark Ages with *all* of us.'

There was a certain hypnotic effect in the cadences of McInnes's voice. It lulled and it soothed even as it provoked. Pagan could see how thousands of people in Ulster were swayed by the man. You had to give it to Ivor. He put on a damn good show. Even the hand movements, which were expressive and sinewy, must have impressed people in a society not known for great conversational use of the hands. There was something

Mediterranean about it all, something exotic. And in drab, burned-out Belfast it must have had enormous appeal.

Now Pagan wanted to bring this conversation, which Ivor had taken up to roof level, back to the ground floor. 'We were talking about Fitzjohn.'

'I was talking about my enemies,' McInnes said.

Pagan sighed. 'You claim you don't know Fitzjohn. But my London office has different information. We have a photograph of yourself and Fitzjohn together taken outside your church. It's quite a chummy little composition.'

A photograph? McInnes couldn't recall ever having a picture taken with Fitz, whom he hadn't seen since the man had emigrated. 'You're bluffing me,' he said.

'Hardly, Ivor.'

McInnes thought of Houlihan. Bloody Seamus, who had to go and kill a man and then turn around and call the FBI! It was the one flaw in the whole mosaic, the one tile that didn't quite fit right, and it could so easily have been avoided. Damn. Damn Houlihan. Everything should have been perfect. Now there was one spidery crack. And it wouldn't be sealed because bloody Pagan wasn't going to leave it alone.

'Do you have the photograph, Frank?'

'Not in my possession. But I can get it.'

'I wouldn't mind seeing it. I'm sure there's some mistake.'

'I don't really think so, Ivor. This picture shows you and Fitzjohn standing side by side. You have an arm round Fitz's shoulder and he's looking happy as the day is long.'

McInnes blinked. 'I don't deny I may have *met* the man, but I don't remember the encounter. As for the photograph, I'd have to see it before I could comment. If there is such a picture, which I doubt.'

He stood up, but Frank Pagan caught him by the wrist and tugged. Pagan's grip was very strong.

'Don't run away, Ivor. Stay and chat.'

'I've got work to do, Frank.'

'What kind of work?'

'Research.' McInnes saw that Pagan's eyes, which were hard and distant, resembled the small grey moons of some icy planet. It was a look he didn't like.

'Why was Fitzjohn in Albany?' Pagan asked. His tone of voice was chilly now, and harsh. It was the voice of an interrogator demanding answers in some basement room.

'How the hell would I know?'

'Who killed him?'

McInnes made a flustered movement with his hands. 'Frank, for God's sake. You keep harping.'

'Did you know the IRA was in America?'

'How could I know something like that?'

'Did you know they planned to bomb the church?'

McInnes shook his head. 'You're losing control, Frank.'

Pagan stood up. He released McInnes now. Ivor took a couple of steps away.

'You're scared of something, Ivor. What is it?'

McInnes smiled thinly. His wrist hurt from Pagan's tight grip. 'Irrational people upset me, Frank.'

Irrational people. Pagan thought that was pretty good, coming from McInnes.

'It's the photograph, isn't it?' Pagan asked. 'That's what's worrying you now. You can't remember where or when it was taken, and you're desperately trying to think up some lie to cover it.'

McInnes shook his head. 'I don't believe in this photograph, Frank. So how could it worry me?'

Pagan came very close to McInnes now. There was hardly an inch separating the two men. 'You and Fitzjohn,' Pagan said. 'You must have been close, Ivor. Two good pals.'

McInnes stepped back. He rapped his rolled-up newspaper against his leg. Bloody man, he thought. Hard man with his tough talk. But Pagan knew absolutely nothing. He was all bluster, all empty performance. A man on a fishing expedition, that was Frank Pagan. There was no photograph. There couldn't have been.

'Why don't you do something important, Frank? You said Jig was here in America, didn't you? Why don't you go out and *catch* him?'

Frank Pagan smiled, but barely. The expression was little more than a slit on his face. 'Nice comeback, Ivor. Very nice,' he said in a grim way. 'But remember this. Whatever it is you're doing here, I'll find out. I'm good at finding things out. In other words, Ivor, keep looking over your shoulder.'

'I'm used to that, Frank.'

'You may be used to it, Ivor. But you better be good at it.'

McInnes turned away. He moved in the direction of his hotel, walking without glancing back, even though he knew Pagan was still watching him. He wasn't going to let Pagan shake him. Damn the man! But today of all days he wasn't going to be upset by Pagan. He entered his hotel, passed the telephone banks, tempted to make one call, *aching* to make one call, longing to hear the voice of reassurance that would tell him his plan was fine, that it wasn't going to go wrong, that Frank Pagan couldn't stop it.

He kept moving.

When he entered his room, he locked the door. He opened his briefcase and searched the lining for the streetmap of New Rockford. He spread the map on the bed and stared at the thick black pen-marks, meticulously drawn arrows that indicated the route the bus always travelled. He concentrated on the arrows but what he kept hearing was Frank Pagan's bloody voice saying *I'm good at finding things out*.

Not this time, McInnes thought. Not now.

Pagan exited from Central Park on Fifth Avenue at Sixtieth Street and walked to the place where he'd parked his rental car, a very mundane Cutlass. He'd abandoned the Cadillac because it was too conspicuous. The Olds, on the other hand, was the colour of excrement and melted into the background, which was the kind of camouflage he wanted. Last night, when he'd dumped the whole FBI in the shape of Tyson Bruno, he'd walked all the way to the Village, where he'd checked into a rundown hotel and passed a bad night on a mattress that felt like the surface of Mars. He had half-expected Zuboric to break down the door.

He drove up Sixth Avenue, clogged with bad-tempered Monday morning drivers. There was a great deal of rage on the streets of New York City. At a stoplight, he pressed the scan button on the digital radio and found a rock station with which he felt comfortable. He listened to the Mersey Beats singing *Sorrow*, and although he wasn't a big fan of the old Mersey sound, the music was restful. More restful, certainly, than the little scene with Ivor, which had proved only that the Reverend was a man with a secret he was grimly determined to keep even when confronted by a potentially damaging photograph.

A secret, Pagan thought.

Was it *possible* Ivor knew of an IRA presence in the USA?

Was it possible that he had come to America *knowing* the IRA was about to launch a mysterious offensive?

And was it Ivor's intention to direct covert operations against the IRA, using America as a battlefield? Had Fitzjohn been one of Ivor's foot soldiers who came to grief in a skirmish with the IRA?

Pagan shook his head. He wasn't sure where this line of speculation was going. If it was true, it would mean that both the FUV and the IRA had forces present inside America. But why would the IRA *suddenly* export its violence? Why bring it to America in the first place? That made no sense. The only foreign soil on which the IRA had ever operated was England. And there was nothing to be gained from acts of terrorism inside America because they would certainly alienate the Irish-Americans who provided both sympathy and money. The main attraction of the Cause, after all, was that it conducted its affairs at a distance of some three thousand miles and was therefore not something to sully your own backyard. The Irish-Americans appreciated that, and the IRA understood it, and there was agreement on that basis. So why the hell spoil a decent understanding by blowing up a church, even a Protestant one?

It was all wrong. It was all out of balance.

Pagan braked at another stoplight. Ivor wasn't a stupid man. He had a cunning capable of creating byzantine situations. Jig, for instance. McInnes had surely known all along Jig was in the country, but he'd consistently denied it. Just as he denied any association with the Free Ulster Volunteers. These links and connections, these skinny threads, made painful knots inside Pagan's brain. And he had the feeling that it was all utterly simple, something so damned obvious it was staring him in the face only he couldn't see it.

He squeezed the Olds between a taxicab and a garbage truck, a manoeuvre that caused several cars behind him to brake quickly. He made a right turn, sliding away from the chaos he left in his wake. He wondered what Artie Zuboric was doing right now. But he didn't wonder for very long.

New Rockford, Connecticut

Patrick Cairney lay flat on his stomach. The long blades of grass around him were coated with a thin film of ice. Overhead, the branches of bare trees were illuminated by a weak sun, a frosted disc with no colour. Cairney edged forward through the grass until he could go no further because the hill became sheer suddenly, a grassy cliff, a long hard drop to the road below. He blinked into the sun.

He'd seen such a sun before and he remembered it, remembered participating in a raid with Libyans inside the border of Chad. Twenty men, himself included, had attacked a convoy of trucks about two hundred miles from Sebra, the last Libyan command post before Chad territory. It was a dawn attack, filled with surprise. The Chad drivers, their trucks loaded with old machine-guns, had been travelling straight into the sun and they hadn't seen the small force descend on them, weapons blazing. It was over in a matter of minutes, and what Cairney recalled best was the sense of anti-climax after the long night of anticipation.

He peered across the road below at the big house, which was located at the end of a narrow driveway. It was a sprawling house, additions made here and there with no particular theme in mind. He brought his binoculars up to his eyes and swept the grounds. A car sat in the driveway, Earlier, a woman had escorted two children into a station wagon and, followed by a pale-blue sedan, had driven down the driveway and vanished along the road. Neither the wagon nor the sedan had returned.

Before coming to New Rockford, Cairney had gone to a newspaper office in Stamford, Connecticut, which had an entire section in its morgue dedicated to the adventures of the Dawson family. America, it appeared, couldn't get enough of the Dawsons. Tons of newsprint were devoted to Tommy and Kevin and Martha and the daughters. The daughters especially. In the absence of presidential offspring, Kitty and Louise Dawson were the next best thing. They went to a local school. They were ordinary kids, the kids next door. Unspoiled, nicely flawed. Little princesses, the Republic's answer to the royalty it had cast off two hundred years ago and still pined for.

Cairney assumed that the big dark car was a Secret Service vehicle. The grounds, so far as he could see, offered very little opportunity for any kind of cover. Winter had stripped the trees with the result that anybody travelling up the driveway could be seen clearly from the windows of the house. He realised that if he was to get to Kevin Dawson without being seen he'd have to wait until nightfall. His coat was damp from the grass and his feet were cold. His breath hung on the chill air. This wasn't going to be a snap. This wasn't going to be anything simple, like slipping inside Nicholas Linney's home or mingling with the half-drunk crowds at Jock Mulhaney's court.

He brought the binoculars back up to his eyes. He saw a tall, dark-haired man get out of the big car and light a cigarette. The man crossed the lawn slowly in front of the house, surveyed the grounds, stubbed his cigarette underfoot, then returned to the car. Cairney lowered his glasses. Nightfall, which was many hours away, many dead hours away, was going to be his only chance. He crawled backwards from the edge of the hill and when the house was no longer in view he stood up, shivering. He was tense, and his sense of solitude strong.

Hours to kill. He was thirsty and hungry now. He walked back down the slope to the place where, behind a stand of trees at the end of a faded path, he had parked his car. He'd seen a diner some miles back near the freeway. He'd go there, eat and drink quickly, then come back here to his post on the hill. He drove through the sombre Connecticut landscape, which reminded him more than a little of certain parts of Ireland in winter.

The diner was an aluminium tube with an air of the Depression about it. Cairney parked the Dodge and went inside, where he sat up on a stool and ordered coffee and a sandwich. He picked at the sandwich, no longer as hungry as he thought he was. Then he looked round the diner. A married couple with a child sat near the window. Two linemen for the phone company occupied a back booth. It was all very ordinary. For a moment he wondered about conventional lives, little acts of love and hatred, commitments and belongings and yearnings. He wondered about the bricks of everyday life and how people managed to balance them. Mortgages and library books and envelopes with cellophane windows in them and alarm clocks ringing on chilly mornings. He wouldn't have been very good at such a life. He was alone the way Finn had always been alone, married to an abstraction called the Cause. And the only freedom from the marriage lay quite simply in the last divorce of all, which was death.

The Cause, he thought. What would become of it if he didn't get the money back? The blood would cease in the veins of the Cause, and the heart would stop pumping, and the brain would atrophy and die. And what would he have given his life to if the Cause withered on his account – *because he couldn't get the money back?* There was a small, panicked voice in his head now.

He stepped down from the stool. He was anxious to get back to the hill overlooking Kevin Dawson's house. He had the strong intuition that the money was there, maybe because he wanted it to be there. Maybe because he longed for the end of this particular road.

He moved towards the front door of the diner. Then paused. There was a telephone in a small alcove to one side. He stared at it. Then he was going towards it even as he resisted. Even as he thought *No, I don't need this now. I don't need this ever.*

John Waddell sat at the wheel of the rental truck. He had braked at an intersection where there was a four-way stop sign, an American traffic peculiarity to which he was unaccustomed. He was reluctant to edge the vehicle forward because he was uncertain of what the sign meant exactly. Did he or did he not have the right of way? There was no other traffic in sight, just rows of frame houses and porches. On one porch an elderly woman was watering a potted plant, bent like a worshipper at a shrine. She looked up once, glanced at the truck, then went back to her watering-can.

'What are you waiting for?' Houlihan asked. 'The fucking weather to change?'

Waddell eased the truck forward. He was flustered by the unfamiliarity of the vehicle and the strangeness of driving on the right side of the road. Houlihan, who sat beside him, was extremely impatient this morning, more so than usual, always snapping when he talked. On his lap Houlihan had a sheet of paper on which he'd scrawled the directions he'd been given over the telephone. He'd been in the phone booth a long time and when he emerged he'd looked dark-faced and determined, the muscles clenched furiously in his long Irish jaw. The sheet was a mess of black lines and scribbled words.

Waddell reached the other side of the intersection. The old lady raised a hand and waved, and he thought *Missus, you wouldn't be waving if you knew, if you really knew.* He drove slowly for a block, then Houlihan said, 'This is Makepeace Street. Turn right.'

Makepeace Street, Waddell thought. If ever a street was wrongly named. He swung the truck right and followed the street, which looked the same as all the back streets of New Rockford, until Houlihan instructed him to turn left. Nantucket Street. Here the houses were starting to thin out. At the end of the block there was a school behind a wire fence. Three yellow school buses were parked just inside the fence. Waddell glanced at a playground with basketball hoops, a soccer field, and a set of wooden swings. In the distance, at the end of the field, a group of small kids chased a ball around, and the sound of their play reached Waddell's ears. It was a sound he found particularly unsettling because it reminded him of his own history, of a time when he'd stand on the sidelines of muddy fields and watch his boy play soccer, when his nerves would be taut on behalf of the kid who played with the clumsy determination of a child with two left feet but an enormous heart. The kid had heart all right.

Waddell held his breath. He hadn't really thought about the boy in a long time. There wasn't much point in bringing all that up again, because he'd buried the pain along with the bodies, but you never really buried pain, did you? He blinked out across the field. He just wanted to be away from this place.

Houlihan looked at his notes. 'Keep going,' he said. 'When you get to the end of this road, turn left.'

Waddell put his foot on the gas pedal. He followed Seamus's instructions. Now, beyond the school, there were no more houses and the road was very narrow, barely wide enough for one vehicle to pass. Trees grew on either side, mature trees whose lower trunks were covered with deep green moss. The branches made a bare arch overhead, reaching out to touch other trees, creating all manner of shadows. Waddell kept driving until Houlihan told him to pull over. There was a flat area, grass worn by old tyretracks, at the side of the road. It was a rectangular patch of land surrounded on three sides by woodland. Waddell thought there was something forlorn about the place.

Seamus Houlihan opened the door and jumped down. He went to the back of the truck and released Rorke and McGrath, who had obviously been sleeping because they emerged unsteadily, rubbing their eyes and yawning. Rorke cleared his throat and spat out a ball of phlegm and looked very satisfied with his output.

Houlihan walked over the rectangle of land. Here and there candy wrappers lay around.

A kid's discarded sneaker, weatherbeaten and abused, was caught in the tangled branches of a bush. Waddell stepped down from the cab and watched Houlihan, who stood with his hands on his hips, his face turned towards the woods beyond the clearing. John Waddell shuddered. The wind blowing out of the trees was biting.

'Over that way.' Houlihan said, directing Rorke and McGrath into the trees. The two men moved between the trunks, waiting for Houlihan to tell them when to stop. When they were about twenty yards away, Seamus told them to halt. 'That's far enough,' he said.

Waddell looked at Rorke and McGrath. They were hardly visible there in the woods. If they were to bend down you couldn't see them at all. Houlihan whistled tunelessly a few seconds, then approached Waddell and slung his big arm round Waddell's shoulders.

'You'll be over there with me, Waddy,' Houlihan said.

Waddell licked his lips. The surface of his tongue was very dry. He was trying to make his mind go far away, sending it off on a journey, as if it were a javelin he could toss through the air at will. Anywhere but here.

He followed Houlihan into the trees, then stopped when the big man came to a halt. Waddell wanted to ask why they were out here, what it was that Houlihan was planning now, but he didn't want to know. Something was going to come this way, he understood that much. And it was going to be ambushed.

'This is where we'll be,' Houlihan said, squinting back the way they'd come. He dug the heel of his boot into the ground, making a mark. Waddell wanted to think it was a game, kids playing in the woods, cowboys and indians, a game of hiding, anything at all but what it really was.

Waddell turned up the collar of his jacket. The wind blew into his eyes and made the branches overhead rustle. It had to be pleasant here in the summer, he thought, leafy lanes, bowers, a romantic spot. But it wasn't pleasant now, not even with the yellowy sun streaming behind the threadbare trees.

'When the time comes, we'll have the weapons in our hands,' Houlihan said. 'The real thing, Waddy.'

Waddell shifted his head slightly. He peered through the trees to where Rorke and McGrath were situated. The real thing, he thought.

'Are you up for it, Waddy?'

Waddell tried to imagine standing here, hidden from the road, with a machine-gun in his hands. The prospect alarmed him.

'What are we going to be shooting at?' he asked.

Houlihan smiled. He tapped his nose with his index finger, a gesture indicating secrecy. 'You'll know when the time comes.'

'Is it a vehicle of some kind?' Waddell asked.

'You're an inquisitive wee bugger, Waddy.'

'Do we just stand here and open fire on it?'

Houlihan nodded. 'That's all you have to do.'

Waddell stared up into Houlihan's eyes. The look he saw there was the same he'd seen that night in Finn's house when the old man lay trapped and dying between the strings of a bloody harp. It was beyond cold, more than the mere absence of light. There was nothing in the big man's eyes but a vacancy, a frightening void where everything that breathed and had life perished.

'What chance will this vehicle have?' Waddell asked.

Houlihan said, 'None.'

Waddell was quiet a moment. What was it Houlihan wanted to ambush? A truck? A car? 'How many people will be inside it?'

Without answering, Seamus Houlihan walked away. When he'd gone about ten yards, the big man turned back and said, 'Let's get the hell out of here. It's time to get some lunch.'

New York City

Leonard M. Korn looked at the huge wall map that had been hung in Zuboric's office. A few coloured pins, each indicating a place where Jig had either been seen or had allegedly operated, were stuck into the surface. There was one for Lower Manhattan, another for Bridgehampton, one for Albany, and a fourth in White Plains. Since coming to New York City by helicopter from Washington, Korn had dispatched six field agents to each of these locations to do what he called follow-up, which consisted mainly of going over the territory and asking questions of inhabitants who might have seen Jig without actually knowing it. It was a blunderbuss operation, in fact. You scattered men all over the place, compiled hundreds of pages of notes, fed the raw information into computers and hoped that some kind of pattern, capable of predicting Jig's movements, capable of sketching a variety of scenarios, would emerge from deep within the electronic brain after a process of analysis, comparison and collation. In addition to the twenty-four agents presently in the field, Korn had also sent six explosives experts to White Plains to sift through the charred remains of the church. A further ten agents were involved in checking the backgrounds, movements and financial records of Nicholas Linney. All in all, it was exactly the kind of operation the Director enjoyed because it gave him the opportunity to leave his mark everywhere.

Korn turned in his chair to look at Arthur Zuboric over the bank of special telephones, each a different colour, that had hurriedly been installed since his arrival. Agents came and went along the corridors, rushing to feed data by direct computer link to Washington, making phone calls, keeping tabs on the men in the field. Zuboric, who no longer recognised his own office, was impressed.

Korn said, 'This should all have been done before, of course.'

Zuboric nodded slightly.

'Still,' and Korn rose in his platform shoes. 'Better late than never. Our President's motto.' A small smile played on Korn's mouth. He folded his hands in front of his body and swayed back and forth on his heels a moment. 'But we're not here to criticise our elected officials, are we?'

'No, sir,' Zuboric said, in a dry voice.

Korn turned to the window and looked out at Manhattan with disapproval on his face. He was a Washington man through and through and generally unhappy with any city that wasn't the Nation's Hub.

'Frank Pagan,' he said.

Zuboric had been waiting for this. The full wrath of the Director could come down on him now. It crossed his mind that this would be a highly appropriate moment to suddenly say that he'd decided to resign from the Bureau. The perfect time to run away. He caught a tantalising glimpse of freedom beyond the reach of Korn's mighty arm. Out there, away from the Bureau, was another country, a pleasant sort of place where he might be happily and peacefully married to Charity. And broke, too.

'Frank Pagan has a history of curious behaviour,' Korn said. 'I assume you've read his file.'

'Yes, sir.'

'He should have been put out to pasture a long time ago. But who can understand the British? Instead of firing Pagan when he didn't fit in at Scotland Yard, they gave him his own little dominion with his own powers of rulership. Crazy. And now he has to go and have a breakdown in the USA.'

A breakdown. Zuboric flexed his fingers. The Director was silent for some time. It was spooky, and unnerving.

'A Lone Ranger complex,' Korn finally said, sighing, shaking his head. 'Didn't you notice? Didn't you see the signs?'

Zuboric stared at the floor. If he admitted he'd seen signs of what Korn called a breakdown, then it would be tantamount to confessing his lack of insight into human behaviour and consequently an inability to predict situations. If he didn't admit it, then he was damned on the grounds of insensitivity. Either way he was lost. He opened his mouth to say something, but Korn cut him off.

'The point is, he's out there somewhere,' and one of the Director's white hands flew up in the direction of the map. 'Presumably with the intention of capturing Jig. If he succeeds, well, that would be an unacceptable state of affairs. How would we look then, Zuboric? How would the Bureau look if this lone man brought in Jig?'

Zuboric shook his head. He knew the answer to that question.

'Does Pagan know something we don't?' Korn asked.

'Not to the best of my knowledge, sir.' But Zuboric wasn't sure. Lately he'd had the disturbing feeling that Pagan was hiding something, although he hadn't been able to put his finger on it.

Leonard M. Korn sat down and said nothing for a time. Then, 'The point is, Zuboric, Pagan's expendable. Just as expendable as Jig.'

Expendable. Zuboric thought the word had a fine ring to it. He liked the idea of it being applied to Pagan. When he thought of Frank Pagan attacking Tyson Bruno he was enraged. Apart from the assault on a Federal agent, Pagan had made Zuboric's operation look very bad indeed, clumsy and inept.

'What I'm saying, Arthur, is that while Frank Pagan doesn't rank priority as far as I'm concerned, it wouldn't be altogether a tragedy if he had an accident of some kind during the course of our investigation.' Korn shrugged. 'If he gets in our way, that is.'

A death-warrant, Zuboric thought.

'On the other hand, it would be more *tidy* if he were simply bundled up and shoved on a plane for Heathrow.' The Director ran a hand over his shaved head. 'I really don't care one way or another. You do understand what I'm saying, don't you?'

'Yes, sir.' Zuboric moved his feet around.

'His photograph has been circulated to everyone involved in this operation,' the Director said. 'Let's talk about something else. Let's talk about you, Arthur.'

Here it comes, Zuboric thought. His heart fluttered. He knew that Korn had something in mind for him, perhaps one of those banishments into exile for which the Director was notorious. If it wasn't the bat caves of Carlsbad, it could be the frozen tundra of the Dakotas. He suddenly had an insight into Korn's powers. This small man, with the shaven head and the voice that barely rose above a whisper, was privy to all manner of confidential information, and had all kinds of power over others. At a whim, he could consign you to oblivion, ruin your career, wreck your whole life. With the stroke of a pen, Leonard M. Korn could make it seem as if you'd never existed. Zuboric wondered what that sort of power did to a person.

'I think you need to spend a little time out of the city, Arthur. Rural Connecticut might be pleasant.' Korn smiled, a sly little expression. 'Our President has a brother, as you know.'

Zuboric wondered where this was leading.

'It appears that Kevin Dawson and his family are planning to take a trip this afternoon. The President wasn't specific when he talked to me.' Korn paused. He took a pen from the pocket of his suit and fiddled with it. 'Whatever. Our President seems a little anxious about brother Kevin's safety these days. Don't ask me why. Perhaps it's an occupational hazard of being a Dawson. Somebody's always got it in for you. Anyhow, the upshot of this is that I agreed to provide a little extra protection for brother Kevin and his offspring. Namely, you.'

'Me?' Zuboric wasn't sure if this assignment meant exile and removal from the Jig affair or something else. You could tell nothing from the Director's face, which was inscrutable in the way of most men who have played political games all their lives.

'It's a simple matter. There are already three Secret Servicemen deployed at the Dawson house. Our President feels a little added security wouldn't be a bad thing. He turned, of course, to the Bureau with this request. He trusts the Bureau.' Korn stood up, looking at Zuboric. 'Naturally, the Secret Service would know about your presence, and so would Kevin Dawson. You'd simply keep a low profile around the household, and when the time comes for the family to leave for the airport you'd escort them. That's all there is to it.'

Zuboric relaxed a little. It wasn't banishment entirely. And even if it were exile, it wasn't going to be a very long one. It would give him a day away from Jig and Frank Pagan and anything else pertaining to twisted Irish matters. He could stand around the Dawson house in Connecticut and think up ways to persuade Charity to marry him.

'The Dawsons plan to leave at four. You could get up to New Rockford by early afternoon if you left now.'

'Do I go alone?' Zuboric asked.

'Take Bruno with you,' Korn answered. 'Presumably he needs a break from the city as much as you.'

Zuboric moved towards the door. He saw a flurry of white-shirted agents in the corridor. From somewhere came the clacking of a printer. Phones were ringing in the offices. One Irish killer had created all this bedlam. One man. Zuboric turned, looked back once at Leonard Korn, then stepped out into the corridor. The countryside was suddenly very appealing to him.

'Remember, Zuboric. Keep your profile so low your chin is scraping the ground. Understand?'

'Understood,' Zuboric said.

Leonard M. Korn watched the agent leave. When the door closed the Director removed his jacket and hung it neatly over the back of the chair. He rolled his sleeves up, turning each cuff exactly four times. He looked at the blank TV, a small portable, which he'd had placed in the corner of the room. The White House was going to issue an official statement some time today. Not Thomas Dawson himself, but one of his faceless spokesmen. The subject would be the presence in America of the IRA terrorist known as Jig and the bombing of the church in White Plains. It would mention how the Federal Bureau of Investigation was presently pursuing every available lead. There might even be a confident hint that the capture of Jig was imminent.

The prospect of all this publicity satisfied Leonard M. Korn. But he gained even more satisfaction from the fact that Thomas Dawson had capitulated, that all the needless secrecy was at an end. There was still something else that made Korn feel very good about himself – Thomas Dawson had telephoned him not more than an hour ago with the request to supply, as *quietly* as possible, a little extra protection for brother Kevin. Korn, even as he wondered why Kevin might need extra muscle, had asked no questions. He knew the President had reasons of his own for not drawing on the Secret Service pool, and he suspected that they had to do with his nervousness about this whole Irish situation, but he wasn't going to examine them. Later, if he thought it necessary, a little exploratory surgery into the life of brother Kevin might be useful. It would do no harm to know why Kevin needed added protection. But for the moment he'd agreed gladly, almost obsequiously, to the request, understanding that some kind of trade-off had been made with the President.

Thomas Dawson had given Korn his manhunt.

And he'd quietly given Tommy Dawson, in the process of tit for tat, favour for favour, two FBI agents. It was called backscratching and it was how Washington worked. A handshake, a tacit agreement, a little discretion. And voilà! You had a system that functioned. Besides, it was always a pleasure to oblige the person in the White House, even if all you were doing was supplying two agents, both of whom were tired and hungry and no longer needed at the heart of things.

Roscommon, New York

Celestine Cairney picked up the telephone on the second ring. She was seated at the kitchen table, a phonebook open in front of her and a cigarette burning down inside an ashtray. When she heard Patrick Cairney's voice, she picked up the cigarette and tilted her chair back at the wall and held the receiver in a hand that had become moist.

'You sound like you're miles away.' It was the first thing that came into her mind.

'New York City isn't so far,' he answered.

She stared up at the ceiling where a wintry fly, black and glossy, circled the unlit fluorescent lightstrip. She tried to picture Patrick now, his surroundings, what he was wearing. But no images came to her.

'You called yesterday, didn't you? But you just hung up.'

Cairney said he hadn't. There was a voice behind him, background noise, a man shouting something about eggs over easy. So he was in a restaurant, a café, somewhere. She shut her eyes tightly and sucked cigarette smoke deep inside her chest, then tried to relax as she exhaled, stretching her legs, letting one arm hang limply from her side. But there was turmoil within.

'I wanted to talk to my father,' Cairney said.

Celestine said nothing for a long time. That wasn't why he'd really called. She wasn't convinced by him. He'd called because he needed to hear her voice as much as she needed to hear his. She wanted to say this, but she didn't. She wanted to say *I want you, Patrick. Before it becomes impossible.*

'Are you still there?' he asked.

'Yes.'

'Something's wrong, isn't it?'

'Yes.'

'Is it my father?'

Celestine made a pattern with the telephone cord, pressing it against her thigh, pushing it deep into the soft flesh in an absent-minded fashion. She felt a catch in her throat, like a small air-pocket, a vacuum lodged there. She opened her eyes and looked round the stainless-steel kitchen. Her heartbeat was loud in the hollow of her chest.

In a very deliberate voice she heard herself say, 'He had an attack last night.'

'Is it serious?'

'Tully said so. I had to call him in.'

'How bad is serious?'

'Bad enough. Tully says one of the lungs is completely collapsed and the other isn't doing too well.'

'He ought to be in hospital.'

'Tully doesn't want him moved yet,' Celestine said. She looked through the open kitchen doorway into the hall. The silences of the big house seemed ominous to her just then, shadows and still places and huge empty rooms. It was like a child's idea of a haunted house, phantoms on stairways, apparitions in windows.

She said, 'If he gets stronger, he can be moved. But not before.' She raised her hand, slipped it beneath her blouse, pressed the palm flat against her stomach and made small circular strokes.

'*If* he gets stronger?' Cairney asked.

'Patrick, this is touch and go. This is a bad situation. He can hardly breathe. Tully has him inside a portable oxygen tent.'

'Is Tully still there? I'd like to talk to him.'

'He left an hour ago.'

'Is he coming back?'

'He said later.' She was quiet. She raised her legs, propped her feet up on the table so that her skirt slid back. She wore no underwear. She imagined Patrick Cairney touching her between her legs.

'Can you come home?' she asked.

Cairney sighed. 'Maybe tomorrow. I'm not sure yet.'

'It would mean a great deal to Harry if he could see you.'

'I know.'

'Your own father has to be more important than some goddam gathering of academics.' She raised her voice. She hadn't intended to. But she had to show him she was unhappy and frayed and couldn't handle this situation on her own.

'I'll do what I can,' he said.

'Of course you will.'

The voice of the operator came on the line, asking in a faintly metallic way for Cairney to insert more money. But then the line was dead and Cairney was gone. Celestine replaced the receiver, stood up, wandered round the kitchen. She paused by the window which had a view of the woodlands behind the house.

Then she stared down at the open telephone book on the table. All morning long she'd been calling different educational institutions, colleges and universities throughout the state. She'd even contacted a group that called itself the Archaeological Society of New York. One polite voice after another had told her what she needed to know.

There was no symposium anywhere at the time. Not in New York City, not in the suburbs, not in any of the large or small cities of the state, not even in any of the obscure colleges that proliferated in rural areas. There was no such thing as the event Patrick Cairney claimed to be attending. If she'd had doubts about him before, she had absolutely none now.

She lit another cigarette.

She stepped out of the kitchen and stood in the hallway, looking up the staircase, which ascended by stages into gloom. She felt extremely tense as she gazed upward, He would come home. Because he felt guilty about what had happened, because he wanted to see her again, and because of his father. Yes, he'd come back. He had good reasons. And what would she do then?

Only what she had to. There was no choice.

She put her foot on the first step. A small web of smoke drifted away from her lips. She raised her face when she heard a sound from the top of the stairs. Harry stood up there in his bathrobe, his bare flesh the colour of paper.

She smiled up at him. He was whistling quietly to himself. His white hair was wet from the shower, and the smell of his aftershave was strong enough to reach her at the foot of the stairs.

'By God, I can smell spring this morning,' he said. He'd been morose for most of last night, distant and preoccupied in a place where she couldn't reach. But now, even if he was forcing it slightly, he seemed cheerful.

'It's in the air,' she replied.

'My stomach's rumbling. There's nothing quite like spring to stoke an old man's appetite.'

She watched him descend. He seemed almost sprightly today. There was a slight lift to his step. When he was halfway down he spread his arms and rolled his eyes and in a fake Irish baritone sang, *'I shall tell her all my love, all my soul's adoration. And I think she will hear me and not say me nay.'*

Celestine clapped and said it was a good impersonation of an Irish barroom singer. Harry put his arms around her and hugged her strongly as he finished his song.

'It is this that gives my soul all its joyous elation. As I hear the sweet lark sing in the clear air of day.'

22 New Rockford, Connecticut

Frank Pagan drove through the business district of New Rockford, noticing banks and insurance offices and real estate brokers as well as the usual fast-food franchises with signs that created an ungodly jumble along the road. The sign that welcomed you said New Rockford had a population of some 57,540 souls.

Beyond the business district were suburbs of frame houses. Here and there a flagpole protruded from a house or stood unadorned in the middle of a lawn. There was a sense of neatness and quiet patriotism here, an orderly world well-preserved. But then appearances changed, and the grids of the streets yielded to pockmarked dead ends, alleys, abandoned warehouses, weeds, after which woodland stretched away for mile after mile.

Pagan parked the Cutlass outside an industrial park and studied the streetmap he'd bought in the town. He made a circle with a ballpoint pen, folded the map, drove the car on to the thruway and continued until he came to Leaf Road, which was the exit he wanted. It began promisingly enough, then dwindled to a one-vehicle thoroughfare with a barbed-wire fence running along one side. Beyond, punctuated by the occasional meadow, were tree-covered hills, which seemed to gather all the available sunlight and squander it, so that the prevalent impression was of shadows and dank places. It wasn't an encouraging landscape.

When a house came in view, Pagan slowed the car. It was a large, ungainly house, set some way from the road at the end of a driveway. It was overlooked by a series of small hills. There was no number anywhere, no name. If this was the wrong house, then he would simply ask directions and leave.

He turned the car into the driveway.

Before he had gone twenty feet a man wearing a dark suit and black glasses emerged from a clump of shrubbery and waved him to stop. Pagan braked. He had an uncomfortable moment when it crossed his mind that the man might be associated with the FBI – but then he realised he was being paranoid. Zuboric couldn't have traced him here. How could he?

Pagan rolled his window down and smiled. He was about to ask if somebody called Dawson lived here when he saw a gun in the man's hand. A very large gun, trained directly on Pagan's forehead.

The man, who was built like a weightlifter, reached for the car door and opened it and Pagan got out with absolutely no reluctance at all. A second figure, somewhat taller than the first but with exactly the same kind of shades, appeared at Pagan's side. Pagan was expertly frisked, then pushed face first against the side of the Olds. Whoever they are, these characters had done a certain amount of frisking in their time. Pagan wondered how long it might take him to reach his own gun, if the situation called for it. His pistol was in the glove compartment and too far away. It was a maxim of his that a gun was only useful in direct proportion to its proximity. And his was presently redundant.

'Get his ID,' the taller man said.

The other, waving the gun near Pagan's face, plunged his hand inside Pagan's jacket and took out his wallet.

The taller man reached for the wallet and flipped it open. 'He's a long way from home,' he said.

'Yeah,' the other man said. 'You ever seen ID like this before, Marco?'

Marco stepped so close Pagan could smell his aftershave. 'Never did,' he said.

'Me neither.' The wallet was flipped shut. 'We got absolutely no way of knowing if it's authentic.'

'I came to see Dawson,' Pagan said.

Marco laughed. 'They all say that, don't they, Chuckie?'

'Mr Dawson doesn't just see people who wander in off the street, fella,' Chuckie said.

'Unhappily, I didn't have time to make an appointment.'

'Call the cops,' Marco said.

'Before you call anybody, you better tell Dawson I'm here, because he's going to be damned unhappy with you if he doesn't get to hear what I have to say.'

Marco came closer. He pushed his knee into the back of Pagan's leg, pressing deep into the crook. Pagan was obliged to bend under the pressure. He loathed being shoved around, and if it had been Marco alone he might have taken a swing.

'I don't have the time nor the inclination for this kind of intimacy, Marco.' Pagan spoke his best accent, trying hard to sound the way Foxie did. He wasn't very good with upper-class accents and he wouldn't have convinced anyone in the gentlemen's clubs along Pall Mall or Piccadilly, but neither Chuckie nor Marco could tell he was faking it. It was a strange thing about Americans. They had a kind of self-imposed sense of inferiority, possibly some old colonial hangover, that put them in awe of Oxford tones, as if the accent of a BBC newscaster were the way God talked. Pagan had noticed this phenomenon before. It worked now, at least to the extent of Marco removing the pressure from Pagan's leg.

'Buddy, you and a thousand other guys come here wanting to see *Mister* Dawson,' Chuckie said. 'Your fancy ID isn't going to cut it here, bozo.'

Pagan turned around and faced the pair. 'Look. Take my ID card. Show it to him. Tell him it has to do with certain Irish funds. Do that for me.'

'Irish funds?'

'You heard me.'

Marco reached out and took Pagan's ID. He flexed the powder-blue plastic card between thumb and forefinger, as if he meant to snap it in half. Then he glanced at Chuckie, who shrugged. It was a bad moment for Pagan. If either of these characters took the trouble to run his name through a computer, and if he was already imprisoned in the complicated circuitry of the FBI's electronic brain, then he was in deep trouble. The only thing to do was to be insistent with Marco and Chuckie. And authoritative, if he could summon the dignity for a decent performance.

'If Dawson doesn't want to see me, I'll be happy to let you turn me over to any cops you like,' he said. He sounded as if he had a plum in his throat. 'But I know he'll want to talk to me. It's up to you.'

Marco hummed. He looked at Chuckie again. The black glasses glinted, four sombre discs.

'I'll take your card inside, fella,' he said. 'But Chuckie here is going to keep his gun pointed right at your brain, understand?'

Pagan nodded. Marco, who obviously didn't want Pagan to think he was a softie just because he'd consented to something, performed his knee trick again, only this time he pressed so hard that Pagan had to go down on all fours.

'*Understand*? Marco asked.

'I understand,' Pagan replied. He felt like a barnyard animal pawing earth.

'If he moves shoot him, Chuckie.'

Chuckie said he'd be glad to. Pagan rose slowly, watching Marco go off in the direction of the house, which was very still, silent, the windows reflecting the glacial sun. He moved his feet in an uneasy manner. Marco could at this very moment be running his name across the telephone wires and into the ear of a computer operator. That would be the end of this solo performance, Pagan thought. He brushed little streaks of mud from his overcoat and waited.

Marco appeared in the doorway of the house. He waved an arm. Chuckie, who still had his gun trained on Pagan, jerked his head.

'Move,' Chuckie said.

Pagan moved. Chuckie walked behind him. When they reached the house Marco said, 'He'll see you.'

Pagan smiled. Marco ushered him inside and across the hallway with a great show of reluctance. Outside a closed door Marco paused and slipped off his black glasses and stared at Pagan with eyes that were almost the same colour as the lenses.

'We'll be right here, Pagan,' he said. 'Right on this spot.'

'Of course,' Pagan said.

'Go in.'

Pagan pushed the door open and stepped inside a large sitting-room which was furnished in a fussy Victorian way, heavy furniture and belljars, and which was scented with violets. Children's toys and books were scattered on the floor, as if there had been small untidy intruders in the museum. A blind was drawn halfway down on a window, tinting the room a faint yellow. The man who stood by the fireplace cleared his throat and looked at Pagan unsmilingly. Kevin Dawson was taller than his photographs suggested. He held Pagan's ID card in one hand.

'Let's get one thing straight. I don't know anything about any Irish funds,' Dawson said.

The defence of ignorance. Kevin Dawson talked like a man conscious of a hidden tape-recorder, somebody who wanted to leave an exonerating cassette for posterity. He understood Dawson's attitude – after all, the brother of the President of the United States couldn't confess to a complete stranger that he had any involvement with the finances of the IRA. There were laws against the unreported export of huge sums of cash. And Kevin Dawson couldn't be seen to break the law.

'So why did you agree to see me?' Pagan asked.

'Your ID made me curious,' Dawson said. 'But if you've come here to question me, I think you're going to be very frustrated.'

'I'm not the one who's going to be frustrated,' Pagan said. He moved to the window and looked out beyond the trees at the surrounding hills. It was a view he found depressing and somehow fascinating in a melancholic way. He rapped his fingertips on the pane of glass. 'I don't give a damn one way or another about IRA money or the misguided people who collect the stuff. I'm only interested in Jig, who is either going to come here looking for you, or else is on his way to a place called Roscommon to see Harry Cairney. I'm guessing here, but I may be completely wrong. If he *does* come here, I want to be somewhere nearby. I don't want your buffoons out there getting him first.'

'Hold on, Pagan. You're losing me. I don't know anything about the IRA. I don't know who Jig is. The only connection I have with Ireland is that I'm third-generation American-Irish. That and the fact I've visited the place a couple of times. Nothing more.'

Pagan smiled. Dawson's deadpan expression wasn't very successful. The man was palpably uneasy. If he was in control of himself, it was only with a great effort. There was sweat on his upper lip.

'Regardless of what you say, Jig's going to get here sooner or later. He wants his money back, and he's not going to be in the most pleasant frame of mind by this time,' Pagan said.

Kevin Dawson made a small gesture with one hand, a flutter. 'I don't know anything about any money.'

'That's what you say. But Jig isn't going to believe that one.' Pagan glanced through the window again. This whole side of the house was exposed to the hills. And something about those hills kept drawing him. The shaded pockets in the landscape, the sunlight. They had a certain mysterious quality, similar to the landscape of the English Lake District which Pagan had always found brooding and hostile. A landscape for poets and manic depressives.

But it wasn't just those qualities that made him keep looking up there. He was thinking about something else. He placed an index-finger on the glass and drew a tiny circle, which he peered through as if it were the sight of a gun.

'Good view,' he said.

'Some people think it's too severe,' Dawson remarked.

Dawson moved to the mantelpiece and adjusted a photograph. Pagan saw that it was of two girls, presumably Dawson's daughters. Dawson turned around, faced Pagan. 'This Jig,' he said, then paused a moment. 'Do you have any hard evidence he's in the vicinity? Or is it only guesswork?'

'Nicholas Linney wouldn't think it was guesswork,' Pagan said.

'Who?'

'It doesn't matter.' Pagan glanced back up into the hills. Sunlight turned to deep shadow in the high hollows. Dawson was a very poor liar. He didn't have the flair for it. Therefore he had no future in politics, Pagan thought. 'How did you get into it in the first place?'

'Into what?'

'You know what I'm talking about. How did you get into the patriot game?'

'When did I stop beating my wife?' Dawson said. 'It's that kind of a question.'

Pagan felt a small flare of anger. People like Dawson played at being Irish. They bought their way into it from the safety of their big houses in America. They sent money as if they were investing in offshore developments. Well, their houses just weren't so safe any more. 'Do you have any idea of the sheer human misery your money can buy in Ireland? Do you know what explosive devices can do to a person? Have you ever seen the victim of a machine-gun? Or did you just get caught up in the *romance* of it all?' And Pagan made the word 'romance' sound obscene. 'If people like you didn't send money there in the first place, maybe there wouldn't be weapons, and maybe we'd be moving in the direction of some kind of peace. Who knows?'

'There are always going to be weapons,' Dawson said.

Pagan shrugged. 'Here's the funny consequence of it all, Dawson. If you run into Jig, you'll be looking directly down the barrel of a gun that you probably paid for yourself. How does that thought grab you?'

'Is your lecture over?' Dawson asked.

'It's over,' Pagan replied. Ease off, he told himself. You're here looking for Jig, not to moralise on terror in Ireland. He felt a cord of tension at the side of his head. There was stress in him, and fatigue, and he felt like a traveller who wasn't sure he'd come to the right place anyway. No, he couldn't afford to go off at tangents like that. He'd come too far and he had the feeling, that astonishing light bulb of intuition, that he was on the right track.

'I'm sorry if I can't help you,' Dawson said, 'Maybe you'll have better luck at the other place you mentioned.'

'You mean Roscommon?' Pagan asked.

'I believe that's what you said. Roscommon.'

'Where Harry Cairney lives. But you don't know that name either, do you?'

Dawson shook his head. 'I know it in a political context. That's all.'

'And I suppose Jock Mulhaney means nothing to you?'

'He's some kind of union figure,' Dawson said.

'You might say that.'

Dawson stepped towards the door. He pulled it open, looked at Pagan with a smile that was almost all desperation. He couldn't be honest, couldn't admit his connections. Denials were vouchers for limited amounts, valid for limited durations. And no matter how hard Dawson denied his involvement, it wasn't going to make a damn bit of difference to Jig. If Jig came here and somehow sneaked past Mannie and Moe outside, if he got into the house and confronted Dawson, he wasn't going to be even remotely convinced by Dawson's squeaky claims of innocence.

'Good luck, Pagan,' Kevin Dawson said.

'I wish you the same, only more of it.'

Pagan stepped out into the hallway where the two bodyguards were waiting for him. Behind him, the door of the room closed, and Kevin Dawson was gone.

'We'll see you out,' Marco said.

'No need.' Pagan headed to the door. Chuckie and Marco tailed him anyhow.

Outside in the thin light Pagan studied the view of the hills again. They seemed to him the most interesting aspect of his visit to this place.

From the place where he lay concealed in the hills, Patrick Cairney stared down at the house below. He saw Frank Pagan walk to his car.

Frank Pagan. Always Frank Pagan. Always one step behind him. He wondered where Pagan's information came from. Maybe Mulhaney had talked. Maybe Mulhaney had told Pagan the same thing as he'd told Cairney. *Kevin Dawson took the money. Dawson is the one.*

Ten minutes ago he'd seen Pagan arrive. There had been a confrontation with the two men who guarded the house, then Pagan had gone indoors. Had he come to warn Kevin Dawson about Jig? Was that it?

Now he saw Pagan get inside the car, then drive along the narrow road. Cairney followed him with the binoculars until he was out of sight. He swung the glasses back towards the house and tried to concentrate on how he was going to get inside. He had to get past the two guards. How, though? And how long was it until nightfall now? His body was cold, and he felt cramped. He lowered the binoculars and looked along the ridge, his eye sweeping the wintry trees and the dead grass that swayed limply in the wind. He couldn't concentrate. His mind kept slipping away from him and the wind made him shiver.

There were spectral images. *His father trapped under an oxygen tent like something immersed in ectoplasm*. He couldn't shake this one loose. Harry Cairney, close to the end of his life, propped up inside an oxygen tent with tubes attached like tendrils to his body. There was a terrifying sadness inside Patrick Cairney, and a sense of loss – it came from the thought that he might never see Harry again. It didn't matter whether he loved his father or not. It didn't matter whether he even respected the man. Like any son facing the imminent death of his father, he felt he was about to lose some essential part of himself.

One of the men below stood against the hood of the car and smoked a cigarette. The other wandered round the side of the house, then returned. They stood together, both now leaning against the car, and they presented an impenetrable obstacle between Cairney and the house. Cairney rubbed his eyes. He focused on the house, the two men, but still the landscape wouldn't yield up an easy way to get inside that place down there.

Think. Think hard. The money might be inside that house and you're lying up here wondering about your father and your thoughts won't make a damn bit of difference whether he lives or dies.

His truant attention strayed again, and he was thinking about Roscommon once more, seeing Celestine sit by the sickbed of his father. Maybe she spoke softly to the old man. Maybe she was reading to him. Or perhaps she just sat there watching him motionlessly, her hands in her lap and her lovely face expressionless and her hair pulled back so that she looked gaunt and distressed and prepared for the ultimate grief.

Cairney focused on the men below. His head pounded now, and his hands, when he lowered the binoculars, shook visibly. He sat back against the side of the hollow, wondering at the responses of his own body. It was as if strange blood flowed in his veins and the heart that pumped so loudly in his chest were not his own. He was seized with the feeling that he shouldn't be here in this place at all, that he should never have been sent from Ireland unless it was to kill a specific target, a certain individual. Unless it was to do the very thing he did best, better than anyone else.

Why didn't you send somebody else, Finn? Was your precious Jig the only candidate?

He crawled to the lip of the hollow. From where he stood he could see almost the whole length of the hills. Slopes swooped down into shadows where the sun didn't go. These shadowy places, like sudden pools of unexpected water, troubled him. He wasn't quite sure why.

And then, because he understood how to read landscapes, how to tell human movement from the motion of the wind, how to feel when a landscape had been subtly altered, he knew.

New York City

At ten minutes past two, the Reverend Ivor McInnes entered the office of a car rental company on East 38th Street. He spoke to the clerk at the desk, a young man with red hair arranged around his skull like a corona. McInnes reserved a 1986 Continental because he liked the idea of travelling in some comfort. He looked at the desk-clock as the clerk filled out the various papers. He was glad it was one of those digital affairs. He didn't think he could tolerate the idea of watching the agonising movements of a second hand. It was twenty past two by the time the young man completed the copious paperwork. McInnes said he'd pick the car up around six. He had to return to his hotel first and pack.

He left the agency at approximately two-thirty. He thought of Seamus Houlihan and the others as he stepped out on the street. They'd be taking up their positions by this time.

He walked slowly along the street, looking now and then in the windows of stores. He felt the way he had done before White Plains, except it was heightened somehow.

In about twenty minutes, if the information he had received was correct – and he had absolutely no reason to doubt it, because of its reliable source – the vehicle would be making a turn into the isolated stretch of road where Houlihan and his men were waiting.

Twenty minutes.

Twenty long minutes.

McInnes reached the intersection of Thirty-Eighth Street and Fifth Avenue. He looked in the window of a jewellery store. Rings, necklaces, bracelets. It would take his mind off it all if he went inside and lost himself in browsing through the glittering array. Nineteen minutes. He wandered between the glass cases, tracked by a sales clerk who insisted on pointing out the merits of this or that stone.

McInnes stopped in front of an emerald ring. He asked the clerk to bring it out and show it to him. The clerk said it was an excellent piece and any woman would be *delirious* to have it. Ivor McInnes held the stone up to the light. Its greenness was stunning and deep. McInnes closed his hand over the ring. The stone felt very cool against his skin.

'I'll have it, he said. *Eighteen minutes.*

'Excellent choice,' the clerk said. 'Cash or credit card?'

'Cash.'

The clerk, who was a small man with eyes that themselves resembled gems, smiled. 'Is it a gift, sir? Shall I gift-wrap it?'

'Why don't you,' McInnes said. As he watched the clerk cut gift-paper with long scissors, he stared across the floor to where there was a clock display. All kinds of timepieces hung on the wall, every last one of them showing a different time. The effect was of stepping outside the real world and into one where the passage of seconds and minutes and hours couldn't be measured with any semblance of accuracy. McInnes had to look away. Real time was important to him now.

Seventeen minutes.

He tried not to think about time. He tried to put it out of his mind. But it kept returning to him and his nervousness increased. Sixteen minutes.

Sixteen minutes and it would all be over. And by tomorrow, if everything went as planned, he'd be out of the country entirely.

New Rockford, Connecticut

John Waddell crouched in the shrubbery. He held an M–16 against his side. He glanced out across the clearing at the place where Rorke and McGrath were concealed, but he couldn't see them. He felt Houlihan tap him lightly on the shoulder and he turned. The big man was offering him something, and it took Waddell a moment to realise it was a stick of chewing-gum. Waddell shook his head.

'Helps you relax,' Houlihan said.

Waddell looked through the barren trees. He had the odd feeling that he wasn't here, that some other entity had been substituted for him and that the real John Waddell was back in Belfast, strolling across Donegal Square and wondering where he'd stop for a pint of Smithy's. But Houlihan nudged him, and the illusion disintegrated.

'Are you all right, Waddy?' the big man asked.

'Fine,' John Waddell said.

'Gun loaded?'

Waddell nodded. He looked down at the M–16 in his hands.

Seamus Houlihan, who also held an M–16, tapped his fingers against the stock. This drumming increased Waddell's anxiety. He looked up at the sky. Clouds drifted in the region of the sun.

Houlihan looked at his wristwatch. 'Two-forty,' he said. 'Ten minutes.'

Waddell tightened his grip on his gun. What he hoped for was that something unexpected might happen and that the exercise would have to be postponed. A freak storm, for example. Or the appearance of other people. But this was such a damned lonely place he couldn't imagine anybody coming here by choice. And what kind of vehicle could it possibly be that made a stop here anyhow? He tried to slacken his grip on the gun but his fingers remained tight and stiff.

Houlihan made a sniffing sound. He wiped the back of his sleeve over the tip of his nose and cleared his throat. Waddell thought for a moment that he detected a certain jumpiness in Seamus, but he decided he was wrong. The big man never showed any unease at times like this. he was always cool. Always in control. Chewing gum, looking composed – Jesus, Seamus might be contemplating a stroll on a Sunday afternoon. Waddell felt a branch brush his face, and he was startled.

'You're a twitchy wee fucker,' Houlihan said.

'I'm okay,' Waddell replied.

'Look, there's nothing to be nervous about. Point the bloody gun when I tell you, and fire. That's all. Nothing to it.'

Ten minutes, Houlihan had said.

Waddell wondered how long ten minutes could be. He glanced at Seamus, then he looked through the trees. 'I wish to God we were out of here,' he said. 'Out of this whole bloody country.'

'Soon.' Houlihan removed his chewing-gum and flicked it away.

'How soon?'

Seamus Houlihan, keeper of secrets, didn't answer. He checked his gun, traced a finger along the barrel. What did it take to be that relaxed? Waddell wondered. What kind of ice-water ran in Seamus's veins?

'Five more minutes,' Houlihan said.

Eternity. Waddell wanted to urinate. He concentrated on his weapon, wishing it was lighter, less of a burden. The weight of the thing made it all the more menacing.

'Four,' Houlihan said.

By Jesus, he was going to count the bloody minutes down! Waddell tried not to listen. Houlihan could keep his countdown to himself. Waddell preferred to hear nothing.

'Three.'

Waddell saw McGrath's face briefly across the clearing. Then it was gone. Momentarily a cloud masked the sun.

Two.

In the distance there was the sound of a vehicle.

'It's early,' Houlihan said, swinging his weapon into a firing position. 'Get ready.'

The sound grew. Waddell held his gun at his side and waited. The vehicle seemed to strain, gears clanking and grinding, as it came closer. Waddell stared beyond the clearing but he couldn't see the vehicle yet because there was a bend in the road. As the motor laboured and whined, the noise grew. Waddell gripped his gun tightly.

'Ready,' Houlihan said.

Waddell shook his head. No, he thought.

No.

'Ready,' Houlihan said again.

Waddell – baffled by the sense of unreality he suddenly felt, almost as if time and motion had ceased to exist and the whole world had frozen in its flight-path and he was the only person left alive – stared at the vehicle as it appeared in front of him. It was a big yellow school bus, and it was coming to a dead stop in the clearing, and the faces pressed to the windows were those of children, and they were smiling even as Houlihan stood up in the shrubbery and levelled his weapon at them.

Frank Pagan drove two miles from the house of Kevin Dawson, then turned the Oldsmobile off the road and down a dirt track that led between the wooded hills. When the car would go no further, when the track had become too narrow and rutted and overgrown with weeds, he got out, taking his gun from the glove compartment. It had been a long time since he'd climbed any hills and he wasn't sure his physical condition was terrific, but he was going up anyway. He went between the trees, straining over fallen logs and mounds of wet, dead leaves that had been buried under snow since fall. Here and there patches of old snow, hard as clay, still clung to the ground.

Halfway up the hill Pagan had to stop and catch his breath. He leaned against a tree trunk. The sun, trapped between spidery branches, was a frozen, listless globe. When he'd been staring at these hills from the window of Kevin Dawson's living-room, Pagan had imagined that this landscape was the perfect one for Jig. There were pockets in which to hide, trees and shrubbery for cover. If Jig wanted to observe the Dawson household, what more suitable place from which to do it? He knew that if *he* were Jig, this was the kind of spot he'd have come to without hesitation. But that was only a guess. Just the same, Pagan felt he had nothing to lose by climbing up here, save perhaps the future use of lungs and legs.

He climbed again. There were no tracks, no pathways, only the sullen trees pressing against him and crisp twigs cracking underfoot. His breath hung on the air like cobwebs. Up and up and up. Any higher, he thought, and he'd need an oxygen mask, a Tibetan guide, and dried food for a week. He could see the road below and, off to his left about a mile, Kevin Dawson's house, which looked isolated in the landscape. Ahead of him, running the entire length of the range, was more woodland. He paused, looking down the slopes. There were a thousand places where Jig could hide and wait for the right time to make a move on Dawson's house.

Pagan blew on his hands for warmth. A gnawing wind had begun to rush across the slopes, carrying smells of moss and deadwood and rotted leaves. He moved through the trees, gazing down every so often. From certain places the Dawson house couldn't be seen because trees obscured the view. But here and there, in clearings, every detail of the structure could be observed in miniature. Windows, eaves, smoke rising from a chimney.

It was a lifeless landscape, almost morbid in its quiet and lack of colour. He walked a little further, then stopped again, wishing he had paid more attention to the art of tracking and reading signs when he'd been a Boy Scout. How many stories could a crushed leaf or a broken branch tell you if you knew how to interpret the damn things? A decent Boy Scout could find a whole bloody library of information in this place. But Pagan, a city boy, had never had any great affinity for rustic places.

He kept moving. The wind came up, blowing directly into his face and shaking all kinds of sounds out of the trees. Pagan turned his face away from the fullness of the blast, which whipped his hair and his coat.

Then the wind died and the place was still again.

Pagan moved quietly. Underfoot, dead leaves crackled, frail wood popped. It was impossible to stir in these woods without announcing yourself.

He came now to a hollow in the land, a scoop masked by crisscrossing branches. Somebody could conceal himself successfully in such a place. Pagan looked beyond the hollow. There, immediately below on the other side of the road, was Kevin Dawson's house. The perfect view. But the hollow was empty and still.

He went down carefully, his gun held forward.

He didn't register the noise he heard. It was a whisper on the far edges of his awareness. He thought it might have been an animal, a rabbit emerging from a thicket. He was about to turn his face around when he heard the voice say, 'Toss the gun a few feet to your side, Pagan. If you don't, you get a bullet in the back of your head.'

Pagan threw the gun a couple of feet away. He saw Jig come forward to pick it up.

'I heard you coming. I heard you coming for the last twenty minutes.'

Pagan stared at his own gun in the man's hand. Fool, he thought. You should have finished reading Baden-Powell's *Scouting For Boys*. You should have studied tracking and bent blades of grass and little heelmarks in the soil and all the rest of it.

Jig said, 'A brass band would have made less noise. Put your hands in the air where I can see them, then have a seat.'

Pagan did as he was told. He sat down inside the hollow and stared at Jig, who had a gun in either hand. Pagan wondered if this were the place, this lonely ridge overlooking a lonely house, where he would die.

Until he saw the yellow school bus rolling towards the clearing and understood he was meant to open fire on the vehicle as soon as it stopped, John Waddell had never thought of himself as a terrorist. In his world, terrorists were always Arabs who blew up airports and planes, or IRA fanatics who planted bombs inside supermarkets and pubs. But suddenly, as if he had been given a stunning insight into his own condition, he realised he was no better than any of the thugs who committed these outrages. He wasn't a soldier in a credible struggle, he wasn't in the glorious vanguard of Ulster freedom, he wasn't even a *man*, because a man didn't fire an automatic weapon at a crowd of kids in a school bus. It was a monster's work. All the sensations that had been depressing him since White Plains became more strident, more compelling. What business did he have firing a fucking gun at a bunch of kids?

He watched the bus pull into the clearing and stop, and he heard the hiss of the automatic door as it slid open. He was conscious of a light blue car behind the bus, smoke from its exhaust rising into the frigid air. There was a man inside the car although Waddell hardly registered this fact because he was drawn to the faces of the children at the windows. A boy of about eleven appeared in the door of the bus, satchel over his shoulder. He was about to step down from the doorway but he hesitated, turning to say something to a friend. There was laughter and a good-natured insult and somebody tossed a rolled-up ball of paper at the boy's head.

Houlihan, thus far unseen by the kids in the bus or the driver of the blue car, was standing with the M-16 in firing position. Waddell was screaming inside. He wanted to stop this whole thing before it started, but now Seamus Houlihan was snapping at him to stand up and start firing, and the hell of it was he couldn't move, didn't want to move, wanted to remain crouched in the damned shrubbery and make believe this was all a nightmare. The kids all had the same face, and it was the face of John Waddell's own dead son, and he couldn't bear the image.

He looked up at Houlihan, and he shook his head.

'Get up. Get up on your fucking feet, God damn you.'

Waddell stared at the big man with his mouth open.

'Fucking eedjit,' Houlihan said. He poked Waddell in the chest with the barrel of the weapon and John Waddell understood that Seamus, his friend, his avenging angel, his mentor, would blow him away without even thinking about it.

Houlihan pulled the gun back, swung around, and opened fire. From the bushes at the other side of the clearing Rorke and McGrath began their volley as well. Waddell watched in white terror as the windows of the yellow bus exploded. He heard the shrieks of children and saw the boy in the doorway fall forward, lying half-in and half-out of the vehicle. He saw the driver of the vehicle slide out of her seat and disappear in a sudden spray of blood. The firing continued, on and on and on, until there wasn't a window remaining on the bus and the yellow panels had been riddled with holes. But now Waddell understood something else. The man in the light blue car was shooting back. He'd crawled out of the car and was concealed now behind the vehicle, a pistol in his hand, and every so often he'd send a shot into the trees. Houlihan changed his magazine and started firing again. Waddell stared at the bus. It was shattered, a great yellow shell, and now there were no faces at the windows, only jagged slices of glass hanging in frames at angles that defied gravity.

Houlihan made a roaring sound. A battle-cry. He was firing at the blue car with a savage determination. Waddell heard the shots ricochet off the metal. Then he stared down at the gun in his hands. He realised he should have shot Houlihan. It was the sane thing to do. He should have turned the weapon on the big man before all this started, but now it was too damned late.

Houlihan grunted, fired, his whole body shaking from the relentless kick of the gun. Waddell saw the blue car catch fire and explode all of a sudden. One moment it was there, the next it had gone up in a cloud of flame and smoke. And then there was a secondary explosion, louder than the first, and the clearing was showered with glass and plastic. The driver of the car lay face down some yards from the yellow bus.

It was over.

The clearing was silent. The whole afternoon, so sulphuric and cold, was terribly silent.

John Waddell dropped his weapon. He felt Houlihan grab him and pull him to a standing position. He was cuffed roughly by the big man, stinging blows that made his eyes water and brought blood into his mouth.

'You're a dead man, Waddy,' Houlihan said.

John Waddell said nothing.

Houlihan had an odd little grin on his face. 'It's war, John. It's this bloody war. And I can't have a man beside me who doesn't have the guts for it. You understand that, don't you?'

John Waddell nodded his head slowly. He looked in the direction of the dead boy who lay in the doorway of the yellow bus. His satchel had burst open and sheets of coloured paper spilled from it. Waddell thought he'd never seen anything as sad as that. He turned back to look at Houlihan, and he understood, in the final moments of his life, that Seamus was fighting a war that he never wanted to see finished. For as long as he lived, Seamus Houlihan would never be able to liberate himself from this conflict. He was trapped in violence because he was consumed by his love for it.

'Maybe you'll go to heaven' Houlihan said. He'd taken his pistol from his belt, and he pressed it against John Waddell's heart, and he pulled the trigger quickly. Waddell fell into the shrubbery, where he lay with his face turned up towards the sun.

23 New Rockford, Connecticut

'What now?' Frank Pagan asked, looking up at Jig who stood on the rim of the hollow.

Jig's expression was grim. 'I'm thinking of shooting you,' was what he said in the voice Pagan had heard a thousand times on tape. The accent was not exactly Irish. Nor was it American. It came somewhere between the two. It was the accent of a man who was neither one thing nor the other, as if he'd spent much of his life wandering indecisively between two nations. And the face, which Pagan had tried to imagine so many times and which he'd glimpsed only briefly before at St Finbar's, was handsome and yet inflexible, almost as if all the muscles were locked in place. It was not the kind of face one could envisage smiling in a relaxed fashion, or in calm repose. The eyes were vigilant and guarded, the mouth defiant. Jig reminded Pagan right then of something wild, a creature forever conscious of traps and pitfalls, who sees enmities everywhere, who expects hostilities. But there was another quality, one so hidden it was difficult to detect at all, and Pagan had a problem defining it. In some other circumstances, he thought that this face – presently so hard and set – might be capable of showing sensitivity and concern. But not now. Certainly not now.

'Let me know what you decide,' Pagan said.

'However, I'm not in the habit of shooting defenceless people, Pagan. Unless they're guilty of crimes against Ireland.'

'Am I included in that category?' Pagan asked. He stared past Jig and up into the trees through which the afternoon sun created white flickers. He had to gather his thoughts, all his resources, and decide how he might turn this situation to his advantage. It was a possibility that seemed ludicrously, laughably, slim.

'As far as I'm concerned, you're just another English policeman. And that's enough to make you guilty.'

'What about two young Cambodian girls in a house in Bridgehampton? What crimes had they committed against Ireland?'

Jig was quiet a moment. 'They were killed by a man called Linney.'

'It's not what the FBI believes, Jig.'

'I don't give a damn what the FBI believes. The same applies to you, Pagan. I've never been interested in what people say or believe about me.' The wind, blowing down through the trees, stirred Jig's tightly curled hair almost as if a hand had passed over his skull. Pagan thought he had never seen a person so tense as this one. You could almost see glowing wires just beneath the surface of his skin.

'The FBI also believes you were responsible for the explosion in White Plains.'

'What explosion?'

'You've been out of touch, Jig. Somebody blew up a Presbyterian church in White Plains.

They made a pretty thorough job of it. Then they called the FBI to claim it as an IRA score. And where the FBI is concerned, you're the only IRA factor in the vicinity, ergo you're the one responsible.' Pagan looked to see what effect this information would have on Jig.

Jig's expression didn't change. 'I've never been in White Plains,' he said, without any emotion in his voice. 'I'd have no reason to blow up a church. Presbyterian or otherwise.'

'They also claimed you killed a man called Fitzjohn in Albany.'

'I get around, don't I?'

'It would seem so.'

'I haven't been in Albany either.'

'Tell that to Leonard Korn. I understand he's a good listener.'

Jig stared at Pagan. 'I don't know of any authorised IRA activities in this country that would involve bombing. It doesn't make sense.'

'My feeling exactly,' Pagan said. 'What makes it even more interesting in the case of Fitzjohn is that he was a member of the Free Ulster Volunteers. But it gets better still.'

'I'm listening.'

Pagan said, 'Ivor McInnes is in New York City.'

'And what is that holy man doing there?'

'I'm not absolutely sure. But I have a feeling he could clear up some of the mystery if only he would talk. Ivor can be very close-mouthed when he wants to be. He knows a hell of a lot more than he's prepared to say. Whatever's going on, Ivor has a dirty finger in it somehow.'

Jig's face changed slightly., The set of his mouth altered, but Pagan couldn't tell what it meant. He even wondered if any of what he was talking about interested Jig remotely. The man's mind was seemingly elsewhere, his manner distracted. It was the house below, Pagan realised. All Jig's focus was fixed there.

Then Jig turned to look at Pagan. 'I'm wondering why you're here on your own, Pagan. I'm wondering if maybe there aren't more of you up in these hills and you're sitting here smugly waiting for them to turn up. Don't you have a little gang of associates? On Canal Street, you said you had a score of men.'

'I dumped the Bureau.'

'Did you now?'

'They want your balls nailed to Leonard Korn's bulletin-board. Which made me a little unhappy. I have my own ideas about justice.' Pagan paused a moment. 'They're turning over every stone they can find. It has all the makings of a massive manhunt. After all, you're a killer. And you can't hide under the umbrella of Irish romanticism, not after the barbarism in White Plains.'

'Irish romanticism,' Jig said disdainfully. 'There's no such thing, Pagan. Is Belfast romantic? Are checkpoints romantic? Do you find anything enchanting in the sight of a country that's dying from schizophrenic hatred?' He looked down at the guns he held in both hands, turning them over, examining them in a thoughtful way.

He said, 'So the mighty FBI is looking for me, is it?' I don't know if I should feel proud or humbled by the notion.'

'Nervous would be a more practical response,' Pagan said. He was wondering how he could get the weapons away from Jig. Idle speculation. There was no way in the world Jig was going to be fooled by a surprise attack.

Jig pressed the barrel of one of the guns against the side of his face and scratched. 'You could be telling me a complete fairy-tale, Pagan. You could be sitting here right now and making all this up. You could be thinking that some convoluted story about bombings and murder and an FBI manhunt might fluster me enough that I'll call off my mission and go home quietly. You obviously know what I'm looking for in this country, and it would suit your purpose – and your Government's – if I didn't find it. No money, therefore no weapons. The Cause would be strapped for cash, which would delight Whitehall.'

Pagan shook his head. 'The only way I want you to go home is handcuffed to me.'

Jig smiled for the first time. 'How do you propose to accomplish that?'

Pagan stood up. 'Let me put it another way, Jig. If you decide to go down to see Kevin Dawson, you're dead. You're finished. There's absolutely no way in the world you're going to get within a hundred feet of that house without somebody blowing your bloody head off. I know that for a fact. Your only real chance is with me, Jig. I'm the only person who believes you're not the monster the FBI is itching to kill.'

'And what makes you think so highly of me, Pagan?'

'I know you. I've studied you. I know how you operate, and I know how you kill. I also know that you're out of your depth in this country, Jig. Too much is stacked against you here. This isn't your kind of operation. This isn't the old one-two, the quick in-and-out that you're used to.' Pagan made a sweeping gesture with his hand. 'This isn't some future ambassador stepping out of his mews cottage and into his Jaguar. This is something else altogether.'

'What exactly are you saying, Pagan? That I give myself up to you? I'm standing here with two guns in my possession and I'm supposed to give myself up to an *unarmed* man because he's got some intriguing stories to tell? Back to Britain and a cosy berth in one of Her Majesty's lodging-houses? I came here to recover some lost property, Pagan. I don't intend to go home without it.'

'It isn't going to be a matter of just that, Jig. You're looking at the prospect of going home inside a plain wooden box. Take another look down at that house. There are two Secret Servicemen with guns they're just aching to fire. Be realistic.'

'You call it realistic to listen to your story?'

'It's the truth.'

'I'm never sure what it means when people say they're telling the truth, Pagan. I've heard a lot of different truths lately.'

Frank Pagan was silent. If he were in Jig's shoes, would he have believed the narrative? Probably not. Probably he'd have reacted in precisely the same way, with incredulity. In Jig's profession, the only counsel you ever listened to was your own.

Pagan turned and looked down at the stretch of road which lay between the hills and Kevin Dawson's estate. In the distance there was the sound of a car. He narrowed his eyes and looked off in the direction of the noise. He saw a car come into view at a place where the road ran between the folds of hills.

'Give me the glasses a moment,' he said.

Jig, slipping one of the guns inside the waistband of his pants, passed the binoculars to him. Pagan held them up to his eyes and saw the car approach the entrance to the Dawson estate where it was stopped, just as Pagan himself had been, by the Secret Servicemen. Pagan tightened his grip on the glasses. He saw two men get out of the car. One was Tyson Bruno. The other Artie Zuboric. Pagan thrust the binoculars back at Jig, who held them to his face and studied the scene below.

'Surprise, surprise,' Pagan said.

'The tall one is a friend of yours,' Jig said.

'Zuboric. You saw him at St Finbar's Mission. The other is an FBI agent called Tyson Bruno.'

Jig lowered the glasses. He looked at Frank Pagan. His face was unrevealing. Pagan was suddenly aware of how close Jig stood to him. How very near the weapons were. One frantic grab, he thought. He rejected the idea immediately. One frantic grab was likely to be his last.

He said, 'The only reason I can think of for that pair to come here is that somehow they know you're in the vicinity. Which means we can expect even more men turning up pretty damn soon. Now do you see? There's no way into that house. What makes it worse from your point of view is that they apparently know you're around. So what happens when more men arrive and suddenly these hills are swarming with people who all want a piece of you? What happens when it's open season on Jig?'

Jig said nothing. He sat down and frowned. Pagan was puzzled by the sudden appearance of Zuboric and Bruno. Did they *really* know Jig was in the vicinity? Or had they come here expecting to find only Frank Pagan? How could they have known that Pagan was here, though? Unless Dawson had made a phone call to somebody in authority, but the timetable was all wrong. If Dawson *had* called the FBI, there hadn't been time for Zuboric and his sidekick to get here from New York City. Mysteries.

'Even if I believed your story,' Jig said, 'what difference would it make? Even if everything you said is true, do you think it would make me roll over like some lame dog and let you take me back home for my own protection?'

'You might find things a little different at home,' Pagan said. 'Especially now.'

'Meaning what?'

'Meaning simply that you might find yourself out in the cold with your own people. After all, you blew up a church and a whole bunch of innocent people along with it. You might find a change in the tide. Some people will go along with a hero only so far. They tend to dislike it when they find their hero is capable of the same scummy acts as any ordinary thug, no matter what side he happens to be on.'

'You can't goad me, Pagan.'

'I wasn't aware of trying.'

'I had nothing to do with that church.'

'I know that. But what does my opinion count for? People died in that explosion. Innocent kids as well as adults. People who had nothing on their minds except the usual Sunday rapport with God.'

Jig looked through the binoculars at the house. Pagan thought of a man calculating the movements of his own future, weighing this possibility against that one, trying to decide on a course of action.

'It doesn't matter a shit if I happen to believe you, Jig. The FBI has other ideas. Soon the public will have those ideas as well. And the public is notoriously fickle, my friend. You're a hero one day, the next you stink. The great Jig is reduced to killing harmless people. The bold Irish assassin turns common gangster. It's going to make nice reading. How does that make you feel?'

Pagan wondered what Jig's reputation meant to the man. Did the newspaper articles and the songs sung in Irish bars and the reverence afforded Jig mean anything to him? Was his ego such that he couldn't allow his reputation to be eroded by the actions of other people?

Pagan waited for his words to sink into Jig's brain.

'What do you really want, Pagan?'

'Two things.'

'What two things?'

'First, I'd like to know who's going round committing these acts you're being blamed for. And I keep coming back to good old Ivor. It was courtesy of the Free Ulster Volunteers that I found out you were in America in the first place. And it's a fair bet that Ivor was instrumental in making sure I received that bit of information. If he knew that much, maybe he knows why Fitzjohn was killed and why somebody bombed the church.' Pagan paused. He had one more dart to shoot in Jig's direction. 'Maybe he even knows something about that lost property of yours.'

Jig passed his gun from one hand to the other. If this last remark of Pagan's swayed him any, he certainly didn't show it. 'That's a lot of ifs, Pagan.'

'I agree. But what else is there?'

'You think you can make him talk?'

'Between us, I suspect we could get something out of him.'

'Between us? You're actually asking for my help?'

Pagan shrugged. 'Don't you *want* to know who's been taking your name in vain? Don't you want to know if McInnes has any information about your money?'

Jig affected to ignore this question. 'What's the second thing?'

'You know what that is.'

'Me,' Jig said.

'Correct.'

Jig stared off into the trees. 'You've got to understand one thing, Pagan. I'll never let you take me. No matter what.'

Pagan nodded. 'You're the man with the weapons. I make it a cardinal rule never to argue with guns.'

Jig looked back down the slopes towards the road. Pagan tried to imagine the inner workings of the man. Obviously Jig suspected a trap. But at the same time perhaps he was beginning to realise the hopelessness of getting access to Kevin Dawson. On the other hand, maybe he didn't know the meaning of hopelessness, maybe he had such a supreme belief in his own capabilities that he didn't think in terms of insuperable obstacles. But it didn't work that way, not in the real world. Not when you were faced with determined people who wanted nothing but your death.

'If I understand you, Pagan, you're calling a truce,' Jig said.

'In a way.'

'I don't like truces. Especially when I have all the advantages.'

'Take your pick.' Pagan gestured towards the house.

Jig turned his face from the anxious wind that came fretting once again down the slopes.

'Go down there,' Pagan said. 'See if you can get an interview with Kevin Dawson. Try it. I wish you all the luck in the world.'

Jig stared at Frank Pagan. 'Do you really think it matters to me if I get the blame for things I didn't do? Do you think I *care* about anything so bloody shallow as my reputation? If some group of IRA idiots has gone free-lance, that's not my problem. Whatever blame attaches to my name is irrelevant in the long run. Personalities don't enter into this.'

The old terrorist cant, Pagan thought, with some disappointment. The usual humbug of the fanatic. History is more important than people. Movements outweigh personalities. Pawns in the larger game. Etcetera and amen. He had expected something more out of Jig, although he wasn't sure what exactly. In his experience of terrorists, they were mainly men and women who approached life without humour. They were emotional fuck-ups. And even when they experienced human feelings that weren't related to their particular cause, they didn't know what to do with them. Maybe Jig came into that category.

He said, 'I misjudged you, then. I thought you'd see it as your problem, Jig.'

'We don't have matching objectives, Pagan. And we don't come from the same perspective.'

Pagan sat down. 'Fine,' he said. 'But what if the people who attacked the church are going to kill again? What if they already have. What if it's something even more monstrous than the church this time? Whatever it is, Jig, it's going to be attributed to you as surely as if you'd left your fucking fingerprints at the scene. And when Jig gets tainted by these actions, how does it reflect on the things he's supposed to stand for? How does it rub off on his Cause? The plain fact is, Jig, somebody's out there making a fucking asshole out of you and every bloody thing you stand for'. Pagan was quiet for a time. 'Okay. Go down there to Dawson's house. Be a martyr. Isn't that what the Cause expects of you anyhow? Doesn't the Cause expect all its good soldiers to die totally fucking senseless deaths?'

Jig wandered to the edge of the hollow. For a second Pagan thought he was about to step down the slopes and between the trees and, as if it were a personal act of defiance, like a unicyclist setting out on a frayed wire, go immediately in the direction of the house. But then he stopped and stood motionless. Pagan wondered what was going on in his mind now. Had anything Pagan said made a dent? Was he going to agree to the truce? It was a desperate kind of proposal, Pagan realised. But he had no other cards to play. It was reasonable to assume that Jig wouldn't be happy with any activities that sullied his precious Cause, but would he go as far as Pagan wanted him to? If he did, and if they went after Ivor the Terrible together – and the idea of nailing Ivor appealed greatly to Pagan, with or without Jig's help – it would at least have the advantage of keeping Jig within Pagan's reach. It wasn't much, but it was something as far as Frank Pagan was concerned. And down the line somewhere he'd have to make his play, he'd have to get the weapons away from Jig. If an opportunity occurred it was going to be a small one and he'd have to be alert and act faster than he'd ever acted in his life. Jig wasn't going to doze off, that was certain.

From somewhere down the road, like the cry of a wounded animal, there was a noise that echoed through the hills. Jig tilted his head, listening.

Frank Pagan stood up.

The noise was growing shriller, more urgent. Pagan looked off into the distance, where he saw red and blue flashing lights creating a small extravaganza against the backdrop of the dour hills.

'Looks like more reinforcements,' Pagan said, wondering about all this activity. 'I suppose we can expect the cavalry next.'

There was a very thin smile on Jig's face, but the eyes were deadly serious. He continued to look at Pagan and the look was one of scrutiny, uncertainty, like that of a man testing the ground beneath him for the presence of a mine.

He said, 'The air around here is unhealthy.'

Pagan agreed. 'And getting worse.'

'Remember what I said, Pagan. You don't take me. Under any circumstances.'

'I've got that.'

'Don't let it slip your mind. You're dead if you do.'

'I like living,' Pagan said.

Jig looked one last time back down at the estate. Then he sighed and asked, 'You really think Ivor McInnes knows, do you?'

'I'd bet on it.'

Jig was silent a second. Then, 'What hotel is he staying at?'

Artie Zuboric didn't like the Secret Service because he thought its agents had an overblown concept of their own importance. They guarded Presidents and visiting heads of state, admittedly, but Zuboric thought they had it easy when you got right down to it. He stood outside Kevin Dawson's house in the company of Tyson Bruno and felt frustrated because the two SS characters who'd greeted him had told him in a rather airy fashion to keep himself occupied in the grounds. There was more than a little condescension in their manner. This was their little world, and they didn't like intruders because they could look after Dawson damn well by themselves, and besides, they considered the FBI screw-ups in general.

Zuboric stood with his hands on his hips and gazed at the house. The two SS characters stood some distance away, smoking cigarettes and looking extremely proprietorial. They hadn't even allowed Zuboric inside the house, and so far there hadn't been any sign of Kevin Dawson.

Zuboric turned and examined the hills. Tyson Bruno cleared his throat and said, 'I keep thinking about that fucker. The way he decked me. I should never have let that happen.'

Zuboric shook his head. He hadn't thought of anything except Frank Pagan during the drive up here. He looked at Tyson Bruno and said, 'Enjoy the countryside.'

'I hate the fucking countryside,' Bruno answered.

Zuboric looked back at the house. He felt he should have been invited inside and introduced to Dawson, which was what his position merited. Instead, he was being left out in the cold. All because the SS guys protected Kevin Dawson with the zealous tenacity of insecure lovers. 'Let's walk,' he said. 'Take a look around.'

They walked between the trees as far as the narrow road. Dawson's estate was about eighty acres, most of it meadow but wooded here and there. It seemed to Zuboric that it was secure, given the vigilance of the Secret Service fatheads, which prompted the question of why he'd been sent up here in the first place. He felt like an underused extra in a movie, a body, something superfluous.

Tyson Bruno lit a cigarette. 'I'd rather be back in the centre of things,' he said. 'Do you think this is Magoo's way of punishing us?'

Zuboric didn't answer. He was looking at the house. Smoke rolled down the roof, blown out of the chimney by a gust of wind. So far as pastoral prettiness was concerned, this whole area wasn't exactly in the blue ribbon class. It was too forlorn, too uninviting. He stuck his hands in the pockets of his coat. He was thinking of Pagan again, and he'd resolved not to because it created a knot of sheer anger in the middle of his brain.

He tried to relax but Pagan came again, returning to his thoughts like a ghost you couldn't exorcise. He would have liked to see Pagan one more time, just one more time, and give the man a dose of some very bad medicine. He'd never trusted Pagan from the beginning, never warmed to the guy, and now he was filled with a churning need for revenge that might have to go unsatisfied unless he happened to run into the limey again. After all, hadn't Korn practically given the green light to the final solution of the Pagan problem?

'Magoo thinks we screwed up, so he's giving us a little taste of exile. Call it a warning,' Bruno said.

Zuboric frowned. So far as he was concerned the assignment wasn't such a bad one and certainly couldn't be construed as a severe knuckle-rapping. After all, Kevin Dawson was the President's brother, and Magoo wouldn't take that fact lightly. On the other hand, the Director's inscrutability was legend. You didn't make it to the top if you were an easy guy to figure. Zuboric gazed up into the hills, then looked back at Tyson Bruno, who appeared quite uncomfortable.

'Spooky landscape,' Bruno said. 'What makes a guy want to live way out here anyhow?'

Zuboric shrugged. 'Privacy, I guess.'

Tyson Bruno made a snorting sound of derision. It was clear he didn't think much of privacy. He tightened his drab plaid scarf at his neck and narrowed his eyes as he looked across Dawson's estate. In Zuboric's mind, Tyson Bruno was a perfect example of the old school, a graduate of the J. Edgar Hoover Academy for numbskulls. He was dependable up to a point, but not very inventive. Until Frank Pagan had come along, he'd been a rather reliable watchdog. Frank fucking Pagan. Ireland, fucking Ireland. He found himself wishing that the whole goddam island would sink under a tidal wave, drowning Frank Pagan with it and all the problems he'd laid, like so much crap, on Zuboric's doorstep. Problems Artie most certainly didn't need. He had a whole shitload of his own. Charity had started talking about some rich physician who was paying a lot of attention to her lately. How could Zuboric compete with that?

Zuboric walked between the trees. At his side, Tyson Bruno was scanning the landscape, his head swivelling on the thick stalk of his neck. He reminded Zuboric of a bullfrog in certain ways.

'I could use a nip of gin,' Bruno said. 'This damn cold is getting to me.'

Zuboric stopped quite suddenly. In the distance he'd heard something, a sound that never failed to raise the level of his adrenalin. It was the shrill siren of a police car, and it was growing louder, sending scared birds whining out of branches. Zuboric turned his face towards the road. He could see flashing lights, two small points a couple of miles down the road.

He leaned against the trunk of a tree and watched. The cop car was still blasting its siren as it swung into the driveway and went towards the house, where the two SS agents were already taking up a defensive position behind their car, weapons drawn. The police vehicle came to a half, the siren died. It was all very quick. Two uniformed cops jumped out of the car. The SS men, trusting nobody, especially callers in uniform – who could easily have been fakes – emerged with their guns ready.

'What the fuck,' Bruno said.

Zuboric, who knew the signs of trouble when he saw them, started to walk back towards the house. The cops and the agents, having apparently arrived at an understanding, had gone inside the house already. Even before Zuboric had reached the house, Kevin Dawson was hurrying out, the agents flapping behind him. All three got into the Secret Service car, which whipped past Zuboric at top speed and tore down the driveway, spewing dirt as it travelled.

Puzzled, Zuboric looked at the two uniformed cops. He flashed his ID and asked what was going on. The two state policemen appeared flustered and uncertain.

The older of the pair studied Zuboric's ID a second. His hand trembled.

'I can't really describe it,' was what he said, and his voice, like his hand, shook.

Patrick Cairney shaded his eyes against the harsh afternoon sun that burned against the windshield of the Dodge Colt. He glanced at Pagan, who was behind the wheel, then looked down at the gun in his lap. As he did so, he remembered something Finn had once said about how the Cause would one day wither because it lacked nobility. And it lacked nobility because it had no heroes any more. *I'll make my own bloody hero out of Jig,* Finn said. My own bloody hero. What would Finn think of him now that he'd entered into this pact with Pagan? Would he call it an error of judgement, damned from the very beginning?

Finn's advice might have been to withdraw from the vicinity of Dawson until the heat had gone out of the situation and an approach to Dawson involved less risk. Maybe. But Finn would also have been angry about somebody maligning the Cause by blowing up a church. And Finn's outbursts of anger were fierce things to behold, as if the whole person were on the volcanic rim of exploding into lava. Finn might have done precisely the same thing as Jig was doing now. *Let's find out what bloody McInnes is up to and put a stop to that bastard once and for all.*

Cairney turned the gun over in his hand. He was unsure of the decision he'd made. Thoughts crowded him, cramped him. His sick father. The missing money. The possibility that Ivor McInnes might know something about it. The notion that Pagan could be setting a trap.

And Celestine. The last thought he wanted or needed right then. But there was her face, her face floating through his mind, the remembered feel of her mouth, the vibrant warmth of the woman. There she was, a bright, enticing intruder on his thoughts. He closed his eyes for a second. The retreat into darkness. The calm centre of himself. It wouldn't come. He couldn't find it.

He opened his eyes, looked at Frank Pagan's face as Pagan drove the winding road that led narrowly through the hills. He suspected Pagan was telling the truth about McInnes being in New York and the attack on the church, but he wasn't certain if Ivor McInnes knew anything about the money. How the hell could he? And how could the FUV have informed Pagan about the American trip anyway – something only he and Finn knew about?

This last question buzzed in his head. The obvious answer – that there was a traitor within the ranks of The Association of the Wolfe – was disheartening. But Frank Pagan might have been lying from start to finish, fabricating everything he'd said. He'd have to be wary from here on in, supersharp, each one of his senses prepared for some sudden occurrence – a move from Pagan, a car following too close behind, anything. If Pagan was as tenacious as he thought, this truce was going to be as substantial as ice in springtime. And if it melted – if it melted he'd shoot Frank Pagan without any further thought.

What had Pagan said? *Be a martyr? Isn't that what the Cause expects of you anyhow?* That remark had stung Cairney more than anything else, because Pagan had somehow managed to centre in on the one thing that was anathema to Jig – the idea of martyrdom, the notion that that was what the Cause was all about finally. To succeed you had to be dead. To win you had to have died a soldier's death. A loser's death. To win you had to have old women light penny candles to your memory in cold churches and old men drink Guinness over your sanctified name. The old Irish ways, your name immortalised in song and dredged up on every anniversary of your death, which was usually premature and always fruitless.

And something else Pagan had said had struck a chord inside him. *You're out of your depth in this country, Jig. Too much is stacked against you*. Maybe. But it didn't matter now. It was too late for it to matter. Finn had sent him into this, Finn with his hopes and ambitions, his conviction that Jig could do anything. He'd prove Finn right in the end. When he went back to Ireland with the money it would prove that Finn's decision to send Jig to America had been the right one all along, that Finn's faith in him was completely justified.

'I wonder why Kevin Dawson left in such a hurry,' Pagan said. He was turning the Dodge into a sharp bend, driving in a fashion that was a little cavalier. The squeal of tyres on pavement seemed to delight him.

Cairney said nothing. He'd been just as curious as Pagan at the sight of Dawson hurrying out of the house and racing off in a car with the two Secret Servicemen. Shortly after, the FBI agents and the two state cops had also departed. If Cairney had been indecisive about his next step, then the knowledge that Kevin Dawson had left the house made up his mind for him. What was the point of watching an empty house when you had no way of knowing if and when Dawson was coming back?

Pagan swung the Dodge into a hairpin turn and looked at Cairney as he did so. 'Does my driving make you nervous?'

Cairney shook his head. He wouldn't give the Englishman any small satisfaction. Pagan, as if Cairney's refusal to be upset rattled him, put his foot harder on the gas pedal and the car went whining into the next turn. Pagan took his hands from the wheel for a second. The speedometer was approaching seventy-five and the small Dodge was quivering.

Cairney pressed his gun hard into Pagan's ribs. 'I see how it would suit you if we were pulled over by the highway patrol. But I don't think I'd care for that personally. Anyway, guns behave unpredictably at high speeds, Pagan. Keep that in mind. Never play games with me.'

Pagan caught the wheel, braked gently, and the car slowed. 'I'll drive like a senile dowager,' he said.

Cairney pulled the gun back from Pagan's body. 'So long as we have an understanding.'

Pagan nodded. 'I'm sure we have,' he said. He was concerned about the tension in Jig, the extreme wariness. He didn't like the proximity of the gun either, the way Jig had it pointed directly at his side. He sighed, jabbed the radio, heard only static. Jig reached out and turned the radio off.

'Let's get some groundrules straight upfront, Pagan. No noise. No music. No conversation. If we get to New York and I find out all this is bullshit, you're dead. On the other hand, if Ivor *does* know something, I decide the next step. Is that clear?'

'Clear,' Pagan said, thinking how he wasn't cut out for this chauffeur business. He hated being in an inferior position.

On either side of the road now the hills were flattening, drifting down gently into meadows. Roadsigns appeared, indicating the thruway some miles ahead. Older signs pointed out backroads, cattle crossings, deer warnings. Everything was lit by the same filmy ivory sunlight, which had an illusory quality. Here and there an old farmhouse or barn was visible, framed by trees. There was a bucolic assurance about everything, a timelessness.

The road curved suddenly, a long sweeping turn that almost took Pagan by surprise. He braked lightly as he took the Dodge into the curve. And then, surprised by what he saw ahead of him, he slowed the speed of the car so abruptly that Jig was momentarily thrown forward. Not enough to make him careless with the gun, but enough to irritate him.

'For God's sake, Pagan – '

And then Jig saw what it was that had so surprised Frank Pagan, and his first thought was that if *this* were the trap, then it was elaborate and cunning, involving all kinds of incongruous vehicles – a shattered school bus, a sedan that issued a thin cloud of smoke, a couple of state police cruisers, two ambulances, and several other vehicles all parked carelessly around the pathetic relic of the yellow bus, whose windows had been broken and side panels blitzed. Then Jig became conscious of something else, the sight of bodies lying in a clearing between the trees, with men in white coats hovering over them. The realisation that many of these bodies were unmistakably children caused his heart to freeze. He put his hand involuntarily up to his mouth. *Kids*. And his mind was spinning back to a street-scene he'd once witnessed in the Shankill Road area of Belfast when two kids, both bloodied from random gunfire, had been stretched out on a sidewalk, small casualties of a conflict that was beyond their understanding – but that had only been two kids, now he was staring at about ten, a dozen, he wasn't sure. He heard his own blood pound inside his skull, and ice laid a terrible film the length of his spine.

Pagan was travelling past the scene at about ten miles an hour. A cop came across the road and waved an arm impatiently at the Dodge, gesturing for it to pass and mind its own goddam business. Pagan's nostrils filled with the stench of burning rubber and gasoline.

'Keep moving,' Cairney said. He poked the gun into Pagan's hip, concealing the weapon under the folds of his overcoat.

Pagan winced. 'I've got no bloody intention of stopping. Do you imagine I'm going to try and turn you over to some local cop? Take that fucking gun away from me.'

Pagan pressed his foot on the gas pedal as the car drew closer to the cop. Smoke drifted thickly across the road, obscuring the cop for a moment. When it cleared the policeman was about fifteen feet away, still waving his arm. Pagan stared past him at the clearing. What the hell had happened here? It looked as if the school bus had been used for target practice. It was an unreal scene, yet the air of authentic tragedy hung over it. Those small bodies under sheets. The ambulance lights flashing. The men sifting around the wreckage. Pagan's eye was drawn quickly to an area at the rear of the clearing.

Artie Zuboric was standing there, ash-coloured, his usually upright body set in a slouch, as if the weight of whatever had happened in this place were too heavy for him. At the centre of the clearing, flanked by his Secret Servicemen and a group of cops, stood Kevin Dawson.

'Jesus Christ,' Pagan said horrified by the scene, by the awful expression on Dawson's face.

Jig, who had also recognised Dawson, asked, 'What the hell's going on here?' And his voice was hushed, his question phrased in a tone Pagan hadn't heard from him before.

Pagan barely had time to absorb the whole situation before the scene dwindled in the rearview mirror and was finally lost beyond a curve in the road. But the look on Dawson's face stayed with him. It was that of a man shattered, a man bewildered by events that defy description, someone who has seen his world tilted on its axis.

It was grief.

It was a look Frank Pagan had seen on his face, when reflections in mirrors threw back the countenance of a stranger undergoing an impossible trauma, an experience beyond the language of loss. It was an alien voice whispering in your brain over and over *Roxanne is gone, gone, gone.*

Dawson's daughters, Pagan thought.

It struck Pagan then with the force of a hammer.

Somebody had ambushed that school bus which must have had the Dawson girls on board otherwise why would Kevin Dawson be there looking so utterly grief-stricken?

Somebody.

Dear God. He felt his stomach turn over.

Somebody, he thought again. It was violence as pointless and as brutal as that done to the church in White Plains. And what he heard suddenly was Ivor McInnes's voice saying *If it's the IRA, it's not going to stop with some church. Once those fellows get the taste of blood, they don't know when to stop.*

Pagan had a raw sensation in his heart.

There is going to be a telephone call. A man will speak in an Irish accent. He'll say that the bus was attacked by members of the Irish Republican Army.

And Jig, who was still looking at Pagan, still waiting for an answer to the question he'd asked minutes before, was going to be blamed for this new monstrosity. It had all the texture of the completely inevitable. Jig would be blamed, then crucified.

Pagan thumped his foot down hard on the gas pedal. Had Ivor McInnes known about this outrage? If he'd known, as Frank Pagan felt he did, about an IRA presence in the USA, had he also known that *this* was going to happen?

A small nerve began to work in Pagan's cheek as he thought of McInnes, that smug, bloody man with his poisonous hatreds. And something moved through Pagan's brain, an anger he hadn't felt in years, a turmoil of rage, a searing emotion that he couldn't bring entirely under control. He knew this much – he knew he was looking forward to tearing that mask away from Ivor's face and getting down to the truth of things. It would be a slippery descent, because in McInnes's world truth was never something you ascended to, it was a quality concealed in deep places, dank places, down at the fetid bottom of the man's heart.

'I asked you a question,' Jig said. 'What the hell do you think *happened* back there?'

'I can only guess,' Pagan said.

'Let me hear it anyway.'

Frank Pagan told him.

Harrison, New York

Seamus Houlihan called the FBI from a phone booth at a shopping plaza at twenty minutes past five. The man he spoke with attempted unsuccessfully to keep Houlihan talking. But Houlihan delivered his terse message without hesitation, then hung up. He looked across the plaza to the place where the yellow Ryder truck was parked. It was strange, Houlihan thought, not to see John Waddell's face staring out through the windshield. Waddy had deserved to die, it was as simple as that. Like Fitzjohn, he'd been weak when strength was needed.

Houlihan entertained no regrets at the act. There was hardly anything in his life he regretted. Since Waddell had been his friend, though, he felt it was his duty to give the man a decent burial. That was the very least he could do. He had, after all, his own sense of honour.

He paused, staring into the window of a Carvel ice-cream shop. He went inside, ordered a single scoop of vanilla. He had to repeat this order three times because the eedjit girl behind the counter didn't understand his accent. He came out, licking the ice-cream, which was too soft for his taste. By the time he reached the Ryder truck the ice-cream was already melting, running down the sleeve of his jacket. He tossed the cone away in disgust.

He gazed a moment at the discarded confection. It created a bright white puddle on the concrete. He thought of McInnes's instructions to discard all weapons at the time of getting rid of the truck. They were to be cleaned thoroughly of all fingerprints and then dumped in some isolated place, after which Houlihan and the others were to return to Canada, and from there back to Ireland. The part Houlihan didn't like was throwing the weapons away, especially his own handgun, a Colt Mark V he'd become attached to. What did McInnes know anyway? The man wasn't out here doing the fucking dirty work, was he? He wasn't getting his hands grubby. He'd probably never even fired a gun in his whole bloody life, so how could he understand the personal relationship you could develop with a weapon? Besides, what would happen if the weapons were dumped and *then* a bad situation cropped up? You'd be totally naked, wouldn't you!

Houlihan made up his mind to disobey McInnes. It made him feel good. It gave him a pleasing sense of his own authority. He'd keep the guns, *all* the guns, until he was good and ready to toss them. And he wouldn't tell McInnes about this decision when he telephoned him next time. He looked at his watch. He had thirty minutes to kill before he was due to call the Reverend again.

He reached up and opened the door of the cab and slid in behind the wheel.

'What's next?' Rorke asked.

'Another phone call, then a good night's sleep,' was how Seamus Houlihan answered.

24 New York City

In his room at the Essex House Ivor McInnes stared at the TV.

A man named Lawrence W. Childes was speaking from the small coloured screen. The President's Press Officer, he was a solemn figure whose gatherings with the press were reminiscent of a convention of undertakers. He told the assembled journalists that the Government had learned of the presence of the Irish assassin Jig in the United States. That Jig, working either alone or with a group of fellow IRA terrorists, had been responsible for the bombing of the Memorial Church in White Plains. That Irish terrorism, so long contained within the borders of the United Kingdom, had come to the USA. He spoke of an extensive ongoing investigation being conducted by the FBI in association with a variety of local law-enforcement agencies. He was convinced that Jig would soon be apprehended and brought to justice.

After the introductory remarks, Childes was besieged by questions. Hands were upraised, papers clutched and shaken, cameras thrust forward, as journalists vied for attention: Lawrence W. Childes accepted a question from a fat woman with an Irish name. She represented a wire service. She wanted to know why the Irish were operating within the continental United States, a question Childes hummed at but couldn't answer.

McInnes had been packing his suitcase on the bed. He stopped, moving a little closer to the TV. The fat woman was still pursuing her line of inquiry despite the protests of other journalists who, like hopeful adolescent suitors, had claims of their own to press for Childe's attention.

I have no information, Ms McClanahan.

All of a sudden Irish terrorists start operations inside our borders and you don't know why? What exactly is this Administration hiding, Mr Childes?

McInnes smiled. He folded a shirt, put it inside the suitcase. He knew that this press conference was going absolutely nowhere, no matter how shrill were the hyenas of the media in their fullblooded curiosity. He rolled a necktie, placed it neatly beside the shirt. The radio clock on the bedside table said it was 6:39. Since Houlihan had already called, McInnes knew the big man had succeeded in the afternoon's endeavour and had made his call to the FBI on schedule. Which meant that either Lawrence W. Childes wasn't being entirely open with the press or else the information about the school bus hadn't reached him yet. Maybe it had been decided, at levels above and beyond Childes, that an attack on schoolkids wasn't something the American public was geared as yet to hear. What difference did it make? McInnes asked himself. Sooner or later news of the latest outrage would reach them, because a thing like that couldn't be contained forever.

McInnes adjusted the volume control.

A man with a florid face, a boozer's face, was asking if there were any important political figures in the congregation of Memorial Church at the time of the bombing.

So far as we can tell, the answer is negative, Childes replied.

Then what we're talking about is plain random violence and destruction?

It would appear that way.

McInnes placed a pair of pants on top of the shirt. Then he picked up the folder that contained the notes he'd made on the history of Ulster workers in the construction of the railroad and put it inside a side-pocket of the suitcase. He went into the bathroom and splashed some cold water on his face, and when he returned the press conference was still in progress.

Graf, Detroit Free Press. Is there any evidence to suggest that the IRA plans future attacks?

We have no such evidence at this time, Mr Graf.

But why would they come into this country just to blow up one church and then leave again?

As I said, we have no evidence to support the view that the IRA plans further terrorist activities.

McInnes sat on the edge of the bed. He saw Lawrence W. Childes move away from the podium, and he gathered that the press conference had come to an abrupt end. There was one of those uncertain moments when the cameraman loses his focus and the camera swings wildly, shooting a ceiling, an empty doorway, the faces of flustered journalists – but then Childes was back behind the podium again, holding a sheet of paper in one hand. He was calling for quiet and the picture was steady now.

McInnes leaned towards the TV.

Lawrence W. Childes said that he had just learned of a new development. He cleared his throat and read.

At approximately two-fifty this afternoon a school bus was attacked outside New Rockford, Connecticut, by gunmen who claim to be members of the Irish Republican Army.

On board this bus were the nieces of the President of the United States. The President has no statement to make at this time.

There was a long silence. Then the questions, held in check a moment by the fragile sea-wall of concern and decency and outright shock, came bursting forward. Were the Dawson girls injured? How many were on board the bus? What was the number of casualties? Was this the same group that had destroyed the church in White Plains? Was this the work of Jig? Lawrence Childes, face drained and voice shaking, clasped his hands and said that he had no information to add to what he'd already said. Tracked by reporters, who now showed all the demeanour of crazed ladies at a hat sale, he moved away from the podium. Security officers blocked the newsmen as Lawrence Childes vanished down the hallway without looking back.

McInnes turned the TV off.

There. It was out now. It was common knowledge.

And McInnes experienced a feeling that was jubilation suffused with relief. The road had been mapped and travelled and was behind him now. He had won. He zipped up his suitcase, then turned the small key in its lock. He tossed the key in the air and snapped it up in his hand as it fell back down. He uttered a small whoop of exhilaration.

It was out now and all America knew it. The Irish Republican Army had blown up a church and then attacked a school bus. The IRA had sunk to a level that defied description. Already, McInnes was anticipating the next day's headlines and editorials, the anger and dismay that would yield to the call for blood, for violent responses to violent men, an eye for an eye. He could hear the knives being released from their sheaths and sharpened. Revenge, when it came, would be devastating.

He didn't hear the knock on his door at first. Even when he became conscious of it, it barely registered. An intrusion from another world. He turned. Whatever it was, whoever, he could handle it. He could handle anything now. There was nothing that wasn't beyond his capabilities.

He opened the door. Somehow he wasn't altogether astonished to see Frank Pagan. The presence of a second man, somebody McInnes had never seen before, did surprise him, but he quickly took it in his stride. He was in a place where even Frank Pagan couldn't harm him.

'Why, Frank,' he said. 'And you've brought a friend. How very nice.'

Pagan's face was dark. His forehead was broken into deep ridges and his jaw was set at a belligerent angle. His large hands were clenched and they hung at his sides, as if restraining them required effort. The other man had drawn a gun. Curiously, though, he didn't aim it directly at McInnes. Instead, he seemed to point into the space between Pagan and McInnes as if he wanted to cover both men. McInnes stepped back.

'Talk to me,' Pagan said. 'Start at the beginning and talk to me.'

'We've talked already,' McInnes replied. He glanced at his suitcase.

'Packed, are we? Ready to leave?' Pagan asked.

'Quite ready.' McInnes looked briefly at the gun in the young man's hand. 'There's nothng left for me to do here.'

'Wrong, Ivor. You've got unfinished business.'

McInnes shook his head. 'Tell your friend to put his gun away, Frank.'

'I can't tell him anything like that,' Pagan said. He widened his eyes and smiled. 'Bad manners on my part. I forgot to introduce you. Ivor McInnes meet Jig.'

McInnes felt a pulse throb at the back of his throat. He looked into the young man's eyes, which were harder even than Pagan's, and had an odd sideways quality, a shiftiness. McInnes wondered how this state of affairs added up. Pagan and Jig. Now there was a combination that God and Scotland Yard and the FBI hadn't exactly intended. How had it come about that Frank Pagan and Jig were together? How had this pair managed to find one another, and who was the quarry, who the hunter now? It wasn't supposed to happen like this. Not at all.

'Jig isn't pleased, Ivor,' Pagan said. 'He isn't pleased at all. Which goes for me too.'

McInnes saw a narrowing of Jig's eyes. It was hardly perceptible, but it was as obvious as a neon to McInnes.

'I'm sure you're making some kind of sense, Frank,' he said. 'But it escapes me.'

Jig spoke for the first time. 'Tell us about the church, McInnes. Tell us about the school bus.'

'Terrible things,' McInnes said, shaking his head.

'We're all agreed that they're terrible things,' Pagan said. 'But we haven't come here to make little sympathetic noises, McInnes.'

'What do you know?' Jig asked.

'What do *I* know?' McInnes smiled. 'Only what I see on TV.'

'Try again,' Pagan said.

There was a smell of violence about both Pagan and the other man, and nothing quickened the brain quite like that odour. McInnes stepped to the window and looked out at the park. The ghost of a decision was beginning to take shape at the back of his mind. Sometimes, from out of nowhere, he had an inspiration, a flash, an insight that seemed to transcend the usual laboured workings of logical thought. He had one now.

Pagan stepped closer to him. And then one of Pagan's hands was clamped on his shoulder, turning McInnes around as if he were nothing more than a sack of frail kindling.

McInnes hated violence. On one broad level it was a political tool of some use, but when it descended to the personal arena it was loathsome. It wasn't even cowardice on his part either. He'd boxed one year when he'd been a university student in Liverpool, accumulating a fair record, but something about crunching his glove into an opponent's face had repelled him. As indeed he was repelled now by the way Pagan was holding him.

'We're reduced to this, are we?' he asked.

Pagan held a fist beneath McInnes's jaw. 'This is nothing,' Pagan said. 'I haven't even worked up a sweat yet, Ivor.'

'I don't think there's any need for this, Frank.'

Before McInnes could say anything, Pagan had swung the fist in a low trajectory. It dug into the fleshy lower part of McInnes's belly, doubling him over, expelling all the air from his lungs and causing his eyes to register fiery sparks.

McInnes gasped and sat down on the bed and blinked up at Frank Pagan.

'It's like I said, Ivor. We don't have time for any further bullshit. It's pain and more pain from here on in.'

Through layers of pain, McInnes realised he had perceived the outline of a plan that would serve two purposes at once. It would get Pagan off his back, which was admittedly a priority right now. But more than that, it would rid him of Seamus Houlihan, whose work was finished and whose continued existence could easily become an embarrassment over the long run. Besides, Seamus had shown a tendency to take the initiative in situations where intervention on his part wasn't needed. The man was a thug, a cold-blooded killer, and McInnes perceived no kind of future for such a man in his scheme of things. Houlihan was like some kind of primitive weapon that Ivor McInnes had no further use for.

Frank Pagan reached down and grabbed the lapels of McInnes's jacket.

'Easy,' McInnes said.

'Don't stop me, Ivor. Not unless you've got something sensible to say.'

McInnes raised a hand defensively.

'Do we talk, Ivor?' Pagan asked.

McInnes nodded. He was struggling to catch his breath. The lie that had presented itself to him was ingenious, all the more so since it would contain elements of truth. All the best lies had fragments of truth in them.

'We talk,' he said.

Pagan folded his arms against his body. Jig, who had been observing this situation without comment, still had his gun trained in front of him.

McInnes rubbed his stomach where it hurt. He turned the lie around in his mind, preparing to float it in front of these two hostile men. 'I heard a story in Belfast,' he said. 'I have my sources, you know.'

'Go on,' Pagan urged. His tone was sceptical.

'Give me a minute, Frank. Breathless.' McInnes stood up now, just a little unsteady. He took a couple of deep breaths. 'I heard an interesting little yarn about a group of disaffected IRA men who were planning an action in America.' McInnes paused, looking first at Pagan, then at Jig. Both of them were bloody poker-players, he decided.

'It appears that this IRA cell, unhappy because money wasn't coming down the pipeline as fast as they wanted it, decided to branch out. Well, you have some idea of how the IRA is, don't you? They're forever splitting into factions. They're always squabbling and going for each other's throats. Anyhow, this group, which needed finances for various projects – presumably of a criminal nature – came up with the notion of doing a couple of outlandish things in America. The idea behind their thinking was quite simple. They felt that if they went off at a tangent in America, they'd be making a point with the powers back in Ireland. It would be a form of blackmail, you see. They'd come here and make a mess, which would be like holding a pistol to the head of the people in the IRA who mind the purse. Are you with me?'

Frank Pagan didn't move a muscle. No nod, no expression. McInnes swallowed and continued. 'This little group of the disaffected decided on outrages. Human outrages. Acts that would alienate public concern. A church would be first. What's more innocent than a church after all? They they thought of the answer to that one, didn't they? They came up with something even more vile. A school bus. Better yet, what if that particular bus carried two rather important children? You see the wicked way some people think.'

'Spare me the moral judgements, Ivor.'

'Well, apparently they've come here and they succeeded in doing what they set out to do. Now they think they'll go home and suddenly the purse-strings will be wide open for them because if they're not then it's an easy matter to come back to the United States and do something else." McInnes paused. He wished he had a litmus paper he could dip into Frank Pagan's brain to check the effect of his story on the man. 'You understand what I'm telling you, don't you?'

Pagan said nothing.

McInnes went on, 'Blackmail, Pagan. Blackmail on a terrible scale. You and I might not understand that way of thinking, but certain people come to it quite naturally. And the people responsible for these horrors are quite capable of anything. As you well know.'

'Where do you fit in, Ivor?'

McInnes stood up, a little shaky. A lie was always more convincing if it involved a detail that cast the liar himself in a bad light. And this was the tactic McInnes pursued now. 'I know how many people perceive me, Frank. They think that because I'm socially and philosophically opposed to Catholicism, that I'm behind Protestant violence.'

'Get on with it, Ivor.'

'You're an impatient man, Frank Pagan.'

'You have that effect on me.'

McInnes smiled slightly. 'Well, to be perfectly honest, I saw an opportunity to do myself some good. Call it selfish thinking. I'm not without a certain vanity, after all. Most people have some. What I genuinely believed was that I could come here, make contact with these people and perhaps negotiate something that wouldn't involve the violence we've seen in the last few days. In other words, I misled myself into thinking I could contact these men and reason with them. It didn't matter that I was on a different side from them. The point was, I thought I could sway them, I thought I could make a gesture that had nothing to do with the partisan nature of life in Ireland. I believed I could spare the United States a taste of the strife that has torn Ireland apart for so long.'

McInnes paused. He stared at Frank Pagan with a look of grief and misery in his eyes. 'I failed, obviously.'

'You thought you could be a saint, did you?'

'Not a saint, Frank. Just the voice of reason.'

'The voice of reason,' Pagan said flatly. 'Do I applaud now?'

'Applaud?'

'Quite a little performance, Ivor.'

'You don't believe me?'

'In another world I might. In a world where cows played bagpipes and money grew on trees, I might be convinced.'

McInnes shrugged. 'I'm telling you the truth.' He looked at Jig, who had been listening motionlessly to the story.

Pagan said, 'Let me see if I can get this straight, Ivor. You came after these men, without telling anyone in authority, because you imagined you could do your Henry Kissinger bit and get them to sit down like reasonable men at a table? You imagined some blood-thirsty IRA characters were going to pay attention to the man they think of as the Protestant anti-Christ?'

'I thought I could do myself some good,' McInnes said. 'Call me vain. Call me egocentric. Call it a normal human response.'

'Call it bullshit,' Frank Pagan said.

McInnes looked down at the floor. He felt suddenly very calm, in control of things. Even the sight of Frank Pagan's incredulous face didn't trouble him.

'You asked for the truth,' McInnes said.

'And what did I get? Tripe.'

'Have it your own way, Frank.'

Pagan glanced at Jig, then said, 'What about Fitzjohn? How does he fit into this fable of yours?'

McInnes looked sheepish. 'I'm afraid I lied to you there, Frank.'

'Well, knock me down with a feather,' Pagan said.

'Fitzjohn was acting on my instructions to arrange a meeting between myself and this IRA faction.'

'Your personal emissary.'

'Exactly.'

'And?'

'They killed him. They aren't reasonable men. I thought they were. But I was wrong again. Poor Fitzjohn.'

Frank Pagan sat down on the bed now. 'If any of what you're telling us is true, you're covered in blood. You're up to your thick neck in blood. You claim you knew in advance of situations that could have been prevented if you'd gone to the authorities. Jesus Christ, we're talking about innocent kids here! We're talking about kids travelling home on a school bus.'

'Ask yourself this. Would the authorities have listened to me?'

'I don't believe a word of this. That's the problem I'm having, Ivor.'

Jig moved slowly across the floor. McInnes imagined that the gun in the young man's hand was going to come up through the air and smack him straight across the face and he braced himself for it. But it didn't happen.

Jig asked, 'How did your source happen to come upon all this information in the first place?'

McInnes's mind was like a needle laying threads across what had already been embroidered. He knew how he could convince Jig of his story at last. He knew which name to drop into the conversation for maximum effect. He said, 'I can't reveal that. But I can tell you this much. A man called Padraic Finn was in control of finances, which didn't please certain people. It obviously didn't please the faction I'm talking about, the ones who are here in America right now.'

'Finn?' Jig asked.

'That's right.'

Jig stared at McInnes. There was a flicker of interest in his eyes now. 'How did your source know about Finn?'

McInnes smiled in a weary way. 'There's a very old craft called infiltration, Jig. No doubt you're familiar with it.'

Jig absently fiddled with the tuner of the bedside radio. 'What do you know about the missing money?'

'Money?' McInnes replied.

'Money from the *Connie O'Mara*,' Pagan said.

'I'm a couple of steps behind you,' McInnes said in a puzzled way. 'You're talking in another language.'

There was silence inside the room.

'I don't believe Finn was infiltrated,' Jig said finally.

McInnes gazed down at his suitcase. 'He wasn't just *infiltrated*, my friend. No, it was more than that.'

Jig stared at McInnes. 'What more?'

'This same IRA faction *murdered* Padraic Finn at his home near Dun Laoghaire.'

Jig didn't move. McInnes saw the face change. He saw the lips open and the skin turn white. He saw all the light sucked from the eyes, drawn backwards into some unfathomable area of the skull. McInnes had never seen a face alter so quickly, so profoundly.

Jig shoved his gun directly at McInnes's head, the barrel pressing in a spot just above McInnes's ear.

'You lying bastard, McInnes.'

McInnes tried to move away from the weapon, but Jig was pressing it hard.

'I'm not lying,' McInnes said.

'They *couldn't* infiltrate Finn. They *couldn't* murder him.'

'But they did. They went at night to his house. They'd already bribed the watchman, George Scully. With nobody to protect the house, it must have been easy for them.'

Jig took the gun from McInnes's head as suddenly as he'd placed it there. He opened his mouth to say something, but no words came. He was like a man trying to still some awful internal turmoil to which he was totally unaccustomed. A man experiencing some new and terrifying sensation that he couldn't name, couldn't identify, didn't want to believe.

'*No*,' Jig said, and his voice was hollow.

McInnes said, 'I know where these killers are. Their leader is somebody called Houlihan. There are four in this group, so far as I know. They travel in a rented Ryder truck. And they're presently staying at a place called the River View Motel near Hastings.' McInnes paused. He could see that Jig was absorbing this information quietly, but Frank Pagan – ah, always the sceptic – was looking incredulous, a big frown distorting his features.

McInnes thought a moment about Houlihan and the others. It was *perfect*. If there was a confrontation in the course of which Houlihan and his pals were killed, it would be splendid. What did it matter if they were later discovered, after fingerprints were run through computers, to be Free Ulster Volunteers and not IRA? He'd simply say he was mistaken, if Pagan asked. He'd simply say he'd received the wrong information and had passed it along in good faith, that he'd believed the men in the River View Motel were IRA. Pagan couldn't prove otherwise. He could interrogate until doomsday, but he couldn't prove a damn thing. There was just no way. And, since Houlihan had dumped the guns and the remote-control devices that triggered the explosives, there was absolutely *nothing* to tie some dead FUV men into the barbarism in New Rockford or the bombing in White Plains. All anybody would ever know was that four men from Ulster, their purpose in America mysterious, had been killed in a motel in Hastings, New York.

The weakness in this scheme was the possibility of Pagan taking prisoners – the slight chance that Houlihan or one of the others might talk. But it was such an unlikely possibility that McInnes dismissed it. For one thing, Houlihan and the others would never talk. Houlihan's strange moral code precluded betrayal, no matter the circumstances. He'd never give anything away. He was a miser when it came to revealing information. He'd never say anything about his reason for being in the USA. Even if he wanted to talk, was he likely to *admit* that he'd gunned a school bus and bombed a church?

But it would never come to that, because McInnes knew Houlihan well enough to guess that Seamus, even though he'd dumped the incriminating automatic weapons, wasn't going to discard his beloved handgun quite so promptly – he'd never go anywhere without his pistol. Which was fine. The handgun had played no part in the attack on the school bus. And if the pistol was all he had, Seamus would gladly go into battle. He'd never turn his back on a good fight, especially if he still had his precious handgun. And Seamus would never be captured because he'd rather blow out his own brains than go back to jail again. Anyhow, if the expression on Jig's face meant anything, the possibility of prisoners being taken was remote, a courtesy that Jig in his present mood wouldn't entertain. The young man had a desperate killing look. He was ready to do violence. He was ready to kill. The battle was inevitable and, to McInnes's way of thinking, a neat solution to his problems with Seamus Houlihan and the FUV. But it would be the last one. After this, he thought, there would be no more violence.

Jig picked up the telephone. McInnes watched him. The hand that held the receiver was tense, skin drawn, knuckles bleached. McInnes heard the young man ask for a phone number in Ireland.

After about thirty seconds Jig hung up.

'No answer?' McInnes asked. He thought *Dead men don't answer telephones*.

Jig appeared not to have heard the question. He once more picked up the telephone and asked for the number of the River View Motel.

McInnes smiled. 'You don't think Houlihan registered under his own name, do you?'

Jig said, 'It's easy to find out if a party of men arrived in a Ryder truck.' His voice was clipped, shorn of intonation, like that of a deaf person who had never learned the nuances of speech.

McInnes stretched out one hand. 'Go ahead,' he said. 'You'll find out I've been telling the truth.'

Frank Pagan stared at Jig. 'You can't be giving serious consideration to any of this shit,' he said in dismay.

Jig said nothing. He dialled the number.

McInnes smiled at Pagan, who had the look of a man chewing on fragments of an electric light bulb, a trick he'd never master no matter how long and hard he worked at it.

New Rockford, Connecticut

Artie Zuboric had very little experience of handling grief, his own or anyone else's. Now, as he stood in the living-room of Kevin Dawson's house in the company of Tyson Bruno and the two Secret Servicemen, he was conscious of a tide of grief flowing throughout this large house.

Upstairs, in a darkened bedroom, Kevin Dawson was standing at the bedside of his sedated wife, Martha, holding her hand and muttering something unintelligible over and over. Earlier, Zuboric had looked inside the bedroom through the open door, but his awareness of pain was too much for him.

In the hallway outside the living-room people came and went. Physicians. Family members. Employers in one or other of the Dawson industries. There was word that Thomas Dawson himself was on his way here. Zuboric went over to the fireplace and looked at the framed photographs of the two Dawson girls on the mantelpiece, but he couldn't bring himself to look for long. He stepped out into the hallway and stood at the foot of the stairs. Tyson Bruno came out to join him.

Neither man spoke for a very long time. Grief, Zuboric noticed, imposed silences, made you speak only when you had to and then in hushed whispers. Grief was like sitting in the reading-room of a large library. He glanced up the long staircase a moment. He was anxious to be out of this place, out in the cold night air, but instructions had come directly from Korn that he was to stay where he was until the Director himself had arrived. Already, the site of the attack was being combed thoroughly by a dozen FBI agents and a score of State cops, all feverishly working under floodlights. Forensic experts were going over the bus in punctilious detail. But what could that tell them except what they already knew – that twelve children out of a total of eighteen on the wretched bus had been murdered, including the daughters of Kevin and Martha Dawson?

'It's a fucking nightmare,' Tyson Bruno said.

Zuboric wandered to the front door of the house. He pushed it open. It was a nightmare all right, and it made him horribly impatient. Somewhere in the darkness was the man responsible for it all. Somewhere there was Jig. Zuboric wondered what kind of man was capable of an act like the massacre of schoolkids. He knew terrorists courted indecency with a passion. He knew they understood no limits. But *this*. This was something else.

Tyson Bruno came and stood beside him. 'I'm thinking,' he said quietly, 'I'm thinking Korn's going to be a very angry man, Artie. He sends us up here to keep an eye on Dawson, and what happens?' Bruno made a sweeping gesture with one plump hand.

'He can hardly blame us for this,' Zuboric answered. 'Christ, we weren't responsible for looking after that school bus. That wasn't our brief, Ty.'

'Tell that to Korn,' Bruno said. 'He's going to be looking for heads to roll. And we're the most convenient ones.'

Zuboric drew a fingertip through his moustache. He felt most uneasy. It was more than the grief that eddied through this house. It was more than the wall-to-wall misery of this place. There was an element of truth in what Tyson Bruno said. The Director, who took every dent in the FBI armour personally. It didn't matter in the long run that guarding a school bus hadn't even been mentioned. The Director had one of those selective memories that could reach back and revise any conversation. The Director could say that he'd told Zuboric to protect the bus. Zuboric wouldn't put that kind of thing beyond the man. The Bureau was everything. People didn't matter. They were nothing more than fuses that burned out and could be replaced.

Zuboric stepped out of the house. He scanned the bleak darkness and the cars parked outside. 'It's the wrong time to start thinking about our own skins,' he said.

'It's never the wrong time for that,' Tyson Bruno replied.

Zuboric made an impatient gesture with his hand. That was something else about grief. It precluded all other matters and feelings, regardless of their importance. You went into a state of suspended animation. Everything was put on hold. You couldn't act. Couldn't think.

A sound by the living-room door made him turn around. He saw the two Secret Servicemen coming out of the room. They moved almost in unison, like a married couple who have become attuned to one another's vibrations over the years. They carried with them a scent of cologne, somewhat stale, as if it had been trapped in their suits for a very long time. Without their dark glasses, their faces looked strange and blank, a pair of unfinished masks.

The one called Marco stepped outside the house and lit a cigarette. Zuboric had to move aside to let him pass. The other, Chuckie, remained just inside the door, drawing the night air deeply into his lungs.

'It's a hell of a thing,' Marco said.

There was a muted murmur of agreement among the four men.

Then silence. Marco pulled on his cigarette and said, 'They were the prettiest kids. Given the fact they were Dawsons and got a lot of attention, they were damned nice. Jesus.' He dropped his cigarette and crushed it with unrestrained energy. 'I'd like to get the guy that did this.'

Zuboric looked away. There was a half moon over the hills.

Marco said, 'It's sickening. That's what it is. It's like somebody kicked me in the gut. I can't get over the feeling.' He blinked out at the sky. 'Some motherfucker comes here and shoots up a bus. I keep thinking, what the fuck has Ireland got to do with those two kids, huh? What did they know from Ireland, for fuck's sake? And not just those two. A whole gang of kids.'

Chuckie blew his nose into a big white handkerchief. Zuboric thought the moon was the saddest he'd ever seen.

'Poor Jack Martyns,' Chuckie said, referring to his dead Secret Service colleague. 'He thought he had it easy. Went to school every day. Came home at three every afternoon. What a schedule. Nothing to do but look after a couple of kids.'

Marco furrowed his brow and sighed. 'Jack was a good man.'

Zuboric now caught another scent on the air. It was that of cognac, and it came over strongly on Chuckie's breath. This pair had been drinking on the sly. That's why they were suddenly loose and communicative and open.

Marco smoked a second cigarette. Two people came down the stairs and went silently out in the direction of their car. Zuboric recognised the woman as Kevin Dawson's younger sister, Elaine, who was always in the newspapers because of her celebrated boyfriends. He didn't recognise the guy who went with her, though. Tinted glasses, silver hair, prosperous. He looked just like all of Elaine's other boyfriends.

Zuboric watched the beige Rolls-Royce slide softly down the driveway. Marco was still puffing furiously on his cigarette and Chuckie was studying the centre of his large handkerchief. They put Zuboric in mind of two uncles at the funeral of nieces they'd never known very well. They had been drinking to accelerate their feelings and open their pores up in general.

Marco said, 'Yeah, it's a kick in the gut okay.'

Chuckie agreed. He folded his handkerchief. 'I was wondering about that guy who came this afternoon.'

Marco made a loose little gesture with his shoulders. 'What about him?'

'Well, it was kinda coincidental,' Chuckie said. 'He comes here, talks to Kevin Dawson. Next thing we know, the bus is attacked. Who the hell was he? I mean, what the hell did he want anyhow?'

'Okay, I'm with you,' Marco said in the unfocused way of a man who has drunk one small glass too many. 'The Englishman?'

'Englishman?' Zuboric asked. He had a strange feeling, almost as if a hat-pin had been pushed into his heart. 'What Englishman.'

Both Chuckie and Marco surveyed Zuboric coolly. They appeared to have forgotten his existence and now, forcibly reminded of it, weren't altogether pleased by the fact.

Marco stubbed his half-smoked cigarette underfoot. 'Okay. An English guy comes here. Shows us some fancy ID. Wants to see Mr Dawson on urgent business. Mr Dawson says it's fine. They talk in private for a while. Then the limey leaves.'

'What *Englishman?*' Zuboric asked.

'The name was Pagan,' Chuckie said.

'Pagan?' Zuboric asked. '*Frank* Pagan?'

'Friend of yours?' Chuckie asked.

'What did he talk about with Dawson?'

'Don't know,' Chuckie said. 'It was behind closed doors. Seemed like it was urgent, though.'

Zuboric looked at Tyson Bruno. Then he studied the flight of stairs that led up to the other rooms of the house.

Bruno shook his head. 'I don't think you should, Artie. Bad timing.'

Zuboric barely listened to his colleague. He was already moving quickly towards the stairs, wondering how he could approach Kevin Dawson, how he could get to a man who was totally lost in grief, how he could find out what Frank Pagan had been doing here only a few hours ago and whether there was any kind of information on the face of the whole planet that might redeem him in the thunderous eyes of Leonard M. Korn.

Grief or no grief, it was worth a shot.

New York City

Ivor McInnes stood in the lobby of the Essex House and dialled the telephone number of the River View Motel in Hastings-on-the-Hudson.

A man's surly voice came on the line. 'River View.'

'Connect me with Mr Houlihan please.'

'*Momento*.'

McInnes waited. When he heard Houlihan's harsh accent he said, 'This is the last call I'll make until we meet in Canada, Seamus. I have to be absolutely sure you've followed all my instructions to the letter.'

'Don't I always follow your bloody instructions?' Houlihan asked.

'Not always.' McInnes saw a lovely girl in a knee-length fur coat wander down the lobby. He watched the loose motion of her body under the folds of the coat. He imagined the bareness of her back and the way her spine would fall in diminishing ridges to her buttocks. She smiled at him in an absent fashion. He was reminded of another smile, another face.

'This is important, Seamus,' he said.

Houlihan sighed but said nothing.

'You've dumped everything I told you to dump?'

'We got rid of the remote control devices yesterday. Nobody's ever going to find them. Nobody's ever going to pin that church on us.'

'I'm talking about the guns, Seamus.'

Houlihan paused before answering. 'They're gone,' he said.

'Every gun?'

'Every last one.'

'Are you absolutely positive?'

'Is there a point to this conversation?' Houlihan asked.

'Did you toss your handgun as well?'

'I did. With great regret.'

McInnes caught it then. The lie in the big man's voice. Seamus still had his pistol. Therefore he'd fight. 'You're clean then.'

'As a fucking penny-whistle.'

'There's absolutely nothing left that can connect you with any of your recent activities?'

'Not a damn thing,' Houlihan said.

McInnes was quiet for a moment. Then he said, 'You did a wonderful job, Seamus. See you in Canada.'

He hung up, smiling. The girl had gone now. The lobby was empty. McInnes felt a deep glow of anticipation. He had almost reached the end of it all now. Only the final pieces remained to be put in place.

In the rear seat of the helicopter Thomas Dawson sat huddled inside his overcoat. Below, there was one of those staggering views of Manhattan, all lights, like a huge cathedral of electricity. He closed his eyes and sat with his head tipped back. He wasn't looking forward to an encounter with his brother's anguish. He patted his gloved hands against his knees and sighed and gazed out of the window again as the chopper banked abruptly, swinging away from the canyons of the city.

There had been a great deal of sorrow in the Dawson family history. His older brother Joseph, to take one example, had shot himself through the head with a revolver at the age of twenty-three because he'd been depressed over some affair of the heart that hadn't worked out. And his youngest sister, Sarah, had died in a sanatorium from an overdose of heroin. But there had never been anything quite like this, the deaths of two small children in the most violent way imaginable. Sarah and Joseph had been neurotic, highly strung, the kind of people who perceived every slight in the most magnified fashion and perhaps their self-inflicted deaths were not so terribly surprising.

But the two girls –

Dear Christ, they'd been nothing but innocent children! What had they *ever* done to deserve such deaths? Dawson, not unnaturally, searched his mind for somebody he might blame for this tragedy. It was easy to say that he might have done more personally, could have been more persistent in forcing Kevin to take his family out of the country. He might also have acted more decisively in dealing with the presence of Jig. By the same token, the FBI could have been more vigilant, worked a little harder at bringing Jig to justice. When you started down the blame trail, it was hard to stop. Kevin himself – for God's sake, he should have seen the danger in his involvement with the Irish. Now, if he understood that at all, it was just too damned late. Goddammit. You could lay blame all over the place with thick brushstrokes, but nothing would ever restore those two small girls to life.

Thomas Dawson took out a cigarette and lit it. He exhaled the smoke slowly in the direction of his fellow passenger, Leonard M. Korn, who'd come aboard in Manhattan.

'We could have done more,' Dawson said. He couldn't keep a certain quiver out of his voice. 'God, we should have done more.'

Korn said nothing. He nodded his shaven head. He wasn't a man who felt the kind of pity most human beings do, but in the presence of Thomas Dawson's obvious grief, he was touched a little. It wasn't his main concern at this moment, however. He was also thinking of ways in which he might perform some damage control. Admittedly, the Secret Service had been directly responsible for the two children, but there *had* been an FBI presence in the vicinity, and that was bad. He'd have the scalps of the two agents, of course. He'd nail them to a wall in public. But this kind of bloodletting would only go so far to protect the Bureau from charges of negligence. There was really only one thing that might turn the situation around somewhat.

And that was the death of Jig.

Korn looked at the President. 'We haven't prepared for terrorism from this quarter,' he said. 'From the Libyans, of course. From some of the Arab countries, certainly. We routinely keep such people under scrutiny. But the Irish . . .' And he flapped one of his small white hands.

Thomas Dawson wasn't interested in what Korn had to say. He was remembering the previous summer when he'd taken his nieces out on the Presidential yacht and they'd cruised Chesapeake Bay. He was remembering a quality in those girls which had struck him as rather unDawson-like. They were without guile, that's what it was. You couldn't imagine them conspiring about anything. This had to be on account of Martha's influence. Dawson gulped down more smoke, which was harsh at the back of his throat. He wondered how Martha was doing. She was a steadfast little woman, one with reserves of strength, but how could anybody pull out of a situation like this?

The Dawsons would survive. They always did. They had their own shock-absorbers for family tragedies. They retrenched, regrouped, and came out stronger in the end. But there was a very bad time ahead. He stared from the window. The lights of Manhattan had gone and there were stretches of black landscape below.

'We could have done more,' he said again. He wasn't really speaking to Leonard Korn, but rather to himself. As far as he was concerned, Korn's career was coming dangerously close to an end.

Korn could see, even in the darkened cabin, that Thomas Dawson had all the mannerisms of a shellshocked man. The tremor in the fingers, the toneless voice, the way his eyes were quite without life.

'I give you my solemn vow, Mr President,' Korn said, 'that we'll settle this Irish business – '

Thomas Dawson interrupted. 'The British have been saying the same thing for centuries, Korn. And what have they actually achieved?' Dawson turned so that the instrument lights around the pilot's seat threw eerie little colours, stark reds and chill greens, against his face. 'The answer is nothing. In several centuries, the British have accomplished absolutely nothing.'

Korn chewed on a fingernail. It was hard to talk to a man in Thomas Dawson's present distraught condition.

The President put out his cigarette and continued to speak in the same unemotional voice. 'Tomorrow, the next day, I'll meet with the British and Irish ambassadors. I won't push the matter too strongly – at least not yet – but I'm coming very close to recommending that they consider some form of American assistance in combating the IRA.'

'An American presence?' Korn asked. 'In Ireland?'

Thomas Dawson nodded. 'A handful of advisers, in the beginning. People with some expertise in counter-terrorist tactics. Twenty, say. Twenty-five. Whatever the situation calls for. Later, of course, we could add to that number if need be.'

Korn asked, 'Will the Irish and the British accept this?'

Dawson shrugged. 'Who knows? It's a friendly suggestion. One ally to a couple of others. They haven't exactly handled it well on their own, have they? Besides, I'm not talking about sending in armed forces. Advisers only. There's a big difference.'

Korn sat back in his seat. He wasn't interested in the President's plans for Ireland.

Thomas Dawson said nothing more on the subject. He was conscious of the helicopter losing height. He looked out of the window and saw, like a submarine rising on an empty dark sea, the pale lights of an isolated dwelling. And then he was dropping towards it, down and down to his brother's house of sorrow.

25 Hastings, New York

The River View Motel was a brown brick building located five miles from State Highway 87. It was inappropriately named. Unless you had an excellent telescope and a forty-foot high platform on which to stand, you'd never get a glimpse of any river. The view, such as it was, was obstructed by the rooftops of surrounding houses and by trees. Seamus Houlihan stood on the balcony outside his room and looked out across a concrete forecourt at two small neon lights that said OFFICE and VACANCY. He saw the shadow of the man who sat behind the window there. Then, changing his angle of vision, he saw the yellow truck. It was the only vehicle in the whole bloody place. Scratched and dented and spattered with mud, it resembled some old wagon of war.

Houlihan leaned against the rail. So far as he could tell this place had no other residents besides himself and Rorke and McGrath. He yawned, turned around, stepped inside his room. He locked the door, sat down in the armchair, picked up his M–16 from the floor and wondered why bloody McInnes had been so insistent when he'd called a while back. The man had turned into a nag. He was like an old woman, Houlihan thought. Worrying over this, over that, fretting and whining. He'd be taking up crochet next. Dump the weapons indeed!

Houlihan heard Rorke and McGrath move along the balcony. They knocked quietly on his door. He got up, slid the chain, let them come inside. Rorke was carrying a sixpack of Genesee Cream Ale, and McGrath had a pint of Johnny Walker Red Label.

Houlihan produced a deck of cards from his duffel bag and shuffled them. 'Want to play a few hands?' he asked.

'Aye, why not,' McGrath said. He and Rorke sat down at the small table by the window. Houlihan popped one of the beers and proposed a game of three-card brag, nothing wild.

They played a hand for American pennies and Houlihan won it with a queen high. Rorke had a ten, and McGrath the worst hand possible in brag, a five high. Houlihan smiled and sipped his beer, which tasted like soapsuds in his mouth.

Rorke dealt a second hand, which Houlihan also won, this time with a pair of eights.

'Shitty cards,' McGrath said, turning over a four, a six and a nine.

McGrath dealt another hand. Houlihan received three threes, called a prile, the highest hand in the game. He had quite a collection of pennies by this time, a small coppery heap in front of him.

'You're a lucky sod,' McGrath said.

Houlihan scooped the pennies towards himself. He liked the simple pleasure of winning.

Rorke yawned. McGrath shuffled his feet. Neither of them ever enjoyed playing cards with Houlihan for long. Seamus had a way of always winning. When he started to lose he'd begin to cheat, palming cards in the most obvious fashion. Nobody ever complained when he cheated.

From the forecourt below the window there was the sound of a car. Houlihan stepped to the drapes, parted them deftly, saw a small red car go past the truck and then it disappeared around the other side of the building. After that there was silence again. Houlihan dropped the curtains back in place.

'Anything wrong?' Rorke asked.

'Just a car,' Houlihan replied.

McGrath ran a tattooed hand through his short brown hair. 'I don't mind saying, I'll be glad when we're out of this place. It gives me the willies being the only people in this whole dump.'

Even though the car had gone, force of habit kept Houlihan listening. He experienced a small shrill sensation of unease, and he had been trusting such instincts for a long time now. He reached down and picked up his automatic weapon, a movement that was almost involuntary.

He looked at the other two men. 'Where are your guns?' he asked.

'In our room,' Rorke replied.

'Get them and come back here.'

'Get them?' Rorke asked.

'Do as I tell you.'

Both men turned towards the door.

'One of you,' Houlihan said. 'It doesn't take two men to pick up the weapons.'

McGrath went outside, closing the door behind him. Houlihan, stepping back to the drapes, saw him move along the balcony. Outside, the forecourt was still, lit only by a couple of pale lamps and the neon signs burning above the office.

'What's wrong?' Rorke wanted to know.

Houlihan didn't answer. He wasn't sure anyhow. There were times when he had feelings he just couldn't explain. Some people called it a sixth sense, but to Seamus Houlihan it was nothing more than a survivor's caution. One time, in Armagh Jail, he'd known in advance that some Catholics were lying in wait for him in the lavatories. Nobody had actually told him this. He hadn't seen anything unusual either. It had simply *occurred* to him. There had been a slight pricking sense of danger, nothing he could truly identify, but he'd heeded the sensation with enough attention that when he stepped into the lavatories he was armed with a lead-pipe wrapped in a rag. The Catholics had been there all right, but when they saw what he was carrying they dispersed quickly. Consequently, Seamus had a healthy respect for his own antennae. With his fingers holding the drapes about a half-inch apart he scanned the forecourt.

'What's wrong?' Rorke asked again.

'Probably nothing,' Houlihan answered. 'But I'm not in the business of taking chances.'

'How do you know this isn't an elaborate trap?' Pagan asked. 'How do you know that this isn't something McInnes and I cooked up between us? We play out a dramatic scene. I get to punch Ivor. But it's all fake. It's all done for the purpose of luring you here to Arsehole-on-the-Hudson so we can kill you. How do you know that isn't true?'

Patrick Cairney stared through the windshield of the Dodge at the side of the motel building. He wasn't really listening to Frank Pagan. He was looking up at the balcony. At the lit windows of one room. There was a pain inside him that throbbed endlessly. He shut his eyes a second, and what he saw pressed behind his lids was Finn, Finn the indestructible, the immortal. Finn in his baggy cords, standing by the window in the room of harps. Finn's finger tunelessly plucking strings. Everywhere he searched his mind he saw images of Finn.

Cairney opened his eyes and stared hard at the yellow rectangle of window above.

When he'd called the house near Dun Laoghaire, an unfamiliar voice had answered the telephone. Not Finn. Finn, who always answered the phone himself because there was never anybody else in the house to do it, would have picked up the receiver *if he'd been there to do it*. And he wasn't. The strange voice had been hard and sharp and edgy. *Who is this? Who's calling?* Patrick Cairney had a mental image of Garda officers going through the house, and somewhere lay Finn's body covered in a plastic sheet, surrounded by photographers and fingerprint men and all the other officials who attended so clumsily to violent death. A murder investigation, Finn's house ransacked by careless fingers, files opened and read, correspondence analysed for clues.

Finn was dead.

Patrick Cairney tried not to think. But this one incontrovertible fact kept coming back at him. Again and again. It surged up out of all the hollows he felt inside. It echoed, died, returned with vigour. *Finn was dead*. He'd never felt loneliness like this before.

'You haven't answered my question,' Pagan said.

Cairney couldn't take his eyes from the window. He needed to kill. It was the first time in his life that he felt he really *needed* to shed blood. Beyond that lit window were the men who had slain Finn. The butchers. 'McInnes is telling the truth. This isn't a trap.'

Frank Pagan sighed. It was when McInnes had mentioned Finn that the atmosphere of the room in the Essex House had changed. Jig bought the whole story. Everything. Lock and stock and all the rest of it. He remembered Finn's name from his files, recalled the mystery of the man who was said to have controlled the finances of the IRA, and what he wondered about now was the nature of the relationship between Jig and Finn. Ever since McInnes had pronounced the man dead, ever since that phone call had been placed to Ireland, Jig had gone into a place that was beyond Pagan's reach. A place where with every passing moment it seemed to Pagan that something quite volcanic was going on inside of the man. Pagan thought about taking his chance now, grabbing the gun in Jig's hand and seizing it. But he wasn't going to be lulled by Jig's apparent distraction or the volatile nature of his mood.

Cairney said, 'McInnes was right about Finn. He was right about the Ryder truck.'

'He said four men checked into this hotel. The guy at the desk says three.'

'McInnes got his numbers wrong. That's all.'

Pagan asked, 'Have your ever heard of this Houlihan?'

Cairney pressed his fingertips to his eyes. There was a dull pain behind them. He thought he heard the sound of his whole life collapsing inside him. 'Pagan, I don't know the name of every person associated with the IRA. We're talking about a large and secretive organisation arranged in cells. It's highly unlikely that I'd know the man.'

Patrick Cairney continued to study the motel. A balcony ran the length of the upper floor, studded here and there with dim overhead lights. Across the forecourt two neon signs shimmered. One read VACANCY. The tension he felt was strong, like acid rising inside him. He tried to relax, tried to put his mind in a place beyond Finn. There isn't time for this, he thought. Finn wouldn't want you to grieve over him. What Finn would want was retribution, plain and simple. *Get on with it, boy. Don't dwell on death. People come and people go, only the Cause remains*. All at once Cairney was standing in Glasnevin Cemetery and Finn was handing him a revolver, and Cairney wished now that he'd reached out – just once in the whole time he'd known Finn – and goddam *held* him. On that day. Or any other. Just once. Somewhere. But death took everything away, sealed all the hatches, killed all the possibilities, and whatever he felt now for Finn could never be said.

'You've only got McInnes's word,' Pagan said, with the air of a man making one last plea which he knows in advance will be useless. 'You've only got his word that the men in this motel are responsible for all the violence. In my book, Jig, that's a damn frail thing to go on.'

Cairney looked at Pagan. 'Your own story was also frail, if you remember. And I accepted it, didn't I? I accepted the story you told me about McInnes, didn't I? It was me who decided to take a chance on you, Pagan, and go back to New York City.'

'There's a difference,' Pagan said. 'I don't lie.'

Cairney returned his eyes to the balcony. Then he glanced across the parking-area at the yellow truck. It dully reflected the neon signs.

'So what now?' Pagan asked. 'Do you go in? Is that your scheme? Do you go in with your six-gun drawn and your fingers crossed?'

Pagan lowered his face wearily against the rim of the steering-wheel. He was tired of arguing the case against McInnes. Besides, Jig was running this show. Jig had the guns. It was Jig's baby. And if Jig wanted to believe Ivor, if he wanted to believe that the men inside this motel were some renegade faction of the IRA, well that was the way it was going to be, and there was nothing Pagan could do or say to change it.

Cairney tapped the barrel of his gun against the dash, a quiet little tattoo. 'You're going in with me.'

'Right,' Pagan said. 'Unarmed, of course.'

Cairney reached inside the pocket of his overcoat and took out Pagan's gun, the Bernardelli.

'I can't do this alone,' Cairney said.

Pagan stared at his own gun. He made no move to take it from Jig's hand.

Cairney realised that this gesture could easily backfire. He was holding the gun out, reaching across a gulf that was far more than the handful of inches separating him from Frank Pagan. But what was the alternative? If he went in alone against the three men, his chances were very thin. Besides, that would entail leaving Frank Pagan right here in the car – and Pagan might just sneak away to make a phone call, bringing in reinforcements. It was possible. Cairney, who knew he was gambling, dangled the Bernardelli in the air.

'I can't do this alone,' he said again.

'Goddam,' Pagan said.

'I *need* you, Pagan. Take the gun.'

'Then what?'

Cairney said, 'I don't think you're going to shoot me in the back, Pagan. You had a chance at that already on Canal Street.'

Pagan still didn't take the weapon. He kept his hands clamped to the wheel.

Cairney thrust the Bernardelli forward. 'There are three men in this place, Pagan. They shot up a school bus, and they bombed a church. More than that, they killed Padraic Finn. That's all I need to know.'

Pagan suddenly hated the idea that he was transparent to Jig. Jig saw straight through him. Jig understood there was no way in the world, given Pagan's private code of behaviour – which was bound up with such antiquated notions as decency and honour and justice, the very sounds of which suggested they belonged in their own room in the British Museum – that Pagan would turn the weapon on him. Frank Pagan wished he were devious, that he had hidden lodes of cunning and could simply take his gun back and shoot Jig through the eyes and drive away from this place, forgetting the three men allegedly responsible for so many deaths. Praise from the Yard. Love and kisses from Furry Jake. Fuck them. Fuck them all. He didn't need their pressures. He'd do this thing his own way. And if it meant going up to that balcony with Jig, then that's what he'd do.

He raised his hand, brought it out towards the gun, didn't touch it.

'Imagine this, Jig,' he said. 'We go in there. There's gunplay. We come out again intact. What then? Do you expect me to hand this weapon back like a good little boy? Because I have no bloody intention of doing that.'

Cairney didn't respond to the question. He couldn't see that far into the future. Nor did it matter. He turned his face back to the balcony.

'It's one of those unanswerable questions, is it?' Pagan asked. 'We play it as it comes.'

'There's no other way.'

Pagan took the pistol from Jig's fingers.

Jig opened the door of the Dodge. The night air that came in was cold and smelled of damp leaves and the musty odour of the river. Honour and decency and a sense of justice, Pagan thought. They weren't always wonderful qualities to bring into a situation. Why couldn't he have been more *sly*? He opened his own door now and started up in the direction of the balcony. Another man might simply have shot Jig there and then. But he wasn't that man, nor could he ever be.

A figure appeared overhead.

Cairney and Pagan, drifting into the gloom beneath the balcony, heard the footsteps rap on concrete. There was the sound of a key turning in a lock, a door opening, closing. Some yards away a flight of iron stairs led to the upper storey. Cairney and Pagan moved quietly towards them.

Jig started to climb. Pagan was surprised by the way the man moved, swiftly and yet without a whisper of sound. He was like a bloody shadow rising, something created by the moon amid latticed metalwork. He appeared not to have substance, weight. Pagan felt clumsy and leaden and *old* by comparison. When they reached the balcony Jig stopped. Two lit windows threw lights out at an oblique angle ten yards ahead of them.

Pagan pressed himself flat against the wall, echoing the way Jig moved. He didn't like the idea of creeping towards the window where the lights now seemed rather bright to him. If *he* had been running this show, he might have chosen to wait outside in the parked car until morning, when at least there would be the definite benefit of visibility.

There was a noise from along the balcony. A door swung open. Framed faintly by electricity from the room behind him, a man appeared. He was holding what looked like two automatic rifles, one stuck under either arm. He struggled to remove a key from his pocket, which he did do in an awkward way, then he turned and somehow contrived to lock the door.

When he'd done this to his satisfaction he started to move towards the place where Pagan and Jig stood. Then, seeing them for the first time, he stopped dead. His features were indistinct but Pagan had the impression that the man's mouth hung open in astonishment.

For a long time there was no movement. It seemed to Pagan that the place had been drained of air, that there was nothing to breathe. Then the man stepped forward and, as if it were the most natural thing in the whole world to be carrying automatic weapons under your arms, moved to the door of the room adjacent to the one he'd just left. He raised his knee and rapped it upon the wood panels.

Somebody opened the door from inside. Pagan saw a heavy shadow fall across the threshold. The character holding the weapons made to step inside when Jig, suddenly going down on one knee like a determined marksman, fired off a shot. Pagan heard it whine in the dark, glancing against concrete. The man with the weapons turned and faced them and this time Pagan was certain that the expression on his face was one of pure astonishment. The man dropped one of the rifles and clutched at the other, trying to swing it into a firing position. Before he could even get a decent grip on the gun, Jig had shot him.

The man was knocked sideways, sprawling against the handrail. The rifle flew out of his arms and clattered across the balcony. Somebody ducked out of the room, grabbed the automatic weapons up, then vanished back inside, slamming the door shut.

All this happened so swiftly that Pagan felt like a spectator at a deadly game. He looked at the body lying halfway along the balcony, face tipped back, legs crooked. Jig was still incautiously pressing forward, his spine flat against the wall. There was more determination than foresight in the way Jig was conducting business here, and Pagan didn't like it, but he felt trapped inside a sequence of events over which he had no control. He weighed his own gun in his hand and realised that the back of Jig's skull made a perfect target for him. The simplest thing in the world, he thought. One shot. One well-placed shot. *Finis*. But it wasn't simple at all.

He saw Jig going towards the light that spilled out of the open doorway five yards ahead. Pagan crouched and followed.

Seamus Houlihan shoved one of the weapons into McGrath's arms. It was rammed with such force into McGrath's body that the man was momentarily winded.

'Who the fuck is out there?' McGrath asked. His face was white. One minute there had been cards and beer and the prospect of going home to Ireland, the next gunfire.

'The enemy,' Houlihan replied. He went closer to the door, opened it a fraction.

'What bloody enemy?' McGrath asked.

'You name it, McGrath. People like you and me don't have many friends.' Houlihan sniffed the air coming in through the open door. He could see, even though the angle was narrow, the outline of Rorke's body lying some feet away on the balcony. When he'd stepped outside a moment ago to retrieve the weapons there hadn't been time to assess the strength of the enemy. Houlihan had been conscious only of the need to get the guns as fast as he could, which he'd done successfully because the enemy was concentrating on Rorke at that point.

Seamus Houlihan picked up the pint of Johnny Walker from the table, took a long swallow, then slid the bottle to McGrath. McGrath drank. When he was finished he set the bottle down on top of the playing cards. He noticed that his last hand, which had gone unplayed, was a reasonable flush. Good hand. But Houlihan would have beaten it somehow. The big man always did.

'We better get the fuck out of here,' Houlihan said.

McGrath appeared hesitant. 'We don't know how many are out there,' he said.

'Does it make any difference? Do you want to sit here and let them come for you? Fuck that!' For a long time now Houlihan had expected to die a violent death. His whole world had been so circumscribed by violence that the notion of a peaceful death, of slipping away in his sleep, was a bad joke. His father had been shot by the IRA in Derry. His brother, Jimmy Houlihan, had been blown up inside a Protestant bar in Belfast at Christmas 1975. Why would he expect his own end to be any different? He clutched the M–16, checked the clip.

He'd gone out once before, and his luck had held. But he wasn't going to risk going out again unless he had the gun blazing in front of him. He had absolutely no fear of death. It neither mystified nor terrified. He had chosen combat as a way of life, and the simple fact was that you lived through combat or you died in the throes of it. Death had no metaphysical implications for him. He believed more in an M–16 than in any God. He was thinking suddenly about Waddy, who'd held some superstitious beliefs, and what he hoped was that he could live through any forthcoming conflict because he'd promised himself that he'd give Waddy a decent burial. Poor wee Waddy.

Houlihan went closer to the door. It occurred to him for the first time that he and the others had been sold out. And that the seller had to be McInnes. Even this realisation neither distressed nor surprised him. In his world treachery was just another fact of life. People said one thing, then did the opposite. It had always been this way, and it always would be. He just wished he'd been better prepared. But at least he hadn't obeyed Ivor's demand to toss the guns. At least there was that, and he was glad he'd made that decision. He looked out into the darkness. There was perfect silence. The night held all sounds like a bloody miser, giving nothing away. He glanced at McGrath, whose face was colourless. Then he turned his eyes back to the door.

He heard something then.

It was barely audible, but there it was.

A movement on the balcony. Leather on concrete.

McGrath whispered. 'There could be twenty men out there.'

'Either we go out or we sit back and let them come in,' Houlihan said. He stepped towards the doorway.

'Who goes first?' McGrath asked.

'We go together.'

McGrath moved to Houlihan's side.

'Just think,' Houlihan said with a smile. 'If you were a Catholic you'd be crossing yourself right now.'

Frank Pagan saw the shadow fall in the doorway. He brought his pistol up, caught his breath, waited. He stared at the shadow, which was massive and still. Jig, who was perhaps two feet in front of him, stopped moving. The open door was three or five yards away at most.

Pagan lost his concentration a second. He wasn't sure why. Tension probably. He gazed down at the motel office where the two neon lights had gone out. Had the clerk gone to sleep? Had he slept through the sound of Jig's gun? Lucky man. It was another world down there, something that came to Pagan as if through filters, gauzy and indistinct. He stared back along the balcony at the dead man, who lay in his very awkward position. Death could be highly unflattering. Pools of liquid, urine and blood, had gathered around the body. Frank Pagan thought he could catch the odour of urine from where he stood.

The shape in the doorway appeared to grow, but then Pagan realised it wasn't a solitary shadow at all, it was the darkness cast by two men who stood very close together. He tightened his grip on his gun. Fear, he understood, didn't have that legendary cold touch at all – rather, it was a warm thing, the temperature of your blood rising and the surface of your skin turning hot.

The shapes moved again. Deliberately, slowly. Pagan glanced at Jig, who was going down as close to the balcony floor as he could. Frank Pagan did likewise, feeling hard concrete against his face.

And then the silhouettes took on flesh and substance, emerging from the doorway, turning from two ghostly things to forms that had an imposing reality about them. The sound of Jig's gun was suddenly loud, ferocious in Pagan's ears, and he must have flinched or briefly closed his eyes because when he looked again and fired his own gun he was aware of a man falling back into the doorway and the fierce rattle of an automatic weapon, which sprayed the air randomly as the man went on falling. The second man, who had been behind the first, shot from his hip in a series of small flashes, and Pagan heard Jig groan, a sound that was less pain than one of surprise.

Pagan rolled on his side and fired his handgun again even as the automatic weapon continued to stutter, pocking the concrete and zinging off the handrail, creating a tympany of destruction. Pagan kept rolling and turning until his body was jammed against the metal rail. His eyes were filled with dust and small chips of shattered concrete and he had difficulty focusing, but he understood that the one man left standing had either used up the clip in his gun or the damned thing had jammed on him and he was now reaching into the pocket of his seaman's coat for something else, another clip maybe, another weapon. Pagan didn't wait to find out. He fired quickly, striking the tall man somewhere in the region of the shoulder. The man spun around and, clutching his shoulder, began to move along the balcony in the direction of the stairs.

Pagan got to his feet. He was conscious of several things simultaneously. The man running. The fact that the two lights below had come on.

And Jig, sitting with his back to the wall, his head tilted back and his mouth open in pain.

Pagan gaped at him a moment and then ran towards the stairs, which the man in the seaman's jacket was already descending loudly. Pagan's feet encountered the M–16 the man had discarded, which slid away from him on contact and went out beneath the rail to clatter on the court below.

The running man was heading for the yellow truck. He stopped suddenly, took a gun from the pocket of his jacket, turned and fired. A window exploded in a place just beyond Frank Pagan's skull. Pagan reached the bottom of the stairs, and the man fired again – a hasty shot that went off harmlessly into the darkness. Now the man was reaching up to the door of the cabin, apparently fumbling with a key in the lock. Pagan ducked beneath the overhang of the balcony where he was absorbed by shadows, and he took very careful aim. His shot went wide, hammering into the side panel of the truck.

He moved out from under the shadows and took aim again. Before he could get a shot off, the big man had fired twice in rapid succession. Both shots went whining past Pagan's head. Then the big man was climbing up into the cabin of the truck, grunting as he moved.

Pagan levelled his pistol.

This time his shot struck the man directly in the side of the face. He staggered out of the cab, flailing his arms as he fell to the concrete. There was one terrible cry of pain and then a silence that stretched through the night.

Now, Pagan thought. *Now Jig.*

He raced up the stairs.

There was no sign of Jig.

Pagan looked the length of the balcony. The two dead figures lay where they had fallen, one slumped in the open doorway of the room, the other close to the rail.

But no Jig.

Frank Pagan hurried to the other end of the balcony. He realised there was a thin trail of blood underfoot, which must have spilled from the place where Jig had been hit. He reached the stairs. Then stopped.

The red Dodge was pulling out of the parking-lot below. Pagan saw the tail-lights dwindling as the vehicle moved away.

Pagan went quickly down the stairs. He sprinted towards the yellow truck. The keys dangled from the doorlock. He climbed up into the cabin, stuck the key in the ignition, turned it, listened to the big engine come to life. As he backed the ungainly vehicle out of the forecourt he thought he knew where Jig was headed. It was inevitable. Since he couldn't go back to Kevin Dawson's, and since he wasn't likely to go into hiding and leave his quest for the missing money in some unacceptable limbo, that left only one place – the last address of all.

Roscommon, New York. The home of Senator Harry Cairney. Where else would he possibly go after Mulhaney and Linney? Where else after Kevin Dawson?

Pagan found Highway 9, which went north. This truck was no match for the Dodge, which meant Jig would reach Roscommon before he could. But there was nothing he could do about that. He'd drive as hard as he possibly could and hope that whatever wounds Jig had sustained would slow his progress north.

When he reached a sign that said Tarrytown, he became conscious of something that lay on the floor of the cab, something bulky stuck between the seat and dash. At first he assumed it was a sack of some kind, but when he passed under the sudden glare of a roadside light, he realised that his guess was quite wrong.

This particular sack had eyes.

Shocked, Pagan braked very hard, pulled to the side of the road. He turned on the overhead light. The face he saw half-turned away from him was chalk-white and ghastly. The eyes were open in a way that suggested some cruel realisation at the abrupt end of life. They had about them a certain knowing quality. The mouth was twisted and stiff and the one hand that was visible was bent in a spastic fashion. Frank Pagan reached out and touched the side of the corpse's jaw, almost as if to reassure himself that this figure had once been flesh and blood and not always the wax effigy it resembled now. A ghoulish moment. He pulled his hand away quickly.

He recognised the man. And as he did so, as he realised that this was the body of one John Waddell, whom he had interviewed last year in connection with the murder of an IRA member in London, he perceived a pattern of events, a meaning in the mosaic that was Ivor McInnes's bizarre story, a flood of understanding. He wondered how he could possibly have missed the truth for so long. Because like most truths, it had been self-evident all the way along.

Blind, Frank.

Very blind of you.

He dragged the body out of the truck and laid it among a clump of bushes at the edge of the highway. And then he was driving again, thinking of Ivor McInnes and the man's scheme, which was luminous in its simplicity and savage in its execution.

26 Roscommon, New York

Celestine Cairney had been unable to sleep. It was five past three and totally dark when she decided she'd tossed and turned on the bed long enough. She got up, went to the window, looked out across the blackness of Roscommon. Earlier, there had been a wisp of a moon in the sky, but even that had gone and the waters of the lake were invisible. She sat in the window-seat and listened to the uneven sounds of Harry breathing.

She looked at the luminous figures on the dial of her watch. When you were excited, when anticipation touched you like this, time had a way of prolonging itself. She got up from the seat and moved through the darkness of the bedroom. She rubbed her hands together because she was tense. She wanted Patrick Cairney to come. She wanted to see Patrick Cairney alone.

She caught this thought and held it.

She was remembering Patrick Cairney again as she'd seen him that night in his bedroom. And suddenly she felt sad. There were times when you wished everything had been different. Birth and circumstances, the history of your heart, every damn thing about you.

She sat in the armchair in front of the cold fireplace, legs crossed, placing her hands flat on her stomach. Her nipples were hard, and the very soft hairs that grew on the lower part of her belly stirred.

Patrick Cairney.

She wanted him to be the first to get here.

'Can't sleep?' Harry's voice startled her.

'A little restless,' she said. She lowered her hands to her side and clutched the silk of her nightgown, bunching it in the palms of her hands. It felt like Patrick Cairney's flesh to her.

Harry turned on the bedside lamp. He reached out for a Kleenex and blew his nose. It was a trumpeting sound, an old man's sound. Even this room smelled like an old man's flesh. She had the urge to get up and throw the windows open and let the cold Roscommon night perfume the air with winter.

'Come here,' Harry said.

She rose slowly, went to the bed, looked down at him. He wore maroon pyjamas with his monogram stitched into the breat pocket. HC, in fine gold thread.

'A kiss,' the old man said.

She lowered her face, brushed her lips against his, stepped back from the bed. 'Get some sleep. You need it.'

'What about you?'

Don't worry about me.'

Harry Cairney watched her with eyes that never ceased to be adoring. She rearranged the bedsheets, turned off the lamp, returned to the window. The room seemed even darker than it had before. She placed one hand under the cushion of the window-seat, where she'd concealed Harry's old Browning, and she removed it. There was a terrifying certainty about the gun, the weight of it, the hardness in her hands. She turned it over a couple of times, then returned it to its hiding-place.

Make him come here, she thought.

Just make him come here.

Soon. Soon now. Soon she'd be gone from this house.

She laid her cheeks against the glass and looked out across the night, and thought how hard she'd tried to pretend she cared for Harry Cairney. And how close she'd come to the peril of actually believing she felt something, when all she carried in her heart for him was no more feeling than a slug had when it slinked insensately through blades of grass and left a trail of crystal. When you pretend to be something for long enough, you become that thing.

But she'd done her duty. She could always say that about herself.

Poughkeepsie, New York

Patrick Cairney pulled into a closed gas station and turned off the engine of the car. The pain he felt was searing, as if the flesh were peeling away from the bone. He reached down and turned up the left leg of his pants and gasped because even something so simple as the brush of clothing against the wound was excruciating. He drew his hand back up. It was covered in blood. He knew that a bullet had passed through, close to the shinbone, burrowing a ragged hole in his flesh. Pretty soon he'd feel numbness around the wound, and then there would be the sensation of uselessness in the limb. He wondered how much blood he might have lost since leaving the River View Motel.

He struggled to take off his coat, which he tossed into the rear seat. Then he removed his shirt and tugged at the sleeve, managing to separate it from the rest of the garment. With this improvised bandage twisted around a ballpoint pen he found in the glove compartment, he made a very crude tourniquet which he applied to the wound. It was extremely painful to do so, but he realised his choices were more than a little limited. He could bleed to death or he could attempt to stem the flow of blood with anything he had at hand – and hope he'd make it to Roscommon before he became weak and delirious.

He rolled the window down and breathed night air deeply into his lungs. He had to keep a very clear head. When he reached Roscommon he'd make up some kind of story – something about an accident. He wasn't sure quite what yet. That was the easy part anyway.

For a moment he sat with his eyes closed and his head tipped back against the seat. It was odd how, when he thought of Finn now, he was unable to bring into his mind an image of the man's face. It was lost to him suddenly. He could hear the voice still and he imagined he was listening to Finn whispering quietly in his ear. *I asked too much of you this time. I sent you in there on a wing and a prayer. I was only thinking of the money. I wasn't thinking about the danger to you. Nobody could have done anything better in the terrible circumstances. I'm sorry, boy.*

Cairney shook his head, opened his eyes.

Roscommon. He'd go there and see his father. He'd go there and heal for a time. It was a safe place for him now. He'd avoid Celestine. He wouldn't think about her. When he passed her in the hallway or ran into her at mealtimes he'd be polite but aloof. She'd get the message quickly.

Goddam, the pain was agonising. He bit on his lower lip hard There was a way to transcend this kind of pain, if he could only reach inside himself deeply enough. The trick was to remove yourself from your physical cage and soar. To cross that bridge between the corporeal and the spiritual. To divide yourself.

Bullshit. Pain was pain, not matter what you tried to think.

Groaning, he retrieved his overcoat and drew it around his shoulders. Then he turned the engine on. You're young and strong and the wound will mend. And after that you can go looking for Finn's money again.

Finn's money, he thought. He'd been sidetracked, detoured, that was all. When he'd healed, he'd go back to Kevin Dawson's house. And if Dawson didn't have the money, then the President's brother might be able to give him a lead to the character Mulhaney had called the Old Man. When his wound was better, he'd go back out again, he'd find the money and take it back to the house near Dun Laoghaire.

The empty house.

The room of muted harps. Finn's old wall posters, collected over the years. There were a couple from the Irish general election in 1932. *End Unemployment! Vote Fianna Fail. Vote*

Cumann na nGaedheal! Cairney recalled them with clarity, the way he remembered the whole whitewashed house, the airy rooms, the crooked hallway, the stairs that went up to Finn's immaculately spartan bedroom, which was like a monk's cell. But he still couldn't see Finn's face. He wondered if he'd ever be able to bring it to mind again or if, like the man himself, it was lost to him for all time.

He drove the car out of the gas station and headed back in the direction of the highway. For the next twenty miles he wasn't even conscious of the pain. He'd found a useful trick to deal with it. He kept thinking of his father, the sickbed, the claustrophobic enclosure of an oxygen tent – and these images dispelled at least some of his own anguish.

Not all. Just some. Maybe enough to keep him plugging through the miles still head.

Danbury, Connecticut

Inside the diner, Artie Zuboric waited impatiently for Tyson to finish his coffee but Bruno was obviousy reluctant to hurry. He'd been like this all the way from Kevin Dawson's place, hemming and hawing, wondering aloud if what they were doing was the right thing. It never occurred to Bruno that what they were doing was the *only* thing and that questions of right and wrong didn't come into it.

Tyson Bruno dropped a sugar lump into his coffee and said, 'When Korn finds we've split, he's going to shit bricks.'

Zuboric was tired of hearing his colleague talk about the things Leonard M. Korn was going to do. 'Look, you want out, that's fine by me. I'll go on alone.'

Tyson Bruno shook his head. 'I've come this far.'

Zuboric was very anxious to be on his way, but Bruno had insisted they stop for coffee. Now, though, Zuboric felt the kind of urgency that had the relentless quality of a runaway train. He knew he'd overstepped his authority, that he'd defied the personal instructions of the Director, but he hadn't seen much point in hanging around Dawson's house and waiting for Korn to show up just to vent his considerable wrath on himself and Bruno.

This was all or nothing time now.

It had taken nerve to walk away from the situation. But then his own reserves of nerve had astonished him. He'd *actually* gone upstairs in the Dawson home and *interrupted* Kevin in the middle of his grief, gently taking him aside, pulling him away from the figure of his sedated wife, saying he had a couple of questions to ask and they had to be answered even though the time was wrong, but the process of justice couldn't wait, sorry sorry, a million apologies, but that's how it had to be. Zuboric didn't want to go through all that again ever. Kevin Dawson had responded to the questions like a man submerged in ten feet of stale green water.

'If we bring in Jig,' Zuboric started to say.

Bruno interrupted. 'If we bring in Jig we'll get medals. And if we also happen to bring in Frank Pagan, hey, write your own citation.' A bruised little smile appeared in the middle of Tyson Bruno's face. 'But you can't open a bank account with ifs, Artie. First off, you got to keep in mind that Kevin Dawson wasn't exactly at his best when you talked to him. The man's in an awful lot of pain and turmoil. In that condition, you don't always get your facts right. Second, you could be making a trip way out to the sticks for absolutely nothing, because by the time you get there Jig might have been and gone, and Frank Pagan as well. If either of them was ever headed there in the first place, that is.'

'I've got nothing to lose,' Zuboric said. 'Neither have you.' And he thought of Charity taking off her copious bra and her G-string for the gratification of sick old men.

Tyson Bruno finished his coffee, pushed his cup aside. 'That's the truest thing you ever said.'

Zuboric started to get up. Tyson Bruno tugged at his coat sleeve. 'I want you to know it took a lot of balls to talk to Kevin Dawson the way you did.'

'I did what I had to,' Zuboric answered.

Both men stepped outside into the parking-lot of the diner.

'It would be neat if we happened to find both these guys in the same place,' Bruno remarked as they reached the car.

Zuboric said nothing. He surreptitiously patted his shoulder holster, a man taking inventory of himself. He got inside the car on the passenger side and Tyson Bruno sat behind the wheel.

'Drive,' Zuboric said. 'Drive like your life depends on it.'

'It does,' Bruno said.

Rhinebeck, New York

The old guy in the twenty-four-hour convenience store did everything slowly and deliberately. When he said the word 'Roscommon' Pagan thought he counted at least fourteen syllables.

'You mean old Franz's place,' the man said. 'Used to belong to a brewer before Harry Cairney came along.'

'That's the place,' Pagan said.

'Can't figure why you'd want to go there this time of day.'

'I'm looking for a friend.' Pagan kept the impatience out of his voice.

The old guy stepped out of the store to the sidewalk. The cold apparently didn't bother him. 'Go down thataway,' he said, pointing one long bony finger down the main street of Rhinebeck, which was sleepy and clean. 'You want three oh eight for five miles. There's a crossroads down there. You take the left fork. Quiet road. There's no signs. Keep going maybe two miles. You can't miss it. Big house about a hundred yards back from the road.'

Frank Pagan thanked the old man and went towards the truck. He climbed up inside the cab and turned the key in the ignition. His whole body, still shaking from the vibrations of the vehicle and all the miles he'd travelled, felt like a tuning-fork. Fatigue gnawed at him. There was some small corner of his brain that was still alert, but it was like a room lit only by a twenty-watt bulb. It was a room occupied by two people. Jig sat in one corner. Ivor McInnes, the Terrible, was silent and surly in another. *I know what you're up to, Ivor,* Pagan thought. And all your silences, all you denials, won't save your white Presbyterian arse now.

But first there was Jig.

He backed the truck up, headed out through Rhinebeck, passing the unlit windows of small stores. He adjusted his rearview mirror, catching a quick flash of his own reflection. He looked like something disinterred and carted home by a dog and dumped in the middle of the Persian rug to the general dismay of the whole family.

Frank Pagan, an old bone.

But an old bone with a mission.

Roscommon, New York

There was a weak suggestion of dawn in the sky when Patrick Cairney drove through the gates of Roscommon and passed the security jeep that was parked between the trees. The driver of the jeep recognised him and waved him to continue.

Cairney, who felt disoriented because the pain in his leg had been crippling for the last twenty miles, slowed the car in front of the house. He made no move to get out at once. He reached down and grabbed the leg, massaging it lightly, trying to ease the pain with his fingertips. The cuffs of his pants were soaked with blood, his sock squelched inside his shoe, and there was barely any feeling left in the limb itself. It might have been a stranger's leg, a graft that hadn't worked. He pushed the car door open and got out awkwardly, standing in front of the steps that led up to the front door. The injured leg pulsated, several scalding little spasms. Cairney moved towards the steps, dragging one foot.

She materialised there in the shadows, a sudden bright spectre in the gloom. She wore a blue robe and her hair was tied up on her scalp with a simple rose-coloured ribbon. Cairney stared at her expressionlessly. He didn't move. Nor did he want her to see him in pain because he didn't need her concern or any offer of assistance. He didn't want her to touch him, a supportive hand on his elbow, the nearness of her body, her perfume, anything. No contact. No connection.

He gazed at her. She was standing very still, her arms at her side. She looked remote. He had absolutely no way of knowing if she was pleased to see him. But then she wasn't *going* to smile, was she? There was a sick man inside the house, it wasn't a situation for merriment or pleasure. It wasn't a time for happy reunions, even if he'd wanted one.

He moved up on to the first step.

It was a brave effort, but he couldn't pull it off. The leg buckled under him and he went down, and suddenly she was coming down the steps towards him, her arm held out and her look one of worry.

She saw the blood on his clothes. She went down on one knee and moved the cuff of his pants aside and her touch, which he still didn't want, was pleasantly cool, almost a cure in itself. She raised her face, looked at him. Cairney closed his eyes. Pain could be seductive at one end of its spectrum, it could lull you out of your body, carry you away into a numb place.

'What happened?' she asked.

'I had an accident.'

'We better get you indoors,' Celestine said. She helped him stand, let him support the weight of his body against her. They went up the steps, bound together as surely as if they'd been roped one against the other. She aided him inside, took him along the hallway, made him lie down on the living-room sofa. His blood came through the useless tourniquet and soaked the velvet material of the couch.

She decided to undo the tourniquet he'd created. She tossed aside the bloodstained ballpoint pen, the sleeve of the shirt, and then she was studying the raw wound itself. She saw at once that it was a gunshot wound, but she didn't say anything. She looked at him, and what she felt was pity for him.

She didn't want to feel such a thing. If she entertained pity, then it would only make everything more difficult. She lowered her eyes and examined the wound again. She touched it gently. Cairney winced, drawing his leg aside.

'Sorry,' she said.

He struggled to control the pain. 'How is he?'

'As well as can be expected.'

'I need to see him.'

'It can wait.'

Cairney moved his leg. Celestine pressed firmly on his shoulders. 'Stay where you are,' she said.

'I can get up. I can make it upstairs.'

'Patrick,' with a warning in her voice.

Cairney swung his leg to the floor. She wasn't going to stop him from going upstairs. He tried to stand, but the leg gave way and he had to sit down again.

'I told you,' she said.

Cairney stared at her. He hated feeling so damned feeble in front of her. He hated the idea of being at her mercy.

She said, 'There's a way to take your mind off pain, Patrick.'

She undid the buttons of her robe and leaned towards him, her small breasts swinging very slightly.

Cairney caught her by the hair and turned her face to one side. Her ribbon came undone and the hair spilled out over his hand and he remembered how, when she'd come to his bedroom, she'd woven that same hair around his penis in a gesture that was perhaps the most intimate he'd ever experienced. Desire and pain. There was a strange interlocking of sensations inside him right then, as if desire and pain had fused together in one feeling that was indescribable and fresh and beyond any emotion he'd ever registered. He shut his eyes, let his hand fall away from her hair, felt her fingers move over his thighs.

'Trust me,' she said.

It was a whisper, barely audible. He felt her breasts against the palms of his upturned hands.

She undid his belt slowly. Then she slid her fingers against his groin.

'Trust me,' she said again.

He felt her mouth, the slight friction of lips, the motion of her tongue. He retreated into the darkness of himself, a refuge of pleasure, a place where all the pains subsided like dead tides. She was climbing up into his lap, and he could feel the edge of her open robe rub the side of his face, then she was taking his hand and directing it between her legs, where she was moist and warm and open for him.

He opened his eyes, looking directly into her face. There was a quality of opaque glass to her beauty, he thought. Just as you thought you could see straight into her, a glaze moved over her eyes, leaving you with nothing.

'Love me,' she said. 'Love me just one time.'

He closed his eyes again and felt himself float out through the estuaries of pain as if on some very frail raft of himself. He wasn't thinking now of Finn nor of the sick man who lay upstairs at this very moment nor of the money stolen from the doomed *Connie O'Mara*, he wasn't thinking, he was out of the range of his own thoughts, beyond the radar of conscience or guilt, moving his hips while Celestine tilted her head back and her hair toppled in disarray over her bare shoulders. It was a fragile moment, and an intense one, and he wanted to believe he was capable of this treachery, that nothing else mattered to him except this woman who straddled him now and in whose body he had lost himself. That the man who lay ill upstairs meant absolutely nothing to him. He had lost Finn – what was the loss of his father compared to that? Besides, he had spent years creating and maintaining fictions. What was one more? He could imagine all the events of recent days collapsing behind him into oblivion. Here and now, nothing else.

And then it passed. The moment was gone. Cairney sighed and fell motionless against the back of the sofa.

Celestine stared at him. She was also conscious of a precious moment passing away. She had an empty feeling, a realisation that this particular segment of time was never going to come again, no matter how long she might live. And it couldn't be otherwise. She slid away from him, lowered herself to the carpet, looked up at his face.

'I asked too much,' she said very quietly. 'Or maybe I didn't ask enough. Go see your father now.'

How could he go upstairs and into the old man's sick room with the smell of Celestine on his fingers? How could he stand by the bed and look into that dying face and not feel the weight of a terrible guilt? He stared down at his wound. Dear God, he'd been so determined to avoid this woman, so intent on staying away from her – and then this had happened, this travesty, this bastard intimacy.

His father's wife.

He stood up slowly.

The leg didn't yield this time. But his eyesight blurred, and he felt very weak.

He turned towards the door, where he stopped and looked back at her. 'There's a name for people like us,' he said.

'I'm sure there is.' Kneeling on the floor, her robe open, Celestine looked impossibly lovely. He understood he was always going to see her the way she was right then. She had a curious smile on her face.

'It was my last chance,' she added. 'I didn't want to waste it.'

That finality in her voice. It was odd. He wanted to know what she meant by her statement, but he didn't ask. He didn't think he could stand the sound of his own voice.

He began to move towards the stairs. He climbed slowly, stiffly, hearing the sound of Celestine at his back.

'I'm sorry,' she said.

She caught up with him on the landing. Ahead, the door of Harry Cairney's bedroom lay half open. Celestine reached for him, caught him by the wrist.

'I'm sorry,' she repeated.

'You don't have to be. It takes two.' He paused. 'In this case, the wrong two.'

He moved towards the bedroom door. He raised his hand to the wood and pushed the door open very quietly.

'You don't understand,' she said. 'How could you?'

Frank Pagan saw the jeep come out of the trees towards him. It moved quickly, blocking the truck on the driveway, then it stopped. Two men stepped out of the vehicle. They carried shotguns and moved cautiously but with a certain dead-eyed determination. Pagan saw a grim quality about the men. Like security guards everywhere, they had enemies all over the place. A mailman, a delivery boy, a milkman – anybody who came to this place was a possible carrier of destruction.

Pagan took his gun out of his pocket and held it concealed between his knees. He gazed past the oncoming guards into the first few bars of dawn that had slinked across the sky, and he thought it was a hell of a way to begin a new day. Two men with shotguns. He hoped it wasn't downhill from here.

He didn't move. He didn't roll his window down. He just watched them coming. They wore plaid jackets and had baseball caps, and they reminded Pagan of archetypes in the American nightmare, those rednecks who seasonally take to the forests and wage a bloody one-sided war on anything with four paws or a beak. Beyond them, through bare trees, he saw the house itself, a big grey stone building that lacked the one quality every country house should have – enchantment.

His attention was drawn back to the two men.

They approached the cab of the truck. One of the men rapped on the glass with the barrel of his shotgun. It was an ominous gesture. Frank Pagan braced himself. He smiled, reached for the door-handle, hesitated. He wasn't going to let such a trivial matter as two men with shotguns spoil his day.

He turned the handle. This was going to take all the scattered elements of his concentration. This was going to need everything he could find in himself.

'Where the hell do you think you're going, buddy?' one of the men asked.

Now! Pagan shoved with all his might and the door flew open, swinging back swiftly on its hinges. It hit the first man with terrific force in the dead centre of his chest, and the window smashed into his face, and he dropped to his knees, clutching himself and groaning. It was a violent collision of metal and glass and bone, and Pagan felt the connection shudder through him. The second guard quickly brought his shotgun up, but he was a pulse too slow because Frank Pagan was already out of the cab and pointing his gun at the man in a deliberate way, the expression on his face as severe and forbidding as he could make it.

'I'll use it,' Pagan said. 'Make no mistake.'

The guard with the shotgun appeared subdued. His look suggested that of a hunter confronted by a duck with an M–16. He stared into Pagan's pistol and dropped his weapon and stepped back from it, raising his hands in the air.

'Cooperation,' Pagan said. 'I like that.'

The man who'd gone down was staring up at Pagan through eyes that showed nothing but intense pain. Pagan kicked both fallen shotguns into the shrubbery and said, 'Get up.'

Moaning, the guard got to his feet. He was a short man and he moved with uncertainty, in the manner of somebody betrayed by his limbs. He wouldn't stop groaning as he shuffled. He raised a hand to his nose and touched it in a tentative way, afraid that it had been broken. Pagan saw slicks of blood gather in his nostrils.

'Get inside the truck,' Pagan said. 'Both of you.'

He herded the guards forward, unlocked the rear door of the truck, pushed them inside. They complained and threatened, telling him what terrible things they were going to do to him when they got out. He slammed the door behind them, locked it, smiled to himself. He hadn't altogether lost his touch, which was a nice thing to know. When he had to act, he could still be swift and purposeful. There was no better way to begin a day than with some striking insight into your own capabilities. To know that, despite the oncoming winter of forty, a season he feared would be drab and filled with dread, you still had the fire inside.

He turned away from the truck, listening to the muffled noise of the imprisoned guards beating on the interior panels, and walked quickly up the driveway to the house. Outside, he saw Jig's red car parked at an awkward angle near the foot of the steps. He paused then, noticing that the front door of the house lay open. He didn't care for the open door. It suggested that the inhabitants of the place had become so distracted by other things that they'd forgotten to close it behind them. Distracted by what, though?

Pagan, whose recent surge of adrenalin was fading, stood very still at the bottom of the steps. He stared up at the grey windows of the house, which reflected very little of the dawn light. It really wasn't a welcoming kind of house. The windows suggested dark rooms beyond them, large rooms with high ceilings. Pagan just knew there would be chilly crawlspaces and an arctic attic, and, in the dead of winter, the whole house would have corners that no heat could ever reach.

He had to go inside. He had to get out from under the windows, which were beginning to make him feel vulnerable. He went up the steps slowly, stepped inside the large hallway, stopped. There was a silence in the place, the kind of quiet that breeds indefinable fears. Pagan looked in the direction of the staircase, an ornate mahogany construction that went up and up into the shadows.

Patrick Cairney stopped as soon as he entered the room. *This was all wrong, this was all somehow askew, his expectations wrenched out of synch with reality. There was no oxygen tent, no tubes and appendages, no sick man lying on the bed*. Harry Cairney was kneeling on the floor by the fireplace, stuffing rolled-up newspapers into a grate that was creating black smoke. He was trying to build a fire, and the stereo was playing an old John McCormack recording, which filled the room with a familiar melancholy.

She was lovely and fair as the rose of the summer

Yet t'was not her beauty alone that won me . . .

It was totally wrong.

Patrick Cairney stood still. He clenched his hands at his side. The song, usually so sentimental and sweet, struck him with terror. He stared at the back of his father's head, conscious of Celestine moving in the corner of his vision, stepping across the room towards the window. Patrick Cairney felt very cold all at once, and the pain in his leg flared up again and with renewed ferocity. He had the sensation of drifting inside a dream, when all your known realities and all your expectations are perceived through the misshapen reflections of trick mirrors, bevelled surfaces, frosted glass.

Harry Cairney turned. His face was lit by surprise. 'Patrick!' he said. 'Dear God, nobody told me you were coming!' He dropped newspapers and matches in a flurry and stepped across the room and embraced his son and held him for a long time. Patrick Cairney clasped his father and it was still dreamlike. Even the touch of the old man had no real substance, no depth.

'Patrick, Patrick,' the old man said. 'Welcome back. Welcome home.'

Patrick Cairney stared over his father's shoulder at Celestine, who was framed by the window. He couldn't read her face. Suddenly he wanted to know what was written there, what her expression said. He thought of the lie she'd told him about his father's sickness, and it made him feel as if his heart were squeezed in a vice. There was something wrong here, very wrong, and he couldn't figure it out. He'd been lured back to Roscommon. He'd fallen into some awful trap. And even though he knew this, he couldn't find the resources in himself to respond to the bewilderment of the situation.

He closed his eyes a moment, feeling his father's breath on the side of his face. The old man smelled of burned newspapers and spent matches.

Harry Cairney released his son, stepped back.

'Celestine knew you were coming, didn't she?' Harry asked. 'This is one of her surprises, isn't it?'

'She knew,' Patrick Cairney said. He heard his own voice echo inside his head. It was the sound of something stirring at the end of a long tunnel.

She's always surprising me.' And Harry Cairney smiled across the room at his wife. She was standing beside the window-seat.

Patrick Cairney reached out and hugged his father again. He held him very tightly this time.

'You'll suffocate me,' the old man said, laughing.

Patrick Cairney slackened his hold. It seemed to him that the only real thing in this room, the only anchor, was his father. He felt the pain burn, rising the whole length of his leg. He fought to gain control over it, but his will wasn't fully functioning.

Celestine, he thought. *What have you done*?

Harry Cairney took a step back, studied his son, noticed the bloodsoaked cuffs of the pants. 'Jesus. What happened to you?'

'I had an accident,' Patrick said.

Celestine moved at the window.

Oh, no, 'twas the truth in her eyes ever dawning

That made me love Mary, the Rose of Tralee . . .

There was the wretched scratching sound of the needle being struck across the surface of the record and the song stopped. Both Patrick Cairney and his father looked in Celestine's direction. The silence in the room was suddenly overwhelming. Nobody moved. Celestine created a slim shadow against the window.

'Why did you do that?' Harry Cairney asked. He went to the record player and took the disc off and examined it. 'You've ruined it for God's sake. Do you know how hard it is to get a duplicate of that particular recording?'

Celestine said, 'I don't care.'

The look on her face was one Patrick Cairney hadn't seen before. It was fearfully cold, and ruthless, and there was a tiny spark of amusement in the eyes.

He also saw the gun in her hand, concealed by the folds of her robe.

Dizzy, he reached for the back of a chair and leaned against it and the pain in his leg went shooting up into his skull, where it was molten and white-hot like lead in a furnace.

'What are you doing with my gun?' Harry Cairney asked.

Celestine pointed the Browning directly at her husband. 'Harry. Dear Harry. Have you met John Doyle?'

Patrick Cairney gripped the back of the chair. He had the strange impression that the ceiling was lowering itself, that the room was diminishing and the walls were going to crush him.

'John who?' the old man asked.

'Your son,' Celestine said. 'John Doyle. Also known as Jig.'

Harry Cairney laughed. 'What the hell has gotten into you?'

Celestine looked at Patrick Cairney. Her face seemed to him as though it were a fuzzy television image travelling through miles of static. He had no control over his pain now. Wave after wave, each one sickening and depleting, surged through him.

'Pat,' Celestine said. 'Didn't you know your father headed the organisation that raised funds for the IRA? Didn't you guess that your own father was on your wanted list? Doesn't it strike you as superbly ironic, Jig? Doesn't it strike you as funny?'

Patrick Cairney shook his head, glanced at his father. *The Old Man* he thought. Harry Cairney raised an arm slowly, turned his hand over in a little gesture of puzzlement.

'You don't know what you're saying, Cel.'

'But I do, Harry.' Celestine smiled. 'Ask your son. Ask him if he's Jig.'

Harry Cairney looked at his son. He opened his mouth, but he didn't say anything. He couldn't bring himself to talk. He gazed down at the blackened blood staining Patrick's leg, then raised his eyes to the boy's face. Jig, he thought. The whole thing was some terrible mistake, a joke, any moment now Celestine would pull the trigger of the gun and a flag would pop out with the words *Ha ha, fooled you*, but it wasn't April the First, and the way his wife looked didn't seem remotely whimsical to him.

Patrick Cairney said, 'You're lying, Celestine.'

She tossed her hair back with a gesture of her head that reminded Cairney of a small girl bothered by flies. 'You're careless, Patrick. You carry a passport made out in the name of John Doyle. You don't take the precautions you should. You're not as good as people say you are. The great Catholic avenger. The Irish freedom fighter. But you're weak, Patrick. Weak where it really matters. Shall I tell your father how weak you really are? Would you like that?'

Cairney stared at her. He understood that it didn't matter to her whether she hurt Harry or not. 'I'd prefer it otherwise,' he said feebly.

The old man had a fleck of spit at the cranny of his mouth. He reminded Patrick Cairney of a man plunged down in the centre of some totally unfamiliar spectator sport whose rules he has to guess. He stepped towards his wife and asked, 'Even if he happens to have a passport in somebody else's name, how the hell does that make him Jig?'

'Because Jig travels under that name at times.'

The old man's face was suddenly florid. 'How do you know that? How do you know any of this?'

Celestine ignored his question. The look on her face dismissed him, relegated him to some unimportant corner of her life. She turned her attention to Patrick Cairney.

'I liked the archaeological symposium bit,' she said. 'It's a pretty good cover. It explains all the trips you must take if anybody ever asked, but it's fake. Totally fake. Tell your father, Patrick. Tell him the truth.'

Cairney felt the room spin around. He wondered how much blood he'd actually lost. He wanted to sit down but didn't move. He had the feeling that if he did sit he'd never rise again. He gazed at the gun in Celestine's hand and experienced an odd little hallucinatory moment when it seemed to him that metal and skin had become fused together. He blinked, rubbed his eyes, focused on Celestine's face, trying to associate what he saw there with the woman who'd whispered *Trust me, trust me* on the sofa downstairs. He had the thought that if she was capable of sexual treachery, what else could she bring herself to do? There were no limits, no boundaries. Anything was possible.

'You've been wasting your time from the start, Jig,' she said. 'It's been a lost cause from the beginning. But you must be used to lost causes by this time. You'll never see that money, Jig. You know that, don't you?'

Harry Cairney, who felt betrayed by all his senses, couldn't take his eyes from his wife. 'What do you know about the money?' he asked.

'Harry, Harry,' she answered. 'We used your boat to steal it.'

'My boat?'

Celestine shrugged. 'Why not? You hardly ever find any use for it, do you?'

Harry Cairney was trembling. 'Who used the boat? Who are you talking about?'

'Ask your son,' Celestine said.

'I'm asking you,' the old man said. 'I'm asking my wife.'

'Your wife,' Celestine said.

'Yes. My wife.' The old man held his arms out. 'The woman I love.'

'Funny. I never really thought of you as my husband.'

Harry Cairney was moving forward, propelled by notions of love, convinced even now that all this was a travesty, some kind of breakdown on Celestine's part, something he could put right the way he'd put things right all his life. In his time he'd been capable of fixing anything. It didn't matter what. And he could fix this, whatever it was. Hadn't some of the most powerful men in the whole goddam nation come to him at one time or another and asked him to bail them out of their problems?

'I don't want to hear that, I don't want to hear you say that kind of thing.' He had both hands extended in front of himself. 'We've been happy. I know we have.'

'Dear Harry,' she said. 'We've had our moments. But they're finished now.'

'What are you saying?'

Celestine was very quiet. Patrick Cairney watched her, knew what was coming, understood he was powerless to do anything about it. He watched Celestine shoot the old man through the side of the neck.

Harry Cairney cried out and dropped to the floor, turned over on his back, raised one hand up in Celestine's direction, and then he was finally still. Celestine turned the gun towards Patrick.

Cairney said, 'You're on their side.'

'The right side, Jig. The side of the angels.'

Cairney kneeled beside the body of the old man. He lightly touched the side of his father's jaw. There was a grief in him, but he realised he wasn't going to live long enough to express it. The tightness behind his eyes, the awful parched sensation in his throat. *Do something.*

'You are the bonus,' Celestine said. 'I never expected you. Not in this house.'

Without looking at her Cairney said, 'They put you here. You told them about the money. The ship.'

'Yes,' she said quietly. 'I told them a lot of things, Patrick. I told them about the money. The route taken by the *Connie*. It wasn't difficult to find out. Your father always thought he was such a hotshot at keeping secrets, but he wasn't. Not really.' She paused a moment. Then, 'I also told them about the route taken by a certain school bus – that New England trip I mentioned, remember? Does that surprise you, Jig?'

A school bus. Cairney felt very cold. He was fumbling towards the sense of it all, groping for a revelation that he knew was going to be denied him.

He opened his eyes, turned his face towards her. 'Who the fuck are you?' he asked, thinking maybe, just maybe, he could fish his weapon out of his pocket, if he could be quick enough, slick, but even as he reached for it she took one step forward and fired her gun a second time.

Cairney didn't feel the entrance of the bullet into his chest. He fell back, knocking a chair over as he dropped, and he lay face down on the rug. He was barely conscious of hearing her footsteps as she approached him.

She bent down to touch the nape of his neck. 'We had some moments too,' she whispered.

Calmly, carefully, Celestine changed her clothes. She stepped out onto the landing, without once looking at the two figures who lay on the bedroom floor. The heels of her boots made soft clicking noises on wood floorboards as she entered Patrick Cairney's bedroom. She stood by the window, gazing out a moment.

She saw a car come up to the front of the house.

She pressed her face against the glass, then she turned away. It was time now. It was time to leave this place.

She opened the closet in Patrick's bedroom and began to remove old books, boxes that contained ancient boardgames, a battered microscope, running shoes, a football, crumpled pennants, a dusty framed wall map with the title LEGENDARY IRELAND in Celtic script. *The relics of Jig*, she thought.

There was a satchel stored at the very back of the closet. She reached for it and drew it towards her. And then she turned around and, with one last glance at Patrick Cairney's bed, she left the room.

27 Roscommon, New York

Frank Pagan was standing at the foot of the stairs when he heard the first gunshot. When he heard the second, he turned and moved back along the hallway. He stepped inside the living-room and closed the door, leaving only a small space through which he could observe the staircase. It was a limited field of vision, but it was infinitely more safe than doing something completely reckless, like charging up the stairs with his gun in his hand. If he waited here, sooner or later Jig was going to come down. He wondered about the gunfire. He assumed that Jig had had to shoot Senator Cairney, although he couldn't understand why *two* shots had been fired.

He waited.

The room in which he stood was elegantly furnished. There were old prints on the walls, each depicting a Dublin scene at the turn of the century. Kingstown Pier. The Custom House on the banks of the Liffey. Horsedrawn carriages on St Stephen's Green. He glanced at them a moment, then returned his attention to the stairs.

Pagan heard a sound from above. A door opened and closed faintly, a slight noise diminished by the mass of the house. Then there were footsteps for a moment. After that there was silence again.

Pagan waited. Earlier, when he'd been poking cautiously through the downstairs rooms, he thought he'd heard a man's upraised voice, but he hadn't been certain. The brickwork of this old house trapped sounds and diffused them and created auditory illusions. He passed his pistol from one hand to the other because there was a sudden small cramp in his fingers. The palms of his hands were sticky with sweat.

Now he heard footsteps in the hallway. They were coming from the front door, not from the stairs as he'd expected. He couldn't see anything in that direction. He heard them come close to where he stood. Heavy steps. A man's steps. They stopped some feet from the door behind which he was standing.

Frank Pagan held his breath, listened. Now there was more movement, from the stairs this time. He glanced up into the dark brown shadows.

The person coming down wasn't Jig and it wasn't Senator Harry Cairney either. Wrong sex.

It was a woman dressed in black cord pants and a black leather jacket. She wore tinted glasses and her yellow hair was held up by a black ribbon. In one hand she carried a small overnight bag, also black, in the other a large satchel. She created a sombre impression as she moved, taking the stairs slowly. Where the hell was Jig? Pagan wondered. And who was this woman?

She reached the bottom step, where she set her bag down and took off her dark glasses. Her smile was suddenly radiant. She had the bluest eyes Pagan had ever seen. She held her arms out. The man who had entered from Pagan's blind side stepped forward and Pagan could see him for the first time, and he felt a certain voltage around his heart.

'Celestine,' the man said.

His voice was unmistakable.

Pagan watched as the couple embraced. There was laughter, the kind of laughter you associate with a reunion. There was relief and happiness in the sound and a maudlin tinge.

'Too long, too bloody long,' the man said.

'Yes,' the woman whispered. 'Far too long.'

The woman slid her glasses back over her eyes.

The man made a gesture towards the stairs.

'It's over,' the woman said.

'Both of them?'

'Both of them.'

The man laughed again. 'You were right about Jig then,' he said. 'You're a bloody wonder. You know that?' The man was quiet before he added, 'I think I'd like to go upstairs, take a look at the body. I'd like to be sure.'

The body, Frank Pagan thought. Was he talking about Jig? Jig's body? Pagan felt a cold hand inside his brain.

The woman turned and looked up the flight of stairs. 'Take my word for it. He's dead. Let's get the hell out of here. I've been in this place too bloody long. I want to go home to Ireland.'

The big man reached down to pick up the overnight bag.

Frank Pagan stepped out from behind the door, holding his pistol in front of him.

The big man turned around, saw Pagan, and for a second his expression was one of disbelief, but it changed to a restrained kind of amusement. 'Frank Pagan,' he said. 'I can't seem to shake you.'

'People always tell me I've got a dogged quality, Ivor,' Pagan replied.

'People are right.' Ivor McInnes sighed and turned to the woman. 'This, my dear, is Frank Pagan. I mentioned him to you once or twice, I believe.'

The woman removed her glasses and stared at Pagan. She didn't say anything. She gazed at Pagan's gun, then turned her face back to McInnes. She shrugged, almost as if Pagan's presence made no difference to her.

Ivor McInnes was still smiling. 'What brings you all the way up here to this wild place, Frank?'

'Jig,' Pagan said. He found it difficult to take his eyes away from the woman's face. She had a rare beauty that seemed somehow innocent to him and he couldn't begin to imagine what her association with McInnes might be. There was intimacy between them, in the way they stood close together, the way they'd embraced before. And, almost as if some of this woman's beauty had affected Ivor McInnes, the man looked suddenly handsome there in the hall, distinguished and proud and pleased.

'Jig's dead,' McInnes said. 'And his father along with him.'

'His father?' Pagan asked.

'Senator Harry Cairney.'

Pagan was quiet. The fact that Harry Cairney was Jig's father took a very long time to make its way into that part of his brain that absorbed information. It had to pass through filters of disbelief first. It had to make its way around the confusion of emotions Pagan felt at the news of Jig's death. Disappointment. Anger. And sorrow – was there just a touch of sorrow in there or was he simply sad that the chance to take Jig back to London with him had gone? He wasn't sure of any of his feelings right then.

'I see it perplexes you, Frank,' McInnes said.

'To put it mildly.'

McInnes shook his head and made a long sighing sound. 'It would seem that neither man knew of the other's activities,' he said. 'It's what you might call a lack of communication. The son doesn't know what the father's doing. And the father has no idea about his son. Ah, modern families.'

Pagan didn't say anything for a while. He'd come a long, long way to take Jig back to England, and now there was nothing left of that ambition. But there was Ivor still, and Ivor would have to suffice. There was also this woman, Ivor's accomplice. Somehow, though, he felt strangely empty. He felt he was moving through the demands imposed upon him by a role, a job of acting, doing the things expected of him even if his heart weren't entirely in it. He'd been after Jig too long, and now Jig was gone.

He looked at the woman and said, 'You killed them.'

The woman gave him a look of mild disgust. 'Do you expect me to admit that?'

Frank Pagan didn't know what to expect. He stared at her a moment, then turned towards Ivor. If he couldn't have Jig, then by Christ he'd bring McInnes to some kind of justice.

He said, 'I almost didn't see your plan, Ivor. I almost missed it. I was looking for the complex when I ought to have been looking for something simple.'

Ivor McInnes moved just a little closer to the woman, cupping her elbow in the palm of his hand.

'You brought your thugs into this country,' Pagan said. 'You orchestrated acts of violence and placed the blame on the IRA.'

'Is that what you think, Frank?'

'Its what I *know*,' Pagan said. He was hoarse all at once, depleted. 'I only fully realised it when I found the body of John Waddell. You lied to me from the start, McInnes. And then you compounded your lies with even more lies. Bullshit about trying to make some kind of peace with an IRA faction. I was in no position to argue with him at the time. You set out to discredit the IRA in the most callous way imaginable. You set out to turn public opinion totally against them by directing the FUV to act as it did.'

McInnes was quiet for a moment. He said, 'Northern Ireland is a sad society, Frank. You've been there. You've seen it. You've seen what happens when warring factions can't find a peace plan. And the sorry thing about it is that there's no possibility of any peace in the future unless the IRA is squashed.'

'Along with the Free Ulster Volunteers,' Pagan said.

'I agree with you, Frank. In the Ireland I want, there's no place for hoodlums.' McInnes glanced at the woman. 'When you want to provoke outrage, you strike at the innocent, Pagan. It does no good in this day and age to assassinate a President. People expect that kind of atrocity. They're numbed by that. But blow up a church and then massacre some children on a school bus, and suddenly you've got the public attention. They howl. Jesus, how they howl! And then they strike back with a vengeance at the perpetrators. In this case, Frank, the Irish Republican Army is the culprit.'

Pagan felt a numbness in the hand that held the gun. He was thinking now of the school bus and the dead children and the fact that Jig had been murdered and all the deaths congealed inside him, a knot in the centre of his chest. He realised he wanted to kill McInnes then and there. Shoot the man on the precise spot where he presently stood. Shoot him directly between the eyes. All along McInnes had been manipulating events, plotting destruction.

'You knew the names of the Fund-raisers, didn't you, Ivor?'

'Of course I did.' McInnes smiled at the woman. 'Mrs Harry Cairney kept me well informed.'

'Mrs Cairney?' Pagan asked.

The woman smiled coldly at Pagan from behind her dark glasses. Frank Pagan wondered what inestimable treasons had been going on in this large gloomy house.

'You could have made my life easier if you'd supplied me with the names, Ivor,' he said.

'I'm not in the business of making my enemy's life easier, Frank. Why tell you their names? It was nice to think of you busily running around to find out. It kept your mind off me for a while.'

'And you knew Jig was coming to the States,' Pagan said.

'All along, Frank. From the moment Finn first sent him. We knew he was coming here to find the money. We told you about that. We wanted you to have a gift from your friends inside the FUV, Frank. We wanted you to come over here and catch him. We were much too busy to be sidetracked into getting him ourselves. Besides, we didn't have the expertise for that. And I assumed you did. You and the FBI. But you failed to catch him. You let me down there. It doesn't matter now, of course. We didn't expect to find Jig was part of this particular household, but you know what they say about gift-horses. And Jig did us a favour by rendering the Fund-raisers obsolete.' McInnes was lightly rubbing the woman's neck. 'Besides, Jig wasn't what I was after. Jig was only a part of a larger entity. I want the IRA in its entirety, Frank. Not just one assassin.'

Pagan said nothing. He kept looking at the woman's expressionless faces. *Mrs Harry Cairney.*

McInnes looked suddenly solemn. 'The trouble is, Frank, your government hasn't done a damn thing about the IRA. They pussyfoot around the problem. They send in bloody soldiers, young kids who're too scared to act. And then when they do get their hands on the IRA, it's your court system that protects the bastards. It's your courts that say these gangsters have rights. They can't be hanged. They can't be flogged. They can't be tortured. Good heavens, don't lay a hand on them or else they'll be sending out for their lawyers and making depositions to the bloody Court of Human Rights in Strasbourg. Jesus Christ! The IRA aren't people, Pagan. They aren't human beings. They're rodents. And you people don't have a clue about what to do with them.'

Rodents, Pagan thought.

McInnes said, 'I'm sick and tired of violence, Pagan. I want an end to it. I want an end to the IRA. I want to see peace in Belfast and through the rest of Ireland. And if the British can't do it, then perhaps the Americans will.'

The Americans. Frank Pagan rubbed the corner of an eye. Here he was now, standing on the precipice of Ivor's dream and looking down a dark slope into the abyss. 'Was that it, Ivor? You brought violence into the United States because you hoped it would outrage Americans enough that they'd send some troops over there to wipe out the IRA?'

'It's going to happen,' McInnes said. 'People in this country are sick to death of terrorists and their threats. They're tired of all the anti-American activities that go on throughout the world. The Americans hate two things, Frank. They hate being put on the defensive, especially in their own country. And they hate to be inconvenienced. My God, do they ever hate that! They can't go to Europe, because they're afraid. They can't cruise the Med, because the bloody Libyans will likely hijack their ships. They can't do business in the Middle East without fearing for their lives. They're tired of it all, Frank. And now they're ready to hit back. And they've got a target all set up for them. The IRA. It's going to happen because there's a weak President in the White House who's going to be swayed by public outrage. A man who's personally suffering at this very moment from his own loss. His two nieces, Frank. His brother's children. The IRA killed his own flesh and blood. Tell me he won't react to *that*.'

Pagan thought McInnes had to go down as the worst kind of monster. The monster who dreams and who doesn't care what his dreams destroy or who they touch or the lives they shatter. He thought about Kevin Dawson for a second. He thought about dead kids and a shattered school bus and a silent country house near New Rockford, Connecticut. For the rest of his life Kevin Dawson would only have pictures of his daughters to look at. Pictures on a mantelpiece.

'You want your own fucking little Vietnam in Ireland.'

'I don't think so,' McInnes said. 'It wouldn't take the Americans long to crush the IRA.'

'No, Ivor,' Pagan replied. 'It would take forever. You don't see very far, do you? The IRA would thrive in the end because it's always thrived in one form or another. The English couldn't kill it. The Irish themselves couldn't stamp it out. It passes between father and son. It goes from one generation to the next. The Americans might subdue them for a while, but sooner or later the Americans would have to go home. That is, if the governments of Ireland and Britain approved of their intervention in the first place, which is highly unlikely.'

'No, Frank. It's the logical step for this country. And do you think the governments of Ireland and Britain are going to turn down a helping hand when it comes to a problem they've been battling with miserable success one way or another for centuries? I don't think so.'

Pagan was quiet again. Ivor's dream, grandiose, elaborate, made a jarring sound inside his head. He said, 'If it hadn't been for your own troops killing Fitzjohn in Albany and calling the FBI, the name of the Free Ulster Volunteers wouldn't ever have entered into the picture, would it?'

McInnes nodded. 'It was a bad moment for me, but it doesn't matter now,' he said.

The woman, who'd been listening to this in a distant kind of way, tugged at McInnes's sleeve impatiently. McInnes looked at her, taking his hand away from her neck. It suddenly occurred to Frank Pagan that this pair expected to walk out of the house and take their leave as if nothing had ever happened here, as if McInnes had nothing to answer for.

McInnes said, 'You'll excuse us now, Pagan.'

'Don't make me laugh, Ivor. Where the hell do you think you're going?'

McInnes looked at the gun. 'I haven't seen my wife in two long years, Frank.'

'Your *wife*?'

McInnes slung an arm round the woman's shoulder. Pagan couldn't see her expression for the dark glasses.

'You sound surprised, Frank.'

'You said she was Mrs Cairney.'

'So I did, so I did.' McInnes smiled. 'You can figure it out for yourself, Frank. I know you're capable of it. But you shouldn't sound so surprised. Why shouldn't an old warhorse like me have a wife as beautiful as Celestine?'

A match made in hell, Pagan thought. He stared at McInnes's large hand on the woman's shoulder.

'Two years is a long time,' McInnes said. 'And I've come a long way to take her back home, Frank. I'm sure you understand.'

'The only thing I understand is that you're going straight to jail,' Pagan said.

'I don't think so,' McInnes smiled. It was an infuriating little movement of the lips. 'For one thing, Frank, you've got nothing in the way of evidence that links me with anything. For another, my dear wife here had no part in the tragedy that took place in this house. Father finds out about son, shoots son, turns gun on himself. You've seen the headlines before, I'm sure.'

'There are some corpses in Hudson,' Pagan said. 'The valiant men of the Free Ulster Volunteers. The people you betrayed. How would you explain them away?'

'Do I have to? They had nothing to do with me. Show me a connection, Frank.'

Pagan hesitated. He saw it now. He saw the flaw in Ivor's scheme, and he circled it in his mind briefly before pouncing on it joyfully. 'They had *guns*, Ivor. Presumably the same guns used in the attack on the school bus.'

'Guns?' McInnes appeared surprised. 'They didn't have any guns!'

'What's the matter, Ivor? Did you expect them to be unarmed? Was that what you wanted? That they wouldn't have anything that might tie them to the school bus? Tough shit. What happened? Did they decide not to follow your orders?'

McInnes said, 'They were supposed to get rid of the goddam weapons.'

'Terrible how unreliable the hired help is these days,' Pagan said. 'It isn't going to be difficult to show that these men weren't members of the IRA. As soon as they're fingerprinted and run through the computer, everybody's going to know that they were connected with the FUV. Fingerprints and weapons will prove conclusively that the attacks weren't carried out by anyone associated with the Irish Republican Army. *How does that grab you, Ivor*? If only they'd tossed their weapons away, everything would have been neatly blamed on the IRA.'

McInnes was quiet for a time. He seemed rather pale to Pagan. 'It might change things a little,' he said and there was a certain raspiness in his voice.

'It might change things quite a lot,' Pagan said. He was savouring this moment, the punctured expression on Ivor's craggy face, the way the man's mouth had slackened, his smile erased. 'It demolishes your notion of blaming the IRA. And there goes your case, Ivor. If you hadn't betrayed your own chums in Hudson, my friend, you might *just* be able to walk out of here. But you were so bloody anxious to get rid of your own thugs you didn't stop to think. You didn't want them around as a potential embarrassment, did you? You slipped up there. You should have let your killers leave the country.'

The woman asked, 'Is he serious, Ivor?'

'Deadly,' Pagan replied. 'Don't you hear it? That long drawn-out sound of a man's scheme dying?'

McInnes made a small fumbling gesture with his hand. He looked lost, but then he appeared to gather himself together again.

'It could still work,' McInnes said. 'I know it could still work.'

'Ivor,' Pagan said. 'It's not going to work.'

'Jesus,' McInnes said angrily. 'I'm telling you it could still work. I'll think of a way. I'll think of something.'

'How, Ivor? How is it going to work now? You can't think of anything that could make it plausible now. There are corpses in Hudson. You can't fucking wish them away, Ivor.'

The woman placed her hand on McInnes's wrist as if to calm him down. She had a small smile on her face. 'They still can't link you with any killings,' she said. 'They can't tie you into anything that's happened, Ivor.'

Pagan looked at her. It was obvious she provided some kind of support system for McInnes, which made her as crazy as he was. The little wife comforting the distraught husband, laying out his slippers in front of the fire and massaging his weary shoulders. The lethal little woman. But Ivor looked despairing again, a chess-player who has overlooked some simple strategy, who has made a bad pawn move at a bad time.

Pagan thought for a moment. 'Even if you could walk out of here, I could make a case, Ivor. You know I could do it. I'd backtrack. I'd go over all your movements. All your associations. I'd go back ten years if I had to, but you know I'd make a damn good case.

There are links between you and the killers because somewhere you had to sit down and plan this whole thing out with them. I'd find those links. And when I did, I'd squeeze you like a fucking cherry.'

The woman said, 'We're going. We're leaving, Ivor.'

'I have a gun,' Pagan said.

The woman slipped off her glasses. There was a cruelty somewhere in that beauty. The mouth was heartless. The eyes seemed subtly insane. 'Use it then, Mr Pagan.'

She linked her arm through McInnes's.

'Use it,' she said again. 'Shoot me.'

Frank Pagan marvelled at her calm. He raised the gun, levelled it. He didn't want these people dead. He wanted them tried and imprisoned. Imprisoned for a very long time, the rest of their lives. Death was altogether too quick, too generous.

The woman smiled at him. 'Goodbye, Mr Pagan.'

'I'll shoot,' Pagan said.

The woman, who had infinitely more nerve than McInnes, put her hands on her hips. It was a gesture of defiance. She had seen into the heart of Frank Pagan, and she understood that he wasn't capable of cold-blooded murder. She knew she was free, that all she had to do was walk with Ivor McInnes to the door.

The smile on her face chilled Pagan.

'Goodbye,' she said again.

Ivor McInnes placed his arm once more around the woman's shoulder.

And then he lurched suddenly, sinking to his knees, a horrified expression on his face. His face travelled down the length of the woman's leg as he slipped. Blood spilled from the side of his jaw. The woman screamed. She turned, kneeled alongside McInnes, and then the back of her scalp was shattered with a sound Frank Pagan could *feel* in his own head. She toppled forward over the body of McInnes, and she lay there motionless, hands outstretched.

Pagan turned and looked up the flight of stairs.

The shots had come from the landing up there. From the shadows, Pagan thought he saw somebody move. He went towards the stairs quickly.

It was Finn's voice Jig heard, it was Finn's voice inside his head. A sea breeze, a gull's wing, it floated through his brain with a soft insistence, quiet and reassuring and coming from a place nearby. *Even when you don't think you've got it, boy, you'll always find some strength from somewhere.*

The strength.

He didn't have any strength left.

What life he still had was going out like the tide in Dublin Bay.

He didn't hear the shots he fired, nor the sound of the gun slipping out of his fingers and toppling down the stairs. He didn't feel any kind of pain. He saw Celestine, the lovely, venomous Celestine, look clumsy in death.

Dying isn't any great business. When you took the oath, you committed yourself to death. It's nothing to fear because it's been a close companion all along.

Dear Finn. He had loved Finn more than he'd ever loved his father. More than any other human being.

Jig closed his eyes. He lay down on the landing. He wondered what death was going to be like.

It was all weariness now, and fatigue such as he'd never felt before.

He didn't see Frank Pagan come up the stairs, didn't hear him. He didn't feel Frank Pagan's fingers touch his arm.

And he never heard Frank Pagan turn away and go back down the stairs because all the doors to his mind had closed tight shut and there was only darkness – and somewhere, at the very last, a sweet note that might have been plucked on the string of a harp, one of Finn's harps, echoing and echoing, then finally silent and still.

Frank Pagan opened the dead woman's satchel, looked inside, saw what he guessed was there all along, then went out onto the steps of the house. Over the lake lay some low clouds, heavy and thick. Pagan walked towards the shore, moving very slowly. He had a bad taste in his mouth and his head felt as if it were filled with stones. When he reached the reeds at the shoreline he sat down.

He tossed a pebble out into the water lethargically. He was beyond tiredness now. His condition felt more serious. There was a numbness inside him. It was almost as if he were out of contact with himself. He couldn't get in touch with ground control. He heard the lyrics of a song he'd listened to only a day or so before on his car radio.

With your long blond hair and your eyes of blue
The only thing I ever get from you
Is sorrow . . .

Celestine Cairney. Sorrow and treachery.

Treachery, he thought. It bruised you, left you shaken. It shouldn't have surprised you, but it always did. Call me naïve, Pagan thought. What is it about you that keeps bringing you back to the untenable idea that the human soul is not so awful as it sometimes seems?

He flipped another stone out into the sombre lake.

He would go home, and he'd take nothing with him, unless you counted a narrative of deception and violence. At least it was something he didn't have to declare at Customs. And he was dissatisfied too, because the total story eluded him. The bits and pieces you could put together only after you'd started to dig around. He wasn't sure he had the energy for that. He wasn't certain he had the inclination to go around tagging the corpses, trying to understand the roles of people who no longer had any part left to play.

He thought of Jig's face in death. How to describe that? Composed? Indifferent? He wasn't sure. He shut his eyes and felt the frosty morning breeze scurry across the surface of the lake, blowing through his hair, against his face. It might have been refreshing in other circumstances. But not now. He hardly felt it.

He opened his eyes when he heard the sound of footsteps coming towards him. The swishing of reeds. He saw Artie Zuboric and Tyson Bruno looming up, two men in a raging hurry, flustered and out of breath. Artie's moustache hadn't been combed, and it drooped sadly. Tyson Bruno needed a shave. His jaw looked like sandpaper.

Pagan smiled at them. 'Welcome,' he said.

Zuboric took a gun out of his raincoat. 'You're up shit creek, Frank.'

'A place I know well,' Pagan replied. He turned away from the two agents and looked out at the gloomy lake. He was going to pretend that Zuboric didn't have a gun in his hand. He wanted to see how far that might get him. A little make-believe.

But Zuboric wasn't going to be ignored. He shoved the barrel of the gun into the back of Frank Pagan's neck.

'Artie, please,' Pagan said. 'It's a tender spot.'

'I'm trying to think of one good reason why I shouldn't shoot you.'

'I'll give you one,' Pagan said. 'I don't want to die.'

'Not good enough, Frankie. Not convincing.'

Pagan pushed the gun away with his fingers. He hated anyone calling him Frankie.

Tyson Bruno, no doubt remembering the day Pagan struck him, plucked a reed out of the ground and bent it between his hands. 'Shoot him,' he said with a certain exuberance. 'You've got the authorisation to do it. Shoot him. Nobody's going to give a fiddler's fuck anyway.'

Zuboric poked the gun back into the nape of Pagan's neck. Frank Pagan stood up, feeling the edge of irritation. These characters had quite spoiled his lakeside meditation.

'One fucking good reason,' Zuboric said again.

Pagan stared into the agent's face. He didn't like what he saw there. Meanness, a lack of imagination, a narrow human being at best. Artie and Tyson, a couple of lovely specimens. Pagan looked out once more across the water. He wasn't absolutely sure if Zuboric intended to use the gun. He had no confidence in his own predictions when it came to Zuboric.

'You been in the house?' Pagan asked.

'Not yet.'

Pagan smiled. 'You should. Jig's dead.'

'Dead? How?'

'Does it matter?' Pagan asked. He had a thought just then. It was cynical and thoroughly without any redeeming qualities, unless you happened to be Artie Zuboric. When it occurred to him he wanted to laugh out loud. But Artie had a gun, and Pagan didn't want to make any sound the agent might misinterpret. He didn't want to die right here and now.

'Artie,' he said. 'How would you like to be a hero?'

Zuboric looked mystified. 'What are you trying to say?'

'How would you like to be known as the man who killed Jig?'

Zuboric said nothing. He was scrutinising Pagan, his whole face filled with mistrust.

'You'd like that, wouldn't you, Artie? Think of it. Think of the fame. Your standing in Korn's eyes. Your stock would go up overnight. You'd be a big bloody hero.'

'I'm not with you,' Zuboric said.

'It's dead simple, I saw you do it, after all. I'm your eyewitness. Jig was about to kill me, when all of a sudden you just popped up and saved my life.'

'Are you serious?'

'Never more so, my old dear. Never more so.'

Tyson Bruno cleared his throat. 'It sounds like bullshit to me. I'd shoot the sonofabitch, Artie.'

'Wait,' Zuboric said.

'It's a nifty idea,' Pagan remarked. 'I'll tell you what. For good measure, I'll throw in Ivor McInnes as well. I'll say you gunned him down because he drew a pistol on you.'

Zuboric narrowed his eyes. 'McInnes?'

'Absolutely,' Pagan looked at Tyson Bruno. 'You could pick up a consolation prize, Ty. We can say you were forced to shoot McInnes's wife because she'd just shot Senator Cairney. Christ, there are enough bodies to go round. Regular funeral parlour up there.'

'Senator Cairney?' Bruno asked.

'The very same,' Pagan said.

'Hold on,' Zuboric said. 'Just wait a minute. What about ballistics tests? They'll find out I never fired this gun at anybody.'

'A piece of cake,' Pagan said. 'It's all a question of logic. Who had what gun and why.

I don't think such a story is beyond us, is it? Not if we put our heads together. It's no sweat.'

'I still don't like it.' Tyson Bruno snapped another reed. he folded it between his hands and blew into it, creating a humming sound.

'Ty. Think. Merit badges. Maybe promotion. A rise in salary. A leg up the ladder. Advancement.'

Zuboric had a curious smile on his face. There was a faraway look in his eyes. 'How can we trust you, Pagan?'

Frank Pagan shrugged. 'You've got two choices. You can shoot me. Or you can use me to back up the authentic story of your heroic deeds. What's it to be, Arthur?'

Zuboric was silent. He was looking at Tyson Bruno. There was some form of mutual decision-making going on here. Pagan stared up at the sky. A sound forced its way through the cover of clouds, throaty and deep. There, far over the trees on the other side of the lake, two helicopters appeared. Whirring, skimming treetops, they were coming in towards Roscommon like a pair of enormous gnats.

'Visitors,' Pagan said. 'Friends of yours?'

Zuboric peered up. Tyson Bruno did likewise, making slits of his puffy eyes. The helicopters came in across the lake, making the water into tiny whirlpools. They were travelling very low.

The chopper in front banked slightly. There was the unmistakable sight of Leonard Korn's shaved head in the cabin. He was gesticulating, pointing down towards the three men hunched by the edge of the lake.

'Your Master,' Pagan said. 'Better make up your mind quickly.'

'One thing, Frank. Why don't you want credit for Jig yourself?'

Credit, Pagan thought. It was a funny word. 'I couldn't do that,' he replied. 'I couldn't deprive you, Artie.'

Zuboric nodded. 'Okay. It's a deal. Tyson?'

Bruno looked suddenly quite brutal. 'It's okay with me. But there's something I got to settle first.'

'Like what?' Zuboric asked.

'I owe this sonafabitch,' and Tyson Bruno turned to Pagan, making a hammer out of his fist and raising it in the air with the intention of bringing it down somewhere on Pagan's face.

Frank Pagan reached up and caught Bruno's fist in his hand and twisted, just enough to make Bruno gasp and step back.

'Not today, Ty,' Pagan said. 'I'm not in the mood. Believe me.'

There was a wicked look in Pagan's eye, a murderous light that made Tyson Bruno refrain from trying a second time.

'Besides,' Pagan added, 'I make it a point not to fight with heroes.'

Zuboric and Tyson Bruno looked at one another as if to be sure they had reached agreement regarding Pagan's proposition. They had. Then they turned and started to walk towards the house.

As Pagan watched them move away, he remembered the satchel in the house. He remembered how it lay alongside Celestine's body. It contained several million dollars of IRA money. He considered calling out to the two agents, but he didn't. Let them discover it themselves. Let them decide what to do with all that cash. He thought he knew anyway. They were about to become heroes, after all. And heroes deserved something more in the way of remuneration than any salary the FBI might provide. He shrugged and looked up at the helicopters. Jig's cash. And Jig was dead. The fate of the money – money that had brought death and treachery, and, for himself, a depression he couldn't shake, an isolation that penetrated him, money that was bloody and tainted and only valuable now to men without scruples – didn't matter a damn to him.

He saw the choppers come in low over the front lawn just as Zuboric and Bruno disappeared through the open doorway and were swallowed by the gloomy interior of the house. He sat down among the reeds. The surface of Roscommon Lake, recently disturbed by the great blades of the helicopters, was placid again, and as desolate as Frank Pagan felt himself.

EPILOGUE

New York City

On the evening before St Patrick's Day, Frank Pagan went inside a bar on the West Side of Manhattan that belonged to a man who had made a good living out of performing Irish folk songs in a rich baritone voice. Pagan ordered a Guinness and scanned the large room. There was a great deal of easy laughter in this place. If there were any tension, if anybody had paid any mind to the editorial writers who had called for the cancellation of the St Patrick's Day Parade this year, it didn't show. You might just as well have tried to cancel New Year's Eve. Everybody here was having a fine old time.

On a small stage behind Pagan a fiddler was tuning up his instrument. Pagan turned to watch. The fiddler, a tiny man with large ears, had a gnomelike demeanour. When he played the fiddle, his stubby little fingers danced in a blur. Pagan, who had booked a flight for London first thing in the morning, closed his eyes and listened to the opening bars of *The Rose of Aranmore*. Somebody at the back of the room sang the lines

But soon I will return again
To the scenes I loved so well
Where many an Irish lass and lad
Their tales of love do tell

It was a thing about the Irish. They were always leaving Ireland and then composing homesick songs, songs filled with the prospect of a return to their birthland. A melancholy crowd, he thought. They were never entirely at home anywhere. And even if they did return to Ireland after years of exile, they were usually eager to be gone again as soon as they could. Who could figure them out?

He finished his drink, decided to have a second. Only four days had passed since the events at Roscommon. In that brief period of time Leonard Korn had been quoted as saying that only the 'tenacity' of the Federal Bureau of Investigation had brought about a resolution to an unhappy business, a Senator from Arkansas had introduced a Bill in the

House calling for tougher screening when it came to Irish immigrants and their political affiliations, sanctimonious editorialists everywhere had demanded a moratorium on Irish public assemblies for an indefinite period, and investigative reporters, like the good little hotshots they were, had gone scurrying off to dig into the lives of Ivor McInnes and Patrick Cairney and anybody else who might have been associated with them.

Pagan was tired. For four days he hadn't been able to rid himself of a disturbing sense of hollowness. It was as if something quite important had gone out of him. Energy, dedication to his work, he couldn't pin it down. He read the signs in himself and decided they were nothing more than the responses of a man burned-out by the events in which he'd participated. What he needed was a vacation from his life, a period where he wouldn't be Frank Pagan at all, but some anonymous tourist with a camera, somebody strolling a sunlit Caribbean beach and sipping tall drinks on a terrace while a great red sun went falling into the blue horizon. A little amnesia. A place where he might forget the question and answer sessions with Leonard Korn that had occupied the last couple of days. *Had he really seen Zuboric shoot Jig? How far was Jig standing from Zuboric when the fatal shot was fired? How did he explain the fact that Zuboric had killed Jig with an old Browning registered to Senator Harry Cairney*? Korn liked the role of Grand Inquisitor. But the Director was too carried away by the possibility of public rapture to be really good in the part. If there were holes in the story – which was reluctantly narrated by a weary Frank Pagan, who wasn't good at lies, and told them with a kind of white-hot resentment of the FBI because he had nothing but contempt for that organisation and the man who ran it – Korn didn't pay them the kind of close attention he might have because Leonard M. Korn needed a convincing story that put the FBI in a good light more than he needed the truth. Pagan supplied the flattering light, wondering all the while how Jig would have reacted to the fable that he'd been killed by a valiant FBI man in the line of duty. Maybe it was best that nobody knew he'd been shot by his own bigamous stepmother. God knows, there was scandal enough in all of this.

Arthur Zuboric had enjoyed his moment in the sun. He'd been called a hero, a description he modestly turned aside. He was only doing his job, he'd said to the reporters who'd clamoured around him. *But why was he retiring*? they wanted to know. Artie said it was time to take a long break. Besides, he had money from his pension, and he could live for a time before making a career decision. *A long vacation*? Yes, Artie had said. Perhaps a month or two in Rio might be nice, especially in the company of Charity, his new fiancée. Tyson Bruno, who was uncommunicative and therefore unattractive to reporters, had taken an extensive leave of absence and was said to be fishing in the wilds of Canada.

Pagan smiled. Rio. Canada. Faraway places.

He turned his glass around in his hand. The fiddle music was strident and loud in his ears. He thought about the Dawsons. The press had been very subdued about Kevin and Martha, apparently respecting their need for privacy, although there was a spate of articles about the lack of security afforded the unfortunate Dawson girls. Kevin and his wife had gone into seclusion at some country estate in Virginia. If the reporters knew of Kevin Dawson's association with Irish matters, they were discreet enough not to write about it.

Pagan shut his eyes a moment. A beach was a tempting prospect. But he wouldn't want to vacation alone. He was afraid of solitude suddenly. He'd had enough of it. He looked at his wristwatch, took another sip of his drink.

The other Dawson, Thomas, was off in the Southwest somewhere, campaigning under the rubric of law and order, and generally bearing up under what one journalist called 'the stress of recent grief'. He had given an interview to *Newsweek* on the Irish question, during the course of which he wondered about the possibility of the US playing a greater role in bringing peace to Ireland. He wasn't specific, for which all his advisers were thankful.

Pagan shook his head. The world moves on, he thought. It keeps turning. And you couldn't keep the Irish down for very long.

The fiddler had begun to play that great Irish weepy *The Rose of Tralee*. Sometimes Pagan thought that there were only about twenty Irish songs in existence and they just kept circulating endlessly. The crowd in the bar was singing along with the musician. Pagan finished his drink. Tomorrow, London. A report for the secretary. Question and answer sessions. Reporters at the airport. He couldn't shake the feeling he'd come all this way for nothing. Screw London. Why didn't he change his plans? If he decided to step on another plane destined for a remote sunny place, what could anybody do to stop him? London seemed a drab prospect to him now, a cold season, wet streets and rooftops, sad little parks.

He looked inside his glass. He wondered if you could possibly tell your future from the pattern left by the froth of a Guinness. *You're going on a long journey, Frank.*

He pushed his empty glass away. He was thinking of Ivor McInnes and the woman called Celestine. Foxie, who had done some legwork in London, had called with the information that Ivor had indeed married the woman in a private ceremony in the Ulster town of Enniskillen in 1978. As for Celestine, it appeared that she'd been born in Belfast but raised in Boston by Irish-American parents, both of whom were fervent anti-Catholics. What she had drummed into her from the start was hatred. The hard-line stuff. Catholics are evil. They breed like rabbits. One day they'll dominate the world. We have to do something about them. Celestine Cunningham, as she was known, went back and forth between America and Ireland, where she became attached to the concept of Protestant supremacy in Ulster. She had bought the whole package, hatreds intact, bigotries in place. She was naturally suited to Ivor. And she was a natural for the Free Ulster Volunteers – indeed, their only female member. Northern Ireland wasn't a place where women went in great numbers into terrorist groups. Their role was expected to be more domestic.

Celestine and Ivor McInnes. Pagan tried to imagine the inner workings of Ivor McInnes. It was tough, Pagan could see the obsession somewhat, but he knew his insights were superficial and limited. There was no way in the world he could grasp the depths of Ivor, the byzantine workings of the brain, nor did he understand what the heart was made out of. There had to be as much patience as there was loathing in Ivor. That plan of his, for instance. Devious, time-consuming, having to make each play slowly. The bigamous marriage of Celestine to Harry Cairney – how long had it taken for McInnes to orchestrate that affair? He had somehow contrived to put Celestine Cunningham in Boston, in a position where she'd inevitably meet Harry Cairney and where her beauty would overwhelm the old man to the extent that he'd want to marry her. Pagan supposed that he might never know now how McInnes had latched on to Harry as one of the Fund-raisers in the first place. Maybe it had started with nothing more than a rumour, an item of gossip produced by one of McInnes's sources of intelligence, a thin possibility that Celestine, as soon as she was ensconced at Roscommon as the bride of the former Senator, confirmed for him. It had to be a strange precarious existence for the woman, watching Harry's activities, listening, spying, and then somehow reporting back to Ivor. Clandestine phone calls. Secret letters. Pagan realised he'd never know the extent of the communication between them.

He wondered if there were ever moments in McInnes's life when he lay awake thinking about his absent wife or if his cause were more important than the matter of sexual jealousy. Did he lie in a dark room and envisage his wife in Senator Cairney's bed? Did he sweat and clutch the bedsheets and stare at the window in anger and envy? Or was he more pragmatic than that, more patient, was his love for the woman subjugated to her usefulness to him? Pagan would never know.

And Jig.

Frank Pagan didn't want to think about Jig. He ordered a third Guinness, sipped it slowly. He could see, if he wanted to, the set of Jig's face as he lay dead at Roscommon. He could see the blood soak into the rug and the closed eyelids and the way the shadows on that landing left small scarlike marks across the skin. But these were images and had nothing to do with the substance of the man. And besides, he didn't want to entertain them. All he knew was that in some inexplicable way he felt a strange sense of loss. Strange because he hadn't known Jig well. Hadn't really known him at all.

He drank from his glass.

The fiddler was playing *The Mountains of Mourne*, Pagan thought he could have taken bets on that one. Later, it would be *Kevin Barry* and *Galway Bay* and *Johnny I hardly Knew Ye*.

He didn't intend to hang around for those tunes. He looked at his watch. He'd finish his drink, and if nothing had happened by then he'd leave. He didn't care if he never heard another Irish tune. He drained his glass, reluctant to set it down and go. But he couldn't linger here.

He thought of how Foxie had told him that all the known members of the Free Ulster Volunteers were being rounded up in Ireland and questioned about the *Connie O'Mara* and the missing money.

The money, Pagan thought. Long gone. Artie was on his way to Rio and Tyson Bruno was in Canada and the money had disappeared in such a manner that soon it would have the substance of legend and, like any lost treasure, attract all kinds of crackpots who claimed they had half of a map to its burial place and needed only the other section to disinter the cash. They came out of the woodwork when huge sums of money were inexplicably missing.

He saw his face in the bar mirror and thought, *Pale, Pagan. Far too white.* He wanted sandcastles and tides and exotic drinks and a woman's mouth.

He turned around when he felt the girl's hand on his sleeve.

She said, 'Sorry I'm late. I couldn't get my money to add up. I was short about nine dollars.'

'A hanging offence,' Pagan said.

She nudged him and smiled. 'It's quite serious.' She removed her shoulder-bag, which somehow managed to slip out of her grasp and tumble on the bar, where it fell open, showering out tubes of lipstick, a wallet, combs, hairgrips and tissues.

'Christ,' she said. 'It's like I can't help myself. Butterflies.'

'It's endearing. Don't worry about it.'

The girl scooped up the items back inside her purse. Pagan, thinking about his beach, turning over the sorry prospect of London in his mind, asked her what she wanted to drink.

'Something green,' she said.

'Green?'

'For St Patrick's Day.'

Pagan looked into her eyes. He felt a strong affection for this clumsy girl. He placed his hand over hers, surprised by his movement, his boldness. It was strange to be touching a woman after so long a time. It was strange and exciting and it took his breath away.

'You're not Irish, are you?' he said.

'With a name like Mandi Straub? You've got to be kidding.'

'So why a green drink!'

'Everybody's a little bit Irish on St Patrick's Day,' she replied.

Pagan put his hand inside the pocket of his coat. He took out an emerald ring he'd found in the hallway of the house at Roscommon. It had been lying close to the body of Ivor McInnes, hidden in the shadows of the staircase. He wasn't even sure now why he'd bothered to pick it up. He didn't know to whom it had belonged. It was a souvenir he didn't want to keep.

'This is green,' he said. He gave it to the girl. 'I want you to have it.'

She held it in the palm of her hand and smiled. 'I can't accept this.'

'Why not?'

'I hardly know you.'

Pagan was silent for a while. Before the night was out, he would somehow remedy that situation. He reached for her hand and closed her fingers gently over the ring.

'Keep it,' he said.

'Are you sure?'

'It's the appropriate colour.'

The girl smiled at him. 'Are you a little bit Irish too?' she asked.

Pagan considered this question for a time before he said, 'Only a little.'

Mazurka

I would like to thank Major R. B. Claybourne (USMCR) for his fine technical help; Mr Bruno Laan for being an indefatigable source of information who patiently answered my questions even when they were on arcane matters; and the Joint Baltic American National Committee for generously providing information that helped with the background to this novel. I would also like to thank Harriette Pine for kindly showing me Brooklyn and Brighton Beach in the dead of winter.

For the children – Iain, Stephen, Keiron and Leda

You must take a good look at reality and understand that in future small nations will have to disappear ... The Baltic nations will have to join the glorious family of the Soviet Union.

— V. M. Molotov,
Soviet Foreign Minister to V. Kreve-Mickevicius,
Deputy Prime Minister of Lithuania, July 1940

The fate of the three Baltic states is unique in human history. Nowhere else in the world are former parliamentary democracies occupied, annexed and colonised by a conquering power.

— The Copenhagen Manifesto, July 1985

The established habits and ideas are disintegrating before our eyes. The disappearance of something customary provokes protest. Conservatism does not want to give way but all this can and must be overcome ...

— Mikhail Gorbachev, *Perestroika*

Mazurka (n.) A Slavic dance in triple measure.

1

Edinburgh, Scotland

There were too many things wrong with Edinburgh in late August. The crowds that filled Princes Street and spilled over into the old thoroughfares leading up to the Castle, which floated in the drizzling mist like a great galleon, gave Jacob Kiviranna a sense of claustrophobia. He was distressed by crowds, especially those that consisted mainly of American and Japanese tourists, restless as magpies, searching for quaint bargains in stores with none to offer. And then there was the weather, which was wet and joyless. It had been raining in a slow, merciless way ever since he'd arrived in the city the day before and checked into a small hotel behind Hanover Street – and now he couldn't rid himself of the feeling that his lungs were waterlogged.

He looked at his watch, an old Timex, and saw he had thirty minutes until the train arrived at Waverley Station. He moved along Rose Street, Edinburgh's famous street of bars, passing open doorways through which he could see flocks of hurried drinkers. He stepped inside one of the pubs, sat on a stool at the far end of the counter – a solitary spot – and ordered gin.

In the mirror behind the bar he gazed at his reflection. The eyes were deeply set and bright and somehow made people uneasy when they looked into them. The few acquaintances Jacob Kiviranna had made in his lifetime – other than analysts and therapists – had invariably found pretexts for drifting out of his orbit and slipping from sight. There was an intensity about him, an other-worldliness, that deterred friendships. Even as he sat now in the bar his lips moved almost imperceptibly in the way of people who have lived lives of extreme loneliness and who converse, if at all, with the voices they hear in their own skulls.

Stitched to the left shoulder of his khaki combat jacket was a Disneyland legend, the face of Mickey Mouse. On the right sleeve was a small American flag. Kiviranna's ponytail was held tightly in place with a brown rubber band. He wore a wispy beard and looked like a superannuated hippie, a relic of another place and time. To a casual onlooker, he might have seemed like a raddled casualty of the drug culture, somebody who had taken one trip too many and hadn't quite managed to make it back and who now lived, poor soul, in a crazy world of his own making. And yet there was something more to Kiviranna than just this impression of being out of touch. There was something purposeful in his air of vague bewilderment, the kind of look aspirant saints carried back with them from the wilderness.

He sipped his drink, looked once again at his watch. If British Rail obeyed its own inscrutable timetables there were now twenty-five minutes until the train arrived on platform three at Waverley Station. He reached inside the pocket of his jacket and touched the gun. It was an Argentinian nine-shot Bersa 225. When he'd handled it in his hotel room this morning, he'd liked the icy blue finish of the pistol, the silken, almost fleshy sensation.

Twenty minutes. He left the bar without finishing his drink. It was a mere ten minutes to Waverley Station, hardly any distance at all, but he'd stroll there slowly.

On Princes Street he stared up at the Castle. It reminded him now of a natural artifact, something hacked by nature out of wind and rock and still in some weird process of change. Along the gardens of Princes Street flags fluttered bleakly. Posters advertising this or that Festival event were limp and soggy and indifferent. Avant-garde plays. Mime shows. Mozart. Pipe and drum bands.

Ahead, Kiviranna saw the entrance to the station. He paused, jostled on all sides by people with umbrellas and shopping-bags. A group of boys wearing the green and white scarves of a local soccer team went banging past him, singing something unintelligible and irritating. He put his hand against the outline of the gun as he moved closer to the station. There was a familiar pain that had come out of nowhere to take root deep in his head.

He heard the shunting of a locomotive and the shouts of newspaper vendors and the screeching brakes of maroon double-decker buses. For the first time now he felt a sudden fluttering of nerves, something that moved around his heart and made him cold. Something that had nothing to do with the external weather. He adjusted his backpack, stopped to look at the headline on one of the local newspapers, then he moved on.

He took a thin guidebook out of his jeans, pretended to examine it, flipping through the pages but seeing little.

Edinburgh has always been known as the Athens of the North.

The print seemed to slither in front of his eyes. The words might have turned to grey liquid. He put the guidebook away. He went down the steps that led to Waverley Station. He touched the gun once more, a small reassuring gesture. He wiped slicks of rain from his face, ran one hand through his damp beard. And there it was again, that sense of nervousness, of a tremor going through his heart, like some extra pulse added to the rhythms of his body. He'd have to bring that under control. He couldn't afford any rebellion inside himself.

He entered the station, a place of enormous confusion, late trains, loudspeaker announcements, stacks of luggage, discarded newspapers. Porters stood around like impatient gravediggers awaiting the end of a eulogy they'd heard a million times before. Kiviranna wandered through the huge station, scanning the platforms. The loudspeaker announcements bewildered him. Strange place names were uttered in strange accents. *Inverkeithing, Kirkcaldy. Kinghorn.* He studied the arrivals and departures board.

The pain in his head pulsated now and his jawbone felt locked. He hated the sensation because sometimes in the past it had given rise to the irrational fear, the suffocating fear, that his mouth would one day close and never open again. *Anxiety, Jake, sheer anxiety.* All the shrinks he'd ever encountered in institutions had told him that. And they gave him drugs with mellow names to assuage his fears, and sometimes they worked, sometimes not, and when they failed he'd sit for long, insomniac hours on the edge of his bed, wrapped in a blanket, shivering, imagining all manner of terrible things, hearing all kinds of weird sounds float up from the hostile street below the window of his apartment.

He moved to the gate of platform three. A ticket inspector glanced at him, then looked away. Another Yank. One of the impoverished ones. A middle-aged student doing Europe in five and a half days. The inspector had seen them all in his time. He'd seen fellows who looked exactly like Jacob Kiviranna, 'beatniks' – which was how the ticket inspector thought of them – coming from Amsterdam with marijuana in their shoes, shifty-eyed scruffs who muttered to themselves.

Kiviranna looked along the platform, which was stacked with mail sacks and trunks. He went to a newspaper stand where he browsed for a time. Then he wandered round the concourse of the station and studied the arrivals board again. Seven minutes. Seven minutes that were going to be very slow ones. Seven minutes before he could dispose of the evil that was presently sliding over slick railroad tracks toward Edinburgh.

Despite a bitch of a hangover, Frank Pagan was enjoying the task of escorting Aleksis Romanenko to Scotland. Normally Pagan had no real fondness for trains, for the musty compartments which, even in first class, were extremely uncomfortable. And views from carriage windows were less than breathtaking – the backs of granite houses and sorry little gardens and ramshackle greenhouses. Now and then a face in a rainy window gazed at the passing train as if such an event were the week's highlight.

But today Pagan felt detached from his dislikes. He had spent the previous evening riotously and quite unexpectedly drinking vodka with Romanenko in the Savoy Hotel in London, and now he was numb, and amazed by Romanenko's resilience. The Russian was in his middle fifties and yet he had the ability of a much younger man to bounce back from all the booze he'd drunk the night before.

Pagan, lulled by the rhythm of the train, looked across the compartment at Romanenko, who was holding forth in an exuberant way about the future of the computer industry in the Soviet Union. He demonstrated freely with his strong red hands, he shrugged, rolled his eyes, smiled a great deal – the kind of energetic man who couldn't keep still for very long and whose enthusiasms had a childlike, contagious quality.

Pagan tried to remember where last night had gone. It had begun with a courtesy call, he recollected that much. He'd visited Romanenko's room at the Savoy to discuss the timetable for this trip, and matters relating to security. Romanenko, with that demanding hospitality common to many Russians, produced a bottle of vodka and two glasses and insisted on drinking a toast to 'my new friend from Scotland Yard, my security guard, the very first Brottish policeman I am ever meeting in my life' – a toast that inevitably spawned another, then another, until finally a second bottle was opened and Pagan had the feeling he'd known Romanenko all his life. There had been warm handshakes, embraces, enthusiastic talk about a new purpose, a new spirit, inside the Soviet Union. *You will see differences, Frank Pagan, such as you have never dreamed of. Big changes are coming*. And here Aleksis had looked almost sly, a man privy to information Pagan could not have guessed in a thousand years. Given to winks and nudges and physical contact, he had the manner of somebody bursting to reveal crucial information and yet prohibited from doing so. *Big changes. Big surprises. Wait and see, Frank Pagan.*

Pagan thought he remembered the Russian crying tears of joy somewhere along the way and how the toasts had become more and more fulsome, with references to coexistence and peacefulness and how the 'Rosha' of the future was going to be. *A country, my friend Frank Pagan, for the twentieth century! Yes! Out of the Middle Ages and into the wonderful world of the computer! Yes! A hundred times yes! Let us drink another toast to the new Rosha! And to you and me, Frank Pagan, let us drink to a new friendsheep!* And then they'd gone together down to the bar, because Romanenko had the urge to strike up more *friendsheeps*, this time with women, and all Pagan could remember of the trip was Romanenko's ruddy face surveying the bar with lecherous intent, then the way he'd dragged a reticent young woman out of her chair and danced with her between the tables, his arms thrown around her waist and shoulders and his great laughter sweeping aside her delicate protests.

Pagan had a foggy recollection of making it home in a taxi – but the memory was too dim to fix with any certainty. Now, bright-eyed and irrepressible, Romanenko was laughing as he told some horror story about industrial sloth in the Soviet Union. He had a huge repertoire of jokes on the subject of the inconveniences of Russian life, and he related them with an actor's gusto in an English that was often muddled yet always charming.

Apart from Pagan and Romanenko, there was a third man in the compartment. Danus Oates was a middle level official from the Foreign Office, a young man with a pleasantly bland face and a plummy accent that suggested Eton or Harrow. Oates, whose function was to act as a kind of tour guide for the Russian, wasn't a great conversationalist. His talk was limited to such topics as the weather and some background chat about the history of Edinburgh, which he delivered like somebody who has swallowed a recorded message.

In the corridor of the train there was a man from Special Branch and a sullen character, presumably KGB, from the Soviet Embassy. Security surrounding the Russian wasn't especially tight. There hadn't been any death threats or virulent anti-Soviet propaganda in the newspapers or any outpourings of nationalist sentiment from the rabid groups that despised Russia. And Romanenko, after all, was just one anonymous official from a Russian outpost in the Baltic. The protection afforded him was little more than a courtesy, but it was Frank Pagan's responsibility to make sure that the Russian attended the Festival, heard the music he wanted to hear, Prokofiev's Classical Symphony, and was returned to London the following day in one piece – and Pagan took the job as seriously as he could.

'Are we close to Edinburgh?' Romanenko asked, gazing out of the window with some excitement. Like a boy on his first trip overseas, Pagan thought. The flushed expression, the voice a little too loud.

Danus Oates said that it would be another ten minutes or so. Romanenko smiled, lit a cigarette, a Player's, and fell silent for perhaps the only time since the train had left London.

Pagan stared out of the window. It was one of those leaden Scottish afternoons – drab skies and a low heaven, beneath which the granite houses, stained by rain, looked squat and depressing.

'Wish we'd had a better day,' Danus Oates remarked. He had an upper-class Englishman's attitude to Scotland. It was an English colony where there were only two things of conversational significance – grouse-shooting and salmon-fishing.

The Russian shrugged. 'Rain is not a problem to me, my friend. In Rosha, finding a good umbrella – that's the problem.'

Pagan smiled, closed his eyes, drifted for a time.

Romanenko and Oates were, of all things, discussing roses now, a scarlet clutch of which Romanenko had just noticed in a backyard. Oates didn't know a rose from a rhododendron but he'd been trained in the craft of small talk and he made it with consummate ease. It transpired that Romanenko's hobby was rose-growing and he discussed it with the same enthusiasm he had for everything else, his hands caressing the air around him as if it were a delicate flower. He apparently had quite a garden at his dacha on the shores of the Baltic.

He took a wallet out of his pocket and showed Oates some photographs. Oates went into his head-nodding mode.

Pagan, who needed to stretch his legs and check to see if his hungover circulation was still functioning, excused himself and stepped out into the corridor, where he slid one of the windows open and enjoyed the feel of cold rain on his skin.

The man from Special Branch who stood in the corridor considered Pagan eccentric. To his way of thinking, Pagan didn't belong in the club. His clothes – brown shirt, beige necktie undone, a slightly baggy two-piece tan suit, brown canvas espadrilles – were wrong. His manner was wrong. He didn't have the right attitude. The man from Special Branch, who was called John Downey, resented the idea of Pagan being in charge of the security around Romanenko and so he thought sullen thoughts when it came to Frank.

With the special kind of malice that is often found inside a bureaucracy, certain members of Special Branch had been jubilant when Pagan had returned empty-handed last year from the United States where he'd gone in pursuit of an IRA gunman. There were even a few who had rowdily celebrated the disbandment of Pagan's own anti-terrorist section over drinks in a pub called The Sherlock Holmes. From the accounts Pagan had heard, it was an evening of gloating merriment. For his own part, Pagan didn't give a damn what his colleagues thought of him. He had never lived his life to please other people and he wasn't about to let the opinions of morons trouble him now.

John Downey's waxed moustache suggested something faintly colonial. He had the face of a man who might have watched the last flag of the British Empire come down from the flagpole at the final outpost. He had the deflated cheeks of an old bugler.

'I had better plans for Saturday than this,' Downey said. 'Spurs are at home to Arsenal. I wanted to be at White Hart Lane.'

Frank Pagan didn't share the great British passion for soccer. He watched the daylight disappear as the train plunged briefly into a tunnel, then the darkness was gone again and Downey's face came back into focus.

Downey peered into the compartment at the Russian. 'He's not much to look at for a First Secretary of the Communist Party.'

Pagan wondered if Downey would have been more impressed by a hammer and sickle tattoo on Romanenko's forehead. He found himself gazing at a globule of moisture that clung to the impenetrable hairs of Downey's moustache. The sight amused him.

'It's a job, John,' Pagan said. 'Think of yourself as a delivery boy. One Russian brought to Edinburgh, then hauled back to London again. And everybody's happy.'

Downey appeared to consider this, as if he suspected a buried insult in the reference to a delivery boy. Then Downey's face changed to a leer. 'At least he's not Irish. Is he, Frank?'

Pagan smiled in a thin way. Men like Downey, when they had the hold of a bone, never quite managed to let it go. For many months now, Downey had brought up the subject of Ireland on any pretext. It was infantile, Pagan knew, but it appeared to feed some deep, ludicrous need inside Downey's heart. What a life Downey had to live, Pagan thought. He had his football games and the task of waxing his bloody moustache and what else – beyond making tasteless remarks at Pagan's expense? It was a life that was difficult to imagine in its entirety. And yet not difficult, perhaps just appallingly easy. Despite himself, despite his resolve never to respond to sorry barbs, Pagan had an urge to slash back at Downey in some way – but that required an energy he hadn't been able to find in himself lately. He was treading water, going through the motions, listless. The death of the IRA gunman had pleased some people inside the hierarchy at Scotland Yard. They could at least claim that the man known as Jig was no longer a menace. And there had been a half-hearted attempt to make Frank Pagan some kind of hero, but it was doomed to failure because it was a role Pagan didn't have the heart for. Besides, credit for the gunman's death – if credit was an appropriate word – had been attributed to the FBI. In the end, there had been nothing remotely heroic in the death of the Irish assassin, and it had left Frank Pagan with a sour taste in his mouth.

Now, following the dissolution of his own Irish section, he'd been doing odd jobs for months, mainly guarding visiting dignitaries from African and Commonwealth countries, or Communist tourists like Aleksis Romanenko, who came to Britain to do a little business and squeeze in some sightseeing in this quaint green land.

He stared at Downey. 'As you say, John. He's not Irish.'

Downey's smile was like a bruise on his face. He enjoyed scoring points against Pagan, especially when Pagan failed to rise to his own defence. 'Because if he was a mick, Frank, they wouldn't let you near him with a ten-foot pole, would they?'

Pagan slid the window open a little further and rain blew into Downey's eyes, making him mutter and blink and reach for a handkerchief in his coat pocket. Such a small triumph, Pagan thought. The trouble with a man like Downey was how he reduced you to his own idiotic level. He watched John Downey rub his face with the handkerchief. Moisture had caused the wax moustache to lose some of its glossy stiffness, and now it curled above Downey's upper lip like a furry caterpillar.

'Sorry about that, John,' Pagan said. 'I hope you brought your waxing kit with you,' and he shut the window quickly, stepping back inside the compartment. The train was already beginning to slow as it approached Waverley Station.

Romanenko looked up expectantly. 'Are we there?' he asked.

'A minute or so,' Pagan replied.

'Excellent, excellent.' Romanenko stood up, clutching his briefcase to his side. He wore a very British Burberry raincoat and shoes of fine Italian leather, soft and gleaming.

'Do we see the Castle soon?' Romanenko asked.

'Very,' Danus Oates answered.

Pagan watched the platform loom up. When the train came finally to a halt, Pagan opened the door of the compartment and climbed down. Romanenko came immediately after him and almost at once John Downey fell into step beside the Russian, who was sniffing the air deeply and saying how railway stations smelled the same the world over, an observation with which Oates, whose experience of railways was minimal, readily agreed. The sullen man from the Soviet Embassy walked several feet behind the group looking this way and that, his head, reminiscent of a pumpkin, swivelling on the thick stalk of his neck.

Pagan stared the length of the platform, aware of people disembarking from the train, being met by relatives, little reunions, porters hauling baggage, mail sacks being unloaded – too much activity to follow at one time. Too many people. Pagan, who was walking about five or six feet ahead of the Russian, looked in the direction of the ticket-barrier, some twenty yards away. Beyond the gate there were more crowds. The bloody Festival, he thought. And a local soccer game into the bargain. There was no real control here. The environment wasn't properly sealed. And that made him uneasy. But uneasiness was something that plagued him these days, a sense of groundless anxiety. He supposed it was part of his general mood, his indecision, the feeling that his life and career were a pair of bloody mongrels going nowhere in particular.

'I understand we have a car waiting outside the station,' Danus Oates said. 'We're to dine at the George Hotel, which is said to be the best in the city. The chef is preparing Tay salmon in an unusual manner in honour of your visit.'

Pagan wondered what was meant by 'unusual' in this case. He hoped it wasn't going to be some nouvelle cuisine monstrosity, salmon in raspberry sauce with poached kiwi fruit. He had a sudden longing for plain old fish and chips smothered in malt vinegar and eaten out of a greasy newspaper, preferably *The News of the World* with its lurid tales of child-molesting vicars. He had an urge to whisk Romanenko away from any official arrangements and plunge with him into the side-streets of this city, into the dark little pubs and alleyways and courtyards, into the places where people really lived their lives. This is the way it really is, Aleksis. This is what you don't find in the restaurant of the George Hotel.

'We must visit the Castle after we've eaten,' Romanenko said. The eagerness in his voice was unmistakable. He had a thing about the Castle.

'Of course,' Oates replied.

Pagan looked towards the ticket-barrier. Crowds were milling around. Loudspeaker announcements reverberated in the air. Through the station exit, some distance beyond the barrier, Pagan saw a square of rainy grey sky. A bleak Saturday afternoon in August in what he considered the most austere of European capitals. Behind him, Romanenko was staring up at the vast glass ceiling of the station.

They reached the ticket-barrier, Pagan still a few feet in front of Romanenko and the others. Which was when it happened.

When Jacob Kiviranna saw the train come to a dead halt, he was standing about six feet beyond the ticket-barrier. He took a few steps forward, pushing his way through the crowd, his hand covering the pocket that contained the gun. It was strange now how utterly detached he felt.

He watched Romanenko's group approach the barrier. There were five in all. Romanenko was talking to a man in a camel-hair coat and pinstriped suit. On Romanenko's left side was a well-built man with a dark moustache. In front of the Russian was a tall short-haired man in a tan suit, who moved with a watchful sense of purpose. And in the rear was the fifth man whose overcoat and haircut identified him as Russian, most likely KGB.

Kiviranna focused on Romanenko as he came through the barrier. Then he stepped closer, squeezing himself between a porter and a group of genteel elderly Scottish women with walking-sticks and umbrellas who were trying to induce the porter to carry their luggage. Kiviranna reached into his pocket and removed the Bersa, concealing it in the palm of his hand. He needed one clear shot, that was all. One clear shot at Romanenko.

Kiviranna brought the gun up. The sound of loudspeaker announcements detonated inside his head and then dissolved in a series of meaningless echoes, because he was conscious now of nothing save the short distance between his pistol and Romanenko's face.

With an expression of horrified disbelief, Romanenko saw the gun and raised his briefcase up in front of his eyes, a futile attempt to protect himself. Kiviranna fired directly into the Russian's heart, and as Romanenko screamed and collapsed on the ground and his briefcase slithered away from him and panicked pigeons flapped out of their roosting places in the high roof, Kiviranna turned and started to run. But the tall man in the tan-coloured suit, who had hesitated only a second in the aftermath of the gunfire, seized him roughly around the waist in the manner of an American football or rugby player and dragged him to the ground.

Frank Pagan, struggling with the gunman, disarming him, clamping cuffs on his wrists, was conscious of old ladies yelping and porters hurrying back and forth and the appearance of two uniformed policemen who immediately began to keep curious onlookers away – including a group of soccer fans who had apparently decided that the violence in Waverley Station was more authentic than any they might see on a soccer field. There was chaos, and that was a state of affairs Pagan did not remotely like. There was chaos and gunfire and he hadn't been able to prevent this awful situation from happening and that galled him as much as anything.

Pagan left the handcuffed gunman face down beneath the watchful eyes of one of the uniformed policemen, then he turned to look at Romanenko, who lay flat on his back with his eyes open, as if it were not death that had paralysed him but a catatonic trance. There was a dreadful wound in Romanenko's chest, and Danus Oates kept saying 'Oh my God, my God,' as if the killing would mean a demotion for him inside the Foreign Office.

John Downey, who at least knew how to behave around a murder scene, was wading into the spectators and cursing as he roughly pushed them back. It was all madness, that special kind of disorganised lunacy which surrounds any scene of blood. It was the way flies were drawn to feed and bloat themselves on a fresh carcass, and in this case the carcass was one Frank Pagan had been supposed to protect. But he'd failed and Romanenko, the ebullient Romanenko, the enthusiast, the new friend, lay dead.

You weren't supposed to let this kind of thing happen, Pagan thought. This was going to be an easy job. The kind of work any nanny should have been able to accomplish without breaking sweat. And now suddenly it was a mess and he felt the muscles of his stomach knot. Oates, like a somnambulist, was reaching down to pick up Romanenko's briefcase, which had fallen alongside Aleksis's body.

The man from the Soviet Embassy, who hadn't uttered a word all the way from London, said, 'Please, the case,' and he made a move in Oates's direction, stretching out his hand to take the briefcase away from the young Englishman.

Pagan stepped between Oates and the Russian. He seized the case from Oates and held it against his side. 'It stays with me,' he said.

'On the contrary, Mr Pagan,' the Russian said in immaculate English. 'It goes back to the Soviet Embassy. It may contain business documents that are the property of the Soviet Union. Private material. Confidential matters.'

'I don't care if it contains the Five Year Plan for the whole of bloody Siberia,' Pagan said. 'It stays with me. A man has been murdered and the case may contain material evidence of some kind. If it doesn't, you'll get it back.'

Danus Oates muttered something about the possibility of a diplomatic incident, as if there were no words more blasphemous in his entire vocabulary. Pagan gripped the briefcase fiercely.

The Russian looked at Oates. 'Explain to Mr Pagan that the briefcase is Soviet property. Explain international law to him, please.'

Oates stammered. His tidy little world had collapsed all about him and he appeared unsure of everything – diplomatic protocol, international law, perhaps even his own identity. He had the expression of a man who suddenly discovers, late in life, that he's adopted. 'I'm not sure, it's outside my province,' was what he finally blurted out. Pagan almost felt sorry for him. Good breeding and all the proper schools hadn't prepared Danus Oates for violence, other than the kind in which pheasants were despatched by gentlemen with shotguns.

'I keep the case,' Pagan snapped. 'And that's final.' The Russian wasn't easily appeased. He reached towards Pagan and tried to pull the briefcase away. Pagan placed a hand upon the Russian's shoulder and pushed him back – a moment of unseemly jostling that might quite easily have led to further violence had it not been for the fact that there were policemen everywhere now, plainclothes men from the Edinburgh Criminal Investigation Department, uniformed cops dragged away from soccer duty, sirens whining, ambulances roaring through the rain. Pagan, clutching the briefcase to his side, was suddenly drained by events – and at the same time angered by what he saw as his own delinquency in performing a task that should have been as simple as sucking air.

A tall man with white and rather theatrical side-whiskers appeared at Pagan's side. He introduced himself as Inspector Dalrymple of the Edinburgh CID. He had a melancholy manner and he surveyed the scene with the unhappy expression of a drama critic at an amateur performance. Pagan took out his ID and showed it to the Inspector, who looked suitably impressed.

'I wish this hadn't happened in respectable old Edinburgh, Mr Pagan. Gives the place an awfully bad name.' He stared first at the corpse, then at the handcuffed gunman, who lay motionless on the ground. 'I'll give you a hand getting the body out of the way. The least I can do. Keep Edinburgh clean, eh? Don't frighten the tourists. After all, this isn't Glasgow,' and Dalrymple chuckled briefly, because Glasgow's reputation as a rough, criminal city was something Edinburgh people never tired of gloating over.

The Inspector, stroking his copious whiskers, began to issue orders to various policemen. Ambulance men, those attendants of injury and death, had appeared with a stretcher. Pretty soon there would be nothing left, no traces of the violence that had happened in this place. Pretty soon there would be nothing but dried bloodstains and a memory of murder. Pagan watched the body of Romanenko being raised on to a stretcher with a certain finality. But nothing was final here at all and Frank Pagan knew it.

John Downey had appeared out of the crowd and stood beside him. Crow, Pagan thought.

Downey blew his nose loudly, then studied the centre of his handkerchief, grotesquely fascinated by his own effluence. 'Well, Pagan,' he said, folding the handkerchief into his pocket. 'This is what I'd call a fine kettle of fish.'

'One thing I always liked about you, John, is your original turn of phrase.'

Downey smiled, and it was a brutal little twist of his lips. 'You're up shit creek, Frank. Romanenko was your baby and you let him slip down the plughole with the bathwater. The Commissioner's going to need an extra dose of the old digitalis to cope with this one, chum.'

Shit creek, Pagan thought. It was a stagnant waterway he knew intimately. He stared at Downey. There was an urge to strike out suddenly, a longing to stifle the man. He resisted the desire even as he realised that it was the first really passionate yearning he'd felt in many months. There was spirit in him yet, he thought – and despite the chaos around him it warmed his blood and it made his nerves tingle and it kicked his sluggish system into some kind of life. All this might be a mess, but it was his own to straighten out. He had become the proprietor of a bad situation, like a man who has unexpectedly inherited a house he later discovers has been condemned.

The goon from the Soviet Embassy, who had been lingering close to Pagan as if he might still get a chance to snatch the briefcase away, said, 'I promise you, Pagan. Unless you hand over the case, you have not heard the last of this.'

That promise was the one thing of certainty, Pagan thought, in an uncertain state of affairs. He turned and walked back to the place where the handcuffed gunman lay motionless.

The big man who stood that same night on the ramparts of Edinburgh Castle wore a charcoal suit especially made for him by an exclusive tailor who operated out of basement premises on East 32nd Street in Manhattan. He also wore a matching fedora, pulled down rather firmly over his head. He had a craggy face dominated by a misshapen nose. It was the kind of face one sometimes saw on former boxers but the eyes were clear and had none of that dullness, that dead-dog quality, that afflicts old fighters. He was sixty years old and still muscular and hard the way he'd always been because condition was important to him. In the past, it was condition that had saved his life. He was still proud of his body.

He removed a cigarette from a silver case and lit it with a gold Dunhill lighter on which his initials, M.K., had been engraved in a craftsman's script. He never inhaled smoke. He blew a cloud from his mouth and looked down across rainy Edinburgh, marvelling at the damp nimbi that glowed here and there in the night and the floodlit monuments. The rain, which had been sweeping relentlessly across the city, had slowed now to little more than a drizzle and the night had a quite unexpected beauty, almost a magnificence, that touched the man.

From the distance he could hear a sound of bagpipes and although it was strange music to him, nevertheless the despair in the notes, the unfulfillable longing, moved him. Scotland was not his own country – but very little separated him from his native land. The North Sea, Scandinavia, the Baltic. It was hardly any distance at all. He felt a painful twinge of homesickness. But then he'd grown accustomed to that sensation over the years and whereas it had troubled him deeply in the past, now he was in control of it. But only up to a point, he thought. Because every so often he was still astonished by the way the sensation could creep up on him and, like some wintry vulture, claw his heart.

He crushed his cigarette underfoot. Tonight was not the night for those old predatory birds. Tonight was not the time for remembering that he hadn't seen Estonia since 1949, when he'd been captured by Soviet forces and shipped inside an overcrowded freight car to Siberia, where he'd survived along with other Baltic freedom fighters, along with many thousands of the dispossessed – brave Latvians, valiant Lithuanians, headstrong, determined men who might have lost the battle but would one day win the war, because they had a secret weapon Stalin and all his butchers could never strip away from them. They had hatred.

He moved along the ramparts, wishing – dear God, how he wished – he was strolling along the cobblestones of Pikk Street, past Mustpeade clubhouse, through the Suur Rannavarav and down to Tallinn Harbour to look at the ships. Or passing the medieval Kiek-in-de-Kök cannon tower and the Linda statue to reach Hirve Park where he had walked hand-in-hand many times with his wife Ingrida on those summer nights in June when it seems the sun will never sink in the sky. It had become a dream to him, a dream of a dead city, a beautiful corpse bathed in pearly light.

But he wasn't going to yield to memories. In any event he'd heard how the Tallinn of his recollection had changed with Soviet occupation – the Russians had torn historic buildings down, renamed streets, and erected those dreary blocks of high-rise apartments that were so deadeningly characteristic of Communist architecture.

He checked his wristwatch. It was almost nine. He had been waiting for more than an hour. But what was a mere hour when weighed against the forty-three years that had passed since the Russians had 'liberated' his country? Old men learned one thing. They learned how to sing in the soft voices of patience.

He looked at the young man who stood alongside him. In the young man's blue eyes the lights of the city were reflected.

'He's not coming, Mikhail,' the young man said. He was extraordinarily handsome, at times almost angelic, but he had no self-consciousness about the perfection of his looks because external appearances meant very little to him. When he entered a restaurant, or stepped inside a crowded room, he turned heads and fluttered hearts and caused glands to work overtime – he affected people, mainly women, in ways that rarely interested him. This coldness, this seeming indifference, only enhanced his physical desirability. He wasn't merely a handsome young man, he was a challenging presence in the landscape, and difficult to conquer.

Mikhail Kiss looked away from his nephew and made an indeterminate gesture with his enormous hands. He had killed with those hands. He had dug graves with them and buried his dead comrades with them. 'If he isn't coming, then he's bound to have a damn good reason.'

'Like what?'

Mikhail Kiss shrugged. Who could say? Meetings were hard to arrange, and sometimes things went wrong, timetables became confused, time zones were overlooked, planes were delayed, trains ran late, a hundred accidents could happen. Nothing was perfect in this world anyway – except revenge, which he carried protectively in a special place deep inside his heart. He nurtured revenge, and fed it carefully the way someone might tend an exquisite plant. Vengeance was precious to him, and vows that had been taken long ago were not forgotten. He was a man who still breathed the atmosphere of the past.

He moved closer to the young man, seeing the way a muscle worked tensely in the cheek and how the blond hair, which lay lightly upon the collar of his raincoat, was speckled with drops of very fine rain.

'Something must have gone wrong, Mikhail.'

Mikhail Kiss squeezed his nephew's shoulder. He didn't say anything. He never allowed himself to think the very worst until there was no alternative. Leaping to conclusions was a sport for the young and tempestuous.

The young man, whose name was Andres Kiss, leaned upon the stone parapet and looked down through the darkness that rose up around the rock on which the Castle had been built. He restlessly rubbed the rough surface of stone with the palm of one hand. A person with a sense of history might have imagined, even for the briefest time, the touch of the mason who had put the stone in place many centuries ago. He might even have imagined calloused skin, a face, a concentrated expression, and marvelled at how the past created echoes in the present. But Andres Kiss's sense of history went back a mere forty years, and no further.

He turned his face away from the sight of the city spread out beneath him, and he looked at his uncle. 'I have a bad feeling in my gut,' he said. 'I don't think he's going to come.'

A gust of wind blew soft rain at Mikhail Kiss's eyes, and he blinked. He felt exactly as his nephew did, that something had gone wrong, that down there in the shadowy pools between lamps and neon signs something altogether unexpected had happened to Aleksis Romanenko.

2

Zavidovo, the Soviet Union

The cottage was a simple three-room building located on the edge of Zavidovo, a one hundred and thirty square mile wilderness some ninety miles from Moscow. The house was surrounded by trees and practically invisible until one was within twenty yards of the place. It was reached by means of a mud track, which was severely rutted. Dimitri Volovich had some trouble holding the car steady on the awful surface, especially in the dark. He parked a hundred feet from the cottage, then stepped out and opened the rear door for Colonel V. G. Epishev, who emerged into a blackness penetrated only by the soft light from one of the cottage windows.

Epishev ran a finger inside his mouth, probing for an annoyingly stubborn particle of the apple he'd eaten on the way from Moscow. He had a pleasant round face, the kind you might associate with a favourite uncle. It wasn't memorable, which suited him very nicely. In the West he could have passed for a stockbroker or a certified public accountant. His manner, which he'd cultivated over years of service in one or other Directorate of the KGB, was indeed avuncular, sometimes kindly in a way that disarmed even people who were his sworn enemies. And he was known among these enemies – a diverse group that included political dissidents he'd imprisoned or practising Christians he'd dissected or errant Jews he'd shipped in the opposite direction from Israel and into a colder climate than they desired – as Uncle Viktor, although no affection was implied by the term.

He turned towards the lighted window, hearing Greshko's music issuing from the house. An incongruous sound in the Russian night. He wondered what it was that the old man found so absorbing in American country songs. It was a weird taste Greshko had acquired in the late 1940s, when he'd spent six months as *rezident* in Washington at the Soviet Embassy.

Epishev, followed by Lieutenant Volovich, entered the cottage. Neither man was at ease in this place. As officers of the KGB, they had no compelling, official reason to visit Greshko, who had been removed a year ago from his position as Chairman of State Security. He was therefore non-existent, *persona non grata* inside ruling circles – even if there were those who feared him still and who awaited news of his death with considerable impatience.

The nurse appeared in the doorway of the bedroom. She was a small black-haired girl from the Yakut, and her oriental features had a plump-cheeked innocence. Epishev was never sure about her. She went about her business briskly, and her Russian was very poor, and she seemed to think it perfectly natural that Greshko would have visitors – but you could never tell. The Colonel, who had lived much of his life promoting a sense of paranoia in others, didn't care to experience the feeling for himself.

'He's awake,' the nurse said. Her uniform was unnaturally white, almost phosphorescent in the thin light of the room.

Epishev and Volovich went towards the bedroom door. The music filled the air, a flutter of fiddles, a scratching Epishev found slightly painful. The bedroom was lit only by a pale lamp on the bedside table and the red and green glow of lights from Greshko's sophisticated stereophonic equipment, which the old man had had imported from Denmark.

Greshko's face emerged from the shadows. Once, it had been large and round, reminding Epishev of an angry sun. Now, changed by terminal illness, the skin was transparent and the eyes, still brightly piercing, were the only things that suggested any of Greshko's former fire. Angular and terrible, the features appeared to draw definition from the shallow pools of light in the small room. When he spoke, Greshko's voice was no longer the harsh commanding thing it had been before, a dictatorial instrument, imperious and thrilling. The cancer had spread to his throat and when he said anything he did so laboriously, barely able to raise his voice above a rasping whisper. A length of plastic tubing ran from Greshko's body to a point under the bed. It was transparent and would fill now and then with brown liquid, the wastes of Greshko's stomach. Or what was left of it.

Epishev moved nearer the bed. He tried to ignore the smell of death that hung around the old man. He concentrated on the dreadful music, as if that might help. A man with a nasal condition was singing.

As I walk along beside her up the golden stair,
I know they'll never take her love from me.

'Poor Viktor,' Greshko said. 'You never liked my music, did you? You made passable attempts at trying, didn't you?'

Epishev was held by Greshko's eyes, as he'd been trapped so many times in the old days. If Epishev had ever had a true friend in a life that was almost entirely solitary, it had to be Vladimir Greshko. Only Greshko's patronage and protection had spared Epishev the whimsical wrath of Stalin, at a time when Stalin was launched on still another purge of Soviet society and Epishev had been a young man of twenty-two, barely at the start of his career. His youthful ambition, so far as he'd ever been able to comprehend, had been his only 'crime'. And Greshko's intervention with the Great Leader had saved Epishev the long one-way trip to Siberia. Epishev remembered this with a gratitude that would never diminish. He had repaid the debt with years of unquestioning loyalty to Greshko.

Greshko made a small gesture with one thin white hand. 'Come closer.'

Epishev sat on the edge of the bed. This close to Greshko, he thought he could see death, as though it were a shadow that fell across Greshko's face. 'Listen a moment,' the old man said. And his hand, a claw of bone, dropped over Epishev's wrist. 'Listen to the music.'

Epishev shut his eyes and pretended to concentrate.

If tonight the sun should set
On all my hopes and cares

Greshko said, 'Do you hear it, Viktor?'

Epishev looked into the old man's eyes. He wasn't sure what he was supposed to hear.

'Ach,' Greshko said impatiently. 'You're too young. Too young.'

It was an odd thing how Epishev at the age of fifty-five always felt young and inexperienced in Greshko's presence, always the neophyte in the presence of the old master. Nobody knew Greshko's real age, which was somewhere between eighty and eighty-five.

'You never knew what it was like to build the railways in the 1920s, how could you? The great spaces. The sky, Viktor. That endless sky.'

Epishev couldn't see the connections here, couldn't tell which way the old man was going. Since his sickness and removal from office, Greshko had increasingly rambled in directions that were hard to follow at times. Epishev had heard how, as a young man caught up in that first dizzying outbreak of Bolshevik success, Greshko had gone into the wilderness beyond Sverdlosk to lay railway tracks. It was a period of his life the old man reminisced about frequently.

'That's the sound of it all,' Greshko said. 'In that music, there's the sound of the endless sky. And the wind across the plains, Viktor. That's what I always hear. I don't understand all the words, but the feelings – always the feelings. Why does it take an American to capture something so plaintive?'

Epishev glanced at Volovich, thin and motionless and uncomfortable in the doorway. To Volovich's right was a stack of record albums, perhaps a hundred or so in some disarray. Epishev, who had an excellent command of English, could read the names of certain singers. Hank Williams. Johnny Cash. Bill Monroe. Smiling men in cowboy hats. He wondered how they could smile so, when they produced such miserable sounds.

The music came to an end and there was a silence in the bedroom, broken only by the sucking noise created by the plastic tube.

'What has Birthmark Billy been doing recently, Viktor?' Birthmark Billy was the derogatory way Greshko referred to the new General Secretary of the Party, a man he loathed so much he could never bring himself to use the proper name. 'Tell me the latest news. Has he been tearing things apart again?'

'He had the Director of the KGB in Krasnoyarsk arrested on a charge of corruption.'

'Krasnoyarsk? That would be Belenko. Belenko was one of my own.'

'Yes,' Epishev said.

Greshko was suddenly restless. His hands fluttered in the air. 'Soon there won't be a single institution, a single law, a single custom he hasn't attacked and changed. This whole society will have been altered beyond recognition. Don't doubt this, Viktor, but one day in the very near future these changes are going to affect you as well. You'll go into your office as usual and you'll find the furniture has been moved around and a total stranger is sitting where you used to sit. And they'll send you to Gorki where, if you're lucky, you'll find yourself directing traffic. And if you're unlucky, Colonel Epishev . . . ' Greshko's hands dropped to his side and something – some spark of life – seemed to subside inside him. He lay very still.

Epishev had heard this speech before in one form or another, and now he waited for the fire to build in Greshko again, as he knew it would. He was also puzzled why he and Volovich had been ordered to come to this place at such an hour, but he couldn't hurry Greshko, who never volunteered information until he was ready to do so. The old man sighed and turned his face toward the lamp and Epishev could see the scar on his throat where the surgeon had gone in with a knife.

'God damn him,' Greshko said quietly. 'God damn him and his cronies.' The old man stared at Volovich. 'Close the door, Dimitri.'

Volovich did so. With the door closed, the air in the room was charged with the electricity of conspiracy.

Greshko said, 'The Russian people need the whip of authority. They don't need some quack who comes along and drops tantalising hints about how there are going to be some new freedoms. Elections! A free press! More consumer goods in stores! You don't find the Russian spirit in democracy and better nylon stockings and finer toothbrushes and imported French wines! The people don't understand these things. They don't want them because they don't know how to use them. And even if they deceive themselves into thinking they do want these things, they're not ready for them.' Greshko paused. His breathing was becoming harsh and laboured.

The strange voice was subdued now, almost inaudible. 'What the new crowd fails to understand is that the Russian people need a little fear in their lives. They need emotional austerity. Stalin understood it. Brezhnev, who was a lazy bastard in many ways, also understood it. And I understood it when I ran the KGB. But this new gang! This new gang thinks they have a magic wand and they can wave it and everything will change overnight. They fail to realise this isn't the West. Democracy isn't our historic destiny. Adversity is the glue that has always held Russia together.'

Greshko raised himself up once more with an amazing effort of will and looked towards Volovich.

'Put something on the turntable, Dimitri,' he said.

Volovich found an album and played it. It was a man singing about his life in a place called Folsom Prison and it was very maudlin. Epishev wanted to get up from the place where he sat and put a little distance between himself and the wretched plastic tube, but he didn't move. Even as he lay dying, there was a magnetism about Greshko, perhaps less well-defined these days but still a force Epishev knew he couldn't resist.

Greshko licked his dark lips, stared up at the ceiling, seemed to be listening less to the sounds from the speakers than to some inner melody of his own. He moved his face slowly back to Epishev and said, 'Romanenko is dead.'

So that was the reason for this midnight summons! For a moment Epishev didn't speak. Greshko's sentence, so baldly stated, floated through his mind.

'Dead? How?'

'Shot by a gunman in a railway station in Edinburgh about six hours ago.'

'A gunman? Who?'

'I have no more information,' Greshko said. 'I only learned about the assassination less than two hours ago,' and he twisted his neck to peer at the bedside telephone, as if he expected it to ring immediately with more news. So far as Greshko was concerned the phone was both a blessing and a threat. His various contacts and sympathisers around the country could always keep in touch with him, but at the same time they always had to be circumspect when they called, because they were afraid of tapped lines and tape-recorders, and so a curious kind of code had evolved, a sub-language of unfinished sentences, half-phrases, substitutions, a terminology whose caution Greshko disliked. He had always preferred forthright speech and down-to-earth images and now it seemed to him that more than his exalted position had been stripped from him – they'd taken his language away from him too.

Epishev asked, 'How does this affect us?'

Greshko smiled, a weird little expression, lopsided, like that of a man recovering from a severe stroke. And then suddenly he looked bright, more like the Greshko of old, the one who had regarded the delegation of authority as a fatal weakness. This was Greshko the ringmaster, the man who guarded the computer access codes of the State Security organs with all the jealousy of an alchemist protecting his recipe for gold, a man as cold as the tundra and whose only love – and it was love – was for his precious KGB, which was slowly having the life sucked out of it by the new vampires of the Kremlin. Epishev imagined he could hear the brain working now, whirring and ticking, then taking flight.

Greshko said, 'Our main concern is whether Romanenko's message has fallen into the wrong hands or whether it reached its intended goal. If it was intercepted, then by whom? And what did the message mean to the interceptor? The problem we have is that we were never able fully to ascertain the content of the message. The only way we might have done that would have aroused Romanenko's suspicions, and that wasn't worth the risk . . . ' Greshko drew the cuff of his pyjama sleeve across his mouth and went on, 'We know Romanenko had planned to pass it along in Edinburgh to his collaborators, we also know the message was an indication that all the elements of the scheme were successfully in place – but we don't know the extent of the information it contained. Was it some vaguely-worded thing? Or was it more specific? Could a total stranger read it and understand *exactly* what events are planned inside the Soviet Union a few days from now? Was it written in some kind of code? You see the threat, of course, Viktor. In the wrong hands, this information could be disastrous for all of us.'

Epishev was silent. From his long association with Greshko, he knew that the old man's questions were not intended to be simply rhetorical. Greshko had no time for verbal sophistry. When he asked questions, he wanted answers. The correct answers. It was really that simple. Romanenko had gone to Edinburgh to deliver a message. Greshko needed to know what had happened to it. A great deal depended on finding out. Epishev placed his palms together, rubbed them. There must have been a look of some uncertainty on his face because Greshko said, 'You still haven't overcome your fear, have you, Viktor? You're still unconvinced, aren't you?'

Greshko reached for a small bottle on the bedside table. He opened it and held it up to his mouth. It contained Brezhnev's old remedy for all illnesses, valerian root and vodka flavoured with *zubravka* grass. Greshko was convinced that it was the only thing that kept him alive.

'I'm not afraid, General,' Epishev replied. But he wasn't absolutely sure.

'Everybody feels fear at some time or other, Viktor. There's no shame in saying so. I know you, Viktor, and I know what runs through your mind. Romanenko was an enemy of the State. He was involved in a conspiracy against our beloved country. Right? And since you are being asked to take part in this same conspiracy against a State you've served so faithfully for most of your life, the words treachery and sedition pop into your mind, don't they, Viktor? But that's muddled thinking! The State you served no longer exists, Colonel. The Russia you love is being dismantled in front of our eyes – and if something isn't done quickly, it will cease to exist in any recognisable way.' Greshko paused and snatched a couple of deep breaths, his shrunken lungs filling to their inadequate capacity.

'Viktor,' Greshko said, and his hand went out once more to touch the back of Epishev's wrist, a chill connection of flesh that made Epishev want to shudder. 'Any major blow against this new regime has a damned good chance of destroying it and that should be a cause for rejoicing. Romanenko's conspiracy can only hasten the end of those charlatans who've seized power. They've encouraged certain freedoms. They've told those ethnic minorities that their rights are to be respected, haven't they? They've manufactured a climate in which every dissident moron feels it his duty to argue and squabble with the State. So let them suffer the consequences of what they've created in this country. The quicker they're booted out of office, the better. The means don't matter a damn.'

Greshko paused a moment. 'And the beauty of it is that there are no files on Romanenko in any KGB office! There's nothing on any of the computers! There's absolutely no trace of Romanenko's association with this conspiracy! We've been watching Romanenko for years, and we've known what he's been planning because he lived in our damned pockets and never suspected a thing because we were always careful . . . ' And he laughed, because his own foresight delighted him. When he'd seen the changes coming after the death of Brezhnev, and then later the demise of the hapless Chernenko, he'd taken the trouble to remove all kinds of information from the KGB, knowing a day would come when it would be useful to him. And that day, Epishev thought, had arrived with a vengeance.

'Are you with me, Viktor? Are you still loyal to me?'

Epishev replied, 'I've never been disloyal to you, have I?'

'There's a first time for everything, Colonel.'

'Not where you and I are concerned, General.' The idea of disloyalty would never have entered Epishev's mind. It was more than just the fact of his gratitude to the old man and the years of their alliance, it was a question of shared beliefs. Like Greshko, Epishev thought that the Soviet Union was heading hurriedly toward disintegration. As if it were some massive star whose course has been suddenly changed, the republic was doomed to explode from internal pressure. Those fresh winds everyone said were blowing through the country were as poisonous as radioactive clouds. And Epishev, like Greshko, had absolutely no desire to breathe them.

'Then we're agreed, Viktor. Romanenko's plan must be carried through to the end. Regardless. We may not like the idea, but we have no choice except to go along with it if we want to see our country restored to what it was. In other words – *the plan must succeed.*'

Epishev knew what was coming now. He had known it ever since Greshko had announced Romanenko's murder.

'When you go back to Moscow tonight, you'll see the Printer,' Greshko said.

It might have been routine, except for the fact that Greshko had absolutely no authority any more, save for what he bestowed on himself. It might have been standard operating procedure. But it wasn't. Greshko though, like a great actor, was able to create the illusion of all his old power.

'When the Printer has your papers ready, you leave the country.' Greshko was buzzing now, barely able to keep his hands still. 'You have that authority. You don't need a written order. You'll find out what has happened to Romanenko's message. If it fell into the right hands, then we have nothing to worry about. If it's in the possession of the wrong party, and the outcome of the whole scheme is threatened, you will eliminate that threat. It's simple, Viktor. There are no ambiguities.'

Eliminate that threat. Epishev wondered if he still had the heart for that kind of task. When he was younger, it had come easily to him. Now, even though he enjoyed such tasks as interrogation, even if he didn't object to rubber-stamping papers that condemned people to imprisonment or death, he wasn't sure about killing somebody directly, somebody whose breathing you could hear, whose eyes you could look into, whose fear you could smell. He hoped it wouldn't come to that. Perhaps Romanenko's paper had arrived at the appropriate destination. Perhaps everything was already in its rightful place and Greshko's precautions were, although understandable, nevertheless unnecessary.

He stood up, stepped away from the bed. He looked a moment at Volovich, but it was impossible to tell what Dimitri was thinking. After all the years together, he still couldn't read Volovich with any ease. Was Dimitri going along with this? Greshko, with all his old arrogance, had obviously assumed so, otherwise he wouldn't have been so open. Dimitri hadn't been made privy to everything because Greshko had insisted on limiting the Lieutenant's knowledge as a matter of routine security, but he knew enough to understand what he was involved in.

'We're not alone, you know,' Greshko said. 'There are hundreds of us, Viktor. Thousands. I'm in daily contact with men, some of them in positions of great authority, who feel exactly as we do. And these men are ready to take over the reins of power at a moment's notice. Some of these men are known to you by name. Some of them you can call on for help overseas. You know who I mean. Others prefer to remain anonymously in the background. I mention all this to make you feel less . . . solitary, shall we say? We're all dedicated to the same thing. We're all patriots.'

Epishev went a little closer to Dimitri Volovich. He caught the sickly citric scent of Volovich's Italian hair oil. It was awful, but anything was better than the odour surrounding Greshko's bed.

'This is the most patriotic thing you have ever been asked to do,' Greshko said. 'If it helps, think of yourself as a loyal officer of a small, élite KGB that operates secretly inside the larger one. Think, too, of how this élite KGB is connected to some of the most powerful figures in the country, men who are just as discontented as ourselves.'

Epishev was already thinking of the drive through darkness back to Moscow and the visit to the Printer. He was thinking of identification papers, a passport, airline tickets.

'Remember this,' Greshko said. 'If there are complications and you're delayed outside the country, I want to be informed. I want news, no matter how trivial it may seem. Don't call me directly on my telephone. Volovich here will be the liaison. Every day, Viktor. I expect that much. But let's be optimistic. Let's hope the business is straightforward and our worries needless.'

There was a sound from the bedroom door. The nurse stepped into the room, carrying a tray which held small medicine bottles. 'I need my patient back,' she said, and she smiled cheerfully.

'It's feeding time at the zoo,' Greshko remarked. He winked at Epishev, who turned away and, without looking back, left the bedroom.

On the road to Moscow a fog rolled out of the fields, clinging to the windshield of the car. Volovich drove very slowly even when he'd turned on the yellow foglamps. Epishev sat hunched in the passenger seat. He blinked at the layers of fog, which parted every now and then in the severe glare of the yellow lights, only to come rushing in again.

'Does it constitute treason, Dimitri?'

Volovich stared straight ahead, looking grimly into the fog. 'I never think about words like that.'

'I'm asking you to think about them now.'

Volovich shrugged. 'I take my orders directly from you. Always have done. I'm a creature of habit, and I'm not about to change at this stage of my life. If you're asking whether I'm loyal, the answer is yes. Besides, I never think about politics.'

Epishev leaned back in his seat. He closed his eyes. Politics. This was no mere matter of politics. If Volovich chose to simplify it for himself, that was fine. But it came down to something that was far beyond the ordinary course of Party personalities and rituals. What was going on here was a struggle between the old ways and the new, and Epishev who loved his country as fiercely as Greshko knew where his own heart lay. There were flaws in the old ways, but it was a system that worked in its own fashion, one that people had come to accept. And if there were failings, they were temporary, and inevitable, because the road to Communism wasn't exactly smooth – or even straight. The Revolution had never promised an easy path. Epishev, who had been a Party member for more than thirty years, and before that a dedicated child of the Komsomol, knew what the Revolution had intended. Like an ardent suitor with a faithful passion, he had committed his life to this one mistress. He tolerated all her failings and loved all her glories. And sometimes, when he thought about the Revolution – which he saw as an ongoing process, unlimited, as demanding as it was endless – he experienced an extraordinary sense of iron purpose. He was in the slipstream of history. Everything he did, every task he carried out, no matter how distasteful, had been shaped by the historic forces that had overthrown the Romanovs in 1917.

But to toss all this away! To open windows and throw the old system out! To change the purpose of the Revolution! And to do all this with such indecent haste! Heresy was hardly the word.

Epishev stared into the fog and sighed. He had absolutely no choice but to go along with Greshko. Anything else would have been complete hypocrisy. It didn't matter if Greshko was motivated by pure patriotism, or the promptings of a dying man's monumental ego, because Epishev knew his own reasons were good. He was, as Greshko had correctly pointed out, a patriot. He knew no other way to be.

The fog was thinning now. Epishev glanced at Volovich. 'When I need to telephone, I'll contact you at your home. I'll use the East Berlin link. It's safer.'

Volovich switched off the foglamps. The car began to gather speed. Between thin pine trees, a half-moon had appeared, suspended in a way that struck Epishev as forlorn. He was thinking now of Romanenko, the First Secretary of the Communist Party in the Estonian Soviet Republic, and trying to imagine a shadowy gunman in a railway station. When he'd first heard Greshko speak of the organisation that called itself the Brotherhood of the Forest and how this old association of Baltic freedom fighters had been the driving-force behind Romanenko's plan, when Greshko had patiently explained the merits of the conspiracy and how it might be used against Birthmark Billy and his cronies, Epishev's first instinct had been to distrust the entire undertaking. Romanenko was an Estonian, a Balt, and Epishev trusted absolutely nothing that originated in any of the Baltic countries.

More than fifteen years ago he had spent nine months in Tallinn, the capital of Estonia, where he'd been sent from Moscow to purge the city of Estonian nationals with suspect sympathies. The Balts were a clannish crew, annoyingly supercilious at times, and they tended to protect one another from the common enemy, which they saw as Russia. He remembered Viru Street now, and Tsentralnaya Square, and the 5th October Park. A handsome city, a little too Western perhaps and its native population too irreverent, but there was a pleasant atmosphere, at times almost a buoyancy, in the cafés – places like the Gnome and the Pegasus – that one found nowhere else in the Soviet Union.

More than buoyancy, though. There was defiance throughout the Baltic. One encountered it in Latvia and Lithuania as well. There were strikes, and well-organised protests, and various groups babbling publicly about their rights and singing forbidden national anthems. It was as if all three Baltic nations still believed themselves to be independent of Russia. So many Baltic nationals even now resisted – and loathed – the absorption of their so-called 'republics' into the Soviet Union. And they were encouraged in their dreams by émigré communities overseas, mainly America. He thought of the social clubs in Los Angeles and Chicago and New York where old men played cards or shuffled dominoes and wrote angry letters to their Congressmen about 'prisoners of conscience' behind the Iron Curtain. All that was harmless enough. All that was empty noise and the fury of frustration. Dominoes and cards and folk-festivals and national costumes amounted to nothing. Conscience, after all, was cheap.

But now it had gone beyond simple conscience. The Balts had engineered a plot which had been in the planning a long time and, if Greshko had his way, stood every chance of success. And if it did succeed, it would release all kinds of turmoil, all manner of ancient frustrations and ethnic demands for sovereignty and self-determination throughout the Baltic. What Greshko hoped for was an apocalypse – a popular uprising inspired by the success of the plot and unified by its symbolism, mobs in the streets, tanks and soldiers of the Red Army fighting the local populations of Tallinn and Riga and Vilnius, the disintegration of Soviet influence in satellite republics, a decomposition that might spread beyond the Soviet Union itself and into Poland and East Germany and Czechoslovakia, an anarchic state of affairs that would doom the upstart brigade who ruled these days from the Kremlin. What Greshko desired was nothing less than a new Revolution, one that would replace the bastard liberalisation of the Politburo with an older, more reassuring socialism. What Greshko really wanted was yesterday.

Epishev put a finger inside his mouth and finally located the sliver of apple that had been stuck between his back teeth for the past hour or so. He examined it on the tip of his finger. He had a way of staring at things that suggested the concentration of a coroner inspecting an unusual corpse. He wiped the pellet from his fingertip and sighed, looking out at the moon, which had a curiously hollow appearance, as if it were simply an empty sphere. And he had a sense of uneasiness for a moment, because he felt he'd become exactly the kind of person he'd spent most of his life hunting down and destroying. He had become an enemy of the State.

But the uneasiness passed as quickly as it had come, and Epishev watched the fog return, spreading like acid across the face of the moon.

When the nurse had gone Greshko lay alone in the darkened bedroom. On certain nights, his fiery pain was beyond any of the opiates the nurse administered. And then there were other nights – and this was one of them – when he felt free of the burden of his cancer. There was calm and stillness and even the prospect of a future to anticipate.

He stared at the window. Outside, the night was completely quiet, and the quiet was that of his own death. But he could hold it at bay, he could keep it from entering this bedroom, he was too busy, too curious to die. Besides, his hatred would not allow him to expire. He needed only to live long enough to hear the noises of chaos and destruction. He needed only to live for five short days, if the Baltic scheme ran according to its own timetable. And Viktor would make sure that it did.

He turned his thoughts to Epishev. A good man, a good Communist, if perhaps a little too ruminative at times. But there was also an element of brutality to Epishev and he'd go to the ends of the world for Vladimir Greshko. What more could you ask for?

Epishev would probably use a Hungarian or West German passport and leave Eastern Europe through Berlin, perhaps passing himself off as a commercial traveller or, as he'd once done many years ago, as a piano tuner. A piano tuner! Sometimes Epishev could be inventive. And if that wasn't always a desirable quality, there were times when it was admirable, especially when you combined it with a streak of ruthlessness and complete commitment to the class-struggle of Leninism – something Greshko himself had come long ago to regard with utter cynicism.

More important than imagination, though, was the fact of Epishev's bottomless loyalty, which Greshko had bought cheaply years ago with a simple lie about how Joe Stalin wanted to purge Viktor from the KGB and the Party. Stalin hadn't been remotely interested in Epishev. Indeed, the old *vozhd* hadn't even heard of the young man. But Greshko had dreamed up the fiction, thus presenting himself as Epishev's saviour, as the man who had intervened *personally* on Epishev's behalf. From that time on, Viktor had never questioned a single order issued by his deliverer. A lie, but justifiable within a system where power depended on a network of unquestioning loyalties you forged in any way you could.

Greshko smiled. The idea of setting in motion events that would alter the self-destructive course of this great empire delighted him. He shut his eyes and stuck his hand out to touch the surface of the bedside telephone. He knew he hadn't been given the privilege of a phone out of charity or kindness. He had a telephone for one reason only – so that his conversations could be eavesdropped, his intentions monitored. But Greshko also knew that only a token attempt was made to record his messages because he had called in an old debt from a certain I. F. Martynov, Chief of the Internal Security Directorate, who also happened to be a closet homosexual with a dangerous liking for those lean and lovely teenage boys of the Bolshoi School of Ballet. There were choice tidbits about Martynov's life in Greshko's possession, unsavoury items that Martynov, a married man with overwhelming political ambitions, could not afford to have made public. A little mutual backscratching, a couple of unspecified threats, and Martynov had agreed that only a small proportion of Greshko's conversations would be monitored strictly for appearance's sake, and that even these would be sanitised by Martynov himself.

So Greshko used the telephone freely, though not without some caution. He might have a lock on Martynov, but such locks could stand only so much pressure. His callers, on the other hand, who knew nothing of Martynov's editorial wizardry, were always wary. A retired admiral in Minsk, a former UN ambassador in Kharkov, a Party boss ingloriously ousted in Perm, a retired Minister of Foreign Affairs who called from his dacha in Stavropol, a former Deputy of the Supreme Soviet from Moldavia, and many others – Greshko's callers were men who had previously been in power and who were now living reclusive lives filled with bitterness and a desperate yearning for what they had lost. But there were other supporters too, the kind who wished to remain anonymous because they were men who still had prominent positions they wanted to keep. A Deputy Chairman on the Council of Ministers, a dozen or so members of the All-Russian Congress of Soviets, a Vice President of the Supreme Soviet, several KGB *rezidents* overseas, and a variety of personnel in five different Directorates who owed their promotions to Greshko's patronage in the past.

These men did not risk telephone calls. They smuggled notes to Greshko, messages brought by visitors, terse words of support, commitments, promises for the future, loosely-worded statements that, read carefully, left no doubt about their feelings concerning Birthmark Billy and his gang. It was a subterranean network, an amorphous one in need of strong organisation, but nevertheless huge, and what gave it strength was its resistance to change, its longing for the way things had been before. It was growing daily, drawing recruits from the ranks of the dissatisfied, or from those whose power-bases had been eroded or whose privileges had been removed. It was growing quietly and in secret, pulling in politicians, army officers, bureaucrats, ordinary workers, and it would continue to do so, just as long as things continued their decline inside Russia.

Greshko suddenly perceived the vastness of the Soviet Union, the great plains, the mountain ranges, the lakes and rivers, the *taiga*, in a flash of illumination and love. What was that line the Americans used in one of their songs? From sea to shining sea . . .

They were such apt songwriters, the Americans.

3

London

Martin Burr, the Commissioner of Scotland Yard, had spent several years of his life in the Royal Navy and had lost his right eye during a vicious skirmish with a Nazi U-boat at Scapa Flow in 1943. He wore a black eyepatch which gave him a jaunty, seasoned appearance. The one good eye, green and bloodshot, surveyed the world with weary intelligence.

Pagan respected the Commissioner. At least he wasn't a politician. He was first and foremost a policeman and loyal to those he commanded. And if sometimes he was imperiously paternal, then that was almost forgivable in view of his enormous responsibility, which was to keep the peace among the thousands of men – some of them highly-strung – whose careers and destinies he controlled.

Now, as he hobbled around his large office with his walnut cane supporting his bulk, he kept glancing sideways at Pagan, and there was just a hint of explosiveness in the good eye. Pagan, who had returned from Edinburgh by plane only a few short hours ago, still wore the suit that had been made grubby during his scuffle with Romanenko's killer.

'There will be some form of protest,' said the Commissioner. 'No doubt there's some damned First Secretary from the Russian Embassy already brow-beating the Foreign Minister. They'll bitch every chance they get, Frank. Bloody Bolsheviks.'

Bolsheviks, Pagan thought. That was a quaint one. He noticed that the Commissioner's office was without windows. The light in this room was always artificial, issuing from recessed tubes of fluorescence that made objects seem ghostly.

The Commissioner sat down and looked gloomy. He rapped the carpet with his cane and for a second he reminded Frank Pagan of an English country squire. It was deceptive. There was nothing sleepily bucolic in Martin Burr's character. And his public-school speech patterns concealed a sharp brain and a streak of ruthless determination. 'Let's see what we've got here, Frank, before I come up with some bland yarn to feed to the wolfhounds of Fleet Street.'

Pagan longed for a window, a view, a sight of the city. This office oppressed him, despite the collection of sailing ships in wine-bottles and the small models of British destroyers that littered a shelf, the only items of a personal nature in the whole place.

'Romanenko gets himself shot. And I'm not blaming you because a man can't have eyes in the back of his head, after all. But a lot of people, and I include the press as well as the Russians, are going to think us incompetent idiots. Be warned, laddie – some people are going to say you might have been more vigilant.' The Commissioner looked at Pagan and shrugged. 'Some people are already saying it, Frank. When the Yard isn't solving crimes, it's doing the thing it does best. I'm talking about gossip. I'm telling you I sit atop a pyramid of bitchery like some bloody pharaoh who's got nothing better to do than listen to the whining of his courtiers and the moaning of his soothsayers.'

The Commissioner smiled and Pagan wondered if there was some sympathy to be detected in the expression. Sometimes, when he didn't want you to observe his true expression, the Commissioner had the habit of turning his face to one side so that only the inscrutable eyepatch was visible, which gave him the crafty demeanour of a pirate who possesses one half of the map to the secret place where the doubloons are buried.

'Now the briefcase, Frank. According to the wallahs along Whitehall, it's theoretically the property of the Soviet Union because Romanenko was a representative of that country. Therefore it has to be returned. However, I'm not in any great hurry to oblige. One doesn't want to be scurrying around doing the Russians favours, does one?'

Pagan stared at the briefcase, which was propped against the wall. Alongside the case, there lay the contents of Jacob Kiviranna's backpack and the weapon, the Bersa, that had been used to kill Romanenko. It was a sorry little collection of items and Pagan had some difficulty in associating these things with the violence that had happened only a few short hours ago in Edinburgh. There was a harsh dreamlike quality to the experience now, and yet he could still hear the sound of the gun being fired as if it were trapped inside the echo-chamber of his skull.

'But first,' the Commissioner said, 'before you talk to this fellow Kiviranna, let's examine his cargo.' He hobbled toward the backpack, staring at a couple of shirts, a pair of jeans, socks, underwear, a guidebook to Edinburgh, a rail ticket, two hundred and seven dollars, a prescription bottle that contained several capsules of Seconal, and Kiviranna's American passport.

Pagan picked up the document and stared at the photograph. It showed a man with a rather sulky expression, a petulant set to the lips, hair drawn back tightly against the sides of the head. The ponytail couldn't be seen because of the direct angle of the shot.

'He entered London at Heathrow three days ago. It's the only stamp.' Pagan flipped through the blank pages in the manner of a man scanning a murder mystery to reach the denouement without having to wade through the locked rooms and the poisoned sherry and all the other red herrings. 'And somewhere along the way he acquired the Bersa.'

The Commissioner said, 'And since it's damned near impossible to smuggle a weapon into any country these days, it stands to reason he had an accomplice who provided him with the weapon. So what are we dealing with, Frank? And who the hell is Jacob Kiviranna anyway? Is he part of some bloody mad right-wing cult? And did he really expect to shoot our Soviet friend in broad daylight and make an escape? These are questions we need to have answered, Frank. And I'm tossing it all, lock stock and bloody barrel, into your court.'

Where else could it be tossed? Pagan wondered.

The Commissioner continued. 'Besides, what was so important about Romanenko that he deserved to be shot? As I understand it, he was nothing more than the First Secretary of the Communist Party in some Baltic Soviet Republic, which is not exactly a place where hotshot Party comrades make a name for themselves. And all he came here for was to discuss some humdrum business proposition pertaining to computers, for heaven's sake. It isn't quite the kind of thing that marks a man out for assassination.'

Frank Pagan replaced the passport alongside Kiviranna's other possessions. It was

Romanenko's briefcase that absorbed his attention now. He wanted to open it, but he realised he was going to have to wait for the Commissioner to give him permission. The Commissioner seemed to be savouring the closed briefcase, wandering around it, and once actually prodding it with his walnut stick.

'I wonder if there's anything in this case that might suggest a reason why Romanenko was shot,' Burr said.

'I've been wondering myself.'

Burr paused a second, then said, 'Do the honours, Frank.'

Pagan picked up the case, which was of good brown leather. It was locked, but he easily forced it open with the use of the Commissioner's sharp brass letter-knife. He dumped the contents on the desk. Papers, files, documents in Russian, a schematic diagram of a computer which looked like a maze in a child's book of fun. There was a packet of Player's cigarettes, a disposable razor, a hairbrush, and a shirt, purchased in the Burlington Arcade in London, that was still enclosed in its original cellophane wrapping. There was also a sealed envelope with no address on it.

The Commissioner sifted through the papers. 'It's a pathetic assortment, Frank. Apart from what looks to me like business documents, it's just the kind of stuff a man might carry if he plans a quick overnight stay in another city.'

Pagan spread the papers on the desk. He knew no Russian at all and he felt, as he always did when he encountered a language with which he was unfamiliar, that he'd been stripped of a vital cognitive sense. He might have been staring at a complicated code. He was also touched a little by sadness, because he'd liked Romanenko. Pagan had always had an affinity for people who courted excess.

The Commissioner, whose own Russian was limited to the word *nyet*, looked perplexed. 'We're going to have to call in one of the smart boys from the Foreign Office. Otherwise, this is gobbledygook. And I'd personally like it translated before we turn it over to the Soviets.' The Commissioner sniffed. 'I'd like to know what's inside that sealed envelope, though.'

Pagan picked up the envelope and held it up to the light. He longed to tear it open.

The Commissioner asked, 'Do we use a steam kettle? Or do we simply slice the thing with a knife?'

Frank Pagan grinned. 'Go for broke,' he said, and he ripped the envelope open. It contained a single sheet of yellowing paper covered in a language completely alien to him. Disappointed, he stared at the strange words, written in faded blue ink, as if they might be made to yield up some kind of sense simply by an act of concentration. The Commissioner peered at the sheet with a look of frustration on his face. He even pressed his nose close to it, sniffing the old sheet of paper which smelled musty, like something stored for many years in a damp attic.

'What language is that?' the Commissioner asked.

'I haven't got a clue,' Pagan said. He glanced at a couple of words – *Kalev, Eesti, tooma*. The handwriting wasn't very good. 'Danus Oates is something of a linguist.'

'Then let's fetch the lad,' said the Commissioner.

'He's somewhere in the building,' Pagan said. 'Last time I saw him he was swallowing Valium in the canteen. Events in Edinburgh unsettled his delicate constitution.' As they had unsettled his own, Pagan thought, which was a lot less sensitive than Danus Oates's.

'Fat lot of good Valium's going to do him,' said the Commissioner. 'In the meantime, you ought to have a word with our American friends in Grosvenor Square, Frank. See if they've got anything on this Jacob Kiviranna. The fellow to contact over there is a chap called Teddy Gunther. See what you can get from Kiviranna first, although from what I hear he's either rather surly or two bricks shy of a load.'

Pagan arranged Aleksis's papers in a neat pile.

The Commissioner said, 'So far as Romanenko is concerned, if you want to find out if there's anything that made him a suitable candidate for assassination, the man to see is Tommy Witherspoon. He's got something to do with the Foreign Office, though if you ask me that's only a cover. I think Tommy really liaises between the FO and some of our intelligence agencies. Tommy lives and breathes Russia. I'll give him a call and tell him you might have a question or two for him.'

Pagan looked down at Romanenko's papers a second. The dead man's effects. The bits and pieces of a life. A life that had been blown away right in front of his own eyes. He felt acutely depressed, as if he might have done something to prevent the catastrophe. It was too late for regrets – but then when were regrets ever timely? He remembered the hours he'd spent drinking with Romanenko, how the Russian's booming laughter filled the hotel room, the conspiratorial way Aleksis had said *You will see differences, Frank Pagan, such as you have never dreamed of. Big changes are coming*. The biggest change so far had been Aleksis's murder, which was surely the last thing Romanenko had had in mind.

'By the way, if the press gets on your arse, you've got nothing to tell them. Keep that in mind.' The Commissioner paused a moment. 'Whole thing's a bit of a bloody mess. But you've had worse, haven't you, Frank?'

Frank Pagan looked up at one of the fluorescent tubes which, slightly flawed, blinked now and again. 'Maybe,' he answered. He moved towards the door. 'Don't you want to sit in on my interview with Kiviranna?'

The Commissioner shook his head. 'As I said, Frank, I'm leaving it entirely to you. In any case, I'm sure to have some Russians to deal with very shortly.' He adjusted his eyepatch. 'One last thing. Change your suit first chance you get. You look like something the cat dragged in.'

Jacob Kiviranna was being held in an interrogation room on the second floor, a bare chamber with no windows, a table, a couple of uncomfortable chairs. He chain-smoked, tilting his chair back against the wall and blowing rings up at the ceiling. He'd undone the ponytail and now his long brown hair fell around his shoulders. He had a glum expression on his face, disturbed only by the occasional tic of a pulse beneath his right eye. Pagan's impression was of a man whose life was a closed book which, once you opened it, would contain a drab little story of childhood neglect, lonely adolescence and fruitless adulthood, a serial of failures and pitiful vignettes.

He glanced at the young uniformed policeman who stood, arms folded, in the corner of the room, then sat down facing Kiviranna and tossed the US passport on the table. It fell open at the photograph. Pagan wondered about the ethnic origin of the name Kiviranna.

'Jake or Jacob?' he asked.

'I don't care,' Kiviranna replied. He had a flat, lifeless voice, like that of a man whose verbal interplay with others has been strictly limited.

'Let's start with the biggie, Jake. Why did you kill Romanenko?'

Kiviranna didn't answer. He dropped a cigarette on the floor, crushed it with his ragged sneaker.

'It's going to make my life a whole lot easier if you answer my questions, Jake,' Pagan said.

Kiviranna shut his eyes, placed his arms on the table, then lowered his face. His mouth hung open and he made exaggerated snoring noises. Bloody comedian, Pagan thought.

He glanced again at the cop who stood in the corner. The young man looked about nine years of age. Every year's influx of new recruits seemed younger than ever and they made Pagan, at forty-one, feel old and weatherbeaten.

'Let's try another question,' Pagan said. 'Where did you get the gun?'

Kiviranna opened one eye. He smiled at Pagan but remained silent. He had brown teeth misaligned in his dark gums. Pagan studied the man's combat jacket, the Mickey Mouse patch on one sleeve, the small US flag on the other. He gazed at the beard, which was shapeless. He had the feeling he was peering into the past, confronting a species that, if not extinct, was at the very least threatened. You rarely encountered hippies these days. Now and then an old DayGlo van would chug past you on the street and it would be plastered with faded peace signs and weathered bumper-stickers bearing mellow messages, or you'd see some clapped-out forty-year-old flower-child sliding quietly along the sidewalk – but they didn't seem to come in bunches any more. Pagan remembered a time when he'd admired the lifestyle, before it became ugly and drugged.

He wandered around the room, pausing when he reached the door. 'I wish you'd talk to me, Jake,' he said. 'If it's something simple, if it's just that you don't like Russians and you think the only good Commie's a dead one, I wish you'd say so.'

Kiviranna sucked on a cigarette. There was some tiny response just then when Pagan had mentioned the Russians, a very slight thing, a small change in the man's expression.

Pagan decided to pursue the opening. 'By the way, Jake, they want you. Did I mention that already? They'd like to talk to you. In the circumstances, I can't say I blame them.'

'Who wants me?'

Pagan went back to the table and sat down. 'The Soviets. They'd like me to turn you over to them. They're being pretty persistent about it. And I'm not sure I can prevent it.'

'You're out of your mind,' Kiviranna said. 'No way would you hand me over.'

Pagan shrugged. Sometimes when you interviewed a person you got lucky very quickly and you managed to touch a little nerve of fear. And it was apprehension that showed now on Kiviranna's gaunt face.

'I don't know, Jake. You shot one of their own. They're not happy with you. Come to think of it, I'm not exactly delirious about you either. Take your pick. Either you talk to me, or you take a short car ride to the Soviet Embassy, where you get to sit in a dark room and they shine lights in your eyes and smoking isn't allowed. You'll meet some men whose coats seem just a little too tight and who make loud noises with their fists.'

Kiviranna sat upright now. 'I killed the guy on British soil. I know the law, man.'

'You *think* you know the law, Jake. But when it comes down to tricky stuff like the death of a Russian, it starts to get pretty complicated. Diplomatic considerations raise their ugly little heads, chum. Her Majesty's Government might owe the Soviets a favour, let's say, and that favour might just turn out to be you.'

Kiviranna leaned back against the wall. 'I set one foot inside that Embassy and I'm history. I'm past tense.'

'Right, Jake. It's not a healthy prospect.'

'It's a fucking political game. And I get shuffled like a pawn.'

'Pawns don't get shuffled, Jake. You're thinking about cards.' Pagan smiled, and leaned across the table so that his face was a mere six inches away from the other man's. 'Let's just talk, okay? No more rubbish. Let's start with motive.'

'Motive?'

'Why did you kill Romanenko? Money? Political conviction? Or was it something else?'

'He was a fucking asshole, man.'

Breathtaking. Pagan had expected some high-flown political cant, the kind of platitude assassins and terrorists so enjoy, that overblown rhetoric which was ultimately meaningless. *He was a fucking asshole, man* wasn't the kind of thing he'd anticipated at all. He stared at Jacob Kiviranna for a while before he said, 'If that was sufficient cause to blow a man away, the streets would be practically empty.'

'Okay. He sold out to the Russians. Is that enough for you?'

'Exactly how did he do that?'

'You name it. He carried out Kremlin policies in Estonia. He kissed all the Russian ass going. Guy was never off his fucking knees. An order came down from Moscow, Romanenko was the first to implement it. Didn't matter what it was. He'd get the job done. He was the Kremlin's rubber stamp. It didn't matter he was born in Estonia, he was the Kremlin's boy through and through. Which made him a goddam traitor.'

Pagan listened to the man's toneless voice, then picked up the US passport, flipped the pages. 'You're an American citizen, Jake. How come you give a damn about Romanenko anyway? I don't see how he could have affected your life.'

'I got family left over there,' Kiviranna said. 'Cousins, a couple of uncles, aunts.'

Revenge, Pagan wondered. Did it come down to a motive as basic as that? 'Had Romanenko threatened your family? Had he done something to them?'

Kiviranna didn't say anything for a time. He smoked another cigarette and the small windowless chamber clouded up and the young cop by the door coughed a couple of times. Kiviranna gestured with the cigarette and looked very serious. 'He didn't have to do anything personal to them, man. He was a Communist and a traitor to his own people. That's enough. We're talking about evil. I eliminated evil. That's the only thing that matters. You see evil, man, you wipe it out. The more evil you get rid of, the more good there is in the world. That's what it's all about. It's logical.'

Evil – now there was a fine melodramatic word you didn't hear a great deal these days unless you frequented certain extreme religious sects or moved in mad terrorist circles, where it was used to describe anyone who didn't believe in either your choice of a God or your cause. Pagan studied Kiviranna's face again, wondered about his background. Had this wild-eyed character, who impressed Pagan as the kind of man you saw speaking to himself in the reading-rooms of public libraries, come three thousand miles to commit a murder because he believed that Aleksis Romanenko was evil? Was he driven by a missionary sense of bringing goodness and light into the world? Had he planned this killing all alone? Had he walked around with a dream of death in his head for weeks, perhaps months on end? An obsessive, a sociopath, the kind of guy who suddenly pops up with a handgun and makes a name for himself by killing a person of some standing in a political system he thought deplorable. *I eliminated evil.* Jake the avenger, the equaliser, the mad angel of light.

'So wiping out this evil was your own idea, Jake? Is that what you're telling me?'

'You got it.'

Pagan was unhappy with this reply. It didn't answer the question of how Kiviranna had come into possession of the gun. Somebody had presumably passed the weapon to him after his arrival in Britain, and when you had two people you had a conspiracy, and so much for a lone killer theory. For another, Pagan had the feeling, which he couldn't readily explain and which surfaced in his mind at the end of a chain of unanalysable instincts, that Jake, albeit lonely and out of touch, was basically a gullible soul, and that the killing of Romanenko was an idea that had been *encouraged* in him. It wasn't a conclusion he'd reached without some kind of assistance, some kind of *persuasion.*

'How did you know Romanenko was going to be in Edinburgh, Jake?'

ad it in a paper, I guess.'

'An American paper?'

'I guess so, I don't remember.'

Pagan's eyes were watering in the smoky room. It was hardly likely that Romanenko's visit to Britain had been mentioned in any US newspaper. It wasn't entirely newsworthy in America to print a story about an obscure Communist Party official making a quick business trip to the United Kingdom. It was even less likely that any press item would mention something so utterly unimportant as the side-trip to the Edinburgh Festival. So here was another question: *how had Jake come across his information?* There was only one answer – it had come from the same person or persons who provided the gun.

Pagan got up from his chair and walked round the room.

'Let's go back to the weapon. How did you get it, Jake?'

'I bought it here in London. I don't remember the store.'

Pagan wheeled around quickly and strode back to the table. 'You don't just walk into a shop and buy a gun in this country, Jake. You fill in forms, there's a waiting-period, the police run a thorough check on applicants. You haven't been in England long enough to acquire a weapon legally.'

Kiviranna looked down at the surface of the table. His hands shook, and he pressed his palms together to keep them steady. 'I need a favour,' he said.

'Let's hear it.'

'I had some medication in my backpack. I'd like it.'

Pagan nodded at the young policeman, who went out of the room to fetch Kiviranna's medicine.

'Nerves trouble you, Jake?'

'I have some problems, man. I'm getting over them.'

Pagan looked sympathetic. 'Back to the gun, Jake.'

Kiviranna shut his eyes and rocked his body back and forth for a time. 'Okay. I got it in Soho. I went into a club, I asked around, guy sold me the gun. It was easy.'

'You're trying my patience, Jake. You don't walk inside some club in Soho, a complete stranger, an outsider, and find somebody to sell you a gun. It doesn't happen that way. You need an inside track. Think again.'

Kiviranna was silent. He stroked his beard. 'I got a real bad headache.'

The door of the room opened and the young policeman stepped inside, handing the brown prescription bottle to Pagan, who laid it on the table and rolled it back and forth as he studied Jake's anxious face.

'Tell me about the gun and you get one of your pills.'

Kiviranna was silent a moment. 'Okay. The gun was in a luggage locker at that station – what's it called? King's Cross?' He stuck a hand out towards the bottle, but Pagan covered it quickly with a palm.

'How did you know the gun was going to be there, Jake? Who told you? Who gave you the key to the locker?'

Kiviranna didn't take his eyes away from the bottle in Frank Pagan's fist. The look on his face was one of subdued desperation and Pagan, clutching the pills Jake was aching for, felt a surge of sympathy for the man and a slight disapproval of his own cruelty.

'He was an old guy I met in New York.'

'Did he just walk up to you on the street? Did he say here's a key, fly to England, fetch the gun, shoot Romanenko?'

Kiviranna shook his head. 'He got my name from somewhere, he called me. We met a few times. I never knew his name, and that's the truth.'

'How come he approached you, Jake? What made him choose you?'

'I guess he heard I had certain sympathies.'

'Were you offered money?'

'Expenses, that's all. I wasn't going to take money for ridding the world of a guy like Romanenko.' Kiviranna sounded a little offended by the suggestion. 'We met a few times, we talked, I agreed to do the job.'

'Where did your meetings take place?'

Kiviranna was speaking more frankly now. 'Different places, man. Sometimes Manhattan. Sometimes Brooklyn. One time we met at Coney Island, next to the old parachute jump. Another time the boardwalk at Brighton Beach.'

'Tell me the man's name, Jake.'

'I don't know it, I swear. He wasn't anxious for me to know, and I wasn't anxious to find out.'

Pagan took the cap off the bottle. 'Why did he want you to kill Romanenko?'

'Because he felt the same way I did.'

'Tell me more about this mystery man.'

Kiviranna's forehead glistened with sweat. 'What's to tell? He was maybe seventy, in there somewhere. He spoke with a thick accent. Shabby clothes. He didn't look like he had two nickels to rub together. But I guess he got money from somewhere, enough for my expenses anyway. I don't remember much more.'

'And even if you could remember more, you wouldn't tell me,' Pagan said. He tilted the bottle and a few capsules slid on to the table. He examined them carefully, checking the name of the manufacturer, Lilley, imprinted on the side of each one.

'I've told you everything,' Kiviranna said.

'I don't think so, Jake.' Pagan pushed one of the pills across the table to Kiviranna, who picked it up quickly and tossed it into his mouth. 'Enjoy. We'll talk again tomorrow. Maybe you'll find your memory has improved after a good night's sleep.'

Pagan put the medicine bottle in his pocket together with Kiviranna's passport, stood up, walked towards the door. He was struck by fatigue but he knew that it was something he was going to have to carry around with him for some hours yet.

'What if I don't have anything new to tell you in the morning?' Kiviranna asked. 'What then?'

Pagan turned, looked at the man, smiled in a thin way. He didn't answer the question but hoped that his smile, so devoid of mirth, suggested an unspeakable threat. Closing the door, he went out into the corridor and dipped his face into a drinking-fountain, letting a jet of lukewarm water splash against his eyes and forehead. A gun in a left-luggage locker, a nameless man in New York who'd sent Jake all the way to England – maybe it was all very simple, nothing more than a straightforward political assassination planned by Jake's anonymous acquaintance and carried out by Kiviranna who, through his own strange filter, saw the world in terms of black and white, evil and good. Maybe that's all there was to the affair.

But there was a dark area at the back of Pagan's mind, a room in which assorted problems lay like unlit light bulbs awaiting a surge of electricity to illuminate them. And in this room there lived Pagan's muse, his own inner policeman, his personal inspector, who was rarely satisfied with simplicity and who hated darkness passionately. He loathed puzzles too, such as the plain white envelope, sealed and unaddressed, that Aleksis Romanenko had carried in his briefcase.

4

London

Thomas Maclehose Witherspoon, who had a first-class degree in Political Science from St John's College, Oxford, was walking his cocker spaniels in Green Park when Pagan met him shortly after eight-thirty. He was a tall man with an adam's apple that suggested something stuck in his windpipe. He wore a navy blue blazer with some kind of crest on the pocket and white flannels, as if he were a fugitive from a cricket game. Witherspoon's thin hair was combed flat across the enormous dome of his head. The pedigree spaniels, named Lord Acton and Gladstone, were romping in the distance, and ignoring Tommy Witherspoon when he called their names.

When Witherspoon spoke, in a voice that might have been sharpened by razor blades, there was a scent of port on his breath. Pagan wondered if he'd dragged Tommy away from some polite little dinner party, causing the man a terrible inconvenience.

Witherspoon picked up a fallen branch and called after his dogs again. 'Highly-strung buggers,' he said.

Pagan thought a good kick in the arse might have induced in the creatures a sense of obedience, but he didn't say so. Witherspoon tossed the branch in the air and watched it fall.

'So you're the notorious Frank Pagan, eh? Heard about your Irish business.'

Pagan, wondering when his name would cease to be associated with Ireland, made no reply. He studied the sky a moment, watching the August sun slide down between trees of an impossible greenness. London could still amaze him at times with its verdancy.

'So you lost Romanenko,' Tommy Witherspoon said, in a weary way, as if Pagan's problems were a total bore. 'I must say I thought it damned careless of you.'

Pagan, irked by Witherspoon's manner, wanted to come back with a barbed comment, but resisted the temptation. He sniffed the air instead. There was a smell of diesel, ruining all this summer greenery and presumably pumping toxic materials into the bodies of nightingales.

Tommy Witherspoon asked, 'What can I do for you anyhow?'

'What do you know about Romanenko?' Pagan asked.

'Isn't that an irrelevant question, Pagan? The fellow's dead and I understand you have the assassin in custody, and I don't see how any further knowledge of Romanenko could possibly be of assistance to you.'

What an unbearable toad, Pagan thought. 'There are some things I want clarified, that's all,' he said.

'Ah, clarified,' Witherspoon said. 'You're on a personal quest, are you, Pagan? A man with a burning mission?'

'Personal?'

'The old ego. The policeman's pride. Can't stand the idea of being involved in a royal fuck-up, so you've got to start poking around to make yourself look somewhat less useless, eh?' There was raw snideness in Witherspoon's tone.

Pagan had a sense of something chill coiled around his heart. Maybe all it came down to was the inescapable fact that – as John Downey had so cruelly and succinctly put it, and as Tommy Witherspoon had echoed it – he'd fucked up. And maybe he was doing nothing more than turning over stones and trying to look busy because the more conscientious he appeared the better he'd feel. It was a sorry little insight and he hoped there was no truth to it. What came back to him again were Aleksis's drunken words – *big changes, big surprises*. He supposed the big changes referred to the reconstruction of Soviet society, but what were the big surprises? What had Aleksis, with his sly winks and nudges, intended to suggest with that expression? *Wait and see, Frank Pagan*, Romanenko had said. Wait for what? It was one of the problems of death – it left silences and unanswered questions behind.

'Look, Romanenko was shot and I want some background,' he said. He put a little steel into his voice now, a cop's impatience.

Witherspoon yawned. 'Well, Pagan, if it's going to calm you down, I'll give you the quick tour. Romanenko was First Secretary of the Communist Party in Estonia. Estonian national, in fact. Don't be too impressed with his grandiose title, though. It's common practice for Russians to put nationals in charge in their colonies, but the real power always lies with the Second Secretary of the Party, who's invariably a Central Russian, a Soviet, handpicked by the Kremlin. Romanenko was just another titular head, a symbol, a sop. You find people like Romanenko all over the Russian Empire. Latvia. Lithuania. Georgia. Armenia. You'll find them in every one of the fifteen so-called autonomous republics – which is a laughable name for colonies – of the Soviet Union. It's designed to keep the natives restful and the dissidents asleep at night if one of their own is nominally the boss. It's a bloody sham, of course. Chaps like Romanenko don't have much in the way of real power. And they can't blow their own noses unless they get a direct order from the Kremlin – provided the Five Year Plan has manufactured enough hankies to go around.' Witherspoon smiled at his own little joke.

'If Romanenko was so unimportant, why would anybody want to shoot him?' Pagan asked.

'Now that's hardly a taxing mystery,' Tommy Witherspoon said in an offhand way. 'Consider this. There are certain parties outside the Soviet Union, let's call them exiled malcontents, who have very long memories and carry grudges the depths of which would astonish you. Romanenko would be an obvious target for any Baltic exile loony fringe, because he was so clearly in cahoots with the Russian lords and masters. Ergo, the fellow's perceived as being a first-rate rotter, selling his own country out to Moscow. Do you see?'

Witherspoon, in his own aloof way, was echoing what Kiviranna had already told Pagan, which was something of a disappointment because Pagan had somehow expected a different answer, one with more substance, a little more meat on the bones of the affair.

'Now,' Witherspoon said, 'I'll throw a little extra fuel on the general bonfire, Pagan. Given the current changes inside the Soviet Union – which may or may not turn out to be window-dressing and only time will tell – there has been something of an upsurge of nationalism in the Soviet colonies. Lithuanians demonstrate for independence. Latvians collect signatures on petitions. Kazakhs gather in Red Square to wave their flag. Given this perception of some freedom, which may be merely an illusion, certain exiled parties feel the time is right to throw some external support behind the nationalist movements inside the Soviet Union. Are you with me?'

Pagan saw Witherspoon's dogs come bounding back, pink tongues flapping. Witherspoon patted them, fed them some kind of tidbits from a cellophane bag. 'Good lads,' he said to the eager creatures in the kind of voice a man might have reserved for his two very young sons.

'You're saying that the killing of Romanenko might be a message for the boys back home that they're not alone in their quest for independence. That there's support in the West.'

Witherspoon arched an eyebrow. 'Quite. And that's all there is to this business, Pagan. In your shoes, I wouldn't start looking for skeletons in closets. If it amuses you to dig for little mysteries where none exist, be my guest. But if I were you, I'd put aside your policeman's pride, admit you were less than vigilant, thank your lucky stars that the assassin was sufficiently an amateur to be so easily caught, and sit down in some quiet corner to compose your report.'

Pagan ignored Tommy's patronising tone. Amateur was a fair description of the manner in which Kiviranna had shot Romanenko. No telescopic rifle fired from a concealed place, no attempt at diversionary tactics, no planned route of escape. A passionate amateur, someone with at least one oar out of the water, who considered Romanenko a stain to be wiped out. Was Witherspoon right? Was Pagan being dictated to by his bruised ego, his failure in Edinburgh to protect a man he'd felt a certain fondness for? Was it on so flimsy an edifice as his own injured vanity that he was playing detective?

'Must be off,' Witherspoon said, leashing his spaniels. 'Trust I've been of some help,' and he walked away from Pagan without looking back, straining to keep his mutts in line.

Alone in the centre of Green Park, Frank Pagan continued to watch the sun as it slid inexorably down into darkness, and it was the kind of nightfall in which leaves cease to rustle, and the stillness suggests all kinds of impenetrable secrets. When the sun had finally gone, leaving a brassy layer of thin light over London, Pagan walked in the direction of Mayfair. He wondered about the identity of the person in New York who'd sent Jacob Kiviranna on his mission – if indeed such a man existed or was simply a figment of the killer's imagination. And the feeling hit him again that there was more to this whole business than the easy surfaces of things suggested, but he was damned if he could pin it down.

It was completely dark by the time Pagan reached the American Embassy in Grosvenor Square. He'd walked all the way from Green Park and up through the streets of Mayfair, lost in the kind of aimless speculation that turns a man's mind to blancmange. There were a couple of lights in the American fortress but, apart from a Marine guard and a few clerks on the upper floors presumably performing nocturnal tasks of a clandestine nature – probably the cipher boys of the CIA – the place was lifeless and almost ghostly. The guard, a handsome black with an accent that suggested Alabama, had been expecting Pagan and escorted him inside the building where the man known as Theodore Gunther was waiting in the lobby.

Ted Gunther was a short man with a crewcut. He wore thick-lensed glasses and a striped seersucker suit that hung on him rather badly, crumpled by the humidity of the night. He shook Pagan's hand, glanced at the grubby jacket, but was apparently too well-mannered to mention Pagan's sartorial condition. Frank Pagan sat down and as soon as he did so an exhaustion coursed through him and he could feel the demon of sleep hover on the edges of his mind.

'Bad business in Edinburgh,' Gunther said.

Pagan agreed. A very bad business.

'Martin Burr mentioned something about a passport I might check out for you.'

Pagan took the document from his pocket. Gunther flipped quickly through the pages, looking for God knows what. He stared at Jacob Kiviranna's photograph then, like a connoisseur sniffing a wine, held the document up to his nose and smelled the binding. He held the passport between thumb and forefinger and bent it slightly, a bibliophile assessing the authenticity of a first edition.

'It seems one hundred per cent the genuine article,' Gunther said. 'It hasn't been tampered with. It even smells good. Sometimes the paper smells wrong when it's a fake. I doubt it's a forgery. But if you don't mind, I'll hold on to it in the meantime and take a more clinical look-see.'

'Be my guest,' Pagan said, gazing across the lobby where a dim light burned.

'I guess you want a little more from me than verification of Kiviranna's passport. You'd like to know something about his background, if he belonged to any organisations, whether the FBI has anything on file. A radical association. A crime or two.'

'Anything you can turn up,' Pagan said. 'He claims he has an accomplice in the United States. I'd like to know if you can shed a little light on the identity of the mysterious associate. Maybe there's even more than one. I can't get a handle on whether Kiviranna's telling me the truth or whether he's making up stories as he goes along.'

Theodore Gunther took off his glasses and rubbed his eyes. 'I'll help you all I can, of course. Always glad to be of some use to our allies, Frank. You can count on it.' And Gunther smiled for the first time. It was one of those open American smiles that suggest placing each and every relationship on an easy first-name basis because formalities have no place in friendships between historic partners.

'Tell me, Frank. What kind of fellow is this Kiviranna anyhow? How does he strike you?'

Frank Pagan shrugged. 'He wouldn't be on anybody's guest-list for an intimate dinner-party, I'll say that much. And I'm not going to be astonished if you find a background of mental illness and/or drug problems. He looks more harmless than vicious, but that's not a compliment. I get the distinct impression he's out to lunch more often than he's home.'

Pagan tilted his head back in his chair. He was reluctant to get up and return to the streets of Mayfair. Ted Gunther took a packet of mints from the pocket of his limp jacket and placed one on his tongue. He said, 'It's a sorry fact, but there are all kinds of fringe outfits back home who see Communism as the numero uno enemy of the free world. Most of them are harmless, thank God, but every now and then some weird fish slips through the net. Perhaps that's all Kiviranna will turn out to be. A weird fish who wriggled through a hole.'

Pagan rose from his comfortable chair. He saw the Marine guard from the corner of his eye, the stiff uniform, the boots that shone like two black mirrors, the glossy visor of the cap pulled down flat against the nose.

'I'll get back to you as quickly as I can,' Gunther said.

'I'd appreciate it.' Pagan walked across the lobby and Gunther, who had a funny little stride, like a man with artificial hip sockets, came after him. Together, both men went out of the Embassy and stood on the steps.

Pagan looked across Grosvenor Square, that corner of London that had virtually become an American colony. He wasn't sure, at the time or much later, why his attention was so suddenly drawn to a dirty yellow Volkswagen beetle which was turning left on the Square even as he watched it. Perhaps it was the pall of exhaust smoke that hung behind it like a dark shroud. Perhaps it was the rattling sound made by the loose exhaust pipe or the horrible squeal of faulty brakes. Or perhaps it was the face of the pretty young woman at the wheel – who glanced at him briefly as the grubby little car passed out of sight, leaving nothing behind but the odious perfume of its passing.

Gunther held out a hand to be shaken. Pagan took it, thinking it was slack and pawlike and, despite the humidity of the evening, a little too damp just the same.

'I'll make some calls right away,' Gunther said. 'Rouse some folks out of bed.'

'Which will make you popular,' Pagan remarked.

'I'm more interested in answers than winning any popularity contest, Frank,' and Gunther smiled again, the very essence of Anglo-American friendship.

Pagan walked down the steps away from the Embassy, crossed Grosvenor Square, searched the traffic for a taxi. When he reached the other side of the Square he looked back at the darkened Embassy and saw Theodore Gunther go inside the building, the glass doors swinging shut behind him.

Moments later, just as Pagan successfully hailed a cab and was about to step into it, a light went on in a second-floor window. Pagan glanced up and saw Gunther's silhouette pass briefly in front of the glass.

Panicked, Jacob Kiviranna woke in the dark holding-cell, his body drenched in sweat, yet he was cold and his teeth rattled together and he couldn't keep his hands still. He sat on the edge of his bunk, his blanket wrapped round his body. He was afraid, more afraid than he could remember having been in his life before. Was it this sense of terror that made him so fucking cold? He wished he had more downers because the first one had worn off and now he was frazzled and disoriented and it was only with a great effort that he could remember where he was.

He shut his eyes and rocked his body back and forth and remembered the face of the old guy who'd given him the key to the luggage locker and the airline ticket and an envelope that contained five hundred dollars for expenses. He remembered the tiny glasses the guy wore, and the way they were perched on the end of his long nose, and how frayed the cuffs of his jacket were – but that was all he could bring to mind. And when the cop called Pagan came back in the morning to ask for the old guy's name, he wasn't going to believe it when Kiviranna told him once again that he didn't know it, that he'd never known it, never asked. He could point out the places where he'd met the old guy, he could take him to the boardwalk or show him the apartment building in Manhattan where the guy lived or where they'd walked at Coney Island, or even his own coldwater apartment in the Village where the old guy had come one time. But when it came to a name, forget it. There were some situations when you just didn't want to know names, when secrecy was everything.

And Pagan wasn't going to believe that.

Without batting a fucking eyelid, Pagan would turn him over to the Russians. And the Russians would stick him on board an Aeroflot flight to Moscow, and that would be the end of it. Kiviranna opened his eyes and looked around the dark little cell, vaguely making out the door, the unlit lightbulb overhead. There was no way he was going to Russia. Under no circumstances. Never. What they'd do to him over there – they'd interrogate him and beat him and then finally prop him up against a stone wall and shoot him. His perceptions of the Soviets had been shaped by stories he'd heard from older relatives in the USA, men and women who'd survived Stalin's various holocausts and who remembered wholesale executions and famine and even rumours of cannibalism during the 1930s and who told horror stories about how, to this very day, immigrants sometimes disappeared from their homes in New York City and were smuggled back to Russia by the KGB. And they were never heard from again.

He got to his feet and, still draped in the blanket, wandered up and down the cell. In the corner of the room was a porcelain washbasin and a paper-towel holder. Kiviranna ran the hot water faucet until it scalded his palms. That was one kind of pain, and he could just about stand it, but he knew the Soviets had ways of inflicting unthinkable agonies. No, he wasn't going to Russia to be executed for the murder of Romanenko – which wasn't murder at all, but a justifiable act, a moral act. That's what the old guy had drummed into him every time they met. *Romanenko doesn't deserve to live. Look what he's done to our people. He's scum, he's not human. There's a good word for him. And that's evil. He sold us down the goddam river. You kill him, your name's going to be legend. A hero.*

Kiviranna, who had been attracted by the possibility of heroism, went back to the bunk. He pulled the mattress to the side, revealing the metal frame, the springs. He touched the frame, his hands trembling. Sweat ran from his forehead into his eyes and he blinked because the salt stung. He stepped back from the bed, stared up at the lightbulb. The thought that came into his head just then seemed totally logical to him. He bent over the bed, laid a hand on the interlocking pieces of thin wire. Totally logical. He was surprised he hadn't thought about it before.

In a life that had often been puzzling, and lonely, and brutally drab, in a cold world where most people inexplicably shunned or avoided him, he understood he'd reached a pinnacle by killing the monster known as Romanenko. A summit. It was as if he stood on the crest of a hill and could see his whole past stretched out below him, a sequence of worthless menial jobs, a couple of jail stretches for petty offences, months of hospitalisation in institutions without windows where he was given injections and subjected to all kinds of humiliating tests, a clumsy infatuation with a woman who despised and ridiculed him. He could see all of this vanishing towards the horizon and he knew that his existence had amounted to a total waste of goddam time. Until the killing of Romanenko.

What was the rest of his life going to be like after that high? He shivered under the blanket. He went down on his knees and began to unhook the metal springs attached to the frame of the bed.

He wasn't going to Russia. He was sure of that.

5

Fredericksburg, Virginia

The large white house, built in neo-colonial style, was located in a narrow leafy street on the edge of Fredericksburg. Its former owner, an Australian who had made a vast fortune publishing a horse-racing sheet, had sold the property in 1985 to a man who said his name was Galbraith and who hinted vaguely that he had retired from a lucrative career in the aerospace industry. Both the name and the career were fabrications. The property, all seven wooded acres of it, changed hands for one million dollars in a transaction so smooth and quick it surprised the Australian handicapper, who took the money and moved to Boca Raton.

The house, set some distance from its closest neighbour, had undergone considerable changes under the direction of the new owner. Steel shutters were hung on the windows, an elaborate security system installed, and several new phonelines added – although not by technicians employed by the Bell telephone company. A huge mainframe computer was hooked up in a room on the second floor, which had been remodelled for just that purpose. The interior walls were painted a uniform oyster-shell colour. Mature trees were planted all around the property and, as if these did not quite satisfy the owner's lust for privacy, a ten-foot brick wall, electrified along the top, was also constructed. Galbraith, an enormously fat man with an addiction to things English – such as croquet, crumpets and Craven A cigarettes – was rarely seen in the neighbourhood, perhaps only occasionally glimpsed as he went past in a stately Bentley with darkly tinted windows.

At two a.m. US Eastern District time, two hours after Frank Pagan had left the American Embassy in London, a beige BMW drew up at the gates of the dark house, which slid open to admit the vehicle. The car moved up the circular driveway, then parked directly in front of the house. The driver, a man called Iverson, emerged from the German automobile and climbed the steps to the front door. Iverson inserted a laminated card into a slot, and was admitted after a moment. Inside, he headed at once for the door that led to the basement.

Iverson had bright blue eyes which were heavily lidded and his chin appeared to have been carved in stone. His blond hair had been cut so close to the skull that the scalp seemed blue-tinted. He was in his late forties, but the lack of lines and creases, the lack of animation in the face, made it impossible to guess. It wasn't the kind of face that accommodated expressions with any ease. There was severity and a sense of singlemindedness about the man. He descended the stairs to the basement in the stiff-backed manner of someone who has been for most of his life associated with one or other arm of the military.

Galbraith, dressed in the kind of loose, monklike robe he found very comfortable, his feet bare, sat on a brown leather sofa in the basement. He sipped espresso from a demitasse, then set the cup down on a smoked-glass table and raised one hand, which resembled a small plucked chicken, in a rather weary greeting.

'Sit,' Galbraith said in an accent that was Boston, but had been tempered to suggest the other side of the Atlantic. 'Welcome to *As The World Turns.*'

Iverson sat. He stared at the various consoles on the wall, some of which depicted the darkened garden outside, while others flashed a variety of data transmitted from the mainframe on the second floor. Some of this information, which was coded, concerned the flight-plans of American fighter aircraft on NATO assignments in various parts of Europe. Other data, which constantly changed, listed such things as troop manoeuvres in Eastern Europe and the Soviet Union, the movement of ships and submarines in the Soviet Baltic fleet, the orbits of Russian spy satellites, the location of Russian radar installations, and a whole lot more besides, much of it irrelevant in global terms.

Galbraith had a whole world brought into the basement by the consoles. He was like some fat spider in the dead centre of an intricate electronic web whose strands stretch around the globe. He sat sometimes for hours, observing the relentless flow of information that travelled from space satellites and other complex computer links at great speeds along the filaments of his web. Iverson studied the consoles in silence, glancing now and again at Galbraith's face in which the eyes were mere slits surrounded by ravioli-like pillows of white flesh.

Galbraith, who weighed two hundred and eighty pounds, breathed noisily as if sucking enough air for three men. His laboured breathing had been one of the arguments he'd used when he'd first gone before a secret session of the Congressional Select Committee on Intelligence Operations to demand funds for the purchase of this property in Fredericksburg. *The air in DC, gentlemen, is becoming increasingly hard to live on. It dulls the senses and clouds the mind. Fresh air means increased alertness, and a happier, healthier crew. And cost-effective, too, a lower tax base, cheaper utilities, less expensive housing.*

Galbraith was as persuasive in argument as he was imposing in girth. Few politicians ever liked to contend with him, and fewer still demanded a reckoning, although there were always a couple who longed for his blood, small-minded men who called themselves – proudly, mind you – 'moralists' and who waited a chance to pounce on the fat man, catching him in some ugly covert operation with blood on his palms. These were men, usually from states where the electorate was corn-fed, who had a smell of old bibles and damp pulpits about them, and who drew their constituencies from the same people who donated money to TV ministries. They were stupid men, and narrow-minded, but they were not to be underestimated because they wielded the kind of power that could punish intelligence efforts where it really hurt – in the old pocketbook. And they waited, with withdrawn fangs, for Galbraith to commit a public faux pas, or fall into an espionage scandal. But not even these critics realised that Galbraith was effectively separating himself from the DIA – the Defense Intelligence Agency – to establish an autonomous branch, an inner sanctum, in the tranquil countryside of Virginia. The operation became known, to those who knew such things, as the GIA, Galbraith's Intelligence Agency.

The funds were approved and Galbraith moved the computer operation out of the capital, although he left most of his staff behind in the old quarters. He took with him only a handful of specialists, men and women trained to interpret the data provided by the computer. These were people he'd hired personally and who tended to see the world through the same prism as Galbraith himself did, which was one of self-preservation and what the fat man thought of as 'sophisticated' patriotism – to differentiate it from 'frontier' patriotism, which he considered a mindless kind of thing, a redneck instinct, a mere wormlike reflex. Galbraith's version was grounded in the simple assumption, which needed no drum-rolls to accompany it, no National Rifle Association to maintain it, that the continued existence of the United States as the primary power in the world guaranteed the continued existence of the world itself.

'Good of you to come at this hour, Gary. Smoke?' And he pushed a box of Craven A across the glass surface of the coffee table. Iverson declined. With a remote control device, Galbraith switched off the consoles. Iverson noticed the absence of electronic humming in the room now.

Galbraith said, 'Here's a fine illustration of the limits of modern technology, Gary. While we sit in this lovely house and can keep track, say, of a couple of penguins merrily fornicating in Antarctica, we still haven't reached a situation where we can do a damn thing to predict human behaviour. In other words, just as we think we have matters under control, up pops some human idiot to scramble the whole equation.'

'Which human idiot do you have in mind, sir?'

Galbraith stood up. His huge robe flowed around him like a collapsing tent. He went to a closet, opened it, took out a packet of English chocolate digestive biscuits and nibbled on one. Then, disgusted by his own needs, he tossed the half-eaten biscuit into a wastebasket. 'They've ordered me to diet again, Gary. Which makes me cranky as hell. It came down from no less an authority than the White House physician, who speaks in a voice like God's. Galbraith, he says, there's a svelte person inside you, and he's dying to get out. Either you let him out, or you die. Svelte, I ask you. Do I look like there's a thin bugger inside me pining for freedom?'

Iverson said nothing because he'd never known how to make small talk. Years of military service and discipline had robbed him of most social graces. He was all business. He smiled uneasily as he looked at the fat man, knowing full well that Galbraith's obesity was his trademark as much as Aunt Jemima's face on a packet of pancake mix. On the Washington dinner-party circuit, at least along that inner track where the real powerbrokers wined and dined, several people had perfected an imitation of the Galbraith waddle, which the fat man responded to in a good-natured fashion. None of his impersonators knew for sure what he did for a living, an ignorance Galbraith fostered by behaving in a self-deprecating way. He made fat jokes at his own expense. My obesity, he'd once told Iverson, is my cover – in more ways than one.

Iverson said, 'You were talking about a human idiot, sir.'

'Yes, so I was.' Galbraith returned to the sofa and plumped himself down. Iverson's presence was comforting to him because Gary was a man without hidden emotions. No neuroses, no festering depths. Galbraith sometimes thought that Iverson was a relic from the Eisenhower years, when no shadows disturbed the American psyche, a time when the boy next door was exactly that, not some secret cock-flasher or dope fiend or peeping-tom. Iverson made Galbraith positively *nostalgic* for the simpler days of the Cold War, the apple-pie days.

'I'm talking about an idiot who has scuppered our friend Vabadus, and has thus threatened White Light.'

'Scuppered?'

Galbraith looked wan suddenly. 'Vabadus is dead, Gary. He was shot by someone unknown to us.'

Iverson went straight to the only point that mattered to him. 'Before or after the connection?'

'Before, alas. It wouldn't have mattered had it happened after. Then we'd know everything was secured.' Galbraith made a fist out of one of his plump hands in a rare gesture of irritation. 'It's my understanding that dear old Scotland Yard has become involved, which may pose problems for us.'

'Of course,' Iverson said.

'With luck, they may miss the point. They may simply overlook it. On the other hand . . . '

'On the other hand the Yard may become a little too alert,' Iverson said.

'Precisely, Gary. And we can hardly tell our British allies what's going on, can we? Nobody tells them anything these days in any event, so why awaken them from their well-deserved slumber now and talk to them about White Light?' Galbraith sat back and sighed. He turned the name White Light around in his head for a moment. It was the in-house code for the Baltic project. Galbraith, who had grown up in intelligence agencies at a time when code-names were bestowed on anything that moved, had christened this project White Light in memory of his one trip through the Baltic countries at the height of the so-called Khrushchev 'thaw'. What the fat man most remembered, aside from a rather depressing socialist shabbiness in the capital cities of the Baltic, was the extraordinary length of summer nights and how the sky was suffused by an odd white clarity.

'So what do we do?' Iverson asked.

Galbraith stared at the younger man. 'I think the only reasonable thing is to keep a very close eye on the situation in London and if it gets out of hand – if, say, certain persons at the Yard get a little too alert – then we may have to do a dark deed.'

Iverson, who knew what was meant by the phrase dark deed, nodded his head slowly. 'What do we know about the killer?'

Galbraith took a folded sheet of paper from the pocket of his huge robe and passed it to Iverson. 'So far only a name, which I've written down for you.'

Iverson stared at the name. 'You want me to look into his background?'

'I think it's essential.' Galbraith picked up the remote device and pressed a button and all two dozen screens flickered back to life. He stared at one screen in particular, which showed a list of all fighter planes, mainly F-16s, allotted to NATO, and their schedule for that day. 'At least I don't see any problem with this aspect of the matter,' and he waved a hand at the screen.

'That's the easy part,' Iverson agreed.

'I love smooth sailing, Gary. I love it when the parts click nicely together. It's like solving Rubik's Cube by sound alone.' Galbraith tapped the remote device on the surface of the table. 'But I just hate unexpected problems. And I especially hate the idea of anything unfortunate happening to Scotland Yard personnel, God knows. Sometimes, though, self-interest takes precedence over sentiment, Gary. It's that kind of world these days. I wish it were otherwise. But we're all realists in this neck of the woods.'

Iverson agreed again. It was another thing Galbraith liked about Gary. He was such an agreeable fellow. Galbraith dismissed him, heard him go back up the stairs, then there was the sound of the door closing. Alone, the fat man stared at his black and white electronic universe in an absent manner. He was thinking about Vabadus again. He felt he'd lost a friend, even though he'd never met the man. Vabadus, in Estonian, meant freedom. Galbraith thought it a very appropriate choice for the late Aleksis Romanenko.

London

Frank Pagan's flat in Holland Park had more than a touch of squalor about it. It was the kind of place in which a man clearly lived a solitary life. Somehow, Pagan had the feeling that it was always late in this apartment, always dark, as if sunlight never managed to find its way through the curtains. When he stepped into the living-room, the first thing he did was to pour himself a glass of Glenlivet. He surveyed the chaos of things like a stranger who finds himself suddenly tossed into another man's world. There was a milk bottle with curdled contents and three slices of hardened toast and a glass of orange-juice that had alchemised into an antibiotic. Pagan shut his eyes and savoured the drink.

In Roxanne's day, of course, everything had been different. But there was an abyss of self-pity here Pagan didn't want to encounter. Recollections of a dead wife were at best numbing, at worst excruciating. Loneliness had a gravity all its own and it pulled you down into its bleak centre. He stepped into the bedroom and wondered how long it had been since he'd laid flowers on Roxanne's grave. Weeks now, he supposed. There had been a time when he'd gone daily to that terrible fucking place and stared at the headstone as if, through the sheer mystic effort of will, he might conjure the dead woman up out of the cold earth and love her again.

He sat on the edge of the unmade bed and stared into his drink. He wondered if he was somehow getting better, if he was finding a quiet place to put his grief, like some safe-deposit box of the heart where it could be left locked and hidden. He'd removed Roxanne's photograph from the bedside table three months ago but in some odd way it was still there and he imagined it always would be. He closed his eyes again and sipped his drink and tried not to think about his wife and the way she'd died that Christmas because of the festive activities of a mad Irish bomber who'd detonated a killing device on a crowded London street. All he knew was that the planet without her was not exactly a better place. And perhaps this was the loneliest and most dreadful realisation of all – the world was reduced, diminished, by her absence.

These painful recognitions dismayed him. He rose, wandered to his stereo, found a record and set it on the turntable. It was an old Bo Diddley tune named *Mona*, with the kind of hard, driving rhythm that was almost a form of anaesthetic. He turned up the volume and let the noise crowd the room. Pure therapy, raucous and uncomplicated. Then, as if compelled to move by the music, he strolled around the room.

Consider simpler things that are not connected to love and grief. Consider the violence that had taken place at Waverley Station – when? Had it only been ten hours ago? The music had stopped now and the apartment was eerily quiet and he poured himself a second Glenlivet.

Perhaps it was more than his injured ego that made him want to impose a mystery on the event in Edinburgh, that made him want to look for hidden depths where Tommy Witherspoon claimed there were none. Perhaps it was the fact that his life, which had been about as exciting as that of a guppy mooning around inside an aquarium, had taken an interesting turn. It might be nothing but a brief illusion of mystery – even that was more intriguing than the blunted way things had been before.

He turned his thoughts once more to the contents of Romanenko's briefcase and as he was wondering whether Danus Oates had translated the material, he was surprised to hear the sound of his doorbell ringing. He went to the intercom and turned it on.

A woman's voice, distorted by the outmoded electrical system, said, 'Mr Pagan?'

'Speaking,' was all Pagan could think to reply.

'I know it's late, but I'd like to see you.'

The accent was American. Pagan looked quickly around the apartment. How in the name of God could he have a visitor in a dump like this, especially a woman?

'My name's Kristina Vaska,' the woman said. 'I realise we don't know each other, Mr Pagan.'

'Can it wait?' Pagan asked. 'It's been a long day and I'm tired.'

'I appreciate that. But it's very important I see you. It concerns Aleksis Romanenko.'

'You better come up. I'm on the second floor.'

He pressed the buzzer that unlocked the front door. Immediately he began to clear some of the mess from the dining-room table, a futile effort because no sooner had he carried the glass of penicillin and the milk bottle into the kitchen than he heard the woman knocking lightly on his door.

She was in her late twenties, possibly early thirties, and as soon as he looked at her Pagan realised it was the person he'd seen driving the yellow VW around Grosvenor Square. He was struck at once by the intensity of her eyes, which were that shade of brown that comes close to blackness, the absence of light. And yet there were lights, tiny flecks that seemed almost silver to Pagan. She had a wonderful square jaw that suggested tenacity. Her dark hair, cut very short, was curled tightly against her head. There was no makeup on her face. She wore a white linen jacket and blue jeans, all very casual, and she carried a bulky shoulder-bag. She was lovely in the effortless way some women seem to be, as if by pure chance, a happy collision of disparate elements. The word Pagan wanted was serendipity.

'My humble abode,' he said, thinking he might make some excuse about how his cleaning lady had the pox and couldn't come, poor old dear, and he was sorry about the shambles.

Pagan stared at breadcrumbs on the soiled table linen and cursed the odd nervousness that had afflicted him suddenly, the unease. It was almost as if the ghost of Roxanne Pagan sat in the bedroom, resentful at the intrusion of a woman into the apartment. Pagan underwent a mild sense of guilt. It was pure bloody nonsense, he thought. It was something a man had to grow out of. The spirits had their own lives to lead. And the living had living to do. But why was it so *difficult?*

The woman held out her hand and Pagan shook it a little too quickly. Her skin was cool against his own.

'I'm sorry it's this late,' she said.

Pagan was too restless for sleep anyway. He gestured towards a chair and Kristina Vaska sat down. He noticed she was very slender in the way dancers sometimes are, that she moved as if her body were an instrument she played unconsciously. Pagan was so unaccustomed to company in this place that he didn't think to offer her a drink. Besides, now that she had impressed him with her appearance, now that he'd looked carefully at her, he had a more important question to ask.

'Do you usually follow people around?'

Kristina Vaska smiled. 'Would you believe I was in Grosvenor Square at the same time as you by pure chance?'

'I've been known to entertain a few weird beliefs in my time,' he answered. 'That wouldn't be one of them.'

'I wanted to talk to you.'

'And so you followed me.'

She nodded her head, still smiling. It was the smile that did it, he thought. He'd always been a sucker for a mischievous grin, for that certain elfin quality. He saw at once that Kristina Vaska was the kind of woman with whom you couldn't be angry for very long, which put him at an emotional disadvantage because he'd lost one of his more potent weapons – the forceful annoyance, the irritated flash of the eyes, which sometimes made people very wary of Frank Pagan because they sensed dangerous levels inside him.

'I've been following you ever since you left Scotland Yard. I trailed you all the way here. Then I got nervous. So I drove around for a while. After that, what the hell,' and she shrugged. 'I just pulled out the old courage and rang your doorbell. I figured I had nothing to lose.'

The quality of persistence, Pagan thought, and a suspicion formed in his mind that he didn't much like. 'Let me guess,' he said. 'You want a story. You want Frank Pagan's eyewitness account of murder in Edinburgh. Sorry to disappoint you, love, but I don't talk to the press.'

Kristina Vaska gazed at him, and her look was as cool as her hand had been a moment before. 'I don't have any association with the press, Mr Pagan.'

Pagan said nothing for a moment. He had a sense of sheer awkwardness. He fussed with the tablecloth, moving crumbs around. Empty gestures. He wished he could find something terrific to do with his hands. 'You mentioned Romanenko,' he said finally. 'Is there something you want to tell me?'

'Let me ask you a question first,' she said. 'What do you know about him?'

Pagan had an interrogator's dislike of having questions directed against him. 'Not much,' he replied.

'What do you know about the country he came from?'

'Russia?'

Kristina Vaska shook her head. 'Estonia, Mr Pagan.'

'I only know it's part of the Soviet Union \ "

'*According to whom*?' The tone of her question was as sharp as the point of a needle.

Pagan saw it coming. He knew what he was in for and he felt himself cringe. She was going to be one of those slightly cracked ladies, all spit and intensity, who had a firm political stand she shouted about at every opportunity, a portable platform she could assemble in no time at all out of the carpentry of her convictions. Apolitical himself, despite some left-wing leanings that had been stronger in his twenties, Pagan was very uncomfortable with zealots. In his personal experience they were either dangerous or deranged, and sometimes both at once. They had a habit of shaping the world to meet their own political requirements. To Pagan's way of thinking, zealots were first cousins to terrorists. It was just a matter of degree.

'The United States doesn't recognise Estonia as Soviet territory,' Kristina Vaska said. 'Nor does your own country. So far as the US and the UK are concerned, the Soviet Union illegally seized all three Baltic nations in 1940, after they'd been independent for twenty years.'

Pagan started to interrupt, but it was impossible.

'The pretext – and the Russians aren't exactly subtle when it comes to such matters – was that the Baltic had to be defended against the Nazi menace. When World War II started, the Germans drove the Russians out of the Baltic, which was only a temporary condition. The Russians came back in 1944 to take up where they'd, left off – as the great liberators of Estonia, Latvia and Lithuania.' Kristina Vaska paused a moment and what Pagan saw in those dark eyes was more than anger, it was a deeply-held resentment, the kind that lodges unshakably in the soul. She stood up and walked around the room now and Pagan, entranced by her movements, that indefinable harmony of motion called grace, watched her.

'The point is, Mr Pagan, the people of the world are very familiar with Nazi atrocities. They know about what happened to the Jews of Europe. But when it comes to Soviet atrocities in the Baltic, there's a kind of ignorance that frustrates the hell out of me. I'm talking about the mass deportations of Baltic nationals to Siberia. I'm talking about hundreds of thousands of people from three separate nations with their own language and cultures who were uprooted and shipped out of their homelands and if they were lucky enough to survive inconceivable journeys in railroad cars, they found themselves in labour camps, where most of them died anyway. This is a horror story, Mr Pagan. This is genocide, plain and simple. And it's going on to this very day. It's going on, perhaps in more subtle ways, but it's still happening because the KGB sees to that. The KGB makes sure, at every level of Baltic society, that the native peoples of the Baltic countries are being Russified – which is just a polite fucking word for extermination.'

She stopped moving and stared at him. He had the feeling he'd been hit across the skull with a stout wooden plank. She went on about how native languages were falling into disuse, cultures dying, how TV stations broadcast only in Russian, how young people were being conscripted into the Soviet Army and shipped to Afghanistan to fight a war they didn't care about on behalf of a system they despised, and Baltic peoples were being dispersed to other parts of the Soviet Union, and anybody who raised his voice to complain had the nasty habit of disappearing from view.

There was an aura of energy about her, almost a force-field. Pagan, who could think of nothing to say because she'd somehow managed to make him feel a little ashamed of his own neglect of recent history and uncomfortable with what she surely perceived in him as insensitivity, wondered about her background. She talked with an American accent, but what was her family history?

'I'm sorry,' she said.

'Sorry?'

'Sorry you don't know more about it. And sorry I went on at you. I hate to lecture.'

'And I hate being lectured,' Pagan said. But he was intrigued just the same. He had run into many of the disenfranchised persons of Europe in his life. The Poles, the Hungarians, the sad exiles who formed social clubs in London suburbs and held dances and sometimes wrote letters to newspapers. It was just that he hadn't considered the Baltic nations as countries with identities as singular as those of Poland or Hungary or Czechoslovakia. He'd always thoughtlessly assumed they were indivisibly a part of the Soviet Union and if he ever considered them at all it was a process that took place on some far edge of his awareness, a subject that never troubled him, never came into focus in a place where he could see it clearly. Every now and then he'd read about a student riot in Latvia or some form of protest by the Catholic Church in Lithuania, every now and then he'd absently read about petitions delivered to the United Nations by people with strange, unpronounceable names – but there was a distance to these things, as if he were seeing them down the wrong end of a telescope. It was, he realised, unforgivably parochial of him. And it was no real justification to tell himself that cops weren't exactly famous for their interest in affairs beyond their own particular parish, which was usually small and well-defined, a tidy little patch where you knew all the scams that were going on.

'People forget,' Kristina Vaska said. 'That's the problem. When a wrong isn't righted immediately, it becomes the status quo, and people just don't think about it any more. It's easy, you see. It's the complacent way.'

'And I'm complacent,' Pagan said.

'And ignorant. Which pisses me off.' She looked around the room. 'And you also live like a pig, which pisses me off even more.'

Pagan smiled. Her earnestness had suddenly gone and there was levity in her expression and he could see, behind the features that had become so damned stern a moment before, a sense of humour, a warmth. 'I'm not here a great deal,' he said feebly.

'I can't say I blame you.' She glanced through the kitchen door, which unfortunately Pagan had left open. 'Now there's a room where some bodies might be buried. I bet you lie awake at nights and hear things moving about inside the refrigerator.'

Frank Pagan closed the kitchen door. 'I thought you came here to talk about Romanenko,' he said.

'You needed a little edification first.'

'Which you provided.'

'I'm not exactly through with the background yet, Mr Pagan.'

'I had the feeling,' he said. The education of Frank Pagan, he thought. And so we grow.

Kristina Vaska wandered to the window and ran the palm of one hand down the edge of the curtain. Then she let her hand fall to her side and turned to face Pagan. 'I don't know how serious you are, Mr Pagan. And I don't know how seriously you take me. Sometimes you seem just a bit flippant. Maybe it's something in your manner.'

'I'm listening,' Pagan said. 'Seriously.'

'I don't suppose you've ever heard of a man called Norbert Vaska?'

Pagan shook his head. 'A relative of yours?'

'My father.'

There was a silence in the room suddenly. Pagan was aware of the quietness of the night pressing against the house, the darkness laying a still film upon the window. And Kristina Vaska, who could go from impassioned enthusiast to bantering domestic critic in a matter of seconds, had changed yet again. Her eyes were directed into herself and Pagan knew that whatever she was looking at it wasn't anything in this room.

'My father taught engineering at the Tallinn Polytechnical Institute in Estonia,' she said. 'He was a good engineer. At least he was a better engineer than he was a Communist. He didn't believe in the system. He had status, you understand, and materially his life was fine. A car. A good apartment. A refrigerator. Things we take for granted in the West. Unlike some people, though, my father couldn't continue living under a system he considered malignant just because he happened to be one of the privileged ones. In 1966 he joined a group called the Estonian Movement for Democracy which developed ties with similar groups in Latvia and Lithuania.'

She glanced at Pagan, as if she wanted to be absolutely sure of his attention. He thought how grave she looked now.

'He became an editor of an underground newspaper, the *Estonian Independent Voice*. This involved considerable risk to himself. Maybe you can imagine that. Aside from writing articles and distributing the newspaper furtively, he often had to make trips to Riga in Latvia, or he'd go to Vilnius in Lithuania. I've tried to imagine how terrifying it must have been for him – attending underground meetings in the dead of night in somebody's apartment . . . a group of men whispering about how to fight the Soviet occupation of their countries. I've often tried to picture that scene and I always feel the same cold fear. Here was a man with a position, prepared to risk it all for his personal beliefs.'

She looked at Pagan, almost as if she wanted to be sure he was listening. 'He was arrested by the KGB on April 14, 1972. I remember it clearly. There was a knock on the door after midnight. Now there's a simple little phrase that's utterly terrifying, Mr Pagan. There's something people like you and me don't have to live with. A knock on the door after midnight. Three men took my father away. They had no warrant. Who needs a goddam warrant if they're KGB anyhow? They ransacked the apartment. They trashed the place. They left my mother and me behind. We heard nothing more about my father for three months. He'd been put in what's called "special confinement". That's a goddam awful phrase. You see nobody. You talk to nobody. You get nothing to read. You sit in a windowless room and you know nothing because nobody tells you anything. After three months, we heard he'd been sentenced to life imprisonment in the city of Perm in the Soviet Union. It was one of those places that pretend to be psychiatric institutes. You've heard of them, no doubt.'

Frank Pagan said he had and that he was sorry to hear about her father. But he wondered where this was going, how the dots were going to be connected, what the relationship was between Romanenko and Kristina Vaska's narrative.

'After, we heard he'd been transferred to a labour camp in the Arctic Circle. Then, without any warning, my mother and I were expelled from the country and flown to Helsinki. All this was done, you understand, without one single word of explanation. Nothing. A car came to fetch us. We were told to pack as much as two suitcases would hold. We were given passports. We were handed expulsion papers, which meant we were stripped of Soviet citizenship – although that didn't exactly cause a great gnashing of teeth. After a month in Helsinki we went to the United States. On September 12, 1972, we arrived in New York City. I'm good with dates, Mr Pagan. Certain dates just seem to stick in my mind. For example, I haven't seen my father since April, 1972. It's a long time. It's too long.'

She moved across the room. She came very close to Pagan as she passed. He was aware of something stirring in the air around him. Call it electricity, he thought. Whatever it was, it took him by surprise. It was an unexpected reaction and he wasn't sure how to deal with it.

'I know it's brave of me,' she said. 'But I'm going to risk your kitchen. I'm dry. I need water.'

She opened the kitchen door. Pagan heard her rinse a glass, then there was the sound of ice-cubes being pried loose from the freezer. When she came back she smiled at him. 'There's a process known as defrosting a freezer, Mr Pagan. A polar bear could live in yours.' She sat down, sipped her water, stared at him.

'I was never very good at science at school. I don't understand the principles of freezers.'

'I don't think it takes an Einstein,' she said, shaking the slightly furry, opaque cubes in her glass.

Pagan turned the subject away from his embarrassing domestic life. 'Have you heard from your father?'

'He's not exactly in a place served by a postman, Mr Pagan. As for his location, I'm not sure. The last time I heard any news about him he was in a labour camp near Murmansk in Siberia. That was more than a year ago. According to my source, he was very ill. He had pneumonia and he wasn't getting the right kind of medication. There's no such thing as a malpractice suit in a Siberian labour camp.'

Frank Pagan said, 'I keep reading in the papers that things are supposed to be getting better for political prisoners in the Soviet Union.'

'Sure, if you're a famous physicist or you've got influential friends in the West. But not if you're simply a former professor of engineering at the Polytechnic in Tallinn. Norbert Vaska doesn't have clout. He's just another forgotten prisoner, another number among thousands. It's going to take years and years if men like my father are ever going to be released under some general amnesty programme. It takes a long time for anything to change in Russia. There are too many people with a vested interest in the system. People who don't like change at any price.' She drained her glass, set it down on the table. 'Which brings me – finally – to Aleksis Romanenko. You were probably wondering.'

'It had crossed my mind,' Pagan said. And for some reason he couldn't name he felt an odd little tension go through him. He had the feeling that whatever conclusion Kristina Vaska was approaching, it was somehow going to complicate his life. He saw her reach inside her large purse. As she did so, the telephone rang and Pagan put out his hand towards it, annoyed by the sudden intrusion of the world outside, irritated by any interference at the crucial point of the woman's story. He had an unhappy rapport with phones at the best of times. Now it was a sheer bloody nuisance and he was tempted just to ignore it and go on listening to Kristina Vaska. But he didn't.

The urgent voice he heard was the Commissioner's.

'Young Oates has turned up something that might pique your interest, Frank. I suggest you drop whatever – or whoever – you're doing, and get your arse over here on the double. I'm keeping a very unhappy Russian diplomat at bay, and I don't know how long I can stall him before the Third World War breaks out.'

'I'll be there,' Pagan said. When Martin Burr used the phrase 'I suggest', it was always a command meant to be obeyed immediately.

'Come in that fast American car of yours and pretend we've just abolished the speed limit, would you?'

'Give me ten minutes,' Pagan said.

'Make it nine. And I'm not joking. There's been another development here, quite apart from Oates's translation, that might come as something of a surprise.'

Pagan put the telephone down. Shit. How could Martin Burr's timing be so damned bad? He looked at Kristina Vaska, who was watching him expectantly. He wondered what kind of surprise Burr had in mind.

'I'm sorry, he said. 'I've just been summoned by the Commissioner. It's like getting a message from God.'

'Then you don't want to keep God waiting,' she said. 'I'll put the end of my story on hold, Mr Pagan.'

'How do I get in touch with you?'

Kristina Vaska shrugged. 'I haven't made a hotel reservation.' There it was again – that smile which changed her entire face and made her eyes light up and dissolved all the gravity of her expression. 'I could easily wait here. I mean, if you don't mind. If you don't think I'll be in the way.'

'I don't know when I'll be back,' Pagan said.

'I'm not in any hurry.'

Pagan, who was seized by a feeling of total discomfort, gestured toward the sofa. 'It opens out into a bed,' he said. 'You'll find blankets in the bedroom if you need them.' He thought of this woman stepping inside his bedroom, and the image was an odd one, like a picture hanging aslant on a wall.

'I'll be okay. Don't worry about me, Mr Pagan.'

He hesitated a moment in the doorway. It was obvious that she sensed his awkwardness and found it amusing.

'Just don't go anywhere,' he said. 'I'm anxious to hear the rest of your story.'

'I promise you'll find it very interesting.'

Pagan opened the door. But he was still hesitant. It was all very strange to him. A woman in his apartment, an attractive woman waiting for his return. Somebody with an unfinished narrative that was connected to the disaster in Edinburgh. Why hadn't Martin Burr waited just a few minutes more before telephoning? Pagan hated interrupted stories.

'Don't worry. It's perfectly safe to leave me here,' she said. 'Cross my heart I won't steal the silverware. It's probably lying in the sink anyway, too dirty to steal.'

Pagan smiled. 'I wasn't thinking about the silverware.'

Kristina Vaska said, 'I bet you don't have any anyhow. You look like a man who uses disposable plastic cutlery, Mr Pagan.'

'Call me Frank,' he said. 'And if you want to know the real truth, I eat with my hands.'

Saaremaa Island, the Baltic Sea

It was almost dawn when Colonel Yevgenni Uvarov stepped out of his quarters and walked quietly across the concrete compound. He passed under the shadows of the radar scanners, which turned silently, ominously, in the early light. Anything that moved out there on the Baltic would send a signal back to the scanners, which would then feed the signal into the one-storey building Uvarov now entered. There was a row of small green screens that received the radar transmissions. They were largely inactive and the technicians who stared at them were bored in the manner of men who spend their days in expectant vigilance that more often than not fails to produce excitement. They watched the screens and their eyesight invariably became bad over a period of time. Uvarov had the thought that the men under his command were prisoners of the green screens, hopelessly addicted to studying radar signals.

Uvarov crossed the large room, pausing every now and then to examine one of the screens, or to check the progress of a trainee operator. He reached his desk, located at the back of the room, and he sat down. His chair was hideously uncomfortable. The surface of his desk was clear. There was nothing of a personal nature to be seen anywhere. He kept a photograph of his wife and children inside the desk. Every now and then, as if to remind himself of the reason for his decision, he'd open the drawer and glance at the photograph – and what filled him was a sense of devotion and gratitude and love. He had only to look at the photograph, which was a stiff studio shot done in slightly unreal colours, to make himself believe that his course of action was the correct one. Just the same, he often felt a fear so great be was convinced it showed on his face, that other people couldn't fail to notice it. And sometimes the fear yielded to a kind of despair – he had spent fifteen years of his life in the Army and within the next few days he was going to throw it all away. The whole thing had the texture of a bad dream, a nightmare in which he was trapped as surely as a fly in the jaws of a spider.

His wife and two teenage children lived in Moscow. Uvarov only saw his family whenever he was granted leave. It didn't happen often. Last year, when his wife had fallen ill, he'd requested compassionate leave, and he'd been denied. The refusal galled him. The service to which he'd devoted so much of his adult life should not have denied him such a simple plea. But it was the system, it was the way the system worked, with a lack of understanding for human needs. Uvarov felt he'd been denied more than compassionate leave. He'd been denied his humanity. And his family had suffered needlessly.

A year ago. How much had changed in that short time, he thought. He yawned because he'd slept badly. He always slept badly these days. He stood up, walked around the room, observed the operators at their screens. Then he went outside.

He could hear the slow Baltic tide that came and went upon the beach beyond the wire perimeter. A few gulls, scavenging the shoreline, flapped in the dawn light. This depressing island, thick with military installations, rocket-bases and airfields and anti-ballistic missile interceptors, was another factor in his sense of general disappointment. Now and then an opportunity arose for brief leave on the mainland, which meant perhaps a twelve-hour visit to Tallinn – certainly never enough time to travel to where his family lived. Whenever he returned from Tallinn, a pleasant medieval city, a place with a sense of life and colour, it took days before he could suppress his restlessness and discontent.

He raised his face to the sky. Overhead, six MIG-27s flew in formation, breaking the cloud cover and then vanishing in the direction of the mainland. An impressive display, he thought. A show of force and strength. Suddenly Uvarov felt small and insignificant and the task he'd agreed to do struck him as overwhelming. He wouldn't go through with it, he couldn't, he didn't have the nerve. But then he wasn't alone in the undertaking, there were others involved, officers like himself who were ready to act at the appointed time – or so he'd been told by the man he'd met several times in Tallinn. What if it was a lie, a kind of sadistic ploy to test his loyalty? What if the man in Tallinn was some kind of inspector of internal affairs whose job it was to detect the potentially disloyal, the weak, those who had no commitment to the system?

Uvarov felt a tightness in his heart. He moved back in the direction of the low, grey-stone building, passing once again under the radar scanners. He sometimes had the feeling he was doomed to spend his whole life in this wretched place, forever commanding the men who endlessly studied the green screens and waited for the sky to reveal signs of danger. It was an awful prospect, one he couldn't tolerate.

He opened the door, crossed the room, returned to his desk. He sat down, studied the reports of NATO activities that had been recorded in yesterday's logs, the usual harmless catalogue of flights, the practice bombs dropped beyond Russian territorial waters, the idle strafing of the Baltic, nothing out of the ordinary. Then he pushed his chair back from his desk and thought of the photograph in the drawer – which reminded him of the very thing he didn't want to think about, the brown envelope concealed under the floorboards of his family's apartment in Moscow, the package that contained three US passports and fifty thousand American dollars in small bills that had been given to him by the man in Tallinn, the man he knew only as Aleksis.

6

London

The surprise Martin Burr had mentioned turned out to be depressing and sickening. Frank Pagan stood motionless in the doorway of Kiviranna's cell while the Commissioner hobbled around inside the small chamber, his cane making quiet ticking sounds on the floor.

Burr said, 'Have to hand it to him. He was an ingenious bugger.'

Pagan crossed the threshold, thinking how the cell was too small to contain three men, even if one of them was dead. Jacob Kiviranna lay across his bunk. The mattress had been removed and was propped up against the wall. A long length of wire, one end of which lay close to Kiviranna's lips, was attached to the light-fixture in the ceiling. The bulb had been unscrewed and lay on the floor. Kiviranna's eyes were closed and there were black burn marks around his lips and nostrils. Urine soaked the blanket he'd wrapped himself in. The cell, poorly ventilated, smelled of scorched flesh.

'He unhooked the bedsprings from the frame, patiently straightened out a length of wire, stuck one end into his mouth then the other into the electric socket,' Burr said, and peered up at the wire that dangled from the ceiling.

Pagan looked down at the corpse, then turned away, went out into the corridor. Martin Burr followed. Pagan peered the length of the corridor for a time, saying nothing, trying to imagine Jake placing the wire between his lips, laying it over his moist tongue, then standing up on the bed-frame to unscrew the lightbulb and twist the free end of the wire into the socket. He felt a fleeting nausea. Suicide always struck him the same way – a sheer bloody waste. What had prompted it, what madness, what fears had come to Jake in the darkness of the cell and driven him to such an act?

Both men were quiet for a moment before Burr said, 'Let's go back up to my office. We'll have a glass of something, then look at what young Oates has produced.'

Frank Pagan hesitated a second before he followed Martin Burr in the direction of the lifts. He was thinking how tidy it all seemed now. Too tidy. Both assassin and victim were dead, which – if Jake had been telling the truth – left only an enigmatic accomplice in the United States, somebody who might already have disappeared into the shadows from which he'd first namelessly emerged. Somebody who, if Ted Gunther failed to turn anything up, might always remain an anonymous mystery.

Pagan stepped inside the lift, beset by an unexpected sense of anger at Jacob Kiviranna. He closed his eyes as the cage climbed in the shaft. Whatever answers Jake might personally have been able to provide were forever lost now.

It seemed more stuffy than usual in Burr's uncluttered office. Pagan picked up the sheet of paper the Commissioner had laid on the desk. For a second all he saw as he stared at it was the sight of Kiviranna, an after-image dishearteningly impressed upon his retina. He drained the shot of Drambuie Burr had poured for him, then set the glass down. He knew you were supposed to savour the stuff, but he wasn't exactly in a sipping frame of mind.

'Poetry, Frank. Why would Romanenko carry around a piece of poetry inside a sealed envelope? I can understand a man travelling with a *volume* of poems, let's say, if he wants to while away some boring hours on a trip or if he needs to read himself to sleep. But what I *don't* understand is sealing a few lines of the stuff inside an envelope.'

Pagan studied the sheet of paper that was covered with Danus Oates's cramped, scholarly handwriting. Here and there words had been crossed out and alternatives written carefully in the margin, indicating how Oates must have struggled over an exact translation. He'd also provided alternative words in parentheses.

> But the day will (tomorrow?) soon be breaking/When all the torches will be burning/ Throwing flames in widening circles/Which will free (untie? lit: cut the cord of) the arm embedded/In the mighty chains of rock./Kalev will be coming home/To bring happiness (contentment/freedom?) to the people/Of a new Estonia.

He placed the sheet on the Commissioner's desk. He didn't consider himself a judge of poetry, but he thought he knew enough to recognise bad verse when he saw it. 'I assume something's been lost in the translation,' he said.

'I agree it's somewhat overstated, but it sounds to me like a patriotic poem, and that kind of thing has a tendency to be bloated,' the Commissioner said, plucking at the edge of his eyepatch. 'The point is, who the hell is Kalev? And why was Romanenko carrying this particular poem around, Frank? It looks as if he'd had it in his case for half a bloody century too. The paper's practically falling to pieces. And here's another odd thing – Oates tells me it was written in a language I'd never heard of before, something called Livonian, which is almost extinct. According to Oates, it's related to modern Estonian, and to some elements of Latvian.'

Pagan looked at the poem again. He had difficulty concentrating. 'It could be a message Romanenko intended to deliver before he was killed. Maybe he was supposed to make contact with somebody in Edinburgh, somebody who'd understand the significance of those lines. Why carry something around in an envelope if you don't mean to deliver it?'

'A possibility,' the Commissioner remarked.

'It could also be a code of some kind.'

'I thought about that. If it's a code, where does one start? Codes are a bit out of our province.'

Frank Pagan had a moment in which he felt sleep flutter somewhere at the back of his head. 'What else did Danus Oates translate?' he asked.

The Commissioner indicated a small stack of papers at the side of the desk. 'That poem's the only unusual thing. There's some technical stuff as well as correspondence between Romanenko and a man called George Newby, the director of a microchip company in Basingstoke that was apparently tendering a bid for Romanenko's business.'

Pagan said, 'If Romanenko was supposed to meet somebody in Edinburgh, who was he? And what exactly did this individual do when Romanenko didn't show up? Did he just shrug his shoulders and walk away? The more I think about Aleksis, the more he slips between my fingers.'

He set the poem down on the desk, although he continued to stare at it. Kalev, he thought. It was the kind of name given to extraterrestrial characters in the comic books of his youth. Kalev! Emperor of Saturn ! Master of Cosmic Wisdom! Pagan could have used a little of that cosmic wisdom himself right then. He took his eyes away from the poem because staring wasn't bringing him any answers.

The Commissioner rolled his walnut cane back and forth on the surface of his desk. 'To make matters somewhat more intricate, there's an impatient little sod called Malik from the Soviet Embassy waiting downstairs for me. He's come to collect the briefcase. According to the Foreign Office, the case and its contents go back to the Russians. *Immediately.* I've been stalling Malik as best I could until I talked to you about this enigmatic poem. But if I don't return the material sharply, Malik's going to lodge an official protest with the Foreign Secretary, which would be a bore.'

Pagan stood up and walked around the windowless room. 'Do you intend to return the poem?' he asked.

The Commissioner smiled. It was the expression of a man who was no stranger to mischief. 'My feeling is that the Russians have got enough on their plate without having to worry about a bit of bad verse. And if anybody ever asks, we've never even heard of the bloody poem.'

Pagan saw something enjoyably conspiratorial in his superior's face. It was an aspect of the Commissioner's personality he liked – this sneaky way he had of taking risks, of defying authorities even higher than himself.

Pagan carefully placed Oates's translation of the poem, and the brittle original, back in the envelope, and stuck it in the inside pocket of his jacket. The Commissioner swept Danus Oates's other translations into a drawer, picked up a telephone, said something to whoever was on the other end of the line.

After a minute, Malik entered the room. He was a short man with enormous eyebrows and a face that suggested a rocky promontory. Pagan observed that the Russian, who wore a lightweight Aquascutum overcoat of a decidedly bourgeois nature, had a certain self-righteous expression on his face. He was the offended party, the victim of the tactics of capitalist law-enforcement officers, and consequently of monstrous capitalism itself, and nothing was going to change that. If need be, he'd play this injured role to the hilt. His eyebrows quivered as he spotted the briefcase.

'Are you ready to hand it over?' he demanded. His English was excellent.

'We've come to our senses at long last,' Pagan said.

Malik stared at Frank Pagan, obviously unsure of Pagan's tone, which was sarcastic. The Commissioner said, 'What Frank Pagan means is that you can take the briefcase. It's all yours, Mr Malik.'

Unceremoniously, Malik grabbed the case and held it against his chest. 'Your methods leave much to be desired, gentlemen,' he said. 'It's not enough that you fail to protect the life of a high Soviet official – you then confiscate the property of the Soviet Union, which you keep in your possession, without good reason, for twelve hours.'

The Commissioner made a soothing noise, although it was clear to Pagan that his heart wasn't in it. He was going through the motions of commiseration. Pagan leaned against the wall and folded his arms.

Malik patted the case. 'We are also going to make an official request to interrogate the killer of Romanenko. This will be done through the proper channels, of course.'

Both Pagan and Martin Burr were silent. Then Burr said, 'I'm afraid that won't be possible.'

'You're going to refuse the request?'

'I don't have a choice,' the Commissioner replied.

'And why is that?'

Martin Burr explained. Malik shook his head in disbelief. He said, 'First you allow Romanenko to be assassinated. Then you make it possible for the criminal to escape justice by committing suicide. What kind of organisation are you running?'

'I resent your tone,' Burr said. 'We hardly made it possible, as you put it, for Kiviranna to take his own life.'

'A suicide,' Malik remarked. 'How utterly convenient for you. Now the killer is no longer around to answer questions that might be embarrassing to you. Are you certain he took his own life?'

'What are you suggesting?' Burr asked. His face had turned the colour of a plum.

'His death spares you the need for a public trial, Commissioner. It spares you the awkwardness of putting the man in the witness-box, where he becomes the perfect symbol of your inadequacy to secure the life of a Soviet official. Who knows? Perhaps you even encouraged the unfortunate man's demise.'

'You're an outrageous twit,' Burr said, and thrust the tip of his cane into the rug, a wonderful little gesture of restrained savagery. His sense of fair play had been insulted but what else could he have expected from a Bolshevik anyway? They had their own rules and sometimes they defied the understanding of a decent man.

Malik moved toward the door. He clutched the briefcase at his side. 'Goodnight, Commissioner.'

The Commissioner harumphed. If the Russian was going to flaunt good sense, then he, Martin Burr, was most assuredly not going to observe good manners. So far as he was concerned, the Bolshevik didn't deserve common courtesies.

The door closed behind Malik.

'Little shit,' Burr said. 'Have you ever heard such balderdash in your life? The sheer gall of the man is appalling.'

The Commissioner sat down and sighed. He looked rather depressed all at once. 'What have we really got, Frank, when all is said and done?'

'We've still got Kalev.'

'Whoever he is,' Martin Burr remarked dismally.

Pagan was thinking of Kristina Vaska. He was thinking how he wanted to hear the rest of her narrative.

'I may have a way of finding out,' he said.

The Commissioner stared at his desk lamp. 'Let's hope so, Frank. I hate being in the dark.'

Frank Pagan agreed. The dark, with all its secrets, all its inaccessible corners, was not his place of choice. He thought about Aleksis – drunk, laughing, joking, dancing with a reluctant partner, an embarrassed English rose, in the subdued bar of the Savoy, a man of mirth and boundless energies. But it was clear now that there had been other sides to the man as well – secretive, submerged, hidden from view. And whatever they were they'd led to his own murder, a suicide, and the arrival of a woman, with an unfinished story, in Pagan's apartment.

Aleksis, Pagan thought, you may have been an insignificant Communist Party leader in some minor Soviet colony – *but what were you really up to?*

Zavidovo, the Soviet Union

Vladimir Greshko heard the sound of a car and turned his face to the window of his bedroom, seeing the first yellow light of dawn press upon the glass. He was always a little surprised to have lived through another night. Death, with all its dark finality, had been much on his mind during the last couple of weeks. He didn't believe in an afterlife. What would a man do with eternity anyhow, except scheme against his fellows? To form Marxist action committees and provoke Revolution in heaven? To convert angels to Engels and replace God with Communism?

He raised his face, rearranged his pillows, covered the plastic tube with the edge of his bedsheet. The obscene sucking sound of the device filled him with disgust.

He saw the bedroom door open. The Yakut nurse stepped in, nervously wiping her tiny hands in the folds of her white uniform. Behind her stood General Olsky. *Olsky – of all people!* The sight of the new Chairman of the KGB quickened Greshko's tired blood. He wondered what had brought Stefan Olsky all the way from Moscow to this godforsaken place.

Olsky wore a dark pinstriped suit. Greshko considered him a pencil-pusher, a clerk, a man without an ounce of flair in his soul, a colourless bureaucrat so typical of the new breed. He was Birthmark Billy's protégé and therefore a member of the Politburo's inner sanctum. When Greshko had run the organs of State Security, Olsky had been a mere Deputy in the Third Directorate. His rise, engineered by the General Secretary, had been spectacular. At the age of forty-one he was the youngest man in Soviet history to be Chairman of the KGB, which was another source of resentment for Greshko, who hadn't assumed control himself until his sixty-first birthday.

'You look well,' Stefan Olsky said.

Greshko said nothing for a moment. He seethed whenever he imagined Olsky occupying *his* office, sitting in *his* chair. He knew Olsky had had the office redecorated, that all the old paintings had been returned to storage and replaced by charts – charts, sweet Christ! – that the old phone system had been renovated and the six phones Greshko had enjoyed supplanted by a single device that allowed Olsky to hold what were known as 'conference' calls. Every day new changes. Every day something else swept away.

'I look as well as a dying man can,' Greshko said. 'You're trying to be kind, Stefan.'

Stefan Olsky approached the bed. This was his first visit to Greshko's cottage, and he'd heard about the old man's condition, but he hadn't been prepared for the smell that hung in this room – this commingling of human waste and disinfectant, this deathly odour.

Olsky stepped to the window, looked out. He had recently taken to shaving his head, as if to make himself look older, more experienced. He ran a palm self-consciously over his skull. His wife had pleaded with him to let the hair grow back. She said she didn't want to wake each morning and find an egg on the pillow next to her.

'It's pleasant here,' Olsky said. 'Greenery. Fresh air. Very nice.'

What had Olsky really come here for? And why so early in the day? Greshko surveyed the Chairman's face. Unmarked by experience, the old man thought. How could such a face frighten anybody? To run the organs you needed *presence*, you needed to be able to instil awe in other men. If Olsky had presence, if he had charisma, it was of a kind Greshko couldn't possibly understand. He was even a *teetotaller*, for God's sake, which fitted very nicely with Birthmark Billy's anti-vodka crusade. But what the General Secretary didn't realise was that vodka was the *fuel* of Mother Russia. To take vodka away, to reduce its production and price it beyond the means of a worker, was a natural disgrace, like yanking an infant from its mother's tit. But none of the new gang had any affinity for the heart of the country, at least not the way Vladimir Greshko, a poor peasant boy from the Stavropol Territory, perceived it. What did they know about the unending struggle against the bitter climate and a countryside racked by famine in the 1930s? They were all college boys, chicken-hearted, cologne in their armpits, educated by the benefits of a Revolution they were now attempting to dismantle. *Ingrates!*

Thoughts of Olsky provoked rage. What made things worse was that Greshko, at the time of his abrupt removal from office, had come into possession of information which alleged that Olsky had investments in Western European money-markets held, of course, in fictional names, dummy corporations and the like – but if the allegations were true, what kind of Communist did that make Stefan Olsky?

Greshko wished he'd been able to present this information to the Politburo, which would have been distressed by the furtive capitalism of Comrade Stefan, but by the time he decided to do so it was too damned late. All the doors had been slammed shut in his face with a finality that even now sounded through his brain. Too slow, old man, he thought. And perhaps just a little too complacent. But he still had the information, and a time might come when it would prove useful. One of the lessons of his long life was that you never threw *anything* away.

Olsky turned from the window and smiled. He had dark eyes and high cheekbones and a wide mouth that was rather pleasant and generous. 'I imagine it could get lonely here,' he said. 'You're lucky to have a great many friends, Vladimir.'

'I've been blessed,' Greshko remarked. What was Olsky driving at? 'I'm not completely forgotten by my old comrades.'

'Some of whom are very dedicated to you. Some of whom travel considerable distances to visit you,' Olsky said.

'Only to pay their last respects, Stefan.'

Olsky had always found Greshko to be slippery and devious. There was a certain charm about the old fart, which Olsky acknowledged rather grudgingly, although he'd never been a fan of Greshko's way of running the organs – autocratic, secretive, possessive. Olsky had heard Greshko referred to within the Politburo as King Vladimir, and not always jokingly.

Like a monarch, Greshko had ruled the KGB as if it were a court, with courtiers who curried favours and engineered palace intrigues in an atmosphere of distrust and malice. What underlay this regal technique of management was paranoia and fear – which had also forged durable loyalties between Greshko and many of his former subordinates, a fact that troubled Stefan Olsky. He didn't intend to run the organs the way Greshko had done. He believed in inter-departmental cooperation and an open-door policy – concepts that were not readily grasped by the old guard, who grumbled and complained at every little change and sometimes even reminisced openly, brazenly, about how things had been different under the control of General Greshko. It was going to be difficult and slow, and very demanding, to change the KGB.

'Is that why you've come, Stefan?' Greshko asked. 'To pay *your* last respects?'

'Not entirely. The fact is, some of your visitors . . . disturb me, Vladimir.'

Greshko smiled. 'Don't tell me you *spy* on me?' he asked in mock horror. He knew that some of the foresters who worked around Zavidovo sent information back to Moscow about who had been seen in the vicinity, what they'd done, where they'd gone. During his own tenure he'd received information from the same men who nowadays provided the service for Olsky.

'Reports have a way of reaching me,' Olsky said. 'Rumours are like homing pigeons.'

'And what do you hear, General?'

'Some of your friends have nostalgic longings. Some of them belong to certain organisations, Vladimir, that call themselves by such names as "Memories" or "Yesteryear" – consisting of men who have a dangerous yearning for the way things were. War veterans. Factory managers. Party members. And they have some sympathetic ears inside the Central Committee. Obstructionists, Vladimir. People who cling to the past.'

'I can't be held responsible for the sympathies of my friends,' Greshko said. 'People are slow to change their ways, Stefan. Give them time. Sooner or later, they'll get used to this new Russia you're building.' *This new Russia*. Greshko had uttered these words in a way that was almost sarcastic.

'What about you?' Olsky asked. 'Are you getting used to it?'

'I'm dying,' Greshko answered. 'I don't have time to get used to anything.'

Olsky was quiet a moment. The old boy could put on a good act, he could smile and look altogether innocent, but Olsky was wary. 'There's talk of a conspiracy, Vladimir. I hear rumours in Moscow. I hear them too often.'

'Conspiracy!' Greshko laughed, a rich, hearty sound. 'Listen to me, Stefan. A few old friends get together here and there. They talk about the old days. They drink vodka, get sentimental, they weep a little. Where's the conspiracy in that? One of the first lessons you must learn is that Moscow has a hidden rumour factory. My advice to you, comrade, is not to listen. Or if you must listen, be selective.'

Olsky walked back to the window. He had been Chairman for only five months now and the last thing he needed as he reorganised State Security was a conspiracy of hard-liners, diehards, old reactionaries whose imaginations could carry them no further than the idea that the greatest of all Russian leaders had been the murderer Stalin. Rumours, whispers, shadows – sometimes Olsky had the feeling he was listening to voices inside a closed room, voices that fell silent as he approached the door. He turned his face once more to Greshko. Even sick and dying, the old man managed to give off a glow that suggested residual power. What you had to remember about Greshko was that he still had friends in high places, that when you approached him you did so cautiously.

'Is that why you came here?' Greshko asked. 'To warn me about the company I keep?'

The atmosphere in this room was cloying. Olsky was anxious to go, to get inside the car and have his driver return him to Moscow. That night he'd promised to take his wife, an amorous woman called Sabina, to a new drama at the Sovremennik Theatre. For some reason, perhaps because of their air of freedom and licence, experimental plays always excited her, an excitement she brought back home to the bedroom. Olsky never tired of his wife's advances.

'There's one other thing,' he said.

'Go ahead.'

'I've been conducting an inventory, Vladimir. Of files. Computer data. Current cases.'

An inventory. Greshko thought how sadly typical it was of Olsky to make the organs sound like a damned haberdashery. 'And?'

'A certain file is unaccounted for, Vladimir. I don't have to remind you of how serious that is.'

'You don't have to remind me of anything.' Greshko thought of the documentation he'd removed and he felt a quick little shiver of tension. 'Clerks and computer operators are notoriously slipshod. They've probably made some kind of idiotic mistake.'

Olsky was silent a moment. 'We were able to establish that the missing file was that of somebody called Aleksis Romanenko, First Party Secretary in Tallinn. Whoever removed the file forgot to delete the name and number from the central directory.'

Damned computers, Greshko thought. He'd never really grasped all this new technology. He wondered if this was something that should worry him. Did it matter that Olsky knew Romanenko's file had been removed? Probably not. So long as he didn't know what was in the file, then it wasn't worth bothering about.

'What makes you so sure that the file was *removed*, Stefan? Sometimes there are glitches, and computers destroy their own data. Or so I've heard.'

'True,' Olsky said. 'But in this particular instance there was a date when the file disappeared. The computer recorded the date automatically, which it would not have done if the program were malfunctioning. So I'm led to believe the material was *deliberately* taken.'

'By whom?' Greshko asked.

Olsky shook his head. 'I have no idea. I thought perhaps you might be able to throw a little light on the matter. You had charge of the files at the time when this particular data was taken.'

'One file among hundreds of thousands? Are you serious? I've never even heard of this fellow – what did you say his name was?'

'Romanenko.'

Greshko looked incredulous. 'Really, Stefan. What's so damned important about one missing file in any case? What's such a big deal that the Chairman himself has to worry about a trifle like this?'

Olsky went to the door, which he opened. He looked across the kitchen at the Yakut woman, who was stirring food in a saucepan over the wood stove. She turned her face, regarded him briefly, then looked away again.

Olsky said, 'Normally, it might mean nothing. But Romanenko was assassinated yesterday.'

'*Assassinated?*'

'In the circumstances, the missing file struck me as an odd coincidence.'

Greshko placed his hands together on the surface of his quilt. 'Ah, now I understand your puzzlement.' He tapped the side of his skull. 'The name means nothing to me, but if I remember anything, I'll be sure to get in touch with you. The trouble is, my memory's like some damned dog that won't come when I call it. I'll try, though. I promise you. I'll try.'

'I'd be grateful,' Olsky said. There was a long pause before Olsky looked at his watch. 'I have to return to Moscow.'

'Of course,' Greshko said.

'Goodbye, Vladimir.'

As he stepped out, Olsky watched Greshko's face, which in shadow appeared enigmatic. But perhaps not. Perhaps there was some other expression barely apparent in the shadows, a hint of amusement, of pleasure, like that of a man enjoying some hugely private joke.

Olsky had no illusions about the way Greshko despised him. He left the house and stood for a moment under a large oak, which shielded him from the morning sun. He listened to the drone of flies, the cawing of rooks, the sound of a horse whinnying in the distance. Then he looked in the direction of his car, wondering if it had been a mistake to come here in the first place. Simple vanity – was that it? Had he wanted the old man to see that the organs of State Security were at last in strong young hands? That the dried-out old ways were inevitably passing and a new generation was changing things? To impress and perhaps worry a sick old man – was that why he'd mentioned conspiracy and his knowledge of Greshko's friendships? If so, he'd underestimated the former Chairman, who wasn't likely to be in the least concerned by references to intrigues and acquaintances of dubious loyalties. A dying man was beyond ordinary fears.

Olsky moved out from under the tree. When he reached his car, he looked back at the cottage. No, he thought. It was the missing file that had really brought him here from Moscow, a file whose removal could have been achieved only by Vladimir Greshko himself or by somebody who'd been given that authority by the old man.

It was strange, he thought, how the old man hadn't asked a single question about Romanenko's assassination – no interest in place and time, no interest in detail, the means the assassin had used or if he'd been apprehended. Absolutely nothing.

Either Greshko didn't give a damn about the killing or else he'd already learned the details of Romanenko's murder from another source. If the latter was true, then he'd been lying when he'd denied ever having heard of Romanenko.

Olsky got inside the car, settled back in his seat and closed his eyes, unable to shake the feeling that Greshko, in his wily way, had been playing a game with him for the past thirty minutes, a game based on subterfuge and concealment. And Olsky felt the frustration of a man trying to introduce new rules when certain players stubbornly prefer sticking, no matter what, to the old ones.

Ten minutes after Olsky's departure, Greshko spoke into the telephone. 'Has Epishev gone?'

'He left five hours ago, General,' Volovich replied. 'On the first available flight.'

Greshko set the receiver down. He looked at the calendar on the wall. There were now four days left. Sighing, longing to smoke one of the cigars his physician had denied him, he tried to content himself with squeezing a small rubber ball he kept in the bedside table. It was a poor substitute for drawing rich tobacco smoke deep into one's lungs. By God, how he would have loved to light one! He tossed the stupid ball aside in a gesture of contempt, then he opened the flask that contained the special mixture.

He sipped, thought of Olsky, smiled. It was fascinating to watch the new Chairman fish in waters too deep for him ever to penetrate. *You're keeping the wrong kind of company, General Greshko. A certain file is missing, General Greshko. Wipe my arse for me, General Greshko.*

Greshko laughed aloud. He would love to nail Olsky, to crucify that shaven-headed upstart, to see him hung out to dry like a bundle of wet kindling.

Four days. He corked his flask, knowing he could live that long.

7

London

Kristina Vaska was amused by Pagan's apartment. She wandered through the rooms slowly, thinking disorder was almost a law of nature here, from the untidiness of the bedroom to the flaky state of the bathroom, where towels and discarded socks formed a small, lopsided pyramid. But Jesus, there was something touching in all this mess, something that, in spite of herself, provoked a maternal response. It was an easy reaction and she didn't trust it. If Pagan couldn't look after his domestic life by himself, why should she even think of doing it for him? She'd long ago given up the notion that there was something engaging about men who needed to be looked after. Like careless boys, they couldn't fend for themselves – but she was damned if she was going to find such helplessness attractive. Pagan was already appealing enough in his own hesitant way. He didn't need the assistance of charming ineptitude.

In the bedroom she came across a silver locket that hung from the lampshade by a thin silver chain. On the back of the ornament were the initials R.P. She fingered the item for a time, wondering about the initials. Somebody P. Somebody Pagan.

In the drawer of the bedside table she solved the problem. She found a framed photograph of a woman, a lovely woman with an intelligent face. Across the bottom of the picture were the words *With all my love, Roxanne, September 83. Our Third Anniversary.* Kristina Vaska put the photograph back and wondered what had become of Pagan's wife that she was nothing more than a picture stuffed in a drawer and a locket hung from a lampshade.

She crossed the bedroom and opened a closet, where several suits and sports coats hung on a rack. This was obviously Frank Pagan's neat corner, his tidy place. The suits and jackets were enclosed in transparent plastic bags, set aside from the general chaos of the apartment. An island of order. The suits were good ones, well-tailored in a modern way, and some of the sports coats were, well, slightly ostentatious. There were also several shirts whose patterns might have been designed by a coven of drunken Cubists. Frank Pagan was clearly a man of some vanity who tried to keep in touch with sartorial trends. On the bottom of the closet were shoes, most of them casual slip-ons, all neatly aligned.

She shut the closet and sat on the edge of the bed, staring through the open bedroom door into the living-room, where a stack of long-playing records was arranged against one wall. The first thing she'd done when Pagan had left was to go through the collection of albums, because she believed you could learn about a person from his or her choice of music – a theory tested by Pagan's collection, which consisted entirely of what she considered noise. Every record was early rock and roll, ranging from well-known stuff like Little Richard and Jerry Lee Lewis, to material she found obscure, Thurston Harris and the Sharps, Freddy Bell and the Bellboys. What could she learn about Pagan from this assortment except that he liked loud simplicity and indulged in massive, possibly lethal, overdoses of nostalgia?

She rose, wandered back into the living-room. Clues to a man's life, she thought. The music. The prints on the walls which were mainly old concert posters – The Rolling Stones at Wembley Stadium, Fats Domino at the London Palladium. As if they'd been hung by a hand other than Pagan's, perhaps that of the absent Roxanne, there were also delicately faded prints depicting scenes of 19th century English country life. It was quite a contrast between the rowdy and the bucolic.

She walked to the window, where she parted the curtains and looked down into the street. Across the way was one of those quiet squares that proliferate in London, a dark area of trees beyond the reach of streetlamps. Branches stirred very slightly in the soft night breeze. She imagined incongruous animals foraging for food out there – a badger, a field mouse, creatures disenfranchised by the city. Then she moved toward the sofa and lay down, closing her eyes.

When she heard the sound of Pagan climbing the stairs, then the twisting of the key in the lock, she sat upright. He came inside the living-room with a vaguely unsettled expression on his face, like that of a man who suspects he's stepped inside the wrong apartment. She was amused by his awkwardness, by the way her presence in his territory affected him.

'How was God?' she asked.

'Flustered,' Pagan said.

'I thought Gods were unflappable by definition.'

'They get anxious when something's not quite right in their domain.'

Like Martin Burr, Pagan was also flustered. Like Martin Burr, Pagan had the feeling that something was not quite right in his domain. Part of it was due to this woman's sudden entry into his life. He looked around the room as if he expected to see changes, small rearrangements she might have made in his absence. But everything was the same as before. What would she move anyway? The bloody furniture? It was a ridiculous notion. She probably hadn't even risen from the sofa all the time he'd been gone. He was entertaining some silly thoughts, and he wasn't quite sure why.

'Are you too tired for the rest of my story?' she asked.

'I want you to take a look at this first.' He removed the poem from his pocket and handed it to her. There was a tiny connection of flesh as his hand encountered hers. 'Tell me if it means anything to you.'

She read it, looking solemn. 'I know it better in the original,' she said, and there was a catch in her voice. '*Küll siis Kalev j̃ouab koju, Oma lastel õnne tooma, Eesti põlve uueks looma.* It's been a long time since I recited anything in Estonian. And it's been a long time since I read those lines.'

Pagan had never heard Estonian spoken before. What it reminded him of was Finnish, which he'd heard once or twice, finding it a little too arctic to be mellifluous. He looked at Kristina Vaska. She had her eyes shut very tightly and two thin tears slithered down her cheeks. He felt suddenly helpless – what was he supposed to do? Go to her, put his arms round her, comfort her? He wasn't sure how to behave.

'I'm sorry,' she said.

'It's okay.'

'It's not okay. I don't like to cry. I don't like feeling homesick and I can't stand being weepy.' She opened her eyes and forced a tense smile. Then she dipped into her purse and took out a paper tissue, which she pressed against her eyelids. Pagan watched in silence. He had a longing to hold her hands.

'Can I get you a drink?' he asked.

'I'm okay.'

'You're sure?'

'I'm sure.' She smiled again, a pale effort, and gazed at the poem. 'I haven't read *Kalevipoeg* since I was a kid.'

'Can you explain the poem to me?'

'It's from an old legend. Kalevipoeg was the son of Kalev. Kalev, who founded the kingdom of Estonia, was the son of the god Taara. According to the story, Kalevipoeg impressed the gods with his upright character, so they severed his legs at the knees then they embedded his fist in the stone surrounding the gateway to hell. Which is where he is to this day – preventing the return of the Evil One, the Devil.'

'The gods have a strange way of showing their appreciation,' Pagan said, wondering if a little half-arsed levity was even remotely appropriate. 'So Kalevipoeg is some kind of local hero.'

'A symbol of goodness.'

'And he's expected back when things get really rough?'

Kristina Vaska said, 'Yeah, but I doubt if he's ever going to return. He's had plenty of opportunities. And if he hasn't come back by this time, I'd say he's simply not going to show. Gods are notoriously unreliable.'

'They have their own timetables, that's all.'

Kristina Vaska scanned the poem again, her hand trembling slightly. 'I assume Romanenko had this in his possession, Frank?' she asked. It was the first time she'd used his name and she did so almost coyly, in a way Pagan found appealing – as if she were speaking a very private word.

Pagan nodded. 'The question is, why was he carrying it around with him? It was written in something called Livonian and stuck inside a sealed envelope.'

'Maybe I can shed a little light on why Romanenko would have this poem with him.'

'How?'

'By telling you something about the man, which is the reason I'm here anyhow,' she said. 'As I recall, I was getting to the end of my tale when I was rudely interrupted. Shall I continue?'

'I'm listening.' Pagan was impatient now.

Kristina Vaska took a deep breath. 'Okay. I was up to the part where Romanenko was about to make an appearance. First, a question. Have you ever heard of an organisation called the Brotherhood of the Forest?'

Pagan, sensing an unwelcome detour, shook his head.

Kristina Vaska said, 'The Brotherhood fought the Soviet occupation until 1952, maybe 1953. Mainly they had nothing but rifles and guts. But what really finished them off were Soviet reprisals against the farmers who supplied the Brotherhood with food and shelter. So they disbanded. Some were executed, others imprisoned. A few fled from the Baltic. My father, who was a member of the Brotherhood when he was sixteen years old, threw his rifle away and managed to slip back into society, which wasn't easy for him – given his views. I suppose he thought he could continue the struggle by political means. It wasn't a period of his life he talked about, you understand. He let one or two things slip when he was in an expansive mood or if he'd been drinking, but never anything of substance and only in front of the immediate family.'

Frank Pagan watched her. The darkness of the eyes, the mouth that was a little too large for the face and yet somehow absolutely right, the soft curl of eyelashes – a skilled portrait artist or a poet might have done justice to her idiosyncratic beauty. Pagan, neither artist nor poet, was content to look and appreciate.

'I want to show you something, Frank.'

She opened her purse. She took out a small, cracked photograph, an old black and white affair with a scalloped edge. She handed it to him. Pagan saw two young men, boys – one neatly bisected by the crack in the picture – standing in shirtsleeves under the branches of a tree. They both held rifles. Their faces were misty with that nebulous quality old photographs often have and their expressions weren't easy to read. There was toughness in them, and grimness, but they were both grinning in a stiff fashion as if the photographer had bullied them into smiling when neither of them felt like it.

'The man on the left is my father,' she said.

Pagan looked at the face of Norbert Vaska, seeing no resemblance between the man and his daughter.

'The man on the right,' she said, then paused.

Pagan raised his face from the picture and waited.

'Don't you recognise him, Frank?'

Pagan, puzzled by her question, looked at the picture again. How could he possibly recognise a Baltic rebel in a photograph that had to be forty years old, a soldier in a forgotten war fought when Frank Pagan had been barely five years old?

'Look closer,' Kristina Vaska said.

Pagan did so. There was something, the foggy edge of recognition, but then it slipped away from him. 'I give up,' he said.

'The man on the right is Aleksis Romanenko.'

'Romanenko?' Pagan stared at the photograph. Time had eroded the resemblance between the man with the rifle and the one who'd been assassinated in Edinburgh. There was some mild similarity, nothing more. 'Are you sure?'

Kristina Vaska was emphatic. 'Beyond any doubt.'

'I'm having a hard time with this, Kristina,' he said. 'You're telling me that Romanenko, the First Secretary of the Communist Party in Estonia, was once a guerilla who fought against the Soviets? That he was a member of this Brotherhood?'

'That's what I'm saying.'

Pagan laid the photograph on the rug. Romanenko's face gazed up at him – and now Pagan thought he saw another quality there, a certain defiance, a challenge from the past. 'I need more,' he said quietly.

Kristina Vaska stood up and walked to the window. She parted the curtains and gazed out at the park in the square. 'Aleksis Romanenko was one of my father's best friends. Even when he began his climb in the Party, he was still Norbert Vaska's friend. Until the early 1970s he would visit our house. The visits stopped after my father's arrest in 1972.'

Pagan caught something here, a slight stress in her voice. He asked, 'How was Romanenko able to rise in the Party?'

She turned from the window. 'He obliterated his past, Frank. He recreated his own history by falsifying records. You've got to remember how the war scattered people all over the Soviet Union. The deportations alone accounted for millions of people uprooted and shipped elsewhere. Think of the confusion. Wholesale turmoil. Badly kept records, documents destroyed in air-raids, birth-certificates and identity papers burned. An ingenious man like Romanenko could take advantage of the situation.'

She paused, looked distant, even a little forlorn. There was at times, Pagan thought, a certain delicacy to her features. 'He must have lived with the constant fear of being found out. Which is the way my father lived. In the end Norbert Vaska couldn't work within the system any longer. But Romanenko did.'

'Worked within or worked against?' Pagan asked.

'Both. The phrase we want is a double life. Aleksis may have been the Party Secretary, but he believed in the independence of the Baltic countries. And secretly, he did everything he could to support that goal.'

Pagan remembered the way Romanenko had held his briefcase against his chest in the railroad station, the way his face had looked when the gun was fired. Contorted, horrified, a man stepping suddenly into a nightmare and seeing all his fears, which he has nurtured for thirty years or more, suddenly rear up at him in the form of an assassin's gun. A double life, he thought. So that was Aleksis's secret world, his hidden depths. The idea that Aleksis had worked against the Soviet system gave Pagan a small glow of pleasure.

'Then we can assume the KGB found out about Romanenko and killed him.' But as soon as he'd said this Pagan thought how trite it was. How pat. Simplicity had a certain elegance, but in his experience simple things often turned out to be deceptive, layers yielding to other layers, each revealing a fresh complexity.

There was Jacob Kiviranna, for example, an American who had travelled three thousand miles to shoot Romanenko, and there was the mysterious associate who'd arranged for the gun to be made available in London. Could Kiviranna and his accomplice be a part of some devious Soviet solution to the problem of what to do with the two-faced Romanenko? A hired gunman fetched from overseas to kill Romanenko in Edinburgh, which at least had the merit of complying with the old axiom that you never shit on your own doorstep?

Pagan dismissed this and not simply on the grounds of its simplicity. The idea of Jake Kiviranna being recruited by the KGB didn't ring any bells for him. Jake hadn't impressed him as the type on whom any clandestine organisation would take a chance. It was possible that Jake might have been used unwittingly by the KGB, but that raised another question Pagan found puzzling.

He looked at the woman and said, 'The problem I have when I blame the KGB for Romanenko's death is this – why was he allowed to leave the Soviet Union in the first place? If the KGB intended to kill him, it would have been less messy to do it quietly at home. A lonely road, a car accident, something out of the public eye. Why go to all the trouble of shooting him in a railway station in Edinburgh? But then if it wasn't the KGB who organised his murder, who did?'

Kristina didn't answer. She stared at the window and saw dawn, the colour of a cloudy pearl, in the London sky. Pagan watched the same quiet light, enjoying the silence in the room for a while before turning back to her.

He said, 'Maybe Romanenko had changed his views over the years. Maybe he'd become tired of the deception involved and settled down as a loyal servant of the Party. In which case, he might have been killed by some people he'd let down badly.' It was a frail little kite, but Pagan, mired in possibilities and speculation, flew it anyhow.

Kristina Vaska said, 'I doubt Romanenko would have changed his loyalty. You have to keep in mind the fact that Aleksis belonged to the Brotherhood. And the bonds of the Brotherhood just don't go away. These are men who simply won't forgive the Soviets for murdering their nation. They kept in touch with each other over the years, Frank.'

The Brotherhood, Pagan thought. If it existed now, what else could it possibly be but a band of ageing men thriving on dreams? How could it be anything other than a harmless kind of social club, games of bridge or gin-rummy interspersed with patriotic songs and some bilious grumbling and toasts of loyalty made with wizened hands?

'Okay. Even if this outfit is alive and kicking, what makes you so damned sure Romanenko still had anything to do with it?'

Kristina Vaska said, 'Because of the poem.'

'Ah, our old mate Kalev.'

'Exactly.'

'Enlighten me, Kristina. Make it as clear as you can.' She smiled. 'It's very simple. The poem had very special meaning for my father's cell of the Brotherhood. Aside from its obvious patriotic content, the poem was used when they wanted to send a message secretly. Anybody reading it would understand its meaning immediately. Anybody who received these lines always knew what they stood for. They're a green light, Frank. They mean go. They mean everything is in place and it's okay to go ahead.'

'Go ahead with what?'

'With whatever the plan happens to be.'

'What plan?'

'I don't know in this case. The only assumption I can make is that it's something directed against the Soviets. Given the background of the Brotherhood, knowing how they feel about the Russians, what else could it possibly be?'

Something directed against the Soviets. Pagan stared into his empty glass. Bafflement was a tiring business. Even as she explained some things, Kristina Vaska made others even more obscure. Was it part of this mysterious plan for Aleksis to pass the envelope to a contact in Edinburgh, as Pagan had thought before? Was the connection to be made at the Castle? Was that why Aleksis had expressed such an interest in visiting the place – because somebody had been waiting for him up there in the dark fortress? And would this man, this spectre, read the lines, inspiring lines resonant with nostalgic echoes of an old guerilla war, and know precisely what he was supposed to do?

Pagan had the feeling he was being moved further and further away from the core of things. Like some object on a fretful tide, he was being sucked back from the safety of the shoreline. Deep waters, he thought. And growing darker as he trod them.

He asked, 'If the poem's a message, and Aleksis was the messenger, who was the intended recipient?'

Kristina Vaska had no answer to this question. Pagan rubbed his eyes. What he needed was the light of a fresh morning, a new day, a brain that didn't feel like a leaden mass locked in his skull. He looked towards the half-open bedroom door and wondered if he could find sleep.

He shrugged. 'Maybe we can talk again at breakfast.' *Breakfast*. He wasn't sure if he had anything more to offer than some stale Rice Krispies floating in milk of a dubious vintage.

'Is that an invitation to stay?' Kristina Vaska asked.

'If you don't mind the sofa.'

'The sofa's fine, Frank,' and she seemed to linger over his name, as if she were inviting Pagan to read something into her tone of voice.

'I'll get you some blankets.' He stepped into the bedroom, foraged inside a closet, then carried a couple of blankets back to the living-room, where the woman had already taken off her shoes and was lightly massaging her toes. He set the blankets down, watching how she smoothed her flesh with long, supple fingers.

She raised her face to him and smiled. 'I appreciate your hospitality. Really.'

Pagan went back into his bedroom and closed the door. He could hear her move around. He wondered if she slept naked, a disturbing speculation.

He stared at the ceiling. Sometimes he could sleep on a problem and then, as if he were visited in the dark by his muse, he'd wake with some kind of answer. He didn't feel optimistic this time, though. He suspected that his muse, normally fond of cryptic problems, had vacated the premises with the haste of an unhappy tenant.

He reached out, killed the light. But he couldn't put the idea of the woman out of his mind. The more he contemplated her, the more irksome questions and doubts arose. It would have been comforting to accept Kristina Vaska at face value, to be certain that she was no more than she claimed to be – the angry daughter of a man imprisoned and destroyed by a brutal system, somebody who had simply entered Pagan's life because she wanted to help.

But Pagan took very little at face value, no matter that the face in question happened to be bewitching, and lovely, the kind that might plunder and pirate your heart and simply sail away with it.

He kicked off his shoes, and shut his brain down – although it continued to murmur still, like some busy river he could hear in the distance.

It was twenty-five minutes past noon when V. G. Epishev stepped inside the Roman Catholic church in the Fulham district of London. The humid air in the church had the texture of flannel. He sat down at the rear and looked absently at the altar. A dolorous clay Virgin peered off into the middle distance. Behind her, concealed in shadow, a large crucifix hung on the back wall. Rows of candles in glass jars created small flickering islands of light. Here and there, supplicants kneeled in front of the jars and crossed themselves, or else genuflected as they passed the altar.

The whole effect, Epishev decided, was tawdry and sentimental. The mystery of Christianity distilled in cheap candles and icons – was this all there was to it? Did people actually find hope and sustenance here? He wondered if the appeal lay in the fundamental simplicity of it all, the easy cycle of sin and redemption.

He sat back in the pew. His forehead was sticky. Even the slight draught that cavorted through the candles was thick and warm. He wasn't altogether uneasy in this place, rather more puzzled. Years of interrogating believers, years of exploring their hearts, hadn't brought him any closer to an understanding of their faith. He knew that faith, which transcended the limits of reason, was a great leap they all claimed to have made. And, like the curator of a museum in possession of an interesting artifact he cannot identify, Epishev was mystified, and fascinated, by the nature of this commitment.

He wiped sweat from his forehead. As he did so, he was aware of Alexei Malik slipping into the pew beside him. Epishev took off his glasses quickly and put them in his pocket.

'Why did you choose this place?' Malik asked.

'I have a warped sense of humour.' Epishev, who wanted to get down to business immediately, noticed the briefcase Malik was holding. 'I assume that's Romanenko's?'

Malik nodded. 'It's Romanenko's.' A short pause, then, 'But the message is gone.'

Epishev was silent for a long time, fanning the heavy air with a hand. 'Who removed it?'

Malik's voice dropped to a whisper, like that of a man whose words are constantly monitored, constantly eavesdropped upon. 'I think we can be certain it was done at Scotland Yard, either by the Commissioner or a policeman called Frank Pagan. It's very likely that the Commissioner delegated the entire matter to Pagan. A man by the name of Danus Oates was also present in Edinburgh. Oates is something of a linguist and if Romanenko's message had to be translated he'd be the man to do it.'

Epishev massaged his eyelids. The flight from Moscow to Berlin, then from Germany to London, had tired him. Some kind of spiced-up eggs had been served on board the second plane and he could feel them burning a hole in his stomach. 'We must find out what the damned message said. The General wants to be one hundred per cent certain that the plot is not about to be derailed, Alexei.'

Epishev watched a middle-aged woman kneel quickly before the altar. A priest emerged from shadows and engaged her in conversation, hovering over her like a large black bat.

'What about the assassin?' Epishev asked. 'What do we know about him?'

Malik stuffed his handkerchief away. What he disliked about Colonel Epishev, with whom he'd worked in the past, was the way the man asked questions. They were always phrased directly, always posed in a tone that made you feel as if you were taking an oral examination, and that every question could be answered in only one acceptable way.

Malik said, 'The assassin somehow managed to take his own life a few hours ago.'

This item of news surprised Epishev. 'In custody?'

'In custody,' Malik replied.

'How careless of the custodians,' Epishev said and returned his gaze to the front of the church, noticing for the first time a stained-glass window depicting Christ in his last agony. 'What have you learned about him?'

'Very little,' Malik answered. 'His name was Jacob Kiviranna, an American.'

'With a Baltic name,' Epishev said. 'Was he acting alone?'

Malik said, 'We think so. According to the Soviet Mission in Manhattan, the killer didn't belong to any dissident groups in the United States. And he certainly had no known affiliations here.'

Malik, whose official function was to serve as assistant to the Ambassador (a liberal recently installed by the new regime in Moscow), had a whole network of informants throughout the United Kingdom, a varied crew of alcoholics, homosexuals, loners, sociopaths, blackmail victims, fellow travellers, exiles, and fantasists numbed by the Welfare State who needed the romance of thinking themselves spies. He'd spent a long time building this network, and much of the intelligence that reached him was reliable. If he said Kiviranna had no allegiance with any organisation inside the UK, he was offering an assessment that was reasonably accurate.

'These might be useful,' and Malik took a sheet of paper and a photograph from his pocket, passing both items to Epishev. 'I was unable to get a photograph of Danus Oates, only an address. However, I did acquire a picture of Frank Pagan. His address is on the back.'

Epishev stuck the paper inside his wallet, then studied the photograph briefly. The likeness of the man called Pagan was blurry, but what Epishev saw was a lean, determined face. The picture appeared to have been taken without the subject's knowledge because

Pagan was looking off into the distance, away from the camera, and his expression had no self-consciousness about it. It was a hard face in some respects, but there was a slight suggestion of humour around the eyes, as if this man took himself seriously only to a point.

Epishev put the picture away. He was impatient to be out of this church now. It had begun to affect him adversely. It was a place where people came to share a common belief, and Epishev, who had shared very little with anyone in his life, felt a quiet little ache of unease. He stood up. 'Did you bring me the other thing I wanted?'

Malik said that it was outside in the car. Both men left the church. The early afternoon sky was overcast, the air suffocating. Malik's car was an unexceptional Subaru, a rental. A car with diplomatic plates might have been more than a little obtrusive parked outside a Catholic church in a working-class district of Fulham.

When both men were seated in the Subaru Malik reached across and opened the glove compartment. Epishev took out the gun, which was a brand-new Randall Service Model with a silencer. He held it in his palm, admiring it a moment before placing it in the pocket of his coat.

He put a hand on Malik's shoulder. 'You've been very helpful, Alexei.'

Malik smiled. 'We're on the same side, Viktor. We want the same goal. The kind of things happening in Russia . . . ', Malik paused, searching for the correct expression. 'They're not Russian.'

Epishev stepped out of the car, feeling the gun's weight drag at his coat pocket. 'You're right, Alexei. Whatever else they might be, they're not Russian.'

He didn't look back at Malik as he moved away from the car and along the pavement. The same side, Viktor. The same goal. The restoration of the Revolution's credentials.

He stopped on a street corner outside a small grocery store. He took Malik's slip of paper from his wallet, memorised the address written there, then tore the sheet into fragments. He turned Frank Pagan's photograph over, committed the address on the back to memory, then ripped the picture into four pieces. He placed all this litter, rather fastidiously, in a wastebasket affixed to a lamp-post.

Moscow

General Stefan Ivanovich Olsky and his wife lived in a large apartment in the Lenin Hills on the outskirts of Moscow. It was a modern home, filled with Western appliances and decorated in the kind of blond wood surfaces one associates with Scandinavian houses. It was located on a street that was off-limits to most Muscovites, guarded at each end by uniformed militia men.

Unlike most Russian women married to powerful men, Sabina Olskaya kept herself informed about her husband's work and discussed it with him. But mainly she listened, because she knew her real strength came from her sympathetic ear. She was also ambitious on her husband's behalf, imagining a day when he might ascend from the Chairmanship of the KGB to General Secretary of the Party.

She lay in the bedroom, listening to the sound of her husband running water in the bathroom. It was early evening, and they'd taken a light meal together, and now they were going to make love, which was something they invariably did at this time every Sunday. The General's demanding schedule meant that their time together was both precious and sacrosanct, and Sabina guarded it jealously. She was a slim woman with long black hair and a wide mouth and front teeth which protruded slightly – a flaw in her appearance Stefan Olsky found very attractive.

He came out of the bathroom wearing a silk robe. As he approached the bed, Sabina rolled on her side, reaching out to slickly untie the cord, so that his robe fell open. She could tell from the expression on his face that he was preoccupied and she knew from experience that when he was absorbed in something he was as distant from her as a man walking on the surface of the moon.

She sat with her back against the pillows, her legs crossed. She had wonderful thighs. Before her marriage, she'd been a ballet dancer in the corps of the Kirov, and she still exercised every day. Now Olsky stroked her thigh absent-mindedly, unconscious of the years of training that had gone into creating such fine muscle tone.

She reached for an apple that lay in a bowl on the bedside table and bit into it loudly.

'So,' she said. 'You let that old fart Greshko upset you?'

'Am I upset?'

'Let's say you're distracted, shall we? He's a sick old man, he lies buried in the country-side, why should he worry the Chairman of the KGB?'

Stefan Olsky closed his eyes. Inside the bedroom there was a caged bird, a small yellow canary that sang in a tuneful way. The General listened a moment, aware of a warm breeze blowing in through the open window, stirring the long curtains. His beloved wife, the playful breeze, the songbird – all the elements were present for happiness, for contentment. Why then was it so unattainable? He opened his eyes, ran the palm of his hand across his shaved skull. At his side, Sabina practised turn-outs with her feet, then raised her long legs in glorious extensions.

Stefan Olsky said, 'Fact. Greshko removes Romanenko's file. (Or authorises its removal, the same difference.) Fact. Romanenko is killed by an assassin. Fact. Greshko associates with people known to be unsympathetic to the General Secretary and his programme.'

Sabina, who knew just the kind of people her husband was referring to – and especially their wives, those shapeless, tight-lipped spouses, those unfashionable old biddies who lived like wraiths in their husbands' shadows – made an expression of disgust and said, 'They're toothless decrepit shits.'

'They can still bite with their gums, dear heart.' He had a strong feeling he was missing something, something that kept slipping between his fingers, some gap in a logical sequence, except he wasn't sure what. He had three separate facts, but they didn't provide him with a syllogism.

He thought of how he'd taken over the KGB during this period of enormous social reconstruction, and how the General Secretary made excellent speeches about infusing Soviet society with a new dynamic but the actuality was difficult, the practical implications complicated. Inside the KGB, for example, the old guard, some of them Greshko loyalists, went to great lengths to make pernickety complaints. It was as if the very word new had the same effect on those thick-skulled old-timers as sunlight on vampires.

Change was struggle, an uphill struggle. Sometimes it couldn't be forced, it couldn't be pressured, it had to be coaxed along. Sometimes it only happened through attrition – and you needed patience while the old guard died or retired. Patience, persistence, these were the qualities in himself that Stefan Olsky most admired.

He clasped his wife's hand and held it to his lips. He nuzzled her knuckles, but he was still behaving absent-mindedly.

Sabina Olskaya watched her husband's face. She was very much in love with him and proud of the role he was playing in retraining this cumbersome elephant that was Russia to her. During her career with the Kirov she'd travelled to the West a score of times, and she'd adored it for more than the great stores and the elegant restaurants and the fashion-able people walking on the splendid boulevards. What she'd become enamoured of was a certain spirit – she could think of no other word – that existed in the West. It was something she discovered in newspapers and books, in cinemas and theatres, in late-night conversations she had with friends in those countries – an exhilarating freedom, a giddiness which at times left her breathless, a world of choices, a world seemingly without limits. The Soviet Union she always came back to depressed her, a lumbering beast in drab colours. But now it was being turned around, a dash of colour added here, a touch of spice there, and Stefan – her husband – was one of the men helping to make the alterations. She kissed his forehead just then, more from gratitude than lust. She wanted to live in a new Russia, not the one typified by those old dodos who made Stefan's life so difficult at times with their underhand ways, and their outmoded dogma.

The telephone was ringing on the bedside table. Olsky picked it up. He heard the voice of his personal assistant, Colonel Chebrikov, a stuffy young man whose principal attributes were unqualified loyalty and an ambition that was not markedly acute.

'A man known as Yevenko was arrested a couple of hours ago, General,' the Colonel said. 'He was in possession of counterfeit currency.'

'Yevenko?' Olsky asked. 'Should the name mean anything to me?'

'Perhaps not, sir. He's been involved in various currency scandals in the past. In more recent years, his speciality has been forged documents. Sometimes he's known as the Printer.'

'And?' Olsky watched his wife rise from the bed and walk to the window, where she stood balanced on one leg. The gown she wore caught the breeze and blew away from her thighs.

'Well, sir, he has information.'

'What kind of information, Colonel?'

'He'll only tell it to you. And then only on the condition that you . . . that you are lenient with him. The information concerns a man you asked me to make a report on recently with a view to retirement or reassignment. One of Greshko's people. Colonel Viktor Epishev.'

Olsky said, 'I'll meet you in twenty minutes, Colonel.' He hung up the receiver quickly. He got up from the bed and crossed the floor, catching Sabina by the shoulders, kissing her on the mouth. Then he stepped back from her.

She asked, 'Will I stay awake for you?'

Even though Stefan Olsky said yes, yes she should stay awake for him, he wondered how many hours of his time would be absorbed by his other wife, the one infinitely more demanding and more complex than Sabina, the one called Mother Russia.

8

Brooklyn, New York

Andres Kiss, his blond hair moved by the breeze, hurried along the boardwalk at Brighton Beach. Even in his haste he walked with grace. People who noticed him, and many did, were impressed by his poise. There was nothing clumsy, nothing angular, in the way he hurried. If he suggested a blur, it was a streamlined one. He wore a three-piece suit of dark brown silk. His white shirt was open at the collar because he hated the restriction of neckties. He paused once, scanning the Sunday afternoon crowds that had come out to promenade and sniff the ozone.

Old Russians, many of them Jews, sat in the doorways of shops and jabbered or played cards. There was loud music coming from various sources, a clash of sounds – balalaikas on somebody's tape-deck, rock and roll from a ghetto-blaster hoisted on the shoulder of a passing skateboarder, the drone of some 1950s Soviet crooner limping out of battered speakers that had been set up on a vendor's table where you could buy tapes bootlegged from the original Russian records. Here and there people were huddled in earnest political discussions about the direction of Soviet society or in serious debate about the inadequacies of Blue Cross and Blue Shield. Old ladies walked dogs through the salted air and sometimes paused to let their pets poop.

Andres Kiss knew this scene so well he didn't analyse it, didn't think about the mix of cultures or the way foreign languages and dialects filled the air around him. He walked until he reached the closed door of what had once been a hot-dog shop during the golden age of the boardwalk, that halcyon time when nearby Coney Island, now a haven for druggers and muggers, had been a safe place for family outings.

The window of the shop was filthy and the faded lettering on the glass barely legible. Andres Kiss reached deftly into the pocket of his pants and removed the key the old man had reluctantly consented to give him only a few weeks ago.

He glanced up and down the boardwalk before inserting the key into the lock. You couldn't be too careful. Brighton Beach, with its enormous immigrant community from Soviet Europe, was a hotbed of gossip. Stooped old women with shopping-bags babbled on street corners, eyes hooded and lips flapping. They were as efficient as any telegraph system. Then there were the scum from the so-called Russian diplomatic mission in Manhattan who infiltrated the neighbourhood so they could collect information on who was saying what, data they shipped back to Russia where it was used to put pressure on families still over there. Andres hated the KGB with a passion so profound it rendered him speechless.

He turned the key, then stepped inside the bleak room beyond, closing the door at his back and smelling the dank scent of the place, a fusion of sawdust and mildew. Sunlight hardly penetrated here. His eyes slowly became attuned to the dimness and he made out the old refrigerator, a prehistoric job which had no door. Then a couple of battered chairs. There was an ancient menu on the wall. Hot-dogs were 15 cents. Soda cost a nickel.

'You call this punctual? For this you wear a fancy wristwatch?'

The voice that came out of the gloom was thickly accented. Andres saw Carl Sundbach emerge from behind the refrigerator. In what little sunlight filtered through the grubby window, Sundbach appeared fragile. He wore an antique raccoon coat, the way he always did from the first of September to the last day of March, regardless of the temperature. His face was thin and angular and there were glasses attached for safekeeping to a threadbare string that hung round his scrawny neck. He was one of the richest men in the whole of Brooklyn, probably in all New York State, but he was so frugal he made Scrooge seem like a charitable foundation.

Sundbach came a little nearer. He scanned Andres's face a moment, his little eyes flicking back and forth.

'You don't know time, huh?' And he seized Andres's wrist in his hand, tapping his fingernails on the dial of the Rolex. 'Thirty-two years old and still you don't know time. Even when we got a calamity going on.'

Andres took his hand away and said, 'I'm ten minutes late. So what?'

'So what? Maybe the world is falling to pieces and you want to know so what?'

'Nothing's falling to pieces, Carl,' Andres said.

'I hear different, sonny. I hear bad news. You get to my age, you trust your instincts. And what they're saying isn't good. You know what I think? It's all over. It's finished. The whole thing's going to be cancelled. Which maybe isn't such a bad idea.'

'It's a goddam stupid idea,' Andres said. 'Nothing's going to be cancelled. No way, Carl. Not now.'

'A terrible thing happened in Scotland. A man is dead, for God's sake.'

'I know, Carl. I just got back from Edinburgh. Remember?' Andres was always made impatient by Sundbach. It was tough to practise the composure Mikhail Kiss advocated. *Give him respect, Andres. He's an old man now, but he used to be a real fighter.* Andres forced his mouth into a smile, which brightened his handsomely sullen face. He looked quite angelic right then, the cherubic boy who'd been the joy of the boardwalk as a baby, clucked over by *babushkas*, stroked by teenage girls overwhelmed that anything could be so beautiful, a golden little heartbreaker who always held on tightly to Uncle Mikhail's hand.

'We didn't reckon on *murder*, Andres.' Carl Sundbach, whose raccoon coat reeked of mothballs, peered in the direction of the window where he could make out, barely, the old gilt letters on the glass. Some of the letters were missing now, scratched out by weather and vandals. *Brook yns Best H t Dogs. Roo Beer.* Once, he'd fantasised about reopening his shop when the boardwalk returned to its former glory, but in recent years he'd become disenchanted. It wasn't going to happen. Now now. Not ever. All the good days were gone. What you had now were kids guzzling beer and humping under the boardwalk, leaving their battered cans and discarded condoms, which looked like hollowed-out snails, all over the place.

Nevertheless, he kept this place, and he came here sometimes, usually on Sundays when Andres picked him up, riding by train all the way down from Manhattan, where he had a rent-controlled apartment on the lower East side. He'd sit in the space behind the refrigerator and he'd reminisce about the days when Sundbach's had been a going concern and sometimes he even imagined he heard the ringing of the cash-register.

Sundbach shivered. He was perpetually cold, even in sunlight. Andres went to the door and opened it, glad of the sea air. He clutched the old man's spindly elbow as they moved along the boardwalk. Every now and then Carl would nod his head at an acquaintance or he'd tip his ancient hat at a passing female who caught his eye. He still fancied himself something of a lady's man, a *seelikukütt*, a hunter of skirts.

They walked slowly to the side-street where Andres had parked his Jaguar. He opened the passenger door for Carl Sundbach and watched him climb in.

'You ought to drive an American car,' the old man said when Andres had the Jaguar going along Brighton Beach Avenue, past the Russian delicatessens and the pharmacies and under the shadow of the El. 'The English don't know how to make cars no more.'

It was always this way. Always the complaints, always something to whine about. Andres glanced at the front of the Black Sea Bookstore where a couple of guys leaned against their bicycles and argued. Politics, Andres thought. What else would they argue around here? He was of the opinion that such arguments were finally pointless. Talk achieved nothing. What you really needed was another kind of vocabulary – one of action.

Andres rolled his window down. The stench of camphor was clogging his nostrils.

Sundbach said, 'I had a British car, a Rover, in Tallinn. Before the Russians came into the Baltic. After the *tiblad* arrived, you couldn't get parts. You couldn't get gasoline. The English knew how to build cars in those days. I must have driven that Rover thousands of miles. Kahula to Narva. Tartu. *Mu jumal*, Tartu was beautiful then.' Sundbach sighed. 'I used to have this feeling I'd see the old country again one day. Now,' and he made a small fluttering gesture with his hand, 'I know better.'

Carl Sundbach could go on and on, rambling, reminiscing. Pretty soon he'd be remembering the time he ate the rancid *heeringas hapukoorega* – herring with sour cream – at a roadside restaurant in Jogeva and came down with food-poisoning bad enough to kill a dozen weaker men, or the day the Brotherhood blew up a Soviet munitions dump outside Haapsalu in 1949. He had one of those memories that resurrect every small detail of the past, every trifle, the kind of clouds that were in the sky on such and such a day or the colour of a guy's eyes. When he told a story, Carl Sundbach digressed encyclopaedically, feasting on a sumptuous banquet of recollections.

What the hell, Andres Kiss thought, when you'd hauled yourself up from being a poor Baltic immigrant to one of the wealthiest men in the state, when you owned a chain of motels and fast-food restaurants, when you had property all over Brighton Beach, maybe you deserved the luxury of indulgent nostalgia. Andres had often heard the story of Carl's financial success, the sheer toughness involved, the ambition, the way business enemies had been bulldozed. There was still this suggestion of flint to the old man.

Andres said, 'You'll see it again, Carl.'

Sundbach shook his head. 'I'm trying to be a realist, boy.'

'You sound more like a defeatist.'

'There's a difference?' Sundbach asked.

The younger man never tried to answer Carl's rhetorical questions. He took the Jaguar on to the Interborough Parkway, heading out to the Island. He stared through the window at a sign for the Harry S. Truman Expressway. Overhead, in a cloudless, sunny sky, a small silvery twin-engined Piper flashed. Andres Kiss, filled with a longing to be up there at the controls of the craft, watched it until it went out of sight.

He took a pair of dark shades from the visor, where they'd been clipped in place. He put them on. He liked the way the sun was dulled now. Too much unfiltered brightness could damage your eyes. When he'd been in the Air Force he'd known men who were grounded because of poor eyesight. Andres wasn't going to run the risk of hurting his vision because there wasn't a thing in the world like soaring up there – not sex, not drugs, nothing. It was undiluted freedom when you were twenty or thirty thousand feet high and rolling through cloudbanks. What thrilled him was the idea of defying gravity, of being suspended in a frail craft that could, if the engine stalled, come crashing down through space. And sometimes, as if he were locked in a delicious place between life and death, Andres imagined that fall and was fascinated by the prospect. To smack the earth at eight hundred miles per hour seemed to him an appropriate way to check out, the flyer's way.

In Glen Cove he travelled leafy back roads until he reached the house, which occupied several acres of prime Long Island real estate. Grey and huge, with turrets and cupolas, and a lawn so immaculate it might have been groomed by a hairdresser, it was situated at the end of a gravel driveway. He parked the Jaguar alongside a black Mercedes. Then he opened the door of his car and looked up at the front of the house. A lime-green awning hung over the porch. Sundbach, who'd dozed for much of the journey the way he usually did, opened his eyes.

'We're here?' he asked hoarsely.

'We're here,' Andres Kiss replied.

In the sun-room at the back of the house, where glass walls overlooked prolific rose gardens that blazed with colour, Mikhail Kiss poured tea from a silver pot into dainty china cups. His big hands made the china seem like something plundered out of a doll's house but he poured almost tenderly, a man engrossed in a ritual he respects.

He looked up when Carl Sundbach and Andres came into the room. He thought of the contrast between the young man and the old warrior, the present and the past, strength and frailty. It was important to remember how closely linked past and present were, how much they owed to each other. Without that sense of history, everything they were involved in, everything they'd planned, would be no more than an act of vandalism, a mindless terrorism of the kind that so appalled him.

Carl Sundbach reached for a tea-cup, poured a shot of cognac into it, and sniffed the steam. Andres, declining the offer of tea, stared out into the garden. Through the open doorway a faint gust of wind blew the seductive scent of roses into the room.

Mikhail Kiss, who believed in coming straight to the point, asked, 'This tragic event in Edinburgh – is it going to influence us?'

Carl Sundbach made a windy little noise of surprise. 'You have a habit of asking questions in the wrong order. What you're asking now isn't what I'd ask myself first. The most important question is obvious. Why was Romanenko killed? Then comes the next question. Who shot him?'

Mikhail Kiss, weary after the long sleepless flight back from Britain, regarded Sundbach's questions as irrelevant. But Carl had poured thousands of dollars into this whole affair and felt he'd purchased the right to ask any questions he wanted.

'Your priorities are wrong, Carl,' he said.

'*My* priorities are wrong?' Sundbach asked. 'Tell me, tell me how you figure that.'

'Carl, does it make any difference who killed Aleksis, or why? It was probably some dangerous oddball with a crazy notion and a gun. What would you have me do? Stop everything? Send out messages saying everything has to be halted? Have you any idea how complicated that would be?'

'I hate complicated,' Carl Sundbach said. 'Give me simple every time.'

'Nothing's simple,' Mikhail Kiss said. 'All this has taken a very long time to stitch together, and I can't undo the whole embroidery now, even if I wanted to.'

Sundbach took off his raccoon coat. His concave chest gave the impression of a man in the throes of malnutrition. He was sweating slightly. 'Suppose this killer knew what Aleksis was up to. Let's say this killer knew everything there is to know. Imagine that. Just try. Tell me you don't see the consequences.'

Mikhail Kiss said, 'Only a scared man worries about consequences he can't possibly predict, Carl.'

'One thing I hate is a man sounds like he just read a fortune-cookie,' Sundbach replied. 'This is my point – if Aleksis was killed, then it was because *somebody knew what he was involved in*. Which makes it likely the whole damn scheme's blown. Forgive me, but that's too risky for me. This was supposed to be a big secret – but I told you all along it was too complicated to keep quiet. I kept saying. Make it simple. Short and simple. No, you knew better, didn't you? You had to have grand plans.'

Mikhail Kiss stood up and looked out into the garden, turning his back to the room. The way sunlight struck roses always touched him. He remembered how Aleksis Romanenko had been proud of his flower garden around his house on the bank of the Pirita River. *My peasant instincts*, Aleksis used to say. *If I don't grow things I betray my heart and I die a little* – the theatrical kind of thing Aleksis was given to saying.

In the late 1940s and early 1950s both Kiss and Romanenko had been active in the armed struggle against the Russians in the Baltic. There had been some of the predictable differences between two strong-willed men locked in a useless struggle, but they had common bonds – a passion for the land, and a profound attachment to the Brotherhood of the Forest.

Kiss remembered how, during the cold spring of 1951, Aleksis had planted marigold seeds on a wooded hillside north of Kuusiku. Grubby, lice-ridden, undernourished, facing the prospect of annihilation at the hands of Soviet patrols, Aleksis had planted his precious seeds with all the poignant care of a man who expects eventually to see the flowers grow. He also remembered Carl Sundbach, at that time a gaunt man in his late thirties, saying that if seeds could grow to be rifles, he'd be sowing them himself day and night. But since war was not a horticultural event, why bother?

Derision hadn't fazed Aleksis. It was almost as if he'd wanted to bring some flourish of his own, some form of hope, into a situation of despair. And it had been despair, because daily the Russians were burning farms and shooting farmers who'd supported the fight of the Brotherhood. And they'd been increasing the ferocity of their patrols, pouring more men and more arms into the fight so that the only possible outcome for the Brotherhood was starvation and defeat. In the midst of this turmoil Romanenko had planted his seeds, an act of optimism and grace that Mikhail Kiss remembered, all these years later, with great clarity.

It was odd to think of Aleksis dead now. It was like trying to imagine the inside of a vacuum. He had been closer to Aleksis than to any other member of the old Brotherhood. And now another memory touched him, and his eyes moistened, and he felt a tightness at the back of his throat. He remembered the *Kalevipoeg* and how, on the day when they'd parted company, when their cell had disbanded – hungry, lacking weapons, crushed by a weariness no amount of courage could overcome, numbed by an impossible struggle – he'd given Romanenko a handwritten sheet of paper with four lines of verse on it, written in Livonian, a Finno-Ugric language Kiss had once studied as a student at the university in Tartu. A secret souvenir of a doomed freemasonry, a reminder in an almost extinct tongue, a cryptic memento of a struggle that was dying around them.

When we rise again, Aleksis had said, *this paper will be the one true sign*. And so Romanenko had kept the sheet for years, more a symbol of a resurrection than a souvenir of a lost cause. It was this same paper that Kiss was supposed to receive on the ramparts of Edinburgh Castle on the night of Aleksis's death – the same four lines of the old patriotic poem that would indicate the time had come for the rebirth. It was a seal to be embossed on the plan, a guarantee from Romanenko that everything was finally in place for the assault, an imprimatur.

Now Kiss recalled the cold shock, the grief, of hearing about Romanenko's murder on British television and the sudden dilemma the murder posed. To proceed or – as Carl Sundbach was advocating – to forget the whole thing. His first reaction had been to abort, but then he knew that if he were to cancel the operation now, he'd live the rest of his life with regret – and what was more appalling than sinking embittered into old age? The architecture of the scheme was too careful, too intricate and lovely, for it to be shelved and forgotten.

He barely listened to the way Sundbach was whining. Carl's trouble was simple. He'd used up all his guts and stamina in his drive to become rich in America. And with riches had come a cautious, conservative way of looking at things.

Kiss looked at Carl who was going on about this grandiose – pronounced *grandyoose* – plan, wondering aloud why he'd gone along with it in the first place, pouring in money, then more money, and still more money, greasing palms and arranging passports for those who'd have to find a way of fleeing the Soviet Union after the event. Why wouldn't a simple assassination have been enough? Why hadn't they just decided to kill somebody, some Russian high-up, and been content with that? Depleted, finally speechless, Sundbach wiped flecks of spit from the corners of his mouth.

Kiss, who had invested money of his own in the scheme, who had spent freely on arms, money he'd earned on the stock markets of the world, said, 'Assassinations mean nothing these days. Any crackpot with a gun can go out and shoot anybody he likes. They don't even make the front page, for God's sake. Never at any time did we seriously consider assassination.'

Sundbach clasped his skinny white hands on the surface of the table. 'Listen, if you go ahead now, if you ignore the danger signs, you might be signing the death warrants of everybody involved, including our friends inside the Soviet Union and maybe even ourselves if those KGB scum at the Russian Mission also learn about us.'

In a quiet voice, one of restrained impatience, Andres Kiss said, 'What Mikhail's saying is that the game is too far along for anything to be changed. All the pieces are in position. Everything is ready. And if we go with the plan, we have to go now. Otherwise, forget it.'

Carl Sundbach said, 'I disagree, Andres. The pieces are not all in position. There is one vital piece we don't have and we all know what that is. I'm talking about Romanenko. I'm talking about the very big fact that we don't know if Romanenko was going to tell us to play our hand or throw in our cards. And since we don't know this, it's my opinion we take the loss. All the wasted time. We say it was quite an experience, quite a dream, and we back away.'

Andres Kiss smiled his most brilliant smile. 'It's not a dream for me, Carl,' he said. And it wasn't. He had anticipated the conclusion of the scheme so many times that it had come to have something of the texture of an event already past, already history. In a sense, Andres Kiss had lived his own future.

Sundbach fingered the string to which his eyeglasses were attached. 'I say we get out now. If it fails, too many people may die. Listen to me. Maybe Aleksis was going to tell us to wash our hands of the whole business. Maybe he was going to tell us that something had gone wrong. How can we know anything for sure?'

Andres Kiss stood up. 'It's a pity you're not a gambling man, Carl. Then you'd realise there's a fifty-fifty chance Aleksis was going to give us the okay to proceed.'

'And you'd take that chance?' Sundbach asked.

Andres nodded confidently. 'I'd take it.'

Sundbach looked at Mikhail Kiss. 'And you?'

'Without hesitation,' Kiss replied.

'You're both crazy,' Sundbach said. 'Both *hullud*. What is it with you pair? You both in love with tragedy? Personally, I don't like the feeling of putting my goddam head under a guillotine. I figure suicide isn't one of my options. And I don't want to be responsible for the deaths of other people either.'

There was an awkward silence in the room. Then Sundbach sighed. It was an old man's sigh, filled with sorrow and disbelief. He stared out into the roses, thinking how their bright colours seemed suddenly gloomy, like flowers round a sickbed when the patient is terminal. He had the feeling his was the only voice of reason here.

'So,' Sundbach said. 'This is the way it goes. Aleksis is dead in Scotland, you don't know who killed him, you don't know if he was carrying the message, *but you're going ahead anyway.*'

Neither Mikhail Kiss nor his nephew said anything. Their silence was eloquent, and united, a combination against which Sundbach couldn't compete.

Sundbach put out one thin hand and laid it on the back of Andres Kiss's wrist. 'What if they're waiting for you? Bang! You fall out of the sky. No more Andres Kiss.'

The young man said, 'I'll take the chance, Carl.'

Carl Sundbach poured himself a little tea. His hand trembled. He sipped quietly, then looked over the rim of his cup at Mikhail Kiss. 'I never made a bad investment before. I never lost a dollar on anything. You know why? Because I never gambled. That's why. Except for this,' and he made a sweeping gesture. His eyes were suddenly moist. 'Forgive this little display. I was remembering how you came to me years ago, Mikhail. You said you had a plan. I listened. I was the only one who believed in the chance of your success. The others – I'm thinking of Charlie Parming and Ernie Juurman, all the rest of them – they didn't even want to know. They turned their backs on you, Mikhail. Your own countrymen, fellow *patrioots*, they turned their backs. Alone, I supported you. But now . . . '

Carl Sundbach drew the sleeve of his shirt across his face. 'I wish you luck. Myself, I'm too old for a doomed adventure. I'm out.'

'Reconsider, Carl,' Mikhail Kiss said, though not with any enthusiasm. In the last analysis, Sundbach was like Charlie Parming and the others. They had all grown old badly. They spoke easily about vengeance when they'd been putting vodka away, or when they got together for reunions that were invariably boastful in the beginning then finally tearful, but when it came down to action they had no iron left in their hearts. America had made them prosperous and soft. Sundbach was a scared old man who'd gotten in over his head, that was all.

Sundbach said, 'Reconsider? No. What I want is a situation I can leave with no regrets. I want Andres to drive me back to the boardwalk. Then I can get on with my life.'

Sundbach rose slowly, grabbing his raccoon coat, struggling into it. He thought how the death of Aleksis hadn't changed a thing. Maybe there was still a chance Mikhail Kiss would come to his senses, maybe he'd be able to look at things clearly and understand that his scheme had been only a gorgeous dream. For a while, for too long, he'd believed in Kiss's plan himself – but what was he except an old man with too much money, too much time, somebody who wasn't listening to the way the heartbeat of the world was changing? Then he'd started to listen, he'd started to take the pulse of things, and now he understood that Kiss's way was the way of doom. There was another way, and it didn't involve such destruction, only patience.

He looked at Andres Kiss. 'I'll wait for you in the car.'

A few minutes after Sundbach had stepped out of the house, Mikhail Kiss and his nephew went upstairs to the room Kiss called his office. It was stacked with books and pamphlets of the kind issued by the various Baltic Independence societies in Western countries. The Committee for a Free Estonia. The World Legion of Lithuanian Liberation. The Baltic World Conference. Kiss considered all these organisations well-intentioned but powerless, feeble groups of people who did nothing more than release a flood of unwanted paper, diatribes against Russian activities in the Baltic that nobody wanted to read – petitions to the United Nations for recognition of the sovereignty of the Baltic states, telegrams to world leaders, letters to United States congressmen and Australian senators and British MPs, who sent polite supportive replies marked more by impotent indignation at the plight of the Baltic than anything honest and practical. But what did all this verbiage amount to in the end? The answer was, alas, zero.

Kiss had belonged to a number of freedom organisations in the past, but he'd always resigned from them out of a sense of frustration. Endless talk and petition-signing and the drudgery of committees served the purposes of some people – but not those of Mikhail Kiss, who was tired of how the whole Baltic tragedy had been ignored by world opinion, relegated to the backwaters of old men's memories, a dead issue.

Did nobody care that cultures and languages were being deliberately destroyed and that a completely illegal form of government had been forced upon three nations? That the Baltic was now little more than an arsenal where the Soviets had installed a vast array of weapons and rockets? What Kiss remembered – and this was where the hurt and pain still lay – was the way the three Baltic nations had flourished in that gorgeous period between the wars, a time of economic progress and honest political experiment, of literature and art, a golden age of self-determination, a time for hope and optimism when for twenty short, brilliant years freedom, not fear, had been in people's hearts. Gone now, all of it, down the slipstream of history.

He stared at a framed photograph on the wall. It showed him in 1974 presenting a petition to President Gerald Ford outside the White House. Ford had made a brave little speech that day about how America would always support the integrity and rights of the Baltic states, a nice speech, but one with all the significance of a *munakook*, a sponge cake. And then Ford had vanished inside the White House and the petition disappeared into the attaché case of a Presidential aide, where it would lie forgotten the way all such idiotic papers did. Even then, on the day of Ford's speech, Mikhail Kiss had already surrendered any belief he'd ever had in the usefulness of paper protests. Even on that fall afternoon he'd understood that the plan, first considered between himself and Romanenko in the middle of the 1960s, was the only possible direction to take.

Kiss moved to his desk where he sat down, picking up a paperweight in the form of a miniature Edinburgh Castle, a recent acquisition whose significance struck him as gruesome now.

'Do you trust him not to talk?' Andres Kiss asked.

Mikhail Kiss looked surprised. 'What kind of question is that? If Carl wants out, we let him leave. It's that simple.'

The young man said, 'I don't like the idea of Carl walking around with the kind of information he has.'

Kiss didn't care for the clipped coldness in his nephew's voice. 'I've known him a long time. Say what you like about his faults, he can keep his mouth shut. Besides, who's he going to talk to? The nice men at the Soviet Mission in Manhattan?'

Kiss put the small bronze castle down and looked at his nephew. He'd raised Andres from the moment he'd been born, immediately after the death of his widowed sister

Augusta in childbirth. It was a responsibility for which Kiss, accustomed to a life of solitude, a life devoted to making money for himself and his Wall Street clients, wasn't prepared. He often wondered if he'd discharged his obligation in the best way, if he'd done everything he might have to raise Andres.

He shut his eyes against the sunlight streaming into the room. He sometimes thought he'd placed too much emphasis on old stories of the Brotherhood, instilled in Andres too much of his own hatred of the Soviets. He'd told him tales of what it felt like to lie on a forest floor while Soviet warplanes bombed the place where you were hiding. He'd told sad stories about farms burning and farmers being dragged into fields and shot, about the sorrow of having to bury a dead comrade or the elation when the Brotherhood successfully destroyed a Russian convoy. He'd told him of the time he came across an abandoned farmhouse in the attic of which four small children, with piano wire round their necks, hung from the rafters and the way their blackened blood stained the floor beneath them and how he'd never managed to rid his mind of this image, which chilled him still and made his loathing of the Soviets even more intense, if that were possible.

Andres had absorbed all his uncle's hatred of the Soviets and their system, but there were certain things he couldn't grasp. He heard war stories and thought only of revenge. He had no insight into the spirit that had existed in the Brotherhood, no idea of the fellowship. How could he have? What could Mikhail Kiss have told him about the compassion between men, the bonds forged in the crucible of a hopeless war? How could this young man, born and raised in America, have understood the kind of camaraderie nurtured by conditions that had never existed within the United States?

Kiss thought that there was a very real sense in which he hadn't been a good teacher because he'd failed to make the young man's understanding complete, with the result that some element was missing from Andres's personality, an elusive quality Kiss wanted to call 'heart' or 'humanity'. As a human being Andres was all angles and abrasive edges, tightly-focused, somebody whose physical beauty concealed his tough-mindedness. He had, at times, a certain charm, but there was something borrowed about it, as if he were a man trying to speak in a foreign language he hadn't properly learned. He'd never formed close relationships with women, preferring the quick and the casual, simple encounters in dark places. He'd entered the US Air Force at the age of nineteen, ascended through the ranks with chill brilliance, a Major at the age of thirty-one who flew F-16s on NATO missions. On his thirty-second birthday he resigned his commission, because he'd drained the Air Force of all the information he needed to have. It had nothing else to offer him.

The young man's life was an equation in which his military career was one factor, his inherited hatred of the Soviets another. An equation made in steel, Mikhail Kiss thought, durable and unchanging. It was this steel that made him important in the Brotherhood's plan, but it was the same alloy that would prevent him from being the kind of man who loved and inspired love in others. And Mikhail Kiss felt at times a little guilty because of the way, inadvertently or otherwise, he'd moulded his nephew – not into a rounded human being, not into a person with compassion and understanding, but into the destructive instrument of the Brotherhood.

Now Kiss rose from the desk. 'Carl's waiting for you,' he said.

Andres stood in the window, and the sun made his hair gold. Although he was used to obeying his uncle, he thought Mikhail too trusting. He wanted to say that Carl shouldn't be dismissed this way, that an old man who'd turned his back on the Brotherhood shouldn't be allowed to walk away unconditionally – but he knew Mikhail would counter with a sentimental argument about the history he shared with Sundbach. So he didn't argue. He never quarrelled with Mikhail. He kept his objections quietly to himself. Men like Mikhail and Carl Sundbach, with their old attachments, their facile nostalgia, made him impatient. He walked to the door, opened it, gazed across the landing towards the stairs. There he paused.

Seeing the young man's hesitation, Mikhail Kiss said, 'Trust me. Carl won't speak to anybody.'

Andres Kiss looked about as relaxed as he ever did. He stepped out of the room, drawing the door shut behind him. He went down the stairs and out on to the porch. Sundbach sat in the passenger seat of the Jaguar. His glasses glinted in the sunlight. He turned his head impatiently and said, 'What kept you? I was going to send a search-party.'

Andres Kiss moved in the direction of his car. He clenched his fists at his side as he moved, his fine hands turning an angry white colour.

Fredericksburg, Virginia

Galbraith said, 'I love the way they shape the world according to how they think it ought to be. They refuse to contemplate disagreeable alternatives. Kiss and Kiss are going ahead *no matter what!* They want to make a statement about that diddlyshit corner of Europe the Soviets stole and half the world hasn't heard about and the other half can only do some pooh-poohing over because it's a goddam *fait accompli* anyhow. I love their dedication.'

The fat man, who wore a small acupuncture stud in his right ear – placed there only that morning by a Filipino practitioner everyone in DC swore by – reached up to rub the little globe of metal, which was said to curb the craving for food. With growing exasperation he rubbed for about thirty seconds, then dipped his hand inside a box of Black Magic chocolates by Rowntree Mackintosh, and said, 'So much for the ancient healing arts of the goddam East.'

He stuffed a chocolate into his mouth, then he reached out to the tape-recorder and rewound the reel to the part where Andres Kiss could be heard to say *It's not a dream for me, Carl.*

'There,' Galbraith said. 'That's probably my favourite part. You can hear the kid gloat when he says that. His voice practically drips. Frankly, I'm glad Sundbach dropped out. I was never convinced he had the right stuff. A little too fond of the cherry brandy. I always felt he'd come undone eventually.'

Iverson, seated beneath the banks of video consoles, heard old Carl say *I don't like the feeling of putting my goddam head under a guillotine*. The meetings in the house in Glen Cove had been taped for more than a year now, and Galbraith had come to regard them as regular Sunday afternoon listening.

'Does he worry you, Gary?' Galbraith asked.

'Sundbach?' Iverson frowned, gave a little shrug.

Galbraith nodded. This morning he was dressed in a dark suit instead of the robes he usually favoured. He wore a blue carnation in his lapel. 'He worries young Andres. You can tell that much.'

'Andres worries about everything, sir,' Iverson said. 'When he was in the Air Force he worried about making the grade. Nothing was more important to him than learning to fly. He spent more hours in an F-16 simulator than any man in the history of the Force. He worried about his physical exams. He worried about his eyesight. The clue to Andres is his compulsive personality. He's a perfectionist.'

Which is why we have him,' Galbraith said. He had discovered one of his favourite chocolates, a dimpled, strawberry-centred rectangle that he popped into his mouth before closing the box and shoving it across the glass-topped table. At least he was *trying*. 'The trouble is, Sundbach worries *me*. I don't like the idea of the old fellow walking out at this stage of the game.'

Galbraith killed the tape-recorder just as Mikhail Kiss was saying, *Trust me. Carl won't speak to anybody.* He wandered around the room for a while. Iverson watched him. For a fat man he moved smoothly, seeming to glide at times, like a hydrofoil on a cushion of air. He finally returned to the sofa where he sat down, glanced at his watch.

'I have an afternoon tea affair on the roof in about five minutes, Gary. Do we have anything to discuss before I leave?'

Iverson took out a small notebook, flipped the pages. 'One, there's nothing new from London. A cop called Frank Pagan's in charge of the affair, but I haven't heard anything more.'

Galbraith said, 'Keep on that one just the same.'

Iverson said, 'Two. I don't have anything new on Jacob Kiviranna except for sketchy details. Where he went to school, where he was born, the fact he spent a couple of years in jail for offences ranging from public nuisance to aggravated assault. We should know more any moment.'

'Aggravated assault? That's promising. I think we need to know if Vabadus's killer was a psycho or something else. So keep pressing on that one. Make sure any information we get on Kiviranna reaches Scotland Yard too. It ought to keep this Pagan busy around the edges of things in the meantime. Clear the material with me first, though, won't you?' Galbraith stood up. 'We might also do ourselves a small favour by keeping an eye on Carl Sundbach. I'm only thinking aloud now, you understand, but I'm also wondering if it might be necessary to do a dark deed where Sundbach's concerned. Call it a feasibility study, that's all. I don't want you coming in here with blood on *your* hands, Gary.'

Galbraith looked thoughtful. Ever since a DIA employee – they were never known to Galbraith as agents, a term he considered theatrical – had been apprehended last year carrying a case containing one point three million dollars into Cuba, money earmarked for certain persons who were anxious to see Fidel unseated and who needed weaponry, ever since this embarrassing little fiasco had been hinted at in a variety of newspapers and periodicals, Galbraith had become hypercautious and overprotective when it came to his department of the agency. He had devised a new policy, which was to use only outsiders, if possible, when it came to the truly dirty deeds. Doing something nefarious wasn't the problem. Being found out was.

'You might want to probe Andres,' Galbraith said. 'You might want to take his temperature, see if he really thinks Sundbach's a danger. After all we don't want to jump in and do something irrevocable if the old fellow's simply harmless, do we?'

Iverson agreed.

On his way to the door, Galbraith stopped. 'Do you think Andres ever suspects anything?' he asked.

Iverson considered this, then shook his head firmly. 'I really don't think he's gifted in the area of peripheral vision, sir.'

Galbraith looked thoughtful a moment. He stroked his little acupuncture stud and said, 'The one thing I wish is that these Balts weren't so goddam sentimental. It's the only problem I have with them. I was never very happy with the sealed envelope business and the poem. To them it's like some holy relic. To me it's unadulterated nostalgia and inefficient to boot. I can see the Brotherhood getting off on using their old call sign – but I keep thinking it would have been so much more damn simple if Romanenko had just telephoned Kiss when they were both in London.' Here Galbraith stared morosely at the chocolate box, his expression that of an addict pondering a cure. 'Still, who am I to interfere with the rituals of men whose purpose I support and admire wholeheartedly? If that's the way they felt they had to do things, who am I to criticise their habits, Gary? Anyhow, I hate to give you the impression I'm ungrateful to the Balts, because that's far from the truth. On the contrary, I regard their cause as sacred. Without it, where would White Light be?'

Galbraith, smiling, climbed out of the basement. The effort made him short of breath. He rode in the private lift to the roof, which had been transformed into a garden, surrounded on all aides by bulletproof glass. Three satellite dishes scanned the skies silently. There was a view of the countryside around Fredericksburg, a secretive, green landscape. Galbraith walked to the centre of the roof, pushing aside a variety of shrubs and flowers – dense, spreading acacia, red bougainvillaea, dwarf pomegranate bearing inedible dwarf fruit, bromeliads. It was all a little too much, Galbraith thought. When he'd asked for a garden up here, some greenery to give the roof aesthetic appeal, he hadn't taken into consideration the ego of the gardener, a man who considered himself no mere potter of shrub and fern but a 'landscape architect'. It had become a world in which ratcatchers were rodent-control agents, and plumbers sanitation consultants.

In the centre of the roof a table had been set up for afternoon tea in the English style. Silver teapot, china plates, scones and assorted jams, small cucumber sandwiches. Two men in dark suits sat at the table. One was Senator Crowe, a Texan, the other Senator Holly from Iowa, both senior members of the Senate Committee on Foreign Relations. John Crowe had been in Washington so long that it was said he'd been consulted on the original plan for the White House. He was an emaciated man with the demeanour of an undertaker. His face, which consisted of hundreds of tiny squares of wrinkled flesh, a parchment patchwork, always made Galbraith think of the Dead Sea Scrolls. Holly, on the other hand, was younger, pot-bellied, a man with a smile that apparently left his face only when he slept. Galbraith thought of him as Jolly Holly, even thought there was something vaguely sinister in the fixed grin.

'These sandwiches have no damned crusts,' John Crowe snarled in the throaty voice that made him famous and widely impersonated.

Galbraith sat down, thinking how Crowe always had a vaguely depressing effect on him. Access to the kind of power Crowe had – in the intelligence community, the Foreign Relations Committee, and the Senate Committee on Military Expenditure – had made him a grave, gloomy figure, and wraithlike. He reminded Galbraith of a satirical, spectral version he'd seen of the figure of Uncle Sam in a rabid left-wing movie on the Vietnam War some years ago.

'It's an English affectation,' Galbraith said.

Crowe, nodding his head in acknowledgement of this information, put his sandwich back on his plate as Galbraith poured tea. Galbraith noticed there was a slight tremor over the old fellow's upper lip and a waxiness to Crowe's complexion, as if he'd been dipped in a melted candle.

Senator Joseph Holly picked up a knife, neatly dissected a scone and opened it. He spread the surface of one of the halves with Dundee marmalade. When he spoke he did so in a nasal manner, his voice seeming to emerge from the cavities behind his eyes. 'So this is where the taxpayer's money goes,' he said.

'This is window-dressing,' Galbraith replied. 'Where the money really goes is elsewhere, Senator.'

Holly kept on smiling. 'You spooks know how to spend.'

'Keeping the world safe for democracy is no Macy's basement, gentlemen,' Galbraith said in a cordial way. He hated fiscal matters, penny-pinching, keeping accounts, all the tedious chores involved in his relationship with official Washington.

John Crowe said, 'The cost is goddam high, and getting higher.'

'By the minute,' Galbraith agreed cheerfully.

Joseph Holly ate a small mouthful of scone. A bee floated close to the open jar of marmalade and the Senator swatted it away. It promptly returned, clinging to the underside of Holly's saucer. Holly asked, 'Are we being recorded right now?'

'This is the one place where I don't allow recordings,' Galbraith replied. It was true that he wasn't taping any of this conversation. He might have done so by activating a small button located on the underside of the table. But this wasn't the kind of talk Galbraith wanted to have any record of – quite the opposite.

'Good,' Holly said. 'Senator Crowe and myself – we're not interfering, keep that in mind, Galbraith – we want to know if this operation is still go on the scheduled date. We hadn't heard from you – '

' – And I consider your silence arrogant, Galbraith,' Crowe said. 'You don't bite the goddam hand that feeds you. You don't misinterpret the freedom we give you as a goddam licence to do whatever the hell you like. You keep us posted, for Christ's sake.'

Galbraith raised his eyebrows. 'I can only plead pressures of office. No excuse, I know, gentlemen.' He twiddled his fingers and watched the slow movement of the satellite dishes. He understood Crowe and Holly had come down to Fredericksburg to throw a little weight around because they'd been pressured by their allies – a group that included two generals, three congressmen, and a smattering of anonymous industrialists – to find out what the hell was going on. Besides, Crowe was the nominal Director of the DIA and Holly his titular assistant, although neither man was involved in the daily business of the agency.

Was the bird going to fly? That was the question they wanted answered. That was why they were really here in Fredericksburg. Galbraith smiled. He looked plumply reassuring. 'Senators, everything is going according to schedule. There are no snags, no snafus, no unexpected scenarios. The clockwork ticks even as we sit here surrounded by all this pleasing greenery.'

Crowe leaned across the table, blocking the sunlight. 'I'm happy to hear you say that, Galbraith. I'm very happy. I haven't been sleeping lately. Worry, I guess. I liked the world the way it was, Galbraith. I liked the old world better. The way things are going now . . . ' Crowe didn't sustain his line of thought. He faded out into a dark silence, his mottled fingers playing with a disc of cucumber that had fallen out of his sandwich.

Galbraith said, 'We all liked that world better, Senator. It had a certain predictability about it, which was extremely comforting.'

'It surely was,' Holly said.

'And well-balanced,' Galbraith added.

Crowe suddenly picked up his unfinished thought and added, 'We're going to hell in a goddam handbasket. That's where we're headed.'

Galbraith watched the bee slide out from under Senator Holly's saucer. He said, 'I think that trip to hell is something we intend to stop, Senator Crowe.'

John Crowe raised his waxy face. Galbraith noticed a film of membranous material covering one of the old man's eyes.

Crowe said, 'One of the problems is the quality of the people these days. Men who aren't big enough for their jobs. Dwarves and midgets, Galbraith.'

Galbraith made a sound of agreement.

Crowe went on, 'And I'm not just talking about Washington, no sir. I'm talking about the other side as well. I'm talking about how difficult it is to replace a Brezhnev. Even an Andropov. When we had the Chernenko interregnum I really thought we were in hog heaven. And Christ, we had such goddam high hopes for Vladimir Greshko until he fell ill and they gave him the boot. He was a mean sonofabitch and you couldn't trust him further than you could spit, but he knew his goddam place. I'll tell you this, if he was running the show over there we'd be in a damn sight better position. All this hanky-panky we get nowadays wouldn't be going on. Greshko never had the time for that bullshit.'

Galbraith plucked a gooseberry-tart from a plate and nibbled it. Its sourness made him wrinkle his face a moment. He said, 'What I liked about Greshko was how you couldn't trust him, but you could always count on him.'

'Damn right,' Crowe said. 'How is the old bastard anyhow?'

'Alive, so I believe,' Galbraith replied.

Neither Crowe nor Holly needed to know more than that. The secret of success as Galbraith perceived it lay in controlling the spigot of information, knowing how much to release, how much to hold back. When it came to politicians, who traded in the currency of gossip, you withheld the maximum amount possible and doled out a mere trickle. You slaked a thirst, you didn't release a flood.

Galbraith finished his tea, wiped his fingers in the folds of his napkin. 'I think we can safely say, Senators, that the status quo will be restored before the week is out.'

Crowe looked happy. Holly smiled his unchanging smile – at least until he stood upright suddenly and slapped the palm of his hand upon his neck.

'Shit,' Holly exclaimed. There was a squashed bee, still living, fluttering, in the dead centre of his hand. 'Bastard stung me.'

Galbraith clucked sympathetically. 'At least you have the certain pleasure of knowing your assailant is mortally wounded, Senator. Wouldn't it be wonderful if politics worked with such admirable symmetry?'

9

London

Danus Oates lived alone in a three-room flat in Knightsbridge, not far from Sloane Square. The other tenants of the house were a pair of elderly sisters, both quite mad, who kept macaws in enormous cages, and a retired coffee plantation manager from Kenya whose face had the texture of cowhide left too long in direct sunlight. It was a quiet house and Oates moved about it with stealthy consideration. He was well-bred and well-mannered and, until the horror yesterday in Edinburgh, had always considered his life rather humdrum. He had a future in the Foreign Service, so he was told, and he hoped one day to emulate his father – Sir Geoffrey Oates, Her Majesty's Ambassador to Norway. Like many patriotic men dedicated to public service, he was neither greatly ambitious nor overwhelmingly imaginative, but he was pleased, in a general kind of way, with his existence.

His one extraordinary talent was for languages, which came to him with an ease that was inexplicable, all the more so since there was no history of this affinity in his lineage. He spoke not only the usual languages of commerce and diplomacy – French, German, Russian – but he had an excellent knowledge of Greek (ancient and, modern), Spanish, Italian and Swedish. He could read and speak two of the three Baltic languages – Estonian and Latvian (in its Upper dialect) – and he understood to a useful degree some of the arcane forms associated with them, Livonian and Low German. He had a smattering of the Carpathian dialect of Ukrainian, more than adequate Hungarian, and he was fluent in Moldavian, which was really a version of Rumanian. He was presently teaching himself Ottoman Turkish, or Osmanli, from cassette tapes provided by the Foreign Office Library. Quite often Oates dreamed in foreign tongues.

Because he'd spent hours translating the Livonian material at Scotland Yard, he hadn't returned to his apartment until six a.m. that Sunday morning. He'd been made groggy too by the twenty milligrams of Valium he'd taken in an attempt to restore his ruined nerves. Consequently, he fell into a sound sleep as soon as his head hit the pillow, and he dreamed for an odd reason of the Estonian word for 'potato' in some of its various grammatical cases. *Kartul* meant potato, but because prepositions in Estonian were suffixes, *kartuli* meant 'of the potato' and *kartuliga* meant 'with the potato' and *kartulil* 'on the potato'. His long sleep and his strange dream of *kartulid* – potatoes, plural – was interrupted at approximately four o'clock in the afternoon by a hand clamped over his mouth.

Oates woke abruptly, and found himself looking up into a kindly face, that of a man who might generously toss coins in the cup of a blind beggar. Oates couldn't breathe because the hand was forced very hard over his lips. His sleepy mind, shocked into alertness, considered a number of possibilities. He was being burgled. Or he was about to be raped. Or this intruder with the gentle face was in reality a madman who'd slit his throat any second with a razor.

Oates kicked at the bedsheets and tried to twist his head away, but the older man was astonishingly strong.

'The rules are simple, Mr Oates. I ask some questions. You answer them honestly. You understand?'

Oates blinked his eyes furiously. The stranger took his hand away and Oates sucked air into his lungs. With the return of oxygen to his brain came a defiant urge. After all, what the hell was this chap doing in Oates's flat? What gave him the bloody right to come stealing inside another fellow's bedroom? Oates, who wore black and red striped pyjamas, a present last Christmas from his fiancée Fiona, stepped out of bed, brushing past the intruder.

'Where are you going?' the stranger asked in his accented English.

Oates didn't answer, just kept moving. He was thinking of the telephone in the corner of the bedroom. Calling the gendarmes. Getting some law and order established around here. He'd almost reached the phone when he felt it – a searing pain between his shoulder-blades. It rocked his spine, settled somewhere in the middle of his skull like a small glowing coal. He collapsed on the floor and moaned. He looked up at the man, who stood directly over him, shaking his head in a gesture of regret.

'Take me seriously, Mr Oates. Don't force me to strike you again.'

Danus Oates moved his head very slightly. The idea of violence terrified him. He stammered the way he'd always done when he'd been a schoolboy at Harrow and an object of cruel fun. 'What d-d-do you want?'

'Your cooperation,' the stranger said. He squatted beside Oates, who felt paralysed, though whether through fear or because the intruder had struck some vital nerve centre he couldn't tell.

'I believe you may have done some translating, Mr Oates.'

That bloody Livonian stuff! So that's what all this was about! Oates was a little relieved to discover that the fellow wasn't an escaped lunatic after all. But only a little. He looked up into the sympathetic brown eyes, the concerned expression.

'What precisely was it you translated?'

'Business d-documents, some business c-c-c-correspondence.'

'Is that all?'

'There was also a p-poem,' Oates said. He saw no harm in admitting this. After all, he was a budding diplomat, and if this was all some kind of cloak and dagger nonsense he wanted no part of it.

'Tell me about it, Mr Oates.'

Oates felt a little surge of security. He was on familiar ground now. 'There were four lines of verse,' he said. 'They were written in a form of Livonian, which is rather obscure. Do you know anything about that language?'

The intruder shook his head. 'I don't have time for an academic discourse, Mr Oates. The contents of the poem, please. That's all I ask.'

Oates said, 'I'm simply trying to tell you the poem was written in a language few people speak any more. There were one or two words of modern Estonian mixed in, but mainly the vocabulary was Livonian. So far as I can gather, the poem referred to somebody called Kalev who apparently has the ability to bring joy to Estonia.'

'Kalev?'

Oates nodded. He struggled into a sitting position. The pain had diffused itself, and was no longer centralised, but had broken into little tributaries that flickered along his nerve-endings. He rubbed his arms, which for some reason tingled.

'In your opinion was the verse some form of code?'

'Code?' Oates blinked. 'That sort of thing is really rather outside my province.'

'This poem wasn't returned to the Soviet Embassy by Scotland Yard. Do you know why?'

Oates, remembering how the strange lines of verse had so intrigued the Commissioner, shook his head. 'I'm no expert on how Scotland Yard works.'

The man pinched the bridge of his nose a moment, sighing as he did so. 'Does Frank Pagan have the poem in his possession?'

Danus Oates said he presumed so except he couldn't be sure, all he'd done was to translate the material, then pass it back to the Commissioner, who would have assigned it to Pagan. He thought the Commissioner wouldn't have given it to anyone else because Burr had said he didn't want the existence of the poem bruited about, so the circle of those who knew about the verse was probably very small. But, good Christ, Oates didn't know anything for certain – he hadn't even understood the damned poem, he said. In fact he wished he'd never been in Edinburgh in the first place. He had an unwanted memory of Romanenko mentioning how railroad stations smelled and then the loud roar of a pistol and Frank Pagan throwing himself bodily at the assassin. His brain was like a large box in which everything made loud rattling noises.

Oates made it up as far as his knees, but he was unsteady, and swayed a little. The intruder helped him to his feet, then back to the bed. Oates sat on the edge of the mattress. He still felt curiously dizzy, at one remove from himself. The red stripes of his pyjamas seemed to pulsate at the corner of his vision. The older man had to have the strength of a damned ox to fell him like that. He looked at the man, who was gazing round the bedroom, which was decorated with antique furniture and nineteenth-century equestrian prints, family heirlooms.

Then the stranger walked to the window and looked out. There was a view of a quiet Sunday street, parked cars, a pub called The Lord Byron on a far corner. Oates gnawed on his lower lip. The man's silence was unnerving, even menacing. Surely, though, this was the end of the business. Oates had no information to give, he didn't have a clue about why the poem wasn't returned to the Russians, he was actually of very little use to this stranger – who, if he were a reasonable man, would recognise the fact and simply depart. Oates prayed he was exactly that: a reasonable man.

'I mean, if I didn't happen to know the language, I wouldn't have been involved in any of this,' and Oates attempted a nervous little laugh, which emerged as a girlish giggle, a sound he didn't quite recognise as his own. 'As for the poem, well, it didn't make any damn sense to me, but I can't speak on Frank Pagan's behalf, perhaps it means something to him.' He babbled on, driven by his nervousness, words streaming out of him. The stranger turned now, and smiled. It was a warm little expression which chilled Danus Oates to the bone. A few spots of rain struck the window and slithered down the glass. Oates's attention was drawn to them momentarily, and he thought how very banal the raindrops seemed, how ordinary – but then everything struck him as commonplace all at once, this bedroom, the bed, his striped pyjamas, the things in his room. Everything was sublimely prosaic except for the gun in the intruder's hand which Oates had noticed when the man turned from the window but had refused to register. A delayed reaction – only now it struck him like a tiny comet flashing through the darkness of his head, and the everyday quality of his surroundings was altered beyond recognition, and all the anchors securing him to the familiar were cut loose.

'L-l-look here,' Oates said. 'You're not going to use that thing.' His tongue adhered to the roof of his mouth and he had no control over the sudden tic under his eye.

The stranger moved closer to the bed. He seemed to be turning something over in his mind. Whatever it was, Danus Oates knew it was connected with his own future, a concept that was rushing away from him with the sound of air escaping a punctured balloon.

The man pushed the gun into the soft flesh below Oates's ear. Oates imagined he heard the weapon ticking like some awful clock measuring his frail mortality. He shut his eyes and tried to swallow.

'P-p-p,' but the word please wouldn't come out at all.

The intruder came so close now that Oates could feel the man's breath upon the side of his cheek, and he could smell the gun, the peculiar metal odour of it, the hint of oil. He opened one eye and thought how vast the weapon seemed from his perspective.

'Are you telling me everything you know, Mr Oates?'

'*Absolutely,*' Oates whispered.

The gun was eased away from his neck and for a moment Oates was flooded with a relief so intense he felt light-headed. It was a sensation that lasted only a fraction of a second. The stranger fired the silenced gun once and Danus Oates, who had no more ambition in life than to become the British Ambassador to a civilised country like Austria or Holland, fell from the bed and toppled to the floor.

V. G. Epishev, struck by vague regret, didn't look at the body. He put the gun in his coat pocket, then stepped quietly out of the apartment, hearing from far beneath him the scream of a bird. And he thought of Vladimir Greshko and the way the old man lay like some bird himself, an aged buzzard with wings folded, eyes shut, talons always ready to strike.

He moved down the stairs quickly, let himself out into the street. Thin clouds floated over the wet slate rooftops of Knightsbridge. A dreary Sunday, an afternoon in which autumn could be smelled on the air like lead. An afternoon for death and dying.

He walked until he came to the place where he'd parked his hired car, a Ford, then he drove away, watching rain slide over the windshield. He was certain that Oates, poor doomed Oates, had been telling the truth. What had he been in any case but an innocent bystander, an accident of history? The option to allow Oates to live hadn't really been viable, although Epishev had considered it. As soon as Epishev had left the apartment, the young Englishman would be on the telephone to Scotland Yard, babbling about his mysterious intruder and all the questions he'd asked.

Verse, Epishev thought. A few lines of poetry. If these were a code, then it might be something simple, something a man like Frank Pagan might be able to figure out. Something that contained dates and times and places, the particulars of the Brotherhood's plot.

He parked his car under a damp tree on a quiet side-street. He pinched the bridge of his nose, a characteristic gesture of concentration. His instruction from Greshko had been simple. Eliminate the threat. Epishev made no distinction between real or imagined threats – they were equally menacing. What did it matter if the poem contained a code or not? The important thing was the idea that it might. Uncle Viktor, who had lived for a long time in a world of menace, had a word for this kind of elimination. He called it precautionary.

Frank Pagan and Kristina Vaska left Pagan's flat and walked across the square, through dripping laburnum and under wet laurels, following a narrow path that led past empty wooden benches. Pagan had wakened with a headache and an urge to walk in the rain, to get out of the apartment and away from the telephone calls from the scribblers of Fleet Street, who wanted his eyewitness account of the murder in Edinburgh.

Kristina Vaska had asked to accompany him and now she stepped along at his side wearing a raincoat she'd borrowed from his wardrobe. It was far too large for her. The sleeves hung three inches beyond her hands, the hem trailed the wet grass. She looked frail and childlike in the oversized coat, but Pagan knew this fragility was more apparent than real.

He surveyed the square, pausing at a place where the pathway divided. It was bleak here, and private, his own rain-shrouded enclave in the heart of Holland Park. The path led past a shelter, a simple wooden edifice with benches that was a retreat for the old people of the neighbourhood. Today it was empty and smelled of damp wood and wet moss. Kristina Vaska paused by the shelter.

She asked, 'How long have you lived a life of chaotic bachelorhood?'

Pagan said, 'I was married once.'

'What happened?'

'She died.' Two words. *She died*. Pagan wanted to leave it there, simple and terse, unexplored. He didn't want to go into that history of pain. He looked the length of the square. The only other life forms were an elderly woman, an eccentric in plastic raincoat and hat, walking an enormously fat, boisterous dalmatian.

'I'm sorry', Kristina said.

'It's not anything I want to talk about.' He moved past the shelter, listening to the tick of rain on leaves. 'Let's talk about Kristina Vaska instead.'

'I can think of more interesting topics. What do you want to know?'

'Where you live. What you do for a living. The usual stuff.'

She smiled. 'I live in New York City. I work as a researcher.'

'What kind of research?' Pagan was unhappy with vague terminology, and the word 'researcher' fell into a category of occupations that included financial consultants, management analysts and Members of Parliament.

'Let's say a writer or an organisation wants information. They come to me, tell me what they need, and I find out. I spend a lot of time in libraries. Is there anything you need to know about Sargon the Great, King of Akkad? Are you having a problem about the habitat of Leadbeater's possum? Do you have an urgent desire to find out how the Ashanti live and what they worship? Then I'm the person to see.' She looked at him with her head tilted a little to one side. 'Among other things, I've also done considerable research –

unpaid, entirely on my own initiative – into the Brotherhood, which wasn't altogether easy because the literature isn't extensive.'

Pagan tried to imagine her hauling heavy volumes from dusty shelves in obscure libraries and somehow couldn't fix a clear image in his head. 'What brought you to England?'

'Am I being interrogated, Frank?'

Pagan shook his head. Had it been so long since he'd carried on any ordinary discourse that he'd forgotten how? Was there a tone in his voice that suggested he suspected everybody he met of *something*? 'I didn't mean to make it sound that way. Force of habit, I suppose.'

'I guess in your line of business you think everyone has ulterior motives. So you don't take anybody on trust. Including me. I sneak into your little world – a mine of information, a source of intrigue, only you don't know exactly who I am or what my motives are. What makes it even more perplexing is the way I turn up at the same time as Romanenko – and wham! You're sitting on one of those really bizarre coincidences cops aren't supposed to swallow. Correct?'

Pagan, thinking how close Kristina Vaska had come to describing his state of mind, picked up a damp stick and tossed it through the air and watched it fall with a mildly expectant look on his face, almost as if he expected an invisible dog to fetch it for him. 'When I get information, I like to know as much as I can about the source.' He sounded more defensive than he would have liked.

'Makes sense,' she said. She walked ahead of him now, leaving the path and pushing through damp shrubbery. He went after her, noticing the way her hair was flattened by rain against her scalp. One of the most provocative images in Pagan's sexual cosmology was the sight of a woman stepping from a shower or coming up out of the ocean after a swim, her hair wet and uncombed and falling carelessly. Something in the randomness, the basic disarray, appealed enormously to him. As she parted damp shrubbery and rain blew across her face and hair, Kristina Vaska was attractive to him in just that way.

She stopped moving, turned to him, grinned. Her whole look teased him. She raised her hands in a gesture of surrender. 'Okay. You got me cold, Pagan. I confess. I was the one supposed to meet Romanenko in Edinburgh. I was his contact. He was supposed to pass the poem to me. I'm the Brotherhood's messenger. Please don't send me to the big house, I don't want to grow old and wrinkled in a cell, please find some charity in your heart.'

She clutched the lapel of his coat and shook him slightly and he laughed aloud at her sudden pantomime, thinking how the sound cut through his unease. Then she released him and turned away from him once again and moved between the trees. He walked behind her, blinking against the rain.

She stopped between two elegant willows whose branches trailed the ground. In this location, this secret heart of the park, it was impossible to see the houses around the square. It was an intimate place, a green island afloat on the wet afternoon, and Pagan felt the unexpected impulse to reach out and touch the woman, perhaps something as simple as laying his fingertips against her lips. With some difficulty he resisted the urge.

She wiped raindrops from her eyelashes and smiled at him. 'Actually, the real truth's boringly simple, Frank. I came to London because I hoped I'd get a chance to talk with Romanenko. I read in somewhere that the Soviets were interested in buying computers in the UK, and that Romanenko was being sent. I had a notion he might just be able to use his influence to help get my father released. I wasn't sure how I was going to engineer a meeting, because I know the KGB's usually in attendance – but I thought it was worth a shot. Unfortunately, I never got the chance to see him. I went to the Savoy, but he'd already left for Edinburgh. Then I figured I'd wait for him to return. The rest you know.'

Pagan listened in silence. There was still a shadow across his mind. 'Why do you want to help me? Why bother to tell me about Romanenko and the Brotherhood? Altruism? Or am I missing something?'

'You're not missing anything. Your viewpoint's just a little jaded, that's all. You don't expect people to be helpful. I don't have any concealed motives, Frank. I heard about the killing on TV, I thought you might need information you weren't going to get anywhere else. Here I am. That's it.'

He stepped a little closer to the woman. She ran her fingers through her wet hair. Pagan felt an odd sense of longing. The last yearning he'd had like this belonged in quite another lifetime, in the dead seasons of his past. Eroticism in the rain, he thought. A fine sexual fever under the damp trees. She was bewitching in the oversized coat, a child-woman.

She ducked a little too quickly under a branch, moving beyond his reach, heading out of this leafy corner and back in the direction of the path. Pagan was a little startled by his feelings, which Kristina Vaska must have read in his eyes – given the haste with which she'd stepped away from him. Was he supposed to feel foolish now? Embarrassed by his obviousness?

Saying nothing to each other, they walked back along the path. Pagan gazed at the empty lawns, the damp flowerbeds, the low sky that hung above the square and emphasised the desolation, the emptiness, of the place. The fat dalmatian and the elderly woman he'd seen before weren't visible now, even though the barking of a dog could still be heard through the rain.

'Can you remember where you read about Romanenko's visit?' he asked.

She smiled as if his suspicions were a constant source of amusement to her. 'You're priceless, Frank. What difference does it make where I read about it?'

'I'm curious, that's all.'

She closed her eyes, looked thoughtful. '*The Economist*. US edition. Any more questions?'

Pagan gazed at the small wooden shelter in the centre of the square. 'I don't think so,' he said.

'Did I pass the test?'

'Was there a test?'

'From the moment I first stepped inside your flat.'

They were approaching the shelter now. Pagan stared beyond it, through the trees, seeing the dim windows of his own apartment. The curtains were still drawn from the night before. He could see the narrow street lined with parked cars. Kristina Vaska was perfectly correct, of course. He'd been testing her all along, and he hadn't quite finished yet. He might be attracted to her, but he wasn't going to get downright careless on that account. An earlier version of Pagan, a younger self, might have had a more romantic lack of caution, a willingness to be indiscreet with his heart – but at the age of forty-one Pagan had crossed a demarcation line on one side of which lay blind ardour, on the other wariness.

'Let's go back indoors,' he said. 'I need a drink.'

V.G. Epishev sat inside the parked car, listening to the quiet sound of the engine running. He watched Frank Pagan and the woman crossing the square in the direction of the street. It was the presence of the woman that threw him off balance. He hadn't expected a companion in Pagan's life. For some reason he'd assumed Pagan's life would be as solitary as his own.

His view of Pagan and the woman was impeded for a moment by a shelter in the middle of the park, then they re-emerged, pausing to exchange some words. They inclined their heads towards each other, and Epishev detected intimacy in this gesture. He wondered if Pagan and his companion were lovers. He tried to imagine them that way, but it was like the taste of an exotic food he hadn't sampled in a long time – and yet he could vaguely remember the tantalising flavour.

Something about the woman disturbed him. She provoked a strong sense of familiarity in him. It was the kind of feeling you had when a word lay on the tip of your tongue but you couldn't quite utter it. He thought he'd seen her before somewhere. No, he *knew* he had.

Pagan and the woman were still moving towards the exit. They walked about two feet apart from each other and there was no apparent intimacy now. Epishev put his hand into the pocket of his coat that contained the gun. He rested the other hand on the door-handle, looked along the quiet, rainy street.

It kept coming back to nag him, this feeling that somewhere in the distant past there had been an encounter with the woman. He was sure of it now. He gazed across the grass at her face, which was partly hidden by the upturned collar of her outsized raincoat. A lovely face, but tantalising. She made a gesture with her hand, threw her head back, laughed at something Pagan said. Epishev turned the handle of the door.

Pagan and the woman were about a hundred yards from the low stone wall that surrounded the square. Now the woman was staring almost directly at the car and Epishev brought his hand up to his lips and coughed into it, a reflex action, a gesture to conceal himself from her attention.

Who was she? And where had he seen her before?

He had a little memory trick he sometimes used. It was to envisage the environment in which he'd seen a particular face. It was to recall physical details – dress, weather, the colour of wallpaper, the curtains – and then set the remembered face against these recollections.

Tallinn, he thought. He had the feeling it had to be Tallinn. He recalled a flight of stairs, a bicycle propped against the wall on the landing, an open doorway that led inside a large apartment, a well-furnished set of rooms.

He almost had it then. But the memory was like a badly-tuned television station, a picture that fluttered, blemished by static. Damn. Now Pagan and the woman were a mere fifty yards away and they were walking more briskly than before. They wanted to get out of the rain, of course. To dry themselves off. Epishev undid the safety catch on the gun, and ran the tips of his fingers over the surface of the weapon. He'd step out of the car, approach Pagan with the gun, and the rest would be easy, a matter of getting back Romanenko's mysterious verse, which was presumably inside Pagan's apartment or even on his person, and then he'd dispose of both the Englishman and the woman, right here on this street if he had to –

A young girl in braided hair, a yellow print dress, bare feet in sandals, a child sobbing . . .

Pagan and the woman were approaching the stone wall now, the exit, the pavement. For a second they were lost behind a clutch of dense trees, then they reappeared.

A child sobbing.

And that was when it came to him, reaching across the years, echoing out of the past, it came to him with sudden clarity. He could see a young girl's face and the way her hair was braided and how she'd cried and scratched viciously at his hands as her father was being led out of the apartment in Tallinn on a cold morning more than fifteen years ago. Fifteen long years ago – how had Frank Pagan come into the orbit of the daughter of Norbert Vaska, the child called Kristina?

She turned her face towards the car then, for some reason. She turned, looking damp and pale, her black hair plastered across her scalp, her mouth a dark circle. Epishev wasn't sure whether it was recognition that crossed her face, whether his appearance provoked memories inside her of that same chill morning so long ago, when she'd been twelve, perhaps thirteen. He saw something in her features change, and then she was reaching for Pagan's arm and pulling it, and hurrying him across the street to the house. Pagan, running alongside her, his overcoat billowing around him, looked puzzled and reluctant as if the woman had drawn him suddenly into a game he couldn't follow.

Epishev, his sense of timing skewed by the sudden movement of the couple, tightened his grip on the gun and was about to step out of the car when he was aware of the enormous black and white dog thumping and pounding along the pavement towards him, a massive spotted creature, perhaps two hundred pounds in weight, pursued by a woman in a plastic raincoat. This monstrous animal had sighted Epishev stepping out of the car and now it charged with crazed canine friendliness toward him, a dumb light in its eyes, paws upraised, tail flailing the air like a whip. Epishev drew the car door shut and watched the creature slobber against the glass before losing interest and padding huffily away. The damned English and their damned pets! But he'd lost the initiative, the element of surprise, even before the appearance of the mutt.

Across the street Pagan and Kristina Vaska had vanished inside the house, and the dark brown door was shut behind them. Epishev cursed, stared up at the windows. Had she recognised him? Of course – how else could one explain the speed with which they'd crossed the street and entered the house? How else to explain that urgency?

Epishev drove the Ford along the street, passing the dalmatian, which had its leg cocked against a wall. He glanced once more at Pagan's house, and then he was turning out of the narrow street, wondering what had brought Kristina Vaska into the policeman's world, and what it would mean if indeed she'd recognised him.

Inside the apartment Frank Pagan poured two shots of scotch and gave one to Kristina. She was silent, listening to the rain upon the window. Pagan watched her sip the drink, then he went to her and rubbed one of her cold hands between his own. She trembled. He walked to the window, looked down at the street, saw nothing below but the woman in the plastic raincoat caressing her spotted dog. There was no sign of the stranger who had so suddenly spooked Kristina and made her claw at his coat-sleeve in such a panicked manner that she'd dragged him across the street and inside the house before he'd even had time to register the existence of the man.

Kristina moved to the sofa and sat down. She was motionless for a long time.

'His name's Epishev,' she said in a quiet voice, almost a whisper. 'Some people call him Uncle Viktor, and they don't use the name fondly.'

Pagan sat down beside her. He wanted to reach for her hand again, but he didn't. 'How can you be sure it's the same man?'

'Because it's fucking hard to forget the face of the KGB officer who arrested my father in Tallinn.'

Pagan didn't doubt her fear. He could read it in her eyes as plainly as bold print. But there was something else here that troubled him, a convergence of more echoes from the past, actors from an old melodrama that might have been revived purely for his personal bewilderment. Uncle Viktor and Norbert Vaska. The KGB and the Brotherhood of the Forest. It was as if a faded photograph had been retouched, making it appear fresh and new. And it had been thrust rudely into his face, forcing him to look directly into it. He had the thought that his life, which had been simpler only recently, was taking strange, complicated detours. The problem with these departures was the feeling that he had no control over any of them.

He stared for a while at the prints on the walls. 'Why would the KGB send somebody here?' he asked. 'Why send somebody to spy on me?'

'Spy? I don't think Viktor Epishev would have anything as innocent as spying in mind, Frank. That's not what he does. Let me put it to you this way. If he's been sent over here because of you, he's got a more sinister purpose than simply watching you.'

'He wants me out of the way,' Pagan said rather flatly, more a statement of fact than a question.

'I'd hazard that guess, Frank.'

'Hazard another one and tell me why.'

'I don't exactly know. Let's look at what we've got. Romanenko carries a message he doesn't get the chance to deliver. We assume the message was intended for another member or members of the Brotherhood. Let's say the gist of it is to go ahead with a plan, which we believe is a plan against the Soviets. The message however, falls into your hands.'

'And Epishev wants it.'

'Presumably.'

'And he wants to silence me into the bargain.'

'Yes.'

'It's not adding up for me,' Pagan said. 'If the KGB thinks I have knowledge of some anti-Russian business, the logical thing would be for them to ask me directly. Frank, old comrade, what do you know about this Brotherhood stuff? That would be the rational approach. The notion of somebody being sent here to kill me – apart from scaring me quite shitless – seems a little extreme.'

They were silent for a while. Then Kristina said, 'Here's another possible consideration. Maybe the KGB already know what the Brotherhood's up to – only they'd prefer it if you didn't.'

'Which would imply the KGB is in bed with the Brotherhood, wouldn't it?'

Kristina Vaska nodded. 'And that's an impossibility. The likelihood of the Brotherhood fornicating with the KGB is about as remote as finding a civil rights lawyer in Moscow.'

'Here's a question for you. How would somebody go about finding out exactly what it is the Brotherhood's up to?'

Kristina Vaska shook her head, moved to the window, looked out into the rain. With a fingertip she drew a thin spiral on the glass. Pagan went towards her. He gazed over her shoulder and across the square.

'I wish I knew more,' she said.

'When you researched the Brotherhood, what did you find out about them?'

'I researched their past, Frank, and that was tough enough. Their present's even more difficult. They don't advertise for new members. They don't put ads in newspapers giving the times and locations of their meetings. They're not in the business of promoting themselves.'

'If I wanted to find one of the members, where would I start looking?'

'Jesus, I wish I had a specific answer to that one. The truth is, they ended up all over the place. Australia. New Zealand. Scandinavia. There's probably even a couple of old members right here in London. But mainly they made it to the United States. Chicago. Los Angeles. Mostly they came to New York City, Brooklyn in particular. But since many of them arrived as young men, they presumably married, raised families, and – like all good upwardly mobile Americans – prospered and moved out into the suburbs. Like I said, they don't advertise their whereabouts.'

'If you researched them, surely you must know some of their names?'

There was frustration in Kristina Vaska's voice. She looked at Pagan as if he'd asked the one question that had bewildered her for years. 'They weren't stupid men, Frank. They didn't fight under their own names. They used pseudonyms. *Noms de guerre* to protect their families if they were captured. They left nothing but dead-ends behind them when they dispersed. I spent a long time trying to track old members down when I was doing my research. Elusive's an understatement when it comes to their identities. I'd keep running into references to men who operated under names like *Rebane*, the Fox. One man called himself *Kotkas*, the Eagle. Another was *Hunt*, the Wolf. I could never pin anything down about the true identities of these characters. Apart from Romanenko, I never learned any real names. And I tried goddam hard, believe me. It's like I said, Frank. Records – even when they exist – are difficult to obtain and after a while you get so frustrated you can't do anything else but give up. If the men of the Brotherhood took such pains to conceal their identities, what right did I have to come along and try to force open old doors anyway? So I stopped looking. I quit.'

Pagan was silent. He stared into the trees. He remembered the way he'd yearned for her down there in the square, that brief flare of longing, as if he might find in her an escape hatch from the lonely condition of his life. He looked at the delicate shadow in the nape of her neck. Now now, he thought. Maybe never. He wondered what it would be like to make love to this woman.

There was a long silence broken only by the metronome of the rain. She turned from the window and said, 'Epishev scares me. He scared me when I was a kid, and he scares me now. I have this memory of the way he patted me on the head and told me everything was going to be all right. I can see him and his goons take my father out of the apartment. I can still see the way the bastard smiled.'

'Do you think he recognised you?'

'I hope not.'

Pagan thought of the pistol, the Bernardelli he kept in a shoebox under his bed. He said, 'We're safe here.'

'For how long, Frank?'

Pagan didn't answer the question. He was thinking of somebody out there in the rain, somebody who'd been sent from the Soviet Union, a man whose purpose only added to a general mystification that Frank Pagan didn't like. He reached inside the pocket of his jacket and removed the poem, the original version, and he stared at the blue writing on the cracked sheet of paper. Dry old words, dry paper, foreign to him in more ways than mere language.

Saaremaa Island, the Baltic Sea

Colonel Yevgenni Uvarov practised the signature, which he'd seen hundreds of times. He wrote slowly, in the manner of an unpractised counterfeiter. Every time he covered a sheet, he studied it then wadded the paper up as tightly as he could. When he had it compressed into a tiny ball, he took it to the bathroom and flushed it. Once, a little tipsy on the Georgian wine he sometimes acquired, he imagined a secret laboratory where all flushed paper was fished from the sewers and dried out and examined by the KGB, a special department of effluence commissars who were puzzled by the fact that somebody kept signing the name *S. F. Tikunov* over and over, and then tossed the papers down the toilet.

His hand became cramped. He capped his pen, rolled the sheet of paper until it was no larger than a walnut, then turned his face away from the lamp beside his bunk. He stood up, put on his jacket, left his quarters. He passed the leisure room, which was a spartan affair containing an old black and white TV and three ancient easy chairs. Once, Uvarov recalled, a technician called Samov had rigged a makeshift antenna for the TV, and for three nights a station from Finland had been visible, tantalisingly so, bringing another world into this drab place. American programmes, Scandinavian ones, even some pornography – these were watched secretly until Samov's aerial was reported and its inventor sent elsewhere.

There was a full moon outside, and the radar antennae were superimposed strangely against it, as if they were odd cracks that had developed on the moon's surface. Uvarov walked to the shoreline, took the paper out of his pocket, threw it into the tide. He gazed for some time across the silvery water, thinking of his wife and children. He saw a Kirov guided missile cruiser, a floating palace of lights, about a half mile from the shore.

He walked back in the direction of the control centre that housed the radar screens and the computers. Two of the computers were inoperative, and had been for days, despite the arrival of a maintenance crew from Moscow, argumentative men who'd tinkered without success, squabbling among themselves, blaming one another for the failure. At any given time two of the four computers failed to function because of flaws in their basic designs – they were bad copies of Japanese originals. They were scheduled to be phased out, and replaced, but the programme was already five weeks late.

Uvarov entered the centre, smelling the dead, stale air of the place, absorbing the green screens, the uniformed men who sat before them. Nothing was happening on the waters of the Baltic. He spoke to a couple of the technicians, pleasantries, little else. In recent months he'd tended to remain aloof. He saw no future in forming friendships.

He walked to his metal desk, sat down. He pretended to work, to study papers, but in reality he was examining a computer manual which had been circulated by the Defence Ministry. It had been printed in a limited edition, and access was restricted to men above the rank of Colonel. The manual detailed the interfacing between the computers at this installation and those located at other Air Defence posts in the Baltic sector of the Soviet Union and in Moscow itself. He read for a while, then closed the manual, placing it for safekeeping in the drawer with his family's photograph.

The timing had to be unerring. He rose from his desk, walked along the banks of consoles, hands clasped behind his back. He paused when he reached the wall. Where a window might have been located, there hung a large portrait of Lenin. Uvarov felt an odd sense of constriction, of being caged in an airless space. The surface of his skin was hot, and there was a dull ache behind his eyes.

Nerves. Nothing more than nerves. He was living so very close to the edge these days that physical reactions were not entirely surprising. He glanced at the face of Lenin, then walked back the way he'd come. The radar screens were lifeless. Everything here was lifeless. Uvarov suddenly longed to hear his children laughing, or the sound of his wife playing her piano.

He reached his desk, leaned against it, folded his arms over his chest. On the wall some yards away was the Orders Board. He turned toward it, gazing at a variety of instructions, orders, revised orders, revisions to those revisions, procedures. They came in batches every day from Moscow, and they were all signed by the same man – the Commander in Chief of Soviet Air Defences, Deputy Minister S. F. Tikunov.

Uvarov breathed very deeply, tried to relax. The sheer magnitude of what he was involved in made his heart pound and his pulses go berserk. A week ago he'd asked the physician for something to help him sleep, but the doctor had been unwilling to prescribe drugs and Uvarov didn't press the matter. Why have *insomniac* on your record? It would be perceived eventually by somebody in records as a weakness and then it might result in a whole battery of those psychiatric tests everybody had become so fond of lately. And Uvarov had neither the time nor the inclination to be the subject of any kind of inquiry.

The telephone rang on his desk and he was startled for a second by the intensity of the sound. It pierced him. He reached for the receiver and held it to his ear. From the amount of static on the line he knew the call was long distance.

A man's voice said, 'Colonel Uvarov?'

Uvarov said, 'Speaking.'

The voice responded, 'Aleksis told me to contact you.'

10

Moscow

After Lieutenant Dimitri Volovich parked and locked his car and removed the windshield-wipers as a precaution against theft, he looked the length of the quiet street, which was located between the Riga Railway Terminal and the Sadovoye Ring. It was a pleasant street and Volovich's apartment building was new, built from brown brick and flanked by spindles of newly-planted trees. The sixty apartments were allotted to people with *blat*, the influence necessary to live a life of comfort within the Soviet Union.

As a middle-ranking officer of the KGB, one with many years of faithful if unenterprising service, Volovich was entitled to a few perquisites. The two-roomed flat, with its 13.2 square metres of living space – a little more than the average decreed by the State – was one of them. His automobile, a black Zhiguli, was another. In Soviet terms, he was a man of some means. He was also a person with no particular ambitions beyond loyalty to the organs of State Security, which from a practical point of view meant loyalty to his immediate superior, Viktor Epishev. But it was this allegiance that troubled him as he moved towards the entrance to the building. And it troubled him less in terms of any conspiracy against the State, but more at the level of his own survival. His life, he had to admit, wasn't such a bad one. And he wanted to keep it.

As he was about to step inside the building, he was aware of a long dark car approaching the kerb. It was a Zil with tinted windows and imported whitewall tyres. Volovich stared at the whitewalls. He knew whose car this was. The rear door opened and he moved towards it even as he fought panic down, like something hard in his throat.

'Come in,' a voice said from the back of the car.

Volovich stumbled into the dark interior. He couldn't make out any details in the dimness of the big car save for the shadowy outline of somebody who sat tucked in the corner. He knew who it was in any case, and he was overwhelmed.

'Close the door, Dimitri.'

Volovich did so. The car, whose driver was invisible beyond a panel of smoked glass, drove away immediately.

'In all Moscow, what is your favourite drive, Dimitri?'

Volovich licked his lips. He couldn't think. He stared at the shadowy figure and said, 'I've always enjoyed the ride to Arkhangelskoye Park, sir.'

I'm not guilty of anything, he thought. *Keep telling yourself that*. He breathed deeply and quietly, conscious of the way General Olsky was observing him. The General reached forward to flip a switch set into a panel in the door.

'Driver,' he said. 'Take us to Arkhangelskoye Park. Go by way of Petrovo-Dalniye.'

Volovich gazed out through the tinted windows. He saw the Sovietskaya Hotel and the Dynamo Stadium, almost as if he were viewing them through eyes that weren't his own. He was trying hard not to display any kind of uneasiness or fear, but it was difficult. He was conscious of the Aeroflot Hotel, then the Metro station at Alabyan Street, but these impressions belonged in another world. Volovich's world, which had dwindled abruptly, was confined to this car and the man who sat on the seat next to him.

General Olsky said, 'It's an ugly building. I always think so.'

Volovich stared at the Gidroproekt skyscraper, which was lit even though nightfall wasn't complete. He had no opinion one way or the other, but he agreed with Olsky in any case. The Zil was travelling along an underpass, beyond which was the road to Arkhangelskoye.

'It's good to have an opportunity to talk to you, Dimitri,' he said. 'Sometimes a man in my position loses touch with the rank and file, you understand.'

Volovich craved a drink. Water, vodka, anything. The surface of his tongue was like the skin of a peach.

'How long have you worked with Colonel Epishev?' the General asked.

Volovich was filled with sudden dread. Olsky wouldn't have mentioned Viktor's name unless he was leading towards something disastrous.

'Twenty years, more or less.'

'You're very close to him, I assume.'

Volovich sat very still. He wondered how he looked to Olsky, whether his panic was visible somehow, whether he'd given himself away – a line of sweat on his upper lip, a nervous tic somewhere. He wasn't sure. 'We work together,' he managed to say.

'I have a question,' the General said.

There was a long pause. Volovich looked through the window. He understood the car was in the vicinity of the Khimki Reservoir, but suddenly he'd lost his bearings.

'Where is Epishev?' the General asked.

It was the question Volovich had expected and feared. He said, 'Unfortunately, General, he doesn't always keep me informed of his whereabouts.'

'Nobody seems to know where he's gone. It's very odd. I know my predecessor gave Epishev certain freedoms, and I understand they were close . . . a little like teacher and pupil. But the fact remains, I have no way of accounting for Epishev's absence. He's not in his office, he's not at his home, he left no information with his secretary.'

Volovich remembered stories he'd heard about the General's wife, rumours of her sexual prowess when she'd been a ballerina. He'd seen the woman once, waiting for her husband inside a parked limousine. A woman of stunning beauty. 'I wish I could help, General,' he said.

Olsky changed the subject suddenly. 'Reconstruction is taking place in our country, Dimitri. We must remember to keep open minds at all times. We must be alert. We must be strong enough to shed a strong light on our shortcomings. Change of this magnitude is always painful. But many people, even those who basically agree but argue that we're doing things too quickly, are going to have to adapt – or perish.'

Olsky said the word 'perish' softly, almost in an undertone. Volovich thought he'd never heard it pronounced in such a menacing way.

'Certain people belong in another era,' the General went on. 'They're like dinosaurs. For example, my predecessor, a man of undeniable patriotism, outlived his usefulness. He was quite unable to adapt to new thinking. Is Epishev a dinosaur?'

Volovich didn't know what to say. Nor did Olsky appear to expect an answer, because he went on without waiting for one. 'We need men who are flexible, Dimitri. Men who can alter their dried-out old attitudes and work for change – as well as their own advancement, of course. Do you see yourself as such a person?'

Their own advancement, Volovich thought. He liked the phrase. 'I try to keep an open mind, General.'

'That's all we ask.' Olsky flipped the switch on the panel and told the driver to stop the car. There were small sailboats floating on the surface of the reservoir. Volovich remembered there was an aquatic sports club nearby.

'To the best of your knowledge, Dimitri, is Epishev still in the country?'

Volovich made a little gesture with his skinny fingers. Since he'd already said he didn't know where Viktor was, what more was he supposed to add?

'He didn't say anything to me about going abroad, General.'

'When did you see him last?'

Volovich felt this question eddy around him like a treacherous little whirlpool. 'Perhaps a week ago.'

'A week.' Olsky appeared to think this over. His look was inscrutable, though, an impression exaggerated somehow by the formidable shaved head. 'So far as you're aware, Dimitri, does Epishev have any contact these days with General Greshko?'

Another tough one. Something delicate hung in the balance here. Volovich hesitated. 'I don't believe so,' he chose to say.

Olsky smiled. 'Thank you, Dimitri. I've enjoyed our little talk. Would it be inconvenient if I dropped you here?'

Volovich wondered how many miles it was back to his apartment and whether a bus or a Metro ran that way. It had been years since he'd travelled by public transportation. 'It's no inconvenience, General,' he said. After all, what could he have answered? *It's a fucking nuisance, Comrade Chairman*?

He opened the door, stepped on to the pavement. He watched the big black car vanish down the street. He had a sense of unfinished business, realising that his lie wouldn't hold up for long if General Olsky decided to scrutinise it. If General Olsky fine-tuned his microscope and placed Volovich's statement on an examination slide, the lie, fragile tissue as it was, wouldn't hold up *at all*.

When the car was on the Volokolamsk Highway, General Olsky opened the smoked-glass panel that segregated him from his driver, Colonel Chebrikov, and leaned forward.

'He's the same man,' the Colonel said, without turning his face.

'Are you absolutely sure?'

'Completely, General. Lieutenant Volovich visited General Greshko in Zavidovo last night, accompanied by Colonel Epishev. The meeting lasted about an hour.'

Olsky sat back in his seat again, staring out at the streets, mulling over Volovich's lies. Here he had the bits and pieces of a puzzle, like one of those twisted metal problems you were supposed to solve by separating the parts. Volovich and his Colonel, the enigmatic Viktor Epishev, visit Greshko late at night. Within three hours of that meeting, Viktor Epishev goes to see a man called Yevenko, a criminal, in Moscow. Yevenko, the Printer, is instructed to make a passport bearing Epishev's likeness though not his name. The passport is West German, the bearer's name Grunwald. Epishev takes the false passport, leaves.

'Do you believe the Printer's story?' Olsky asked.

Chebrikov said, 'The man's in a tight spot, General. He needs all the leverage he can get. Currency crime isn't a joke. He's facing twenty years hard labour, perhaps even the firing-squad. Besides, he did have those photographs. And the stamp.'

Olsky shut his eyes, remembering how he'd gone to the Printer's place of business only an hour ago, a grubby basement room in a very old building, a windowless space that smelled of strong chemicals and dyes. There, Yevenko, a dirty little man with ink-stained fingers and the blackest nails Olsky had ever seen, had produced copies of passport pictures he said he'd taken of Colonel Epishev very early that day. He'd forged the German passport, put Epishev's photograph inside, then embossed it with the official passport stamp of the Federal Republic of Germany – which he then also produced with a flourish, flashing it under Stefan Olsky's nose, as if to prove something beyond all doubt.

Yevenko's place was a treasure-house of stolen artifacts. Official stamps from various countries, blank passports from such places as Turkey and West Germany and Malta, three blank identification cards from Interpol, one from the US Federal Bureau of Investigation, and another from the Irish Garda. A man could visit Yevenko and walk out within ten minutes with a new identity and even a job in a foreign police force.

'So where did this mysterious Grunwald go?' Olsky asked.

'We're working on an answer to that one, General.'

Olsky opened his eyes. 'What does Volovich remind you of, Colonel?'

Chebrikov was quiet for a time. Then he said, 'A fish.'

'I thought he was a little more wormlike, personally.'

'An eel, then,' said the Colonel.

'Close enough. Now take me home.' Stefan Olsky closed the smoked-glass window, enjoying the sense of isolation he had in the back of the limousine. It was a place where a man might be alone to think. He wasn't allowed such a luxury because his telephone rang and he reached for it at once, hearing the voice of the Major in charge of all KGB computer operations.

'I believe we've discovered what you're looking for, Comrade Chairman,' the Major said.

Olsky thanked the man, hung up the receiver, then informed his driver that his destination had changed.

London

It was almost dark, and the rain had stopped, and the wind in the square had died finally. Frank Pagan made a phone call to Tommy Witherspoon, who was not in his office. A plummy voice informed Pagan that Mr Witherspoon, in an emergency, might be found in his club on Piccadilly. The voice added a reminder that this was Sunday, the day of Mr Witherspoon's rest, and any interruption of the man would have to be thoroughly justified.

Pagan put the receiver down. He looked inside the bedroom where Kristina Vaska lay on the bed, her back turned to him, a blanket pulled halfway over her body. Earlier, complaining of fatigue, she'd gone to lie down. Pagan wasn't sure if she was sleeping. He stepped quietly inside the bedroom. She turned her face towards him, blinking in the square of light that fell from the living-room. *A woman in my bed,* Pagan thought. *Somebody I hardly know, somebody attractive to me*. It was a novel consideration.

He sat on the edge of the mattress. 'I have to go out for a while.'

'Do you want me to stay here?' she asked.

'I don't want you to disappear on me.'

'I don't like the idea of being alone, Frank. What if Epishev decides to come back?'

Pagan doubted that the Russian would return. By this time, Epishev might have concluded that Pagan's apartment was the last place of all to visit, that if Kristina Vaska had recognised him then Pagan would have taken precautions. Perhaps Epishev even imagined that policemen were cunningly concealed in the neighbourhood, ready for a reappearance.

'I'll arrange for somebody to keep an eye on you,' Pagan said. He reached under the bed and took his gun from the shoebox. He stuck it inside a holster, which he strapped to his body so that the gun hung at the base of his spine. 'But I really don't think he's going to be careless enough to come here again.'

She still looked doubtful. He picked up the bedside phone, punched out the number of the local police station and asked for a certain Sergeant Crowley. When the Sergeant came on the line, Pagan used his intimidating Special Branch voice to ask that a patrol car be placed outside his home. Crowley had an ordinary cop's attitude toward Special Branch, which was the resentment of a commoner for the aristocracy. So far as Crowley, a decent if plodding man, was concerned, the princes of Special Branch thought the sun shone out of their bloody royal arses. But he agreed to Pagan's request anyway.

Pagan put the receiver down. 'That takes care of that.'

'How long will you be gone?' she asked.

'An hour or two.' Pagan gazed down at her. Then he leaned over and kissed her forehead impulsively. She didn't seem at all surprised by the gesture. She caught his hand and held it and looked up into his eyes. There was something troubled in her expression, a guarded quality.

It was wrong here, he thought. This was the room the dead had claimed, and it was damned hard to wrest ownership from a corpse. He stepped away from the bed, releasing himself from her hand.

'Hurry back,' she said.

He crossed the living-room floor and stood at the window until he saw the patrol car appear. It parked in the street below. He returned to the bedroom. 'When I leave, slide the deadbolt in place.'

'Be careful, Frank.' She sat upright, brushed hair away from her forehead. She looked just then as lovely as he'd ever seen her, and he was held in place a moment by a sudden enchantment about which there was a frailty, a sense of illusion, as if she might simply vanish were he to go any closer to her. Pagan, unexpectedly touched by his own reaction, stepped out of the flat.

When he reached the foot of the stairs he heard the sound of the deadbolt being slammed firmly into place. He went cautiously out to the street, glancing at the police car, and the faces of the two young cops, as he walked to his Camaro. The dark square across the way, the lit windows of houses, the still trees – all this familiarity, changed by his consciousness of a man called Epishev, pressed uneasily against him.

Tommy Witherspoon had a slow, disdainful laugh, a *hor hor hor* sound Pagan associated with wealth. If it were possible for somebody to laugh down his nose, Tommy Witherspoon was that person. He wore a black blazer and white slacks and an old school tie Pagan was proud not to recognise. Tommy belonged in his club, you could see that. He merged with the antique wood and the soft lamps and the ancient portraits of past members that hung from the walls and the indefinable ambience of old money and yesterday's empires.

'I mention Epishev and you get hysterical,' Pagan said, uncomfortable in this whole milieu, which reeked to him of privileges that, in most cases, hadn't been earned, but rather bestowed, passed down from father to son along the infallible circuitry of blood.

Tommy Witherspoon was drinking madeira. His lips were stained, which indicated he'd been imbibing most of the day. Half-drunk like this, he was even more haughty and less charming than he'd been during Pagan's last encounter with him in Green Park. Alcohol brought out all his worst traits – loftiness of manner and a bristling unshakable self-confidence.

Witherspoon said, 'I laugh, Pagan. But there's some slight pity in the sound.'

'Pity?'

'If your man is really Epishev, as you lay claim, then I'm sorry for you, old chap. He's a tough cookie, if I may venture an Americanism. I wouldn't like to have Eppie poking around in my neck of the woods.'

Eppie, Pagan thought. Tommy Witherspoon's way of talking suggested he was this close to where all the skeletons were buried. Keeping secrets along Whitehall, striding discreet corridors all day long, did something to a man. It made him smug, and pompous, and insufferably patronising.

'Just tell me what you know, Tommy. I absorb it, get up, shuffle off into the night. Dead simple.'

Witherspoon sipped his madeira and frowned. When he spoke he did so off-handedly, like a man accustomed to believing that his utterances were pure pearls and all his listeners swine. 'There are those who say, Pagan, that Uncle Viktor is a creation of the Central Committee. Some argue that if he didn't exist in actuality, the Central Committee would have invented him. A man with Epishev's set of mind, which one may accurately call neanderthal, could well have been created by the inner members of the former Politburo. If they wanted to bring forth a model of Communist man, a sort of Marxenstein, if you catch my drift, they might have hammered together dear old Uncle, who has bought lock, stock and bloody barrel the whole Marxist-Leninist waffle. With jam on it.'

Witherspoon leaned across the small round table. Pagan noticed how he propped an elbow into a faint ring of wine left by the base of his glass. Two old dodderers, relics of Empire, moved past the table, muttering something mean-spirited about women.

Witherspoon said, 'Uncle has been kicking around for a good many years, usually performing dirty tasks assigned to him by the soon to be late, if not lamented, General Greshko.'

'I read somewhere that Greshko had retired,' Pagan remarked, remembering a couple of newspaper articles that had appeared in recent months about the General, who had been something of a survivor, guiding the KGB through several Soviet regimes. Pragmatic, cunning, one of the old guard – these were the words and phrases that had been applied to Greshko.

'Retirement is a euphemism, in Soviet fashion, for being ousted. Epishev was well and truly Greshko's boy. Greshko played the pipes and Uncle danced to any tune going. Some of the melodies were more than a little unpleasant, Pagan.'

'Such as?'

Witherspoon caught the waiter's eye and had his glass refilled. 'Greshko assigned him the task of rooting out and silencing, usually for all eternity, anyone who raised his or her voice against the system. I understand Uncle carried out his tasks with the zeal of the true believer. Murder, blackmail, deportations to labour camps without possibility of parole – Uncle used everything in his copious bag of tricks to silence the small voices of dissent. He was very very good at this. He's responsible, one way or another, for thousands of deaths. As for imprisonments, well, the figures are beyond computation.'

'A butcher,' Pagan said.

'Ah, the endearing simplicity of the policeman's mind. My dear Pagan, you can't just hang one of your banal little labels on the fellow. Butchery is only a part of Epishev's repertoire. As I understand it,' – and Witherspoon gave the impression that his understanding was the only correct one – 'Epishev is something of a chameleon. He blends with backgrounds. He changes colours. He's apparently not without charm, albeit of a deadly nature. He's the sort of chap who smiles apologetically as he tightens the garotte round your adam's apple. More than a butcher, Pagan. He has much blood on his hands, undeniable*eee*, but he has a system of very hard beliefs that justify anything he does. And when did you last hear of a butcher slaughtering a cow because the animal didn't happen to share the butcher's philosophy?'

Pagan didn't enjoy being talked down to by Tommy Witherspoon. He was being made to feel like a kid learning the alphabet by staring at letters on wooden cubes. 'What's his situation since Greshko was put out to pasture?'

'Who can say? Uncle Viktor belongs in the old camp, Pagan. Whether he can survive the new regime is anybody's guess. Maybe the new boys will want to sweep him under the rug because he's a leftover from the past, and therefore embarrassing. But if he's running around our green and pleasant land, as you say, then presumably he still has a function to carry out.'

Pagan gazed across the large room. The long windows were dark. On Piccadilly streetlamps were lit.

'I must say, though, I find it *awfully* hard to believe Epishev's here.'

'You mean you find it hard to believe you didn't know about it, Tommy.'

Witherspoon fixed Pagan with an inebriated grin that was very cold. 'I really can't see anybody sending him overseas unless it was Greshko. If the organ-grinders of the KGB wanted somebody to do some dirty work in London, I have the feeling they'd have sent a younger chap, somebody completely unknown to us.'

'Is it possible Greshko did send him? Is it possible Epishev came here on business that wasn't officially sanctioned by the present leadership of the KGB?'

Witherspoon looked suddenly befuddled, half-gone in an alcoholic haze. 'Anything's *possible*, Pagan. Greshko had a vast power base, and that doesn't just simply *disintegrate* in a matter of a few months. A great many people over there aren't enamoured of the new boys in the Kremlin, don't forget. But the general impression I keep getting is that resistance to the new chaps isn't terribly well-organised, more a kind of choral moaning than anything else. But I can't imagine Epishev aligning himself with a dying old man like Greshko.'

'If Greshko didn't send him, and if Epishev's an embarrassment to the KGB these days, then who gave him orders to come here? Did he make the trip of his own free will?'

'As I keep trying to intimate, Pagan, Soviet intentions are frequently too murky for our Western minds to fathom. Especially, it would seem, the mind of a policeman. Cops are fine when it comes to handing out speeding tickets, I daresay, but let them loose in the big world of political subtleties and they're quite at a loss.'

Pagan stood up. He wondered how much more of Tommy he could take without doing something utterly uncivilised. 'Is there a photograph of him?' he asked.

Witherspoon laughed until his eyes watered. 'Lord, no. A photograph of Epishev! I know people in the field who'd give a year's salary for a likeness of Uncle Viktor!, A photograph of Epishev! Really, Pagan. What do you think this is? Do you think the KGB supplies us with pics and bios of its top people? Dear oh dear oh dear.'

Pagan placed his hands on the edge of the small table. He had one more question. He waited until Witherspoon's derisive laughter had finally subsided before he asked, 'Is the name Norbert Vaska familiar to you?'

'Afraid not. Should it be?'

'Just curious, Tommy.' Pagan started to turn away. As he did so, he couldn't help yielding to a mischievous temptation. He allowed his hip to collide with the table, spilling Witherspoon's glass and sending a fair amount of madeira into the man's lap.

'*Ooops*,' Pagan said, a little dazzled by his own pettiness. But it was more than just a small strike at Tommy Witherspoon, it was a reflection of his general frustration, the unanswered questions that crowded his head.

Witherspoon stood up quickly. 'Oh, really, Pagan. That was frightfully clumsy of you,' and he began to dab at his groin with a handkerchief.

'Sorry, Tommy. Really.'

Witherspoon glared at him. 'Did you do that deliberately?'

'Hardly. What do you take me for?'

Witherspoon let his wine-red handkerchief drop on the table. He looked highly doubtful. 'I've got an answer for that, Pagan. I take you for somebody who's completely out of his league. I take you for somebody Uncle Viktor could have for his bloody breakfast and still not be satisfied. I've got a suggestion for you – let intelligence handle all this. Let the big boys cope with Epishev. You're strictly second division, old chap.'

Pagan smiled. 'Your nastiness is showing, Tommy. If you're not careful, they'll blackball you out of this place for failing to show civility to your guests.'

'Guests? I didn't ask you here, Pagan.'

'If you had, Tommy, I wouldn't have come.' And Pagan turned, moving past the nodding heads of dozing old men in the direction of the lobby. When he looked back he saw a waiter hurrying towards Witherspoon's table with a dripping sponge.

Business as usual, Pagan thought. The servant classes cleaning up the mess made by the overlords. Wondering bleakly when this whole calcified system might change, Pagan stepped out into Piccadilly.

Ninety minutes after Frank Pagan had gone, Kristina Vaska lay in the darkened bedroom with her eyes closed. What she was remembering was the way Pagan had looked at her, first in the park, then just before he left the apartment, an unmistakable look, a light in the eye that had all the hard clarity of a gem. Frank Pagan, who liked to think he played his cards close to his chest, who imagined he went through the world with tight-lipped wariness, had dropped his defences – he had become, on both occasions, *obvious*.

There was a quality to Pagan that drew her, a combination of self-confidence and a lack of polish, a sense of rough and smooth coming awkwardly together in the man. He reminded her of a stone she'd once found on the bank of the Pirita River, a curious stone that seemed to have been welded out of two distinct elements – glassy on one side, gritty on the other, an unlikely amalgam, a small paradox of nature. That was how she saw Frank Pagan.

She hadn't intended to like him. She hadn't set out to be drawn to him. She wondered what kind of lover he'd be, and she imagined honesty, an absence of subterfuge, quiet consideration.

She sat upright, looked at the bedside clock. It was ten o'clock. She took off her clothes and dropped them on the floor and headed in the direction of the bathroom. She glanced at the door as she passed, unconsciously checking the security of the deadbolt. She was going to be safe here. Epishev had no means of getting inside. And if Epishev couldn't come through the front door, then her past couldn't gain entrance either, that nightmare that had taken concrete shape in a rainy London street fifteen years and a thousand miles from where it had first begun.

She imagined her father's face, but there were times when she couldn't see him with any clarity. There were panicked moments when the face wouldn't come to her, but remained in shadow, an ancient ghost she couldn't summon. And then she had a sense of internal slippage, as if her memories had begun to disintegrate. She shut her eyes, imagined Norbert Vaska's hands, strong and firm, the long fingers that brushed a strand of hair from his daughter's face or held her by the waist and drew her up from the ground – the fingers, yes, but the face, she couldn't see the face except in brief glimpses, like a holograph fading.

As she drew back the shower-curtain, turned on the faucet, adjusted the temperature, she heard the telephone. Her first impulse was to ignore it. Then she thought the least she could do was to take a message.

She wrapped herself in a towel, went back into the living-room, lifted the receiver. 'Frank Pagan's residence,' she said. Residence was too genteel a word for what Pagan had here. It conjured up visions of order, serenity, well-oiled servants going smoothly about their duties.

The man who answered introduced himself as Martin Burr. He said he had an urgent need to talk to Frank Pagan.

11

Riga, Latvia

Three Soviet Army trucks with full headlights burning clattered along Suvorov Street toward the Daugava River. It was dark and the covered vehicles moved with the illusory urgency peculiar to military trucks, a briskness that suggested high speeds to anyone watching. In reality, the trucks were travelling at no more than forty miles an hour. They crossed the river and entered the area of Riga known as the Pardaugava, the industrialised left bank of the sprawling city. They passed an isolated green area, a rather rundown park, and then an old cemetery, beyond which there stretched a district of factories and warehouses.

Some of these factories were new, but there was a general deterioration the farther the vehicles travelled. They left behind the kind of showplace industrial plants so beloved by Intourist officials and Party chairmen and penetrated a darker, less attractive area of early twentieth-century warehouses and factories and sites where old buildings had been gutted. The air smelled of mildew, and the corrosive aroma of rust, and from elsewhere, borne on a breeze, the salty suggestion of the Bay of Riga. The trucks rolled down streets that became progressively more narrow, little more than lanes built in an age when horse-drawn cabs pulled factory owners from one business to the next, and men filled with inchoate hatreds and resentments planned revolution in sweatshops.

Killing their lights, the trucks stopped finally in a dead-end street, the kind of place city mapmakers conveniently overlook and then ultimately forget and future generations of city planners rediscover with total amazement. For many minutes nobody emerged from the vehicles, which were parked close to a decrepit building that over the years had housed companies manufacturing window-shades, then shoelaces, then tobacco pipes, and most recently camera lenses. It was abandoned now, although four years ago it had been briefly used as a rehearsal studio for an outlawed rock and roll band called Gulag.

A door opened and a man appeared with a flashlight. He blinked it twice, switched it off. The drivers, dressed in the uniforms of the Soviet Army, emerged from the trucks and hurried towards the building. From the rear of each truck, from under canvas, other soldiers appeared. A mixed crew – a couple of corporals, a sergeant, a major, and a colonel.

The interior of the old factory had a basement, reached by descending a staircase that hung on the crumbling wall in a precarious way. The man with the flashlight went down carefully, warning the soldiers to follow him with caution. The basement, lit by a single kerosene lamp, was filled with all the detritus of all the industries that had ever occupied the building – lengths of twine, slivers of broken glass, unfinished pipes and stemless bowls, tassels of the sort that hung to blinds. There were also thirty wooden crates, the only things in the basement that interested the men.

The man with the flashlight kicked aside the lid of one crate and the uniformed men gathered round in the yellow-blue paraffin flare to look. The weapons, American M-16 rifles, Swiss SIG-AMT and Belgian FN auto rifles, lay in no particular order. There were handguns in some of the other crates – Brownings, Colts, Lugers – and ammunition. One crate contained Czech-made grenades, another Uzi pistols. It was as if whoever had purchased this supply of arms had scoured all the darker bazaars of the international weapons market, buying a lot here, another lot there, an oddment in a third place.

The men were thoroughly delighted with the delivery. They knew the number of weapons was comparatively puny, the task ahead of them overwhelming, but the guns represented support from a world beyond the Soviet Union, and that made the men both glad and touched, and less isolated than they'd ever felt before.

The man with the flashlight, who was known only as Marcus, said they had better hurry. He didn't like staying in this basement any longer than he had to, and the crates had to be moved and the sooner the better. His nervousness was contagious. The uniformed men worked quickly and silently, carrying the crates up from the basement and placing them in the trucks, under canvas. The whole operation took about five minutes before the trucks were ready to roll again. One was headed for Tallinn in Estonia, a second for Vilnius in Lithuania, and a third had only a short distance to travel – a concealed place in the forest around Kemeri, some thirty miles from Riga.

The men took only a few moments to part, even though they knew it was highly unlikely they'd ever meet again. There was handshaking, some edgy laughter, some back-slapping, but mainly there was a sense of grim fatalism about them. Their trips were hazardous ones, their ultimate actions bound to be deadly. But they had no qualms about dying. Even so, there was a moment in which the agitated banter stopped, a profound silence of the kind in which people realise, as if for the very first time, the exact nature of their commitment.

And then the trucks left the area, travelling in convoy for several miles until they reached the bank of the river again, the place where each vehicle went its own way. Headlights flashed three times in the dark, a signal that might have meant good luck or farewell. They moved away from one another now through the streets of the city, past the dark windows of closed shops, unlit office towers, silent houses, past the eyes of patrolling militiamen who, if they paid much attention at all, would see only army trucks hurrying on some military task, and the faces of uniformed men in the high cabs.

These same militiamen wouldn't have any way of knowing that the trucks had been stolen weeks ago, that their cargoes were illegal and their registration plates fake, that the transportation dockets carried by the men were forged and that the men themselves were no soldiers – but a collection of assorted dissidents in stolen uniforms, Baltic deserters from the Soviet Army in Afghanistan, some students from the University of Vilnius, a couple of patriots from the last days of the old Brotherhood, and a few men who had spent time in Soviet jails for their democratic beliefs.

Nor could the uninquiring policemen have any idea of how the weapons inside the trucks were to be used or the blood that might be shed a couple of days from now.

Manhattan

Dressed in a grey Italian suit and matching homburg, Mikhail Kiss moved along Fifth Avenue. It was ten o'clock and the night had shed some of the clamminess that had characterised the day. He looked down at his wedding-ring as he headed in the direction of Columbus Circle, which loomed up just before him. He hadn't removed the ring in more than forty years and as he gazed at it he realised he'd come to think of it as a natural part of himself. It was a source of heartbreak, even after so much time had passed. But time didn't erase everything. Quite the opposite. Sometimes, through the years, things grew instead of diminishing. And Ingrida's face floated before him, spectral and lovely, and then he felt it, the old pain, the cutting sorrow, the sharp glass in his heart, and what he pictured was how she'd died, with a Soviet bullet buried in her chest.

He squeezed his eyes shut as he paused at a Don't Walk sign. He hadn't seen Ingrida die, and what he knew was only what he'd pieced together from rumour and gossip in the early years of the 1950s. She'd been taken in a truck, along with other women whose husbands were suspected of guerilla activity against the great Russian Empire, to a meadow outside the town of Paide in central Estonia. There, the women had been made to stand in a line, and then a machine-gunner, hidden by trees, had opened fire. Kiss wondered if death had come as a surprise to her or if somehow she'd known it was going to happen, if she'd stepped into that meadow and come face to face with the certainty of her own end even before the gun had fired. What the hell did it matter now? He had an image, and it wouldn't leave him, and it was of Ingrida's face turned up to a wintry Estonian sky and blood flowing from the corner of her mouth and a fat fly, waxy and obscene, alive, landing on her lips. *Ingrida, mu suda, mu hing. Ma tunnen puudust sinu jarele.* Ingrida, my heart and soul. I miss you.

For a very long time, even after he'd found his way to the United States via Germany, he'd had a fantasy in which he encountered the machine-gunner. Accidentally – on the street, in a store, anywhere. And what he did in this murderous hallucination was to tear the man apart, to rip his limbs from his body, fibre by agonised fibre. After years had passed, the fantasy started to assume other forms. The gunman, after all, was only obeying orders. And the official who issued the orders to the gunman did so only because he was following policies set by the Kremlin. Therefore, individuals weren't to blame. It was the system, evil and corrupt, which operated from behind the thick walls of the Kremlin that was to blame. So Mikhail Kiss's fantasy had become channelled elsewhere.

He passed the Lincoln Center, moving under lit streetlamps. Then he turned into a narrow street where he paused. Perhaps it was nothing more than the absence of lights, perhaps something he thought he detected in the shadows of doorways, but he was suddenly afraid. He looked back the way he'd come. He realised that the feeling didn't lie in the notion that some local KGB agent might be following him – instead, it was buried inside himself, in the coils of his own nerves. What if Carl Sundbach had been right and this whole affair was doomed? What if Romanenko had been carrying a message that was meant to cancel the project because something *had* gone wrong?

You grow old, he thought. You're thinking an old man's thoughts, fearful and silly. The truth of the matter was simple – he just didn't want to ponder the motives behind Aleksis's murder. Some disaffected emigrant, some crackpot with a pistol, a madman with a political axe to grind – Aleksis's killer might have been almost anyone. He didn't want to think, even for a moment, that anything could have gone wrong with the scheme *itself*. It would go ahead as planned. He and Romanenko had spent too long a time welding their network together, joining each link in secrecy, from the Finnish businessman who carried Kiss's letters to Helsinki to the radical human rights activist from Tartu who placed each communication inside an old windmill at the Wooden Buildings Museum on Vabaohumuuseumitee Road about two miles from Tallinn, from which place it would be retrieved by one or other of Aleksis's trusted associates and delivered to Romanenko. Sometimes, in moments of paranoia, Kiss wondered if along the way there might be a weak link, a treacherous coupling, somebody who revealed the letters to the KGB. But since the operation hadn't been stopped, and Romanenko hadn't been arrested, Kiss always assumed the network had never been penetrated.

He came to another narrow street now and the fear passed as suddenly as it had come. He was in the vicinity of Fordham University, where expensive apartment buildings flourished on side-streets. He might have taken a more direct route to this neighbourhood than he'd done, but he never came here the same way twice. He crossed Amsterdam Avenue and went inside an old building, a former warehouse converted into studios and apartments.

He climbed to the third floor. At the end of the hallway he knocked on a door, which was opened almost at once by a man Kiss knew only as Iverson. He was probably in his late forties, but the lack of lines and creases, the lack of *animation* in the face made it impossible to guess. Kiss couldn't recall Iverson ever smiling or frowning. There was something decidedly spooky about the man, as if he had no inner life whatsoever, and that what you saw on his face was all there was. Kiss always thought of him as a *kulm kala*, a cold fish.

The suite of rooms was completely devoid of furniture. There was white fitted carpet throughout and the walls were glossy white, reflecting the recessed lights. It was a strange apartment, Kiss thought, neat and always spotless, and yet without any sign of ever having been lived in. He assumed that Iverson used it only for these meetings. Kiss took off his homburg and wiped his damp forehead with his palm and considered how perfectly this empty apartment matched Iverson's personality.

'Do we go or don't we?' Iverson asked.

Always straight to the point, Kiss thought. For a moment he hesitated. He walked to the windows, which had a view of the dark river. A barge, bright yellow upon the blackness, floated past. *Do we go or don't we*?

Kiss turned and looked at the man. 'We go,' he said, *There. It was done. And there was no going back.*

'You've had confirmation?' Iverson asked.

'Yes,' Kiss lied.

'I never had any doubts.'

Kiss smiled now. What he felt was a rush of pure relief, like a chemical flooding through his body. It was the sensation Americans called 'high'. He had a tangible sense of the network he'd created, an adrenalin flowing out of this building and through the darkness, a powerful vibrancy that went untrammelled across land and sea to stop, finally, in Moscow. He had a sense of all the links he'd spent years hammering into place coming together at last, as if each link had been galvanised suddenly by a surge of lightning.

Iverson leaned stiffly against a wall. Even the pinstriped suit he wore was bland and unremarkable. He was a man who courted the prosaic avidly. 'All you have to do is make sure your man is in Norway. We'll take it from there.' For the first time in any of their meetings, Kiss thought he detected an emotion in the man.

Iverson said, 'Now it's finally happening, I've got this strange feeling in my gut. You ever ride a rollercoaster, Kiss? It's that kind of thing.' And he allowed a very small smile to cross his lips. It looked as if it had been airbrushed on to his face.

Kiss had to come to understand that Iverson – who was either an officer in the United States Air Force or had been at one time, an anomaly Iverson deliberately failed to clarify – feared the Russians. But Kiss, whose focus was limited to three countries with an area of some sixty thousand square miles and a population of eight million, had no particular interest in Iverson's motives. Andres, who had maintained all kinds of connections in the armed forces, had brought Iverson in about eighteen months ago, saying he was a completely dependable man who could provide an essential service. And that recommendation was enough. Whether Iverson was acting alone, or whether he represented a consortium of men who shared his views, some shadowy congregation of figures who preferred to stay offstage, Kiss didn't know, even though he sometimes felt that Iverson was merely a spokesman. But without Iverson's help the whole scheme would have been more difficult, perhaps even impossible.

Strange bedfellows, Kiss thought. An old Baltic guerilla fighter and a mysterious figure with military connections who saw a way to undermine a regime he feared.

'Well,' Iverson said. 'I guess we don't see each other again.'

He held his hand forward and Kiss shook it. Iverson's clasp was ice-cold, bloodless.

'*Nägemiseni*,' Iverson said. Goodbye.

Kiss was touched by Iverson's effort to learn a word in Estonian, a language totally alien to him.

'I practised it,' Iverson said.

'You did fine.' Kiss, smiling, went towards the door. There he turned and said, '*Head aega*,' which was also goodbye.

Iverson said, 'One thing. We never met. We never talked. This apartment ceases to exist as soon as you step out the door. If you ever have any reason to come back to this place, and I hope you don't, you'll find strangers living here. And if anybody ever asks, Kiss, I don't know you from Adam.'

London

Frank Pagan looked at the corpse of Danus Oates only in a fleeting way, before turning his back. Oates's splendid silk pyjamas were soaked with blood. Martin Burr, who had come up to London by fast car from the depths of Sussex – where on weekends he lived the life of an English country squire – gazed down at the body with sorrow.

'Damned shame,' he said to Pagan and he swiped the air with his cane in a gesture of frustrated sadness. 'I wish the cleaners would get here and remove the poor lad. Let's go into the living-room.'

Frank Pagan followed Burr out of the bedroom. The Commissioner sat in an armchair, propping his chin on his cane and gazing thoughtfully through the open door of the flat. A uniformed policeman stood on the landing and three neighbours – two emaciated women and a leathery man, the latter having discovered the body while making a social call – were trying to sneak a look inside the place with all the ghoulish enthusiasm of people who consider murder a spectator sport.

'Shut that bloody door, would you?' Burr asked.

Pagan did so. When they'd first come to Oates's flat, Pagan had told the Commissioner what he'd learned about Epishev from Kristina Vaska, and Burr had absorbed the information in silence. Now Pagan said, 'The way I see it is Epishev came here because he'd learned Oates had worked on the translation. He wanted to know what Oates had found out. The answer was, of course, very little – a few lines of verse in an obscure language. What else could poor Oates say? Maybe all he could tell Epishev was that I had the thing in my possession – who knows? Epishev, covering his tracks like any dutiful assassin, killed him. And I was the next name on the list, because I'd come in contact with the verse as well.'

'The damned poem's like a bloody fatal virus,' Burr said angrily. 'You touch it, you have a damned good chance of dying.' He was genuinely shocked by this murder and the presence of a KGB killer in London, and the fact that his own dominion was tainted by international political intrigue. He liked, if not a calm life, then one of logic and order and watertight compartments.

Pagan stuck his hands in his pockets. 'If it's a virus, it acts in very peculiar ways. The thing I haven't been able to figure out is why the KGB would want to come after people like Oates and myself. Obviously, they imagine I know something, and they don't *like* me knowing it, whatever the hell it is. But what's the big secret? If the Brotherhood's working on an act of terrorism against the Russians, let's say, why would the KGB want to destroy the people who might have evidence of it? Unless the KGB is involved in the plot as well – or at the very least doesn't want it to fail.'

'And that's a rather odd line of reasoning, Frank.'

Pagan agreed. He moved up and down the room in an agitated manner. He was remembering now how Witherspoon had talked about a struggle between the old regime and the new, and how Epishev had belonged in the Greshko camp along with the old power-brokers, those who had been sent scurrying into reluctant redundancy. It was an elusive thought, a sliver of a thing, but perhaps what was unfolding in front of him was some element of that power-struggle, some untidy aspect of it, the ragged edges of a Soviet situation that had become inadvertently exported to England. He turned this over in his mind and he was about to mention the thought to Burr when the Commissioner said, 'This Vaska lady. Do you think her information is on the level?'

'I had a few doubts at first,' Pagan replied.

'But not now?'

'I'm not so sure.'

'But you want to believe her.'

'I think what she says about this Brotherhood and Romanenko's part in it is true. And I believe her when she says she came here in the hope of seeing Romanenko about her father. I also have the strong feeling she wasn't mistaken when she identified Epishev.'

Oates's living-room was cluttered with very tasteful antiques. There was a photograph on one wall that depicted Danus, around the age of fifteen, in the straw-hat of a Harrow schoolboy. Fresh-faced, rather chubby at the cheeks, all innocence. Pagan paused in front of it, shaking his head. You couldn't begin to imagine Oates's doomed future from such a guilelessly plump face. It was all going to be sunshine and a steady if unspectacular climb up the ladder of the Foreign Office.

Martin Burr was quiet for a while. 'If what she says about this Epishev chap is correct, I don't think this whole business belongs to us any more, Frank. I really don't think this is anything we can keep. If Epishev is KGB, it's no longer our game.'

Pagan felt a flush of sudden irritation. 'We give it away? Is that what you're saying?'

Martin Burr frowned. 'I don't think we *give* it away, Frank. Rather, it's *taken* from us. There's a certain kind of skulduggery that doesn't come into our patch, Frank. We're not equipped. And you may bitch about it, but sooner or later you have to face the fact that intelligence will want this one. No way round it, I'm afraid. Besides, I understand our friend Witherspoon has already dropped the word about Epishev in the appropriate quarters.'

'Good old Tommy.'

'He was only doing what he perceived as his duty, no doubt.'

'I bet.' *Frank, you should have seen that one coming*. What else would Tommy do but run to his pals and gladly confide in them that Uncle Viktor had surfaced in England and that a certain incompetent policeman was handling things? Pagan could hear Witherspoon's voice, a cruel whisper, maybe a snide laugh, as he chatted to his chums in intelligence. *La-di-da, don't you know?*

'You want me to forget Epishev, is that it?'

'Frank,' the Commissioner said. 'Don't make me raise my voice. I'm trying to tell you how things are. Consider it a lesson in reality.'

'I may forget about Epishev, Commissioner, but is he going to forget about me? I've got something he believes he wants. Keep that in mind.'

Martin Burr shook his head. 'Ah, yes, I'll expect you to turn your translation of the poem and the original over to intelligence when they ask for it – and they surely will – and then wipe the whole damned thing out of your mind.'

'Commissioner, if Epishev shot Oates, that makes it murder in my book, and I don't give a damn if Epishev's KGB or an Elizabeth Arden rep, he's a bloody killer. What makes this very personal, sir, is the fact that this killer has my number. And you want me to turn him over to some characters who call themselves intelligence – which so far as I'm concerned is a terrible misnomer. Anyway, Epishev's going to believe I've got what he wants whether I turn it over or not.'

Martin Burr ran a hand across his face. 'Sometimes I see a petulantly stubborn quality in you that appals me.'

Pagan knew he was playing this wrongly, that he was coming close to alienating the Commissioner, who was really his only ally at the Yard. He took a couple of deep breaths, in through the nostrils and out through the mouth – a technique that was supposed to relax you, according to a book he'd once read on yoga. But spiritual bliss and all the bloody breathing exercises in the world weren't going to alleviate his frustration.

The Commissioner said, 'It upsets me, too. I want you to know that. I wish there was some other way.'

'Then let me stay with it.'

'There's nothing I can do. I wish it could be otherwise. But sooner or later, Frank, I'm going to feel certain pressures from parties that I don't have to name. And I'll bow to them, because that's the way things are. Those chaps know how to press all the right buttons.'

'I could always work with them,' Pagan said half-heartedly.

Martin Burr smiled. 'The idea of you working with *anyone* is rather amusing.'

'I could give it a try.'

The Commissioner shook his head. 'Damn it all, how many ways can I tell you this? Intelligence doesn't like the common policeman. Let's leave it there.'

Pagan opened a decanter of cognac that sat on an antique table. He poured himself a small glass. There had to be some kind of solution to all this, something the Commissioner would accept. But Martin Burr, even though he'd complained about Pagan's stubbornness, could be pretty damned intractable himself. It was a knot, and Pagan couldn't see how to untie it. What he felt was that he was being brushed carelessly aside, and he didn't like the sensation at all.

The Commissioner reached for the decanter now and helped himself to a generous measure. He returned to his armchair and turned the balloon glass slowly around in his hand. He said, 'I like you, Frank, perhaps because I think your heart's in the right place. Even at your worst, I've never questioned either your heart or your integrity. But this – ' and Martin Burr made a sweeping gesture with his hand – 'this tale of a Baltic clique that a young gal weaves and the presence of this Epishev and a dead Communist up in

Scotland into the bargain, all *this*, my dear fellow, is not your private property, alas. Do we understand one another?'

'Perhaps,' Pagan said, and drained his glass. The cognac had eased only a little of the pressure inside him.

Martin Burr smacked his lips. 'Let's take some air, Frank. I don't want to be here when the cleaners and the fingerprint boys come. They tend to reduce death to a business, which I always find unseemly.'

Pagan followed the Commissioner out of the flat and down the stairs, past the goggling neighbours and their questions. Outside in the early morning darkness, Martin Burr stood under a streetlamp and leaned on his cane. The neighbourhood was silent and sedate in that way of well-heeled neighbourhoods everywhere.

'Is she pretty?' the Commissioner asked suddenly.

'What's that got to do with anything?'

'Touchy, touchy, Frank. All I'm saying is that human nature, being the general old screw-up it is, sometimes allows a fair face to turn a man's head. Has she turned yours?'

'Hardly,' Pagan replied.

'Just watch yourself. Subject closed.' The Commissioner smiled like a one-eyed owl. 'As for this Brotherhood, how much does the young lady know?'

'Less than I'd like.'

'Intriguing, though. The idea of some old fellows plotting against the Russians after all this time. Makes you wonder what they're up to. And then there's the wretch Kiviranna. Who sent him to kill Romanenko? Too many unanswered questions, Frank.'

Pagan detected something in Martin Burr, a quality of curiosity that wouldn't leave him. Even if he was about to turn the Epishev affair over to the lords of intelligence, Martin Burr was still intrigued by it all, more so perhaps than he really wanted to admit. The old cop, Pagan thought. The scent in the nostrils. The mysteries. The rush of adrenalin. Martin Burr was animated, perhaps even hooked.

'I'm still thinking aloud, you understand, Frank, but if Epishev is hunting down this piece of paper, then he knew that Romanenko left the Soviet Union with it in his possession – reasonable assumption? Question – if it's so damned important that it gets Oates killed, why was Romanenko allowed to leave with the poem in the first place? Answer – because the KGB *wanted* him to make the delivery. Is that also reasonable? It implies that Aleksis, either willingly or unwittingly, was working for the KGB.'

'Or at least for certain KGB personnel,' Pagan remarked quietly.

With a rather thoughtful look, Martin Burr stared up into the light from the overhead lamp, where a flurry of moths battered themselves to pulp against the bulb. 'Are you positing the existence of factions within that venerable organisation, Frank? Can of worms, old chap. Somebody else's can.'

'I don't know exactly what I'm positing,' Pagan replied. Can of worms, he thought. He kicked a pebble from the pavement and heard it roll across the narrow street. For somebody about to give up a case, Martin Burr was fretting over it more than a little.

'Pity to turn it over, Frank.'

'Pity's not strong enough,' Pagan said. How could he conceivably walk away from this? More to the point, how could Martin Burr expect that of him?

The Commissioner glanced at his wristwatch. As he did so, a taxi came along the street, slowing as it approached the lamp-post where Pagan and Burr stood. Ted Gunther, the man from the American Embassy, emerged from the vehicle. He paid the driver and the cab slid away. Gunther, wearing a suit over striped pyjamas that were plainly visible at his cuffs, looked apologetic as he entered the circle of light.

'They said at the Yard I'd find you here.' He blinked behind his thick glasses. 'I hope I'm not interrupting anything.'

'Nothing that can't wait,' the Commissioner said in the manner of a man whose weekend has been totally ruined anyhow.

Gunther scratched his head. He'd obviously been roused from his bed and had hurried here. His crewcut was flattened in patches across his skull and there was an excited little light in his large eyes. He was also slightly short of breath. 'I just received the information you asked for about Jacob Kiviranna, and I thought you'd want it right away. I pulled a few strings, called some old favours home.'

'You got some poor schmucks to work on a Sunday for you,' Pagan said.

'More or less. I sent an inquiry out over the wire immediately after we talked and I made a couple of phone calls.' Gunther took a couple of sheets of paper from his coat pocket and tipped them towards the glow of the streetlamp. He reminded Pagan of somebody raised in the dead of night to get up and make an impromptu speech, somebody who has welded together a few odd phrases but hasn't had time to develop a theme.

'Let me just read you what I've got,' Gunther said. 'Kiviranna lived in Brooklyn – '

'Brooklyn?' Pagan asked. He remembered that Kristina had told him that some members of the Brotherhood had settled in Brooklyn in the 1950s. He found himself stimulated suddenly, his interest aroused the way it always was when he confronted correspondences and connections, even when they consisted only of thin threads, such as this one.

'Brooklyn,' Gunther said in a slightly testy way, as if he resented having his narrative interrupted. 'He had no known family – he was apparently smuggled out of the Baltic as a baby by relatives who are now dead. We don't know anything about his parents. He worked as a freelance carpenter, drifting from job to job, making sure he was paid in cash for his labours. Cash is always hard to trace, and it's easy not to declare it, which meant that Kiviranna managed to steer clear of the scrutiny of our Internal Revenue Service. In other words, for all his adult life, Kiviranna paid no taxes. In fact, I'd say he might have avoided all public records of his existence if it hadn't been for his jail sentences. To begin with, he did five days in 1973 for public nuisance.'

'Meaning what?' Pagan asked.

Gunther read from his sheets. 'He urinated on a diplomatic car registered to the Soviet Mission in Manhattan then he tried to punch his way inside the Mission itself.'

'He didn't like Russians,' Pagan said drily, and glanced at Martin Burr, whose face was expressionless. But Pagan had the distinct sense that something was churning inside the Commissioner's head, that even as Gunther recited Kiviranna's history Burr was partly elsewhere.

'It's a running theme in his life,' Gunther agreed. 'In 1974 he attacked a policeman outside the Soviet Embassy in Washington. In 1977, he drove a motorcycle into a limousine occupied by the Soviet Ambassador, causing considerable damage both to himself and the vehicle.'

'A kamikaze sort,' Pagan remarked.

Gunther swatted a moth away. 'He did five months for that little escapade and underwent psychiatric evaluation. Which . . . ' Here Gunther shuffled his papers. 'Which revealed that Kiviranna was something of a loner, didn't join clubs, didn't make friends, felt inferior, that kind of thing.'

Predictable, Pagan thought. Assassins tended to be loners. They weren't usually renowned for having social graces and joining clubs.

'In 1980 he became involved in narcotics. He was busted for possession of heroin. Probation, more psychiatric evaluation. Then he appears to have behaved himself until

1984, when he formed an attachment with a woman, or thought he did – the lady thought otherwise. Kiviranna became obsessed with her. When she spurned him, he slit his wrists. He was committed for a period to a psychiatric unit in upstate New York and diagnosed as schizophrenic.'

Schizophrenic. What else? Pagan felt impatient. Nothing he'd heard here was compelling enough to explain Gunther's appearance after midnight. There was nothing spectacular in any of this. Why hadn't Gunther waited until morning? The eager ally, Pagan thought. Throwing on his suit over his pyjamas, making haste in the darkness. Pagan thought suddenly of Kristina Vaska in his apartment, and the patrol car in the street, and he realised he wanted to be away from this place and back home with the woman. A little twinge he recognised as something akin to panic rose up inside him.

'He was released in 1985, tried to contact the woman in 1986, was rejected a second time, then he attacked the Soviet Ambassador to the United Nations. Somehow, he managed to smuggle himself inside the UN building, waited for the Ambassador to appear, then stabbed him with a flick-knife. The wounds were superficial, thankfully. He got two years for that one. He was released only five months ago.'

Gunther folded the sheets. 'That's the story, gentlemen.'

Pagan sniffed the night air. He knew why the narrative didn't satisfy him. There was a missing element, and that was the shadowy figure who'd been Kiviranna's accomplice, the person who sent Jake overseas to a rainy Scottish city with a gun in his hand. It was like looking upon the bare bones of a life, a bloodless synopsis from which all detail has been omitted and an important character suppressed.

'You've been very helpful,' Martin Burr said to Gunther.

Pagan made a small noise of gratitude because he felt he had to, but he still couldn't keep from thinking that this brief history was hardly worth getting up in the middle of the night to deliver. It rang a slightly false note, only he wasn't sure why. It was as if Gunther had been commanded to deliver this scant information by the powers over him. A sop to the Yard from its Americans chums, Pagan thought. Sheer condescension. No, it was his own state of mind, he decided. It was frustration that made him create whole chapters out of thin nuances.

The three men were quiet for a time as a slight wind picked up along the street and blew through greenery. Martin Burr took a small cheroot from his jacket and lit it, cupping one hand against the breeze.

He smiled at Ted Gunther and asked, 'Do we know the name of the woman who treated poor Jake so callously?'

'I don't have that information,' Gunther answered.

'Is it something you can find out?'

'I guess. I don't see a problem there.'

'Mmmm.' Martin Burr tossed his cheroot away, barely smoked. He prodded the pavement with the tip of his cane, then he turned to Frank Pagan, who recognised the Commissioner's *mmm* sound. It indicated an emerging decision, a step he was about to take – but only after due consideration of the protocols involved. Pagan was apprehensive all at once, waiting for Martin Burr to continue.

The Commissioner said, 'There's a nice American word to describe Kiviranna, and I think it's patsy. Somebody used him to kill Romanenko. Somebody used Kiviranna's apparently bottomless hatred of the Soviets. Directed him, shall we say, although he clearly needed very little direction. The question I have is this – did the chap who sent Jake all the way to kill Romanenko *know* what Aleksis had in his possession? Was that the reason he wanted Romanenko dead? Did he want the message to go undelivered? And if that was the case, how did he know Romanenko was carrying anything in the first place?'

Burr looked up into the lamp, staring at the suicidal mazurka of moths. Then he said, 'Do you see where I'm leading, Frank?'

It was dawning on Pagan, and he wasn't sure he liked the light that was beginning to fill his brain. *You sly old bastard*, Martin, he thought, but he said nothing.

Martin Burr grinned. He glanced at Gunther, as if he'd just remembered the man's presence, then he returned his mischievous one-eyed stare to Pagan. 'I may have to hand Epishev over to other parties, Frank. But I don't have to give them Jacob Kiviranna, do I? He's dead, after all. And intelligence isn't likely to give a tinker's curse about him. I rather think Kiviranna, who did commit a murder, is our pigeon, and ours alone. The man wasn't some bloody KGB villain, after all. He was a common killer, exactly the kind we specialise in.'

The Commissioner pressed his fingertips against his eyepatch. 'We're perfectly entitled to examine Kiviranna's background, Frank. We're perfectly within our sphere of influence to look into his mysterious life. Nobody's going to take that away from us. And who knows? Perhaps something in the fellow's history will clarify certain matters that are baffling us at the moment. Perhaps you'll even learn more about this odd fellowship – what's it called?'

You know damn well what it's called, Pagan thought. 'The Brotherhood, Commissioner.'

Gunther had discreetly drifted several yards away, and stood beyond the reach of lamplight, as if he sensed a private conversation he shouldn't be eavesdropping.

Pagan saw it all now, and he wasn't exactly happy with it. 'You get me out of the way, which leaves things open for intelligence. And at the same time you're offering me a bone which may just have some meat on it – enough at least for me to chew on for a time.'

'You're an insightful fellow,' Martin Burr said. 'Like I said, Frank, you may turn something up that will surprise us all.'

'You want to have your cake and eat it,' Pagan said. 'You should've been a politician.'

'I'd slit my throat first.' Martin Burr looked at Gunther. 'How's the weather this time of year in New York, Ted?' he asked.

V.G. Epishev stood for a time in the centre of the darkened square. The rain had blown away, leaving the darkness damp. There were few lights in the windows of the houses around the square – but in what he took to be the windows of Pagan's apartment a lamp burned behind a thick curtain. Epishev parted a tangle of shrubbery, hearing his feet squelch in soft black mud. Nearby, a flying creature – bat, bird, he couldn't tell – flapped between branches.

He moved under trees, stepping closer to the street, glancing up at the lit windows, then observing the police car which had been parked in the same place for hours. He made out the shapes of two policemen inside the vehicle. One, smoking a cigarette, let his hand dangle from the open window. Epishev walked close to the low stone wall.

That afternoon, when he'd first seen Pagan with the woman, he'd driven back to his hotel in Bayswater – a greasy room, an anonymous box overlooking an overgrown yard – and he'd lain for a long time on the narrow bed, pondering the presence of Kristina Vaska. The conclusion he came to was simple: if Pagan had known nothing of the Brotherhood before, he almost certainly knew something now, courtesy of Miss Vaska. Whether the message was coded or not, the fact remained, so far as Epishev was concerned, that Kristina Vaska would have provided Pagan with some insight into the Brotherhood, at least as she understood it. The question that burned Epishev now was the extent of the woman's understanding.

Did she know of the plan? If not all of it, did she know any part? Did she know enough to cause the destruction of the scheme? Even if she didn't – could Epishev take that kind of chance?

All such speculation was finally fruitless. How the woman had come into Pagan's life, the nature of her information – he could dwell on these matters to infinity and still solve nothing. The solution didn't lie in further pointless rumination. The answer lay elsewhere – in action.

He skirted the wall. He reached the street, looked up once more at the lit window, then he gazed along the pavement at the police car. He stood very still, merging with the trees behind him, becoming in his stillness just another inanimate shadow. He saw the red glow of a cigarette behind the windshield, then the spark as the butt was flicked away. It was very simple. He'd walk straight towards the car. He wouldn't look extraordinary at all, just a man taking the night air. He moved out from beneath the branches.

He put his hand in the pocket of his raincoat and curled his fingers around the gun. Then he paused, conscious of the flare of a match inside the police vehicle and the sound of a man's voice carrying along the pavement – *I told the missus, I said the last thing we needed was another bleedin' crumbsnatcher*, and then there was silence. Epishev kept going. He was about twenty-five yards from the patrol car now. He took the gun out of his pocket and held it against his side, so that it was concealed by the folds of his coat. Fifteen yards.

One of the policemen was staring at him now from the car. Epishev had the impression of a face half-lit by a streetlamp. Cigarette smoke drifted out of the open window. Epishev called out 'Maxwell! Maxwell!' and kept moving until he was only a couple of feet from the vehicle. Then he called the name again 'Maxwell! Here, Maxwell! Come to me!'

The policeman with the cigarette asked, 'Whatsamatter?'

Epishev stopped at the window of the car, lowered his face, looked inside. *There were only two of them, nobody concealed in the rear seat.*

'I am missing my cat,' he said. He wondered if he sounded suitably concerned. 'Brown male with white paws. Very distinct markings. Impossible to overlook.'

The smoking policeman turned to his partner. 'Seen any cats, Alf?'

Alf shook his head. 'Sorry, chum.'

Epishev shrugged. He smiled apologetically, as if he were ashamed to have wasted the valuable time of these two guardians of law and order, then he brought the silenced pistol up very quickly and fired it twice into the squad car. It was brutally efficient. The policeman closest to Epishev dropped his cigarette and slithered sideways and his head slumped on his partner's chest. Alf, the younger of the two, lowered his face like a man dozing. Blood stained his blue shirt in the region of his heart.

Epishev stepped away from the car and crossed the street swiftly to Pagan's house, climbing the steps, stopping outside the brown door, checking the lock. It was a simple affair and easily forced, nothing more than a little quiet surgery undertaken with a penknife – and then he'd be inside, he'd be climbing the stairs to Pagan's apartment, where perhaps both Pagan and the woman were in bed even now, making love. Two quick shots, Epishev thought. The ultimate orgasm.

He took out his knife, selected a short thin blade from the selection of ten or more available to him, forced it into the lock. He turned it gently, listening for the inner mechanism to be released. Then, breathing in the patiently shallow way of the safecracker, he heard the lock click and felt the door move. He nudged it a little way. A darkened hallway faced him, a stairway. He didn't step into the house. He was wary of the silences and the lack of light.

He put his knife away, took out the gun again. The hallway smelled of stale air and a hint of damp. All he had to do was to stride along the hall and rise quietly up the stairs – and yet he hesitated, because his instincts told him something was not quite right here, something was out of joint and he wasn't sure what.

He didn't move. It was only when he heard the sound of the car draw up and he turned his face back to the street and saw the bright headlamps that he knew –

Frank Pagan wasn't at home.

He'd gone out, leaving the woman with the police to guard her, and now he was back. Epishev heard a door slam and he saw Pagan get out of an American car and come quickly along the pavement, then pause in the manner of a man who has forgotten something. Pagan turned away. *He walked back across the street to the police car.*

Epishev saw Pagan incline his face to the window of the police vehicle, then he raised his pistol even as Pagan, stunned by the sight of the dead policemen, turned his face in the direction of the house. Two things occurred to Frank Pagan almost simultaneously – one was the realisation that a man was about to fire a gun at him from a darkened doorway across a narrow street. The other was that this same man might already have been up to the apartment where Kristina was alone –

Pagan threw himself to the ground, rolling as soon as he hit concrete, twisting his body in the manner of a burning person trying to douse flames, sliding for the safety of the underside of the squad car. He saw powdered concrete rise up inches from his face, dug out of the ground by the violent impact of a bullet. And still he kept twisting, until his body was jammed against the exhaust system. He reached behind him for his own weapon, a manoeuvre that called for a certain double-jointedness in the cramped space between exhaust-pipe and ground. He fumbled the weapon free and fired it twice but his angle was low and useless and his shots struck a garbage-can on the pavement. They were loud though, wonderfully loud, spectacularly so, and they echoed along the street with the intensity of a car backfiring, except worse.

The gunman took another shot from the doorway of the house and Pagan heard the bullet slice into one of the tyres of the patrol car, which immediately deflated so that the vehicle listed to one side, making Pagan's position even more uncomfortable. But it was the last shot of the brief encounter because now windows were being thrown open along the street, and lights were turned on, and cranky voices, disturbed in sleep, were calling out a variety of obscenities.

Pagan squeezed himself out from beneath the car as the gunman, afraid of all the public attention, started to run. Pagan glimpsed the man's sallow face briefly under a dim streetlamp – somebody you wouldn't look at twice in the street. Then the gunman headed for the darkness of the square, jumping the stone wall and vanishing into the trees. Pagan got to his feet and considered the idea of giving chase, but his mind was on Kristina Vaska now, and he hurried towards the house, rushing the stairs, finding the door of the flat locked, pounding on it, then hearing the deadbolt being drawn and seeing Kristina Vaska standing there, bright and freshly-showered, in one of his robes, an old paisley thing that had never been worn with anything like this kind of elegant sexuality –

'I thought,' he said. The relief he felt was like a narcotic. He was stoned by it.

'Thought what?' she asked.

Pagan put his arms around her and pulled her towards him and felt her wet hair pressed against his cheek. He wanted her with a ferocity that astounded him. And he knew it was reciprocated, he could feel her heart beat against him and the heat of her breath on his skin, he knew that he would only have to slide a hand between the folds of the robe and touch her lightly on the breasts – he understood he'd have to travel only a very short distance before he'd be lost.

He stepped back from her. He was thinking of the two young cops in the squad car, how they lay so very close together in a position of intimacy that only death had the chilling skill to choreograph. Two young cops – and they'd been murdered because of a situation they knew nothing about, something that should never have touched their lives, events from a history of which neither of those two men would have been aware.

It was waste, bloody waste.

In a frustrated gesture, Pagan pressed his large hands together until the knuckles were white. He walked over to the window. Below, people were milling around the squad car. Gore drew them out. Violence magnetised them.

He was aware of Kristina Vaska standing at his side. He said, 'Two young cops are dead down there. Uncle Viktor's handiwork.'

Kristina Vaska shut her eyes and bit very gently on her lower lip. Pagan put an arm round her shoulder and thought how this intimacy provided no real defence against the brutality of the street below.

12

Trenton, Nero Jersey

In the early 1950s the facility had been an active USAF airfield but now it was used solely for training pilots and mechanics. Three vast hangars, located nineteen miles from downtown Trenton, contained a variety of aircraft in different stages of dismemberment. Young men worked under the guidance of their instructors, welding, soldering, exploring the mysteries of electronic circuitry.

Some distance from the three main hangars a fourth was situated at the place where the field was surrounded by barbed-wire. This construction, smaller than the others, contained an F-16 simulator. Andres Kiss stood with his hands on his hips and a certain arrogant expression on his face – though the look was less one of arrogance than of supreme confidence, that of a man so sure of his abilities he is contemptuous of any attempt to test them. He swept a strand of blond hair from his forehead and smiled at Gary Iverson, who produced a length of black cloth from his pocket and dangled it in the air. He knew Kiss would pass the blindfold test without difficulty, but Galbraith, whom Andres Kiss had never heard of, had to be reassured because the fat man's eye for detail was like that of an eagle for its food supply. Galbraith could spot an overlooked detail or a sloppy piece of business with uncanny accuracy.

Andres Kiss climbed inside the simulator, which was a working cockpit of an F-16 fighter plane. He studied the panel layout, but it was all so familiar he could have sketched it from memory. He took the blindfold from Iverson's hand and pulled it over his eyes, knotting it at the back of his skull. Because there wasn't enough room in the cockpit for two, Iverson had to stand on the platform attached to the simulator, from which position he could verify the results of the blindfold test.

'We don't need to go through this,' Kiss said.

'Do it for me, Andres.'

Andres Kiss adjusted the blindfold. He perceived Iverson as a necessary conduit for the Brotherhood's plan. Without Iverson, the scheme would have been nothing more than the sentimental yearnings of old men. What Iverson brought to the plan was reality in the shape of an aircraft, which might have been otherwise impossible to obtain.

Kiss and Iverson went back some years together to a time when Andres had first learned how to fly a fighter plane and Gary Iverson had been his instructor. Kiss was the most willing student Iverson had ever had, the most adept. The young man's affinity for flight was unnatural. Earthbound, Andres Kiss wasn't the kind of man you'd want to spend an evening with. Pub-crawling with Kiss became an exercise in profound tedium even for somebody like Gary Iverson, whose own social graces were tepid at best. But when you put Kiss inside an aircraft he was transformed, some miracle of transmutation took place, and Kiss was touched by a radiance, an ease he otherwise didn't have.

Now Kiss rubbed his fingers together like a man about to shuffle a deck of cards. 'Go,' he said.

'Manual pitch override switch,' Iverson said.

Kiss moved a hand to the left console, touched the switch. He did this without hesitation.

'Antenna select panel,' Iverson said.

Kiss smiled and reached for the right console, his fingers passing over the engine anti-ice switch to the place Iverson had requested.

'Master caution light.'

Andres Kiss reached forward to the instrument panel. With blindness imposed upon him like this, he relied on an inner vision which in its own way was even more clear than ordinary eyesight. It was as if there existed in his brain an illuminated map of the cockpit. He touched the master caution light in the centre of the instrument panel.

'Oil pressure indicator,' Iverson commanded.

Kiss found it to the right of the panel. It was all so goddam easy. Iverson asked for the ejection mode handle and Kiss went to the right auxiliary console without thinking. He did the same for the fuel master switch on the left console, the autopilot switch, the cockpit pressure altimeter – everything Iverson asked for Andres Kiss found without hesitation.

'Can I take this goddam thing off now?' Kiss asked.

Iverson said he could. Kiss undid the blindfold, crumpled it in his hand, passed it back to Iverson. Then he climbed out of the simulator. Both men stood in silence for a time, dwarfed by the height of the hangar. There was a very small skylight set in the roof and morning sun shone through. Andres Kiss experienced the same kind of awesome sensation in a hangar that a devout Christian might in a vast cathedral.

Iverson made a fist of his right hand and glanced at the antique Air Force ring he wore on his fourth finger. He'd bought it twenty years ago in a pawnshop. It was at least a half a century old and it gave Iverson a sense of continuity, of belonging to an exclusive club. Now he remembered Galbraith's instruction to probe Andres about Sundbach, to feel him out. He relaxed the fist and smiled at the younger man. 'When I saw your uncle last night I got the impression of . . . I want to say, uneasiness, Andres.'

'He's getting old, Gary. That's all. Old men are apprehensive.'

Iverson thought of the meeting yesterday in the house in Glen Cove and the way Carl Sundbach had walked out. 'It wasn't apprehension. I got the feeling he was keeping something back from me. I mean, you guys aren't having problems, are you? Is there anything I'm not being told, Andres?'

Andres Kiss said he couldn't think of a thing. He'd never understood how much Iverson knew about the Brotherhood, or how much research he'd done into the nature of the plan. He assumed Iverson wouldn't have made a plane available without doing a deep background check – but how deep was deep? Did he know about Romanenko and the whole Soviet side of the affair? Did he know about the undelivered message? There was guardedness on both sides, and secrecy, and that was only correct. Security sometimes depended on areas of mutual ignorance. But every now and then there was tension because of this need for secrecy. For instance – who did Iverson work for? Kiss knew he'd gone to work at the Pentagon somewhere along the way, but he didn't know if he was still employed there. And why was he so keen to make an F-16 available? There were old loyalties at work, of course, and a shared past in the Air Force, but these were not enough to make somebody give you a present of a very expensive aircraft. Andres Kiss might have pursued these questions if he'd been a different kind of man. Somebody more reflective, somebody more widely focused, might have explored and probed for satisfactory answers. But Kiss didn't have that kind of scope. On the bottom line, Iverson was supplying a plane that Kiss was desperate to fly – did anything else matter?

Kiss recalled now how Iverson had first entered the plan, how a chance encounter with Gary Iverson at an air show in Atlantic City two years ago had revitalised an old friendship, one Iverson pursued with an enthusiasm that surprised Kiss, an ardour that even flattered the younger man. Iverson issued dinner invitations, or asked Kiss to join him for cocktails in midtown hotels, or sometimes even invited him to make up a foursome at which the women were invariably handsome and silent and eager to please. The friendship turned eventually, as friendships do, on an axis of mutual trust. On one inebriated night Kiss had talked openly about Mikhail, about the men of the Brotherhood, of lost causes and resurrections – not in a specific vocabulary but in a general one that caused Iverson to be intrigued. It began like this, in vague ways, and it grew until Iverson's F-16 had become a pivotal piece in the jigsaw, and Iverson himself a mysterious force behind the success of things.

'Let me be straight with you, Andres,' Gary Iverson said. 'Some of my people – and I can't name names, you know that – are concerned about one of your personnel.'

'Who?'

Iverson admired Kiss's cool, his smoothness, his way of failing to mention such major incidents as the rupture at yesterday's meeting in Glen Cove and the assassination of Aleksis Romanenko. 'It's Sundbach. We worry about him.'

'Sundbach?' Andres Kiss felt a sense of relief. For a moment he imagined Iverson was going to bring up the matter of Romanenko's murder, and say that it was an obstacle, an incident that had made his people unhappy, that support for the mission was beginning to evaporate. But if he hadn't mentioned Romanenko, then it was because he hadn't learned of Aleksis's role in the scheme. Therefore Iverson's knowledge of the plan's groundwork was limited.

'I wasn't aware you'd ever heard of Sundbach, Gary. You've been doing some digging.'

'I didn't leap into this business without doing some research, Andres.'

'If you'd dug a little deeper, you'd have learned that Sundbach's out.'

'Out?'

'As of yesterday.'

'Out? Like how?'

'He quit.'

'Let me get a handle on this. He just walked away. Just left the room? So long, it's been good to know you?'

Kiss was silent for a long time before he said, 'That's right.'

Iverson examined a slick of oil on the floor. From another hangar came the roar of a plane's engine being pushed through its paces by enthusiastic apprentice mechanics. 'I'm a little surprised, Andres. I'm surprised he walked. There's a lot at stake here, friend, and an old guy like Sundbach . . . ' Iverson paused. 'Let me be right up front with you, Andres. Point one, Sundbach's a little too fond of his drink. Point two, an old guy who drinks can be indiscreet. Point three, we don't need indiscretion at this stage of the game. Point four, he knows a lot . . . '

'Mikhail says he isn't a threat.'

'Maybe Mikhail's right. Who knows? Maybe Mikhail knows Sundbach better than anyone else. All I can tell you is some of my people don't like the notion of this old character having so much information, no matter what Mikhail thinks. Some of my people have this affliction called high blood pressure.'

Kiss studied the other man's face carefully, wondering if he were meant to read something into the absence of expression, something that couldn't be uttered aloud but was to be understood, between friends, in silence. Was he being tested? Was this mention of Sundbach meant to be some kind of examination of his feelings, the way the simulator had been a test of his knowledge? More than feelings, though. Was he being asked to demonstrate some initiative, to carry out a task Iverson didn't want to spell out directly? It was subtle, and quiet, and the nuances of the situation troubled Kiss. He felt like a man looking into a fogged mirror.

'People who outlive their usefulness can be damned tricky,' Iverson remarked. 'Sometimes, though, they just don't do diddley. They potter in their gardens and grow things they can't eat. Is Sundbach like that?'

Kiss said, 'He doesn't have a garden.'

'Doesn't have a garden,' Iverson said, more a private little echo than anything meaningful. He moved towards the hangar doors and pushed them open, looking out across the concrete expanse of old runways, cracked now and weeded. 'Well, maybe he'll find something else to pass the time.'

'Maybe,' Andres Kiss said, and some of the fog began to clear from the face of the mirror.

Manhattan

It was one o'clock in the afternoon when Frank Pagan arrived at John F. Kennedy Airport. He had expected to be met by somebody from the New York City Police Department, because Martin Burr had arranged a liaison, but nobody turned up. It was an insufferably humid afternoon. As he rode in a cab towards Manhattan, Pagan sat with his eyes shut and the window open, feeling a feeble little breeze blow upon his sweating face. You could drown in this kind of weather, he thought. Even the prospect of Manhattan, a city he adored, a city whose electricity sent people scurrying around like galvanised particles, didn't take the edge off his sense of brooding isolation – a condition exaggerated by four scotches on the plane and the absence of Kristina Vaska who, stuck with a ticket she hadn't been able to exchange, wasn't scheduled to arrive in New York until tomorrow.

Kristina Vaska. He could still see that uneasy juxtaposition of images, wet-haired Kristina in the old paisley robe and the two dead cops in the street below, and he was caught between the erotic and the dismal, a place that had all the appeal of an occupied mousetrap. He opened his eyes, stared out at suburban streets beyond the highway, neat boxed dwellings surrounded by neat boxed shrubs. And he remembered the horror he'd felt when he'd looked inside the squad car, when he'd put his face to the window and was about to ask something simple like *Anything happening?* and he'd realised that both occupants were dead, one with his face on the other's chest, the driver with his mouth wide open and blood around his lips.

The two dead cops had caused Martin Burr an apoplectic depression. Pagan couldn't remember ever having seen the Commissioner look so grim, all colour drained from his face and all mischief gone from his one good eye. The cops were hurriedly removed, the car towed, but not before the scandalmongers of Fleet Street, alerted by neighbours, had come upon the scene. Martin Burr had been obliged to hold an impromptu press-conference in the course of which his voice had quivered once and he'd gone silent, holding his emotions in check. No, he told the reporters, he had no idea of the identity of the killer. And no, he had no idea why they were parked opposite Frank Pagan's apartment nor what their nightly routine might be – lies, of course, lies that wouldn't slake the scribblers' voracious appetites for too long.

Later, in the privacy of his office, Burr had said *Don't feel bad about it, Frank. Don't blame yourself for those two coppers.* It was a struggle, and Pagan didn't think he'd win it, because obviously the two young men would still be alive if it hadn't been for the fact that he'd called the local police station for a couple of watchdogs. They'd still be alive, and married, and raising their kids. He stared from the window of the cab, feeling as grim now as Martin Burr had looked in London only a few hours ago. Resentful too, because he was being pitched out of the centre of the action, expelled like some truant schoolboy.

I want you on the first available plane, Frank. I want you out of here and far away from this lunatic. Leave him to MI6. Get what you can on Kiviranna and come home again.

Pagan had been unable to resist saying that he was being shuttled off to do something any responsible cop in New York could do. It would've been simpler to use some local cop and have him talk to the woman who'd scorned Jake Kiviranna – a lady, according to information supplied at the last minute by the ever helpful Ted Gunther, called Rose Alexander who lived in Brooklyn: Simpler and cheaper. Telexes, Commissioner, don't cost much. Burr had chosen to ignore him.

Pagan looked up into the cloudy sky. He was thinking of Brooklyn, a place he'd visited before and had no real desire to see again. Martin Burr had wanted him to rent a hotel room there, but Pagan had firmly drawn a line of his own when it came to his place of residence. The Commissioner might be the great architect, he might be the one who sent men hurtling across oceans in accordance with his own designs, but there was no way he was going to impose a Brooklyn hotel on Frank Pagan. Pagan had booked a room in the Warwick, which wasn't exactly top-notch, but his per diem covered it. Barely. *Very well, Frank. I don't care where you stay, so long as it's out of trouble.*

He thought of Kristina. Before leaving London he'd booked her into a room in a quiet hotel in Kensington, far from his apartment. He'd driven her to the place by a circuitous route, then made certain she went to her room, which was chintzy in a very English way, cosy, guaranteed to soothe. *Look at those curtains,* he'd said. *How could anything bad happen in a room with curtains that look like they'd been designed by Pollyanna?* She'd laughed, but there was a tension in her, and she was just as depressed as Pagan by the deaths of the policemen. She'd be safe in the Stafford Arms Hotel in Kensington for one night, Pagan thought now. Tomorrow she'd be back in New York. He was missing her already – a new sensation in his life. Previously, he'd missed only the dead. Missing the living was filled with all kinds of possibilities.

He escaped from the cab outside the Warwick on West 54th Street, plunging into the air-conditioned lobby, where he checked in smoothly and went up to his room on the sixth floor. He stood for a time at the window, watching the sky above Manhattan. He went over the puzzles again, seeking connections, trying to pull together various conjectures.

He sat on the edge of the bed and scribbled words on a notepad. *Kiviranna. Epishev. The Brotherhood of the Forest. Romanenko.* Then he drew a series of connecting arrows, linking each name with the other, until the sheet was covered in a maze of lines resembling a complex spiderweb. Faction was the word he came back to, the idea that within the KGB there was some kind of support for Aleksis's Brotherhood, that a group of individuals – large, small, he couldn't possibly know – was actively encouraging the Brotherhood's scheme. The death in Edinburgh and the failure of Aleksis to play the role of postman, these things had created sudden detours for the supporters of the Brotherhood and their plan . . . whatever it was. A rush went through Pagan, the familiar feeling he got when he had a flash, an insight, when he saw hitherto unmapped terrain from a point above. All right, he thought, there's a power struggle inside the KGB, even within the Politburo itself – but so what? If it were true, it provided only a context for those events that touched him personally. Political realities within the Soviet Union were as distant as Mars and had nothing to do with him. It was as if somebody had shaken the tree of the Kremlin and a couple of strangely-marked leaves had fallen in Pagan's lap, that was all. He could examine the leaves, and dissect them, but he could never see the larger picture, the architecture of the tree.

He sighed, pulled the sheet from the pad, tossed it inside the wastebasket. Which was when he heard a sharp knock and he rose, opening the door. The man who appeared in the doorway was about five feet seven inches tall and wore a polka-dot bow-tie that drooped from his collar. He had on a light tweed jacket, the elbows of which were patched in leather. He resembled a scholar, Pagan thought, the kind of gnome you saw behind a stack of books in a library, eyes glazed over with that shell-shocked look of too much knowledge. He had uncontrollable feathery red hair which seemed to rise, like puffs of thin, gingery smoke, from his skull.

'Frank Pagan? I'm Klein,' the man said. 'Max Klein. NYPD.'

Pagan closed the door after Max Klein had entered the room. The bow-tie was all wrong, Pagan thought. What kind of NYPD cop wore such a thing for God's sake? And the green leather patches didn't complement the brown material of the jacket. Pagan noticed the leather sandals in which Klein's bony feet were bare. The word *eccentric* floated into Frank Pagan's head. How did this character, with his odd appearance and scholarly face, fit into the macho scheme of things in the NYPD? Did Klein belong to some special department? The Office of Misfits? Pagan had an image of a large room in which sat cops like Max Klein, men who didn't look and feel like policemen, outcasts and dwarves and innocents, errors of recruitment, who had somehow lost their way in the political labyrinth of the police department.

Pagan shook Max Klein's hand. 'Glad you could come,' he said.

'I was going to meet you at the airport,' Klein said. 'But things got away from me. Story of my life.'

Pagan sat on the edge of the bed, looking at Klein, who was scratching his foot through the strap of a sandal.

Klein said, 'I've got an address for you somewhere,' and he dipped into the pocket of his jacket, pulling out an assortment of paper, slips, creased notes, a couple of dollar bills, matchbooks, lint. He placed his collection on the floor, then he got down on his knees and started to sift through it.

Organised man, Pagan thought.

Klein said, 'I'm filled with good intentions. I keep meaning to buy a wallet and put things inside it in an orderly fashion. I never quite get round to it.'

There was a certain childlike quality about Max Klein as he sorted through the detritus on the rug, a *niceness* that showed on his good-natured face.

'Here it is,' and Klein brandished a slip of paper. 'Rose Alexander.'

Pagan took the piece of paper and looked at it. There was an address in Brooklyn and a telephone number. The paper had other scribbles on it, truncated words, dates, a variety of doodles, some of them in the shape of noses, mouths, eyes, all rather skilfully rendered.

Pagan asked, 'What do you do in the Department?'

Max Klein stuffed everything into a pocket, then climbed back up into his armchair. 'I don't exactly fit any category with ease. Right now I work Fraud in Brooklyn. But I joined the force as an artist – '

'An artist?' *They send me an artist*, Pagan thought.

'I draw faces,' Max Klein said and blinked his gingery eyelashes. 'I put together drawings from witness descriptions.'

Frank Pagan was quiet a moment.

Klein said, 'Yeah, I know. I know what you're thinking. You're saying to yourself you've been fobbed off with a guy whose basic skills aren't especially useful.'

'Well.' Pagan shrugged.

Max Klein fidgeted with his bow-tie. 'If it puts your mind at rest, I *do* know my way around Brooklyn. I was raised there, went to school there. It's my territory. So don't write me off just because I'm not some hotshot investigator who's seven feet three inches in his bare feet.'

Pagan smiled. 'How much did they tell you?'

'They said a Communist official was killed in Scotland by a guy from Brooklyn. That you were here to check on the assassin's background, which they said was kind of shadowy.'

Shadowy, Pagan thought. Max Klein said, 'I've got a Department car outside, if you're ready.'

Pagan pulled on his jacket, slipped into his shoes. 'I'm ready,' he said.

Carl Sundbach clutched his grocery sack to his chest and crossed Third Avenue in the direction of Twenty-Ninth Street, where his apartment was located. He skipped nimbly through traffic, thinking he might evade the man following him. He wasn't supposed to know he was being tracked, but the guy wasn't exactly hotshot at his trade and besides Carl had a nose for such things. His years in the hills and forests of Estonia had honed certain skills he'd never altogether lost, and one of these was an instinct, rather like a small alarm, that told him when he was being watched. He'd turned once, glimpsed the fellow, a medium-sized anonymity in a dark blue suit, then he'd reached the sidewalk and hurried towards Twenty-Ninth Street.

When he unlocked the front door of his building he shut it quickly behind him, peering through glass at the street. But the man was nowhere to be seen. Sundbach climbed the stairs to his apartment, four rooms on the second floor. Out of breath, he let himself in, bolted the door behind him, slumped into a chair in the kitchen and let his groceries – veal, pig's knuckles, celery stalks, onions, all the ingredients for the dish called *sult*, jellied meat – roll from the paper bag in his lap to the floor. He tilted his head back, breathed through his open mouth, shut his eyes.

He'd first seen the man only that morning when he'd gone for his newspaper. Then, minutes ago, he'd been conscious of the same face in the aisles of the supermarket. *Kurat!* The man looked so out of place among the shoppers that Sundbach spotted him at once. He looked like a *lurjas*, a sneak. He'd pretended an interest in the produce section, fingering leeks and pressing zucchini, but it was an unconvincing performance. Sundbach opened his eyes. *Who was having him followed?* That was the big question.

He rose, a little shakily, and walked into the large living-room of the apartment. It was furnished in what one might have called émigré chic, stuffed with chairs and sofas Sundbach had bought from Baltic dealers in New York, old sepia prints of Estonia that depicted the University at Tartu, the steeple of the Oleviste Church, and an aquatint of Tallinn done in 1816 by an artist called A. Schuch. There were also shelves of china, some of it family heirlooms Sundbach had managed to salvage from the old country. There were tea kettles and brass plaques and a collection of Estonian books and underground literature smuggled out of the Baltic over the years. On one wall there hung a gallery of American photographs, each of which showed Carl Sundbach in the company of influential Americans – Sundbach shaking hands with Robert Kennedy during that doomed Presidential campaign to which Sundbach had contributed a small fortune (Carl recalled Kennedy saying he'd make room on his agenda for the whole Baltic issue, only a madman's bullet had put an end to that little dream), Sundbach with then Governor Rockefeller during the ground-breaking for a new Sundbach hotel in Albany, Sundbach with an unhappy-looking Ramsey Clark during the Democratic primary in 1973. There were photographs of Carl in the company of entertainers like Wayne Newton, Liza Minnelli, and Robert Goulet, taken at charity luncheons or dedications of hospital wings to which Carl had donated large sums of money. The whole gallery was an immigrant's dream of making good in America, of making not only large sums of money but also of moving in the company of the blessed. Carl was proud of what he'd achieved in his new homeland. By sheer hard work, and equal measures of guts and cold determination, he'd shaped his own dream.

He picked up the telephone that sat on his old roll-top desk. The receiver was an ancient black one, and heavy. He dialled the number of Mikhail Kiss in Glen Cove. Kiss came on the line after the fifth ring.

Carl Sundbach said, 'You having me followed, Mikhail?'

'Followed?' Kiss sounded incredulous.

'A man in a blue suit. Everywhere I go, he goes.'

Kiss laughed softly. 'Why would I send somebody to watch you, Carl?'

Sundbach opened the middle drawer of his desk. Inside lay an old revolver and a photograph album with an ornate leather cover. He flicked the album open, gazed absently at pictures, many of them old black and white shots that belonged in another lifetime. He said, 'You want to keep an eye on me. Make sure I give nothing away. Make sure I don't speak to the wrong people or go to the wrong places.'

Kiss laughed again. 'Take my word for it. I haven't sent anybody to keep an eye on you, Carl. I'm insulted by the suggestion.'

'Then who is he? Who sent him?'

Kiss was quiet for a time. 'I can only think of the Russian Mission.'

'No,' Sundbach answered quickly. 'A *vanya* I'd smell at five miles. He doesn't dress like a man from the Mission, Carl. He's not Russian, unless the Soviets are starting to wear better suits. So who is he? Who sent him if it wasn't you?'

'Perhaps you're imagining it,' Kiss said.

'*Kuradi perse!*' Sundbach slipped into an Estonian curse with the ease of a man who has never left his native country, and who thinks all his thoughts in his native tongue. 'I'm imagining nothing, Mikhail.'

'Listen to me. You just bought a nice place in Key West, go down there for a few weeks, relax.'

'Thanks for the suggestion. I'll keep it in mind,' Sundbach said. He hung up and sat for a while with his hand on the receiver. Then he rose, walked to the window, looked down at the street. Across the way a group of teenagers sat on a stoop, passing back and forth a bottle of wine in a brown paper bag. But there was no sign of the man in the blue suit. Florida, for God's sake! He'd bought the Key West condo for tax reasons, he wasn't going to fly down there and sit in the bright sunlight with people who'd lived their lives and had nothing better to do than grow fat and brown.

He was about to turn from the window when he saw the man in the blue suit pass the stoop where the kids sat drinking. The man said something to the kids, then turned his face up in the general direction of Sundbach's apartment. Carl dropped the lace curtain and moved back from the glass, catching his breath in his throat. If Kiss hadn't sent the man in the blue suit, then who the hell had?

Sundbach sat down, opened the desk drawer, took out the old revolver, weighed it in the palm of his hand. It was a good, secure feeling, the connection of flesh with cold metal. He stuck the gun back, shut the drawer, stood up, looked absently around his living-room.

The thought struck him then, it came out of nowhere like lightning on a calm summery night – the man on the street, the man who was watching him, might have some connection with the murder in Edinburgh. But how could that be?

He pressed his fingertips upon his eyelids and sighed and felt just a little scared. He'd have to sit very still and think it all through, step by step, searching for any small thing he might have overlooked.

Brooklyn

Klein's car was a late-model Dodge, bruised and dented, a sponge on four wheels. Klein drove like a man afraid for his life, his hands tight on the wheel. He had none of the average New Yorker's contempt for pedestrian life-forms and traffic signals, because he slowed at crosswalks and observed the lights cautiously.

It was after six by the time he parked in Brooklyn, and there was a clouded sun hanging in the sky over Sheepshead Bay.

'This is the place, Frank,' Klein said. It was a street of old grey tenements. 'This used to be an okay neighbourhood, which is hard to believe now. I grew up a couple blocks from here. I used to think this neighbourhood was for very rich people. I always felt dirt poor when I came down this street.'

Pagan realised he was disoriented, that he had absolutely no idea of his location because he hadn't been able to follow Klein's route to this place. He stepped out of the car and stood on the sidewalk, watching the small man ease himself from behind the steering-wheel.

'Number 643, apartment seven,' Klein said. 'That's the joint we want.'

Pagan moved toward the entranceway of a tenement. Klein followed nimbly, with a motion that was close to skipping, as if his sandalled feet never quite made contact with the sidewalk.

The hallway smelled of fried food. Two bicycles were elaborately chained to a radiator. Pagan stepped around them, pausing at the foot of the stairs which stretched up through gloom to the next floor. Then he started to climb, and Max Klein followed.

Apartment seven was on the second floor. Pagan waited for Klein to reach the landing, then he knocked on the door. The woman who opened it was about forty, rather appealing, dressed in blue jeans and a peasant blouse. There was a slightly spaced-out expression on her face, as if she'd been interrupted in the lonely act of contemplating her inner landscape. She wore her long brown hair parted in the centre and a metal charm bracelet dangled from her wrist. Pagan had an impression of zodiac signs, Celtic crosses, peace symbols, a whole series of miniatures that shivered as she moved her hand.

Klein flashed his badge and asked, 'Rose Alexander?'

The woman nodded, pushing a strand of hair out of her face. 'Last time I looked,' she said.

'This man' – and here Klein nodded at Pagan – 'this man has some questions to ask you.'

The woman turned her face to Pagan. 'Who are you?'

Pagan told her. He showed her his ID, which she stared at for a long time. She touched the laminated surface of the card and Pagan had the distinct impression she was either stoned or else had done so much dope in her time she'd failed to return from one of her trips. She was caressing Pagan's ID as if it were a lover's poem. Pagan thought there was something anachronistic about a doper caught in middle-age. Rose Alexander was a prisoner of a time-warp, a fugitive from the late 'sixties, the peasant blouse, the blue jeans that he saw now had been patched with little squares of rainbow-coloured material, the peace-symbols hanging from her wrist.

'Scotland Yard,' she said. 'You've come a long way.'

'Mind if we come inside?' Klein asked.

'Be my guest.' She held the door open for them.

There were posters on the wall that belonged to the purple age of psychedelia – Jimmi Hendrix in neon three-D, Bob Dylan in an art-nouveau rendering, The Beatles in their Sergeant Pepper finery. Pagan, remembering these times, was plunged back into a world of Nehru jackets, incandescent gurus, scented hand-made candles, and blissed-out songs by Donovan.

On a table in front of an electric fire the inevitable stick of incense smoked in its own little Nepalese brass container, throwing the sickening scent of patchouli into the room. Rose Alexander sat down cross-legged on the floor. She struck a match, lit a cigarette, held the smoke in her lungs a long time in a doper's manner, her small mouth tense.

'Lemme guess,' she said. 'Since I haven't broken any laws I'm aware of, you must be here to talk about Jake Kiviranna.'

Pagan wondered if events in Waverley Station had made it into the newspapers over here. Even if they had, it was doubtful that Rose, ensconced in her own little universe, kept abreast of world affairs. Rose, it appeared, had been expecting news of Kiviranna to surface at some time or other in her life – the bad penny that keeps turning up, as brightly abrasive as ever, no matter how many times you toss it away.

'He shot a man in Scotland,' Pagan said.

'It figures.'

'You don't seem surprised.' Remarkable calm, Pagan thought.

Rose Alexander stared at Pagan coolly. He caught a glimpse of her as she might once have been, young and carefree, even beautiful, strutting the crowded streets of the Haight in San Francisco or getting high at Woodstock, her long hair hanging over her shoulders and her jeans flared above bare feet and zodiac signs painted on her cheeks and forehead.

She said, 'If I don't seem surprised it's because I'm not. Do you know Jake?'

'I met him briefly . . . ' And here Pagan hesitated. He had half of a sentence still to complete and he was reluctant to do it. 'I don't know if you're aware of the fact he committed suicide.'

Perhaps a vague flicker crossed her face, Pagan wasn't sure. But she still looked unperturbed. 'Don't get the impression I'm a cold bitch. But nothing you've told me so far surprises me at all. I'm not amazed he killed somebody and I'm not exactly blown away by news of his suicide either.'

Pagan glanced at Klein, who was fiddling with one of those lamps with a transparent base filled with expanding liquid. Great pink bubbles rose up hypnotically. Rose Alexander lit another cigarette. Pagan sat down in a beanbag chair, which immediately reassembled itself around him like a loose fist.

Rose Alexander said, 'I had to get a court order restraining Jake from coming near me. Not once, but twice. He forced his attentions on me when I didn't need them and I didn't ask for them. Jake became a nightmare for me.'

Pagan, who wasn't interested in Jake's obsession with this woman, wanted to steer the conversation in the direction of anything Rose might know about Kiviranna's trip to the United Kingdom and the identity of the man who sent him on that fatal voyage. But Rose had other ideas and she wanted to talk about Kiviranna no matter what Frank Pagan desired.

'When I met him first I felt sorry for him,' she said. 'It was in some bar on Brighton Beach Avenue. He had a lost look. And I've got a thing for lost creatures. I got drunk and Jake got infatuated. For most people, this would be no big deal. Like a slight cold. You sweat it out, it goes away. Not to Jake Kiviranna. Jake's thing for me was colossal. Flowers. Cards. Gifts. Poems. I couldn't turn around without finding Jake in my shadow. It's nice at the beginning. But it gets old real fast, man. I tried to point this out to Jake, I tried to let him down gently, I was kind – but there are some people you can't get through to and Jake Kiviranna was one of them. They hear only what they want to hear. Nothing else makes a dent.'

Pagan glanced at Klein, who was going through Rose's collection of record albums. Familiar old names flicked past. The Grateful Dead. Jefferson Airplane. Big Brother and the Holding Company. Names out of a history that seemed more distant than a mere twenty years.

'Jake wouldn't go away. I figured if I couldn't let him down gently, I'd try some reality therapy, so I dated a couple of guys, and I hoped Jake would get the message, but the only message he ever got was the desire to beat me up. Which he did. Two, maybe three times. A couple of broken ribs. Three teeth. A split lip. It might have been worse. He'd beat me, then he'd shower me with flowers. That gets pretty fucking stale. I had to go to court to get a restraining order. The next thing, Jake slashes his wrists. He was a sick sonofabitch. He sent me a poem written in his own blood. Think about that one. Slits his wrists and still finds the time to write verse. Bad verse.'

Pagan was quiet for a time, wondering if Rose Alexander had run her course. She stubbed her cigarette out and looked at the rings adorning her fingers, then she tipped back her head and looked at the ceiling and said, 'I never wanted to hurt him, you understand.'

'I believe you,' Pagan said. He struggled up out of the beanbag chair, which made a rasping sound as he rose. 'When did you last see Jake?'

'Couple of months ago.'

'In what circumstances?'

'He was waiting for me in the street one night. Standard stuff for Jake. He liked to spy on me. He liked to find me with other guys.'

'Did he say anything about how he was going away? Did he mention anything about leaving the country?'

Rose Alexander smiled. 'One of the problems with Jake was how you could never tell when he was talking bullshit or when he was being on the level. Sometimes he'd talk in this real wild way, sometimes he'd be calm. But you couldn't tell from his manner if he was into fantasy or reality. I don't think I listened, Mr Pagan. I didn't want him around. Even after I got the restraining order, he'd still call me or try to see me. The bottom line is, Jake scared me.

Pagan was quiet for a time. He had a mental image of the way he'd seen Kiviranna in the cell in London. The scorchmarks, the elaborate electrocution carried out with a madman's patience, a death that was both simple and ugly. 'What did he talk about the last time you saw him?'

'He was completely out of it,' she answered. 'He said he was going to make some kind of statement against international Communism – he had this things about how the Russians had murdered his parents and grandparents in one of those stupid little countries that don't exist any more and how he had to do something about it. I wasn't exactly happy to see him, Mr Pagan. Forgive me if I'm forgetting anything – I wasn't a captive audience. He was talking crazy. I just wanted to get the hell away from him.'

'Did he say anything else? Did he talk about friends?'

The woman laughed. 'Friends? Jake didn't have any, Mr Pagan. Friendships were off limits to him. How could anybody befriend a guy who was sweet one day, then out of his tree the next? Would you want Charlie Manson for a friend?'

Pagan was frustrated. If this proved to be a dead-end, if Rose Alexander knew nothing about any accomplice, he might as well fold his tent and go home. He said, 'Think. Anything at all might be useful.'

She was pensive for a time. 'Okay. Here's something. The last night I saw him he asked me to give him a ride. He had to be in a certain place at a certain time. The guy he was meeting had a thing about punctuality. Remember, I wanted him out of my life in a hurry, Mr Pagan. So I said I'd drive him where he had to go. Which is exactly what I did. And that was the last I saw of him.'

'Where did you take him?'

'To the boardwalk at Brighton Beach.' Rose Alexander lit another cigarette, which she held in a hand that fluttered like a small injured bird. It was obvious that any conversation about Kiviranna agitated her.

'Did he say who he was going to meet?'

She shook her head slowly. 'He didn't say. It was just somebody he had to meet on the boardwalk, that's all.'

Pagan noticed for the first time that she had a collection of freckles around her nose and cheeks. 'But no names.'

'No names,' she said.

Pagan looked across the room at Klein, who had an expression on his face of frustration. 'Did he give you any kind of impression of the person he was supposed to meet?'

The woman blew a long stream of smoke and for a moment her face was lost to Pagan. She said, 'Sorry. I draw a blank. I guess if he told me anything I must have suppressed it. Or else I never really heard it in the first place.'

Pagan was disappointed. He stood very still a moment, looking at a picture on the wall, a sepia-tinted mushroom, a doper's picture, and rather ominous. 'If I need to ask anything more, I'll be in touch,' he said. 'Thanks for your time.'

She smiled in an insipid way. 'Yeah, sure.'

Pagan stepped out of the apartment with Klein. Then he started to go down the stairs. He was aware of Rose Alexander watching from the open doorway.

'I just remembered something,' she said, and her voice echoed in the stairwell. 'It's not very much, but you never know.'

Pagan stopped, turned around, climbed back up to the landing. The woman had her hands in the pockets of her jeans and was leaning against the door frame, her hips thrust forward in a way Pagan found mildly provocative, all the more so for the lack of self-consciousness in her manner.

'Like I said, it might not be much, but here it is.' She smiled at Pagan, perhaps a little sadly, as if all she were throwing him was a scrap. 'Jake was going to meet the guy in some kind of old shop on the boardwalk. He mentioned that in passing. Maybe it amused him, I don't know. It just came back to me. I didn't ask any questions about it, because I didn't want to know.'

Pagan thanked the woman again. Outside in the street he walked toward Klein's car. He got in on the passenger side and Klein climbed behind the wheel. Pagan said, 'Suddenly I'm overcome by an urge to get some good sea air into my lungs.'

'You got it,' Klein said.

Klein drove the Dodge in the direction of Brighton Beach Avenue and the boardwalk. Neither he nor Pagan noticed the pea-green Buick that moved half a block behind them, a stealthy vehicle, the kind of car nobody ever wanted except for people whose need for total anonymity overwhelmed their desire for attention and their good taste. It followed, always half a block behind, all the way to Brighton Beach.

Fredericksburg, Virginia

Galbraith dined in a moody way alone on the roof, consuming a simple Indian meal prepared for him by the chef of a famous Washington restaurant and sent to Virginia by fast car. He ate spinach rice coloured with saffron, tandoori prawns, cucumber raita and mariel mimosas, those delightful little puff pastries that contain grated coconut, sultanas and cardamom seeds. He pushed his plate away, sat back, belched delicately into his napkin, then gazed across the roof at the satellite dishes. He stared beyond, into the mysterious sky the dishes scanned and analysed. He dropped his napkin on his empty plate, rose, crossed the roof and re-entered the house, climbing down and down into the basement.

His digestive juices made rumbling sounds. The Indian meal lay uneasily inside him. He ought never to have eaten in his present mood. And the spicy food he'd just consumed – well, really, he ought to have known better. He moaned as he settled down before the consoles, which he regarded with impatience.

When Iverson came into the room Galbraith didn't turn his face to look. He drummed his stubby fingers on his knees in a gesture Gary Iverson took to be one of exasperation. Iverson also knew, from long experience of Galbraith's behaviour, that the fat man would be the first to speak, that any question on Iverson's part would be utterly ignored.

Galbraith made a plump little fist, misleadingly cherubic in appearance. He spoke in a very flat tone of voice. 'I am an anxious man, Gary. Do you want to know why I'm such an anxious man, Gary?'

Iverson mumbled something meaningless.

Galbraith smacked the coffee table with his fist and an ashtray jumped. 'Where do I begin? Ah, yes, let's deal with the home front first, shall we? Let's discuss our own shortcomings. A telephone conversation between Carl Sundbach and Mikhail Kiss was logged here two hours ago. It appears that Sundbach has spotted our man. A man of ours, presumably a professional, has been rumbled by an old fellow whose eyesight isn't the best and whose reflexes are arguably threadbare – and yet *he made our man*, Gary.'

Iverson looked up briefly at one of the consoles, absently noticing a NATO message, white letters on a black background, a detailed outline of the next day's strategic naval manoeuvres.

'Incompetence, Gary,' Galbraith said. 'I will not stand for that kind of thing. Now we have Sundbach worrying about who in the name of God is watching him. Do I overreact, Gary? Do I hear you think that? Consider. Sundbach knows he's under surveillance. He can't figure out who's doing the watching. He's an old guy, maybe he gets scared, what does he do?'

Iverson shook his head.

Galbraith hopped up from the sofa, causing vibrations and making motes of dust rise. 'I am dealing in possibilities, Gary, which is what I always do. And here's one to stick in your throat. Sundbach, a terrified old man, a man with a gun licence, decides to shoot his pursuer. It's not beyond feasibility, Gary. *The mess! One of our operatives dead in the street!* I am speaking here of shame, Gary. The involvement of the local police. Homicide detectives. *Newspapermen*. Horror!'

Iverson considered this scenario unlikely, but didn't say so. He had seen Galbraith react this way before in situations where he thought the professional reputation of the agency was endangered or where the threat of exposure lurked. He was more than normally sensitive, it seemed, when it came to his beloved White Light project.

There was a silence in the basement. Galbraith, who had the kind of vision that enabled him to see around corners, who had the sort of imagination that allowed him to explore possibilities even as he juggled them, who liked to predict human behaviour as if his brain were a series of actuarial tables or psychological logarithms, returned to the sofa and sat down and his monk's robe flopped open, revealing enormous hairy white thighs.

'Take that useless surveyor out of the street, Gary, and send in the Clowns.' Clowns was the in-house term for those highly-skilled and expensively-trained employees whose functions within the Agency were many and various, but always clandestine. Sometimes the Clowns were called upon to erect smokescreens or manufacture diversions when such strategies were needed. They staged car wrecks, set alarm bells off, lit fires, fucked up telephone lines, forged documents, tampered with computer networks, pretended to be insurance salesmen or window-cleaners or Swiss bankers or Italian lawyers or whatever role was required in a given situation. When specialised surveillance was needed, when the ordinary watcher in the street had been exposed, the Clowns were the people you sent for. They were inventive men and sometimes just a little arrogant in the way of all specialists. Galbraith had introduced the concept of the Clowns years ago – a budgetary secret concealed under the vague rubric of Miscellaneous – and they'd been useful on many occasions. They prided themselves on the fact that only rarely had they resorted to real violence. Theirs was a pantomime world, a place of appearances and illusions, flash and noise when needed, or quiet play-acting if that was preferred.

'Did you probe young Andres?' Galbraith asked.

Iverson nodded. 'I did.'

'And?'

'He quotes Mikhail. Mikhail trusts Sundbach to behave himself.'

'And Andres goes along with that?'

'To some extent,' Iverson said.

'But not all the way?'

Iverson shrugged. 'It's hard to say. He defers to Mikhail, at least on the surface, but I get the feeling he might do something different if Mikhail wasn't around.'

'How different? Would he do violence to Carl Sundbach?'

'Maybe. It's hard to tell with Andres. He's like a man completely covered in very tight

Saranwrap. You look at his face and you think Prince Charming, and then a kind of glaze goes across his eyes and you know you've lost him. And you don't know where he's gone.'

'I want him to stay out of mischief, Gary. That's the only thing that matters. He's got to be on board that plane to Norway at ten o'clock tomorrow night, and it's too close to the end to have a royal fuck-up now.' Galbraith rubbed his acupuncture stud. It was said to relieve stress, which so far it hadn't done. 'I move now to another matter, perhaps even a little more disconcerting. And that is dear old London, Gary. It appears that Colonel Viktor Epishev of the KGB is running around causing havoc over there, having shot two young policemen on duty. His real target is none other than Frank Pagan, who arrived in New York this very day. (I am having Pagan watched, of course. Let us pray for competence in this instance.) I want to keep Pagan busy diddling round with Kiviranna and out of harm's way, but I really can't have Epishev causing all this grief over in London.'

Galbraith paused. He was suddenly conscious of the delicate balance of things, the wheels spinning within wheels, the equilibrium so finely calibrated that even the light touch of a spring breeze might blow it all to kingdom come. He had been given a heavy responsibility, and he was determined to carry it out. The future of mankind, even if mankind were a class among which he found a thousand things despicable, a thousand things grubby, was no small affair. He cleared his throat and surveyed the consoles a moment.

'I really don't know what Vladimir Greshko thinks he's up to by sending his man to London,' Galbraith said. 'But I believe it's time we found out. Agree?'

'Yes,' Iverson said.

Galbraith made a steeple of his fingertips and held it under his lower lip in a contemplative gesture. 'I love smooth surfaces, Gary. Porcelains. Silks. Certain kinds of stones. Glass. Mirrors. I like surfaces so smooth you can't feel any kind of seam. What I hate is sandpaper. And what I'm beginning to feel right now is a certain amount of grit forming beneath my fingernails. I don't like the sensation, Gary.'

Galbraith dropped his hands to his side. 'It's time to make Ted Gunther earn his salary, don't you think?'

13

Zavidovo, the Soviet Union

Because it was a beautiful dawn the Yakut nurse – a firm believer in the benefits of early rising and crisp air, even if the patient was terminal – had helped Vladimir Greshko into a wheelchair and pushed him out into the garden, where he sat in the shade of a very old oak, surrounded by pines and wildflowers and all the rest of what he considered nature's repetitive graffiti. It was, for him, a bucolic nightmare. Despite his rustic origins and the sentimentality he often felt for the land, he had become a city person, somebody made nervous by the racket of birds.

He watched the nurse go back inside the cottage and he glowered at her. To have been detached from his tube, disgusting as the thing was, was like being yanked from an umbilical cord. Twenty minutes, the Yakut bitch had said. Twenty minutes, no more, as if she were bestowing a precious gift on him.

The trouble with nature, Greshko reflected, was its unsanitary condition. Little things chewed on even smaller things. Ants scurried off with disgusting larvae in their jaws. Wild animals and birds crapped where they felt like it. He loved the tundra, those great prairies with their romantic isolation and impenetrable mystery, but when it came to thick trees and the awful green density of this place, he experienced a suffocating claustrophobia.

He closed his eyes, opening them only when he heard the sound of an automobile approaching from the distance. He turned his face to the pathway that led to the cottage, peering through the twisted posts of the old wooden fence. His first thought was that Volovich was coming to say he'd received news from Viktor, but when he made out the shape of the Zil – unmistakable! – he knew his visitor was General Olsky.

He saw Olsky get out of the long black car and come through a space in the fence, where a bramble bush snagged the sleeve of his well-tailored suit. Greshko stared at the bald head as it ducked under the thorns. And then Olsky was crossing the thick grass to the wheelchair in short springing steps. He wore this morning amber-tinted sunglasses, a horrible Western affectation as far as Greshko was concerned. They caught the dawn sunlight and glinted as if two copper coins had been pressed into his eye sockets.

Olsky asked, 'How are you today, Vladimir?'

'Unchanged, Stefan. You find me as you found me when you were last here. Two visits in as many days! I feel very honoured.'

Olsky circled the wheelchair, pausing immediately behind Greshko. As a technique, Greshko thought it ludicrous. Was he supposed to twist his head round in order to see the little shit? Was this meant to place him at a disadvantage? Greshko wanted to laugh. When it came to technique, when it came to the body language of interviews, he'd written the book.

'Let's walk, Vladimir,' Olsky said. 'I'll push you.'

'As you wish.'

Olsky shoved the chair over the thick grass, a shade too quickly perhaps, as if he meant to unnerve Greshko. Olsky wheeled him towards the pines, where the ground was rougher and the chair shook. Then Olsky stopped, catching his breath and sitting down with his back to the trunk of a pine. He snapped a stalk of long grass and placed it against his teeth.

'Do you like it here?' Olsky asked.

'This green prison? What do you think?'

'I can imagine worse places, Vladimir.'

'I suppose you can.'

Olsky stared in the direction of the small house. 'You've got a decent place to live. Your own medical attendant. It could be a whole lot worse. At least the sun is shining and the weather's warm.'

Greshko smiled. Just under the surface of Olsky's words, he could hear it – a quietly implied threat, a hint of how the last days of the old man's life could be made utterly dreadful by removing him from this place and sending him in some cramped railroad carriage to the distant north. *Am I supposed to be scared shitless? Am I meant to nod my head and drool with gratitude?* 'Why don't you come to the point, Stefan? Dying men don't have time for circumspection.'

Olsky was quiet a moment. 'Where is Colonel Epishev?'

Epishev, of course. Greshko said, 'I assume he's at his desk. Unless you've misplaced him, of course. Which would be damnably careless of you.'

Olsky took off his glasses. 'Where have you sent him?'

'Sent him? You forget, General, I have absolutely no power in the organs these days.'

'He came here. I have that on good authority. He came here with Lieutenant Volovich. I can only assume you issued instructions to him.'

Olsky watched a woodpecker as it fastened itself on to a pine trunk and rapped its beak with sublime ferocity of purpose. *Rap rap rap.* Epishev and Volovich had been spotted coming here. An, the risks one ran! The trees had ears and eyes and every goddam blade of grass was a potential microphone.

'I receive so many drugs, Stefan. I sleep a lot. Sometimes I have no idea of time. Sometimes people come to see me and I don't remember them ever having visited. And so many people come, I have more friends than I can count.'

'I want an answer, Vladimir. Why did Epishev and Volovich come here? And where have you sent Viktor?'

Greshko wondered if somehow Volovich had been made to talk. But if Dimitri had confessed, then Olsky wouldn't be here asking these questions. Things would be different if Olsky really knew anything. Things would be rather more straightforward, perhaps even a little brutal. Greshko would have been removed from this place without ceremony. Besides, why should Volovich admit anything that might incriminate himself? The man might be nothing more than Epishev's toady, but he was surely no fool when it came to survival.

Olsky replaced his glasses. 'Are you denying you were visited by Epishev and Volovich?'

Greshko smiled in spite of the sudden pain that knifed through his abdomen. Pain like this, you were never prepared for it, it went through your nerve-endings like a dagger through old papers. 'How can I deny something I can't remember?'

Olsky felt oddly tense in the old man's presence, even though he knew he had no need to. Sabina was forever reminding him of his own new authority – *Sweet Jesus, you are the Chairman of the KGB, you don't need to be in awe of anyone, my love.* And of course she was right. But there was something in Greshko's demeanour, a quality connected to Greshko's history, the sense of the man's legend that now and then unnerved Olsky. Greshko had walked the same stages, stood on the same platforms as Stalin and Khrushchev and Bulganin and Malenkov, the luminaries of modern Soviet history. Greshko had been at the centre of things for so many years that his absence created a vacuum which, for most Soviet citizens accustomed to seeing his face on state occasions, was almost unnatural – as if the moon had failed to wax.

'First you lose some computer data,' Greshko said. 'Then you lose one of your Colonels. If I was running the organs – '

'But you're not, General – '

'When I did, *General*, I controlled everything, the tasks of my key personnel, the access codes to the computers, nothing ever slipped away from *me*.' With some effort, Greshko raised his voice. 'I knew where everything and everybody was, day and goddam night, I lived the organs, *General*, twenty-five hours a day, eight days a goddam week. Don't come here and make accusations that I gave an order to Epishev! You know I don't have *that much* power these days,' and here the old man snapped his fingers. 'If I did, by God you'd see some iron in the backbone of this country!'

Olsky stood in silence for a time. He had cards to play, but he wanted his timing to be correct. He was prepared to let Greshko rant for a while. He watched globules of white saliva appear on the old man's lips. Then Greshko yielded to a prolonged fit of coughing, doubling over in his wheelchair, wiping his sleeve across his lips. His skeleton seemed to rattle. Olsky, noticing how crystalline mucus clung to the material of the old man's sweater, turned his face away for a moment. The paroxysm passed and Greshko, white-faced, was silent.

Olsky wandered some feet from the wheelchair. With his back to Greshko, he said, 'A man called Yevenko was arrested yesterday, General.'

Greshko, whose chest felt raw, his lungs on fire, closed his eyes. He had the impression of a thousand wasps buzzing through his brain. Yevenko, he thought.

'More commonly known as the Printer,' Olsky said. 'A criminal type whose speciality is forged papers, passports, and even the occasional rouble. He was arrested on suspicion of currency irregularities. It was a routine kind of arrest, but it had an interesting aspect to it. The Printer, it seems, had a story to tell about recently being called upon to make a West German passport for a man known as Grunwald.'

Greshko was sarcastic. 'Fascinating. Tell me more.'

'Grunwald, according to the Printer, is in reality our comrade Epishev.'

'Really,' Greshko remarked. He showed absolutely no emotion on his face. 'And you take the word of this criminal?'

'He was in a tight spot. He was ready to barter. People like him usually tell the truth when they face the prospect of lengthy incarceration.'

Greshko wheeled his chair a couple of feet. 'Let's suppose for just a moment this criminal is telling the truth – although, as you may be aware, General, criminals rarely do. Viktor might have needed a forged passport in the normal line of duty. He works in some very grey areas, after all. He infiltrates underground groups, he may need false ID, a cover of some kind.'

'It's possible.' Olsky paused. 'I'm reliably informed that the man using this passport left the Soviet Union on an Aeroflot flight to East Berlin. He then caught a connecting flight to London.'

'London? Why would Viktor travel to London?' Greshko asked. 'This is all very thin, General. What evidence do you have that the man called Grunwald is Epishev in any case?'

Olsky said, 'The photograph in the forged passport was Epishev's. The Printer assured us of that.'

'And you believed him?' Greshko infused scepticism into his voice, the tone of the experienced old master contemptuous of the apprentice's naivety.

Olsky didn't reply to this question. 'Did you send Viktor to London, Vladimir?'

'Why would I send him there? Why would I send him anywhere, for God's sake? Besides, I couldn't send him abroad, he'd need clearance from a superior officer.'

Olsky, who knew Epishev had the authority to go in and out of the Soviet Union at will, a clearance given him by Greshko years ago, glanced through the trees for a time. There was something just a little pathetic in backing Greshko into a corner. Something almost sad, although that was an emotion Olsky couldn't afford to feel. He wondered why he wasn't savouring this moment. 'Comrade General, when I visited you before I mentioned missing computer data relating to a man called Aleksis Romanenko.'

Greshko, like some old parrot, cocked his head and listened. What now? What links was this upstart Olsky trying to make?

Olsky said, 'I mentioned that the data had been deliberately removed. But in this particular instance we had a stroke of quite extraordinary good fortune.'

'Good fortune?' Greshko asked. There was a lump, like stone, in his throat.

'Indeed. We were able to reproduce the missing data from some back-ups that a clerk took the precaution to make.'

'Back-ups?' Greshko asked. *He hadn't thought of this possibility. He hadn't imagined any clerk conscientious enough to make a goddam duplicate of the data.*

Olsky went on, 'It's fascinating material. It appears Romanenko had well-developed ties with a subversive organisation both inside and outside the Soviet Union known as the Brotherhood of the Forest. I must make the assumption, Vladimir, that since this data existed when you were Chairman of the organs, you must have known of it.'

'I never heard of it. It means nothing to me.' Greshko leaned forward in his chair. The damned pain went through him again, making it difficult to concentrate. His eyes watered and he gasped quietly. *Back-ups. Duplicates.* He wondered which wretched clerk was responsible for such a thing. It was his own damned fault because he'd never really understood the intricate ways of the new computer system, he'd always been puzzled by it and overawed, and like any man terrorised by a new technology he'd failed to grasp its potential.

'Come,' Olsky said. 'A traitor like Romanenko, a man in a high position – and you never knew about him? You with your omniscient knowledge of the organs? Really, General. How can I believe you?'

Greshko spoke quietly, giving the distinct impression of a man surprised by nothing. 'Obviously some useless clerk, some slipshod moron, forgot to bring the material to my attention. Or perhaps during the changeover to the present computer system, the data was overlooked.'

Olsky laughed quietly in disbelief. 'But you never overlooked anything, General, did you? And surely you didn't employ morons?'

Greshko listened to the woodpecker again. Rap rap rap. The sharp beak of the creature might have been poking at the timbers of his own brain just then. He became silent in the manner of a man who has unexpectedly just lost a piece in a game of chess, a knight trapped and seized, a bishop ruthlessly snared.

Olsky said, 'On the day Romanenko was shot, Epishev came to visit you. Early next morning he vanished using a fake passport. He went to London. Why the sudden rush to visit England? An overwhelming yearning to see Westminister Abbey, General? Or is there some other reason he needs to be there in the wake of Romanenko's murder? And now here's a brand new element – the former Chairman of the KGB, the all-seeing General Greshko, admits he knew nothing of Romanenko's subversion! *And asks me to believe this story.*' Olsky raised a finger to his lips and spoke in a mock whisper filled with comic astonishment. 'Or could it be that General Greshko had a good reason of his own to leave Aleksis Romanenko in position as a high Party official? Is that it?'

Greshko waved a hand in the air. 'You're full of hot air, Olsky. It's a wonder you aren't floating away over the damned trees.'

'I ask myself. Was General Greshko involved with Romanenko in a subversive scheme? Is it that simple? Is this a deeper echo of the sounds of conspiracy I keep hearing?'

'I'd be very careful if I were you, Stefan.'

Greshko saw the Yakut woman come out of the house and approach the wheelchair. She was carrying a tray of medication. He was relieved to see her.

Olsky looked at the nurse as she came striding across the grass. Then he tapped the face of his wristwatch, as if he'd just remembered an appointment. 'I'll keep in touch, of course, Vladimir. I know you're interested in the outcome of my investigations.' And then he turned and moved toward the parked Zil, sliding through the fence and deftly avoiding the bramble bush that had snagged him before. Greshko watched him step into the large car, then heard the sound of the engine turning over.

'Pill time, General,' the nurse said.

Greshko observed the car as it vanished between trees, leaving only a vibration behind. He felt the nurse stick a capsule into his mouth. He swallowed it, listening to the Zil until it became indistinguishable from the drone of insects. Back-ups, he thought. The need for duplicates that sometimes obsessed the petty clerical mind. So be it. He squeezed his eyes shut tightly and concentrated, tracking things through his mind, wondering what his next step would be if he were General Smartass Olsky. What would you do next, Stefan? The answer came back at once. *I would put the squeeze on Volovich. I'd twist Volovich like a damp rag until he told me everything he knows.* The question was how much Volovich knew. He hadn't been told the precise extent of the Brotherhood's plan, but he certainly knew enough to cause enormous trouble.

Greshko glared into the sun as if he might stare it down. Back-ups and duplicates, by God! Well, he had a back-up of his own which, like a palmed card, he'd play when the time was ripe. And that ripeness, he felt, was upon him.

He smiled at the nurse and she regarded him in a wary manner. 'Why are you smiling?' she asked.

'Why not?'

'You want something. That's when you smile, General. When you need me.'

Greshko shrugged, turning his face from the sun, which was the colour now of a blood orange. 'Perhaps,' was his response to the Yakut woman.

Tallinn, Estonia

Colonel Yevgenni Uvarov disembarked from the launch in Tallinn harbour just after daylight and walked until he reached the Mermaid monument, where he sat on an empty bench beside a clump of shrubbery. He pretended to be interested in the monument, gazing up at the winged woman that stood atop a stone structure, but he couldn't concentrate on it. He read on a plaque that the statue had been erected in memory of the crew of the *Russalka*, which sank in the Gulf of Finland in 1893, but every so often he'd turn and look away, back across the shore to the harbour, where the tall stacks and funnels of ships looked dense and tangled in the dawn sky.

He was unable to still the nervousness he felt. He got up, walked round the green wooden bench, scanned the shoreline, fidgeted. Since he'd taken the phone call last night on Saaremaa Island he'd been living as if at some distance from himself. He hadn't slept. The idea of sleep was foreign to him. He hadn't eaten breakfast, not even a simple cup of tea. He'd risen in that strangely chill dark just before sunrise and gone down to the fast launch that went back and forth between the island and Tallinn, ferrying mail and supplies, and he'd stepped on board and nobody had asked him any questions even though he'd waited for the captain of the vessel to approach him for ID papers or an official pass. He calculated he could be gone for only six or seven hours before he was missed from the radar base – although in reality his absence might be noticed at any time, especially if there were some unforeseen emergency. But he thought he'd covered himself as well as he possibly could, by informing his adjutant – perhaps the laziest man in the whole command – that he had to travel on unspecified official business to Kuressaare on the southern part of the island.

He stared at the sea, waited, wondered if he'd done the right thing by coming here, or if he'd just walked into a trap that would cost him his life. He could imagine it – discovery, the disgrace of a court-martial, public humiliation, a death sentence. And what would happen to his wife and children then? Branded, destined to a terrible life, a world in which doors would be closed to them.

Uvarov returned to the bench, sat, waited, smoked a cigarette. The man on the telephone had mentioned Aleksis's name and the importance of meeting – but he hadn't identified himself, and now Uvarov, whose heart would not stop kicking against his ribs, wished he'd never met the man known as Aleksis, that he'd never accepted the US passports and the enormous sum of money, but Aleksis had been persuasive, and convincing, and finally impossible to refuse, with his enchanting pictures of life in a free world, a future for the children, a place where a man might advance through his own merits – Aleksis had painted a portrait of a desirable place that Uvarov's wife Valentina lusted after. *Freedom, Yevgenni. A new life. To bring up our children as we choose, Yevgenni. The risks are worth it.*

Uvarov heard the sound of a car door slam nearby. He stared at the statue, couldn't sit still. He heard footsteps on the cobblestones and he raised his face just as a man came into view.

The voice on the telephone had said, *I read* Sovietskaya Estonia. *I always carry a copy with me.*

Uvarov saw *Sovietskaya Estonia* folded under the man's arm, looked away at once, sucked the sea air into his lungs, felt his eyes smart and begin to water. The man came to the bench, sat down, tapped Uvarov's wrist with the rolled-up newspaper. The Colonel felt a fist close inside his stomach as he looked at the newcomer – who was perhaps in his late forties and wore a thick moustache that covered his upper lip. He was dressed in the uniform of a Major in the KGB, a fact that caused Uvarov to grip the bench tightly.

'Don't believe everything you see, Colonel,' the man said. 'The uniform is borrowed.'

Uvarov pressed his palm to his mouth. The man smiled and reassuringly touched the back of Uvarov's hand. 'You don't look so good, Colonel. Let's walk some colour back into your face.'

Uvarov rose. The man took him by the arm and they strolled round the monument in the direction of Kadriorg Park. The sun, low over the harbour, cast all manner of strange shadows between the anchored ships.

'Learn to relax, Yevgenni.'

Uvarov stopped moving. He stood under a tree, lit another cigarette, tried very hard to smile. Relax, he thought. Tell me how. Show me!

'Call me Marcus.'

'Marcus,' Uvarov said.

'You suspect a trap. Ask yourself this, my friend. If this were a trap, would I appear in this particular uniform? I'd be in civilian clothes, trying to put you at your ease, wouldn't I? I'd be trying to lull you, no?'

Uvarov made a feeble gesture and the man named Marcus, whose expression was one of weary strength, smiled. 'You all suspect you're about to be arrested. Each and every one of you feels the same when I make contact.'

Uvarov looked back in the direction of the harbour. A pall of black smoke rose from the funnel of a ship, spiralling slowly upward like a funereal scarf. Each and every one of us, he thought. 'How many are involved?' he asked.

'In the armed services of the Soviet Union, less than a score, perhaps less than a dozen,' Marcus answered in an enigmatic way. 'Outside the services, the number is impossible to estimate. Patriots come and go, Yevgenni. One day you can count thousands, another day hundreds. Mercenaries on the other hand tend to remain stable.'

'You're vague,' Uvarov said. He didn't like to think of himself as a mercenary. He was going through this nightmare for his family's sake, not because he wanted to accumulate riches in the West.

'I need to be.' Marcus looked toward the dark smoke now. He had a face that was pocked and pitted, the result of some childhood disease. It gave him a seasoned appearance, a toughness.

'Why are you making contact? Where is Aleksis?' Uvarov asked.

'Aleksis's part is over, my friend.'

Uvarov clutched the man's wrist. 'My family – '

'In wonderful health, Yevgenni.'

'You're sure?'

Marcus stroked his moustache. 'They long to be with you. They long for freedom.'

Uvarov felt his anxiety fade, but only a little. He took a handkerchief out of his coat pocket and blew his nose because the mention of his family had choked him and he felt like crying. Marcus, in a gesture of kindness, placed a hand on Uvarov's shoulder.

'Soon, Yevgenni. Very soon,' Marcus said. 'Now listen to me carefully. I could not give you your final instructions over the telephone, for obvious reasons. As soon as you have performed the function Aleksis hired you for, a small launch will be waiting for you at the jetty that services your installation. It will look like any ordinary military launch except for this one fact – the vessel will not be flying a flag. It will wait for exactly five minutes, no longer. When you get on board, you'll be taken to Hango in Finland.'

'And my family?'

'Your family will be in Helsinki many hours before you arrive in Hango. They'll be safe. I promise you.'

'They're travelling alone?'

'Of course. But they have passports. They'll leave Russia through Leningrad.'

Somehow Uvarov had expected different arrangements, that he'd be going with his wife and children when the time came, but that was fantasy. Obviously, if he wanted to join his family he'd have to go through with Aleksis's task – otherwise, he'd be stranded in Soviet territory while his family was safe in Finland.

'What if something goes wrong?' he asked.

Marcus crossed his fingers and held his hand in front of Uvarov's face. 'If we perform our tasks efficiently, nothing can possibly go wrong.'

'If is the strangest word in the language,' Uvarov said.

Marcus moved a couple of feet away. 'Keep your nerve. Don't lose it.'

Uvarov wanted to detain Marcus now, because he found comfort in the notion of a fellow conspirator. But he couldn't think of anything else to say.

'In Helsinki, my friend. Your wife and children. And a further fifty thousand American dollars.' The man known as Marcus walked between the trees and didn't look back.

Uvarov watched him go. If, the Colonel thought. *If* everything went according to plan. *If* all the nameless conspirators Marcus had mentioned played their roles and adhered to the timetable. If. How many other Army personnel were involved apart from himself? Less than twenty, perhaps less than a dozen, according to Marcus. A small number of men. The smaller the number, the less chance of something going wrong.

Uvarov was slightly cheered by this thought.

The man called Marcus walked to the place where he'd parked his car, an inconspicuous black Moskvich. He took a dark overcoat from the back seat and wore it over the KGB uniform, then he sat behind the wheel. Marcus, whose real name was Anton Sepp, formerly a sergeant in the Soviet Army in Afghanistan, looked back at the figure of Yevgenni Uvarov as he drove away from Tallinn harbour. Then he headed through the streets of the city, passing along Toompea Street in the medieval part of Tallinn, where a network of narrow alleys ran between crooked houses. Already there were a few early tourists moving listlessly, the ubiquitous Japanese with their cameras, a couple of Americans – you could always tell the Americans from the cut of their clothes and the slightly condescending looks on their faces as they studied quaintness – and a few Finns who came for riotous weekends of vodka drinking. The tourists would rummage in the souvenir and craft shops or they'd walk to the foreign currency stores on Tehnika or Gagarini Streets. They'd wander the museums and at night, sated by history, they'd sit through a Western-style cabaret of forced cheerfulness in the basement of the Viru Hotel.

Marcus was happy to drive out of the city, past blocks of new high-rise apartments, which were surrounded by mountains of cement and sand and the occasional thin tree These were depressing areas, and boring – the more so when you contrasted them with the rich medieval architecture of old Tallinn – and yet people were expected to live their lives in such prefabricated tedium. He kept driving until the city was behind him and the sun was rising over the landscape and the countryside around him was rich and green. He turned the car off the highway about thirty-five miles from Tallinn and drove down a narrow track between pine trees. On either side of the track, obscured by thickets of trunks, dark green meadows stretched out and the surface of a narrow lake was visible. The car rocked and swayed over ruts for three or four miles, then the pathway twisted and an old farmhouse came in view.

Whitewalled, shuttered, it appeared at first sight to have been abandoned. But fresh tyre-tracks in the forecourt suggested recent activity and, under a tarpaulin that had been hung across a roofless outbuilding, were three vehicles – a grey Volvo station wagon, a small Zaporozhet, and a Soviet Army truck that only a day before had been in Riga in Latvia.

Marcus parked the Moskvich, entered the house, stooping as he did so because the ceiling had been built at a time when human beings were smaller. The room in which he stood was furnished only with a table and four roughly-carpentered chairs. Marcus removed his overcoat. He heard the click of a magazine being inserted into an automatic rifle, a slight echo from another room. A figure appeared in a doorway, a young man with an M-16 rifle held in the firing position.

'Relax, boy.' Marcus smiled, sat at the kitchen table, rolled a cigarette from a leather tobacco pouch. He was tired and it showed on his face. He smoked, watched the young man approach the table, saw the automatic weapon being propped very carefully against the leg of a chair.

The young man drummed his fingertips on the table. It was less a sign of nerves than it was of restlessness. He was ready to go into action. He'd dreamed of nothing else for a long time now. Marcus watched the young man, and his thoughts drifted to Aleksis Romanenko. When tasks had been allocated, functions delegated, Aleksis's role had been to make certain that those members of the Soviet armed forces he'd recruited wouldn't fail at the last minute, and that their escape routes were firmly in place. This role had suited Aleksis because it involved travel – both in the Baltic and in Russia itself – and as a ranking official he could go almost anywhere without question. Now, with Aleksis dead – gunned down, or so it was rumoured: hard news was a precious commodity – Marcus had been obliged to assume Aleksis's part, like an understudy stepping in at the last moment. Marcus, a deserter from Afghanistan, didn't have freedom of movement. As a fugitive, his style was cramped. His original role had been to make sure the weapons smuggled into Latvia from the United States were distributed between the Baltic countries, and that the various groups would move in unison when the hour came. But now he was exhausted at having to play Aleksis's nerve-racking part.

Thirty-four hours. He sat back in his chair, enjoyed the cigarette, gazed at the young man, whose rather innocent face concealed a certain ferocity, a dark purpose. The boy, who called himself Anarhist, meaning Anarchist, had spent two years in the Soviet Army in Chabarovsk on the Chinese border and a further two years in a military prison for distributing pamphlets of a nationalist nature, calling for freedom for all the nationalities – the Balts, the Georgians, the Armenians, the Kazakhs, the scores of other races – harnessed by the Russians. There were hundreds like this boy throughout the Baltic, brave and determined and patriotic, and many of them were waiting for the moment.

Marcus crushed his cigarette out. He thought of the trips he had already made – to Riga, Haapsalu on the Baltic coast, Moscow itself – and the final arrangements he had concluded with the people Aleksis had bought. They were all like Uvarov, scared and yet mildly defiant, ambitious to leave a country and a military system that both terrified and stultified. And they were all impatient men too, filled with the belief that the Soviet system was changing but at an intolerably slow pace which couldn't satisfy their needs. A few had indisputably genuine philosophical differences with the system. Others had grievances, complaints that the system was unfair, or uncaring, that it didn't listen to the small if reasonable voices of dissent. Some had grudges that went back years, often to a time before they were born, back to grandparents who'd been purged by Stalin, relatives conjured out of existence by a political programme that could never conceal its inherent barbarism, no matter how much cosmetic surgery was done. Some resented the way their careers had failed to take fire, that their wives were discontented, their homes inadequate, their long separations from family intolerable. A few had material aspirations, their minds filled with pictures from glossy Western magazines. What they all shared was the belief that they were innocent inmates in a drab prison, and that the only light they could see, if one existed at all, was at the end of a very long tunnel. And none of them knew the nature of the plan, although some might have guessed it, but if so they'd repressed the knowledge, blinded themselves to their own conclusions.

Aleksis had chosen these people masterfully. He had tapped into deeply-rooted discontentments, old grudges and fears, and he'd assembled a team of key personnel, keeping them afloat on money, and passports, and promises. He'd also manipulated them through their families, providing passports to wives and children, making sure the families travelled out of Russia the day before the action was scheduled, thus locking the husbands firmly into the plan. It was, Marcus had often thought, a scheme of quite extraordinary insight, and he could only marvel at the patience with which Aleksis had put it together, the energy involved, the charm and persuasion needed, the clandestine meetings conducted in an atmosphere of fear and distrust and uncertainty.

He rolled another cigarette. A third person stepped into the room now, a girl of about twenty with short yellow hair and light blue eyes. She had just awakened from sleep and she looked bleary. She wore an old American combat jacket, khaki pants, a black t-shirt. Her feet were bare. She sat down at the table and put her feet up on the rough wooden surface, rubbing her eyes as she did so. She was hardly more than a child, Marcus thought, but she had already spent eighteen months in a psychiatric hospital for her role in editing and distributing an underground newspaper critical of Russification. She'd been given electric-shock treatments, the only permanent effect of which had been to leave her with a rather attractive laziness in one eye. Marcus knew her only as Erma. There was an intimacy between them, something that wasn't fully realised as yet, but it was the kind of closeness developed between people with a common cause.

She rolled a cigarette from Marcus's leather pouch, smoked in silence for a time. She was impatient, and anxious. Her spell in the so-called psychiatric hospital hadn't instilled patience into her. Marcus reached out and laid his hand over the girl's.

'You can't hurry time,' Marcus said.

The girl stared at him, as if his truism were beneath her dignity. Tucked in the belt of her pants was a Colt automatic. She let her hand drift over the butt of the pistol. Marcus felt it then – the youthful eagerness of this girl, the desire that was in her to fight, something she could barely restrain.

'I had a dream,' she said.

'Bad or good?'

'I dreamed the time came and all the streets were empty.'

The boy, Anarhist, made a snorting sound. 'Dreams don't mean anything,' he said.

Marcus stood up, stretched his arms. He would go upstairs now, and try to nap, to settle his mind down in that place where it lay perfectly still. But lately he'd been having a difficult time sleeping. He'd shut his eyes and try to make himself comfortable but then the images would come back in at him the way they always did. He'd be standing on dry, rocky terrain under a terrible yellow sun, his mouth filled with dust and his eyes stinging. Three Afghans kneeled some yards away, their faces turned from him, their hands tethered behind their backs. Marcus noticed – a detail that never escaped him, no matter how many times he played this dreadful movie in his head – how the ropes cut into the skin of the bound men. He blinked his eyes as the wind blew over the rocks and his nostrils filled with dust and somebody, on the edge of his vision thrust a revolver into his hand, which he took, understanding what he had to do with it. The wind flapped the headgear the Afghans wore and in the distance was the noise of rockets screaming. *Shoot*, somebody said. And Marcus raised the revolver and fired into the heads of the three men, who fell forward into the dust even as the wind, whistling through the cavities of rocks, still made their clothing flap against their bodies. The same memory, always the same bloody memory, images of a pain he couldn't exorcise. He'd been involved in other things in Afghanistan – the shelling of villages, blowing up bridges and highways, direct combat – but they didn't match the execution of the three guerillas, neither in shame nor in terror.

He climbed upstairs in the old farmhouse, hating his own recollections, but hating the Russians more for having created them in the first place.

London

V. G. Epishev, who operated on the principle that a man in constant motion left a confusion of trails, had checked into a hotel in Earl's Court, a few streets behind the underground station. It was not a great hotel, but it had the merit of obscurity, located as it was at the end of a warren of narrow thoroughfares. He had a room on the top floor, one of the very few rooms in the establishment with its own telephone. *It's extra, you know,* the woman at the desk told him, as if she were pleased by his little touch of extravagance and proud that her hotel could provide the opportunity. *But it's ever such a convenience, dear.*

Epishev lay on the bed, turned his face to the window. It wasn't quite light outside yet. He thought of making a call to Dimitri Volovich, but what did he have to report so far? The prospect of going through the rigmarole of raising the international operator, then being put through to East Berlin, and from there patched to Volovich in Moscow only to speak in terse, uninformative phrases, had no appeal. Greshko could wait. What choice did he have anyway? There was something enjoyable in the idea of exercising a little power over the old man, of being Greshko's eyes and ears, his brain, in a foreign country. And Epishev was determined to savour the novelty of the feeling.

Besides, he'd been struck once or twice lately by the suspicion that this whole project, this undertaking that had forced him to travel hundreds of miles and had involved him in murder, was less a patriotic task than it was the construction of an epitaph for a sick old man who wanted to be remembered as the saviour of Russia. Perhaps it wasn't the well-being of the nation that primarily interested Greshko, perhaps it was more the prospect of some gratifying words on his tombstone that compelled Vladimir Greshko to sit in Zavidovo like some conniving spider.

Epishev got up, performed some routine exercises, toe-touching, then some brisk sit-ups. He went to the window, opened it, breathed deeply. When the telephone rang, he picked it up on the second ring, understanding it could only be Alexei Malik, since he'd told nobody else of his whereabouts.

'I'm in the lobby,' Malik said.

Epishev hung up. He walked down the six flights of stairs to the foyer, which was a threadbare square of a room that smelled of very old carpet and dusty curtains. The desk was unmanned, the foyer empty save for Malik, who stood close to a curtained window. Epishev crossed the floor, noticing a red double-decker bus clatter past in the street. The hotel was shaken a moment by vibrations.

'Let's walk,' Malik said. He moved to the door, held it open for Epishev. Outside, there was a slash of milky light in the sky over Earl's Court. Both men moved in silence through the streets, pausing in front of a newsagent's shop which displayed bold headlines concerning the violent slaying of two policemen. Malik paused to survey the tabloids, shaking his head as he read.

'The English don't like it when their policemen are killed, Viktor,' he said. 'It touches something raw in the British psyche.'

Epishev said nothing. He had no interest in Malik's perceptions of British society. He walked away from the newspaper display, the headlines that shrieked about the murder of policemen and the deterioration of law and order throughout the island in general and how gun-control laws had to have every remaining loophole closed.

Malik fell into step beside him. 'I had a meeting with two men from British intelligence, Viktor,' Malik said. 'They called me at the Embassy, insisted on an urgent conference.'

'And?'

'Your name came up several times. They seem to think you're responsible for the killings.'

'Preposterous,' Epishev said.

'As you say.' Malik looked up at the sky in the manner of a man who thinks he feels rain in the air. 'I denied all knowledge of your existence, Viktor. What could I possibly know about KGB personnel in any case?'

Epishev stopped on the corner of Earl's Court Road. He saw people plunging into the underground station, workers heading towards their places of employment in the half-dark. He turned to look at Malik. 'You want to know how they came up with my name, of course.'

'I'm curious,' Malik said. 'Did they pull it out of a hat like a rabbit? Did they conjure it out of nowhere?'

'British intelligence is hardly known for its powers of extrasensory perception, Alexei.' Epishev, who didn't like the idea of standing on a main road, moved in the direction of the side-streets again. 'The explanation is very simple,' and he told Malik about Kristina Vaska, about how she'd recognised him outside Pagan's apartment.

Malik and Epishev turned into a quiet street of trees. From somewhere nearby there was the rumble of an underground train, breaking the silence.

'It's unfortunate,' Malik said eventually. 'Mistaken identity, of course. Besides, how could this woman recognise you after all this time? When the men from British intelligence come back, and they're bound to, I'll tell them I made further inquiries and that the only KGB operative by the name of Viktor Epishev is enjoying his retirement in the Crimea, or something to that effect. Therefore, you couldn't possibly be in England.'

'That's only going to work so long as they don't start making some inquiries of their own through their network in Moscow. If word gets back to the Chairman that I might be in London . . . ' Epishev had no need to finish this sentence. He was conscious of how fragile everything was.

'I shall be completely convincing, Viktor.'

Epishev was impatient suddenly. He hadn't accomplished what he'd come all this way to do. He hadn't ensured the security of the Baltic plan. And now there was the disturbing connection between Pagan and Kristina Vaska. He felt exposed, endangered, saddled with complexities he didn't need. His memory of the gunplay in the street last night didn't help his mood much either. Pagan had moved too quickly, squeezing under the car with such alacrity that Epishev hadn't had time for accuracy. It was a good thing to learn for future reference that Pagan's instinct for survival was extremely sharp. It was something to take into account.

Malik looked at his wristwatch. 'I need some breakfast. Let's go somewhere for coffee.' He clasped Epishev by the elbow and steered him gently back in the direction of Earl's Court Road. Epishev went with reluctance, following Malik into a coffee-bar a few blocks from the underground station, a busy, smoke-filled room run by Turks.

'Why this place?' Epishev asked. He was uncomfortable in this crowded room.

'There's somebody I want you to meet,' Malik said.

Feeling vaguely alarmed, Epishev asked, 'Meet? Meet who?'

Malik spotted an unoccupied table and headed towards it, drawing Epishev with him. Epishev asked his question again, but Malik was already gazing at the menu, a grease-stained, typewritten sheet, and seemed not to have heard.

'*Who?*' Epishev asked a third time.

'A friend,' Malik replied. 'Do you want coffee? Toast? Eggs?'

'Friends should have names,' Epishev said with some anger in his voice. 'I don't like being introduced to people without warning, Alexei. I don't like having things sprung on me.'

Malik shook his head in vigorous denial of any underhand behaviour. 'I'm talking about an ally, Viktor. An important one.'

Epishev was about to say something when Malik stood up and waved an arm in greeting. Epishev turned his face towards the door, seeing the newcomer step in. The man, who wore thick glasses and a lightweight suit, smiled at Malik and came across the room, threading through the clutter of tables and the harried waitresses balancing trays with the agility of circus performers. The man reached the table and pulled up a chair. He shook Malik's hand. Epishev, displeased by what he perceived as subterfuge on Alexei's part, unhappy at the notion that Malik was bringing in an unknown third party, absorbed only a brief impression of the stranger before turning his face to the side.

'Viktor,' Malik said.

Epishev looked at the newcomer again. He saw round, rather flabby features, a button-down shirt, a seersucker jacket of pin-striped design, a crewcut.

'Viktor, I want you to meet a very good friend of ours.'

The newcomer smiled warmly. 'Gunther,' the man said. 'Ted Gunther.'

There was a long silence during which Epishev studied the American's face. There was a certain kind of face which Epishev didn't care for. And Gunther had it – a face as obvious as an open sandwich.

'I think it's time to clarify things,' Ted Gunther said, and he rubbed his hands in the congenially cautious manner of a diplomat about to do some business in détente. 'The last thing we want is misunderstandings, right?'

Epishev, still staring at the American, said nothing.

Brighton Beach, Brooklyn

It was dark and the moon was rising on the ocean when Frank Pagan and Max Klein stepped on to the boardwalk at Brighton Beach. The night, hot and close, filled with smells of sweat and the collected suntan lotion of the day and fried foodstuffs, crowded Pagan like some great damp creature risen up from the water. Both men walked slowly to the end of the boardwalk, drifting through the crowds, the roller-skaters and skateboarders, the cyclists, the old couples moving arm-in-arm, the kids popping beercans and jousting for the attention of girls with hairdos fashioned by stylists from other planetary systems – seething activity, clammy heat, the ocean almost motionless. Pagan, sweating, leaned against the handrail and looked out at the water.

'Welcome to Brighton Beach,' Klein said, and he waved a hand at the sky, as if the very constellations were a part of Brooklyn.

Pagan studied the storefronts that lined one side of the boardwalk. Here and there a vendor sold soda and hot-dogs, but what really intrigued Pagan were those places that seemed to serve as social clubs, establishments without signs. You could see through open doorways into cavernous rooms where men, mainly old, played cards or studied chessboards. Slavic music drifted out into the darkness, oddly nostalgic, even sorrowful. Though he couldn't understand a word of what was being sung, Pagan found the sound touching anyhow.

Klein said, 'These places used to be stores. Some sold tourist trinkets, others greasy foods. But they gradually got taken over by emigrant societies. Mainly the Russians, although you sometimes find Ukrainians or Moldavians or Latvians – you've got to be careful with the distinctions, Frank. Come here some Sundays it's like Babel, guys talking in Russian or Latvian or Georgian. You name it. Odessa Beach, USA.'

Pagan started to walk. Klein, nimble in his open sandals, kept up with him. Now and then, like a nautical blessing given in a miserly way, a faint breeze would come up from the ocean and blow aside the humidity for a moment, then the swamplike dark would reassemble itself. Pagan paused in the open door of a clubhouse and saw a middle-aged man in a loose-fitting suit dance with a large woman who wore pink-framed glasses and had her yellow hair up in a beehive. The music was big-band stuff that might have been recorded in the early 1950s.

Klein said, 'The people that come to America from the Soviet Union tend to keep to themselves. It's almost a force of habit with them, Frank. They come from countries where everybody was a snoop. Even your next-door neighbour was a potential informer for the KGB. What I'm saying is you can't just walk around here asking questions. If some Balts have organised themselves into a fraternity with a sinister purpose, which is what you tell me, they're not going to be shouting it from the rooftops.'

Pagan moved out of the doorway. 'Rose Alexander mentioned an old shop.'

'Take your pick,' Klein remarked. He gestured with a hand, indicating three or four stores that hadn't been occupied in a long time. Some had windows protected by metal grilles, others padlocked doors, one had a faded To Rent sign with a realtor's name bleached by the sunlight. Pagan had a sense of decline here, of an age that had passed, a world receding. There must have been dignity here once, but it had been reduced to the kind of seediness he associated with decrepit English seaside resorts.

He walked a little way, trying to imagine Kiviranna coming along these same slats of wood. It would be dark, and Kiviranna's contact would be waiting for him in the shadows, perhaps inside one of the vacant shops, and Jake would move along the boardwalk in a stealthy manner, taking care that nobody saw him. Pagan conjured up these tiny pictures, almost as if he were forcing himself to see the ghost of Kiviranna appear before him now, leaving a spectral trail for him to follow. He tried to eavesdrop an old conversation. *The man's name is Romanenko. You have to kill him. This is the key to the place where you'll find the gun.*

Would Jake have asked why Romanenko had to be killed? Would he have bothered with a mere detail like that? Suppose he had? What would his contact have answered? *He's carrying something that can't reach its destination, Jake. That's all you need to know.* And Jake might have nodded his head, absorbed the information. But it probably hadn't happened that way at all. Jake's connection would only have to say that the world would be a better place if a treacherous Commie like Romanenko was taken out of it and that would be enough for Kiviranna. Pagan walked to the handrail, leaned there, gazed out over the dark water for a time, seeing the moon that sent a column of shivering silver across the sluggish tide. Then he turned back to the empty stores whose dark windows suggested rich mysteries.

'I suppose it wouldn't be difficult to track the owners of these places down,' he said to Klein.

Klein guessed it would be a matter of public record. It would take maybe a phone call or two, a little legwork. Pagan wanted to know how quickly this could be accomplished and Klein, wondering at the Englishman's dedication, his apparent immunity to jet-lag, figured it might be done first thing in the morning when people with regular jobs were at their desks. There was a hint of sarcasm in Klein's speech, nothing objectionable, enough to make Pagan smile to himself.

He continued to stare at the windows. Some had faded signs inscribed on glass, old lettering barely legible in the thin light from the lamps that burned along the boardwalk. *Roo beers. H t dogs. C t on candy* – like half-finished answers in an elaborate crossword puzzle, or words in an alphabet designed to be read only by initiates. Frank Pagan, feeling fatigue creep through him at last, glanced once more at the moon, thought about Kristina Vaska – in whose half of the world this moon would already be fading – then he asked Klein to drive him to his hotel.

They walked back to the place where Klein had parked the Dodge. Once again, either on account of fatigue or darkness, neither man noticed the car that travelled behind them all the way back to Manhattan. It was not this time the pea-green Buick, which had been replaced by a navy blue 1983 Ford Escort, a car unremarkable in every way, and just as anonymous as its predecessor. The pea-green Buick had gone in another direction, back to the apartment building in which Rose Alexander lived.

London

The moon that had taken Frank Pagan's attention had disappeared completely from the sky when Kristina Vaska woke in her hotel in Kensington. She rose at once, went inside the small bathroom, splashed cold water across her face, brushed her teeth. She dressed, packed her suitcase, then she sat for a time on the edge of the narrow bed. She had three hours until her plane left Heathrow. She checked her ticket to be absolutely sure, then put it back in her wallet. She remained motionless on the bed. A morning newspaper had been shoved under the door of her room, one of the hotel's little courtesies, but she couldn't bring herself to pick it up. From where she sat she could read the headline, or at least that half of it which hadn't been folded.

TWO POLICEMEN SHOT IN

That was all she could make out. She turned her face away.

Those men were dead because Frank Pagan had asked them to protect her. It was a world of blood in which men kept dying.

She found it an unbearable thought to get around, an obstacle in the dead centre of her brain. She got up, covered her face with her hands in such a way that an observer might have imagined her to be weeping – but she wasn't, even if she felt like it. She picked up the phone on the bedside table, dialled the hotel operator, asked to be connected with Mrs Evi Vaska at a number in upstate New York. While she waited Kristina imagined the antique phone in her mother's tiny downstairs living-room, the room she called the parlour, she pictured Evi Vaska in her white makeup moving through the small boxlike rooms and down the crooked stairs of the old house, past the shelves of fragile china figures, all the glass reindeer, the crystal ducks, the porcelain gnomes and elves that crowded the little house and that always seemed to be growing in number, as if they bred in the dark. Kristina imagined she heard the lacy gown Evi always wore whispering on the steps as she moved. From her house in the foothills of the Adirondacks, Evi Vaska wrote impassioned letters to Congressmen and Senators and British Members of Parliament concerning Norbert Vaska's incarceration, conducting a relentless campaign she thought would win her husband's freedom.

Relentless, Kristina thought. And doomed.

'Hello?' Evi Vaska's voice was distant.

For a second Kristina was tempted to hang up without saying anything. She hesitated. 'Mother.'

'Kristina!' Evi Vaska's voice became breathlessly excited. 'Are you still in England?'

'Yes,' Kristina said. She pictured the house, the hundreds of miniature figures that rendered the place even more claustrophobic than it was, with its narrow passageways and cramped staircase and low ceilings. Even the garden, a wild green riot, pressed in upon the house as if to isolate it before finally consuming it. Kristina had the thought that the house and its garden were like her mother's mind, a place of lifeless figures and disarray.

'Is there news, Kristina?'

'We'll talk when I come home, mother. I'll drive up to see you and we'll sit down together and we'll talk.'

Kristina pictured her mother's flour-coloured face, the black eye makeup, the deep red lipstick, the dyed yellow hair that lay upon her shoulders like the broken strings of a harpsichord. 'In other words there's nothing, is that what you're saying, Kristina?'

'That's not what I'm saying, mother. Look, I'm flying back today. At the weekend I'll drive up to you. I'll come up to the Adirondacks.' She tried to keep impatience and exasperation out of her voice, but she wished she hadn't called in the first place. She sighed. She didn't have the heart for this talk. She didn't have the heart for any of it.

'You didn't see Aleksis? Is that what you're trying to tell me, Kristina? So there's no news of your father? Is this what you're keeping from me?'

Kristina Vaska put the receiver down. She walked to the window, pressed her forehead upon the glass, looked down at the street below. She felt as if she were a victim suddenly, a casualty of history, wounded by forces from the past – forces that had killed some people and driven others, like Evi Vaska who sat in a world of her own creation, totally out of her mind. And her eyes watered, but she didn't weep, no matter how tight the constriction at the back of her throat or the ache around her heart. She was beyond tears. She needed dignity, which came through retribution rather than grief.

14

Virginia Beach

There were days when Galbraith needed to get out of the house in Fredericksburg, when he suffered from a rarified form of cabin-fever and had to step away from the consoles and the never-ending flow of data. A man might choke to death on so many tiny bones of information. Sometimes he sat in the back of his chauffeured car and was driven to Cape Hatteras or Williamsburg or Richmond. On this early Tuesday morning he chose to go to Virginia Beach, city of soothsayers and palmists, tea-leaf readers and cosmic masseurs, hitch-hiking gurus and astral travellers, faith healers and tarot interpreters and astrologers and other fools. It was a city Galbraith found refreshingly silly, all the more so since it took its 'metaphysics' with grave seriousness. On his last visit here Galbraith had had his chart done by a fey astrologer – just for the hell of it – who told him that the heavenly portents were far from pleasing. Galbraith listened to talk about one's moon being in Venus, and how an absence of earth signs indicated a certain abstract turn of mind, utter nonsense over which he nodded his head grimly. He declined the opportunity to have his past lives revealed for the further paltry sum of twenty bucks. One incarnation, in Galbraith's mind, was more than enough. Anything more was arguably masochistic.

He surveyed the ocean from the back of the Daimler, or at least those stretches of it one might spot between high-rise hotels. It was a sunny morning and the sea was calm, and the yachts that floated out towards the Chesapeake Bay did so with slack sails. Galbraith observed the streets, the summer festivities, people strolling through sunshine, men and women in bermuda shorts, kids in funny hats, the kerbs clogged with Winnebagos from faraway states. The great American vacation, he thought. He wouldn't have minded a vacation himself. He hadn't taken one in fourteen years, unless one considered a trip four years ago to Monaco but that had really been business. And this quick jaunt to Virginia Beach, which had the superficial appearance of a leisurely drive, was still connected to work. Nothing Galbraith did was ever done without purpose. Aimless was not in his vocabulary.

The chauffeur, a black man called Lombardy, turned the big car away from the strip and through streets that quickly became dense with trees. Graceful willows hung over narrow inlets of water. There were expensive homes here, many of them refurbished Victorian affairs filled with brass and stained glass and heavy with a ponderous sense of the past lovingly restored. Galbraith watched the Daimler plunge down a lane and listened to branches scratch the windows. Lombardy parked the car outside a house which was so well-camouflaged by trees that it couldn't be seen from the road. The black man opened the door and Galbraith slid out of the back seat, puffing as he waddled towards the front of the house.

Galbraith pushed a screen-door, entered a yellow entrance room which led along a yellow hallway to rooms the colour of daffodils. He felt like a man plummeted without warning into a strange monochromatic world, a place of yellow sofas and chairs, yellow lampshades, yellow rugs, a house in which even the mirrors had a faint yellow tint. The effect, he decided, was to make one feel rather jaundiced.

'I liked it better when it was red,' Galbraith said.

The small man who appeared at the foot of the stairs wore a saffron kimono. 'Red is rage,' he said. His black hair, heavily greased, had been flattened on either side of the centre parting.

'And yellow's mellow, I daresay,' Galbraith remarked.

'Yellow is springtime and rebirth, Galbraith. Yellow is the colour of pure thought.'

'Also yellowjack fever and cowardice.'

The man inclined his head. He had some slight oriental lineage that showed in the high cheekbones and the facial colouring. He had exceptionally long fingers.

'Colour and harmony, Galbraith. In your hurried world, you don't take the time to plan your environment. You eat fast and hump fast and read fast and think fast. What an ungodly way to live. The gospel according to Ronald MacDonald.'

'When I want to hear about taking time to sniff the goddam flowers, Charlie, I'll read Thoreau. Meantime, I've got other things on my mind.' Galbraith wandered to the window and released a blind, which sprung up quickly, altering the monotonous light in the room. 'Do you mind?'

'What if I did, Galbraith?'

'I'd ignore you anyhow.' Galbraith wandered to a sofa and lay down on his face, closing his eyes. 'It hurts here and here,' and he pointed to a couple of places at the base of his spine. Charlie tugged Galbraith's shirt out of his pants and probed the spots. Charlie, who had built an expensive clientele among the richly gullible, and employed a hodge-podge of massage techniques together with some oriental mumbo-jumbo, always managed to fix Galbraith for a couple of months or so.

'You're too fat,' Charlie said. 'No wonder you hurt.'

'I didn't drive down here to be abused, Charlie. Mend me. Spare me bullshit about the Seventh Temple of Pleasure and the Six Points of the Dragon and the Jade Doorway to Joy and all that other piffle you fool people with, just fix me.'

Charlie pressed his fingertips into the base of Galbraith's spine and the fat man moaned. 'You're carrying around an extra person, Galbraith. For that you need two hearts. Do you have two hearts, fat man?'

Galbraith closed his eyes and felt little waves of relaxation spread upward the length of his spine and then ripple through his buttocks as Charlie went to work with his sorcerer's fingers. For a while Galbraith was able to forget his usual worries, drifting into a kind of hypnotic state. There were times in his life when he needed a retreat from the vast panorama of detail that was his to oversee, an escape from the insidious pressures of his world, the network of responsibilities that each year seemed to grow more and more elaborate. Power, he realised, was an ornate construction, delicate membranes imposed one upon another, creating strata that sometimes perplexed him, sometimes made him nervous. He'd realised in recent years that he couldn't carry the weight of his job alone. He had to rely on other people. There was no escape from this fact. The best you could do was make sure you didn't delegate important matters to total idiots. If Galbraith had one dominant fear it was the idea that a dark deed would be traced back to his own outfit, even to his own office, and that some form of public exposure would follow. Sweet Jesus – there were fresh-faced youngsters in Congress who fancied themselves investigative officers of the people, *ombudsmen* for the commonfolk, and they were like hounds out of hell if they had the smell of any illicit expenditure of the taxpayer's money, the more so if it were used in a covert manner.

He came suddenly alert when Charlie said, 'Your associate is here, Galbraith. I'll leave you now.'

Charlie draped an ochre towel across the exposed lower part of Galbraith's body before he left the room. Galbraith twisted his face to see Gary Iverson looking uncomfortable in the middle of the floor. Galbraith had almost managed to forget that he'd arranged to meet Iverson here.

'Pull up a pew, Gary,' Galbraith said. If he had more men like Iverson – reliable, loyal, patriotic, devious – he might eat less and sleep more. A svelte, well-rested Galbraith – it was quite a thought.

Iverson dragged a wingbacked chair close to the sofa where the fat man lay. He'd come directly from New York, travelling by helicopter to Norfolk and from Norfolk by car. It seemed to Iverson that he spent most of his life in motion, like a pinball in Galbraith's private machine, banging between Fredericksburg and DC and New Jersey and Manhattan and Norfolk.

'Ever had one of Charlie's specials?' Galbraith asked.

Iverson shook his head.

'Remind me to give you one for Christmas.' Galbraith rolled over on his back. 'He issues gift certificates good for one bath and a rub-down. Highly recommended, Gary. Besides, this is probably the most discreet place I know. Charlie appreciates how much some people treasure privacy.'

Iverson looked round the room. Yellow wasn't his colour. He gazed at the square of window where the blind had been released. He was very glad to see greenery brush against the pane. He said, 'Early this morning Frank Pagan and his sidekick Max Klein made inquiries concerning certain vacant properties on the boardwalk at Brighton Beach.'

'Did they now? Whatever for?' Galbraith sat upright. He had the feeling he wasn't going to like anything he heard from Gary.

Iverson said, 'They went to the boardwalk last night after interviewing Rose Alexander.'

'Ah, yes, Kiviranna's unwilling friend. I recall her name from your report. And she sent them scurrying off to Brighton Beach?'

Iverson nodded. Galbraith closed his eyes a moment. He had times in which he could literally see trouble as one might witness thunderheads gathering on a distant hill. There were connections here that made him very unhappy indeed.

'Do we know what she told them, Gary?'

'An inquiry was made, sir.'

Galbraith frowned. Inquiry was a word that could conceal a multitude of sins. 'I trust this inquiry was peaceful?'

'The woman was cooperative. She had nothing to hide. She told us exactly what she'd told Pagan. Shortly before he left for London, Jake Kiviranna had an appointment with somebody on the boardwalk – in one of the old shops.'

'Ye gods,' the fat man said. 'You don't suppose there's coincidence here, do you?' Galbraith asked this question with heavy sarcasm. He thought of coincidence the way an atheist might think of God. Acceptable if you were naive enough to have faith, preposterous if you gave it only a moment's consideration. He stood up, adjusting his pants, discarding the towel. 'You understand where this is leading, don't you, Gary?'

Iverson nodded. He had a quick eye for complexity. Galbraith raised a finger in the air and said, 'Jake goes to an old shop on the boardwalk. Carl Sundbach just happens to own such an establishment. Carl Sundbach also happens to know that Romanenko is due to arrive in Edinburgh.' Galbraith paused, then paced the room, speaking very slowly. 'Sundbach tells Kiviranna . . . go to Edinburgh . . . shoot Romanenko . . . '

'Why though?'

'Why indeed? Why participate at considerable expense in the Brotherhood only to make an attempt to scotch the entire goddam operation by using a hired gun? Do you see any sense in that?'

Both men were silent for a time. Galbraith said, 'We know Sundbach wasn't happy with the plan. Good Christ, he walked out on it. It's all there on the tape of that last meeting in Glen Cove. But was he so unhappy with it that he decided he'd ruin the goddam thing himself if he could? And then when he realised he couldn't halt the Kiss express, no matter what, he walked away . . . '

'A change of heart,' Iverson said.

'Fear maybe. An old man's terror. Old age and terror – there's a combination made in hell. And utterly unpredictable.' Galbraith looked thoughtful for a while. 'What worries me, you see, is this fellow Pagan getting too close to the flame of the candle. I don't want him singed, Gary, unless it's essential. And if it's essential, I don't want us to be involved. Not even remotely.'

In an unhappy voice Iverson said, 'It may very well be essential, sir.'

'Meaning?'

'I've heard from London.'

'And?'

Iverson gathered his thoughts, parading them in an orderly manner in his mind as if they were foot soldiers with a tendency to be unruly. He noticed a pitcher of iced water, rose, poured himself a glass, returned to his chair. 'It seems that Frank Pagan has been travelling in some interesting company, sir. The daughter of a former member of the Brotherhood, a man who vanished into Siberia some years ago, has become a companion of Pagan's. The assumption is that this young lady, Kristina Vaska by name, has provided Pagan with some information about the Brotherhood. We're not sure what. But Pagan may be able to come to certain conclusions. He knows something about the Brotherhood, he's about six inches away from Sundbach – it's a situation fraught with danger.'

Galbraith loved the *fraught*. He adored the way Iverson spoke in general, with a kind of polite precision. But he worried now over Frank Pagan who was meant to remain on the safer fringes of things and stay well clear of the centre. It really was too bad. He said, 'So Viktor Epishev has been running amok over there in an attempt to silence this potential menace.' He pulled at his lower lip and looked for all the world like a petulant choirboy who has just been told that his voice is about to break and his singing career is kaput.

'Apparently,' Iverson replied. 'His initial objective was to make sure that nothing inhibited the scheme, that Romanenko's message wasn't deciphered – '

'*Deciphered?*'

'It seems Greshko told Epishev the message might contain a code of some kind, which in the wrong hands – '

Galbraith interrupted, his jowls quivering with sudden anger and his eyes popping. He was rarely touched by rage but when it happened it was an awesome sight. Iverson was hypnotised by the fat man's volcanic display of temper.

'*Classic Greshko*! No matter what you tell that old fucker, no matter how goddam hard you try to ram something into his head, he runs it through that paranoid brain of his and comes up with something off the goddam wall. He was *told* there wasn't a code. I told him that *personally.* I told him there was nothing hidden in that message, nothing secretive, nothing that needed to be analysed. It's a simple bloody message, I said, and it couldn't mean a damn thing to anyone outside the Brotherhood. But oh no, *oh no*! – that wasn't good enough for *him*. Classic goddam Greshko! Trust nobody, especially your friends, especially your American friends! Always look at the world through the prism of suspicion. Always think the next fellow is trying to put one over on you. He probably thought I was trying to slip a nuclear weapon past him, for Christ's sake! Or drop some fucking bombs on his beloved railroad tracks! Sweet Jesus!' Galbraith shook his head. 'The truth of the matter is he didn't need to send Epishev to London at all. He didn't need a man running around over there doing that kind of damage. *All he had to do, Gary, was to leave everything alone*. And that's the one thing he's never been able to do in his entire goddam life. He's never been able to leave anything alone! And that includes White Light!'

Both men were quiet for a few moments. Galbraith walked to the corner of the room where an old-fashioned upright piano was located. It had been lacquered in high-gloss yellow and was almost painful to behold. He sat down and thumped out the first few bars of *St James Infirmary Blues*. He broke off and, feeling a little less tense now, looked at the keys pensively. He was thinking of that summer in Monaco in 1984, the leisurely mornings spent reading on the beach, the splendid dinners at Les Lucioles in Roquebrune or La Couletta in Eze-Village, the magnificent room he had at the Hotel de Paris on the Place du Casino, the white sunlight on a blue ocean. He was remembering evenings in the Grand Casino, walking through the verdant gardens or strolling the gambling rooms, casually playing roulette here, blackjack there, *chemin-de-fer* – rare moments for Galbraith, who hardly ever left anything to pure chance.

He dropped his hands from the keyboard, thinking of how Vladimir Greshko, travelling as incognito as incognito can get, hadn't appeared in Monaco until the third day. Their encounters had all taken place indoors at night – in dark little bars, hotel rooms, secluded restaurants. Their talks at first had been guarded. After all, they had little in common on any superficial level. What could Galbraith, with his Ivy League sophistication and wealthy background, share with the Chairman of the KGB, a rough-edged peasant more cunning than intelligent? The only novel Greshko had ever read, for example, was *Crime and Punishment*. Galbraith on the other hand was a Henry James aficionado. He loved the convoluted sentences and the cultivated world James described. What could he possibly feel for a yarn in which the central event was the sordid murder of a moneylender by a broodingly unsympathetic student? All that Russian gloom, dear Christ!

The only true bond between them was a world view, a global vision which, although different in some respects, nevertheless consisted of many common elements – a well-defined balance of power between the two supernations, an intermittent détente characterised by periods of warm progress and years of arctic chill, a status quo that, precisely because it achieved nothing real other than to promote national anxieties and keep the arms manufacturers of the world on cheerful terms with their shareholders and bankers, was more acceptable than any of the proposed changes both men knew were coming, and both loathed. And their hatred of change, of disruption, of any erosion in their spheres of influence, glued them together with a fastness unusual between men of such different backgrounds.

It wasn't exactly an easy camaraderie. It had its origins in a meeting concerning international terrorism that took place in Geneva in the fall of 1983, when it had seemed to Galbraith that Vladimir Greshko was sending invisible signals across the conference room. An enigmatic note was slipped under a hotel door, a couple of terse phone calls were made in the ensuing months, and the eventual outcome was the secret meeting in Monte Carlo.

Greshko had said *I am on the way out, Galbraith. Now we will have a world where our much-*

admired new General Secretary will alter the fabric of things. He wants to create a Russia that neither you nor I will recognise. One we will not understand at all. A dangerous place for me, and for you, Galbraith . . . because you will not know where America stands when Russia changes. And I will not know. And all the people you have become so used to dealing with over the years will be sent to the glue factories like tired old horses. You replace old horses with hardworking young ones, Galbraith. With colts and stallions who have new feeding habits. Think about it . . .

And Galbraith did think about it, and he cared very little for any of his thoughts. Under the sun of Monte Carlo, both men discussed what might be done to preserve a world both had become accustomed to, a world they considered safe and manageable. Endless talk, demanding and exhausting, two days without sleep, periods of high excitement followed by dismay, too much coffee, too much vodka. What they needed was a plan, something they could remain aloof from and yet somehow take part in, what they needed was a scheme they hadn't themselves designed but one they'd inherited, and could shape to their own ends. Something which, if it happened to go wrong, couldn't possibly be laid on their respective doorsteps. It was two more years before such a situation presented itself in the form of an old friendship between Gary Iverson and Andres Kiss.

And still there existed a mutual lack of trust between Galbraith and Greshko, a situation that would diminish with the years but never entirely dissolve because Vladimir Greshko was programmed never to trust a fat capitalist. Galbraith brought his fingers down on the keys, creating a melancholic minor chord that echoed for a while through the room. With just a little more trust, Greshko might never have sent his man Epishev to London. The old fart must have imagined something was being kept from him, that the devious Americans were up to their usual nefarious nonsense, that the message contained coded details which were to be denied him, and that in the end the Americans wanted to throw a little sand in an old man's eyes. And nobody – *nobody!* – was allowed to make a fool of General Vladimir Greshko.

Galbraith ran off a few more chords, then he played the chorus of *Nobody Knows You When You're Down and Out*. He turned to Iverson. 'Epishev is still in London?'

'Yes,' Iverson replied.

Galbraith looked contemplative. 'I'm thinking aloud, you understand. But he might be useful.'

'Useful, sir?'

'He wants Pagan, doesn't he?'

'Yes.'

'And Pagan's here, about to make a nuisance of himself . . . '

Gary Iverson nodded his head slowly.

'And Epishev's in London,' the fat man said quietly. 'Not any great distance as the crow flies.'

Glen Cove, Long Island

Mikhail Kiss lay on a deck chair in his sunlit garden. He wore dark glasses and a cotton shirt and khaki shorts that revealed the thick silvery hair covering his muscular legs. He glanced at his watch. It was just after eleven a.m. In eleven hours from now, Andres was going to step on board a Scandinavian Airlines flight from Kennedy. Eleven short hours. Kiss felt nervous suddenly.

He sat upright, looked back at the house, saw the shape of young Andres inside the glass-walled room – he was so damned cool, so cold, you might think the trip that night was no more than a casual tourist affair.

For his own part, Mikhail Kiss couldn't silence his nerves. Maybe it had something to do with the dream, the awful dream that had come to him in the darkness and filled him with dread. In this dream he'd been sitting in a restaurant with Carl Sundbach and Aleksis Romanenko, a very strange place with neither menu nor cutlery, a still room where no waiter ever came to serve. The three men had sat in a silence broken only by a thin music coming from a distance, the unrecognisable music that existed only in dreams, neither melodic nor familiar but shatteringly atonal. And then, from nowhere, a shadow had fallen across the table – but Mikhail Kiss hadn't raised his head to look at the newcomer, at least not immediately.

He got up from the deck chair and he thought *Dreams mean nothing. Dreams are not the harbingers of future happenings.* He walked towards the house, stepped inside the glass-walled room, saw Andres skim through the pages of a news magazine. Mikhail Kiss filled a glass with water and drank quickly. Then he sat down, taking off his dark glasses.

'How are you?' he asked.

'How should I be?'

The older man shrugged. 'A big night ahead of you, I thought . . . '

'It's just another night.' Andres kept flicking pages.

Just another night. Mikhail Kiss thought how difficult his nephew had been ever since Carl had walked out on Sunday, how distant and aloof, locked inside his own head. *It's not just another night for me, Andres. I've lived a long time with this idea. I've breathed it. I've slept with it and nursed it. I've travelled thousands of miles to make it real. Even when it looked impossible, I still kept going.* He wanted to say these things to Andres, but he couldn't form the words in any way that would give them the hard conviction he felt in his heart.

Andres Kiss smiled, seeing the odd expression on his uncle's face and thinking how old men could be like little kids. He patted the back of Mikhail's hand. 'There's nothing to worry about, Mikhail,' he said. 'Everything will go according to plan.' And he thought: *Especially now. Now that he had the idea.*

Mikhail Kiss wondered about the certainty in his nephew's voice. The confidence. Andres had always had that supreme self-assurance that almost seemed at times to be indifference, as if he thought of himself as specially blessed, a magical being, a beautiful young man protected by the gods. Experience hadn't caused him any suffering. What he knew of pain and sorrow he'd learned second hand. Kiss searched the smooth face, the eyes, the perfect mouth, for some sign of uncertainty, some little touch of concern, a feeling, anything – fruitless. Andres Kiss gave nothing away. Mikhail Kiss realised that his nephew scared him sometimes.

Andres closed the magazine and laid it down. The idea had come to him during the conversation with Iverson in Trenton. It had begun like a vapour drifting slowly at the back of his brain, and then it had taken shape and become hard as it floated into the light, and then he'd known with certainty what he had to do with Carl Sundbach. Besides, hadn't Iverson practically *instructed* him to do the thing? Hadn't Gary Iverson done everything but *spell the goddam business out*? To protect himself, to protect his own position, to cover his ass, Iverson obviously couldn't come right out and say *Do it, Andres.* But he'd left Kiss in absolutely no doubt. *Sundbach's a menace, therefore. . .*

Therefore. It was obvious. The young man stood up and looked at his uncle a moment before he said, 'I have to go out for a while.'

Mikhail Kiss heard something in the young man's voice, only he wasn't sure what. A false note, a distortion. 'Out? *Now*?'

Andres Kiss nodded. 'I'll be back in plenty of time for you to take me to JFK. Don't worry.'

Mikhail stood up. 'You shouldn't go anywhere. Not today. You should stay here. You should be relaxing.'

Andres turned away, and Mikhail went after him, following him out of the sun-room and into the hallway. 'I don't see what's so important you have to go out.'

Andres didn't reply. He walked towards the front door.

'What is so damned important you have to go anywhere, especially today, for God's sake?'

Andres opened the door, turned to look at his uncle. 'I'll be back, Mikhail.'

Mikhail Kiss watched the door close, then heard Andres's car in the driveway. For a long time after the sound of the automobile faded, Kiss stood motionless in the hallway. Then he went back to the sun-room, sat down, lit a cigarette, closed his eyes. He felt a strange little nerve, a cord, flutter in his throat.

And there was the dream again. There was the shadow on white linen, the eerie music. He saw himself raise his head up, saw himself look into the eyes of the fourth man, the one who approached the table, the one who stood over the other three and said nothing. Distanced by the dream, Kiss rose and extended his arm, his hand held out to shake that of the fourth man – who had said nothing and done nothing, except to offer a small, spectral smile.

That smile. That face.

Why had Norbert Vaska come back after all these years to make Mikhail Kiss shudder in the warm morning light?

Manhattan

Of the four properties vacant on the Brighton Beach boardwalk, two belonged to a massive mortgage company in New Jersey, one to a pair of brothers who lived in a retirement home in Manhassett, and the last to a company called Sundbach Incorporated, with corporate offices given as an address in lower Manhattan. On the basis of geographical convenience, Frank Pagan decided that the address in Manhattan was the first one to check, then the retirement home in Manhassett, and finally, if need be, the mortgage company in New Jersey. He had Klein drive him from the Warwick down through the midday sunshine of Manhattan. It was one of those gorgeous late summer days that bless the city all too infrequently, the air marvellously clear, a blustery breeze blowing through the canyons, no humidity, blue skies, skittish little clouds more suggestive of spring than fall.

The address in lower Manhattan turned out to be a rundown brownstone carved into three or four apartments. An assortment of bells were arranged at the side of the door, but the names written on small cards were faded. Pagan squinted at them, locating one that had the name Carl Sundbach on it in very faded blue ink. He glanced at Klein, who said that as corporate edifices went this one was more than a little inauspicious, then pressed the button. After a while the face of a man appeared behind the glass panel set in the door. He stared at Pagan and Klein without opening the door.

'Who is it? What do you want?'

Pagan took out his credentials and pressed them to the window and the old fellow, putting on spectacles, stepped forward to look. Klein did the same thing with his NYPD badge, but still the old guy didn't open the door.

'What do you want with me?'

'Just a couple of questions,' Pagan said.

'Go ahead. Ask!'

Pagan, exasperated by having to shout through a closed door, said, 'It's going to be a whole lot easier if you open up and let us come inside.'

Carl Sundbach stared at the two cops, whose appearance bewildered him, especially the one with the Scotland Yard ID. He was inclined to panic a little, because if somebody had come all the way from London then it had to be connected with Kiviranna. What else? Now he had the thought that the man who'd been following him in the streets and markets was also a cop. For one dark moment, Sundbach had an urge to throw the damn door open and spill the whole story, keeping nothing back. But he couldn't do that, not even if he lived through a thousand years of torture.

Pagan pressed his face against the pane. 'A few questions, that's all. We'll take five minutes of your time at the most.'

Sundbach wondered if the failure to open the door was going to be construed as suspicious, if the most reasonable course of action was to admit this pair of jokers, remain extremely cool with them, and send them away satisfied. Cups of tea, perhaps, some quiet hospitality. This was the behaviour of a man with nothing to hide. Lurking behind a locked door, on the other hand, was probably a strategic mistake.

'Okay. Five minutes,' and he opened the door, turning towards the stairs even as the cops entered. 'This way,' he said, leading them up into the gloom. He took a key out of his pocket, opened the door to his apartment, and showed the policemen inside, smiling now and bobbing around them. 'You fellows drink on the job? I got some nice Yugoslavian wine somewhere.'

Both Pagan and Klein declined. Pagan looked around the apartment, absorbing the sheer quantity of items here, the overstuffed furniture, the heavy curtains, the shelves of books, the scores of old prints that covered everything save for what must have been Sundbach's special wall, reserved for photographs of the old fellow in the company of celebrities. It was a suffocating apartment, overloaded with Sundbach's possessions, many of which must have had nostalgic significance for him. Pagan had the strong feeling of having stepped into another era – back, back to the turn of the century, when people lived around their possessions in rooms where you couldn't breathe and where you just knew a tubercular child lay white and still in a shuttered attic bedroom. There was dust here, and the dampness of old paper, a sense of an unindexed life collected and stored in these rooms.

Carl Sundbach took the stopper from a fine old decanter and poured himself a glass of dark red wine. The glass, he said in a thick accent, had once belonged to the last Tsar's uncle, General Alexei Alexandrovich. He was making conversational noises. Pagan wandered to the bookshelves, glancing at titles, most of them in foreign languages. *L'Entente Baltique. Die Nationalen Minderheiten Estlands.* And pamphlets, scores of them, stacked in bundles, held by string or elastic and stuffed with sheets of notes. They were mainly in languages Pagan couldn't identify. He stepped away from the shelves and gazed at various prints on the walls even as Sundbach was proudly explaining some of his celebrity photographs to an interested Klein.

'This was taken when Bobby came through here on his campaign. A young man, much vigour. I had raised money for him, you understand. You see where he signed the picture? Look there. To my friend Carl, it says. Now this one over here, taken with Perry Como, that came about when he opened the wing of a hospital in Brooklyn. I give a little to charity now and then. America's been good to me.'

Pagan found himself looking at a copy of an engraving made by a certain Merian in 1652. It depicted a walled city with steeples and according to the brass plate attached to the frame the city was Tallinn. There were others, views of castles, tall ships in a harbour, churches, all carefully framed and labelled, all pictures of old Estonia. *Bingo*, Pagan thought. He had an equation, a connection between Carl and Jake Kiviranna, an ethnic bond. But it was too easy, too thin. Unless anybody could prove beyond doubt that Sundbach had sent Jake overseas on a mission of murder, unless there was solid evidence of the kind so loved by prosecutors and judges, Carl could fly the Estonian flag from his window day and night and it wouldn't mean a damned thing. It certainly wouldn't connect him to a murder in Edinburgh.

Carl poured himself a second glass of red wine. The New York cop was simple to deal with. He was the kind of American impressed by celebrity. He probably read *People* magazine. The tall *inglane* on the other hand worried Sundbach because he prowled, taking everything in with a quiet, hooded look. And those grey eyes were cold and unreadable. Warmed by the wine, Sundbach felt a flood of confidence. Let them ask their questions and be on their way. He had nothing to hide. He sat down at his desk.

Pagan asked, 'What exactly is Sundbach Enterprises?'

Carl Sundbach replied, 'A few hotels, a couple of small-town newspapers, a little real estate here and there.'

'And you operate this yourself?'

Sundbach smiled. 'Nowadays, no. Sundbach Enterprises is part of a big corporation called Van Meer Industries, which is part of something else. IBM for all I know! It's too complicated for me. I got nothing to do with it other than some financial interest.'

'You own an old shop on the boardwalk,' Pagan said. 'Is that yours personally or part of this big corporation?'

Sundbach sipped his wine. The old shop, he thought. They knew about it. So what? It wasn't exactly a secret. 'That I keep as my own,' he said.

'Any reason?'

Sundbach stood up and, a little flushed, pointed to a framed dollar bill that hung above his desk. 'This, my friend. Look carefully. The first dollar I ever made in my own business in this country and I made it on the boardwalk. So I keep the shop. It's sentimental. Do you understand me?'

Pagan nodded. 'When did you come to America?'

'Early 1950s,' Sundbach said.

'Have you kept up an interest in the politics of the old country?' Pagan asked.

'The old country?'

'Estonia,' and Pagan waved a hand at the prints.

'Pardon me, I don't think there's any such place. There used to be, and it was a wonderful country, but now it's called the Estonian Soviet Socialist Republic and soon you won't even see that much on a goddamned map.' Sundbach smiled sadly at the Englishman. 'You said you had questions, Mr Pagan. Maybe you could come to the point?'

Pagan turned to look at the old man. Shoot from the hip, Frank. 'Do you know a man called Jacob Kiviranna?'

Sundbach, whose heart skipped only a little, looked puzzled. 'No, I don't.'

'Think,' Pagan said.

'What's to think?' Sundbach asked.

'Somebody saw you with Kiviranna on the boardwalk.'

Sundbach shook his head. He stared at the *inglane*. This was all bluff, it had to be. Even if somebody had seen him with Kiviranna, what did that prove? 'I don't know the man. Your information's wrong.'

Pagan came a little closer to the old man. He smelled the wine on Sundbach's breath. 'Kiviranna shot a man named Aleksis Romanenko.'

Sundbach turned over the palms of his hands. There was a forced smile on his face. What he wondered was how any kind of connection had been made – had that *perse*

Kiviranna talked? But what could Jake have said anyhow? Sundbach had always taken the greatest care to conceal his identity from crazy Jake, who wasn't a man who asked too many questions anyhow. They'd held their very first meeting at the shop on the boardwalk and Sundbach had made a great pretence at forcing entry, as if he wanted to show Jake Kiviranna that he was beyond the law, he broke into abandoned shops, he had a bandit's disregard for other people's property. He was a goddam anarchist, the kind of guy Jake could trust without losing any sleep.

Carl Sundbach cleared his throat. 'Aleksis who? You got any more names to throw at me?'

'Just those two,' Pagan said.

Carl Sundbach made his chair swivel as he reached for his wine. 'I like to help policemen, Mr Pagan. I think they do a great job without much thanks, you understand. But you've given me nothing except puzzlement. I don't know the men you mention. And a shooting – what would I know about a thing like that? I'm a retired businessman, not a gangster.'

Pagan said nothing for a time. He studied Sundbach's face in silence. The old man was pouring a third glass of wine in a composed fashion. Pagan wandered round the room, glanced through open doors, saw a bedroom with a vast four-poster bed, an enormous bathroom with an antique tub, a kitchen with an old-fashioned black stove. There was the scent of camphor from somewhere. Pagan imagined closets packed with clothes and mothballs.

Sundbach, he realised, could maintain his innocence until the sun froze over. Perhaps he was telling the truth anyhow, perhaps he knew nothing about the killing in Edinburgh, but Pagan had one of those niggling little instincts that told him otherwise. He stopped moving, leaned against the wall, folded his arms. *It's all here, Frank. Everything you're looking for is in this room. Crack the bastard open.*

'Talk to me about the Brotherhood, Carl,' he said.

The Brotherhood. How did the English policeman know about the *vendlus?* How had he stumbled into that one? Sundbach, the essence of serenity, sipped his wine. 'The what?'

'Tell me why you wanted to wreck the Brotherhood's plan, Carl. Why did you send Jake to Edinburgh to murder Romanenko? Are you KGB? Is that it? Did you get an order from Russia? Or straight from the Soviet Mission in New York?'

Sundbach, as if astonished, blew a fine spray of wine through his teeth and laughed. He looked at Klein in the manner of a man appealing to reason. 'Is your English friend here on a day-release programme from some kind of institution? Does he have to check back in at six o'clock every night?'

Pagan stepped quickly towards the desk, looming over the figure of Sundbach, who was still seated. 'Does the KGB tell you what it needs, Carl? Does it tell you what hoop to jump through – the hoop in this case being the murder of Romanenko? You get poor Jake Kiviranna to do the job because you know there's something loose in his attic, therefore he's a loony, exactly the kind of fellow to pull a political assassination. You don't get any blood on your hands that way. Keep them nice and clean, don't you, Carl?'

Sundbach had an urge to scream at the *inglane* and to tell him how very wrong he was, how his conclusion might be correct but his reasoning was all bent out of shape – but that would have meant telling the truth about the Brotherhood and he wasn't going to do that. The trick was to let the moment pass, let this man's accusations fade into silence, and stay very calm.

'You through, Mr Pagan?'

'I'm through,' Pagan said.

'I lost my two brothers between 1945 and 1949,' Sundbach said. The anger he felt made it difficult to talk. 'The KGB killed them. And you accuse me of working *for* the KGB. I don't want to say any more to you. I don't want you in my house. Go. Go now.'

Pagan walked towards the door. He longed for fresh air and sunlight and the breeze scampering along the streets. In this apartment it was hard to draw air into your lungs unless, like Sundbach, the air you breathed was from the past. He opened the door and stepped out on to the landing, and Klein followed.

Sundbach, decanter in one hand, glass in the other, stared across the room at both men. 'I would die before I worked for the KGB,' he said. 'That's the truth.'

Pagan drew the door shut and stood for a second on the gloomy landing before turning and going down into the street.

Pagan sat in the passenger seat of Klein's car, which was parked four or five doors from Carl's building. He stared across the street at the windows of Sundbach's apartment. Klein said, 'I think I heard one of the old guy's blood vessels pop. You backed the wrong horse there, Frank, when you said the magic letters KGB.'

Pagan rolled down his window, let his hand hang out of the car. He didn't question the genuineness of Sundbach's emotional reaction to the mention of the KGB. He said, 'I agree. But I've got a feeling he's lying about all the rest of it. He hired Kiviranna, arranged the trip, set everything up. The only thing I got wrong was the KGB connection.'

'If that's true, who's he working for?'

Pagan was silent a second, looking up at the apartment as if the curtained windows might be made to yield an answer. 'Maybe himself,' he said.

'And the motive?'

Pagan pressed his fingertips into his eyelids. 'Who knows? Maybe he just didn't agree with the Brotherhood's plan. Which tells us something definite – he knew all about it.'

'Which means he's either one of the Brotherhood, or he's got an inside source,' Klein said.

'Precisely.'

Klein undid his bow-tie, which collapsed and fell in two thin strands across the front of his chest. 'What now?'

'I think we let old Carl marinate for a while,' Pagan said. 'Then we'll go back over there and we'll put some real pressure on him.'

Max Klein, who wondered what Pagan meant by 'real pressure' but didn't want to ask, took a pipe from the glove compartment and lit it, filling the car with a richly-perfumed tobacco smoke. Pagan watched the street, noticing a gang of kids outside a corner grocery store, a couple of men passing a bottle back and forth, a TV repairman's van. A young man with blond hair that fell to his shoulders got out of a parked Jaguar on the corner and walked past the clutch of kids and the men drinking. In his white cotton jacket and pants – casual chic, obviously expensive – he had the appearance of somebody who'd made a wrong turning along the way. He looked as if he'd happened upon this drab street purely by chance, which was why Frank Pagan tracked him idly as he came along the pavement.

The man went directly to the building where Sundbach lived, climbed the steps, rang one of the doorbells, waited. Pagan saw Sundbach come to the door, open it, and the young man entered the building after exchanging a couple of words with Carl, who seemed reluctant to let him in. An intriguing pair – the old man in the shabby cardigan and the well-tailored visitor who had the looks of a fashion model. What could they have in common?

Pagan glanced at Klein, who had also seen the young man enter Sundbach's building.

'They make an unlikely couple,' Klein said. He took a small notebook from his pocket and wrote down the registration of the Jaguar. The notebook was stuffed with loose slips of paper, suggesting the enormous, if finally futile effort of an untidy man to impose order on his world.

Pagan settled back in his seat. 'Give it ten more minutes. Then we'll go back for the pipe you just happened to leave behind in Carl's apartment.'

'Gotcha,' Max Klein said brightly.

Andres Kiss drank a glass of the old man's horrible Yugoslavian wine. This apartment, which he'd visited only once before, was unsufferably cluttered. He put the wineglass on the table, then smiled across the room at Carl, who was sipping quietly. Although there was a sociable grin on the old man's face, he was puzzled, even troubled, by Kiss's presence.

'You go tonight,' Sundbach said. 'It's still the same?'

Andres Kiss looked at his glass and reminded himself to clean it before he left the apartment. 'The plan hasn't changed, Carl.'

Sundbach realised he was slightly drunk, that his reactions were coming to him through a series of filters, just like the daylight that fell first through muslin then damask at the window. His head was like the inside of the apartment, murky and overloaded.

'You go be a hero, Andres. Myself, I think there are other options.'

Andres Kiss smiled. He put a hand in the pocket of his pants. 'Such as?'

Carl Sundbach shrugged. He was remembering the meetings with the madman Kiviranna, the night on the boardwalk, the time they met in Penn Station, or the afternoon they'd walked through the Metropolitan Museum of Art – five, maybe six encounters in all. *You shoot Romanenko, Jake. That's all there is to it. You'll be a goddam hero.* Jake Kiviranna, another asshole, a *tagumik*, with a hero complex, hadn't even asked questions. Romanenko was a Communist, a turncoat, and that was all there was to the business. He deserved to die. Perfectly logical. Perfectly natural. Jake's mind didn't have compartments that spilled over into each other. There were no complications when it came to Kiviranna. Of course, it would have been a different matter if Jake had known that he was assassinating one of the leading figures in the anti-Soviet underground in the Baltic.

One of the leading figures . . .

Carl Sundbach was suddenly depressed. The murder of Romanenko wasn't a decision he'd taken lightly. He and Aleksis had fought side by side for years, not always liking each other, and not always agreeing, but they'd developed a mutual trust, a dependency. And the Brotherhood's plan had always seemed feasible to Carl, although less so with each passing year. It wasn't just that his memory of his native country was beginning to fade around the edges and had begun to recede in importance to him. It wasn't even the fact that age had depleted his energy, his sense of commitment. It was the idea that fresh new voices were being raised in the Soviet Union which had caused him to stop and think and to debate whether the Brotherhood's way had any merit in the end, or whether it was time to put the scheme under wraps – at least until the new directions in Russia had come into focus. Perhaps the directions would be good, perhaps not. But it was a chance worth taking, especially when the consequences of the Brotherhood's scheme could bring about wholesale slaughter – and not simply inside the Baltic countries.

Carl, who knew Mikhail Kiss was beyond reasonable argument and could never be persuaded to give the Kremlin a chance, saw only one way to make the plan grind to a halt. Aleksis had to die. He had to die because nothing short of his murder would make Mikhail Kiss consider abandonment. *And it hadn't worked.* If anything it had backfired, because both Kisses were simply more determined than ever to go ahead. Especially this young one, this terrifying boy with the yellow hair and the face that wouldn't melt *margariini*, this young creature with ice in his veins.

'I asked a question, Carl,' Andres Kiss said.

'There are alternatives that are less destructive. That's all I'm saying. I'm talking about reality.'

'I'm listening,' Andres said. 'Reality fascinates me.'

'You don't hear the pulse, sonny. You and Mikhail, you're deaf men. You don't want to hear.' Sundbach picked up the decanter, but it was empty.

'Tell me about this pulse, Carl. I'm curious.'

The old man wandered round the living-room in an unsteady way. 'Things are changing over there. The time for this plan has gone, Andres. It's time to put violence in cold storage.'

'You really believe what you're saying?'

'Listen to me,' and here Sundbach placed a bony hand on the young man's wrist. 'We can't get our country back the way it was. But we can get *something* back. We can get some kind of self-determination over there but only so long as we stay inside the system. So maybe it's not independence. Maybe it's not the way it was. But it's the best goddam shot we've got! Your way is doomed, sonny. Your way is pure romantic bullshit – a fart on the wind, Andres. I didn't always see it like that. But I'm prepared to give this new regime a chance.'

Andres Kiss shook his head. 'You swallow their crap about all these terrific changes?'

'I believe it can happen. Slowly, sure. But it can happen.'

'Nothing's so cheap as words. The Russians can talk up some fine intentions. After all they've put us through, you're still ready to trust them?'

'Up to a point – '

'You've grown soft in the head, Carl.'

'Listen,' Sundbach said. 'Try to have patience. Don't go ahead with this foolish scheme. Things will get better in the old country. More freedoms will come. Why not let the new system have a chance? And if it doesn't work out, you can go back to the plan later.'

'In your world, Carl, cows will fly.'

Sundbach sat down in a very old grey leather armchair. 'You're an impossible boy, Andres. What do you know? From where I sit I can smell milk on you.'

'You want us to fail, don't you?' Andres asked. 'You want the whole fucking thing to fall apart!'

Sundbach said nothing. Why bother to answer the question? It was wasted breath. Tomorrow, over the Baltic, Andres Kiss might have his moment of truth.

'What did you feel when Aleksis was shot, Carl? Glad?'

'Glad isn't the word,' Sundbach said.

'What is the word, Carl?'

Sundbach was quiet a moment. 'I thought it would be a time for quiet reconsideration. Why rush into violence? Why go ahead with something so drastic if another way could be found?'

Andres Kiss stepped closer to where the old man sat. He saw Sundbach turn his face to the side and look across the room. Andres folded the hand in his pocket around the length of soft, silky material that lay concealed there. It wouldn't take long, he thought. A minute perhaps. A little more. He gazed into Sundbach's discoloured eyes, detecting nervousness in them, something furtive.

Andres touched Sundbach's shoulder very lightly. 'You listen to the Russians, you think you're hearing something new. But there's nothing new. It's the same old song only with a new singer. Freedom isn't in the melody, Carl. The words haven't changed. The only thing that's changed is your mental condition.'

'All I said was we give it a try. Postpone –'

'Postpone nothing.'

Sundbach began to rise from his chair, but Andres gently pushed him back into it. It wasn't a violent gesture, but Sundbach interpreted it that way, as the first trivial skirmish in a situation that would escalate. He tried to rise again, but again Andres pushed him back down. Carl Sundbach, who had always been a little afraid of this young man, albeit in an abstract sense, was surprised to find how quickly the fear could become a concrete thing.

Andres Kiss said, 'With Aleksis dead, you thought the plan would be abandoned, didn't you? That's how you wanted it to be.'

Sundbach didn't speak. He sensed violence all around him, the very air of his apartment electrified by it. He saw it in this young man's cold eyes and mirthless smile. So much beauty and no heart.

'You thought if Aleksis was killed, Mikhail would lose his nerve and give up.'

Sundbach shut his eyes. The sound of a gun fired in a railroad station echoed through his imagination. He didn't believe he'd been mistaken in arranging for Aleksis to be murdered. But he'd failed to change anything, and it was a failure purchased at a very high price.

Andres Kiss took the soft length of material from his pocket. It weighed nothing in his hand. He let the thing dangle against the old man's lips. Carl opened his eyes quickly.

'What's this?' He pushed it away from his mouth.

'What do you think it is?'

'A stocking, a lady's nylon.'

'You got it, Carl.'

'Mikhail sent you here,' Sundbach said. 'Mikhail sent you here to be my goddam assassin!'

Sundbach, panicked into movement, tried to get up out of the chair but Andres struck him quickly on the mouth, knocking him dizzy. Sundbach felt the nylon go around his neck and he kicked vigorously at the young man, striking Andres Kiss on his cheek. The old man got up, rushing across the room to the door. Andres caught him there. He pinned him against the wood and shoved his palm up under Carl's chin and thrust the old man's face back. Sundbach gasped and made a claw of one hand and dug it into Andres's forehead, scratching the flesh, breaking the skin. For a moment, shocked by pain, Andres Kiss released his grip and Carl was able to get a hand on the door-handle. But before he could pull it open Andres struck him on the back of the head with his clenched fist.

Carl slid to the floor and moaned.

Kiss went down on his knees, twisting the nylon stocking around Carl's neck even as the old man flayed at him feebly with his fists.

'For the love of God, Andres.'

Andres crossed the ends of the nylon. He pulled them very tightly, hearing Carl groan and feeling Sundbach's hands, which fluttered desperately upwards, pressing against his mouth. Andres held his breath and kept tightening the stocking.

And then Carl was finally silent and his neck, caught in the fatal tourniquet Andres Kiss had applied, hung at an odd angle to his body. Kiss, out of breath, stood up.

'I think it's time,' Frank Pagan said, and got out of the car, slamming the passenger door shut. He took a step in the direction of Sundbach's building, conscious of Klein sliding out from behind the wheel, aware at the same time, from the edge of his vision, of the TV repair van pulling away from the pavement.

Later, Pagan might marvel at the gall of the operation, but his first impression was of the van swinging in a squealing arc, making an illegal turn on a one-way street. Then the vehicle clambered up on the kerb and struck a fire-hydrant, which immediately sent a great jet of water rainbowing into the air behind Klein's Dodge. Pagan, halfway across the street, watched the van continue in its destructive path, seeing it plough into the trunk of Klein's car, which crumpled like construction paper. Klein, emerging from the driver's side, was tossed forward by the impact. He fell face down under the glittering cascade of water that rose out of the ruptured hydrant. Pagan hurried back to the sidewalk and leaned over Klein, who was sitting up and dazed, looking at Pagan with the expression of a man on thorazine.

'*Holy shit*,' Klein muttered. 'Was it lightning?'

The van, which had the logo *Rivoli's TV & Radio Repair* on the side panel, wheeled into reverse and pulled away from the smashed Dodge. It came to an abrupt halt half-on, half-off the sidewalk and then, roaring madly, lunged straight towards Pagan, breaking open plastic garbage sacks and strewing the air with fishbones and potato peels and clouds of feasting, breeding flies. *Dear Christ!* Pagan, half-blinded by water, threw himself to the side as the van rocketed towards him. He slid down a short flight of steps to the door of a basement apartment, twisting his head in time to see the van roar along the street. He rose, raced back up to the pavement. The van was already turning the corner at the end of the street, leaving a pall of blue exhaust like something conjured out of existence by a flamboyant magician.

He walked to where Max Klein sat. 'You okay?'

'I'll live,' Klein said.

Pagan helped Klein to his feet, then stared through the sunlit water at the empty space where the Jaguar had been. Slick, he thought. The whole thing, dead slick. He looked up at the windows of Sundbach's apartment and something caused him to shiver, and he thought he knew what.

'You want to go after the van?' Klein asked.

Pagan saw the way Klein's feathery red hair had been plastered across his scalp with water. 'Let's go back to Carl's.'

Saaremaa Island, the Baltic

Colonel Yevgenni Uvarov walked between the computers and the consoles, passing the stern portrait of Lenin, whose eyes seemed to follow one no matter where one moved. The Colonel gazed across the wide expanse of floor towards his desk, then up at the clock on the wall. He couldn't put this moment off for long, not now. He checked his watch, returned his eyes to the clock, as if he were all at once obsessed by time – but he was in reality stalling, delaying the moment from which there was absolutely no return. Burning the bridges, Uvarov thought. Setting them all aflame.

He moved towards his desk. A technician named Agarbekov stepped in front of him. Uvarov was startled by the sudden movement and it must have shown on his face because Agarbekov gazed at him strangely.

'Console eight isn't working, sir,' Agarbekov said.

Why was he being bothered by this utterly trifling detail now? Uvarov wondered. 'You know the procedures, Agarbekov.'

Agarbekov was hesitant. 'I followed procedures, comrade Colonel, and nothing was ever done. The repairs were never made. Don't you remember?'

Uvarov put one hand up to the side of his face. He was flustered suddenly, thinking he heard reproach in Agarbekov's voice. He couldn't remember, it was really that simple. For weeks he'd been operating on a level where ordinary things receded, and his memory malfunctioned. He was living – not in the now, the present – but in the immediate future. He looked at Agarbekov, a white-faced twenty-year-old from Kiev with a lock of greasy black hair that fell over his forehead and which he kept pushing away.

'Are you unwell, comrade Colonel?' Agarbekov asked.

Uvarov shook his head. 'I'm perfectly fine, Agarbekov. I have so many things on my mind. I can't be expected to concern myself about one small repair. Go through the usual procedures a second time.' The sharpness in the voice, the impatience – Uvarov wondered if Agarbekov detected stress in his behaviour. He smiled and tried to appear calm. He placed a hand on Agarbekov's shoulder and made a mild little joke. 'Procedures are designed by Moscow with only one purpose, Agarbekov. They weren't written to help you, only to test your ingenuity in getting around them. Didn't you know that?'

'I had my suspicions, comrade Colonel,' Agarbekov said.

Uvarov walked to his desk. He sat down, looked at the clock on the wall. He was aware of Agarbekov watching him from across the room. Had the small joke alerted Agarbekov to something? Uvarov wondered. How could it have done? It was innocent, a simple act of sympathy for Agarbekov, who was caught up in the often stupid rules and regulations and procedures that were a part of military life. Uvarov shut his eyes and wondered if Agarbekov was KGB, if he'd been stationed here to observe men in sensitive positions. He opened his eyes, and now there wasn't any sign of Agarbekov. KGB! You see them everywhere. You imagine them all over the place.

He opened the middle drawer of his desk and quietly removed a sheet of typewritten paper. He scanned the words quickly even though he knew them by heart. Then he looked at the top of the page where bold letters read: *From the Office of the Deputy Minister.* Uvarov picked up his pen and his hand shook and he had to work hard to still it. He carefully signed the name S. F. Tikunov across the bottom of the page, then he rose and walked to the Orders Board, where he pinned the sheet up. He could barely breathe. He looked at the sheet hanging on the board and he had the thought that his forgery was utterly childish, anybody could see through it, it would be spotted at once by the operators who religiously took note of all new material on the Orders Board.

His face covered in perspiration, he went unsteadily back to his desk. He passed the computers, two of which were out of order still, and lay exposed to his view – circuit boards, yards of thin wire, the intestinal confusion of broken electronic equipment. He looked at the clock again. At midnight, the message he'd placed on the Orders Board would be routinely transmitted by computer from this installation which – as the major tracking station in the area – was an electronic post office for all pertinent orders issued in Moscow by the Deputy Minister, and relayed to a score of lesser installations along the Baltic coast.

Uvarov sat down. He was conscious of Agarbekov watching from the other side of the enormous room. The young Ukrainian's face was white and expressionless, floating in the bleak fluorescent lighting like a balloon. *Don't stare at me,* Uvarov thought. But then Agarbekov had turned away already and had vanished beyond the banks of screens, leaving Uvarov with a strange sense of unfocused discomfort.

The Colonel looked in the direction of the Orders Board. Even though he couldn't read anything from this distance, he felt that the sheet he'd just pinned there was very distinct, the letters large and bloated. He imagined he could read it plainly. *Routine Electronic Maintenance Order Number 09 06, 1600–1700 hrs Wednesday September 6.*

Uvarov got up. For a second he was tempted to remove the notice before anyone had seen it. But he'd made his mind up, and he couldn't cancel now, and besides one of the operators was already standing in front of the board and looking at the faked order pinned there. Uvarov, who expected his forgery to be detected there and then, was filled with relief when the operator turned away from the order without any unusual expression on his face.

Uvarov stepped out of the building. The night air was chilly and he shivered. He listened to the soft sound of the tide, and he thought of the dark waters beyond the range of his vision, and how for one short hour tomorrow the defences of the Baltic coast would be stripped of their eyesight, and in this state of temporary blindness astonishingly vulnerable.

15

Manhattan

Frank Pagan's room had that dreary unlived-in look of hotel rooms all the world over. As soon as he stepped inside, he removed his jacket, still damp from the fire-hydrant, then his shirt. From the inner pocket of the jacket he took out a long brown envelope, which he set on the bedside table. Then he lay across the bed and pondered the ceiling.

He felt the weariness that is an accumulation of things. Travel, frustration, loneliness. And murder. He'd known roughly what he was going to see inside the old man's apartment, he'd guessed it, but even so he hadn't been prepared for the sight of Carl Sundbach with a nylon stocking knotted round his throat. There, surrounded by all his Baltic memorabilia, the old man lay in the middle of the room as if he were himself just another useless, albeit grotesque, keepsake. The broken spectacles, the false teeth scattered over the rug – murder had a way of diminishing a person, of breaking somebody down into his less admirable components. And the killer, assisted by whoever drove the kamikaze van, had slipped neatly away.

Pagan went inside the bathroom, doused his face with cold water, returned to the bedroom, turned on the radio – what this room needed was *noise*. He found a station playing Frankie Ford's classic *Sea Cruise*, and he walked to the window, looking out over mid-afternoon Manhattan. The sun, made hazy by pollution, was the colour of a bruised daffodil. A frolicsome wind flapped along the cross streets and died out in the avenues. Pagan pressed his forehead to the window. Since there existed no such company as Rivoli's TV & Radio Repair – surprise, surprise – the problem now was whether Max Klein could extract some useful information from the registration plate of the Jaguar.

Max had made inquiries just as soon as Sundbach's body was discovered, only to learn that the Jag belonged to an auto-leasing company on Long Island that had leased the car to an entity called Rikkad Inc, with corporate offices in Merrick. It was not apparently leased to any particular individual, but rather to the corporation as a whole, and when Klein had tried to telephone the number of Rikkad Inc he'd received a recorded message saying that Rikkad, a division of something called Piper Industries, was closed for the day and thank you for calling. Piper Industries, with offices in New Platz, had no information to give about Rikkad and suggested Klein try the Merrick number again in the morning.

Pagan turned from the window, suspecting that Klein, if he discovered anything, was going to find himself ensnared in one of those corporate mazes, an auditor's nightmare, where the structure of ownership is complicated and one corporate entity is laid upon another – the point being to obscure responsibility and evade direct culpability in the event of law-suits or tax claims. Klein had decided to look at records in the offices of the Corporation Commission and Pagan, needing some quiet time alone, had walked back to the Warwick.

He wondered what he was left with after the death of Carl Sundbach. Certain facts, certain connections, but they suggested empty railway cars connected to a locomotive going nowhere. He'd hoped that Sundbach was going to be the entryway to the Brotherhood – but that particular little light had been blown out and the entryway was a cul-de-sac in darkness now. And if he was no closer to the Brotherhood, then he was also no nearer to an understanding of their scheme, nor why certain Russians apparently stood in the shadows behind it.

He turned from the window, picked up the envelope on the bedside table, sat on the edge of the mattress. He stood up when he heard the sound of somebody knock lightly. When he opened the door and saw Kristina Vaska there, a small charge of electricity coursed suddenly through him, a voltage almost adolescent in its intensity.

'Frank Pagan?' she asked, smiling.

'The very same.'

She stepped inside, closing the door behind her. She sat on the bed. 'I wanted to get here sooner, but I went to my apartment to drop off my luggage.'

Pagan, filled with the desire to touch her and yet postponing the moment, had ignored the essentials of the woman's life. She lived in this city, therefore she had to have an apartment. Somehow the information surprised him, as if he'd stumbled into a concealed corner of her world. You go in this direction, he thought, and before long you're asking all the old, half-scared questions – is there a boyfriend somewhere? is there somebody else? a rival? even more than one?

'I don't even know where you live,' he said.

'Eighty-sixth and Amsterdam.'

'How was the flight?' he asked, dismayed by his own question. *How was the flight? Was it raining in England? Did you have the plastic stroganoff for lunch on the plane?* He was staggered by his sudden knack for the inane.

There was a long silence in the room, an abyss into which all sounds were abruptly sucked, as if this narrow hotel bedroom were an island of sheer soundproofed quiet afloat on the turbulence of Manhattan. Pagan stepped towards the bed.

Kristina said, 'Oh fuck the flight, Frank. I don't want to talk about airplanes and luggage. That's just stuff. Sit down beside me. I want to forget *stuff*.'

He sat down. He reached for her hand and held it. She twined her fingers through his and he couldn't recollect any gesture more intimate in years.

'Look at me, Frank. I'm *trembling*, for Christ's sake.'

How unlike Roxanne she was, he thought. Roxanne, with a certain coyness, had been passionate in less direct ways. She would have gone at her desire indirectly, using touches, gestures, as if she couldn't quite trust speech to convey her needs. Kristina, less subtle perhaps, was no less exciting. She lay back, curling her legs under her body. There was a lull, a quietness, one of those intolerably enjoyable moments of anticipation. He remembered when he'd walked with her in the park. He remembered the dampness of laurels and laburnum, moisture on old wood, raindrops on a coat. The effusiveness of recollected perfumes. The swift touch of passion he'd felt, the urge to invade this woman's world.

She held one hand out in front of her face and laughed. 'I'm shaking like a schoolgirl. I feel idiotic.'

Pagan kissed her and the warmth of the kiss, the confident way she returned it, shook him. He undid the buttons of her shirt and slid his hand over a breast and saw how she raised her face back and upwards, her mouth open and her throat in shadow, and it was one of those sublime perceptions he knew would return years later even after this passion had gone, one of those pictures that are immediately luminescent in the memory and against which other encounters are inevitably judged. He was hungry, emptier than he'd ever imagined, driven by an excitement and urgency that surprised him.

Naked, she was perfect. He ran his hand between her breasts and down over the surface of her stomach to her thighs, astonished by the sweet geometry of her body and by his own need to enter her. *Now,* she said. *Do it to me now, Frank.* And her voice was hushed and hoarse, like that of a tantalising stranger. She was a verbal lover, whispering over and over, sometimes his name, sometimes words that might have been vulgar in other situations but now seemed magical to him, sometimes simply making sounds in his ear that drove him to utter distraction. He buried himself in the act of love. He buried himself in a place beyond all the mysteries, beyond Romanenko, beyond the Brotherhood and their secret poetry and old wars, beyond Epishev and gunfire in a railway station. It was a place where all the clamour and the mysteries dissolved and the only truth was this woman and the intimacy he shared with her.

They made love slowly, each trying to be more generous than the other, as if they were exploring each other's limitations only to find none, discovering instead a lovers' world of infinite possibility which Pagan, grown stale in his years of loneliness, had long ago forgotten. When it was over, he propped himself up on an elbow and looked down at her. He realised, with something of a surprise, that he wanted her again. Immediately too, as if he'd discovered untouched realms of stamina and impatient desire in himself.

Moscow

Vladimir Greshko felt death in the back of the car as though it were an invisible passenger. He sometimes studied the darkened landscape, staring across flat fields and through trees and seeing the occasional light of a farmhouse, but mostly he kept his eyes shut and listened to what sounded like death's persistent song – a distant music, a couple of fragmented notes that might have been blown on a wind instrument, seductive and enchanting. He squeezed the small rubber ball he carried in a pocket of his overcoat. *The solace of solid things*, he thought.

The Yakut nurse drove with great caution, easing the car over ruts as gently as she could. Now and again she would make a remark about the folly of this journey, but the General had long ago ceased to listen. Wrapped in a heavy greatcoat which the nurse had demanded he wear, he saw fields give way to construction, to scaffolding and great piles of bricks that littered the landscape. New Soviet housing was going up, those hideous blocks of flats that reminded Greshko of tombstones marking the burial-grounds of a race of giants. There was a thought here he might have pursued at some other time, a symbolism that might have amused him with its irony, something to do with the death of giants – but not now, not tonight.

And then the new construction yielded to finished apartment blocks, drab and lifeless, and the Yakut nurse announced the outskirts of the capital. Greshko felt the rush of energy that Moscow, in her great generosity, always gave him. This was his city. This was where he'd risen to power. He knew the streets, the neighbourhoods, he knew the criminals and informants and spies, he knew where the black-marketeers met to sell currency or buy weapons or dispose of stolen cars. He knew its pimps and whores, ambassadors and bureaucrats, politicians and gangsters. There was nothing he couldn't acquire in Moscow, nothing – American dollars, rare works of art, imported cars, automatic rifles, you name it. If you knew where to look, Moscow had everything a man could possibly need or want. From his office on Dzerzhinsky Square he'd once controlled this amazing city, understanding it the way no other man could – especially not a man like General Olsky, who didn't have the rhythms of Moscow in his blood.

But it wasn't *his* Moscow to which he was returning now. It had been taken from him, seized by usurpers, and purged of all his old cronies, who had been shipped to country cottages or seaside villas to rot away the last years of their lives and to dream of how they might regain the power they'd lost. He stared at the buildings, which were old friends. The Central Revolutionary Museum on Gorky Street, the Hotel Minsk, the Yermolova Theatre.

He made the Yakut stop the car a moment. He rolled the window down and sniffed the air, so unlike the countrified stuff he was forced to breathe these days, then he told the woman to drive on. He gave her the address where he wanted to go and settled back in his seat again, restless, animated by his return, which may have begun quietly and was completely unannounced – but which would end differently, if he had his way.

He shut his eyes, reflected on Epishev a moment. Viktor hadn't yet made contact with Volovich, whom Greshko had telephoned only a few hours ago, a nervous Volvovich, terse, talking like a man whose teeth have been welded shut. The conversation had been brief, elliptical. Volovich, undeniably loyal to Viktor, was a rabbit nevertheless, and even if he'd never been told the *entire* extent of the Brotherhood's undertaking, just the same he knew enough to create problems if he came under pressure.

Viktor's failure to make contact troubled Greshko. Either he had no information to impart (a fact he might have relayed by telephone, as a simple courtesy at the least), or else something had happened to him. Whatever, his absence had come under the scrutiny of Olsky. And that was undesirable.

He opened his eyes, peered through the window. The car was travelling along the Komsomolsky Prospekt towards the Lenin Hills.

'Take a right turn here,' he said to the nurse.

She did so, swinging the car into a narrow street that was dense with foliage under bright streetlamps. The houses here were large, constructed within the last forty years. They had copper roofs and elegant gardens and although they'd been converted to apartments during the past twenty years, they were considered among some of the finest residences in the city. You didn't live in a place like this if you were nobody.

'Here,' Greshko said, and he indicated one of the houses that was almost completely concealed by trees.

The nurse turned the car into a driveway, parked it.

Greshko buttoned his greatcoat and stepped out of the vehicle. The Yakut woman came out to assist him, but he brushed her aside. He had to enter this house unassisted, and pain and frailty and the hole in his stomach be damned. There was dignity in him still, and fire in his blood, and he wasn't going to give anyone the satisfaction of seeing him hobble with the help of a nurse. But he hurt like hell.

'Get back in the car,' he told the nurse. 'And stay there.'

Alone, he went shakily up the steps to the door of the house. He rang a bell, waited.

There wasn't an answer. He didn't ring a second time. He opened the unlocked door and found himself in a long, broad hallway with a high ceiling. A staircase led up into darkness.

Nikolai Bragin appeared at the end of the hallway. He wore a baggy three-piece suit and his hair, wild and unruly, sprung from his high skull in uneven tufts. It was the hairstyle of a man who habitually ran his fingers across his scalp. He wore glasses that pinched the end of his nose and he chain-smoked.

'My dear Vladimir,' Bragin said. There was a brief embrace. 'It's been – what? – two years?'

'It feels like a lifetime,' Greshko said.

'Can't stay away from Moscow, eh?'

'I need to get laid,' Greshko said, and winked. 'One last time.'

Bragin laughed. 'And you think this is where all the whores are, eh?'

'Indisputably,' Greshko said.

Bragin led him into a large drawing-room, which might have been a stage-set for some pre-Revolutionary drama. Both men sat at a sofa by an unlit fire. The fireplace was ornately carved with the figures of eagles alighting on prey. Presumably the piece had been removed from an aristocratic mansion. Greshko thought the place smelled of prosperity, much of it plundered from Russia's history – icons on the walls, old books stacked on the shelves, an ancient silver samovar seated on a gilt-leafed table.

'Tea?' Bragin asked.

'I'm at that stage of my life when only vodka does me any good, Nikolai.'

'You shall have some.' Bragin rose, took a bottle from a cupboard, and poured two small glasses that Greshko thought were niggardly. Greshko tossed his back immediately, then helped himself to a second, which he also disposed of quickly. It was first-rate stuff and it roared in his blood.

'Now, Vladimir. What brings you all the way to Moscow? You were enigmatic on the telephone.'

Greshko poured himself a third vodka and swallowed it in one gulp. Three vodkas and he could hear those American songs in his head! He leaned across the table. *Sweet Christ, how he hurt*. He held the liquid in his mouth before swallowing it. It did what it was meant to – it numbed his nervous system, making the pain seem distant and just tolerable.

He said, 'I come here a dying man. Therefore, what I am about to tell you should be seen in the light of detachment, the lack of self-interest common to dying men. I have no personal axe to grind, you understand.'

Bragin looked a little embarrassed. Greshko, who wondered if he appeared drunk to the other man, pushed his empty glass away. Too much vodka too quickly was a prescription for disaster. And on an empty stomach that wasn't really a stomach at all these days – merely half of one, or a quarter, he was never very sure what the surgeons had left him of his digestive tract.

'There's a plot,' Greshko said quietly. 'It involves national security.'

'A plot?'

Greshko nodded. 'Before I go any further, I want you to know in advance that I can't identify my own sources.'

'Of course,' Bragin said.

'I know editors and journalists like yourself hear that phrase all the time,' Greshko remarked. He paused, looked down inside his vodka glass. Nikolai Bragin, an editor of the daily *Izvestia*, had been a journalist since the mid-1950s and now, at the age of fifty-five, was one of the most prominent newspapermen in the Soviet Union and enjoyed unprecedented access to the highest chambers in the land. For years, Bragin had dutifully toed the Party line. His reputation had been built on dull acquiescence rather than daring. His prose was said to be more effective than any Soviet tranquilliser – of which the Russian pharmaceutical industry had produced few in any event. He printed what the Party wanted him to print. The word 'investigative' was not, in his vocabulary, an adjective used to describe a certain kind of reporting. He had pursued the bland and the inoffensive with a very blunt pencil. And then, in the last two years, lo and behold! a transformation, a small miracle had taken place. Bragin had published a long piece critical of the Government's handling of the pollution of Lake Baikal, and followed it with a three-part series on judicial corruption. Like a lifetime teetotaller introduced regrettably late to the beauties of wine and determined to compensate for the dry years of self-denial, Bragin had been reborn in the journalistic freedoms generously permitted by the Kremlin, trading his blunt pencil for a rapier, and shaking off the blinkers that had restricted his vision for almost thirty years. Nikolai Bragin saw himself as a hero of the press, a protector of the rights of small people against the elephantine clumsiness of central government. He was therefore a natural choice for Greshko. If there was to be some holy new form of openness in Soviet society and in the press, Greshko had asked himself, why not try to make some use of it? Why not test it? Turn it against its adherents? Set it upon itself? Why not give it some ammunition and see if it self-destructs? Everything free, Greshko thought, had also the freedom to destroy itself.

'Certain parties within the organs of State Security are involved in a plan directed against our country, Nikolai.'

'Be more specific, please.'

'It's my understanding that General Olsky, Chairman of the KGB – a trusted servant of the State, a man with grave responsibilities – is involved in a scheme with certain dissident factions overseas to perpetrate an outrage against our country.'

Bragin was quiet for a second. 'And what is the nature of this outrage, Vladimir?'

'That is unknown to me, unfortunately.'

'You're being very vague.'

The old man reached across the table, laying one hand on Bragin's wrist. 'Listen to me, Nikolai. General Olsky, acting against the interests of the State, has sent his emissary Colonel Viktor Epishev out of the country to liaise with a Baltic movement whose primary goal is to achieve independence from the Soviet Union. These forces, as you well know, have existed inside Russia for most of this century. Blackguards and malcontents. Scoundrels. Baltic scum.'

Bragin took a pen from his pocket and wrote something down in a tiny notepad. Then he looked at Greshko. 'You're making a very serious accusation about the Chairman of the KGB. Can you substantiate any of this?'

'Certain KGB files are missing. These files, which are damning to Olsky because they link him with outlaw elements in the Baltic states, have obviously been destroyed by him in an effort to cover his crimes. Viktor Epishev is also missing. If you were to ask Olsky about Epishev's whereabouts, he'd deny knowledge of them. And that would be incriminating enough. Since when does the Chairman of the KGB not know the whereabouts of one of his own Colonels, for God's sake? When I ran the organs, I always knew where all my officers were. Night and day, it didn't matter, I always knew.'

Nikolai Bragin lit a cigarette from the butt of one he was already smoking. His fingertips were orange and the front of his waistcoat soiled by spilled ash. His darkly-jowled face was constantly vanishing behind smoke clouds. 'It's not enough, Vladimir. If I start asking questions to substantiate your story, people are going to say your personal view of Olsky has caused you to concoct a scheme to discredit the man.'

Greshko shook his head. 'I expect that, of course. But it might prove enlightening if you were to ask General Olsky why he came all the way from Moscow to see me the other day.'

'And why did he?'

Greshko took air into lungs that were barely functioning. 'He tried to enlist my support in his scheme. Unsuccessfully, I might add. It's my understanding that he has been secretly trying to muster support from formerly influential people – people, shall we say, that are no longer in power but are ready to rule again if called upon to do so, people whom he thinks might be relied upon to form a new government. Olsky wants to discredit the present regime and replace it with another. With himself, no doubt, in the role of General Secretary. That's his goal. And in collusion with reactionary forces inside the country as well as outside, that's just what he intends to do.'

Greshko, who had begun to wheeze, took a handkerchief from his pocket and applied it to his lips.

Bragin said, 'General Olsky is held in high esteem within the Politburo. You're walking through a mine-field.'

'I'm used to mine-fields,' Greshko said.

'The trouble is, Vladimir, I only have your word for all this. Who can prove Olsky belongs in a conspiracy? Is there documentation? Is there evidence? I'm sorry to say your word doesn't carry weight these days, Vladimir. For me to consider this story, I'd need more to go on. I can't blunder around asking awkward questions without some foundation.'

Greshko sat back in his chair. His heartbeat was monstrous all at once, a frantic drum locked in his chest. He had trouble swallowing and the surface of his skin was clammy. Was this the moment? Was this death coming in? He closed his eyes. How could he exit without nailing that fucker Olsky to a cross? He trembled, concealed his shaking hand under the table.

'Do you need water, Vladimir?' Bragin asked. Greshko shook his head. He opened his eyes. Steadying his hands, he gripped the edge of the table. 'Let me ask you, Nikolai. Is General Olsky a good Communist? Is he ideologically sound?'

'I would imagine so.'

'My ass,' Greshko said. And he reached for the inside pocket of his greatcoat, which felt heavy and suffocating, removing several photostat sheets. He shoved them disdainfully across the table. *'There's your good Communist, Nikolai. There's your ideologically sound Olsky.'*

Bragin picked up the papers and Greshko smiled. It was a good moment, one of the best he'd had in years. He watched Bragin go through the sheets. Bragin made a humming sound between his closed lips as he read. When he'd finished he didn't raise his face up from the papers.

Greshko said, 'One hundred and sixteen thousand English pounds in a money-fund organised by Coutts Bank in London. Three hundred and thirty thousand American dollars in a trust run by the Wells Fargo Bank of California. Six million Swiss francs deposited with the Credit Suisse in Zurich. Transaction receipts, records of deposit, all of Comrade Olsky's good Communist activities are right there in front of your very eyes, Nikolai.'

Bragin looked up now from the documents.

Greshko said, 'I've given you photocopies. If you're interested in the originals they can be found locked in safety deposit box number 1195 in the vault of the Oxford Street branch of the Westminster Bank in London.'

Bragin said, 'You've done your homework, Vladimir.'

'I had excellent sources once,' Greshko said. There was a long silence. Bragin got up. Greshko gathered the sheets together and tapped them on the table.

'This is something of a surprise,' Bragin said.

'I imagined it might be,' Greshko remarked. 'I admit this documentation in itself doesn't connect Olsky to any seditious movement. But it raises some distressing questions about the General. If he can dabble so freely in capitalist enterprises, and indulge himself in a system he professedly hates – well, who can say what he might or might not be capable of? And how did he amass the money in the first place?'

'Your point is taken,' Bragin said, and there was some hesitation in his voice.

Greshko rose. He was no longer unsteady. 'What will you do next, Nikolai?'

'One doesn't leap into something so sensitive as this, Vladimir.'

'I understood you journalists could come and go as you please these days. I believed you had a mandate to write about dry-rot in the system, Nikolai, no matter where it might be found.'

Bragin ran his thick fingers through his hair. 'We have some new freedoms, of course. But we haven't been given a licence to kick doors down, Vladimir. We don't destroy reputations in a malicious manner. If Olsky is guilty the matter will come to the surface.'

Greshko stepped towards the door, where he stopped, turned around. 'You're saying you would need Party authorisation before you could investigate my information, is that it?'

'Hardly,' Bragin replied. 'However, if I assembled a story with indisputable documentation, the Party would want to examine the evidence before giving its approval to publication – especially in an area such as this one.'

'In other words the Party still tells you what you can print?'

Bragin shook his head from side to side. 'Vladimir, I have more freedom now than at any other time in my career. But some sensitive matters need to be cleared in advance, that's all.'

'Are we talking about censorship?'

'Censorship? I wouldn't use that word. It's out of fashion.'

Greshko opened the door. 'I'll leave the papers with you. I have copies of my own, of course. I'll see myself out.' He paused, turned back. 'When you write this story, please be sure you mention the original source of it.'

'I won't forget, Vladimir.'

Greshko opened the front door. He felt rather jaunty all at once. He paused on the steps, smelling the air. Then he went confidently towards his car, where the Yakut nurse sat behind the wheel. He got in on the passenger side and told the woman to drive him now to the Moskva Hotel on the Karl Marx Prospekt for his second and final appointment of the night. He sang quietly under his breath as the car moved through the dark streets.

He was under no illusion that Bragin could simply write the story as he saw fit. What Greshko had really done was simple. He'd planted a seed to discredit Olsky, certainly. But much more than that. When the Baltic assault took place the very next day, when the extent of the plot became apparent, when those clowns who ran the Politburo were swept away on great tides of discontent and humiliation and public wrath and injured patriotism, Greshko was certain that Nikolai Bragin would remember the man who had forewarned him. Greshko had protected his own reputation. When it came time to analyse his career, when one hundred years from now autopsies were performed on his life and work, he would be remembered as the man who had exposed treachery in the highest echelons of power, who had uncovered corruption in the very heart of State Security. A Soviet saint, canonised by history. And wasn't that what life was all about when you got down to the bitter end of it? Your reputation? Your place in the scheme of things? Your name?

The car halted in front of the Moskva Hotel, and Greshko stepped out. He told the Yakut woman to wait for him. He glanced at the doorman as he entered the hotel, The doorman, touched by a shiver of recognition from the recent past, didn't question the old man muffled in the heavy overcoat as he entered the foyer. Greshko went up to the third floor. The room he entered was dull and a little shabby, the woodwork in need of paint, the wallpaper faded.

A young man sat at a card-table in the middle of the floor. He wore a plaid shirt open at the neck and blue jeans and the cigarettes he smoked were unfiltered Capstans, empty crumpled packets of which were scattered around the room. Greshko smiled at the young man and thought: *My insurance policy.*

The man, whose name was Thomas McLaren, stood up. He appeared a little awed in the presence of the former Chairman of the KGB. He was a ciphers clerk at the British Embassy, somebody Greshko had once caught in what is politely called 'an indiscretion'. A married man, McLaren had been ruthlessly seduced by a female KGB officer called Tamara. A sad affair, really, because McLaren had fallen in love with the woman and she had become fond of him – but permanence was impossible, of course. Photographs were taken of couplings in hotel rooms, meadows, borrowed apartments. McLaren, who understood he'd been manipulated, had been placed on ice for a day when he might be needed. And that day was now.

Greshko sat at the card-table and McLaren fidgeted.

The General said, 'I will be quick and to the point. I am going to give you certain documents. You will make sure these fall into the hands of respectable journalists in your country.' He took documents from his overcoat, copies of the same papers he'd given to Bragin, and he laid them on the card-table. 'They refer to the conduct of General Olsky, Chairman of the KGB.'

The young man put a hand out, but Greshko stopped him. 'Read them when I leave. There's no time now.' Greshko paused because new pain fluttered across his chest and up into his throat and he felt dizzy. He was quiet, waiting for the pain to pass. McLaren, who had black hair and eyes intense with fear of blackmail – a fear he'd carried with him day and night ever since Tamara had been revealed to him as KGB – watched the old man warily.

'General Olsky, handpicked by the General Secretary to run the KGB, is deeply involved in a foreign plot to undermine this Government. A good journalist may ask himself, what kind of human insight does the General Secretary lack that made him appoint this treacherous person? And if Olsky is a traitor, are there others in the present Politburo? Has the General Secretary made other . . . shall we say unfortunate appointments? Is he a man so lacking in insight that he's easily fooled?'

'What kind of plot do you mean, General?' McLaren asked.

'You'll know everything very soon. All I ask is you ensure delivery of these documents to reliable sources. And make absolutely sure you mention my part in bringing you the information. You must also point out to your writers that I made every effort to make our present leadership aware of this corruption, but I was ignored. I tried again and again, always with the same results. Newspapers all over the world will publish the story. The new Russia falls to pieces! All the bold new promises go down in flames of betrayal and treason! Wonderful headlines, eh?'

Greshko, tired now, fell silent. He studied McLaren for a moment. 'Please. Try to relax. This room isn't bugged. I still have a little influence, McLaren. I made sure it was safe here before I came.'

McLaren looked relieved. He opened the documents Greshko had given him, glanced at them. General Greshko stood up.

'Do as I ask, and all incriminating photographs, as well as negatives, will be destroyed. You understand me?'

McLaren understood.

Greshko walked to the door. For a moment he lost all his strength and had to grip the door-handle to keep from slipping. Then he stepped out into the corridor and walked towards the lifts, stiff-backed, moving with all the dignity he could find. He went down to the lobby, thinking it had been quite an evening, and that if his story failed ever to see the light of day in the Soviet Union, it would at least be published elsewhere in the world, and whispers and rumours, like quicksilver passages of air, would slip back inside Russia, quiet at first, then growing louder, and more shrill, and finally undeniable. After the success of the Baltic plot, Olsky would be removed, and the Politburo purged of Birthmark Billy and his cronies who had tried to fabricate an obscene new Russia, a hybrid society hacked out of half-understood socialism and an uneasy yearning for the stuff of the capitalist world. A bastard place, a nightmare land of varying political beliefs and separate nationalities, Greshko thought as he walked towards his car. But he'd done everything he could to confer legitimacy upon his precious country once again.

Manhattan

Pagan rose from the bed and looked down at Kristina Vaska. She had one knee uplifted, and the other leg stretched flat, so that the pubic shadows, always gorgeous mysteries, were even more inviting. It was a precious moment, and like everything precious fragile, and Pagan wasn't sure what he was supposed to say about what had just happened, or if speech would somehow alter the delicacy of things. He walked across the room to the window, pulling his robe around him as he moved. The afternoon sun was still hazy, slanting through the spires of midtown and yet failing to touch the streets below, which were already locked into that premature twilight characteristic of New York City.

He turned. Kristina was watching him. Pagan went back to the bed and sat down, letting his fingertips rest very lightly on the woman's hand.

'You surprised me, Frank Pagan.'

'I surprised myself.' And he had, he had.

She stretched in a lazy way, closing her eyes. She hadn't expected to end up in this bed. She hadn't anticipated that rush of feeling, nor had she imagined the extent of his desire, which touched her, filling her with an awareness of how deep his loneliness must have been. At the same time, her own complicity in his release had amazed her, because he'd activated responses in her that, like someone miserly with her emotions, she didn't want to feel.

Pagan inclined his head, let his lips touch the back of her hand, thinking how strange it was to be drawn after all these years into romance, and how much simpler life might have been if he'd relegated this encounter to the bargain basement of uncluttered sex, a one-shot thing, a brief fling, and then silence and amnesia. But it was undeniable – Kristina Vaska, whom he barely knew, had touched him inwardly, in places that hadn't been touched for God knows how long.

He raised his face. 'I'm thirsty. Do you want me to call room service?'

'I was under the impression,' she said, 'that we'd just had room service.'

Pagan smiled, reached for the telephone, ordered coffee and sandwiches. He replaced the receiver, remembering the brown envelope that had slipped to the floor during the recent amazing excesses on the bed. He didn't want to touch it, didn't want to be reminded of Carl Sundbach and a world that existed beyond the walls of this room. But he picked it up, even though he didn't open it at once. He held it as a man might hold something contaminated, reluctantly and with great distaste. He was suddenly nervous at the idea of asking Kristina to look at the photographs and wished he didn't have to. He kissed her, laid a hand flat against the side of her face, and thought how sweetly fragile she seemed right then.

'I want you to look at something,' he said quietly.

'Suddenly you've got a grim tone in your voice, Frank. I've heard it before and I don't think I like it. What are you asking me to do?'

'I've got some old photos here,' and he opened the flap of the envelope, tipping the contents on to the sheets. 'Before you look at these, does the name Sundbach mean anything to you?'

She thought a moment, then shook her head.

Pagan said, 'One other thing. Before you pick up these pictures, I want you to be prepared for the fact that your father's in a couple of them.'

'My father?'

Pagan nodded. 'I found the pictures in the apartment of a man called Carl Sundbach who was just murdered.'

She reached for the photographs. There were three in all. Pagan looked over her shoulder as she gazed at them. They were all similar, as if they'd been taken within minutes of each other. Similar and very familiar.

The first depicted three men in shapeless jackets, photographed against a backdrop of wintry trees. The men had rifles, which they held loosely against their sides. One of the men had a bandoleer strapped over his jacket. In the second photograph, there were also three armed men, but one of them was different from the first picture, as if the person he'd replaced had gone behind the camera. In the last photograph there was still another permutation of three men. In each picture the same stark trees formed the background. Taken quickly, Pagan thought. Hasty souvenirs of war snapped by cameramen in rotation. Guns and four tired, grubby men. Guns and weariness. And a sense of camaraderie, as if the men in the photographs were prepared to die together in a common cause.

In two of the photographs Norbert Vaska and Aleksis Romanenko stood side by side, looking exactly the way they had in the snapshot Kristina had shown Pagan days ago. In the third picture Vaska was missing, and Romanenko, who looked impossibly youthful, had been photographed between the other two men. It was this picture that Pagan picked up now.

He said, 'The man on the left is Carl Sundbach. The one in the centre is Romanenko. Have you ever seen the big man, the one on the right?'

She shook her head. 'Never.'

Pity, he thought. There had been a chance that if she'd been able to identify the stranger, she might have presented Pagan with a clue to the Brotherhood, a step closer to the elusive core of things. Since Sundbach and Romanenko were dead, and Norbert Vaska in Siberia, that left only the big man with the broken nose and the high forehead. Was he still alive? If he wasn't, then the Brotherhood would remain what it had always been – a locked room.

'I've never seen Sundbach either,' Kristina said. 'Who was he?'

Pagan went inside the bathroom, ran a glass of cold water, returned to the bedroom and sat down again. He said, 'He was associated with the Brotherhood – but he was also seemingly instrumental in bringing about Romanenko's murder. Presumably this treachery was frowned upon, and it got old Carl eliminated.'

'Who killed him?'

Pagan shrugged. 'I can give you an eyewitness description of the alleged killer, and I can tell you the make and registration of the car he was driving, but that hasn't helped much so far. A young man with some tricky back-up in the vicinity – which perhaps suggests the Brotherhood is still doing active recruiting.'

Kristina ran the palm of her hand over the surface of the old pictures. She touched her father's face with a fingertip, then she gathered the pictures together quickly and put them back in the envelope. 'So Sundbach betrayed the Brotherhood,' she said.

'It looks that way to me,' Pagan remarked.

Betrayal. Kristina got out of bed and went to the bathroom. She closed the door. She sat on the edge of the bathtub, her head tilted slightly to one side. She sat this way for a long time, turning the word *betrayal* over and over in her mind, remembering the very last thing Norbert Vaska had ever said to her, and she saw her father as she'd last seen him and remembered the way he'd whispered to her before they took him away and she heard his grim words again and again. An unchanging litany of whispered echoes. She wondered if she was doomed to listen to those same echoes for the remainder of her life. Or if Frank Pagan was going to provide the means to silence them once and for all.

She opened the door. Pagan came to her and held her very tightly.

'You make me feel good,' she said. 'I want you to know that, Frank.'

'It's one of those reciprocal things,' Pagan replied, infusing his words with a flippancy that wasn't remotely appropriate to his feelings. But he was an amateur at the heart's games and he'd lost once before and he didn't think he could stand losing again. And already he was beginning to feel the first soft warmth of seriousness.

There was a knock on the door. He assumed it was room service but when he opened the door he saw Max Klein standing in the hallway, looking a little agitated.

'We should talk,' Klein said.

Pagan said, 'One moment.'

He shut the door, surveyed Kristina Vaska's splendid nakedness. It was almost a crime against nature to cover such wonder up, but he suggested she get dressed. She gathered her clothes together, stepped into the bathroom, and then into the shower. Pagan could hear the sound of her singing *Are You Lonesome Tonight?* over the thunder of falling water as he admitted Max Klein into the room. She had a good strong voice, but she didn't know the words.

Moscow

The telephone rang in Dimitri Volovich's apartment – once, twice, a third time before Volovich answered it. He knew as soon as he lifted the receiver, as soon as he heard interference that sounded like wind whistling through a wet tunnel, that this phone call was coming from a great distance. He wasn't surprised, then, when Viktor Epishev's voice came across the line.

'I'll be brief,' Epishev said.

'I can hardly hear you, Viktor!'

'Tell him this . . . ', The voice was swept away for a few seconds. '*. . . reason to believe there may be a threat to the plan . . .*'

'A threat?'

'*Just tell the old man that I think I can make things secure in time . . .*'

'How bad is the damage?'

'*. . . can't hear a thing . . .*'

'Viktor? Viktor?'

The line had gone dead in Volovich's hand. He put the receiver down and stood motionless for a moment. The palm of his hand was damp with sweat. He looked around his living-room, the functional leather armchairs, the table piled with books and newspapers, the old family photographs on the wall. He moved, somewhat listlessly, into the narrow kitchen, made a cup of tea, and considered the prospect of having to deliver Epishev's message to the old man. All the bloody way to Zavidovo with so slim a message, for God's sake! And the risk involved! Exactly what was this threat he'd mentioned? The old man was certain to ask, and Volovich didn't have the answers to give.

He carried his tea into the living-room and made himself comfortable in one of the leather chairs. He loved this apartment, enjoyed the kind of tenants who lived in the other flats. Right now, for example, he could hear the child called Katerina Ogoridnikova practise her piano on the floor above – a sweet sound that drifted gently down, a little Mozart. A talented child, young Katerina, and very pretty, the daughter of a man who operated a chemical plant and a woman who translated foreign journals for one of the ministries. The tenants in this building had a certain social standing, and Volovich appreciated the fact. He had no great desire to go out into the darkness, leaving all this comfort behind, to make the trip to Zavidovo, but he supposed he'd do it in any event since it was his duty to inform Greshko of any communication from the Colonel.

He set his empty tea-cup down on the table. He went inside the bedroom for his overcoat. Sighing, he did up the buttons, placed his key in his pocket, then stepped across the living-room to the door.

He opened the door, went out on to the landing, turned to lock the door. Startled by shadows that moved behind him, he dropped the key and heard it clatter on the floor, a sound that seemed to reach him from a long way down, like a stone dropped in a very deep well. He turned his face in the direction of the shadows.

There were two of them, and they wore the uniforms of corporals in the KGB. Volovich recognised neither of them, but they didn't immediately worry him because of their inferior rank. He glanced down at his key, seeing how it shone under the lamp on the landing.

'Comrade Lieutenant,' one of the corporals said. He was a chubby man with a Stalinesque moustache. 'You are ordered to stay in your apartment tonight.'

'Ordered? By whom?' Volovich infused his voice with a certain indignation, but he wondered if he succeeded or whether he sounded unconvincing to this pair. *Ordered*, he thought. He didn't like the sound of the word at all.

'We have our instructions, Comrade Lieutenant,' the same corporal said.

'And who issued these instructions? Show me paper. Show me documentation. If you don't have it, step out of my way.'

There was a sound from the stairs now, the click of heels upon linoleum, and Volovich turned his face in the direction of the noise. A figure loomed up and a face took shape in the light that fell across the landing.

'Let us talk, Dimitri.'

Volovich, his heart pounding, stepped back against the wall. He watched General Olsky, in full uniform, bend down to pick up the key, which he then placed in the lock of Volovich's door and twisted. The door creaked open.

'After you,' the Chairman said.

16

Manhattan

Gary Iverson stood in the empty apartment in the vicinity of Fordham University, conscious of starkness, white-painted empty rooms and high bright ceilings. The lack of furniture caused a lack of shadow, hence of texture, and he always had the feeling in this place that he was about to be prepped for surgery. He could hear the sound of the other man's voice coming from one of the rooms at the back, and then the voice was silent, and a door opened at the end of the hallway.

Iverson looked at the man who came along the hallway to the living-room. He had an uninteresting face, if somewhat kindly, but it wasn't in any way memorable. Had anyone asked Iverson to close his eyes there and then and describe his companion, he would have found the task difficult.

'Did you get through?' Iverson asked politely.

'Terrible connection. Impossible to hear anything.'

'Too bad.' Iverson stepped inside the open-plan kitchen, looked in the refrigerator, found a couple of bottles of ginger beer. A recipe on the label informed him that this soda was an ingredient in something called a Moscow Mule – highly appropriate. He took out two bottles and gave one to his companion.

'I wish we had something stronger, Colonel,' Iverson said.

Epishev opened the bottle, swallowed, made a face. Then he wandered to the large window that looked out across the river, which had a strange lemon tint in the early evening sun. He had been in the United States on two previous occasions – once to provide security at the Soviet Mission, the second time to investigate the activities of the Soviet Deputy Ambassador to the United Nations, a man suspected of being soft on the West, and therefore a possible security risk. Epishev liked the country, or the little he'd seen of it. He understood he wasn't going to see a great deal of it this time either.

Iverson chugged his ginger beer. Then he said, 'Welcome to America,' and smiled in an artificially charming way. It was also a slightly strained expression because this apartment never failed to make Iverson a touch uneasy – he was forever conscious of Galbraith, ensconced in his basement in Fredericksburg, listening to everything that was said in these rooms. And today he was more than usually sensitive because he knew that Galbraith, having heard of the death of Sundbach at the hands of the unpredictable Andres Kiss, was bound to be wrathful. And when the fat man was angry, it wasn't a pretty sight.

V. G. Epishev turned from the window. He was still dislocated from the trip, the suddenness of it, his own lack of preparation and insight. He'd known about US involvement in the plan all along, of course – where else was an American plane going to come from if not from the Americans? – but it was only when Malik had introduced him in London to the man known as Gunther that he became aware of the extent of American interest, how it reached inside the US Embassy and spread, if Malik was to be believed, into the upper reaches of American military circles and God knows where else. *There's more to all this than you and I have ever been told, Victor,* Malik had said. *US involvement doesn't begin and end with an Assistant Ambassador at the US Embassy. It goes higher, and it goes deeper, and some of the most influential men in America are involved . . .*

What was painfully obvious to Epishev was how Greshko had kept a certain amount of information from him, but that fact shouldn't have surprised or irritated him. Greshko had done what he always did so very well. He'd concealed information, and juggled it, doling a little out to one person, some to another, so that the total picture was known only to himself. Devious Greshko, master of deception and legerdemain, creator of his own myth, saviour of Russia. Love and hatred, Epishev thought. Greshko inspired extreme responses in other people, as if any form of relationship with the old man took place on a moving pendulum.

Epishev, who always imagined he occupied a special place in the old man's affections, felt resentful of Greshko just then. The old man had excluded him. Yet – and here lay the hold Greshko had, the true nature of the loyalty Epishev felt – he was no less anxious to please Greshko than before. It was a kind of magic, Epishev thought, a sorcery. At a distance of four thousand miles, Greshko's grip was as strong as it had been at a mere six feet.

He stared at Iverson and said, 'Why is there no furniture in this apartment?'

'We keep it for meetings,' Iverson said. 'Nobody lives here.'

Epishev said, 'In the Soviet Union, this kind of apartment would be occupied by two families.'

Iverson shrugged and drained his ginger beer. He wasn't sure what to say to this. He had a script written for him by Galbraith and he had no desire to deviate from it. He put his empty bottle down on the kitchen counter and said, 'Let's talk about Frank Pagan, Colonel.'

'And the girl,' Epishev said.

'Of course.' Iverson walked across the room, putting a little distance between himself and the microphone he knew was planted in the vent above the kitchen stove. It would pick up his voice anyhow, but he enjoyed the idea of Galbraith straining to listen. What he didn't know, but on one level of awareness suspected, was that the entire apartment was one enormous eavesdropping device. The walls had been specially treated with a chemical that amplified any sound and relayed it to a series of hypersensitive pick-ups lodged in the ceiling. A sigh, a whisper, the touch of a handkerchief to a lip, a quiet fart – Galbraith heard it all in Fredericksburg.

Iverson leaned against the wall, arms folded. He had no way of knowing how much he had in common with Viktor Epishev of the KGB, how they both served masters given to authoritarian whim, strong-willed men who guarded their dominions jealously, who resented intrusions and meddlesome outsiders, and who found trust difficult. Iverson and Epishev – both obedient and yet at times capable of some mild straining at the leashes that held them in place, both loyal, both patriots, both pedestrians in the hall of bevelled mirrors that was international political ambition and intrigue.

Iverson said, 'According to our information, Pagan and the girl are staying at the Warwick Hotel here in Manhattan. Pagan – presumably because of information given to him by the girl, and because he's come to some understanding of the coded *meaning* in Romanenko's message – has started to drift very close to the Brotherhood. Only this afternoon we were forced to intervene in a situation . . . ' *In a situation I might have foreseen but didn't*, he thought.

Gary Iverson, turning the word 'coded' around in his mind, admiring Galbraith's cunning, glanced at his wristwatch and went on, 'I don't have to tell you how disastrous it would be at this stage if Pagan and Kristina Vaska interfered with things. There's a third person in the picture as well, a New York policeman called Max Klein, who's been assisting Pagan. It's a sensitive situation, as you can well understand.'

Epishev said, 'But the solution is very simple, Iverson.'

Iverson hesitated. 'As you say, Colonel, it's very simple.'

'Then what's holding you back?'

Iverson paced the floor, stopping at a place where sunlight slicing through the windows struck his face and made him blink his eyes. 'We need your help, Colonel Epishev.'

Epishev was hardly surprised by the request. He hadn't been issued a quick visa and flown first-class to the United States on the first available plane just to play tourist. He'd known his help was needed from the start, from the moment when Gunther had stamped his passport in his offices in the US Embassy and told him that Pagan and the girl were now in New York City – 'pursuing investigations' was how Gunther had phrased it, his face rather mysterious, as if there were more he wanted to say but didn't have the authority to say. Epishev knew what the Americans wanted of him. He wanted the same thing for himself.

'You need to keep your own hands clean,' Epishev said.

'The situation's delicate,' Iverson replied.

Epishev gazed back out over the river. A tugboat came in view, a small dirty vessel spewing out dark smoke.

Iverson went on, 'Killing a New York policeman – to say nothing of a man from Scotland Yard – isn't something we do with great enthusiasm. You, on the other hand, don't have . . . ' Iverson let his sentence hang unfinished.

'Killing isn't anything I relish myself,' Epishev said quietly.

'Nobody relishes it,' Iverson said.

Epishev smiled. 'And your superiors have qualms.'

'Qualms, sure,' Iverson remarked. 'But it's more than that. They're afraid of unwanted complications. They don't like the idea of this triple elimination coming back on them, sullying their good name, if you understand what I'm saying.'

'They're afraid of ghosts,' Epishev said, a slight scoffing note in his voice.

'You might say. Congressional ghosts. Journalistic ghosts. We're a country of inquisitive spectres, Colonel. It's part of the price we pay for freedom and democracy, you see.' Scoring a point, Iverson thought, and why the hell not? He hated Communism. He hated Communists. He didn't like this character Epishev coming to the USA with such ease, and he was unhappy with the idea of any collusion between America and the Soviet Union. But he wasn't the scriptwriter, Galbraith was the creator when it came to situations and scenes, Iverson was merely an actor in the drama. At least he had the advantage of knowing how this particular drama was going to end, and it pleased him to think of the small aircraft floating in darkness with all the density of the Adirondacks lying mysteriously below . . . He derailed this train of thought. Anticipation might be amusing and enjoyable, but as Galbraith was constantly saying, *The future is the province of soothsayers, Gary. We mere mortals have to make do with the moment*.

Epishev said, 'Your superiors don't have much power, if the killing of three insignificant people causes them such worry.'

'Oh, they have power, Colonel. But they also believe that discretion is one sure way of holding on to it.'

'Why do dirty work if they can get somebody else to do it for them?'

Iverson nodded. 'You were given an order from your own superior, Colonel. As far as I understand it, your mandate was to eliminate any threat to the plan. That's all you've come to America to do. Your duty. Plain and simple. Everything you need will be supplied to you. Immediately after the success of your undertaking, you'll be flown from New York to Germany. You'll re-enter Russia, your orders will have been carried out, people will be pleased on both sides. You'll have all the help we can place at your disposal. You can even have the use of our personnel – up to a point.'

'And what point is that?'

'The point where their culpability might be established.'

'By the ghosts you fear so much?'

'Exactly,' Iverson said.

Epishev watched the old tugboat vanish from his sight. Then the yellowy river was empty and the sun hung behind factory stacks on the opposite bank. Greshko's face floated up before him, the smell of the sick-room, the aroma of death that clung to the walls with the certainty of dampness.

'I have guarantees?' he asked.

'Cast-iron,' Iverson replied. 'Remember. If General Greshko trusted us enough to enter into this partnership, well . . . '

Epishev considered this. If Greshko had trusted these people, then Epishev had no reason to feel otherwise. Greshko's trust, as he well knew, was given only sparingly, and then never completely – but if he'd made an important compact with the Americans, then it was because the advantages in it for him were too attractive to refuse. There was a long silence in the room, broken finally by Iverson, who looked solemn as he said, 'You can count on our backing all the way.'

'You have Pagan and the girl under surveillance?' Epishev asked.

'Constantly,' Iverson answered. 'We never sleep.'

Moscow

'Tea, General?' Volovich asked, but his tongue was heavy in his mouth. He watched Stefan Olsky cross the floor to one of the armchairs, where he sat, crossing his legs and removing his cap.

'I don't think so,' Olsky said.

'It's no trouble – '

Olsky held one hand up, palm outward. 'I said no, Dimitri.'

Volovich hovered in the doorway to the kitchen. Pain throbbed behind his eyes.

Olsky said, 'I like this apartment. I imagine you're fond of it too. Convenient location. Pleasant rooms.'

'It's comfortable, General.'

Stefan Olsky was quiet a moment. 'You were going somewhere when I arrived.'

Volovich, whose mind suddenly had the texture of an ice-skating rink, a thing of slippery surfaces and frozen depths, nodded his head imperceptibly. 'A stroll, a late-night stroll,' he forced himself to say.

Olsky said nothing for a moment. 'You took a call from Viktor Epishev a few minutes ago. The call was patched here through a KGB switchboard in East Berlin. It originated in the United States. My listeners are located in the basement of this building – does that surprise you?'

A tapped telephone. It was a nightmare and Volovich was hurled into it and, as in all nightmares, no immediate escape was apparent, no relief forthcoming.

Olsky said, 'Viktor Epishev mentioned a threat to the plan, Dimitri. What is the nature of the plan?'

'Plan?'

'Don't play games with me. I hate games.'

Volovich shook his head. Being stubborn would finally prove futile, but there were old loyalties and they would sustain him, if only briefly. 'I don't understand what you're talking about, General.'

'I know you and Epishev visited Greshko last Saturday. I know Epishev left the country the next day. I know you're all involved in some kind of Baltic conspiracy – don't waste my time or insult my intelligence, Lieutenant.'

'I have nothing to say.'

Stefan Olsky stood up and strolled around the apartment. 'You have a comfortable life here, Dimitri. A good apartment, a car, a job that isn't terribly taxing. And yet you risk throwing it all away – for what? Why do you feel you have to protect Greshko and Epishev? Do you imagine they'd protect you if the situation were reversed?'

Volovich, who saw the logic of the question, didn't answer it. He looked down at the floor like a scolded schoolboy. He heard General Olsky move around the apartment, but he didn't look. Once, Olsky passed just behind him, so close Volovich could feel the General's breath on the back of his neck and smell his sweet aftershave lotion.

'I admire your loyalty, Dimitri. I understand your need to protect your superiors.'

Volovich still didn't speak.

'But sometimes old loyalties have to give way to new ones, Dimitri. Just as old systems have to yield to new ones, if there's going to be progress. Olsky was quiet a moment. 'I don't approve of some of the methods used by my predecessor. I admit they got quick results, but the cellars of Lubianka are damp and they don't feel quite right to me any more. Too medieval. Too crude. This is the late 20th century and Greshko's barbarism is outmoded. I much prefer the idea of solving this business between us in a civilised way . . .'

Stefan Olsky sat down again. He looked at the darkness upon the window, the slight light cast there by a streetlamp. A faint wind rustled the thin young trees outside. He turned his eyes back to the wretched Volovich. He felt an odd little sense of pity for the man.

'Tell me the nature of this plot.'

'I don't know,' Volovich said, raising his face to look at the General.

'Nobody told you, Dimitri? Am I to believe that?'

'Nobody told me. Correct.'

Olsky said, 'I understand you have a mother, Dimitri.'

'Yes.'

'You were able to use your influence to have her admitted to a KGB-operated rest home on the Black Sea.'

'I only did what a great many people do.'

'I'm not quibbling with that. But you used your influence in the wrong way, didn't you? Some people might construe it as misuse of privilege. Even a form of bribery.'

'Bribery?'

'In which case your mother would be obliged to move.'

'She's sick, General.'

'There are hospitals.'

'If she were in a hospital, she'd be dead now.'

Volovich glanced inside the kitchen where a kettle had begun to boil. He pictured his mother, who suffered from incurable emphysema, being moved from her light, airy room in the sanatorium and taken to some dreary state hospital in a small drab suburban town, where care would be minimal and medication unavailable and nurses rude.

'Make your tea, Dimitri. You need it.'

With hands that wouldn't stop shaking, Dimitri brewed tea, then stood inside the living-room and sipped it. He was quiet for a very long time, struggling with himself, seeing the sheer hopelessness of his situation. He said, 'I don't want her moved, General. She's comfortable where she is.'

'I imagine she is,' Olsky said.

Volovich swallowed hard. He might have had a pebble in his throat. 'I'd tell you if I knew, General. But I don't know. They kept me in the dark.'

'You must have some knowledge.'

'I understood Romanenko was delivering a message to a contact in Britain. Then Romanenko was shot, the delivery didn't happen and Epishev was sent to make sure nothing else would go wrong.'

Olsky felt a little flicker of fatigue go through him. All afternoon long and throughout the evening, he'd been dispatching KGB agents to the major cities in the Baltic countries, to Riga, and Vilnius, and Tallinn, hundreds of agents, under strict orders to act with stealth and the appropriate discretion in their inquiries. Dissidents, refuseniks, political deviants – these had been rounded up quietly and taken from their homes and questioned, then returned as swiftly as possible. Apartments were ransacked, files removed, documents studied. The operation brought forth a number of unexpected prizes, although none of them was related to the Baltic plot. A musician in Vilnius had an illegal mimeograph machine, a Jewish writer in Tallinn was in possession of a large amount of foreign currency, a cache of heroin had been discovered in the apartment of a physician in Riga, and in the Latvian city of Valmiera a professor of physics had a collection of several hundred precious icons. At any other time, Olsky would have been pleased with these results, but not now. They brought him no closer to the truth he really wanted.

'You must have gathered *some* impressions, Lieutenant.'

Greshko and Epishev, who sometimes seemed to share a common language Volovich couldn't penetrate, had never really made him an intimate part of the plan. 'A few,' Volovich said. 'The truth is, *I really didn't want to know.*'

'A conspiracy against your country, and you didn't want to *know?*'

'I worked with Colonel Epishev for twenty years – '

'And you're close friends – '

'Yes, we are – '

'And you couldn't let him down – '

'Correct, General.'

Olsky sighed. 'Tell me your impressions.'

Volovich put his tea-cup down. 'I understood the plot's aim was an act of terrorist aggression inside the Soviet Union.'

'But not in the Baltic republics?'

'I don't think so, General.'

Olsky asked, 'Where in the Soviet Union? And when?'

'I don't know.'

'Moscow? Leningrad? Kiev?'

'I swear I don't know – '

'And what kind of terrorism? Bombs? Assassinations?'

'My impression is that there's a plane involved. The attack will come from the air – but I'm guessing now.'

'From the air?'

'Yes, General.'

'But that's impossible,' Olsky said, just a little too quickly. Ever since a foolish West German teenager had contrived to fly a small aeroplane directly into Red Square two years ago – to the general humiliation of the authorities – defences had been strengthened. It was boasted now that they were impregnable, even if Olsky knew that 'impregnable' was one of those illusory words of which the military was so fond.

'One would have thought so,' Volovich said. 'I just wish I knew more.'

Volovich lapsed into an uncomfortable silence. General Olsky walked around the room, examining books and phonograph records. He picked up a copy of *Trud* from the table and flipped through the pages. He believed Volovich because he understood that a minion like Dimitri would not be made privy to essential information. He'd drive cars, and carry messages, and act as liaison, and he'd pick up information here and there, but his role would never be very significant. Greshko, even more possessive in old age than he'd ever been, more like a sharp-clawed cat than before, would have seen to that.

'What happens to me, General?' Volovich asked.

'Until I decide, you're under house arrest. You'll answer your telephone as you usually do, and if anybody calls from your office you'll say you're sick with cold, whatever. Apart from having this very severe chill, you'll sound otherwise perfectly normal.'

'And when my cold is cured?'

Olsky didn't answer the question. He stepped out of the apartment and stood on the landing. He looked down the stairwell, seeing through pale lamps the shadow of Colonel Chebrikov waiting in the foyer. Olsky descended, nagged by the realisation that he'd been looking for the sources of this Baltic business in all the wrong places. Common dissidents, writers, dreamers, Jews, applicants for exit visas – he had reached into the predictable areas for suspects, when he should have been looking elsewhere. *An aeroplane*. What kind of people were in a position to help an aeroplane carry out an act of aggression, an act of terrorism, against the Soviet Union? The answer was obvious, and yet painful because it involved powerful men who were sensitive when it came to their domain, which was nothing less than the air defences of the country.

He crossed the lobby to where Chebrikov was standing. The young Colonel, who stood at attention whenever Olsky was within his line of vision, said, 'There was a call for you on the car radio, General. From the Kremlin. The General Secretary wants to see you. Urgently, sir.'

Manhattan

'I'm sorry, I didn't know you had company, Frank,' Max Klein said when he stepped inside the hotel room and heard the sound of Kristina singing in the bathroom. He fidgeted with his bow-tie, a polka-dot affair that drooped, then sat down in one of the two easy-chairs in the place. He had a way of entering rooms, softly on sandals, that suggested the movements of a retired cat-burglar a little embarrassed by his habitual stealth. Even his feathery hair seemed stealthy on his skull, as though it would whisper secretively were a breeze to blow through it.

'It doesn't matter,' Pagan said. He didn't have time for explanations of Kristina. He might have told a narrative of Soviet repression, the story of a man whose family had been destroyed years ago, and how Norbert Vaska was imprisoned in Siberia, but Pagan had no real urge to familiarise Klein with all this background, nor with how Kristina Vaska had swept into his world. The sound of the shower stopped, but Kristina didn't emerge and there was only silence from the bathroom for a long time.

Klein stared at the bathroom door a moment, then took some papers out of his jacket. Like everything else that found its way into his pockets, the papers were crumpled and creased, and he had to spread them on the table and smooth them before they were manageable. 'Do you know how easy it is to set up a corporation in this country, Frank?'

he asked. 'It doesn't take much, I'll tell you. A lawyer draws up articles of incorporation, you pay the guy his fee – anything from three hundred to a thousand dollars – and you file the articles with the Corporation Commission, and that's it. Unless you're a known felon, you're the President of your own company within a matter of moments. A piece of cake.'

Pagan leaned across the table to look at the papers Klein had spread out. Klein said, 'These documents represent a triumph of corporate maze-making, Frank,' and he pushed some photostat sheets toward Pagan, who was hoping only to hear a bottom line, not a digression on the illusory nature of corporate structures.

'Carl Sundbach operated a company called Rikkad Inc.'

'Then *he* was responsible for hiring the Jaguar?'

'Not quite,' Klein said. 'He turned ownership of Rikkad over to another company named Piper Industries – they make belts for vacuum cleaners – but he stayed on as Chairman of the Rikkad board. Rikkad, incidentally, supply paper products to hotels. Not only was he Chairman of Rikkad, he was also CEO of Piper, so he'd sold his company to himself. High finance baffles me, so don't ask questions about tax strategies, because I don't have answers.'

'Where is this going, Max?'

'I'm getting there, I'm getting there.' Klein turned over some more sheets of paper. 'Look at this. Piper Industries, in turn, is a subsidiary of something called – drum rolls, please – Sundbach Enterprises, which was sold five years ago to none other than Rikkad Inc. The snake swallows its own tail and Carl was lying when he said he'd sold his company to another outfit. When you look at the names of the corporate officers in each case, only two names reappear. Carl's, and somebody called Mikhail Kiss, who is apparently the financial VP of all three companies.'

'But who the hell leased the bloody Jaguar?' Pagan asked.

'To find the answer to that baby, we have to ask Kiss, don't we? If he's financial Vice President, he's got to have some kind of information about what flows in and out. And since it costs approximately eight grand a year to lease a Jag with insurance from the company on Long Island – I checked it, Frank – it's the kind of expense he's not exactly going to overlook.'

Corporate mazes, funny paperwork, networks that swallowed themselves. Pagan gazed at the papers just as Kristina stepped out of the bathroom. Affected by slight awkwardness, Pagan made the introduction. Kristina, with a social charm he hadn't noticed about her before, shook Klein's hand and showered him with attention, as if he were suddenly the most important thing in her world – it was quite a knack and the small man looked as if he'd had an encounter with an angel. Pagan marvelled at the easy way she made small talk with Max Klein, then the grace with which she apologised for interrupting. She drifted to the window, turned her back on the two men, saying she hadn't meant to disrupt them. Max Klein protested – *her kind of interruption, hey, he could stand that any day of the week.*

Pagan watched her, saw the way her shirt tapered into the narrow belt of her blue cotton pants, and how her damp hair glistened in the fading sunlight. He was struck by wonder at the way she commanded his attention, by her grace and quiet elegance, and how the sunlight made a soft outline of her at the window.

'I've got an address for Kiss,' Klein answered. He opened his notebook and found the page he needed. He showed it to Pagan, to whom the address meant absolutely nothing.

'He lives in Glen Cove, on the Island,' Klein said. 'The phone's unlisted. I could get it if you needed it.'

'I don't,' Pagan said. 'I'd rather go in person.'

'Now?' Klein asked.

'Why not?'

Kristina moved directly behind Pagan, one hand laid on his shoulder with a proprietary intimacy he enjoyed. She said, 'I'll wait for you here if you like, Frank.'

Pagan stood up. He looked directly into the woman's dark eyes, seeing sympathy in them, and insight, and he realised nobody had looked at him in quite that way since Roxanne. He was moving in other dimensions here, and enjoying them, even if he wasn't sure where they were ultimately taking him. She kissed him lightly on the side of his face.

'Take care,' she said.

Moscow

The office of the General Secretary of the Communist Party of the Soviet Union was located in the Palace of Congresses at the Kremlin. It was painted in shades of brown and lit by concealed spotlights, each of which played quietly and artfully on the man's large desk, creating the impression that the Secretary was on a stage, the central player in an unfolding drama. The room, though vast, was stark in its furnishings. Thick brown curtains hung day and night at the window and the outer edges of the room were forever in gloomy shadow, and impenetrable. The General Secretary was middle-aged, the youngest leader of the Soviet Union since the Revolution, and wore no medals upon his chest in the fashion favoured by his bombastic predecessors. His style of governing was relaxed, at least in public, and low-key, and he enjoyed the rapport he'd established with the ordinary people. He took frequently to the streets, plunging among the workers, shaking hands until his flesh was bruised, listening to complaints and disappointments and promising to put things right. His was a new Russia, a different kind of Soviet society which, while forging ahead into unmapped regions, had to take pains not to offend and isolate the old – a difficult and rather delicate balancing-act, and a conundrum whose solution would take many years.

But the General Secretary was a determined man, and steely, and he'd been playing Party games for most of his adult life and so knew how to bend Party opinion in his direction, at least much of the time. He knew how to use patience to work the older members, those quietly sullen men who remembered Lenin and had survived the ravages of Stalin's ways. He knew how to use charm when he encountered stubbornness, and when charm failed him he knew the best way to be rid of the 'ideologically backward' was to send them to distant *oblasti* where they assumed grand titles and exercised absolutely no power. He knew how to use persuasion when it came to slowing down those of his own followers who wanted to hurry everything, men of excess and unbounded impatience, whose qualities of dedication were needed but whose temperaments were not.

Now, raising his face from the sheets of paper that contained the working draft of the speech he intended to deliver to the Praesidium in twelve hours' time at the Palace of Congresses, he capped his fountain-pen and looked at the figure of General Olsky, who sat facing him.

'This speech, Stefan, which may be the most audacious I've made,' – and here the General Secretary tapped the papers with his pen – 'is going to be called incautious by some, bold by others, and heresy by all the rest. The hardline Marxists are going to say I'm soft on Western capitalism, which is anathema to Communism. The so-called democrats among us are going to say I've bent over backwards to appease the Marxists and leftover Stalinists who got our economy into a mess in the first place. I want to make unemployment a fact of Soviet life, for example. A bad worker should be fired. Others should compete for his job. Isn't that perfectly natural? And the old men will nag me and say there can be no official unemployment in a socialist society. And the military – I see apoplectic generals when I announce my intention to cut military spending by twenty per cent over two years. I take a little from some, give a little to others, and hope it balances in the end.'

The General Secretary took off his glasses. It was two a.m. and he was weary. He surveyed the banks of telephones on his desk. Directly below his office was the main auditorium of the Palace where Communist Party Congresses had been held ever since 1961, when the Palace had been constructed. It was an impressive building, containing eight hundred rooms and a banqueting hall that could seat a couple of thousand people, but it wasn't the General Secretary's favourite building at the Kremlin by any means. He much preferred the sumptuous halls that housed the possessions of the Royal Family – the Regalia Hall with its extraordinary thrones and crowns, or the Hall of Russian Gold and Silver where there were elaborate candlesticks, goblets, rings, earrings and likenesses of saints. These displays stimulated a quiet yearning for Russia's past that most people might have found strange in a progressive General Secretary, but he'd read widely in Russian history, and perceived his own roots in these readings, as well as his own designs for the future. This great sluggish bear that was Russia, bogged down in its own muddy past, had to be set free to survive.

Olsky, always awed in the presence of the General Secretary, gazed across the massive desk. Socially, he was comfortable with the Secretary when they met for drinks, or once in a great while to play cards, but when it was a matter of official business he could never bring himself to feel easy.

The General Secretary said, 'About an hour ago, I spoke with Nikolai Bragin. At his insistence, let me add. He was most anxious.' He opened a drawer in his desk and drew out some photocopied sheets of paper, which he slid toward Olsky, who read them slowly, once, twice, three times. He tried to keep his hand from shaking.

'I'm obliged to show them to you, Stefan.'

'They're forgeries, of course,' Olsky said calmly. 'Where did you get them?'

'Would it surprise you to know they came from Greshko, who tried to interest Bragin in a story of scandal and corruption inside the Politburo?'

Olsky sighed. 'I'm not surprised.'

'According to Greshko, there's some kind of plot against the State going on. He told Bragin there are Baltic factions involved and he claims . . . And here the General Secretary paused, searching for the right phrase. 'He claims that you're part of the whole thing, Stefan. He also claims that a certain KGB Colonel, Viktor Epishev, has been sent abroad under your express orders to participate in the scheme.'

'Do I *have* to answer these ridiculous charges against me?'

The General Secretary smiled. It was one of the most famous, most frequently-photographed smiles in the world. 'I'm not satisfied there's any need for official action, Stefan., Do you know the exact nature of the so-called plot?'

'Not yet. But I'm close to knowing.'

The General Secretary picked up the documents and arranged them in one neat pile. 'Greshko's like a wild boar. Insane when wounded,' he said. 'I've always had a grudging admiration for the old fellow. I suppose that's a terrible admission to make, but he used to tell some entertaining stories.'

'A dinosaur's charm,' Olsky said.

The General Secretary made his chair swivel. 'I wonder about his life these days. I wonder what it's like to be completely stripped of power and sent out to pasture.'

Olsky said, 'His mind wanders. He can't tell reality from fantasy. The old Greshko wouldn't have done anything as ludicrous as running to the press with forgeries. He's slipping.'

'Slipping or not, he claims to have copies of these documents, Stefan. What worries me is the idea that he may have distributed them to people less scrupulous and more gullible than Bragin. A foreign journalist, for instance. Somebody in a foreign embassy, perhaps. You might make inquiries.'

The General Secretary was quiet for a second. 'I don't like the idea of Greshko shooting his mouth off to people about these documents, whether they're forgeries or not. My whole administration has advocated exposure of corruption. How does it look if articles appear in foreign newspapers about the Chairman of the KGB dabbling in capitalist money markets? The fact that the stories are false is irrelevant. People believe what they read, Stefan. And then the news comes back into this country over the Voice of America, or through Scandinavian radio, and before you know it we're discredited in front of our own people by rumours. It goes well beyond malice on Greshko's part, Stefan. It affects us all. It affects our standing in this country, all the way up from the smallest workers' soviet to the Central Committee itself – and we need all the support we can get these days. Any kind of weakness, any suggestion of corruption from within – I don't have to spell out the possible damage to us.'

Olsky didn't know what to say. He'd underestimated Greshko, but he wasn't the first man ever to do that. He'd been humiliated by the old man, and his position placed in jeopardy. He felt a quickening of anger, a warm flush spreading across his face. The idea that his reputation had been attacked, and in the most questionable way, enraged him. But he maintained the appearance of control, if only because a display of emotion in front of the General Secretary would have been unseemly.

He said, 'His physicians expected him to die months ago. I read their reports. Nobody expected him to live this long.'

'He was bred into a tough generation,' the General Secretary said. 'The fact remains, he's still alive and doing damage. The problem for you, Stefan, is to make sure the damage isn't fatal.'

'And how do I achieve that?'

The General Secretary took the cap from his fountain-pen and began to edit his speech. It was as if Olsky had ceased to exist in the room. After a moment, the General Secretary stopped writing, and looked across the desk at the Chairman of the KGB.

'You have to deal with it as you think fit, Stefan.'

Olsky wasn't quite sure what the General Secretary was saying to him.

'There are a great many people in this country, Stefan, who want to hurt us. Greshko happens to be in the vanguard of our enemies. They are also the enemies of progress. Therefore, they are acting against the Party's interests. But you're the Chairman of the KGB. Why ask me for advice?'

Olsky stood up. He turned his cap around between his hands. As he moved his face, he was struck directly by one of the concealed spotlights. He blinked.

'And this alleged plot?' the General Secretary asked. 'Can the Chairman of the KGB deal with that also?'

Olsky moved out of the light and stood in shadow. Was there something quietly mocking now in the General Secretary's voice? He wasn't altogether sure.

'I can deal with Greshko and his damned plot,' Olsky said, sounding all the more angry for the fact that he didn't raise his voice.

'Spirit!' the General Secretary said. 'That's why you got this job in the first place, Stefan. Spirit.'

Olsky moved toward the door. He understood he'd just discovered a use for Lieutenant Volovich. Yes, and it was appropriate, something the wretched Volovich was schooled to do. It pleased Olsky on one level, even as it dismayed him to think he'd reduced himself to the level of his predecessor, but it was a game of cunning now, and survival, and all the rules of decency were suspended.

'A question, Stefan.'

Olsky stopped, turned around, listened.

'They *are* forgeries, aren't they?'

'Yes,' Olsky said.

The General Secretary looked at the photocopied documents. 'Clever ones, though,' he remarked.

17

Near Tallinn, Estonia

Somewhere in the hours of darkness the girl called Erma came into the small room Marcus occupied at the top of the house and slid inside his sleeping-bag and put her arms round him, teasing him gently out of a sleep that hadn't been deep to begin with, a dreamless state, a dark floating. She curled her fingertips beneath his testicles and touched him, feeling him stir. She enjoyed the ease of her own power.

Marcus woke. He'd been expecting the girl to come to him for some time, and so he wasn't altogether surprised to find her beside him. He touched her breasts, which were soft, weightless, adolescent. He ran the palm of one hand – his skin was rough and this shamed him because he felt the girl flinch very slightly – down her flat hard belly to her groin, where the pubic hair grew light and shapeless. He moved a finger softly back and forth until she'd become very moist. She straddled him, rocking above him, invisible in the complete dark of the room. Blind like this, Marcus was conscious of how his other senses were extended – the slight milky smell of the girl, the unbearable softness of her flesh beneath his fingertips. It had been a long time since Marcus had been with a woman, and the girl could tell. He came quickly and she with him, shuddering, biting her lip to be silent because other people slept in this house, and she felt his sperm explode through the dark spaces of her body, thinking of it as a series of coloured lights popping deep inside her.

Then she rolled off him and lay beside him, holding his hand. She said, 'I'm scared, Marcus. If you want the truth, I'm terrified.'

'We're all scared,' Marcus whispered. 'We all pretend we're not because we have to. But deep down.... You'll find you're no different from the others.'

'Are we going to die?' she asked.

Marcus was quiet, listening to the dark, the sound of insects, the occasional flutter of a bird in a nearby tree, the light wind that blew from time to time upon the old shutters. He looked at the luminous dial of his watch. It was almost two a.m. This was the day, and he didn't want it to be, he wanted to stall for another day, perhaps find time to enjoy this girl a little longer. But there was no changing the calendar of events. Here in Estonia, and in

Lithuania, in Latvia, in Moscow – this was the day they'd planned and worked for, through years of secrecy and fear, through euphoria and gloom, trust and paranoia. He listened to the tick of his old watch, then turned the dial away so that the sharp green light wouldn't annoy him. He put his hand around the girl's shoulder. She trembled.

He gazed at the window and saw a thin moon sailing behind a garland of clouds. Tonight he was more tense than usual. But so were all the others who occupied this old house. Erma, the young man who called himself Anarhist, and the old fellow named Bruno, who occupied the attic and snored deliriously in his sleep and who'd been fighting the Russians one way or another since 1945 – they were all anxious in this damp, silent place.

What made Marcus more uneasy than the others was the fact that he'd gone to Tallinn earlier in the day for some food, and he'd sensed it at once in the streets, a change, a poisoned atmosphere – and then he'd seen the number of KGB cars in the city centre, and the officers who moved through side-streets and alleyways, and it became apparent to him that the KGB was conducting one of its periodic assaults on the city, ferreting out names on one of its notorious lists of 'hooligans' and suspected criminals. They moved on this occasion with unusual stealth, Marcus had thought, and he saw nobody handcuffed, nobody harried or pressed unwillingly inside automobiles – almost as if the order had come down from Moscow to do things quietly and with the least possible fuss. But the timing was bad for him. A concentration of KGB officers in the city was the very last thing he needed, and he couldn't help wondering if their presence had anything to do with the plan.

Fear, Marcus thought. And he listened to the night, to the sounds that grew in the dark.

'I want to fight, but I don't want to die,' the girl said.

'Nobody wants to die.' He could see her small face by moonlight and thought how beautiful it was in silver and how tragic the world was that this young girl, brutalised by the Russians, was ready to take up arms – when in another reality she might have been falling peacefully in love. An ordinary existence, a husband, children. 'Listen to me. You could leave now. Nobody would think badly of you. You've got a long life ahead of you.'

'What kind of life, Marcus?'

It was a good question, and Marcus had no answer. A life of repression, a life of careful utterances, of never knowing who was watching you, who was saying things behind your back – he might have mentioned all this but he didn't. He slid out of the sleeping-bag and went to the window and looked down into the courtyard.

'Not much of one,' she said, answering her own question. 'If I could keep my big mouth shut, and go about my business and notice nothing – but that would be like death.'

Marcus gazed at the outbuilding where the vehicles were parked. He saw it then, or thought he did, the cold hard disc of a flashlight, something that burned brief and yellow in the dark before vanishing, something alien that shouldn't have been there. He turned to the girl and said *Ssshhh*, then he dressed very quickly and told her to do the same thing. After that she should go wake the others immediately and tell them to move around with no noise. Armed, he said. They must be armed.

'*What did you see?*' she asked.

Marcus picked up his automatic rifle, his Uzi, and made a gesture with his hand, a swift, chopping motion that meant the girl was to hurry. She scampered quietly out of the room and Marcus went back to the window, where he looked out cautiously, seeing once again the glow of a flashlight and hearing the noise of the tarpaulin that covered the vehicles being moved slowly aside. Now there were shapes that came to him in the thin moonlight – three men, maybe four, but he couldn't see clearly. He heard the attic floor creak, then the noise of Bruno on the narrow staircase, followed by the sharp sound of the boy's voice as he was awakened from sleep by the girl. *What*? he asked, but the girl must have silenced him then.

Marcus turned when the old man came in the room. He had a pistol in one hand and a Browning Magnum rifle in the other, and he carried himself with his chest thrust forward, his shoulders back, the stance of an old fighter ready to renew hostilities with an eternal enemy.

'In the yard,' Marcus whispered. 'Three, maybe four. I can't tell.'

Bruno approached the window, peered down. He was licking his lips nervously, dehydrated by the possibility of gunplay. Marcus studied the darkness, seeing a figure emerge from the outbuilding with a flashlight, and immediately behind him two others, both illuminated briefly by the moon, young men, boys, dressed in KGB uniforms.

'Do we fire from here?' Marcus asked. He could smell liniment from the old man, which he habitually rubbed into his muscles every night, believing it kept him young and supple.

'*Mida rutem seda parem*,' Bruno said. *The sooner the better.*

The three figures below were coming towards the front door of the house now. They would knock first, Marcus knew, but only once, and then they'd force their way in. They had grounds for forced entry, even though they needed none. Four vehicles concealed under tarpaulin, highly unusual, even suspicious. It was enough.

Erma and the young man came into the bedroom. Anarhist had his M-16 strapped to his shoulder, the barrel slung forward. Erma carried a Uzi pistol, which seemed too large for her to hold. Tucked in the waistband of her pants was her other weapon, the Colt automatic. She looked fierce suddenly, no longer the scared girl who'd made love to Marcus moments before. Anarhist looked down from the window and Marcus could sense it in the young man, the urgency to fire his gun, the desire that drove him.

'Not yet,' Marcus whispered. 'There might be others in the vicinity. We need to be sure.'

'Wait? Screw it.' Anarhist raised the barrel of his rifle and Marcus gripped it with his hand. The angle was narrow now, because the men below were clustered around the front door and the boy would need to hang from the window to get a decent aim, and then he'd be exposed.

'Go to the top of the stairs,' Marcus said. 'When they come in, fire. You'll have a better chance.'

The boy went out of the room, followed by Bruno, whose anxiety was as sharp as the young man's. Marcus stayed at the window, watching, thinking that sounds of gunfire would bring others to the scene – if there were others nearby. And if they came, they'd enter this courtyard, and he could fire down on them. He smiled at the girl, who crossed the room and stood at his side. 'I'm ready,' she said.

Marcus touched the side of her face. It came to this moment, he thought, all the years of longing, the years of hatred, they came to a point in time when they couldn't be contained any longer. He seemed not to exist, or if he did it was in some form he couldn't recognise, shapeless, out of his body, an entity floating in the scant light. He held his breath, heard the sound of something hard on the door below, perhaps the barrel of a weapon – and then the door was forced open and the intruders were inside the house.

Marcus heard the gunfire, the terrible roar of it, and he saw through the open bedroom doorway the boy and the old man firing down into the entranceway, and the old man was saying *Kaunis! Kaunis!*, meaning, *beautiful, beautiful*. The fire was returned from below in a brief outburst, and Marcus saw the boy hit in the skull and thrown backwards against the wall. And then somebody was running from the house. Marcus, standing in the window, fired into the courtyard and the running figure stumbled, ran a few more paces, fell, crawled, and Marcus fired again.

The silence that flooded the dark was immense, oceanic. Marcus stepped out of the bedroom, glanced at the dead boy, then at the white face of the old man. The girl was making an odd little whimpering noise, her sleeve drawn up to her face like a mask. Below, at the foot of the stairs, lay two KGB men, one atop the other as if in death a strange intimacy had been imposed. Marcus went down the stairs, stepped into the courtyard, walked to where the third KGB man lay. The side of his skull was gone and his face, beneath the glare of Marcus's flashlight, had about it an unreality, like something left only half-created. He killed the flashlight, listening to the dark, concentrating. There was still only silence. He went out of the courtyard and walked until he came to the rutted track, and there he paused. A car was parked to the side of the track. He approached it cautiously. There was nobody in it, and no sign of any other vehicles. He sat down on the ground, his back to the front tyre of the car. He was shaking. He stuffed his hands in his pockets but the trembling went on, even after he'd risen and walked back to the house and climbed the stairs to look at Anarhist, who lay slumped against the wall.

Marcus reached down to close the boy's eyelids, conscious of the girl watching him, and of the old man standing nearby, clearing his throat in the manner of somebody about to make a speech. But Bruno thankfully said nothing.

'I don't know if they came here purely by chance or if somebody tipped them off, but we leave here now, Marcus said. 'We'll go elsewhere until it's time.'

Nobody disagreed.

Fredericksburg, Virginia

Galbraith had been furious – and his unleashed fury was like a mad panther loose in a room of fine china – when he learned of the risk Andres Kiss had taken by going to Carl Sundbach's apartment and unexpectedly killing the old man. The carnival in the street, the water display and the battered cop car, hadn't exactly delighted him either. It often seemed to him that the Clowns took their in-house name too seriously, and had some adolescent need to perform acrobatics and gravity-defying stunts in cars and the like, which Galbraith found distasteful altogether. True, they'd managed to divert Pagan from Andres Kiss, creating a triumph out of the almost disastrous coincidence of Kiss and Pagan being in the same area at the same time, but *still* . . . The whole situation need not have happened. *And it had arisen because Gary Iverson had failed to fathom young Kiss's killing potential.* He'd failed to read the man with any accuracy, and Galbraith was annoyed by the fact that his own trusted servant, the loyal Iverson, *his right fucking hand*, had proved less than perspicacious in an important matter.

Dressed in his robe, Galbraith was lounging in his basement, gazing at his consoles, tapping into the vast data banks of the planet. The grimness of his mood was caused as much by Andres Kiss's unnecessary risk as by his own apprehension, his tangible sense of anticipation. The clock was running down, and Frank Pagan was out there and he still had the potential to do damage.

Galbraith studied the consoles, albeit in an absent way, because he was thinking of Epishev. Listening to Gary's conversation with the Russian in New York a couple of hours ago, Galbraith had been struck by a chill note in Epishev's voice, and a curious reticence on the man's part – as if he suspected some kind of trap. Perhaps his long association with Greshko had made Epishev just as paranoid as his superior. It was only because of Greshko's suspicions that Epishev had become involved in the first place – and since Galbraith hated waste, it occurred to him that Epishev's talents should be put to the best possible use. It was one of Galbraith's most important gifts. He knew how to use the talents of other people to perform tasks he'd never undertake himself.

He looked at the consoles. There was a message from the US Embassy in Moscow, destined for the State Department, but picked up by Galbraith's technology just as it plucked everything out of the sky.

> The General Secretary will address the thirty-eight member Praesidium of the Supreme Soviet at approximately 1600 hours Moscow time. He is expected to push through a progressive programme on both social and economic matters although there is likely to be strong criticism from certain elements in the Party, who consider his innovations too drastic. It is thought that he has sufficient support, although the outcome will be close. End end end.

End end end – but of what? The world as he knew it? Galbraith wondered. He checked his wristwatch. It was almost seven. In three hours time Andres Kiss would be catching his plane to Norway. Three hours. Galbraith picked up one of his telephones, the white slimline one which looked incongruous amid the other five receivers, all of them standard US government issue. He punched in eleven digits, and almost immediately heard Gary Iverson's voice.

'Where are we, Gary?' Galbraith asked.

'On the Long Island Expressway,' Iverson replied. His tone was muted, a little remorseful. He clearly felt he'd failed Galbraith, and Iverson was a man who rarely failed at anything. Except, Galbraith thought, simple human understanding.

'And where's Pagan?'

'Pagan and Max Klein are about four cars ahead on the outside lane, sir. The girl is not travelling with them.'

'Their destination is Glen Cove?'

'Apparently,' Iverson said across a connection that was remarkably clear. 'I imagine Max Klein's researches at the Corporation Commission provided him with Mikhail Kiss's name. I guess they tracked down the number of Andres's Jag, and that got Klein rolling.' A pause. 'I'm sorry about that one, sir. I had no idea Andres would do what he did. If I'd known . . . '

Sorry, Galbraith thought. Being sorry wasn't going to cut it. Being sorry was a dead-end street. This was where the miscalculations had led. This was what Iverson's illiteracy in reading the human heart came down to. This panic, this last-minute crap, this needless pursuit and the inevitable slaughter. 'Call the Kisses. Tell them to leave for the airport.'

'My information is they've already gone, sir.'

'Fine. Where's Epishev?'

'He's directly behind me in a van.'

'And the MO?'

'It's his own idea and I think effective. It dispenses with both men at once.'

Galbraith said, 'I don't want you anywhere near it Gary. Is that understood?'

'Understood. What about the girl?'

'I'm not interested in her in the meantime. When Pagan's no longer . . . well, *around*, we'll keep her under surveillance for a while to see what she does. Not that it's going to matter, because it's after the fact by then, Gary. Keep me posted. And no fuck-ups. No near misses. No collisions. No calamities. Are you receiving me?'

Galbraith hung up. He chewed on a fingernail. There was at least no caloric intake in this kind of oral activity. He was still nervous, and there were phone calls to return from Senators Holly and Crowe, that fretful Tweedledum and Tweedledee. He lay down on the sofa, thinking how unfortunate it was that a man like Frank Pagan, whose file he'd pulled from the Scotland Yard interface, whose attributes he admired, was doomed to die because he'd been in the wrong goddam place at the wrong goddam time.

The fat man shut his eyes. He contemplated the design of White Light, the mosaic which, despite the unwillingness of certain pieces to fit, was nevertheless a fairly attractive thing to behold. He was pleased in general with the pattern, and the fact that neither he nor his department was even remotely involved in events which by tomorrow night would have echoed around the world. He even liked the sound of the very name White Light – which had about it a certain shimmering intensity, a mysterious quality, something that raised it above the mundane manner in which clandestine projects were normally christened. He thought of Operation Mongoose, and Operation Overlord, and Project Bluebird, and he decided that White Light was superior to all of them.

He opened his eyes when he heard the sound of somebody knocking on the basement door. He called out *Entrez* and saw the ugly little woman known rather cruelly around the building as Madame Avoidable.

'The papers you asked for,' she said. She wore a green wool cardigan and matching skirt and her glasses kept slipping to the end of her nose, causing her to make constant adjustments.

Galbraith took the documents and thanked her.

She said, 'These are in the system.'

'And the genuine ones?'

'Expunged as per your request.'

'Mmm mmm mmm, a million kisses of gratitude,' Galbraith said. He flipped through the pages, about six or seven in all. He watched Madame Avoidable leave, then he spread the sheets on his table and gazed at them. They were very good, very convincing. It was Andres Kiss's military record, and it read like a case-study in schizophrenia. He absorbed such phrases as 'delusions of grandeur', 'failure to accept any authority other than his own', 'a sense of a personal mission against the Soviet Union', and 'unwillingness to comply with Air Force regulations'. At the bottom of the page was the signature of a military psychiatrist (since deceased) and the stamped legend DISHONORABLY DISCHARGED. It was a nice little piece of fabrication and it would go down well with the gentlemen of the press when the time came.

Long Island

Max Klein had replaced the battered Dodge with another department car, a tan Ford of unsurpassed anonymity, the kind of vehicle used by narcotics officers making undercover buys. Pagan noticed scratchmarks across the back seat where handcuffed suspects had presumably scuffled around vigorously. Klein, who hadn't said much all the way from Manhattan, was curious about the woman in Pagan's room, but reluctant to ask questions. He had the feeling the Englishman wasn't exactly a man who opened up for you. Likeable, tough, the kind of guy to have with you in a crisis, Pagan gave the impression of a closed person, difficult to know, hard to reach.

As the Ford passed an exit for Flushing, Klein decided to take a chance. He said, 'I thought you came to New York on your own, Frank.'

'I did.'

'Don't think I'm prying. The woman, I mean.'

'I don't.' Pagan enjoyed the friendliness he found in Americans, the quick camaraderie, the casual way first-name relationships were formed, all of which made a bright contrast to the taciturn English, whose hearts you had to drill open as if they were safes containing something too precious to touch. The down side of this easy manner was the way certain Americans thought they had the freedom to go rummaging around in your life, which was what Klein was edging towards now. But Pagan was going to be firmly polite.

'I don't want to go into it, Max. I don't want to complicate your life.'

'Complicate my life?' Max Klein laughed. 'My life's already complicated. I'm thirty-seven years old and instead of hanging in the Museum of Modern Art I'm driving a goddam cop car on the Long Island Expressway. You think that's a simple transition?'

Withered ambitions, Pagan thought. He stared at the highway before him and the way the sinking sun glinted from passing cars. Did he want to hear about Klein's life? Apparently he had no choice because Klein was talking about his paintings, his days in art school, the months he spent dragging a portfolio of his stuff around midtown galleries, only to encounter the severity of rejection. At least it steered the subject away from Kristina, Pagan thought, half-listening to Klein's good-natured banter about the rebuffs he'd received at the hands of gallery owners and art critics. Max had developed a shell of self-mockery, referring to his paintings as the work of a quick-sketch artist with delusions of mediocrity. Pagan, smiling, looked in the mirror on the passenger side, seeing the flow of traffic behind.

'I used to be in demand with my sketches,' Klein said as he deftly changed lanes. 'Give me a witness, a half-assed description, and I'd whip out a picture of a suspect in no time flat. Nowadays, they can use computers or a pre-made ID kit. They don't need my particular skills. So they push me here and there, one department to another. Fraud last month. Juvenile the month before. Before that it was missing persons. You want an insight into sheer misery, Frank, missing persons is the cream.'

Pagan made a noise of sympathy. He saw the exit for Great Neck. 'How much further?' he asked.

'A few miles,' Klein replied.

Pagan glanced once more in the side mirror. A large cement-mixer rattled behind, and then tucked at an angle in the rear of this monster was a dark blue van whose windshield glowed golden in the sun. He looked at the greenery along the edge of the expressway, imagining simple pleasures, walking with Kristina Vaska through a meadow or along a sandy shore or lazing by the bank of some stream. *Sweet Jesus, Frank* – had it come to this so soon, these little halcyon pictures, these banal images of romance? He was almost embarrassed by the direction of his own mind. *You've been too lonely too long*.

Klein swung the car off the expressway now. Pagan saw the exit sign for Glen Cove and then the greenery that had bordered the expressway became suddenly more dense and leafy, and white houses appeared to float half-hidden in the trees. Klein slid from his pocket the piece of paper with Mikhail Kiss's address on it, and looked at it as he braked the Ford at a red light. Since he didn't know where Brentwood Drive was located, he said he'd have to stop at a gas station and ask.

Pagan turned his head, seeing the same cumbersome cement-mixer and the dark blue van behind him, and suddenly, without quite knowing why, he was uneasy, perhaps because he remembered the van outside Sundbach's building, which had been the same make as the one behind him now, perhaps it was because the van hadn't attempted to overtake the slow-moving cement-mixer for the last twenty miles. It's in the air, Frank, he thought, this general wariness, this low-level fear that you'll go a step too far and upset somebody to the point of madness – something you might have done already.

He tried to relax, rolling his window down and smelling the perfume of new-mown grass float across the evening. He had a sudden glimpse of water, a narrow inlet that penetrated the land from Long Island Sound, and then the water vanished behind trees. Klein pulled the Ford into a gas station and Pagan saw both the cement-mixer and the dark blue van go past, and he felt a quick surge of relief because he'd already begun to construct unpleasant possibilities in his mind.

Pagan took the slip of paper from Max Klein. 'I'll get directions,' he said, and he stepped out of the car, glad to stretch his legs. He walked toward the glass booth where the cashier sat. He pushed the paper towards the woman, who was middle-aged and wore her hair in a slick black bun. She had the slightly flamboyant look of a retired flamenco dancer. She started to give directions, then interrupted herself to answer the telephone.

Pagan, staring across the forecourt, past the pumps, past Max Klein in the tan Ford, folded his arms. He could hear the distant drone of a lawn-mower, a summery sound, lulling and comforting, as if the very essence of the suburb was encapsulated in that single familiar noise. There was nothing alien here, nothing extraordinary, just this unchanging placidity.

He shut his eyes a moment, caught unaware by a sudden tiredness, then he shook himself, opened his eyes, saw the dark blue van come back along the road, moving slowly, the windshield still burnished by sunlight. It came to a halt on the side of the street opposite the station. Pagan felt curiously tense as he watched the vehicle.

The van moved again, but slowly still, making an arc in the direction of the gas station. Pagan put his hand behind him, reaching for his gun in the holster, but not yet withdrawing the weapon because this might be nothing, an absolutely innocent situation, a van driver deciding he needed gasoline and turning back to get it, nothing more than that. Frank Pagan fingered the butt of the Bernardelli, watched the van cruise toward the pumps, and he realised how jumpy he'd become. He saw Klein behind the wheel of the Ford, his head tilted against the back of his seat in a weary manner.

The van kept rolling forward. It was about twenty feet from the station now. It stopped again, hidden somewhat from Pagan's view by the thicket of gas-pumps. The cashier hung up the telephone and said, 'Now where was I? Oh, yeah, you take a left at the second light,' but Pagan wasn't really listening. He saw a hand emerge from the blue van and something dark flew through the air, crossing the bright disc of the evening sun a moment, flying, spinning, falling, and it was a second before Pagan realised what it was, a second before he opened his mouth and shouted *Max!*

He saw Klein's face turn towards him even as the van hurried away and the driver was briefly visible. Then the Ford exploded and a streak of flame burst upwards, blue and yellow and red fusing into one indescribable tint, and he heard the sound of glass shattering into something less than fragments, something as fine as powder, then a second explosion which caused Klein's burning car to rock to one side. For a moment all light seemed to have been sucked out of the sky, as if the sun had dimmed. Pagan wasn't sure, but he thought he heard Max Klein scream from behind the flames that seared through the car, the burning upholstery, the black smoke that billowed from under the wrecked hood. He rushed forward, thinking he might have a chance to haul Max out, but the intensity of heat and the choking smoke drove him back, scorching his face and hair, blackening his lips. He saw Klein through flame, burning like a straw man, one fiery hand feebly uplifted, as if he might still find his way out of this furnace – and then the flames engulfed him. Pagan, drawing a hand over his face, was forced to step back. The air was unbreathable and the smoke that rose furiously out of the car stung his eyes and blinded him. A mechanic rushed out with an extinguisher but he couldn't get close to the car because of the heat. Besides, it was far too late to help Max Klein. Inside the glass booth the cashier was calling the fire department, also far too late for Max Klein.

Pagan moved back from the sight of the burning car and sat down against the wall of the gas station, paralysed by utter dismay. He hadn't acted quickly enough, hadn't drawn his gun when the van had first aroused his interest, hadn't done a goddam thing to alert Klein. He listened to the sound of the car flaring and he turned his face to the side because he could still feel the awful blast. The cashier came out of the glass booth and touched him on the shoulder and asked if he was hurt. Pagan shook his head. He hadn't even suffered a superficial burn. The woman pressed a wet cloth into his hand and he covered his face with it. Poor fucking Max Klein, the department handyman. Whoever had tossed the grenade hadn't meant it to be for Klein alone, he was sure of that.

Whoever. He rose, threw the damp cloth away, drew his sleeve across his forehead. For an instant, just before the blast, before the rich, deathly smoke had covered everything, he'd seen the face of the van driver with striking clarity, and he remembered the last time he'd seen that face on a London street. Viktor Epishev, impassive behind the wheel of the van, his expression one of complete concentration, like that of a man who loved control. Pagan wondered bitterly if Uncle Viktor had ever done anything in a spontaneous way. Had he ever seduced a girl? Fallen hopelessly in love? Yielded to a casual whim like rolling up the cuffs of his pants to walk the edge of a tide or gone out and bought a brightly-coloured shirt just for the sheer hell of it?

Control and violence.

Pagan, shocked by the suddenness of things, numbed by his last image of Max Klein behind the screen of fire, wandered inside the men's room and filled the wash-basin with cold water and plunged his head into it, holding it there until he thought his lungs might explode. Gasping, he raised his face up from the water, and grabbed a handful of paper towels, then he walked back out to where the Ford was burning like some awful pyre whose colours kept changing. He shook his head from side to side, wondering if Epishev had mistakenly thought both Pagan and Klein had been in the Ford. Perhaps, blinded by sunlight, he hadn't seen clearly. Perhaps even now Epishev imagined that Pagan was dead in the ruined car. Whatever, it was painfully clear that Pagan was to be prevented at any cost from visiting the house of Mikhail Kiss – whose address he held, scribbled on a piece of creased paper by Max Klein, a name and a number surrounded by half-sketched faces and interlocking circles and three-dimensional squares, the work of the failed artist.

Throat parched, Pagan watched as a bright red fire-engine drew into the gas station, a flurry of sirens and dark hoses unrolling and men who worked at a speed that suggested the whole gasoline station was going to blow up at any moment. In silence Pagan watched them blast the blazing car with their high-pressure sprays, but then he walked away because he didn't want to be anywhere nearby when they doused the flames sufficiently to pull the remains of Max Klein from the crematorium.

Kennedy Airport, New York

Mikhail Kiss found the bright lights of the terminal painful to his eyes, and he blinked a great deal, although sometimes he wasn't sure if it was the harsh light or the prospect of tears he was struggling against. He watched Andres at the Scandinavian Airlines desk, the check-ink procedure, the way the female clerks fawned around him. He didn't have a suitcase, only an overnight bag. There was no luggage to go on board. Andres returned to the place where Mikhail sat and took the seat next to him, saying nothing, just tapping his fingertips on his knees or every so often checking his boarding-pass.

Mikhail Kiss lit a cigarette and for the first time in many years inhaled the smoke deeply into his lungs. He took his eyes from Andres and looked across the terminal floor, seeing two security cops move side by side with vacant looks on their faces. They passed through the glass doors and out into the failing light. Mikhail Kiss examined the departures board. Soon they'd begin boarding the plane that would take Andres to Norway. Mikhail stubbed out the cigarette and sighed. Why was there nothing to say? Why, at the very point he'd worked so long and hard to reach, were words so reluctant to form in his mouth? He laid his hand on his nephew's sleeve, a gentle gesture, perhaps more meaningful than any words could be. But it was a small thing, and it didn't go very far to dispel the feeling of estrangement from the young man that Mikhail Kiss experienced.

Something was wrong, and he couldn't define it. It was more than the goddam dream that kept coming back at him like a bad taste. The face of Norbert Vaska. The music in that white restaurant. *They don't go away,* he thought. *They come back to haunt you, no matter what you do,* What did he feel? he wondered. Was it sorrow? Or resentment at the tenacity of ghosts? But it was more than just the persistent image of Norbert Vaska that troubled him, and he searched his mind fruitlessly.

A bad feeling. Like the one he'd had that night in Edinburgh. That was close to the sensation.

Andres Kiss smiled. For a second Mikhail thought he detected a slight tension in the expression, and he was caught in a memory of when Andres had been a young boy, ten, maybe eleven, stepping into a boxing-ring for the first time, his face hidden behind a protective headpiece too large for him, his hands dwarfed by enormous gloves. He remembered how Andres had turned to him at the last moment and how frightened he'd looked and Mikhail, touched by this vulnerability, had felt needed then – but the moment passed and Andres went inside the ring and demolished his opponent with fierce speed and Mikhail realised that night he'd never really be needed in this young man's life, that Andres could achieve everything he wanted on his own, without help. And so it was now.

There was an announcement that the flight to Oslo had begun to board. Mikhail looked at his watch. 9:30. Andres examined his ticket and boarding-pass again, saying, 'Round-trip. I appreciate your optimism, Mikhail.'

Was this meant to be a small joke? 'I wouldn't send you anywhere one-way, Andres,' and he reached out to embrace the young man, whose body was stiff and unyielding, as if human contact distressed him. It was then Mikhail noticed a scratch on his nephew's forehead, which had apparently been covered by some kind of makeup, a powder of the kind women use, and he was going to ask about it. But now there wasn't time. And he didn't want to know anyhow.

Andres Kiss stood up. 'I guess this is it,' he said.

Mikhail Kiss felt moisture forming behind his eyes, but he blinked it away. It was a time for strength, not for useless sentimentality. He wished Carl Sundbach could have been here, because there was a sense of incompleteness, of somebody missing from the circle. Maybe he'd call Carl later, tell him that Andres was on his way to Norway, keep him informed. And maybe by this time Carl would be over his weird paranoia that somebody was following him through the streets and watching his apartment. Old age, Kiss thought, feeling the phantom of it move through him. It rendered men absurd, magnified their fears, expanded their anxieties.

Andres said, 'The day after tomorrow, Mikhail. Until then.'

'Until then,' Mikhail Kiss said quietly. He watched Andres walk to the gate, then pass through without looking back. Mikhail had an attack of sudden panic and was filled with the urge to go after his nephew and call him back and tell him that everything was cancelled, there was no need to fly. Even if he'd done so, it would have been a futile gesture because the scheme had a life of its own now, a force that couldn't be halted, not even by the man who'd first set the whole thing in motion. It had grown, and matured, like a child over whom you no longer have dominion.

His work was finished. He walked out of the terminal. He stepped under lamps and signs and moved between taxis and buses. He felt his age again, a decay, a sense of internal slippage. And his memory was surely going. He'd forgotten to say to Andres at the last moment the words *Vabadus Eestile* – freedom for Estonia. But it was too late now even if the unspoken words seemed very important to him. He walked into the parking garage and took the stairs up to the second level, where he'd parked his Mercedes.

It was time to go home and wait.

18

Glen Cove, Long Island

Without waiting to answer awkward questions from investigators, Frank Pagan, sickened by the stench of fire that clung to him, had walked away from the burning Ford and moved through narrow streets, following the general directions the cashier had given him. These were impressive streets where branches of old trees interlocked overhead, creating barriers against the sky. The houses here were large, built on enormous green lots. These were streets in which money didn't speak, it hummed tastefully. Pagan paused when he reached the corner of Brentwood Drive, where the greenery was even more dense and the houses virtually invisible behind crowded stands of trees and thick hedges.

There was something secretive about the street, the impenetrable shadows, the way the houses were concealed from view. People here wanted to live private lives, and so they'd created their own wilderness in the suburbs of Long Island. A pedestrian in this place stood a pretty good chance of being arrested, because it was the kind of area where walking was something only criminals and cranks ever did.

He looked at the driveways of homes as he passed them. Numbers were so discreetly displayed you had to search for them among shrubbery. He found number fourteen. A hedgerow grew around the property and a gravel driveway disappeared among foliage. The only part of the house that could be seen was the red-tiled roof. Pagan took a few steps along the driveway, which curved suddenly and the house came in view, an ornate turreted construction set just beyond a well-kept lawn. A green awning hung above the columned porch. There were no cars in the driveway, no signs of life. He glanced at the windows, noticed nothing, no face behind glass, no curtain shivering.

He walked up on to the porch. The doorbell was one of those old-fashioned brass affairs that you pulled toward you. He could hear the bell echo within the house, but nobody came to answer. He moved slowly around the back of the house where an impressive rose garden was located. The flowers grew in lavish, meticulous beds.

Pagan looked through the glass walls of a sun-room, which had been added to the original structure. But he saw nothing, only the vague outlines of furniture. Then he stared across the rose beds for a time, where there was a white-latticed gazebo draped by willows, and beyond that a thick stand of oleander. None of the surrounding houses was visible because of the dense foliage, which gave this particular dwelling a sense of isolation, of loneliness – as if nobody had ever lived here.

Some of this isolation touched him. He had an urge to sit down and sleep and withdraw, making himself numb to the death of Max Klein, numb to the question that had begun to nag at him ever since he'd strolled away from the gas station – *how had Epishev known he was in the United States?*

Maybe it was no great mystery. He imagined how it might have happened that Epishev came across his information. John Downey, for instance, who was known to have connections in Fleet Street, and who was often the so-called 'reliable source' in newspaper stories about the Yard, might have run into an intrepid reporter anxious to get some eyewitness details about events in Edinburgh and Downey, after a few of the Newcastle Brown Ales he so enjoyed, might have let slip the fact that Frank Pagan was off on some junket to New York City. As soon as the scribbler had his information, it would then travel along the Street, passed from the mouth of one crime reporter to the next, from one pub to another, where sooner or later the item would reach the ears of one of those accredited, if vaguely shadowy, journalists who gathered information for the Soviet press. From there it was a cinch that the knowledge of Pagan's trip would find its way back, sooner or later, to a source at the Soviet Embassy. A whisper in the ear of Epishev, and there it was . . .

Pagan could imagine this sequence, which was less one of malicious exposure than of bloody careless talk loosely bruited about in places where cops and reporters met to sink a few jars.

Epishev, Pagan thought. Everywhere Uncle Viktor went there was death in the vicinity. Everything he touched shrivelled and turned black. It was quite a knack to go through life laying things to waste all around you.

His head still filled with the memory of flames, Pagan peered once again through the glass walls of the sun-room. Then he tried the door, which yielded. Whoever owned this house, whoever Mikhail Kiss might be, he clearly felt he had nothing to fear from burglars, that the quiet authority, the rich seclusion of the street, was enough of a deterrent in itself. Pagan pushed the door, entered the room quietly, stood motionless. There was a strong smell of cut flowers in the air.

He stepped out into the hallway. To his left a flight of stairs rose up into darkness. Ahead of him, across the entranceway, were other rooms. Doors lay open and the half-darkened surfaces of wooden furniture gleamed quietly. The silence here was deep and impressive and the dying sunlight that managed to find its way inside rooms, squeezing through drawn-down blinds, was slightly unreal, like light from another planet.

Pagan went to the foot of the stairs, looked up a moment, then walked inside the room just ahead of him, a dining-room with an oval table and rather spare contemporary prints on the walls, a room with a certain sterile quality that suggested meals were never actually eaten here, nobody sat down to dine. It reminded Pagan of a window display in a furniture shop. Unlike the home of Carl Sundbach, with its clutter and disorder and a sense of an unarranged life being lived in its rooms, the house of Mikhail Kiss was imbued with absences and silences.

Pagan entered another room, a sitting-room, expensively done, white leather sofa, matching chairs, chrome, and again the same spacious emptiness. He walked to the stairs, climbed quietly, reached the landing. Two bedrooms, an office, a bathroom. The first bedroom was large and uninteresting, the bed made up, a book open and face down on the bedside table, an easy-chair under the bay window. Pagan glanced at the book, which was in a language he didn't understand, then he noticed a photograph of a woman on the mantelpiece across the room. He didn't pick up the framed picture. The woman wore her hair in the style of the late 1930s. It was a good face, probably beautiful if you liked the gaunt, rather haunted look. Written on the picture, and barely legible, was an inscription – again in a language Pagan couldn't read – and the signature *Ingrida, 1938*. For a reason he couldn't begin to explain, Pagan was touched by a momentary sadness, perhaps caused by the look in the woman's eyes, or the sense he suddenly had that he was gazing upon a picture of the dead. Why did some photographs create the impression that the subject of the picture was dead?

He stepped out of the bedroom, then into the adjoining one. A narrow room, a single bed, prints depicting a variety of aircraft, and trophies – shelves of silver cups and medallions and plaques, awards decorated by miniature figures, a boxer, a runner, a javelin-thrower. It was quite a collection. Pagan picked up a statue of a boxer and read *To Andres Kiss, First Prize in the Junior Boys Section, Long Island Boxing Association, 1969*. All the awards here were to the same Andres Kiss, and there were scores of them, attesting to a disciplined, athletic life, an achiever's life, the kind of existence defined by very definite goals. Did Andres ever have time for fucking around? Pagan wondered. Presumably not, if he spent all his adolescent years training for competitions and winning trophies.

Andres Kiss. Was he Mikhail's son? Pagan replaced the trophy, crossed the room, looking for photographs of the boy wonder. Trophies galore, but no pictures, no casual snapshots. He looked at the posters of aircraft. They were all US and British fighter planes from World War II. So Andres liked athletics and aeroplanes – what did this tell you, Holmes?

Pagan went to the window, looked out across the garden at the back of the house, seeing how darkness, almost complete now, robbed the roses of their colours. He let the curtain fall back in place and was about to turn out of Andres Kiss's room when he noticed some framed papers on the wall above the bed. He had to turn on the bedside lamp to read them. Interesting stuff. A certificate issued by the United States Air Force to Captain Andres Kiss on the occasion of his promotion. An award from the USAF to Captain Andres Kiss for compiling one thousand hours of flying time. An honourable discharge to Major Kiss, dated September 1985. So young Andres went from being a juvenile terror in the boxing-ring to a wizard of the airways, a high-flyer. Pagan turned off the bedside lamp and stepped out of the bedroom to the darkened landing.

He was about to go inside the room that was clearly an office when he heard the front door opening and the sound of a key being tugged out of a lock, then the *chink-chink* of a chain in the palm of a hand. Frank Pagan stood very still at the top of the stairs, watching as a light was turned on in the hallway, illuminating the big man who stood in full view for only a moment before he stepped out of Pagan's vision.

Pagan held his breath. He heard water running inside a glass, then the rattle of ice-cubes, the sound of liquid being stirred. He descended slowly, quietly, watching the square of yellow light falling out of the kitchen and into the hallway. The big man's shadow appeared briefly, then was gone, and a door closed somewhere. The sun-room, Pagan thought. *He makes himself a drink, takes it to the sun-room, sits down, relaxes.*

Pagan reached the foot of the stairs, where he paused. Through an open door he could see the man sitting on a wicker sofa, his legs crossed, his head tilted back, a drink held slackly in one hand. Pagan, taking his gun from its holster, moved into the doorway that led to the glass-walled room.

The man stared at him in surprise. Ice-cubes made faint knocking sounds inside his glass.

'Don't bother to get up,' Pagan said. It was the man in the photograph, the one who'd been snapped beside Romanenko and Sundbach. Altered by time, his hair white, his body rearranged by the years, but it was undeniably the same man.

'Mikhail Kiss?' Pagan asked.

'Who wants to know?'

Pagan flashed his ID in front of the man's face. Mikhail Kiss, who had looked alarmed, seemed to relax now, reassured by Pagan's identity card.

'I thought you were, I don't know, a burglar,' he said. 'I'm Kiss.'

'You left your side door open, Mr Kiss.'

Mikhail Kiss stood up, sipped his drink, smiled. 'I grow careless with age Mr Pagan. Do me a small favour. Put the gun away.'

Pagan returned the Bernardelli to his holster. 'A precaution,' he said.

'Sure. I might have pulled a gun and fired on you. After all, we live in an age of guns,' Kiss remarked, still smiling, running one large hand through his white hair.

Pagan glanced a moment through the glass walls, seeing the ghostly shape of the gazebo out there in the darkness. Then he turned to look back at Mikhail Kiss, who seemed completely at ease now, and hostlike, as if he were wondering what kind of treats he could find to force upon his visitor.

Pagan had an uncomfortable moment suddenly, a light-headed sensation, a flashback to the sight of Max Klein in the burning car, and he wondered if this image was going to recur, if it was going to come into his head when he didn't want it, or enter his sleep when he didn't need nightmares. He pushed the picture from his mind and looked at Kiss, wondering if the big man had noticed his discomfort.

'You've come a long way,' Kiss said. 'What can I possibly do for a man from Scotland Yard?'

Pagan needed to sit down. He moved to one of the wicker chairs. He studied Kiss's face, thinking it was good-natured, and cheerful, the face of a man who doesn't come to subterfuge easily. Where to begin? Where to make the first incision? Start with the car. Start with something simple. Go slowly at first.

'I'm trying to trace the driver of a certain Jaguar,' Pagan said.

'A Jaguar?' Mikhail Kiss asked.

'The car was leased to a company called Rikkad, of which you're the financial Vice President.'

'Rikkad,' and Kiss looked like a man ransacking his memory, a man who hears a faint bell ring at the end of a long corridor.

'Rikkad is one of your business ventures with Carl Sundbach,' Pagan said in the manner of a theatrical prompter. There was an act going on here, and Kiss had slipped into some kind of amnesiac role, but Pagan wasn't in the mood to be a gullible onlooker in the balcony.

Mikhail Kiss drained his scotch, set his empty glass down. 'We've had so many business ventures, sometimes I forget,' he said. Why in the name of God was an English cop interested in the Jaguar? Only Andres ever drove it, and he'd returned it to the offices of the leasing company late that afternoon, so why was Pagan asking questions about it?

'But you remember now,' Pagan said. 'And you remember the Jaguar.'

'Yes, of course, it comes back to me.'

'Did you drive it?'

Mikhail Kiss shook his head. 'Too sporty for me, Mr Pagan.'

'Who used it then?'

'My nephew mostly. Andres Kiss.'

Pagan sat back in his chair, and the wicker creaked under his weight. *Andres Kiss, Superboy.* 'I'd like to talk to him.'

'Unfortunately, that isn't going to be possible.'

'Why not?'

'He just left on vacation.'

'When?'

'Tonight,' Kiss said.

'Where did he go?'

Mikhail Kiss shrugged. 'Europe,' he answered.

That, Pagan thought, was fucking useful information. 'Where exactly?' he asked.

'He said he was touring. You know the young, Mr Pagan. They don't make plans.'

'He flew, did he?'

Mikhail Kiss nodded. He had a tight, claustrophobic feeling, and it made his chest ache. What did an English policeman want with Andres, for Christ's sake?

'Where did he fly to?' Pagan asked.

Kiss laughed. 'I'm only the boy's uncle, Mr Pagan. He tells me nothing.' He lit a cigarette. 'Why are you asking these questions about Andres?'

Pagan didn't answer at once. He liked the silence, the way it built, the suspense that lay at the heart of quietness. He got out of the wicker chair and looked across the darkened gardens. The gazebo was no longer visible, the sky moonless.

'Carl Sundbach was murdered this afternoon,' Pagan said, and he turned to look at Mikhail Kiss's reaction.

Kiss was waxy suddenly, and pale. 'Murdered?'

Pagan nodded. It was obvious that Kiss, unless he was more talented an actor than Pagan imagined, hadn't heard this news before.

'And you suspect my nephew? Is that why you're here?' Kiss asked. He had to fight the blackness that was inside him now, the sense of inner control receding, the wave of nausea that rolled through him. He remembered the unexpected way Andres had gone out, the moodiness of the boy later at the airport, he remembered aloofness and ice.

Pagan said, 'A young man drove a jaguar to Sundbach's street. He parked it, went up to Sundbach's apartment. Twenty minutes later Sundbach was found murdered. The young man and the Jaguar had gone.'

Kiss asked his question again. *And you suspect my nephew?*

'Yes,' Pagan said.

'Why would he kill Sundbach, for God's sake?'

Pagan had a small enjoyable moment, like the kind a conjurer might savour before pulling a multitude of things out of a hat he has shown the audience to be empty. Silks, rabbits, doves, pineapples, an unexpected world.

'My guess is he learned that Sundbach had arranged the murder of Aleksis Romanenko,' and here Pagan took one of the photographs from his pocket and tossed it into Kiss's lap. It was done with flair and great aplomb and the timing was a joy. Three faces stared up from the photograph – Sundbach, Romanenko and Mikhail Kiss, three young warriors fighting on behalf of a lost cause.

Kiss shut his eyes and laid one hand over the picture and he thought *You old fool, Carl.* Of course there had been pictures, and he remembered the bravado of the day when they'd been taken, and how they'd gone out that morning – four of them, the nucleus of the group – and ambushed a Russian patrol, a successful enterprise, and how Sundbach, who was never without his pre-war Kodak, had insisted on photographs. Souvenirs, he'd said. *Mälestusesemed*, things of remembrance. Something to show our grandchildren, he'd said. Now, after all this time, the pictures, which Kiss had told him several times to destroy, had resurfaced and a prying Englishman had seen them. It was strange, almost mystical, the way the past clung to the present. And it was there in the old photo, a connection that couldn't be denied.

Mikhail Kiss looked down at the picture. He could smell the dampness of the forest, he could feel the wet earth against his face as he lay in a hollow while the *tiblad* patrolled nearby. Now what was this Englishman telling him? what nonsense was this about Sundbach arranging the death of Romanenko? and Andres killing old Carl?

'I think you're mistaken, Mr Pagan. I can't believe Sundbach would have anything to do with the death of Romanenko.'

Pagan, glad that Kiss wasn't going to dispute the authenticity of the photograph and deny it was his own younger image there, reached down, picked the photograph up, looked at it. 'Quite the opposite. I think there's a strong possibility Sundbach arranged it because he discovered Romanenko was controlled by a certain faction within the KGB.'

'Controlled by the KGB? You're out of your mind.'

'I don't think there's any doubt, Kiss. The KGB knew what Aleksis was carrying to Edinburgh, but they didn't stop him leaving the Soviet Union. And you want to know why they didn't? Because they want the Brotherhood's plan to work.'

The Brotherhood. Mikhail Kiss, who had a stricken look on his face, walked quickly into the kitchen. Pagan followed, watching the big man make himself a second drink. Ice-cubes slid from his hand and fell to the tiled floor and cracked like glass. Kiss kicked the broken cubes aside and looked at Frank Pagan and wondered how this Englishman had heard about the Brotherhood. He sipped his drink and tried to remain calm. He said, 'I think you've made a grave error. Especially in your suspicion about Andres.'

Pagan admired Kiss's control, even though he sensed it was superficial. The man's manner was cool, smooth, and there was something of perplexed innocence in his expression.

Pagan said, 'I suppose I could always put the matter beyond any doubt by looking at a picture of your nephew. Do you have a photo?'

Mikhail Kiss stared at the Englishman, who had one of those faces that can be deceptive, a mask drawn across true feelings. But Kiss saw it in Frank Pagan's eyes, a core of conviction that what the Englishman was saying was the truth. Kiss turned away, fighting a chill he felt. He heard himself ask how Carl had been murdered, and Pagan replied with the single word *strangulation* and Kiss remembered the cut on Andres's forehead, which perhaps Carl, the old fighter, the *vöitleja*, had managed to inflict at the end of his life. Something dark raced across Kiss's heart when he thought of this boy he'd raised, this killer of old men. He shut his eyes tightly. He wondered if he could deny the boy's existence, if he could deny the very thing he'd created.

'I don't have a photograph,' he said.

'I didn't think you would.' Pagan poured himself a glass of water from the faucet and drank it quickly. He could still taste smoke in his mouth. 'What is the Brotherhood's plan, Mikhail?'

Kiss turned to the Englishman. 'Plan? What plan?'

'The one the KGB seems to like,' Pagan replied. 'The one the KGB has found some use for.'

Mikhail Kiss shook his head. There were edges here, boundaries he couldn't chart, as if the landscape Pagan described were too chaotic to grasp. There was no way in the world that the KGB could have controlled Romanenko. There was no way the KGB would encourage the scheme. They'd destroy it, not use it. Everyone connected with it, himself included, would have been disposed of in some way.

'When you talk about the Brotherhood, you seem to ascribe to it a sinister quality it doesn't have. I admit we're a group of loosely organised patriots who regret the seizure of our country – but we're not planning anything, you understand. And if we did, it wouldn't be anything the KGB would approve of, I can tell you.'

Pagan folded his arms, leaned against the sink. There was a flatness in the way Kiss talked, a lack of vigour. It was as if his understanding of his nephew's crime had diminished him in an important way, and now he was simply going through the motions of concealing the Brotherhood's scheme.

'Too many people have died,' Pagan said. 'Too many people have died for me to buy your bullshit. Is it terrorism? Is it political assassination? What the hell is it?'

Mikhail Kiss walked out of the kitchen and back into the sun-room, the glass walls of which were pitch black now. Pagan followed him, frustrated by the big man's evasiveness. What was he supposed to do? Pull a gun and force Kiss to tell the truth? Pagan had the distinct feeling that guns wouldn't convince Mikhail Kiss to do anything he didn't want to do.

'How do you feel, Kiss, about the fact that your plan is being put to use by the KGB? How do you feel about serving up something useful for your enemies?'

Mikhail Kiss sat down, looked sadly at Frank Pagan. 'Please, Mr Pagan. No more. No more questions. I'm tired now.'

Goading wasn't much of a strategy either, Pagan decided. He moved a little closer to Kiss and said, 'Romanenko is dead. Carl Sundbach is dead. Two London policemen are dead. A young English diplomat was killed. And tonight a New York cop was burned to death inside his car. This plan of yours is running up quite a total, Kiss. Somebody gets in the way of it and whoops – the fucking KGB makes sure they're not around to do any more interference. You make a great team. The Brotherhood and the KGB.'

Kiss said nothing. He wasn't really listening to Pagan. He was thinking of Andres Kiss killing Carl Sundbach. He was trying to imagine that, seeing pictures, Sundbach perhaps rolling on the floor while Andres tied the cord tighter and tighter still, the old man struggling, fighting, gasping at the end of it all.

Pagan brought his face close to Kiss's ear. 'Is Andres part of it, Mikhail? I understand he's a hotshot flyer. Is he part of the scheme? Is he going to fly a plane for you? Is that it? A bomb, Mikhail? Is he going to drop a bomb?'

'For God's sake.'

Pagan was trying to come in from all angles here, as if this buckshot approach might confuse Kiss, might draw an answer out of him that he didn't want to give, but Kiss was too quick for this tactic.

Kiss rose from his chair, brushing Pagan aside. 'You bark up the wrong tree, Pagan. Go home. Go back to London. Let it be. It doesn't concern you. Countries you know nothing about, countries occupied by the Soviets, why should you interfere with them? The British had their chance in the 1940s, Pagan, and sold the Baltic cheaply to Stalin. I'm telling you now, it's too late to sit up and take a fresh interest in my people. Forget it. Go home. Leave it to people who care, people who understand. What the hell do you understand about it? Mind your own damned business.'

'It's become my fucking business, Kiss!'

Kiss stepped into the hallway, and Pagan went after him. There, under the hall light, Mikhail Kiss stopped moving, and stood very still. Pagan, surprised to the point of silence, felt an odd tension at the back of his throat.

She was standing by the front door. She wore a plain white t-shirt and blue jeans and her shoulder-bag hung at her side. There was very little makeup on her face. When she smiled at Pagan she did so in a thin way, and he thought she looked beautiful, but in some way changed, except he couldn't define it.

'Frank Pagan's right,' Kristina Vaska said. 'This whole thing *has* become his business, Mr Kiss.'

Moscow

General Olsky went to the window of his office and parted the slats of the blind, seeing a strange red sun in the morning sky which, in a theatrical manner, lit the old women sweeping the street below, so that they had the appearance of a Greek chorus keeping itself busy. Then he closed the slats and turned to look at Deputy Minister Tikunov, who sat on the other side of the desk.

Ever since the meeting with the General Secretary, Olsky had despatched hundreds of additional agents into the field, in Moscow and Leningrad and Kiev. He'd ordered them to enter the offices of the Defence Ministry and examine the files of personnel deployed in sensitive positions at radar installations, which he considered a logical place to start if Greshko's scheme involved the flight of a plane into Soviet airspace. It wasn't a decision Olsky had taken lightly, and it infuriated Tikunov.

Tikunov, Deputy Minister of Defence, was also Commander-in-Chief of the Soviet Air Defence Forces. He was a squat man who bore an uncanny resemblance to the late Nikita Khrushchev. To Tikunov's way of thinking, the KGB had too much influence, both in civilian and military life, and he frequently found himself hoping that if genuine reforms were to be made in the Soviet Union they would first of all be applied to the kind of authority commanded by the organs of State Security.

Tikunov said, 'I assume, comrade General, you can explain the swarms of your men in my headquarters? I assume you can explain the nature of your business?'

Olsky regarded Tikunov's large red face, a peasant face given to Slavic volatility, extremes of emotion not easily hidden. His face was an accurate barometer of his feelings at all times. Olsky didn't feel obliged to give an immediate explanation. There were delicate and rather ambiguous questions of rank at issue here, and Olsky was conscious of the fact that Tikunov had been Commander-in-Chief of Air Defences for a longer time than he, Olsky, had run the KGB. Olsky, though, was a candidate member of the Politburo, and closer to the General Secretary than Tikunov, which compensated for the matter of longevity.

'I'm operating with the full authority of the General Secretary,' Olsky said, which was stretching a truth slightly. The General Secretary had simply said *Deal with it as you think fit, Stefan.*

Deputy Minister Tikunov wondered if he should ask to see some kind of written authorisation. He had every right to do so, of course, but the Chairman of the KGB, no matter who occupied the position, was never a man one questioned lightly. And so he hesitated a moment, considering his options and trying to bring his temper under control.

'Let me ask you a question, Minister,' Olsky said. 'How difficult is it these days for an aeroplane to penetrate our airspace undetected, Minister?'

'What the hell kind of question is that?' Tikunov asked.

'A simple one.'

Tikunov bristled a little. He hadn't come here to discuss hypothetical matters with the Chairman of the KGB. He simply wanted all those bloody snoops, those supercilious upstarts, those fucking gangsters, out of his buildings and out of his domain. 'It's possible. Hardly likely.'

'In what circumstances is it possible, Minister?'

Tikunov raised a hand and counted on his fingers. 'One, if the plane flies beneath our radar. And two, if the radar is malfunctioning. In the former circumstances visual contact would be made sooner or later.'

'Are any of your radar installations malfunctioning?'

'To my knowledge, absolutely not. If such a thing happened I'd know about it.'

'Automatically?'

Tikunov nodded. He wondered where this was leading. He had the feeling he'd allowed Olsky to take control, and he didn't like it.

'Are there circumstances, aside from malfunctions, when a radar installation would be inoperative?' Olsky asked.

'During routine maintenance, of course.'

'And is there any such maintenance presently going on?'

'There's nothing scheduled.'

'Could maintenance take place without your knowledge?'

'Hardly. Only the smallest of jobs could be done without my permission. Anything that affected the grid as a whole would need my approval.'

'Let's say, for the sake of argument, that certain men under your command decided to render radar inoperable and didn't want you to know? Is that possible?'

Tikunov, who liked to think he treated his officers with respect and believed he was respected by them in turn, was shocked by the suggestion. 'I'd have such men shot, General. Are you questioning the loyalty of my officers?'

Olsky nodded. 'I think there's a possibility your system may have been tampered with, Minister.'

'Unthinkable,' Tikunov said.

'To you, perhaps. But I insist you check the status of all the radar installations in the Baltic sector.'

Tikunov felt he had to assert himself here. This whole conversation had begun to sound like an extended personal insult to him. 'I'll be perfectly happy to check the status of my radar and investigate possible disloyalty among my officers – just as soon as you show me a written order from the General Secretary, comrade Chairman.' Tikunov, his face growing more red, his cheeks quivering, was adamant. What he really despised about the KGB was the way they eroded one's sphere of influence. They could strut in and take over your whole life. 'I'd also like to get a grasp on the reason behind your questions, General. Do you know something I don't know? Have you heard of an unauthorised plane intending to violate Soviet airspace?'

Olsky moved round his office in a restless way. 'I've received information that leads me to believe an aircraft is planning an attack on the Soviet Union.'

'What kind of aircraft?'

'I don't know.'

'Perhaps you know where it might be coming from?' Tikunov asked in what he thought was the tone of voice used to humour people, but it was a clumsy effort made by a humourless man.

Olsky shook his head.

'By God, General, you're an encyclopaedia of information,' Tikunov said. 'Just the same you think you have enough to send your agents into my province and cause all kinds of mischief. Where did you get this so-called information from anyhow?'

'I can't answer that,' Olsky said. 'And you know better than to ask.'

'The only possible enemy aircraft in this region capable of delivering any kind of strike against us would be from NATO,' Tikunov said. 'Are you saying that we can expect a plane from NATO to attack us? One plane? One little plane, General?'

'I'm not saying that,' Olsky answered.

'Then what the hell are you saying, Olsky?'

Olsky wished he had answers to Tikunov's questions, but all he had to go on was Volovich's vague information, and that wasn't enough. A plane, but what kind of plane?

and from where? He picked up a pencil and tapped the surface of his desk with it, conscious of how he might have appeared to Tikunov – as a man coming apart slowly under the pressures of office.

'I can't take chances, Minister,' he said. 'Which is why I ordered my men to search the quarters of every member of your staff in any kind of sensitive position, and not only in Moscow.'

Tikunov spluttered and his red hands – which despite their colour suggested iciness – became welded together. 'I'm goddamned appalled, General! First your thugs ransack my personnel files and tamper with my computers – '

'Hardly thugs, Minister,' Olsky said. 'They know what they're looking for. They're interested only in those officers whose positions might allow them to interfere with radar operations – '

Tikunov ignored this. 'Then I find they've been given carte blanche to rummage through the accommodations of my officers. The whole situation's gone beyond intolerable.' He walked to the door and made a gesture of exasperation. 'I'll communicate my displeasure to the General Secretary at once, of course.'

'Your prerogative,' Olsky said. 'But I still suggest you check the status of your installations before you start making angry phone calls, Minister.'

'Don't tell me what to do, General,' Tikunov said. 'I quite understand that the business of the KGB is other people's business, but keep your nose as far out of mine as humanly possible.'

Olsky watched the Deputy Minister slam the door as he rushed from the office. After a few moments, Colonel Chebrikov came into the room, carrying some papers in his hand.

'There's something here that will interest you, sir,' the Colonel said. 'Three KGB officers were found murdered twenty miles from Tallinn.'

'Murdered?' Olsky slumped back in his chair. It was going to be one of those days, he thought, when bad news creates a force all its own, and keeps rolling, accumulating more and more unfortunate items like some great black snowball turning to an avalanche.

'They were apparently suspicious of an abandoned farmhouse about twenty miles from the city, and they went to investigate – acting under your general orders to locate dissidents and apprehend them. The farmhouse, it seems, was used by itinerants from time to time. When the officers didn't re-establish contact with Tallinn HQ, a search of the area was made. All three of them were found wrapped in tarpaulin and stuffed inside an old well. They'd been shot. The farmhouse had recently been occupied – signs of food, a couple of sleeping-bags. A vehicle was left behind, an old Moskvich. The ownership hasn't been traced.'

Olsky leaned across his desk. 'Could there be a connection? Could there be some kind of link between the assassins and this alleged conspiracy?'

'Perhaps, General. On the other hand, you always find extremists in the Baltic countries. They come with the territory. Every now and then we pick somebody up because he's been distributing anti-social documents and we find he's got an old gun tucked away someplace. A war souvenir, usually. Maybe the occupants of the farmhouse come into that category, loonies who happened to have guns. They're not necessarily linked with a major conspiracy.'

Not necessarily. It was the kind of vague response Olsky didn't want to hear. He needed definite information, hard facts. He was suddenly restless. There was an architecture to all of this, a blueprint he couldn't read, a design he couldn't grasp, a logic that eluded him. A plan, a widespread plan, something carefully contrived, years in the making, years of patience and the kind of single-minded determination that is the legitimate child of obsessive hatred. The Balts hated the Russians – a fact of life, something that didn't diminish with each new generation of Balts, no matter how many Lithuanian children were pressured into joining the Komsomol or how many young Latvians were members of the Party or how many youthful Estonians learned Russian in schools. The hatred went on and on, seemingly without end. Olsky, who would gladly have found some suitable accommodation with the nationalists in the Baltic if the choice had been his to make, was depressed. Three dead officers in Estonia, a terrorist conspiracy within the Soviet Union, Viktor Epishev in the United States, Greshko cruising Moscow in the hours of darkness and spreading rumours – these things impinged upon him all at once, creating a knot in his brain.

And then there was Dimitri Volovich.

Poughkeepsie, New York

The airfield had once belonged to a private flying club that had gone bankrupt, amid rumours of embezzlement and some public scandal, a few years ago. Now the hangar doors flapped in the breeze and the perimeter fence had rusted and kids sometimes played baseball on the old runway. The runway was cracked and weeds came up through the concrete here and there, irregularities that caused the single-prop Cessna to bounce and shudder as it came down to land.

Iverson, feeling a slight chill creep through the dark, drew up the collar of his lightweight overcoat and glanced at Epishev as the plane bumped and taxied toward the place where they stood.

'Unseasonable cold,' Iverson remarked.

Epishev said nothing. He gazed at the plane, which was smaller than he'd expected. He'd arrived first-class and now, with his work done, he was leaving through the back door, being flown from Poughkeepsie – which was God knows where – to Canada, and then back to the Soviet Union. He would have preferred to depart in more comfort, as befitted a man who had completed an important task.

Iverson saw the little craft come shivering toward them and he reached out, touching the back of Epishev's arm.

'You did very well,' he said. 'My people are pleased. I hear General Greshko is delighted.'

Epishev listened to the dark wind make rustling sounds as it slithered through the broken fence. A light went on in the cockpit of the Cessna and the silhouette of the pilot became visible.

'Who flies the plane?' Epishev asked.

'One of our own pilots,' Iverson answered.

'Is he good?'

'Are you nervous, Colonel?'

'Small planes . . . ' Epishev didn't finish his sentence. The plane, which bore a false registration number, was moving nearer.

'He's a good man,' Gary Iverson said. 'The best.'

The Cessna had come to a stop now. Epishev took a step towards it, hearing the propeller turn slowly. He was unhappy with this. The small airfield, the ridiculous plane, the way he was leaving the United States. He felt he deserved better.

'You'll be comfortable, Colonel,' Iverson said. 'I promise you that.' He took a small flask from his pocket and poured a shot into the silver cap, which he passed to Epishev. 'A short toast to the friendship between our countries, Colonel. To cooperation.'

Iverson raised the flask to his lips.

'What are we drinking?' Epishev asked.

'What else? Vodka.'

Epishev tossed the shot back, returning the cap to Iverson, who immediately stuck it back on the flask.

'The girl,' Epishev said. 'What will you do with the girl?'

'Our general feeling is that without Frank Pagan she's been rendered ineffective.'

'That's all? You see no danger?'

'She'll be kept under surveillance for a while,' Iverson said. Now that the toast had been drunk, he was impatient to be gone from this dreary place. 'But she's no danger to our plan now.'

Epishev shrugged, then walked toward the Cessna and climbed up into the cockpit. He waved at Iverson, who returned the gesture, even if Epishev couldn't see it in the darkness. The plane made a circle, bouncing back onto the runway, and then it was racing along, up and down, wobbling, finally rising just before the runway ended. Up and up, slow and noisy, vanishing into the blackness. Iverson watched until the wing-lights were no longer visible, and then he walked to his car.

He used the car telephone to make a connection with the house in Fredericksburg. When Galbraith came on the line, Iverson said, 'He's gone, sir.'

'He drank the toast, I trust?'

'Of course.'

'I think it's better like that, don't you? Are you going to spend the night in New York? Or are you headed back down here?'

'I'll stay in the city,' Iverson said. 'I'm tired.'

'Sleep well, Gary.'

Galbraith hung up. Iverson replaced the telephone and sat in the darkness of the abandoned airfield and thought he could still hear the distant thrumming of the small plane. He turned the key in the ignition, looked at the dashboard clock.

Approximately thirty minutes from now the tasteless sedative in the vodka would send Epishev into a sound sleep. The pilot would parachute from the Cessna at a prearranged spot close to the town of Troy, and the craft, with the comatose Epishev on board, would crash in the Adirondacks, quite possibly in the sparsely-populated region beyond Lake Luzerne, where it might lie undiscovered for many years.

Without a trace, Iverson thought. And he was filled with renewed admiration for Galbraith, who had seen this whole scheme in one flash in the yellow house in Virginia Beach, one blinding insight, the way a grandmaster will see checkmating possibilities twelve devious moves ahead. *Use outside talent whenever you possibly can, Gary. Just make sure it never gossips about you. People who tell you a dog is man's best friend are wrong. Man's best friend is silence.*

19

Glen Cove, Long Island

The question that formed on Mikhail Kiss's lips was one he didn't have to voice aloud. He knew the answer anyway, because the family resemblance was too forceful, too striking. He knew who this young woman was even before she said, '*Küll siis Kalev jõuab koju . . .* ' with that thin, misleadingly playful smile on her face.

She stepped past Kiss and Pagan and entered the glass-walled room, where she stood in the middle of the floor. There was something just a little arrogant in the way she stood, Pagan thought, a quality he hadn't seen in her before – but then she was apparently full of surprises, and one more shouldn't have troubled him. He had a depressing sense suddenly of being caught up in a drama whose first two acts he'd missed or, at best, had seen only obliquely from the corner of his eye. He was very aware of an unresolved conflict between Kiss and Kristina, a situation he couldn't bring into sharp perspective. He was standing outside, his face pressed against the glass, and the room into which he tried to look was out of focus.

Mikhail Kiss said, 'I used to wonder what had become of Norbert's daughter. I tried to stop thinking about her, and sometimes I succeeded.'

'It's taken me a long time to find you,' Kristina said.

Mikhail Kiss's mouth was very dry. 'I think I've been expecting you for years, one way or another. I had a dream about Norbert last night.'

There was a strange crossfire here, and Pagan knew he didn't belong in it. He'd gatecrashed. Shadows moved on the edge of his mind, and he didn't want them to take recognisable shape, because he didn't want to see what they really were when they emerged into the light. There was one unmistakable conclusion, and he needed to avoid it.

Kristina moved closer to Mikhail Kiss and asked, 'Do you know the last thing Norbert Vaska ever said to me?'

Kiss shook his head slowly.

'*They've betrayed me*,' Kristina said. Her voice trembled. '*The Brotherhood betrayed me*.'

'Betrayal's an easy word,' Kiss said. 'It's too simple.'

'What would you call it?'

'I would call it sacrifice.'

'Sacrificed by his old comrades. His friends. His own Brotherhood.'

Kiss ran the palm of his hand across his eyes. 'You have to understand the circumstances,' he said quietly.

'Why? Would they justify everything?'

'They may help you understand, Kristina.'

'I doubt it,' and she was fierce, unrelenting, her expression more intense than Pagan had ever seen it. She was talking to Kiss as if Pagan – having served his purpose in leading the way to the heart of the Brotherhood, a feat she apparently couldn't achieve on her own, a goal obscured by the passage of time and the pseudonyms the Brotherhood had assumed, old trails that had faded, old pathways too weatherbeaten to follow had ceased to exist. Gone. Shoved aside. Used. Just like that. He didn't know whether to be outraged or bewildered by his own negligent heart. He didn't know whether to admire this woman's tenacity of pursuit. This talk of betrayal and sacrifice – was it vengeance she wanted? He moved his hand very slightly, letting it hover behind him, concealed from view but close to the location of his gun.

'Briefly, it comes down to the fact that Romanenko was in serious difficulties some years ago,' Kiss said. 'He occupied, as you may know, a position that created problems for him. He led two lives. And sometimes they came in conflict with each other. You understand this much, of course.'

Kiss paused. Was the story worth telling now? It was fading, because that was how he wanted it, a threadbare memory, something whose shame was no longer so bright and blinding. He glanced at Pagan, aware of the *inglane*'s look of confusion, and what was apparent to Kiss was that Pagan and Kristina had enjoyed some kind of relationship, perhaps they'd even been lovers – but Pagan hadn't expected the woman to turn up here in this house, of all places. And there was a shadow of hurt on Pagan's face, an imprint of anxiety on those features that were so used to concealment.

'I'm listening,' Kristina Vaska said. Now she did look at Pagan, and offered him a brief smile, nothing of consequence. Frank Pagan wondered if he was going to be fobbed off with this trifle. He put out a hand towards her, laying the palm on her arm, but she appeared not to feel his touch. She was concentrating on Kiss.

Kiss went on, 'There was a time, when our plan was in its earliest stages, when Aleksis realised he was coming under suspicion from certain factions in the Party. And the KGB had begun a particularly tough campaign in Tallinn. Aleksis's loyalties were in question. There were rumours about his life. Questions he couldn't afford, Kristina. A man in his position had to be above any kind of suspicion, because he was important to the cause.'

Kiss paused. This was the tough part. This was the part he didn't want to utter aloud. But ghosts were pressing against him, forcing him to speak. 'It was decided that he had to prove his loyalty to the Party. He had to stop the questions, the whispers. What good would he be if he were arrested and imprisoned? How could he contribute to the cause from a jail cell? Therefore, whatever he was going to do would have to be drastic.'

'I can guess the rest,' Kristina said.

'Maybe, maybe not. Romanenko and I had a meeting in 1971 in Helsinki. Our meetings, you understand, were difficult to arrange and often held hurriedly in strange places. This particular meeting – and I don't remember it with any pleasure, believe me – took place on the ferry to Suomenlinna. I remember the day – it was cold and rainy. Fitting weather for what we had to do. Aleksis outlined a plan to protect his reputation and I agreed to it. Between us, we decided to give Norbert Vaska to the KGB. Everything. His participation in a democratic society. His part in running an underground newspaper. Aleksis gave the information to a certain Colonel Epishev, who then arrested your father.'

There was silence in the room for a long time.

'You did a terrific job,' Kristina said eventually. 'You must have been very proud of yourselves.'

'We did what we had to do to save the plan. You must try to understand that, Kristina. It was a matter of survival. It was either your father or the death of everything we had ever hoped for and worked for.'

'You made the wrong choice,' Kristina said.

'Choice isn't the word. The solution was forced on us. Dear God, do you think what we did was easy for us?'

Pagan thought how painful it was to see a man obliged to speak a truth he'd clearly contrived to keep from himself for years, the forced words, the pauses, sentences dragged up from a place deep inside. He was filled with a sense of anticipation now, wondering what Kristina would do next. There was an air of unpredictability about her.

Kiss said, 'There. I've told you. I owed you that.'

'What do you want now?' Kristina asked. 'Absolution?'

'I sometimes think that if he knew, Norbert would understand why we did what we did. But I don't expect forgiveness from you.'

'Forgiveness is the last goddam thing I could give you even if I wanted to,' Kristina said. 'I didn't come here to do you favours, Kiss. I came here to look at you. I came here to see what kind of man betrayed my father.'

Mikhail Kiss stared uncomfortably at the floor. He said, 'I'd do it again if I had to, Kristina.'

Kristina Vaska walked across the room and looked out at the darkness. She said, 'You ruined my family, Kiss. It wasn't Epishev who wrecked it. What did he care? He was only doing his fucking rotten job. But you and Romanenko, you gave my father away, you practically made a donation of him to the Russians. And my mother . . . '. She paused here and there was a slight catch in her voice and Pagan had the urge to go towards her and comfort her, but he didn't move. The space between himself and Kristina had filled up with unexpected obstacles.

'My mother sits in a forlorn little house upstate and she writes letters, Kiss. She writes letters to the Kremlin and the White House and Number Ten Downing Street. Begging letters. *Please help me get my husband released from Siberia*. Year after year she sends off the same letters and it's deadening to go through the same process endlessly – petitions, forms, the whole dumb rigmarole that you know in advance isn't going to work, but you do it anyway because you don't have any other channels . . . '

Kiss sighed. His mind had drifted away from this room, this house, this girl who had opened the door for ghosts. He was thinking of Andres high above the Atlantic. The journey, the arrival.

Kristina Vaska opened her purse, took out a pistol, turned it on Mikhail Kiss. Pagan stepped toward her, and she waved him away, gesturing with the gun. Her expression was hard and uncompromising, as if whatever beauty she had was destroyed by her murderous intention. Kiss looked at the pistol, watched the way the woman came forward, saw how she held the barrel of the gun towards his head, then he felt the pressure of metal against the side of his face. She pushed it hard into his flesh.

'Kristina,' Pagan said.

'I looked for a long time, Frank. Ever since I first came to this country, I've been looking. Sometimes I thought I was getting close, then it would slip away. I'd get only so far before I'd run into blank walls,' she said. 'When I was running out of options, I found you. And you found Kiss.'

Pagan wanted to reach for her and take the weapon away. He saw Kiss's flesh fold like paper where the barrel of the gun made a deep impression in his face. Kiss had his eyes shut. There was the sound of the safety being released and it echoed inside Kiss's skull like the noise of somebody shouting in a tunnel.

'Kristina,' Pagan said. 'He's the only link I've got with the Brotherhood's plan. If you shoot him . . . '

She stared at Pagan. 'What do you think I care about that, Frank? What are they going to do? Say boo to the Russians? The Russians will squash them the way they squash everything.' She pushed the gun harder and Kiss, flinching, moaned at the way metal cut into his flesh.

'Let me at least talk to him,' Pagan said.

Kiss, moving his face away from the gun, tapped the side of his skull. 'Talk until you're blue in the face, Pagan. The plan is locked in here, and that's exactly where it stays.'

Pagan stepped closer to the old man. 'Stay away, Frank,' she said. 'Keep out of this. It's got absolutely nothing to do with you.'

'People keep telling me that. And I don't seem to hear them properly.'

'You better start listening,' Kristina said. She tightened her finger on the trigger, conscious of the vulnerability of Kiss's flesh, the veins at the side of the skull, the fragile arrangement of bone and flesh and tissue she could blow away in a fraction of time. And then it wasn't Mikhail Kiss she was seeing, suddenly it was her father, it was Norbert Vaska, and she envisioned him in his white wasteland and wondered if he'd died there, or whether he was alive and still remembered his daughter, if he remembered love and all the things that had been taken from him. She imagined him with his eyes shut in death and then she had an image of gravediggers spading half-frozen ground, not yet thawed after winter but softening in the growing warmth of spring, and then they laid Norbert Vaska into this chilly earth. She shut her eyes a second. These pictures were more than she could bear. The frozen white hands, crystals of ice clinging to eyelashes, the lips silent and blue, the eyes – perhaps open – staring into an arctic nothingness. She thought she heard his voice say *The Brotherhood betrayed me*. Is this what you want me to do, father? she wondered. Do you want me to pull this goddam trigger? To avenge you? Or would you tell me now that Kiss and Romanenko did what they had to, that in any war – even a lost one like this, even a pathetic little struggle like this – all useful tactics are justifiable? Confused suddenly, enraged by her own bewilderment, Kristina Vaska stared at the side of Kiss's face, seeing one expressionless blue eye, a faint shadow of white hair on the damp upper lip. *Kiss and Romanenko riding a ferry in the rain, and planning Norbert Vaska's death* – how plain, how straightforward, how civilised. Would you have agreed with them, Norbert Vaska? If it had been you and Romanenko on that ferry discussing Mikhail Kiss, how would you have behaved? There was madness here, the madness of patriotism, of men fighting for a totally hopeless cause, creating their little make-believe reality in which they see themselves bravely evicting the Soviets, pitchforks against submachine guns, Molotov cocktails against tanks, sorry dreams. Anger went through her, a dark red rage filling her brain. It was uncontrollable.

'*Kristina*,' Pagan said.

She saw him reach for the gun and she said, 'Get the fuck away, Frank.'

'Kristina,' he said again.

'Goddam you!' Her eyes were moist and she couldn't quite see Kiss clearly now, but enough. She said, '*You piece of shit, you useless piece of shit*,' and she understood she couldn't shoot him. She couldn't do it. She smacked him across the lips with the pistol and as his head tilted away from her she struck him again, bringing the barrel of the gun down upon his forehead, and his whole face swung back, blood pouring from his brow, from his split lip. She raised her hand up and started to bring it down a third time in a violent arc, a mindless movement, but Pagan caught her hand in the air and took the gun from her, and all her terrible fury collapsed and she slid to the floor where she sat cross-legged, staring at Mikhail Kiss, who had his face covered with his hands. She thought *A worthless piece of shit, and I can't even shoot him*, and she closed her eyes and imagined she felt the misty rain fall across the Suomenlinna ferry where two men planned her father's betrayal. And she had the thought that even though he was absent, even though he knew nothing about the plot against him, just the same Norbert Vaska *would have agreed, he would have given his consent to his own condemnation because he lived with the taste of the Brotherhood in his mouth, he lived in the past, when the enemy was somebody you could see at the end of your rifle and your native land hadn't altogether yielded to the Russians*.

Mikhail Kiss, his hands covered in his own blood, sat down in a chair. He was breathing hard. Pagan bent over him.

'When is it going to happen?' Pagan asked.

'Go fuck yourself,' Kiss replied quietly.

'When and where, Mikhail?'

'*Vabadus Eestile*,' Mikhail Kiss whispered.

Moscow

In her apartment near Izmailova Park, Valentina Uvarova hurriedly packed clothing. She'd been told to travel lightly which was no great problem because there wasn't much she wanted to bring along with her in any event, there was nothing here worth remembering, or keeping, except for a couple of toys – sentimental favourites of the two children – and a few necessary items of clothing. She was a small woman with a tiny oval face and cheekbones so high her eyes seemed deeply recessed into her head. People who knew her spoke most often of her determination. *Valentina's such a determined person*, they'd say, as if grit were a fault. But her determination concealed something else, a basic discontentment with the barren prospects of her life.

She stuffed the case, closed it, noticed how nervous she was. She sat on the bed and smoked a cigarette, listening to the sounds of the children in the kitchen. They knew they were going on a trip, she simply hadn't told them where. They knew Daddy would be joining them wherever it was, and this made them happy. Valentina touched the small crucifix she wore round her neck and said quietly to herself *Dear Jesus, help us now.* She let her hands fall into her lap and she pressed them together.

We're going away, we're going away, we're going away!

This was the girl's voice, shrill and penetrating. Valentina Uvarova had warned the children to say nothing to anybody. Not to their friends, their relatives, not even to their grandmother. They were to keep completely silent, but for a kid secrets were impossible to maintain. She walked into the kitchen and silenced the children. The boy, who looked like a miniature of his father Yevgenni, was easy. The girl was the spirited one.

'We must keep very quiet,' Valentina said.

The girl asked, 'When are we leaving?'

'In a couple of hours.'

'Why can't we go now? Right now?'

'Why? Do you want to wait in the railway station?'

'Yes,' the girl said. 'I like stations.'

Valentina considered the prospect, but she didn't want to hang around a station, passing hours before the train arrived. If she stayed here, at least there were still things to keep her occupied. There were dishes to clean. There was rubbish to be removed. Even though she might be leaving this apartment forever, she couldn't possibly leave it in disarray. They'd talk about her after she'd gone, and they'd say *She left the place like a pigsty,* but what can you expect from a traitor's wife anyway? She wouldn't leave the place dirty. Not Valentina Uvarova. She couldn't stand the idea of the women in the neighbourhood saying bad things about her.

She went to the sink, turned the faucet, and lukewarm water spluttered out, and the old gas-heater wheezed on the wall above her.

We're going away, the girl said in a whisper. *We're going to see Daddy.*

Valentina shushed the child again. She ran some dirty plates under the water, wiped them with a cloth, set them aside to dry. A new life, she thought. The phrase kept running through her head like an inescapable melody. A new life.

She dried her hands on a towel. And that was when she heard the heavy knock on the front door. She felt it then, blood draining from her face, from her hands, her heart turning a somersault in her chest.

Somebody's at the door, the boy said.

She looked at her son's small upturned face, the eyes that were suddenly wary, and then she stepped along the hallway. She opened the door slowly. It was not one visitor, but two, and they wore uniforms that filled her with dread.

Glen Cove, Long Island

If there was any evidence of what the Brotherhood planned to do, Pagan thought the logical place to find it was in the only room he hadn't so far explored, the office on the second floor. He switched on a light, surveyed the room. It was the desk that interested him primarily, and he walked towards it, scanning the papers spread across the surface. He began to flick them, beset by a sense of urgency. A need to keep busy, that was it. Keep going. Don't stop. He was aware of Kristina Vaska entering the room and he thought, *Ignore the woman.*

He didn't look up. He heard her cross the floor, felt her hands on his shoulders. He didn't move. Her touch stirred him and he resented his own response.

'You must accept one thing, Frank.'

'Tell me about it,' Pagan said.

'I care about you. I didn't want to, but it happened. And that hasn't changed. At first, I just thought you were going to be useful to me, you had resources I could use. But it changed. It became something else, Frank.'

'Terrific,' Pagan said.

'I've hurt you.'

'You're an insightful sort of person. I like that.'

Pagan shuffled the papers around. They were written in Estonian. What else could he have expected? He kept shuffling them anyway, looking for something he might understand.

'Frank, listen to me. I never intended to cause you any harm.'

'I'm not harmed,' he said sharply. 'Disappointed, yes. Up to here with you, yes. Disgusted with the idea you used me, absolutely. But harmed? No, love. Not harmed. It's like having something in my eye. It smarts for a few minutes, but a little water flushes it away.'

'I want to talk to you. Look at me.'

He did, but only briefly, then went back to the papers. There were bills, credit card vouchers, letters, but nothing that yielded up the kind of information he could have used.

'I admit,' she said. 'I wanted to kill him. Or I thought I did. But when it came right down to it, Frank . . . ' She touched his arm. 'I thought I wanted to kill Romanenko too, but I don't know if I would have been able to do that either. Circumstances prevented me from finding out anyway.'

He said, 'Look, you drift into my life. We spend a couple of pleasant hours passionately fucking – '

'It was more than that, and you know it – '

Pagan shook his head. Taken for a ride, he thought. The careless heart. The alchemy of attraction that transmuted blatant lies into shining truths, changed dross into lovely little gems. He remembered one of the first things she'd ever said to him. *I don't have any concealed motives, Frank. I heard about the killing on TV, I thought you might need information you weren't going to get anywhere else. Here I am. That's it.* And you bought it, Frank. You laid your money out and you bought the whole gooseberry patch. She's been working you from the very start, twisting you and shaping you, oiling you so you'd run smoothly along the right tracks. And, boy, didn't you ever? Wind my clockwork, sweetie, see how I run.

He looked at the typewriter on the desk, scanned a sheet of paper in it. That damned language again. He swivelled the chair around, turning his face away from Kristina Vaska.

She said, 'It doesn't have to end like this, Frank. We could walk away. We could leave this place right now. What goddam difference does the Brotherhood's plan make to us? Does it matter if it succeeds or fails? Who cares?'

'I care,' he said.

Mikhail Kiss appeared in the doorway, a blood-stained towel clutched against his face. When he spoke he did so through swollen lips and a mouth that no longer felt associated with his face. 'Feel free,' he said. 'Papers, letters, documents – look at anything you like, Pagan. I'm a hospitable man, but you'll find absolutely nothing.' And then Kiss turned and went into his own bedroom, where he sat on the edge of the bed with his eyes closed and the towel pressed to his lips.

Pagan watched him go. There was something smug in the way Kiss had spoken and Pagan wondered if there was a bluff going on. Ransack my office all you like, you won't find a goddam thing. No, it wasn't a simple bluff. If Kiss had kept anything important in this house he wouldn't have gone out and left the place unlocked, and he wouldn't be allowing Pagan easy access to this office. He tore the sheet of paper from the typewriter and handed it to Kristina and asked her to translate it. She looked at the paper a moment before she said it was a recipe for a dish called *mulgikapsad*. She looked at the other papers that lay across the desk, the ones Pagan had leafed through, and they were all recipes, every single one of them.

'He must be compiling a cookbook,' she said.

Pagan got up and walked to the window. *A cookbook. A bloody hobby.* He parted the curtains and looked down into the darkness of the garden. *Think. Just think. You're supposed to have some kind of knack for hunches, little flashes of intuition. They served you beautifully when it came to Kristina Vaska, didn't they?* He heard the woman come up behind him and lay her hands on his shoulders and he loved the way she touched him, despite himself.

'Forgive me, Frank.'

Forgiveness was hard. There was always the spectre of deceit. My little actress, he thought. But it couldn't all have been an act. There must have been moments of truthfulness. He wanted to think that the lovemaking – at least that had been real. Besides, what had she done but harbour the desire to avenge her father's betrayal? It wasn't as if she'd found in herself the capacity to kill anybody, was it? Pagan turned to look at her, but gazing into her face was as difficult as finding forgiveness. He'd been fooled, and that was a tough one to digest.

'How long is it going to take?' she asked.

He raised a hand and lightly touched the side of her face a moment. 'If you'd been straight with me from the start – '

'And you would have helped me, Frank? You would have gone out of your way to help a crazy lady with vengeance on her mind? I thought my way was better. The anxious daughter worried sick about her father's health – I figured that was the one most likely to succeed. And if it sounds calculated, you're absolutely right. It *was* calculated. I could have used a goddam slide-rule.'

Calculated, he thought. He walked back to the desk. Through the open door and across the landing he could see inside Kiss's bedroom. Kiss still sat motionless on the edge of the bed, the red towel pressed to his mouth, his eyes shut. He seemed absurdly calm, removed from the situation, secure in the knowledge that Pagan would find nothing in any of the rooms of this house.

Pagan sat on the edge of the desk. *Think, Frank. Relax, and think.* Kiss doesn't want to tell you where Andres went. Why not? Answer: because he's up to something and Kiss doesn't want you to know. Such as? Such as? Answer: he has to be part of the plot.

Unavoidable conclusion. What part, though? What role? Pagan walked out of the office and went inside Andres's bedroom and Kristina followed.

Pagan sat on the edge of the bed. On the bedside table there lay a couple of books, a paperback novel detailing the exploits of a deformed avenger in post-holocaust America, a daily meditation book, and a world atlas. Frank Pagan glanced at the paperback and read *Bosco kicked the door down and fired his machine-gun, splattering the hooded figures until the room turned red with blood and spilled brains*. Pagan set the book down, flipped through the meditation book and saw underlined the sentence *How many of the world's prayers have gone unanswered because those who prayed did not endure to the end?* Pagan put the book aside, then glanced at the atlas. On the map of Europe somebody had drawn thin red lines seemingly at random, inscribing them over Britain, then across the North Sea, where they ended in Scandinavia, a whole meaningless tangle of lines. He closed the atlas, stood up. The clues !o Andres Kiss, he felt, were all here, except that he couldn't read them.

And when you couldn't find inspiration, you fell back on that other policeman's tool which, though blunted from constant repetition, was still a useful device. You fell back on that old standby – the sheer doggedness of inquiry. He returned to Kiss's office and dragged the telephone directory out of a drawer and turned to the section marked Airlines, dismayed when he saw how many there were. He'd start with the As and just keep working until he could locate the airline on which Andres Kiss had left the country – provided he *had* flown overseas, as Mikhail had said. Provided, too, that he was travelling on an authentic passport under his own name. Long shots, long odds.

Pagan picked up the telephone. He glanced through the open door and across the landing, seeing Mikhail Kiss observe him with mild interest as he dialled.

Tallinn, Estonia

The man known as Marcus drove the Red Army truck along Gagarini Street in the direction of the harbour. He saw KGB agents everywhere he went. He saw them milling around the railway station, some of them in uniform, others trying to look inconspicuous in plain clothes. By now, of course, the murders of the KGB officers would have been discovered, and consequently more men would be poured into the streets. By mid-afternoon Tallinn would have the atmosphere of a convention city accommodating a thousand or so KGB. It was not a festive thought.

He checked his wristwatch. Four more hours. He thought of his comrades in Latvia and Lithuania and wondered how many of them were presently looking at their watches and counting minutes away into hours and feeling the same apprehension as he.

He drove the army vehicle in the direction of the harbour. The rendezvous was to take place in an old warehouse close to the docks. He entered the narrow street where nothing moved but plump pigeons flying out from the protection of eaves. Nothing out of the ordinary. He passed the building, a dilapidated brick structure. He slowed the vehicle, swung it round, went back the way he'd come. When he reached the warehouse again, he parked the truck, making sure the engine was still running. He approached the large door of the warehouse, pushed it open, then drove the truck inside the building.

There was a score of people inside already. Among them, Marcus saw Erma and the old man Bruno, who had made their way to this place separately. Marcus opened the tarpaulin that covered the back of the truck. The three boxes contained rifles and handguns. He passed them out quickly and quietly, thinking how there was nothing left to say because everything had been said already, the speeches had been made, the toasts drunk. He looked at the faces of those present, and he saw grim expectation in the expressions, and a certain fatalism. What they were going to do in a few short hours was inevitable – and so was the outcome.

Glen Cove, Long Island

It was dawn when Frank Pagan, who had spent hours having airline personnel wakened from their sleep, finally received the information he wanted. He put the receiver down and rubbed the back of his neck wearily. He looked at Kristina Vaska, who was curled in a chair, half asleep. Mikhail Kiss stood in the doorway of the office.

'You're a persistent man, Pagan,' he said.

'Sometimes.'

'What good will it do you to know where Andres has gone?'

'I don't know yet,' Pagan said. He picked up the telephone again. 'I'll have the answer to your question as soon as I've called the police in Oslo.'

Mikhail Kiss stepped closer to the desk. 'And they'll stop him?'

'They'll hold him,' Pagan replied.

Kiss, alarmed, put his hand over the telephone, firmly pressing the cradle down. 'No,' he said. 'I can't allow you to do this.'

Pagan looked into the big man's bruised face and what he saw there was desperation. 'You can't stop me, Kiss.'

Kiss, who was strong, tried to yank the telephone from the wall. Pagan caught him by the wrist. For a moment neither man made an impression on the other, neither man budged because there was an equivalence of strength, a balance. It might have remained this way for many minutes except for the fact that Kristina Vaska got up from her chair and struck Kiss on the elbow with her gun – a quick blow, delivered sharply and with admirable economy, which made the big man shudder and loosen his grip. He sunk into a chair, clutching the bone at the place where he'd been struck. Then he immediately rose again and reached out for Pagan, but Kristina Vaska pointed her gun directly at him and shook her head from side to side.

Kiss saw the determination in her face and stood very still. His blood-stained hands hung at his side. He was beset by a sense of futility, of having built the last twenty years of his life on an edifice that was quivering under him now, shaken by the Englishman, by the young woman with the gun, by the ghost of Norbert Vaska.

Pagan drew the telephone towards him. He dialled the number for the international operator.

'Say thanks or something,' Kristina Vaska said. 'I just helped you out.'

'Thanks or something,' Pagan replied.

'Smartass.'

Olso, Norway

Andres Kiss was met at the airport in Oslo by a dark blue Volvo, whose driver barely glanced at him.

'You'll find a suit in the back seat,' the driver said. 'When we're out of the city I'll stop in some quiet place and you can put it on.'

Andres Kiss placed his hands flat on his knees. He settled back in his seat, hearing the driver talk about the recent heatwave that had afflicted Oslo, but he wasn't really listening. He had other things on his mind.

'You'll have a clear afternoon for flying,' the driver said.

Andres nodded absently. 'Good,' was all he said, and his voice was strong and confident. It was a fine thing to go out to and meet your destiny untroubled by any hint of fear.

20

Mossheim, Norway

Andres Kiss thought the plane looked beautiful on the ramp. He approached the craft with the awe of a man who is as close to perfection as he is ever going to get in his lifetime. There was a magnificent austerity about the F-16 B, its vicious potential concealed in smooth, aerodynamic lines. If you narrowed your eyes and looked at the plane sideways, you might think it a sharp-beaked hawk. Andres, who wore a fire-retardant Nomex suit, a G-suit, and a survival vest, strolled round the aircraft, almost hesitant to go up the ladder and into the cockpit, as if he wanted to prolong the joy of anticipation.

He sniffed the sweet morning air into his lungs. It had been three years, three long years, since he'd been in this place. Three years since he'd flown an F-16 on missions in the Baltic, when his squadron, based at Luke Air Force Base in Arizona, had been deployed by NATO to participate in routine tactical manoeuvres.

The man who had picked him up in Oslo stood with the shadow of a wing falling across his face. He appeared very anxious to Kiss, in a hurry to get the bird off the ground. Andres, on the other hand, felt no such urgency. He'd climb into the plane, and he'd put on the helmet, attach the harness, and go through all the necessary steps before takeoff, all those logical little moves you made prior to flight. Andres adored the checklist, the jargon, the sense of belonging to an elite group of men who knew how these birds worked. When he spoke the secret language of flyers, he felt eloquent. It was as if he were a member of a select freemasonry, privy to all kinds of arcane information.

'Here,' and the man handed Andres a set of charts.

Andres Kiss took them, studied them briefly. The flight plan, but he knew it already. Besides, it wasn't a directive he intended to follow. Not all the way. Only up to the point where he would digress radically from it.

'Let's move,' the man said.

Andres was still unhurried. He stared across the runway, seeing other planes sitting motionless here and there on the base, each casting elongated shadows. He saw the barbed-wire fence beyond the hangars, and the security checkpoint, through which he and his companion had passed without any difficulty. It was a good feeling, Andres reflected, to know that Iverson's promises had all been kept, that his part in the scheme was working perfectly.

He followed the other man around the plane, wondering how much his companion knew, if he was part of the whole tapestry or simply somebody following an order that had come down from Iverson in the United States, an unquestionable command that, although irregular, he had to execute.

They moved together to the forward fuselage on the lefthand side of the plane, checking the canopy, the external jettison handles, the Side Winder missile on the leftwing tip. They went next to the nose wheel, and circled to the righthand side of the craft and the outboard station on the wing that housed the second Side Winder. Andres Kiss looked automatically for leaks, for any kind of fluids that might have dripped from the craft, but he saw none.

Then the fusing of the Mark 82 bombs was checked on the underside of the plane. After that it was time to go to the cockpit. Andres felt the first little shiver of the day, a slight tremor of anticipation.

He climbed the ladder and squeezed himself inside the cockpit. He stared at the instrument panel, the radar display panel, the vertical velocity indicator, the airspeed mach indicator, the autopilot switch. On the left console was the G-suit hose connection, the fuel master switch, the throttle. On the right was the oxygen and communications hook-up, the oxygen regulator panel, the stick. Andres stared at the dials with an expression of intensity. There were so many of them, each dedicated to the perfect functions of the craft, each related to the other in a sequence of irrefutable logic, and he knew them all, and they made him feel comfortable.

The other man, who had given Andres no name but who was obviously employed at this base in the capacity of crew chief, reached inside the cockpit and attached the fittings that linked Andres to the ejection system. Then, still working in silence, he plugged Andres into the oxygen system and handed him his helmet, which Andres put on.

Cockpit check. Andres studied all the switches to make sure they were in the off position. *Verify fuel master on guard down. Engine feed knob normal. External power unit switch normal. Fuel control in primary position. Throttle off. Brakes locked. Landing gear handle down. Master armament switch off. Air source knob normal.* Andres went through this procedure, realising that what had been missing from his life was this sense of well-defined purpose – and now here he was following all the old rules rigorously.

The other man climbed down the ladder from the cockpit. He didn't give Andres the customary thumbs up OK sign, as if he wanted no further part in the whole affair. Andres looked down at him, still smiling. He turned the main power switch to battery. The batteries discharged, the invertor output was good. Everything was fine.

Andres spoke to clearance delivery in the control tower. 'Mossheim Clearance. Louisiana Alpha 07, IFR Round Robin, clearance on request.'

There was a brief pause before Andres heard the response. 'Louisiana Alpha 07 Mossheim Clearance, clearance on request. Forty-five past the hour. Stand by this frequency.'

'Louisiana Alpha 07, roger.' Andres placed the jet fuel switch to Start 1. He checked the back-up fuel control caution light, which registered OFF. Then he stared at the RPM gauge. Throttle advance to idle. The hydraulic oil pressure lights went off, and RPM stabilized at normal ground idle. Functioning, Andres thought. Everything in position. The sweet integrity of the plane.

The voice in the tower said, '07 you are cleared by the Mossheim One departure direct to the Stockholm 140 at 50 climb and maintain flight level 250, squawk 2545, departure control frequency will be 345.5.'

Andres repeated this and the voice in the tower said, 'Read back correct. Contact ground for taxi.'

Andres contacted ground control and was told to taxi to runway 03. He felt the rumble of the craft vibrate through him as he looked from the cockpit and gave the wheels out signal. The man on the ramp alongside the craft hurriedly removed the chocks and Andres increased the throttle slightly and released the parking brake. He taxied to the arming area, conscious of the muted power of the plane, the way its ferocity was held momentarily in check. In the arming area he let his hands hang from the cockpit as the ordnance crew chief attached a variety of electrical leads to the bombs, the missiles and the 20-millimetre cannon, which made the weaponry operational. The ordnance chief gave the thumbs-up sign, indicating proper configuration.

Andres thought, *Let's go. Let's just fucking go.*

He taxied to the edge of runway 03, where he initiated the automatic on-board test system, which checked fifty-seven separate functions of the craft. It was all beautiful. He checked the flaps. Normal. Trim centre, both ailerons, horizontal trim and rudder. Fuel control in the primary position. Speed brakes closed, canopy closed. He checked the harness, the attachment of the G-suit to the console. Verified that external fuel tanks were feeding the main tanks. Ejection safety lever, oil pressure, warning and caution lights.

'Mossheim Tower, Louisiana Alpha 07 takeoff one with clearance.'

'Louisiana Alpha 07, Mossheim Tower, taxi into position and hold runway 03 right.'

The moment, Andres thought. The final check. 'Roger. Posit and hold.' He verified engine oil pressure and saw that the generator lights were out. Ready to go.

'Louisiana Alpha 07, Mossheim Tower cleared for takeoff, runway 03 right contact departure.'

Andres accelerated the engine through 80% and released the brakes. The aircraft accelerated to one hundred and fifty knots and he eased back on the side stick to establish an 8 to 12 degree takeoff attitude. At approximately one hundred and fifty-six knots, the plane was airborne. It was a rush, a great surge of adrenalin. Andres felt his stomach tighten and his heart leap. He was home at last.

He said, 'Mossheim Departure, Louisiana Alpha 07 airborne, passing 7,000 feet for flight level 250.'

The message came back, 'Roger 07, Mossheim Departure, right turn now direct to Stockholm. Maintain flight level 250.' The F-16 was climbing at a speed of 10,000 feet a minute. Andres Kiss, in complete control of the craft and himself – if indeed there was any distinction between the two at this moment – looked down on a diminishing landscape turning yellow in the early afternoon sun. So far as anyone on the ground was concerned, this flight was just another exercise carried out by an American fighter plane attached to NATO. Routine, simple – drop a few bombs and fire the cannons at targets on the uninhabited little Baltic island that was used for target practice, then return to base. That's what all the paperwork would say.

Andres, climbing still, soaring, knew otherwise. This exercise was in no way routine. When he reached Russian territorial waters, when he arrived at the place where he could go no further without violating Soviet airspace, he wasn't going to turn back. Nor had he any intention of squandering his weapons on some uninhabited little island. No way.

Glen Cove, Long Island

The speech of the police inspector in Oslo had a curious kind of formality to it, as if he'd learned the English language from teachers in tuxedos. He apologised profusely, perhaps with more politeness than the situation warranted, saying that Andres Kiss had been picked up at the airport by a man in a Volvo, prior to the arrival of the Oslo police, and taken elsewhere. And, according to a reliable female eyewitness taken by Kiss's striking good looks and thinking him a rock star, the car that had picked Kiss up was registered to a certain Flight Sergeant at Mossheim Air Base, which was a North Atlantic Treaty Organisation base – and, perhaps Mr Pagan would understand, the Oslo police had no real desire to enter the base unless Norwegian security was 'indisputably' at stake. There were, ah yes, ah-hum, political considerations involved as well, and surely Mr Pagan would also understand that much too. Frank Pagan thanked the inspector and hung up.

He went inside Andres Kiss's bedroom and looked at the world atlas. He found a map of Norway and Sweden, discovered Mossheim about twenty miles from Oslo, close to the Swedish border – and two hundred miles' from the Swedish border was the Baltic Sea.

He closed the atlas, thinking it was no distance at all from Norway to the Baltic, and from there to the coast of the Soviet Union. In the kind of plane Andres Kiss was presumably accustomed to flying it was a distance that could be covered in thirty minutes. Another thirty minutes across the Baltic, and you were practically in Leningrad. If you chose to enter the Baltic through Latvia, then it was only a matter of about an hour's flying time until you reached Moscow from Riga.

Pagan went back to the office. Mikhail Kiss was looking out of the window, his back to the room. Below, in the early light of day, the roses had begun to assume their colours again, bold, almost defiant in the dawn.

'Are you going to tell me?' Pagan asked. 'Or am I going to have to guess?'

Mikhail Kiss turned. It was hard to see him in the softly-lit room because the sun hadn't yet penetrated it. 'What do you think, Pagan?'

'Life would be easier if you told me,' Pagan said.

Kiss was quiet a moment. 'I put it all together from nothing. It would only be fair to see you reconstruct it from nothing.'

Pagan shut his eyes, rubbed the lids. 'Andres is going to fly a plane from Mossheim. He's going to enter Soviet airspace somehow. Then, presumably, he'll deliver some kind of bomb or rocket. Is that close enough?'

Kiss smiled. 'You expect an answer to that?'

Pagan went on, 'My guess is that he's going to strike a symbolic target, something that's going to displease the Soviets no end. I think he's more interested in damaging Soviet prestige than anything else.'

Soviet prestige, Kiss thought. He was thinking now of the fighters waiting in the Baltic cities, the men and women ready to rise up and do battle. He smiled. 'You're still cold, Pagan.' And he remembered Pagan's story about how Romanenko had been used by the KGB, which now struck him as a preposterous bluff on the Englishman's part, a ploy to lure Kiss's secrets out of him. Well, if Pagan could play games, then so could he!

'You wouldn't tell me if I was warm anyway,' Pagan said. He gazed across the room at Kristina Vaska, who sat huddled and shivering, because there was a chill in the air at this time of day. She was pale and tired, as if all her energy had evaporated during that one moment of fury against Kiss. But it was more than a moment, Pagan thought. She'd carried it with her for years.

'How does he get an aeroplane? How does he manage to do that? Does he steal one?' Pagan asked these questions in the manner of a man thinking aloud. 'How does he get inside a NATO base and steal a bloody plane, for Christ's sake?'

Mikhail Kiss shook his head. 'You work it out, Pagan.'

'Inside help is the only way.'

'You're sure of that?'

'I'm not sure of anything. Especially the target.'

'Maybe there's no target,' Kiss said.

Pagan sat behind the desk, shut his eyes. He'd forgotten the last time he'd slept, the last time he'd lain down – and then it came back to him. It must have been the hours spent with Kristina.

He said, 'No more games, Kiss. No more guessing games.'

'You're out of stamina, Pagan?'

'I've got stamina,' Pagan said. 'At least enough to make another phone call.'

'You've already called half the civilised world,' Kiss said. 'Where this time? What's left?'

Frank Pagan reached for the receiver and called Directory Assistance. Without taking his eyes from Mikhail Kiss's face, he asked for the number of the Pentagon.

The Baltic

Andres Kiss, who had refuelled in the air over Gotland Island, a tricky manoeuvre he handled deftly, looked down on the grey-green waters of the Baltic. The F-16 carried 13,500 pounds of fuel, and he'd need every last pound of it if he was to get in and out again according to plan. As soon as he'd disengaged the F-16 from the airborne tanker, and seen the amber disconnect light on his panel, he suddenly pulled the nose of his aircraft up, simulating an out-of-control situation.

The plan called for him to broadcast an emergency message, which he now did. 'Mayday, Mayday, LA Alpha 07, I've got a fire light.' And he continued his rapid rate of descent, plummeting to 10,000 feet, then 5,000, then 2,000. Down and down, rolling, swooping through cloud banks and seeing vapours disperse as he plunged.

'LA Alpha 07, state your position.'

Andres Kiss didn't reply to the voice in his headphones.

The request came again, and Andres ignored it a second time. He turned off the IFF switch, which would indicate to any radar probe that he'd hit the water below and was beyond any possibility of communication. Radar operators would assume that the emergency bleeper hadn't gone off because he hadn't ejected before the craft struck water.

So far, Andres thought, so good.

The plane was now about a hundred and twenty miles from the city of Riga in Latvia and travelling at six miles a minute. He kept descending, stabilising the craft when he was a mere hundred feet above the surface of the Baltic in Russian territorial waters. He could feel the effect of the water, a series of vibrations that disturbed the flight path of the craft. Using the Inertial Navigation Set, he flew east. As a back-up he had charts which would allow him to make visual verification of the information provided by the INS.

The island of Saaremaa, which the Soviets had seized from Estonia, loomed up to his left. A faint early morning haze hung around it. Andres Kiss thought of Mikhail now, and wondered what he was doing at this precise moment. He might be sitting in his sun-room, looking out into the garden. Or he might be pacing nervously, counting down the minutes.

Andres smiled, glanced down at the water, watched spray churn up from the surface. At this height he was flying below the point at which he might be picked up by the Soviet radar – provided the radar systems were operating. If the plan was running smoothly, they would not be. By flying this low, Andres wasn't taking any chances. If something had gone wrong inside the Soviet Union and the air defence systems *were* functioning normally, he'd still evade detection by radar.

Sun burned on the water, broken by the disturbed surface into millions of little sparkling lights. Andres checked the instrument panels again. He was travelling at three hundred and sixty knots per hour, a speed that conserved fuel. He was already far beyond the reach of any NATO aircraft that might have picked up his mayday signal. It was about ten minutes now to the Soviet mainland. Ten minutes through the Gulf of Riga – and then on, inevitably, towards Moscow.

Fredericksburg, Virginia

Galbraith had one of those numb moments of bewilderment, a time in which all brain activity seems suspended. What he was hearing made no immediate sense to him and might have been uttered in a foreign tongue. He opened his eyes – he'd been snoozing, dreaming of tropical places, sand dunes and palms and free-flying parrots and great date clusters – and heard the sound of Gary Iverson's voice coming through the telephone speaker on the bedside table.

'Name of God,' Galbraith muttered sleepily. 'Tell me again.'

Iverson repeated what he'd said a moment ago, when Galbraith had first been stirred from his all-consuming slumber by the buzzing telephone.

'Fucking Epishev,' Galbraith said, tossing back the bed covers. 'God damn his soul.'

'He erred, sir,' Iverson said, his voice made hollow by the echo in the speaker. 'He must have assumed there were two men in the car. But the man who used Mikhail Kiss's telephone to reach the Pentagon was Frank Pagan – '

'Assume! We assume nothing in this business, Gary,' and Galbraith, stark naked, stepped out of bed. 'We never assume. Assume is not in our vocabulary. Assume is a word for goddam politicians and priests. Assume is a word for people who have faith in things that cannot be seen, Gary. For example, you assumed Andres Kiss would obey Mikhail and leave Carl Sundbach untouched, did you not?'

'Yes, sir.'

'You see my point.' Galbraith, breathing hard and vowing anew to diet, climbed into a vast pair of pants with a waist wide enough to encompass two, perhaps three, slender adults. 'What will we do now, Gary? What will we do?'

'A dark deed,' Iverson suggested quietly.

'It's a frightful thought,' Galbraith replied, though without much conviction. 'There has been a traditional alliance, Gary, which I don't have to point out to you, between our two nations and their law-enforcement agencies. There has been shared information, even if in recent years there has been a falling-out between clandestine services in the two countries. Nobody trusts the Brits, do they? Well-intentioned men whose security has had the integrity of a colander. Nevertheless, Gary, the idea of *my* agency doing a dark deed on Frank Pagan . . . ' Here Galbraith pulled on a tent-like white shirt. 'I think I'll speak with this tenacious fellow and see if I can make him see sense, and if I can't do that, then perhaps – Well, I daresay the Clowns can have him, but only if they dine with discretion. We can't leave the man free to walk about, can we?'

'No,' Iverson said. 'We can't do that.'

Galbraith, looking sorrowful, forced his feet into a pair of black leather pumps. He was hugely unhappy that Epishev had failed, because the onus was squarely back on him, and he didn't like that at all. He stood up, stamped his feet inside his shoes, and suddenly remembered the mention of something in the dossier he had on Colonel Epishev. Of course, the silly bastard was far-sighted and had to wear glasses, which he was seemingly too vain to do! Idiot vanity! Galbraith thought. If Epishev had worn his glasses as he was supposed to, then perhaps Frank Pagan wouldn't be around right now, doing damage, threatening the outcome of White Light.

Iverson said, 'I took the liberty of arranging to meet Pagan at Grand Central Station, sir, an hour from now.'

Galbraith thought of the fast chopper that would hurl him through space at a speed of some two hundred miles an hour. He hated the deafening roar of the blades and the headache that always gripped him and the miserable sense of being tossed around in midair. But he knew of no faster way to Manhattan from Fredericksburg. His flying time would be approximately one hour and twenty minutes.

'I'll be there as quickly as I can,' he said.

Moscow

General Olsky handled the contents of the envelope as if they were fish that might or might not be dead. What he had in his hand were three American passports and fifty thousand American dollars. He flicked one of the passports open, stared inside it, then set it down. He tossed the bundle of money on to his desk in a dismissive fashion. He looked at Colonel Chebrikov.

'The woman actually *denies* knowing how the passports and the money came to be hidden under her floorboards?' Olsky asked.

'Yes,' said the Colonel.

'Even after it was pointed out to her that the passports bear photographs of herself and her two children?'

'She claims it's a malicious practical joke, General.'

'I don't see the joke at all,' Olsky remarked. 'Perhaps Mrs Uvarova has a strange sense of humour. What about her husband, Colonel?'

'He's going to be brought in for questioning, General.'

'Has Deputy Minister Tikunov been informed that the family of one of his "trusted" officers has foreign money and foreign passports in its possession?'

Chebrikov said, 'I imagined you'd prefer to make that call yourself, General.'

Olsky smiled. 'How right you are,' he said.

New York City

It was five-thirty a.m. when Frank Pagan entered Grand Central Station. When he'd finally reached the Pentagon by telephone and had been put through to a duty officer there, he'd been told to hang up and wait. Somebody would call him back. What Pagan detected in this procedure was the kind of paranoia patented by the military mind. Ten minutes later, the telephone had rung in the kitchen of Mikhail Kiss's house and a voice that did not belong to the first duty officer asked Pagan for details.

It wasn't a situation in which details were exactly plentiful and Pagan's narrative, he realised, had about it a demented tone. Was he being relegated to that category of nuts who call the Pentagon or the CIA in Langley with schizoid tales to tell of dark plots? Was he just another lonely loony calling to hear himself speak?

Apparently he was taken with some seriousness, enough at least for the listener to suggest a rendezvous in a mutually suitable place, which turned out to be, at the suggestion of the listener, Grand Central Station. It wasn't altogether convenient to drive from Glen Cove back to Manhattan, but Pagan – forced by old habits – broke the speed limit all the way, using Kiss's large Mercedes instead of Kristina Vaska's Pacer, which reminded him of a fishbowl equipped with wheels. Whether Kristina was still in Glen Cove, or whether she'd gone by now, Pagan had no way of knowing. She'd wanted to come with him to Grand Central, an offer he flatly refused. He kept insisting, for his own benefit, that he didn't give a damn anyhow. Seal it and bury it, he told himself. Inter the whole bastard thing. *Put it in a coffin and deep-six it*.

He moved across the concourse, seeing a sparse gathering of early morning travellers, a couple of derelicts, a few drunks wondering what fibs to tell their wives who'd been waiting up all night in the suburbs. He'd been told to look for a man carrying a copy of *The Cleveland Plain Dealer*, a clandestine touch he found amusing. He stood outside a shuttered news-stand, which was the appointed place, and there he waited.

He gazed across the station, impatiently tapping a foot on the ground. He thought, *It began in a railway station and it may end in one, among the litter and the discarded tickets and muffled voices out of loudspeakers and the air that's dry and hard to breathe*. And then he was thinking of Edinburgh and a trail that had begun with the assassination of Romanenko. But it had begun long before that in a forgotten guerilla war in countries which, to all intents and purposes, had been erased forever from the minds of mapmakers.

He moved along the front of the news-stand, hearing the shunting of a locomotive nearby. Then he saw his contact, a tall stiff-backed man with a copy of *The Plain Dealer* held against his side. Pagan stepped forward to greet him. The man looked at Pagan, smiled. He had a pleasantly bland face and fair hair that was cut very short across his skull.

'Frank Pagan?'

Pagan nodded. The man, who had very pale blue eyes, studied Pagan's face a moment, as if he were searching for visible signs of lunacy. The man started to walk, and Pagan followed, thinking it apt that no name had been given, no handshake, no rank, no affiliation. Secrecy was a way of life in military circles. And when it was impossible to keep something secret, you did the next best thing, you stifled it in incomprehensible jargon.

They walked together towards a bar, which was closed. The man peered through the windows and said, 'Your story's fascinating.'

'I'm happy you think so,' Pagan said.

'Goddam fascinating.' The man turned and clapped one firm hand on Pagan's shoulder. 'And unfortunately vague. A plane flies out of Norway. What kind of plane? And who authorised it to fly? Or was the plane stolen? You got any idea how difficult it is to steal a military aircraft? It's all pretty damn thin, but it gets worse, doesn't it? You don't know the specific target, you don't know the nature of the alleged strike. Boil it down, Frank – mind if I call you that? – and you're not left with much, are you? Just a few guesses, basically. And to be perfectly candid, if you hadn't been affiliated with Scotland Yard – I checked you out, by the way – your story would be in the slush pile already. NFA – no further action.'

Pagan wondered if he was supposed to have documentary evidence of his story, if it had to be suitably notarised. He said, 'It shouldn't be beyond your resources to find out if a plane has been stolen from the base at Mossheim.'

The man shrugged. 'There are always NATO exercises around the Baltic, and they involve scores of aircraft. It's not as simple as you might imagine to locate one particular craft, especially since we don't know exactly what we're looking for.'

Pagan was disappointed by the man's lack of enthusiasm. He struggled to be patient and calm. 'I understand it might be difficult, but in the circumstances don't you think you should be making some kind of bloody effort? Don't you have a computer tracking system?'

The man's smile seemed an immutable thing, living a separate life from his face. 'Don't get me wrong, Frank. I'm not going to dismiss your story. I'll look into it. I promise you that. But it's going to take a little time.'

'Look, I have a feeling we don't have time. This character Andres Kiss is already on the base at Mossheim. He might even have flown by this time – '

'Frank, Frank, Frank. We checked Andres Kiss out and he used to be a USAF Major, just as you said. But why do you make the assumption he's gone to Mossheim to steal a plane, for heaven's sake? Some of his old squadron members are based there right now, the guy could be paying a visit, a vacation. It doesn't have to be anything nefarious. Like I said, Frank, if you had just a little documentary evidence, well, it would make a hell of a difference.'

Pagan said, 'I'm beginning to get the impression that my narrative isn't quite setting you on fire. If I were a suspicious man, I'd say you weren't exactly interested in it.'

'Of course I'm interested in it,' the man said.

'Then why aren't you doing something about it?'

The man laid his hand on Pagan's shoulder again. 'Here's what I suggest, Frank. You trot on back to your hotel and leave it all to me. Don't worry about a thing. It's in good hands.'

'I'm not about to trot anywhere,' Pagan said. Especially not at the suggestion of someone as patronising as you, Blue Eyes, he thought. There was an insincere quality to this nameless man, and Pagan didn't like it, didn't trust it. He didn't like the way he was being stalled either.

'Jesus, you're a hard man to convince, Frank. You imagine I'm going to ignore the whole goddam thing? You imagine I don't believe you? I'll take the appropriate steps, I promise you that.'

'When?'

'Frank, let me give you the simple ABCs of it. This is a military matter. We're all goddam grateful you brought it to our attention, believe me. But it's out of your hands now.'

'I don't think so,' Pagan said, and he stared at a row of phone booths a hundred yards away. What was the time in London? he wondered. Martin Burr would be at his desk and if Pagan couldn't get this supercilious bozo to do something quickly, he'd cheerfully call the Commissioner, who would most certainly contact the NATO command in Europe. But why in the name of Christ was there such reluctance here?

He said, 'If you don't want to follow up on my story – and I mean *now,* sunshine – I'll make a phone call to somebody who will. That way, if I'm completely off the wall, if I'm suffering from a brainstorm, then at least I'll have the benefit of relief.'

The man followed Pagan's line of vision in the direction of the phones. 'I wouldn't,' he said, and the smile finally was gone.

'Give me a damn good reason not to,' Pagan said.

'We've got a communications problem here, Frank, and it bothers me. What I'm trying to say is that as far as you're concerned, those phones are off limits.'

'Off limits?'

'Precisely.'

'If I want to make a call, you stop me, is that it?'

The man said nothing.

Pagan briefly closed his eyes, hearing the sound of something he should have caught minutes ago, something that echoed in his head and throbbed. Realisation, a cold dawning, the noise of a frozen penny dropping inside his brain. He looked into the man's face, which had all the animation of a stiff mask.

'You *want* it to fly,' Pagan said quietly. 'You *want* the fucking plane to make it!'

The man continued to be silent.

Pagan could still hear the coin tumbling down the chutes of his mind, gathering momentum as it moved, and he was reminded of a game he used to play at carnivals as a kid, when you stuck a penny in a slot and watched it roll towards a variety of possible destinations – some of which returned your coin, most of which kept it. Christ, what had he stumbled into? Where was the rolling coin destined to go? You call the Pentagon, you report the possibility of a stolen plane, an impending disaster, and the duty officer turns you over to Blue Eyes, who's seemingly in no great hurry to prevent destruction. What the hell was going on here?

'Let me see if I can guess it,' Pagan said. 'Are you and Andres Kiss working together? Is that it? With a little help from some friends inside the Pentagon? Am I right? Is it some kind of elaborate military conspiracy?'

The man shook his head. 'That's too simple, Frank. There's no military conspiracy. There's no vast involvement at the Pentagon.'

'What is it then? Just a chosen few? A helping hand here, a little support there? Why don't you spell it out for me, friend?'

'I want you to meet somebody, Frank. Somebody who can give you a better perspective on this whole matter. He's waiting outside. He doesn't like public places.'

Pagan hesitantly followed as the man began to walk across the concourse in the direction of the exit. Outside the station a long black limousine was parked in defiance of No Parking signs. Pagan understood he was to move towards it. The back door was opened from inside. Pagan hesitated.

Blue Eyes said, 'You'll be fine, Frank. Go ahead.'

Pagan looked inside the car. A fat man, his face in shade, occupied most of the back seat. There were two televisions, a couple of phones, decanters of scotch and sherry.

'Go ahead,' Blue Eyes said again.

Pagan concentrated on the fat man's face, the eyes that were hardly more than two very narrow gashes, the cheeks that appeared to be stuffed with food – as if the man were a hibernating animal preparing himself for the long sleep of winter.

'Frank Pagan,' the fat man said, and patted the space on the seat alongside him. 'I've been looking forward to meeting you. But we can hardly talk like reasonable men if you insist on standing in the street, while I sit in the comfort of this car. What's it to be?'

'You step out,' Pagan said.

'Humbug. It's more comfortable in here.'

Pagan shook his head. The fat man sighed and emerged from the limousine, looking just a little testy but forcing a smile anyhow. Blue Eyes moved some distance away, browsing through newspapers at a news-stand.

'Stubborn, Pagan,' the fat man said.

'So I've been told.'

They walked a few paces. The fat man asked, 'How is Scotland Yard?'

'Is this going to be small talk? I already told your man out there that I had a situation I thought should be checked out. He appeared completely reluctant.'

'He's a good man. Don't be hard on him. He takes orders well.'

'From you?'

The fat man nodded. 'I understand you want to stop a certain plane flying to the Soviet Union, Frank.'

'I had a notion,' Pagan said. He was suddenly very impatient.

'Question, Frank. How much do you know? How much have you glued together?'

Pagan studied the man's face. He had a small mouth and rather tiny teeth. Pagan thought for a moment before he said, 'Why should I tell you what I know? I don't even know who you are, for Christ's sake.'

'My dear fellow, I'm a great fan of Scotland Yard. You and I, old man, we're on the same team. Nobody's going to hurt you, Frank. We're friends here. My affiliation is a wee bit difficult to explain.'

'I bet it is.'

'National security.'

'Whose national security?'

'The whole Western world, Frank. I'm not speaking only of our own backyard, my friend.'

Pagan started to move away. He was tired of obfuscation, weary of allusion, sick to his heart with mystification. All he wanted to do was to go back inside the station and call the Commissioner. The fat man caught the sleeve of his jacket and held it.

'Don't rush away, Frank. Tell me what you know. Besides, you've got nothing to worry about, have you? You're armed. I'm not. I've read your dossier and I know you carry a

Bernardelli in a rear holster. And I wouldn't be seen dead near a gun. All I'm interested in is your version of the situation.'

Pagan assembled his thoughts, which raced here and there like doomed summer butterflies eluding a net. He said, 'The KGB found some use for a group of Baltic freedom fighters. At least certain factions in the KGB and their friends did. The Balts don't seem to have a clue they're being used by the very people they despise most. I assume the KGB motive is related to a power-struggle inside the Soviet Union – old against new. That's my best guess. I can't see any other reason for the support of the Balts. But now I get the distinct impression from your friend over there that there's more to this than I imagined. Now it appears that the Balts aren't only getting help from the Soviets, they're also getting assistance from certain Americans as well, some of whom have military connections.'

The fat man shrugged. His small eyes were very bright and hard like two polished brown stones. He appeared to be just a little amused now.

Pagan said, 'American and Soviet collusion. It explains some things. Such as how Epishev knew I'd come to the United States. The Americans told him. How Andres Kiss could steal a NATO plane and fly it inside Soviet territory. The Americans could provide the aircraft, the Soviets the means of entry.'

'Ingenious,' said the fat man. He pressed his chubby fingers to his mouth.

'What I don't entirely understand is American involvement,' Pagan remarked.

'Think about it, Frank,' the fat man said. 'I'm sure it's on the tip of your tongue.'

Pagan was quiet a moment. Traffic chugged past the entrance to the station, taxicabs honking at the black limousine that impeded their movement. Pagan observed that the limo wasn't equipped with the usual licence plates. Instead, it had the kind of temporary plates used by car dealers.

He said, 'My best bet would be that some Americans would like to see the new Soviet regime replaced. I'm naive enough to wonder why.'

'Replaced is understatement. Try removed and forgotten, Frank. Buried with all its manifestos of good intentions. Interred with all its spurious nonsense about democracy and freedom. That's closer to the mark. It's a matter of protecting our civilisation, for want of a better word.'

'So Andres Kiss flies an aeroplane inside the Soviet Union and *that* act of terrorism protects our civilisation?' Pagan asked.

The fat man grinned and his eyes vanished off the planet of his face. 'You know, Frank, some of us long for the old days when we knew who the Russians were. We had a set of rules, and we could get along with the Soviets because they were predictable. We understood how they operated. We knew their level of incompetence. Government by geriatrics. What do old men love more than anything else, Frank? I'll tell you. They adore the status fucking quo, that's what. But all these goddam changes have upset things more than a little. When the old farts started dying off, we always assumed other old farts would take their places. We thought the Soviets had an endless supply of old farts. We didn't see a new breed rising, did we? We didn't think ahead. Now we don't know where they stand these days. And worse than that, we don't know where *we* stand either.'

Pagan said nothing. He felt restless. Was the fat man trying to stall him? Detecting Pagan's restlessness, the fat man raised his voice.

'When they talk about reforms, and how they're going to change the Soviet Union from top to bottom, that really troubles me. Ye gods! who knows what they're going to release? Vast reservoirs of untapped talent lying around, skills that have gone unused because nobody gave a fiddler's fuck about a system that disregarded basic human rights. But give people a sense of dignity, give them some comforts, make them think they're really important, and we might see a goddam Russian renaissance in technology, science, energy. *And then what?*'

The fat man took a handkerchief out now and blew his nose in short, trumpeting sounds. 'The big question is, can this fragile globe stand a *really* powerful Russia? Will the old power pendulum swing over to the red zone? What kind of world would it be if the Russians dominated it? I get chills up and down my spine. You see, I liked things the way they were, Frank. I think what we're doing can help us keep the upper hand. We're not discussing some lunatic right-wing bullshit here, Frank. Let's just say a few people, with different motives but a common goal, put their resources together. Certain Americans don't like this new Russia. More importantly, a good number of Russians don't like it either. Change, they say. Screw change. We want things the way they were. Let's have it back the way it used to be. What a nice coincidence, don't you think? Here's something the Americans and the Soviets can get together on finally. A joint Soviet-American venture to destroy all this unwanted *newness* in Soviet society. A collaboration, Frank, between ourselves and some sympathetic Russians. Fraternity and cooperation.'

'With the Balts playing the fools,' Pagan said.

'That's your choice of description, Frank.'

'When you say *ourselves*, who are you referring to?' The fat man fell silent now. Pagan knew his question was going to go unanswered. The fat man was something within something within something, connected to the US government, but tucked away, and well-hidden, and finally beyond the pale of the federal bureaucracy.

'And this plane?'

'It's going to cause a commotion, Frank. And we're gambling that it will bring down the present Politburo leaving a nice empty space for some reliable old faces.'

'If I might use an Americanism – the whole thing sucks.'

'Pray tell.'

'It's a volatile plan. You don't know the precise consequences of it. If you attack the Soviet Union, if a NATO plane violates Soviet airspace and drops a bomb – how can you tell there won't be retaliation of some kind? Even if that doesn't happen, I don't like the idea of people needlessly dying, which I imagine will happen if this plane flies.'

'Needlessly, Frank?'

'I don't want to argue with you. Your outlook's unreal. The world changes, and you can't stop it. You can't interfere.'

'Oh dear,' the fat man said. 'I thought you might reach a more balanced judgement than that, which is why I gave you the benefit of this nice little chat. Think again, Frank. I do wish you'd keep in mind the fact that an arthritic Russia is a containable one. Anything else is, well, a little too unpredictable.'

Pagan shook his head. There was nothing in the world so astonishing to him as the compulsion of organisations and fraternities and secret societies that think they can alter history, nothing that reduced him quite so quickly to speechlessness. Partly it was the conceit of it all, the terrible arrogance. Partly it was the desperation of these men, and their obsessions, which lay beyond reason. For Kiss and Romanenko it had been vengeance. For the fat man and his Russian cronies it was nothing less ambitious than trying to preserve a Russia to which they'd become complacently attached for their own reasons. Anything new, anything that might bring about a different Soviet Union, even a progressive one – God help us all – was not remotely acceptable.

'You think you can get away with it?' Pagan asked.

'Get away with it? We can get away with anything. Shuffling paperwork so that a plane can be taken without authority – by a former pilot who's utterly deranged, of course, as all the records will show – that's child's play. Don't worry about us.'

Pagan was quiet a moment. 'I don't walk away from here, do I?'

'Frank, really. Step out of my life. I never met you. You never met me. And you never will again. Simple. I love Scotland Yard, and I wouldn't dream of harming one of its people. But I do wish you'd stay a little longer and chat some more with me. I'd like to talk about more pleasant things. London, for example. Tea at the Ritz. Dinner at the Connaught. The South Coast. I have so many fond memories. There's a small town in the West Country, Bideford, and I recall –'

'Some other time,' Pagan said.

The fat man smiled, looked at his watch. Then he shrugged. 'Goodbye . . . ' He snapped his fingers in frustration. 'Christ, I've already forgotten your name.'

Pagan stepped away from the man. He felt tense, dehydrated. The fat man returned to the big black car, stepped inside along with Blue Eyes. The car pulled away, vanished. Pagan moved back in the direction of the station entrance. Back to the telephones.

But he knew he wasn't going to be allowed. He wasn't going to make it that far. He sensed it. Even the morning air around him was charged suddenly with the electricity of fear. He moved slowly towards the station, passing under the shadows of the building, turning his face from side to side, seeing nothing, but *knowing*, just knowing that somebody was about to prevent him from reaching the phones.

He didn't see the sniper on the roof of the station. He didn't know he was being closely observed through a telescopic lens by a sharpshooter, a former Marine champion, who held a Weatherby auto rifle. Pagan only knew that as he walked towards the entrance he was exposed and vulnerable, but at the same time didn't want to break into a run, he wanted to look totally calm. Halfway towards the station entrance he paused, looked from left to right, saw nothing unusual, nothing concealed in shadows, nobody seated in parked cars. Just the same, *he still knew.*

He kept moving. He didn't see the glint of the rifle as the early sun struck the walnut stock, or the way the sharpshooter took out a pair of dark glasses and pulled them over his eyes. Pagan had to stop because several cars blocked his way into the station. But he didn't think to look up, he was concentrating on the station entrance, the idea of making it as far as the telephones. When the traffic passed, he stepped off the pavement. He had perhaps fifty yards to go. He hurried now for the first time, unaware of the fact he was trapped in the dead centre of a lens, a moving target neatly bisected by crosslines.

And then something, an inexplicable impulse, made him raise his face and look up, and he saw the way the sunlight caught the weapon, although for a second he wasn't absolutely sure of what it was that glinted high above him, and he thought of a bird carrying a piece of silverfoil, or a sliver of broken glass. When he understood what it was he knew the realisation had come a little too late for him.

He barely heard the voice from behind.

'Frank!'

He did the only thing he could think of. He threw himself forward, hearing the noise of a gun, realising it was too loud to have come from the roof, that it originated from a point just behind him. It was followed by a second shot, then a third, and the sound echoed around him. He raised his face and gazed up at the roof, but the gunman was gone, scrambling out of view, leaving behind him only an expensively modified weapon that bore no registration number, no marks of ownership, and no clue to the identity of the person who'd altered the weapon.

Pagan rose slowly to his feet, aware of cars crowding around him, irate drivers, delayed commuters, the screaming of horns. And there, standing alongside her idiotic little car, her Pacer, stood Kristina Vaska, looking very solemn and quite lovely in a pale, tired way, one hand on her hip, the other wrapped loosely around her pistol, a tiny smile on her face – enigmatic, and quite unfamiliar to Pagan, but nevertheless at that moment the most welcome gesture he'd ever received from another human being.

He returned the smile and then he went inside the station and walked towards the telephones.

Moscow

Deputy Minister Tikunov, who hated to admit he was ever wrong about anything, and who thought crow the most disgusting taste a man could carry in his mouth, spoke into the telephone. 'It appears that your information is genuine, General. An F-16 was stolen from a NATO base in Norway. It's heading for Russia.'

'Stolen?' Olsky asked.

'That's the official NATO statement. I've just had their Commander on the line from Brussels.'

'Then do what you have to do,' Olsky said. 'But do it quickly.'

Tikunov flicked a switch on a communications console on his desk. He ordered a top priority check of every radar installation between Moscow and the Baltic. He also ordered squadrons of MIG-29s and MIG-25 Foxbats to fly immediately on a seek and destroy mission.

21

Saaremma Island, the Baltic

When he saw the F-16 go flying past in the far distance, Colonel Yevgenni Uvarov hurried in the direction of the beach. The falsified maintenance order he'd issued meant that any radar sightings, which would normally have been relayed to his control centre and from there to Moscow, were effectively contained inside the computers under Uvarov's command. Because technicians worked on the computers, the line of communication from Saaremaa Island to Moscow was severed for the hours of their labour. Uvarov had short-circuited the system, and since no sightings could be reported to the Ministry in Moscow, no order could be given to destroy the intruder. Only the Minister, or the Deputy Minister, or somebody authorised by them, could issue such an order.

Uvarov reached the beach and ran towards the stone jetty, looking for the launch. There was no sign of the vessel. Panicked, he raced to the end of the jetty and scanned the water. There was a faint haze rising off the sea. He thought he could still hear the roar of the F-16 as it raced – barely above sea-level – towards the coast, but he couldn't tell since the plane was out of sight.

Where was the damned launch? Uvarov anxiously scanned the water. Nothing. No sight of anything. What if he'd been tricked? What if there was no such vessel? What if Aleksis had been lying all along? Uvarov, so panicked he could barely breathe, peered out into the haze, his eyes stinging from salt spray. He looked back the length of the jetty, seeing the barbed-wire strung around the control centre and the radar dishes that turned ceaselessly, probing the sea and the sky. *Where was the fucking launch?*

And then he heard it. He heard it! It appeared through the haze, a small vessel that churned up an enormous wake as it speeded towards the jetty. Uvarov raised his hand, waved impatiently. Hurry, he thought. Dear God, hurry. He glanced back at the control centre once more. There was another sound now, and one he couldn't altogether identify because he was concentrating on the launch, which had cut its engine and was drifting towards the quay. *Hurry, hurry.* Uvarov started down the steps, seeing two figures on board the small green craft. One of them was preparing to toss a rope towards Uvarov, uncoiling it. And then Uvarov felt it, the turbulent passage of air, the breeze that swept his face and ruffled his hair, and he looked upwards, drawn to the great turning blades of the helicopter. The rope came towards him and he clutched it hastily as the launch drifted nearer to him – ten feet, seven, five – dear Christ, he'd have to leap. He braced himself, jumped, clutched the side of the launch and was hauled on board even as the helicopter descended like some predatory creature and the man who appeared in the open doorway of the chopper started firing at the launch with a machine-gun. On and on and on, blitzing the deck of the small craft, a crazy kind of firing that seemed to have no end to it. Uvarov fell, conscious of a wound in his side – a distant awareness, beyond any immediate pain. What he felt more than anything was sadness and regret.

He shut his eyes and even though he didn't see them he experienced the heat of the flames that had begun to billow out of the launch's fuel system, which had caught fire during the machine-gun assault. The launch smoked and smouldered before it finally exploded, sending debris up and up into the salt air.

Tallinn, Estonia

In the middle of the afternoon, the man known as Marcus met three other men, each of them carrying a concealed weapon, outside the Hotel Viru. At the same time another three men assembled near the Tallinn Department Store on Lomonossovi Street. The Viru Hotel, a modern twenty-two storey construction on Viru Square, could be seen from the department store. Marcus and his companions crossed Estonia Boulevard where the afternoon traffic was dense and the pedestrians, swollen by hundreds of tourists, created a slow-moving crowd that made progress along the pavement difficult. Marcus looked once at his watch as he reached the corner of Lomonossovi Street. Thirty minutes.

The three men who had gathered outside the department store were following some yards behind. Marcus had the thought that they all looked suspicious, that anyone observing them would notice that they all carried hidden weapons, but this was the result of his own tension and fear. In fact they looked just like anyone else strolling through the afternoon sunshine under a blue Tallinn sky.

Marcus paused, lit a cigarette, caught the eye of a pretty girl moving past. Her ash-coloured hair, tugged by an ocean breeze, blew playfully up around her cheeks and she pushed it aside in a gesture Marcus found unbearably sweet. In thirty minutes he'd probably be dead. In thirty minutes, simple things, beautiful things like the girl's hand caressing her own hair, would be beyond his experience.

He thought of the girl Erma and the old man Bruno, who were part of a second group forming on Suur-Karja Street, some distance from the old Town Hall. This unit, consisting of twenty people, would enter the Central Post Office and order the clerks to close the doors for the rest of the day. In Latvia and Lithuania similar insurrections were taking place simultaneously. In Riga, groups were scheduled to seize the Post Office on Lenin Street, the Latvian State radio offices, and the TV tower located on one of the islands on the Daugava River. In Vilnius, the targets were the Central Post Office on Lenin Prospekt, the State Television studio, and the railway station. From the post offices in all three cities, telegrams would be sent to a variety of cities in the West – including Stockholm, Paris, London and New York. These messages would be the same in every case – a declaration of Baltic independence, evidenced by this robust resistance, no longer passive, no longer a matter of mere flag-waving, to Soviet occupation – and by the daring flight of a patriot into the heart of Russia itself. A message was being delivered to the world, and it was one of freedom.

Marcus stopped on Lomonossovi Street. He checked his watch again. Synchronisation was important. He would deliver his own message at precisely the same time as the aeroplane launched its attack. There was impressive power in such orchestration. Chaos would convince nobody. Who would respond to a disorganised rabble? If there was to be a general revolt throughout the Baltic countries, those who decided to participate in it had to be convinced that the leaders were proficient as well as patriotic. They had to have confidence in the organisation. Everything had to be done the way Aleksis had planned it, with attention to detail, to timing. Aleksis had once said that revolutions often failed because they weren't punctual, a statement Marcus had thought amusing at the time. Not now . . .

Marcus continued to walk. Up ahead was the building that housed the Estonian Radio and Television studios. He lit another cigarette, glanced at his companions, noticed how they bantered among themselves like working-men going home at the end of a long day, men who perhaps had stopped at a café for vodka or beer. Marcus put a hand inside the pocket of his overcoat. The gun felt very good to him. He was aware of crowds jostling him, the smells of colognes, bread from a bakery, gasoline fumes, so many scents. Was it like this when you knew your life was almost over? Were you suddenly sharper, keener, more receptive to the world you were leaving?

He put his hand around his gun. He looked back at the men following him. He smiled, a tense little movement of his lips. Now, he thought. It was almost time.

The Soviet Union

Andres Kiss flew low over marshy countryside, noticing here and there small rounded hills and the occasional river, now and then a farmhouse. He avoided towns and villages. He was still flying at a speed of six miles a minute. He set the radar on 'range only', which permitted him to look approximately eighty miles ahead and thirty thousand feet above, then he placed the master arm in the ON position, so that he was armed and ready in the event of an attack – if there had been a visual sighting of his F-16, and he prayed that there hadn't. He continued to fly between the low hills and through shallow valleys, keeping to the shadows where the sun didn't penetrate. If he hugged the landscape this way, the chance of any high-altitude craft spotting him was severely limited. He saw nothing above him in his radar, and ahead the landscape was dreary. His luck, so far, had held. But luck, he knew, was a fickle bitch, and could change her mind at any time.

Not today, Andres Kiss thought. He had a feeling that fortune was with him.

He was heading due east now. He was approximately 180 miles – thirty minutes' flying time – from Moscow. And the Kremlin.

He studied the landscape around him, seeing it flash past at the kind of speed he loved. Blurs, brown-greens, a landscape that suggested spilled paint. Cattle whizzed past, and grain silos, and houses, and the stacks of the occasional factory. Reservoirs, dams, electricity pylons. It was crazed speed and impressions came at him faster than his senses could truly register them.

This, Andres thought, was power.

Tallinn, Estonia

The first casualty was the uniformed guard who stepped from behind his desk to question Marcus.

'You need a pass, comrade,' the guard said. 'And an appointment.'

Marcus said, *'Ya ne panimayu parooski,'* which meant he didn't speak Russian, which was a lie. He asked the guard to speak in Estonian. The guard, a surly young man from Minsk who loathed the Baltic, and who was homesick for his native city, said he didn't speak Estonian. He did, but only to a small degree. Today, though, he didn't feel like wrapping his tongue round those strange sounds, and he didn't like the look of this fellow who'd just strutted inside the building. The young man put his hand on his holster.

Marcus shot him then. The guard fell backwards and a girl began to scream at the end of the hallway. Marcus turned, saw his companions enter the building with their guns drawn. He hadn't expected to kill the young man, but this was too important for scruples now, too important for hesitation. He hurried along the corridor, seeing doors open on either side, the troubled faces of men and women, employees of the State Radio and Television Company which regularly flooded the air with Soviet-approved trash and which took its editorial direction from the Ministry of Communications in Moscow. The girl who'd been screaming before was silent now, covering her face with her hands and kneeling on the floor.

'You're not going to be hurt,' Marcus said. 'Direct me to the broadcasting studio.'

The girl pointed towards a staircase. 'Up there. Studio Two is radio. Studios One and Three TV.'

Marcus moved toward the stairs, leaving five of his men posted in the hallway. He took the stairs quickly, followed by two men who were brothers from the district of Tallinn called Mustamae, a place of monstrous Soviet apartment houses. He checked his watch again as he moved.

Ahead, a second guard stepped out of an office into the corridor. He had a pistol in one hand and he fired it directly at Marcus. The shot struck one of the brothers, who fell silently. The guard didn't get the chance to fire again before Marcus had shot him in the forehead. And then he was hurrying along the hallway, looking for the door of the studio he wanted. He didn't want TV, he preferred radio because he believed more people listened to music on the radio in the afternoons than watched the tedious graveyard that was Tallinn television.

More people were filing out of their offices. Marcus didn't know how long he had. Sooner or later somebody was going to pick up a telephone and call the militiamen and then the building would be invaded by cops. The five men posted in the hallway below could hold them off for quite some time, although Marcus wasn't sure how long that might be. He took the prepared message from his pocket as he rushed along the corridor. Studio One. Three. What had the hysterical girl said? Studio Two? Marcus noticed a red light above the door of Studio Two. He pushed the door open, stepped inside the soundproofed room.

Two women were seated round a microphone discussing how best to pickle herring. In a glass booth beyond the women sat three technicians. The women stared at Marcus as he entered, then – utterly perplexed by this unscripted occurrence, this intrusion into their domestic programme – looked at the technicians for guidance. Marcus waved his gun and made his way to the control booth, shoving the door open.

'I want to read a statement,' he said.

The technicians didn't know how to behave. One, muscular and bearded, asked, 'On whose behalf?'

'The Movement for Baltic Independence.'

The bearded man smiled. 'Be my guest,' and he gestured towards the microphones where the two silent women sat.

The Soviet Union

Fifty-four miles from Moscow. His predetermined initial point. Nine minutes of flying time. And so far it was working, everything, working like a goddam charm. Even the landscape seemed welcoming to him, a carpet laid out for him to fly over. Magic, Andres thought. Pure magic.

And then he was tense. Flying low over a flat landscape was one thing. Flying between stunted hills, that was a piece of cake. But Moscow was looming up, and Moscow was going to be something else.

He punched the on-board clock, starting from zero and counting up to eight and a half minutes. He pushed a small white button which armed the station where the three Mark 82s were located. Weapons live. Bombs live.

Now, he thought. The last lap. The big city.

Counting up. Still counting up. Five minutes. Six. Seven. But then time was becoming meaningless to Andres now, because he felt he was beyond such measurements. He was in a place without clocks. He was airborne and free and time was a ball and chain you tossed down through the clouds.

When eight minutes had elapsed, he began to climb rapidly, creating an angle of eventual descent. Three hundred feet. Five hundred. One thousand. Fifteen hundred.

Andres's face sweated in his helmet. He could see Moscow – *Matushka Moskva* – spread before him in the afternoon light. He could see towers and apartment buildings and spires and a gleaming stretch of the Moskva River and the movement of traffic on the streets. As he climbed, he said in a soft voice the Estonian version of the Lord's Prayer, which he'd learned from Mikhail Kiss in childhood. *Mei isa, kes sa oled taevas . . .*

Tallinn, Estonia

Marcus looked at his watch. It was time to read his statement. He sat nervously at the microphone and spread the sheet of paper out on the table before him. For a second he couldn't quite make out the words. He rubbed his eyes, cleared his throat, stared at the technicians in the glass booth. Two were expressionless, but the bearded man looked encouraging.

'Any time you like.' The bearded man's voice was loud inside Marcus's earphones.

Marcus took a sip from a glass of water and began to read. His statement, carefully composed by Romanenko many months ago, concerned the travesty of international justice that was the Soviet occupation. It concerned the rights of nations to self-determination. It concerned old non-invasion treaties, compacts made between the Russians and the Baltic countries, that had been cynically disregarded by the Kremlin. It concerned the revolutionary movements in Latvia and Lithuania that even now were broadcasting to their own people in Riga and Vilnius. And finally it concerned the daring flight of a young pilot into Moscow and how that single act of unselfish bravery was the standard against which all patriotic acts had to be judged, the spearhead of a new movement towards freedom, the call to liberty, the ultimate symbol.

Marcus stopped reading. He didn't realise that his speech hadn't been broadcast, that the transmitter had been rendered inoperative by technicians after he'd read the opening three sentences, and that the five men left to guard the downstairs hallway had been shot and killed by an invasion of militiamen. He had no way of knowing that the young man from Mustamae, who had been standing guard outside the door to Studio Two, lay dead in the corridor, shot by militiamen. Nor could he know that the group that had seized the Post Office at number 20 Suur-Karja had been killed in a thirty-minute gun battle with the KGB.

Marcus raised the water glass to his lips and looked at the bearded man, who winked at him through the glass. Marcus ran a hand over his face. He set down his glass just as the studio door opened. He reached at once for his gun as two militiamen, armed with automatic rifles, entered the room with their weapons already firing.

Marcus slumped across the table, spilling his water glass. A stream of water slithered across the paper on which his speech had been written, causing the ink to run in indecipherable lines, as if a bird with dark blue claws had alighted on the paper.

Moscow

At two thousand five hundred feet Andres could see Red Square, and the Kremlin – and there was the Palace of Congresses, where the Communist Party conferences were held.

Andres Kiss's target. Mikhail Kiss's target. The target of the Brotherhood. The place where destinies were decided, the malignant heart of the system the Brotherhood had despised. Andres Kiss could see the great columns that surrounded the building and he thought of how, within its vast auditorium and spacious offices, men decreed the fates of people within all the Soviet Republics, how decisions taken here filtered down into everyday life in the countries of the Baltic, and affected the way people lived. Here the party bigshots planned to bury the Baltic nations. Here they planned to turn Balts into third-class citizens in their own countries. Here the party engine functioned, pumping out poisons that had to be swallowed by people who had absolutely no desire to feed on Russian lies or to embrace a system that was alien to them, one that killed the spirit and demolished the soul.

It was Andres's intention to drop the first bomb at one end of the building, the second in the middle, the third at the other end, and then turn the aircraft in the direction of Leningrad and the Gulf of Finland, which was his one chance of getting out of the Soviet Union before he was attacked.

That was his intention.

He was about three miles from the Kremlin when he nosed the F-16 downwards, conscious now of the way the city tilted through his cockpit, as if the buildings all listed impossibly to one side. Down and down now. Fifteen hundred feet above ground level, twelve hundred. That was when he saw three MIG-29s in the eastern sky, perhaps no more than two miles from him. That was when he realised, with a start that made his heart shudder, that something had gone wrong with the plan.

Without thinking, operating entirely on old instincts and training, he manoeuvred the F-16 into firing position and released one of the forward quarter heat-seeking Side Winders. It exploded on contact with the MIG-29 nearest to him: a flash, a violent plume of smoke, and the Soviet aircraft was gone. Andres fired the second missile and made a direct hit on another of the MIGs, destroying the plane with startling immediacy. The afternoon, so placid, before, was filled with trails of smoke and turbulence and destruction.

The third Russian plane zoomed above him and attacked him with cannon. The F-16 trembled and vibrated in the storm of fire but didn't receive a hit.

Andres, still believing in luck, still believing that the angels were on his side, rolled back into his dive on the Palace of Congresses as the remaining MIG-29, the Fulcrum, fired down on him from above. Let him catch me, Andres thought. Let the fucker do his worst. He'd already brought two of them down and he wasn't about to be stopped by some goddam Ivanovich shooting at him. He was about two miles from his target now and he had his hand poised over the bomb button, and when the bombs fell upon the Palace they'd explode after a fifteen-second delay.

At one thousand feet two SA-11 missiles, fired from a site three miles beyond Moscow, came screaming towards him, disintegrating the fuselage of the F-16 and turning the aircraft into a mass of fiery debris that splintered in the sky and fell, like the tail of the most glorious firework that had ever lit the air above Moscow. Andres Kiss, harnessed to his seat, helmeted, still saying the closing lines of the Lord's Prayer, his hand reaching for the bomb button, felt nothing save a very brief moment of burning discomfort before he was falling and falling, along with the flaming remains of his aeroplane, into an empty soccer stadium a mere two miles from the Palace of Congresses.

Zavidovo, the Soviet Union

It was almost midnight when Dimitri Volovich arrived at Greshko's cottage in Zavidovo. The Yakut nurse opened the door for him. Without waiting for any response from her, he stepped inside. 'I'll need a glass of water,' he said.

'Of course.' The nurse fetched him the glass. He didn't drink from it. Instead, he pushed open the door to Greshko's bedroom.

Curtains had been drawn against the windows. The only source of illumination was a tiny reading lamp affixed to the wall above Greshko's pillows, but this was barely more than a pinpoint of electricity.

Greshko, who had been lying with his eyes shut, opened them when he heard Volovich enter the room. Because of the bad light, he could barely make out the Lieutenant's face. He propped himself up on his elbows, rubbed his eyes. He saw a glass of water in Dimitri's right hand.

'Come closer, Dimitri.'

Volovich did so. Obedience to the old man, he thought, was a hard habit to break. But General Olsky said it had to be broken. It was the only way.

Greshko frowned. There was something here that wasn't quite right, something askew. Perhaps it was the flat tone in Volovich's voice, an edge, barely noticeable, which sounded abrasive.

He sat upright now, expecting pain, which had gone through him all day long like a blade, but surprisingly there was none. When there was no pain he imagined he'd held death in abeyance once again, that he'd overcome his oldest adversary – but why did he feel no sense of exaltation, no joy, no triumph?

Volovich approached the bed. Greshko stared at the glass of water. 'You have a message from Viktor?'

Volovich sat on the edge of the bed, crossing his legs. 'No message, General.'

'No message?'

'None.'

Greshko gestured toward the stereo. 'Put some music on, Dimitri.'

Volovich shook his head. In this small act of disobedience, Greshko suddenly saw the limits of his power. So this was it. After all these years, this was the moment. Losing wasn't the thing that troubled him, because a gamble was a gamble after all. It was the way they'd changed the rules of the game that irritated him. He imagined Olsky and Nikolai Bragin, a cosy little chat, a handshake, a secretive smile. Perhaps even Birthmark Billy had been involved. Of course he should have foreseen such collusion against him, he should have known that the rules would be altered – but what was life if you didn't take bloody risks? A toss of the dice, a turn of the cards. But the dice had been loaded, the cards unfairly marked.

'How did they get to you, Dimitri?'

'It doesn't matter.'

'Money? No, I doubt that. Threats, then. They threatened you.'

Volovich nodded.

Greshko smiled. 'And if you kill me, you'll be protected.'

'Yes.'

Greshko uttered a hoarse laugh. 'And you believe this? You believe your protectors are honourable men, Dimitri? You believe they'll let you keep your job, your perks, your nice uniform?'

'I have no choice.'

'How is it to be?' Greshko asked. 'Does the General commit suicide while depressed over his incurable physical condition?'

'No suicide.'

Greshko watched Dimitri Volovich raise the glass of water.

'Something to drink, is that it?' he asked.

'Yes,' Volovich said.

'Ah,' Greshko said. 'A heart attack. Cardiac arrest. Weakened by his long illness, the General succumbed peacefully at midnight.'

Volovich removed his wallet, opened it, shook a small capsule out. He cracked the plastic casing, dropped white powder into the water, and swirled the glass around in his hand.

'Mix it well,' Greshko said.

Volovich looked at the clouded water. He held the glass to Greshko's lips. The old man didn't drink immediately. He smiled over the rim of the glass.

'Drink,' Volovich said.

Greshko sipped the liquid. It tasted slightly bitter. He felt it burn at the back of his throat, but then the sensation passed.

'I wish Olsky had administered this himself,' Greshko said. 'But he's such a gutless little shit. He wouldn't have the courage to come here.'

Greshko closed his eyes, smiled. Then, through the fluttering of his eyelids, he saw Dimitri Volovich, who appeared to be floating a very long way off. Fading. Darkness. Sweat. It was like falling through water whose temperature increased the deeper you sank. He raised a hand in the air, a weightless thing of skin and bone. This sense of life closing down, of blinds being drawn, wasn't so bad except for the terrible heat that had begun to burn inside him.

'And what becomes of Russia, my dear Volovich?' Greshko asked.

He lay very still. Dimitri Volovich stood up and left the bedroom. He told the Yakut nurse that the old man was sleeping, and then he stepped outside into the darkness, hearing the trees rustle and night creatures foraging in the forest, sounds that filled him, for some reason, with an odd sense of fear.

Epilogue

Sussex, England

Frank Pagan stretched out in a deckchair and stared up into the sunlight of the early afternoon. It was one of those brilliant mid-September days that condescend to visit England infrequently, warm and yet with a hint of the autumn still to come, that glorious time before the leaves change and drift in a brittle dance to the ground, and the landscape turns melancholy. He enjoyed the feel of sunlight on his eyelids, the drone of insects, the sound of a cricket-bat colliding with a leather ball, a timeless click, placid and unthreatening and peculiarly English.

He looked across the playing-field at the white-suited figures who stood motionless on the rich grass. It was one of those games you didn't have to pay attention to, because very little ever happened. Occasionally a batsman was out, and occasionally some daring soul would swing his bat at the ball and send it flying over the boundary, but attention wasn't a necessary condition of enjoyment. Serenity was the soul of all village-green cricket games. Peace and detachment, idleness, a glass or two of beer, a suggestion of unimportant pageantry. He edged himself up in his striped deckchair and watched the bowler approach the wicket and make his delivery, and he followed the leisurely flight of the red ball as it spun towards the batsman. The ball went harmlessly past the batsman, and the wickets, into the enormous gloves of the wicket-keeper.

Pagan reached for his beer, which had turned warm under the sun, and he sipped it slowly. He stared beyond the playing-field to the oak trees on the other side, where the scoreboard was located, and a small ramshackle pavilion stood. The score, to Pagan, was utterly irrelevant. There were some animated old men in chairs around the pavilion, and here and there an interested youngster, but in general the event was observed with nonchalance and the kind of patience required by any cricket spectator. Nothing mattered here. Nothing that happened here would change the course of the world in any way. And he liked that sensation. He liked the notion of being removed from anything that was hectic, and he liked the peacefulness of doing absolutely nothing.

And watching cricket. And drinking flat beer. And not thinking about Kristina Vaska, whom he hadn't seen or heard from since the events at Grand Central Station. He owed her his life, he understood that much. And he was grateful. But he had the feeling that other possibilities had slipped away, that other conceivable futures had cancelled themselves, and this thought – try valiantly as he might to ignore it – left him depressed.

He looked along the row of deckchairs that stretched on either side of him, shielding his eyes from the sun and seeing Martin Burr – who carried two glasses of beer – come towards him from the striped marquee where beverages were sold. Pagan had come here at Burr's invitation, an invitation he'd accepted gladly because for the six days since he'd returned from the United States he'd done very little but make a report and linger aimlessly in his apartment. He cleaned the place up, but that took only a day and a half. He shuffled pictures on the wall, made some minor changes, moved furniture around, dusted his record albums, and that took another day. Coming down here to Martin Burr's little corner of the world was a break from the dreariness of London.

Burr looked out at the cricket players. A batsman had just been declared out and there was a smattering of subdued applause from the pavilion area. The Commissioner made an adjustment to his eyepatch and turned towards Pagan.

'I have some news that may interest you, Frank.'

Pagan didn't want to hear what it was. He wanted to lose himself in laziness and detachment. He wanted to believe that Burr had invited him down here for rest and relaxation, that the Commissioner had no ulterior motive. Life had to be simple, for God's sake.

'I mention it in passing, Frank,' Burr said. 'If you're interested in loose ends.'

Pagan looked at the Commissioner. Martin Burr sipped his beer, leaving a ring of foam on his upper lip, which he made no attempt to wipe away.

'It's from Witherspoon. Thought you might be curious, that's all,' and Martin Burr looked rather sly all at once.

'All right. I'm curious.'

Burr leaned a little closer. There was something mysterious about the Commissioner, Pagan decided, as if this cricket game were just a front, an excuse, for something else. He wasn't sure what.

'We keep getting news about revolts all over the place. In Latvia. Lithuania. Estonia. It seems that armed bands rose up and were quickly put down again. There's nothing very firm, you understand. Some eyewitness accounts, some diplomatic reports. A couple of telegrams purporting to be from the Movement for Baltic Independence were received in Paris and Stockholm. And the BBC monitored a speech on Estonian radio about the fight for freedom, but the speaker was cut off in the middle of it. That's all. The Soviets are officially saying nothing, of course. But it appears that these rebellions were timed to coincide with the attack of that plane. One massive display of defiance and courage. One huge cry for independence.'

'Which didn't quite make it,' Pagan said. It would have been quite a symphony, he thought. Quite an arrangement, everything succeeding at the same time. He remembered Aleksis and he thought of the bravery, the effort, the sheer damned ambition of Romanenko and Mikhail Kiss. He thought of their commitment, that zealous attachment to their cause that overwhelmed everything else in their lives – even such things as simple loyalty to an old comrade like Norbert Vaska. Commitment and vengeance. And betrayal. There was a level on which Frank Pagan admired that kind of courage even if he didn't agree with its ultimate chaotic aim, a bloody war all across the Baltic nations, a war that could have only one outcome. But finally he felt a certain ambivalence toward the Brotherhood and if there was a sensation he hated in himself, that was the one.

'Damned good effort, though.' Burr was quiet. 'The Americans are saying the pilot was a complete schizophrenic. History of mental illness. To be expected.'

Pagan nodded. 'Of course.' He was remembering Mikhail Kiss and the big house in Glen Cove and the empty rooms. He wondered if Andres's trophies were still in place, his certificates still hanging on the walls.

Burr watched the game a moment. 'Perhaps even more mysterious is the way Epishev has simply vanished from the face of the earth. My feeling is that the Russians are playing that one really close to their chests. They probably took him out and shot him for his role in this subversive drama.' Burr sipped his beer. 'Tommy also says there's an unpublicised shake-up going on in air-defence personnel, which is to be expected, of course. According to his sources, about a score of officers have been arrested already and more are expected.

Most of them were in possession of large sums of American money and false passports. Presumably these came courtesy of that Brotherhood of yours, Frank, which must have spread more than a few dollars around the place.'

Martin Burr set his glass in his lap. He was silent for a time. 'And General Greshko is dead. A timely sort of death, wouldn't you say – given the role he's supposed to have played in this failed revolution. Heart-attack. Naturally, it would be. Unless it was a car crash. Prominent Soviets usually only succumb to those things.'

Pagan smiled. Burr drained his beer and added, 'One of the last chaps to see him was one of our own, a fellow called McLaren at the Embassy. Greshko told him the most outrageous story of financial skulduggery and sedition on the part of the new Chairman of the KGB. There were documents too.'

'Documents?'

'Apparently. The PM doesn't want them bruited about. Can't embarrass our Soviet friends. We're allies these days. Expect you've heard that, Frank. We're like that with the Bolsheviks.' Martin Burr closed his index and middle fingers together, then belched in a restrained way. 'As for your fat man – well, no trace, absolutely no trace at all. He just doesn't exist, it seems. A spooky thought, Frank. Somewhere in the hidden government of the United States, in one of those subterranean outfits that really run the show over in America, there lurk figures prepared to plan the future direction of the human race, without regard to reality. Makes you think, Frank.'

Pagan watched him for a time because he couldn't escape the uncomfortable sensation that Burr was withholding something else, a topic he didn't want to mention, words he couldn't quite get right. He had the look of a man rehearsing in his head. Pagan knew it would come out eventually. It always did where the Commissioner was concerned.

'Lovely day,' Burr said.

The weather. But that wasn't what was on Martin Burr's mind, Pagan was certain. Burr stood up, prodded the ground with his cane, surveyed the field of play a moment.

'I feel like something to eat,' Burr said. 'A sandwich perhaps.'

'I'm not hungry,' Pagan remarked.

'Walk with me anyway, Frank. Keep me company.'

Pagan rose from the deckchair and followed Martin Burr in the direction of the marquee, making his way past people who dozed in chairs, or who lay indolently in the grass, past toddlers and young lovers, and others who were simply sunning themselves on this rare day. The marquee, pitched on the edge of the green, was a colourful affair of red and white striped canvas. Pagan could see people milling around inside, cluttered at the drinks table or buying sandwiches and pork pies.

He followed Burr into the large tent. The light here was muted, filtered through heavy canvas. He had an impression of beer kegs and sandwiches under glass trays and a muddiness underfoot where beer had been spilled. He had another impression too, and he couldn't quite define it, but for no good reason a slight sense of expectation went through him, as if this were the place where Martin Burr intended to reveal the thing he'd so obviously been reluctant to mention. He walked behind Burr to the food table and the Commissioner, after surveying an unappetising array of tomato and cucumber sandwiches, turned with a serious look on his face.

'I'm not sure how you're going to feel about this, Frank,' he said.

'Feel about what?'

The Commissioner gestured to the far side of the marquee. For a second, Pagan hesitated, didn't follow the Commissioner's direction. He stood very still, not wanting to look, and yet knowing beyond any doubt what he'd see when he did turn his face. He felt strange, just a little disoriented, and all the sounds inside the tent became magnified in his head and echoed there.

'You may consider it unfair of me,' Burr said. 'Or you may think it's presumption on my part to interfere in your life, Frank. But there you are. I was tired of seeing you moon about. I think you need to give the girl and yourself a break.'

Frank Pagan turned his face slowly.

She was wearing a plain lemon dress and a wide-brimmed hat that cast a shadow over her features. She was looking directly at him and there was the slightest suggestion of a smile on her lips, but he couldn't be sure of that. She was motionless, and lovely, and he felt odd, out of touch with himself, all the pulses in his body unsynchronised. And then his attention was drawn to the figure who stood just behind her, a man of indeterminate age, slightly stooped but clear-eyed, a man who held himself erect as if only with enormous effort.

Even if he'd never seen the man's photograph before, Pagan would have known that it was Norbert Vaska.

Pagan didn't move. He heard Martin Burr say, 'She's on her way back to the States, Frank.' Burr paused. 'Just came to collect her father in Berlin. And I thought, why not? I'm not, you understand, playing bloody Cupid.'

Pagan returned his gaze to Kristina Vaska, wanting to go towards her but not moving even though every urge in his body commanded him to cross the space that separated him from her.

She stepped towards him. She said, 'We didn't say goodbye before.' She moved her hand, laying it on the back of his wrist and this touch, so casual, reminded Pagan of what had been lost along the way.

'You got your father out, I see,' he said.

'It all happened very quickly. I received a phone call telling me to meet him in West Germany.'

'I'm glad.'

'I owe it to you, Frank.'

'Me?'

'It seems the Soviets were happy that you warned them about Andres Kiss. That's what I gather. My father's a kind of gratitude present.'

'You saved my life. So that makes us equal.'

Kristina Vaska nodded her head. She looked, Pagan thought, almost unbearably beautiful.

'I guess so,' she said.

Pagan stared at Norbert Vaska. He was white, withered, but there was a spirited quality in the eyes. It was the same determination he'd seen in Kristina many times, that grim sense of focus, of purpose.

She took his hand and shook it. It was a prosaic gesture that made him ache.

'Frank,' she said. 'Is there a chance for us?' What a question, Pagan thought. He wasn't sure how to answer.

'It's just that I'd like to think so,' she said.

'We'll see,' was all he could find to say. 'Let's give it some time.'

He turned and walked out of the marquee into the bright afternoon sun and he moved, somewhat blindly, back in the direction of his chair.

Burr appeared, settling himself into the chair beside Pagan. 'Have I missed anything?' he asked, gazing out across the cricket field.

Pagan smiled. 'I've never known you to miss a thing, Commissioner.

Mambo

This book is dedicated to Thomas Congdon, for his continuing support, encouragement, and friendship.

I would like to thank for their help: Lieutenant Nelson Oramas of the Miami Police; Sergeant Bob Hoelscher of the Metro Dade Police; Richard Brams; Ed Breslin and Nick Sayers for their considerable editorial counsel; Dr Dov Levine; Major R. B. Claybourn (USMCR); Richard and Arthur Pine; and Eddie Bell for his faith at the right moment. I would also like to thank Erl and Ann Wilkie for the tour of the auld place.

1 London

On a cold October night, two vans and three cars moved in slow procession down a narrow street of terraced houses. The street, already poorly lit, was darker in those places where Victorian railway bridges straddled it.

Frank Pagan, who rode in a blue Ford Escort directly behind the leading van, had the uneasy feeling that this neighbourhood, perched on the farthest edge of Shepherd's Bush, was about to fade into nothing. The houses would give way to vacant sites, half acres of rubble with perhaps here and there some forlorn allotments on which stood broken-down greenhouses. It was not a picturesque part of town, but its drab anonymity and sparse traffic made it as safe a route as any.

It was all theory as far as Pagan was concerned. He knew from his own experience what every policeman knew: there was no such thing as complete security. What you had at best was an illusion of safety. You created diversions, surrounded yourself with some heavy protection, and kept your fingers crossed that good fortune, even at its most positive a fickle administrator of human affairs, would be on your side. Tense, he gazed at the small houses, the television lights thrown upon curtains, the half moon over the roof-tops dimmed by pollution, and he had the thought that in a few years this decrepit neighbourhood, like so many formerly dreary London districts, might even be on the rise, resuscitated by estate agents, the terraced houses refurbished and sold to young professionals who did one thing or another in the City or at the nearby BBC.

For the present, though, it was a labyrinth of slum and shadow, exactly the kind of place through which to transport the monster who sat alongside Pagan in the back of the car, the monster whose name was Gunther Ruhr.

Pagan glanced at Ruhr for a second. He was uncomfortable being this close to the man, uneasy at the touch of Ruhr's leg against his own. Ruhr had one of those faces that suggest flesh long buried in damp earth, a maggot's pallor earned the hard way, hours killed hiding in cellars or somebody's attic. You might imagine that if you cut Ruhr's skin something as viscous as transmission fluid would seep from the veins. Certainly not blood, Pagan thought. Whatever connected Ruhr, with his enormous capacity for brutality, to the rest of the human race, wasn't immediately apparent to Pagan.

The German press, with its unbridled sense of melodrama, had been the first to call Gunther Ruhr *Die Klaue*, the Claw, a reference to the peculiar prosthetic device Ruhr had been wearing on his right hand at the time of his capture and which had immediately been confiscated from him. Ruhr's right hand was missing both middle fingers. The other two fingers, the first and the last, appeared abnormally distant from each other and unable to move more than a quarter of an inch in any direction and then only stiffly. The deformity, exaggerated by the perfect curve of the thumb, was compelling in its way. Like a morbid man enticed against his better judgment by a freak show, Pagan found himself drawn reluctantly back to it time and again.

Some said Gunther Ruhr had accidentally blown his hand up with one of his own homemade explosive devices back in the days when he was still learning his trade, others that the deformity was a birth defect. Like everything else connected to Ruhr's life, neither story had any supporting evidence. Ruhr was a mythical monster, created in part by the screaming excesses of the European tabloids but also by his own pathological need for secrecy and mystery. Without these qualities, nobody could ever have become so successful a terrorist as Gunther Ruhr had done. Nobody, saddled with such a recognisable disfigurement, could have carried out so many atrocities unhindered for so long unless his life and habits were so deeply hidden they couldn't be quarried even by the best specialists in terrorism, who had tracked him for fourteen frustrating years.

The explosion of a Pan Am airliner over Athens in 1975, the mining of a crowded cruise ship in the Mediterranean in 1978, the bombing of a bus carrying teenage soccer players from Spain along the Adriatic Coast in 1980, the destruction of a resort hotel on the shore of the Sea of Japan in the summer of 1984 – the list of atrocities which Ruhr had supposedly masterminded was long and bloody. The hotel had been destroyed on behalf of a group of anti-American Japanese extremists; the Spanish boys were said to have died at the command of a violent Basque coalition; the cruise ship had been mined because its passenger list consisted mainly of Jews and Ruhr's employer was rumoured to have been a Libyan fanatic. What Ruhr did was done, plain and simple, for money. He had no other master, no political position. His services went to the highest bidders at those secret places where Ruhr's kind of labours were auctioned.

And now Frank Pagan, through one of those small accidents that sometimes brighten a cop's life, had him under arrest and was transporting him through the back streets of London and on to Luton, where he was to be flown to the maximum security prison of Parkhurst on the Isle of Wight. *Under arrest*, Pagan thought, and scanned the street again, seeing TV pictures blink in rooms or the door of a corner pub swing open and shut.

Under arrest was one thing. Getting Ruhr – with all his connections in the violent half-world of international terrorism – to his destination might be something else.

Pagan stared at the two men in the front of the car. The driver was a career policeman called John Torjussen from Special Branch, his companion a thick-necked Metropolitan cop who had once been a prominent amateur wrestler known as Masher. Ron Hardcastle was the man's real name and he spoke with that peculiar Newcastle accent. There was something menacingly comforting in Hardcastle's presence.

Pagan looked at the van ahead, which contained four officers from Special Branch and an assortment of rifles and communications equipment. Turning, he glanced next at the two cars behind, then the van at the very back – each vehicle was manned and armed and alert. Menacingly comforting, Pagan thought again. All of it. Everything designed to keep Gunther the Beast safe and secure until he could be firmly caged on the Isle of Wight.

And yet Frank Pagan felt a strange streak of cold on the back of his neck, and the palms of his hands, normally dry and cool, had become damp. He shut his eyes a moment, conscious of the odd way Ruhr breathed – there was a faint rattle at the back of the man's throat as if something thick had become lodged there. The noise, like everything else about Ruhr, irritated Pagan.

The puzzles of Gunther Ruhr, Pagan thought, and looked briefly at the German. Why had he come to England? What was he doing in Cambridge, of all places? Planning a doctoral thesis on atrocities? Giving tutorials on bloodletting? Ruhr had been interrogated for three days after his capture but he had a nice way with his inquisitors: he simply ignored them. When he condescended to speak, he contradicted himself three or four times in the space of half an hour and yet somehow managed to make each version of his story equally plausible. What Gunther Ruhr did was to surround himself with fresh fictions, recreating himself time and again. Even if there were a real core to the man, nobody could ever gain access to it, perhaps not even Ruhr himself.

The Claw, Pagan thought with disdain. He hated the way such nicknames took up residence in the public imagination. After a while they exerted a fascination that often had nothing to do with the acts of the villains themselves. Jack the Ripper was still good for a shudder, but how many people brought to mind the images of disembowelled girls, intestines in tidy piles, hearts cut out, everything bloody and just so? How many really pictured the true nightmare? The tabloids had a way of taking a scumbag like Ruhr and elevating him to a celebrity whose name alone doubled circulation for a time. And somewhere in the course of the international publicity circus the real nature of Ruhr's deeds would be lost and a patina of myth drawn over the man, as if he were some wildly appealing combination of Ripper and legendary terrorist, somebody who made pulses beat a little quicker. It was the wrong side of fame, Pagan thought with some resentment. Ruhr deserved another fate altogether: total oblivion.

In the front seat, Ron Hardcastle lit a cigarette and the air in the car became congested.

Ruhr spoke for the first time since they'd taken him from his cell at Wormwood Scrubs. 'You will have a decoy column, of course?' he asked. He had impeccable English, a fact that irked Pagan, who wanted Ruhr's English to be broken and clumsy and laughable.

Pagan didn't answer. Ruhr blinked his very pale eyelids and said, 'Personally, in your position, I would have a second column somewhere close at hand. Perhaps even a third, although I would put that one on the motorway, I think, and have it travel at high speed. Then my friends – assuming I have any – would be very confused. "Where is Gunther? Where can he possibly be?" ' The German was silent for a second. 'Of course, deception's a highly personal thing,' and here he smiled, as if he were making some polite little joke for Pagan's benefit. But there was a supercilious quality in the look that caused Pagan to bunch his hands tightly in the pockets of his overcoat and turn his face back towards the street. Ruhr was partly correct. A decoy convoy was travelling in the vicinity of Paddington and Marylebone, but there was no third parade.

'Your voice gets on my bloody nerves, Ruhr,' Pagan said, then immediately regretted this unseemly display of hostility because it gave Gunther Ruhr obvious satisfaction, which took the form of a smile as crooked as his bad hand.

There was a miserable silence inside the car, broken only by the hiss of the radio and the message *Nine-twenty, all clear. Proceeding due east on Elm Avenue.* Ah, the dear banality of Elm Avenue, with its dim shabbiness, a small broken-down corner of what had once been another England. Now heroin and crack replaced tea and crumpets of an afternoon.

Pagan opened the window a half-inch, releasing some of Hardcastle's smoke. The small houses were misshapen by moon and shadow. The occasional pub or fish and chip shop looked unnaturally bright.

'You are so very tense,' Ruhr said in a soothing voice. He might have been a physician calming a nervous patient. 'Surely you don't expect somebody is going to rescue me, do you?'

Pagan said nothing. It was best not to be drawn, to stay aloof. There were levels to which you could descend, places where all you ever encountered was your own worst self, and Frank Pagan had no desire to slip that far down. His temper had a sometimes abrasive edge and he was getting a little too old to keep cutting himself on it. Do the bloody job, get this scum to Luton, go home. But just don't let it get personal. You hate a man like Gunther Ruhr, and you loathe the forced intimacy of this small car, and breathing the same damned air is repulsive – but what did feelings, those expendable luxuries, have to do with it?

'Such people would have to be mad,' Ruhr said. 'Or very clever and daring.'

Pagan shut the window. Ron Hardcastle turned in his seat and glared angrily at the German. 'Just say the word, Frank, and I'll do this bastard for you. Be a right fooking pleasure.'

There was a generous quality in Masher Hardcastle's offer of violence, and Pagan didn't doubt that big Ron would enjoy inflicting physical damage on Ruhr. Despite some temptation, it was a sorry equation all the same. Pagan couldn't see Ruhr's taste for violence matching with that of Ron Hardcastle, law enforcement officer and former wrestler. There was increased tension in the car now, as if it had found its way in from the darkened street like a thin vapour. It had a name, Pagan thought: impotence. You might want to unleash the snarling dog inside Hardcastle, you might even want a piece of Gunther Ruhr for yourself, but the laws *Die Klaue* flouted so viciously afforded him some protection from brutality.

Pagan put a weary smile on his face and looked at the German. It was an amusing consolation to think of the circumstances of Ruhr's apprehension in Cambridge, how the elusive terrorist, whose newspaper reviews had called him 'the man without a shadow' and 'the phantom beyond human needs and desires', had been captured in a bedroom in a lodging-house near St Andrew's Street. The memory was a perfect diversion from stress.

'I've got you, Gunther,' Pagan said quietly now. 'And that's what it comes down to in the end. *I've got you,* and all because you couldn't keep your pecker in your trousers.' He waited for Ruhr's expression to change to one of discomfort, perhaps even wrath, but Ruhr was too good at this game to give up control of that awful white face. He merely looked at Pagan with a raised eyebrow.

'Was she worth it, Gunther?' Pagan asked. 'Was she worth the risk? Or can you only get it when you pay for it? Too bad she didn't want to go the rest of the way with you – you wouldn't be here now if she'd kept her mouth shut, would you? You wouldn't be here if she'd been a sicko like you.'

If these were low blows, if they were supposed to vent some of Pagan's annoyance, they certainly weren't causing the German any pain. Ruhr, whose hands were cuffed in his lap, laughed and said, 'I never have to pay for anything, Pagan.'

'Until now,' Pagan said. Christ, he was feeling vindictive and petty.

'Die Reise ist nicht am Ende bis sur Ankunft.' Gunther Ruhr spoke quietly. Pagan, whose grasp of the German language was poor, recognised only a couple of words. He had no way of knowing that Ruhr's phrase fully meant *the journey is never over until the arrival,* nor did he intend to ask for a translation. He wasn't going to give Ruhr even the simplest kind of satisfaction.

There was a pub on a corner, a place called The Lord Nelson. A voice came over the car radio. *Proceeding west along Mulberry Avenue. All clear.* Pagan looked at the pub, then saw some modern blocks of flats rising beyond, where thin lawns and stunted trees grew under pale lamps, many of which had been vandalised and cast no light. It wasn't a good place. It looked wrong and it smelled wrong and the extended reaches of darkness bothered him. He sat forward in his seat, anxiously studying the unlit areas and thinking how vandalism was a way of life in a neighbourhood like this. Public phones, shop windows, anything that was both motionless and fragile was a target for a kid with a stone in his hand and nothing in his mind save breakage. But then the high-rise buildings receded and there were more streets of 1930s terraced houses and the voice on the radio was saying *Proceeding due east along Acacia Avenue* and Pagan felt the quick little tide of unease ebb inside him. If there was going to be an attempt made to rescue Ruhr, the dark places back there would have been eminently suitable. Acacia Avenue, narrow and comparatively well lit, was benign by contrast.

He sat back again, observing the parked cars along the kerb, and hearing the sound of what he took at first to be a light aircraft. But it was louder than that, and close, a throbbing that had its source two or three hundred feet above the rooftops. Ron Hardcastle turned his big red face around to look at Pagan questioningly.

'What the bloody hell's that?' he asked.

Pagan tried to see through his window, but his angle was bad. Then the voice came over the radio again: *There's a helicopter above at approximately one hundred and fifty feet and descending rapidly.*

The sound of the low-flying chopper became thunderous now, deafening, vibrating with such intensity that the car shook as if it were travelling over ruts. Pagan leaned forward and shouted into the radio. 'What the hell does it want?'

The pilot won't identify himself. I've asked for ID three times and he doesn't bloody answer, Frank.

Pagan had briefly entertained the hope that the chopper might belong to Scotland Yard, something the Commissioner had finally decided to add to the convoy at the last moment. Now he was worried. He looked at Ruhr, who shrugged and said, 'I know nothing about it.'

It was a statement Pagan didn't have time to question, because suddenly the darkness was transformed. What had been nothing but slight menace and an unidentifiable anxiety was suddenly changed. Pagan saw the leading van, fifteen feet ahead, catch fire as flares were dropped on it from the sky. The shape of the helicopter was visible for a second, but in an unreal way, like an after-image on a retina. The Ford Escort braked just as an enormous column of unruly flame roared out of the van, and streaked up and died in a vast series of starry sparks.

And then everything was ablaze in the most spectacular way. All the cars parked along the kerb exploded and burned as if they'd been timed to ignite simultaneously. Acacia Avenue was illuminated by flames as bright as daylight. Pagan opened his door, his first shocked instinct that of rushing towards the burning van in front of him because he thought he heard somebody scream inside the wreck, but the heat thrust him back at once. *Dear Christ*, it was a force of nature, seeming to melt his skin and weld it against his bones. He couldn't move any closer, nor did he hear the screaming again. Who could survive that inferno? Those four poor bastards would have been charred almost at once. The rear van and the other two sedans, also fire-bombed by the helicopter – which had wheeled away, whirring up toward the moon and disappearing – were alight too, their occupants scrambling out into the street, shadowy figures desperately trying to avoid the flames surrounding them. Confusion and chaos and smells sickeningly intermingled – burning rubber, smouldering upholstery, kindled shrubbery, scorched flesh. Gunshots too, as policemen fired upward in the general path of the chopper.

Pagan did the only thing he could think of. He grabbed Ruhr by the shoulders and dragged him out of the Escort because no matter what, no matter the extent of the calamity, it was still his job to secure the German. The Ford, stalled and engulfed by smoke, wasn't going anywhere. The only possibility of movement now was on foot.

Pagan pushed Ruhr forward in the direction of the pavement, seeking a space between burning cars, feeling his eyes smart and his nostrils fill with smoke. Nothing could be breathed here without searing the tissue of your lungs and throat. Conscious of Hardcastle at his back, and Torjussen moving just ahead, Pagan shoved Ruhr again, because the German was lagging, as if, like some demented bug, he wanted to linger close to the brightness of the flames.

'Move, bastard,' Ron Hardcastle said, and made one hand into a thick fist, which he smacked directly into Ruhr's spine. Ruhr gasped and his legs buckled as Pagan hauled him through the dense smoke to the pavement. This whole damned place reminded Pagan of old photographs of wartime London just after a heart-breaking air assault. People were screaming and hurrying out of their houses now, windows shattering, doors kicked open, a landscape of flame and bitter smoke and red-hot metal, total ruin made all the more appalling by the way it had bloomed so violently out of a commonplace night on a commonplace street.

Ruhr must have known, Pagan thought. He must have been waiting for this moment. He must have expected a rescue effort. In his own heart, Pagan had half expected it too. He just hadn't anticipated anything on this destructive scale. But who could have foreseen this? Who could have looked into the old crystal ball and come up with this fiery scenario? Pagan recalled raising the subject of air surveillance at one of the many meetings concerning the transportation of Ruhr, meetings complicated by the noisy extradition demands and political requirements of Spain and Greece and the United States, but the notion had been overruled as being too ostentatious, too obvious, by a committee of well-meaning men who thought the secret route to be travelled by Ruhr was perfectly safe, something that could never be penetrated. And wasn't stealth more appropriate than the high visibility of a police helicopter rattling the slates of suburban roof-tops? These were men who lived in a dream world. They weren't out here on the streets now. Besides, there was never a way to cover every possible occurrence. You could plan until your jaw dropped off, but in the end a man had to be moved, and, from the moment Gunther Ruhr had ridden out of Wormwood Scrubs, the risk had grown. Whoever wanted Ruhr free wanted him with an extravagant sense of destruction Pagan had encountered only once or twice in his lifetime.

Pagan shoved the terrorist quickly along the pavement, seeking safe passage through the furnace that devoured cars on one side, hedgerows on the other. The blast of heat was solid and crippling. He had the notion of getting to the next intersection, a place beyond the flames, and then commandeering somebody's house, calling in reinforcements and new vehicles. It was vague, more of an instinct than a plan, but he had to get Ruhr off the streets quickly. The perpetrators of this elaborate attack weren't about to go home empty-handed.

Hardcastle had his gun out now, and so did Torjussen, who was a step ahead of Pagan and Ruhr – a party of four locked in a fiercely hot dance amid the crackling of wood and the *whooshing* made by fuel tanks exploding. Smoke, thicker than any fog, blinded Pagan and scorched his face.

He saw the assault squad only briefly when a wintry breeze scoured the street and cleared the air.

Five, six men, he couldn't be sure how many. They wore ski or ice-hockey masks – it was another detail of which he would never be certain. They were dressed in camouflage and carried automatic rifles. Pagan was conscious of Gunther Ruhr throwing himself face down on the concrete and then Ron Hardcastle firing his gun in the direction of the squad, but smoke billowed in again, obscuring everything. There was more gunfire, much of it random and wild.

Ron Hardcastle fell. Torjussen disappeared somewhere and Pagan reached down to grab Ruhr and drag him back along the pavement, thinking there might yet be some safe corner of the world in which to hide his prisoner. Away from here, away from all this destruction, a small, safe place.

But the weather conspired against the plan. The wind came a second time. It whined over the houses and blew the length of the burning street and cleared the smoke. With his gun in his hand, Pagan faced the squad over a distance that might have been no more than a hundred feet.

Gunther Ruhr, who lay on the pavement, smiled up at Pagan in an odd way. Pagan raised his weapon, a Bernardelli, but he was cut down by gunfire before he could get off more than two shots in the direction of the group.

He'd known pain before. But he'd never felt anything quite like this, so crucifying and raw. It had no specific location in his body. It consumed all of him.

He had a blinding moment when he registered the fact that his legs no longer existed and his heart had been yanked out of his chest; and another when he understood that this kind of pain was a reservoir of very hot tar in which he could only go down and down, round and round, drowning under a black surface.

2 Miami

Magdalena Torrente crossed Calle Ocho, the main street of Little Havana. She looked up once at the sky, which was clouding toward darkness and heavy with the possibility of warm October rain, then she headed west. She passed Eduardo's furniture store, a bright island of art deco sofas and lamps, an expensive anomaly in this neighbourhood of *farmacias* and little cafés selling *café cubano* in paper cups. She ignored the approving comments and whistles of men who stood outside the cafés and took time out from their constant preoccupation – how to assassinate that *barbudo hijo de puta*, Fidel Castro – to register and appreciate the beautiful, mature woman passing quickly in the humid twilight.

She made her way through traffic at an intersection where the air smelled of coffee and fried foods, and then turned right, entering a narrow street darker than Calle Ocho. Here windows were boarded and barred and small houses had the appearance of undergoing a siege; in this city of easy death and abundant drugs and murderous addicts who thought burglary every doper's birthright, it was a very real impression. She'd parked her car several blocks away at the Malaga Restaurant, thinking it best to move on foot in case her licence plate was noticed and remembered by one of the spies Fernando Garrido was always lecturing her about. Now, given the hazards of the district, she wondered if she'd made the right decision. The car would have been some kind of protection. Without it she felt vulnerable, despite the gun she carried in the pocket of her leather jacket.

From an open upstairs window a man shouted down at her 'Hey, hey bebe,' and then laughed in a fractured drunken way – 'ka ha ka ha,' a sound that dissolved in a cough like a baby's rattle. Latin music, fast, tropical, overheated, played from a radio in an open doorway where several shadowy figures, lost in the ether of drugs, stared out at her. She hurried now, pausing only when she reached the Casa de La Media Noche, a restaurant that specialised in Cuban food. It was said to serve the best *langosta enchiladas* in all Miami. Through the window she could see a crowd of diners, waiters bustling back and forth, busboys hurrying with carafes of ice water. Festive Cuban music was playing loudly on a jukebox.

Magdalena Torrente stepped into the alley that ran behind the restaurant. She knocked on the back door, which was opened by a tall man of about seventy. He wore a panama hat and a crisp white suit of the kind called a *dril ciel*, made from an Irish linen so special that only one mill in the Republic of Ireland still supplied it. Fernando Garrido took her hand and kissed it, a brushing of lips on flesh, a simple courtesy in a world grown weary of good manners and civilised behaviour. Then he led her toward a box-like room without windows, where cans of tomatoes and bags of beans formed pyramids in the middle of the floor.

'There's no place for you to sit, Magdalena,' Garrido said. He spoke Cuban Spanish, with its generous vowel sounds.

'It doesn't matter,' she said.

He shrugged, and she thought there was some small despair in the gesture, that of a man disappointed by the directions of his life. Once, in another world, Fernando Garrido had been the mayor of Santiago, the second largest city in Cuba. He'd had political ambitions. He'd dreamed vibrant dreams of replacing the sequence of malignant dictatorships, those dreadful reefs on which Cuba had foundered and rotted, with democracy and social justice. And then his notions had been overtaken by Castro's revolution, which he'd supported at first in a wary manner, more out of relief at the end of the dictatorship of Batista than any great faith in the stated ideals of Fidel, whom he'd never trusted and personally didn't like.

In July 1960, one year after the Revolution – which had accomplished nothing except to trade one set of gangsters for another – Fernando Garrido had been arrested by Castro's security forces. He was charged with the sort of 'crime' so common in Communist societies, undefined and unfounded, absurd and yet sinister. It was a crime devised by dull Marxist imaginations and framed in such a vague way that it could never be grasped by its 'perpetrator'. This kind of nebulous offence was often called 'counter-revolutionary', a term that had any meaning the regime attached to it. So far as Garrido could tell, his only misdemeanour was to have been a politician during the reign of the dictator Batista. Guilt by association – and for that he'd been imprisoned for seven long years on the Isle of Pines, severely beaten, given electric shocks, then released and expelled from the country without explanation! The experience had left him with a tremor in his hands, a recurring nightmare of violence, and a hatred of Castro that was acute and constant, like shrapnel in his heart.

Garrido moved to the centre of the room, where a lightbulb hung from an old cord. To Magdalena Torrente he looked like a plantation owner in an old sepia picture, benign yet strict, generous but careful with his kindness. He took off his hat. His hair, dyed an incongruous brown and brilliantined, an old man's vanity, glistened under the light like a wary skullcap. He had lived for almost thirty years in exile and the weight of that expulsion showed on his face. But his dreams, which would not lie still and let him savour in peace the fruits of his thriving business, were still powerful. He wanted the one thing all exiles crave and few achieve – a triumphant return to the motherland, a vindication.

'This neighbourhood,' he said. He appeared to lose his train of thought a moment. 'It gets worse every day. Drugs. Violence. I remember when it was a good place to have a business. Now it gets too dangerous.'

Magdalena didn't want to listen to Garrido's regular complaints about how the massive influx of Cubans from Mariel in 1980 had altered the fabric of life in Miami for the worse. She already knew how Castro had shipped out all his undesirables, his criminals and addicts, his deranged and schizophrenic, and unloaded them upon an angry Florida. She already knew how drugs and murder had poisoned the Cuban community. She wanted to pick up what she'd come for and leave, but something about Fernando Garrido always made her linger. She knew what it was: he was a link to her father, the last one left to her. The thought made her feel lonely for a moment.

Garrido lit a small cigar and blew a stream of smoke up at the lightbulb. 'Did anyone follow you here?'

It was his regular question. She shook her head. Her long black hair was thick and fibrous. 'Nobody followed me.'

'You're a beautiful woman and very noticeable, Magdalena. You can never be sure. Castro's agents infiltrate very well. They're good at anything underhand. Never underestimate them.'

She said she didn't. She told him firmly that she didn't take chances. He smoked quietly, surveying her face, watching her with an intensity that made her uncomfortable. She knew from his expression what he was going to say, and she was anxious to avoid the long, flowery comparisons with her dead mother. Garrido would reminisce about the old life in Cuba when they'd all been very young, himself and Humberto Torrente and the lovely Oliva, oh, they'd been a great threesome, an inseparable trio going everywhere together, *aieee*, beaches and restaurants and nightclubs. Garrido's Latin sentimentality, his ornate phrases, irritated Magdalena because the past wasn't what mattered to her any more. Then Garrido would always say the same thing half-jokingly: *Your mother's only fault was she married the wrong man in Humberto. Honourable as Humberto was, Oliva should have listened more closely to my entreaties.* And he'd smile and kiss Magdalena's brow, and sometimes there would be tears in his dark brown eyes.

She looked at her watch. She had hours before she was due at the airport but she wanted to give an impression of haste. There was laughter from the restaurant; the music grew louder.

'You're anxious to leave,' he said.

She nodded her head, glanced again at her watch. The small room was stifling. She watched him walk in the direction of some bare metal shelves where two pistols lay side by side. He removed a section of shelf in a very deliberate way, then set it on the floor.

'My secret place,' he said.

The wall had a concealed panel built into it. Garrido slid it aside, reached into the black space and took out a briefcase. 'Before I give you this, I must ask a question you may find unpardonable,' he said. 'Do you really trust him? After all, our association with him goes back four years. One might be pardoned for expecting results very soon.'

A tiny night moth fluttered against Magdalena's lips and she brushed it gently aside. 'The question's perfectly understandable, Fernando, and the answer's simple. I trust him. How could she not? she wondered'. If you loved, you had to trust: one was a basic corollary of the other. A fact of life. 'Besides, something this intricate takes time.'

Garrido tapped his fingernails on his front dentures, a *click click click* that indicated thought. 'Do I detect something else? Something a little more than trust? If so, I caution you to go carefully.'

'I'm always careful.' She raised a hand to her hair. His insight surprised her. Was she that obvious? Did she wear her feelings like a necklace? She was a little embarrassed. She'd always imagined she knew how to conceal herself from the world. But Fernando had been familiar with her since childhood; he'd become accustomed to reading her expressions. Defensively she said, 'I don't mean to be rude, but my private life isn't really any of your business, Fernando.'

'You're right, of course. I shouldn't try to counsel you. If you trust him, that's good enough for me.' Garrido stepped closer to her. He pressed the handle of the case into the palm of her hand. Even though there was nobody else present in the room, the gesture was surreptitious. It was force of habit. Garrido had spent years living in fear of Castro's spies in Miami, years raising funds for nocturnal raids and acts of sabotage inside Cuba, blowing up power stations and electric pylons, dynamiting naval installations and airfields, or spraying beach-front tourist resorts with guns fired from sea-going craft. He'd participated personally in many of these manoeuvres until his nerve had gone. It was a game for the young and valiant.

Garrido inclined his face in a rather formal way, pressing his lips upon her cheek, an avuncular kiss. She smelled mint and tobacco and something else, something alcoholic, on his breath. She held the briefcase casually, as if it contained nothing of any importance. Then she stepped toward the door, but Garrido caught her by the wrist. His skin was damp.

'We have enemies,' he said quietly.

'I know.'

'Even among our friends. Remember that.'

Garrido dropped his hand and backed away from her, smiling for the first time now. His dentures, the colour of his suit, gleamed. 'But I don't need to tell you anything, do I? You're not a child any more. I have to keep reminding myself you're not Humberto's little girl.'

Humberto's little girl. Garrido had a good heart, a heart as big as Cuba itself, but he could never overcome his old-fashioned patronising manner. Wouldn't he ever grasp the fact that she was thirty-nine years old, for God's sake? That she was dedicated to the same cause as himself and had an important voice in it? That the role she played in the political schemes of the exile community here in Miami was just as important as his own?

'I haven't fit that description for a very long time, Fernando.'

Garrido was very apologetic. 'The trouble with growing old is that you don't want things to change. You want everybody to stay the same age because it means you don't grow old yourself. It's a nice folly. Forgive me for it.'

Magdalena reached the door. Well-mannered as ever, Garrido opened it for her. In the dark hallway a massive figure emerged from the shadows. Carlos, a taciturn giant from Las Tunas Province, Garrido's watchdog. He wore a shoulder-holster beneath his dark jacket. He moved slowly and quietly, his musculature evident under his clothes; a powerful man, sleek and silent. Magdalena thought there was something a little spooky about Carlos. He had the look of a man who has been involved in more than a few premature deaths.

'Where did you park, Magdalena?' Garrido asked.

'At the Malaga Restaurant.'

'Carlos will escort you there.'

She was about to say she had a gun, she didn't need protection, but she didn't utter a word. Carlos would follow her anyway. Garrido wasn't going to allow anybody to carry that briefcase through the streets of Little Havana without an armed escort.

She smiled her best smile, which dazzled Garrido, then she raised a hand as she left. Garrido, seemingly frozen in the doorway of the small square room, stood without moving for a long time. He listened to the silences that followed Magdalena's departure. Then he took a cigar from the pocket of his jacket and lit it.

Garrido, once known in politics as El Ganador, the winner, closed his eyes. He sucked smoke into the back of his throat and remembered how it had felt to be that man of victory. The man who controlled Santiago de Cuba in the early 1950s, the young reformer – ah, the golden naïvety of those years – who wanted to change a festering system. All that sweet energy, that devotion to his calling. How remote it all seemed to him suddenly, and

Cuba so very far away; and yet, as if affected by some untreatable malaria of the heart, he could still shiver when he thought of going back to his homeland.

He shut the door of the room. He thought about Magdalena out there in the darkness, the long trip in front of her. Jesus! The way she trusted! He hadn't trusted anything in that uncluttered way for years! Nor would he do so now. Especially now. He would do precisely what had to be done, what should have been done a long time ago; and Magdalena might never need to know.

He listened to the music that played on the jukebox and prayed Magdalena would take the same kind of care with her heart that she would with the contents of the case.

Magdalena Torrente drove her grey BMW from Calle Ocho to the Rickenbacker Causeway and then Key Biscayne. Here, on the shores of Biscayne Bay, were opulent houses protected by elaborate security systems and regular patrols which echoed the same state of siege that existed in the poorer neighbourhoods of Miami. It was as if the siege had simply risen several notches on the social scale, and the differences between Key Biscayne and areas like Little Havana were finally only cosmetic.

At eight-thirty she parked in the drive of the house she'd inherited from Humberto Torrente. Surrounded by lush palm and bougainvillaea and rubber trees, it was located some yards inland from the shore, where a motorboat was tied to a wooden slip. Magdalena unlocked the front door, went inside, crossed the tiled entrance hall, passed under a large skylight filled with stars. Across the living-room, an enormous bay window framed dark water. There was an unobstructed view of Miami, lights and neon, approaching aircraft, traffic on the silvery causeway: a glittering city trapped under a canopy of humidity.

She climbed the stairs. Her bedroom was plain. She had no taste for the bright shades, such as the gold curtains and red rugs, you often found in Hispanic homes; nor were there any of the customary religious artifacts, the gory Christs, the saints with their cartoon placidity, the prim Virgins, the whole panoply of blood and pain, chastity and redemption.

The only decoration in the bedroom was a black and white picture depicting Humberto Torrente in the uniform of a Colonel in the Cuban Air Force, taken in 1956 at some social function at the Havana Yacht Club. At his side stood his wife Oliva, dark-haired and exquisite, in a white cocktail dress. They looked prosperous, healthy, in love, and yet there seemed to be a glaze across their smiles, a sadness half-hidden, as if they knew that within six years of the snapshot both of them would be dead.

Magdalena gazed at the photograph for a time – 1956: she'd been five years old then. She was ten when her parents died their separate deaths. For her whole adolescence she was fated to a life of guardians, some of them nuns in boarding-schools, others widowed aunts in Miami Beach. She'd spent her fifteenth year in Garrido's custody at his big house in Coral Gables. Time and again he had explained his view of Cuban history, one of endless struggle, endless betrayal. He insisted that Humberto's death captured in miniature the tragedy of Cuba. Hadn't Humberto struggled for liberty with all his passion? And hadn't he been betrayed in the end?

Magdalena didn't buy all the way into Garrido's melodrama. Where Cuban politics were concerned, she tried to temper her passion with a certain objectivity. But it was the passion, inherited from Humberto, which had led her restlessly during her twenties and early thirties from one exiled group to another – to those with arsenals stashed in the Everglades and others who had bomb factories in South Miami and others still with safe houses in the Keys where semi-automatic weapons were converted to the real thing. She'd enjoyed the feel of guns in her hands and the idea of belonging to a secret army – the elaborate security precautions and the passwords and the intensity of the young men who trained with the kind of total concentration that made them good soldiers though poor lovers. She'd made love to many of them, and couldn't differentiate one from another now, those quick, silent boys, all of whom put the death of Castro above complete enjoyment of life. It was as if they were destined to live every day of their lives with a shadow of their own making across the face of the sun. So long as Fidel lived, there would always be this eclipse.

After ten years of association with one exile movement or another, Magdalena Torrente's experience of direct, anti-Castro action had consisted of an effort to dynamite crates of Soviet weapons in the heavily guarded Havana harbour (there were no weapons, only boxes of agricultural machinery; intelligence had been wrong), and the delivery of explosives to underground members in Pinar del Rio. She had flown the twin-engine Piper herself, a skill she'd learned from exiled pilots, while her three companions dropped the supplies by parachute to men and women waiting in darkened tobacco fields below.

Both sorties into Cuba had been thrilling, both heavy with the clammy menace of capture and death. Both had brought Magdalena closer to an understanding of what the cause meant. It was no mere abstraction, no games played in bomb factories, no simple rhetoric of freedom. It was life and death, and in particular her own life and death, that the cause demanded. And yet these adventures lacked something. She had the feeling of futility that might have dogged a person attacking an elephant with a can of mosquito repellent. One could sting Castro with nocturnal assaults, but they were never fatal.

In her middle thirties she'd realised that to be a soldier was not enough in itself. You had to be closer to the centre, to the place where strategic decisions were made. You had to be near the power. To fire weapons in the Everglades or assemble guns in the Keys (from where, frustratingly, you could practically smell Havana on the wind) was useful; but useful wasn't enough. The ability to fire a gun or fly surreptitiously into Cuba were not going to keep a dream alive. So she had entered the political world of Fernando Garrido and his cronies. It was a tiresome group at times, one that squabbled endlessly in the Cuban way, but influential and rich and committed without question to the destruction of Fidel.

Magdalena had won a reputation in these political circles as an energetic voice, somebody to be listened to, someone whose role was less illusory, and perhaps more practical, than knowing the parts of an M-16 rifle. Here, too, she came to realise she had deeper ambitions than to scurry in and out of Cuba under cover of darkness. And so she attended committee meetings, and she whispered in the ears of powerful figures in the exile community, and she listened to the pulses that beat in the darkness and smelled the breezes that blew through Miami and tracked their direction – and she detected in herself an immeasurable impatience. She wanted things to change in Cuba quickly. Not tomorrow. Not the next day. Now.

When Castro finally fell . . .

She touched the photograph of her parents, fingertips on glass, tentative, loving. She remembered her father as a serious man whose rare displays of levity were all the more precious for their scarcity. Sombre, hard-working, Humberto Torrente had been dedicated to a patriotic ideal. He'd chosen the wrong way to realise it, that was all. His mistake was to place all his hopes on American military assistance and he'd died for that false expectation in 1961 at the Bay of Pigs, the B-26 he piloted shot down by Castro's artillery over San Blas in Cuba. What Humberto failed to realise was that outside forces alone could never have unseated Castro at that time. The Americans, led by a vacillating Kennedy, had chickened out at the Bay of Pigs, withholding air support and naval artillery, leaving Cuban freedom fighters stranded on beaches. No, outside assaults could be useful up to a point, but the successful overthrow of Castro could come only from within Cuba, from men who hated the whole suffocating regime and who had the means and the courage to replace it with a free society.

Magdalena's mother, Oliva, hadn't been interested in Humberto's goals. Her own world was limited, constructed as it was around husband, home and child. The way Magdalena had turned out would have shocked her. What good was a woman who hadn't borne children? who didn't know how to cook? who didn't have a man to keep house for? What good was this kind of woman?

Shortly before Christmas 1961, Oliva Torrente, unhinged by her husband's death, swallowed an overdose of barbiturates. As if to emphasise how little she cared for a world without Humberto, she'd elected the sin of suicide over the burden of living a widow's life.

Magdalena considered the past an irrelevant encumbrance. Only the future mattered, only the task ahead. She turned away from the photograph. She took the gun from her pocket, removed the leather jacket, locked the weapon in her bedside table. She put Garrido's briefcase on the bed, opened a closet, removed a full-length suede coat. She placed the chocolate-coloured coat beside the case, then opened the case. The money was tightly bundled. There were stacks of hundred dollar bills. Under these were other stacks in one thousand dollar denominations.

The total was close to a million dollars, collected throughout the Cuban community from donations made by respectable doctors and lawyers and bank officials, cash skimmed from the *bolito* games and jai-alai betting and gathered quietly in Cuban bars, illicit money from drug dealers whose astronomical profits had endowed them with an indiscriminating sense of charity. It came from all manner of sources and was amassed, as it had been for the last four years, in the Casa de la Media Noche by Fernando Garrido, head of the group that called itself the Committee for the Restoration of Democracy in Cuba, an organisation whose wealthy members preferred anonymity to public notoriety.

In a sense the cash was dream money, the money of ancient pains and grievances, dollars thrown up by the need for vengeance against a system that had broken families and plundered property, capital dampened by the blood of those who'd already been martyred in a cause growing old and impatient. The cash was destined for Cuba, there to be used by the democratic underground movement for its operating expenses, which included illegal radio transmitters, pamphlets and newspapers. It bought food and guns for those obliged to hide in the mountains. It clothed and fed the children of these fugitives. It also purchased explosives used in acts of internal sabotage. Counter-revolution was an expensive business.

Magdalena undid the buttons of the coat. The lining, specially prepared for her by a seamstress in Hialeah, was divided into a series of pockets, each of which would hold a large number of bank-notes. It was skilful tailoring. There was no way a casual observer could tell the coat contained anything other than the body of the person who wore it; a smuggler's garment, designed for one purpose only.

Magdalena transferred notes from the briefcase to the lining of the suede coat. It took her twenty minutes to empty the case. She tried the coat on: weighty but tolerable. She looked at herself in a mirror. She didn't appear in any way different, no artificial plumpness, no unseemly bulges. She would be nothing more than a beautiful black-haired woman travelling alone on a long flight. Her looks – the way her thick hair fell mysteriously on her shoulders and how the lean line of her jaw emphasised a delightful mouth, the eyes that were knowingly dark and secretive, like those of a torch-singer – would draw attention as they always did. But the coat wouldn't cause anybody a second glance, which was all that mattered.

From the closet she removed a small suitcase she'd packed that morning. She went down the stairs, turned off the lights. Outside, the night was heavy with moisture. Over the Rickenbacker Causeway silver lightning flashed, then thunder crackled as if the sky were a vast radio receiver picking up static. Magdalena stepped inside her car, backed it out of the drive.

Across the street, Carlos sat in a black Pontiac parked under a twisted rubber tree. When she drove past she gave him a thumbs up sign, then for amusement tried to lose him in traffic, but Carlos, with his watchful black eyes and unsmiling features, was an expert at bird-dogging. Slipping coolly through traffic, he managed to stay directly behind her all the way to Miami International Airport.

Norfolk, England

It was dawn, and cold, when the girl rode the chestnut mare to the top of the rise. The ground was hard with frost and the horse's hoofs thumped solidly. The animal's breath hung on the chill air, tiny clouds turned red by the first touch of sunlight. The girl rode with all the confidence of someone who has been mounting horses since early childhood. This particular mare was a special favourite, a big mellow horse that loved to be ridden.

The girl reined the animal at the top of the rise and looked out across the countryside. This corner of England, more than a hundred miles from London, was almost exclusively flat, fields stretching toward a horizon that seemed very far away. Here and there isolated antique villages of the kind so adored by tourists interrupted the monotony of the furrows; occasionally a marsh or pond seeped up through meadowland and created a watery diversion. The girl, whose name was Stephanie Brough, had lived all her fourteen years in this vicinity. The nearest cities were Norwich to the north and Ipswich to the south, and in between, as she sometimes phrased it, was *sheer bloody boring nothing*.

She dismounted in a stand of thin birch trees. The rise sloped down to bare fields that would become muddy as soon as the frost melted. She liked all this – riding in the early dawn, avoiding the *awful* breakfasts with her parents and that twit of a brother Tim (who sometimes flicked pellets of soggy Corn Flakes at her when he thought nobody was looking; *Timmy Twit*, she thought. Everybody expected *him* to go up to *Oxford* in two years! He couldn't find his way to the bloody loo without a map! And her parents doted on him in such a sickening way: *Tim's so clever, oooh, fawn and scrape)*. She liked the huge secrecy, the feeling that the world belonged only to her at this time of morning before school.

A casual onlooker would have seen a slim, pretty girl, trim in her blue jeans and white cotton sweater, her small breasts barely evident, her yellow hair cut very close to her scalp in a fashion that was almost boyish. But nobody was watching Stephanie Brough, not at this hour of the morning.

She gazed down the slope. She had a clear view of the place she'd come to see. About three hundred yards from where she stood was the whitewashed farmhouse that belonged to a family called Yardley. Old Man Yardley had died last year and his sons, delighted they didn't have to work the land for the old tyrant, had upped and left for London. (Such smart buggers, she thought.) Ever since then the place had been empty. Steffie had supposed it would always remain that way – who'd want to rent or buy that old dump with the black fields surrounding it? It was isolated and rundown and the willow trees that drooped around it made it look creepy.

Yesterday, though, to her great surprise, something was different. During her morning ride she'd seen a dark-blue Range Rover outside the house. Intrigued by the possibility of some new happening in a part of the world where fresh occurrences were rare, she'd come back to see if the vehicle was still there, or perhaps even catch sight of the new occupant. In this rustic environment information was a prize, something to be seized then passed along to the next person, like a great favour. Oh, *by the way, there's some new people at the old Yardley place. You didn't know?*

The vehicle was parked where it had been the day before. But the house still looked disappointingly empty, the windows dark and bare. A crow was scratching around in the soil. Leaves, fallen from the willows, had become piled against the east wall of the property. It was all rather desolate. Steffie enjoyed little mysteries, and, in her mind, the dead appearance of the old house was exactly that – something to be solved. Why was there a Range Rover and no sign of life? Why was there no smoke from the chimney, no dog in the yard? Everybody had dogs around here.

She wanted a closer look. She left the mare chewing on a clump of grass, then moved down the incline a little way. She stopped after a few yards, uneasy at the idea of trespassing on other people's property. Divided between her natural curiosity and her sense of intrusion, she wasn't sure if she should go any further. But really, what harm could it possibly do to pop down there and just sniff around? If anybody discovered her she'd just tell them she lived on her father's horse-breeding farm three miles away, and then introduce herself as the next-door neighbour – practically.

She was halfway down when she heard the noise – a penetrating *crack*. Her first startled reaction was that a jet from an airbase nearby had shattered the sound barrier, a common occurrence round here. But then she realised the noise was closer than that and more focused: it had come from the house. The raven, cawing harshly, rose in the clear air.

If it hadn't been a supersonic plane –

She suddenly realised what had caused the sound. She turned back up the rise, moving quickly, her heartbeat rapid. The noise had faded but she could still hear it perfectly inside her head. *Crack*. Just like that. When she reached the top of the slope she glanced one last time down at the house.

The building was as lifeless as it had been before, the windows opaque in the chill dawn.

But somebody had to be inside. Somebody had to have fired the gun. Guns did not go off by themselves. Unless there were spirits, and Steffie was too sophisticated to believe in anything like that.

She rode the mare hard between the birches, intrigued more than ever, and afraid in a way that was quite new to her and strangely interesting.

Crack.

She'd come back tomorrow. She couldn't leave the mystery alone.

3 London

When his wife Roxanne had been killed seven years ago by an IRA bomb detonated in a London street, Frank Pagan had lived for some time in a world of incomprehensible pain, a bleak place where his will to live was smothered. It was the sort of pain that lingered in bewildering ways long after the event. A resemblance on a street, a phrase from a certain song, the creak of a floor in his flat – these things stirred the ghost, and the pain returned, always swift, never less than savage. He'd come to accept that this emptiness was a lifelong thing. He'd combated it to some extent, but there was always the residue. Sometimes he'd caught himself waiting for the approach of Roxanne Pagan's memory. The anticipation of pain, a gentle masochism.

That was one kind of hurt.

In this white hospital room, whose translucence suggested an hallucination, he was beginning to understand another form of pain altogether. When he raised his face, hot threads tightened malignantly in his chest. When he had to get out of bed and go to the toilet – he defiantly refused to take the wheelchair, which was transportation for the damned only – he walked like a man negotiating a field of broken glass. Any sudden motion sent a violent response up through his bandaged chest. At times his heart seemed charged with electricity, as if copper wires were conducting a brisk current through it.

He really hadn't needed to be reminded so forcibly of his own mortality. What also shook him was the sense of violation, his body breached by a force that might have destroyed him. This notion was shocking: he'd been shot at before, but never hit, and perhaps he'd come to think it was one of those things that happened to other people, never to oneself.

It didn't matter that his Pakistani doctor, Ghose, a sweet chain-smoking man with fidgety hands, kept telling him he was *wery wery* lucky. After all, six policemen had died during the carnage four days ago in Shepherd's Bush. Another inch to the left, Ghose had reminded him, another short inch, and the total would have been seven. *Imagine it, Mister Pagan – the tiny distance of infinity.* The idea of six dead policemen, four inside the leading van, one in the third car, and poor Ron Hardcastle from a devastating head wound, took something away from any contemplation of his own luck. Even the knowledge that two of the assailants had also been killed didn't quite cut the gloom.

On the morning after Pagan's admission to the hospital, Ghose had held up X-rays in his smoky-orange fingers, pointing enthusiastically to the pathway of the bullet, which had gone straight through the right lung. *Absolutely no functional disturbance*, Ghose had said. *No fractured ribs. No debris. Very little crushed tissue. A wonderfully clean exit. I'm utterly delighted. I rarely see such symmetry. You must thank God for the insignificant yaw of the bullet.*

Yaw: now there was a nice little word. Pagan had wondered why, if it was such a terrific wound, aesthetically so pleasing to Ghose and with a low yaw factor into the bargain, he was in such terrible *pain* those first three days.

Initially he'd been injected with morphine. A thoracostomy tube had been inserted in his chest to reinflate the lung, and then attached to a chest-draining unit. The wound had been closed on the third day. He'd been given anti-tetanus therapy and antibiotics and Ghose prescribed Pethidine, so that this fourth day was the most comfortable Pagan had spent. But comfort in the circumstances was merely relative: he was more glazed by drugs than truly soothed. Just when he thought the pain had subsided it would come back and lance him, causing him to gasp and his eyes to water.

And then, Christ, there were the dreams. In most of them he was back on that terrible street again, surrounded by searing flames, hearing the same explosions. Sometimes he rushed toward the burning van and tried to get the door open to release the trapped men, but he never quite made it. Infuriating dreams, frustrating and tragic. He always scorched his hands in these nightmares. At other times he dreamed of Gunther Ruhr, hearing over and over the drily uttered German phrase Ruhr had used in the car. *Die Reise ist nicht am Ende bis zur Ankunft* – endlessly repeated, echoing. He reached out in anger to silence Ruhr, but invariably the German had vaporised, courtesy of that special chemistry of dreams and Pagan would wake sweating, filled with a sense of desperation.

What he really needed was to be discharged from this place. He couldn't do anything from a hospital bed. He couldn't bring the outside world into this boring room of tubes and charts and starched bedsheets. He couldn't begin to get at Ruhr, who had disappeared without the courtesy of a clue. He'd asked Ghose only that morning to release him. With that inscrutable look all doctors must learn in medical school, the doctor said he'd consider it.

Restless, Pagan turned his face to the window, where a rare October sun shone on the dusty glass. A tree, gloriously lit by autumn, pressed against the windowpane and tantalised him. There was a high breeze outside, the kind of spirited wind that dries laundry. All this contributed to his impatience. All this made him doubly determined to find a way out of here before it was night again and nurses came to dispense sleeping-pills with the persistence of drug-dealers. *Now, Frank, you really must swallow this, do you the world of good.* Or, *Come on, Frank, be a good boy.* He didn't *want* to be a good anything. He wanted to be a cantankerous pain in the arse to doctors and nurses alike. He wanted out: he wanted Gunther Ruhr.

When the door of his private room opened he saw Martin Burr step inside. Burr, the Commissioner of Scotland Yard, carried a bottle of that universal panacea called Lucozade and a small bag of fruit, both of which he set down on the bedside table. Haggard from insomnia, he'd been coming twice a day ever since Pagan had been rushed here by ambulance. The Commissioner propped his walnut cane against the bed and sat down, smiling at Pagan, who noticed how a streak of sunlight struck the dark-green plastic patch over Burr's blinded right eye.

'How are we today, Frank?'

'We're a long way from wonderful,' Pagan replied. 'We would like to get the hell out of here.'

Burr reached for his cane and tapped it on the floor, sighing as he did so. 'You're always in such a damned hurry, Frank. Accept the fact you've been wounded, and even if you're released from this place you need time to convalesce. You still look awful.' Burr looked round. 'Rather nice place. Room to yourself. TV. Magazines to read. Enjoy the privacy, Frank. Think of it as an enforced leave.'

'With respect, what I need is to get back on the job.' Burr's smile was small and strained, barely concealing the stress of a man who had just spent the worst four days of his life. There had been endless news conferences, and questions raised in the House of Commons about events in Shepherd's Bush. A commission of inquiry was being set up, which meant that a bunch of professors and civil servants would be asking all kinds of bloody questions. And the press, good God, the press had squeezed the tragedy for everything it was worth and more. The breakdown of law and order. The incompetence of British security forces. The supremacy of the 'super-terrorist'. On and on without end. A mob was howling for blood, preferably Martin Burr's. And the Home Secretary had commanded Burr to attend a private interview, which could only mean that the Commissioner's job security was somewhat in doubt. These were not good times. The temper of the country was bad; the citizens were horrified when policemen were killed.

Burr said, 'What would it accomplish if you returned to work? You'd wear yourself out within a day, Frank. You'd be back in this bed in no time flat.'

'I don't think so. Basically I think I'm in good shape.'

'Notwithstanding a hole clean through your chest. Think of the shock to your system.'

'I can't just lie here.'

'Afraid you have to,' Burr said. 'Anyway, everything that can be done is being done.'

'And Ruhr's back in custody?'

'Below the belt, Frank.'

Burr leaned towards the bed. He laid both hands over his face and massaged his flesh in a tired way. When he spoke there were hollows of fatigue in his voice. 'Let me bring you up to date. Our explosions people say the parked cars that exploded along Acacia Avenue were detonated by a timing-device and the explosives used were of Czech origin.'

'Brilliant work,' Pagan remarked drily.

Martin Burr gave Pagan a dark look. 'I realise you have very little patience for the kind of systematic work technicians have to do, Frank. Nevertheless, it has to be done.'

Pagan shut his eyes. There was a tickle in his nostrils. A sneeze was building up. If it succeeded, it would send uncontrollable bolts of pain through his chest. He struggled to overcome it, reaching for a tissue just in case.

Burr continued. 'Twenty-six cars were detonated simultaneously. Nobody we interviewed in the vicinity saw anybody plant the explosives in the first place. The whole thing was done with an extraordinary degree of stealth.'

Pagan opened his eyes. The sneeze had faded. He lowered the tissue and looked at Martin Burr. 'I think we can take stealth for granted,' he said. *That tone* – it was close to petulant sarcasm. He'd have to be careful not to push it. Alienation of Martin Burr wasn't a good thing.

Burr fingered his plastic eye-patch, which he did when he was annoyed. 'I understand your impatience, Frank. I also understand that a gunshot wound affects a man's perceptions. However, I didn't come here to listen to your cutting little asides. I've got enough on my plate as it is.'

Whenever he was irritated, Burr resorted to a patronising tone that Pagan disliked. Chided, Pagan stared at the window, the gorgeous sunlight, and resolved he'd leave this place today no matter how the considerations of Doctor Ghose turned out. He'd swallow some Pethidine and walk out of this bloody hospital under his own steam. By mid-afternoon he'd be back in his office overlooking Golden Square in Soho, where his anti-terrorist section was located. Lord of his own domain again.

'Now where was I?' Martin Burr said. 'Ah, yes. I was coming to the two terrorists killed in the assault.'

Pagan felt his interest quicken. 'Is there anything new?'

'We haven't been able to identify one of the men. The other, however, was an Australian citizen by the name of Ralph Masters.'

'It doesn't ring any bells,' Pagan said.

Burr sat back in his chair. 'Born Adelaide 1940. Served in the Australian Army in 1960. Nothing for a long time. Then he turns up again in Biafra, nowadays Nigeria, in 1967. He was in the Congo in 1968. After that, he makes an appearance in Nicaragua in the mid-1970s.'

'The mercenary circuit.'

'Indeed.'

'Is there anything more recent on him?'

Burr shook his head. 'So far as we know, he'd been sitting quietly in Sydney. He installed telephones for a living.'

'That must have bored him senseless. Some people can't settle after they've tasted war. Is there a record of him entering this country?'

Burr shook his head. 'We don't know when he came in, nor how he got here. We don't know who employed him.'

'The same people who employed Gunther Ruhr. Who else?' Pagan plucked a purple grape from the bunch Burr had brought. He popped it in his mouth and bit into the soft skin.

'Whoever they are.' The Commissioner was morosely silent. Pagan had never seen him quite so dejected. He felt an enormous sympathy for Burr, who took the death of the policemen hard. Recent events had obviously been a heartbreak for him, visiting the widows, the fatherless kids, mouthing platitudes that amounted to nothing in the end. The Commissioner, a candid man who had no glib political skills, was not above genuine tears.

'I keep thinking about how our security was breached, Frank. I come back time and again to that. That aspect of the whole thing depresses me. It's not only the dead officers, although God knows that would be monstrous enough in itself.'

'Too many people knew the route,' Pagan said. 'And somebody blabbered.'

'The itinerary was decided at the highest level. The Home Office was involved. It was decided by all parties that instead of an ostentatious escort we would transport Ruhr quietly by a highly secret route. An awful mistake, as it turned out.'

A secret was hard to keep in a world of committees, Pagan thought.

Burr made circles on the tiled floor with the tip of his cane. 'I seem to remember you were the only one who raised the subject of air cover, Frank. I wish the rest of us had paid more attention.'

Pagan shrugged. None of the Commissioner's wishes could alter the past. Both men were quiet for a long time before Burr went on, 'I'd like to think that if somebody gabbed out of turn then it was from sheer carelessness rather than outright treachery. I don't like the idea of a mole.'

'But it's a distinct possibility,' Pagan said.

Burr got up from the chair and walked to the window. He was a big man, wide-shouldered and heavy around the centre. He looked out into the sunlight and blinked. 'Ten people knew the route, including ourselves.'

'I don't think you can stop at ten, Commissioner. If you include secretaries and assistants, who have an odd knack of getting wind of everything, the number's probably closer to thirty, thirty-five. And out of that lot somebody – by accident or design – had a connection with Ruhr's friends.'

Pagan paused. His mouth was very dry. He sipped some water before going on. 'The trouble is, it's difficult to run a really thorough investigation of some thirty individuals, especially if it has to be done quickly. And since Ruhr's obviously up to something in this country – otherwise the big rescue makes no sense – time's a factor. He's not over here to sit around twiddling his thumbs for weeks, is he? He's an expensive commodity. Somebody paid for him to be here. That same somebody spent a lot of money on the rescue. I suspect we're looking at a matter of days before Ruhr does whatever he's here to do. Perhaps less.' Pagan hadn't spoken more than a couple of short sentences since his wound and now he was hoarse. There was an ache in his chest, a brass screw turning.

Burr stared at him. 'If you're saying that our red priority is to find Ruhr and put the security breach on the back burner, I wholeheartedly agree. Easier said than done, alas. Half the police force of England is looking for him right now, Frank. We've had reports of the bugger in Torquay and Wolverhampton and York and all the way up to Scotland. In terms of false sightings, Gunther Ruhr rivals unidentified flying objects.'

Pagan had a mild Pethidine rush, a weird little sense of distance from himself. At times he floated beyond everything, spaced-out, drifting, a cosmonaut in his own private galaxy. It was a pleasant sort of feeling. It was easy to see how people became addicted to

Pethidine. It relegated terrorists and dead policemen and gunshot wounds to another world.

Pagan shut his eyes and tried very hard to concentrate. 'Ruhr specialises in destruction. The question is, what is he here to destroy? And why was he in Cambridge? What's so interesting about the place?'

'Not a great deal, Frank.' Martin Burr, an Oxford man with no high regard for the rival university, helped himself to a small glass of Lucozade. He drank, made a face, wondered about the masochism of whole generations of British people who had sought good health in the oversweet liquid.

'What about the countryside around Cambridge? Aren't there a couple of military bases?' Pagan asked.

'There's a NATO installation about forty miles away in Norfolk. Also a number of RAF bases within a forty-mile radius of Cambridge, plus a couple of army camps. We've been doing a spot of map-reading.'

'I thought the NATO base was going out of business.'

Martin Burr nodded. 'To a large extent. The terms of the American-Soviet disarmament treaty call for mid-range ballistic missiles to be removed from bases, shipped back to the United States and then destroyed – with Russian observers on hand to ensure fair play. There's a laughable contradiction in terms. I've yet to hear of a Bolshevik who understood fair play.'

Pagan rarely paid attention to the Commissioner's bias against Communism. It was a facet of Burr's personality: a form of phobia, and really quite harmless.

'Any one of those places is a candidate for Ruhr,' Pagan said.

'They've all beefed up security heavily in the last few days for that very reason. They wouldn't be easy targets for our German friend.'

'Is there anything else that might attract him to the area?'

'I've been thinking about that too. Ruhr's target could be a person rather than a place. Or a group of people. In which case, where the devil do we begin? At least three international conferences are coming up in the next week or so in Cambridge. The city's going to be filled with all kinds of experts. Environmentalists, meteorologists, chemists – and that's only in Cambridge. What if Ruhr's target lies in Northampton? Or Bury St Edmunds? What then?'

Pagan considered the Commissioner's remarks for a moment. Ruhr had become endowed with almost supernatural powers: he was everywhere, and capable of anything. 'Here's another possibility to make things a little more complicated: Ruhr was just passing through Cambridge on the way to somewhere else – London, Birmingham – and he stopped to have some fun, if you can call it that.'

Pagan remembered the girl who had been with Ruhr at the time of his capture. A skinny little thing, anaemic, small-breasted. Her name was Penny Ford and she lived in a one-room flat where she'd taken Ruhr after a casual encounter in a pub. When Pagan had interviewed her she'd said that she wasn't in the habit of inviting strange fellows home, you understand, but Ruhr had been, well, bloody persistent and anyhow he didn't have a place to stay, and she was only human after all. And her rent was almost due into the bargain and she was a bit short of the readies. She'd imagined a straight screw, Pagan thought. Uncomplicated sex, a quick exchange of money, end of the matter. Ruhr had other notions.

Penny Ford hadn't been able to tell Pagan why Ruhr was in Cambridge or how he had travelled there or where he was living. She knew nothing about him. She was informative only when it came to his sexual demands. Pagan remembered the girl's quiet voice.

We had sex, and I thought that was the end of it . . . I went inside the lavatory and when I came back he was sitting up on the edge of the bed and looking at me . . . well, in a funny kind of way . . . And he was making this dry whistling sort of noise, you know, tuneless like, but weird, like he wants to whistle only he doesn't know how . . . He asks me to come over. Which I did, because I thought he wanted another go. He asks me to sit on his knee. Which I also did.

And then?

He has this terrible disfigured hand, of course. That made me sympathetic to him at first. I see him take something out of his jacket, which is hanging on the back of a chair. It's a metal contraption with a leather strap, strangest thing I ever saw. And ugly as sin.

Ugly as sin, Pagan thought. What had so spooked Penny Ford was an unusual artifact consisting of a strap and two long steel protuberances, both sharpened at the end. At first glance the contraption had no apparent function, until you realised – as Penny Ford did – that it was the prosthetic device Ruhr fastened over his deformed hand. The two sharp metal columns, each about six inches long, took the place of the missing fingers.

He wants me to spread my legs so he can stick that bloody thing inside me, honest to God . . . Can you imagine what that sharp steel would have done to me? I mean, sex is one thing, but that was evil . . .

Evil: Pagan remembered thinking it was an impressive word. Penny understandably resisted Ruhr's request and the German had become threatening, catching her by the hair and trying to force her to obey him. She'd struggled and screamed. Ruhr might have been able to silence the girl and slip away easily, but by sheer chance two plainclothes detectives were already inside the house questioning a first-floor tenant about a recent burglary. They responded to the screams immediately, imagining at worst a domestic dispute. They hadn't expected to corner the world's most wanted terrorist with his trousers hanging round his knees and his underwear at half-mast. Pagan had found this image very entertaining before. In the shadow of recent events it didn't seem remotely amusing now. Ruhr was sick and vicious. Worse, he was also at liberty, and Frank Pagan was not.

Pagan sat upright. 'Christ, I want out of here.'

Martin Burr shook his head. 'There are persons in the morgue with more colour than you. Accept your fate and be still.'

'I need some fresh air, that's all.'

Burr smiled. 'Even if you were able to leave, you don't have anything here to wear. When they brought you in, your suit was totally ruined.'

'Ruined?'

'Bloodstained and torn.'

The suit, made specially for him by a tailor with basement premises in Soho, had cost Frank Pagan a month's salary. In normal circumstances he would have lamented the wreckage of a fashionable beige linen suit, but not now. 'I'll leave in a bloody bedsheet if I have to.'

'Frank Pagan wandering the West End in a bedsheet. The mind boggles.'

'All I do is lie here and feel useless. Sometimes Ghose teaches me new words. I just learned "haemothorax", and that's the highlight of the whole day.' Pagan looked at Martin Burr with disarming intensity. 'I need to be in on this one. You know that.'

Martin Burr ignored Pagan's plea and took a pocket watch from his waistcoat. He flipped the silver lid open. 'I must be running along, Frank. Busy busy. Things to do. I'll see if I can come back again tonight. Can't promise.'

'And I stay right here?'

'Exactly.'

Pagan watched Martin Burr go toward the door. 'Is that an order, Commissioner?'

Martin Burr sailed out of the room neither answering Pagan's question nor acknowledging it, even though he must have heard it. Was it some sly tactic on the Commissioner's part? Was he telling Pagan to take total responsibility if he discharged himself? Pagan listened to the click of Burr's cane as it faded down the tiled corridor. Then he lay very still for a time before he smiled and reached for the telephone at the side of the bed.

4 Glasgow

Two men sat in the glass-walled conservatory of the Copthorne Hotel overlooking that heart of Victorian Glasgow called George Square, a large open space dominated by statues and the massive edifice of the City Chambers. On this rainy afternoon in October the Chambers, built in the Italian Renaissance style, looked vaguely unreal and uninhabited, as if the local government officers who were its usual occupants had fled in a scandalous hurry. The whole rain-washed square gave the same empty impression despite the occasional pedestrian hurrying under an umbrella.

The older of the two men, a small white-haired figure called Enrico Caporelli, gazed pensively through the wet glass. Every five minutes or so he could see his black limousine pass in front of the conservatory while the driver killed time circling the area. Caporelli, five feet tall and sixty years of age, swung his dainty little feet in their expensive Milanese shoes a half-inch off the floor.

Everything about the Italian was tiny, except, it was said, his cunning and his sexual organ. He'd been legendary for his dalliances with showgirls in his old Havana days. Whenever he thought of the floor shows at the Tropicana or the Nacional – before the *barbudos* had come down from the hills and screwed everything and everybody on Cuba – he remembered them with fondness and loss. He rubbed his hands, which were smooth as vellum, and said, 'I've always enjoyed the statues here. Things were built to last back then. They were expected to be *doorable.*'

The younger man nodded, although the statues in the square didn't appeal to him. They lacked flair. Passion, uncommon in damp presbyterian climates, was missing.

Caporelli gazed at Queen Victoria a moment, then turned his face away from the drenched stone likeness of the monarch. He changed the subject suddenly. 'Nobody on God's earth is worth such a price.'

'Normally I would agree with you. But not in this case. Believe me.' The younger man, Rafael Rosabal, was tall and muscular, handsome in a manner that was particularly Latin. He had the kind of face, symmetrical and perhaps a little too perfect, that at first beguiles most women, then later begins to trouble them in some indefinable way.

Rosabal was cold in this climate. He'd been cold ever since he'd left Havana ten days ago. Despite the heavy woollen overcoat he'd purchased in Moscow, he was still uncomfortable. He wondered why Caporelli always chose unlikely cities for their meetings. Saint Etienne, Leeds, now Glasgow. Presumably Caporelli had business interests in these places.

'If he's as smart as I'm always being told, how come he got himself in this godawful mess in the first place?' Caporelli posed questions with an authority that came from years of giving orders and having them obeyed. He had the often haughty dignity of a cardinal accustomed to having his ring kissed.

Rosabal shrugged. 'He has tastes, peculiarities. Sometimes he gives in to them.'

'I don't want to know.' Caporelli raised a hand. He had no interest in the sexual foibles of other people. 'A man that allows his tastes to overcome his head – I don't like that kind of man.'

'I saw him yesterday. He's in a safe place. I assure you the problem is under control.'

Caporelli spoke gravely, his voice without cadence, his accent an odd hybrid of Calabria and Long Island. 'At great expense, I gave you the financial backing you said you would need for the operation. My generosity resulted in tragedy. Who likes dead policemen and hysterical newspaper headlines? I'm too old for anger, my friend. It's a drain. I only have so much energy. I want to spend it contemplating pleasant things.'

Rosabal plucked a cube of sugar out of the bowl and placed it on his tongue, an old habit. He was amused by the way Caporelli talked about his 'generosity', as if everything had been an act of charity, a personal donation from Enrico's private account, and there was going to be nothing in this for the Italian but a sense of well-being. San Enrico. All heart. The patron saint of terror.

'We got him back,' Rosabal said. 'That's the important thing, Enrico.'

'We should never have been placed in such a position to begin with. Having to bail out a man who's supposed to be doing a job for us – tsssss, that's not how to do business.'

Rosabal silently cursed Gunther Ruhr's proclivity for strange sex. It was the only cavalier aspect of Ruhr's life, which was otherwise single-mindedly dedicated to terror. 'Nobody else can deliver. That's the important thing to remember.'

All this violence made Caporelli touchy. He liked the idea that he was too civilised for violence. After all, didn't he own some of the world's finest paintings? Hadn't he invested in great sculptures and financed operas and symphonies and ballet companies? A number of cities in North America and Europe were unknowingly indebted to Caporelli for their cultural lives.

So it was no source of joy for him to be associated, even remotely, with men who were little better than animals, scum like this German who had had to be rescued four days ago in London. A goddam bloodbath, he thought. Who needed it? Even if this Kraut was the only man in the goddam known universe capable of doing the job, who needed the heartache?

When Rosabal had requested many thousands of dollars to rescue the German, Caporelli, turning the same blind eye he'd turned all his life whenever profit was threatened, had managed to convince himself that the cash was for a vast amount of grease, *la mordida*, bribes for prison officials, guards, cops. In his wildest fantasies he couldn't have come up with what the British newspapers were calling The Shepherd's Bush Massacre. He had developed a form of immunity to the realities of violence and an awesome capacity to distance himself from any personal culpability. Like many men whose hearts are basically vicious, Enrico Caporelli had discovered the ultimate hiding-place: denial.

He said quietly, 'I don't like the idea of new widows. I hate it when women cry. I'm suckered by tears. Orphaned children eat my heart out.'

Hipócrita, Rosabal thought. A few orphans, a few widows, what did these really matter to the Italian? Caporelli sometimes strutted the stage of his life as if it were a melodrama. Rosabal said, 'I'm not delighted either. But it couldn't be avoided. The alternative was to dump Ruhr.'

'What I also don't like is this manhunt I read about. Every cop in the country is looking for Ruhr. He's too hot.'

'Nobody is going to find him.'

'Still. My gut tells me we should look elsewhere, get somebody else.'

The Cuban said, 'From now on, no more accidents, Enrico. No more mistakes. Smooth,' and he planed the surface of the table with his palm for emphasis. 'You have my word.'

Rafael Rosabal glanced at a nearby table where two middle-aged women drank tea. They had the furrowed brows and glazed eyes of habitual eavesdroppers and they bothered the Cuban, who regularly experienced the sensation that he was being watched or followed. In the Soviet Union recently he knew he'd been observed by the KGB, which was standard practice. Here, in Britain, there might be surveillance from the internal security arm of intelligence. He hadn't seen anyone suspicious, but that didn't mean he *wasn't* being watched. He leaned across the table, closer to Caporelli, whose fussy caution annoyed him. Rosabal understood that the stakes were too high for Enrico to abandon Ruhr at this stage. Caporelli would go with the German in the end, but first there had to be this song and dance.

'We have to trust each other, Enrico,' Rosabal said. 'I need to know that when I return to Cuba you won't change the way things have been set up. I need that assurance. If you drop Ruhr now, you abandon everything. That's the bottom line. Keep this in mind – we want the same thing. We have the same goals.'

The same goals, Caporelli thought. The rich, gravy-filled pie that was Cuba. He said, 'I asked for this meeting because I wanted to find out what safeguards you could give me. But my cup of confidence isn't exactly overflowing, Rafael.'

Rosabal plucked another sugar cube from the bowl. 'What would you have me do? Put Ruhr in a straitjacket until the time comes? He isn't going to be a problem. He's on his best behaviour. I give my word. I stand or fall by that. If my word isn't good enough for you . . . You want to drop the plan, tell me now. The first stage is only two days away.'

Caporelli pinched the bridge of his nose. What were two days when you weighed it against the thirty years that had passed since the barbarians had taken control of the island and given everybody the shaft with their so-called Revolution? Two days: if the first stage went without flaw then he and his associates would see things through to the end.

He looked at Rosabal and what he perceived in the young Cuban's face was bottomless determination and in those dark eyes an intensity of fierce ambition such as he hadn't seen in a long time. He liked these qualities. He liked this young man's conviction. In a world where trust was a debased currency, he trusted Rafael Rosabal, even if he had the feeling that the Cuban sometimes wasn't sure how to walk the fine line between restraint and impatience. A flaw of youth, that was all. A little too much fire in the belly.

'How is the Vedado these days?' he asked. The Vedado was his favourite part of Havana, where the large hotels and enormous private residences had been built. He'd always thought of it as his own sector of the city, his personal domain, and he'd ridden the streets with a proprietorial attitude. He'd been an intimate of former President Batista, who'd conferred honorary Cuban citizenship upon him. He still had a photograph of the ceremony. Government ministers had owed him favours.

He'd owned a magnificent baroque house near the University – cobbled courtyard with bronze statues, mango and pomegranate trees growing against the walls, the smell of the ocean through the open windows of the huge master bedroom. The bathroom had been built out of the finest Italian marble with gold taps, in the shape of gargoyles, created by the kind of proud craftsmen who no longer existed in Castro's shabby socialist paradise. He'd heard that his beautiful house, confiscated in 1959 on behalf of the bullshit Revolution, was now occupied by a department of MINAZ, the Ministry of the Sugar Industry, or one of those other godawful bureaucracies the *fidelistas* were so fond of creating.

He wanted that house again. He wanted it back so badly he ached. He lusted after it with an intensity that was beyond simple greed. It was *his* house; he had always imagined dying in it one day. He could hear the sound of his heels echo in the tiled entrance hall and the laughter of girls in the upstairs room. Tall women, huge breasts, invariably blonde, that was how he'd always liked them. Back then, he'd been blessed with amazing stamina and a lot of lead in his pencil.

But it was more than just the house.

'The Vedado could use a coat of paint,' Rosabal said. 'Like everything else in Cuba.'

Enrico Caporelli rose from his chair and took a pair of leather gloves out of the pocket of his black overcoat.

'Then we must see if we can give it one, Rafael,' he said. 'Fresh paint is one of my favourite smells.'

The rainclouds over Glasgow grew darker and heavier as the limousine left the city and approached the coastal road to Ardrossan and then south to Ayr. On the Firth of Clyde, the stretch of water that eventually became the Irish Sea, the rain turned to mist, drawing a lacy invisibility over the Island of Arran and the imposing mountain called Goat Fell. Once, in a dramatic way, the peak pierced the mist like a fabulous horned creature, but was gone again before Caporelli was sure he'd seen it.

He dozed in the back of the big car, waking every so often to look out at the rainy green countryside or some small town floating past. At Ballantrae, fifty miles from Glasgow, the car turned away from the coast and headed inland on a forlorn road that was rutted and pocked. This narrow strip passed between tall hedgerows. Here and there, where the hedges parted, overgrown meadows sloped toward a distant stand of thick, misty trees. How could any place be this green? The darker the green, the more secretive the landscape. Caporelli had the sensation he was travelling into a kingdom of rainy silences. A secure kingdom, certainly; he saw at least two men with shotguns stalking the spaces between trees.

The house came finally in view, a large sandstone edifice built in the early part of the twentieth century, although its style echoed much earlier times. Circular towers suggested fortresses of the late sixteenth century. Darkened by rain, the house had shed some of its red stone warmth, and looked uninviting. The limousine entered the driveway and came to a stop at the ornate front door, which was immediately opened by Freddie Kinnaird, whose florid face appeared to float through the rain like a balloon escaped from a child's hand.

Caporelli waited until the chauffeur, a taciturn man called Rod, had opened the door for him before he got out. Then, ducking under an umbrella Rod held, he stepped toward the house where Freddie Kinnaird shook his hand vigorously. 'Welcome to Kinnaird's folly.'

They were improbable associates, the beefy red-faced Englishman with hair the colour of sand and the tiny white Italian. Kinnaird placed a hand on Caporelli's elbow and steered him inside the enormous flagstoned hall of the house where a fire burned in the baronial fireplace. Caporelli spread his palms before the flames, thinking he didn't much care for the size of this room or the stuffed animal heads that hung high on the walls – elks, boars, deer. They had the glassy, haunted look of all animals slain before their time.

'Why did you buy this place, Freddie? Did you need something small and intimate?'

Freddie Kinnaird poured two small sherries from a decanter and smiled a generous white-toothed smile. 'It has some obvious benefits. One hundred and twenty acres of thick green countryside, spot of nice fishing, no inquisitive neighbours, which makes security inexpensive. I picked the whole thing up for a song a few years ago. Upkeep's high, but it makes a splendid change from the hurly-burly of dear old London.'

Caporelli took one of the glasses and clinked it lightly against Kinnaird's. There was the standard Society toast, the simple *To the success of friendship*. No matter the language – English, Italian, German or, more recently, Japanese – the form never varied. Freddie Kinnaird tossed a log on the fire and it blazed at once, sending sparks up into the chimney.

'The others are upstairs.' Kinnaird raised his face and looked up at the mahogany gallery. Constructed halfway between floor and ceiling, it ran the length of the wall. 'The Americans arrived half an hour ago.'

'Good,' Caporelli said.

'What did Rosabal say?' Kinnaird set down his empty glass.

'He gave me assurances. I accepted. I like this Rosabal. He's so desperate to deliver I can smell it on him. There's no scent so strong as the musk of sheer goddam ambition. And I trust him. After all, he provided us with the locations of Cuban military defence units and their strength and only an ambitious man, a man who knows what he wants, would go to that kind of trouble. For him it's a simple equation. If he keeps Ruhr under control, he stands a chance of getting his hands on the political machinery of Cuba and all the benefits and patronage that go with the job. President Rosabal. He's in love with the sound of that title. As for us, if the first act doesn't play, we withdraw. We take our losses, check out alternatives.'

'Not a notion I relish. The mere idea of starting all over again overwhelms me.'

The Italian smiled. 'I don't think we'll have to.'

Kinnaird picked up his empty glass and studied it, looking like a professor of archaeology surprised by some odd find. 'Before we go up, Enrico, you should be prepared for some opposition to Ruhr.'

Caporelli dismissed the threat. 'Tssss. I think I can convince them to wait and see. Where do you stand, Freddie?'

'With you,' Kinnaird said. 'But the holocaust in Shepherd's Bush has left me with a very bad taste in my mouth. Nobody expected that, least of all me.'

'You can do one of two things with a bad taste,' Caporelli said. 'Swallow it. Or spit it out. What you can't do is gargle it, Freddie.'

'What have you done with yours?' Kinnaird asked.

'I swallowed the sonofabitch.'

They climbed upstairs to the gallery and moved through a warren of rooms, most of them unfurnished and only half-decorated. Ladders and rolls of wallpaper and paint cans were scattered everywhere. Plaster had been stripped, revealing lathe underneath. Kinnaird made excuses for the state of things. Local workmen were slow, and supplies sometimes had to be ordered from Glasgow or London. There was more than a touch of *mañana* in this part of the world. Caporelli followed his host, noticing how the high ceilings were lost in shadow. Long windows were rattled by rain squalls. Outside, trees shuddered in the black wet wind.

Finally Kinnaird led the way inside a room that resembled a corporate boardroom. Men sat at a large oval table and the air, thick with tobacco smoke, hung over their heads like ectoplasm. Velvet curtains had been drawn across the windows and little fringed lamps were lit, imparting an atmosphere of genteel clubiness. A drinks cabinet provided a variety of expensive Scotches and vintage brandy. What made this gathering different from any board-meeting was the fact that the table was bare. No papers, no notepads, no folders, no pens. The men here didn't take notes. They were forbidden by their own statutes to create reminders or memoranda of these gatherings.

Enrico Caporelli moved to the empty chair at the top of the table, his place as Director. He sat down, looked round. There was uncertainty here, but Caporelli knew he could play his colleagues like an orchestra. In the past he'd steered them, by sheer force of personality and some theatrical ability, into decisions they'd been reluctant to make.

Apart from himself, there were six dark-suited men around the table; of this number, only the Americans presented any kind of real obstacle. The German, Rudolf Kluger, a sombre, bespectacled man with the smooth discretionary air of a banker from Frankfurt, usually agreed with Caporelli. The French representative, Jean-Paul Chapotin, who was a handsome silver-haired man in his late fifties, generally came into line after some initial Gallic posturing. Freddie Kinnaird, by his own admission, was a foregone conclusion. The thin, unsmiling Japanese member, Kenzaburo Magiwara, who had the appearance of a man who carries important secrets in his skull, frequently agreed with the majority because he believed there was strength through unity. Otherwise why had the Society of Friends endured? Caporelli reflected on how the Japanese had only recently been admitted, a gesture in the direction of changing times.

And then the Americans! Who could predict the reactions of Sheridan Perry and his companion, the gaunt man known as Hurt? They had that quiet arrogance found in some Americans. It was the understated yet persistent superiority of people who think they have invented the twentieth century and franchised it to the rest of the world.

Sheridan Perry, flabby in his middle age like some fifty-year-old cherub, and Harry Hurt, lean as only a compulsive jogger can look – how could they appear so dissimilar and yet both emit a quality Caporelli found slightly sinister? They were an ambitious pair with the ease and confidence of men who come from a reality in which ambition is to be encouraged and pursued. It was no dirty little word, it was a way of life.

Hurt was an athlete who had graduated from Princeton and then spent many years in the military, rising to the elevated rank of Lieutenant-General. Later, he'd been an advisor in such outposts as Nicaragua and El Salvador. He sometimes seemed to be issuing orders to invisible subordinates, men of limited mental capacity, when he talked. Perry, whose jowls overhung the collar of his shirt, came from old midwestern money: railroads and banks and farmlands. He had been educated at Harvard Business School but there was still the vague suggestion of the provincial about him. True sophistication was just beyond him, something that lay over the next ridge. He reminded Caporelli of a man who knew how to talk and how to choose his suits and shirts but in the final analysis some small detail always betrayed him, perhaps his cologne, perhaps his mouthwash.

Caporelli observed the two Americans a moment. He had himself spent many profitable years in the United States and still maintained homes on Long Island and in Florida. He had a great fondness for Americans despite his aversion to their rather unshakable conviction in the correctness of their own moral vision. In this sense, Hurt and Perry were typical. But this narrowness of perception, this self-righteousness, also made the two Americans good capitalists. Unfortunately, though, they tended to think of the Society as something they deserved to own.

Now Caporelli cleared his throat and ran quickly through some items of business that in other circumstances would have been considered important. The manipulation of South African diamond prices, the request of a deposed Asian dictator to launder enormous sums of stolen money, the opportunity to purchase a controlling interest in a score of troubled American savings and loans banks, the question of funding a weakening military junta in a South American republic notorious for political turbulence. These were the usual affairs with which the Society concerned itself during its long and sometimes argumentative half-yearly meetings.

Today Caporelli dispensed with all this quickly. He knew there was only one real item on the agenda and the members were impatient to get to it. He spoke in the kind of voice he reserved for wakes. He summarised the situation, moving nimbly over recent 'unhappy events in London' and insisting on the need to look at the larger picture. He reiterated his faith in the plan that had been concocted years before. Why tinker with running clockwork? He admitted Ruhr had brought a volatile element into the situation, but Rafael Rosabal, a trustworthy man, had pledged his word: everything was in place. And the timing was ah, *perfetto*. How long could the Soviets go on funding Castro's private little reality at a time when they were tightening their purse strings all over the globe? Cuba, already an economic leper, was certain to be disowned by its niggardly Russian masters. An orphaned Cuba, weak, neglected. Who could wish for a better opportunity?

When he saw doubtful expressions on the faces of some members he became eloquent, reminding them of the prize to be won. An island paradise presently run by 'animals', Cuba was a prime piece of Caribbean real estate, a tropical delight, a licence to print money. His delivery was good, his manner confident. As a final gesture in the direction of the Americans, Caporelli spoke of the moral imperative involved in the plan. What could be more right than the end of a corrupt regime?

He sat down. He sipped from a glass of water. Not such a bad performance, he thought.

Sheridan Perry spoke in one of those flat voices in which you could hear two things: the winds of the Great Plains and an underlay of Harvard Yard. He said, 'As you point out, Enrico, the elements are present. But how can you be sure Ruhr is under control?'

Enrico Caporelli shrugged. 'I can't say with one hundred per cent certainty he's going to be a pussycat, Sheridan. There's never such certainty in anything.'

Sheridan Perry had a nice smile and perfect little teeth. 'Ruhr screwed up with the hooker in England and God knows he might do it again. Why didn't you let him rot in jail? Why compound the problem by giving the go-ahead to some completely reckless rescue – planned, incidentally, by Rosabal, your man of honour?'

'I exercised my judgment as Director. There were excesses.'

Sheridan Perry raised his eyebrows. 'Judgment, Enrico? Excesses? The London incident has shocked all of us in this room. The Society can't condone that kind of violence. Matter of interest, how much did your Shepherd's Bush extravaganza cost us?'

Enrico Caporelli mentioned a figure that was in excess of two hundred thousand pounds. 'A drop in the ocean,' he added. 'Compared with what's at stake.'

Harry Hurt talked now in his patient, slightly professional way. 'Money aside, we don't kill defenders of law and order, because it promotes anarchy. The Society has never done that. We stabilise regimes. We don't *undermine* them. Unless they're run by bandits.'

'Like Cuba,' Sheridan Perry said.

In spite of Perry's hostility, Caporelli had the feeling the Americans would support the plan finally, but they were after something in return. He'd known Perry and Hurt for too many years not to recognise the signs: the air of collusion, the sense that they'd rehearsed their position before the meeting. Caporelli remembered Perry's father from fifteen years ago, a banker with a rough tongue who'd imparted both his position in the Society and his self-righteousness to Sheridan.

'We want your word.' Sheridan Perry stared at Caperelli with an evangelical look, very sincere, as if he had salvation to sell. 'We want your *solemn* word, Enrico. If Ruhr blows it again, you'll offer your resignation. We want that promise.'

So that was it. Caporelli wasn't entirely surprised. Perry lusted after the Director's chair, which he'd missed by only two votes last time.

'I give it gladly,' Caporelli said. The Directorship didn't enthrall him. It had some advantages. It gave one a certain freedom to make a decision on one's own. But that same freedom was also a heavy responsibility and he wasn't intrigued by titles these days anyway. All he really wanted was what was owed him – with interest. Accounts had to be balanced before they could be closed, and his Cuban account had gone unsettled for far too long.

Caporelli solicited the other members around the table. A vote was taken: the plan would proceed. If the first stage wasn't completed, the scheme would be aborted. The Director's promise of resignation was noted.

Caporelli, who felt he'd won a tiny victory, looked at Hurt. 'Let's go on to the next item of business – Harry's report on the situation in Central America.'

Harry Hurt had jogged all round Kinnaird's estate earlier. Then he'd showered, and meditated for twenty minutes, and now he exuded the glow of sheer good health. He sat at the table like a human lamp. 'There are no problems. Everything's primed. Officially, the Hondurans accept the story we're constructing a resort fifty miles from Cabo Gracias a Dios. Unofficially, they know we're doing something else. It's costly to bridge that gap between the official and unofficial perception in Central America. Everybody's schizophrenic down there. We forge ahead, greasing palms as we go. The airstrip's finished. We're rolling.'

'How many men are assembled now?' Chapotin asked.

'Twelve hundred,' Hurt said.

'And what will the total commitment be?' Magiwara asked.

'Fifteen. But we could go with twelve.' Hurt smiled his jogger's angular grin. 'In point of fact, we could take the whole goddam Caribbean first thing in the morning and still have time for ham and eggs in Key West. If we wanted.'

The room was silent. Caporelli looked at the faces, waiting for further questions or comments. Harry Hurt always spoke with such authority that he left no doors open. When it came to military matters, he was the resident expert. It was known that he had friends in high places in Washington who had assisted, if only indirectly, in the creation of the military force in Honduras.

Caporelli stood up slowly. He declared the meeting adjourned.

He left the room as drinks were being poured and chairs pushed back. The formality of the meeting diminished in more relaxed small talk. What Freddie Kinnaird had called 'the holocaust in London' had already been assimilated by the members and subjugated to the prospect of profit, as if it were nothing more than a delayed cargo or an adverse stock market or a foreign currency plummeting, just another item of business. The Society of Friends had absorbed many shocks in its history. It had always survived them.

Freddie Kinnaird, a gracious host, had placed a bedroom at Caporelli's disposal. Perched at the top of a tower, it was round with slit-like windows. Caporelli removed his suit and silk underwear and lay down naked, listening to the relentless rush of wind and rain on the tower. He closed his eyes.

He remembered Cuba.

He remembered that April morning in 1959 when the three *barbudos* had come to his house in the Vedado. They wore green fatigues. With their beards they might have been cloned from a sliver of Fidel's flesh. They carried revolvers and their boots thudded on the Italian marble entrance. They'd been drinking, still celebrating Fidel's success. It was a twilight time, Caporelli recalled, between hope and fear of disappointment. Soon the Revolution would deteriorate in mass arrests, firing-squads, disgusting show-trials, expulsions, Communism. For the moment it was still something to celebrate, if you were a *fidelista*. The *barbudos* were led by a man who called himself Major Estrada, a fat man with a black beard and a face pitted with old acne. He wore green-tinted glasses. Even now, Caporelli could envisage him with astonishing clarity: the pockmarks, the flake of spinach or parsley lodged in the beard, the brown teeth, the black eyes hidden behind cheap green glass.

Major Estrada flashed a crumpled piece of paper under Caporelli's face, a 'document of transfer' so hastily printed the ink was still damp. It was as if the Revolution had rushed to bestow legality on itself. In the name of the Revolution, all Caporelli's property was to be confiscated. This included the house in the Vedado, the Hotel St Clara located on Aguir Street near the Havana Stock Exchange, the apartment buildings on A Street and First, the large General Motors dealership at the corner of 25th and Hospital. They wanted it all.

Major Estrada took his revolver from his belt and waved it in the air. Caporelli, he said, was little better than a parasite sucking the blood of the poor. Caporelli had been thirty years old at the time, brashly confident that his powerful associates could clarify this misunderstanding quickly. But he'd misread the Revolution. Those of his friends who hadn't left the island had smelled the wind and were busy stashing such money as they could before Castro took it from them.

Caporelli made futile phone calls while Estrada's two soldiers ransacked the house. They created a destructive passage through the place – broken glass, mirrors, overturned vases, silk curtains hauled from windows, statues riddled with gunfire.

The American girl asleep in the upstairs bedroom, a dancer called Lynette, a passionate young woman Caporelli had stolen from a floor show, was wakened by the noise of the soldiers. Caporelli remembered hearing her swear at them and then she appeared, wrapped in a peach-coloured silk robe, at the top of the stairs.

'What the hell's going on, Enrico?'

'Tell the young woman to shut up and get dressed,' Estrada said.

Caporelli shrugged. Either he defied the Major to impress the girl, or he obeyed Estrada and looked feeble in his own house.

The girl said, 'Enrico, can't you get rid of these guys?'

Estrada said, 'Why don't you do that, Enrico?'

Caporelli turned to look at the Major, who was smiling, enormously pleased with the situation. Then he faced the girl again, whose silk robe shimmered in the sun that streamed through a skylight above her. Angelic, Caporelli thought. How could he disappoint this angel?

He was about to say something when Estrada tried to press the piece of paper into his hand. It was of extreme importance to the Major to serve the document. He was a bailiff of La Revolución, a process server for the new order, and he took the task seriously.

'You must accept the paper,' he said. 'As for the girl, tell her to get dressed and leave. She has no future here.'

From the top of the stairs the girl put a little whine into her voice and said, 'Enrico, what the hell do these characters want? Can't you do something about them? They're tearing your house apart.'

Caporelli looked at the paper, refused to accept it. 'Stick the document up your ass,' he told Estrada.

It was a moment in which Enrico Caporelli was pleased with the sheer beauty of defiance, a heightened moment wherein he had a sense of his own unlimited potential. He perceived himself through the eyes of the girl and he was beautiful and cocksure and eternal.

Major Estrada struck Caporelli across the face with his pistol. The girl screamed, a shrill noise that reverberated across marble surfaces. Nauseated by pain, embarrassed, Caporelli slipped to the marble floor. He couldn't remember now if he'd lost consciousness for thirty seconds or five minutes: there was a dark passage at the end of which was Estrada's hand holding the gun, pushing the barrel between Caporelli's lips.

Caporelli felt the warm gun against the roof of his mouth. He was aware of the smell of booze on the man's breath. Alcohol and revolutionary fervour. The Major was capable of anything. On the landing, the girl was holding the corner of her silk robe to her mouth. She'd believed Caporelli was protected by the powers in Cuba, that he had the kind of clout which made him impregnable. Last night he'd been tireless, a demon lover, coming at her time and again with a remorseless quality that was extraordinary even in her wide experience. Now he was reduced. He looked tiny to her down there in the entrance hall, and sad.

'Take the paper,' Estrada said, and released the safety catch. It was the most lethal sound Caporelli had ever heard. Nevertheless, he defied the Cuban again. He said *Piss off*, his tongue dry upon the steel barrel.

'*Payaso*,' Estrada said, and shoved the gun hard. Caporelli made pitiful retching noises. Later, he thought how little dignity there was in the situation. Stark fear diminished you, reduced you to nothing. Everything you imagined yourself to be was peeled away from you, and nothing else mattered but the proximity of the weapon and the fact that your heart was still beating and you were prepared to strike any kind of deal to keep it pumping. The presence of the girl was already forgotten. The idea that she witnessed this shameful incident meant nothing to him just then.

Estrada took a rosary from his tunic and ran the beads through the fingers of one hand. 'God have mercy on you,' he whispered. '*Adios*.'

And then the little scene, poised so bleakly on the edge of death, dissolved in laughter as Estrada wrenched the gun out of Caporelli's mouth. The two soldiers, who had reappeared, were also laughing; it was the raucous laughter of drunks enjoying a great joke. Caporelli shut his eyes. His stomach had dropped. His mouth flooded with viscous saliva. He thought he felt a warm trickle of urine against his inner thigh, and he prayed it wouldn't show.

Estrada said, 'Now, Enrico. Take the paper.'

Caporelli reached out without opening his eyes but Estrada, teasing, held the document away from the outstretched hand. The girl was immobile on the landing.

'Let me hear you beg a little, Enrico, or I stick the gun back in your mouth. Only this time no joke.'

'I beg,' Caporelli said. Although he couldn't see her, he was conscious of the girl moving now, the hem of her robe brushing the marble staircase.

'For what?'

There was dryness in Caporelli's mouth. 'I beg you. Give me the paper.'

Caporelli's hand closed around the document. Estrada reached down, patted him on the head. Like a dog, a pet that had misbehaved and was now to be banished.

'Big shot, eh? Friend of Batista, eh? You think you own Havana! The Revolution is stronger than you and all your friends, *compañero*. The Revolution will bring you and your friends to their fucking knees! Now you've got ten minutes to get the hell out of here. Pack what you can carry in a small suitcase and go. Cuba doesn't need you. Cuba doesn't need your women.'

Caporelli listened to the sound of the three men strut across the courtyard. He remained on his knees for a long time afterwards, humiliated, ashamed by his failure of nerve. Why hadn't he gone on defying Estrada? Why had he caved in and begged? The answer was devastatingly simple: he'd been to a place he'd never visited before in his young life, the borderline between living and dying. It was a place without sunshine and women, a terrifying place where all your money and power didn't amount to shit. Life was better than death, even if humiliation was the price you paid.

When he stood up he saw the embarrassing trickle of urine on the marble, and he cleaned it with a white linen handkerchief monogrammed with the initials EC. The girl was standing over him.

She said, 'Oh Enrico,' and then she was silent and he couldn't decide what was in her tone, whether disappointment or horror, embarrassment or sympathy.

Thirty years later, he could still hear the mocking laughter of the men. He could see Estrada's scarred face and the expensive handkerchief stained with piss. He could still feel the pistol against the roof of his mouth and smell the girl's perfume. He trembled with rage when he remembered Estrada's control of the situation, and his own disgrace in the presence of the girl.

He sat up, took his wallet from his jacket. He flipped it open, removed a crumpled sheet of paper. He smoothed it on the bed, his hand trembling the way it always did when he remembered Major Estrada. It was the document of transfer, the *traspaso de propiedad*. He had made up his mind a long time ago that he wasn't going to destroy this forlorn keepsake until he was back in Havana.

He closed his eyes. How could you count what Cuba had cost him? In monetary terms he'd been robbed of three million dollars in 1959, worth about seventy million thirty years later. But he had a melancholy sense of having lost something other than money: Estrada had stripped him of honour. But Estrada wasn't the real culprit. It was Castro, whose shadow fell like that of a great dark vulture across Cuba. It was Castro who had robbed him and it was Castro against whom he would have his revenge.

5 London

Frank Pagan's unit, officially known as SATO, the Special Anti-Terrorist Operation, occupied two floors of an anonymous building in Golden Square in Soho. The unit had come into existence in 1979 as a specific response to Irish terrorism. In the middle of the 1980s it had been disbanded and integrated into the structure of other Scotland Yard departments. Last year, however, at the direction of Martin Burr, the unit was revived and its charter expanded beyond Irish matters. Pagan, despite internal opposition at Scotland Yard from men who resented the publicity he'd generated in his career, had been named officer in charge. Small minds, Burr had said. Small people. Pagan had a screw you attitude to these gnomes who criticised his personal style, his fashionable suits and coloured shirts, the American Camaro he drove, the rock and roll he favoured. He did not fit comfortably into the Yard hierarchy, which was not known for its flexibility in any case. He possessed a streak of energetic individuality, considered very close to anarchy by those who disapproved of him.

On this cold evening in October, Pagan sat at the window of his office and looked down into the darkness of Golden Square. He had secured his release from hospital that same afternoon by the simple if painful expedient of rising from the bed, dressing in the clothes brought to him by his assistant Foxworth, and strolling past the nurses' station. He'd been assailed at once by the staff nurse, a bollard of a woman who ruled the wards with a tyrant's flair. She'd prevented Pagan's exit until Dr Ghose could be summoned. When the physician arrived, he'd berated Pagan for taking things into his own hands, but he'd seen a strong resolve in the Englishman that was outside his experience. What else could he do but permit Pagan freedom on the condition that he change his bandage once every day, take his painkillers and antibiotics, refrain from any energetic activity, and return within three days for a check-up?

Loaded with gauze and bandages, armed with prescriptions, uttering lavish promises, Pagan stepped out into the late afternoon a free man. The adrenalin rush of liberty hadn't lasted long before he discovered that his freedom wasn't from pain. Inside the taxi on the way to Golden Square he doubled over, clutching his chest and alarming Foxie, who didn't know what to do. Pagan swallowed a painkiller and the fit passed shortly thereafter, but it drained him, leaving him paler than before.

Now, sitting at the window of his office, he poured himself a small shot of Auchentoshan, a Lowland malt whisky of unsurpassed smoothness he'd begun to drink lately. Combined with Pethidine, it banished all misery. It encased the brain in a velvet envelope.

'How do you feel?' Foxworth asked. He sat on the opposite side of Pagan's desk. He was a tall man, the same height as Frank Pagan. His bright red hair was cut short, but it still resembled an unmanageable bush.

'I feel like something a dog might throw up. But I thank my lucky yaw I'm still alive,' Pagan replied.

'A good yaw's priceless,' Foxie remarked. He'd been Pagan's assistant during SATO's first incarnation. Pagan had recently rescued him from the Forgery squad to bring him back into the fold. Foxie had been horrified by the shooting in Shepherd's Bush. Pagan's wounding in particular was too close to home, too unnerving. A darkness had coursed through the whole unit at the news. Detectives, even those who disliked Pagan, moped in their partitioned offices, awaiting hospital bulletins.

Now that Pagan had come back work was in progress again, but Foxie thought his return premature. Frank was pallid, and the diet of malt whisky and drugs wasn't likely to be beneficial, no matter how strong his constitution might be. It was vintage Pagan. He couldn't keep away. Gunther Ruhr was preying on him, burning a hole in his brain.

Foxie studied his superior a moment. There was a new gauntness about Frank's features. He looked like a bleached-out holograph of himself, as if he were on the edge of fading away entirely. There was the usual flinty light of determination in Pagan's grey eyes but it seemed faintly manic to Foxworth.

Pagan stood up. His shadow fell across the massive pop-art silk-screen of Buddy Holly that dominated the wall behind him, a splash of extraordinary colour in a room that was otherwise white walled and merely functional. 'Let's start with this dead Australian,' he said.

'I'm a little ahead of you, Frank,' Foxworth said. He reached for Pagan's in-tray and retrieved a telex that had come from Sydney only that morning. 'It's not exciting.'

Pagan stared at the report. it said only that the man killed in Shepherd's Bush was one Ralph Masters, age fifty, a former sergeant in the Australian Army. There was a brief mention of the man's mercenary activities, but no criminal record. He lived alone, no known relatives. 'A bloody bore,' Pagan remarked. 'Is that the best they can send us? Excuse me if I nod off.'

'I'll follow it up by telephone later,' Foxie said.

Pagan looked across the square. It was eight-thirty and the streets were quiet and a faint mist adhered to the lamps. By altering his angle slightly he could see taxis cruise along Beak Street. In the other direction he could see the glow from the harsh, frosted lights of Piccadilly.

'I'll need the usual list.'

'It's already here,' Foxie said, patting the in-tray. 'Updated this very morning.'

'You're fast, Foxie.'

'Greased lightning. That's me.'

Pagan stared at the lengthy computer print-out Foxworth passed to him. Prepared by the Home Office and available to a variety of law enforcement agencies, it was a list of people who had entered the United Kingdom recently, and whose names appeared on the Home Office data base under the category 'questionable'. This included visitors involved in political activity in their homelands, alleged radicals, Communists, businessmen employed in dubious concerns (for example, suspected of having narcotics connections), anti-monarchists, and assorted others. The list showed a high preponderance of Libyans, Irishmen, Iranians, Palestinians and Colombians. None of those named had been denied entry into the country. They weren't considered 'undesirable' enough for that measure. The 'undesirables' belonged on another catalogue altogether and were usually detained, interviewed, then deported before they had more than a couple of lungfuls of British air.

'Have you run these names through our own computers?' Pagan asked. The length of the print-out depressed him. There must have been more than four hundred individuals. Was all the world's riff-raff cheerfully entering this green land?

'It's being done even as we speak,' Foxie said.

'You're really on top of things here, aren't you? I should have stayed in hospital.'

'Which would have shown remarkable judgment, Frank.'

Pagan squeezed out a small smile and sat down. He went into a slump for a moment. Where the hell did you start? Where did you go to find Ruhr? It struck him as an overwhelming task. Looking for a terrorist in hiding was going to be the kind of thing where luck, that grinning bitch, would play a significant role. Or sheer doggedness. Pagan much preferred flair, the sudden insight, the flash of knowing, to all the humdrum police procedures of knocking on doors and slogging the streets and interviewing people who thought they were about to be arrested for old parking fines.

'Are you sure you're all right?' Foxie asked.

'Do me a favour, Foxie. Stop looking at me as if I'm going to collapse in a coma.'

'Sorry.'

'I'm not about to keel over. Understand?' Pagan rattled the print-out, just a little annoyed by the concerned look on Foxworth's face. Was he destined to be scrutinised at every turn by his fellow officers looking for signs of infirmity? 'Where was I?'

'The list, Frank.'

'Right. The list. The trouble is, the people who rescued Ruhr aren't likely to show up on any damned list. The Australian didn't. Why should we expect any of the others to be co-operative enough to make an appearance? It's just not on. I don't think we can expect any leads to Gunther from the print-out. Besides, the people who rescued Ruhr might be home-grown talent, Foxie, and they wouldn't be on this index. The only import might have been the Aussie.'

'Could be.'

'What the hell, it's procedure, and we'll follow it, but I'm not getting my hopes up.' Pagan put the print-out aside, sipped his drink. He set the empty glass down. 'Another thing, Foxie. I don't want any information leaving this office unless it's cleared by me personally. If there's a leak, I don't want it being traced back here. I want a scrambler on my line to the Commissioner's office.'

'Noted,' Foxworth said.

'Do you have reports on the search for Ruhr? Is there any pattern?'

Foxie shook his head. 'The usual hysteria, Frank. The good people of the land peer from behind lace curtains and think, Ah-hah, Gunther the Beast is lurking in the shrubbery. The mass imagination. Wonderful thing.'

Pagan sighed. 'Where does that leave us, Foxie?'

'There's the rub. Where indeed?'

Pagan gazed through the window again. He was thinking of the terrorist groups and their supporters in the darkness of this great city, loose clans of rightists, leftists, Leninists, Marxists, Marxist-Leninists, white supremacists, radicals who plotted to overthrow the monarchy (a notion with which Pagan sometimes had a modicum of sympathy), Libyans who sat in Mayfair and paid vast sums of money for explosives and weapons, Palestinians in Earl's Court scheming to get their homeland back – they were out there in the dark corners, murmuring, planning, talking to themselves, in an atmosphere of paranoia.

Pagan had had encounters with a great variety of them, from the silly groups that consisted of two or three very lonely people putting doomed homemade bombs together in garden sheds to groups like the Libyans, some of whom lived in bullet-proof apartments in the West End and controlled banks and had access to funds beyond reckoning. He knew their worlds. He knew that if there was to be any useful information about Ruhr and his associates it would be out there among the sympathisers and the financiers and fellow-travellers. It could be anything, an item of gossip, a whispered rumour, the kind of information that never percolated up from street level to official channels. And he wasn't going to get it sitting in Golden Square.

'I think I need a ride in the fresh air, Foxie. Will you get us a car?'

'A car?' Foxie thought that an early night would be the best thing for Pagan, but didn't say so.

'Car. Four wheels, chassis, internal combustion device – you remember?'

Foxie smiled, picked up the telephone.

The car was a Rover and Foxworth drove, following directions given to him by Pagan, who constantly consulted a small red notebook. This, Foxie realised, was Chairman Frank's famous Red Book, in which were said to be inscribed the names and addresses of all Pagan's connections in the terrorist network. It was Foxie's first sight of the legendary book.

They went first to an apartment belonging to Syrians in Dover Street, Mayfair, then to a Libyan house in Kensington, disturbing people who watched TV or prepared evening meals. At the Kensington house a black-tie party was going on, ladies in cocktail dresses, delicate little sausages on toothpicks. Pagan didn't care that his timing was terrible. He was, Foxie noticed, in full flight and for the moment at least like the Pagan of old. No formalities, no niceties of etiquette, were going to get in his way. He helped himself to coffee, swallowed a sausage, and looked around as if the dinner-party wasn't taking place at all. There was a lot of surly conversation, the kind that originates in suspicion and outright resentment. *We don't know Gunther Ruhr. We don't know anything about him or his friends. We are innocent of any illegal activities, Mr Pagan – kindly leave us in peace or speak to our lawyers.* They all had lawyers nowadays, Pagan thought. They all had smooth-faced men in pricey pinstripes who manipulated legal niceties for hefty fees. Lawyers appalled Pagan. They had the moral awareness of toadstools and the untrammelled greed of very small spoiled children.

Next, a basement flat in Chelsea occupied by a group of very intense men who called themselves The Iranian Revolutionary Front aka TIRF. Acronyms were like test-tubes in which radicals appeared to spawn. If you didn't have a decent acronym you didn't have an image, and without an image no new recruits. TIRF opposed both the new Ayatollah and American imperialism. Pagan tried to goad them by asking about the ideological confusion in such a position but they didn't want to be drawn into a dialogue with a reactionary policeman, the representative of a monarchy. They'd suffered under the Shah and to them the Queen of England might have been Pahlevi's wicked sister. The Iranians barely raised their faces from their bowls of rice, avoiding eye-contact with both Pagan and Foxworth. A sulky zero there.

Across the river after that, to a house overlooking Battersea Park where a bald West German in a velvet smoking-jacket spoke in a knowledgeable manner about the terrorist connections between Europe and Northern Ireland. *Perhaps Ruhr's working for the Irish, Mr Pagan,* the German suggested. Why import Ruhr? Pagan wondered. The Irish had their own gangsters.

From Battersea to Wandsworth. In a prim semidetached house a lovely young Czech woman, who had been arrested once for her membership in a gang of terrorists that had made an elaborate attempt to bomb the Russian Embassy in Bonn, brewed cups of herbal tea and denounced Gunther Ruhr for 'excessive violence'. She didn't know where to find him, nor had she any idea who had rescued him. In pursuit of the quiet life, she'd lost touch with her former associates. Now she grew organic vegetables and consulted the *I Ching* and breast-fed a baby that had begun to cry in an adjoining room. Like everyone else encountered during this strange tour of Pagan's London, she knew nothing, heard nothing. All was blind silence and frustration. Houses in Camberwell and Whitechapel, inhabited by Lebanese and Palestinians respectively, brought similar results. Absolutely no information about Gunther Ruhr or his employers or his rescuers made the underground circuit. Final.

On the way back to Golden Square Pagan said, 'A waste of bloody time.'

'At least you put the word out,' Foxie said.

'A fat lot of good, Foxie. Whoever employs Ruhr works in complete secrecy. And the rescue operation might have been carried out by phantoms. Nobody knows a damn thing.'

Pagan and Foxworth rode in the lift, an ancient iron coffin that clanged and rocked up to the second floor. Inside his office Pagan had another small taste of Auchentoshan and settled down behind his desk. He was out of breath. He'd gone beyond mere fatigue. He was in another world where you couldn't quit trust the evidence of the senses. It was like jet-lag magnified, almost as if you saw the world reflected in bevelled mirrors. He stared at the darkened window, listening to the faint whirring of the three computers on the floor below. It was just after midnight and the silence of the streets accentuated the noise of the electronics, which were sinister to Pagan because he had no affinity with them.

I got up from my deathbed for you, Ruhr, he thought. I got up and I walked. You could at least provide me with a hint. You could at least tell me how much time I have left before you do something monstrous. The time factor! It was unsettling to be adrift on a planet whose only clock belonged to Guitther Ruhr.

Foxworth came into the office with a computer printout. 'This is what you wanted. Our computers analysed all four hundred and seventeen names on the Home Office list, all people who arrived in the United Kingdom in the last month. Out of that lot, there are twenty-nine on whom we have active files of our own.'

Pagan scanned the sheets with blurred eyes. Twenty-nine match-ups. That was practically a crowd. He had only eight investigators at his disposal. It wasn't possible to conduct twenty-nine investigations simultaneously. Even if he managed it somehow, by borrowing men from other departments, how could he be sure he wasn't wasting manpower and time? Since it was almost a certainty that neither Ruhr nor his associates had entered the UK legally, the names on the list would yield nothing. Twenty-nine!

'I think I'll stretch out on the sofa,' he said. 'Get some of the weight off my feet.'

Foxworth frowned. 'Wouldn't you be better off going home, Frank? Happy to drive you.'

Pagan shook his head.

Determined bastard, Foxie thought. Frank had to have the constitution of a Clydesdale.

Pagan walked very slowly to the couch in the corner of the office. It was an old horsehair piece, overstuffed and creaky and cratered. Even though he lay down with great care, a shaft of pain pierced him and he moaned slightly. When you thought you had it silenced for the night, back it came just to remind you you're no longer master of your own system.

'I'd like a map,' Pagan said. 'A decent one that covers the whole Cambridge area.'

'I have one in my own office.'

'Bring it in here and pin it above my desk, will you?'

'Right away.' Briskly, eager to please, even to pamper him, Foxie stepped out.

Flat on his back, Pagan raised the computer print-out above his eyes and squinted at the list of names. Beneath each name was nationality, followed by the reasons why the person had been entered in SATO's computers in the first place. There was a Dutchman called Vanderberg known for his skill in building custom rifles, an American who had some questionable connections in the Lebanon, an Italian journalist notorious for his radical left-wing sympathies and his 'exclusive' interviews – florid and sycophantic – with fugitive terrorists. If Pagan couldn't find the time and manpower to run a check on the people who had access to the allegedly secret route used on the night of the Shepherd's Bush disaster, how could he justify the investigation of these twenty-nine, not one of whom suggested a plausible bridge to Gunther Ruhr?

And yet how could he know for sure? Thoroughness was a bloody dictator. If you were Frank Pagan, you were imprisoned by your own exactitude. Everyone on the list would have to be contacted, interviewed, even if only briefly, or watched. The likely outcome was that all twenty-nine would be eliminated from having any association with Gunther Ruhr. End of the matter. Heigh-ho. The joys of police work. The enviable glamour.

He was about to set the print-out aside, and ponder the matter of delegating the inquiries to cops purloined from some other department, when he noticed a name at the foot of the second page.

It blinded him at first. He thought he'd hallucinated it, a set of letters created by the morphine-like effect of Pethidine. He shut his eyes, hearing Foxie come inside the room, hearing Foxie say something about a map, noises off-stage, off-centre, as if Foxworth had stepped toward the outer limits of the world and could barely be heard. Pagan opened his eyes. It was still there. Unchanged.

Dear Christ, how many years had passed?

Pagan turned his face toward Foxworth, who was standing on a chair and tacking the map to the wall.

'Foxie,' Pagan said.

Foxworth stepped down from the chair and moved across the room to the sofa. He thought Frank looked very odd all at once, as if more than pain troubled him.

'What's the matter? Is something wrong?' he asked.

Pagan pointed to the name on the sheet. Foxie looked closely. It meant nothing to him.

'I'd like to know where this person can be found, Foxie.'

'It may take a little time.'

'Do it.'

There was an uncharacteristic note in Pagan's voice, the grumpy irritability of somebody confronted by a puzzle he couldn't understand, one he thought he'd solved a long time ago.

Foxie wrote the name down.

From the window of her hotel room, Magdalena Torrente saw the expanse of darkness that was Hyde Park. Black and whispering, it created a shadow at the heart of London. It was a long time since Magdalena had been in England. It would be pleasant to come one day as a tourist, spend some time, see sights. This trip, like the last one, was going to be brief.

The last time here: she didn't want to think about that.

She shut the window, looked at her watch. It was two a.m. She moved across the room, pushed the bathroom door open, saw her own reflection in the fluorescent glare of the tiled room, dark circles under her eyes and colourless lips. She considered make-up, but he didn't like her in cosmetics. A real woman, he sometimes said, doesn't need to paint herself into falsehood.

She lay on the bed. The lift rumbled in the shaft along the corridor. It stopped; the doors slid open. Magdalena closed her eyes and listened carefully. The thick carpet in the hallway muffled the movement of anyone passing. *Do you trust him?* She wondered why Garrido's objectionable question came back to her now. Old men knew how to ask tiresome questions. Old men with ambitions, like Garrido, could be especially taxing. Running out of time, they needed answers in a hurry. All their questions were blunt ones. *Do you trust him?*

She heard the key turn in the lock. She pretended to sleep. It was part of a lover's game. He would kiss her awake from a sleep he knew wasn't genuine. He came inside the room very quietly and crossed the floor and she felt the mattress yield as he sat down beside her. He raised her hands to his lips. She felt her pulses jump and her heartbeat rage. He did this to her without fail. The touch of his flesh made her fall apart, a sweet disintegration that was like nothing else she'd ever felt. She lost herself along the way, imploded, turned to fragments. Sometimes she couldn't remember her own name. Love's amnesia. She had no patience when it came to him. She took his hand and guided it between her legs. Her short skirt – he liked them short – slipped up her thighs. She wore nothing under the skirt. His hand went directly to the core of her and she gasped because she felt as if he'd penetrated some secret she'd been keeping from the rest of the world. He knew her in the most intimate ways, the deepest ways. She spread her legs, astounded by her own wetness. His finger went inside her and she moaned, biting on her lip because she knew she'd scream if she didn't keep her mouth closed. She turned slightly, reaching out for him. He was hard and ready and beautiful. Her lover. Her love. She said his name once, twice, lingering over syllables until they became meaninglessly joyful, less like sounds than delicate tastes in her mouth.

He tugged the skirt from her hips, slid the blouse from her shoulders. He kissed her breasts, her throat, her mouth, and each time his lips touched her skin she felt a delightful giddiness. She was in flight and soaring. She closed the palm of her hand around his cock and stroked it softly, drawing it closer to her own body as she did so. Sheer impatience made her bold and aggressive. She spread her legs as widely as she could and led him inside her, then she locked her heels on his spine, rocking him, hard, then harder, as if she were trying to trap something that couldn't quite be caught: an essence, an elusive moment.

Hard, harder still, she held on to him, and the dance grew quicker and simpler and more forcefully intimate until nothing separated her from him. There was only love and this insane free-falling bliss. She bit his shoulder and clawed his back, arching her hips, lifting herself up to intensify the connection, and then she came and kept coming until she was quite drained and he'd gone limp inside her. They collapsed together in silence, both breathless, both very still, paralysed.

When finally she got up from the bed, her thighs felt weak, her legs distant. She walked to the window and gazed out over the park. A match was struck, a cigarette lit. The room filled with the acrid smell of tobacco. She turned, seeing his face in the pale red glow of his cigarette. She moved back towards the bed. It was always this way; she immediately wanted him again, as if the first encounter had been nothing more than preamble, a surface scratched. There were other levels to reach, other satisfactions to be had. He drew on his cigarette and the reddish glow illuminated his bare chest.

'Your goodies are on the bedside table,' she said.

She saw him smile. It was a good smile, lively and attractive, open and genuine. She loved his face. If she were blinded she would have known the face by touch alone, its familiar topography. She shivered because the intimacy of all this overwhelmed her. At times, her careless sense of love frightened her. Only if you consider futures, she thought. The trick is to live in the moment. That way you can't think of fate. Fate is what happens tomorrow.

'You're too thoughtful,' he said.

'How can anybody be too thoughtful? I like doing things for you. I think about you all the time. I can't get you out of my head. I try, you know. I wake up and I tell myself – I must have a day, one lousy day, when I don't think about him. And it never happens.'

He was quiet for a long time. He stubbed out his cigarette. Then he said, 'Do you think it's any different for me?'

'I hope you suffer the way I do.' She tried to make this sound light-hearted but it came out with more gravity than she'd intended. She sat on the bed and took his hand, pressing the palm over a breast. 'I want us to be together. Always together. I hate the way we're kept apart.'

'It's a matter of time.'

'Patience isn't one of my virtues. I have to practise it. Every time we meet I panic when I think of how little time we have together. I want it to be different.'

'Soon. Everything will be fine soon.' The welcome certitude in his voice filled her with hope. Things would work out in the end because they had to. She had the same uncomplicated belief in the triumph of love some people have in the prophetic qualities of the stars. Other men paled by comparison now. She thought of how he dominated her imagination. In the few times when she considered this love clearly, she saw it as some form of addiction, as demanding as any narcotic.

'Did you have any problems?' he asked.

'With the money?' She shook her head. 'I sailed straight through. I knew I would. I have this look I sometimes do – haughty and regal. Nobody meddles with it. Especially customs officials.' She gestured toward the closet. 'It's all there. I put it in a briefcase. Exactly the way you like it.'

'You do everything the way I like,' he said.

She laughed. She had a laugh that was a little too deep to be ladylike. 'I want to please you,' she said.

He stroked her breast almost absent-mindedly. He had moments like this when an essential part of him disappeared. She was frightened by these times. They undermined her, riddled her already frail sense of security. She went to the bathroom, filled a glass with water, returned to the bed.

'Garrido isn't sure about you,' she said.

'At times Garrido's an old woman.'

'He's still sharp. He's intuitive. He knows what I feel for you, but I'm not sure he approves.'

'Garrido worries me, Magdalena. His age – '

'You can't go back on your promise,' she said. 'Garrido and everyone else on the Committee expect some kind of positions of authority. They think of themselves as the provisional government in exile. It's been that way for years. He sees himself as the Minister of the Interior or something just as elevated. It's the only thing he lives for. He's a hero in the community. You can't even *think* of excluding him.'

He sighed, patted the back of her hand. 'It's going to be all right. I'll keep my word.'

The atmosphere in the room had changed slightly. There was a vague darkness all at once, almost a gloom. She knew what it was. She'd opened the door and allowed Garrido to come inside, Garrido and all the politics of *el exilio*. This bedroom was sacrosanct, a place for lovers only, not for politics, and dreams, and plots.

She wanted to dispel the melancholy. Lightness, something trivial. She reached to the bedside table and picked up the small silver bowl containing cubes, each nicely wrapped with the name of the hotel written on them. She undid one, held it out, popped it in the man's mouth. It was another game they played together, another tiny familiarity.

She laid the tip of her finger between his lips. Then she kissed him. The small crystals of sugar that adhered to his tongue made the kiss wildly sweet.

'I love you,' she said. She whispered his name several times. She'd been taught as a child that when you said a word often enough you understood its true meaning, its innermost reality. So she repeated her lover's name, searching for an intimacy inside an intimacy, a revelation, the blinding insight that she was loved as much as she loved. She wanted the ultimate security.

He made her sit on the edge of the bed, then he gently parted her legs. She watched him, with anticipation and delight, as he kneeled on the floor, his mouth level with her knees. She continued to observe his face as it disappeared into the shadows between her thighs and then she trembled, throwing back her head and closing her eyes, her hands made into slack fists, her mouth open.

A voice that was not her own said *I love you, Rafael. I love you.*

New York City

It was ten p.m. local time and drizzling lightly all across the eastern seaboard when Kenzaburo Magiwara arrived at Kennedy Airport. He passed nimbly through customs and immigration where his passport, densely stamped, much-used, caused the immigration officer to make a mild joke about how Mr Magiwara should have a season ticket to America. Magiwara never smiled. It was not just that occidental humour eluded him, which was true, it was more the fact that the mask of his face had not been built for easy merriment. To most Europeans, Magiwara bore a strong resemblance to a younger version of the late Emperor Hirohito. Small saddles of flesh sagged under his eyes and his mouth was arrogant. He emitted a sense of power, although its precise source was hard to locate.

Did it come from the sharp little eyes and the impression they'd seen every hand of poker ever played? Was it from the disdainful mouth, about which there was some slight secretive quality? Or was it something more simple – like the assured way the man moved, as if he knew doors were going to be opened for him before he reached them, as if he understood that flunkies were going to attend to his baggage and transport and that all the insignificant details of his life were taken care of by others?

A chauffeured limousine was waiting just outside the Pan Am terminal. It transported Magiwara in the direction of Manhattan. He sat in the back, feeling a little sleepy, looking forward to his arrival at the apartment he owned in Central Park South. It had been a good trip, at least in the sense that the Society of Friends had seen fit to continue on its present course.

Magiwara was the first Japanese ever to have been invited to join the Society, which connected him to a world wherein enormous profits could be made and fortunes increased beyond dreams. It was a form of freemasonry, although he had no prejudices in that direction. Quite the contrary, secret societies had existed in Japan for centuries and Magiwara had been associated with a few of them in his time – business groups, fraternities of a political nature, religious organisations.

But the Society of Friends was different. It had no secret handshakes, no secret languages, no rituals of indoctrination, no masonic trappings. The Society, although profoundly secretive and jealous of its own anonymity, had gone beyond those forms of playacting. It promised more than fabulous wealth, it pledged a share in power, in shaping the destinies of countries like Cuba, sinking under the miserable weight of Communist mismanagement. The Society assured personal contact with history. It rendered senseless the notion that men were powerless before destiny. Some men, such as the members of the Society, could make an amazing difference. That they could make incalculable fortunes at the same time was not unattractive.

Magiwara gazed through his glasses into the drizzly streets. He believed he had a great deal to contribute to the Society, some of whose members bore him a residual resentment for his race. Caporelli, for example, had always seemed vaguely indifferent to him, and the two Americans, whom he didn't trust, treated him with the condescension of men who have eaten sushi once and, finding it deplorable, have condemned all of Japanese culture as being crude.

Magiwara knew he'd overcome these obstacles in time. He'd never yet been defeated by a hurdle placed in his way. At the age of fifty-eight he had amassed a personal fortune of seventy-three million dollars. Membership in the Society of Friends would increase that sum a hundredfold. The legality of the Society's business didn't perplex him. He knew there were grey areas, under-explored by routine capitalists, in which creative men might construct profitable enterprises. Such as Cuba, he thought.

He had studied the Society's history, at least the little that had been made available to him in the archives, stored in a bank-vault in the Italian town of Bari. These documents provided a broad outline of the Society's development, from the late nineteenth century when it had come into existence as a banking adjunct to the Mafia, laundering Sicilian money, investing it discreetly and legally, managing it as it grew. Through the 1920s and 30s, the Society, reorganising and naming itself for the first time The Society of Friends, a title whose ironic religious resonance escaped Magiwara, had seen the urgent need to move away from the violent excesses and the adverse publicity generated by men like Capone. The Society, far more secretive than the Mafia – which had become a public corporation, a soap opera, its innermost workings exposed for all and sundry to relish – now existed quite apart from the organisation that had spawned it. Few contemporary

Mafiosi even knew of the Society's existence. If they'd heard of it at all it was only as ancient history, an obscure group that had gone out of existence before the Second World War, having 'lost' considerable sums of the Mafia's money in 'regrettable market trading'. In fact, the missing money had been embezzled cleanly by officers of the Society and now the Society owned banks and investment houses that had once belonged to the great financial barons of the West, managed funds, manipulated massive amounts of the currencies that flowed between the stock exchanges of different countries. It influenced prices on the world's markets, funded anti-Communist movements in Central America, Asia, and Africa. It never avoided its fiscal responsibilities. Its various fronts – banks, financial houses, shipping companies – all paid taxes in the countries where they were located. Whenever difficulties arose, whenever there was a tax dispute, these disagreements were always somehow settled very quietly, man to man, banker to revenue officer, and the Society of Friends was never mentioned. It moved unobtrusively and swiftly like a great shark seeking the shadowy places where it might be glimpsed but never identified. Sinewy, elegant, contemptuous of weakness, indifferent to ethics, it was firmly entrenched in the structure of world capitalism. And Kenzaburo Magiwara was a part of this great organisation.

He looked out of the limousine. Almost home. He laid his hands on his thighs, drummed his dainty fingers. There was a skeletal delicacy about his whole body, as if his skin were no more than one thin membranous layer stretched tightly across bone. The delicacy was more apparent than real. Magiwara was hard and acquisitive and ambitious. Apart from accumulating a personal fortune, he also owned two United States congressmen, a British Member of Parliament, a Christian Democrat in Italy, two members of the Austrian Nationalrat, and assorted police chiefs in European and Asian cities – all useful acquisitions.

The big car slowed to a halt at a traffic signal. The rainy street was quiet, practically empty save for a small car, a black Dodge Colt that slowed alongside the limousine. Magiwara paid it no attention.

The light changed from red to green. The limousine didn't move. Magiwara leaned forward and tapped the smoked-glass partition separating him from the driver. There was no response. He pressed the button that rolled the partition down.

It was the strangest thing. The driver wasn't behind the wheel. Magiwara raised himself up, peered into the driving compartment, thinking that his driver had suffered something – a heart attack, say – and slithered to the floor. But he wasn't anywhere in the vehicle.

Puzzled, not panicked, Magiwara frowned. He was aware of the Dodge Colt alongside, which also hadn't moved. A side window opened in the small car. Magiwara anticipated a face, but none appeared.

The rolled-down window revealed only a darkness in which something metallic glinted. It took him only a moment to recognise the object. It was blunt, terrible, archaic, and he was seized by a sense of unreality, of some awful mistake being perpetrated here.

The blast of the sawn-off shotgun rocked the limousine. It crashed through the glass and all Magiwara heard just before it blew his face away was the piercing sound of shaved air and eternity.

6 Norfolk, England

Gunther Ruhr listened to the tiresome sound of a ping-pong ball clicking on the surface of a table. He rose from the narrow iron bed and went to the doorway of the living-room, on the far side of which two men were casually playing table tennis. Everything here irritated Ruhr, not just the noise of the ball but also this isolated house surrounded by mud and broken chicken coops and the bitter smell of dry rot that filled his nostrils night after night. A chill rain fell predictably every afternoon, but mainly what depressed him was the company he was obliged to keep.

There were four men in all. They had taken part in Ruhr's rescue from the English police, and he admired their reckless courage – but on a simple social level they tended to talk in single syllables, or when speech failed them, as it often did, they grunted. When you'd been stuck for days in a run-down farmhouse with no fellowship save the noise of the rain on the window and nothing to read but a mildewed Baedeker's 1913 *Handbook for Paris* (the only volume he'd found in the whole house), you needed some kind of diversion.

The two preening Argentinians, Flavell and Zapino, were dark-faced characters who spent a great deal of time running combs through their slick black hair. Now and again they'd congratulate themselves for the successful rescue of Ruhr, as if they were men at a school reunion remembering old pranks. When there was nothing to interest them on the old black and white TV, they dismantled weapons and cleaned them. They looked like contented lovers at such times. Yesterday morning Flavell had accidentally discharged a pistol, firing it into the ceiling and causing great consternation.

The other pair, the ping-pong players, were the Americans, one a cadaverous man called Trevaskis (the most articulate of the four; no great compliment), the other a pale white giant known, rather ordinarily, as Rick. The Americans kept to themselves, conversing in a form of English that Ruhr found hard to follow. Street patois, slang, mangled words. Trevaskis, who was all bone, and whose eyes shone with a missionary fervour, looked across the room at Gunther Ruhr.

There was contempt in the look. It was an expression Ruhr inspired in many people, one he'd seen all his life. People tended to step away from him, as if they intuited some terrible quality in him, a thing both lifeless and contagious. When they were too stubborn to move, they gazed just as Trevaskis was doing now, trying to stare down the demon. It amused the German. He sometimes thought of himself as a prism in which other people might glimpse a blackly intimidating aspect of the human condition.

Trevaskis, something of a joker, said, 'Sleep well, Mr Claw?'

The giant Rick, dressed in white T-shirt and blue jeans, smiled. He smiled at everything Trevaskis said. The two Argentinians put their combs away and turned to look. Ruhr remained in the doorway, folding his arms across his chest. The Claw. He neither liked nor disliked his nickname. It had been created by the press, merchants who traded in revulsion.

The same press had bestowed the status of legend on him, and he was pleased by that. He kept clippings under the floorboards of the tiny attic apartment he secretly maintained in the Sachsenhausen area of Munich. These invariably referred to his lack of moral values and his coldness toward human suffering. He was called barbarous, a monster. He sometimes leafed through the cuttings and felt removed from these descriptions. They missed the point. It wasn't so much his lack of certain qualities, it was more the fact that he considered ordinary human virtues undesirable. Everybody wanted love and affection: therefore they were commonplace and debased. Everybody deplored needless violence: therefore it was acceptable. Ruhr's logic was based on perversity. What other men might strive for, Ruhr wanted to destroy. What some men might exalt, Ruhr ridiculed. The sea of his feelings ran contrary to any common tide. Even his physical deformity, which he liked because he thought it mirrored the inner Ruhr, separated him from other people. He was alone in the world. He'd never felt any other way.

Ruhr stepped into the living-room. He raised the perfect hand to his face, stroked the firm jaw. An intriguing aspect of the recent misadventure in Cambridge was that suddenly, after years of anonymity, he had recognisable features! He was a public figure whose photograph had been printed in newspapers all over the world! His face was almost as well known as that of any movie star, which was not an altogether unpleasant novelty. He liked it the way any actor, formerly obliged to perform as a masked character, might enjoy recognition after years of doing his best work in the shadows.

He caught the ping-pong ball in mid-air and closed his left hand around it. 'We have work to do. Tomorrow is the day.'

The four men were silent. They watched Ruhr closely. They were more than his rescuers, more than the soldiers in his command, they were also his guards, instructed by the Cuban to keep him from harm, to limit his movements and make sure he didn't repeat the disastrous business in Cambridge. Ruhr had nothing but disdain for the men who bought his services. He had no sense of being an employee. Instead he considered himself the master of those who hired him. Nor did he ever trust the men who paid him because they were usually slaves of one ideology or another, lackeys to this obsession or that. They seldom had themselves under control; consequently, they were unable to control anything around them.

The Cuban, for example: Ruhr no more trusted him than he believed in God. You could see all the Cuban's wretched ambition in his eyes, in every word he spoke, every gesture he made. He'd come here two days ago, breathing fire, warning Ruhr not to screw things up, trying to hide the fact he was afraid because his aspirations were menaced, and Ruhr had played the obedient little dog with a theatrical contrition the Cuban, wrapped up in his own aims, apparently missed. Yessir, yessir. I'll be good, sir.

What the Cuban did not know was that Gunther Ruhr always took precautions for his own safety; documents, papers, numbers of bank accounts, copies of cashier's cheques, diaries describing assignments and naming names – these were in sealed boxes in the possession of a certain Herr Wilhelm Schiller, a lawyer in Hamburg, who had instructions to open them only in the event of Ruhr's death or disappearance. Ruhr believed in protecting himself.

Now the four men were watching over him, sentries circling the cage of an unpredictable madman. Ruhr was thrilled by the idea of creating tension in other people.

'Get the map,' he said.

The Argentinians produced a detailed Ordnance Survey map. Ruhr spread it on the table. He had an amazing memory, a mind that seized the essential details of anything and stored them for instant recall at any future date. He had studied this map once and he didn't need to look at it again for his own sake. He was rehearsing the others.

He pointed to a minor road that ran between woodlands. There was a windmill to the east, a canal in the west. A mile past the windmill was the crucial fork in the road. A thin pathway ran in one direction toward a dairy farm; the other tine, smooth and concrete, sliced through more woodland, lovely and dense and unfenced, affording marvellous opportunities for concealment and surprise. Here and there on the map were villages and hamlets. The only village of interest, Ruhr said, was the one known as St Giles. Six miles beyond it was the airfield of the East Anglia Flying Club. This was the most crucial location in the whole operation. If Ruhr and his men were somehow prevented from reaching the airfield, they would separate. If they were not already dead, Ruhr added, and smiled in his usual thin way, the expression of a man whose sense of humour, misunderstood by all, had doomed him to a life of smiling alone.

The Argentinians asked questions about time. They both wore very expensive watches and they believed that these instruments had to be 'seenchronised'. Ruhr told them that time was his own business, something he kept to himself for security reasons. The South Americans understood and became silent.

Ruhr folded the map. He went inside the kitchen. Eggshells, bacon rinds, twisted pieces of cellophane, matches, cigarette butts, open jars of meat paste – trash everywhere. Ruhr filled a glass with water, drank slowly. He didn't like the chaos in this room. He preferred a world of clean angles and well-defined spaces. But it wasn't always possible to live in such a perfect universe. All too often there were intrusions, such as this kitchen and its dirty disorder.

Or the girl in Cambridge . . .

He remembered her unsunned thighs and the way she'd shivered when she'd taken her jeans off and how she'd drawn a thin curtain across the window, trying to look provocative but succeeding only in appearing pathetic. And then the expression on her face when the steel gleamed on his hand – she'd screamed, and after that came the chaos and ignominy of capture.

He remembered the policeman called Pagan who had asked all kinds of questions. Ruhr had made up stories, weaving them off the top of his head. Like any good storyteller, he believed in his fictions. He was a salesman with a line in time-share condominiums, an absentminded Egyptologist on a backpacking vacation, an urbane professor of Swiss Literature (a part-time occupation, you understand, he'd said to an unsmiling Pagan) – identities, some of them amusing to him, flooded Ruhr as fast as he could assume them.

Pagan refused to be entertained by the ever-changing cast of characters. He'd been demanding. Frustrated, he'd thump his fist on the table in the interview room. At other moments he tried to disguise his irritation by falling silent and looking directly into Ruhr's eyes. The Englishman had determined grey eyes, but Ruhr had met their challenge without flinching. And now the English cop was wounded, or so the TV news had said. Lying in a hospital bed, Ruhr thought, frustrated and angry and desperate. A man like that could be extremely dangerous if he were out on the streets. A man like that wasn't likely to be confined too long to a hospital.

But he had the measure of Pagan; he was confident of that. Pagan was dogged, but clearly not inspired. In a contest between himself and the Englishman, his own superiority would triumph every time. Pagan had intuitions, of course, but they would be dull compared to Ruhr's own. Ruhr could slip in and out of other souls; Frank Pagan, at best, could only hope to read – by means of emotional braille – other people's behaviour and, through this slight empathy predict their future actions. Guesswork! Ruhr had no affinity with anything so unreliable. He put his credence only in certainty, and the supreme certainty was his faith in himself.

Ruhr raised his glass to his lips. The memory of the girl was still strong. She hadn't been beautiful, perhaps not even pretty, but Ruhr didn't care about ordinary beauty. Her paleness, her fragility, glass to be shattered – that was what had attracted him. But then he'd become blinded by his need to put the deformed hand inside her and twist it upward into her womb, and hear flesh come away, that soft whimpering sound of skin and sinew torn and muscle cut. Usually the girls fainted. Sometimes they bled to death. At such times it seemed to Ruhr that he wasn't entirely involved in these acts, that he stood outside himself, hypnotised by his own need to dominate and hurt, entranced by the simplicity, the purity, of power. There was another factor too, and that was his curiosity about the female anatomy: the way it worked, the intricate arrangement of womb and tubes, a fascination that had begun when he'd first seen a medical text at the age of eight and glimpsed, in a rose-coloured sectional diagram, the soft pink secrets of the female interior, and its essential vulnerability. The sight of it aroused a perplexing hunger inside the young boy Ruhr had been, and he'd never forgotten those detailed sketches. For a time he had toyed with the notion of becoming a doctor, perhaps a gynaecologist, but the idea had lost its intrigue, vanquished by Ruhr's preference for destruction over restoration.

Now what troubled him was to have been caught in Cambridge so stupidly! Was it slackness? Was he too old at thirty-seven to be as cautious, as vigilant, as he'd always been? Why hadn't he clamped a hand round the girl's mouth and silenced her? Was he becoming simply blasé, arrogant to the point of indifference? Or had it come down to something else: the idea of creating a contest for himself, his own brilliance matched against another mind, a protagonist – Frank Pagan, for example? Was Pagan even worthy of that consideration?

Trevaskis came into the kitchen. 'It's cold, Ruhr. The guys want permission to light a fire.'

'No fire,' Ruhr said. He disliked Trevaskis. The other men were acquiescent, but Trevaskis had an independent streak that was going to prove troublesome in the end. The American would have to be watched over. 'What would happen if somebody saw smoke from the chimney? Perhaps you would rather go up on the roof and wave a big red flag?'

Trevaskis shrugged. Ruhr's sarcasm didn't go down well with him. A silver St Christopher around his neck shimmered. 'This place isn't exactly a day at the beach, Ruhr.'

'As long as I'm in charge, my friend, there will be no fire. When you remember how much you're being paid, Trevaskis, you'll find that discomfort has a way of becoming tolerable.'

Trevaskis fingered his medallion. He had never worked with Ruhr before. He thought the German unstable, like an unpinned hand-grenade in a closed fist. The business with the metal claw – what sort of sick shit was that? And then the goddam rescue, which had cost the lives of the Australian and the other guy, the little Swede called Anderssen – all that stoked Trevaskis' general resentment. He wasn't going to get into a fight with Ruhr, though. When this job was finished, there was going to be a quarter of a million dollars in hard cash, and you didn't blow off that kind of bonanza. You didn't let Ruhr do anything to fuck it up either. The Cuban guy had quietly promised Trevaskis there would be a big bonus if Ruhr behaved himself.

'You're the boss,' Trevaskis said. *The fucking Führer,* he thought.

Ruhr drained his glass and set it down in the sink. He let his left hand touch the pistol tucked into the waistband of his corduroy trousers. 'Keep that fact in mind, Trevaskis.'

'It's like tattooed right here,' and Trevaskis tapped his head. *Asshole*. He shivered in an exaggerated way, blowing on his hands as he shuffled toward the door of the kitchen.

'One other matter,' Ruhr said. 'This room needs to be cleaned. If the men are complaining of cold, a little hard work might quickly warm them up.'

'Great idea,' Trevaskis remarked.

'You're so agreeable I feel I can delegate the task to you with every confidence.'

Trevaskis smiled oddly. 'Spick and span. Shipshape. Every surface like a mirror. Count on it.'

Ruhr said, 'You know what cleanliness is next to.'

'I've heard.'

Ruhr raised his deformed hand suddenly and laid the palm on Trevaskis' shoulder. He watched with some delight the American flinch, then try to conceal his gesture of revulsion behind a stupid little grin.

'Godliness,' Ruhr said. 'If you believe in God.'

Trevaskis didn't move.

'I have no such belief,' Ruhr went on. 'This hand, for example. Would a caring God allow a child to be born with a deformity like this? Why would any God wish to punish an innocent child? What sin could I possibly have committed in my mother's womb to deserve to be born a freak?'

Trevaskis said nothing. Ruhr's touch offended him. But how could he back away without admitting a surrender of some kind?

'I lie,' Ruhr said. 'I wasn't born this way at all, Trevaskis. I was born with five fingers. Perfectly natural. When I was twelve I took my mother's kitchen-knife and I hacked off the two middle fingers. I remember a rather boring juvenile desire to understand pain. So I experimented on the only subject available – myself.'

Trevaskis moved an inch or so, getting out from under the hand. But Ruhr was quick. He brought his palm up to Trevaskis' cheek and laid it there. It was an odd gesture that might have been affectionate in some other circumstances, but here it was sinister. Ruhr's clammy flesh had a strange smell to it, like decay. Trevaskis stood motionless. He wanted to smack Ruhr's hand away. This close to the German you could practically hear him ticking.

Ruhr said, 'I was a child wonder, Trevaskis. A marvel. At the age of eight I had read Kant. I found the Categorical Imperative less of a directive than the urge to discover what lay under a girl's skirt, which I did at ten.' Here Ruhr laughed in a dry, quiet way.

'By the time I was eleven, I knew how to make gunpowder. First the intellectual pursuits, then the sexual, finally the destructive. I learned one thing with great certainty: the effect of a bomb is more immediate than all Kant's philosophy. The only way to kill a man with Kant is to strike him over the head with the Complete Works in German.'

There were elements of truth in Ruhr's brief narrative. He had read Kant at eight, as he claimed, and he had indeed learned to make gunpowder at eleven. But these strands had become so interwoven with myth that they were hard to separate: he no longer knew if he'd been born deformed or caused it to happen. He no longer cared either way. The reality of his past was often mundane, so he altered it. Self-mutilation was much more intriguing than some genetic error.

Ruhr had been born in Munich, the child of itinerant fundamentalists who were members of a proselytising American sect with headquarters in Baton Rouge, hardcore scriptural believers who thought Galileo and Darwin brothers of Satan. Ruhr's parents, both rather distant persons who considered their very bright child something of an unexpected encumbrance, moved around Europe with such frequency that a three-week lease on a cheap apartment was deemed stability. It became clear to Gunther Ruhr that he was needless baggage to his parents – gaunt people with bright, spacey eyes and a disarmingly naïve zest for accosting strangers on street corners and shoving fundamentalist pamphlets into their hands. They despised the child, and he in turn was embarrassed by them and what seemed to him the sham of their religious beliefs: God was a mass of philosophical contradictions, so why bother with Him? Life was simpler without a deity.

Somewhere along the way, Ruhr's parents managed to leave him behind. Either they simply forgot him in their religious obsession or were too troubled by his outspoken cleverness, and his inclination toward atheism, to want his company. He was boarded out at a variety of schools where his natural brightness overwhelmed all around him. Abstract subjects were grasped in moments and committed forever to a memory that was a well-tooled trap. Other students bored him, wasted his time. He befriended nobody. At the age of sixteen he qualified for a place at the University of Hamburg, which he entered during a time of social unrest when student activists were erecting barricades in streets. Attracted by destruction, thrilled by streets made foggy from tear gas and the daily battles against the police, Ruhr came to life as he'd never before. He discovered in himself a knack for subterfuge, an affinity for the cellars where people made up revolutions and schemed to bring society down. He was a natural.

At the age of seventeen, he took part in his first bank robbery, led by a student radical shot and killed in the course of the theft. Ruhr took the fallen leader's place without asking or being asked. For the next two years he and his gang robbed banks throughout Europe. During this time Ruhr developed all manner of alliances that would later form the foundation of his terrorist network.

In 1974, he was contacted in Rome by a representative from a certain Middle Eastern nation who needed some 'demolition' work done – the bombing of an aeroplane, to be specific. Ruhr, amazed that he was being offered such a large sum of money to undertake a task he might have done for nothing save expenses, accepted the assignment.

It was his first *real* act of mercenary terrorism. By contrast bank robberies were trifles, small local jobs with no international significance. The aeroplane, with crew and one hundred and eighteen passengers, exploded on the ground at Tel Aviv. Ruhr remembered the fascinating newspaper pictures, the TV shots. It was at this time he began to make a scrapbook of his deeds. The press, interested in Ruhr's terrorist activities for some time, uncovered his role in the tragedy and began to delve into what little was known of his history. With that strange fascination newspapermen always reserve for people of high intelligence gone somehow 'wrong', journalists turned Ruhr into that archetype of brilliance and violence combined, the 'mad genius', 'the sick boy-wonder'. It was at this time too he first wore the strange stainless steel prosthetic device and discovered that his taste for destruction, that unfathomable need, went beyond the bombing of aeroplanes.

Now Ruhr smiled at Trevaskis, then let the hand fall back to his side. 'You hated me touching you, didn't you?'

Trevaskis' mouth was dry. 'It didn't faze me, Ruhr.'

Ruhr said, 'You're a bad liar. Nobody likes me to touch them. I can feel their revulsion. This interesting appendage' – and here he turned the hand over and over – 'creates abhorrence in other people, which they try either to disguise as sympathy, or ignore. Such fools. I see through people, Trevaskis. I read the fine print on their hearts.'

Trevaskis moved toward the kitchen door. He wanted to get away from Ruhr. Sometimes you looked into another man's eyes and what you saw there was unknowable. It was like dark mysterious water when you had no sounding instrument to probe the depths. Ruhr, whether truthful or lying, gave Trevaskis the impression of an unpleasant illusion done with mirrors.

'Now clean this horrible place,' Ruhr said.

The giant Rick appeared just then, bending his head a little to clear the top of the door. He had watery brown eyes and a mouth too small for his enormous white face. He gave the impression of great physical strength without a mind to direct it.

'There's somebody out front,' he said. His voice was a whisper.

'Who?' Ruhr asked.

'I didn't get a real good look. I saw somebody step across the front yard and go behind the vehicle.'

'One? More than one?' Ruhr asked.

'Only saw one,' Rick replied.

Ruhr moved quickly out of the kitchen. He went from the living-room to his bedroom, the window of which looked directly out into the yard. He parted the damp yellow blind an eighth of an inch: all he saw was the Range Rover in the heavy, slanting rain. And yet he had a feeling of a scene recently disturbed, a stillness through which some trespasser has moved. He couldn't say why, simply an old instinct. He took the pistol from his waistband and returned to the living-room. When he moved with stealth and speed he was impressive, graceful, a man whose quiet elegance had been honed by more than fifteen years of surreptitious acts.

The Argentinians had automatic rifles clutched in their arms. Trevaskis and Rick carried handguns.

'Flavell, Zapino, stay at the windows, but don't show yourself,' Ruhr said. 'Trevaskis, you and Rick cover me from the kitchen.'

'You're going out there?' Trevaskis asked.

Ruhr didn't answer. He was already moving to the kitchen. There was a side-door that opened on to the place where the run-down chicken hatches were located.

'Wait,' Trevaskis said. 'Let somebody else go outside. You oughta stay here.'

Ruhr heard nothing. When he was involved in action he closed his senses down to anything extraneous. Action was everything, single-minded, demanding all one's concentration. He opened the kitchen door softly. The cold mid-afternoon rain stung his face. He loved the sensation. Trevaskis stood behind, whispering his useless objections.

Ruhr stared across the mud. Raindrops rattled the old coops. He took a step outside. He was insubstantial now, merging with the elements, a kind of transformation that Trevaskis could only admire from the kitchen doorway. This was no ordinary man sneaking through the rain with a gun: Ruhr melted into the greyness of the weather, as if the rain created a funnel of camouflage around him.

Ruhr reached the corner of the house. He looked at the Range Rover. The muddy yard was empty. He stood motionless against the wall of the house. Water ran from his thin hair over the lids of his eyes. Then he heard the sound, something that lay under the incessant squabble of the rain, a wet noise but different, a squelching pressure on soft mud.

And there she was.

A child, a girl dressed in school uniform, short black skirt and maroon blazer and long maroon scarf trailing over her shoulder. She was running, breaking free from the cover of the Rover, but the black mud fettered her movements and disturbed her balance. She was heading towards the slope that rose up behind the farmhouse, arms stretched on either side for equilibrium, a dancer in the slime. Ruhr went after her, enjoying the certainty of catching her. He moved with long strides, strong ones, cutting down the distance between himself and the girl at will. Her beret flew off. Her short blond hair quickly became soaked with rain.

Ruhr grabbed her around the waist before she was even halfway up the slope. He swung her round to face him and she blinked from all the rainwater in her eyes. Through her soaked blouse could be seen the small white brassière she wore. She tried to tear herself away, but Ruhr, laughing, moved behind her and locked one arm tightly under her chin, forcing her tiny face back.

'Why were you spying?'

'You're hurting me.'

Ruhr applied more pressure. 'What were you doing sneaking around my house?'

'Nothing . . . cross my heart . . . let me go!'

Ruhr released her and she rubbed her neck at the place where he'd bruised her.

'I can hardly breathe,' she said.

'You'll be all right.'

'I live a few miles away, I wanted to say hello, introduce myself, but you're obviously not friendly – '

Ruhr said, 'If you're so innocent, why did you run?'

She shook her wet hair. 'Scared.'

'Scared? Of what?'

'The gun in your hand,' the girl said. She walked a few steps, reached down to pick up her beret, turned it round between her fingers. Ruhr watched the short skirt rise upon her young thigh. The expanse of flesh between the knee-length socks and the hem of the risen skirt was all the more provocative for its innocence. She was slim, and pretty in the awkward fashion of the young; insecure about her own looks, uncertain about her place in the world.

Ruhr put the gun in his waistband.

'I'll leave,' the girl said. 'I won't bother you again, I swear it.'

'Tell me your name first.'

'Steffie.'

'What a very ugly name,' Ruhr said.

'Stephanie then.'

'That's better.' It occurred to Ruhr that he could let this girl walk away. By tomorrow morning he'd be gone from this place anyhow. What did it matter? He looked down at the house; he thought he saw the shadows of the two South Americans in the windows.

'Well,' the girl said, and there was a flutter of fear in her voice. 'I suppose I'd better leave.'

Ruhr watched her face. There was renewed anxiety in her eyes and her mouth had become very tense. And of course he knew why.

'I can't let you go.'

She backed away. 'I didn't see anything. I swear I didn't.'

He stepped toward her. She slipped as she moved backward. She lay in the mud, the skirt above her waist, white underwear showing, her legs raised and bent at the knees. He stood over her.

'You know who I am, don't you?'

She shook her head, tried to rise, slipped again. 'Please,' she said. 'I won't say anything. Not to a living soul. I promise.'

'You saw my picture in the newspapers. You saw this,' and he raised his right hand.

Tears rolled over her cheeks. 'I only want to go home.'

'We all want that, Steffie.'

He reached for her arm, hauled her to her feet, led her down the slope to the house. She wouldn't stop crying; he hit her once, rather softly, across the side of her face. After that she sobbed in silence, as if something inside her had begun to break. He pushed her into the house, slammed the door shut.

'What the hell is this?' Trevaskis asked.

'A little gem,' Ruhr said. 'Isn't it surprising what a man can find in an otherwise dreary English landscape?'

At the summit of the slope, under bare, sodden trees, the girl's horse whinnied, a sound obliterated by wind and rain.

Nobody in the farmhouse heard.

London

Martin Burr dreaded visits to the Home Secretary's office. It was a vast oak-panelled room hung with faded oil paintings of politicians past. Under the scrutiny of the portraits the Commissioner felt like a defendant in the dock of history, judged by the stern faces of an awesome jury – the first Earl of Chatham, Gladstone, Lord Acton, Sir Robert Peel. Their faces glowered disapprovingly into the room as if abruptly summoned from a long, well-deserved sleep. Martin Burr looked round the room for a sign of something less imposing, less official, and found it parked in a dim corner – a small, bedraggled canary in a brass cage. The little bird shivered in misery.

Burr turned when the door opened and the Home Secretary came in. 'Sorry to have kept you waiting, Martin.' He tossed some folders down on his enormous desk, then rummaged in a drawer and brought out an eye-dropper filled with clear liquid. He went to the bird cage and pushed the dropper through the bars, letting fluid drip into the canary's food dish. 'Bird's got some kind of flu. This stuff's supposed to help it. It's touch and go, I fear. We live in hope.' The Home Secretary gently rattled the cage, bringing his face very close to it and whispering to the canary. 'Don't we, Charlie? Don't we live in hope?'

He walked back to his desk, sat down. 'Now then. This bloody Ruhr business. Where are we exactly?'

Burr, who half-expected to be axed, gazed at the window. The afternoon sky over the Thames was low and leaden. 'Not as far along as I would have liked, Secretary,' he said. 'The search continues. Sea ports are being watched. Air terminals. Railways. All public transport. Ruhr's picture is plastered everywhere. Frank Pagan's office is examining all known terrorist connections.'

'Pagan? Shouldn't he be in hospital or something?'

'He's a stubborn bastard,' Burr said. That damned Pagan. 'He discharged himself yesterday.'

The Home Secretary turned his face toward the window and appeared to consider this information. Then he turned back to the Commissioner. 'What news of the leak, Martin?'

Martin Burr imagined he saw Sir Robert Peel frown. He glanced up at the portrait of the man who had founded the London police force in 1829. Then he looked elsewhere. 'I've imposed unusually strict limits on the number of people who have access to the paperwork generated by the Ruhr investigation. Memoranda and confidential reports on the affair no longer circulate in the usual way. Pagan has tightened his own departmental security – restricted access to computer data, telephone scrambling devices, that sort of thing. When we communicate with each other in the future, we do so directly, either face to face, or on a safe line. No third parties.'

'But you haven't sniffed out the culprit?'

'No, but that isn't our top priority, Secretary. After all, the damage caused by the leak is already done. We're concentrating exclusively on Ruhr. When we catch him, then I can turn my attention to our internal shortcomings.'

The Home Secretary was silent for a time. 'Sound approach, Martin,' he said finally.

This unexpected vote of confidence startled Burr. He poked his walnut cane into the weave of the Secretary's Persian rug. He had come here expecting his own execution or, at best, a severe reprimand. The Home Secretary wasn't famed for a kind heart. A compliment from him had been known to make otherwise sombre men light-headed for weeks. Perhaps the Secretary's mild approval was merely a way to soften the inevitable blow. Burr braced himself.

'Do we have *any* idea why this German is here?' the Secretary asked.

Martin Burr shook his head. 'There's a list of possibilities that grows longer by the moment.'

'Possibilities or guesses, Martin?'

'Guesses,' Burr said.

The Secretary was quiet for a time. 'When six policemen die, when we have an atrocity of that magnitude, it's common to look immediately for an individual to take the total blame. The obvious choice, Martin, would be you. Commissioner of Scotland Yard, the man in charge of Ruhr's transport, the responsible commanding officer, etcetera etcetera. The great masses, who have quite a taste for the blood of fallible officials, would not be unhappy with a public hanging.'

Burr sighed and nodded his head. A public hanging: he saw himself turned out of office, a long retirement at his house in the Sussex countryside. He saw himself stooped and ancient, pottering around in a garden whose fruits and flowers didn't remotely interest him but were merely things one grew on the way to the grave.

'What damn good is a scapegoat?' the Home Secretary asked. 'Your record is distinguished, Martin. And I stand squarely behind you. I will say so in public at any time.'

Surprised, Burr brightened at once. 'I appreciate that.'

'I am one of your staunchest supporters, Martin. And I am certain the Commission of Inquiry will exonerate you in due course.'

Burr felt a surge of gratitude that rose to his head like blood. He wasn't sure what to say. He saw the Home Secretary reach across the desk and extend his hand, which Burr shook. It was a vigorous grip between two men who have sworn to uphold the laws of a nation.

'Go back to work with a clear mind, Martin,' the Home Secretary said. 'I don't want you to be hindered by criticism. I don't want the Commission of Inquiry to distress you in any way. Remember this. You have an ally in me.'

'I'm very grateful, Secretary.'

'No need. If you were an incompetent buffoon I would have you out of office in two shakes of a lamb's tail. But you're not. Your record speaks for itself.'

Burr rose from his chair. A weight had been removed from him and he felt quite spry all at once. Even the portraits appeared less uncompromising, as if Burr had passed some kind of test and his examiners were, for the moment at least, pleased with him.

The canary cheeped bravely. The Home Secretary walked to the cage and looked inside. 'Bird's first sound in days. Perhaps it's a good omen.' He drew a fingernail over the bars, making a dull harp-like noise. 'Keep me posted daily, Martin. That's all I ask. When anything comes up, I will expect to hear from you.'

'Of course, Sir Frederick.'

The Home Secretary smiled. It was the easy expression of a man who, though born into wealth, prides himself on having the common touch. For this reason he was never called Sir Frederick in the newspapers. It was always the more colloquial Sir Freddie.

He walked Martin Burr to the door.

'Good luck, Commissioner.'

'We'll need it,' Burr said.

Still smiling, clapping Martin Burr on the back, Sir Freddie Kinnaird closed the door.

7 London

By mid-afternoon on his first full day of freedom, Frank Pagan had coaxed extra help from a variety of departments. Men had been called in to do extra shifts or work their day off. A few had been summoned from the twilight world of semi-retirement and sent out into the streets, grumbling yet grudgingly pleased to be useful. Officers travelled to a score of different places, Ealing and Wembley, Poole and Ramsgate, anywhere the names of those on the computer list had been located. It was a thankless undertaking, but what alternatives were there? Ignore the twenty-nine names? No. Pagan wanted to cover as many bases as he could. Later, there might be the consolation that he'd done everything possible and hadn't skimped. He had three officers checking private airfields in the Home Counties for any evidence of the helicopter used in Shepherd's Bush; another bloody long shot.

By four o'clock, Pagan had also sent two men to Cambridge to analyse potential targets in the area with the Chief Constable. Another five had been ordered to met the security officers of military bases throughout East Anglia, from Colchester in the south to Hunstanton in the north, an area some eighty miles wide and sixty miles long. Bounded by The Wash and the North Sea, it was a region of waterways, leafy lanes, ancient churches. Villages, some of them surprisingly remote, still had timbered houses. Across this flat green landscape, Air Force jets screamed out of bases and left fading trails in the sky.

In Golden Square two officers were employed full time taking phone calls from people who claimed to have seen Ruhr. These came from every corner of England; The Claw had been observed by a lonely old man in Hull, a young drunk in Plymouth, a very proper lady in Sevenoaks, an octogenarian in Radlett. He had also been spotted on Westminster Bridge, and in a restaurant on the Grand Parade in Eastbourne by a short-sighted French waiter who'd never forgotten the humiliation imposed on France by the Germans at the Maginot Line. Ruhr, it seemed, was as common as hedgerow, and his movements just as tangled.

Even though officers were scurrying all over the place, and business was being conducted briskly, Pagan was still beset by a sense of having overlooked something very simple, except he wasn't sure what. It was a flavour in his mouth he couldn't name, a word he couldn't get off the tip of his tongue. Too many Pethidine, too little sleep on the hideous office sofa. He had the feeling that his brain, knocked off-centre, was dealing with the German only in a peripheral way. And the deficiency of his muse had really nothing to do with insomnia or pain. Face it, Frank, he told himself in that stern inner voice he kept for self-honesty: you've been bollixed by the last name on the bloody list.

The twenty-ninth name. As he looked down into the darkening afternoon in Golden Square, he was uneasy.

He wished he could set the past aside, lock it inside a box labelled oblivion. But it was a sneaky intruder, and it came upon you with the quietness of a shadow. He thought that perhaps Foxworth hadn't been able to track the person down, and maybe that would be a relief, but all the particles of his curiosity were wildly activated. Sometimes the urge to visit your own history was overwhelming and so you walked old neighbourhoods regardless. The reckless heart, Pagan thought. It went where it wanted to go, striding to its own timetable, and there was nothing you could do but follow, even if the journey took you into the red-light district of your memories.

Foxworth entered the office, whistling slyly. 'Has anybody mentioned your resemblance to Quasimodo?' he asked.

Pagan shook his head. 'I must be missing something.'

'It's how you carry yourself, Frank,' Foxie said. 'Like Charlie Laughton. All you need is a fair-sized hump.'

'I can't think of any other way to be comfortable.' Pagan had placed all his weight on the left side of his body. His right arm hung rather uselessly, and the right shoulder was raised a little. It wasn't a pretty sight, but it was an improvement on total discomfort.

'I'll get you a bell for Christmas.'

'I'd settle for Gunther Ruhr.'

Foxworth stopped whistling. He took out his notebook, flipped the pages. He tore out a sheet, slid it across the desk to Pagan. 'I found the individual you wanted. Wasn't easy, actually. She checked into a hotel in Victoria two days ago, then promptly settled the bill and moved without explanation in the middle of the night. Arrived in a second hotel in Knightsbridge the day before yesterday. Did the same damn thing all over again. Paid the bill, *arrivederci*, upped and moved to the address you now have. Strange behaviour. One might say suspicious.'

'One might.' Pagan looked at the piece of paper, then tucked it in his pocket.

'You'll need a driver,' Foxie said, thinking that what Frank really needed was a nurse and three weeks in a quiet room with an ocean view.

'And that might as well be you, Foxie.'

'I was hoping you'd ask.'

Pagan was silent and nervous in the car as Foxworth drove along Piccadilly and up through the clogged streets of Mayfair. Late afternoon yielded to evening. Feeble sunlight pierced the slate-coloured sky, laying a dirty amber streak across Berkeley Square. Park Lane loomed ahead, and Hyde Park beyond, where evening had already settled among the trees. Pagan folded his hands in his lap. His mouth was very dry. This visit wasn't the most practical thing he'd ever done. He could have assigned somebody else, even Foxie, to make this call. But how could he have resisted and let the chance slip past and then have to kick himself in regret?

The monolithic hotels of Park Lane were ahead now, great slabs of glass and concrete that overlooked Hyde Park. Foxie parked the Rover outside one of the hotels and followed Pagan through the glass doors. Pagan inquired at the desk for the room number he wanted, then shuffled over the thick-piled carpet to the lifts.

'You go the rest of the way alone. Correct?' Foxworth asked.

'Correct,' Pagan said. Sometimes Foxie's face was like a kid's; he wasn't very accomplished in the craft of concealment. He had been very curious about Pagan's odd reaction last night, and he was even more curious today, and now he was to be denied direct access to the secret. Bloody Frank! he thought. Furtive bastard!

'Sit in the bar or something,' Pagan said. 'I don't expect to be very long.'

'I'm disappointed, Frank.'

'Those are the breaks, Foxie.' Pagan stepped inside the lift, pressed a button for the twelfth floor. When he got out in a corridor that was deserted and weirdly quiet, he had the urge to return to the lobby and leave. Empty corridors in hotels unnerved him.

How long had it been? Twelve years? Thirteen? If it had lain dormant that length of time, why disturb it now? it had turned first to dross, and then the years had refined it further, and now there was surely nothing left but dust. *Dust, my arse*! If that was all, why would you be here?

He moved along the corridor. He found room 1209 and knocked on the door. After a few moments it opened about half an inch. The gap was filled with darkness and Pagan could make out only the eyes at first, but that was all he needed to see. They were unmistakable, blacker than he'd remembered; sad and reflective and deep and lovely, they drew him down into them even as they'd done twelve, thirteen years ago. Down and down; all those years ago there had been bliss at the end of this fall. He smiled uncertainly. He was tense, knotted.

'Frank?' The voice was the same too. Perhaps a halftone deeper, a little throatier. It was a voice made for risqué jokes and laughter in a bar just before closing time.

A ghost touched him. He had the overpowering desire to put his hand out and feel her – no innocent contact between his fingers and her cheek, nothing smacking of mere fondness, but a truly intimate touch, his fingers on her nipples, her belly, between her legs. This was how she'd always affected him, and time apparently hadn't altered that. It was fascinating to find an old passion lodged in the blood still. Remembered love was the most tantalising of all, flavoured with things that might have been; small regrets, unfulfilled desires, sorrows.

'Frank Pagan. I can't believe it.'

'Can I come in?' he asked.

A beat of hesitation. Then she said, 'Could I stop you if I wanted to?'

He shook his head. There was a time, he thought, when I would have done anything for you. Rational, irrational, good, bad – these terms lost all meaning when love had you dazzled. He took a few steps forward. Curtains were drawn, a TV playing, no volume. A smell of cigarette smoke and perfume lay in the air. This was something new; she hadn't smoked in the past.

She wore a green silk robe belted not at the waist but lower, slinking around the hips. She wore clothes like few other women. She gave them a personality entirely her own, smart, a little sluttish, conspiratorial in a way, because she wanted you, and only you, to know what soft secrets lay under the garments. She always looked as if she were about to disrobe, as if clothes fettered her natural urge to go naked, which gave her an edge of unpredictability. And Pagan, twenty-eight years of age at the time of his passion for this woman, had thrived on this brink even as it had threatened him. He'd known bottomless jealousy and terrifying insecurity; when you loved Magdalena you lived with fear of loss, but you lived gloriously just the same. She made all your nerve-endings taut and your blood never stopped singing strange and unfamiliar tunes. Siren, whore, lover, friend – she'd bewildered the young Pagan with her permutations.

'How did you know I was in London?' she asked.

'Your name's on a list. Everything's on a computer these days,' he said.

'A list? You make it sound very grim. I take it this isn't a social call?' She sat on the unmade double bed and glanced past him across the room. The door to the bathroom was shut. A band of light glowed in the space between floor and door.

'Not entirely,' Pagan said. He wanted to go closer to her, but he stood some five or six feet from the bed, conscious of how his sharp remembrance of old intimacies made him feel awkward.

She pushed a hand through her marvellously thick hair. 'How long has it been?'

'Thirteen years, give or take.'

'Sweet Jesus. I was a child back then.'

'You were twenty-six.'

'And naïve.'

'We were both naïve.'

'Yeah, but didn't we have a time?' She smiled, reached for the bedside lamp, switched it on. He saw now, in the light that flooded her features, small lines beneath the eyes and around the corners of the mouth. But these minor incisions of time took nothing away from her. Quite the contrary, they gave her more depth and softened the beauty that had once been too perfect. She had the kind of looks that turned heads so quickly one could almost hear the separation of vertebrae.

Thirteen years ago Pagan's world had been transformed by this woman. Before his marriage to Roxanne he'd played the field, but his encounter with Magdalena Torrente had reduced that field to a dried-out pasture, consisting as it did of pallid girls whose notion of passion was as thrilling as taffeta. Cups of tea in bed, biscuit crumbs, damp little flats and whining gas-fires. Magdalena Torrente, a creature from another world, had come in like a tropical storm, cutting through Pagan's Anglo-Saxon cool with her ardour. And he'd lost control.

'I've thought about you often,' Pagan said, and wondered at the banal language of reunions. Reunions and grief had that in common: a thin lexicon.

'Likewise,' she said.

'You look wonderful.'

'My hair's a mess. No make-up.'

'When did you ever need it?'

'You've still got that silver tongue, Pagan.'

Pagan's ribcage had begun to hurt. He had to sit down.

'You look sick,' she said.

He told her briefly about Ruhr, and the shooting. He sat in an armchair, swallowed a painkiller.

'How bad is it?'

'It comes and goes. Mostly it comes.'

'Poor Frank,' she said.

He liked the sympathy in her voice. For a moment he wished she'd get up and cross the space that divided them and perhaps hold him, baby him, soothe him. And then he was glad she didn't touch him because when it came to Magdalena he'd never quite been able to get enough of her. She resisted complete possession. Her passions were real and intense, her heart sincere, but he always felt that she kept something in reserve, something unreachable despite all the intimacy between them.

'I behaved badly in those days, didn't I?' he said.

'I don't remember that, Frank.'

'I couldn't take you at face value. I never quite knew how to behave around you. I wanted to own you.'

'But I played you like a guitar,' she said quietly. 'I manipulated you. I was a self-centred monster.'

'I was just as bad. I remember we were in a restaurant, a place in Soho. I thought you were flirting with the waiter and I couldn't stand it.'

'You didn't talk to me all night long,' she said. 'You sat in a huff. As I recall, I slid my foot into your crotch under the table, and you pretended nothing was happening.'

Pagan smiled at the memory. Water under the bridge, he thought. But it wasn't swift-running; it passed under him sluggishly, giving him time to look down at reflections. 'I'd never felt that kind of jealousy before. I couldn't think straight.'

'I felt very powerful, Frank. Control over a hot-shot young cop! What an ego trip.' She stood up, smoothing the front of her green silk robe with the palms of her fine hands. She could perform the most simple manoeuvre and change it; the striking of a match could be transmuted into an erotic gesture, the application of eye-shadow as bewitching as a high-class strip show. She was theatre, and Pagan had been her willing audience.

'How long are you here for?' he asked.

'I leave tomorrow.'

Pagan wondered why Magdalena was still in her robe at this hour of the day, but he wouldn't ask. 'Do you have time for dinner?'

'There's something I can't cancel. I would if I could.'

'How about tomorrow?'

'I can't, Frank. Sorry.'

'Why do I still feel a very old jealousy?'

'Because you're crazy. Because you're a romantic.'

'I'm not sure that's how I like to be defined.'

'You'll always be a romantic, Frank. You'll always occupy a special place in my memory.'

Something sounded sad to Pagan, as if he existed in Magdalena's mind only as a fossil, relegated to the museum where former lovers lay mummified. There was no question so far as he was concerned – he had once loved this woman in a way he'd never quite loved again, a tempestuous affair, probably self-destructive, but dramatic and more turbulently physical than anything else he'd ever experienced. She took him to his limits then pushed him beyond them, forcing him to soar through the barriers of his reserve and aloofness.

'Thirteen years.' She shook her head, as if the passage of time bewildered her. 'I don't think I'm over the surprise of seeing you yet. And the suspicion.'

'Suspicion?'

'You're not here just to reminisce. You said it wasn't exactly a social call.'

Pagan was silent. He wondered if he'd hoped for something that the situation couldn't possibly yield, perhaps a brief rekindling of old sensations, a liaison even; but this was pure bloody fantasy. People moved on. They built other lives. They had other loves.

'The computer kicked out your name,' he said. Jesus, he didn't want to talk about *this*.

'Does that mean I'm up shit creek?' She put a hand over her open mouth; mock horror.

'It depends on why you're in London. The last time you were trying to buy weapons.'

She laughed. 'Don't remind me. I was naïve then.'

'Naïve enough to look for guns on the black market anyway. And get yourself arrested.'

'You were the nicest arresting officer I could have hoped for.'

'Are you still involved in the same cause? Still trying to buy guns?'

'Hey, look at me, Frank. I'm thirty-nine and mellow. Guns in the hands of some Cuban extremists isn't the answer. I changed direction.'

Pagan stared at the TV a moment. A man was mutely reading the evening news. 'What direction are you pointed in now, Magdalena?'

'We still want Castro out. That never changes. But I know it isn't going to happen unless it comes from inside Cuba, and with only a minimal amount of force. I don't know if you've been paying attention, Frank, but there are people in Cuba who believe in bringing democracy to the island. I'm a sympathiser.'

'How is this supposed to be achieved?' Pagan asked.

'What do you think?'

'A coup?'

She didn't answer.

'Bloodless?' Pagan asked.

'I can't see into the future.'

'How could it be accomplished without *some* bloodshed? And what exactly is a "minimal amount" of force? How do you actually measure that?'

Magdalena Torrente said nothing.

'But you believe this coup is a possibility?' Pagan asked.

She didn't answer directly. 'The democratic underground in Cuba keeps growing. People are sick of deprivation. Communism has a big personnel problem. For every good man it attracts, it enlists a hundred bullies who don't know Karl Marx from Harpo. Whenever there's a new problem, which is ten times every day, they think rationing's the answer. No shoes? No baby food? No drinking water? No fish to eat? Tough shit, those are all just mere inconveniences *en route* to the perfection of the state, which is coming. Maybe in a couple of centuries, but it's coming. Meantime, we're sorry we have to grind your face in the dirt.'

Pagan remembered taking Magdalena Torrente into custody after she'd been arrested in 1977 in a gun dealer's flat on Baker Street. He'd been part of a team watching that place for weeks, listening to tapped phoned conversations, waiting for the precise moment to swoop on the dealer, a Belgian whose cover was that of a dealer in nineteenth-century Flemish art. When the raid happened, Magdalena was in the middle of bargaining over the price of one hundred FN rifles intended for a group of anti-Castro rebels in the Escambray region of Cuba. The guns would be channelled through Miami to Cuba by a Florida group who had run afoul of the FBI and therefore had to buy weapons abroad. So Magdalena had been dispatched to London with a huge sum of cash.

When she'd been arrested the money was confiscated. The judge, who thought Communism akin to rabies or a rattlesnake's bite and believed democracy to be the British Empire's one true gift to the planet, had lectured her in the fashion of a stern uncle but he'd refused to imprison or deport her. She had been 'misguided by her own youthful zeal for liberty', a nice judicial phrase, a kindness. Obviously, the good justice had been mildly infatuated with the beautiful young Cuban-American who stood in the dock before him.

After her acquittal, Frank Pagan defied protocol and good sense by spending ten days and nights with her. He'd known it wasn't a bright career move to fraternise with your prisoner, even if she'd been discharged. But that was how she affected him. She made him blind to consequences.

'What brings you here this time, Magdalena?'

'I'm a tourist.'

'A very fussy one when it comes to hotels, I gather.'

She stared at him. She was capable of making her eyes seem like two hard stones, which stripped her face of all expression. She had masks that could be terrifying. 'You've been spying.'

'No. You move so often we had trouble tracking you down.'

'I'm a hard woman to please. A hotel has to be comfortable.'

'Look at it from a police point of view. Maybe you're up to something and you want to make it difficult to be followed. You take the precaution of moving around.'

'You can shove that one, Frank. I didn't like the first two hotels. There's nothing sinister in that. I don't know what you're fishing for. I was in Paris before London. Before that Rome. You know how superficial we Americans can be. Six hours in Barcelona and we've seen everything. Now it's London's turn. Three antique stores, Harrod's, the Changing of the Guard, and I'm out of here.'

Pagan experienced one of those drugged moments in which the strip of electricity under the bathroom door seemed to vibrate. He rubbed his eyes, looked away.

'Do you have any more questions, Frank? Or are we through?'

There, he thought. A sliver of ice in her voice; a little frost. He said, 'Look, I already told you your name had to be checked, that's all. You haven't been singled out especially. There's a whole slew of names.'

'It's got something to do with this character Ruhr?'

'Yes.'

'You don't imagine for a moment that I'd ever be connected with anybody like that?'

'Of course not.'

'But you just had to see me.'

'I had to see you. Did you come here alone?'

'Sure. I often travel on my own. I'm reaching that stage – set in my ways. I like solitude.'

Something troubled him here. An element was wrong, a balance disturbed. Somehow he was having difficulty imagining Magdalena, gregarious Magdalena, travelling alone.

That isn't quite it either, Frank.

He said, 'Sometimes I wonder what would have happened if you hadn't gone back home thirteen years ago:'

'Do you think we ever really stood a chance, Frank? Do you think we'd still be together?'

'Tough question.' He remembered trips along the river to Richmond; strolling in Kew Gardens; walking hand-in-hand around the Serpentine. Bistros in Chelsea; antique shops on the Fulham Road; Petticoat Lane. He'd taken her to a cricket match at the Oval and she'd fallen asleep. Tourists and lovers in starry, brilliant London.

'And totally unanswerable,' she said. 'You're a British cop. I'm a Cuban democrat exiled in Florida. It's a big divide.'

Pagan looked round the room. He didn't want to leave. Screw divides, he thought. Why didn't she ask him to stay a little longer?

He realised with a quiet little shock that he knew the answer to that question, that he'd known it for some minutes now, but hadn't wanted to admit it to himself. The light under the bathroom door shimmered like mercury, then seemed to expand. *Of course*! Bright light in a closed room. The mystery of Magdalena's new-found love of her own companionship. The strange uneasiness he'd felt. It tumbled into place like so many coins slowly falling.

She was looking at her wristwatch on the bedside table; a surreptitious glance. 'It was good to see you again, Frank. But I'm already late for my appointment. I'm sorry we don't have more time. I hope you get your man.'

He finally gave way to an impulse, pulled her towards him, perhaps just a little too sharply, and kissed her. He surprised himself, but she didn't resist, she offered her open mouth and the tip of her tongue, and when he placed a hand inside her robe she didn't immediately push him away. For a few seconds he forgot Ruhr, and the wound, and the way the world trespassed. He remembered what it was like to be inside this woman, that collision of flesh, and how her breasts tasted between his lips. The memory had all the odd luminosity of an hallucination and the poignancy of a dead love.

'Go,' she said.

He stepped into the corridor, turning once to look at her, seeing only one hand raised in farewell as the door closed on her. One hand. A fragment of Magdalena. It was somehow very fitting.

Downstairs in the lobby he found Foxworth sitting impatiently under a vast spidery plant. Foxie stood up.

'I want you to go up to the twelfth floor,' Pagan said.

'Oh?'

Pagan grunted and lowered himself cautiously into the sofa alongside his assistant. The plant created a dark green umbrella over his head. 'The room number's 1209. Keep an eye on it in a casual way. See if you can look like the house detective.'

'May I ask why?'

'I want to find out who's hiding in the bathroom.'

'Bathroom? Can you fill me in slowly, Frank?'

Pagan looked in the direction of the lifts. 'Later.'

Rafael Rosabal dried his face, then tossed the towel aside. 'I didn't know you had friends in this town.'

'It was a long time ago,' she said.

'Yeah? *Poor Frank.* I heard.' He opened the closet, removed a shirt, pulled it on. 'It sounded like it was only yesterday.'

'You're jealous. How wonderful! You're actually jealous!'

Rosabal said nothing. He clipped his cufflinks neatly in place. Silver and diamond, they gleamed in the lamp-light. He was fastidious about his appearance.

She went on, 'You heard him. He came here on a routine matter. There's a hunt going on for this German, whatever his name is. Pagan isn't the kind of guy to cut corners. He sees stones, he turns them all over. Compulsive. I just happened to be one of his stones.'

'Was he also compulsive as a lover? Did he make love to you all the time? Was he insatiable?'

'I don't remember.'

'You obviously still mean something to him. But does he mean anything to you?'

She laughed because she was enjoying this moment. She'd never seen him even remotely jealous before. 'We're planning to run away together. We lowered our voices when it came to that part so you wouldn't overhear.'

Rosabal took her in his arms and held her. Had he really been jealous? He wasn't sure. He thought about Pagan and Magdalena for a moment – a surprising little fluke, a trinket of fate, amusing the way all such concurrences can be, but it meant nothing in the end. There was no way the English policeman could link Magdalena to him; and even if Pagan made such a connection, what did it matter? How could the Englishman possibly discover any association between Rosabal and Gunther Ruhr?

'Is he likely to catch the German?' he asked.

'I don't give a damn. I don't want to spend our last half hour together wondering about some lunatic on the run. We've got better things to do.'

'I was just curious. If he's compulsive, presumably he isn't going to sleep until the man is caught.'

'Who cares? What difference does it make to you?' She unclipped his cufflinks, slid her hands up his arms and felt the fine hair stir as if touched by electricity. She undid the buttons of his shirt, then pushed him back across the bed; he was distracted.

'I'm just interested in the kind of man your former lover is,' he said. 'Natural curiosity. Was he better than me?'

'Forget him. Nobody's better than you.'

She lowered her face and kissed the hairs that grew across his chest. Where the hairs faded, his skin was brown and almost satin to the touch; she opened her eyes, studied a small blue vein that travelled crookedly just beneath the surface of flesh. She said, 'I adore you. I wish I had words to tell you how much.'

Rosabal lay silent, his eyes shut. She felt his fingertips against the back of her neck, small indentations of pressure; he had powerful hands and sometimes he underestimated his own strength. She moved her head and his hands slackened and the pressure diminished.

She opened his fly slowly. She always knew how to arouse him and change his mood. 'My sweet darling,' she said. *Vida mia!*

He saw her hair fall over his thighs. He shut his eyes and held his breath as if he meant to contain the explosion in his fashion, but he couldn't. He heard the way she moaned joyfully, her hands cupped together under his testicles; he came with a surge that rocked him. She raised her face. A glistening thread of semen lay on her lip and she removed it with a fingertip. She held this frail memento towards the light, then it drifted away. There was a profound intimacy she had with Rafael that with any other man would have been unthinkable. Certainly she'd never known it with another lover. It excluded the rest of the world. She found herself doing things she'd never done before, thinking thoughts that would never have entered her mind until now. She looked at him. He was so beautiful at times he made her ache.

They lay together in silence.

Then she said, 'I want to leave before you. I don't like waiting behind after you've gone.'

'Of course.'

She shut her eyes very tightly. At the back of her mind she could already feel the sorrow that always came, like some vindictive wraith, whenever they parted. And there was always the same penetrating doubt, the heartache of wondering if, and when, they would meet again.

'Tell me we're going to win,' she said. This was another troublesome matter for her; she needed reassurances here too. Her love for Rosabal, her political beliefs, her desire to play a significant role in changing Cuba – these were bound together so tightly as to be inseparable.

'Do you doubt it?'

'I like to hear you say it, that's all.'

He turned his face towards her. 'We're going to win. Nothing can stand in our way.'

Her face propped against the palm of her hand, she gazed at him. *The ultimate victory.* There were moments in which she could feel it as certainly as she might some fever in her blood – a raging flood of light and warmth. She had one such moment now as she studied her lover's face. Her fears and doubts drifted away like so much steam.

She turned over on her back, looked up at the ceiling. She thought about the role she would play later, in the time after Castro. Rosabal had brought it up a year ago in Mexico City; the only true democracy, he'd said, was one based on elections that were not only free but fair. And with that delightful smile on his face which contained her future, he told her how he had come up with a special job for her, namely Minister of Elections, a post he'd create for her when the time came, a powerful position that would bestow upon her the responsibility of ensuring elections free of corruption and coercion, elections that would be untainted by fraud as they so frequently were in such countries as Panama and Chile. Cuban democracy would be a model for the rest of Latin America.

Besides, what damn good was a rotten democracy? he'd asked. What good was it if votes could be bought with money or threats of violence? People had to cast their ballots without fear. Her job, as Rafael had enthusiastically described it, would be more than merely overseeing the impartial counting of ballots; a whole nation accustomed to one antiquated system for which *nobody had ever voted* had to be re-educated, an enormous task that affected every stratum of society. Immense propaganda would have to be created in schools, factories, farms. Simple democracy; an alien concept for a whole generation of Cubans who had to be wakened, and shaken, and remade! And he had absolutely no doubt that she had the energy for this; she had the zeal, the dedication, there was no question.

The prospect, and Rafael's faith in her, filled her with excitement; he intended to make her the principal architect of free elections in Cuba. In 1961, at the Bay of Pigs, scores of men, including her own father, had died in pursuit of that ideal. She shut her eyes. She said, 'Do you know what makes me really happy? It's not just the importance of this job – it's the fact *you* understand what it means to me. Even after we're married, you want me to have a life of my own.' She opened her eyes, looked at him.

He said, 'You have too much to contribute. I wouldn't expect you to give up your independence. I've told you that before. In any case, it's part of your charm.' He smiled now. 'Presidente Rosabal and his wife Magdalena,' he added, as if testing the coupling. 'It sounds so very right.'

And it was; what could be more natural? she wondered. Rafael and Magdalena. Lovers. Husband and wife. President and Minister. All along the line they fitted smoothly together. Sometimes this realisation overwhelmed her. She, who had always looked upon marriage as a relic of a simpler age when women blindly entered into unfair contracts – she wanted to be this man's wife; she wanted Rafael as her husband. He had asked her a year ago in Mexico City; her acceptance had been the most tranquil moment of her life. But she had known from the beginning that she'd never be just a decoration at Rosabal's side, never window-dressing. She wanted more. And she was going to get it.

Rafael Rosabal was silent for a long time. Then he pointed his index finger, gun-like, at the ceiling, and made a clicking sound.

'Castro is a dead man,' he said in a toneless voice.

'Yes.' Magdalena Torrente laid her face upon her lover's chest. 'A corpse.'

Dover, Delaware

The house, overgrown with weeds and shrubbery, had no ostentation. It was large and anonymous, rather like its owner John Merkandome, who was known in intelligence circles as the Grim Reaper. Located a couple of miles from the Little Creek Wilderness Area, the house commanded some splendid views of Delaware Bay, but it was otherwise plain and unadorned. Merkandome paid very little attention to his surroundings. He enjoyed the indoor pool in which he presently floated, but, beyond that, he had no time for luxuries.

He breast-stroked to the side of the pool and hauled himself halfway out of the blue water, which dripped from his grey hair into his eyes. He was a lean man with an odd skin condition that caused his flesh to appear marbled. He sat down on a step and blinked as he said, 'All our studies came to the same conclusion. Every single hypothesis led to the same result.'

'With tragic consequences in London.' The other person in the pool was a round-cheeked man called Allen Falk. Falk, who had wavy hair, oiled and styled in a way that suggested the mid-1950s, had advised the last two Presidents and the present incumbent on Central American matters. He was an influential counsellor whose love affairs were as public as his professional life was wrapped in mystery. He was said to have parlayed his leverage in The White House into a crucial role in defining CIA policy in Central America.

Nobody really knew the extent of Falk's power. How far it reached was a matter of ongoing rumour. In his social and sexual life he dallied with actresses, lady novelists, and on one occasion a beautiful pop singer who later had a nervous breakdown. Falk's fame was of a curiously American kind. Those things of substance he might have achieved played no part in it; only the margins of his life – his women, his cologne, the make of his sunglasses – were taken into account by the gods who decide the credentials of celebrity.

Merkandome, who was approaching his fifty-seventh year, got out of the pool. He was in good shape for his age, better than Al Falk, who was slightly plump and relied on tailors more than exercise for his appearance. Falk swam in his ungainly way to the side of the pool. The stench of chlorine was heavy in the air.

Merkandome draped a towel round his shoulders. 'Those are the accidents we learn to live with, Al,' he said in his New England accent. 'Tragedies are an occupational hazard. You should know that by now. You should also know that no study can take into account every possible human factor. In this case, a sick German's sexual peccadilloes. Incomplete input, Al, equals incomplete equation.'

Falk would personally have preferred another plan of action from the start, but Merkandome was the expert in plausibility studies, not he. It was the Grim Reaper who created models and ran them through computers in his private lab in a grubby building owned by a front called Dome Electronics in Wilmington, Delaware. The CIA knew the building well because Merkandome was a major consultant to the agency even though he was no longer on any official payroll these days. For thirty years he'd worked at Langley, an organisation man.

In 1961 he had been involved in planning the operation that turned out to be the fiasco at the Bay of Pigs. For the rest of his life Merkandome lived with the idea that not only had he failed to bring down Castro but he had also provided that sonofabitch with one of his most glorious public relations victories – the chance to gloat over the defeat of American-backed forces.

'I pay bright young graduates from MIT a lot of money to run plausibility studies, Al. They don't leave stones unturned. They're smart fellows. More than that, though, they're *thorough*. And give me thorough over smart every time.'

Al Falk climbed up out of the pool, reached for a towel, began to dry himself off. His pectorals sagged, a gloomy fact he noticed in an absent-minded way. 'If we hadn't needed the hardware, we wouldn't have needed Ruhr,' he remarked. Falk hated conditionals. They cluttered a man's life.

'Sure, but we needed the hardware,' Merkandome said. 'Every single study came up with that, Al. Without hardware, there's no good pretext to go in and get the job done. We worked it through from hundreds of angles. For example. We considered the phony kidnapping of a Senator's son by Cuban agents. We played with the idea of poisoning the water-supply to the US base at Guantanamo and blaming it on Castro. We went through one scenario after another, Al. Some plausible. Some downright stupid. Most of them far too soft. You don't have to hear them all. What it always came back to was the notion of our own shores being menaced. You threaten a fellow in his own back yard, and he becomes irate. Any action he takes to defend his life and property is justifiable. That was the strongest concept of all. But we didn't figure Ruhr's weakness into our equations. How could we? We didn't know about it.'

Allen Falk tossed his towel aside. He looked up at the glass ceiling, beyond which sultry afternoon clouds clung to a weak yellow sun. 'Apparently nobody knew,' he said.

'See? The human factor,' Merkandome remarked.

Fuck the human factor, Falk thought. Why weren't things always cut and dry? Why were they so damned ragged? Falk, even though he was a master of court intrigue and knew how to play the byzantine game of White House politics, nevertheless longed for simplicity at times; a world in which all your plans actually worked – what a terrific place that would be. People always considered Falk a complicated man. They were wrong – he was a simple man in complex circumstances.

Falk got to his feet. He thought of the cops dead in that London suburb, the people injured, the property destroyed. The trouble was that everything had its price. Especially freedom. He had no intention of cancelling the programme now, even if he wanted to, and he didn't. Too much was already involved, too much invested. And not just money.

He glanced at the Grim Reaper and said, 'The show goes on.'

'They said you were a trooper, Al,' John Merkandome replied.

London

Shortly before midnight, at a well-preserved eighteenth-century house overlooking the Thames in Chelsea, Jean-Paul Chapotin slipped his key inside the lock, opened the door, stepped into a narrow hall carpeted in vile red. He placed his briefcase on the three-legged table in the hall, then entered the sitting-room, which might have been decorated by a fop. Eighteenth-century furniture was permissible, to be admired even, but Chapotin loathed the powder-blue walls and ceiling and the curtains the colour of a new moon.

He sat on the sofa, which was too narrow for a man of his bulk, but the whole house was too narrow and cramped. He made a telephone call to his wife Gabrielle in Paris. Gabrielle, who would be wearing whatever absurd garment had been mandated by the queens who ruled *haute couture*, answered in a voice made dreamy by tranquillisers.

'I have to stay here another day,' Chapotin said.

'Then I'll see you tomorrow?'

'Yes, yes.' Chapotin heard a floorboard creak at the top of the stairs. 'Is everything well?'

'Why shouldn't it be?'

Chapotin shrugged. Conversations with his wife had become impossibly dull over the years. What had once been wild adoration had dwindled during the course of their twenty-year marriage to the kind of mutual tolerance that communicates itself best in silence; and when silence failed, there were always domestic trivialities to crowd the minutes. The plumbing in the house near the Bois de Boulogne, the servant problem at the country estate in Provence, the drunken behaviour of a certain stable-hand at the stud farm in the Loire Valley.

'Will I pick you up at the airport?' she asked.

'Send a car.'

The conversation terminated. He was weary suddenly, and stretched his legs. He yawned. Once again, from the upper part of the house, he heard the creak of a floorboard.

He rose, walked into the hall, looked up the flight of stairs.

'Melody?' he said.

It was a silly name, he thought. The only thing remotely musical about Melody was her love of the noise made by cash-registers ringing, the song of money, Chapotin's money. But, dear God, the little English debutante was beautiful in a way Chapotin, normally a sensible man of moderate inclinations, found irresistible.

She appeared on the landing, a vague, skinny girl whose large blue eyes, alas empty, dominated her features. She wore an ostrich boa – selected, no doubt, from one of the 'junk' shops in the neighbourhood and charged to Chapotin's account – and a 1920s flapper dress with shimmering fringes. She had on very bright pink shoes. Her taste in clothing and interior design was, charitably, eclectic. Her moussed hair was pressed down on her skull and artfully arranged around her ears.

'Ahoy,' she said.

Chapotin was always in two minds about his mistress. The accountant in him wanted to dump her; but the libertine couldn't bear to part with this vacuous, sexy girl. She came down the stairs slowly, trailing the boa behind her.

'Kiss kiss.' She stood on the bottom step.

Chapotin kissed her. She tasted of baby soap and vermouth and was completely desirable.

'Take me places, Chappie. You never take me anywhere. Fly me to new continents.'

'Where would you like to go?' he asked. He could hardly wait to undress her and have her; the lust he experienced was impossible.

'Paree,' she said. '*Naturellement*.'

'I have a little problem with that one, *chérie*.'

'Melly's stuck in boooooring old London while Chappie jets all over creation,' she said.

'Soon we'll go to Hawaii.'

'Luaus chill me. Grass skirts demoralise me. I'm not thrilled.'

'Then where would you like to go?'

Melody shrugged and trailed the boa inside the sitting-room. Chapotin went after her. Why did he put up with this child? What kink did he have in his character? It came down to something really quite simple. His regular life was so demandingly sombre and filled with stress that he'd forgotten how to play and have sheer fun – until Melody, like a creature from some far planet, had crashlanded on his staid, tightly buttoned little world.

She sat down on the sofa. Her white stockings had a lacy design. She wore very black eye make-up. Chapotin sat beside her. He laid one hand on her wrist.

'I'll take you on a world cruise.' When would he ever find the time?

'Ocean waves! I would vomit constantly.'

Chapotin wondered how his fellow Society members would react to this girl if they ever met her – which, of course, could never be allowed to happen: the Society did not permit private lives to touch its affairs. Enrico Caporelli, who had a roving eye, might be charmed by the girl's odd sexuality, but the others – especially those prudish Americans and the slightly sinister Magiwara – might sniff with disdain.

Chapotin understood that his devotion to this child would be considered by some a weakness, but he had a romantic's incurable heart and a lust that gripped him like a hot fist.

He put his hand on her knee.

'We'll come to some accommodation,' he said.

Melody blinked her long false lashes. 'We shall see what we shall see, Chappie. In the meantime, I may order new curtains and new rugs to match.'

Chapotin had the gruesome feeling that his mistress would one day come to resemble his wife, that his whole life would be one long barrage of domesticity. Curtains! Plumbing! Carpets! What he needed was the escape route of Melody's sweet young flesh. He lunged towards her but she was as slippery as the material of her dress, and she glided out from under his hands.

'Ah-hah,' he said.

'Ahhah yourself, Jaypee. No foreign junket, no fuckee.'

Chapotin lunged again. Melody nimbly stepped aside. He was amused. He liked the hunt.

'You can't catch me,' she said, and laughed.

Jean-Paul Chapotin struck out his hand and grabbed the dress, which ripped as soon as she whirled away from him, revealing the extraordinary sight of Melody Logue's pale and lovely inner thigh. A tattooed robin, red-breasted, wings spread, nestled close to her vulva. It was so lifelike it had quite startled Chapotin the first time he'd seen it.

'Leave her royal bloody highness and live with me,' she said.

'Leave my wife?'

Yes, he thought. Yes, yes, yes. To get at that bird he'd do anything, anything at all. Chapotin stretched out one trembling hand but Melody slipped away again.

'Say the word and win the bird!'

Chapotin laughed. This romping eighteen-year-old nincompoop who blessed his life – how could he leave Gabrielle for this? On the other hand, how could he not?

He heard the sound of glass breaking, muffled by the thickness of the curtains. Without thinking, Chapotin caught the girl and dragged her to the floor with him. He barely registered the two orbs that rolled across the carpet. He knew what they were, but recognition didn't prompt an instant response. It was a joke, an execrable joke, it wasn't real. The girl clutched him and said *Oooo* just as the grenades exploded.

Chapotin had time only to reflect how strangely quiet the whole thing was, like a noise inside a vacuum. Shrapnel pierced the girl's neck. Her skin-tissue flew through the air into Chapotin's eyes, blinding him. He tried to raise his hands to his face. Severed at the wrists by the hot blast of metal, they were gone.

8 Fife, Scotland

At six-thirteen a.m., a transport plane was cleared for take-off from an air base in Fife on the east coast of Scotland. The plane, a C-130 painted in camouflage, was normally deployed shuttling men and equipment between various NATO bases and the United States. An impressive flying machine over ninety feet long, it was capable of carrying as much as seventy thousand pounds of cargo. On this rainy morning, the C-130's approved flight plan would take it south into England and across the Channel to Germany, where it was scheduled to pick up sixty paratroopers in Wiesbaden and return them to Alabama. The crew consisted of pilot, co-pilot, navigator and flight engineer.

The take-off was smooth. The great plane went out over the North Sea into clouds, then turned back inland and began its climb toward Edinburgh. Cantankerous rain slashed at the fuselage and every so often the craft bucked the turbulence like a whale on the tide. In the cargo area crates of spare parts and tools rattled around and some loose sacking slid back and forth. But something else also moved, unnoticed by the crew on the flight deck, something that had been concealed on board for many hours and waiting, with nervous impatience, for just this occasion.

Directly over the Border Country, that underpopulated and lovely tract of land dividing two nations, three armed men stepped inside the flight deck. They carried automatic pistols and wore fatigues. There were no masks because there was no need to conceal their faces. After all, the men intended to leave no witnesses. The leader of the four was a black-haired man in his early forties called Joseph Sweeney. It was Sweeney who pressed his gun directly into the pilot's skull and ordered him to relinquish the controls. One of Sweeney's men took the pilot's seat. The co-pilot was also ordered to give up his position. He complied. Only the flight engineer complained and he was struck across the mouth for his troubles.

Sweeney led the crew back into the cargo area. It wasn't immediately apparent to any crew member what the hijacker intended to do to them. They feared his pistol, but nobody imagined he'd fire inside the aircraft – if he had any sense. At the worst, they expected to be bound and flown wherever the hijackers might have in mind and then traded or bargained over. Certainly none of the crew anticipated that Joseph Sweeney would do what he did.

He ordered the flight engineer, who was bleeding freely from the mouth, to open the paratroop door. There was a momentary hesitation before the engineer responded: they were going to get parachutes, weren't they?

Sweeney waved the gun and the engineer opened the door and cold misty rain blew inside. Understanding of Sweeney's purpose came swiftly to the crew. They were supposed to jump, yes, but without parachutes. If they didn't, Sweeney would shoot them.

The flight engineer was told to go first. When he resisted, Sweeney fired one shot into the man's groin. Still the engineer wouldn't go through the open door and Sweeney was becoming annoyed by two things – the cold rain that had started to soak his clothing, and the man's stubbornness. The other three crew members had a kind of stunned desperation about them; they began to look for ways out of this horrifying predicament – a stray wrench, a hammer, anything they might grab as a weapon. Sweeney read the signs of resistance and didn't like them. He called for one of his fellow hijackers to come out of the cockpit and join him. A strong surly man who looked Arabic came from the flight deck and struggled with the engineer and finally hurled him out. The falling body made a tunnel through clouds as it dropped from a height of seventeen thousand feet over wet moorlands.

One by one, the other crew members were dispatched from the plane. The pilot resisted with the greatest ferocity and Sweeney had to shoot him between the eyes before tossing him out. Sweeney shut the door. He was shivering.

The plane continued south, flying over Newcastle and the River Tyne and then heading for the industrial Midlands, where pollution and weather conspired to create a perfect canopy of impenetrable cloudiness.

London

It was six-twenty a.m. when Foxworth woke Frank Pagan, who had slept once again on his office sofa. Foxie had brewed strong coffee, which roused Pagan from his Pethidine dreams, which were senseless and inchoate. He woke slowly, reaching for the cup Foxie held before him. Cautiously he moved into an upright position and sipped the hot black liquid. It was good stuff. Foxworth, a well-bred young man with a taste for the finer things, always ground his own Jamaican Blue Mountain beans.

'Nectar,' Pagan said, blinking at the very thin yellow light that had begun to stretch across Golden Square like a skin graft that hadn't quite taken. He had some vague recollection of Magdalena in one of his bizarre dreams, but the form was lost to him.

Foxworth produced some gauze and scissors. 'Today we have the changing of bandages,' he said.

'Let me get this down first.' Pagan drained his cup, then he reached for his painkillers on the window ledge. He drew his hand back. 'I'll see if I can get by without them for a while. I wouldn't want to end up in some treatment centre for drug addicts. I lean toward compulsive behaviour as it is.'

Foxworth agreed with that assessment. 'Let's get the old bandage off.'

'Foxworth Nightingale,' Pagan remarked.

'I was a Boy Scout. I had a drawerful of first aid badges. Now turn to the side, Frank.'

Pagan obliged. Foxworth removed the old bandage and dressing and discarded them. With impressive neatness, he snipped a length of new bandage and placed it around Pagan's chest, then fastened it.

'The exit wound looks raw,' Foxie said. 'The entrance isn't so bad, though. Put this on.'

'A clean shirt?'

'I took the liberty of going to your flat. I didn't think you'd mind. I brought you a clean suit and some underwear. Also shoes and socks. I hope everything matches.'

The suit was brown linen, the shoes black, the socks grey, the shirt pale-blue herringbone. Pagan didn't have the heart to criticise the colour scheme. Besides, he was looking for Gunther Ruhr, not dining at Le Caprice. Foxworth, for his part, had had a terrible time going through Pagan's wardrobe, the shirts that suggested bad dreams, parrots and Hawaiian plants and swirls of vivid colour, the array of shoes that covered the spectrum from bright canvas espadrilles to shiny black leather, the dozen suits of all kinds, linen and tweed and silk, summer and winter, formal and otherwise, single- and double-breasted.

'You'd make a fine gentleman's gentleman, Foxie.'

'I'll keep that in mind.'

'Is there more coffee?'

Foxworth opened a thermos flask and refilled Pagan's cup. 'A couple of overnight items, Frank. I'll run through them for you. First, the usual sightings of Gunther. Sheffield, Morecambe, Newcastle.'

'Now he's travelling north,' Pagan said drily. 'Soon we'll hear he's in bloody Reykjavik trying to take out Icelandic citizenship.'

'He was also seen in Sloane Square and Pimlico and stepping aboard a train at Victoria Station. Also in Brighton, Canterbury and – here's a nice one – Stonehenge, where he was spotted by a couple of druids.'

Pagan shook his head. Druids, he thought. Stonehenge drew all kinds of oddballs, like a giant bug light in the middle of Salisbury Plain.

'What other news, Foxie?'

'We've had reports from our men in East Anglia. They say security at military installations is tight. As for the Chief Constable in Cambridge, he's got every available policeman in the county beating the fields with sticks, in a manner of speaking.'

Pagan stood up now, walked to the window, saw a few early morning drones cross the square in the direction of their offices. He had a sudden sense of dread. All the order he saw beneath him – the streets, the parked cars, this somnolent London square – had a transient quality. A man like Ruhr, if he went unchecked, could demolish a city block with very little trouble.

'Is there any progress from the manhunt?' Pagan asked.

'Drudgery,' Foxie said. 'Door-to-door drudgery. Our men keep knocking and they keep asking, but no Gunther.'

'The bastard's somewhere,' Pagan said.

Foxie picked up a thick manila folder, opened it, took out a sheet of paper. He said, 'By the way, there were two murders last night in Chelsea. It's outside our bailiwick, but I mention it because of the MO. Two grenades tossed through a window. Boom boom and cheerio. The report mentions the fact that the weapons were extremely powerful but homemade.'

'Homemade? Irish?'

Foxworth shrugged. 'It's very remote. The victims were a French businessman called Chapotin and his bit of fluff, a girl by the name of Melody Logue, who happened to be the niece of Lord somebody or other. I don't see any reason the Irish would want to dispose of the pair. I also considered the idea that it could be the work of Ruhr, but homemade isn't his style. Unless he's changed.'

Pagan made a gesture of impatience. 'I'll read the written stuff when I've got time.'

'There's one interesting little snippet about Chapotin.'

'Which is?'

'From 1957 until 1959, Jean-Paul Chapotin was the Deputy French Ambassador to Cuba.'

'Cuba.' Pagan considered this item a moment, but it didn't have a place in the framework of his preoccupation with Gunther.

'Cuba brings me to the last item, of course,' Foxworth said. 'It took some hours and a lot of looking through the Foreign Office's mug shots, but finally I was able to identify Magdalena Torrente's friend.'

'And?' There was impatience in Pagan's voice. He wanted to pretend that Magdalena's room-mate meant nothing to him. It was the kind of inquiry one made on the side. A personal tangent, the geometry of an old love, that was all.

Foxie rummaged back inside his folder and brought out a small stack of flimsy sheets; across each were the words 'For Internal File Only'. Foxie smiled in a way that suggested larceny. 'It took some persuasion and a bit of the old school tie to get these, Frank. Domestic surveillance division of intelligence. Ever since a Cuban diplomat tried to shoot one of our intelligence chaps on a London street in 1988, surveillance of Cubans on diplomatic or any other kind of business here has increased considerably. The watchers don't want to let Cubans out of their sight. Besides, all this surveillance irritates Castro, and everybody loves getting old Fidel's goat – '

'The point, Foxie.'

'The point, Frank, is a man called Rafael Rosabal.'

Norfolk

Stephanie Brough pressed her tongue against the strip of rayon that had been used to gag her. Her arms were tied behind her back with short lengths of rope that cut into her skin, and her ankles were bound so tightly bone was forced against bone. The loose ends of her restraints had been knotted to the frame of the narrow bed on which she lay. There was a window above her. It was dawn and heavy clouds rushed across the sky.

She hadn't slept at all. How could she? Even with her eyes shut she'd been conscious of Ruhr sitting in the corner of the room in an old armchair. He'd been there most of the night, sometimes just gazing at her. You couldn't tell anything from his expression. You couldn't tell what he was thinking or planning. He just looked so chilling.

Oh Steffie, she thought. *Perhaps today they'll release you*. She wondered about her poor mare, which she'd left in the rain. The horse would trot home eventually, she was sure of that. And then Steffie's Dad would go to the police – it was really that simple, wasn't it? He would have gone to the police already, wouldn't he?

She shut her eyes. She heard voices from the kitchen. The skinny man, the American whose name she didn't know, was talking to Ruhr. They were arguing, and she knew it had something to do with her, but she didn't want to listen.

What she remembered was how her father had talked about Ruhr, and the killing of those poor policemen, and how Ruhr was a monster who deserved to hang. She hadn't paid close attention because her father was always saying that so-and-so should be hanged, or that hanging was too good for some people. Her father was a bloody dinosaur, but really quite nice.

She'd seen Ruhr's picture in newspapers and on TV. And yesterday, when she'd recognised him, her heart had withered and something had dropped like a boulder into her stomach. When he'd dragged her back to the house she couldn't help thinking of all the terrible things he was said to have done.

Is he going to kill you, Steffie? Are you just another victim?

She turned her face to the wall. If somebody was going to shoot her, she didn't want to have to see the killer come in the room. Think other things! Think music or books or The Lord's Prayer! The argument in the kitchen was still going on. The harsh voices were almost audible as they rose and fell, Ruhr's especially, high-pitched and nasal. She tried to tune it out. A few drops of rain knocked on the window above, and the branch of a dead tree flapped.

What would it be like to be shot through the skull? Probably nothing. No sensation. The end. Panicked, she struggled for a few seconds against her bonds, but it was hopeless. The harder she laboured, the more painfully the ropes cut. Her eyes watered in sheer frustration.

Ruhr came into the bedroom. He carried a rifle; tucked into his waistband was a handgun. His bad hand was concealed inside a pocket. He approached the bed and smiled, but she couldn't stand to see that smile, which was unreal, like something razored out of his face, a damp slit. He sat down, slid the gag from her lips. She was thankful to him for that at least, but her gratitude lasted only a second.

'Are you hungry?' he asked.

She shook her head. She wouldn't speak. She'd be perfectly quiet, like one of those nuns who had taken vows of silence. It was a small rebellion, but she couldn't think of any other kind of resistance.

'You don't want to speak?' Ruhr asked. He set his rifle down, propping it against the mattress.

Steffie said nothing. Actually, silence was pleasant, like a great estuary of motionless water; she could float and go on floating across its surface. Floating lilies and serene swans and reflections of the sky. She stared at Ruhr, remembering how he'd smacked her yesterday, and suddenly the surface of her silence seemed fragile. He could strike her again and make her talk, if he wanted.

'Little girl,' Ruhr said. He put his good hand on her stomach, the palm flat. She had a firm belly, none of the softness that comes with the collapse of time. 'Pretty little girl. Your friends tell you, no? They tell you how pretty you are. I imagine you have many boyfriends.'

Silence; rain on the window; the branch drumming. She thought, *These are a few of my favourite things*.

Ruhr moved his good hand. He slid it under her blouse – her white blouse, caked with hardened mud, disgusting – and then unhooked her brassiere from the front. She had the thought that if she let him do whatever he wanted then surely he'd set her free. Ruhr tugged the brassière from her body and turned it over in his hand, smiling as he studied it. Then he lowered his face into the garment and didn't move for a while.

'The smell of a young girl,' he said. 'There is nothing quite so fresh and lovely.'

Steffie felt her stomach rise up into her throat. How could she bear it if he touched her again? He was ugly and white and the very idea of being kissed by him – *he wouldn't stop at kissing! he'd screw her*! – filled her with terror. The nearest she'd come to sex was with Jason Turnberry in the summer just past; not the whole way – he'd fondled her breasts and she'd let him touch her between the legs for a second, but Jason wasn't Gunther Ruhr, Jason was a lovely timid boy, and he stopped when you told him to.

'You are so afraid,' he said. 'There is really no need, Stephanie. Sometimes when you are afraid it becomes contagious, and the people around you begin to be afraid also, and then they do irrational things out of fear. Be calm, little girl.'

Steffie licked her dry lips. What bloody good was silence anyway? It was too meek, too feeble. If she was going to get anywhere, she'd have to speak. Her voice was hoarse when she whispered, 'If you let me leave, I swear I'll never say a thing to anybody. I'll make a solemn vow.'

Ruhr said, 'In my experience, people who make solemn vows are usually the first to make betrayals also.'

'I wouldn't do that. I promise.'

Ruhr looked at her for a while. He slowly transferred the small brassière from his good hand to the bad one. 'I am sure you believe what you say right at this moment. But my answer is the same. You see,' – and he patted her knuckles; his skin was like damp slate – 'I have business to conduct and I can't afford to let you go home to your parents. Do you understand that? It would be imprudent of me to release you.'

'When will you let me go? When your business is finished?'

Ruhr stood up. He looked down at her. 'In about twenty minutes from now, we are going to take a short trip.'

'Where?'

Ruhr placed a fingertip to his mouth, a gesture of secrecy.

'But,' was all she managed to say before Ruhr replaced the gag.

Outside the house, Trevaskis and Rick loaded the Range Rover with M-16s, tear gas canisters, rocket launchers, grenades, gas masks. The guns, which had been cleaned yet again last night by the Argentinians, were all in excellent condition. Ruhr's inspection of the weapons had been thorough.

Trevaskis, half-listening to the car radio, said, 'You ask me, it's fucked, the whole situation.'

Rick, as taciturn as he was massive, grunted as he loaded a box of ammunition.

'Some things you don't mess with,' Trevaskis said. 'This kid, now. What's the point? I wouldn't have brought her inside the house in the first goddam place. No way. A quick bullet in the skull, kid's dead, you got no extra baggage.'

'Right,' Rick agreed.

'And if you don't want her blood on your hands, then all you gotta do is tie her up real tight and leave her in the house. Sooner or later somebody's gonna find her.' Trevaskis, who didn't much like the idea of violence being done to a child, was quiet for a moment. 'He's one sick sonofabitch, lemme tell you. Look into his eyes, man. I seen saner guys in county asylums.'

Slicks of rain ran down Trevaskis' face to his neck and slithered over his St Christopher. 'So long as he don't screw up the whole deal, I don't care. I'll tell you one thing for free: I can't stand that bastard. If he crosses me . . . ' Trevaskis let his sentence hang unfinished. Then he added, 'There's only one goddam reason to bring the chick along.'

'What's that?'

'Think about it, Rick.'

Ruhr came out of the house just then. The Americans fell silent at once. Ruhr walked round the Range Rover and stood with his arms folded. He stared up at the dawn sky. The clouds and the rainy haze weren't going to be unfavourable factors. He looked at his wristwatch: six fifty-eight.

'I still say we don't take her with us.' Trevaskis stared at Ruhr, a hard look that didn't impress the German, who simply made an impatient gesture. 'Either we shoot her, or we leave her behind and secure.'

'She goes in the back of the vehicle. We've discussed all this. The matter is closed, Trevaskis.'

'And then what? What happens to her afterwards?'

Ruhr said nothing. Trevaskis wearied him. The American stuck his thumbs in his belt loops and said, 'I just heard on the car radio your man Pagan's back on the job, Ruhr. He's outta the hospital and coming after you. How's that grab you, Mr Claw?'

Ruhr walked some yards from the vehicle. He wasn't even going to dignify Trevaskis' information, thrown at him like some feeble gauntlet, with any kind of comment. Pagan was a policeman and one cop was much like another: they all had dead imaginations. The best one could hope for from a man such as Pagan was that his injury might have made him a more dangerous adversary, that he was looking less to recapture Ruhr than he was to avenge the death of his comrades. A cop on a personal mission was always more interesting than one plodding through dull routine.

But he'd deal with the question of Pagan later, because something else had begun to bother him slightly.

There were times when he stood in a landscape or stepped inside a room and he had an instinct, almost a certainty, an animal sense, that something adverse was about to happen. Often this premonitory ability gave him time to take evasive action. But right now whatever troubled him was so vague it was like a faint scent blown on a haphazard breeze.

He looked up the slope of land that rose from the farmhouse, up through mud and wet trees and clumps of nettles. Whatever made him uneasy lay on the rise, he was sure of that much. He covered the butt of his pistol with the palm of his hand and studied the landscape. The trees dripped, the foliage stirred, the mud was covered with puddles that reflected the sky like so many tiny cracked mirrors.

Ruhr thought about the girl. Her parents would have begun last night by calling their daughter's friends. There would have been no panic at first, a mere uneasiness, perhaps a certain irritation after a time. Then they might have gone out on foot to search for her. Rain and mud and the absence of light would halt them, at least until dawn. They would also have called the local police.

But how many men were available in a country constabulary? And the terrain, covered with muddy fields and ditches and a tortuous network of lanes, could not be combed quickly. Even though it was mainly a flat landscape, it was a secretive one, with hollows, and tall grasses, and dense stands of trees. There were hundreds of isolated farmhouses, weekend cottages for Londoners, windmills, abandoned ruins.

Ruhr took a couple of steps toward the slope. He might have done what Trevaskis had recommended. He might have shot the child. He'd already considered the idea. In time, no doubt, he would jettison her. But he remembered the feel of her skin, and the small white brassière flecked with mud, and he thought about the high cheekbones and the thin oval face and the way her short skirt hardly covered her thighs. He was flooded with a longing both familiar and dangerous. The youthfulness of the child, her silken vulnerability: these were the two elements of an equation whose sum was terror. And what was terror but a means of total control? Besides, when he thought of the girl in Cambridge he had a sense of unfinished business, which he didn't like.

There was another factor in the girl's favour. He imagined a situation in which he might need a hostage, a human shield, a bargaining chip. In his past experience he'd found hostages useful tools. It was astonishing how the forces of law and order would silence their guns when they knew innocent lives might be jeopardised. The terrified face of a hostage was a mirror that reflected the image of an orderly society threatened. Let the hostage be killed and what did you have – the failure of the state to protect its innocents, the dreaded anarchy the forces of law existed to prevent.

Trevaskis might have shot the girl, but therein lay the difference between the American and Ruhr. The former never considered the possibility of finding gold in dross; Ruhr, on the other hand, had a genius for turning the unexpected to his advantage. How else had he survived this long?

Now the wind blew, running through the trees as if a congregation of squirrels had set the branches dancing. Under that rattle there was something else. Not the wind.

Then Ruhr saw.

There, at the crest of the slope, a man pushing a bicycle appeared. He was coming down toward the house; Ruhr at once recognised the man's uniform as that of a police constable. Here, in this rustic corner of England, country policemen still cycled their beat. Ruhr watched the man come down the incline, then he turned slightly, conscious of how Trevaskis and Rick were motionless now, and how the two South Americans stood very still in the open doorway of the house.

The policeman reached the foot of the slope. He was middle-aged and slightly overweight and he wheezed a little.

'Morning,' he said.

Ruhr kept his pistol covered.

'Bloody awful day,' the policeman added. He made sure his bike was well balanced against the trunk of a tree, then he strolled toward Ruhr. Mud squelched beneath his heavy boots as he moved. About six feet from Gunther Ruhr he stopped.

'I'm looking for a girl that's gone missing,' the constable said. 'Seems she was out riding and her horse came home without her last night. I was wondering if you'd seen any sign of the child.'

A horse; the girl hadn't mentioned an animal. 'I'm sorry,' Ruhr said.

'Well then,' the constable said. 'Keep your eyes open, sir, if you don't mind. Always appreciate any information. You new around here?'

Ruhr nodded. He saw it suddenly in the man's face: recognition, disguised behind a large uneasy smile, but recognition just the same. It was unmistakable.

The policeman scratched the side of his face and said, 'We all know how young girls are nowadays. Spend nights with their boyfriends. Parents are the last to know, of course.' The constable had himself in check now. He had control. He could go through the motions without showing the excitement of discovery. This was the terrorist being hunted all across England – and here he was, right in your own back yard!

'Thanks for your time, sir.' The policeman glanced at the house, then walked to his bicycle. 'Sorry to have troubled you.'

He wheeled the vehicle out from under the tree and when he'd pushed the bike about ten feet, Ruhr called out to him.

'Constable. One moment.'

The policeman turned. Ruhr moved toward him. The wind gathered force and shook every tree on the slope and blew a quick flurry of dead leaves through the air.

'Sir?' the policeman asked. A solitary leaf had settled on his shoulder.

Three feet from the constable, Ruhr stopped. In a swift gesture, which looked superficially innocent – a man bending to adjust a sock, a shoelace – he reached beneath the turn-up of his trousers and into the leather sheath he kept strapped to his shin. The knife was in his hand before the constable could move, and, before the weapon registered, the policeman was all but dead. He couldn't move quickly enough for Ruhr, who came up with the knife at an oblique angle and drove the blade into the throat. The policeman cried out, clutched the slash in his neck, then slid to his knees as if, astonished by imminent death, he needed to pray. Ruhr stabbed the man a second time, twisting the blade deep in the ribs.

The policeman fell back, knocking his bicycle over and causing the front wheel to rise in the air, where it spun idly. Ruhr wiped the blade with some leaves.

'Fucking impressive,' Trevaskis said to Rick.

9 Villa Clara Province, Cuba

The house overlooked the ocean and the group of islands known as the Archipelago de Sabana. It was a large white stucco affair constructed around a central courtyard; moonlit water splashed out of a fountain and cascaded over a statue in the shape of a naked girl. The statue was a fine example of social realism, but the Lider Maximo, who stood on a balcony overlooking the fountain, wasn't exactly famous for his appreciation of anything artistic, though he always talked otherwise, since nobody ever questioned his judgments. He surrounded himself at times with swarms of words – like a beekeeper of language – phrases heaped on phrases, intricate and often colourful, yet frequently convoluted and downright enigmatic.

He fought with the urge to smoke one of the cigars he'd given up a while ago. He looked up at the sky. It was a gorgeous Cuban midnight with thin, high clouds and the sound of the tide, a night of coolness and clarity. But the Lider Maximo wasn't in any mood to appreciate such things.

Noises rose from the party in the room below. A piano played. Somebody told a joke to polite laughter. Across the courtyard, beneath arched doorways, armed guards stood in shadows. There were always guards wherever the Lider Maximo went. He even had people who tasted his food before he consumed it.

He turned away from the sight of the statue and walked inside the house, intolerant of this social gathering tonight; the chit-chat, the men who wanted to shake his hand, the requests whispered in his ear, a favour here, a favour there, everything was a bore. He listened a moment to the piano. He had no ear for music – especially now, when he was this impatient.

Where was the Minister of Finance? What was keeping him?

The Lider Maximo went down the stairs. The piano was silent. In the large drawing-room all heads turned as he entered. His unsmiling condition had been noticed earlier and the party had adjusted itself. What might have been loud was muted and discreet. Everybody tried to please the Lider Maximo. They stepped around him as if he lived at the centre of a large pampa of unbroken eggs. Everybody breathed softly in his presence and smiled just a little too eagerly. Women, some of whom underwent a suppressed hysteria in the man's company, were shrill in their pleasantries. But he was more than a man; he was as much an icon in Cuba as the old plaster Christs and Madonnas one still found concealed all the way from the Golfo de Guanahacabibes in the west to Punta Caleta in the east.

Communist Party officials and military leaders and attractive women filled the room. Some spilled out on to a patio where the remains of a roast pig turned on a spit and charcoals glowed and wine bottles stood in disarray on small tables. The Lider Maximo, stroking his beard, stared through the open door and across the patio.

The car would come from that direction.

He tried to be charming to a handsome silver-haired woman, a Danish journalist, who wanted to know some thing about political prisoners – but he was surrounded by his attendants and assistants and the usual Colombian novelist with three names who was something of a house pet. The entourage that swirled about him also included a group of Communist functionaries, some of whom had come from Italy and Spain and India, sightseers of Caribbean Communism: *fidelismo*.

He was too tense for this congregation. He stomped outside and waved his followers away. He wanted a moment's solitude, which wasn't such a selfish desire in a life that had not been his own since 1959. For thirty years he'd been public property, as much nationalised as the sugar industry, or the tobacco companies, or the banks. He was very tired and growing old; he knew that the young people of Cuba referred to him as El Viejo, the old one. Where was the stamina of yesterday? where the legendary strength?

In his starched garberdine fatigues he strutted across the patio. He tore a chunk of flesh from the hot pig and thrust it into his mouth. It had the taste of a highly spiced automobile tyre. He spat it out. The piano began to play again, and there was a round of quiet laughter, more of relief than genuine pleasure. He created a black hole wherever he went tonight; his absence from the main room allowed the guests to relax. He sat slumped in a chair and looked absently at a plate of scorched pig skin, left-overs. In an ill-temper he pushed the plate aside and it clattered to the tiles, where it broke, scattering the discarded food. Nobody turned to look. When El Jefe (as he was also called) broke anything, whether a plate or a law, no voices were raised in criticism.

There wasn't enough food on the island. Every day shortages grew worse. Every day brought some new complaint. Once the criticism had centred around ideology: people asked him questions about the urgency behind universal literacy when reading material was restricted, or why Cuba had aligned itself with the Soviet bloc. Nowadays, ideology wasn't uppermost in the minds of Cubans; they wanted better food, better consumer goods. They heard US radio broadcasts and saw smuggled movies, videotapes, outlawed magazines, and they felt deprived. Ninety miles away in the USA people had everything. In Cuba stores had empty shelves and useless goods and clothing designed in such centres of *haute couture* as Varna, Bulgaria, or Brasov, Rumania.

For the first time in many years, the Lider Maximo was afraid.

He'd known fear before. In the Sierra Maestra in the late 1950s when he'd fought the armies of Batista with only a few men. In 1953, when he'd led an unsuccessful assault on the Moncada barracks in Santiago. Yes, he'd known *el temor*, but he'd never been cowardly. What had they always said about him in Cuba? Fidel, he has the largest *timbales* on the whole goddam island! But this was very different, another stratum of fear; it was as if he could hear the ship of this eight-hundred-mile-long island grind to a halt, the engine broken beyond repair, the fuel tanks empty.

Sometimes, too, the fear yielded to an odd panic. He became easily confused, and amnesiac, and caught himself in the midst of a sentence whose end he'd quite forgotten, or in the middle of an action whose purpose was a puzzle. Now and again he felt slight pains in his stomach, too inconsequential to have his physicians treat. On one occasion, a coldness had seized his heart like a gauntlet of frost, a disquieting sensation that had lasted perhaps for ten seconds. It was age, he thought. Eyesight and teeth went, so did the interior plumbing and the central pump. A man was no more than an intricate machine; and all the blueprints to explain his parts and repair them were incomplete because medicine was still a primitive quasi-science.

Perhaps fear was something else age brought in its merciless wake.

He tilted his head to one side, listening to the croaking of frogs in the distance, so many it was practically a roar. He gazed across the patio, seeing how his armed guards had taken up new positions in the shadows. Inside the house the piano was playing something composed by Silvio Rodriguez, considered a 'safe' musician by the regime. The Lider Maximo knew that if he hadn't been present the pianist would have performed Cole Porter or Irving Berlin or some other Yanqui music. The Lider Maximo was deferred to, even revered. But he knew people carped behind his back and ran him down and accused him of bankrupting Cuba.

There was the sound of a car. He stood up, tugged at his beard. He saw headlights approach. At a point in the road where the concrete twisted toward the ocean, the car lights illuminated white surf. Then the motor died, and a door slammed. The Lider Maximo moved quickly across the patio to embrace the new arrival and whisk him away to a quiet upper room where they might talk, free from the noise of the party.

The room was small, containing only a desk and two chairs and piles of unsorted books. A green-shaded lamp provided the only light. The Lider Maximo said, 'You're very late.'

'There were flight delays,' the visitor replied.

The Lider Maximo waved a hand impatiently. 'Speak to me. Tell me the outcome.'

The visitor said, 'It's just as we feared. The well's running dry.'

The Lider Maximo tossed his head back and looked up at the ceiling where a large motionless fan threw a cross-like shadow; it was possible to see, through the hairs of his beard, the thick double chin. 'They want me out, am I right? They want me to step aside.'

'No, Commandante. They expressed no such desire.'

The Lider Maximo scoffed. 'They wouldn't tell you to your face. The Russians don't operate that way. They smile at you, toast you, and after ten vodkas they hug you. Best of friends. Comrades! Only later do you realise you've been lied to and cheated. Make no mistake, *compañero*, they want me out. I'm too disobedient. Too unruly. They can't always control me the way they would like. If they had a weak man in my position, they might open their purses more generously to Cuba.'

The visitor said, 'I don't think it has anything to do with you, Commandante. They say they'll no longer invest money in Cuba at the levels we've come to expect. The new Politburo has more on its collective mind than Cuba. They'll continue to buy sugar –'

'Oh, this makes my heart glad.' The Lider Maximo's sarcasm was too grim to be amusing. Besides, his sense of humour was always slightly skewed and too heavy-handed to cause much mirth. The charm for which he'd been famous earlier in life had deserted him to a large extent. The world had eroded it.

'– at the present prices. But there will be severe cutbacks in technological help. As many as three hundred advisors will be withdrawn. Joint construction projects already under way, such as the nuclear generating plant at Jurugua, will be halted. No new ones will be started. We can no longer expect – and I quote – favoured treatment.'

The Lider Maximo was angry. 'Favoured treatment!' He spluttered. 'We've always had a special arrangement with them!'

'The Soviets are economising worldwide, Commandante. It's really that simple. They face economic chaos at home. Their whole economy is rotten and cumbersome. The cost of Afghanistan was too high. Now they're turning inward. They're no longer enthusiastic about the spread of Communism in Central America. We're seeing a new era. The Soviet priority is to look after themselves. Their own people are complaining bitterly about the quality of life in Russia.'

'And the *rusos* throw their old allies to the dogs?'

'There will be a bone or two. But that's all. We can't look forward to a continuation of generous past policies.'

'*Cochinos!* Perhaps I should make the trip to Moscow myself.'

'It may make no difference.'

The Lider Maximo was too proud to go cap in hand before the Russians. The begging-bowl held out for scraps! Never! Besides, he had no fondness for the General Secretary, whom he considered a capitalist. He had entertained the man during the Secretary's visit to Havana last spring. Serious talks had taken place on the subject of solving Cuba's indebtedness to the Soviet Union, and there had been a great deal of smiling camaraderie for the benefit of the world's press. But now, when the Lider Maximo needed some extra credits, when he needed cash, when he saw his Revolution founder in an ocean of debt and despair, the Soviets had abandoned him.

Nothing was said for a long time. Faintly, the piano could be heard from the lower part of the house. Outside, the breeze picked up, driving the tide a little harder on to the beach. From the courtyard came the sound of a guard sliding a clip inside his automatic rifle. They were always prepared, always checking their weapons. The Lider Maximo put on a pair of glasses and walked to his desk, where he scanned a batch of papers.

'Do you know what these are, *compañero*? Projections prepared by our finest economists. Graphs and numbers and scientific notations. They were prepared by people in your own Ministry. They forecast continued shortages in basic items. Beef. Fish. Milk. Shoes. Medical supplies. These might be alleviated by an infusion of hard currency. But where is it to come from? Without hard currency, how do we import goods? The shortages will get worse. And our soldiers returning from Angola – how are they to be absorbed into a work force that has no work for them?'

He crunched the sheets in his hands and tossed them up in the air, swatting at them like shuttlecocks as they floated back down. He picked up those that had fallen, balled them even more tightly in his fists and threw them from the window, where they were carried briefly by the breeze. *Papeleo*, he kept saying with contempt. *Papeleo* – red tape. Those sheets he didn't pick up he crumpled underfoot, wiping them back and forth on the floorboards as if they were dogshit that adhered to his soles. Then, his energy spent on this extraordinary display, he sat down at his desk.

'They are out to get me,' he said. 'Not just the Russians, *compañero*. But there are forces in Cuba that would like to see me dead. Outside Cuba, the CIA is still sniffing after my blood. I constantly hear tales of counter-revolutionary armies forming here and there in Central America. And the exile community in Miami – there are a great many who would murder me and feel joy.'

He was quiet. He was remembering the old days when La Revolución had been his youthful mistress, the love of his heart, when she'd been bright and optimistic and constant.

Now she was turning, as many loves do, into a nagging crone whose demands grew more preposterous daily. She'd become brittle, and her breasts sagged, and she was gaunt. She had all the light-hearted humour of a Greek chorus. And yet once, in the delight of her early years, those breasts had been full, and her belly smooth and tight. She had been a glory to behold. Lost inside La Revolución, he had squandered the very best of his seed.

The Lider Maximo said, 'I have few trusted friends. My brother, perhaps. But he's in Africa. My inner circle – but they're too ambitious for me to trust them wholeheartedly. My bodyguards, of course. But even guards have been known to turn. And you. My Minister of Finance. Can I trust you, Rosabal?'

There were rare moments when Rafael Rosabal glimpsed the ghost of a younger Fidel, not this curmudgeon who grew resentfully old but another Castro of flinty determination and irresistible charm. He'd once possessed magnetism enough to persuade men to embark on the frail overcrowded craft called the *Granma* and sail twelve hundred miles on a harsh sea from Mexico to Cuba, the gift of convincing them they could survive not only the voyage but the killing heat and cold and malarial mosquitoes in the inhospitable mountains of the Sierra Maestra. Triumph – you could still see that glint in Fidel's eyes when they weren't otherwise darkened by injuries and betrayals, many of them imagined.

Rosabal said, 'I am on your side, Commandante. As always.'

The Lider Maximo looked thoughtful. 'You see, the problem is simple, but not easy to correct. When we won the armed struggle against Batista, we faced a situation that was beyond our experience. What did soldiers know of the economy? Of government? They could fire rifles, but they couldn't administer the sugar industry, or the tobacco crop, or the mines. So mistakes were made. Bad mistakes. The wrong crops were planted – '

Rosabal thought: *You were personally responsible for those, Commandante. You were the laughing stock of Cuba for your bizarre horticultural ideas.*

' – and essential machinery rotted on the docks in Havana because we didn't have the necessary moving equipment. And perhaps our agricultural reforms took the initiative away from small farmers. We brought capitalism to its knees, Rosabal. But what did we put in its place?'

Rosabal was very quiet. A quiet pulse beat at the side of his head. He knew this pulse, which was often the harbinger of a rage he couldn't always control, a dark sensation Castro often inspired in him. He maintained his poise with enormous difficulty, closing his eyes a moment, concentrating very hard on the black spaces inside his head. He made no answer to the Commandante's question, which had been rhetorical in any case.

The Lider Maximo said, 'People live longer nowadays, and they are better educated, and they have brighter opportunities, but none of this is enough for them. Why?'

Rosabal felt the breeze come through the flyscreen and stir his hair. His bad moment passed; that sense of slippage was gone. He had control of himself again. His voice was relaxed. He said, 'I wouldn't presume to know the answer, Commandante.' He thought: *Because life is drab, and people feel hopeless. And now not even the Russians will support you. You have driven Cuba into disaster and bankruptcy, you stupid old fucking clown in your idiotic gaberdine fatigues.*

Castro said, 'The problem isn't in the system, Rosabal. Of course there are some inefficiencies. But the real problem is that the people are self-centred! They put themselves before the Revolution. If there is a failure, Rosabal, it's because we haven't *educated* the people as well as we might. We haven't educated selfishness out of them. They still don't understand that the Revolution requires extraordinary patience and endurance and self-denial. We've asked them for an enormous effort in the past, but we haven't asked for enough. Now we must demand even greater sacrifices.'

'Greater sacrifices?' Rosabal asked. How typical of the Commandante to turn blame away from himself and apportion it to the people! If only the people had been educated to understand the shortages on the island, there wouldn't be any complaints! How laughable! The populace hadn't understood the Revolution, and in the Lider Maximo's mind that was the real failure!

Castro's lips contorted slightly. There was a swift arc of pain in his intestines; he wondered if he might have ulcers. He waited until the feeling passed before he said, 'In Cuba today, for example, we export all the lobster we catch, and most of the shrimp. As a consequence, the Cuban people don't have these bourgeois delicacies in their diet. The reverse side of the coin is that children no longer have rickets and malaria is practically dead. And if the Russians are no longer going to assist our Revolution, then we must tighten our own belts one more notch, Rosabal. We must ask for more working hours and cuts in pay. We must have more volunteers in the construction industry and in the cane fields. We must export more beef cattle.'

Rosabal was filled with contempt for the Lider Maximo. He was thinking of the small room in the Palace of Congresses in Moscow where Anatoly Tal, the Minister of Finance, had talked to him at great length about how much money the Soviet Union had poured into Cuba – and he'd emphasised the word 'poured' as if he were talking about some precious liquid tossed down the sink. In currency and technical support during the last thirty years, the exact amount was incalculable, but Tal reckoned it in the region of two hundred and fifty billion US dollars. And what had the Soviet Union gained? Hard questions were being asked inside the Politburo. There were members prepared to cut Cuba completely adrift.

Rosabal mentioned none of this to the Lider Maximo. It would prompt a ranting speech that might last for hour after hour, filled with bitter expletives and self-pity, bravado and chest-thumping. One of Castro's speeches, characterised by non-sequiturs and nostalgic drifts, could imprison a listener for four or five hours, and Rosabal had no desire to be locked into such a monologue. Sometimes these speeches took dangerous turns, and the threats increased with the bitterness, and Castro spoke about bringing destruction to his principal enemy, the United States. You could see it then in his eyes, a certain fiery quality, something that shone with the light of old dangers that hadn't quite died away. *There are still teeth in your head, El Viejo,* Rosabal thought. *There is still danger in you. But for the sake of Cuba, you must be forcibly removed.*

Rosabal glanced at his watch; in one hour and twenty minutes from now, the first act would begin in the depths of the English countryside.

'We will initiate a new propaganda campaign,' Castro said. 'Tomorrow, we will announce to the Cuban people that the Russians – who are now friendly with the Yanquis – have deserted their Cuban comrades. There will be a period of patriotic self-denial. Posters. Newspaper articles. I'll make a speech on television. I'll talk on radio. I'll go into the streets and squares.'

Rosabal heard the familiar voice, but tuned out the words. He walked to the window, concentrated on the sound of the piano playing thinly from below. The tune, perhaps inevitably, was '*Guantanamera*'. He gazed across the courtyard, seeing small huddles of guests.

Here and there he recognised sympathisers – an old soldier who had been with Fidel in the Sierra Maestra but had lost all faith, a female journalist whose critical reports on Communism circulated anonymously, an official from the Ministry of the Interior who despised the police state he had helped create.

Rosabal turned back to Fidel, who was still talking. Did the Lider Maximo use language as a means of exorcising his doubts, of chasing despair away? Did he drown truth with the empty rattle of words? Or was it the poison systematically introduced into his system by his personal physician during the last three months that made him babble so freely and with such confusion? Not enough poison to kill, only to confuse and debilitate the bastard. Rosabal didn't want him to die that way. He wanted to look him straight in the eyes at the point of his death.

When that time came, Rosabal would kill him personally.

And then the island would be his, wrested from this pathetic dictator whose time had come and gone, whose policies had not only failed but had torn the heart out of sad, dying Cuba; a corpse barely afloat in pale blue water.

Norfolk

The Range Rover travelled slowly down a narrow lane. On either side meadows stretched toward trees. An unpromising morning sun, now white and watery, hung low on the landscape, destined to vanish behind cloud mass again. A church tower eclipsed the sun a moment and headstones in a cemetery, damp still from the recent rain, gleamed gently. It was lovely and serene, a world of quiet, peaceful corners and birds that called softly. Even the sound of the Range Rover was absorbed by the landscape.

Flavell drove. He did so with great care. No traffic lay behind, none came in the opposite direction. The world might have been empty. Ruhr sat in the front; the two Americans and Zapino in the back. The girl, bound and gagged, was cramped on the floor. She lay very still. She'd seen the body of the policeman – barely covered with dead leaves – and the sight had horrified her. If she'd worried about her own death before it had been at one remove, like a very bad dream. But it was different now because there was no awakening. This was the reality. She kept whispering *Jesus* to herself, over and over.

Ruhr watched the road. He had no need of the map, which lay folded in the glove compartment. He knew where the turns were, the intersections that lay ahead. He checked his watch. It was eight a.m. A signpost announcing the village of Hornside (population 134) approached. A narrow main street, a pub, a grocery, an antique shop, a church and then Hornside, in all its bucolic charm, was gone like an old postcard.

The Range Rover kept moving. Ruhr looked at his watch again. Ten past eight. The narrow lane turned this way and that. A windmill loomed up, its big blades motionless. And then the road forked. Ruhr directed Flavell to drive between trees where the vehicle would be concealed from the sight of anyone passing. Flavell cut the engine and there was silence.

Eight-thirteen.

Ruhr ordered the men to make their weapons ready. Rick, in charge of the tear gas, stepped out and began to remove canisters, which he set carefully in the damp grass. The Argentinians checked the clips in their automatic rifles. Trevaskis fingered his St Christopher for luck, then checked his own rifle. Steffie Brough shut her eyes tightly. She didn't want to look. Not at the men, not at the guns; she wanted to be blind, freed from everything that encroached on her. *Jesus Christ, please help me. I haven't done anything wrong, not really wrong. I don't deserve this. Get me out of this and I'm yours for life.*

Ruhr looked once again at the time. Eight-seventeen.

The landscape was still quiet. But it seemed sullenly menacing now, as if something long dormant were about to emerge from a crack in the earth. Ruhr stared through the trees at the road. He raised his rocket-launcher to his shoulder. He turned his face up to the sky, from which the sun had disappeared. He listened. He could hear it faintly in the distance. The timing was exactly right. Beautiful.

And now there was another noise, a low rumble of gears that sent vibrations through the still air. It was the sound made by an engine whose enormous power was restrained.

'You all know what has to be done,' Ruhr said. If they didn't, it was too late to learn. The time for rehearsals was long past.

Ruhr peered through the green enclosures of the trees. He saw a large truck covered by a dark-green canopy. More than thirty feet long and cumbersome, it travelled at fifteen miles an hour. Directly in front were three jeeps, and on either side of the truck, two motorcycles. In the rear a smaller truck carried a dozen armed soldiers. The larger vehicle's gears groaned, the ground underfoot trembled. Ruhr looked up at the sky once more.

There, like a flying spider, was the black helicopter, the Cobra. Unmarked, windows tinted, it came in at a low angle, barely skimming treetops and sending birds up out of branches. The sky screamed, the day gone suddenly wild; but it was merely a preamble.

Now, Ruhr thought. He pulled his mask over his face.

The first canisters, thrown by Rick, exploded in front of the jeeps. Swirling gas created an unbreathable atmosphere. Ruhr aimed his rocket-launcher and fired at the jeeps even as the occupants, prepared for the contingency of tear gas though surprised by it nevertheless, fumbled for their masks. Trevaskis let his M-60 blaze at the same time. One of the jeeps overturned and slithered into a ditch, where it caught fire.

The blades of the Cobra fanned smoke and petrol fumes. Fire from the guns mounted on the chopper was directed viciously at the motorcycle escort. Fuel tanks on the bikes exploded while the chopper began to fire at the smaller lorry in the rear, where armed soldiers were scattering into the trees and firing their automatic rifles up into the sky.

Ruhr released another rocket, which blew a second jeep apart. Flame, higher than the trees around it, created a vast blue and orange column brighter than any sun. Zapino and Flavell, both masked, ran through the trees toward the long truck. Its drivers were climbing out of the cab and shooting in the general direction of the chopper. The Cobra, hunting the soldiers, eluded the shots and sprayed the woods with quick fire. It was important to wipe out the scattered squadron before radio communication could summon reinforcements. They would arrive sooner or later, of course. Ruhr preferred later. Much later.

He surveyed the action with quiet satisfaction. He saw Flavell and Zapino reach the long truck. He fired his rocket launcher again, setting more trees on fire. And suddenly, emerging from the thick orange smoke, was a green military helicopter, probably part of the original escort, scanning the terrain for just such a contingency as this.

Ruhr watched the Cobra, a huge mysterious raven, churn upwards, drawing the military helicopter clear of the smoke. The Cobra fired its rocket-launchers first and the camouflaged chopper tilted sideways, then downwards, going into an evasive slump. The Cobra persisted like a rabid bat, pursuing the other aircraft with a tenacity Ruhr admired. The air struggle was brief. The military craft exploded and the Cobra wheeled away from the great reaches of flame.

But not quickly enough. Flame and debris blown out of the falling chopper caught the fuselage of the Cobra, which disintegrated with spectacular fury and dropped into a nearby meadow where it burned.

Ruhr, who never allowed himself to be upset by the changing fortunes of war, hurried from the cover of the trees, spraying the area before him with his M-16. He was alive now, attuned to battle, moving, not thinking, running on instinct. Zapino had already gained entry to the cab of the long truck. Flavell, dead, lay directly under the large front wheels. Everything burned – jeeps, motorcycles, trucks, the wreckage of the choppers, trees, an abandoned barn nearby. It was a landscape imagined by a pyromaniac. Everything burned except the one thing that mattered: the large truck with the green canopy.

Ruhr climbed up behind the wheel. He engaged the gears and drove over the body of Flavell and through the wreckage of jeeps and the corpses of soldiers. Gunfire still came from those soldiers concealed in the woods, sporadic, almost indifferent. It was answered by Trevaskis and Rick as they rushed toward the parked Range Rover. Rick was struck in the neck and he fell face down.

In the truck, Ruhr stepped on the accelerator. The Range Rover, with Trevaskis at the wheel, came out of the woodland and followed. Thin gunfire still rattled behind them, growing fainter. Ruhr stamped the pedal to the floor. He couldn't get the truck beyond forty, forty-five miles an hour because of the weight of the cargo as he drove the narrow, empty lanes that led to the airfield. There was an astonishing density to the trees here. They created a mystery out of the quiet meadows and lonely farmhouses that lay beyond them.

Ruhr looked in the side mirror. The Range Rover was immediately behind. The airfield was one mile away. Ruhr tried to get the truck to go faster. At fifty, it vibrated with asthmatic severity. It began to shudder and skip and threaten to die as the airfield came in view.

At the edge of the tarmac sat the massive transport plane, the C-130, engines already running. Ruhr drove the big truck to the back of the plane where a ramp, hydraulically operated, angled out of a doorway in the C-130's underbelly. The Range Rover came to a stop alongside the truck and Trevaskis jumped out.

'Let's get this fucker loaded toot sweet!' Trevaskis shouted.

But Ruhr had something else to do first; he reached inside the Range Rover and lifted out the girl.

'Christ,' Trevaskis said, baffled and angry. Rick was dead and so was Flavell and if somebody had managed to summon reinforcements this whole place would be crawling with soldiers and Ruhr *still* found time to take this girl along. The sick fuck.

Ruhr carried Steffie Brough to the ramp. Her blouse half undone, small white breasts sadly visible, mud-flecked skirt swept to one side. Her eyes were open, bloodshot from the tear gas. If they expressed anything, Ruhr couldn't read it. Her lips, dry and cracked, appeared to have lost colour. Ruhr took her school scarf from around her neck, draped it carefully over the back seat, then raised her small body up, passing her to the hands of the men inside the transport plane, who took this unexpected merchandise without question.

Trevaskis, puzzled by the business with the scarf, guided Zapino as he backed the truck up toward the ramp so that the cruise missile and the separate rectangular compartment, some eight feet by seven, that contained the control system, could be loaded into the plane.

It was a precious prize, the stolen property of the North Atlantic Treaty Organisation.

10 Norfolk

It was shortly after ten a.m., some two hours since the attack. Ambulances came and went in utter confusion along country lanes built for horses and carts. Spectators from nearby villages stood beneath umbrellas and some macabre souls took photographs, despite the entreaties of military policemen. Physicians in wet white coats, an Anglican priest, a group of taciturn military investigators, the inevitable reporters, the general ghouls attendant on every bloodletting – it was a crowded circus, and Pagan, whose chest pain flared despite a recent ingestion of Pethidine in the fast car from London, was filled with several feelings at the same time, all of them cheerless.

Rain fell bleakly. Foxie had his collar turned up and looked like a gambler praying for a winner in the last race of a long, losing day.

'I'm angry,' Pagan said quietly.

When Frank's words emerged like sand through a clenched fist, Foxworth knew Pagan was going into his dragon-like mode. Even the way his breath hung on the chill wet air suggested fire. The business in the hotel last night with the Cuban-American woman and the man known as Rafael Rosabal, who had turned out to be a member of Castro's government, was another problem. Something there cut deeply into Frank, and Foxie wasn't sure what. Pagan had reacted oddly to Foxie's information about Rosabal, as if he were pretending not to listen at all. Was the woman an old love, a potent ghost still? Foxworth was a tireless observer of the signs in Pagan's personal landscape, and he'd developed an ability to read most of them – and even love a number of them – but every now and then Frank vanished inside himself and became camouflaged at the heart of his own terrain. Now was one such moment.

'We have half the police force of the country looking for Ruhr – and he pulls this off anyway,' Pagan said. 'A fucking cruise missile!'

A savage little pulse worked in Pagan's jaw. 'You know what makes it even worse? We've got a couple of eyewitnesses among the soldiers who saw his face clearly before he put on his gas mask. You know what that means? He wanted people to see him. He wanted to be noticed. He's like a bloody actor who just happened to do a quick stint in the sticks here. He wants audience appreciation even in the miserable provinces! Jesus Christ! The man's bored with all his years of anonymity and now he's got a taste of fame and he loves it. Vanity, Foxie. He's suddenly got theatre in his blood. I want him. I want that bastard.'

Foxie surveyed the team of experts that was sifting through the wreckage of the two helicopters. Here and there, in ditches, under trees, hidden by long grass, lay bodies that hadn't yet been taken away. It was a sickening scene. Foxie thrust his hands in the pockets of his raincoat and thought how infrequently he'd seen Frank Pagan this upset. Sirens cut through the rain, flashing lights glimmered feebly. It was a miserable day with a grey sky that might last forever.

'The missile didn't have a warhead,' Foxworth remarked. A small consolation. 'Without the nuclear hardware it's only a bloody twenty-odd foot cylinder of metal.'

'With dangerous potential,' Pagan said. He was watching a soldier being raised on a stretcher; the boy's leg was missing below the knee. Pagan turned his face to the side. There had been a royal battle in this quiet spot whose only usual violence was that of an owl setting upon a fieldmouse, talons open, a quick dying squeal by moonlight.

An official limousine approached the crossroad and squeezed with some authority between parked ambulances. Martin Burr got out followed by the Home Secretary, Sir Frederick Kinnaird. Both men made their way over the damp road to where Pagan stood.

Pagan had no great fondness for the Home Secretary, nor any specific reason for his dislike except that he was not enamoured of politicians in general. They inspired in him the same kind of confidence as used-car salesmen. Vote for me, my Party has been driven only by an old lady and then only on Sundays and never more than thirty miles an hour. Burr did the introductions. Hands were duly pumped. Burr opened a small umbrella and shared it with Sir Freddie. This made Pagan conscious of his damp woollen overcoat and Italian shoes that leaked rainwater.

'Is it as ghastly as it looks?' Freddie Kinnaird asked.

It was on the tip of Frank Pagan's tongue, a mischief; he wanted to say *No, it's been a lovely party but we've run a bit low on the canapes, Freddie, my old sunshine*. But he merely gestured toward the demolition site.

'A cruise missile was taken, I understand,' Kinnaird said.

Pagan noticed Kinnaird's black coat with the slick velvet collar; an exquisite silk tie went well with his striped shirt, made for him in Jermyn Street, no doubt. Kinnaird said something about how the missile had been on its way to Tucson, Arizona, there to be destroyed under the terms of the Russian-American treaty. He spoke in a drawling way, as if his every word were precious, to be lingered over. Now and again he shoved a strand of thin, sandy hair out of his eyes.

Pagan said, 'We assume the missile was driven to an airfield nearby and flown out. There are about half a dozen airstrips in this vicinity left over from World War Two, most of them private flying clubs now. I've got men checking them out. If the missile *hasn't* been flown from the area, it wouldn't be too hard to hide. An underground tunnel, a warehouse, a bus garage.'

'To where could the missile be flown?' Kinnaird asked.

'Anybody's guess,' Pagan said. 'I hope we'll have an answer soon. The RAF has been conducting an air search, but since they haven't told *us* anything, it means they don't have a thing to report. Otherwise they'd be crowing.'

Kinnaird said, 'I understand one would need a fair-sized transport plane to carry the missile. Surely that shouldn't be too hard to spot.'

Foxworth replied, 'And it wouldn't be, except for two things, Home Secretary. The rotten weather and the fact that there's an enormous amount of air traffic in this part of the world. London's only one hundred miles away, and the pattern of traffic there and throughout the Home Counties in general is horrendous. The system is overloaded.'

'Why steal a missile without a warhead anyway?' the Home Secretary wanted to know.

Nobody had an answer to Sir Freddie's question. Rain fell on Burr's black umbrella. The Commissioner asked, 'What about the dead terrorists?'

'We're still working on ID,' Pagan replied. 'We've got four of the buggers. Two died in the assault. Another two inside the chopper.' He was impatient suddenly. He was very fond of Martin Burr, and admired him, but he disliked the way Big Shots drove up from London to ask what progress had been made when it was damned obvious that men were bleeding to death and ambulances slashing through the rain and the whole scorched, smoking landscape looked as if a meteor had struck it.

'Rather fond of helicopters, aren't they?' Freddie Kinnaird said. 'What do we know about this one?'

Pagan had one of those quirky little urges to unbutton his overcoat and show Sir Freddie that, contrary to anything he might have read in the tabloids lately, there was no Superman costume under his shirt. He restrained himself and said, 'We're running checks. We know it was a Cobra and the markings had been painted black. Beyond that, nothing yet. We're working on it. We assume it was the same aircraft used in Shepherd's Bush. But that's just an assumption, and practically worthless.' Pagan had a difficult moment keeping anger and bitterness from his voice. The idea of a second chopper attack, and the sheer murderous arrogance behind it, rattled him.

'Sorry, by the by, to hear about your gun wound. Bloody tragic business in Shepherd's Bush.' There was the famous Kinnaird touch, palm open on Pagan's shoulder, a slightly distant intimacy, as if between nobility and the common man there might be only the merest suggestion of physical contact. It was all right for their lordships to fuck the serving wenches but not altogether good form to become too intimate with the footmen.

Pagan walked toward the wreckage of the Cobra. The dead terrorists were covered with sheets of plastic, under which charred faces might be seen opaquely, as if through filthy isinglass. Men with protective gloves picked through debris cool enough to handle. Pagan watched for a moment. From a mess such as this, hard information would emerge only slowly – a fingerprint here, an engine identification number there, maybe a scorched photograph in a wallet. It would take a long time for this chaos to yield anything useful.

Now Foxie approached the smoking rubble in a hurried way. 'Just got a message from a place called St Giles, Frank. It sounds quite interesting. It's only a few miles from here.'

'I'd welcome anything that gets me the hell out of here,' Pagan said.

'I'll fetch the car,' and Foxie was gone again, nimbly skirting the small fires that still flickered here and there in the gloom.

The airfield beyond the hamlet of St Giles had once been a run-down place, redolent of robust pilots with waxen moustaches dashing off in Spitfires to defeat the Hun, but the old hangars had been painted bright blue and the control tower refurbished in a similar shade. Somebody had taken some trouble and expense to tart the place up. A red windsock flapped damply. A sign attached to the tower said East Anglia Flying Club in bright letters. Small planes, chained to the ground for protection against the wind, were scattered around the edges of the runway.

Foxworth and Pagan got out of the car. It was a dreary open space, exposed to the elements. A thin wet mist had formed in the wooded land beyond the hangars where a group of men stood around a Range Rover. Pagan walked the runway, Foxie following. At a certain point; Pagan stopped and kneeled rather cautiously to the tarmac, dipping his finger into a slick of fresh oily fluid; it was some kind of hydraulic liquid, viscous and green, rain-repellent. He wiped his hands together and walked until he reached the copse of beech trees.

Three men stood near the blue Range Rover, the doors of which hung open. Pagan recognised Billy Ewing, the Scotsman who worked at the SATO office in Golden Square. The other two were uniformed men, probably local. Billy Ewing, who had a small red nose and blue eyes that watered no matter the season, had a handkerchief crumpled in the palm of one hand as he always did. He had allergies unknown to the medical profession. His life was one long sniff.

'We haven't touched a thing, Frank,' Ewing said in a voice forever on the edge of a sneeze. 'It's just the way we found it.'

The Rover was hidden, although not artfully concealed. Whoever had stashed it here between the trees had done so in haste, or else didn't give a damn about discovery. Pagan looked inside. Boxes of cartridges lay on the floor, a discarded shotgun, two rocket launchers, three automatic pistols; quite a nice little arsenal. He looked at the instrument panel. The vehicle had clocked a mere three hundred and seven miles. It still smelled new.

Billy Ewing coughed and said, 'An old geezer who was illegally fishing a local stream says he heard a bloody great roar this morning and when he looked up he saw – and here I quote – "a monster hairyplane near a half-mile long" rising just above him. Scared him half to death, he says. If you need to talk to him, Frank, you'll find him at a pub in St Giles where he went to take some medication for his fright.'

As he listened to Ewing, Pagan reached inside the rear of the vehicle. Lying across the back seat was a wine-coloured scarf of the kind worn by schoolkids as part of a uniform.

He removed the scarf. A small threaded motif ran through it, the stylised letters MCS. The last two might have stood for Comprehensive School.

'What do you make of it?' Foxie asked.

Pagan didn't reply. An odd little feeling worked inside him, something vague moving towards the light, but as yet indefinable. He held the garment to his nose. There was a fading scent of rose.

'Belongs to a girl,' he said. 'Unless boys are wearing perfumes these days.'

'You'll find a few,' Ewing remarked in the manner of a philosopher resigned to paradoxes. 'It's a funny world these days, Frank.'

'What's the scarf doing in this particular car?' Foxworth asked.

The feeling coursed through Pagan again, creating an uneasiness. 'My guess is Ruhr left it there deliberately,' he said.

'Why? You think he's thumbing his nose at you, Frank?'

Pagan gazed through the beech trees. Ruhr's disturbed mind, the surface of which Pagan had barely scratched during their interviews, seemed to present itself in a solid flash of light, like a hitherto unknown planet drifting momentarily close to earth. 'It's possible. I think he's got himself a bloody hostage and wants me to know it. He likes the idea of turning the screw.'

Pagan shrugged; how could he know for sure? The flash of light had gone out and Ruhr's mind was once again a darkened planetarium. 'Let's find out what MCS stands for,' he said. 'Then call in the fingerprint boys and have them go over this car.'

Foxworth shivered as the wind rose up and roared through the beech trees, tearing leaves from branches. He wasn't happy with this deserted airfield, or the spooky beeches, or the girl's scarf. Nor was he exactly overjoyed to see Frank slyly swallow another painkiller, which he did like a very bad actor, turning his face to one side and smuggling the drug into his mouth.

'Keep an eye on things here for a while, Billy,' Pagan said.

'Will do,' the Scotsman answered, and sneezed abruptly into his hankie.

Pagan and Foxworth walked back to their car. The red windsock filled with air, rising quickly then subsiding in a limp, shapeless manner.

Cabo Gracias a Dios, Honduras

The mid-morning was infernally humid; even the sea breezes, sluggish and sickly, couldn't dispel the stickiness. The man who stood on a knoll overlooking the ocean wore very black glasses and a battered Montecristo Fini Panama hat; he carried an aerosol can of insecticide with which he periodically buzzed the mosquitoes that flocked constantly around him.

The man was Tomas 'La Gaviota' Fuentes, a Cuban-American whose nickname, The Seagull, came from his amazing ability to fly seaplanes. Storms, whirlpools, hurricanes – Fuentes flew and landed his planes regardless. He had a madman's contempt for whatever inclement weather the gods sent down.

Fuentes looked along the beach, watching a score of fighter planes come in pairs at 1500 feet, then drop to 1200, at which point they strafed the sands, firing at bulls eyes painted in the centre of white banners. The planes, a mixture of Skyhawks, Harriers, and F-16s gathered from a variety of locations, used the inert practice ammunition known in the trade as blue slugs. Many of the banners remained undisturbed as the aircraft completed the run and veered left. Then fifty amphibious craft, each containing fifteen armed men, rolled with the tide towards the beaches. Every day the men practised wading ashore, hurrying over the sands to the cover of trees, where they disappeared swiftly and quietly.

La Gaviota took off his hat and cuffed sweat from his brow. This place was the asshole of the world. He turned away from the beach and strutted towards his large tent. Despite the fan powered by a generator, stifling air blew in self-perpetuating circles; hell wasn't, as a certain clown of a French philosopher had claimed, other people. Real hell was a canvas tent in a Central American republic surrounded by hungry dung-flies as big as wine bottles.

He poured himself a cold beer from an icebox and gulped it down quickly. He was a big man and all muscle; even the way his forehead protruded suggested an outcropping of muscle rather than bone. Each of his hands spanned twelve inches and he wore size thirteen army boots. He crumpled the can like tissue paper and turned on his radio, which was tuned to a country station beamed out of El Paso. It wasn't great reception, but better than nothing.

The flap of his tent opened just as he shut his eyes and listened to the sweet pipes of Emmylou Harris singing 'Feeling Single, Seeing Double'. The visitor was Fuentes' second in command, a lackey Harry Hurt had sent from Washington. His name was Roger Bosanquet and he was some kind of limey, with an accent you could spread on a scone.

'They're getting better,' Fuentes said. 'They're not perfect, but they're improving.' Here Fuentes added the words 'old bean', which he imagined was the way Englishmen addressed one another at every level of society. His attempt at an Oxford accent was appalling. Bosanquet always responded with a polite half-smile.

Bosanquet said, 'The infantry coming ashore performed with precision. They can't possibly be faulted. The pilots, however, were not as accurate as they should have been. They need a little more time.' He had received training at an army school in England – from which establishment he'd been expelled for reasons Fuentes didn't know, though he had absolutely no doubt the crime was faggotry. All Englishmen were faggots. It was a law of nature.

Fuentes made the basic mistake of seeing only Bosanquet's manicured manners and his quiet subordination. He missed a certain hardness that lay in the Englishman's blue eyes. Nor did he notice the determined way Bosanquet sometimes set his jaw. He consistently underestimated the Englishman, whom he considered a *boniato*, a thickhead. But at some other level, one Fuentes did not care to acknowledge, he envied Bosanquet his education and training. His cool. His *class*.

'They don't have more goddam time,' Fuentes said. 'The clocks are running, *yame*, and they're running just a little too damn fast. The aircraft are supposed to destroy Castro's defensive positions on the beach before the landings, correct? And if they don't, then the poor bastards coming ashore are walking into a slaughterhouse. Correct?'

Bosanquet wiped his brow with a red bandanna. He had served with Latin Americans like Fuentes before now and he disliked their sudden passions; they were brave soldiers but lacked detachment. It couldn't be expected, of course. Impatience and irrationality were programmed into them. They loved theatricality. They threw fits. They were unpredictable. They were not, when all was said and done, Anglo-Saxon. Bosanquet, who had done many dirty deeds for Harry Hurt in his life and who was here in this stinking place to provide a counterweight to Fuentes (and make confidential reports to Harry) spoke in a reasonable way. 'With a little more accuracy on behalf of the planes, everything will work out superbly.'

'*Cojones!* Castro's apes will shoot those poor bastards in the boats like coconuts on the midway,' Fuentes snarled.

'Only if Castro's apes get the chance,' Bosanquet said quietly. 'And we don't believe they will, do we? All we are doing here is to prepare our men for a contingency that isn't going to arise. Besides, it keeps them from getting bored.'

Fuentes, calmer now, mumbled and shrugged. He was into a second beer now, a Lone Star. Like all demanding leaders of men, he always thought the worst of his subordinates. They were misconceived sons of whores and yet he prayed, as any stage director will, that all would somehow be well on opening night, lines would not be fluffed, and some generous magic would inhabit his actors and raise them to the status of gods. In truth, he was reasonably pleased with his forces, but he was damned if he'd ever admit this. You didn't go round handing out Oscars before the performance.

He pulverised a mosquito on his green baize cardtable. He imagined squelching Fidel in just such a way: *schlurp* – out came the blood of Cuba.

Bosanquet opened an attaché case that contained several cashier's cheques and negotiable bonds. Fuentes looked at the stash for a second. He imagined depriving Bosanquet of the loot and making off into the hills, there to vanish and live a life of debauchery eating the pussy of coffee-coloured maidens. It was a temptation easily ignored. Fuentes had been in the Cuban Air Force until 1959; he'd been promoted to the rank of Major in the US Marines following some heroic feats of flying against Castro during the Bay of Pigs. But there was no way he could fit into an American officers' mess. He looked wrong and his accented speech was rough and his manners were uncouth, which added to his resentment of somebody like the well-spoken Bosanquet who always seemed to know the correct thing to say. But you couldn't fault Fuentes when it came to loyalty to his superiors. Besides, Harry Hurt wasn't the kind of guy you wanted to cross. Fuentes had the feeling Hurt wasn't acting alone, that a powerful, wealthy organisation existed around him, and Harry was just another ghost in a mighty machine.

Fuentes popped a third beer and tossed the aluminium tab into the blades of the fan which sucked it in, rattled it, then ejected it. 'You got a lot of bread there, Roger,' he said.

Bosanquet shut the case. 'Today's the day we spend it.'

Fuentes wondered how much longer a man might live in such a shitpile as this. After his retirement from the Marines he'd purchased a six-hundred-acre spread in Texas, between Amarillo and McLean, where he raised Aberdeen-Angus cattle and studied military history in his spare time. Sometimes he thought he should just have stayed home. But lonely old soldiers, like trout, were suckers for old lures. It wasn't even the money. What it really came down to was a break in the predictable tedium of life in the Texas Panhandle. Back home he had nothing but cows. Down here he had an army to drill – mainly Cuban boys recruited with great secrecy from the exile communities in New Jersey and California. A few had come from Florida, but Fuentes had not concentrated on recruiting there for the simple reason that he believed there were just too many big flapping mouths in Miami. He also had some Mexican mercenaries and a handful of Bolivians who all claimed to have been with Che at the end and who believed Fidel had conspired in Guevara's killing. In addition, he had about twenty Americans who had been in Vietnam, at least half a dozen of whom were CIA operatives in undercover roles. There was a considerable amount of hardware too: automatic weapons; grenades; rocket-launchers; a seemingly endless supply of ammunition; and the twenty fighter-planes the amazing Hurt had somehow managed to acquire in the military bazaars of the world. The F-16s had been built in Pakistan, the Skyhawks originated in South America, the Harriers, though American-made, had been bought through South African sources.

Fuentes hated Castro for the way he'd kicked ass at the Bay of Pigs. One of those bruised asses had been Fuentes' own. Cuba without Castro was Tomas Fuentes' dream. He had no idea who would take over the country after Fidel because this was information he'd never been given, nor did he particularly need it. He assumed that the next president and his government would have the support of both the Americans, which in Tomas' mind meant the CIA and some powerfully rich individuals, friends of Harry Hurt and certain important factions inside the Cuban armed forces. What did it matter? Nobody could be worse than Castro. Fuentes would do his own job, and do it to the best of his ability, and the politicians would take over when all the dust had settled.

'Listen,' said Roger Bosanquet.

Tommy Fuentes tilted his head. There was the sound of a small plane overhead. Fuentes stepped out of the tent. The plane, a Lear jet, approached from Nicaragua. It flew toward the airstrip that Fuentes and his army had hacked out of this godless landscape. The plane came in low and silvery-gold, touched down, bounced, then ran smoothly the length of the runway. Fuentes, with Bosanquet trotting at his back, walked down the hillside to the tarmac.

The Lear rolled to the place where Fuentes and Bosanquet stood. When it stopped completely the side-door opened, the gangway slithered down into place, and two men – so similar in height and appearance they might have been twins – stepped out into the insufferable weather. Both wore floral shirts and sunglasses and brand new white linen pants and they looked like novice fishermen of the kind you find drifting in the coastal waters of Florida under the questionable tutelage of some self-appointed, dope-smoking guide. They were called Levy and Possony, and they spoke English with Eastern European accents, developed in the 1960s in Prague where they'd been dazzling physics students together at the University, brighter than all the other students and most of the professors too. They had lived for years in Tel Aviv and Jerusalem and then at a secret research institute in the Negev, where they'd been regarded as scientific treasures of a kind – even if they'd been rewarded on the same salary scale as basic civil servants. It was commonly assumed, and quite wrongly, that they were too obsessed by their little world of scientific exploration to have any interest in material possessions. What was overlooked was the simple fact that Levy and Possony, after lives of poverty and wearisome anti-semitism in Eastern Europe, followed by emigration to a strange land inhabited by people who spoke a language the two Czechs never mastered, longed desperately for something bright in their lives. Tired of penury in pursuit of science, weary of scratching around for grants, fed up with the bulk of their salary cheques being gobbled by patriotic taxes, they both desired less spartan lifestyles – even, to be honest, with a touch of sin thrown in.

Levy and Possony had come to the attention of the Society in the person of Harry Hurt, who saw in them middle-aged geniuses endangered by sexual dehydration and monotony. Neither was married; both were very horny in a manner befitting secular monks who had toiled for many arduous years in the rarified, lonely atmosphere of higher physics. Levy and Possony, like two figs, were wonderfully ripe for picking, and Harry Hurt, who had all the charm of an open cheque-book, plucked them carefully by moonlight, giving them money, briefcases of the stuff, vacations at glamorous resorts in exotic places where access to women was made easy for them. Possony had taken to Brazilian ladies and Levy to fellatio in a hot tub. Then a little indoctrination about how Castro loathed the existence of Israel and was practically an honorary Palestinian – wouldn't it be wonderful and, yes, patriotic, to help bring down a regime such as Fidel's? Levy and Possony, anxious only that nobody be hurt on account of their participation – an assurance gladly given by Harry Hurt, who would have assured Khaddafi a Nobel Peace Prize to get what he wanted – had their consciences swiftly appeased and agreed to a form of defection. In return for what Hurt needed, Levy and Possony would spend very pleasurable lives in some tropical paradise. They would be provided with new passports under new names, and they would be rich. And, if some future urge seized them to return to research, Hurt would cheerfully provide the means.

Now, Levy and Possony shook hands with Fuentes and ignored Bosanquet completely, as if they had intuited his lower standing. They had about them the contempt of tenants of ivory towers for those who toil in the cellars and workhouses of the world. Possony wore thick-lensed glasses through which his eyes, enlarged, unblinking, appeared to miss nothing. Levy, on the other hand, had a certain myopic uncertainty about him which suggested brilliance held in some delicate neurotic balance.

'Only mad dogs and Englishmen,' said Bosanquet, gesturing at the raging sun. It was his little turn at wit, but it went unappreciated. Noel Coward had never played in Cabo Gracias a Dios.

'We have the merchandise,' Levy said. 'You have the money?'

Bosanquet opened the case. Possony counted the bonds and cheques which he did with irritating slowness, like an old-fashioned accountant who has forgotten to pack his abacus.

'Everything is in order,' Possony said.

'Now the merchandise,' Fuentes said.

'On board the plane,' said Levy.

All four men went up the gangway. The Lear jet was air-conditioned, a blessed oasis. Fuentes glanced into the cockpit where pilot and co-pilot sat. They wore holstered pistols. Levy led the way to a compartment at the rear. He unlocked a door, switched on a light. An unmarked wooden crate, measuring some six feet by four, stood in the lit compartment. There were no markings on the box.

'This is it,' said Possony. 'The material is completely configured to the specifications supplied by Mr Hurt.'

'Therefore accurate?' Fuentes asked.

Levy clapped the palm of his hand across his forehead, rolled his eyes and said, 'What am I hearing?'

It was clear to Fuentes that he'd somehow insulted Levy, though he wasn't sure how.

Possony, less histrionic than Levy, said, 'Accurate? Laser technology, Mr Fuentes. The finest electron microscopes. We're not making imitation Swiss watches to sell on 47th Street.'

Fuentes shrugged. He glanced at Bosanquet, who was obviously amused by Fuentes' moment of discomfort. Possony took the attaché case from Bosanquet's hand and said, 'Now have the merchandise removed from the plane so we can leave. Nothing personal, you understand. But obviously we're in a hurry to get the hell out of here.'

Paris

The hotel with the unlisted telephone number was small and expensive, hidden behind chestnut trees on a side street in the Latin Quarter. The private dining-room, panelled and hung with heavy curtains and eighteenth-century oils, was located on the second floor, a gloomy room, discreet in a manner peculiarly French.

Five men sat round the table, the surface of which had been carved with the initials of various luminaries who had eaten in this room. Victor Hugo had been here, and so had Emile Zola, and Albert Camus had dropped in now and again for an aperitif after a soccer game. The literary credentials didn't impress the five diners, none of whom had much of an appetite. A particularly delicious *terrine de foie de canard* had barely been touched. A good bottle of Saint Emilion had gone practically unnoticed and the consommé, decorated with a delicate lacework of leeks and – a jaunty nouvelle cuisine touch – yellow squash cut in florets, was ignored.

When the last waiter had departed, Enrico Caporelli sat very still for a while. Beyond the heavy curtains could be heard the traffic of the fifth arrondissement, but it was a world away. Caporelli tasted his wine, pushed the glass aside, sipped a little coffee, which was roasted Kenyan and excellent. Sheridan Perry lit a cigarette and Harry Hurt, a fervent anti-smoker, fanned the polluted air with his napkin. Across the table from Caporelli was Sir Freddie Kinnaird; on Kinnaird's right sat the German, Kluger, his face sombre.

'First Magiwara, then Chapotin,' Caporelli said quietly as he finished his coffee. He glanced across the room at Freddie Kinnaird, then at Kluger, then Perry. Why was he drawn back, time and again, to the face of Sheridan Perry? Did he think, at some level beyond precise language, that Perry was behind the murders? Admittedly, Sheridan lusted after the Directorship. But lust was a long bloodstained step removed from two brutal murders, or three, if you counted Chapotin's young fluffball, who, it appeared, had connections with the English aristocracy.

'Why?' Caporelli asked. 'Why those two? Did they have something in common we don't know about? Were they involved in something that went very wrong for them? What made them candidates for death?'

Nobody answered. Some silences are polite, others awkward, but this particular expanse of quiet had running through it, at deep levels, many different tides and currents. Mistrust, anxiety, fear. Caporelli looked inside his coffee cup. He shivered very slightly and thought *Somebody is walking on your grave, Enrico.*

Superstitious nonsense, you peasant! Some things you just don't lose. Your background, the way you were raised in the hills with simple people who crossed themselves whenever there was an eclipse of the moon or a calf was born with three legs. All the money and the smart tailors hadn't erased the old ways. You still tossed spilled salt over your shoulder and avoided the space under ladders and you gave black cats a very wide berth.

'Has anybody noticed anything unusual?' Caporelli asked. 'Any cars following them around? Strange people prowling? Perhaps phone calls with no voices at the end of the line?'

Nobody had witnessed anything out of the ordinary. No strange cars, no stalkers, no late night callers.

'How did these killers know the whereabouts of Chapotin and Magiwara? How did they know not only places but times?' Caporelli asked. 'Neither victim led a public life, after all. They were not common names in the society columns. They were private people.'

Harry Hurt sipped some mineral water. 'Here's one possibility. Our Society came into existence because of the Mafia. We all know this. Had our Sicilian brethren shown more restraint and less taste for lurid publicity, we'd still be their bankers. However we went separate ways. Our predecessors, men of some vision, appropriated certain funds many many years ago and followed their own star. The Mafia, which was making more money then than all the Governments of the free world combined, didn't notice that we had "misjudged" the stock market to the tune of some, ahem, 22.5 million dollars. To them this was mere pocket money. To the Society it was a fresh start.'

'We know the history,' Caporelli said.

Hurt raised an index finger in the air. 'Let me finish, Enrico. Suppose some young mafioso, a kid, a soldier, wants to make his name. Suppose he delves. Suppose he sees in some dusty old ledgers figures that don't add up – what then? Would he want revenge? Would he want to wipe out the Society?'

Caporelli was sceptical. 'First he'd want the money back. Then and only then he'd blow a few heads away. He wouldn't shoot first. He'd want to know where the cash was kept before he stuck us in front of a firing-squad.'

Hurt shrugged. 'I'm only looking at possibilities, Enrico, not writing in concrete. Here's another one. Say an agent of Castro's intelligence service is behind the murders. A goon from G-2 or whatever the hell it's called. Somebody who has heard of our scheme. Perhaps somebody who has been spying on Rosabal.'

Caporelli frowned. 'For argument's sake, let's say Rosabal has indeed been followed by an agent of Castro – which, I may add, I discount. The stakes are too high for him to behave like such an amateur. But so what? Where could Rosabal lead such a spy? This agent might see Rosabal and me drinking tea in Glasgow or beer in a hotel in Saint Etienne – but what good would that do for the spy? Rosabal knows only me. He has no idea of the Society's existence. How could he lead some *fidelista* directly to our membership? No, Rosabal's not the poisoned apple.'

Sheridan Perry sipped Saint Emilion with the air of a man who has been told he should appreciate fine wines but doesn't quite enjoy the taste. 'We've always taken great precautions about secrecy. We've always protected our own identities. Security has been high on our agenda at all times.'

Freddie Kinnaird said, 'Not high enough, it seems. For example, none of us has felt the apparent need for a bodyguard.'

'It suddenly seems like a terrific idea,' Hurt said.

Caporelli stood up. He walked to the window, parted the curtains a little way, looked out. Lamps were lit along the pavements; it was a particularly romantic scene, he thought, the pale orbs of light obscured by chestnut branches, a soft breeze shuffling leaves along the gutters. A pair of lovers walked so closely together they appeared to have shed their separate identities and fused here in the Parisian twilight.

All this talk of a mafioso, bodyguards – it left him cold. It didn't come to the point. He lowered the curtains, fastidiously made sure the two hems met and no exterior light penetrated, then turned to look at the faces around the table.

'We've been ruptured,' he said quietly. 'And we must at least consider the unpleasant possibility that somebody in our own membership . . . ' Caporelli poured himself more coffee. He couldn't finish the sentence. The faces in the dining-room were each in some way defiant or incredulous. 'From within or without, the fact is, our security is broken. Somebody knows who we are, and is set on our destruction. I don't think we're going to reach a conclusion no matter how long we sit round this table tonight, my friends. We'll argue, and throw possibilities back and forth, but nothing will be accomplished in this manner.'

'So what are you saying?' Perry asked. His thick eyebrows came together to create one unbroken line of fur above his tiny eyes.

Caporelli gazed at the American for a time. Again he wondered if Sheridan were capable of making a destructive play for control of the Society; and, if so, was he doing it without the complicity of his friend Hurt? Was there a rift between the two? Had Perry's greed and ambition created an abyss across which Hurt was neither allowed nor prepared to walk?

'I am saying this, Sheridan,' Caporelli remarked. 'I am saying that we attend to personal security by hiring bodyguards. I am saying we adhere to no regular schedule. I am saying that we change cars and travel plans as often as we can. Secrecy is a prerequisite of survival. In short, we take precautions, as many as we possibly can. And we are very careful of how we communicate with one another.'

This last statement fell into the room like a stone dropped from a great height. It was unpleasant. The Society had always existed on the basis of mutual trust. Now it was being undermined. Caporelli imagined he could hear old beams creak and rocks crumble in the deep shafts.

'And does all this affect our Cuban undertaking?' Perry asked. 'Do we cancel that project for starters?'

Suddenly agitated, Freddie Kinnaird made a ball of his linen napkin, which he brushed against his lips. 'Have you lost your mind? The cruise missile was successfully stolen this morning and is presently in transit, and since the British police are practically without clues, I don't see any reason to cancel. The investigation, headed by a policeman called Frank Pagan, falls into my domain. When Pagan knows anything, I know it too. A rather lovely arrangement altogether. If Pagan goes too far, I can find a way to tug gently on his rein. Besides, if we take the precautions Enrico has suggested, I think we will see a general improvement in our mood. Prudence, my dear fellow, wins in the end. And whoever has taken to attacking our little Society will be flushed out finally.'

Kinnaird's expression was that of a voracious estate agent who has just placed an island paradise in escrow and whose plans include casinos, resorts, colossal hotels, and as much sheer, silken sin as anybody could stand.

Kluger lit a cigar. He blew a ring of blue smoke and said, 'I personally do not believe that anyone in this room is a traitor.' There was authority and finality in the German's tone, as if he had access to information denied everyone else. 'I think we have been too lax, too complacent, in our security and now we are paying a price. The solution, as Enrico tells it, is very simple. We continue to go about our business – but with this difference. *Extreme precautions*, gentlemen. Sooner or later, the culprit will appear in broad daylight. Sooner or later.'

Kluger stood up. He filled a glass with brandy and extended his hand across the table. The toast was made, glasses clinked together, faces, formerly glum, forced smiles. Cuba was there for the taking. The show would go on regardless.

'To the success of friendship,' said Sir Freddie Kinnaird.

It was early evening by the time the members left the dining-room. The last wistful twilight had gone, and the cafés were bright now, the night life restless as ever, beautiful social moths flitting after this piece of gossip or fearful of missing that particular face. Nothing had been solved in the hotel, but a slightly uncertain consensus had been reached that no Society member was responsible for the killings.

Arrangements pertaining to bodyguards were discussed, recommendations made. Sir Freddie Kinnaird knew of a reliable agency in London; Harry Hurt spoke well of an outfit in Dallas. And Enrico Caporelli, who had an apartment and a great many connections here in Paris, had already made a phone call and had been promised a carload of armed protectors who would arrive outside in ten minutes or so.

The mood, if not exactly terrific, was not as sombre as it had been before, and the news of Gunther Ruhr's successful theft took the hard edge off grief. The possibility of Cuban profits had instilled a small delight that, in the hours ahead, would grow until dead members were almost forgotten.

The five men stepped out of the hotel together. They were to be met by their security people outside a well-lit cafe across the street. They walked very close to a couple of strolling gendarmes; an illusion of protection until the real thing arrived. Kluger was attracted by a girl at a pavement café but decided to be abstemious, despite the luscious red gloss of her parted lips.

All five men crossed the street at a traffic signal. Kluger, puffing on the remains of his cigar, lagged a few feet behind, turning now and again to observe the lovely girl. He could not have seen the truck until the last possible moment; perhaps not even then. It struck him, tossed him ten or eleven feet forward; then ensnared his limp body under the front axle and dragged it another fifty or sixty feet before final release. Kluger rolled over and over towards the gutter, his coat torn, his arms broken, his face devoid of any resemblance to its former self.

The truck driver's name was Luiz Dulzaides, a forty-nine-year-old long-distance driver from Madrid. His eight-wheel rig came to a halt inside the plate-glass window of a large pharmacy, after it ploughed through colognes and powders and perfumes and demolished a menagerie of soft-toy animals. Dulzaides, tested by the police, had drunk the equivalent of three bottles of wine that day. He'd never heard of Herr Kluger, had no recollection of seeing him at the pedestrian crossing, no memory of striking him. Dulzaides was too drunk to stand upright. He was removed in a police car. Caporelli and the two Americans answered the usual routine questions of the gendarmes while Kinnaird, the most public of the members, feared adverse publicity and slipped easily into the large crowd of spectators that had assembled at the scene.

Officially, it was an accident. After all, Dulzaides was blind drunk; was that disputable? Statements were taken, a report filed, a dossier opened and closed.

Enrico Caporelli and the others repaired for drinks to the Ritz, conveyed there in a chalk-white Cadillac driven by two armed men. Freddie Kinnaird joined them there. Each member was sceptical about the matter of the accident; but what was there to say? The police were convinced, the witnesses many, and Dulzaides' blood alcohol level was undeniably dangerous. Perhaps an accident; perhaps not. If an accident, then it was an ironic one given the recent circumstances surrounding the Society.

In the morning Caporelli, who wanted the chance to speak with a sober Dulzaides and perhaps check the man's background, the veracity of his story, telephoned the jail where the driver had been taken. He was informed by a cold voice that Monsieur Dulzaides had, *hélas*, died of heart failure at four-twenty a.m. and the body had already been claimed by relatives. Like garbage under a violent sun, it had been removed quickly from the premises.

11 Norfolk

Middlebury Comprehensive School, located between Norwich and the ancient Saxon town of Thetford, was a new building that resembled a car-assembly plant, as if each pupil were a machine to be bolted, buffed, waxed and wheeled out into the world – which, Pagan supposed, was true in a limited kind of way. According to the headmaster, a man named Frew who had the deep fatalism of the jaded schoolteacher, a pupil called Stephanie Brough had been missing overnight. Steffie's pet horse had returned home, saddled and riderless. Country policemen, defeated by darkness, had begun a systematic search at first light. By three o'clock in the afternoon, seven hours after the theft of the missile, not only had the missing girl continued to elude detection, but a constable on the case had vanished as well.

By five o'clock inquiries made of estate agents in a twenty-mile radius of Steffie's home had revealed the recent rental of a dilapidated farmhouse. The nice old dear who told

Pagan about the tenancy had the quietly confidential air one sometimes finds in people whose occupations involve discretion. She would give nothing away unless the authority that needed answers had unimpeachable reasons. Pagan's needs, backed by his imposing credentials from Scotland Yard, fell into that category.

It was the woman's opinion that the man who'd rented the house was a 'foreigner', although remarkably 'civilised' for all that.

Had there been only one renter? Pagan asked.

The agent remembered no other. Of course, a tenant could do pretty much what he liked as soon as he had a key, especially in a rural area without nosy neighbours. She would be happy to find a copy of the tenant's signature, but it would take an hour or so. Her office was not, she remarked proudly, computerised. Pagan thanked her and said he'd return.

The farmhouse was dismal, buried in a black hollow. Moss grew against walls and the chimney had partially collapsed. Tyre tracks were found outside the house; on the slope behind the building were varied muddy footprints, some large, a few rather small, small enough to be Steffie Brough's. Pagan stood for a while on the rainy incline, a photo of the girl, provided by her school, in one hand. She was pretty, a lovely devilment in the face, a puckish little smile, tiny pointed ears suggesting other-worldliness. A pixie. He tried to imagine Steffie Brough on this slope, watching the farmhouse.

Was this the place where she'd come? And then what? Had Ruhr surprised her? Pagan ran a fingertip across the image of the girl's face. If he squinted, there was a very strong resemblance between Steffie Brough and the girl with whom Gunther Ruhr had been captured in Cambridge. It was an unpleasant realisation: if this child were in Ruhr's possession, then he not only had a hostage but one who was practically a duplicate of somebody he'd desired into the bargain. Pagan pushed this thought aside and squelched back down to the house where Foxie – whose red hair was the only bright thing in the place – was wandering around.

'I don't doubt Ruhr and his chums found accommodation here, Frank,' Foxie said. 'Look at this. Presumably they kept the child here.'

Foxie led Pagan inside a narrow room where an old iron bed had been placed under the wall. Lengths of rope were attached to the frame; somebody had clearly been bound here. On a threadbare bedside rug lay a small white bra, streaked with hardened mud. Foxie picked it up and passed it to Pagan, who handled the garment as if he were afraid of finding blood inside it. He looked for stencilled initials, laundry marks, but found none. He gave it back to Foxworth, who folded it in the pocket of his raincoat.

Pagan gazed at the bed again, the ropes, the strict knots. The idea of the child being imprisoned here upset him. He wandered uneasily through the rest of the house. Except for the remarkably tidy kitchen, the place was a mess. The smell of dampness was overpowering. Pagan went from room to room, most of them small low-ceilinged enclosures with narrow windows. Upstairs several old mattresses lay on the floorboards. Rodents scratched in the attic.

'This must be the terrorist dormitory,' Foxie said. 'Not very well appointed, is it?'

Pagan moved to the window. The view was uninspiring. Flat and dead fields, stricken by the breath of coming winter, stark trees from which a couple of crows arose. Only the big black birds created any kind of movement. Pagan pressed his moist forehead against the window-pane. The motion of the birds – floating, searching – intrigued him, though for the moment he wasn't sure exactly why.

He went back downstairs to the main part of the house. In the living-room dirty glasses stood on a ping-pong table, newspapers were strewn everywhere, spent matches, cigarette butts, beer bottles on the cracked lino. He re-examined Steffie's picture, turning it over and over before passing it to Foxie.

'Ruhr likes them pale and thin, doesn't he?' Foxworth said in a quiet voice.

'That's the way it looks.' Pagan bunched his hands in the pockets of his sodden raincoat. 'When they're finished with the Range Rover, the fingerprint boys better get over here next. The way I see it, nobody's been very careful about hiding their prints.'

'Arrogant lot,' Foxie said.

'With an arrogant leader. I'll tell you what else pisses me right off, Foxie. How could this damned place be overlooked in the general search for Ruhr? How could it be missed, for Christ's sake? It has all the necessary credentials for a hiding-place. Isolated. Recently rented. You'd think it would be obvious to any cop.'

Foxie was silent. He might have said that the countryside was large, the police force relatively small, and this house well concealed but he could see that Frank was in no mood for platitudes, even truthful ones.

Pagan walked round the room, thinking how some places defeated the imagination – they were empty stages, and you could never imagine anybody playing on them. Other houses, by contrast, were vibrant long after their vacancy, and seemed to echo with laughter that although old was cheerful just the same. But this house was a slum, like an abandoned inner-city house where drunks came to defecate, and light could never alter it. The presence of happy people couldn't change the structural gloom. Misery claimed this house, and misery was a clammy tenant, tenaciously silent.

Ghosts, Pagan thought. He stood at the foot of the stairs. For some reason he thought of Magdalena Torrente; at least her intrusion into his mind was a bright occurrence. He tried to imagine how her laughter, floating deliciously from room to room, might make a difference to this hideous dump. He thought of how he'd kissed her before walking away from her, and he could still feel her tongue against his own – another ghost.

How had it come about that Magdalena, who despised Castro's regime, whose father had been shot down and killed at the Bay of Pigs, had become the lover of Castro's Minister of Finance? Rosabal had reputedly been hand-picked by Fidel to mend Cuba's broken finances and restore economic order to a nation allegedly going under. Castro sent him on fund-raising trips to Russia and Czechoslovakia and anywhere else a purse might be forced open for Cuban coffers. Why did Magdalena associate with such a man? Was Rosabal part of some anti-Castro movement? was that the connection with Magdalena? Had she perhaps changed and become a secret supporter of Castro? God, how unlikely that seemed! Perhaps they were simply lovers. He pinched the bridge of his nose and frowned.

Dear Christ, what did Rosabal and Magdalena matter? He had a missing girl and a crazy terrorist to deal with. Steffie Brough had stumbled on to this place, and Ruhr had seized her. A simple story really, a variation on Beauty and the Beast, with the contemporary addition of a stolen nuclear missile. He wondered if Ruhr had hurt the girl yet in any way, or whether Gunther preferred to savour such possibilities and prolong them, getting the timing and the flavour just right before he made his move.

Or did Ruhr understand how the idea of the frail girl's life and security would go round and round maddeningly in Frank Pagan's mind? And did he enjoy the feeling? Of course he did. Ruhr had one of those instinctive minds that quickly pick up on the personalities of others, almost a mimic's skill; in their few encounters he had come to know Frank Pagan somewhat. He would also know where to open Pagan's skin and lay bare the appropriate nerve.

Pagan saw now that the German was doing more than what Foxworth had called 'thumbing his nose': he was torturing Pagan. The scarf, the bra, these weren't mere gestures. It was as if the girl were being forced to perform a slow striptease. And Frank Pagan, like some devoted father desperately searching for his missing daughter through a maze of sleazy nightclubs, was doomed to find only the girl's discarded clothes.

Impatiently, Pagan stepped to the door and looked out across the yard. The birds were on the ground now, pecking with dedicated industry at something concealed under leaves. For one dreadful moment Pagan's heart lurched in his chest as he walked across the mud. He thought that perhaps the birds were feasting on Stephanie Brough, that she hadn't been kidnapped at all, that Ruhr's clues had been cruel jokes. The girl lay here, demolished by black-feathered morticians who picked their corpses down to bone.

Disturbed, the ravens fluttered a couple of feet away, landed, observed Pagan with bleak resentment. They were patient creatures who often had to take their meals cold. Pagan kicked some dry leaves aside. The face that appeared was missing one eye, half the lower lip had been ripped away, a cheek gouged. There was a deep wound in the neck. The man wore a police constable's dark-blue uniform made all the more dark by blood that had dried around his chest. Pagan turned away from the sight, picked up a couple of rocks, tossed them at the big birds, who flew quietly to a nearby tree, there to wait.

Foxie came out of the house and glanced at the corpse. All colour went out of his face. 'Christ,' he said quietly.

Pagan rubbed his hands together. His entire body was suddenly cold.

Foxworth said, 'I've had enough of this place, Frank. Do we need to linger here?'

Pagan got into the car without saying anything. He heard Foxie on the car telephone, reporting the discovery of the dead constable. The afternoon was darkening, the English autumn yielding to the coming winter with customary melancholy. Pagan sat in a hunched position, bent slightly forward to find relief from his renewed pain. Along country lanes a fresh wind blew moist fallen leaves at the car. All the little scraps of a perforated season were falling finally apart.

The office of the lady who had rented the farmhouse was located in a village seventeen miles from Norwich. It was an eccentric operation, manila folders stuffed in drawers, a big old-fashioned black telephone left over from more poetic times when exchanges had proper names. Joanna Lassiter wore her greying hair up, held in place by a marvellous array of coloured pins that Foxworth and Pagan admired. It was as if her skull were a map and the pins pointers to various locations.

She was a pleasantly confused woman who mislaid files and papers. On her desk scores of yellowing receipts had been impaled on a metal spike. The presence of the two policemen unsettled her. She suggested herbal tea, which both men declined. Pagan was impatient to go back out into the darkness of the early evening.

While she searched her desk for the necessary information, Joanna Lassiter said she personally supervised the rental and management of more than a hundred houses and apartments throughout the area, that business was good, and that once – funny, weren't they, these tiny coincidences? – she'd owned a pet dog called Pagan. As she rummaged she flitted breathlessly from topic to topic as if the pins that held her hair in place had punctured the brain itself, destroying the routes along which mental signals were meant to travel. When she wasn't speaking she kept up a sequence of little noises – *mmms* and *arrumms* and *drrmms*. There was battiness here, relief from a grim world.

'He was, I recall, a pleasant sort of fellow. Wore black glasses, which I don't usually like. I only met him once, and then briefly. Our business was done mostly by phone and mail. Can't possibly imagine him connected to any wrongdoing.' Joanna Lassiter poked through a thick folder from which slips of paper fell to the floor and were not retrieved. 'Most of the tenants give me absolutely no trouble. Well, I always say I have an instinct about people, Mr Pagan. I sense vibrations from them, you see. It's a gift.'

And on and on.

Finally she pulled a sheet of paper out of the folder and held it aloft. 'I rather think this is the naughty little chappie we've been seeking, Mr Pagan.' She held the paper directly under her desk-lamp and squinted at it. Pagan leaned across the desk with interest but the handwriting on the sheet was like Pitman's shorthand.

'The man rented the old Yardley place for six months. Paid the whole thing in advance with a money order. I think he said he was some kind of naturalist, actually. Needed a place to assemble his notes on a book. Mmmm. He was only two weeks into his tenancy. Well. It's not an easy property to rent, I'm afraid. Has bad feelings. Don't much like going over there myself. Dreary. Spot of paint might help a bit.'

'Is there a name?' Pagan asked.

'Name?' Joanna Lassiter looked surprised, as if this were a whole new concept to her.

'Did the tenant have a name?' Pagan asked a second time.

When she smiled thirty years fell away from her face. It was almost as if her bone structure altered. She put her fingertips up to her lips. 'Silly me. Of course there's a name, Mr Pagan. Couldn't very well rent a house to a man without a name, could I now?'

'I've heard of stranger things,' Pagan said.

'I daresay you have.' Joanna Lassiter pushed the sheet of paper across the desk. 'There. See for yourself. Funny kind of name. Foreign, of course.'

Pagan picked up the paper and read.

'Does it help, Mr Pagan?' she asked.

Pagan passed the sheet to Foxworth.

He didn't answer Joanna Lassiter's question because he wasn't sure how. He stared through the black window at the village street beyond. The pub sign hanging on the other side of the road, pale and inviting, reminded him of a thirst he'd been suffering for hours.

Marrakech, Morocco

Steffie Brough's head roared and her whole body, locked for ages in one stiff position, felt like iron. Even though somebody had stuffed small pieces of foam rubber inside her ears the great noise of the plane, like that of a locomotive infinitely screaming in an infinite tunnel, had drilled through her skull anyway. She was sick and tired, shaken by the long turbulent flight. Every now and then she'd felt the craft drop suddenly, like something about to fall out of the sky.

She didn't know how many hours she'd actually lain in the cabin of the truck, conscious of cockpit lights up ahead and the shadows of men moving back and forth. It was very weird being conveyed inside one kind of transportation that was being transported inside another.

When the plane began to lose altitude she became aware of pressure building up in the hollows behind her eyes and then rolling painfully through all the dark cavities of her head. Then the plane skimmed over land, bouncing. After that, the silence was wonderful as the craft slid slowly along the runway.

Now, when the door of the truck opened, she twisted her head back and saw Ruhr. Silently, he undid the ropes that bound her and she tried to sit up but her bones seemed to have jammed in place. Her brain throbbed and the ache in her bladder was unbearable.

'I need to go to a toilet,' she said. The rasp in her own voice surprised her. She sounded just the way her Aunt Ruth had before she died last year from throat cancer. She thought *I'd rather be dead from that than trapped in this bloody awful place.*

She glanced toward the back of the big truck, whose cargo was concealed under a long green canvas cover. She didn't want to think what it might be or why Ruhr and his friends had gone to so much trouble to steal it, because then she'd start remembering all the gunfire and how tear gas and smoke had choked her.

But she thought she knew anyway. What else could it be but a missile? What else was there worth killing for in her small corner of the world? She'd always known there were missiles as close as ten miles from her home because she'd watched people walk along narrow country lanes on protest marches but like many things in her young, protected life, missiles were abstractions outside her own limits and interests. They belonged in a world beyond horses and rock music and boys. Now it was different. She could reach up, she could actually *touch* one of the things if she wanted.

Ruhr led her through the aircraft. She was aware of two men sitting in the half-light and how they looked at her as she passed. The air was thick with the smell of fuel and tobacco. The lavatory was tiny, filthy, the floor puddled, and somebody had removed the lock from the door, but she was beyond embarrassment.

She splashed cold water all over her face, then drank thirstily even though the water tasted stale and dusty. She pushed her wet fingers through her hair. Her reflection in a small mirror was white and dreadful. She seemed to have diminished. She looked like a pygmy, a shrunken head. She hardly recognised herself.

She dried her face with paper towels and wished the lavatory had a window so she could look out. She didn't know where she was, she had no idea where she was going. Her parents – oh Christ they would be completely frantic with worry now. Even her stupid brother would have expressed concern in his own stumbling fashion. She raised her face to the mirror a second time. The rough paper towels had at least brought some colour back to her cheeks. And even if she felt like crying, she knew she wouldn't.

Ruhr had a global network of men and women who owed him favours. This airfield, for example, had been made available by an old associate, somebody close to the Moroccan royal family. Situated twenty-five miles from the city of Marrakech, it had, until recently, been used by Moroccan Air Force fighter planes flying against Western Saharan rebels, but its age and condition had caused it to be abandoned.

The huge transport plane taxied over potholes towards an enormous hangar made from prefabricated metal which had rotted years ago. In the fading afternoon sun, the building's vastness was strangely exaggerated. Bats flew in and out of the disintegrated roof, fulfilling some odd rodent urge to veer close to the strips of blinking fluorescent light that hung from the ceiling.

The plane came to a stop outside the hangar, where a large fuel truck was parked. Joseph Sweeney stepped out of the flight deck and moved into the rear cabin, where Ruhr stood. The two men who had come with Ruhr, Trevaskis and the Argentinian, sat against the wall and looked sullen. Sweeney opened one of the paratroop doors and tossed a rope ladder down. Ruhr said, 'Keep your eye on the girl, Trevaskis,' and then swung down the ladder to the tarmac. Sweeney followed him.

When he had his feet firmly on the ground, Sweeney worked a small finger inside his ear. 'That damned roar deafens the hell out of me,' he said. He shook his head a couple of times, then pinched his nostrils and puffed up his cheeks.

Sweeney glanced a moment at the fuel truck, which was moving slowly towards the plane. Born in County Cork and swept off to Boston at the age of ten, he'd worked with

Ruhr a dozen times all over the world and if anybody could be said to know the German it was Joseph James Sweeney. And while Sweeney wouldn't have enjoyed a night's drinking with Gunther, nor let the man anywhere near his teenaged nieces, he had a certain admiration for him.

Sweeney gestured toward the plane. He asked a question he'd been hesitant about. 'I suppose the kid somehow fits your general plan?'

Ruhr said, 'She may provide insurance. Or diversion.'

Sweeney nodded, then dropped the subject. He knew when to persist and when to let go. Ruhr could be incommunicative and distant when it suited him, and it obviously suited him now. Sweeney felt a passing pity for the girl, but like most of his emotions it was allowed to evaporate quickly.

'You had me worried, Gunther.'

'How so?'

'When they took you in Cambridge, I thought it was all over.'

Ruhr made a dismissive gesture and laughed abruptly. 'You know me better than that. I have many lives.'

Sweeney watched the fuel truck park alongside the plane. In half an hour or so they'd be out of this godawful place and flying the Atlantic. Frankly, he'd be glad when this one was over and he could go back to the anonymous life he'd worked hard to build for himself in the USA, a quiet house in a quiet street in Newburyport, Massachusetts. His neighbours thought he was living off land investments, an illusion he gladly encouraged.

He wasn't sure why this particular undertaking made him so goddam uneasy. The presence of the kid obviously contributed to it, but something was different about Ruhr as well. He had a cold distance about him, a weariness. Sweeney felt these were danger signals although he couldn't interpret them. He'd stay away from Gunther as much as he could for the duration.

He watched the hose from the fuel truck extend to the fuselage of the big plane and remembered the thought that had occurred to him a couple of times recently: *in his lifetime, he'd killed more men than he'd fucked women*. Somehow this realisation had shocked him. He said, 'I really think this is my last time, *amigo*.'

'You've said so before. You've always come back.' Ruhr was conscious of Trevaskis watching him in a hostile way from the door of the plane.

'This time I'm beginning to hear the creak of my bones,' Sweeney said. 'And the thrill's not in it any more. Or maybe there's too much for me to handle. I'm forty-two, Gunther. I've lived this life since I was twenty-two and that's a long time. And I'm not including the five years before that when I was in the United States Air Force. How long can a man go on? Can you imagine doing this when you're sixty?'

Ruhr had also been living this life for a long time. Unlike Sweeney, he couldn't imagine retirement. The real trick was to find new ways to keep the game fresh, to introduce new elements. Even new risks. The alternative was dullness and Ruhr couldn't tolerate that. A bat flew out of the sun and flapped close to his face and he lashed out at the thing.

Sweeney said, 'I can get absorbed real smoothly into what they call the mainstream of American life.'

The mainstream of American life. Sweeney must have been reading *Time* magazine. Ruhr said, 'Barbecues and Budweisers and little girls with metal on their teeth and tedium without end.'

'You make it sound comforting.'

'All anaesthetics give comfort,' Ruhr remarked. 'But only on a temporary basis.'

Both men walked some distance from the fuel truck. In the extensive network of reliable men Ruhr had built over the years, none had proved more valuable than Joseph Sweeney. Whenever Ruhr needed something – an individual's name, or a certain kind of weapon, or in this case a plane – somehow Sweeney always managed to find it. He had become, in a sense, Ruhr's quartermaster, resourceful, reassuring.

Sweeney combined the soothing charm of a confidence man with the hardness of an assassin. Since he'd experienced at first hand the staggering ineptitude of the military mind, he knew how to exploit it ruthlessly, how to gain access to military bases and installations; how to impersonate an officer with such authority that no guard or military policeman ever questioned his presence. He was the best at his craft.

It was Sweeney who had identified the Duty Officer responsible for the transportation of missiles at the site in Norfolk; and even if it was Ruhr who had seduced the man into treachery, nevertheless it had been Sweeney who'd first uncovered the essential information: name and rank and serial number; date of birth; marital status; specific duties; known weaknesses.

Known weaknesses, Ruhr thought. He'd never yet found a man without a faultline to be widened; he'd never encountered a man who didn't have a purchase price of some kind. With some it was very simple – a need for money, for drugs, certain kinds of sex. With others it was more complicated – the moment of shame recaptured, the dark skeleton in the unopened closet. The Duty Officer at the site belonged in the latter category.

A thirty-five-year-old man from Nashville, the Duty Officer had a wife and child living in Tennessee. At the same time, he was deeply involved with a woman who lived in Norwich, a mistress with definite ambitions of her own. It was a situation Ruhr considered pathetic; loneliness had driven the Duty Officer into the grasp of a woman whose connivance overwhelmed the man's naïvety. He was basically a nice, easy-going fellow with the kind of dull good looks essential to the success of any garden party. What the mistress wanted was marriage and an escape route out of the damp miseries of Norwich. She was about to write a letter to the wife in Tennessee. If the man wasn't willing to talk divorce, then, by God, she'd force his hand!

Lurid lives, Ruhr had thought. Especially in the quiet suburbs of boring cities, lurid lives. He felt as if he hovered above this human swamp like a minor god, indifferent. And so, after observing his victim for several days, he'd swooped down from his lofty place into the young man's life, both as saviour and deceiver. He found the pub where the officer sometimes drank, engineered an introduction. He posed as a Swiss photographer who'd unfortunately lost his fingers shooting film in Vietnam. It struck a sympathetic chord in the Duty Officer, who'd served in Vietnam too, towards the bitter end – a fact Ruhr already knew, of course, courtesy of Joseph Sweeney.

A quiet companionship grew; it was nothing substantial. A few beers now and again, under circumstances that appeared to be sheer chance. Once or twice they ran into each other in Cambridge as well as Norwich. It's a small world, Ruhr would say, and smile his most appealing smile, the one in which his lips didn't disappear. Gradually the facts of the Duty Officer's life emerged. He was bogged down, the woman in Norwich was goddam demanding, why had he ever let himself in for this godalmighty mess in the first place? Ah, Sweet Jesus! He loved his wife and kid, he didn't want to hurt them or lose them. But his wife, Louanne, couldn't come to England because she had a sick mother in Knoxville. It was complicated, and getting more out of hand every day. Once the Duty Officer had actually said, *I wish I was dead*.

That, Ruhr suggested, was the wrong solution; the wrong party would be eliminated in that event.

Ruhr had thought up something much better.

If there was to be a candidate for a coffin, the choice was obvious: the mistress – who else?

But how? How could that kind of thing happen? the Duty Officer had asked.

Ruhr was sly then, almost coy in his cunning. He offered a few suggestions, crumbs, nothing more. What it came down to was this simple: the woman in Norwich had to be . . . disposed of. The Duty Officer shuddered at the notion. He'd entertained it, of course. Who wouldn't? But in the end he knew he couldn't commit murder – other than in his heart, he'd added, as if to reassure Ruhr of his masculinity.

Then find somebody else to do it, Ruhr had said.

The idea, once planted, grew in the dark. Ruhr, master gardener, nurtured it, made it sprout. And when it was fully grown and luxuriant in the Duty Officer's mind, Ruhr administered the final flourish one night while he and his new American friend were drinking schnapps at a pub on St Andrew's Hill in the centre of Norwich. Ruhr needed something from the Duty Officer. Something simple really. But classified. Ruhr hinted broadly that in exchange for this small item of information the Duty Officer's life could be 'rectified'. He wouldn't ever have to worry about his girlfriend again. Ruhr understood, of course, that the 'drastic' solution he was suggesting might be offensive, alien even, to the young man, and if he wanted to refuse Ruhr's offer, well, what difference would it make to their friendship?

Why did Ruhr want the classified information? the Duty Officer asked in the manner of a pharmacist asking a customer why he needed a restricted medicine for which he had no prescription.

Ruhr answered that it was a trifle really, a journalistic matter, an opportunity to photograph a missile in transit from a site, an exclusive. He was convincing in an odd, hypnotic way. He could use a stock shot of the kind supplied by military press liaison offices, but he resented the idea. No, what he wanted was the real thing on a real road surrounded by a real escort. The feel of authenticity – that was important. The way things truly looked, that was what he was after. For a photo-journalist, veracity was what mattered.

He needed a timetable, a calendar of forthcoming events, places and times, routes. In return for these snippets Ruhr would ensure the total security of the young man's marriage and with it his peace of mind. And what was life when you had no serenity? How could one pursue a career distracted by emotional problems that could be clarified in an instant?

That night of beer and schnapps on St Andrew's Hill, everything was neatly slotted in place. Ruhr knew he'd get the kind of information so exclusive it made him indispensable. He knew what the route of the missile was to be; he knew the exact time and place. Information was power, especially when it was information his employers didn't have.

It was a triumph to turn the young American round, and yet easy too, because the Duty Officer was so vulnerable. Murder and treachery. Now it pleased Ruhr to think he'd made this very ordinary young man, who was neither terribly bright nor terribly stupid, an accomplice in both crimes!

Three nights later Ruhr sneaked into the woman's house and stabbed her directly through the heart while she slept. He waited until he heard her die, then he left. By the next evening, Ruhr had the information he wanted. It had taken him exactly twenty-three days to get it. He never saw the Duty Officer again.

Now the truck had finished refuelling the plane. Joseph Sweeney lit a cigarette. He watched the sun, in a great explosion the colour of burgundy, slide towards darkness on the rocky horizon. A chill was already in the air.

'It's time to go,' Sweeney said.

'I am ready,' Ruhr remarked. 'As always.'

'We should dump the cab first.'

'Of course.'

The cab of the truck that had conveyed the missile and the launch system was uncoupled from the trailer. It was excess weight on the plane, and useless now. It was detached from the trailer and allowed to roll down the ramp to the airstrip, there to be abandoned.

Havana, Cuba

In the early afternoon, Rafael Rosabal walked on the crowded, humid Calle Obispo in Old Havana. The breeze that blew over the sea wall, the Malecón, faded in the streets in a series of quiet little gasps that would barely shake a shrub. Today everything smelled of salt. Today you could practically *hear* metal corrode as rust devoured it. There was rust everywhere, in the decorative iron grilles of windows and doorways, on the panels and underbodies of the old American automobiles cluttering the streets, even in the paintwork of the new Cuban-built buses and the imported Fiats and Ladas. Where rain had run through rust, coppery stains, suggestive of very old tears, discoloured the façades of buildings.

Rosabal reached the entrance to the Hotel Bristol. He was jostled on all sides by pedestrians who filled the cobbled street. Rectangular posters fluttered twenty feet overhead, advertisements announcing an exhibition of modern Cuban artists at the Casa de Bano de la Catedral. Rosabal loathed Cuban art, which he considered dull and derivative. Socialism, as it was conceived by the Lider Maximo, hadn't altogether electrified creativity.

He went inside the Bristol, passing the registration desk where a clerk was reading a copy of *Granma*, the Party's newspaper. According to the headline, the Lider Maximo was going to make a speech sometime that day on TV.

Rosabal kept walking until he came to the small dark bar at the rear, a narrow room lit by two dim bulbs. He asked for a *mojito* only to be told by an apologetic barman that lemon and lime juice were both temporarily out of stock. He settled for a beer, which he took to a table.

Apart from himself, there was one other customer, a tall, bony man in a dark blue two-piece suit. This was Rosabal's contact, Teodoro Diaz-Alonso. The word that always popped into Rosabal's head when he saw Diaz-Alonso was *remilgado*, prim. Diaz-Alonso wore small glasses parked near the tip of his nose. His stiff bearing suggested a professor of the kind you no longer saw in the city. Diaz-Alonso was drinking cola from a tall glass. Rosabal sat down beside him.

Rosabal was a little uneasy whenever he had meetings with Diaz-Alonso in Havana. And yet why shouldn't there be a point of connection between Rosabal's Ministry of Finance and MINFAR, the Ministry of the Armed Forces, for which Diaz-Alonso worked as a senior advisor? Both men were government servants, after all. They knew the same people, went to the same restaurants and parties, enjoyed the same privileges of rank. Besides, Diaz-Alonso was a frequent visitor to Rosabal's apartment in the Vedado. This encounter would look perfectly natural to any casual observer. So why worry about it?

Diaz-Alonso said, 'The General has asked me to convey his greetings, Rafael.'

'Thank the General.'

'I am also to give you a message.' Diaz-Alonso paused and looked like a scholar recalling a quotation. 'The General says that the conditions you require will be ready.'

Rosabal sat back in his chair and tried to relax. It was extraordinary how, when you were so involved with the architecture of a conspiracy, when one blueprint had obsessed you for so long, you forgot simple pleasures – the taste of a beer, the aroma of a good cigar. It was like living in a room with the shades constantly drawn. Nothing happened beyond the shades, no cars passed in the street, no women strolled on the boulevards, no sun, no moon. The room was everything.

'Tell the General this will not be forgotten,' he said. 'Nor will any of the recent services he has provided.'

Diaz-Alonso was expressionless as he remarked, 'The General does not underestimate the importance of his role in this whole project, Rafael. He is not a man who favours false modesty. But for himself he expects no monetary rewards, of course. He is no mercenary. The General seeks only the post of Minister of the Armed Forces.'

'That's understood.'

Diaz-Alonso raised his hand very slightly, as if to admonish Rosabal, in the gentlest way, for interrupting him. 'The General also expects a certain seniority among Ministers, naturally. First among equals, so to speak.'

Rosabal said, 'The General will be accommodated. Assure him of that.' General Alfonso Capablanca, second in command of the Armed Forces to Raul Castro, had always been consistent in what he wanted. Negotiating with the General through his intermediary had been part of the arrangement from the beginning. The General liked the distance. He also thought it observed a certain kind of protocol which even conspirators must obey, lest they become mere anarchists. There was such a thing as form, Capablanca said. If Rosabal was to become one day the President of this nation – with the help of the General and a number of his senior officers, of course – he would understand that form often meant more than substance. Politics, in the final analysis, was not to be confused with the real world. Politics was a matter of appearance.

Rosabal was equal to the General's cynicism. He found Capablanca an extreme bore, but indispensable. Without his inclusion, and the role of his officers, the scheme would fall to pieces. And without the General's ability to acquire the Lider Maximo's signature on a certain document, the plot – if it existed in any form – would have taken a different shape. Therefore Rosabal, out of a gratitude more pragmatic than sincere, met the General's demands, and was very polite even as he looked forward to the day when Capablanca might be 'retired' by a firing squad.

Diaz-Alonso inclined his head a little. The gaunt, tight-lipped face yielded very little emotion. 'The General will also need to know about any changes in schedule as soon as they occur.'

'I expect none.' Rosabal was thinking of Gunther Ruhr now, and the missile. He looked at his watch. Ruhr would be in North Africa, if all had gone well. And since there was no news to indicate otherwise, Rosabal assumed everything was in order. Anyhow, he would have heard from Caporelli if anything had altered. They usually exchanged messages by telephone. Caporelli called Mexico City, and the message was conveyed to Havana by one of the Italian's employees. Rosabal smiled a little as he thought of the Italian. Caporelli's problem was the way he deemed himself smarter and sharper than anyone else.

Diaz-Alonso said, 'These are very strange times for our nation, Rafael. Once upon a time, I remember, we all had high hopes. Very high. Now, everywhere I look I see discontent.' He shrugged and finished his soda. 'Change must come. Every day, a little more pressure builds up, and steam always seeks an outlet. I wish there was a legal way of achieving change, but there is no longer any legality in the system. The Party is the only voice. And the Party is a big problem, Rafael. It is governed by men who cannot hear the voices of the people.'

'Not for much longer,' Rosabal said.

'Let us hope so, Rafael.' Diaz-Alonso set his empty glass down on the table. He rose to his feet. 'You know how to contact me if you have to.'

Rosabal watched Diaz-Alonso cross the room, then took another sip of his beer. He put on his black sunglasses and prepared to leave. As he passed in front of the bar, the bartender asked, 'Did you hear?'

'Hear?'

'On the radio a moment ago. Fidel has cancelled his speech today. They didn't say why. He must be pretty damn sick if he can't make a speech, heh?'

Rosabal, who worked to maintain a low profile in Castro's government because he found anonymity a more useful tool than renown, said nothing. He thought he saw a slight look of recognition cross the barman's face, but then it was gone.

'I heard a story he has ulcers,' the barman remarked. 'Maybe they're acting up. I don't remember a time when he ever cancelled.'

Rosabal replied with a platitude and continued walking past the bar and the reception desk and back on to Obispo Street, where the breeze had gathered strength and shook the posters that hung in the air. *The Lider Maximo was too sick to make his speech*. For the first time in history, Rosabal thought.

He walked past the herbal shop, El Herbolario. The scent of mint drifted toward him, evoking an unwelcome memory of Guantanamo and Rosabal's impoverished childhood there. *Hierbabuena*, which so many people found pleasing, had grown in profusion near his home. His father had been a poor, illiterate cane-cutter, his house a miserable hut through which hot winds blew dust and which, in the rainy season, became flooded and filled with mosquitoes. People were said to be better off in Guantanamo these days, but that was a relative thing. Poverty, no matter what the Communist statisticians told you, still existed. The only difference was that increased life expectancy and low infant mortality meant there were many more people around to enjoy it.

Rosabal, thinking how far he had travelled from his wretched origins and how close he was to his goal, paused on the corner. He was rich now, he had access to vast sums of money and investments all over the world and he rarely ever thought about his background. Who needed it anyway? Who needed to recall the lack of nutrition and the mosquitoes that fed on thin bodies and the sheer hopelessness that the land instilled in people? He remembered his emphysematic father cutting cane, cutting cane, on and on, season after monotonous season, stooped and burned black by the harsh sun in the cane-fields, a prisoner of King Sugar. He remembered his mother, dour, thick-hipped from too many births, dead at the age of thirty-five. She had never smiled, never. These memories bored into him, one despised picture after another, until he felt tension rise in his throat and a hammer knocking the inside of his skull.

He remembered the terrible day in 1962, two years after the death of his mother, when his father had tried to seek political asylum at the American naval base in Guantanamo; he recalled clutching his father's hand and being surrounded by Yanquis in khaki uniforms who asked his father tough questions and laughed at some of the answers. Rosabal recalled the fear he'd felt at the strangeness of it all, the alien language, the unfamiliar uniforms. The cowed look in his father's eyes had haunted him ever since. The Americans turned father and son back. They rejected a dying man and his nine-year-old boy. They spoke of immigration quotas and application forms and the need for sponsors, things neither Rosabal nor his father understood.

A day later, as a direct consequence of his attempt to flee Cuba, Felipe Rosabal was taken away by *fidelistas*. He was never seen again. For years, Rafael Rosabal couldn't decide whom he hated more, Castro or the Yanquis.

He took a handkerchief from a pocket, wiped sweat from his forehead. You had to control these memories. You had to fight them back, suppress them. They were dead and gone, they had nothing to do with you. You escaped from your childhood, from that dank brutality, from humiliation. Every now and again it reaches out darkly as if to drag you back to your beginnings, but it means nothing. It means absolutely nothing.

Thanks to the Revolution, to the opportunities given to you by Castro's regime, you fled your origins. The poverty. The futility.

The irony of this – his gratitude to the Revolution – was pointedly amusing. After all, he intended to destroy the same State that had educated and raised him at its own expense.

He was calm again as his chauffeur-driven black BMW rolled quietly toward him. He opened the back door and stepped inside where a young woman, who had the intense good looks of a flamenco dancer, smiled and reached out to him. She wore her very black hair pulled back tightly across her scalp and ribboned with red satin. Her lips, whose lipstick matched her ribbon exactly, pressed on his mouth, and she placed the palms of her hands lightly against the sides of his face. It was a gesture in part love, in part possessiveness.

'My darling,' she said, a little breathlessly.

Rafael Rosabal held the woman, but not with any great enthusiasm. Her skin smelled of a perfume called Diva, which he had brought back for her from Europe.

'Can we go home for lunch . . . ?' She blew softly in his ear; she behaved as if the chauffeur didn't exist.

'We can go home for lunch,' he said, holding her hand between his own. Later, she would make love with a kind of serenity that was in total contrast to Magdalena, with whom sex was all fire and final damp exhaustion. Magdalena was like a magnificent whore, Rosabal thought. A wife never, a mistress always.

'Do I make you happy?' the young woman asked.

'Yes.'

'You regret nothing?'

'Nothing,' Rosabal said in an absent way.

The gold ring on the young woman's hand caught the light and glinted. She turned her hand over, studying the band from different angles. Until three months ago, the girl's name had been Estela Alvarez Capablanca, daughter of the General. From time to time Estela still thought of herself as bearing her unmarried name. She hadn't yet become accustomed to her change in marital status. Being the wife of Rafael Rosabal was a new condition for her, and one she thought fortunate. It had all happened so quickly, a fast courtship, a very quiet wedding unannounced in newspapers – because Rafael had wanted it that way – a brief honeymoon in Mexico.

Other Ministers' wives, who had sometimes contrived to play matchmaker for Rosabal in the past, considered them a marvellous couple who needed only a baby to make their marriage a perfect union. Certainly Estela wanted a child. She adored children. Sometimes she wept quietly when she read of atrocities enacted upon infants in the war zones of the world, or her heart ached when she saw some poor sad-eyed kid on the streets of Havana.

Every time she felt Rafael's sperm flood her womb, she prayed for fertility. And her prayers, it seemed, had been answered. Only fifteen minutes before her rendezvous with Rafael she'd gone to her doctor to learn that she was pregnant. Now, quietly joyful, she waited for the right moment to share this news with her husband, who was so often distracted these days.

A mother-to-be, yes, a clinging wife no. She wasn't at all the mindless little wife so many people, Rosabal included, perceived her to be. She had some private core to her, an independence she may have inherited from the General, a stubbornness, a native intelligence that was inviolate. She was domestic, in the sense that she enjoyed both the Havana apartment and the country house near Sancti Spiritus, but it would have been a gross underestimation to think that was the complete picture. Estela Rosabal was her own person. A fire burned inside her that few had ever seen.

For his part, Rosabal believed that being the son-in-law of General Capablanca was a profitable connection: it kept conspiracy in the family. It was a great match, even if it had been made more by power brokers and opportunities than by heaven and heart.

The weary man in the grey and blue plaid jacket carried a Canadian passport that falsely identified him as J. S. Mazarek. The document was a good forgery he'd been given in Miami. He had come to Havana on a cut-rate package tour from Montreal. The group with whom he'd travelled called themselves The Explorers' Association, mostly an alliance of single middle-aged men and women whose only interest in exploration seemingly involved one another's bodily parts. Mazarek had already had to avoid the energetic advances of an opera-humming, large-breasted widow from Trois Rivières.

Mazarek, a big man with hair the colour and texture of froth on a *cappuccino*, had been tracking his quarry along Obispo and Mercaderes Streets, surreptitiously taking photographs. He did this expertly because he'd been doing it for much of his life. Usually his cases involved errant husbands and wandering wives, who tended to be more paranoid than the cocksure Mr Smooth, whose face and movements rarely betrayed a sign of nerves.

Mazarek watched the Minister of Finance open the door of the BMW. Then he got off one more quick shot with his tiny camera. He had enough data on Rafael Rosabal. His employer would be satisfied, though perhaps not absolutely happy. In this line of work – often more a probe of men's hearts than mere detection – satisfaction wasn't always followed by contentment.

12 London

At nine o'clock in the evening Frank Pagan sat in his office and listened to the constant ringing of telephones and the clack of printers. Despite all this incoming information, he was frustrated. What had he learned after all? The answer that came back was disheartening: damn little. He hung his jacket on the back of the chair and pressed his fingertips against his tired eyes, ignoring the bothersome sparrow of pain pecking away at his chest.

Foxie came into the room with a bunch of papers in his hand. He took a sheet off the top and scanned it. 'The chopper was stolen three weeks ago from the Moroccan Air Force, who assumed it was seized by West Saharan rebels. The crew members were Syrians. As you could predict, they didn't enter the country with a shred of legality. Known terrorists, according to the Syrian press attaché in London.'

A Moroccan Cobra helicopter, a Syrian crew; terrorism observed no boundaries. It was sovereign unto itself.

'The other men dead at the site were Richard Mayer, a native of Buffalo, New York, and one Roderigo Flavell, a citizen of Argentina. Mayer was trained by the US Army in the fine art of explosives and was renowned for his demolition skills. Flavell is wanted for questioning in connection with the bombing of a synagogue in Paris a couple of years ago. A merry sort of bunch, Frank.'

Pagan shifted his position. It was hard to concentrate on what Foxworth was telling him. His mind, or some dark aspect of it, kept pulling him away. Too many puzzles, each demanding his attention at the same time, nagged him.

Foxie said, 'The prints we got from the Yardley farm belong to Ruhr, Mayer, and another American named Trevaskis, who has a police record in San Diego: extortion, conspiracy to sell explosives and firearms, gunrunning into Mexico. Considered dangerous. We also found prints belonging to the late Flavell as well as a fellow countryman of his called Enrico Zapino. Zapino is also wanted by the French police. Same synagogue bombing.'

The Yardley Farm. Now there was one puzzle that kept coming back like a bad taste. He couldn't figure out the association between the man who had rented the place and Gunther Ruhr. Impatiently he looked at his watch; the tenant's wife had been sent for an hour ago – what was keeping her? She only had to come from The Connaught, which wasn't more than a ten-minute taxi-ride away. Pagan hoped she might be able to cast a little light on the dark area, if she ever arrived.

Since the gunshot wound he'd felt morose. Now he felt even more bleak about the fate of Steffie Brough. He'd met her parents before leaving Norwich, two very unhappy people trying to varnish their sorrow with good old-fashioned English stoicism and finding that the stiff upper lip wasn't all the advertising claimed it to be.

We'll do our best, Pagan had told them. We'll find her.

What makes you think so? Mrs Brough had asked in that kind of ringing voice which is a cousin to outright hysteria. It was a question to which Pagan had no answer. In the policeman's almanac of platitudes, absolutely none was capable of creating a shield against grief. He kept seeing Mrs Brough's face, which resembled an older version of the Stephanie in the school photograph. Sheer anxiety had stripped her features of any expression other than desperation. Pagan was filled with helpless sorrow and an anger he laboured to control.

Billy Ewing appeared in the doorway, half in, half out of the office. He held a slip of thin yellow paper in one hand.

'Item, gentlemen,' he said.

'I hope it's good news,' Pagan said.

Billy Ewing shrugged. 'Good, bad, I just deliver, Frank. You're the swami, you interpret. Now according to this little gem a transport plane was stolen this very morning from right under the vigilant nose of our Royal Air Force.'

'Stolen?' Pagan asked.

'That's what it says here. On a routine, approved flight from Fife to Germany, an American C-130, which had flown unspecified *matériel* into a base in Fife the day before, was apparently hijacked by persons unknown. The location of the craft is also unknown.'

'How did it take so damned long to provide us with that item?' Pagan said.

'Injured pride,' Foxie suggested. 'The RAF is awfully sensitive.'

'I suppose,' Pagan said, but without conviction. There was no real coordination at times between law enforcement agencies and branches of the military. Each was its own little dominion of egotism.

'Lose big plane, look very foolish,' said Billy Ewing.

'How can they lose a big plane?' Pagan asked. 'I can see the hijacking. Fine. Anything can be hijacked if you want it bad enough. What I don't see is the failure to find the thing.'

With the authority of a man who is halfway to attaining his pilot's licence, Foxie said, 'First, bad weather. Clouds, Frank. And many of them. Second, it's a big sky, and one plane is very tiny in it, no matter how big it looks on the ground. Third, the Air Force has only a limited number of interceptors at its disposal. And where do they look? The North Sea? The English Channel? The Atlantic? If the transport plane's flying low enough, radar's no help.'

'Do you think the RAF has informed the Americans?' Pagan asked.

Billy Ewing said, 'What a scene. The Air Marshal going on his knees to the Americans.' Ewing assumed a sharp English accent, upper-class, accurate. *'Sorry, old boy. One of your planes got away from us. Damndest thing.'*

Pagan rose from his chair very slowly. He walked across the room and turned on a small portable radio. He wanted something raucous and mind-clearing, something to shake up the synapses and cover the quiet drumming noise panic made inside his head. If Steffie Brough was still alive, she was inside an aeroplane with Ruhr and nobody knew where. In his imagination he saw Ruhr skywriting the words *Find Me, Frank.*

Little Richard's 'Long Tall Sally' roared into the room. The sound, which to some might have been torture – Foxworth, out of Pagan's vision, winced – was balm to Pagan's troubled heart. Like most great rock music, it was meaningless if you thought about it. But meaning wasn't the point. Rock hypnotised you into a condition where you didn't need to think. That was the beauty of it. Pagan, an old rock buff, knew such arcane things as the names of the original Shirelles, the first hit song recorded by Gene Vincent, and the date and place of Buddy Holly's death.

Billy Ewing left. His musical tastes went no further than Peter, Paul and Mary and his own whisky-inspired version of Auld Lang Syne every New Year's Eve.

Pagan returned to his desk. He couldn't remember when he'd last slept. His eyelids felt heavy. He needed a brisk infusion of coffee. He was about to ask Foxworth to bring a cup of very strong brew, when the woman suddenly appeared in the doorway.

She was in her middle forties and had reached that condition known as her prime. To look at Gabrielle Chapotin was to understand the word in a way no dictionary could ever define. She had a calm confidence about her, and a style found only in women who have both the means and ambition to haunt the salons of high fashion and those expensive clinics where clever cosmetologists concoct creams and lotions to halt the ruin of the flesh. She had the air of a fortress against whose buttresses decay and deterioration may batter but make little headway.

She was beautiful in a daunting way. The high cheekbones, the hollows in the cheeks that suggested a sour lozenge of candy in her mouth, the long, groomed red-brown hair, the tailored trouser-suit that was pinstriped and authoritative; she was a woman who knew herself very well. She reminded Pagan of a former fashion model, somebody of well-trained elegance.

'Frank Pagan?' she asked in very good English.

'You must be Gabrielle Chapotin.' Pagan rose, walked to the radio, turned it off.

Foxie scurried with a chair for her. She nodded to him as she would to all servants, then sat down with a very straight back. She gazed up at the big silk screen of Buddy Holly, as if she were amused.

'My regrets,' Pagan said. He extended a hand. Gabrielle's clasp was slack and quick. She wanted out of here in a hurry.

'Regrets?' she asked.

'Your husband. The tragedy.'

'Some marriages are in name only, Mr Pagan,' she said.

Madame Frost, Pagan thought. He cleared his throat, asked Foxworth for coffee. Gabrielle declined, saying, she couldn't drink what passed for coffee in England. Pagan made a mild joke about the similarity between British coffee and transmission fluid, but she didn't even smile politely. Foxworth brought coffee in a plastic cup and Pagan sipped. The temperature of the room had fallen; the woman had ushered in a brisk chill.

'I have so much to do,' she said. 'There is tape red.'

'Red tape,' Pagan said. 'But your way sounds more poetic.'

'However you say it. Also funeral arrangements. I have to ship my late husband's body back to Paris for burial. You understand, of course.'

'I don't intend to keep you for very long. A few questions, nothing more.' Pagan set his cup down. 'You realise my interest isn't in solving your husband's murder, don't you? This isn't a homicide operation.'

She looked surprised. 'Then why am I here?'

'Because I sent for you, Madame. When I learned you'd come to London, I thought it would save me a trip to Paris.'

'But why, if it has nothing to do with my husband's murder?'

'I'm more interested in your husband's life than his death.'

'Which life would that be, Mr Pagan? After all, he had more than one.'

It was a good point. Which life? Did they overlap? Had old Jean-Paul kept them completely separated? One world in Paris with Gabrielle, another in London with his doomed Melody. Was there perhaps even a third life, something he kept apart from the other two? J.-P. Chapotin, grandmaster of deception.

'Your late husband rented a farm in the countryside,' Pagan said.

'He hated the countryside.'

'Just the same, the information we have is that a farmhouse was leased to him by an estate agency in Norfolk. So far as we know, he never occupied the house, personally.'

'Why does it interest you if he never lived there?' she asked. She was impatient. She sat defensively, as if she thought a prolonged stay in this room might contaminate her.

'I'm intrigued by the connection between your husband and the people who *did* occupy the house. They were . . . criminals. I'm simply trying to work out the relationship between these men and Monsieur Chapotin.'

'Criminals? I don't know why he would associate with such types. I can't help you, Mr Pagan. You see, I know so very little.'

She placed her hands in her lap and looked down at them. They were excellent hands, long fingers, strong nails subtly varnished. They were made for summoning head-waiters and dismissing servants. Gabrielle may have been the spirit of winter incarnate, but she had class.

'Let's try something simpler. What kind of business was he in?'

'I paid no attention to his affairs,' she replied, skating over – perhaps ignorant of – the double meaning.

'You must have some knowledge,' Pagan said.

'I ran his houses for him, Mr Pagan. That is all I did. I was his housekeeper.'

Pagan didn't think she could ever be anybody's housekeeper. Nor could he imagine Jean-Paul concealing very much from this woman. She was strong, self-willed. She wouldn't be easy to deceive. He resisted the temptation to scoff. He would press on as if he hadn't heard a word she'd said. He'd simply tuck his head down and keep charging. The battering-ram principle.

'Did he have business interests in England?'

She looked slightly exasperated. 'I do not know.'

'I assume he had a bank account here. He would have to pay household expenses in Chelsea. I could easily find out. With a little luck, I might even discover the source of his income. If there was an account, deposits had to be made somehow. There would be microfilm copies of cheques. The bank manager would probably help. They usually do when I ask them.'

'I had thought your bankers were more discreet,' she said.

'Nobody's discreet when you start breaking their bones, Madame,' Pagan said.

'Breaking their bones?'

'Figuratively.'

'How very colourful.'

Gabrielle Chapotin was silent a moment. She smiled for the first time, a rehearsed cover-girl smile but gorgeous anyway. 'Speaking of banks reminds me that Jean-Paul had an interest in an Italian financial institution. I don't remember the name. "Commerciante" something. It should not be too difficult to find if you need to. He also had, I believe, some South African investments.'

Ah. Pagan found it fascinating how responsive people could be when they imagined a stranger poking around in their bank accounts. There was always something to hide, and it was usually money. Obviously Gabrielle knew more about Jean-Paul's business than she was saying, at least enough to become communicative when she faced the prospect of Pagan interviewing a bank manager. What other financial irregularities might be uncovered? What fiscal misdeeds might be stumbled upon? Whatever they were – and Pagan wasn't interested in them – Gabrielle surely knew. It was a great smile, though, and it warmed him.

'I'm glad to see your memory's finally working,' he said.

Gabrielle shrugged. 'Sometimes a small connection is all you need. A spark, you might say. Memory is a strange thing.'

'Very strange,' Pagan said. 'What about his business interests in this country? Can we find a spark for those?'

She opened her purse and took out a Disque Bleu. Foxie found a match, struck it, held it to the cigarette. She smoked without inhaling. Blue clouds gathered around her head, making her look wistful. She gazed at Pagan and for a second he enjoyed a certain intimacy with her, the meaningful locking of eyes, the vague feeling that at some other time they might have met in circumstances more conducive to, well, mutual understanding. He was flattered.

He pushed his chair back against the wall, glanced at Foxie, then waited for Gabrielle to go on. She held out her cigarette and Foxie, the perfect butler, produced an ashtray in which she crushed the butt vigorously. Too vigorously, Pagan thought. She was tense.

She looked away from him now. 'He went to Scotland.'

'Do you know why he went there?'

'He had some kind of business meeting, I believe. But I don't know the details.'

'Do you know exactly where he went?'

Madame Chapotin said, 'I understand he flew to Glasgow. I happened to see the airline ticket when his secretary sent it to the house.'

Pagan was sure that things didn't just 'happen' in Gabrielle's life. She probably found the ticket and sneaked a look at it; she would have spied like an expert. He wondered if she'd known about Chapotin's other life all along but chose to ignore it for reasons of her own.

'Did he stay in Glasgow?'

She didn't know the answer. Nor did she know his business there, or if he hired a car, or whether he was picked up at the airport. She only knew the date of his airline ticket, which she was happy to remember. Pagan believed her. The interview was coming to an end. Foxie, who knew what was expected of him in the light of Gabrielle's slender information, had already slipped out of the room. Pagan stood up.

She said, 'You know, the more I think of this, the more I consider it unlikely that Jean-Paul rented the farmhouse. I cannot imagine him ever doing that. He hated quiet. He loathed country living. Perhaps another man with the same name was responsible. Could that not be?'

'Chapotin's a pretty unusual name,' Pagan said.

'You can check it out, no?'

'My assistant obtained a photograph of your late husband from the police conducting the homicide investigation. A copy is on its way to the woman who rented the farmhouse. If it turns out that the renter wasn't your husband, why would somebody want to pose as him? What would an imposter stand to gain?'

Gabrielle Chapotin had no answer for that one. She drifted out into the corridor, where she stood for a time in thoughtful silence. Then she smiled half-heartedly at Pagan and was gone, leaving behind the faintest trace of expensive perfume.

Pagan didn't like the idea of an imposter. He'd assumed that Jean-Paul had rented the place on behalf of the terrorists, that some connection existed between Chapotin and Ruhr. Perhaps Chapotin was even the man behind Ruhr. To introduce the hypothesis of a fraud at this stage was a complication Pagan didn't need. If J.-P. hadn't rented the place, then why would somebody use his name to do it? Of course, there might be two different Jean-Paul Chapotins, but in England the chances were remote.

Foxworth came back into the room. 'I just had a word with the Glasgow Police. They'll get back to me.'

'Soon, I hope.'

'A.s.a.p. I leaned on them, Frank,' Foxie said, enjoying the phrase. He had a familiar manila folder tucked under his arm, his dogeared odds and ends file. He opened it on Pagan's desk and began leafing through sheets. He found what he wanted, plucked it out and said, 'When I heard Madame say Scotland, I thought I remembered this titbit. Tell me it's mere coincidence.'

Pagan looked at the sheet, spreading it on his desk.

It was one of the sheets Foxie had somehow contrived to coax out of his old school pal in intelligence. It reported the movements of Rafael Rosabal, complete with dates and times – when he entered the country, where he went, where he stayed, who he saw. There was no mention of Magdalena, which meant that Rafael had presumably given his followers the slip during that interlude or that somehow they'd lost him for a while. Busy sort, Pagan thought. Buzzing around. *London to Glasgow.*

Pagan raised his face and looked at Foxworth. 'Can you tell me what's so special about Glasgow at this time of year?'

'It must have its attractions,' Foxworth replied. 'Chapotin went there. So did Rafael Rosabal. At precisely the same time too. Do you think they might have met, Frank?' Foxie looked puzzled. His otherwise smooth young forehead was creased with a severe frown.

'What for?' Pagan asked. 'What kind of connection could there possibly be between Chapotin and Rosabal? And if a connection existed, why go all the way to Glasgow to get together? They each had, shall we say, interests of the heart right here in London, so why travel four hundred miles north to meet? Frankly, I'd hate to see any connection between them. I don't want to unravel some damned mess that involves Rosabal because if a Cuban's up to his arse in this mischief it could turn out to be a real can of worms. I'd be quite happy with just Chapotin.'

Pagan looked beyond Foxworth to the window. The darkness over Golden Square was laced with a thin rain that had begun to fall. He tried to imagine Rafael Rosabal and Chapotin meeting in Glasgow – for God's sake, why? (*He remembered the closed bathroom door in Magdalena's hotel room, the light beneath it, the presence of Rosabal: was that why he was so anxious to discount Rosabal – because it meant Magdalena had no involvement either?*) And even if he established a link, so what? How would it bring him any closer to Ruhr?

Too many questions. Too few answers. A coincidence of place and time and people he didn't like at all. He had so little to go on. Chapotin was the only thread he had to Steffie Brough and Ruhr, and a dead man's name wasn't much.

As if he'd just trespassed on Pagan's ragged thoughts, Foxie said, 'One wonders where Steffie Brough is right now.' There was a grim note in his usually cheerful voice.

Pagan was restless. He got out of his chair and walked to the window; everything in the building had gone silent at the same time. No phones rang, no computers buzzed, no printers rattled. A fragile little island of quiet existed. Pagan looked down into Golden Square. Rain, turned to silver by electricity, coursed through the street-lamps. He took from his inside jacket pocket the small school picture of Steffie Brough, and tacked it to his cork bulletin board.

'One wonders,' he said quietly.

Washington DC

It was a fall afternoon of rare beauty. Washington's monuments might have been erected less to honour some democratic ideal and more to celebrate the way leaves turned and how the smoky orange sun, larger than any ever seen in summer, burnished landmarks, seeming to isolate them in flame.

Harry Hurt always felt good in Washington. As a patriot, he considered it his true home. He loved the statues and monuments; he'd stood at the Vietnam Memorial once, reading the names of the dead and feeling a shiver of gratitude toward the fallen. The city touched him like this, made him conscious of his country, the fact he was above all else an American. He had no shame and no embarrassment at being a patriot.

As he walked along a quiet street some blocks from George Washington University, he was conscious of Sheridan Perry trying to keep up with him. Perry was out of shape. Unlike Harry Hurt, he didn't jog, play handball, eat the proper foods. He had no pride in his body.

Both men paused on a corner. Blinded, buffed by a crisp wind that had begun to blow, Harry Hurt stuck his hands in the pockets of his grey cashmere overcoat. His bony face looked more angular than usual; cords in his neck stood out. There was a question he wanted to put to Perry but he wasn't sure how. There was simply no diplomatic way of asking his compatriot if he was the man behind the murders of Chapotin and Magiwara and Kluger. It wasn't the kind of question guaranteed to promote mutual confidence.

Hurt had spent a restless few hours on Concorde from Paris. He hated unanswered questions. Who was killing off the membership? Who had knowledge of their identities? Somewhere over the Atlantic it had occurred to Hurt that Perry, by virtue of his need for control, was as much a candidate as anyone else and that the best way to proceed was to ask a straight question and be damned. Despite the united front he and Sheridan presented to the Society, Harry Hurt didn't care all that much for Perry in any case, thinking him just a little too self-centred.

Besides, Perry's philosophy was suspect. Like Harry, he called himself a patriot, but Hurt thought he was stretching the definition. He'd once listened to Perry explain the greatness of the USA, a diatribe that caused Hurt some dismay.

According to Perry, the Constitution was a wonderful document, sure; but what made

America great was the other marvellous invention it had given the world – the loophole. There were loopholes in the Constitution, in the legal system, in the tax codes; here, there, everywhere a loophole, and Perry thrived on them. America was a wonderful country just so long as you recognised the loopholes. Perry had grown quite animated at the time. Hurt often thought about the cynicism behind The Loophole Speech. The tragedy was that Sheridan Perry didn't think it cynical at all.

The midnight-blue limousine that had been following Hurt and Perry at a distance of a hundred feet rolled a little closer. Three armed bodyguards sat in the vehicle. They observed the two men closely, watched the street, studied windows, shop fronts, rooftops. Hurt had suggested this stroll so that he could phrase his question in private, without having to embarrass Perry in front of the bodyguards. But the car, the protection, was never very far away, while Hurt's sensitive question was further away than ever.

How could he possibly come right out and ask Perry such a terrible thing? *It's a process of elimination, Sheridan. Since I know it's not me, it either has to be you or Caporelli or Kinnaird. Caporelli's a possible, Kinnaird less so, which leaves you and Enrico as the best possible candidates.* It couldn't be asked. Perry would be deeply offended, a wedge of mistrust would be driven between them. It was, Hurt thought, a no-win situation.

The shop front at which Hurt and Perry paused belonged to a tailoring establishment so exclusive it made suits with no labels, no identifying marks save a special little cross-stitch applied beneath the collar, where it was invisible. Had the needlework been evident, it would have been recognised by only a hundred men at most. It was the apotheosis of elitism. The grubby windows were curtained. No fancy displays here. Nor was there a sign to indicate the business of the shop, simply a street number on a plain metal disc. People who came here tended to have Rolodexes filled with unlisted numbers. These men used Charles Katzner & Sons, Tailors, Established 1925, as a kind of club in which they also happened to have their suits made.

Hurt rang the doorbell; the door was opened within seconds by a tall quiet man who wore a black jacket and pin-striped trousers. A tape measure was draped around his shoulders. With a slightly effeminate gesture, he indicated that Hurt and Perry should follow him – between long tables covered with tweeds and linens, wools and silks, up a narrow flight of stairs and through double doors into a large unfurnished room panelled in dark brown wood. The air had the universal scent of tailoring shops, composed of the smells of dozens of brand new fabrics, all so completely intermingled they were impossible to separate. Blinds, discoloured by too many summers, hung against the windows. The little light that filtered through had a strange brownish hue.

A red-cheeked man stood by the only furniture in the room, a long table on which lay a number of bulky volumes filled with fabric samples. The man wore very black glasses and a blue suit. He leafed through the swatches, pausing every now and then when one took his interest.

'This is a nice linen,' he said. 'I've always liked linen, more so in the pale colours.' He spoke softly. He didn't have to raise his voice to make people listen to him. When Allen Falk entered a room people turned to look. Neither handsome nor trim nor elegant, he had the elusive quality known as 'presence'.

Falk closed the fabric book. 'Let me bring you up to date, gentlemen, in case you've missed anything *en route*. Gunther Ruhr seized the missile, as expected. A nice job too, I understand. He managed, however, to introduce a little complexity we didn't anticipate. He's got a hostage, a young girl. It's no big deal. But the unpredictable throws us off balance.'

'A hostage?' Sheridan Perry had been expecting something strange from the German. 'Why the hell did he need a hostage?'

Al Falk stepped in front of the table. 'We'll get back to the child later. The only important thing is the missile arriving at its destination. And Ruhr's plane, I'm informed, is presently only three hours from landing.'

Harry Hurt felt a little tense. He looked at his watch. Three hours seemed to him a very long time. He didn't like the notion of a hostage any more than Perry did, but only because he disliked unscripted occurrences. He had never married and had absolutely no empathy with children. He sometimes saw them out of the corner of his eye and thought they were hyperactive and too robust, too loud. He had no real admiration for Gunther Ruhr – the man's life lacked principle. Personally, thank God, he'd had no dealings with the German. When Ruhr had supplied the complicated technical specifications for his needs they had come to Harry Hurt via Caporelli, who had received them from Rosabal. Such was the complex chain of obligations. In turn, Hurt had supplied the data to Levy and Possony. This was as close as he'd come to Gunther Ruhr, and he was grateful.

Falk continued. 'There should be absolutely no problems to interfere with the arrival. Our spy satellites, which would have identified the plane, have been "malfunctioning" for the last eight hours and will continue to do so for at least another three. Odd timing, don't you think?'

'Oh, very,' Hurt remarked.

Falk smiled his famous smile. His cheeks, already plump, swelled to the size of crab apples, suggesting the face of a very jolly man, which he wasn't. He was too involved in controlling Presidents and starfucking to be either carefree or generous. The smile was secretive, and knowing, that of a man who imagines he alone has the blueprint to the power circuits of the country.

Sometimes Hurt had a suspicion that Falk knew about the Society. If so, he gave no indication that he understood Hurt and Perry were part of any organisation. Perhaps he knew nothing, but only gave an impression of knowing. Or he simply thought that his old Princeton friend, Harold S. Hurt, was one half of a two-man partnership with Perry, nothing more.

'I've received information that Fidel has come down with an unspecified illness,' Falk said. 'Which is exactly what we've been waiting for.'

'Beautiful,' Harry Hurt remarked.

Falk said, 'Brother Raul, who could be a significant problem because he commands loyalty among some officers, is still in Africa. Events will delay him there until it's too late for him to return to Cuba. According to my information, South African mercenaries are scheduled to launch a border attack on Angola of sufficient ferocity to keep Raul bouncing around the continent for a few more days.'

Harry Hurt was always impressed by the intricacy of the plan; it was a remarkable conception that involved not only Falk, but also the fragmented anti-Castro movement inside Cuba, a handful of terrorists under the direction of Ruhr, and the forces Hurt himself had assembled in Honduras. And behind it all, a benign overseer, a great masonic eye, the Society of Friends.

Hurt also assumed a clique existed at the CIA under Falk's control, although like most things involving that organisation it couldn't be confirmed. But how else could spy satellites be manipulated? How else could the presence of a small army at Cabo Gracias a Dios be kept beyond the reach of those inquisitive journalists who were professional Central America watchers? And how could a South African mercenary assault on Angola be so precisely orchestrated?

Hurt had times when he wondered if the President himself were involved, or if he knew about the scheme but could never in a hundred lifetimes admit it, far less endorse it, for fear of alienating the allies and perhaps enraging the Soviets. It was a slippery speculation and there could never be a definitive answer. The Presidency was, as usual, a mystifying law unto itself, more myth than substance, more shadow than actuality. Besides, Hurt had all along known that the United States could only be involved in this whole project in a manner that was, so to speak, on the periphery of the periphery.

Al Falk walked to the windows, where he stood with his back to the room. 'It goes well,' he said. He rubbed the palms of his hands as if he thought he could strike flame from the friction of skin. Hurt had the feeling that Al Falk confidently believed himself capable of anything, walking on water, raising the dead, you name it.

Falk turned round. 'You get Cuba. We get an end to Fidel. What a terrific arrangement.'

Hurt smiled in his usual lean manner. He pondered the success with which different interests had been gathered together under a common banner. The last of *fidelismo*, and the control of Cuba by the Society of Friends fronted by a reasonable and malleable President in the form of Rafael Rosabal. As Falk said, a terrific arrangement. The only shadow across Hurt's otherwise undiluted enthusiasm was the way the Society was being depleted. Apart from the fact that the situation had produced paranoia, Harry Hurt didn't like being a target on anybody's hit list. Of course, new blood could be encouraged, new members carefully inducted into the inner sanctum of the Society – but that was hardly the point. What he *really* wanted to believe was that the killings had come to an end with Magiwara, Chapotin and Kluger, that these three had been murdered by a party or parties they had somehow managed to injure. A thin little hope, but he clutched it anyhow. It was better than paranoia.

Falk released a blind, which snapped up. The light in the room was tangerine now, and cold. Harry Hurt watched the Presidential advisor as the light struck him. Small reddish veins were stitched across Falk's face, like some form of embroidery. The black glasses glowed as if the eyes behind them had turned orange. Falk appeared quite demonic.

He said, 'I've been watching Cuba for more than thirty years. I've watched over it the way a physician monitors vital signs. I've sniffed the wind from the place, and let me tell you it doesn't smell like sugar. It smells the way the dogshit of Communism always smells. That's what we don't need down there. So let's deodorise the Caribbean. And if the United States can't do it *officially*, then let it be done the only way it can.'

Falk paused. His loathing of Communism had surfaced in 1956 during the failed Hungarian revolution; and had seized him with the passion of a first love affair. In 1968, brutal events in Czechoslovakia had strengthened this hatred. Recent occurrences in China confirmed his beliefs.

The silence in the room was broken only by the sound of his wristwatch beeping twice. He ignored it and went on, 'Whenever the CIA tried in the past to assassinate Fidel, it was always ridiculed. The USA was always the oversized bully trying to push little Fidel round the schoolyard, with no justification except for the fact we were bigger than Cuba and could kick its ass all the livelong day. A stinking image, friends. In the feckless court of world opinion, which is the only international court that really matters these days, we had no justification for killing the cretin and clearing the excrement out of Cuba.' Here Falk puffed out his cheeks. 'It's another ballgame now. This time we'll have evidence that's damned hard and incontrovertible. The trick of victory in our day and age is to present to a reproachful world a *fait accompli* which is perceived as utterly regrettable but inevitable. We don't want to upset the Organisation of American States, some of whose member countries have close relations with Cuba, and we don't want to upset our NATO allies, some of whom enjoy lucrative trade with Fidel. We need the mumble of world approval in everything we do because that's how goddam sensitive we've become. A nation of images. We're not people. We're holographs. All we want to do is look good, for Christ's sake.'

Falk paused, swallowed. 'Consequently, we can't go in with a big stick. No, we go in sideways, obliquely, pretending we have absolutely nothing to do with it. We use surrogates. And if by some *slight* chance we are associated with them, we stand in the courtroom and wring our hands, filled with terrible remorse for having helped recover a missile from a sick despot. But what were we supposed to do? That missile was being pointed directly at our goddam throat, after all. So we *gave some assistance* to a small army of Cuban exiles just to show that we weren't bullying poor little Cuba again. And we laid out our photographs of the missile for all the judges to see. Case closed. Amen.'

Hurt, who enjoyed the way Falk talked, looked down into the narrow street. The limousine was parked across the way, engine running. A white Ford Taurus passed, then stopped.

Falk reached under his glasses with a finger and rubbed an eye. 'Now. The hostage. I think a simple message to Ruhr is going to be enough. Something to the effect that no excess baggage is allowed. No hysterical little eyewitnesses. He knows what to do. He's been around.'

Harry Hurt was about to agree when he noticed the Ford Taurus backing up very quickly until it was aligned with the parked limousine. Something was going on down there. Hurt started to mention the suspicious appearance of the Taurus in the centre of the street, a great plume of exhaust hanging behind it like an angry wraith. He got out the words *I wonder what the hell* and then stopped, because the Ford moved forward very quickly, tyres whining on concrete, leaving the limousine exposed to view.

But only for a second. There was a flash of extraordinary light. The limousine exploded. It rose a foot in the air. Windows shattered, metal buckled, a wheel flew off. A great sphere of smoke, dark, thick, rich, billowed around the limousine. Shockwaves blew across the street and shattered the window where Hurt stood. He managed to step away before thin razors of glass lanced into the room. Allen Falk, less nimble, received a scalpful of slivers. Perry, who stood by the table, was unscathed.

'Dear Jesus,' Falk said. Blood flowed over his forehead and down his well-fed cheeks.

Hurt took out a handkerchief and helped Falk mop blood from his face. He glanced at Perry, who had moved to the broken window and was looking down into the street.

The trashed limousine straddled the sidewalk. The hood was gone, the fender mangled, the trunk crumpled. The doors had been blown open. Two motionless men lay in the back, one upon the other. In the front a man was twisted over the steering-wheel.

Hurt said nothing. Clearly somebody had been under the impression that he and Perry were inside the limo. Somebody had thought them sitting targets. Somebody had been mistaken. *This time.*

Falk touched the side of his skull with the bloodied handkerchief. 'We ought to be long gone by the time the police arrive and start looking for eyewitnesses. I suggest we get the hell out of here now.'

Neither Hurt nor Perry hesitated. The room was filling up with vile, rubbery smoke that drifted across the street from the ruined limousine. As Hurt walked toward the door behind Falk, he considered the question: who *knew?* Who the hell *knew* that he and Perry were travelling in that particular vehicle?

On the staircase down he was struck by a thought that would make some sense to him later: *Perry. Perry knew.*

13 Cabo Gracias a Dios, Honduras

Tomas Fuentes was in his tent when he heard the stale air around him vibrate, at first quietly and steadily, as if the evening sky were filled with the drone of a million batwings. He stepped outside and stood with his hands on his hips, listening. The sound, which originated close to the sea, had the texture of a natural force, a tornado gathering strength, say, or an earthquake forcing open a fissure on the bed of the ocean.

Roger Bosanquet emerged from the tent pitched next to Tommy's. The sound grew more profound. Among the trees yellow kerosene lights illuminated pathways between the large marquees in which the army slept. It was Tent City here.

Tommy Fuentes scanned the heavens, but saw nothing moving. Still the sound grew in intensity, a rumbling suggestive of thunder now. Tommy thought the ground under his feet had begun to tremble, but it was only his imagination. This landscape seemed to trap and amplify sounds. It was like being imprisoned inside a loudspeaker.

'There she is,' Bosanquet said and pointed to the sky.

At first pinheads of light, nothing more. Then the shape of the craft could be seen as it lost altitude and dropped so low that spray rose up from the surface of the water into the lights.

Fuentes and the Englishman walked down the slope toward the airstrip. Blue electric lamps, surrounded by agitated mosquitoes, burned the length of the runway. The plane appeared over the trees, the noise so terrible now that Fuentes and Bosanquet covered their ears. They watched the craft roar down towards the strip. It seemed for a moment to stall in the air, but then it was down with a final scream, lunging across the runway, skidding slightly before coming to a halt about twenty feet from where the concrete ended in a clump of trees.

Just before the two men reached the runway, Bosanquet mentioned the message he'd received some fifteen minutes ago by radio from Harry Hurt.

'A kid?' Fuentes asked. 'There's a kid on the plane?'

'Apparently.'

'I don't want the blood of any kid on my hands,' Fuentes said.

'It's Ruhr's responsibility, I would say.' Bosanquet, forever calm, nodded toward the big plane, where a door was, already opening. 'Your hands will be clean, Tommy.'

Bosanquet looked at the light in the open doorway of the C-130, where Ruhr stood framed in perfect silhouette. The plane's endless rocking during the flight had made Stephanie Brough queasy. All she'd had to eat was some dry fruit Ruhr had given her from a plastic bag. Ruhr, who was never very far from her, had watched her continually. His eyes had seemed to her like the lenses of some scanning instrument beneath which she was being dissected and scrutinised. She wished he'd turn away, look elsewhere, leave her alone. So long as she was the object of his brooding fascination, she was reminded of the danger he represented.

She still had no idea where she was and hadn't been able to eavesdrop on any conversations because of her earplugs. The two men, Trevaskis and Zapino, who sat together some feet away, didn't look like they communicated much and Ruhr didn't speak, so there was probably nothing to hear anyway.

Ruhr opened the door. The night air was scented in a way that was unknown to Steffie Brough, whose world had always been circumscribed by Norfolk and the Fenlands. She smelled ancient moss and lichen and something else, something bittersweet she couldn't identify but which made her think of carcasses. She took the plugs out of her ears and was assailed at once by noises completely alien to her, bird sounds she'd heard only in zoos, a great clacking and squawking that echoed on and on.

Ruhr turned from the doorway. 'Do you know where you are?'

She shook her head.

'This is Honduras.'

She tried to remember atlases, maps, but her sense of geography wasn't strong. The Panama Canal, the Gulf of Mexico came to mind, but she couldn't quite place Honduras. Wasn't it close to Nicaragua? She wasn't sure, and this lack of certainty caused her despair. Wherever Honduras was, it was a very long way from anything familiar. And how could she even think of escape? If she got a chance to run from Ruhr, where would she go? She pictured jungles and headhunters, snakes and tarantulas.

She was aware of her crumpled skirt and soiled blouse and some oil stains on her maroon blazer. She needed a bath badly, but she'd come to think that defiance was more important than fresh clothes; not outward defiance, but another form of resistance – in the mind, the heart. Outwardly, she would try to comply with Ruhr if she possibly could. But inside, where it mattered, she'd stay hard and cold and distant. It was an antidote against falling completely apart. She had to be bloody strong, that was all. No weepy moods. No moaning. Given just half a chance, she'd get through this somehow.

Still, she hated the way his hand lay against her lower back as he led her towards the door and the rope ladder that dropped to the ground. An insufferable intimacy; she remembered how he'd undone her bra back at the farmhouse – oh God, the farmhouse was such a long time ago – and blood rose to her head. She couldn't stand his skin against hers, but she'd have to. If she wanted to survive she'd have to do everything he told her.

Just so long as she was untouchable on the inside.

She swung in mid-air, holding the ladder as it shifted with her weight. Ruhr was just above her. She looked up, seeing under the cuffs of his jeans. Around one ankle he had strapped a sheathed knife. She had an image of the dead policeman at the old farmhouse, his body half-covered with leaves and the strange empty way he stared up at the sky. She remembered how his eyes were filled with rainwater and how slicks, overflowing his lashes, ran down his face. It was pointless to remember that sort of thing. She had to survive, and survival meant thinking ahead, not back.

There were men on the ground below. In the distance, yellow and blue lights burned and a faint aroma of paraffin and scorched meat drifted through the dark. Steffie was light-headed. She gripped the rope, fought the sensation away. Then she was down, and the ground felt good beneath her feet. Ruhr came after, and then the other men from the craft, and suddenly there was confusion, men greeting one another, languages she didn't understand, handshakes. For one tense moment, when she realised nobody was paying her any attention, she considered the possibility of flight.

Dense trees, tents pitched here and there among the lamps, shadowy figures moving back and forth, guitar music, a voice singing a Spanish song in the distance – there was nowhere to run. If she did escape, which was unlikely, she'd certainly get lost and die out there. She looked at Ruhr, who was involved in a conversation with the two men who'd met the plane. The voices were low, but Steffie could tell they were angry. Her parents argued in exactly the same muted way when they didn't want her to overhear.

Ruhr broke away from the two men – one of whom wore a Panama hat – and stepped toward her.

'Come with me.'

She followed him across the concrete strip. An olive-coloured tent, pitched two hundred yards from the runway, stood within a thicket of trees. Ruhr opened the flap and Steffie stepped inside the tent. He struck a match, lit a lamp. An odd bluish glow threw misshapen shadows on the canvas walls.

'Sit down.'

A sagging camp bed was located in a corner. She sat, knees together, hands clasped in her lap. Ruhr stepped in front of the smoky lamp, eclipsing it with his shadow.

'They want me to kill you.'

Her throat was very dry. 'Why?'

'You have seen too much and now you are to be discarded. Permanently. It's simple.'

Steffie was quiet for a long time. She had an image of herself dead – a pale white corpse in a mahogany box, white lace ruffles, a gown, an array of soft candles illuminating her delicate features. But it wouldn't be like that, would it? She'd be shot and dumped in the jungle, where she'd rot. And there was nothing poetic or romantic about that kind of death.

'I don't want to die,' she said in a composed way; she was determined to hide her terror.

Ruhr had no problem with the concept of killing the child. What he resented was the idea of being *ordered* to do it. Nobody controlled him. Nobody told him what to do and when to do it. Fuentes would soon discover that Ruhr was very much his own man. He didn't trust Fuentes or the quiet Englishman called Bosanquet; they had something furtive about them, as if they knew something Ruhr did not. But he knew how to protect himself from them, how to guarantee his own future. Besides, he had not yet finished with this girl; he'd barely begun. And if he was going to kill her he wasn't going to do it the way any cheap assassin would. A shot in the back of the skull, impersonal and fast, wasn't his style. No. He'd been observing her the whole trip, and the more he studied her the more impatient he became.

'I will not kill you,' he whispered. 'I will not let anyone harm you.'

He put his good hand below her chin and turned her face up, forcing her to look directly into his eyes. He could smell the fear on her. He gazed at her slender neck and he remembered her school scarf in the back of the Range Rover. He wondered whether Pagan had read the sign. He was surely at a loss by this time; even if he'd discovered the abduction of the child – and it didn't take a genius to get that far – he had no way of knowing where she'd been taken. Frantic Pagan. Ruhr revelled in the idea of the policeman's anxiety. The abduction of the girl was tantamount to driving a nail into the Englishman's heart.

He caught her shoulders, pushed her down on the narrow bed. She lay mute, looking past him at the lamp, which flickered monstrously and cast enormous distended shadows inside the tent. With a finger of the deformed hand he touched her mouth, forced her lips apart, caused a frozen smile to appear. He inserted the finger between her teeth, along the surface of the tongue, the gums. He drew the finger back and forth, in and out. He could feel the child's body go rigid.

And still she wouldn't look at him. She had closed her eyes. He took her hand and led it toward his groin. She made a noise, shook her head from side to side in protest, then bit the finger still inserted in her mouth. Ruhr, pained, drew away from her. There were teeth marks in his flesh.

He slapped her across the cheek with the deformed hand. She turned her face to the wall silently, hearing the slap echo in her head.

'You must do what I want,' he said. His voice was quiet, hushed, kind. If you didn't know it was Gunther Ruhr speaking, you might think it the persuasive voice of a therapist. It was one of the many voices Ruhr assumed.

'I don't want to touch you,' she whispered.

'What choice do you have, little girl?'

She tried to free herself but it was useless to struggle against Ruhr's strength. She shut her eyes, seeking a secret room in the mind, sanctuary. If she concentrated hard she could reach it, unlock the door, go inside. Safe from Ruhr. Safe from harm. She thought: *Somebody must be searching for me. Somebody has to be looking for me*. Be realistic, Steffie. How could anybody ever find you?

She felt Ruhr's ugly hand cross the flat of her stomach, like a crab moving on her skin.

'My sweet girl,' he kept saying. His breathing was different now, harder, louder. 'I will not hurt you. I promise you. You will come to no harm.'

He stroked her breasts, unconscious of the girl's discomfort, unaware of the tautness in her body. To Ruhr, the girl's pale flesh was a soft, white, marvellous world for him to explore and finally exploit. He was a discoverer, a pioneer, creating a new map of engrossing territory. And, like any colonialist, he would inevitably corrupt the terrain he had conquered.

A sound came from the doorway of the tent. The flap was pushed aside. A shadow fell across Steffie's face. She saw the man from the plane, the skinny one called Trevaskis. The pressure from Ruhr's body lifted as he turned his face around quickly, angrily.

Trevaskis, whose gaunt features appeared ghostly in the odd flickering light, pretended he saw nothing. 'They want you at the airstrip. Something about opening a box.'

Ruhr got up from the camp bed. 'Have you no goddam manners?' he asked. He pronounced 'goddam' as 'gottdam'.

Trevaskis glanced down at Stephanie Brough, then looked at Ruhr. 'Don't blame me. I'm only the messenger. They told me to fetch you. Here I am. Fetching. They need you because they have to open the box. Whatever that means.'

Ruhr laid the palm of his hand upon the girl's face. 'Don't move,' he said. 'Don't even think of moving. Is that understood?'

Ruhr stepped impatiently toward the doorway and out of the tent into darkness. He could see in the lights around the airstrip the C-130's ramp being lowered. He stood very still and watched the great shadow of the missile emerge from the underbelly of the transport plane. It had a hardness of line, a cleanliness of form. Incomplete as yet, it required his knowledge, his touch, to make it perfect. The mood with the girl was ruined for the moment anyway. Later it could be recreated.

Trevaskis came out of the tent, closing the flap at his back. He followed Ruhr a little way in the direction of the airstrip. Then he walked in another direction, entering a dark place where the trees grew close together. Ruhr kept going towards the plane. Trevaskis doubled back toward the tent. He undid the flap. The girl was sitting on the bed, her skirt smoothed down over her knees and her blouse buttoned up. She turned her face towards him. She was white and scared – but how the hell was she supposed to look, Trevaskis wondered, after the sicko had been at her?

Trevaskis said, 'Get the hell out of here. Now.'

'Where can I go?' she asked.

'Look, you got two choices. You stay here, you die. No two ways about it. Don't kid yourself. You go out there, you at least got a chance.'

'What kind of chance?'

Trevaskis said, 'Five per cent better than slim.'

Steffie, who didn't need time to think, got up from the bed. Trevaskis held the tent open for her. She ducked her head under his arm; the night was vast and hostile.

'Kid,' Trevaskis said, and he pointed. 'Go that way. You don't run into any tents over there. Keep going in the direction I'm pointing. I think there's a highway over there. Five miles, something like that. I'm not sure. But it's your best shot.'

Five miles through an unfamiliar environment. For a moment the lamp that flickered against the walls of the tent seemed positively cheerful. For God's sake, how could she even think of staying? She turned away from Trevaskis and, saying nothing, not knowing whether to thank him, headed through the trees. She must have strayed from the narrow path because immediately the foliage was dense all around her, and suffocating, like the greenery of some nightmare.

Strange forms reached out to her, tendrils brushed her arms, something small and furry flew directly at her forehead. And the night *clicked* all around her. Strange insect sounds came out of the underbush and the places where ancient roots gathered around her ankles. It was too much; too terrifying.

Frightened, she stopped. She looked back. Trevaskis was standing beside the tent, his shape outlined by the flame of kerosene. Ruhr, half-crouching, conjured out of the night, appeared behind him. Steffie saw Ruhr's arm rise in the air, then fall swiftly, an indistinct brushstroke. Trevaskis cried out, doubled over, slid to his knees. And then she couldn't see him any more.

She turned and tried to claw her way through the foliage. She froze when the beam of the flashlight struck her. She could hear Ruhr breathing as he came toward her.

'He thought I was stupid enough to leave you without supervision,' Ruhr said. 'Do you also think me stupid, little girl?'

He caught her by the hair and yanked her head back. The blade of his knife, wet with Trevaskis' blood, was thrust against the side of her neck.

Gunther Ruhr smiled. 'I am disappointed.'

Steffie Brough couldn't speak.

Tommy Fuentes watched the missile, mounted on the bed of the truck, come down the ramp under the guidance of the aeroplane's crew members, men anxious to be gone from this Honduran paradise. The cylinder rolled slowly a couple of feet on the concrete, then stopped. A small Toyota truck drew up very carefully alongside the missile. The tail-gate was lowered, and the wooden crate that had been delivered by Levy and Possony was carried out by three soldiers. They set the box down about six feet from the missile.

Fuentes trained a flashlight on the crate and two soldiers held lanterns.

'Where is Ruhr?' Fuentes asked.

Bosanquet said, 'It appears that our German friend has all the worst traits of his race. Arrogance and a complete indifference to any timetable but one of his own choosing.'

Fuentes turned his face to look in the direction of Ruhr's tent. Perhaps when he'd had his fun with the unfortunate girl and then disposed of her, the German genius would condescend to come down to the airstrip and do what he'd been paid for.

After all, the ship that would carry the missile to Cuba was due to arrive within twenty-four hours.

London

A deceptive autumnal sun hung over London, a hazy disc that chilled the city more than it warmed it. At eight a.m. Sir Freddie Kinnaird stepped from his limousine in Golden Square and entered the building that housed Frank Pagan's operation. In the lobby he passed a uniformed policeman, who saluted him briskly, then he rode in the old-fashioned lift to the top floor.

He entered Pagan's office without knocking. He considered it his prerogative as Home Secretary to go wherever he liked within his jurisdiction. He often contrived to conceal this presumptuous attitude with a certain upper-class charm. His style in Savile Row suits had made him, according to a frivolous magazine, the ninth best-dressed bachelor in Britain last year. If Sir Freddie Kinnaird had been a book, he would have been on the best-seller lists.

Today he wore a charcoal-grey overcoat with a discreet velvet collar. Pagan, who lay on the sofa, turned his face drowsily towards the man. 'Sir Freddie,' he managed to say. 'What a surprise.'

'No need to get up, Frank. Just passing. Thought I'd drop in and see how things stand.'

Pagan's shirt was undone. A bandage, applied some hours ago by Foxworth, was visible around his chest. He raised himself into a sitting position and looked at Freddie Kinnaird, whose face had been reddened by the cold morning air. *How things stand,* Freddie Kinnaird had said. Well, one of the things that *wasn't* standing was Pagan himself, who had lain crookedly in sleep and now massaged the sides of his aching legs, his knotted muscles.

'What news, Frank?' Sir Freddie said, glancing at the silk-screen on the wall, then surveying the chaos of the office, the litter that had missed the basket, the coffee cups, the stained saucers, the crumpled fast-food wrappers.

Pagan got to his feet, poured himself a cup of coffee from the pot that had been on a hot-plate for God knows how long. 'The investigation chugs along,' he said.

'How does it chug, and where?' Kinnaird asked.

'With all due respect, Sir Freddie, the details are being kept confidential in light of what happened in Shepherd's Bush.' Pagan sipped the coffee, which was the most vile fluid that had ever passed his lips. Stewed did not describe it. He fought a certain turmoil in his stomach. 'Any information you want must come to you directly from Martin Burr. That's the Commissioner's rule. Access is strictly limited. We don't want any more leaks, obviously.'

'Admirable security,' Sir Freddie remarked brightly. 'Naturally, Martin keeps me informed on a daily basis. I simply thought I might drop in and see if there were any recent developments that may not have reached the Commissioner's desk yet. The overnight stuff. The lowdown, as they say. This whole business has caused me quite considerable anxiety, as I'm sure you'll understand.'

Pagan smiled agreeably. He set his cup down and buttoned his shirt. 'Martin Burr knows all, Sir Freddie. Everything that happens in this office comes to the Commissioner's attention. Promptly.'

There was a momentary silence. Pagan looked at this rather conservatively fashionable man who had become one of the most popular politicians in the present government. Prosperous, rumoured to rise even higher in his political party, Sir Freddie had come a long way. Pagan had a faint recollection of how, a dozen or so years ago, the newspapers had made much of the fact that Kinnaird was strapped for cash because of onerous death duties on the death of his father. The old country estate in West Sussex had been sold to a Japanese electronics tycoon, farming lands in Devon had been auctioned, and Freddie himself, plummeted from the comfortable heights of wealth and rank, a diminished version of what he had once been, was obliged to sit on the boards of a variety of corporations. He needed the money, the companies needed his class and style. He had obviously made a terrific recovery from those days.

Kinnaird asked, 'Seen the morning papers?'

'I try to avoid them.'

'What a hullabaloo,' Sir Freddie said. 'The press doesn't know which way to turn. First the stolen missile. Then the abducted child. And if that wasn't sensational enough, there's the hijacked plane into the bargain. They haven't had this much news in one day since World War Two, I imagine. And speculation, my God! Ruhr's in Africa. He's in Iran. He's in the Canadian Rockies. And the one I like – he never left England. He's holed up somewhere in the countryside, laughing up his bloody sleeve.'

Pagan said nothing. He imagined the headlines, he didn't need to see them. He didn't need to read about Stephanie Brough in particular. Whenever he thought about her he was filled with a kind of parental dread. He couldn't even begin to understand what her real parents were suffering, although he had insights into their all-consuming worry.

He'd refused to take phone calls from the press. They were fielded downstairs with bland, tight-lipped comments from other officers. Reporters were given items of information they could have gleaned for themselves without much trouble – the nationality of the dead terrorists, the origin of the helicopter, the number of military casualties. It was the spirit of limited co-operation: more delicate areas of the investigation were inaccessible.

Sir Freddie adjusted his black cashmere scarf and said, 'I think you're doing a wonderful job in the circumstances, Frank. You and all your men. Convey my admiration to them, would you?'

Pagan hated such speeches, which he felt were offered more for political reasons than out of genuine gratitude. A man like Kinnaird, who was always on-stage, confused politics with real life. He probably made love the way he made speeches, with appropriate pauses for effect and great expectations of applause. Pagan wondered if he were ever heckled in bed.

'Keep up the good work, Frank.'

Kinnaird shook Pagan's hand firmly. Then he stepped out of the office just as Foxworth, hair dishevelled, pinstripe suit crumpled, was coming in. Kinnaird nodded to the young man before passing along the corridor in the direction of the lift.

Pagan sat down behind his desk. Foxworth said, 'Company from a lofty place, I see.'

'Pain in the arse,' Pagan remarked. 'He drops in, fishes for some hot news, gives me a bit of a pep talk, expresses his thanks and aren't we just wonderful all round? Spare me, Foxie. Have you slept?'

Foxworth fixed the knot of his striped tie. His complexion was colourless and he hadn't shaved, but his eyes were bright and excited. 'I got in an hour or two, Frank.' He patted his briefcase. 'I also found time to pick up a change of clothes for you.'

Pagan opened the case and looked at the black and white silk jacket, brown trousers, grey socks, blue and white shirt, and he wondered if Foxie had picked them out in the dark. He didn't criticise; he was less interested in the apparel than in Foxie's quietly pleased little look. 'So what are you repressing, Foxie?'

'Repressing?'

'I know your whole repertoire of grins, twitches and glances. Right now, you look like the top of your head is about to explode.'

Foxie leaned across the desk, smiled. 'Fancy that. Didn't know I was so transparent, actually.'

'You're a window, Foxie. Speak. What's on your mind?'

Foxworth took out a small notebook, flicked the pages. 'A couple of recent developments I think might interest you. First, the Norwich police and our friend Joanna Lassiter. Joanna was shown Chapotin's picture and – according to a certain Detective Hare in Norwich – responded with an emphatic denial. Chapotin was not even remotely similar to the man who rented the farmhouse.'

'Did she describe the man who would be Chapotin?' Pagan asked.

'Better than that. Based on her description, Detective Hare had a composite assembled. It ought to be comings on the fax machine at any second.'

Pagan looked at his watch. 'This Hare's an early bird.'

'Provincial living does that to a man,' Foxie said. He turned the pages of his notebook. 'Now for the news from bonnie Scotland. You'll like this.'

Pagan sat back in his chair.

Foxworth said, 'Rafael Rosabal met a man in a Glasgow hotel, according to a report from the Criminal Investigation Division, which had been asked by London to conduct routine surveillance of the Cuban.'

'Was the man Chapotin?' Pagan asked.

Foxie shook his head. 'No. Rosabal met briefly with somebody called Enrico Caporelli.'

'The name doesn't mean anything,' Pagan said.

'Caporelli, an Italian citizen, is known to Glasgow CID because he has business interests in that city, one of which – a string of betting-shops – has been the subject of an undercover investigation recently. Something to do with skimming cash off the top. Tax cheating. Happens in a lot of cash operations. Enrico Caporelli is simply a sleeping-partner in the business. He isn't involved in the daily running of it. I understand he spends most of his time in Europe and America. Probably doesn't even know some of his managers are skimming.'

'What could Rosabal possibly have in common with this Caporelli?'

Foxworth once more turned the pages of his little book; he was clearly enjoying himself. 'Cuba,' he said quietly.

'Cuba?'

'It's a bit of a maze, actually, but according to some homework Billy Ewing has just completed, Enrico Caporelli resided in Cuba from 1955 until 1959, where he made a considerable fortune in various businesses. The Cubans took everything away from him. Expropriation is Fidel's word.'

'How did Ewing dig that up?'

'From our American pals in Grosvenor Square, Frank. Ewing called in a small favour at the Embassy. Back comes the info that Enrico Caporelli, a businessman deported from Cuba in spring, 1959, was debriefed that same year by the Central Intelligence Agency, which was assiduously gathering material on Castro at the time with the intention, one assumes, of assassination. Hence, Caporelli's name is in the files somewhere.'

A bit of a maze, Pagan thought. The phrase struck him as understatement. He was always surprised by the connections that existed between people who, on the face of it, would seem to have nothing in common. Threads, trails left in space and time. A Cuban politician meets an Italian businessman in Glasgow in 1989, setting up a situation that creates echoes in very old files. Join the dots and what do you get? Companions in conspiracy, he thought. But what was the meat of this conspiracy?

'Where is Caporelli now?' he asked.

'The last available information came from a check we ran with the Italian police. According to the housekeeper at Caporelli's house in Tuscany, he's presently at his flat in Paris.'

'I'd love to have a word with him. I'd also like to sit Rosabal down and have a nice little chat.'

'He already left the country. Presumably he's back in Cuba.'

Pagan stood up. Despite the horror of it, he poured himself a second cup of coffee, which he took to the window. Drones crossed the square, hurrying inside offices. Another day was cranking up. In the east, clouds the colour of mud had begun to drift towards the city; below, a funnel of wind sucked up some brittle leaves. Strangely, an untended scarlet kite in the shape of a horse's head, probably tugged from some poor child's hand in Hyde or Green Park, floated across the roof-tops. Could a lost kite be some form of omen? Pagan watched it go, then turned back to Foxie.

'What does it all add up to?' Pagan asked. 'Rafael Rosabal meets this Italian in Scotland. At the same time, Jean-Paul Chapotin arrives in Glasgow. Meanwhile, somebody using Chapotin's name rented a farmhouse in Norfolk, which became the headquarters for a group of terrorists. One solid connection exists between Rosabal and Chapotin and Caporelli: Cuba. It's all bloody absorbing if you're in the mood for puzzles and you've finished the *Times* crossword, but where does it leave us, for Christ's sake?'

Foxworth closed his little notebook. Billy Ewing put his face round the door. 'Fax for you, Foxie,' he said.

Foxworth took the slip of paper from Ewing. He studied it for a moment, then smiled. 'Surprise surprise,' was what he said. He gave the paper to Frank Pagan.

Pagan found himself looking at a police composite, an identikit creation; he thought these things always made human beings resemble pancakes. They rendered features flat and dopey. The constituent parts of the face never bore any relationship to one another, plundered as they had been from a kit of human bits and pieces. The face in this particular picture had black hair and a straight nose and a mouth that was rather tense and unreal. The face also wore sunglasses. Pagan thought of a zombie.

'What's so surprising, Foxie?' he asked.

Foxworth told him. 'The man in this picture, wretched as he may appear, bears more than a passing resemblance to Rafael Rosabal, which may mean only one thing – that he rented the farm under Chapotin's name.

'What kind of sense would that make, for Christ's sake?'

Foxworth shrugged. He didn't know. He said, 'You'd have to ask Rafael that one, Frank. And since he's back in Cuba, it isn't going to be easy.'

'He'd deny any involvement anyway,' Pagan said. 'How could I prove otherwise? This wretched illustration isn't enough. Rosabal would laugh his bollocks off.'

Pagan, who hadn't looked at a likeness of Rafael Rosabal before, hadn't even wanted to, gazed at the picture. So this was Magdalena's lover, this bland face that stared back at him, this prosaic product of a technician's craft. Composites never suggested emotion, certainly not passion; those lips looked as if they might never have kissed any human being. He tossed the drawing on the desk. It was funny how, after all this time, there was a streak of jealousy in him, like the trail of a very old comet, but uncomfortable just the same.

'And what's Rosabal's connection with Ruhr?' he asked. 'Why would he rent a farmhouse for Ruhr to live in?'

'Perhaps because Rosabal hired Ruhr to steal the missile.'

'Perhaps, but also impossible to prove on the flimsy basis of an identikit,' Pagan said. 'Why would Rosabal want his own damned missile to begin with?' He was thinking of another question now, one he didn't want to ask at all, but which he knew would have to be voiced, if not by himself then surely, sooner or later, by Foxworth.

'I wonder how Magdalena Torrente fits into all this?' he said.

'Maybe she doesn't fit anywhere,' Foxie answered. There was some kindness in his voice, as if he intuited Pagan's difficulty with the subject of the woman.

Pagan sipped the spooky coffee. *Maybe she doesn't fit* – but he wasn't convinced and he wasn't reassured and the melody that ran through his brain was composed of bad notes. His instincts told him he couldn't consign Magdalena to some convenient oblivion. Not yet, perhaps not at all. Somewhere along the way he thought he'd have to see her again, talk to her, probe the nature of her affair with the Cuban. Hadn't she hinted in an elliptical way about the prospect of a coup in Cuba? 'Hinted' was too strong a word; rather, she'd failed to answer his direct questions, leaving room for his own speculation. Mysterious Magdalena.

He had mixed emotions about the prospect of seeing her again. But she was Rosabal's lover and there was at least a chance that she knew something about the Cuban's business. Perhaps they shared something more than each other's flesh; little secrets, the kind spoken across pillows and through tangled limbs.

Rosabal. Magdalena. Chapotin. Ruhr. Caporelli. He wondered what was secreted by those five names.

He asked, 'Why Scotland? Why go up there at all? Why did all three men have to be in Glasgow on precisely the same day? Where did Chapotin go when he arrived there? Did he meet somebody? Did he meet Ruhr? Did he meet Caporelli? Did all three of them get together at some point? Is there life after death?'

Foxworth smiled. 'Is there life after Glasgow?'

'Not for Jean-Paul Chapotin,' Pagan said.

Both men were quiet. The sound of a printer drifted through the open door; a telephone buzzed in another room, a man cleared his throat. Pagan's head ached. Too many questions. The more information that reached his office, the more solid grew the whole edifice of mystery. It was time to be dogged, time to be systematic; take each problem as it comes. Time, he thought: did Steffie Brough, wherever she was, have the luxury of time? He was conscious of a clock ticking madly away.

'If I want to interview Rosabal, what official channels do I have to go through?' he asked.

'I can find out. I suspect they're complicated and involve hideous protocol.'

Pagan shook his head in slight despair. It was a hopeless kind of quest really. Rosabal would simply refuse to come back to Britain, and if Pagan went to Cuba, armed with the silly composite, Rosabal would mock him – if indeed he agreed to see him at all. Ministers and their ministries could keep you waiting in ante-chambers indefinitely, whether you came from Scotland Yard or not. It wasn't going to be fruitful to approach Rafael Rosabal in a headlong manner; there was too much tape red, as Madame Chapotin might have said, for that. No, he would have to chisel away at the edifice confronting him, sliver by sliver, like a sculptor intrigued by the form concealed in a block of granite.

'Put Billy Ewing on it. I've got something else in mind for you, Foxie.'

'Paris?' Foxworth asked.

'Glasgow. I'm taking Paris.'

'Why don't we discuss it?'

'Because this isn't a bloody democracy, Foxie. I get Paris, you get Glasgow. It's a matter of seniority, sonny.'

Foxie sighed in resignation. He doubted if Pagan was quite strong enough to travel, but he wasn't going to argue the point. Frank had switched into his headstrong mode and that was it.

Pagan said, 'I'll see you back here tonight.'

'That soon?'

'Soon? That gives you the whole day, Foxie. Use it well. Tell me where Chapotin went and how he's connected to Ruhr. Tell me why Rosabal would use Chapotin's name. Tell me why they selected scenic Glasgow for skulduggery.'

Slavedriver, Foxie thought. 'You want a miracle, Frank.'

'I want more than a miracle, Foxie,' Pagan replied.

Villa Clara Province, Cuba

At four a.m. the Lider Maximo lay in his bedroom with a rubber hot-water bottle pressed flat upon his stomach. He was unable to speak because of the thermometer stuck between his lips. The physician, Dr Miguel Zayas, checked the great man's pulse.

'Now,' Zayas said. He took the hot-water bottle away and prodded here and there the fleshy stomach of the Lider Maximo. 'Does that hurt? Does that? Does this?'

Castro shook his head. How could he speak with a damned tube in his mouth? It would not do for him to moan and admit pain, even though Zayas was fingering some tender spots; especially he couldn't admit anything so human as pain in front of that old buzzard General Capablanca, who was hovering in the room like a greedy relative at a will-reading.

'What have you eaten recently?' Zayas asked, and took the thermometer away.

'Shrimp,' Castro said. He grabbed back the hot-water bottle and laid it over his navel.

'What else?'

'*Moros y cristianos*.'

'Anything else?'

'Plantains.'

The physician tugged the hot-water bottle from Castro's belly. 'This may aggravate your condition.'

'Which is what exactly?'

'Gastric influenza,' the physician said.

Castro slumped back against the pillows. It was ignominious to have cancelled a speech in which he had planned to castigate the new, cosy friendship between the Yanqui imperialists and the 'soft' reformist, quasi-capitalist regime in the Soviet Union, but the attacks of diarrhoea, which left him weak and helpless, were positively humiliating. He had also a fever and he couldn't concentrate. Goddam, it would have been a great speech, perhaps his best, emphasising Cuba's splendid isolation in the world, the kind of exciting speech that would have brought Cubans together in a show of solidarity. Cuba would not be threatened by this obscene new collusion, this game of footsy, between the United States and Russia.

Capablanca, whose thick white moustache covered his upper lip, came close to the bed. Castro was annoyed by the intrusion of the General, a man he'd never been able to stand anyway. Capablanca was a left-over from a class that should have been swept away by the Revolution, but still lingered here and there in pockets despite the Party's best efforts.

Capablanca, who had a set of papers in his hand, said, 'I have come to remind you, Commandante, that tomorrow's troop manoeuvres require your personal authorisation in the absence of your brother.'

'What manoeuvres?' Castro asked. He could remember no mention of troop movements. His was a life totally consumed by detail: how could he possibly recall every little thing? Nor did he trust his own memory entirely. Lately, it hadn't seemed an altogether reliable instrument. He seized the papers from the General's hand.

Peering through his glasses he saw that the documents described a huge military exercise scheduled for dawn tomorrow. It involved the movement of troops from the Santiago de Cuba Province. Infantry battalions, as well as aeroplanes, were to move inland from the coastal region of the province, which lay on the island's southern seaboard. Ships of the Cuban Navy were also scheduled to sail around the tip of the island at Guantanamo, bound for Holguin Province. This would expose the coast of Santiago de Cuba, leaving it defenceless. Not that Castro expected an invasion force; but one had always to be prepared.

The same documents described other military exercises in Havana Province. These were less extensive than the movement of troops from Santiago to Holguin, but they were impressive just the same and involved the transportation of more than seven thousand men from Havana Province to Matanzas; there, in the mountainous region surrounding Matanzas City, exercises would keep these troops occupied at a distance of some fifty miles from the Central Highway.

'All this involves thousands of soldiers and reservists,' Castro said.

'Indeed,' the General answered.

'Why? Why this undertaking?'

'Readiness, Commandante. Alertness. A standing army must flex its muscle, otherwise it withers.'

'Readiness is important, but does Raul know of these manoeuvres?'

'Of course,' said the General. 'It was Raul's idea.' Lies came to him with great difficulty.

Castro tossed the papers back at the General. The pain that shot suddenly through his stomach was like a fierce little cannonball. He imagined it leaving a scalding trail of debris on its passage through his guts. He spoke with some effort. 'I do . . . not . . . recall my brother ever . . . mentioning these exercises before now, General.'

'But Commandante,' Capablanca said. He was tense, slightly panicked. He hadn't expected resistance; he'd imagined that the debilitated and confused Lider Maximo would give his consent willingly. He needed the Commandante's authorisation of the documents; without that imprimatur, those officers loyal to the Party, and to El Viejo himself, would refuse to participate in the exercises. They wouldn't raise a finger unless one or other of the Castros authorised it. Such disobedience on the part of the misguided loyalists would mean chaos, disorder, bloodshed. The General pictured slaughter on the beaches. God knows, there would be unavoidable bloodshed somewhere down the road but the ship coming from Honduras had to arrive without impediment. That was a matter of the utmost importance.

Besides, there was form to consider; and form was one of the General's obsessions. With the authorisation of Castro manoeuvres would have the appearance of legitimacy. This was important because the General did not want history to perceive him as a common adventurer and scoundrel. Everything he did had to be just so, everything by the book.

He had another important reason, one of sly importance, for getting the Lider Maximo's signature on these papers.

A space had been left on the third page for an extra paragraph to be inserted; this paragraph, when the General added it, would contain Castro's authorisation for a cruise missile, formerly the property of NATO, to be fired from a location outside Santiago de Cuba . . .

Of course, no missile would ever fly. The authorisation was the only thing required; the apparent intent was all.

Now Castro waved a hand in a gesture of dismissal. He was reluctant to give his approval to the manoeuvres because he didn't like interfering with his brother's gameboard. Raul played toy soldiers, not he.

'Cancel them, General. Postpone them until Raul returns.'

'Commandante,' said the General, trying to conceal the small panic he felt. 'You must approve these – '

'I do not have to do anything, General. Now do as I say! Postpone the manoeuvres!'

Capablanca glanced at the doctor. Zayas understood the look; he reached inside his black bag and took out a hypodermic syringe. He inserted the needle into a small phial of colourless liquid, filled the syringe, then held the needle close to the Lider Maximo's arm.

'What is it, Zayas? What's in the syringe?' Castro asked. His eyes opened very wide.

'A simple painkiller,' the physician said.

'I am not in pain!' Castro would have decked the doctor, had it not been for the terrible weakness he felt. His belly creaked like the rotted wood of an old ship and he had the feeling of hot liquid rushing through his intestines. He'd have to get up, rush for the hundredth time to the john.

The needle pierced flesh, found the vein; after twenty seconds Castro, who resisted enforced sleep fiercely, closed his eyes. His head rolled to one side and saliva collected at the corners of his lips as he snored.

The doctor raised one of Castro's eyelids, then let it flop back in place. 'Give me the documents, General.'

General Capablanca did so. The doctor, with meticulous penmanship, forged the Lider Maximo's signature. It was a passable fraud.

'I haven't been his personal physician for years without learning a great deal about our fearless leader,' Zayas said. 'Now open the middle drawer of the desk.'

Capablanca, surprised by both the skill and gall of the physician, went to the desk. Inside the middle drawer was the Lider Maximo's personal seal. The General removed it. He took the document from the doctor, who was still admiring his own forgery, and pressed the metal seal over the fake signature.

'There,' said the General, relief in his voice. 'It's done.'

Zayas looked down at the doped leader. 'When he wakes, I'll shoot him up again.'

The General said, 'I'd prefer him dead. But I have my own orders to follow.' He walked towards the door where he stopped, turned briskly around. 'Your role will not be forgotten, Zayas. By tomorrow night, Cuba will be free of this madman.'

'I'm happy to help a new regime, General. People who love freedom must unite against despots.'

General Capablanca stepped out of the room. In the corridor, Castro's bodyguards stood tensely.

'A minor gastric disorder,' said the General in a booming voice. 'In a day or so he will be as good as new. For now, he sleeps.'

The bodyguards relaxed. They trusted Capablanca and they trusted Dr Zayas. They had known them for years. All, therefore, was well.

14 Miami

On this strange dawn enormous cloud formations, lit by a pale sun, formed a purple mass over Miami. Motionless, the clouds might have been solid matter, cliffs and rocky promontories afloat in the sky. Later, the day would grow warmer and the bulk would disperse in violent lightning and rain, the whole discordant Floridian symphony of weather.

Magdalena Torrente, driving her BMW towards Little Havana, took no notice of the heavens. She crossed the Rickenbacker Causeway at the speed limit. Traffic was still light. She'd been drawn out of sleep by the telephone, and had reached for the instrument with a sense of dread. Nothing good ever came from phone calls at seven a.m. Anything that happened before then had to be ungodly. She'd heard Garrido's voice. He needed to see her at the restaurant. He wouldn't say why. The old man had grown increasingly fond of cryptic behaviour. He'd been playing the secret game for too many years. So, still sleepy, she'd showered, brewed coffee, dressed, left her house in Key Biscayne.

She drove on Brickell Avenue, heart of revitalised Miami, leafy between high-rise buildings. The Bayside Market Plaza was new and bold. Drug money had infiltrated everyday life. An illicit, cocky prosperity flourished here. But this was something else Magdalena didn't notice as she drove toward Calle Ocho. What did Garrido want at this hour? Why had he called? His voice was quiet, almost a whisper – she couldn't tell much from it. On Calle Ocho she passed closed shops; a couple of druggies, locked in their own time zone, stared morosely at her.

On the side-street where Garrido's restaurant was situated she parked the car, got out. She wore blue jeans, soft leather boots that came just above the ankles, a black silk jacket, lemon shirt. She was incongruous in this neighbourhood of steel-shuttered windows and graffiti and funky yards filled with empty wine bottles and needles and tyres.

She entered the restaurant by the front door. The big empty room, which wasn't open for breakfast trade, smelled of last night's onions and chillis. Chairs were inverted on tables. Garrido, in the white suit he always wore, sat in an alcove at the rear. Beside him was a hefty man she'd never seen before – unusual in itself because Garrido always preferred to meet her alone.

Garrido looked up when she approached. She felt a dryness at the back of her throat, a sudden pulse in her chest. Something in Garrido's face unnerved her, although she wasn't sure what – the light in the eye, the set of the mouth, something. He was different this morning and she didn't like it.

'Sit down, my dear,' he said.

She eased into the alcove, conscious of the stranger watching her approvingly. When she caught his eye he winked, smiled. She was sometimes amused by the effect she had on men; even Pagan, even dear Frank, when he'd come to see her in London, had been strangely subdued in her presence – except for his bold parting kiss, which had been interesting to her only as a memory. There was nothing left inside her for Frank Pagan or any other man but one.

Garrido kissed her hand. 'My dear, I want you to meet a good friend. A trusted friend. Sergio Duran. He is with us.'

Magdalena barely nodded at Duran, who nevertheless insisted on placing a kiss of his own on the back of her hand and saying how delighted he was to meet her; she was as beautiful as he'd heard, even more so. It was Latin overstatement, that blend of flattery and *machismo*, and she was unmoved by it.

'Why this hour of the day, Fernando?' she asked. 'What's the big deal?'

Garrido was quiet a moment. He looked moody, distant, and even the chocolate-brown dye he used on his hair and moustache appeared to have shed lustre. 'Sergio returned from Cuba last night,' he said finally.

'And?' she asked.

'Perhaps I'll let Sergio tell you himself.'

'Fine.' She looked at Duran, who wore a blue and grey plaid jacket and styled his hair like frothed milk. 'I'm listening, Sergio.'

Duran's voice was deep and low, more a rumble than anything else. It reminded Magdalena of a radio announcer. He took out a cigar, one made by the Upmann Company of Havana, and he lit it. He had huge fat hands.

'Fernando asked me to go to Cuba on his behalf. He needed somebody to check on a few things.'

'Check on what things?' Magdalena asked, and looked at Garrido, who inclined his head as if to say *Listen, Duran will tell you everything you need to know.*

Duran blew smoke upward, steering it away from Magdalena's eyes. 'He needed certain information. He asked me to provide it.'

'Exactly what are your credentials for gathering information, Sergio?' She was on edge now and couldn't say why exactly. The hour of the day was part of it, certainly, but she knew that these two men between them had something to tell her and there was an awkward kind of pussyfooting going on, an evasion of the point. She was impatient, almost rude in the way she threw questions at Duran.

'I am a private detective right here in Miami,' Duran said.

'I see. So you're qualified to snoop around.'

'Magdalena,' Garrido said, a plea for patience and tolerance in the tone of his voice.

'It's okay, Fernando. Miss Torrente is right one hundred per cent. I'm a qualified snoop.'

'And what did you snoop in Cuba, Sergio?' Magdalena asked.

There was silence. Why did she feel she was a patient in the presence of two specialists who have studied her X-rays with the utmost care and whose prognoses are bleak? They were about to tell her she was terminal.

'Considerable sums of money have gone to Cuba in recent years,' Duran said. 'Fernando asked me to ascertain, as far as I possibly could, exactly where the cash had ended up.'

Ah: so it came down to that old bone, Garrido's mistrust of Rafael, his paranoia. She should have known. He wasn't happy about Rosabal – specifically her relationship with him – and so he'd sent his own personal spy to Cuba! She wanted to shout at the old man, and reproach him bitterly for his distrust, but for the moment she kept her silence.

Duran went on, 'The disposition of funds was always in the hands of one man. Rafael Rosabal. It was left to him to assess the needs of the various underground groups and disperse the cash according to these needs. A big responsibility, of course. A job requiring some measure of good judgment.'

'And?' Magdalena asked. Why did she feel so goddam awful all of a sudden? Something monstrous, just beyond the range of her vision, was taking shape in the shadows of this room. Her forehead was flushed and hot. She put the palm of her hand to it.

'I have discovered beyond doubt that a full accounting is difficult – '

'What does that mean? Be precise, if you can.'

'Money is unaccounted for – '

'Why? Why is it unaccounted for?'

Duran sucked on his cigar; what Magdalena read in his eyes was an odd little look of pity. It was visible pity, the kind felt by a man who so rarely experiences such sensations he doesn't know how to hide them. He said, 'As far as I can tell, millions of dollars are missing.'

'Missing? What does missing mean? How can millions of dollars go astray? What are you saying, Mr Duran? How can you even make such an estimate anyway? It isn't the kind of situation conducive to accurate bookkeeping, is it?' Her voice was shrill and rising. She knew where Duran was headed now. She saw it as clearly as if there were a map in front of her.

Duran spoke slowly. 'Rosabal dispersed funds to the various groups, certainly,' he said. 'But in his own way. Sometimes he'd give money liberally to one group and deny it to another, claiming a shortage of funds. At other times he'd give very little to all the groups, and tell them there was nothing in the kitty, that cash hadn't come from the Community in Miami. He relied on the fact that no one group would know what the other groups received.'

'What exactly are you trying to tell me, Sergio? That Rafael pocketed money for himself?' She made a sound of disbelief, a gasp.

'Be patient,' Garrido said, and patted the back of her hand, which she drew away at once, causing the old man to look rather sorrowful.

Duran continued. 'It appears that Rosabal promoted a system in which he sometimes seemed to be favouring certain groups by saying he'd managed to squeeze out a little more cash for them this time around – but he'd always ask them to keep the favour quiet. Don't tell anyone else, he'd say. Don't start squabbles. This way he created confusion and divided loyalties. Am I making this clear for you?'

'Garrido,' and she turned her face to the old man. 'How could you do this? How can you oblige me to sit through this?'

Garrido said nothing. That silence again; it beat against Magdalena with the certainty of a tide.

Duran went on, 'A rough estimate of monies embezzled would run into the millions.'

'You said yourself that an estimate was impossible.' She was Rosabal's advocate now, his protector, defender.

'I said it was difficult, not impossible. It would take a very long time to be exact, I agree. My own estimate is a ball-park figure, that's all. More, less, what does it matter in the long run?'

'How can you malign him in this way?' she asked. 'Both of you, how can you castigate him like this? Don't you understand the risks he's taken for our cause? He met regularly with underground representatives, people in the democratic movement, he carried US dollars to these people, he went to places where discovery would have meant the death-sentence for him – how can you possibly accuse him of embezzlement?'

Duran shook his head slowly and looked depressed. 'There is other evidence, Magdalena.'

'Like what?'

'I'm informed he's been making investments for the last few years through banks in the Channel Islands. He always goes there briefly whenever he makes a trip to Europe. He visits discreet bankers who invest considerable sums of money on his behalf in France and Switzerland and the Far East.'

'How do you know this?'

Duran shrugged. 'We have reliable sources.'

'Spies.'

'Spies is as good a word as any.'

'How do you know he isn't investing money on behalf of the cause? You don't have any evidence he's investing this cash for himself.'

'Not directly, no. All I can tell you is what I already said – funds are being diverted. And the likelihood that the cash has been invested for the cause is, let's face it, slim.'

Garrido, like a patient country doctor schooled in platitudes, spoke soothingly when he interrupted. 'Sometimes too much money is too much temptation. A man can find weaknesses in himself he never suspected.'

'I believe in Rafael,' she said. She was hoarse; tension had dried her throat and mouth.

As if he hadn't heard her, as if he were just too wrapped up in his own ambitions to pay Magdalena any attention, Garrido continued in a mournful voice. 'It's more than just the money. It's the violation of the trust we put in Rosabal. He was supposed to be our representative in Cuba. He was supposed to be spreading funds to make the democratic underground strong. He was the big man, the force behind the movement to overthrow Castro, he was preparing a coup, assembling a democratic alternative to Communism, and when the time came . . . ' The old man paused and looked sad. He touched his lips with a linen napkin. 'I was a part of it. I was going back to Cuba to serve in this new government. Now what? Now what, Magdalena? Where is the dream now? How can we know if there is any kind of strength or unity in the anti-Castro cause? How can we know if Castro is ever going to be deposed? Do you see what Rosabal has accomplished with his treachery, Magdalena? Confusion. Disappointment. Unhappiness.'

Magdalena stood up. She'd listened longer than she needed. What proof had these two men offered her of Rosabal's alleged larceny? It was unsubstantiated talk. It had its roots in Garrido's approaching senility, his unsupported mistrust of Rafael. Probably even jealousy – Garrido resented the younger man for staying in Cuba instead of fleeing, as he himself had done, into the safety of exile.

'Where are you going, Magdalena?' the old man asked.

'Home.'

'Are you going to ignore what Sergio has told you?'

She didn't answer. She stood, her hip pressed against the edge of the table, her weight on one leg. *Castro's a dead man.* She remembered how emphatically Rafael had said that in London. If Garrido and his side-kick, Duran, had heard him then, they wouldn't have entertained any doubts about his trust, and this obscene investigation need never have taken place.

'We're not finished, Magdalena,' Garrido said. 'Please. Sit down.'

She refused. She took small, almost spiteful pleasure in denying Garrido. He said, 'I didn't want to inflict any more on you, dear girl. But since you choose to defend Rosabal still, you leave me no real choice.'

Garrido nodded to Duran, who took an envelope from the inner pocket of his jacket. He opened then inverted it; photographs slid out on the table.

'Please, Magdalena, sit down,' and the old man gestured in a not unkindly manner, but still she refused him. She gazed at the coloured pictures that lay on the table. She had no desire to look at them closely.

'I took these in Havana,' Duran said. He isolated one, pushed it across the table. As if it were alive the photograph made a quiet sound that suggested breathing; it was the contact of shiny photographic paper on the surface of the table.

Magdalena squinted down at it.

'Pick it up,' Garrido said.

Why did her hand tremble? She didn't reach for it. She could make out Rafael's likeness without touching the thing.

Duran raised the picture, studied it. 'This shows Rosabal getting into a car. Look at it carefully, if you will.'

She saw a car, rear door open, Rafael, beloved Rafael, bending slightly to step inside. Then she looked away. She stared across the room at the window; pinkish light lay on the opaque glass. A car backfired somewhere.

'This I took at Rafael's house outside Havana,' Duran said, and selected another photograph. Once more Magdalena glanced at the thing, seeing a flash of colour, shrubbery, a swimming-pool filled with turquoise water, and there was Rafael seated on the edge of the pool, beautiful in his black trunks, face turned slightly away from the camera.

'Lovely home,' Duran said. 'He lives well.'

Magdalena drifted. She floated from this table, this room; she didn't need to see photographs.

'The young woman beside him in the car, the one who is holding his hand beside the pool . . . ' Duran said, then faltered just a little. 'That is his wife. Estela Alvarez Capablanca, daughter of General Capablanca. They were married a few months ago.'

Wife: the word exploded like thunder in Magdalena's head. And, like thunder, it rolled meaninglessly away, echoing even as it faded. Wife: it might have been a word from an alien dictionary, a signal sent out through space, travelling countless centuries before being picked up on this planet, in this city, this room now by Magdalena Torrente. How could Rosabal possibly have a *wife?*

Magdalena reached down, picked up the photographs, flicked through them. The woman was young and handsome in a way that was distinctly Spanish. The few photographs where she appeared she was invariably looking at Rafael with the eyes of an adoring wife, a new wife, one in whom love has barely flowered. Magdalena, dizzy, set the pictures back down. The tips of her fingers were suddenly chill; a sensation of cold tingled upon her spine and neck. A strange pressure built behind he, eyes, and her heartbeat became arrhythmic.

'I am sorry,' Garrido said. 'He has abused you as well as the cause. I am sorry, Magdalena.'

She barely heard Garrido's voice. She was tracking her own thoughts as if they were strangers eluding her. There had to be a simple explanation. There had to be a reason. Why had he never mentioned this woman, this wife, to her? Why, with the love they shared, had he never shared this information too? Reasons, all sorts of reasons – the wife was the daughter of the General, therefore the marriage might be political, a marriage of convenience. How could she know? How could she know anything? Unless she looked him in the face, unless she stared directly into his eyes, how could she know she'd been betrayed? She had only Duran's photographs to go on. And photographs, at best, were limited windows into reality.

But still her heart wouldn't beat regularly, and the cold had spread like a glacier from spine to scalp. Now the pressure was not located so much behind her eyes as it was in the very air around her, as if she were descending through unlit fathoms in a faulty bathysphere. She moved towards the door. She had to get out of this room and away from these two men and their *evidence* of treachery. She needed time alone, the clarity of solitude.

Neither Garrido nor Duran made any move to detain her. She stepped into the street and stood under a sky whose clouds had become an outrageous bright pink, a carnival colour far removed from what Magdalena Torrente felt.

Paris

At midday Frank Pagan arrived at Orly Airport and took a taxi driven by a chain-smoking Parisian who complained for miles about the economic policies of the Common Market, and how migrant workers were the scourge of all Europe. Pagan nodded politely from time to time and muttered *Mais oui, mais oui*, but he wasn't interested, and the man's patois was difficult to follow.

Pagan asked to be let out on the corner of the Avenue Victor Hugo in the sixteenth arrondissement, a little way before his ultimate destination. His eyes watered from cigarette smoke and his head throbbed as he walked in the direction of the Bois de Boulogne, slowly, deliberately, wary of pain.

Paris was overcast, damp, locked in the leaden grip of autumn; the greenery of the Bois had faded. The gutters were choked by fallen leaves. It wasn't a city that held personal associations for him. Once or twice he'd come here on business, but he knew the place only superficially, like a tourist. He checked Enrico Caporelli's address in his notebook. It was an exclusive apartment building about a hundred yards from where the taxi had dropped him. Grey, imposing, opulent in a stately way, it overlooked the Bois with the musty dignity possessed by the old apartment buildings of the very rich.

Pagan was confronted by a uniformed doorman as soon as he stepped inside the lobby. The doorman, haughty, a *Gauleiter* in burgundy cap and uniform with gold epaulettes, insisted on telephoning Caporelli before Pagan was allowed access to the lift.

Enrico Caporelli apparently was not perturbed by the prospect of an English policeman coming to call; Pagan was led promptly to the lift by the doorman, the iron gates were closed, and it rose in the shaft. He got out on the fifth floor. The corridor was dimly lit. Two men, both dark-suited and muscular in a way no subtle tailoring could ever conceal, greeted him – although there was nothing warm in their manner. They checked his identification, frisked him expertly, without apology. He hadn't brought a gun. When they were satisfied they ushered him into the vestibule of the apartment then withdrew, a pair of big gloomy ghosts vanishing in the dimness of their surrounds.

Enrico Caporelli appeared in a doorway. He wore a navy-blue robe and carpet slippers; somebody's diminutive uncle, Pagan thought. The quick handshake was firm and cool, the skin like smooth leather.

'They overprotect me,' Caporelli said. 'Good men, but perhaps a little too diligent. Come with me, please.'

He led the way inside a study where heavy brocade curtains had been drawn against the windows. The room was lit only by an antique desk-lamp. Pagan, a little surprised by Caporelli's calm acceptance of a policeman's presence, sat down on one side of the desk and wondered about the two bodyguards and whether they came with the territory of the rich. Caporelli drew up a chair facing Pagan and pushed a cigar box across the desk. Pagan declined to smoke.

'I have read about you in the British newspapers, of course,' Caporelli said. There was a hint of New York in the Italian accent. A man without a country, Pagan thought. Or perhaps one with many countries. 'You've become quite a famous man, Mr Pagan.'

Pagan brushed this aside. He'd been played up a great deal in the newspapers lately, but if that was fame then it was a kind he didn't want; it was the notoriety of a man who has survived a tragedy – an airline disaster, a sinking ship. In the circumstances, he preferred anonymity.

'First the unfortunate killings, now the business with the missile.' Caporelli looked sympathetic. 'I am a little surprised you have come to see me. I cannot imagine how I can help you. Of course,' and here was the little shrug of a man prepared to do favours, 'I will always help the police in any way I can. In Italy, for instance, I cooperate with the police beyond!he call of any citizen's duty. Ask them. They'll tell you.'

'I'm sure you re an exemplary citizen,' Pagan said. Dark curtains drawn against the light of day, bodyguards in the corridor: what was Enrico Caporelli afraid of? Kidnapping? Violence of the kind practised by certain Italian radicals? 'But I haven't come to Paris to discuss your good behaviour, Signor Caporelli.'

'Somehow this does not surprise me,' Caporelli said. 'How can I assist you?'

'You were in Britain recently, I understand.'

Caporelli tipped his chair back and looked up at the dark ceiling. Painted there, but obscured by the bad light, was an impression of an angel's gold wing, vast and still. 'Yes,' he said. 'Why is that of interest to you?'

Pagan didn't answer. He sailed straight ahead. Unanswered questions often created a useful uncertainty. He took out his notebook and used it as an actor might a stage prop, flicking pages meaninglessly, pretending to search for something in particular. 'You went to Glasgow.'

'I have business there, Mr Pagan,' the Italian said. 'Now and again I like to check on it. I had no idea my movements would attract official attention.'

Pagan longed to draw the curtains and let daylight fill the room. 'Who did you meet in Glasgow?'

'What would happen if I refuse to answer you?'

Pagan allowed this question to pass unanswered also. There wasn't any sharp response to it anyway; Caporelli could refuse to say a word. That was his prerogative. The important thing, from Pagan's point of view, was to keep rolling along. 'Did you meet a man called Rafael Rosabal?'

'Yes.'

'Why?'

Caporelli appeared amused by Pagan's bluntness. 'He keeps me informed of events in Cuba. A long time ago, I lived there. I like to have news of my old friends on the island. Call me sentimental.'

Sentimental, no, Pagan thought. There was nothing soft-centred about Enrico. 'The Cuban Minister of Finance, a member of Castro's government, brings you news of your friends? Isn't that an odd arrangement? How does Rosabal justify this . . . service? Does his government know he meets you?'

'You sound melodramatic, Mr Pagan. It's all very innocent, I assure you. Years ago, I knew Rosabal's family. The connection has never been broken. Besides, Rosabal and I never, never, discuss politics. I have no interest in Cuban affairs.'

Was this a lie? Pagan wondered. Caporelli had a certain easy plausibility about him, but

Pagan couldn't quite get a handle on Rosabal's angle in this. Why would the Cuban ferry news to Caporelli?

'Why did you have to go to Glasgow to meet?'

'It was convenient for me,' Caporelli answered.

'And for him?'

Caporelli gestured in a manner capable of only one interpretation: *I don't give a damn about his convenience, Pagan.* It was easy to see who had the upper hand between the Italian and the Cuban. Rosabal was clearly ready to be inconvenienced. But why? It wasn't adding up; Caporelli was sliding past another element, something that sent Rafael scurrying to Glasgow. A hold, perhaps; or Caporelli had something Rosabal badly wanted. Pagan pressed his fingertips into his eyelids. Guessing games, no bone-hard facts. He needed links solid enough to create a strong chain.

'Rosabal rented a farmhouse in England. Did you know that?'

Caporelli shook his head. 'I do not monitor his life.'

'He never mentioned this farm?'

'Never.'

A quick beat. 'The house was occupied by Gunther Ruhr.'

'Ruhr? The terrorist? Are you sure of that?'

'I'm sure,' Pagan said, *The terrorist*, as if there were other Ruhrs who might come to Caporelli's mind. 'Can you see a connection between Ruhr and your friend Rafael?'

Caporelli moved his face out from the reach of the lamplight. Shadows settled around him. Only his white hair was visible. 'I can imagine no relationship, Mr Pagan. None at all. Your information surprises me. In fact, it astonishes me.'

But Caporelli's face and voice didn't altogether suggest astonishment; Pagan had the feeling he was telling Enrico things he already knew.

'Why would the Cuban Minister of Finance rent a farmhouse and allow a group of terrorists to inhabit the place, Signor Caporelli?'

Caporelli folded his fine little hands on the desk and regarded them as if they were precious. He shook his head from side to side. 'It defies reason, Mr Pagan. I have no ready explanation.'

Pagan was silent now. Quietness gathered in the black hollows of this spacious unlit room. A clock chimed half past the hour with the subdued sound of an expensive mechanism.

'Stranger still is the fact that Rosabal rented the farm in another man's name,' Pagan said.

'Really?'

'He called himself Jean-Paul Chapotin.'

It was obvious at once that Caporelli hadn't known this before. He bit on his lower lip, then backed himself further out of the range of the lamp, and his face became invisible to Pagan. There, concealed, he recovered his composure with a swiftness that was admirable.

He said, 'The name – you did say Chapotin? – means nothing to me. And as for Rafael's private affairs, well, I'm ignorant of them. I am sure this business is all very interesting for you, but I don't share your fascination.'

Pagan had a well-honed instinct, activated whenever he was presented with a lie. Sometimes, like a pulse, it beat strongly, sometimes hardly at all, but he'd heard so many lies in his lifetime – some told to him by experts – that an encounter with yet another fiction was like greeting an old, if unreliable, acquaintance. Caporelli's lie, that he didn't know Jean-Paul Chapotin, wasn't the best Pagan had ever heard, but it was executed with theatrical skill and assurance. The little man popped a tissue from a fancy designer box with a conjurer's flourish, as if it were the climax to his brief performance, and pressed it to his lips.

'You must excuse me now, Mr Pagan. I don't think I have anything more to tell you. Not that I've been of very great help, I'm sure.'

Pagan wasn't quite ready to be dismissed. 'Are you aware that Chapotin was murdered in London, Signor Caporelli?'

'How could I be? As I already said, Mr Pagan, I am not familiar with the man. I'm sorry if he was killed, of course. But what can I say? You really must excuse me. I have business to conduct.'

Pagan rose from his chair. 'Like you, Chapotin had Cuba in his background,' he said. 'It's one of those bloody terrible coincidences that keeps bothering me. You and Jean-Paul and Rosabal. And the common factor is Cuba. I can't get it out of my mind.'

Enrico Caporelli held a hand in the air, palm turned outward to Pagan. His voice was firm. 'You should know when to stop asking questions. You should know when enough is enough.'

'I never do. It's one of my worst traits.'

Caporelli reached for the gold-plated telephone on his desk.

Pagan stretched a hand out over the receiver, preventing the man from picking it up. 'Why are you in such a hurry to boot me out of here, Signor Caporelli? I want to know a little more about you and Rosabal and poor old Jean-Paul. You can't really expect me to believe you didn't know Chapotin. He was in Glasgow the same day you were there. He lived in Cuba at exactly the same time as yourself. And he was obviously known to Rafael. Don't ask me to file all this under coincidence. Don't insult me.'

Caporelli gave an odd little laugh, a brittle note like a tiny hammer falling twice on a recalcitrant nail. He got up from the desk and wandered among the shadowy furniture. 'You have a fine imagination, Pagan. For your own sake, let it rest. Let it lie quietly. Forget it. A little amnesia is often a healthy thing.'

Ah, Pagan thought. Was that a veiled threat, a fist in a soft kid glove? He liked the idea of being gently menaced by Caporelli; it stirred his blood, his combative instincts. He got up from his chair and grinned at the little man, knowing how utterly infuriating this look could be at times.

'Something's going on, Enrico – if you don't mind – and I want to know what. You and Rosabal, for starters. He travels thousands of miles just so you can hear glad tidings from Cuba? Give me a bloody, break, Enrico. I didn't get up with this morning's dew.'

Caporelli was about to object, but Pagan went on regardless. 'Let's think about Gunther next. He lives in a house rented by *your* friend Rafael. What does this begin to smell like, Enrico? The whiff of conspiracy?'

'I tell you again. Too much imagination. Empty your mind. Sleeping dogs must lie.'

'I kick sleeping dogs, Enrico. I like the way they howl.' Pagan heard a dryness in his voice. He didn't have the spit for this pursuit, the wind. His lungs seemed shallow to him, his intake of oxygen poor. He caught his breath. 'Now why does Gunther steal a missile? Not because he wants one for his collection, I'm sure. He's the hired hand. But who's the boss, Enrico? Rafael? He's a good choice. After all, he was Ruhr's landlord. But is Rafael carrying out an order on behalf of some other party?'

Caporelli had crossed the floor while Pagan was speaking. Now he was pressing a wall-button mounted close to the fireplace. Bringing in reinforcements, muscle to kick Pagan out of here.

'Was it you, Enrico? Was Rafael working for you? Did he hire Ruhr on your behalf? Was that what the meeting in Glasgow was about?' Pagan strode across the room, closer to the little man. All this was wild, like shooting from a dislocated hip. But he had a scent in his nostrils still, and it grew more and more exciting. There was joy in mad surmise, in the crazed inspiration that forced you down unusual pathways. Allegations, red herrings, hares, accusations – sometimes, Pagan thought, work could be fun.

Clearly irritated, Caporelli once again pressed the bell on the wall. Pagan reached out, removed the man's hand from the button, gave the bundle of small bones a swift squeeze. 'Let me finish, Enrico.'

'You have finished,' Caporelli said and pulled away his pained hand.

'Not yet. Here's a fresh tack. I asked myself who else could possibly make use of a missile. Could it be Fidel himself? After all, he had a taste of missiles a few years ago, maybe he liked having them. But let's say nobody in the world wants to sell him one. Then let's imagine he decides to steal one and assigns this chore to Rosabal. Rosabal comes to you for help – old pal, old family friend you say you are – and you put him in touch with Ruhr.'

Caporelli's face was expressionless. Aside from the open eyes, hooded under the white eyebrows, it might have been the face of a sleeper.

Pagan went on, 'But we both know why that script's wrong, don't we, Enrico? You wouldn't lift your little finger to give Castro water on his deathbed, would you? You loathe him because he ripped you off for everything you owned in Cuba. The only interest you could possibly have in Castro is to see him either dead or tossed out of office. Therefore, if *you're* involved, the missile wasn't stolen for Fidel's sake. There's some other reason.'

'You amuse me, but my patience isn't unlimited. I must ask you to leave. Now, please.'

Caporelli walked towards the door. Pagan followed, thinking how pointless it was to hope Caporelli would break down and tell all. The Italian was hard as flint. And crafty. He had trained his face to reveal very little. So far the only real surprise that had registered was when Pagan had mentioned Rafael's use of the name Chapotin. Why had that startled Caporelli? Why had that so clearly bothered him? *Because something was going on he didn't know about, Pagan thought. Something that really worried him.*

'I honestly don't give a damn what you're up to, Enrico. I don't care about Cuba, and I don't care about Fidel Castro. Politics leave me cold. I'm interested in them only in as much as they involve an escaped prisoner who happens to have both a stolen missile and a hostage with him. I want the people *and* the missile back where they belong. And I think you can help me. I think you know where they might be found.'

Caporelli acted as if he were no longer listening. He opened the door, looked into the hallway, called out, 'André. Max. Come here, please. Escort Mr Pagan out.'

There was no reply from André and Max. Caporelli made a small hissing sound of irritation, *tssss*, and moved down the hall. Pagan followed. They passed the open doorway of a bedroom, furnished in black lacquer pieces, like something from the pages of a chic design magazine. Next was the kitchen, the largest Pagan had ever seen, vast and tiled, crowded with appliances, slatted red blinds at the long windows, copper-bottomed pans and skillets suspended from the high ceiling, strings of garlic bulbs, a, hanging congregation of red peppers.

'André! Max!' Caporelli, as if he were calling to two miscreant dogs, clapped his hands briskly. Still no response.

Pagan tried to get the little man's attention, but Caporelli shrugged him off as he stalked the kitchen on his quest for the bodyguards.

'If you'll listen to me, Caporelli – '

'I have listened too long already, Pagan.'

'Tell me what you know about Ruhr, that's all I ask.' Caporelli smacked the palm of his hand against the centre of his forehead. 'How many times do you need to hear it? I know nothing. Absolutely nothing! *Prego*. Do me a favour. Go away.'

Pagan stopped moving after the Italian. He leaned against the tiled wall and considered the pointlessness of further pursuit. Enrico was too good, an old fox, cunning. He was giving nothing away. Pagan stepped back into a space that was probably called the breakfast nook, a cranny containing a table strewn with rose petals, and four chairs. He needed to sit down, think over his options.

He moved towards a chair. Then stopped. The cranny contained more than flowers and furniture.

André and Max had been shot at very close range and propped against the wall in the shadowy cavity. One of the men had his big blank face turned toward Pagan, dead blue eyes open, cheek blown away, the abstract expression of sudden death. Pagan, who could still be shocked by murder, looked across the room at Caporelli and was about to tell him that his bodyguards were no longer guarding bodies – but before he had the chance to speak the kitchen door was opened.

'Ah,' Caporelli said. He was waiting for his soldiers. He thought they were coming through the door, belatedly answering his call. He thought they would have the Englishman ejected in a matter of seconds. Pagan shouted at the little man, something like *Get down*! although he couldn't remember later exactly what he'd said. In the doorway stood a man with a silenced pistol; having disposed of André and Max, he'd presumably been roaming this enormous apartment in search of Caporelli.

And now he'd found his quarry.

Pagan had barely time to record a swift impression, and it was neither interesting nor useful – medium height, medium weight, medium everything, dark hair, dark overcoat, dear Christ description failed him in the intensity of the moment, language melted away. He was, after all, cornered in a breakfast nook, and it seemed completely absurd to be shot to death there: a nook had no inherent dignity. Objective observation of the gunman was the last thing on his mind.

'In the name of God,' Caporelli said.

The gunman fired once. The sound was reminiscent of pressurised air fleeing a punctured pipe. The gunman was clearly an expert shot. Caporelli was spun round by the impact of the bullet, which had struck him directly in the heart. He clattered to the tiled floor, an unsmoked cigar in its cellophane wrapper rolling out of the pocket of his robe.

Pagan had time to see the gunman turn his face towards the breakfast area; the pistol came up once again in the man's hand. Aware of the glass door behind him, conscious too of how he was almost trapped, Pagan turned so quickly that he felt the stitches in his chest stretch. Glass would yield if he forced it, if he threw himself at it: one small corner of his panicked brain still recognised this fact. He launched himself hurriedly and without undue fear of falling from a high place because he'd seen, through the slats of the blind, a balcony, a handrail, flower pots, even an empty bird-cage.

The blind buckled and fell to pieces when he charged it, slats bending under his weight, small plastic screws popping. The door itself shattered easily, scattering angular fragments of glass across the balcony. Pagan landed on hands and knees, but he hadn't been caught by glass and he wasn't bleeding. He rose to an ungainly crouching position and surveyed the balcony quickly. Six feet by twelve, it adjoined the balcony of the neighbouring apartment, separated only by an ornate wrought-iron rail, about seven feet high. Pagan rushed toward it and clambered up. Halfway, he realised he had a terrific view of the Bois de Boulogne. With this appreciation came a certain dizziness. He swayed, moaned, heard air buzzing in his ears, kept climbing. There was neither elegance nor equilibrium in the way he ascended.

He clutched the top of the rail, hauled himself up through strata of pain that were numbed for the moment by the adrenalin of fear. He glanced back once across Caporelli's balcony, seeing how the fractured blind slats bent at all kinds of angles – hung out through the broken glass like some spindly creature that has been crushed. There was no sign of the killer; but that meant nothing. He could be striding toward the glass door even now. He could appear on the balcony at any second. He could still shoot Pagan.

Pagan made one final strenuous effort, and pulled himself over the rail. He dropped without subtlety into the adjoining balcony and stumbled just as a door opened and a man appeared. Not the gunman. He was presumably Caporelli's neighbour, this meek-looking, homely man in the tweed jacket.

'*Qu'est ce qui se passe?*' he asked, alarmed. '*Que voulez-vous?*'

Pagan took out his wallet and showed his ID to the man, who peered at it in the bewildered way of somebody whose life, for so long a placid, plodding business, has just taken a very odd detour.

'Ah, Scotland Yard,' the man said as if these two words explained all. '*Oui, oui. Entrez, entrez,*' and he held the glass door open for Pagan, who turned one last time and looked through the metal rail at Caporelli's balcony – empty and bleak, under the flat noon sky.

The detective who responded to Pagan's phone call was Claude Quistrebert from the Sûrété. He was a tall elegant man who wore a black and white pinstripe suit and a splendid blue carnation in his lapel. Pagan admired his style, which isolated him from his three colleagues, rather badly dressed men who swarmed all over Caporelli's apartment with a clumsy enthusiasm that was almost endearing.

Quistrebert and Pagan talked in Caporelli's study. The Frenchman's English, better than the Englishman's French, relieved Pagan of having to translate.

'Your description of the gunman leaves something to be desired,' Quistrebert said.

'There was nothing exceptional about him. I'd recognise him if I saw him again, I'm sure, but as for striking characteristics or features . . .' and Pagan shrugged dismally; he'd almost been shot at by a total nonentity.

'Striking?' the Frenchman asked, a little puzzled.

'Prominent,' Pagan explained.

'Ah. Of course.'

There was a crash from the kitchen, the sound of a heavy pot or a tureen clattering to the tiles. Quistrebert seemed not to notice. Perhaps he was accustomed to conducting investigations where his men broke things in their enthusiasm.

Quistrebert, sharp-faced, equipped with a nose that might have been made for burrowing, was at the window, looking out across the Bois. 'In the circumstances, I don't think we can expect to apprehend the man,' he said, without turning to Pagan. There was a critical little edge to his tone; he wasn't happy with his British colleague's powers of observation. He'd read of Pagan in the newspapers and considered him, with perhaps a twinge of envy, just another publicity-chasing cop. 'Why was Caporelli killed? Do you have light to throw?'

'None,' Pagan replied.

'You had reasons of your own for being here, of course. I will not pry.'

'Routine questioning.' A blanket phrase, a clear signal that meant 'Don't ask'.

'Naturally.' Quistrebert strode across the room on long, stalk-like legs. He sat behind Caporelli's desk and surveyed the papers there absently. 'Caporelli had business interests in France. A paper mill. A perfume company in Nantes. Also some banking. This much is a matter of public record. I understand he had many commercial interests in Italy also. On the face of it, a wealthy businessman. Such a man would inspire a number of enemies, no?'

'More than likely,' Pagan said. Hadn't Madame Chapotin said that her late husband had a banking concern in Italy? Pagan enjoyed these little correspondences.

Quistrebert stroked the flower in his lapel. 'He interests me, this Caporelli. Only a couple of days ago, he was a witness to a fatal accident here in Paris. I read the report.'

Pagan felt his interest sharpen. 'What happened?'

'He saw a man run over by a truck and crushed. It was a very bloody affair. Very bad. As an important eyewitness, he was required to give a statement, of course. In any case, he clearly felt a personal involvement. The victim of the accident was an associate of his, a certain Herr Kluger from Hamburg.'

An associate. Enrico and his associates, Pagan thought, had a knack for unhappy endings. Chapotin, this Kluger, and now Enrico himself. There was a grand design here, murderously neat.

Quistrebert said, 'They were walking after dinner, it seems, when a truck hit the unfortunate Kluger and dragged him under the wheels. A terrible mess.'

'You're convinced it was an accident?' Pagan asked.

The Frenchman looked unblinkingly at Pagan. 'What else? Scores of witnesses say they saw the truck being driven in an erratic fashion. The driver, a Spaniard, was drunk. I may add that he died of apparent heart failure some hours later in prison.'

Quistrebert was silent a moment. 'I will share with you a curious feature of the affair, Mr Pagan. The body of the driver was removed by persons claiming to be his relatives.'

'Claiming to be?'

'They had identification. They were from Madrid. The body was released to them. Again, nothing so very unusual. People want to bury their dead – a fact of life. But then the discovery was made by a diligent officer that the truck had been stolen four days before in Lyon. The driver had carried a false Spanish licence. No such person ever existed. His fingerprints are not on record. Nor can we locate the so-called relatives who came to claim him. We've been investigating the whole affair, but every avenue turns out to be a dead end, provoking what policemen always dread – too many questions. Too many grey areas. No clues.'

This sounded to Pagan as less an accident than a deliberate murder that hadn't worked out as planned. The killer had lost his nerve, as sometimes all men do, and needed the fiercely blind courage of inebriation to go through with the murder of Herr Kluger. The source of the killer's courage had also been the cause of his downfall. Surely he meant to escape after ploughing the victim down but was too drunk to do so. Pagan wasn't about to suggest this to Quistrebert, though. The Frenchman wouldn't take kindly to unsolicited advice; he had a streak of Gallic disdain and stubbornness.

'What do you know about Kluger?' Pagan asked.

'Another businessman. He was Caporelli's partner in the perfume company. But his interests were wide. He was the chief shareholder in a large pharmaceuticals company in Frankfurt, sole owner of a vineyard in California, the proprietor of magazines in Scandinavia – the list is long. A very rich man. Like Caporelli.'

'Can I have a report of the accident before I return to London?'

'Of course.' Quistrebert smiled for the first time since he'd arrived, a fox-like expression. 'Perhaps when you have official business in Paris in the future you will call me prior to your arrival, Mr Pagan?'

'Count on it,' Pagan said.

Glasgow

Foxworth, who had arrived at noon in an unseasonably warm and sunny Glasgow, had one of those little breaks that make a policeman's lot tolerable. It came at about three o'clock in the afternoon after he'd spent several hours with members of the Glasgow Criminal Investigation Division – friendly men, he thought, and level-headed – going over the reconstruction of Jean-Paul Chapotin's movements in Glasgow. There was the usual dogged routine of checking taxi companies and limousine services and car-hire firms, which involved making many telephone calls and waiting for people to get back to you after they'd checked their records and logs. It was a dismal business, actually, and quite uninspiring; or so Foxie thought. He knew dull routine had its place in his kind of work, but he'd inherited something of Frank Pagan's dislike of this plodding aspect of their employment. Give me the bright moment, Pagan had once said. Give me the flash, the sudden insight when lo and fucking behold, you know beyond doubt!

While the investigation of Chapotin's movements had been taking place, a similar inquiry into Enrico Caporelli's trip to Glasgow had also been going on. This had been a little simpler than the Chapotin inquiry in the sense that there was a record, kept by the men observing Rosabal, of Caporelli meeting the Cuban at a hotel in the centre of the city. Caporelli was merely the peripheral figure in this surveillance, an incidental entry in the Cuban's life. But the young detective who'd logged the time and place of the encounter had the brains to record the number plate number of the limousine that had picked Enrico up. Foxie liked this young man's notes, which combined the merit of plain observation with a touch of personal resentment; *subject rode off in a fat limousine, number plate G654 WUS; very small man with white hair and an arrogant strut.* Fat and arrogant; an enjoyable deviation from the prosaic language of police notes.

It was a start – a licence-plate number.

The limousine that had ferried Caporelli away belonged to a company called Executive Motor Cars Ltd, with offices in West Nile Street in the heart of the city. When Foxie called the number, a polite female told him she 'needed a wee minute' to check her log – how often had he heard the word 'log' since he'd come to Glasgow? – and get back to him. Foxie, during his routine telephoning, had already asked this same woman about Chapotin. My, you're awfully busy, the woman had said on the second call. She had a lilting, liquid accent.

The Break itself happened while Foxworth was drinking tea from a thick china mug and waiting for return phone calls. The woman from Executive Motor Cars Ltd called back to say that the driver of G654 WUS had transported Enrico Caporelli to a house 'somewhere in Ayrshire'. As for Foxworth's other inquiry, the one concerning Chapotin, the woman told him that one of the company's other drivers had picked up a man by that name at Glasgow Airport and had taken him *to the same place in Ayrshire.*

Ah-hah! Foxie had one of those rare moments, given only to cops, poets and fishermen, when the object of a search suddenly materialises. Caporelli and Chapotin, transported by the same limousine company, went to the same address in Ayrshire. Since Glasgow wasn't what you'd call Limousine City, it wasn't such a coincidence that both men had been serviced by the same car firm.

'Can I have an address for the house?' Foxworth asked.

The woman was silent a moment as she leafed through papers. 'Actually, sir, I don't have an address. Only a PO box number in Ayr. That's where we send our bills. Payment always comes from a company in London. This is an account we've been servicing for about a year.'

'One of your drivers could give me directions,' Foxie suggested.

'Of course,' said the woman. 'Always happy to oblige, sir.'

When Foxie telephoned Golden Square to report his progress, Pagan was still in Paris, so he left a brief message with Billy Ewing. Then he drove an unmarked police car to West Nile Street. Executive Motor Cars Ltd was located above a philately shop in whose drab window there was a display of stamps from Third World countries: Cambodia, Togo, Rwanda. (He wasn't sure he'd ever heard of Rwanda.) He entered the building and climbed up to the second floor where he was greeted by the woman, Miss Wilkie, who turned out to be perfectly lovely – late twenties, curvaceous, gorgeous features and skin. In other circumstances Foxie might have been inclined to linger.

She introduced Foxie to a dour man called Roderick McNulty – Rod, as he seemed to prefer – who had actually chauffered Caporelli to Ayrshire. Rod was the kind of person, socially rather stunted, who obliges the requests of other people only reluctantly. With thick, nicotine-stained fingers, he very slowly drew a detailed map for Foxie, and then handed it to him in a grudging manner.

Foxie looked at it a moment. The woman, Miss Wilkie – who had neat little breasts the merits of which were not entirely concealed by a green silk blouse – smiled at him. Terrific teeth, Foxie thought.

'I hope we've been able to help,' she said.

'You've been wonderful.' Foxie meant it too. He thought he might come more often to Glasgow.

She stepped close to him, inclining her head near his shoulder to glance at the map. 'Out of the way sort of place,' she said. 'Who'd want to live there?'

Foxie caught her perfume just then, a delightful musk. Unashamedly romantic in affairs of the heart, given to falling in love with women he spotted only briefly on the street and could never hope to know, he wished Miss Wilkie would ride along with him to Ayrshire.

Rod McNulty said, 'Aye. It's an isolated spot all right.'

'Who lives in the house?' Foxworth asked.

'I wouldn't know,' McNulty said, again hesitant, as if his whole life were one mass of confidences he had to keep. The chauffeur who sees all and says nothing.

With one last smile at Miss Wilkie, who raised a delicate hand in response, Foxworth left.

He drove out of Glasgow under a sunny sky. According to the car radio the weather was fine all across south-west Scotland, although the inevitable cold front was on its way. Outside the city, green fields were bright in the sunlight. Along the coast waters sparkled, suggesting another season altogether.

He stopped briefly in the seaside resort of Ayr, a town of white-washed cottages, a harbour, a busy High Street, a racecourse. He had a dinner of marvellous fish and chips then headed south again in the direction of Ballantrae. He wanted to reach his destination before dark.

As he drove through the small town of Girvan, the rocky hump of Ailsa Craig appeared ten miles offshore. Crowded by thousands of gulls, it looked as grim as a penal colony. When he reached Ballantrae, an old fishing village that seemed just a trifle despondent, he examined his map. The road he had to follow went inland. Road was hyperbole. It was a rutted path between tall hedges. His car thumped and rattled and the setting sun dazzled in his rear-view mirror. The shrubbery became darker, denser. Now and then he had a sense of flat fields beyond the hedgerows, but he saw nothing of interest – neither farmhouses nor haystacks nor grazing cows.

He pulled the car over, turned on the interior light, examined the map. The house was about a mile away now. He drove the last stretch slowly. What was he supposed to say when he got there? *I am making inquiries. I am sorry to inconvenience you.* Standard police procedure. He thought a better ploy might be the Lost Tourist Strategy; after all, he didn't have a local accent. He was obviously a discombobulated stranger. Feigning that particular pathos of the misguided traveller was always amusing, the dog-like eagerness to get back on the right path, the profuse apologies. Why not?

But when he saw the house he wasn't sure. He had somehow expected a farmhouse, at best an old Scottish lodge, perhaps a renovated manse, not this sandstone monstrosity, which seemed ill-defined, uncertain of its own boundaries. Turrets, by God! Neither house nor castle, it managed to suggest one of those late nineteenth-century follies erected by an ambitious whiskered Victorian as a monument to his own – and his age's – enlightenment. Foxworth smiled to himself as he turned the car into the long driveway.

Twilight blurred the edges of the unlit house. Now it looked positively spooky, a place of creaking floorboards and squeaking doors and secret passage-ways. Not your inviting prospect, Foxie thought. But policemen, like plumbers, were obliged to go where the job took them. You couldn't just say *I don't like the look of the place, I refuse to go near it.*

Foxie parked the car. It was the only vehicle in sight. He stepped out. The house was deeply quiet. No TV sounds, no piano playing, no shadow at the window peering out.

An echo of Miss Wilkie's question came back to him. *Who'd want to live there?*

Aye, who indeed?

Foxie crossed the drive. He didn't approach the front door at once. He went instead to the side, wondering if there might be lights at the rear, some sign of life. But he found none. It was indeed possible, he thought, that the place was empty, in which case he'd go back to Ballantrae and ask at a local pub if anybody knew the name of the owner and where he might be found.

The sun slid behind trees, its last light diffused by wintry branches. Twilight was going rapidly. No soft, sweet lingering here. No nightingale tunes. Foxie moved between the bushes.

He neither saw nor heard the parting of bushes to his right. Nor did he hear the quietly hostile skweeee made by the barrel of a shotgun forced between resistant branches of shrubbery. Some instinct finally made him turn round. His heart felt like a ball dropped from the roof of a tenement, down, unstoppably down, a slave to gravity.

'I lost my way,' he said to the shadowy figure who stood half-hidden in the foliage.

The barrel of the gun, suddenly massive, came out of the bushes and was thrust against Foxworth's chest as if to say, with vigorous agreement, *You certainly have, chum.*

15 Cabo Gracias a Dios, Honduras

Steffie Brough, dreaming of her own death, woke when a spider crawled over a closed eyelid. She sat upright quickly and swatted the creature aside. Curled defensively inward, it created a huge black furry ball that flew across the air and struck the far wall of the tent then dropped in long-legged disarray. It took Steffie a moment to assemble her thoughts and remember where she was, and the recollection depressed her. *There were men here who wanted to kill her.*

She heard rain strike the canvas overhead. The tent sagged in the centre where it had gathered water during the hours of darkness. She got up, glanced at Ruhr who lay on the cot. She parted the flap, looked out, saw a dismal steamy morning. Rain weaved a mist in the trees and the density of the forest was overwhelming. Unseen insects kept up their constant click-clicking. How could she possibly have imagined escape last night? There was no way out of this place unless Ruhr said so. If she ran now he'd simply find her and bring her back. She was trapped.

Ruhr still slept quietly and yet she had the odd feeling he could wake at will, that he'd trained himself to sleep only in the most shallow way. An unusual noise would bring him around.

Last night, when it had seemed inevitable that he'd overpower her after the pointless attempted escape, he'd suddenly and strangely lost interest, pushed her away, tossed her a blanket and told her to sleep on the floor. It was almost as if she were a game he didn't want to finish, something he needed to linger over because there was more pleasure in it that way. She clenched her hands and stood in the centre of the tent and realised that if she could see herself from a point outside she would probably look like some kind of animal with her stringy, dirty hair. I smell, she thought. I smell horrible.

Ruhr woke. Steffie had never seen anybody who rose quite like him. One minute asleep, the next fully awake, no transition between. He tossed his blanket aside and got up. He wore white underpants, white T-shirt. He dressed without talking, without even noticing her. He brushed his teeth, using water from an old pail, and spat toothpaste out on the floor. He combed his thinning hair and studied his face in a small corroded mirror. There was intense self-interest in the way he did this, a vanity.

He took his knife from under his pillow. He ran the tip of one finger along the blade, testing its keenness, then sheathed the knife and strapped it to his shin. Only then did he look at Steffie Brough, as if the weapon had reminded him of her existence.

'Hungry?' he asked.

She didn't say anything even though she was famished. Ruhr produced a plastic bag from which he took some dried fruit – God, that was all she'd had to eat since leaving England. He gave her two brown rubbery discs that might have been dehydrated apricot or pear, you couldn't possibly tell by their taste. They were awful, but she ate them anyway. When she was finished she understood she felt a vague, though sullen, gratitude toward Ruhr for the food.

But then she remembered how he'd touched her, that humiliating invasion of her privacy, his awful lips on her mouth, his hands all over her body, and her brief gratitude dissolved.

'More?' Ruhr asked.

She declined. She was still hungry but she didn't want him to know it. He had too much power over her already: why give him more? He took out a metal flask from a canvas bag. It contained lukewarm water. She drank. It was ghastly, gritty, tasted of iron.

'Things here are a little different for you,' he said. 'You're used to something else.'

'Yes.'

'No pleasant bedroom. No nice bathroom for you here.' Ruhr smiled. He rubbed his face with the bad hand. Steffie barely noticed the deformity. She certainly wasn't repelled by it in quite the same way as before. *You can get used to anything*, she thought.

'You would like to go home,' Ruhr said.

Why had he said that? she wondered. There was some sly quality in his voice. He was teasing her, only he wasn't very good at it. He wasn't much good at any kind of social interaction, she'd noticed. Even when he moved he did so without poise, like a man who knows he's ugly and feels people are watching him critically. There was an aura about him of loneliness, the same pall she'd seen around those sad, solitary figures who sat for motionless hours in the draughty reading-room of her local library, sometimes leafing newspapers but more often staring into space at nothing. Steffie, raised by decent people who tended to see the best in the human race and the bright side of everything, almost felt sorry for him.

Almost.

He kills, she thought. He kills casually. She remembered Trevaskis and his unfortunate kindness.

'Perhaps policemen will rescue you,' he said, still teasing in his awkward manner. He opened the flap of the tent. There was the pungent smell of wet canvas. 'Perhaps even as we speak, some kind English policeman is closing in on us. Somebody good and cunning. Perhaps Sherlock Holmes, eh?'

'Perhaps,' she said.

'Hope is so wonderfully human, little girl. What person has not been completely betrayed by hope at least once in his or her lifetime?'

She sat on the floor, and hung her head. It was important to fight despair. Sometimes you couldn't find the strength to do so. Nobody was looking for her, nobody was closing in. It was stupid to think so.

He kneeled alongside her, cupped her chin in the palm of his hand. 'Do not be so despondent, child. Keep hoping. What choice do you have?'

She hated him then more than ever before. The way he touched her under the face was awful in itself, but his words were the real killers – *don't give up hope. Don't be despondent*. Should I sing for you, Ruhr, and dance? She closed her eyes, blinked back tears and thought *Fuck you, you won't see me weep, you rotten bastard.*

He stood upright. She didn't look up at him. He said, 'I have some business to attend to. You will stay here, of course. It would be pointless to run again. Where would you go in any case? I expect to be back very soon.'

She heard him push the open flap aside and then he was gone and the tent was silent save for the metronomic ticking of the rain.

The girl could wait. Delayed satisfaction only heightened anticipation. Ruhr walked down through long wet grass and mud to the landing-strip. The transport plane had gone at first light. He wondered briefly about Sweeney, but Ruhr wasn't sentimental about friendships.

He simply didn't have any. All human relationships were inherently doomed, whether by death or declining interest. Why make any kind of commitment?

He had never loved in his life. On those few occasions when he'd felt the tremor of affection for another, he'd dismissed it as a chemical anomaly, a flaw in his system, something to be rooted out. It was simpler to destroy than to love. Destruction was quick and fevered and exciting. By contrast love, as he understood it, could be a protracted torture, a bundle of insecurities, a murderous game of the emotions.

He paused on the edge of the runway, enjoying the rain against his face. Then he crossed the concrete, passing the missile that sat in the truck at the edge of the runway. The green waterproof tarpaulin, running with rain, still covered the weapon. In the distance, their sounds muted by foliage, soldiers went through tedious drills designed simultaneously to dull the critical faculties and raise the temperature of enthusiasm. Pumped up for the overthrow of Castro, they would set sail with an effervescent sense of purpose and a determination sharpened by weeks of preparation here. The idea of discipline, with its unambiguous rules and codes, pleased Ruhr.

He went up the slope to the place where Fuentes' tent was situated. Tommy was inside with the Englishman, Bosanquet. They sat on either side of a card-table on which a map was spread. Ruhr ducked his head, went inside. The air was thick with cigarette smoke. Inverted lids of old coffee jars were being used as ashtrays by the chain-smoking Fuentes.

Fuentes looked up. Bosanquet took off his reading-glasses.

'His majesty,' Fuentes said. 'See how he condescends to visit us in my humble dwelling, Bose *old bean*. Are we flattered? Beat the drums. Roll out the red carpet. The king comes!'

Bosanquet, who thought poorly of Fuentes' heavy-handed sarcasm, stared at the German. He was really a disgusting shit as far as Bosanquet was concerned. Up there with the schoolgirl in his tent – very bad form. It was child-molesting, no two ways about it. He would gladly have cut out Ruhr's throat, and in other circumstances might have done just that. As it was, it was the child who would have to die, because that was how the order had come down from Harry Hurt. In Bosanquet's scheme of things, whatever was sent down the pipeline from Harry had top priority. Harry signed the pay-cheques and Bosanquet's loyalty was the commodity he bought with them.

'You didn't appear last night,' Bosanquet said. 'We waited for you. You were supposed to perform a task and you failed to show up, which is unforgivable.'

'I fell asleep,' Ruhr said drily. He enjoyed the Englishman's restrained display of temper. 'I had had a busy day, you may recall.'

'What about the girl?'

'What about her?'

'Is she alive?'

'For the moment,' Ruhr said.

'For the moment,' Bosanquet remarked. He really had no stomach for the idea of the girl dying. He got to his feet. Her death wasn't his business. Nor was the murder last night of one of Ruhr's henchmen. These things were Ruhr's own affairs. He changed the subject. 'Are you ready to do the work you should have done last night?'

'It's raining,' Ruhr said, as if this might prevent him working.

'Does that make a difference?' Bosanquet rubbed his sweaty face with his red bandanna. He remembered how Harry Hurt had said that the German's needs were to be met at all times, because he was a very important part of the operation. Presumably this order included pandering somewhat to the German's sense of his own shattering superiority.

'Perhaps not,' Ruhr said. 'The tools.'

'Of course.' Fuentes removed a canvas bag from under his card table. It rattled as he handed it to Ruhr. 'Everything you have requested is in there.'

Ruhr unzipped the bag, looked inside, apparently satisfied.

All three men walked to the airstrip. Ruhr glanced at the covered missile on the truck and the large tarpaulined rectangle that contained the weapon control system. He had no intention of doing the work under the eyes of the other two.

The key to survival was the same as it had always been: he had to be indispensable. He'd known all along that this point would be reached, this place where his future was in the balance. It was always this way. Many of his employers had tried to shaft him in the past, to cheat him after the event. None had ever succeeded. He was always prepared, always kept something in hand. He had the documents in the care of the lawyer Herr Schiller in Hamburg, of course, but Ruhr liked to take out even more insurance policies. In this case, he was essential to Fuentes and Bosanquet and Rafael Rosabal and their scheme because of his specialised knowledge. That was the key and neither of the other men possessed it. Only Ruhr.

Fuentes pointed to a wooden crate, sheltered from wetness by sheets of plastic. He said, 'This is what the Israelis delivered.'

Ruhr glanced at the box, then turned away from it. For the moment he wanted to look at the missile. He unrolled the green tarpaulin a few inches, revealing the blunt grey canister. Without the nose cone the weapon lacked a dimension. Armed, it would have a range of approximately fourteen hundred miles; it could travel at five hundred and fifty miles an hour.

Ruhr walked to the wooden crate, asked Fuentes for a tool, a tyre iron. Tomas found one inside a jeep parked nearby. Ruhr gently opened the crate.

Inside was a layer of packing material, which Ruhr removed.

There it was.

A nose cone of dull silver contained the nuclear warhead. A series of metal connecting pins studded the warhead. These fitted corresponding slots in the housing of the missile. Ruhr stared at the thing for several seconds. Instruments of destruction, from the flick-knife to the warhead, had always exerted great fascination for him. In the war museums of the world he'd been hypnotised by displays of old lances, maces, swords, blackpowder muskets, grenades from World War I, tommy-guns, sophisticated automatic rifles. He believed that man reached his creative peak only when the design and manufacture of aggressive weapons was his goal. All the rest, the other products of creativity, the symphonies and poems and philosophical thinking, the computers and scientific theories, all that was just so much dross in contrast to the creation of devices meant to maim and kill.

Slicks of rain slid over the cone. Ruhr replaced the lid of the box. The beat of his heart was just a little faster.

'Now what?' Fuentes asked.

'I will wait,' Ruhr replied.

'For God's sake, what for?' Bosanquet asked.

'For the ship.' Ruhr stepped back from the wooden crate. 'On board the ship I will make the final marriage.'

'The marriage?'

Ruhr smiled. 'Have I used the wrong phrase?'

Bosanquet loathed this smug character. It was damned hard to stay calm. 'You are supposed to attach the warhead to the missile and make all the connections now, Ruhr. That is the plan. The missile is to be loaded in an armed state.'

Ruhr shook his head. 'If you are unhappy, do it yourself.' He knew neither man could possibly perform the task. Even if they brought in an expert, the newcomer could not easily fathom the connections between the warhead and the missile because Ruhr, with the foresight of the survivor, had had the warhead built to his own specifications, which had been given to the Israelis, Levy and Possony. Changes in the wiring inside the missile were required to make it compatible with the warhead, which was a brilliant modification of the device known in the nuclear arms trade as the W84. A wrong connection, a minor mistake, and the fusing would burn out, rendering both missile and warhead useless. And Bosanquet knew that: Ruhr had once again made himself indispensable.

Ruhr had acquired his extensive nuclear understanding from a homosexual West German technician employed by NATO at Wueschein, a base in Germany. He'd learned how the missile worked, and the principles behind it. He'd absorbed this with the ardour of a man in love with his subject. The technician, menaced by blackmail, had been a wonderful teacher, Ruhr an even more marvellous student. The arcane terms, the payload, the velocity, the range, the connections between warhead and missile – Ruhr took it all in without needing second explanations.

Now Fuentes tore off his hat and flung it to the ground. '*Tronco de yucca*,' he said to Ruhr. 'That's what you are, Ruhr. A goddam *tronco de yucca*. Why don't you do the goddam job now?'

'I don't speak Spanish,' Ruhr replied. He enjoyed Fuentes' primitive display of irritation. 'Is that a compliment?'

'I don't think it is,' Bosanquet remarked. He breathed deeply, staying calm. After all, did it really make a difference if Ruhr armed the missile here or on board the ship? So long as the device was ready to fly when it was placed in Cuba – that was the thing of consequence. Ruhr could make 'the marriage' on the ship, if that was how he wanted it.

'It's okay,' Bosanquet said. 'It's going to be fine.'

'I know it is,' Ruhr responded.

He walked across the runway and back up through the long grass to his tent. Guns fired in the misty distance. Target practice. He entered the tent. The girl was lying on the camp bed, her eyes closed.

He watched her. He was ready for her now.

He moved towards her quietly, with a weightlessness years of stealth had taught him. He was about a foot from the bed when she opened her eyes and drew her hands out from under the blanket. She held a piece of broken mirror, a scabbard-shaped length she held like a dagger, and she thrust it at him. He stepped away, watching how the makeshift blade drew small reflections from within the tent – the girl's lips, one of her determined eyes, Ruhr's own face, fragmented images.

She raised her weapon in the air and slashed again and this time he seized her wrist and slammed it down across his knee, forcing her hand to open and the length of mirror to fall to the ground. She wasn't beaten even then. She pulled herself free of him, twisted, kicked, lashed air with a foot that had never been meant to inflict damage, a long foot, a dancer's foot. He caught the ankle easily, and twisted it, and pushed her back across the bed.

She lay there, breathing hard.

He stood over her.

And smiled.

London

The doctor, Ghose, examined Pagan's chest with his head cocked, like that of a bird, to one side. He kept up an ongoing stream of chatter while he studied the stitches. The human body, Mr Pagan, is a miracle of design and efficiency. Consider for instance the lung, the robust delicacy of that organ, the bronchi, the bronchioles, the whole system of highways that we call alveolar ducts. Easily damaged, Mr Pagan, but they mend under the right circumstances. And these include bed rest, no needless activity. Think of yourself as sedentary for a while.

Pagan liked Ghose and the cheerful manner in which the doctor chided him.

'In future you will move, if at all, only slowly,' Ghose said. He replaced the damaged stitches after cleaning the wound thoroughly.

Pagan disengaged himself from the proceedings by thinking about the report of Herr Kluger's death in Paris. He'd translated it slowly on the plane back to London, skipping vocabulary he didn't know. The gist of the thing was that Caporelli and a couple of his acquaintances – the detailed report named them as Harold Hurt and Sheridan Perry, American citizens – had witnessed the event. Were they simply out strolling, taking the night air, four old pals crossing a street when – *wham* – one of them is dragged under a truck? Perhaps they were headed somewhere, a meeting, a café. It was a dead-end. He could check out Hurt and Perry, which would take time unless they had records of some kind at the American Embassy or were otherwise noted in some central law enforcement computer – if they had ever broken any laws in their time. Time: there it was again, an intolerably demanding master.

Ghose bandaged him. 'There. Almost as good as new. I underline the almost. Now go home. Behave yourself. Don't play in the streets. Cars are quicker than you, Mr Pagan.'

Pagan told Ghose he was going directly to bed, but when he left the hospital he took a taxi, through clogged West End traffic, to Golden Square. It was after seven o'clock when he reached his office. He took the bottle of Auchentoshan from his desk, poured a very small shot into a glass. He sifted his messages. There was one from Foxworth, who hadn't returned from Glasgow. Something about a car-hire company he was going to check out. Pagan could hardly read Billy Ewing's handwriting. Steffie Brough's mother had called, just checking. *Just checking*. This terse message, between whose lines lay a world of pain, caused Pagan to feel as if his heart had been squeezed. He glanced at the child's picture pinned to the wall. The elfin features of the kid neither accused nor derided him for his failure to locate her. They seemed indifferent suddenly, as if resigned to exile.

Just checking. Pagan imagined he heard death in those words. He felt as if he'd entered a memorial chapel to find Steffie's mother looking down into her daughter's coffin and whispering to herself those two dreadful words *Just checking, just checking,* a hand laid softly on the child's cold cheek.

I'll get her back for you, Pagan thought. Some way.

He called Billy Ewing, told him to run a check on Harold Hurt and Sheridan Perry. Ewing had some information of his own, which concerned the protocol of Frank Pagan interviewing the Cuban Minister of Finance. It required a shit-load of paperwork, Ewing reported. Reasons had to be spelled out, justifications given. Documents were then submitted to the Cuban attaché in London, with copies to the Foreign Office. The government in Havana would review the request in due course. To put it bluntly, said Ewing, it might take six months, perhaps a year, and even then it didn't sound promising.

Pagan thought about the great bureaucratic mire into which human intentions, reduced to paperwork, were sucked and invariably lost. He hung up. His next call was to the

Commissioner. Pagan asked for a meeting as soon as possible, Burr agreed. They chose a pub in Soho because Burr had an engagement at a restaurant in Greek Street at eight. Pagan then made one other call, this time to an airline company.

On his way out of his office, he encountered Billy Ewing, who had his face buried deep in a big white handkerchief.

'By the way, anything new from Foxie?' Pagan asked.

'Not yet.' Ewing came up for air from the folds of the handkerchief. 'Bloody pollen.'

'If he gets in touch I'll be at the French pub.'

'Then what?'

'We'll see.'

'There goes a man of mystery,' Ewing said, more to himself than to his boss, as Pagan headed for the door with an agility Ghose would not have recommended.

The French pub, so-called because in another incarnation it had been the headquarters for the French government in exile during World War II, was crowded with West End types, a few tourists, theatre-goers finishing drinks hurriedly, and some dubious characters Pagan recognised as having been acquainted with Her Majesty's prisons at one time or another. He squeezed into the bar, careful to avoid potentially painful contact with anyone, and ordered a scotch.

Quite suddenly he remembered having been in this same bar thirteen years ago with Magdalena Torrente. They'd drunk anis from a large glass urn on the counter and then they'd gone deeper into Soho, strolling hand-in-hand down Old Compton Street, up through the food stalls in the Berwick Street market. They'd eaten dinner at a small Greek restaurant on Beak Street. He'd got quite drunk that night. Drunk and passionate, and probably silly in his passion. The touching evening came rushing back to him in little particles of memory that had been scattered and overlooked.

Martin Burr arrived five minutes after Pagan was served. Unlike Pagan, the Commissioner waded into the throng, nudging with his stick wherever appropriate. He was an imposing man. The eye-patch, the bulk of his body, gave him presence and set him apart. He didn't want a drink. Since the place was crowded, he and Pagan went outside into the street. A snappy little breeze blew up from Shaftesbury Avenue and Pagan turned up the collar of his coat.

'How is the wound?' Burr asked.

'I'll survive,' Pagan remarked. He drained his scotch and set it down on the window-ledge of the pub.

'Don't overdo it.'

'I don't know how, Commissioner.'

Martin Burr smiled thinly. Frank was the kind who'd soldier on regardless. Either one admired this attitude or criticised it for being headstrong. Burr was never sure which side he took.

He put his hands in the pockets of his tweed overcoat. 'I'm getting flak, Frank. All the bloody time. This damned commission of inquiry has its first meeting tomorrow. I'm going to have to talk to them about the leak that led to the calamity in Shepherd's Bush. What can I tell them? I know absolutely nothing new about it.' Burr looked up at the night sky over Soho, looking like a one-eyed country squire sniffing the air for weather changes. 'I also just received some other news that may or may not have something to do with the bloody missile. According to an intelligence report that came to my desk, the Israelis have reported two of their most highly rated nuclear physicists as missing, as well as sufficient *matériel* to make a warhead compatible with the cruise missile. Both men are said to be somewhere in South America. The Israelis are blaming professional burn-out for the theft. Both men were said to be, and I quote, "highly strung". But who knows? The information is vague.'

'If there's a connection with Ruhr, then the cruise might be armed by this time.'

'It might be.'

'Which makes the picture even more gloomy.'

'Gloomy indeed. Who is going to blow up what, I wonder.' Burr slipped fingertips under his eye-patch and scratched. 'If it weren't for the fact that I'd feel like some rotten little bugger sneaking off a sinking ship, I'd tender my resignation in a twinkling. No messing about. But I'm like you, Frank. I keep going. Kinnaird's been supportive, I must say. Which I appreciate.'

A roar of buses was blown on the breeze from Shaftesbury Avenue and the theatre district. This was a transient, brightly lit little corner of London, streets filled with drifters, people who idled in the Haymarket and around Piccadilly Circus and wandered toward Leicester Square.

'Kinnaird's the conscientious sort,' Pagan said.

'Calls me three, four times a day, Frank.' Burr looked as if he were wearied by the Home Secretary's attentions. 'What did you want to see me about?'

Pagan arranged his thoughts. He expected an argument from the Commissioner, or at least an objection. He talked quickly, hoping Burr wouldn't interrupt him. He went lightly on the details, his past relationship with Magdalena. He talked about the connections between Rosabal and Ruhr, the evidence of the rented farmhouse. He sketched his conjectures, trying to give them solid weight, about the threads that linked Caporelli and Chapotin to Rosabal, and thus to Gunther Ruhr. *En passant*, he spoke about the deaths of Caporelli and the others. Now, if there was only the vaguest possibility that the stolen missile was armed, it gave the whole investigation even more urgency.

'There are some iffy bits in there,' Burr said.

Pagan agreed and muttered something about the nature of all hypotheses. He glanced down the busy street.

'What do you propose, Frank?' Burr asked. Sometimes he adopted an attitude toward Pagan similar to one that might be held by an uncle toward a favoured, if slightly wilful, nephew. He was tolerant, bemused, gently critical; he knew that Pagan always did his best no matter the circumstances.

Pagan said what he had in mind.

Martin Burr put one hand up to his dark-green eye-patch. 'Are you really sure that this person – this Magdalena – will tell you anything, even if she's in a position to do so?'

Pagan wasn't sure. He thought about the mysterious coup she'd been so reluctant to discuss: if he knew more about that, there might be progress. 'She's the only real connection I have to Rosabal. And I think the road to Ruhr leads through the Cuban.'

'You could travel a long way and have nothing to show for it.'

'I could also sit on my arse around London and have even less.'

'True,' Burr said. A certain look sometimes came to Frank Pagan's face, and the Commissioner recognised it now, determined, and hard, the slight forward thrust of the jaw, aggressive. 'May I remind you, Frank, that you're not in great shape for travelling? On top of that, your activity in Paris today hasn't improved your condition.'

'I feel fine,' Pagan said. And, for the moment, that was true enough. How long this transitory well-being would last was another matter. He had the feeling he was held together by nothing more substantial than Ghose's stitches.

Burr said, 'Very well. Make arrangements to go.'

'I've already made them.'

Burr smiled. 'I should have known.' He was quiet a moment. Pagan's confidence was sometimes an impressive thing. 'There's an old contact of mine in Dade County. A certain Lieutenant Philip Navarro. You might need him. He knows his way around.'

Pagan memorised the name.

'I hope you bring something back, Frank. God knows, we could use a break.'

The Commissioner shook Pagan's hand, then turned and walked in the direction of Old Compton Street. Pagan didn't watch him leave. He didn't have time to linger. He had to go to his apartment, toss a few things together, get his passport and his gun, and be at Heathrow Airport within the next two hours. He was pleased to have the Commissioner's blessing, the official imprimatur.

With or without it, he'd have gone anyway.

Washington

Harry Hurt kept an expensive apartment in an area of Washington that afforded a splendid view of the Potomac. It was a rich man's view, designed to instil in its owner a sense of unbridled superiority. High above the riff-raff, Hurt indulged his patriotism, which fostered the illusion that anyone – anyone at all – could rise to wealth and prominence in these United States. Any Appalachian dirt farmer's boy, any steelworker's son from Bethlehem, PA, could – God, hard work, and the machine willing – ascend to the highest offices in the land. Harry Hurt believed this without question. While he was not an innocent in world affairs by any means, he was nevertheless naïve when it came to some areas of understanding. His romanticised America eclipsed the hard reality.

The apartment had an exercise-room fitted with an electronic bicycle, stretching devices, a Nautilus machine, a variety of weights and a rowing simulator. In this room Hurt burned off calories and kept himself tight and lean.

A spartan bedroom with a certain Polynesian flavour adjoined the mini-gymnasium, and beyond was a large living-room where he sometimes entertained people. A glass-panelled cabinet, centred against the main wall of the living-room like a shrine, contained a variety of weapons – automatic rifles, shotguns, pistols – as well as photographs of Hurt in crumpled fatigues and black glasses when he'd been a 'military advisor' in Central America. A clutch of shrunken heads, gathered in Central American villages, hung alongside the cabinet like a spray of discoloured garlic bulbs. All were reminders of his glory days.

The door of the living-room led into a vestibule furnished in soft white leather chairs and sofas. This room was presently occupied by new guards Hurt had hired. There were three in all, one a former Secret Serviceman. They wore dark-blue suits.

On this particular evening, more than twenty-four hours after the limousine had exploded, Hurt was in the living-room pouring small shots of an inexpensive scotch called Passport from a bottle labelled Glenfiddich. He had some miserly ways and, like most misers, thought he could fool people with transparent deceptions.

Freddie Kinnaird, who had arrived an hour ago on Concorde, sipped his drink and pretended to enjoy it. Sheridan Perry, knowledgeable about malt whiskies, made no objection either. He was accustomed to this odd streak of niggardliness in Harry. The more wealth Hurt accumulated, the more thrifty he became and the more energy he spent jogging and rowing and heaving weights around. It was almost as if he were obeying some strange axiom of his own: *great wealth leads only to parsimonious guilt which can be reduced only through endless exercise.*

Freddie Kinnaird, who had just finished relating the death of Enrico Caporelli, set his glass down a moment. Hurt deftly slid a coaster, filched from the Stanhope Hotel in Manhattan, under the Englishman's drink.

'When does it end?' Hurt asked. He'd already told Freddie about the attack on the limo, glancing all the while at Perry, as if for some sign of his compatriot's guilt.

'When we three are dead, I daresay,' Kinnaird remarked.

'Hold on, hold on,' Hurt said. 'Let's be logical. Let's take this thing apart and put it back together again. It has to lead somewhere.'

Kinnaird picked up his glass and finished his drink. He had so little time to spend here. There was business to conduct back in England, the affairs of his office not the least of it, but he'd come here to show a sign of solidarity with Hurt and Perry. After all, they were members of the same exclusive club. He detected some mild tension between the pair. Had there been a squabble? In the circumstances, though, nervousness was inevitable.

Freddie Kinnaird also had some information to impart at the appropriate moment, which would come when Harry had played out his little string of paranoia.

'For a while, I thought Enrico himself might be behind it,' Hurt said.

'How wrong you were,' said Kinnaird.

'Now, if it's an inside job . . .' Harry Hurt didn't finish his sentence.

'We three,' Freddie Kinnaird said.

'Right,' Perry said. 'If it's an inside job, it's one of us.'

Freddie Kinnaird played with his empty glass. A lock of hair fell across his forehead, creating the impression of a rather red-faced, ungainly boy. He swept it back with a toss of his head. 'Consider the explosion of the limousine,' he said to Perry. 'Who had the information that you and Harry were travelling in the vehicle?'

Perry said, 'Only Harry and me. That's it.'

'Unless *you* knew, Freddie,' Hurt said.

Kinnaird laughed. 'I was many miles away, Harry. I have no crystal ball, something my political enemies in the House of Commons discovered some time ago.'

'You're saying . . .' Perry stopped, looking both indignant and somewhat despondent at the same time.

'It's either you or me.' Hurt turned to Perry. 'That's what Freddie's saying.'

'Wait a minute there,' Perry said.

Kinnaird interrupted. 'It's only one possibility, gentlemen. Consider this as an alternative. Parties unknown to us, parties seeking the destruction of the Society, might be responsible.'

This was what Hurt wanted so badly to believe. But was it really preferable to ascribe the killings to some faceless organisation rather than to Sheridan Perry? Perry he could deal with. An unknown outfit was more spooky. How the hell did you begin to fight back at a shadow? His thoughts returned to the fiery limousine and the striking little perception he'd had when he'd been obliged to flee the tailoring establishment. *Perry knew,* he had thought then.

Now it made some kind of sense to him.

Consider: Perry knew.

Assume: Perry arranged the hit.

The killers Perry had hired to strike the limousine had erred. Maybe they were supposed to blow up the car later, at some time when Perry – perhaps on the pretext of buying a newspaper, something like that – had stepped out of the limo. It made simple, stunning, logical sense. Perry's killers, in their enthusiasm to do the job, had mistimed the affair.

This is what it came down to: Perry wanted it all, the whole ball of wax. He wanted the Society for himself. He wanted Cuba for himself.

Hurt switched on the light in the aquarium standing against one wall. Sudden fluorescence illuminated a clan of silken Siamese fighting fish. When they moved they did so with a kind of narcissism, as if studying their reflections in an infinity of mirrors. Hurt peered into the aquarium. His own image, the angular features, the great bony jaw, the steely close-cropped hair, shone back at him. Seeing himself thus he remembered that control was one of his strengths, that he wasn't the kind of man to leap to unfounded conclusions. Perhaps he was judging Perry wrongly.

He turned to look at his fellow American. Sheridan Perry was pouting very slightly, the shadow of an expression left over from a spoiled childhood. Little Sheridan Perry had been the centrepiece of his parents' marriage. Fawned over, bestowed with riches, his life an endless cycle of tearing apart wrapping-paper to get to the goodies, young Perry had reached his tenth birthday before he realised that in most other houses Christmas arrived but once a year.

Perry said, very quietly, 'It wasn't me. I'm not behind it. I wish you'd quit staring at me, Harry. I'm no traitor.'

He looked convincing to Hurt. He sounded like a man telling the truth. Kinnaird's hypothesis of an unknown party seemed suddenly feasible to Hurt, who couldn't stand the pained expression on Perry's face. How could Perry, no matter the unfathomable extent of his greed, be responsible for wiping out the Society?

Hurt shook his head, astonished by his own ability to vacillate. You simply couldn't have it both ways. Either Perry was guilty or he was not. Indecision was a sin in Hurt's eyes.

'Let us set all this unpleasantness and mutual suspicion aside for the moment,' Kinnaird said in a firm way. 'There's something else that complicates our lives – the fact that a certain London policeman is presently on his way to the United States. A man called Frank Pagan. Pagan is the one who interviewed Enrico in Paris. He was present at Caporelli's unfortunate death.'

'Do you think he knows anything?' Hurt asked.

'Very little, I imagine. At this present time. All I can tell you is the information I myself get from Scotland Yard.'

'How did he get on to Enrico?' Sheridan Perry asked, frowning, looking oddly pale and anaemic in a way no hearty carnivore ever should.

Kinnaird replied, 'Through Rosabal, I gather. I haven't seen Pagan's report yet on his meeting with Enrico.'

'But how the hell did Pagan get on to the Cuban?' Hurt wanted to know.

Freddie Kinnaird stretched his legs, clasped his hands at the back of his head, and tried to look relaxed, but he was faintly nervous here. 'British domestic intelligence has an occasional policy of observing members of the Cuban government visiting Britain – diplomats, ministers, etcetera. Now and then, a Cuban is selected for surveillance. Rosabal's number came up. He was watched in Glasgow. He was seen with Enrico.'

While Hurt absorbed this information, he could hear various doors squeak open in the long murky corridor of his mind. The idea that Rosabal had been followed in the United Kingdom worried him deeply. Perhaps Enrico had also been placed under surveillance on account of his association with the Cuban. And where could that have led?

'Is it possible that British intelligence is responsible for the deaths of our members?' he asked.

Kinnaird smiled. 'I don't think it's likely. That kind of information would have come to my attention one way or another.'

'Unless they're on to you, Freddie.'

'Nobody is on to me, Harry. Believe me.' Kinnaird smiled. The very idea of his exposure was preposterous.

The silence in the room was disturbed only by water passing softly through the aquarium filter and a faint *plup* as a fish briefly broke the surface. Then Hurt asked, 'How good is Pagan?'

'His determination is notorious. He's also known for overlooking the book when it suits him,' Kinnaird said. He recalled the hurried telephone conversation he'd had with Martin Burr just before boarding Concorde. 'Right now he's on his way to Miami. He has a contact inside the Cuban exile community. Mind you, I don't think Pagan knows very much. Nor do I imagine he's remotely interested in Cuba or anything that might happen there. He wants Ruhr and he wants this young girl Ruhr was silly enough to grab. He also wants to know the whereabouts of the missile.'

Hurt walked to the window. He surveyed the other blocks of apartments that overlooked the Potomac. Lights burned in windows and a passing yacht created a bright yellow band on the dark waters. Hurt felt suddenly crowded. It was more than the deaths of his associates, it was the idea of this Frank Pagan. He looked at his watch. Everything was so damned close to completion. How could he allow some British cop to interfere? If Pagan was headed for Miami and the Cuban community there, he was getting a little too close. He was trespassing on Harry Hurt's zone of comfort.

'Who's his contact in Miami?'

'This is the interesting part, Harry. According to my information, Pagan's friend is a woman called' – and here Kinnaird consulted a small morocco bound notebook fished from his inside pocket – 'Magdalena Torrente.'

'So? What's so interesting about that?' Hurt asked.

Kinnaird was quiet a second. Then he said, 'Magdalena Torrente is an intimate friend of Rosabal's.'

'Intimate?' Hurt asked, alarmed by this new connection. 'How intimate? What does that mean?'

Kinnaird gazed at the shrunken heads. They really were monstrous little things. Their mouths hung open as if these were the faces of people who had died in unspeakable pain. 'My dear Harry, I can only tell you what I read in the reports. And police reports are not renowned for their pornographic details. She's a friend, a close friend. Perhaps a lover.'

'What does she know? Did Rosabal tell her anything?'

Kinnaird shrugged. 'I don't have the answers. My information isn't complete. Pagan won't tell me anything directly. And since he's not the quickest person when it comes to compiling reports for the Commissioner, I am sometimes not altogether *au courant*. But I rather doubt that Rosabal would confide in this woman anything so important as our undertaking, don't you?'

Hurt nodded, though a little uncertainly. 'I don't like it anyway you cut it. The fact that Pagan's contact in Miami is an intimate friend of Rosabal – this is not good news, Freddie.'

Sheridan Perry said, 'It's very simple. I've always, followed the old line that it's better to be safe than sorry.'

'You mean what I think you mean?' Hurt asked.

Perry nodded but said nothing.

'You'd eliminate the pair?' Hurt asked.

'Eliminate's a good word,' Perry remarked.

Hurt wondered if Perry's suggestion, lethal and yet so simply phrased, was Sheridan's attempt to turn attention away from any suspicion of murderous betrayal that might have gathered around him. Kinnaird had deftly changed that subject a few minutes ago, putting into abeyance the question with which this meeting had begun. Sir Freddie, diplomat, smoother of tangled paths, had focused attention on another problem, one more easily solved than that of identifying the killer behind the murders of the Society members.

'Who would you get to do it?' Hurt asked.

Sheridan Perry shook his head. 'Harry, come on. I don't have an inside track with the criminal fraternity. I thought you might know somebody. After all, you're the man with connections when it comes to guns and guys that know how to use them.'

Hurt had the feeling that Perry's last remark was a way of casting a little light of suspicion on Harry himself. It was undeniably true that he had contacts among ex-soldiers and mercenaries, men who considered killing as natural a function as, say, screwing. Hurt had kept some bad company in his time, also true. Was Perry trying to damn Hurt by association? Was he trying to say that Hurt was the logical candidate if the murders were an inside job?

Sweet Jesus, Hurt thought. When you stepped on board that great rolling locomotive of doubt and suspicion it just gathered speed and kept moving, never stopping at any stations, it rattled and screamed past objectivity in its frantic journey to confusion and madness. He took a couple of deep breaths, seeking the calm centre of himself.

'I could make a call, I guess,' he said. Why deny it? He had the contacts.

'I wish there were some other way.' Kinnaird's voice was quiet.

'There isn't,' Perry said. 'You let this character Pagan go where he pleases – what then? And if the woman happens to have information . . . No, Freddie. There's; no other way. We can't afford to take chances now.'

Hurt stepped inside the kitchen. Kinnaird and Perry could hear him talking quietly on the telephone. He spoke for a few minutes, then he returned to the living-room.

'It's done,' he said flatly.

There was a silence in the room. In the entrance room, behind the closed door, one of the bodyguards coughed. Hurt strolled to the window. The view was breathtaking. There was more traffic on the river now: launches, yachts, one of which was strung like a Christmas tree. In the windows of other apartment buildings lights were dulled by drawn curtains or tinted glass.

He said, 'Ever since we became involved in this Cuban business, we've had nothing but problems. I remember when everything was easy. Plain sailing. No clouds. Full membership. We didn't have deaths, killings. We weren't involved in all this . . .' He waved a hand. The appropriate word had eluded him. 'Mainly, though, our associates were still alive and well.'

He stared across the expanse of the Washington night. Because of the vast electrical glow of the city, the stars were dimmed in the sky. He was about to turn his face back to the room when a bullet, fired from an apartment tower nearby, pierced the window in an almost soundless manner.

It penetrated his skull.

Harry Hurt put his hand up to his head, thinking for the shortest time possible, the kind of time only a sophisticated atomic clock might measure, that he had a migraine. It was his final perception, quicker than quicksilver. He neither heard nor saw Freddie Kinnaird and Sheridan Perry rush to the place where, face-down, he had fallen.

The Caribbean

The freighter, an old vessel badly in need of fresh paint, flew the red white and blue flag of Cuba. It was not of Cuban origin. Built in Newcastle, England, some forty years before, it was registered in Panama and named – at least for this voyage – *La Mandadera*. It was a vessel of formidable shabbiness. Rust seemingly held the ship together, creating brown bands around bow and stern.

The captain was a moustached Cuban – American called Luis Sandoval who lived in Florida. He had fled Cuba in 1964 with his wife and family at a time when rumours concerning the removal of children from Cuba to Russia had been rife on the island. It was said that Fidel was going to send Cuban kids to the Soviet Union to be educated and raised there as good little Communists. Luis, like thousands of others, had left Cuba for good. For more than twenty-five years he'd plied his trade as a fishing-guide around Miami, impatiently waiting for the moment of his return to the homeland.

Now he was in the vanguard of the liberation movement.

He stood on the bridge of *La Mandadera*, his binoculars trained on the dark shore five miles away. There was a half-moon and some low cloud and the sea was tranquil. Sandoval scanned the shoreline slowly. He wasn't nervous.

There! To his right he saw the sign he was looking for: a red-orange flare that ripped the darkness like a wound opening. It was followed by a constant flame, a bonfire burning on the beach. Luis Sandoval gave his crew the order to proceed. Within a mile of the place known as Cabo Gracias a Dios he would drop anchor and wait for history to take place. It did not escape his vanity that he was one of many co-authors helping to shape forthcoming events.

Twenty-three thousand miles above *La Mandadera*, a United States spy satellite, that until recently had been bugged by a mysterious malfunction, began to take photographs, hundreds of them, thousands, pictures that would be relayed back to a deciphering station deep in the green West Virginia countryside, where they would be processed and analysed and, like little coded mysteries from space, broken wide open. These same photographs also showed a stormy cloud formation, as menacing in its darkness as a black hole, moving across the Gulf of Mexico and the Yucatan Peninsula toward the waters of the Caribbean.

16 Miami

On its descent into Miami the plane was buffeted like paper in a wind-tunnel. Pagan was the first person off. He entered the stuffy terminal, ploughed through customs and immigration, explained the gun and holster in his overnight bag to an ill-mannered officer who wanted to confiscate it, Scotland Yard or no Scotland Yard identification. A quick phone call was made to Lieutenant Philip Navarro of the Dade County Police, the name of Martin Burr was dropped, and Pagan was let through grudgingly.

He found a cab driven by a cheerful Haitian called Marcel Foucault, whose English was as thick as bouillabaisse. Pagan had Magdalena's address from the forms she'd had to complete for British immigration. It was a house in Key Biscayne. Foucault, who howled appreciatively from his window at passing women, and shook with irrepressible mirth when they responded, claimed to know Miami like a native.

Pagan had never been in this city before. Downtown was bright – office blocks blazed and hotels rose like lit glass slabs. Palm trees, tropical shrubs alongside the road, these surprised him with their alien lushness. He rolled down his window, smelled the salt air. Small man-made islands, loaded with mansions, sat in the dark of Biscayne Bay: Palm Island, San Marco, Hibiscus.

Suddenly the taxi was out over black water, suspended impossibly in the air. A bridge, of course. Pagan shut his eyes, fought off a certain dizziness that assailed him. The turbulent flight, a glass of awful Sauternes on the plane, the ache in his chest – all elements that had unsettled him.

Marcel Foucault nodded toward a cluster of lights at the end of the bridge. 'Zat's Key Biscayne.'

The night air rushing through the window helped Pagan feel better. He thought about Magdalena. What was she going to say when he turned up on her doorstep?

He looked at the growing lights of Key Biscayne. Launches along the shoreline were tethered to private jetties that led to expensive houses. American opulence always impressed him; he thought Americans did wealth better than anybody else. They purchased more, collected more, stored more. They also produced more, ate more, drank more, and divorced more. Rich people here lived as if all America were a going-out-of-business sale.

'Yo street, ami,' Marcel Foucault said. He stopped the cab outside a large house barely visible beyond dense shrubbery. Prolific plants obscured the yellow light burning beside the front doorway; thousands of moths threw themselves at the bulb, frenzied participants in mass suicide.

Pagan, a little surprised that Magdalena lived in such a well-heeled neighbourhood, stepped out. Had he expected some crummy cellar filled with anti-Fidel radicals running a leaky old printing-press? He paid the driver, then watched the cab pull away. He was apprehensive now. Given that Magdalena knew anything, was she likely to tell him? What had seemed a good idea in London now felt insubstantial to him. He wondered if pain-killers had fuelled this whole transatlantic crossing, if the idea had been inspired by the actions of the chemicals absorbed in his system – a junkie's trip.

Picking up his overnight bag, Pagan moved along the. pathway to the front door. He rang the bell, waited, rang again. He was aware of the malicious little eye of the peephole: somebody was watching him from inside. He heard a chain drawn back, a bolt sliding, then the door was opened.

'Frank.'

She appeared in shadow, motionless only a second before she stepped forward and, to Pagan's surprise, threw her arms around him. The embrace, unexpectedly fierce, threw him off balance. He supported himself against the door jamb even as Magdalena held on to him tightly. It was a welcome he could never have anticipated. In a black suede mini-skirt and white silk blouse, she was barefoot and delectable. She whispered his name very quietly almost as if she were afraid of breaking some spell.

She led him inside, across a large tiled hall to a sitting-room. She switched on a soft light. The room was starkly furnished – a sofa, a chair, a table, the lamp. One of everything, he thought. She clearly didn't use this room much. It had the waxen quality of a window-display.

Still holding his hand, she led him to the sofa, then sat alongside him, curling her feet up under her body. He noticed some slight puffiness beneath her eyes, as if she might have been crying before.

She took a cigarette pack from a pocket at the side of her skirt and lit one with a black Bic. He couldn't remember seeing her smoke before and she did it in an unpractised way, like a thirteen-year-old schoolgirl. Something was wrong here, he thought, a sadness, a change. Her smile was a terrific effort, but it was more teeth than pleasure.

'You don't seem overwhelmingly surprised to find me on your doorstep,' he said.

'The weird thing is, I just happened to be thinking about you. Lo and behold, here you are. Is it an omen?'

There was a strangeness in her manner. She was present yet absent, here yet elsewhere. 'What exactly were you thinking about me?' he asked.

'How nice it would be to see you. How nice it would be to see a friendly face. I need one.'

'Why so gloomy?' He laid a hand gently on her shoulder.

'I've had better days.'

She blew smoke up at the ceiling. She had a wonderful throat; lined a little now – what didn't time touch? – it was still marvellous and feminine. It needed no adornment to make it enticing.

'You didn't come all this way just to see me,' she said.

'Who else do I know in Miami?'

'You must have some business here.'

'Business and pleasure. The lines get blurred where you're involved.'

The telephone rang. Magdalena excused herself, rose from the sofa, and crossed the room. She turned her back to him as she picked up the receiver; when she spoke she used Spanish. The conversation was brief. She hung up, glanced at her watch, then walked back to the sofa. She didn't sit this time. Instead, she kneeled on the cushion and faced him. She lit another cigarette. Her short skirt slid up her thigh. Her black eyes were blacker than ever before. You could see all manner of sorrows in them.

'You were saying something about business,' she said. There was a new note in her voice, perhaps a little impatience. Maybe the phone call had reminded her of an appointment.

He suddenly felt scattered, weary. 'I need coffee. Do you mind?'

'I made some before. It's probably still hot.' She went out into the kitchen, and returned with a cup. Pagan took it, sipped slowly.

'Now,' she said, and she touched the back of his hand. 'Speak to me.'

Pagan set his cup down. 'It's a tough one.'

'I'm a big girl.'

'It concerns Rosabal.'

'Rosabal?' She feigned innocence, her acting amateur and half-hearted.

'Ground rules,' Pagan said. 'No bullshit. I know more than you think. If we can both tell the truth from the beginning, it's going to save time.'

She was quiet a moment. 'How long have you known about him?'

'Since you were in London,' Pagan said. 'He was concealed – a little ignominiously, in my opinion – inside the bathroom in your hotel room.'

Magdalena smiled. 'I thought that was amusing. But he likes anonymity. He didn't want anyone to see him.'

'A few people did. Including British intelligence. He was followed. Not always carefully. But he was followed.'

Magdalena crushed out her cigarette in a small glass ashtray. 'Okay. You know about Rafael and me. It still doesn't explain why you're here.'

Pagan told her. He did so briefly, without incidental detail. He left out the deaths of Caporelli and his associates, sketching a mosaic in which certain pieces were omitted. Halfway through the narrative Magdalena walked to the unlit fireplace and stood, legs slightly apart, hands on hips, a defensive attitude.

She waited until Pagan was finished before she said, 'One thing I always liked about you, Frank. You have more imagination than a cop should. But this time I think you've gone overboard, baby.' She smoked again. The small black lighter flashed; Magdalena's cheeks hollowed as she drew smoke into her lungs.

'Overboard how?' he asked.

'Rafael and Ruhr. That's a hell of a connection. What could Rafe have in common with that maniac? And I don't see where a stolen missile fits Rafe's life, Frank.' She sat down on the couch.

Rafe – the lover's abbreviation, the intimacy. The magic word that opened doors on to private worlds. Pagan stood up. His circulation was sluggish. He walked round the room. On the mantel were photographs of a man and a woman, presumably Magdalena's parents. Pagan glanced at them. Magdalena more closely resembled her father.

'When you were in London, you mentioned a coup of some kind in Cuba,' Pagan said. 'Is Rosabal involved?'

'You misheard me, Frank.'

'Let me rephrase it. You *hinted* at a coup.'

'I don't think so, Frank. You misunderstood.'

Pagan stepped toward her, looked down at where she sat on the couch. 'We agreed. No games. No bullshit.'

'*You* agreed. You play by your own rules. I don't remember saying I'd comply.'

'Don't fuck around with me, Magdalena. I don't have time for crap.'

'Keep talking rough. I like it.'

Pagan had to smile. His history with this woman, the passion locked in the past – how could he be anything other than transparent to her? How could he act demanding, and tough, and hope she'd be swayed?

She stood up, gazed into his face, then put her arms round him. Her body was limp. This was another little unexpected act. She was full of surprises tonight. What he detected in her was an unhappiness for which she hadn't found the appropriate expression, and so she held him this way, clutched him for consolation, security, light in some dark place.

He said, 'Look, there's a hostage involved. A child who's only fourteen years old. There's a terrorist responsible for more deaths than I want to think about. He may hurt the kid. He may kill her, if he hasn't already. Too many people have died, Magdalena. I want the kid back. I want to know what plans there are for the missile. And I want Gunther Ruhr. I'm betting Rafael knows where to find him. You might call it a long shot, but it's better than nothing. I need to know what you know. I need anything you can give me.'

Magdalena Torrente was very quiet. She disengaged herself from Pagan and walked away. She stopped at the curtained window on the other side of the room, beyond the reach of the lamp. Her features were indistinct. Ash, untended, dropped from her cigarette to the rug. *He may hurt the kid*; she couldn't stand that idea. She couldn't take the notion of any more hurt.

Pagan went to her and touched the back of her hand. She didn't look at him. She spoke in a voice filled with little catches, as though she were having trouble getting air to her lungs. Flatly, without tone, she said, 'Okay, you've come a long way, you deserve to know something. I don't know a damn thing about Ruhr or any missile. All I can tell you is how things were *supposed* to be. Army officers and their troops opposed to Castro were to seize various strategic barracks. This act was intended to galvanise the democratic underground – we're talking about thousands of people, strikes, demonstrations, the occupation of public buildings, public disobedience, armed insurrection. Everything was supposedly well-orchestrated. Rafael was the leader, the organiser. The plan called for him to head the new government after Castro was deposed. The new democratic government, I should say. People, myself included, intended to return from exile to participate in this . . . this brave new Cuba. It was neat, simple, and it might have been relatively bloodless. But it changed.'

'How?'

'The information I have indicates that Rosabal betrayed the cause.' It was in her voice, her face, the burden of terrible disappointment. But more than that, Pagan thought, there was another emotion, and for want of a better word he called it grief. Magdalena wasn't grieving only for a lost cause. She'd been cut where it pained her, in her heart.

Pagan had to press on, he had to get beyond her sorrow. He hadn't come all the way to Miami to learn about the failure of a counter-revolution. He wasn't interested. He didn't give a shit about Cuba. The world stage didn't enthrall him. His own world was small, and its boundaries well-marked, a specialised place in which wrongs were righted whenever that was possible and justice was more than a dry textbook notion.

He said, 'Did Rosabal ever mention Ruhr to you?'

She shook her head. 'Ruhr! You're obsessed, Frank. I still don't see how Ruhr comes into it. I've heard of people barking up wrong trees before now, but you get the blue ribbon.'

Pagan ignored this. 'What other people did our pal Rafe meet in Britain?'

'I don't have a clue, Frank.'

'Think hard.'

'I *am* thinking.'

Now there was an impatient edge in her voice; she was tired of questions. She'd been asking them of herself all day long, ever since the meeting with Garrido and Duran. Question after question; they distilled themselves into one simple inquiry – Why had Rafael betrayed her?

She clenched her hands and strolled the room, confined by walls and ceilings. She'd gone over her relationship with Rosabal for hours, tracing it from the first meeting – Acapulco, instant attraction, common political convictions, sex marked as much by passion as by tenderness, the kind that grew, at least as far as she was concerned, into love – to the last encounter in London. *I love him*, she thought. And she wanted to believe, despite her weakening conviction, that he loved her, that he had justifiable reasons for his apparent treachery, that the democratic revolution was still a possibility. But the obstacles were so damned hard to overcome.

That day she'd walked the streets of Little Havana with dear old Garrido, arm-in-arm under the purple noon sun. Solicitous Garrido, old family friend. Kindly Garrido, his spindly hand wrapped around hers. He talked of love in an airy way, as if it were a book he'd read seventy years ago and all he recalled were pages of parchment now crumbled. He spoke of the manner in which love was often victimised, brutalised, how there were demarcation lines of the emotions across which warring lovers skirmished, leaving the losers battered.

This was not language to which Magdalena Torrente was accustomed. She was no loser. No victim. And she had no intention of becoming one so long as there was a chance still that Rafael loved her; and in that inviolate part of her free of shadows and doubts, her knowledge was certain: *Rafael loved her.*

The great trick was to keep reality from intruding.

In a situation like this, where trust has been so badly violated, there are not many choices; something has to be done, Garrido had said when they were drinking coffee in the Versailles restaurant. He had shrugged then, an eloquent gesture of disappointment and hatred, and yet there was nothing of surprise in it, as if he'd plumbed the human condition so deeply there were no astonishments left to him. He had been cheated, and his dreams abruptly ended.

Pagan held both her hands and said, 'I wish I didn't have to ask you all these bloody questions.'

'I don't, have answers, Frank.'

He was silent for a time. 'How exactly did Rosabal betray you?'

'Begin with the matter of his wife.'

'Wives tend to be problematic. Maybe he intends to leave her. Who knows?'

'I'm told he only just married her, but I love you for your optimism, Frank.' Magdalena looked down at how her hands were firmly held by Pagan's, and she enjoyed the sense of security in the touch. She raised her face, tiptoed, kissed the side of his mouth.

She said, 'I'm just a casualty of the heart. Other people were shafted in their pocketbooks. He's pretty generous when it comes to spreading treachery around. Over a period of three or four years, thousands of exiled Cubans in Miami and New Jersey contributed millions of dollars to the overthrow of Castro. Most of it ended up – guess where?'

'In Rafael's pocket?'

'That's what they tell me, Frank.'

'Here's what I don't get. If he's a common embezzler, he'd take the money and that would be it. End of. But what the hell is he doing involved with Gunther Ruhr? And this whole missile affair – what is his part in that?'

She shrugged. 'You've come three thousand miles for *nada* except to see a poor confused woman whose brain is scrambled eggs. I don't have answers for you.'

Pagan stepped away from her, finished his coffee, set down the cup. He had a hollow moment of sheer fatigue. He went to the kitchen and poured another coffee, then returned. Magdalena stood in the centre of the floor, hugging herself as if she were cold. She seemed smaller now, diminished in a way, as if Rafe, Captain Charm, had stolen more than her love.

He sipped coffee. There was a key here, he was sure of it, a key that would unlock all the doors that puzzled him, that would allow him access to the room that contained Ruhr and Stephanie Brough. And that key was Rafael, pirate of people's money, swindler of feelings.

Rafael had played along with this democratic underground in Cuba and the great outswelling of patriotic sentiment in the exile communities for his own ends, obviously.

But what were those ends?

Frank, what did all ambitious men seek, for God's sake?

Control. Beyond money, that's what they lusted after, dreamed of, salivated over, schemed and cheated for, maimed and killed for. That's what obsessed them and drove some of them to an odd vindictive madness. They became possessed by the very thing they'd tried to own: solitary control, the chance to shape their little comer of the world to their own liking.

Was that it? Did Rafael want Cuba in such a way that he didn't have to share it with any squabble of exiles who believed in something as primitive and muddle-headed as, heaven forbid, *democracy?* His own private sandcastle, his own fantasy, a place where he could rule the tides. Did it come down to that in the end?

Only Rafe would know.

Where did the missile fit? Where did Caporelli and Chapotin and Kluger come into this picture? Why were these men dying?

Missiles weren't for firing in this day and age. They were playing-cards, toys owned by the richest kids on the block, useful when you needed to flex a little muscle, make a demand, or simply just threaten.

Pagan shut his eyes. *Had Caporelli and friends wanted their bit of Cuba too?*

In the late 1950s Caporelli already had a taste for the place; so, presumably, had Jean-Paul Chapotin. Maybe they liked the island the way it used to be – after all, hadn't it made Caporelli wealthy? It probably hadn't exactly hurt Jean-Paul either. But they couldn't turn clocks back as long as Fidel ran the country.

Solution: get rid of Fidel. How?

A missile on the island would have the effect of –

Of what?

Of making a whole lot of people in this hemisphere rather unhappy.

So what?

Shit, it was slipping away from him.

Fatigued, he sat down on the sofa.

Magdalena sat beside him. 'You look exhausted. Why don't you rest for a while? Stretch out here.'

Pagan had the feeling again that he was missing something simple. But Rafe had the answer. Only Rafe.

'I don't have time to rest,' he said. He stood up. Bones creaked: the small embarrassment of age.

She looked at her wristwatch. 'I have to go out, Frank.'

'A late date?'

'Something like that. You can stay here if you like.' She walked across the room to the stairs leading to the upper part of the house. After a few minutes she came back down, dressed now in a tan leather jacket and blue jeans and looking in her paleness rather fragile.

'Where are you going?' he asked. She didn't exactly look dressed for any commonplace date.

'Out.' She had an ambivalent little smile. He noticed a slightly crooked molar, a tiny flaw he'd quite forgotten, and he remembered how he'd once been enchanted by this trifling imperfection because it humanised her beauty. *Smile for me, come on*: had he really said such things back then and loved her so insanely that the sight of a crooked tooth drove him out of his skull?

'And I twiddle my thumbs? Wait for you to come back? I don't have time for that.'

'I don't know how long I'll be gone. And I can't help you. I can't tell you any more than I already have, and even that was more than I wanted.'

He was irritated by her furtive manner, her secrecy, the way she was dismissing him.

She made to move past him. He placed himself in her way.

'Why the great hurry?'

'I'm sick of questions, Frank. I'm sick of the ones you've been asking and I'm sick of the ones I've been asking myself.'

He moved to one side and she crossed the hall to unlock the door to the garage. Pagan followed her. There was a grey BMW in the garage.

'I'm leaving alone, Frank. I don't want company.'

'And I don't want to be stranded here.'

'Call a cab.'

'I'll ride with you. Take me back to Miami. Drop me off at a hotel. I won't get in your way.'

She sighed. 'You're a determined bastard.'

She got in on the driver's side; Pagan slid into the passenger seat. The garage doors opened by remote control. They slid up, revealing the dark garden in front. She steered forward, the door closed behind her. Then she was out on the street, driving with a carelessness that didn't thrill Pagan, who hated being the passenger anyway.

The BMW approached an intersection, darkened houses, dim lamplights. Magdalena slowed just a little when a large Buick entered the intersection out of nowhere and wheeled straight toward the German car; surprised, Magdalena shoved her foot on the accelerator and the BMW thrust forward, avoiding the larger car by a couple of feet. Pagan turned his head, saw the Buick brake, swing in an arc, clamber up on the sidewalk in a series of small sparks, then come back again – directly at Magdalena's car. She evaded the Buick a second time, but only just.

'Jesus Christ!' Magdalena said. 'What the hell's going on?'

Pagan didn't answer. He looked back at the big, powerful Buick as it passed beneath a streetlight. Two figures occupied the sleek vehicle – a gunman and a driver. The gunman leaned from the passenger window. The weapon he held was a Magnum. A single shot cracked the air; it struck the rear bumper of the BMW, ricocheted.

The Buick roared, veering from side to side in an attempt to draw level with the BMW, striking kerbs, scraping the sides of parked cars, propelled by one murderous purpose. The gunman was still hanging from the window, but the Buick was shuddering in such a way that accuracy was out of the question. When he fired a second time he hit the trunk of the BMW, a dramatic noise like that of a drum struck hard.

Now Magdalena was approaching the Rickenbacker Causeway which linked Key Biscayne with Miami, a long stretch over black water. The Buick persisted, tracking the BMW at a distance of some fifteen or twenty feet. It had all the reality of a dream, Pagan thought – this absurd chase, the gunman and the salt wind that rolled through the open windows of the BMW. Indisputably real was the next gunshot, the bullet that smashed this time through the rear window and whined inside the BMW and passed between Magdalena and Pagan and departed by way of the windshield. As close as you want to come to death, he thought.

There was other traffic on the bridge but sparse at this time of day. A few cars came to a halt as the BMW and the Buick screeched past. Halfway across the Causeway the Buick found reserves of speed and moved up alongside the BMW and the gunman fired directly through the passenger window. Pagan heard it, felt it, understood that this particular bullet might have had his name and number on it; but it ripped the air around his neck and sliced harmlessly past Magdalena, who gasped at the proximity of death.

It was time to shoot back. He'd been delaying in the hope that Magdalena would outrun the other car and thus make it unnecessary for him to fire his gun – he hated the combustible mixture of stray bullets and innocent onlookers in their parked cars – but the Buick clearly had muscle and wasn't going to be outmanoeuvred.

The faces of the men in the American car were plainly visible to Pagan under the Causeway lamps. The gunman was square-jawed and blond; he might have been a man peddling door-to-door some religion or sectarian magazine – Mormonism or *The Watchtower*. The driver was a contrast, dark hair, a brutal little mouth.

Pagan shoved his gun through the window and fired. He missed first time. His second shot must have struck the driver because the dark-haired man raised his hands from the steering-wheel as if it had become suddenly too hot to touch and the Buick, without guidance, skidded out of control. There was one heart-chilling moment in which the laws of physics appeared to have been contravened when the Buick went sliding toward the edge of the bridge and rose a couple of inches before rushing through the barrier and soaring out, like some doomed flying-machine from Detroit, into the air above Biscayne Bay. With its horn sounding in panic, it twisted as it fell, as if trying to right itself in mid-air. It struck the spooky black waters, tossed up a vast white garland of foam, and then sunk bonnet-first into the wet darkness. Its tail-lights, lit still, went under like the red eyes of a creature resigned to drowning.

Pagan sat back and caught his breath. He shut his eyes.

At the end of the Causeway, Magdalena turned the car into a quiet street behind Brickell Avenue, a place of darkened office buildings. She laid her face upon the rim of the steering-wheel. Her knuckles were the colour of ivory. She was drained.

'Were they after you or me?' she asked, a breathless quality in her voice.

'I don't know,' Pagan replied.

Magdalena slumped back in her seat, turned her face toward him. 'If they were after you, how did they know you were here? Did you tell anyone you were coming to Miami?'

'Only the Commissioner.'

'And you trust him?'

'Beyond a doubt.' A leak, Pagan thought, even as he answered Magdalena's question. A leak had led to the horror of Shepherd's Bush. Perhaps the same mysterious source was behind the gunman, somebody no scrambled telephones could ever frustrate, somebody privileged, somebody with an inside track.

'If nobody knows *you're* here, it follows that I was the target,' she said.

'Maybe. But who sent the hit man?'

'Christ, I don't even want to speculate,' she said. And she didn't. Magdalena was afraid, but she didn't like to show fear. She could collect herself only if she shut out of her mind the unpleasantness on the bridge. Her brain was running on empty. She'd done nothing but think and brood ever since she'd gone that morning to Garrido's restaurant.

Who could have wanted her dead anyway? The only candidate that came to mind was the last one she wanted to consider: *Rafael*. If he was really through with her, maybe his next step was to get her out of the way permanently. Maybe he thought her a potential embarrassment to him, a risk. She pushed these ideas aside. She had to believe that the intended target was Pagan, not her, to believe without question that Rafael had nothing to do with it.

For his part Pagan was weary of puzzles; he yearned for solutions. Puzzles became jungles and he needed a pathway, a machete.

'You can get out here,' she said. 'You'll find a hotel within a couple of blocks.'

'Maybe we should stick together. The waterlogged pair in that Buick might have friends in the vicinity.'

She reached across him, opened the passenger door. 'Don't worry about me. I'm just sorry you came all this way, Frank.' She kissed him quickly on the side of his face. 'Good luck.'

Pagan stepped out with great reluctance. No sooner had he moved than she pulled the door shut behind him and slipped the car into gear. He gazed at her face behind glass, thinking how forlorn she looked; she stared at him, smiling in an ungenerous way, a distracted little expression. He was irritated for having given in to her without an argument. He should have insisted, stayed with her no matter where she was headed.

But how could he? There was an urgency in him still, a drive to explore his only other connection, even though he thought he might be too late. What had Magdalena told him anyway? Nothing he could use. Nothing that would bring him closer to what he sought.

He watched her grey car pass under dull streetlamps until it turned a corner and disappeared.

The street was now vaguely menacing like all empty streets that lie behind major thoroughfares. Pagan walked in the direction of Brickell Avenue, where it was brighter and busier and the shadows less complex. He found a hotel. As soon as he entered the vast lobby, where enormous palms and ferns reached up to a tall ceiling, he walked to the bank of public telephones beyond the registration desk.

As he flipped through the pages of the phone directory, he realised he'd left his overnight bag at Magdalena's house. What the hell. He still had his gun, wallet, passport, painkillers; the rest was just luggage.

Havana

Rafael Rosabal left his pleasantly spacious apartment in the Vedado at one a.m. His wife Estela, her long black hair undone and spread upon her lace pillow, woke when she heard him move quietly across the bedroom. She whispered to him, but he didn't hear, or if he did he was in too much of a hurry to pay attention. They'd made love some hours before, Rosabal curiously mechanical, distracted, Estela unpractised and still shy with her own and her husband's body. Sex was a disappointment to her; Rafael, who had known many women, loved her as though his mind and body were elsewhere.

Now he was leaving and still she hadn't mentioned the miracle of her pregnancy.

She listened to the sound of a car arrive outside, then the front door of the apartment closed softly. Sometimes Estela suspected a mistress, someone to whom Rafael hurried, someone in whose heated embrace he found the passion he so clearly hadn't discovered in his marriage. The thought terrified her, all the more so because she could never imagine this woman's face. Once, waiting in this apartment for Rafael to come home, she'd envisaged a face without features, smooth and eyeless and terrible.

At other times Estela believed her only true rival was Rafael's ambition, a far more dangerous enemy than any woman would have been. He restlessly spurred himself on, pursuing furtive goals; there was that strange, secretive business involving her father, the General, and his intermediary Diaz-Alonso – who came to the apartment late at night to whisper with Rafael – but Estela, though she eavesdropped, pretended to have no interest in politics and all the intrigues and gossip it entailed.

However, absolutely nothing that happened in this apartment escaped her. Everything she heard she stored away at the back of her mind. She was never noticed eavesdropping because she was never really noticed at all – she poured wine, made coffee; a walk-on role, a serving-girl, the Minister's young and rather vapid wife. But she was smarter than anyone knew. She listened as thoroughly as any bug planted inside a telephone receiver or under the lip of a table or smuggled at the core of a rose, and she memorised what she heard. In a life that was mainly empty, rescued from total vacuity by visits to beauty parlours and hairdressers and those infrequent times when Rafael deigned to screw her, listening and storing up items of information were her principal pastimes.

Whatever was going on, the quiet phone calls, the late-night conferences, the mysterious comings and goings, the talk of ships and military movements, and the mention of this man Ruhr, whose name was whispered as though it were too evil to pronounce aloud, made her uneasy. She worried about her husband; she worried too about her father, whose most recent utterances in her company were venomously anti-Castro.

She despised Castro as much as anyone, but she understood the dangers involved in plotting against the *fidelistas*. People vanished abruptly in the middle of the night and were never heard of again; friends and acquaintances, even those who had once been close to Fidel himself – nobody was immune. She wanted nothing to happen to either Rafael or the General. Nobody had succeeded in overthrowing El Viejo, and Estela doubted that anyone ever could.

She had been a young woman of privilege in a country that had officially abandoned elitism; unofficially, by rewarding those in favoured positions of power, the system had created a new set of iniquities, and Estela had benefited – a school in Switzerland, a year in France, a summer in Spain. She'd been exposed to freedoms in other countries, and ways unthinkable in Cuba, which she saw now as something of a silly little backwater, crude and unfashionable, a slab of miserably humid land in the Caribbean run by ruffians and gangsters and fought over as if it were El Dorado by men who put vanity before peace, martyrdom before liberty.

But nothing in her experience had prepared her for this undertow of doom that racked her as she walked to the window and looked down. Absently she stroked her stomach, flat now but soon to be big like a flower newly opened; and yet even the notion of this beautiful baby did not diminish the sense of dark fate she felt. Moonlight lay across the surface of the swimming-pool. The lights of her husband's car faded between palm trees, and then were gone out of sight. She crossed herself because she wanted divine protection for her husband.

Had Rafael seen her, he might have mocked her idiot superstition.

The car, driven by Rosabal's chauffeur, went as far as Havana harbour, where Rosabal got out. He carefully descended a flight of old stone steps, slippery, studded with barnacles. He paused where the water lapped this ancient stonework. The boat that awaited him was a black, high-speed cigarette-boat, the kind favoured by gun-runners and dope smugglers. It was occupied by two men in shirtsleeves; Rosabal recognised them as attachés to Capablanca. They seemed undignified out of uniform.

He stepped into the boat. The motor started. The craft speeded across the harbour. Rosabal looked up at the sky; the moon was behind clouds. A brisk wind cuffed the surface of the sea. He turned to gaze back at Havana, which was mainly dark. Now and again measures were taken to save electricity. Lifts failed, streetlights went out, homes were deprived of power. This, Rosabal thought, was Communism in the late twentieth century, a compendium of broken promises and lies, a putrefaction held together by the weakening glue that was *fidelisma*.

No more. Before this day was out it would be boxed for burial, with nobody to weep for it.

President Rafael Rosabal. He liked the sound of it. Rosabal's regime would be neither democratic nor, like that of Castro, puritanical and prohibitive. It would be a benign dictatorship, at least in the beginning; somewhere along the way, years from now, there might be a measure of popular participation. But first the people had to be weaned from the mindlessness in which Castro had raised them, they had to be freed from the shop-worn cant of Marxism. The citizens were like little kids who'd never chewed on anything but the mush provided to them by Fidel. They had to be led to the table and shown how to use a knife and fork and eat real food.

Those disgusting agencies of grass-roots espionage, the Committees for the Defence of the Revolution, would be abolished and their leaders jailed. The ministries, bureaucracies gone mad with that special insanity of paperwork, would be stripped to nothing and the ministers demoted or incarcerated. He would be cautious at first about the use of firing-squads: why alienate the West as Fidel had done thirty years ago? The nightclubs would open again and there would be gambling and if a man wanted a prostitute in Havana, that was his own business; the government would take its cut. Sin would be highly taxed.

American and European investors would be courted avidly, Soviet advisors ejected. Nor would Rosabal be blackmailed by the demands of the United States for representative democracy and human rights legislation; in any event, the Americans would be so gratified, at least for years to come, by the end of Cuban Communism, that political and social 'irregularities' would be overlooked.

Rosabal thought of Cuba as a big dark arena; and he had his hand on the generator that would set it brilliantly alight. His hand, nobody else's. And because he controlled the generator, he had access not only to light but wealth, great wealth, obscene wealth, the kind of riches that a boy from Guantanamo Province should not even dream about. He'd milk Cuba; he'd plunder it as it had never been plundered before. And he'd do it with a benefactor's smile on his face for an exultant populace that considered him a hero, the one who had rid Cuba of Castro.

Havana dwindled, the shoreline receded. Twelve miles out a yacht appeared, a dark-hulled fifty-footer, equipped with communications hardware and a mass of antennae. A light blinked three times. Rosabal knew the signal. He was to board the yacht, *La Danzarina del Mar*.

The cigarette-boat moved alongside *La Danzarina*. Rosabal reached for the rope ladder that hung from the side of the yacht and climbed nimbly up to the deck.

'Rafael, my friend.'

The man who stepped toward Rosabal had a pleasant smile, although not one that Rosabal readily trusted. Despite the fact it was night, he wore tinted glasses. He was dressed in a double-breasted blazer and smart grey flannels and expensive sneakers which looked as if they'd never been worn before. They squeaked on the teak deck.

Hands were clasped, warmly shaken. Both men walked along the deck; in the shadows white-shirted crew members kept careful watch, as if they expected a murderous assault from the ocean. Rosabal leaned against the handrail. Havana was almost imperceptible now. There were brief flickers of lightning from the Gulf of Mexico, far to the west.

'It doesn't look like much from here, does it, Rafael?'

Rosabal agreed.

'Just the same, a whole lot of people have gone to a whole lot of trouble over that island, Rafael. A speck on the globe, nothing more. And it gets all kinds of people in a lather.'

'A hundred thousand square kilometres of real estate,' Rosabal said.

'Which makes people very greedy.'

'As you say.'

The man took off his tinted glasses. 'Are you going to give me what I want, Rafael?'

'Of course. You have my word.'

'No Communist experiments. No flirting with the Soviet bloc. You want loans, you want agricultural machinery, you want certain types of weapons, you want technical advisors, you come to Washington. I don't expect you to smell like a rose, Rafael. You're going to be a very rich man, and very rich men never smell quite right somehow. But I expect you to play fair with me and my government. We're prepared to overlook some things – after all, you've got a long teething period to go through. Just don't overdo it. No excesses, no blatant transgressions, and we'll all be happy.' The man was silent, gazing toward Cuba with a proprietorial air. 'Let's face it, the Caribbean is America's swimming-pool, Rafael. Nobody wants litter in their pool, do they? Nobody wants to swim in dirty water.'

'We have a firm agreement. I will not go back on anything.' Rosabal looked closely at the other man. He noticed for the first time a flesh-coloured strip of Bandaid at the side of the man's forehead.

'Been in the wars, Allen?'

Allen Falk patted the back of Rosabal's hand. 'Your people got their timing wrong.'

'I heard about it. What can I say? They're zealous men.'

'They blew up the limo before they were supposed to. I happened to be a spectator. It's nothing.'

Rafael Rosabal smiled. 'We made amends, of course. Harry Hurt was shot some hours ago in Washington.'

Falk slid his hands into the pockets of his blazer. He looked like an amateur yachtsman readying himself for a photograph. 'Poor Harry and that goddam society of his. Greedy men. Men like that always want more. They don't know when to stop.'

'They were very useful. They served a purpose.'

Both men were silent. The wind blew again, flapping Falk's pants against his legs, tossing Rosabal's collar up against his cheek, shaking the antennae on board.

Rosabal enjoyed how he'd played the Society for all it was worth, how he'd borrowed men from General Capablanca's Secret Service, his private corps of élite killers; shadowy, lethal men who had all the feelings of machines, how they'd murdered the members of the Society – each of whom thought his membership such a big secret – one by one. Now the Society was dying, and with it all its hopes of controlling Cuba. Hurt and Caporelli and the others had been used, deceived in the most brutal way; they'd financed an army, stolen a missile, purchased a counter-revolution – and for what?

So that Rafael Rosabal could become the new President of a new Cuba.

Falk said, 'There was one tiny fruit-fly in our nice shiny apple, Rafael. A British cop called Pagan.' Falk looked at his watch, a slender disk on his wrist. 'He wanted to talk to you about Gunther Ruhr, as I understand. Keen sort of guy. Anxious to get Ruhr.'

'Pagan,' Rosabal said, thinking of London, of Magdalena, the hotel room. He remembered Frank Pagan. 'I notice you use the past tense.'

Al Falk, city dweller, accustomed only to the copper-tinted broth of pollution, took an exaggerated lungful of sea air. 'One of Harry Hurt's last acts was to arrange for Pagan's demise. He knew all these Soldier of Fortune nuts who kill for five hundred bucks. Frank Pagan is probably dead by this time.'

Rosabal frowned. Why did he feel a small cloud cross his mind just then? He thought of Magdalena and wondered if she had been a source of information for the English policeman – but what could Magdalena possibly tell Pagan anyhow? Nothing that could ever be proved. She could at best babble about how democracy was on its way to Cuba, and perhaps how she had ferried money for the new revolution, and the part she expected to play in Cuba's future; that was it, that was all. Silly chatter. *Balbuceo*, nothing more. And Magdalena was good at it; she was just as good at babbling about her Cuban dreams as she was in bed.

He asked, 'How did Pagan connect Ruhr to me?'

Falk drummed a hand on the rail and said, 'It's my understanding that you rented a house for the German. You were remembered. Bad move, Rafael. You could have found somebody else to rent the place on your behalf.'

'There wasn't anybody else. Who could I have trusted? In any case, it had to be done quickly. There was no time to think. Every policeman in Britain was looking for Ruhr.'

Rosabal remembered the haste with which he had to find an isolated house where Ruhr could be hidden. He'd been moving too fast to think with any real clarity. When he'd rented the farmhouse, he did so under Jean-Paul Chapotin's name, believing that if the police discovered Ruhr's hiding-place, they would never associate Gunther with the Cuban Minister of Finance. Instead, they might dig into Chapotin's life and find their way into the Society of Friends, which would have served its purpose by that time and become excess baggage. One of those moments, rare in Rosabal's life, when he'd mistaken quick thinking for cleverness; the crazy old broad who'd rented the place to him had a sharper memory than he'd thought. She must have described him well enough at least for him to be identified.

But none of this mattered now.

In a few short hours, dawn would be breaking.

Falk said, 'What about Freddie Kinnaird?'

Rosabal was quiet for a moment, as if he were deciding, in the manner of an emperor, Kinnaird's fate. 'Freddie has been very helpful. He always kept us informed of the Society's plans and the members' movements. Friends in high places are usually useful.'

'I hear a but, Rafael.'

'Your hearing's good. It has to come to an end for Freddie. It's over. I'll issue the order personally.'

'He expected a generous slice of Cuba,' Falk said.

'Then his expectations are not going to be fulfilled. He knows too much. A man with his kind of knowledge can be a nuisance.'

Falk paused a moment, as if Kinnaird's fate troubled him. Then he said, 'Speaking of friends in high places, your friends in Washington send their greetings and look forward to your success.'

'I'm grateful,' Rosabal said.

He turned his face to Florida. Miami was where those troublesome *idiotas* gathered, those roaring political dreamers who banged their drums for freedom and talked in the cafés in Little Havana and in large houses in Key Biscayne about taking Cuba back. They were fools, and potentially bothersome to Rosabal. Men like Garrido and his large network of cronies, the bankers and politicians and restaurateurs, the TV station proprietors and Hispanic newspapermen and rich doctors, all the money men who were in the vanguard of the Committee for the Restoration of Democracy in Cuba – they were his future enemies. After all, he had stolen from them; and what he had taken was more than just cash.

Were they likely to leave him alone after Castro had been toppled?

Of course not. They would turn against him when they understood he had no intention of bringing their kind of democracy to Cuba. Left to themselves, they would go on raising funds and promoting their moronic ideals and stirring up endless trouble for him; they wouldn't leave him in peace.

And Magdalena. Don't forget Magdalena.

She would come to haunt him in time. When she discovered how she had been betrayed, she'd find a way somehow to make his life difficult. These were not guesses; these were certainties he had understood from the very beginning.

He couldn't allow anyone to trouble him. He had come too far. Everything was within his grasp; he had only to reach a little further.

Falk said, 'We have detailed satellite photographs in our possession. All we need now are photographs of the missile *in situ* on Cuba. I don't want anything that looks faked. I want good clear pictures of the missile on its launcher. I don't want anybody to be in a position to accuse us of doctoring anything, if such a situation should ever arise.'

'You'll have wonderful pictures,' Rosabal said.

He turned his face away from Florida. Lightning came out of the west again, illuminating sea and sky with bright silver. Rosabal enjoyed the stark brightness, the light-show. A storm was gathering in that direction and the wind that sloughed round the yacht was stronger than before. He thought briefly of the signed order, purportedly from the Lider Maximo, that Capablanca had in his possession. The signature was a forgery, but what did that matter? Good forgeries went undetected as long as people were desperate to believe they were the real thing. How many forged paintings hung in museums? How many fake historical documents lay in glass display cabinets?

Falk said, 'As soon as the pictures are taken, I expect to receive your message that the missile has been destroyed.'

'I see no problem with that. It's exactly as we agreed.'

'I'm still just a little worried about your technicians, Rafael,' Falk replied.

'Why? They know how to disarm a nuclear warhead. After all, they learned something from their Soviet masters. They're good men. They know exactly what to do. Believe me. Besides, what is the alternative? To send in some American technicians? Direct US involvement?'

Falk, his hair made unruly by wind, leaned against the rail. Open US involvement was not an option. If Rafael was convinced of his technicians' qualifications, why should he bicker and worry? He said, 'Expect the full media treatment, Rafael. The man who dismantled Castro and his missile. You'll be a hero.'

Rosabal said, 'I expect nothing for myself. Only for Cuba.'

Bullshit, Falk thought. 'A certain amount of fame is inevitable, Rafael.'

'Possibly,' Rosabal said. 'But Cuba comes first.'

Falk looked toward the island. His heart fluttered in his chest, as if he'd been given his first French kiss; after more than thirty years of longing, and watching, and waiting, he was going to see Castro fall. In the intensity of his desire he was blind to any other possibilities; failure was not even a consideration. Everything was going to fit together and function. He believed in cycles of history; the circle in which Castro would be crushed was almost closed.

He turned his face back to Rosabal, remembering now how they had first met during a conference of the Organisation of American States in Costa Rica five years ago. The subject of the conference had been the economics of Central American republics, and the massive debts most of them had incurred. Far from the public arena, from the podium where delegates made their angry official speeches and railed at the unjust practices of the World Bank, they discovered a common interest in the future of Cuba after Fidel. They spent many hours together in a quiet resort hotel near the coast, enjoying the excellent pina coladas, the late-night visitations of exquisite call-girls, and – above all else – a sense of conspiracy that was aphrodisiacal. Although both men were initially discreet, circumspect to the point of obscurity, their mutual confidence grew and they talked more openly as the days passed; it was vividly clear to each of them that unless Fidel were 'removed' then Cuba was doomed.

It started with that simple notion: the replacement of Castro with a non-Communist, democratic regime in which bankers and investors might have faith. If the proposition were simple, the execution was not. It required all of Falk's cunning and patience to hammer together the strategy that would bring down Castro and elevate Rosabal. It required financial partners, men like Harry Hurt and Sheridan Perry and their Society, money men whose greed could always be counted upon to overwhelm their misgivings. Hurt and the others had to be brought into the scheme in such a way that they might eventually credit *themselves* with the glorious idea of bringing down Castro in the first place. But the plan required more than Hurt's merry gang – there had to be co-operation in certain Government and intelligence agencies, there had to be a force in Cuba itself that Rosabal could galvanise when the time came. So many elements, so many different instruments; but Falk, concert-master, conductor, knew how to syncopate the music and make it coherently sweet.

Falk stared back in the direction of Cuba. He was under no illusion that Rosabal's regime would exist three or four years from now. All Cuban administrations, no matter how sound in the beginning, sooner or later deteriorated into ill-tempered factions and violence and corruption of a kind the United States could not officially tolerate. But, in the meantime, President Rosabal would be tolerable, and friendly, and the honeymoon between the US and Cuba would vibrate with fresh enthusiasms and some satisfying intercourse. A pro-American government, corrupt or otherwise, was forever preferable to Communism in any form.

Rosabal looked at his watch. 'It's time for me to leave. When we meet again, Allen, it will be in Havana.'

'I look forward to that,' Falk said.

'A new Havana,' Rosabal added, smiling his best and brightest smile, which flashed in the dark.

Miami

Magdalena Torrente parked her car behind the Casa de la Media Noche in Little Havana. The restaurant was closed for the night, although lights were still lit in the dining-room and the jukebox was playing a mambo and a fat man was dancing with a hesitant skinny woman between the tables. Magdalena stepped into the alley behind the building. Garrido, who had been expecting her, opened the door before she knocked. In his white suit he seemed to shimmer. An hallucination, she thought. Like everything else that had happened.

He held the door open for her, then closed it. They went inside the windowless box-room stacked with cans of tomatoes and sacks of rice. She suddenly longed for a view of something, anything at all. A vista. She clenched her hands and said, 'I love him. I've worried it every way I can and I come to the same conclusion every goddam time. I love him.'

Garrido nodded his head. 'I know,' he said quietly. He thought: *It is your love that makes you the only choice, Magdalena. It is your love and pain.* He was filled with melancholy suddenly, as if he were remembering the lost love of his own life, Magdalena Torrente's mother Oliva; it was all so long ago, ancient history. Just the same, he was glad there was so little resemblance between the dead woman and her daughter.

'You look tired,' he said.

'I'm fine, really I'm fine.'

Garrido caressed her hair with his hand. A small electric shock flashed across his palm. 'Are you sure? Absolutely sure? Do you have the energy, *querida*?'

For a second she gazed up into the bare lightbulb that illuminated the room. She remembered the lights of the Buick on the causeway, the way they burned in her rear-view mirror; she heard again the noise of the big car going through the barrier and over the side.

She blinked, then looked at Garrido. She said, 'I'm sure.'

He went to his secret compartment in the wall behind the shelves. He removed a green pouch, which he handed to her. 'Some things you may need.'

She took the pouch but didn't open it.

Garrido kissed her on the forehead; the touch of his lips was dry and avuncular, his cigar breath and the scent of brilliantine on his hair not exactly pleasant. But she had the thought that at least there was no betrayal in the old man's gesture.

17 Miami

Lieutenant Philip Navarro of the Dade County Police was an uncommon kind of cop, articulate, smart, inquisitive, loaded down with none of the weariness and cynicism, the suggestion of emotional numbness you sometimes find in forty-year-old policemen. He had enthusiasm still, a vitality Pagan liked. He was short and slim, his face boyish; to offset this impression of youth he'd grown a thick moustache and wore a sombre three-piece suit of the kind you might encounter in the lobby of a Hilton during a bankers' convention. He listened to Pagan's convoluted story with the look of an impartial, but kindly, branch manager about to make a loan to somebody with no collateral.

Navarro was a big fan of Martin Burr, who had apparently deported a notorious Colombian drug lord from the United Kingdom some years ago, a man Navarro wanted for a variety of crimes in Florida. Burr had smoothed the extradition process, overriding paperwork and red tape, and Navarro had always been grateful. It was this gratitude that Frank Pagan hoped to tap now as he sat in the Lieutenant's cramped office, whose window looked over a lamplit yard containing impounded cars. On the wall behind Navarro's desk hung framed awards commending him for his civic work and his marksmanship.

Navarro said, 'With your British passport you can enter Cuba legally. Fly out of Miami to Jamaica or Mexico City, get a visa, fly to Havana. I don't see any problem there.'

'That takes too much time,' Pagan said. 'I'm looking for a fast alternative.'

'The age of immediacy,' Navarro said, and sighed, as if he longed for slower eras. He rose from his chair and walked to the window where he leaned his forehead against the pane a moment. 'When I got your call, first thing I did was check you out with Martin Burr.'

'And?'

'He asked me to extend the hand of co-operation. Said you were sometimes on the headstrong side but otherwise okay.'

'Good of him.'

'Also you were less than objective at times.'

'Character analysis isn't Martin's strong point,' Pagan remarked. 'Besides, objectivity's overrated. I get involved.'

'At the gut level,' Navarro said.

'Usually.'

Navarro, who had no great regard for professional detachment himself, liked Frank Pagan. He turned from the window. 'I'm happy to extend the hand of co-operation. I'm just not sure how far it should go. If I understand you, what you're asking me to do is break the law.'

'Purely in a technical sense,' Pagan said.

'Easy for you to say, Frank. I live here. You don't.'

'I don't have your connections in this town, Phil. I don't know where to go, whom to ask. If I did, I wouldn't have come here and bothered you.'

Navarro remembered now that Martin Burr had mentioned something about how persistent Pagan could be. Worse than a bloody door-to-door salesman, Burr had said. 'What makes you sure Rosabal can help you?'

'I never said I was sure. Put it another way. I'm running very low on options, Phil. I have to talk to Rosabal. It might be a dead end, but right now I don't have anywhere else to go.'

Navarro sat up on the edge of his desk, swung one leg back and forth, looked sympathetic. He had been in predicaments similar to Pagan's, when you had nothing more than some bare hunch to base your actions on and your superiors quibbled about the adequacy of your instincts. *You can't make a case on your intuitions, Phil* – he'd heard it all before.

Another reason he was sympathetic to Pagan was because the man had been at the very centre of the Shepherd's Bush Massacre, which – according to Martin Burr – had made Pagan understandably anxious, some might even say overly so. A smidgen of kindness would not go amiss, Burr had added. Phil Navarro, surrounded every day of his life with news of murdered colleagues in the continuing drug wars of Dade County, hadn't grown immune to the shock of loss he felt when he heard of policemen slain on duty.

'What you want is tricky,' he said. 'Also risky.'

'I expected that,' Pagan remarked.

Navarro, who had recently quit smoking, took a wooden toothpick from a container on his desk and poked his lower teeth with it. 'Costly too, Frank.'

'That might be a problem,' Pagan said. He had about four hundred dollars in traveller's cheques and a Visa card whose limit was dangerously close. 'I assume that nobody in this clandestine line of business takes plastic?'

Navarro smiled and said. 'The only plastic they understand is the kind that explodes. But my credit's always good in certain circles. There's always somebody happy to please Lieutenant Navarro. You know how it is.'

'I know exactly how it is,' Pagan said. In London he had his own pool of shady characters who were always delighted to score points with him. They reasoned, quite rightly, that it was better to have Pagan on your side than against you.

'Okay.' Navarro snapped his toothpick, discarded it. 'I'll make a phone call. I'm going to have to ask you to wait outside, Frank.'

Pagan understood. He found a chair in the lobby and slumped into it. He shut his eyes. Through the thin wall he could hear the low mumble of Navarro's voice, but the words were indistinct. Two uniformed cops went past, glancing at him with looks of surly curiosity; he felt like a suspected criminal. He sat for ten minutes, then Navarro called him back into the office.

'I'll drive you to meet a man called Salgado. He'll take you.'

'I owe you one, Phil.'

Navarro raised a smooth well-manicured hand in the air. 'Don't thank me too soon. You ever been in Cuba?'

Pagan shook his head.

'It's not terrific under the best of circumstances, Frank, and the way you're entering the country isn't the best by a long shot. You don't have a visa. Your passport hasn't been stamped at any point of entry. You have no return ticket. No hotel booking. Worst of all, you're carrying a gun. You've got to watch for police. You've got to be very careful you aren't seen behaving suspiciously by those charmers who call themselves the Committee for the Defence of the Revolution – they watch everything that goes on. Some of them are old ladies who sit in their windows all day long to see who's coming and who's going.

They report strangers immediately. Be careful. Act normal. Act as if you know where you're going. And for Christ's sake don't get caught.'

Navarro paused and looked at Pagan with concern. 'I can get you in, Frank. When it comes to getting you out, I don't know how I can help.'

'I'll take my chances,' Pagan said. What else could he do?

Navarro was quiet for a time. 'I was born in Cuba. My parents took me out when I was eight and I haven't been back. I've got family still there. It's an unhealthy place, Frank, like any police state.'

They left the office. When they were out in the lobby Navarro said, 'Salgado will deliver you to somebody who can provide you with a car and the address you need in Havana. After that, buddy, you're on your own.'

'I realise that.'

'You get into any trouble, you never saw me, you don't know who I am, you don't know who flew you into Cuba, you know absolutely nothing. You're a clam. Pretend amnesia. Pretend lunacy. But give nothing away.'

'Lunacy should be easy,' Pagan said.

Navarro drove through North Miami and past Florida International University. Pagan was very quiet during the ride. He felt an odd kind of tension, as if Cuba were a haunted house he was about to enter – Navarro spoke now and then about his vague memories of his birthplace – little things, a horse-race he'd seen at Oriental Park in 1958, going with his father to a baseball game played between something called the Hershey Sport Club and the University of Havana in 1957, a brief adventure in shoplifting at a Woolworth store in Havana. Pagan had the feeling that Navarro might have been reminiscing about life in the United States in the 1950s, as though Cuba, in the doomed reign of Fulgencio Batista, had been nothing more than an unofficial American state.

Dark fields loomed up. Navarro became silent as he drove over a rutted track between meadows. He stopped the car, got out. Pagan followed him over the field. Beyond a stand of trees a small plane idled. A dim light glowed in the cockpit.

'This is it, Frank,' Navarro said.

Pagan shook the man's hand, then glanced at the plane. The propellers turned, the craft rolled forward a little way. To Pagan's anxious ear the engine sounded erratic, a heart missing a beat; you're afraid, he thought. Dead scared and hearing things.

'I'm not convinced this is right,' Navarro said.

'Maybe not.'

'What the hell. Sometimes the wrong thing turns out to be right. In your place, I'd do exactly what you're doing. I justify it that way.'

Pagan understood that he was meant to find some comfort in Navarro's approval. What he felt instead was a kind of clammy apprehension and a tightness coiled around his heart.

Honduras

Two hours before dawn the cruise missile and the tarpaulined missile control module were transported to the freighter *Mandadera*. They were raised by shipboard cranes and lowered into the hold of the vessel. Ruhr, demonic by lamplight, supervised every movement, scolding the crew, hovering over the cylinder in a way that reminded Captain Luis Sandoval of a fussing *abuela*, a grandmother. The German, who carried a canvas bag he would not let out of his sight, checked the strength of the crane cables and the integrity of the winch; he was busy here, busy there, vigilant, energetic, fastidious.

Luis Sandoval, anxious to begin the five-hundred-mile voyage to Santiago de Cuba, fretted impatiently, especially over the child in the entourage, a teenage girl whom Sandoval had not expected. He showed her to a small cabin, where she sat on the edge of the bunk with her knees jammed together and her eyes flat and dull. Why was this child aboard, this urchin, this unsmiling *granuja*?

It was not only the sad-faced child that made Luis Sandoval uneasy. A conspiracy of nature also contributed to his discomfort; he had heard over the ship's radio news of a storm front moving across the Gulf of Mexico toward the Caribbean. Scanning the dark sky proved nothing. He saw only a certain starry clarity. But in this part of the world he knew storms could spring up out of nowhere, streaking darkly from skies that only minutes before were clear. They could race across the heavens, dense cloud masses blown by great winds, rains that fell without apparent end, coastal regions submerged under insane tides. He'd seen it many times and, in those circumstances where science was impotent, a man was thrown back on older gods; Luis Sandoval often crossed himself during storms.

When the missile was safely lowered in the hold, Fuentes and Bosanquet disembarked and reboarded the launch that would take them back to the shore. Luis Sandoval gave the order for the freighter to sail a north-easterly course between the Cayman Islands and Jamaica to Santiago de Cuba, a journey of more than nine hours. Not a difficult trip normally, but there was a nervousness about his ten-man crew that Sandoval disliked.

Anchor was weighed, the ship's engines came rambunctiously to life as if iron bones were shaking beneath the decks. *La Mandadera* set sail, turning in a wide, ungainly arc away from the Honduran coastline. Sandoval observed Gunther Ruhr go down inside the hold. A pistol in the German's belt was visible beneath the blue denim jacket he wore. A great square of light rose from the hold, traversed now and then by Ruhr's enormous shadow.

Luis Sandoval stood on the bridge. The ship's awful cargo was something he didn't want to ponder; the cause of freedom sometimes involved undesirable things. He turned his thoughts instead to the child in the cabin, the scared little girl who sat on the edge of the bunk and had, by all reports, refused water and food.

Sandoval had a daughter of roughly the same age as that sad girl who wouldn't eat and wouldn't talk. He sympathised with the waif, even if he didn't understand her predicament entirely – but what could he possibly do to help her? She was Ruhr's property, or so Tomas Fuentes had hinted during the loading process, and she was to be left completely alone. And Sandoval would never interfere with a man like Gunther Ruhr.

In her coffin-like cabin Steffie realised that it was the blood that so appalled her. It had run down her inner thigh and she'd cleaned it with the sleeve of her jacket but now she thought she could feel it again, warm upon her flesh. She wondered if she were damaged inside somehow. For her age she was lamentably ignorant of her body and knew only what little her mother had told her and what she'd picked up from her friends – a mixture of fact and foolishness. She'd never paid much attention in biology class except when Charlie Hapgood, the blushing, timid teacher, had shown nude illustrations. Now she wished she knew more.

She shut her eyes, laid her small white hands in her lap, tried to forget how Ruhr had undone the buckle of his belt and stood over her, how even then she'd scratched and fought and kicked to no avail, how she hadn't been able to avoid seeing him and the way he was aroused.

She'd bit into her lip to keep from screaming as Ruhr forced her to accept him. He was whispering kindnesses, tender words she couldn't understand because they were in

German, but she knew he was speaking to her from his innermost self, as if a part of him was untouched by cruelty –

But the pain! She'd stuffed her mouth with the edge of a blanket as he crushed her into the cot and moved inside her, growing harder and bigger with every motion – and then he gasped, and his words had come faster then, less tender, harsher, and his nails had dug into her hips. He rolled away from her almost at once and lay in silence looking up at the roof of the tent.

Puddles gathered in folds of canvas. Olive puddles, olive light. She'd closed her eyes and turned her back to him, smoothing her skirt down, trying to show she felt no pain. Trying to be brave.

She heard him rise and go out of the tent. When he'd come back it was dark and he told her they were leaving at once. She found it hard to walk, legs unsteady, muscles stiff. He helped her board a launch; the black sea scared her almost as much as Ruhr's touch.

When she was obliged to climb the scary ladder into the freighter, she thought: I hate you. I'll kill you one day. He was immediately beneath her, climbing, looking up her skirt – but what modesty did she have left?

Now she sat without moving inside the small cabin. There was a tiny porthole but no view. What difference would a view make anyhow? Sea was sea. She studied her hands. Broken fingernails, colourless, unvarnished. She'd broken them in the struggle against Gunther Ruhr. Once she'd been proud of her fingernails, attentive to them, painting them this colour and that – how long ago and silly it seemed to her now, such a petty vanity.

She got up, walked around the cabin, and felt the ship lurch briefly. She lay down, closed her eyes, listened to the rhythm of the engines, *dahda dahda dahda*. On and on. She rose again, went to the cabin door, found it locked; surprise, surprise. She walked back to the bunk. Face down now, head buried in the smelly grey blanket.

She felt so incredibly lonely. But she wasn't going to get weepy about it. That wouldn't serve any purpose. She listened to the ship, couldn't really help listening. Ruhr would come back, she knew that. He'd come back and unlock the door and step inside.

She knew he wasn't finished with her.

Something echoed in the back of her mind from days and days ago, a whole lifetime, something she'd glimpsed in a newspaper, the kind of paper with pictures of tits on page three, a paper her parents never purchased, a story about some girl in Cambridge, a prostitute Ruhr had picked up, a sensational tale of how he'd tried to do this terrible thing to her, shove something sharp up inside her, and that was all she'd read because her father had confiscated the paper. She remembered the girl had been reported as saying *I thought he was going to kill me*.

Now she thought, *Something sharp*.

What came to her mind was the sheathed knife that lay strapped to his shin.

In the dank hold which contained the relics of a past cargo – shapeless bananas turned to foul mush – Ruhr worked under a bright lamp. Now and again an inquisitive crew member peered down into the hold, and Ruhr would curse and gesture with his pistol.

He worked with the kind of concentration one might see on the face of a zealous bible scholar studying gospel. It was exacting work and required all his patience. He used wrenches and special screwdrivers from his precious canvas bag. He removed a plate from the side of the cylinder, exposing a confusing bundle of different-coloured wires – reds, whites, yellows, blacks, purples. There was nothing simple in the nuclear world.

These wires were connected to a variety of receptacles, openings into which the pins of the armed nose-cone would fit. Male, female. Since Ruhr had had the warhead specially assembled for him, the regular correspondence of male to female, of pin to receptacle, the precise sequence mandated by a classified technical manual was not going to make the missile functional.

Peering into the guts of the thing, Ruhr began to make his adjustments, carefully severing certain wires and splicing them with others. He did it without reference to any diagram but schemata he carried in his head. He was conscious of nothing except for what lay beneath his hands. Even the bad hand, limited as it was, seemed to shed its deformity and take on new agility as he explored and snipped, spliced and joined – a surgeon, he thought, somebody repairing arteries and redirecting them; an inventor modifying a tested device; an artist bent over a demanding sculpture whose finished intricacy he alone knew.

Erected, ready to launch and travel the distance from Santiago de Cuba to Miami, Florida – some five hundred and fifty miles as both crows and missiles flew – this lethal tube would, if released, destroy the downtown, the bridges, the water supply, the freeways, hundreds of thousands of people in an area that stretched from Coral Gables to Miami Beach. This warhead would inflict upon Miami more devastation than that wrought on Hiroshima in 1945 by the atomic bomb.

If it were ever released.

Of course it would not be, a fact that caused Ruhr a moment of regret. The responsibility for destruction on such a vast scale was something he would have accepted gladly. But he had been paid only to deliver an armed missile, not to light its fuse.

A slick of sweat ran over his eyelids. The intimacy he forged between himself and the missile was more rewarding than any he'd ever shared with a human. He wiped his forehead with his sleeve, thought of the child locked in a cabin above him. She'd fought him, resisted. He admired her spiritedness. He stared into the body of the cylinder, the veins, the sinews, and he thought of how he'd laid this complex machine wide open with simple instruments. There was a parallel here, a correspondence that couldn't possibly escape him – when he was finished with this operation, he'd go upstairs to the locked cabin.

He picked up a screwdriver; it glinted under the powerful lamp. The slight scratch the girl had inflicted under his right eye with her fingernail began, some two hundred and fifty miles out from Cabo Gracias a Dios, to throb.

Pinar del Rio Province, Cuba

It was not a comfortable flight. The black twin-engine Cessna (a doper's plane painted the colour of night) bounced through layers of turbulence like a shuttlecock in an angry game of badminton. Salgado, the pilot, a Cuban-American with the physique of a linebacker, was imperturbable, a fatalistic observer of the elements. 'If we don't have no control, man, what's the point of worrying?' he'd asked a concerned Pagan who sat in the front passenger seat.

The Cessna dropped through clouds; the sea was agitated. Lightning flared over Key West and the Straits of Florida.

'Hey, something nasty's on its way, man,' Salgado said with the confident air of a hardened weather-watcher. Pagan saw the moon being sucked behind speeding clouds. The lights of the Florida Keys vanished. The plane flew south-west toward the Gulf of Mexico where more lightning lit the sky with hard white electricity. Some fifty miles north of Pinar del Rio, Salgado turned south.

Cuba was visible, mysterious and mainly dark. The Cessna tipped, tilted, battered by a sudden uprising of air currents. Pagan stared at the green instrument lights, which meant nothing to him; how absurd it was to be suspended in black air, kept aloft by a device one didn't understand and whose instrument display was baffling.

He nervously pressed the palms of his hands together. It wasn't altogether comforting to know that Salgado, according to his own boasts, had flown surreptitiously into Cuba more than fifty times. A piece of cake man, was how he put it when he detected Pagan's misgivings. He knew how to outfox Castro's observation posts. Just the same, Pagan's throat was very dry. He wondered what the penalties were for armed illegal entry into Cuba. He assumed Communist countries were not in the vanguard of charitable treatment toward prisoners, especially those who violated borders with Pagan's disregard.

The Cessna began to come down more rapidly now. How Salgado knew where he was going to land mystified Pagan. There were no obvious markers, no well-defined runways. The airstrip, such as it was, had been hacked out of a tobacco field. Salgado's guides were thin moonlight and instinct. He flew as if navigating blindfold. The wings of the plane brushed branches and shook foliage before it came finally, thankfully, to a safe landing.

Pagan stepped down. There was a scent of tobacco in the air, strong and vaguely bitter. What was supposed to happen next? Did Salgado fly out and simply leave him here in this dark, lonely place? No sign of habitation anywhere, no lights, just unbroken night. In a few hours it would be dawn.

Salgado came out of the cockpit. 'This is goodbye, man. I gotta get back before that storm becomes real bad. Somebody's gonna meet you here.'

'When?'

'This is Cuba, friend. Time ain't measured by watches in this place. They got their own system.'

'Terrific.' Pagan didn't care for this information at all. He wanted to hear that Cubans were punctual and reliable and kept all their appointments.

'Adios,' Salgado said.

'Wait – '

'Relax, man. Somebody's gonna show. Count on it.'

Pagan was silent. He watched Salgado climb back up into the cockpit. The Cessna turned around, stopped, then began its run, taking off over the field, skimming trees, vanishing, a black plane in a black sky. With the departure of Salgado the night was emptier than before, as if Pagan's one thread back to safety had been snapped and here he was, stuck, uncertain, in an inhospitable country.

The night yielded nothing. The call of disturbed birds, frogs croaking, the wind occasionally rushing through plants, nothing else. He felt blind, robbed of any sense of direction.

Ten minutes, perhaps fifteen, passed before a lantern appeared on the edge of the field, swinging slightly as it came closer. It illuminated the broken-nosed face of a middle-aged man who wore a black shirt and blue jeans and a straw hat.

'You are Pagan?' Pronounced *pah-gan.*

Pagan said that he was. The man came closer, shining his lantern directly into Pagan's eyes. The stench of kerosene was overwhelming. Pagan stepped away from the flame.

'My instructions are to take you to the highway. A car waits for you there.' The Cuban, who said he was known as El Boxeador, spoke an English that was understandable if slowly enunciated.

'How far is the main road?'

'Two miles. Not far.'

Pagan, wondering about the nature of the network that had made this trip possible, the collusion between Salgado and El Boxeador, walked behind the lantern. He decided they had to be part of some drug-smuggling ring that Navarro had exposed but chose, for his own reasons, not to prosecute.

The air was stuffy. The ground underfoot became marsh-like. Here and there a darkened hut was visible, and once a dog barked inquisitively, but nobody appeared to investigate. El Boxeador, who said he was the former welterweight champion of all Cuba – he emphasised all with a sweep of an arm – explained that there were many Castro loyalists even in rural areas, some of them important members of the Committees for the Defence of the Revolution – a name that caused him to hawk up a quantity of phlegm and spit with contempt.

On and on they slogged, through fields and between trees and dense foliage. Pagan felt the familiar ache in his chest and pondered the notion of a painkiller, then decided against it. Now and then El Boxeador switched off his lantern when he heard a noise; then he had to relight it, which was a seemingly complicated task because either the wick was burned low or kerosene was running out, Pagan wasn't sure which. Finally the highway was reached, a narrow, isolated road with a rough surface that had been patched time and again.

Pagan looked along the main road, which twisted just into the blackness on either side of the road, half-expecting a military patrol, rifles, the indignity of arrest. But nothing moved, no traffic passed.

Finally, they came to the place where a car was parked in a grove of trees. It was a late 1950s Oldsmobile, finned, rusted, painted many times, and, like the narrow highway, patched. It had once clearly been in a collision; a clumsy attempt had been made to fibreglass the hole in the boot, but it looked like a scar. There were still thousands of American cars in Cuba, relics of pre-Revolutionary times, loved and cared for by their devout owners.

El Boxeador gestured to the vehicle proudly and said that it ran like a *campeón*; a little quirky, maybe, but it had more than four hundred thousand miles on the clock and the Cuban expected it to run for the same distance again. The upholstery was torn. Springs came up through the seats, bypassing the greasy duct tape used to repair the material. Pagan, a hopeless lover of American cars, looked at the dashboard affectionately.

'In the glove compartment, you will find a flashlight and a map,' El Boxeador said. 'The address you need is there also.' He reached inside the car and pointed to a scrap of paper taped to the back of the glove box, where it was barely visible. 'There is also a map of Havana. In the Vedado, Rosabal lives on the top floor of a new three-storey apartment building. A place for big shots, you understand. It is guarded usually by an armed man in the hall, sometimes more than one. You will have to deal with that situation on your own, my friend.'

Pagan didn't want to anticipate trouble. If and when he encountered an armed guard he'd cope with it somehow. He shook the Cuban's hand and then got behind the wheel.

El Boxeador tapped the window and said, 'The road goes all the way to Havana. Good luck!'

Pagan forced a little smile of gratitude, then stared through the glass at the bleak road ahead. He had come a long way, but suddenly it seemed to him that the three thousand miles behind him were nothing compared to the hundred that lay directly ahead. Neither tourist nor legitimate visitor, he had absolutely no rights in this country. He started the car, which hummed rather smoothly.

This is it, he thought. A point of no return had been passed.

In slightly more than an hour and a half he would be in Havana.

Ohio

Before dawn, Sheridan Perry had left Washington for what he considered his safe retreat, his private sanctuary. Now, terrified by last night's murderous attack and the memory of how he and Kinnaird had fled the scene before the arrival of police, he sat in the back of a Cadillac limousine as it headed through autumnal Ohio. A monotony prevailed in the landscape, a sense of the year moodily turning. A great cold sun the colour of a brand-new penny appeared low on the horizon, sending chilly light across wasted fields and stubble.

Perry, who saw Harry Hurt each time he shut his eyes and heard once again that dreadful gasp Hurt had made as he turned from the broken window and fell to the floor, his skull shattered like a hammered pumpkin, stared at the fields as if hypnotised. He asked his driver to stop at Youngstown because he wanted coffee. Accompanied by his overweight chauffeur and a stout bodyguard he'd hired from the entourage at Hurt's apartment, he sat on a stool at the counter and listened to Raving Dave Dudley sing 'Six Days on the Road' on the jukebox. Today was the day, Perry thought. Today was the day when things happened in Cuba. Too bad Harry Hurt wasn't going to be around to see the fruits of his work.

Perry finished his coffee. He got up from the counter. Shielded by chauffeur and guard, he walked back to the limo.

North of Youngstown, in the vicinity of Ashtabula, was a house Perry had bought some years before, his secret place. Located on the shore of Lake Erie, the house was set amid dense trees and surrounded by an electrified fence. He'd never taken visitors there, never had a woman out at the house. Only a cleaning lady, a fastidious old bat from Ashtabula, and the Polynesian servant Paco, knew Perry lived there.

Now, as he travelled north, Perry flicked through business papers he'd lately been neglecting, but found it hard to work up much interest in the cash-flow problems of a lumber company located in Vittoria Conquista, Brazil. He shut the case, poured himself a small snifter of scotch from the bar, gazed back at the road again.

The car was only twenty miles from Lake Erie. He began to feel more comfortable the closer he got to his home.

The placid waters of Lake Erie appeared. It wasn't the most beautiful stretch of inland water in the world, but just then it looked marvellous to Sheridan Perry.

His house came in sight beyond stripped trees, mainly cottonwoods whose denuded branches suggested fragile clouds of smoke. The house, constructed of fine stained pine, stood on a knoll. A remote device opened the electrified gate in the fence and the limousine went through, then climbed the drive up to the front door.

Perry was glad to be here. He stepped out of the car.

Mrs Stakowski from Ashtabula appeared on the porch, and so did the manservant Paco in his snow-white jacket. They looked nervous. They never expected Perry to visit this house in late autumn. Usually he came only in mid-spring, sometimes very early summer, because he disliked the climate during other months. He stepped up to the porch. The fat chauffeur and the stout bodyguard followed.

Home, Perry thought. Here he had his computers, his modems and fax machines, and current stock-market prices flashed across his TV screens, he had his sizeable hot-tub and vibrating bed and his library of pornographic movies from the Philippines, he had his electronic games and his collection of rifles.

'Welcome,' said the houseboy.

Mrs Stakowski opened the door for Perry to enter. She did so with noticeable reluctance and a slight frown whose meaning Perry could not read. The room was dim; he couldn't make out anything but the shapes of three men who stood near the fireplace. Perry dropped his briefcase. He heard Mrs Stakowski groan and say she was sorry, but she hadn't had any choice, the strangers were armed; then there was a flash of white as Paco scampered across the porch and headed for the woods. Perry, terrified, turned toward the open door, the porch beyond, where the overweight chauffeur stood motionless.

Sheridan Perry was cut down by gunfire from automatic pistols. It was over in seconds. He was shot in the throat and chest and groin and although he made a valiant effort to turn and flee, the attempt was hopeless; he staggered on to the porch, slipped and fell against the thigh of the chauffeur, rose again with a kind of instinctive strength, then toppled over the porchrail into a pile of raked leaves.

Mrs Stakowski was shot once through the skull and fell to the bottom of the steps. The chauffeur tried to flee and was shot in the back of the neck. The bodyguard freed his pistol from a shoulder-holster and returned the fire into the dim recess of the house, but he was caught by several bullets in the windpipe and one in the eye.

The three killers conferred in Spanish. It was decided that the houseboy, Paco, was barely worth pursuing. What could he tell the authorities anyway? Besides, as the Cuban killers guessed, he'd never go to the cops for one simple reason: he had no green card.

Santiago de Cuba Province, Cuba

Before daylight, the first Cuban troops began to move through the countryside around the city of Santiago. They travelled in Soviet trucks. The convoys passed under the shadows of the Sierra Maestra mountains where, more than thirty years ago, Fidel Castro had gathered his revolutionaries together for their assault on the regime of Batista. In the dark before dawn these mountains seemed indomitable and mysterious, lost in shadows and vapours, legends and myths, more iconography than geography.

The troops, a battalion of them in fifty-three trucks, went by road through the ancient city of Bayamo, where the vibrations of the vehicles rattled shop windows and stained-glass and trembled the old bell in the tower of San Juan Evangelista. The convoys, enlarged at Bayamo by thousands of reservists from the Territorial Troops Militia, passed propagandist billboards with pictures of the blue-uniformed teenagers of the Youth Brigade and captions like *En La Educación Y la Salud*. From Bayamo the convoys would eventually reach Holguin, where manoeuvres would begin near Guardalavaca Beach, which would be closed to visitors and tourists for a day or two.

At the same time as the convoy rumbled through the countryside, four battleships of the Cuban Navy – built in Odessa twenty years ago and obsolete by Soviet standards – sailed around Guantanamo towards Guardalavaca Beach. Shortly after dawn, ten aeroplanes, modified versions of Russian MIGs, flew over Santiago towards Holguin. These too were to play a role in the manoeuvres.

Thus was the province of Santiago de Cuba laid defenceless. And the site for the placement of the cruise missile, a mere fifteen miles from the historic Morro Fortress on Santiago's shoreline, was occupied by a score of anti-Communist officers and more than two hundred men, some of them Soviet-trained missile technicians, who had remained behind on the specific orders of General Capablanca. They would be joined later by the invasionary force from Honduras with its sophisticated weaponry and advanced fighter aircraft that would destroy Castro's air force on the ground; and later still, on the road to Havana, by other disaffected officers and their battalions, a number that Capablanca estimated would total more than ten thousand fighting men. Backed by popular support, by peasants prepared to take up arms against Castro, by disenchanted men and women willing to strike and block main roads and occupy public buildings, by the whole underground movement Rosabal said was firmly in place and ready to rise, how could there be any doubt about the outcome?

West Virginia

The near-sighted technician at the isolated tracking-station, which was dome-shaped and stood in wooded privacy like a very large boiled egg, had analysed the early photographs transmitted from the satellite twenty-three thousand miles above the earth. Magnified many times, enhanced by computers, these images depicted various blobs that to any untrained eye would suggest absolutely nothing. The technician was skilled, however; he also knew what he was looking for.

He telephoned a number in Washington DC. A young lady named Karen answered in a silken voice that made the lonely technician experience a certain sexual longing. She asked for the pictures to be sent at once by courier to the office of Allen Falk. The technician, who spent far too many hours without human company, and who found Karen's voice delightful, offered to deliver them personally.

18 Havana

Magdalena Torrente's driver was a thin nervous man named Alberto Canto, a physician. He met her at the darkened airfield between Havana and San José de Las Lajas where her plane from Florida touched down. She hadn't flown the small Piper herself. She had the experience to do it, but if she was having a hard time keeping herself under control, how could she expect to control an aeroplane? Besides, she knew nothing of the terrain, the destination. Both plane and pilot – a tough, leathery little man who worked in Havana as a tourist guide for Cubatur and pretended to be a happy Communist – had been provided by Garrido, who had made Magdalena's travel arrangements with meticulous care, including the arrival of Canto in his small Lada automobile.

Garrido had pulled all the strings in Havana he still could. Old favours were called home; old friendships had new life breathed into them. Long-distance calls were made, surreptitious conversations took place, places and times were synchronised in Garrido's own fastidious way. The process electrified the old man; the discovery of Rosabal's treachery excited him in a manner he hadn't felt since his heyday in Santiago. Instead of bickering with his fellow exiled democrats, and raising funds for a new revolution whose date had always been annoyingly vague, he had something concrete to deal with at last, something with a hard centre: Rosabal had betrayed everything and everybody, and there could only be one kind of justice.

Now, at the edge of the deserted, wind-blown airstrip, Magdalena stepped into the car and Alberto Canto rolled down the window as soon as he saw her produce a cigarette. She lit it anyway. Her hand trembled and she hoped Canto wouldn't notice. She held Garrido's green pouch in her lap, still unopened.

Canto said, 'I will drop you as close to the place as I can. Sometimes there are extra police patrols in that neighbourhood. They make me uneasy. This whole undertaking upsets me.'

'So why did you agree to pick me up?'

'Because I'm on your side. Which is not to say that I have the constitution of a hero. Quite the contrary. I'm just a scared general practitioner. I don't take risks. I don't have the guts. I couldn't do what you just did. I couldn't fly illegally into a country in the dead of night. Especially a country like Cuba.'

You do what it takes, Magdalena thought. *And sometimes it surprises you.* She said nothing, looked from her window. Havana loomed up around her, neighbourhoods of small houses, shacks, apartments half-built, scaffolding and ladders and cement-mixers in disarray. Unkempt suburbs gave way to another Havana, the central part of the city where imposing buildings and monuments crowded the night sky. Here and there new architecture appeared among the old, the occasional dreary high-rise block overwhelming some decrepit colonial mansion.

Her memories of this place, which she'd last seen at the age of ten, were different from the present reality. What she recalled most were warm hazy nights and palm trees and crowds of students, usually arguing politics, strolling along San Lazaro Street. Nobody argued politics in public anymore. She remembered the stands that sold hamburgers and oysters on Infanta Street and the delicious smells that rose in the humid air. The stands were probably gone by now; the oysters almost certainly. She recalled enviably beautiful, well-dressed women on San Rafael and how she longed to grow up and enter that glamorous life, exclusive nightclubs and dance-halls with tuxedoed orchestras.

She glanced at Alberto Canto. Sweat ran down his neck and dampened the open collar of his white shirt. He took a linen handkerchief from his jacket and pressed it against his face.

'You've got a lot to lose if you're caught in my company,' Magdalena said.

Canto looked grim. 'I wonder if there's anything left to lose in Cuba these days. Life doesn't have much quality. It's mostly dreary but one goes through the motions, because suicide isn't an alternative. I'd like some joy, I think. Even a prospect of joy would do. Perhaps I should flee to Miami and play the exile game.'

Was that how Canto saw her and Garrido and all the others in the US – just players in a game? It was a bleak little thing to say, almost an accusation. Magdalena made no response. How could she object? She didn't live here. Her Cuba hadn't been the daily grinding reality of Canto's; perhaps hers had been no more than a dream place, a state of mind, something she thought she could help shake and remake in quite another image.

A state of mind: was that all? A delusion? She wasn't sure. She understood only how odd it was actually to *be* here in her native country after thirty years. Her sense of exile had always been strong and melancholic. What was more terrible than being forced out of your own country and obliged to live in another just because you disagreed with certain principles? Exile was a wretched condition – the yearning, the way you tried to laugh the longing off as some kind of silliness, but you were never convincing.

Now she smelled the Cuban night as if she'd never smelled anything before. This was where she belonged, the place Rafael Rosabel had promised her and then stolen. She was suddenly aware of his nearness: he was ten, fifteen minutes away, she wasn't sure, her sense of direction had eroded with time, amnesia, confusion. What did she feel? what did she really feel? She didn't know.

Canto slowed the car in the neighbourhood of Vedado. Under the outstretched branches of a palm in a dark street, he parked the Lada, turned off the lights but left the engine running.

'Go right at the next corner. Halfway down the street there's a new apartment block. Very small. Exclusive. Rosabal lives there on the top floor. I understand there is usually a security guard in the entrance. However,' and Canto paused, wiped his face with the handkerchief again, 'because we have a few friends here and there, somebody was able to persuade the usual guard to call in sick. Unhappily, his replacement never received the order to substitute for him. A bureaucratic oversight. One of many in Cuba.'

'Convenient.'

'We have our moments.' Canto stared through the windshield. Wind lashed suddenly through the fronds of the palm and they made hard slapping noises on the roof of the car.

'What about Rosabal's wife? Does she live in the apartment?'

'I didn't know he had a wife,' Canto said.

Welcome to the club, Magdalena thought.

She opened the passenger door.

'I'll come back to this spot in ten minutes,' Canto said and looked at his watch. 'If you're not here, I'll come back again in another ten minutes. If you still haven't shown up, I'll make one more attempt ten minutes later provided it's safe to do so. If you're here I'll take you back to the airfield. If not . . . well, I prefer to be positive.'

Before she got out of the car Magdalena opened Garrido's pouch. The gun inside was a loaded lightweight Fraser automatic with a handle of imitation pearl. She slipped the weapon in the pocket of her leather jacket, then reached inside the pouch again. She removed a small brown bottle that contained two unmarked white capsules, which puzzled her for a moment. And then she understood. Garrido, in a melodramatic gesture, had provided her with failure pills, suicide capsules. *Swallow two, lie down, oblivion guaranteed.* He obviously had no doubts about her business in Havana. It was all black and white to him. Either she'd do the job and come back to Miami, or she'd fail and be captured and take the pills. He didn't see the complexity of emotions involved. He couldn't imagine how there might be any indecision on her part. He didn't want to know. As he got older so did his need grow to make the world more simple, more manageable.

She stuck the bottle in the pocket of her jeans, got out of the car. Canto drove away. She walked quickly, then paused in the shadows as if frozen.

Illuminated by a solitary streetlight, two men were talking together on the pavement opposite. One wore a uniform, the other a white *guayabera*. The uniformed man removed his cap, tossed his head back, laughed at something. He had a pistol at his hip and was obviously some kind of cop; she had no way of knowing who his companion might be. Both men laughed now, heads inclined together like conspirators. Then the cop turned and walked away with a wave of his hand. His companion went inside one of the houses on the street, an old baroque structure carved into expensive apartments. The riff-raff didn't live in this neighbourhood.

Magdalena waited until the street was empty before she moved. The apartment building where Rafael lived was small and rather unassuming; presumably the Minister of Finance in an allegedly Communist society had to keep appearances down as much as possible.

Outside the entrance she stopped to gaze up the short flight of steps to the glass doors; there was a desk in the lobby, and a lamp was lit, but nobody was present.

She pushed the doors open, entered the lobby. There was a lift to her left, but she chose the stairs instead. She climbed quietly, swiftly, possessed by an odd light-headed feeling, as if this were not really happening and she was some kind of wraith and the real Magdalena Torrente was back in Key Biscayne. The gun in her pocket knocked dully upon her thigh as she moved. The fourth floor was at the top of the building. Since there was only one door on each floor, finding Rosabal's apartment was easy.

She stepped toward the door, which had no number, no nameplate.

You will have the pleasure of killing him, Garrido had said.

You have earned that right more than anyone else.

She knocked on the door in a gentle way. Then she waited.

Pagan drove uneasily on the main road that linked Pinar del Rio with Havana. Yellowy moonlight on the range of the Sierra de los Organos rendered the landscape unreal. The Oldsmobile was more invalid than automobile, and had begun to make the kind of clanking sound common to terminal cars. But it hadn't died yet.

Near San Cristobal – where in 1962 the Soviets had installed the SS-4 missiles that had led to the Cuban missile crisis – he parked the car beneath trees because a convoy of army trucks was lumbering past with no particular attention to the conventions of the road. They wandered from side to side on the road, their dim lights menacing. When the last truck had gone past Pagan drove on.

On the outskirts of Havana he came to the district of Marianao. In a silent side-street he stopped the car, consulted the map he'd been given by El Boxeador. He played the dim flashlight over it; Rosabal lived in the Vedado district of the city which so far as he could tell lay in the streets behind the Malecon, the sea wall along Havana's coast.

He drove past darkened houses and unlit shops, a Coppelia ice-cream parlour, a shuttered bar; Pagan had the fanciful thought that a plague might have closed the city down. There were no pedestrians save for a noisy clutch of women who came out of one tenement doorway and immediately entered another, leaving the sound of shrill drunken laughter behind.

Streetlights were practically non-existent and where he found them were about as bright as candles. Lush trees stirred in the dark; here and there large ornate buildings stood like neglected palaces. Some of them had been religious colleges or the business headquarters of dispossessed *norte americano* corporations or the homes of the exiled rich. He drove with uncharacteristic caution, hearing the way the worn tyrewalls, as delicate as membranes, screeched whenever he turned a corner.

He reached the avenue known as the Paseo, which was filled with trucks and private cars and people arguing over the cause of an accident in which a '56 Chevy had ploughed into the side of a van. He didn't like all this activity. He turned left, then right, crossed the Avenida de los Presidentes, found himself back in narrow streets again, some of them without names. Finally, inevitably, the Oldsmobile accomplished what it had been trying to do for the last fifty miles – it gasped and shuddered and came to a halt outside a vacant lot behind tenements. Pagan, struggling with a certain panic, pressed the starter button a couple of times. The engine wouldn't even turn over.

Dead. What bloody timing.

He got out of the vehicle, kicked a front tyre in frustration. Then by flashlight he studied his map, trying to memorise the way to Rosabal's street.

He walked for ten minutes, staying close to shadows as he anxiously sought street signs, landmarks, anything that might correspond to his map. Once, from a window over a butcher's shop in which hung an unrealistic slab of plastic display beef, he heard the noise of a guitar playing lazily and a woman's reedy voice singing '*Una desgracia unfortunada*' and elsewhere a caged bird squawked as if in competition. Down cross streets came the damp scent of the sea and very old stone and air that seemed to crackle with the sound of water dripping on salt. He passed under the signs of closed businesses. *Farmacia. Casa Joyería. Restaurante Vegetariano.*

Once or twice taxis went cruising past. A smell of bread drifted from some distant bakery, arousing Pagan's hunger. When had he last eaten? On the flight from London to Miami. Now he couldn't remember what the food had been. Something awful. The smell of bread teased him. He kept walking, concentrating on where he was going, staying close to walls and passing beneath trees. Sometimes a loud carousing wind blew with such ferocity that it took his breath away and he had to turn his face out of its path.

How much further? he wondered. Was he going in the right direction in this dismal city? Now he stopped, took out the crumpled map, examined it again. His flashlight, as jinxed as the car, flickered and went out. Did nothing work on this whole fucking island? He walked until he came to a streetlamp and he stood below it, staring at the map.

Bloody hell – nothing on the map matched his surroundings. According to the route he'd taken he should have reached a small park that was represented on the map by a tiny green square – instead, what faced him was a warren of narrow streets where the houses all looked dilapidated, not at all the kind of neighbourhood in which you might imagine the Minister of Finance to live.

Narrow streets led to others; old houses mirrored one another. A maze all at once, a territorial riddle, like something you might dream during restless sleep and force yourself abruptly awake into the familiar surroundings of your bedroom.

This was no dream, Frank. No chance of waking up from this.

Sweet Jesus, nothing was familiar here. He flapped the map again, examined it, blinked, remembering that he'd heard once how Communist countries deliberately printed devious maps to throw visitors off balance, to mislead them and prevent them from trespassing in places where they didn't belong or from seeing something 'sensitive' – be it a slum or a military camp or the headquarters of State Security. He also recalled hearing somewhere that street names were frequently being changed as one Party official fell from grace and another rose in prominence. Had Garcia Street, for example, become Munoz Street? Was that the kind of thing that happened? He had an urge to crumple the map and toss it, but even if it was misleading, even if it didn't quite reflect reality, it was still the best shot he had of finding Rosabal.

He walked again. The narrow streets, houses oddly quiet, most of them unlit, threatened him in a way that was more than merely vague. Doorways, darkened and silent, suggested presences that observed him as he walked past. And now he remembered something he'd read once about how each neighbourhood in Cuba, each block, had its own organisation of snoops who watched from windows, who reported strangers to the authorities. He tried to force confidence into his step. He belonged here. He was a man going home late. That was all. There was nothing odd about his presence. Nobody would look at him twice. He whistled quietly, then became silent. What if you were lost here forever? he wondered. What if you could never find your way out of these streets? Round and round, up and down, never seeing a street name, a number, a familiar face. One bad fucking nightmare. One endless inner scream of panic.

Then, when he'd begun to feel a quiet despair, the streets became wider. The houses were larger now, richer, the foliage more dense. The warrens vanished behind him, the streetlamps became more generous. Across the way he saw it – the small park he'd been looking for before, his landmark. He felt a sense of enormous relief. A tiny darkened park, a scrap of greenery, nothing more, but for Pagan it was a major discovery. He consulted his map again; all he had to do was walk another few blocks north and he would come to Calle Santa Maria, which was where Rosabal lived – if the map was even approximately accurate.

For a moment his mood changed. He was elated. He'd come this far without impediment. Even when a car slowed alongside him he didn't let this new frame of mind dissolve immediately. He continued to walk, didn't look at the car, kept his face forward. But when he became conscious of a face perusing him from the window of the vehicle, he understood he was being tracked by a police car, and his sense of confidence slipped quickly.

Calm, Frank. Keep walking. Pay no attention. Pretend you're strolling home after a night on the town – or what there is of it in this place.

The car accelerated, went past him. On the next corner it braked, came to a stop. Pagan kept walking. He saw the door of the car open and a bulky figure emerge just ahead of him. *Can't chat, sorry, got to keep moving*. The cop stood in the centre of the pavement with his legs spread slightly apart; he clearly meant to halt Pagan. Perhaps some strange law existed about being on the streets after a certain time. Or perhaps Pagan simply looked suspicious, the late-night straggler whose presence was of universal interest to passing cops.

Shit. There would be questions in Spanish, a request for papers, documents, visas, the whole can of bloody worms. *I am a deaf mute*, Pagan thought. Would that act work?

Pagan didn't slacken his stride. He'd come this far and he wasn't about to be thwarted by any overweight Cuban cop. There was only one way through this, and it wasn't bluff. He stared at the pavement as he moved, raising his face only when he was within reach of the policeman, smiling, looking nice, friendly, even innocently puzzled by the cop's presence. He bunched one of his large hands when he was no more than seven or eight inches from the cop, who was already asking him a question in belligerent Spanish.

The punch was gathered from Pagan's depths, coming up from a place level with his hip, up and up, a fine arc that carved through air, creating an uppercut the policeman saw but couldn't avoid. The connection of knuckle on chin was painfully satisfying to Pagan, even though the overweight cop didn't go down immediately. He staggered back and Pagan advanced, connecting with a second punch, this one – viciously unfair – directly into the thickness of flesh round the larynx, a hard sharp blow that caused the cop's eyes to roll in his head. He went over this time, flat on his back with his legs wide.

Pagan hurried away, knuckles aching. He was pleased with the swift accuracy of the performance – he hadn't lost his touch; but what troubled him was the effort it had involved and the way he felt drained as he quickened his stride through drab streets of a city strange to him.

Cabo Gracias a Dios, Honduras

Three hours before first light Tomas Fuentes gave the final orders for the evacuation of the camp; he brought together the squadron leaders and their men. In their neat khaki fatigues they looked smart and trim, fighting men. Fuentes, who had a very big pistol holstered on his left hip, spoke through a PA system. He wished his men well in events that lay just ahead.

Five hundred of them would be going on board two battleships that were presently anchored off the Cape. Six hundred more would be taking to the sea in frigates and transport ships. There would be extensive air cover from Skyhawks, Harriers and F-16s providing protection for amphibious landing-craft. The landing beaches would be unprotected; military manoeuvres had ensured the absence of Cuban troops, who were on the other side of the island. Bombing and strafing from the air would knock out any small pockets of Cuban air defences that were still manned; munitions stores and lines of communication would be destroyed quickly. Tanks and field-guns, unloaded from the ships, would be deployed on the road to Havana; beyond Santiago de Cuba there might be extensive fighting with the *fidelistas*. It was not expected to result in anything but victory for the forces of freedom, Fuentes declared. Besides – and here Tomas paused for effect –

it was now known that Fidel was incapacitated and couldn't lead his troops, which was certain to be a blow to Communist morale. This brought cheers from the assembly.

This invasion, Fuentes said, was different from before in every respect. This time they were prepared. This time they had amazing support from their freedom-loving brothers in the Cuban armed forces. This time there would be a popular revolt inside Cuba. This time Castro was hated. In 1961 he'd been revered – well, by God, all that was changed. Cuba was miserable and downtrodden and the people sick to death.

Fuentes looked at his watch. Within four hours, the missile would be in place in Cuba, where it would be made ready to fly upon Miami. Shortly thereafter landing-parties would arrive on the beaches and the first air strikes would occur against Communist bases and airfields. As soon as the freedom forces had established their control of Santiago and launched their initial advance along the Central Highway – joined by anti-Castro Cuban troops and the counter-revolutionary resistance – satellite photographs of the offensive missile would be released to every newspaper in the Western world. Fuentes imagined the headlines. *Castro Planned Missile Strike on USA. Aborted By Invasion Force and Popular Cuban Uprising*. Later, there would be pictures of technicians destroying the missile. Fuentes, who had a natural hunger for publicity, would make sure he got into these shots somewhere.

More than thirty years, Tomas said. It was too long a time. More than thirty dry years of wishing and wanting and longing and hating.

Libertad! he shouted. *Viva Cuba Libre!* His amplified voice tumbled away in the breeze.

He saluted his men, who broke ranks and headed in an orderly manner toward the beaches.

Tomas Fuentes, who would fly to Cuba on one of the F-16s and land as soon as the fighter-planes had done their demolition work, went inside his tent for the last time. After today, the whole camp would be a mere memory. Bosanquet followed him. Both men sat for a few minutes in silence. This quiet was broken by the noise of bulldozers churning over the pathways between tents, obliterating all traces of this small temporary city; soon the jungle would have ascendance again, the landscape would take back that which had been borrowed from it.

'I hate this goddam place, but I'll miss it,' Fuentes said with the snarl in his voice of a man who considers sentimentality a weakness.

Bosanquet concurred. In a moment he'd rise and go to his own tent and there dismantle the radio. He wanted to wait until the very last moment to do so, because he had been expecting a message from Harry Hurt – a rousing speech, some fine words of encouragement – but the radio had been silent for many hours now.

Perhaps Harry maintained his silence for reasons of security.

Yes, Bosanquet thought. That had to be it.

Harry believed in security.

Havana

The woman who answered the door was the one Magdalena had seen in Duran's photographs. She was pretty if you liked a certain fine-boned Castilian look. Her hair, which normally she would have worn pulled back like a skullcap and tied, was loose and lustrous and hung over her white shoulders; her deep-brown eyes, the colour of bitter-sweet chocolate, were her best feature. Her mouth was ample and she had a fine straight nose.

'Yes?'

Magdalena, who very lightly touched the gun concealed in her pocket, said nothing for a moment. She realised that she'd been floating along on the possibility that Duran's photographs were fakes prepared by him for some vindictive reason of his own. She hadn't wanted to believe in the existence of this woman, this Estela. Now, faced with the reality, she felt as if her blood had begun to run backward. Her voice was unsteady. 'I want to see Rafael.'

The woman stared at Magdalena as if she'd been expecting her. 'He's out,' she said. 'He should be back soon.'

'I'll wait if you don't mind.' Magdalena stepped into the apartment, which smelled of something very sweet, like lavender water. She hadn't expected Rafael to be absent. She made absolutely sure the woman was telling the truth by strolling uninvited through the apartment. Estela, protesting, followed her. Artwork, reminiscent of old-fashioned Cubism, hung on the walls. The entire place was lit by dull table lamps which cast an odd yellow light through their shades. Magdalena went into the bathroom, then the kitchen. They were empty.

'What are you looking for?' Estela asked. 'I didn't ask you to come in. What do you want here?'

Inside the bedroom Magdalena saw crushed white sheets, a jar of skin lotion on the bedside table, a silk robe she recognised as Rafe's lay across the bed. There was an intimacy here she couldn't take. Rafael and his wife in this bed, bodies locked together: this dreadful picture reared up in her mind. Did he experience the passion with his wife that he did with her? Was it the same? How could it be? Nothing could have that scalding intensity.

Back in the living-room Estela said, 'Are you satisfied now? What did you hope to find anyway?'

'Where is he?'

'He had business to attend to.' Estela sat down again and looked at an electric clock on a shelf. 'Why do you want to see him?'

'Do you really want to know?' Magdalena asked.

'I'm not sure.' Estela was quiet. The clock made a slight humming noise. 'I have a feeling about you. You and Rafael. A feeling. As soon as I saw you on the doorstep. And then the way you just walked through the apartment . . .'

'What kind of feeling?'

'Not a good one.'

Magdalena had one of those small vicious urges, experienced so rarely in her lifetime, to smack this young thing across the face, but she let the desire go. Was it Estela's fault that she was the wife of Rafael? Estela probably knew nothing of Magdalena's existence. Besides, there was something pleasant about Señora Rosabal, an unexpected intelligence in the eyes. This was no air-head, no mindless bimbo, to decorate Rafe's arm. There were depths to Estela Capablanca Rosabal. This realisation only made Magdalena feel more endangered than before; Rafe could love this woman, and it would be almost understandable. It didn't have to be a political marriage, a match of mere convenience: *He might actually love this woman for her own sake.*

Magdalena said, 'We're friends. I've known Rafe a long time.'

'No, you're more than friends. I get the impression . . . ' Estela didn't complete her sentence. She made a small gesture with her hand, palm upturned, as if she despaired of words.

Magdalena was silent. She might have said *Yes, yes, we fuck; we meet in foreign cities and we fuck our brains out*, but she didn't. She had come to confront Rafael, not his young bride.

Estela said a little sadly, 'Sometimes I imagined there was another woman in his life. I didn't know who. You're very beautiful. What's your name?'

Magdalena told the woman. Estela repeated the name quietly a couple of times. 'It has a nice sound.'

Magdalena wandered to the window, drew back the curtain, looked down into the street. It was all too civilised, she thought. This meeting, the way Estela purred over her name and looks, the politeness. She wished Rafael would come back and she could get the confrontation over with one way or another. This apartment where Rafe lived with his young wife was making her feel weird, off-centre. Her head ached. Rafael doesn't live here, she thought. Not the Rafael you know. It's somebody else. A stranger.

'You love him?' Estela asked.

'Yes.' *Despite it all, yes, yes, yes.*

Estela Rosabal hesitated: 'Does he love you?'

'He married you, not me.'

'He didn't tell you he was married, did he?'

'What Rafael told me or didn't tell me is none of your concern.'

'I think it is,' Estela laid her hands on her lap. The wedding ring flashed under lamplight. 'Anything that involves my husband affects me too. That's the way it is. Tell me why you have to see him.'

Magdalena gazed at the street. She could see a small swimming-pool, surrounded by a fence, to her left. A shimmering light burned under the surface of blue-green water.

How reasonable Estela sounded, how collected. What reserves of strength did she have that allowed her to handle her husband's mistress with no displays of hysteria? It wasn't fair, Magdalena thought. She could never have behaved with such dignity and resolve herself. The young woman had grace beyond her years. Magdalena was jealous now, and not just because of the insight she had into the life Rafe shared here with his wife. Something else. The other woman's youth. Her enviable maturity. The quietly reasonable manner that concealed firmness and iron. These were qualities Magdalena realised she had recently lost in herself. In loving Rosabal she had given up more than she'd ever really imagined. *I was going to be independent. My own person. When I married Rafe I was going to be more than just his wife. Married, dear Christ!*

Something cold went through her. Below, wind altered the smooth surface of the pool, creating concentric circles of disturbance.

'Tell me why you need to see him,' Estela said. She got up from the sofa and stood some feet from Magdalena, her arms folded under her breasts. Perfect breasts, Magdalena thought. Perfect skin. Smooth and unblemished, unworried as yet by time. There would be no anxious scrutiny of that fine, strong, young face in mirrors, no depression when age made another unkind incision. In the future, sure; but when you were as young as Estela age was like death and disease – it never happened to you, always to somebody else.

Magdalena was filled with a sudden resentment of Estela so fierce it surprised her. The Señora had youth, she had Rafe, she shared his life, his world, the future in which Magdalena was supposed to figure so prominently. What was left to the rejected mistress? What was she supposed to do with this sense of loss?

A car drew up in the street below. Magdalena moved back from the window. 'Does he have a BMW?' she asked.

'Yes.'

'Then I think he just arrived.'

Magdalena took her gun out, told Estela to sit down and be still.

'Why do you come here with a gun, for God's sake?' Estela asked.

Magdalena went to the door, stood there motionless, listened for the sound of footsteps. Instead what she heard was the quiet hum of a lift ascending.

'Why the gun?' Estela asked again.

Magdalena didn't answer.

'Are you going to shoot him?'

'Shut up.' Magdalena gestured with the gun and Estela, who had begun to rise, sat down again.

'Please. I beg you. Please don't shoot him.'

The lift stopped, a door slid open, closed again, clang. Silence. Somebody stood outside the apartment. There was the faint noise of a key-chain. The tumblers of the lock turned, the door opened.

Rafael came into the room wearing a dark-blue windcheater and jeans and sneakers; handsome as always, unbearably so. And cool. If the appearance of Magdalena shocked him, he didn't show it. A momentary apprehension perhaps, a quick dark cloud crossing the eyes, but hardly noticeable.

'What a pleasant surprise,' he said. His smile filled the room and lit it. He had the gift of illuminating a whole environment with that one white, spellbinding smile. Magdalena resisted an urge to put out her hand and touch his face.

'I assume you can explain,' Magdalena said. There was frost in her voice.

'Explain? Ah, you mean my marriage.'

'You didn't tell me,' Magdalena said.

'Why should I? What claims do you have on me?'

'Several million dollars worth. Let's start with that.'

Rosabal poured himself a small glass of sherry from a decanter. His hand was very steady. 'I don't like guns pointed at me.'

'Too fucking bad,' she said. She hadn't meant to sound upset, hadn't wanted anything to show in her behaviour or language, she wanted to be as cool as Rafael.

'The money went to a worthy cause, dear.'

'Not the one for which it was intended,' she said.

'There are degrees of need,' Rosabal said. 'I tried very hard to be equitable. A little here, a little there – '

'And a little in your own pocket for a rainy day.'

Rosabal shrugged in a rather puzzled way, as if he hadn't understood Magdalena's accusation. He said nothing; he looked silently offended. He sipped his sherry and she thought: *he has a good act, a terrific act. I fell for it time and again.*

From the corner of her eye she was conscious of a troubled expression on Estela Rosabal's face. Secret aspects of her husband's life were being uncovered; she was learning new, unwelcome things about the man she'd married.

'Do you intend to shoot me?' There was a patronising tone in Rosabal's voice. Magdalena remembered that same voice in other situations, in twisted bedsheets when it became a slyly satisfied whisper, in crowded restaurants when it made outrageous suggestions over the pages of a menu, at heights of passion when it spoke of love in a secret language. *God help me,* she thought, *I still want him.*

'Keep this in mind, Magdalena,' he said. 'Kill me, you kill the new revolution.'

'Oh, yeah, sure, I vaguely remember the new revolution. *Our* revolution. But refresh my memory. I want to hear all about it. I'm sure your wife will be interested as well. And the people you cheated, they'd love to learn about the revolution they paid for.'

'You should give up sarcasm, dear. It's beneath you.' He paused, stared into her eyes with the same knowing look he always used on her. He said, 'Castro will be dead within a few hours.'

'Castro dead?' Estela asked, apprehension in her tone of voice. She might have been expressing surprise and dread at the destruction of some ancient icon.

'Dead,' Rosabal said, without looking at his wife's frightened face.

'I don't believe you, Rafe,' Magdalena said. 'You're lying about Castro. You've been lying all along. You've been doing nothing except stealing from people who trusted you.'

Rosabal made a small injured sound, as if the notion of somebody doubting him were preposterous. 'On the contrary, dear heart. While you stand there and wave your gun in my face, officers of the Cuban armed forces have already taken decisive steps to prepare a successful overthrow of the *fidelistas*. You're looking at the next President of our nation.'

Estela said, 'The next President? You?' Rosabal silenced her with a swift, commanding gesture of his hand. She shut her eyes, turned her lovely face to one side and looked sad.

Magdalena reflected on the unexpected solemnity in Rosabal's voice. He'd changed course suddenly, going from alleged felon and confidence trickster to potential President within a matter of moments. It was a fast transformation, and it shouldn't have surprised her as much as it did. She should have been able to see directly into Rafael's heart by this time, but it remained unpredictable territory to her, by turns swamp and glacier, meadow and quicksand.

'Let's assume for a moment you're telling the truth. What happens to the exiles? What happens to Garrido? The people in Miami and New Jersey and California who gathered money for you – what role do they play?' she asked.

Rosabal sat on the arm of the sofa. He looked comfortable now, as if some minor crisis had just been overcome. 'People like Garrido have an important function in my new Cuba. They will not be overlooked. You may remember I gave my word.'

My new Cuba. The proprietary way he'd uttered this phrase bothered her, but she let it pass, just as she chose not to question the value of what Rosabal called his *word*. She was like an impoverished woman confronted with money she knows to be counterfeit and yet hopes, in the face of all the evidence, that it might still be real, it might still offer a way out from a lifetime of hardship.

'What about everything else?' she asked. 'The new society. Democracy. All the things we ever talked about. The future we planned. What happens to all that? Does that still come into existence?'

Rosabal's smile was tolerant, like that of somebody obliged to explain the simple principles of arithmetic. 'In time, my dear. Change can't be hurried. People have to be prepared. You know that as well as I do.'

In time, she thought. Yes, he was right, a whole society couldn't be changed overnight. Then she caught herself: goddam him, she was thinking the way he wanted her to think! She was blindly agreeing with him. Love had petrified her will. Step away from him, she thought, distance yourself, make believe you never loved him, fake the impossible. *Pretend he never asked you to marry him. Pretend there was never any planned future. Pretend the sun rises in the west and the moon comes out at midday.*

'After you throw out Castro's Communism, Rafe – what takes its place?'

Rosabal said, 'I'll rule as fairly as I can. But don't expect me to be weak. I won't allow anarchy any more than I'll permit instant democracy. Down the road somewhere, perhaps five years from now, I may hold free elections.'

'*Five years? Five years?* I imagined free elections within a few months, six, nine at most.'

'Your optimism is touching. But the Cuban people aren't ready to control their own future.'

'And in the meantime?'

'In the meantime, we prepare the people for eventual democracy – '

'With you in total control – '

'Naturally.'

'And your five years might become ten. Fifteen. Twenty. What happens when you don't step down, Rafe? What happens if you don't want to relinquish power? Then nothing has really changed except the name of the dictator.'

Rosabal shook his head. 'You're overreacting. Everything changes. No more Communism. No shortages. No more reliance on the Soviets. Cuba will be a free nation again.'

Magdalena turned away. It was better if she didn't have to look at his face. Even now he could be so convincing. A free nation, she thought. Was that what he'd said? But how could Cuba be free without elections? How was freedom to be achieved if Rafael Rosabal alone controlled the country's destiny? Dictators might all start from different points of view, some might begin with benign notions, even with charity, but in the end greed and power rotted all of them and they resorted to the same kind of apparatus that could be found in a score of countries around the world – secret police, political prisons, the disregard for basic human rights, torture.

She faced him again. He was watching her, counting on her to put the gun down and tell him she'd been mistaken, that she'd overreacted but still supported him.

Fuck you, Rafe. All she wanted was to lash out at him.

She looked at Estela and in a voice that was both flat and uncharacteristically spiteful said, 'He told me he'd marry me. We used to lie in bed together and plan our wedding. We used to meet in Acapulco. London. Barcelona once or twice. But I don't imagine he mentioned that kind of thing to you.'

It was a sleazy little shot intended to cause him discomfort, but he reacted only with a curious laugh, as if he were embarrassed for her. He didn't need to be. She had more than enough embarrassment for herself. Only the way Rosabal had hurt her could have made her sink so goddam low as to proclaim his indiscretions before his innocent young wife. Magdalena suddenly wanted to deny what she'd said. She felt a sense of shame.

Estela started to say something but another gesture from her husband quieted her at once. She hated his habit of silencing her with that bossy, chopping motion of his hand. Did he think he could shut her up any time he liked? Despite her calm appearance she wasn't really any better equipped to deal with this situation than Magdalena, for whom she felt an unexpectedly strong pity. How could she not? Crushed, Magdalena had lost all composure. Only a heart of clay could fail to be touched.

It was obvious he'd lied to this woman who was clearly the mistress Estela had often imagined. And he'd betrayed his own wife. Without apparent shame. Without remorse.

Estela clasped her hands, folded them across her stomach. She was afraid. Afraid of her husband, afraid of what she'd heard in this room. It was more than the personal revelations that scared her, the deceptions of love. After all, she knew these things happened to people every minute of every day, and they brought pain, but life went on because it had to, and people recovered in time if they had resilience, and old scars faded. What scared her on some other level was the understanding that Castro was to be killed and Rafael was to become the new President of Cuba.

This was the secret matter in which Rafael and General Capablanca and that *solterón* Diaz-Alonso were involved. This was what the late-night meetings amounted to. In Cuba, politics was the domain of men, and they were welcome to its animosities and hatreds. She wanted no part of that hazy world. But she knew Castro would not die easily. He would fight. He was a survivor. He'd outlived most of his rivals. She had a terrible image of roads filled with tanks and guns, corpses in ditches, fields of sugar cane blazing, neighbour fighting neighbour, small children suffering as they always did in the world of grown-up violence. Cuba would turn into another Salvador, a Nicaragua. How could the ambitions of men like her husband and her father threaten to engulf the island in destruction? What if their revolution failed? What if Castro emerged victorious? Rosabal would be branded a traitor and she would be guilty by association. *And the baby, this nameless infant inside her, what would become of it then*? She felt sadness, then the kind of anger that always grew in her slowly.

'If you don't want to talk about your proposals of marriage, Rafael, why don't we talk about the missile instead? That ought to be an easier topic for you.' Magdalena decided to come in at Rosabal from another angle now. Her fist was clenched tightly around the butt of the pistol.

How close was she to firing? she wondered. It scared her that she didn't know. But she no longer had any familiarity with the limits of her own behaviour. It was as if an unpredictable stranger lived inside her. She understood that she wanted to keep after Rosabal, haranguing him, paining him if she could, but she also wanted the opposite, to hold and comfort, to love him. *Unhealthy, Magdalena*. How sick am I? 'I suppose you're going to lie about that too. I suppose you're going to say you didn't arrange to have Gunther Ruhr steal it.'

Rosabal set his empty glass down and ran a fingertip drily round the rim. He looked very calm. 'You have some useful sources of information, Magdalena. I'm impressed. I'm not going to deny there's a missile. But it isn't real. It's make-believe. A ruse, a nice ploy to discredit Castro, nothing more. It's merely for show. It's quite harmless.'

'For show?'

He began to explain how the missile would be disarmed and Castro overthrown. His voice took on the kind of enthusiasm he'd always used to sweep her along, as if she were no more than an object floating on his energetic tide.

She interrupted him as soon as she understood. 'You disable the weapon and the whole world loves you for your heroism. Right?'

'Why not? The world loves heroes. We're in short supply, after all.'

You're good, Rafe, she thought. *You lie, you tell the truth, you go back and forth between the two so often that the only outcome is the one you want most: confusion. How much of what he'd said was true, how much false?*

'Okay,' she said. 'So there's a missile, and it's only for show. Let's take that at face value for the time being and move on. Let's discuss something else. The girl. The hostage. What becomes of her in Ruhr's hands?'

'A girl? What girl?' Estela Rosabal asked. The conversation had gone into baffling areas. Missiles, hostages, things she knew nothing about.

Rosabal gestured for silence again, but this time Estela ignored him and got up from the sofa. She approached Magdalena and asked, 'What hostage? What girl? What are you talking about?'

Rosabal was irritated, his façade altered for the first lime. His wife's small act of disobedience had undermined his *machismo* in Magdalena's eyes. 'Mind your own goddam business,' he said.

Once again Estela ignored her husband. She looked at Magdalena and asked, 'You're certain Ruhr has a child as a hostage?'

'Yes,' Magdalena said.

'What age is she?'

'Thirteen, fourteen.'

Estela Rosabal had read in Central American newspapers about Ruhr and the bestial way he was reputed to have attacked young girls in England and elsewhere. There were pictures of his alleged victims. Such sad faces. Such dead eyes. Estela had never been able to tolerate violence, far less the needless kind done to children. It was a crime against innocence, a violation of nature.

She turned quickly to her husband. Her jaw was firm, her eyes fiery. Aggression altered her features, tightening the skin, emphasising the solid strength of the cheekbones. She reached out, caught the sleeve of Rosabal's shirt. 'What do you have to do with this?' she demanded. 'What in the name of God do you have to do with the business of this child?'

'Child, what child?' Rosabal pulled his arm free.

'Tell me the truth, Rafael.'

Rosabal poured another small sherry. He didn't speak.

Estela asked, 'Does my father know? Does the General know about this? I can't imagine him approving of a hostage situation with a child involved.'

'The General is in no position to withhold his approval of anything I choose to do,' Rosabal said.

'Shall I telephone him? Shall I ask his opinion?'

'Do what you like,' Rosabal said, but without conviction. The plain truth was that he needed the General, at least during the next twenty-four hours. And that stiff-backed old bastard, who had never approved of Ruhr to begin with and barely acknowledged the man's existence or his part in the plan, who would have preferred to believe that the missile had materialised out of thin air, was sure to become apoplectic at the idea of a hapless child held captive by the Claw. Rosabal couldn't alienate Capablanca at this stage. He couldn't risk losing the support of Capablanca and his officers. Things would fall apart if Estela contacted her father.

Estela reached for the telephone. She was bluffing. She had absolutely no idea of the whereabouts of her father or how to contact him. The General was frequently on the move and for years his staff had been under strict orders to keep his movements secret. He drew a very firm line between his private life and his soldierly one, a definite boundary that could not be crossed, no matter what.

Rosabal placed a hand over hers, preventing her from raising the receiver. 'All right,' he said. 'There's a kid. But I had nothing to do with it. It happened without my approval. Ruhr kidnapped the child –'

'Then you have to arrange for her release.'

'For God's sake, what difference does one child make anyway? It's one life, that's all. I'm talking about millions of lives, a new Cuba, new freedoms – '

Magdalena said, 'That's not what you're talking about, Rafael. Do you really give a shit about freedoms in Cuba? You already said all the power will lie in your hands indefinitely. If all you intend to do is make some pointless cosmetic changes inside Cuba, the exile community in Florida will fight you the way it fought Castro – '

'You are both being foolish,' Rosabal said, suppressing the anger of a man suddenly assailed by two women who had formed a collaboration that baffled him. 'You understand only this much,' and he held his thumb a quarter inch from the tip of his index finger. So attentive in such matters as kissing the back of a hand, so skilled in the bedroom, he consistently failed to take women seriously.

'Have the child released,' Estela said. 'Do it now.'

'Don't ever tell me what to do and when to do it. I don't even know where the kid is.'

Estela reached once more for the telephone. Rosabal was quicker. He grabbed the instrument, ripped it from the wall, tossed it across the room. It struck a door and broke apart in useless little bits and pieces.

Estela was quiet for a moment before she turned to Magdalena and said, 'There's a ship called *La Mandadera*. If the child is with Ruhr, then she's on board this ship. Because that's where Ruhr is.'

'Don't listen to her,' Rosabal said. 'She knows nothing!'

'*La Mandadera* is on its way to Santiago,' Estela said. 'It is expected to arrive there soon. Within two, perhaps three hours. Rafael is supposed to meet the ship when it docks. I listen to everything. My husband thinks I'm asleep when he sits here and conspires with his associates. But I don't sleep, I hear everything. What else am I supposed to do when I'm lonely? I heard about Ruhr, about the ship – '

Enraged, Rosabal struck his wife across the side of her head. Her legs buckled dreadfully and she almost slid to the floor. She clutched the arm of the sofa for support and looked at her husband in astonishment. Magdalena, shocked by the sudden act of violence yet oddly impressed by this show of force, raised the gun and pointed it at him. Shoot him, she thought. *Shoot him now.*

He held his hand out. He was marvellously cool again, smiling as if nothing had happened. He had the ability to change everything with charm. He looked quite incapable of violence now. All the tension in his handsome face had dissolved. 'Enough,' he said. 'Give the gun to me.' He took a step toward her.

'Stay away from me, Rafe.'

'Magdalena. We aren't enemies, you and I. We've been too close for all this hostility.'

'Don't move.' She tried to stop the hand that held the gun from trembling. He took another step. He stood about three feet from her, calmly running a fingertip over his forehead. His sun-tanned skin glistened. His perfect mouth continued to smile, infuriating and seductive at the same time.

'We can still be together,' he said. 'Our plans don't have to be thrown away.'

'Bullshit, Rafe.' *She wasn't going to fall for any of it.*

'Be with me. Support me.'

'Rafe – '

'We can talk our problems over. We can resolve them, Magdalena. Or else you can shoot me. You can kill me.'

'There's nothing to talk about – '

'On the contrary, there's everything.' He closed his eyes a moment. Lamplight glowed on his eyelids and his long lashes. He did something strange then. He repeated her name a couple of times to himself, as if it were a sound he'd never uttered before, one he found unexpectedly enchanting.

Estela said *Pay no attention to him* but Magdalena didn't hear, she was concentrating on Rafael, whose voice had become a soft whisper, almost an hypnotic caress. And she remembered how they'd undressed each other in hotel rooms in various cities of the world, the thrillingly indecent haste of their love, she recalled the ritual of the sugar cubes and how once, in a moment of erotic splendour she would savour for the rest of her life, he had slid a cube between the warm lips of her vagina and licked it away, crystal by crystal, *dulzura, dulzura,* drawing it out with the tip of his tongue, then playfully pushing it back inside. She remembered intimacies that terrified her because they exposed her, times when she couldn't dream of her world without Rafael Rosabal. Nor could she contemplate such a world even now. It was a barren place, a planet devoid of life.

'Let us put the gun aside, Magdalena,' he said. His tone was firmer now. 'We'll go somewhere and talk.'

'No – '

He stretched out his hand. 'We can work things out, I promise you. But we can't make any progress so long as you hold the pistol,' and he shrugged, as if to say further talk was pointless, and he was disappointed by her.

'Rafe,' she said quietly. She didn't want to weaken. But he overwhelmed her the way he always did. She saw how deeply she needed him, a fact of nature, incontrovertible.

He ran his strong fingers through his hair, then took one more step toward her.

'Rafe . . .'

She had the curious feeling that her peripheral vision had been destroyed, and she could see nothing but his face in front of her. It dominated the room, throwing everything else into shadow. She was sick from the fever of love, and she knew, with all the certitude of her own addiction, that she could no more shoot this man than she could stop loving him. She'd known it all along, from the moment he'd first entered the apartment. She'd find a way to forgive him for the theft of the money, his marriage, how he'd altered the shape of the new revolution and changed the dream, everything. *Shoot him*, she thought. How could you shoot the thing you loved most? Who was she trying to fool?

She lowered the pistol to her side, a movement she performed as if she had no volition. She was no longer listening to her own warning system; the voice of reason had been struck dumb inside her. Even as Rosabal took the weapon out of her hand and put it in the pocket of his jacket, a part of her knew she should have resisted. And when he spoke she infused his words with a warmth nobody else would have heard.

In a voice that might have persuaded birds to come down from trees, he said, 'We'll go someplace quiet now, Magdalena. We'll talk in private.'

Yes, yes, she thought. The idea of intimacy excited her. She wanted to be alone with him.

Estela pressed a hand to the side of her head where she'd been hit. 'Where are you going?'

Rosabal didn't answer. Estela watched him go out of the apartment. This was not the man who had courted her with such bewitching charm. This was not the beautiful man who had observed all the elaborate etiquette of courtship, who had come with flowers and Swiss chocolates and cosmetics and such obvious affection in his eyes.

Rosabal ushered Magdalena to the stairway. She took his hand, clasping it tightly. It would work out, it had to, there was no other option.

'This way, my dear,' he said to her.

When they went down to the empty lobby, the wind was screaming round the building. The glass doors flapped and palm trees creaked. The night was becoming furious.

She turned to look at him. He smiled, then touched the side of her face with an open hand. The contact was tender. She wanted to make love to him here and now, the place didn't matter. She kissed him, sliding a hand under his jacket. She heard the wind rage at the building and one of the glass doors was blown open, but these were sounds from another world far removed from her. He was hard against her. *He wanted her.* She felt his need and it justified her. Giving up the gun had been the right move.

'Not here,' he said. 'This is too public.'

'I love you,' she said, and drew away from him reluctantly.

'And I love you. But we must find a more intimate place.'

They went outside where the air was filled with electricity and moisture, like a damp sheet stretched across the city.

'My car,' he said. He held her by the elbow as he led her toward the kerb.

'Where are we going?' she asked.

'I have a place in mind.'

'And after we make love – '

'After we make love, we settle our differences, if we still have any by then,' and he laughed in an oddly nervous little way. He opened the passenger door for her.

Something made her hesitate, perhaps his uncharacteristic laugh, perhaps a sudden insight into how witless her feelings had made her, perhaps the lightning that flared with stunning brilliance. She had the unsettling sensation of coming out of a sweet dream into a menacingly real world.

'Get in the car,' he said.

She didn't want to. She looked at him. His lips were narrow and uncharitable, his eyes curiously bright, and not with love. Something else, something she couldn't quite read.

'The car,' he said again.

She opened her mouth, which was suddenly very dry. He had the pistol in his hand, aimed at her stomach.

'Why are you pointing that at me, Rafe?' She couldn't get this situation into focus. It was slipping away from her, and she felt panicked.

'Get in the car,' he said.

'Not until you put the gun away.'

He pressed the weapon into her flesh with such ferocity that she gasped. The abrupt chill of understanding she felt horrified her. He was going to kill her, she hadn't seen it coming, she'd been as careless and dumb as any fifteen-year-old girl in love for the first time. 'Rafe, for God's sake – '

'Do as I say.'

'Dear Christ, Rafe – '

'Let me tell you how it really is, Magdalena. You would be a problem to me. Today, tomorrow, a problem. You know too much about me. You know about my connection with Ruhr. Too much. So now we go to a quiet place. It won't take more than a second. A fraction of a second. Painless.'

Painless, she thought. He sounded like a dentist making a promise to a nervous client, but he was talking about murder, her murder. His tone of voice was utterly reasonable, a calm she found even more frightening than the gun. There was a madness in him, and she'd been blind to that the way she'd been blind to everything about him. He didn't want her, didn't need her. She was a problem, therefore she had to be eliminated. He might even have sent the killer after her in Miami.

The notion devastated her. She couldn't breathe, couldn't swallow. Paralysed, she was only vaguely aware of lightning over the city. The thunder when it came was the kind that clapped and echoed inside her head in a mocking way.

'Get in the car,' Rosabal said again. 'I am running out of time, Magdalena. Hurry. Hurry.'

A small vehicle moved slowly along the street. It took Magdalena a second to recognise it as Alberto Canto's Lada. It began to pick up speed. Rosabal turned his face toward the car, which was closing in on his BMW in such a way that a collision was unavoidable. As he levelled the pistol at the Lada, he experienced a moment of indecision. He was beset by doubts about firing the gun in the street. Neighbours. Police. His ministerial status would almost certainly afford him immunity from a murder investigation if he killed somebody, but these were sensitive hours, and he couldn't take the chance of having to answer questions of any kind. Too much lime had been wasted already. He should have been on his way to Santiago by now. The clocks were running.

The Lada mounted the pavement and kept coming. On and on, doggedly, it kept rolling. Rosabal finally fired when the small car was about twenty feet from the BMW. The windshield shattered but the Lada wouldn't stop. It struck the side of Rosabal's car, swerved across the pavement and the passenger door was thrown open. Magdalena reached for the open door, then threw herself toward it with a gymnast's grace; she managed to grab the edge and hang on as the Lada grazed the wall surrounding the apartment building. She closed her eyes. Air rushed against her. The little car bounced off the pavement and back into the street.

Rosabal fired a second time. The sound of the pistol coincided with the roar of more thunder. You couldn't tell one from the other.

Magdalena slumped into the passenger seat. 'You're braver than you thought, Canto,' she said. *Jesus, the pain. The swift knife-like pain.*

'I saw your predicament. What was I supposed to do?'

Magdalena turned her face, looked back, saw Rafael on the pavement surrounded by a few inquisitive neighbours. 'He'll call the cops. He's bound to. Can you stick to back streets?'

'I can try,' Canto said.

'Take me to the place where you found me,' she replied. She was breathing hard. 'The airfield.'

Canto glanced at her. 'You sound terrible. Is something wrong?'

'It's nothing.'

He saw it then: blood stained the front of her shirt. She was holding a hand loosely over the place, as if trying to conceal it.

'You've been hit.'

'It's nothing. It's not important.'

'You're talking to a doctor. I decide what's important.'

'Take me to the airfield. That's important.'

'Not before I've checked your wound.'

'What do you want to do? Stop the car right here in the middle of this street? Bandage me? Drive, Canto. You can fix me when we get to the airfield.'

She stared through the windshield. Imagine Rosabal's bullet didn't hit you. Your lover's bullet didn't pass through your flesh. Imagine nothing happened. You're well. Everything's fine. You're going back to the airfield. Intact. *It wasn't like that, though.*

She moaned, bent forward, held her hand over the wound. It wasn't clean. It was soft and wet, ragged and appalling.

'I'm going to pull over the first chance I get,' Canto said.

'The hell you are.'

'I have a stinking bedside manner at the best of times. Don't argue with me.'

She tipped her head back, closed her eyes, bit on her lower lip. She had a gloomy sense of futility, an emptiness in her heart. Had she come all the way to Cuba only to lose her life? Was this it? Was this the shitty sum of things?

This miserable exit. What a way to go. She wanted another kind of ending. Now she wanted some justice. She wanted revenge the way Garrido had yearned for it. She realised she still loved Rosabal with all the intensity of a victim's love – a pathetic compulsion, a deficiency of her character. She had no more control over the feeling than she would a virus in her blood. A victim's love was not what she wanted. When you loved like that you could never know any freedom.

There was only one way to be free from it.

She opened her eyes and looked at Canto through her pain. 'I'm a fighter, Canto. I always have been.'

'Somehow I don't doubt it,' Canto remarked, although he didn't like the sound of her erratic breathing.

Rain had begun to fall in huge drops when Frank Pagan reached his destination some forty-five minutes after Magdalena Torrente had gone. The street was quiet and empty by then. A badly dented BMW was parked outside the apartment building. Pagan, damp and not very happy, went into the lobby, passed the desk, headed for the stairs. He reached the top floor, took out his Bernardelli. First things first. Lightly he tried the door handle. Predictably locked.

He knocked. He held the gun pointed at the door.

The woman who came to answer was lovely and pale and indifferent. She held a white lace handkerchief, in which was wrapped an ice-cube, to the side of her head. The sight of Pagan's gun made little impression on her. Pagan walked into the apartment.

'Do you speak English?' he asked.

'A little,' she shrugged. She took the ice-cube from her forehead. There was a marked swelling between ear and eye. 'Where is Rosabal?' Pagan asked.

'Gone.' Spoken without interest. '*Solito*. Nobody else is here. See for yourself.'

Pagan looked inside the other rooms of the flat. They were empty. 'Where did he go?'

'What difference does it make to you where my husband goes?'

So this was the wife, this was Magdalena's rival for Rafe's affections. Pagan wondered what had taken place in this apartment that had left her with such a vivid contusion. Was Rafe a wife-batterer as well as a philanderer?

'I need to find him,' Pagan said. There was a shelf of photographs behind the woman. One, prominently displayed, depicted Rosabal in the company of Fidel. Both men were smiling polite smiles. It was posed, artificial.

'Why?' the woman asked.

'I'm looking for a child. I believe your husband can help me find her. She's with a man called Ruhr.'

Estela Rosabal walked to the photograph of her husband and Castro arid picked it up. She studied it for a moment, then she dropped the picture to the rug and twisted her heel in the dead centre of it. Estela gazed at the slivers, the way Rafael's face appeared imprisoned behind bars of broken glass.

Then she looked at Pagan. 'You've come a long way,' she said.

'Yes. A long way.'

'I will help you find the child.'

She told him about *La Mandadera*, about Ruhr on board the vessel, about the destination in Santiago. Sometimes her voice dropped to a whisper and Pagan had to ask her to say things over again.

'How can I get to Santiago?'

'By road is too slow. You must fly there.' She told him it was about five hundred miles from Havana to Santiago. She wasn't sure exactly.

'How can I find a plane?' he asked.

Estela Rosabal shut her eyes and did not answer for a long time, so long indeed that Pagan assumed she hadn't heard the question.

'I will help you with that too,' she said finally.

19 The Caribbean

The storm that had begun in the Gulf of Mexico carved out a wide path as it rolled in a southerly direction. Around Havana winds measured forty miles an hour; over the Isla de la Juventud and south-east between the shoreline of Cuba and the Caymans they were fiercer, reaching fifty and sixty. Later in the morning, when the storm would move due west of Jamaica, hundred-mile winds would rage over the Caribbean.

Had *La Mandadera* sailed from Cabo Gracias a Dios some two hours earlier, it could not have avoided the impenetrable black heart of the storm that would make the sea west of Jamaica a roiling nightmare; as it was, the ship still couldn't escape brutally damaging gales and cold blinding rain squalls that assailed it after it had passed between the Caymans and Jamaica. Captain Luis Sandoval, whose experience of tempests had never lessened his fear of them, estimated the wind at between fifty-five and sixty miles an hour, ten on the Beaufort Scale.

His ship lurched and plunged on huge swells. Leaden clouds darkened the early sun as they raced. Rain, sometimes turning to a hard hail, relentlessly scoured the decks. There was a deranged fusion here of elements and artifacts, weather and steel, cloud and smoke, one became the other in that dire place beyond boundaries. Day turned back to night within a matter of minutes, a weird compression of time, a suspension of natural laws.

Steffie Brough lay on her bunk. The tiny cabin pitched and rolled as if on castors, and the ceiling rose and fell. Waves covered the small porthole. The battered ship creaked. In her imagination Steffie could see bolts and screws come loose and whole metal panels crash into the sea.

She shut her eyes and fought the urge to throw up. She clutched the side of her bunk and held on, thinking that with every pitch of the vessel it would surely capsize and sink to the bottom of the sea.

Once, when she propped herself up on an elbow and tried to rise, she was thrown back against the wall and struck her head, which ached now. She hauled a blanket up over her face and tried to make herself very small – microscopic – as if she might go unnoticed by the vicious weather.

She heard the cabin door open. Gunther Ruhr, soaked, hair plastered across his head, came inside. He was dripping; his feet squelched. She didn't look at him. She kept her face under the blanket. She heard him dry himself with a towel, then he was so curiously silent for a long time that she sneaked a look.

He was standing at the small sink, the mirror – sharpening something – swish, swish, swish, the sound of an old-fashioned razor on a leather strap – swish, swish, swish – she saw it was no razor, but his knife – and he was whistling under his breath, a whistle that was practically a throaty whisper, spooky and tuneless –

The cabin shifted, spun round. *She was back home, she was riding her mare across wintry fields, and she'd never gone near the old Yardley farm, it was just too dull and drab, it didn't attract her, so instead she rode over Crossfields Hollow and into the village where she stopped by the ice-cream shop and had a chocolate cone and then and then and then . . .*

She felt Ruhr pull back the blanket. She turned her face away from him. He held his knife in one hand. Steffie drew herself back as far as she could until her spine was pressed to the wall. Ruhr looked the length of her leg to the place where his fingerprints had left bruises from before. She snatched the blanket, covered herself.

He sat down, placed the knife upon his thigh.

He listened to the way the storm blasted the ship. If there were different kinds of weather to suit different personalities, storms were what most pleased Gunther Ruhr. They created chaos, they broke down peace and order. They raged for hours and drove the sea and the sky together in one cauldron of turmoil. They sank ships. They excited him; liberated him.

Waves rose across the deck; up and down, down and up, the sea tossed *La Mandadera* as though it were a craft made from matchsticks.

Ruhr laid a finger against the scar the girl had inflicted around his eye with her nail. Then he picked up his knife from his thigh and drew the blanket back from Steffie Brough's body; she held the edge of the blanket tightly, resisted, refused to yield even when he slid the point of the blade gently across her cheek and drew to the surface of her skin a thread of blood. She would hold on forever if she had to, she'd struggle no matter what it took –

Without any trouble, Ruhr hauled the blanket back and laughed. He cuffed the child and she cowered, huddling in the corner, staring at Ruhr with hatred and fear and hopelessness.

The knife flashed just as there was a loud knock on the cabin door.

In the dark hold one of the lashes that bound the missile had come undone. The cylinder, with its armed nose-cone, tipped forward at an angle of twenty degrees. A report had reached Luis Sandoval on the bridge that the weapon was listing in an alarming way. A simple man, he did not know that the missile would not explode accidentally. He believed there was every chance of a holocaust and so he sent an agile seaman, harnessed for his own safety, with an order for Gunther Ruhr to descend inside the hold and secure the *proyectil*.

Santiago de Cuba Province

The outer reaches of storm spread inland toward the province of Holguin, where General Capablanca was forced to postpone his diversionary manoeuvres; tanks were stuck on beaches, sodden soldiers sheltered beneath trees, aeroplanes were grounded, ships anchored unsteadily three miles out in the Atlantic.

The ill-tempered gale blew over Bayamo and into the Sierra Maestra, where several hundred anti-Castro rebels sheltered in damp caves with their rifles. Then it slashed across Santiago itself, whipping the Bay, blowing down telephone lines, taking off the roof of the Leningrado Restaurant on San Juan Hill, flattening cabins at the Daiquiri Motel on Baconao Park Road, sinking a fishing-boat two miles out of Siboney Beach.

From the rain-washed helicopter in which Frank Pagan uneasily sat, nothing could be seen of the ground below nor the sky above. The chopper, rocking in wild currents of air, was piloted by a blunt torpedo of a man Estela Rosabal had summoned – former Lieutenant Alejandro Bengochea, a sixty-three-year-old flyer retired from the Cuban Air Force.

It was the worst ride in Pagan's experience. He expected the flying machine to plummet down at any moment through rainy turbulence and explode on the landscape, but Bengochea, as if he had a special contract with gravity and air currents, kept the machine magically airborne. Bengochea, who wore an old revolver on his hip, spoke no English, nor did he appear to question his flying mission – it had come to him from none other than General Capablanca's esteemed daughter, and that was good enough for him. Had Estela asked him to fly through a ring of fire or aim directly for the moon he would have done so.

For most of his adult life, Bengochea had built his world around the Capablanca family. He was a courtier, Estela his princess. He had known her since she was a small child. He even had home movies, which he sometimes watched all these years later in his small empty apartment in Marianao. They depicted him with the princess riding on his shoulders at the age of seven or building sandcastles with her on the beach at Varadero. The Capablancas had been his only family in a life of unbroken solitude imposed upon him by a military career of complete dedication.

Nothing scared Alejandro Bengochea. Notions of immortality were for the very young. He'd fought against the Yanquis at the Bay of Pigs, flown helicopter missions in Angola ten years ago, been imprisoned and tortured in the time of the Batista regime, he had even fallen out of favour with Castro's government in the early 1970s (he was 'a reactionary', they said), only to be spared imprisonment by the intervention of General Capablanca. What was there to be afraid of? His body was scarred everywhere, one eye had been partially blinded under the ministrations of Batista's thugs. Now he wore black glasses as if they were fixtures never to be removed, not even in sleep. He was a human being living beyond his span. Lucky Alejandro he was called. But he knew how to fly this helicopter with amazing skill, how to keep it aloft in gales.

Here and there, between squalls when the wind withdrew, the beaten landscape could be seen – beaches, a shoreline, sand dunes, visible only for seconds then swallowed again. Pagan shut his eyes. The roar of the helicopter was stunning, thudding inside his head. What he'd seen of the ocean appalled him. White, frenzied, it seethed and foamed furiously over sand and sea-walls. He would not have been surprised to see it reach up and drag the helicopter down into its demanding depths.

The storm caught the chopper, raised it in the sky like a leaf. Alejandro Bengochea enjoyed it. The weather challenged, even amused him, as if this were a personal test between himself and the vicissitudes of the planet. He took the chopper up and up, forcing it beyond the reaches of pandemonium into a momentary calm, an oasis in the sky.

Through another brief window in the ragged rain squall Pagan saw that the helicopter was directly over water now. Land was no longer visible. Fall from this place and you were a dead man; in that frightening, tumultuous sea your body might never be found.

He constantly scanned the waters. How was it possible to spot anything down there in that fury? And if you stared long enough and hard, you could even begin to hallucinate the appearance of small islands, or whales, or sea-troubled freighters – greys imposed on greys, and nothing distinguishable. Pagan, whose usual determination was weakening, felt the search was hopeless. But Bengochea loved this sea-hunt with all the devotion of a bird-watcher on the trail of a rare species. He wouldn't give up and go back to the shore.

The chopper rocked, lost height, Bengochea laughed; he had a relationship with destiny quite alien to Pagan. Down and down the helicopter went, until it seemed inevitable it would plunge into the water.

'There!' Pagan pointed downward.

A freighter, camouflaged by the sea, pitched. Waves frothed over the deck. The ship looked appallingly insubstantial on the swell, something that might have been set on a pointless journey by a child's hand.

Blinding rain and spray rose up. There was nothing to see, no world beyond violent water, no sky, no ship, nothing.

The freighter seemed to have vanished entirely, leaving Pagan to wonder if, after all, he'd seen anything.

The intensity of the storm overwhelmed Captain Luis Sandoval. His radio had ceased to function, his navigational equipment was useless. Locked in his sightless, airless bridge, a glass prison, he guessed he was some nine miles from Santiago. His first mate was an experienced old seaman named Zaldivar, but even this seasoned mariner had no idea of the exact location of the freighter. The storm reduced perceptions, destroyed instincts, threw men back on guesswork.

Luis Sandoval cursed this weather, this *tormenta*. When he looked up he prayed for a break, a sign of sunlight – but the rains kept coming and the decks were submerged. From the engine room had come an ominous report that about nine inches of water had collected below and that the pumps were labouring. This goddam bitch of a boat! Sandoval thought. This *puta!*

Zaldivar, his white beard grizzly, his face etched by the acid of too many suns, was a superstitious man who blamed the presence of Ruhr and *el proyectil malvado* for the freighter's predicament. Without the crippled *alemán*, none of this would have happened. Hadn't the day begun quietly? Hadn't there been a clear sky and a quiet sea? *Aiee*, it was the fault of the freak with the vile hand. There could be no disputing Zaldivar's nautical logic, grounded as it was in a system that transcended the empirical. The sea operated under the laws of its own gods, who were furious beyond all reason.

Sandoval ceased to listen to the old man's babblings. He peered from the bridge. Along the deck he saw, as if it were a figure from an hallucination, Gunther Ruhr moving toward the hold. A rope was tied round his waist and snaked behind him to some safe point. He was going to secure the missile. Zaldivar rubbed his beard and shook his head as Ruhr opened the hold and vanished into darkness.

'*El Diablo*,' the old sailor remarked quietly.

Sandoval looked upward. Out there in the dense structure of the squall he saw a flying ghost, a bizarre outline that was gone before he was certain he'd ever registered it.

Ruhr could barely catch his breath in the storm. Only when he reached the hold and lowered himself into the darkness were his lungs able to function again. Exhausted by the struggle along the deck, he sat on the floor, breathing fast and hard until his energies returned. He turned on a flashlight and saw how the cruise missile, having slipped one of the mooring cables, lay out of balance. It was no great matter to secure it again. He followed the line of loose cable to a metal hook on the wall and there he anchored it, making certain it was tight. His hands were cold, his fingers stiff.

The freighter rose in the swell, dropped again. The storm was magnificent still. He hauled himself out of the hold, clutching the rough fibres of the damp rope knotted round his waist. The other end of the rope was tethered to the handrail about thirty feet along the deck. He loved the idea of his life hanging by such a feeble lifeline.

He reached the deck.

Seventy feet above him, a grey helicopter swayed in the gale.

Alejandro Bengochea took the chopper down toward the deck of the ship, but it was hard to hold the machine steady against the energetic frenzy of the wind. At sixty feet he was driven back; the chopper swung in a great circle, then returned to roughly the same point. Bengochea, sometimes bellowing with a sportsman's laughter, sometimes quietly coaxing his craft, fought to hold the machine steady. Both chopper and freighter seemed tied together now as if bound by strands of the same rainy web.

Pagan saw the deck briefly, then it was gone under water; up again, wet timbers, an upturned lifeboat, tar-black smoke zipping away from the funnel. The figure who appeared on the deck seemed to have come out of nowhere; he was roped and threading his way astern like a man following a string through a maze.

Pagan, whose stomach came into his throat, felt the helicopter turn at an awful angle, tilting back down toward the ship before righting itself and hovering one more time, like a demented albatross, over the deck. There was the figure again, looking up this time at the chopper.

Pagan recognised the man. As soon as he did so, he took the rope-ladder from behind his seat and pulled it out. 'I'm going down,' he said.

Bengochea smiled with approval and gave a thumbs-up sign. Pagan, despite the obstacle of being born English, was a man after his own heart.

The chopper dropped another few feet. The daring Bengochea, the crazy Bengochea, would have landed the machine directly on the deck of *La Mandadera* if he'd had the manoeuvrability. Now the helicopter hung some fifty feet over the deck, dangerously close to the masts of the freighter. The ship, rising and falling twenty-five feet on the vicious swell, threatened at times to crest high enough for its masts to crash into the underside of the chopper or to snag the rotor blades. To avoid this calamity required very fine judgment on Bengochea's part, an instinct for prediction in unpredictable circumstances – two feet higher, then three, four, whatever it took to keep the chopper just beyond the reach of the masts.

Pagan opened his door, was almost sucked out into the skies. It was madness, and he knew it. He also knew there were certain kinds of lunacy you could transcend briefly because the fear of the moment carried you over the hurdle of craziness, imposing upon you an illusion of indestructibility. The notion of throwing down a rope-ladder from a helicopter perched precariously above a freighter sailing in a violent sea seemed almost logical to him just then; and he himself the kind of man who, because he was on the side of the angels, the elements would not destroy.

Sweet Jesus! how frail the rope-ladder looked as it unfolded on its way to the deck.

Alejandro Bengochea dropped as low as he could but the wind bedevilled his machine and he had to rise again another twenty feet, and now the deck seemed a long way down and the rope ladder too flimsy altogether. It blew violently back and forth beneath the chopper, more a means of transportation for a trapeze artist than for a London policeman with a wound in his chest and no great fondness of heights.

Pagan took a breath, stepped out into nothing.

Rain swirled in cold haloes about his head. His hands, gripping the fibrous rope, were red and numb. He hung in the air, defying physics and sanity. He imagined the storm picking him off the ladder and spitting him out into the maelstrom of the sea.

He held on tightly; with the determination of a man who has no desire to look death in its seductive eye, he lowered himself. The storm threatened to suffocate him. He could barely get air into his lungs. Turning his face out of the direct roar of the wind, he gasped.

Gunther Ruhr clutched the sixty-foot rope that would lead him back towards the cabin. His balance on the watery deck was poor and sometimes he slipped, tumbled, but always managed to rise again. Once, seeking a moment's shelter in a doorway, he wiped water from his eyes and observed the man who hung from the rope-ladder. The ladder twisted round and was knocked by the sea-wind back and forth, but the man – the man was unmistakable. And Gunther Ruhr smiled.

It was a fine effort on Pagan's behalf. Ruhr, who realised he had underestimated his adversary, grudgingly admired the sight of the Englishman clinging to the ladder and descending rung by miserable rung. toward the deck. Ruhr stepped out of the doorway, and, removing his gun from his belt, he fired once, more as a form of greeting than anything meant to hurt Pagan, who ducked his head and almost slipped from the middle of the ladder to fall the final twenty feet to the deck.

Ruhr continued along the deck, holding hard to the rope. He had thirty, perhaps thirty-five feet to go before he reached the tiny room and the girl. Turning, he looked up again at the acrobat Pagan.

Once, during an August Bank Holiday in Margate when he must have been about nine or ten years old, Pagan had thrown up during a ride on a roller-coaster. He remembered the screaming wind in his face, the shrieks of girls, and the way the thin trail of his vomit had caught the breeze and flown away and how his Aunt Henrietta had shoved a handkerchief into his face with a sigh and a tut-tut and *I should've known you wouldn't have the constitution for this, Frankie. Silly, silly boy, oh dear, oh dear ...*

Where was Auntie Henrietta now when he really needed her? Pagan wondered. What the hell? He needed something more than her big white handkerchief that smelled of mothballs, he needed a bloody weatherproof parachute. The rope ladder was tossed first to the left, then to the right, and Pagan held on, watching Gunther Ruhr move along the deck, waiting for the German to fire the gun again. Ten feet, fifteen, Pagan wasn't sure how far he'd have to drop to hit the deck, but he didn't like his chances anyway. Overhead, the chopper roared and the big blades churned the air; the tumult thrust at Pagan, threatening to blow him back up far enough, so that he'd collide with the blades. Hamburger meat. Mince. Razored neatly out of existence.

Oil drums slithered and clattered across the deck, then bounced overboard; a Cuban flag, looking like a used designer tissue, was sucked away, as if it had imploded. On the bridge, Luis Sandoval shook his head in disbelief. The man who was coming down the rope-ladder was clearly *loco*, and so was the pilot of the helicopter. Who these men were, and what their purposes might have been, were matters of no importance to Sandoval. They were intruders. They were no part of any plan. He unlocked the rifle cabinet. He handed a weapon to Zaldivar, and kept one for himself. Both men loaded the weapons then continued to watch the maniac descend from the chopper which, at any moment, was certain to collide with the freighter's masts – *kaboom!*

'He'll never make it to the deck,' Zaldivar said.

Sandoval shrugged. 'He might. He's crazy enough.'

'I'm not going out there,' Zaldivar said. 'Let the storm take him. Let the storm take the German and his goddam missile as well.'

Inside her cabin Steffie Brough felt the ship tilt, then correct itself again. Water covered the porthole, darkening the cabin. She felt claustrophobic. Even though she knew the deck would be exposed and unsafe, she needed to get out of this wretched coffin. She couldn't breathe. She'd been in this stale little room for too long. She wanted air, rain in her face. Mainly she didn't want to be here when Ruhr came back with his knife. Especially that. It was better to get out and take her chances with the weather than to wait in this place for his return.

She tried the door, but it was locked. She yanked on the handle – nothing. The ship listed again, and she was thrown back across the bunk. She got up, hammered on the door, but of course nobody came to answer because nobody heard her voice.

The only voice in the world was that of the wind.

*

Was the storm faltering? Losing some fraction of its power? It was hard to tell because it was a deceptive thing, dying for thirty calm seconds then flaring up again just as you imagined it was fading. In one such lull Frank Pagan hit the deck, bent his knees, curled his body forward to spare himself the jarring effect of contact between skeleton and wood. He lost his balance at once, slid on his back and skidded toward the side of the freighter, seized a rail, held on, his mouth and eyes flooded with salt water. He blinked, saw Gunther Ruhr some yards ahead.

Staying upright was impossible. Pagan fell again, tumbled forward, came to a halt on his arse. Ruhr looked back, fired his gun, Pagan pulled his head involuntarily to one side but the shot was wide anyway. He stood again and aquaplaned a few feet as the freighter creaked then listed to the starboard side. The ocean swept the deck and Pagan, with as much strength as he could still muster, clenched the rainslicked handrail.

Staggering, he followed Ruhr. He almost missed the hold because its hatch was closed save for a narrow space at one side where it had either been carelessly placed or budged by the storm. He almost missed seeing the section of covered missile below him in the dim light. For the moment he passed it by, rather as a man might hurry past a glass case in a museum that contains artifacts of no fascination for him.

He tried to keep Ruhr in sight. Catching up with him was impossible. His principal objective was not to be washed overboard. Ruhr clutched his rope, his lifeline, hurried, hurried, slid, hurried. Pagan, his breath knocked out of him by the storm, kept following. He took his pistol out, thinking he might wound Ruhr and stop him. He fired but couldn't hit anything on board a ship that bucked like a mad horse. Water streamed across his face and eyes and into his mouth. He thought it was possible to drown without having to sink underwater to do it.

Ruhr glanced back once, then kept moving, holding still to his safety rope. Pagan fired his gun again – useless, useless; and then the wind blew him back and the Bernardelli was jerked out of his hand and carried overboard and he saw it vanish into the heart of the foam.

Ruhr kept moving with the assistance of the rope. Pagan, scudded by water, cuffed, landed on hands and knees. He crawled, rose, glanced up at the helicopter: it looked fragile and exposed and altogether unnatural where it hung. How much longer could Alejandro keep it hovering there? Pagan had to find the kid, get her into the chopper, and get the hell off this ship.

Drenched, blinded, he kept going.

Gunther Ruhr, about twelve feet from the door of the cabin, looked back at Pagan. It was amusing to see the Englishman struggle to stay upright – but then the whole day was one of imbalances and upsets, of symmetry broken down, composure destroyed. Ruhr wiped his eyes with his knuckles, saw the place where he'd tied the rope, saw the cabin door.

He turned to look back one more time at Pagan.

Frank Pagan thought he saw Gunther Ruhr toss back his face and laugh. It was something of which he'd never be certain.

Steffie Brough hammered and hammered on the door until her fists ached. Useless. Then she tugged again and again on the handle.

– Why hadn't Ruhr come back?

– She caught the handle, twisted, cursed, strained.

– The bloody thing wouldn't turn, wouldn't, just wouldn't.

She closed her eyes; small tears slithered out from under her eyelids. There has to be something, she thought. There has to be some kind of way out. She kicked the door panel, nothing yielded.

She took a deep breath, bit her lower lip in sheer determination, puffed out her cheeks, pulled together every fragment of strength she could find. She hauled on the handle, and felt a screw pop out from damp wood, a small, rusty screw, and the handle itself was loose and a second screw fell away and the door, warped by seasons and sea-changes, split slightly. In the core of the wood were tiny worm-holes, small tunnels that released very fine sawdust. Now the entire handle came away in her fist and she opened the door and the sea blast winded her.

She saw Gunther Ruhr coming along the deck.

He was attached to a rail by a length of rope. It was knotted only twelve inches from the open door of the cabin. She was conscious of a second man hanging on to the rail, trailing Ruhr from behind.

She stepped forward. The idea that came to her was both inevitable and compelling. She had to do it.

With frantic fingers she took the loose end of the knot, the kind known to sailors as a double timber-hitch, and passed it through two loops of rope, which undid the knot swiftly. She dropped the rope. She heard Ruhr shout at her in alarm. Released from his anchor of safety he slipped. She saw him fall flat on his back. The rope curled about his ankle and he slithered toward the side, toward the dreadful sea, even as the other man hurried to prevent him sliding out into the waves.

Fingers clamped on Ruhr's wrist, but he kept slipping away.

'I cannot hold,' he shouted. 'I cannot hold, Pagan – '

'You have to fucking hold, you bastard!'

Pagan groaned, clenched his jaw, caught Ruhr's shirt under the neck and pulled with all his strength, dragging Ruhr back from the edge. He couldn't let Gunther go, not now, not after all this distance had been travelled. If he released Gunther, then what had been the point of everything? He owed it to the dead men in Shepherd's Bush to take Ruhr back to London. He owed it to the soldiers murdered during the hijack of the missile in Norfolk. And he owed it to Steffie Brough, to her parents, to all the people Gunther Ruhr had hurt.

He couldn't let Ruhr slide into the sea. Couldn't lose him.

The German wasn't heavy, but the effort of rescuing him drained Pagan. He hauled him away from the rail, then released him; Rhur lay flat and drenched and breathing badly near the cabin dor. Landed, Pagan thought. Like a bloody great fish. Harpooned at last.

Pagan's sense of achievement lasted a second before he felt his heart frost over.

In his good hand Gunther Ruhr held the pistol which he had produced from the belt of his trousers. He pointed the gun directly at Pagan. 'You overlooked this, Frnak. Stupid of you.'

Pagan stepped bak, alarmed. Why had he forgotten Ruhr's gun? Why the hell hadn't he let Ruhr silde into the bloody sea? Too damned anxious, Frank. Too damned keen to play Mr Justice, to take Ruhr back to London and the law. He didn't deserve due process, did he? He was a killer, a terrorist. He had no sense of right and wrong, no charity, no humanity. He didn't deserve his moment in a court of law, for Christ's sake. Pagan glanced at the girl, who was clinging to the cabin door as if her life depended on it.

Ruhr said, 'Wonderful effort, Pagan. But futile – '

The ship bucked suddenly again. The swell, surging under the hull with great might, momentarily forced the bow out of the water. The deck tilted up. Gunther Ruhr, slick and wet, slid seven or eight yards on his back away from Pagan, flailing his arms like a man tumbling down a slippery chute.

It was an opportunity, and Pagan had to seize it before the ship righted itself. There might never be another. Fighting to keep his own balance, he caught the girl by the hand and they ran skidding together towards the rope-ladder which shimmied and flapped as if possessed by a life-force of its own, and was difficult to grasp. Pagan finally gripped it, brought it under control, helped the girl on to the first sodden rung. The climb was strenuous. The ladder blew sideways, the helicopter swayed, all the balances were so delicate that everything seemed destined to fail at any moment from the sky. The girl climbed a couple of rungs, and Pagan came behind. There was a lull then, a few wonderful seconds in which the storm abated a little. Pagan and the girl were able to advance about one third of the way up, which was when Steffie Brough stopped climbing.

'Keep going, for Christ's sake.' Pagan looked down – always a mistake. He saw Gunther Ruhr, upright now, trying to steady himself on the deck for a shot.

'Can't,' the girl said.

'Yes you can.'

'My legs won't work. They won't work. I can't make them work.'

'Bloody hell.' Pagan heard the sound of gunfire; overpowered by a revitalised wind, it was strangely unthreatening. But it came close, and he knew it. So did Alejandro Bengochea, who had been watching Ruhr from the cabin. He turned the helicopter away from the *Mandadera* and out over the water beyond the range of Gunther Ruhr's gun.

Pagan reached up with one hand, placed it against Steffie's spine, pushed gently, tried to ease her further up the ladder. She moved then, one slow rung at a time, panting, terrified of falling. He supported her even when the ladder swung to positions that made climbing impossible.

Once, unable to resist the impulse, he glanced at the sea again. *An evil dream of endlessly falling.*

The chopper kept moving back toward land as Pagan and the girl made their way slowly upwards to the cabin. The rain was falling hard, but the closer the aircraft came to the shore, the more the wind dropped and the sea quieted because the storm was pulling back and rolling out, to renew itself with a vengeance, across the Caribbean. It wasn't completely dead yet. It gusted, still creating havoc as Pagan and the girl pulled themselves up, exhausted, gasping, inside the cabin.

Pagan slumped in the narrow seat, squashed alongside the child. His eyes stung from salt, his hair was plastered to his skull, his clothing and skin so completely soaked he had no idea where fabric ended and flesh began; the storm had welded him to his clothes. His skin was numb.

'We've got to keep the ship in view,' he said to Bengochea.

Bengochea appeared not to have understood. Pagan grabbed his arm, pointed down towards the sea. 'The *Mandadera*. We've got to follow the bloody ship to Santiago. Understand?'

Bengochea shook his head and pointed to the dials in front of him. *'Necesito gasolina. Comprendo?'*

'Gasolina?'

Bengochea rapped a dial in front of him with his fingertips. 'See? *Vacante. Comprendo?'*

The chopper lurched suddenly; the fading storm, as if made petulant by its failure to down the craft, seized the machine and gave it one final, terrible shake. The girl, stricken by panic, pressed her face into Pagan's shoulder. The helicopter dropped rapidly, but then the storm, like a fist at last unlocking, released it; now there was only rain and a slight wind and a green rainswept landscape just beyond the shoreline ahead.

Pagan stroked the girl's wet hair. She was uncertain about his touch, but she tolerated it the way a suspicious animal might put up with a stranger's caress.

Bengochea flew directly toward the coastal road that linked Manzanillo with Santiago. On an airstrip outside Palma Soriano, forty miles from Santiago, he brought the craft down. He got out. Pagan watched him walk towards a one-storey building where he went inside. The girl, her face still pressed against Pagan's shoulder, stared vacantly across the tarmac. She shivered, said nothing. Pagan looked out at the grey sky and listened to the way rain fell sharply on the roof of the cabin. He was bitterly cold, sneezed once or twice, longed for a good fire, warm clothes, dry shoes.

Soon the *Mandadera* would reach the safe harbour of Santiago. Presumably Ruhr and the missile would go ashore there. In her rather glassy, dazed manner, Estela Rosabal had said that the missile – according to her husband – was intended to do nothing more than discredit Castro.

Pagan mulled this over while he waited for Bengochea to return. A missile to discredit Castro, to make him look like a warmonger. To justify his overthrow. To justify the coup Magdalena had talked about. *Fidel has a missile! Look! He intends to use it! He intends to blow up some part of the world! Crazy bastard!* But Rosabal overthrows the old dictator in an heroic coup; nuclear holocaust averted by dashing new President of Cuba. Wasn't that what Estela had whispered? *Rafael believes he will be the next president.*

Question: What nation would be most threatened by a missile on Cuba?

That was obvious. Ergo: by overthrowing Fidel and destroying the missile, Rosabal would be nothing less than a saint in American eyes. American aid would flood the island. American trade would bring riches. Rich tourists. The old guard would flock back to Havana: gamblers, call-girls, pimps, the drug-dealers, gunmen, low-lifers, outlaws, the dubious bankers and lawyers.

Pagan sneezed again and lost his chugging train of thought. His chest throbbed. His eyes watered. His mind was a cold, numb place. What he wanted was dryness, and food, then sleep.

Bengochea came out of the building and walked back towards the helicopter. He was smiling. He had clearly found a source of fuel. He looked up at Pagan and made a thumbs-up sign.

'*Abundancia*,' he said cheerfully. '*Immediatamente*.'

Rafael Rosabal had flown by jet through the edge of the storm from Havana to Santiago. There he'd been met by a half-dozen of Capablanca's officers – two of whom carried expensive cameras to photograph the missile in the launch position.

Followed by a truck containing a score of armed soldiers, Rosabal was driven by jeep out of the stormswept city and along the coastal road toward Siboney. The nice irony did not escape him. It was from a farmhouse at Siboney that Castro had planned his first assault on the Batista regime in 1953, six years before his ultimate triumph. From this place Castro's revolutionaries had carried out a failed attack, a comedy of errors and confused timing, on the garrison at Moncada. Now monuments to the dead rebels lined the roadside and the farm had become a shrine to deify El Viejo. It was one of Communism's many hypocrisies: God was an unofficial entity, forbidden, but men like Castro could ascend to the vacant summits formerly occupied by the deity.

The jeep took Rosabal to a site about two miles from Siboney, a secluded meadow, ringed by trees and sheltered somewhat from the wind, where the missile would be placed. A house – in the possession of a farmer sympathetic to the new revolution – had been placed at Rosabal's disposal. Rosabal sat silently with Capablanca's officers on the screened porch and listened to what was left of the storm and waited.

He would have preferred better weather, but the storm was gradually diminishing; the *Mandadera* would surely reach its destination. The missile would get here. Delayed, but it would still get here.

Rosabal looked at his watch every so often. Now and again he rose and walked up and down the porch and stared out across the meadow, watching rain sweep through the trees. He was tense. The moment he'd worked for was almost here. The time he'd dreamed about for so long was almost upon him. How could he remain perfectly cool?

He thought about Magdalena Torrente.

He was positive he'd hit her with his second shot. He'd seen a look of pain go across her face before she vanished inside the unexpected Lada. When she'd disappeared, he had telephoned influential friends at the Ministry of the Interior, who immediately set in motion an intensive search of Havana for the Lada and its occupants. At Rosabal's insistence, the search, though widespread, was being conducted with a certain discretion. Delicate matters of state, Rosabal had explained, were involved. Make no noise. Do not arrest people carelessly. When the occupants of the Lada were discovered, the female passenger was to be shot on sight.

Magdalena Torrente meant nothing to him anyway. Nor had she ever. She was somebody he fucked, somebody who brought him bundles of cash contributed by the misguided. It was almost as if he were being paid exorbitant sums of money for servicing her.

Rosabal sat down. Suddenly he could feel building inside him the kind of doubts he so rarely entertained these days. What if everything went wrong? What if Magdalena Torrente survived and informed the *fidelista* authorities about Rosabal's revolution? What if this, what if that? He had to keep cool, serene, maintain a calm centre. The poor boy, the cane-cutter's son from Guantanamo, still lived somewhere inside him, that undernourished child who felt he did not deserve any kind of success. He was angry all at once with the ghost of his upbringing. A familiar darkness clouded his vision. It was not the time to be insecure. It was time for resolve, for confidence. It was time to assassinate the past.

Rain pelted the windows, but the heavy skies were less ominous now. The officers smoked cigarettes, studied the rain, said nothing. They too were tense. Now and then a vehicle passed on the road nearby, at which times Rosabal always stared at the meadow expectantly. But the truck carrying the missile did not appear.

When the telephone rang Rosabal's first reaction was one of unease: bad news, he was sure of it. Perhaps the scheme had been discovered and already those forces aligned against Castro had been routed and arrested, and the names of the conspirators given to Castro loyalists.

An officer picked up the phone. The caller wanted the Minister. Rosabal took the receiver and heard the voice of a certain Captain Sanchez of the political police in Havana. The connection was terrible. Sanchez's voice echoed.

'We found the car in San José de las Lajas driven by a certain Alberto Canto. A physician, Minister.'

'And?'

'He was taken for questioning.'

'Has he spoken? Did he mention the woman?'

'He said she was badly wounded. He claims she was going to make her way to Matanzas.

It seems she intended to arrange some kind of black-market transportation back to the United States. He didn't think she could possibly survive. The wound is deep.'

'Shoot the physician. Concentrate on the woman. It can't be impossible to find a wounded woman in the fifty miles between San José and Matanzas.'

'We're looking, Minister.'

'Look harder. Report to me the moment you have killed her.'

Rosabal put the receiver down. So she was wounded, badly so. Poor, ambitious Magdalena, who thought she had it all. He shook his head. Ambition could sometimes be a deceiver. Rosabal smiled to himself, then turned to look across the meadow.

There it was. At last. There it was.

The big truck carrying the tarpaulined missile and the control module came slowly across the muddy path that traversed the meadow. It was followed by a van in which sat a group of technicians who were here to disarm the missile. Gunther Ruhr was visible behind the windshield of the large truck. Next to him was a driver provided by the General.

Rosabal stepped from the porch. Magnetised by the missile, unmindful of the rain – softer now – that fell upon his eyelids, he hurried across the glistening grass to the place where the truck had come to a halt.

20 Santiago de Cuba

Alejandro Bengochea's optimism about refuelling quickly was unfounded. It took almost an hour for a fuel truck to show up and another fifteen minutes during which he haggled with the driver and a bribe was eventually negotiated. Pagan, an impatient man at the best of times, was sorely tested by the length of the transaction. He had images of Gunther Ruhr and the missile disappearing from the face of the earth.

Then, at the conclusion of the deal, the chopper would not start. Plugs and cables in the engine were damp, electrical connections failed to make contact. It took Bengochea another hour of patient labour to bring the machine back to life and fly the forty miles from Palma Soriano to the city of Santiago. He cursed for a while, muttering about low-grade plugs and cables without waterproofing, thieves and cheats and black-marketeers who profited from the re-sale of state petrol.

In the grey morning light the storm's path was made evident by fallen trees and upturned huts and cars that had been tossed on their sides. Inside the city itself were houses without roofs and statues that had been blown ingloriously down and small parks where everything had been flattened – plants, trees, fences. Rain thudded against the skin of the helicopter, but the wind had died to fifteen, twenty miles an hour.

Pagan saw the docks come in view below the railway station. A score of ships were anchored there. They flew a variety of flags – South American, East European, Scandinavian, Panamanian. Alejandro Bengochea directed the chopper up and over the harbour, while Pagan, conscious of the silent child who sat directly behind him breathing in a shallow, monotonous way, scanned the vessels below. Rain blew over unloaded cargo;

discoloured crates littered the docks, unpacked agricultural machinery lay exposed; brand new trucks, recently unloaded, filled up with rainwater.

The *Mandadera* was docked between a Norwegian freighter and a Venezuelan tanker. Bengochea steered the chopper over her deck. There was no sign of life. Ruhr and the missile had already gone.

Bengochea was undismayed by the ship's emptiness. He flew back over the city, surveying the streets, eyes narrowed; how could a missile be hidden from view? Since the ship could only recently have docked, the missile couldn't have gone far. It wasn't the kind of cargo a truck could transport quickly and easily. Bengochea took the chopper up higher, following the line of the coast that led out of Santiago in an easterly direction.

Pagan had the nagging feeling that he should cut his losses and somehow get the girl back home and forget Ruhr and the nuclear hardware. But how could he simply take Steffie Brough back to London and leave Ruhr and the weapon behind? No: he couldn't go back, not now, not after all this; besides, he had the belief, common to men who are more optimist than cynic, that the deeper the shit one had to go through to get to it, the happier the ending had to be.

Hold the thought, Frank.

Bengochea flew out of the city in a northerly direction. He passed over a rum factory and a flour mill and an oil refinery. There was no sign of a truck carrying a missile through the streets. He turned the helicopter around and flew south-west, back in the direction of the sea. *Donde?* he kept asking. *Donde?* Shaking his head in frustration, he flew the chopper low along the shoreline. Then he swung away from the water's edge and back through the rainy haze. The Sierra Maestra mountains, forlorn and unwelcoming, could be seen in the distance.

'It's got to be some bloody place,' Pagan said. The nuclear needle in the haystack.

Bengochea may not have understood the words, but he recognised Pagan's tone. He shrugged sympathetically, then lowered the chopper so that it barely skimmed the tops of trees.

Bengochea turned the aircraft round again. He flew directly over Puerto Siboney, then swung inland away from the beaches, over farmlands and a coffee plantation.

And then the missile was suddenly visible in a meadow surrounded by tall trees. It sat on the back of a long truck and looked incongruous in this rainy pastoral setting. Pagan saw it too. He wanted Bengochea to bring the chopper down into the field, his first quick impulse, but there were too many people on the ground. From a height of fifteen hundred feet Pagan could see men work around the missile, which was being raised by hydraulic jacks into a launch position on the back of a long truck. Uniformed soldiers stood guard in the grassy field.

As a ruse to discredit Castro, Pagan thought, it was elaborate and convincing, right down to the detail of the missile being cranked into a firing position. Somebody down there would have the responsibility of taking pictures, of course. Photographers, not scribes, were the true recorders of history. Nothing in this world was so persuasive as a striking image, one the masses might digest easily: here was Castro's dangerous missile in true living colour, proof of his nuclear calumny. Universal recognition – you didn't even have to be able to read to grasp the horrifying potential of it. And Rosabal would have himself snapped with the missile in the background, naturally. The hero. The saviour. The man who rid the world of crazy old Fidel.

Pagan gestured for Bengochea to circle the meadow again. Looking down, he saw two figures approach the missile-truck. One was Gunther Ruhr. The other might have been Rosabal. Bengochea flew round a couple of times, dropping as low as he thought prudent.

But now there was gunfire from the soldiers in the field. It came uncomfortably close to the cabin. Bengochea pulled the chopper up deftly, but he wasn't swift enough to avoid several shots slamming into the fuselage. Steffie Brough, silent for the last hour, whimpered when she realised the helicopter was being fired upon. Pagan tried to comfort her with some soothing words, but he'd never been very good with kids.

Bengochea went higher as a spray of bullets pierced the window of the cabin and continued past his skull and exited through the roof. Then he took the chopper up beyond the range of gunfire.

Looking down, Pagan saw Rosabal and Ruhr move toward the control module. Was Ruhr about to show Rosabal what the machine was made of? A sightseeing tour? Pagan shuddered at the notion of those two fine upstanding characters controlling a missile. He wished for a grenade, something that would wipe out both Ruhr and Rosabal and render the missile utterly useless at the same time.

He gazed down from a height of three thousand feet into the trees. Think. There must be some course of action to take. He concentrated, but couldn't come up with anything. He understood only that he couldn't ask Bengochea to fly back in again, because he couldn't risk Steffie Brough's life a second time.

In the rain, Gunther Ruhr and Rosabal watched the chopper retreat above the trees, then hover for a time at a safe distance.

'Who is in that goddam helicopter?' Rosabal asked.

Gunther Ruhr said, 'A man called Frank Pagan.'

'Pagan?'

'An English cop. You know him?'

'By reputation. We can take care of him,' Rosabal said.

'Don't underestimate him.'

Rosabal made a dismissive gesture. Pagan was a dogged bastard. How in God's name had he managed to come all the way here? But what did it matter now? Pagan didn't worry him. Automatic rifle fire would either bring the chopper down or drive it away if it returned. Rosabal had no time to be bothered by anything so trivial as an English policeman in a helicopter. He absentmindedly watched one of the cameramen take photographs of the weapon.

Gunther Ruhr looked at the missile. It was beautiful in the rain. 'It's time for me to leave. The missile is delivered and armed. That's what my contract called for.'

Rosabal raised his face, looked at the sky. The chopper was hovering beyond the trees about a mile away. Then he turned to Ruhr, whose colourless face and lips offended him; for a second his attention was drawn down to the ugly hand, which hung at the German's side.

'Don't rush away, Gunther,' he said.

'Why should I wait? Is there some problem? I was promised air passage to Haiti after delivery. I was also promised a considerable sum of money when I reach Port-Au-Prince. I hope you are not thinking of double-crossing me. If anything happens to me, I can guarantee you the kind of exposure that will bring your little world down around your ears.'

Rosabal smiled. 'Nobody is going to double-cross you, my friend. Relax.'

'So why are you asking me to stay?'

'Because this intrigues me. Because I want to know more. Because you're obviously a splendid teacher.' Rafael Rosabal, adept at flattering men whose lives had inspired very little approbation, smiled a warm smile. *We're friends, Gunther, we are in this together,* the smile said.

Rosabal indicated the rectangular control module, from which the wet tarpaulin had been removed. Both men climbed up on to the truck. The door of the module was opened; they squeezed inside.

It was a small chamber some eight feet by seven. There was barely enough room for two men to sit in cramped positions in front of computer screens, directional equipment and the firing mechanism. From the control centre to the missile, which was raised to an angle of some forty-five degrees at the front of the truck, ran sets of cables that relayed commands to the missile's navigational system.

'I am interested in the controls,' Rosabal said. 'Show me.'

Ruhr turned on switches. The screens flickered.

'You enter data here and the missile goes wherever you want to send it,' Ruhr said. 'Within its range, of course.'

'Fascinating.'

Ruhr touched the instrument panel. He loved it. The design was economical, splendidly functional. He ran the tips of his fingers lightly over the console. He demonstrated how one plotted a course for the missile. There was fervour in the way Ruhr talked; it was the attitude of a man bewitched by his subject. Rosabal was more interested in Ruhr's nuclear fascination, his obsession with destruction, than in the technical details with which the German was bombarding him. Technical matters always made Rosabal's eyes and mind glaze over. He really didn't care how a thing worked, only that it did.

'It would be interesting . . . to fly the missile,' Rosabal said.

Gunther Ruhr said nothing. He thought how exhilarating it would be to see the missile riding the skies through the rain, unerring, a twenty-foot steel arrow piercing the heart of its target.

Rosabal pressed the tips of his fingers together, placed them against his lips in an attitude of deliberation; an uninformed observer might have thought he was praying. But Rosabal was imagining Miami, a city he'd never visited, one he'd seen only in books and movies. He was imagining the hotels of the Art Deco district, old men and women sitting on the porches of pink and turquoise hotels, frowning at the hazy sea; he was imagining the exclusive little shops of Coral Gables and the huge hotels on Collins Avenue and the Cuban cafés along Calle Ocho where the troublemakers gathered to squabble about politics in Havana. And then he remembered his sick father who had gone to Guantanamo, to the American Naval Station, and asked for asylum in the United States, how he'd been laughingly turned away, and then made to disappear by Castro's political police afterwards.

Yes, it was right, everything he had planned all along was correct and just. He had absolutely no doubt.

He looked at Gunther Ruhr and he asked, 'Can you make it fly?'

'Of course,' Ruhr replied. He could hardly breathe: *was he being asked to do the very thing he'd dreamed of doing?*

'Then why don't you?' Rosabal asked.

Ruhr felt a shiver of anticipation; the hairs on the backs of his hands bristled. 'What target would please you?'

Some hours before the capture that would result in his execution, several hours before he lied to his interrogators about Magdalena Torrente's whereabouts, Alberto Canto had driven his car to a secluded place and bandaged her side. He'd applied antibiotic cream over the wound, then gauze. The ointment came from Russia, he apologised, and its potency was suspect, but it was all he had in his possession. He wished he had an X-ray machine to assess the damage and fix the position of the slug in her body. The repair he made was a temporary measure, and a poor one at best; she'd need treatment within a few hours at a good hospital. Her breathing was unsteady, her temperature certain to rise. Either she would have to return to the United States or run the risk of a hospital in Havana, where her illegal status might be discovered, and the consequences dire.

She announced she'd fly herself to Florida if a plane could be found. Astonished by her confidence, Canto argued she was certainly in no condition to fly an aircraft despite the painkiller he'd injected into her. Consider the turbulent weather, Canto had said. The darkness. Consider the seriousness of your wound. Your condition is terrible.

Canto had strongly recommended trying to find a pilot to take her. If she had to fly home, she shouldn't be at the controls herself. But she defied him. She could do it alone. She stubbornly insisted. He argued from the medical point of view but Magdalena Torrente, unmoved, had reservoirs of determination that Canto could not even begin to fathom.

At the airstrip outside San José de Las Lajas she stole without difficulty a small plane, a single-engine Beechcraft Bonanza, made in the United States and imported circuitously into Cuba, that belonged to some official in the Ministry of Construction. She'd learned how to steal planes from the old fliers at the exile training camps in the Everglades. Canto still tried to prevent her. There on the rainy field, barely able to hear each other over the scream of the wind, they had argued passionately. It was madness, Canto had shouted. She couldn't fly a plane in her state. If she didn't get to a hospital quickly she might haemorrhage, perhaps bleed to death. But in the end Magdalena's determination overcame the physician's compassionate caution.

She wasn't troubled about flying, despite the weather and her condition. Canto's painkiller kicked in quickly; besides, the storm had begun to diminish by the time she was ready to fly out of San José de Las Lajas. She embraced the physician, expressed her gratitude, kissed him, and left a smear of her own blood on his shirt.

There were maps in the cockpit. The instrumentation was simple. She took off into the driving rain, looking down once for a sight of the physician, but Canto had gone.

She had lied to him. She had absolutely no intention of flying this plane to Florida.

Inside the cramped control module Rafael Rosabal pretended to deliberate a moment before he answered Gunther Ruhr's question about a target.

'I think Miami,' he said.

Alejandro Bengochea landed the chopper in a field a mile from the missile. He got out, checked the body of the craft, which had been struck on the fuselage by rifle fire but the fuel line was intact.

Pagan stepped down from the chopper and gazed thoughtfully into the rain. What was he supposed to do next? His head ached, his mind was an empty room. Armed with an ancient revolver he had borrowed from Bengochea, a gun that should have been retired years ago, how could he possibly slip past soldiers with automatic weapons and get to Ruhr? Even if he did, how could he disable that bloody missile?

He was aware of Steffie Brough watching him. He looked up, half-smiled, tried to appear encouraging, the friendly, reliable London cop who knew which bus to take to Battersea Park or the quickest way to Buckingham Palace. There was some element of accusation in her trance-like expression, as if she couldn't understand why she wasn't going home. She breathed upon the glass and, like a small child fascinated by condensation, drew a shapeless pattern with a fingertip. Then she turned her face away from Pagan, her profile sullen.

Pagan looked across the field. He was wet, but wetness and misery had quickly become conditions of his life, and almost acceptable. He turned Bengochea's revolver over in his hand, and stared once more across the meadow. He shrugged. It wasn't the best idea he'd ever had, but it was the only thing that occurred to him.

'I'm going back there,' he said to Bengochea.

'*Que?*'

'On foot. Alone. *Solo*.'

Bengochea looked puzzled.

Pagan said, 'You stay here. Keep an eye on the girl. If I don't come back, you take her to the British Embassy in Havana. Understand?'

Pagan turned, walked away from the helicopter, looking back once. Steffie Brough wasn't watching him, but Alejandro Bengochea was still shaking his head. He hadn't entirely understood Pagan's words although he was convinced that the Englishman, even if a little *estupido*, was nevertheless a brave man.

Magdalena had flown for three hours at seven thousand feet, trying to keep the Bonanza above the turbulence, but the erratic wind shook the plane. When she climbed higher, clouds obscured the Central Highway she was trying to follow. She didn't want to fly without some kind of direct visual guide. She came down again to about three thousand feet.

Then the painkiller began to wear off. It was hard to find a comfortable position. Maybe there wasn't one. She swallowed two of the codeine Canto had given her, but they didn't quell the fire in her side.

Rain pummelled the plane. Mist and cloud created mysterious shapes around the cockpit. She lightly touched the place Canto had bandaged. Painful. It was weird to realise you had a bullet in your body, a foreign piece of metal in your system. What had it shattered? What had it punctured? Was some vital organ threatened?

But was it any more weird to have a foreign object in your body than to have a broken heart?

Sweat formed on her brow, ran down into her eyes. And yet she was cold, cold inside.

She gazed down at the highway. At some point she would have to fly south-west to Bayamo.

And then Bayamo to Santiago. About a hundred miles. Less than an hour's flying time.

If she could make it.

When she'd flown three hundred miles, the sky had turned to a fuzzy kind of grey. There was light but no sun. The harsh unremitting rain created a bizarre tattoo on the cockpit. She wiped sweat out of her eyes, concentrated on the skies ahead, the road below.

Why was she so damned cold? Then so warm?

She looked down at her bandage. Redness seeped through the material.

I lost more than blood, she thought. I lost myself.

She touched the bandage, brought her hand up; her fingertips were red.

Think good things. But she couldn't keep her head from filling with images of Rafael. His lovely deceptive face kept rising in her mind.

If he materialised here right now, if he appeared beside her in this cabin and asked for forgiveness, what would she say?

Yes.

Yes I forgive you again.

You'd do that, wouldn't you? You'd do it all over again. You never learned a thing. Where Rafael was concerned, her heart always flew ahead of her reasoning like a canary sent by coal-miners into the deep, unmapped caverns of underground shafts to check for poisoned air.

Her love was more than a sickness. She breathed her love for Rafael. It was as necessary to her existence as oxygen. It was inside her the way her bloodstream was. And yet it was poisoned.

She loved him. And she wanted him dead.

She looked down at the grey-green landscape; she could see the ocean flooding over beaches, great clouds of spray.

She flew over Bayamo at one hundred and thirty miles an hour. The pain burned all the way through her. She shut her eyes because it was so goddam fierce. She hadn't ever known anything so intense. Once, years ago, she'd had an abortion, the consequence of a dalliance with a young boy at a military camp in the Everglades, and the doctor had done something wrong and her womb had become infected, and she remembered the way pain seemed to scream inside her; but even that agony, which had been like a hat-pin pressed into the walls of her womb, was nothing to what she felt now.

She dropped her hands from the controls. She was cold, so damned cold, and even though she had no mirror she knew she was pale and the skin under her eyes black. There was sweat on her upper lip and her hands shook and something made from steel, some kind of pincer, clutched her intestines. She cried aloud. She felt herself slip toward blackout; around the periphery of her vision was darkness. She opened a window, let the cold wet air blow at her and keep her awake.

She placed her hands on the controls again and steadied the plane, but her grip was loose and weak and the tips of her fingers numb in a way that filled her with dread. She thought she could hear a spectre whisper, a nearby voice, a hint of a song she'd never heard in her life before now – seductive, distant, bittersweet.

She didn't want to hear that song. She knew what it meant and it scared her, but the fear lasted only a moment before she moved beyond it to some other level of understanding, that place where all outcomes are neither sad nor joyful, good nor bad, but simply inevitable.

Pagan sneaked between the trees that surrounded the field. There was perhaps a score of men, many of them armed, clustered around the missile. Was he mistaken or had the angle of the missile changed since he'd last seen it? It seemed to have been raised to a higher elevation. It pointed toward the sky with a certain dark purpose, angled at approximately seventy-five degrees. Through the rain he could see the open door of the module. Although his angle of vision prevented him from seeing anything more than shadows, he was certain that Ruhr and Rosabal were inside.

Pagan crouched, tried to make himself invisible. If he stepped out of the trees he'd be seen and shot. How was he meant to reach the module? The only possibility that suggested itself – tucking his head well down and running hard at the module – was ludicrous, and utterly suicidal, and he wasn't in much of a mood to slit his own throat. Not yet.

There had to be a better way.

He considered circling the meadow, making an approach from another direction, but the obstacles were exactly the same. Uniformed men carefully watched both landscape and sky in all directions.

It was useless. There was nothing he could do. He could crouch here in the trees five hundred feet away and fire the old revolver towards the missile-truck and perhaps puncture a tyre if he got really lucky. Terrific. But as soon as he fired he'd be shot at: end of Frank Pagan.

He stared at the missile.

It moved noticeably by perhaps a foot, then it stopped. Pagan held his breath. They were playing with the thing from inside the module. Perhaps Ruhr was simply demonstrating it.

Perhaps not. But Pagan didn't like the suspicion that formed in his mind just then.

No, no. They couldn't be planning to fire the bloody thing. Not in a hundred years. Ruhr was just showing Rosabal how it worked, that was all, then it would be dismantled, and defused, and destroyed. Wasn't that the plan? Yes, yes, of course that was the bloody plan, what else could it be?

Pagan felt an extraordinary sense of futility. If the men inside the module intended to fly the bird, he couldn't do anything to stop them – except take a pot-shot at the control module with Alejandro's stupid revolver. What else was there to do?

He aimed the revolver at the control chamber on the back of the big truck; he was very careful, lining up the module in his sight with a kind of concentration that made his head ache. If he struck the module with a shot – perhaps he might hit something important: the wiring, the connection cables, perhaps his bullet might penetrate the shell of the control centre and rupture some essential component inside. You couldn't bank on perhapses, you couldn't pay bills with them.

His hand trembled.

He squeezed his finger upon the trigger.

He fired.

His shot passed through the space between missile and module, harmless, feeble, desperate. The fire was returned, the air split by the vicious spray of automatic weapons. He threw himself flat and crawled toward a clump of shrubbery as he listened to the air whine around his skull.

But there was another sound now, and it came from the sky.

He looked up.

Magdalena had flown three times over the city of Santiago de Cuba before she found what she was looking for. Dimly, she registered the meadow, the ring of trees, the missile-truck fifteen hundred feet below her. It was tiny and it wouldn't stay still in her vision, and spots the shape of amoebae kept prancing in front of her eyes. But it was the chill that bothered her more than anything else, the voracious cold that consumed her. She'd never known such a sensation before.

The death cold, she thought.

The cold of the coffin. Frozen earth.

She passed across the field, wheeled the small plane, made a second sweep; the craft lost height, dropping two, three hundred feet. Then she must have blacked out briefly because she couldn't remember bringing the plane even lower, bringing it down to a height that was only five hundred feet over the missile truck. She clutched her side, drew her hand away, saw how her palm and fingers were covered with blood that had seeped through Canto's bandage. But the bloodied hand was no longer her own, it was some ghostly thing, an appendage without substance. And it seemed to her that the blood froze on her flesh, and changed to crystals, pale pink crystals that were swept from her skin by the draught that rushed through the open window.

Dying, she thought. Dying, dying.

She made another pass over the field.

She was so low now she could see the faces of the men who fired guns at her. Their bullets slammed against the fuselage. She watched the marksmen rush out of her path as she flew no more than fifteen feet over the surface of the meadow.

Dying, she thought again.

It had its own kind of perfect madness.

The truck loomed up in front of her. The missile, angrily poised as if for flight, the open door of the control module – she saw these things rush towards her, and then it was as if everything in the world were being sucked in by her propellers, leaves, blades of grass, men, guns, clouds, everything was disappearing inside the slipstream of her rushing aircraft, crowding her vision, her brain, stifling her ability to take air into her lungs.

Inside the module Gunther Ruhr set the course of the missile. He calculated it would strike directly into the heart of Miami. But accuracy wasn't very important when you were talking about the total devastation of a city; a mile or two either way hardly mattered.

'How much damage will it do?' Rosabal asked. 'How many will die?'

'Consider Hiroshima,' Ruhr answered.

Hiroshima. Two hundred thousand people had died there, many thousands more had become sick from radiation. The city had been totally destroyed. Rosabal said nothing. He heard gunfire outside, ignored it. He merely imagined the chopper was circling the field again. Sooner or later it would be shot out of the sky. Nothing in the external world was important; only this small chamber mattered.

'This will be worse,' Ruhr said cheerfully. 'Much worse. Ten times as many people will perish. Perhaps more.'

'Do it,' Rosabal said.

Ruhr leaned forward over the console. Like a cardshark about to shuffle a deck, a conjurer ready to perform an illusion, he rubbed his hands together a few times as if to stimulate his circulation, then he held both hands over the console. He might have been born for just this moment, his trick of all tricks.

'Do it! Goddamit, do it now!' Rosabal snapped.

Gunther Ruhr smiled; it was perhaps the singular most blissful expression that had ever appeared on his face. His hands dropped toward the console.

In a fraction of time too small for even the finest chronometers to measure, too short for the senses to organise detail from chaos, Magdalena saw Rafael Rosabal in the open door of the module. His face was turned slightly away from her, but his profile was visible, unmistakable. She felt her chilled blood rush to her head and through the window of her small failing plane could smell wet grass and black mud – and then everything came together in that one chaotic reduction of time, module and aeroplane, sky and mud, Magdalena and the man she loved, the man with whom she might now spend eternity if there happened to be one, it all fused, melded, and even as it came together it also exploded and blew apart, white flame conjoining the aircraft and the missile-truck, searing the fuselage, disintegrating the module and the men inside it, setting aflame the cables that married the missile to its control centre, then finally toppling in fire the missile itself, which rolled from the truck and slithered from its erector and slumped, fuses melted and shot, navigational system destroyed, its function rendered harmless, into the soft mud.

Frank Pagan saw Magdalena for only a second as the plane savagely struck the module, and then he closed his eyes against the intense heat he could feel roll across the meadow toward the trees where he stood. When he opened his eyes he looked at how tall flames rose in a great white dance from the truck, a noisy dance set to the strange crackling music of fire. There was a quality of illusion to his perceptions: had he really seen her in the tiny cockpit of that doomed plane? Had he imagined it?

He stepped back under the cover of the trees. The soldiers who had been shooting at him only minutes before were running from the fiery ruin of the truck as fast and as far as they could, some with their uniforms on fire. He saw one wing of the plane collapse like burning paper, but after that there was very little distinction between objects trapped in the furnace. They all glowed with the same hallucinatory intensity.

He turned and ran as quickly as he could to the place where Bengochea and the child waited in the helicopter.

Cabo Gracias a Dios, Honduras

The storm uprooted the tent of Tomas Fuentes and blew it across the airstrip toward the ocean, where anchored boats precariously rode the swell. A freighter that had set sail some thirty minutes before had already turned back, and another small ship was reported capsized. On the airstrip, fighter-planes were chained to stone chocks lest they drift and roll in the wind. Tomas watched his tent go flying off like a great bird with drab olive plumage and the grace of an ostrich, and then it was lost from sight. Bosanquet's tent went the same way, flapping like loose laundry, dragging its guy ropes behind it.

Fuentes studied the roiling sea just as the wind ripped the panama hat from his head and launched it up into the tall branches of trees where it was blown from left to right, up and down, then out of sight, a symbol – if Fuentes wanted to see it this way – of a lost cause.

He preferred to think of it as a cause postponed. There would be other days, and they would be stormless, and the sea clear all the way to Cuba and that *hijo de puta*, Fidel Castro.

21 London

Frank Pagan looked from the window of the Boeing 727 as the electric coastline of Florida faded and the darkness of the ocean replaced land. Then there were clouds, becalmed in the storm's aftermath. He pretended to read the in-flight magazine but his attention was drawn time and again to Steffie Brough in the seat beside him.

She was lost in a glossy magazine of her own, a world of models, a synthetic reality, clearly preferable to the one she'd just experienced. She was oddly quiet most of the trip, unwilling to answer even the most innocuous of Pagan's questions. He realised that sooner or later this little girl was going to need expert help, a counsellor, a therapist. Ruhr had left his mark on her – the question was how much damage had been done?

Pagan, who had no great mastery of small talk, made idle comments, and Steffie Brough responded, if at all, in a dull way. Strangers with nothing to share, Pagan thought, which in one sense was true – he a London policeman, she a horse-breeder's daughter from farmlands, what could they have in common? The girl, though, had a certain dead look in her eyes, as if curiosity were a capacity she didn't have; no questions about Pagan's investigation, no gratitude. Although Pagan sought none, he nevertheless would have thought it natural in the circumstances. She flipped magazine pages, picked at her airline food – chicken pellets with almonds, a glutinous matter masquerading as rice. She was quite lost to Pagan's efforts to reach her, beyond any kindness he showed, any concern he demonstrated. And he tried; despite what he considered a lack of any natural affinity for kids – here he underestimated himself – he made a good effort. Her retreat defeated him.

It was after five a.m. when the flight reached London, a grey English dawn with a spiteful, jaundiced sun. Heathrow was out of the question – too many journalists and photographers waiting for snapshots of that most beloved of human occurrences, the tearful reunion. Consequently, the plane was diverted to Gatwick, and Stephanie Brough's parents were taken there in an unmarked car.

Pagan disembarked with the girl. Outside, in a lounge set aside for the child's return, a small crowd had come to meet her – her parents, a grandmother, a brother (a gangling youth of unsurpassed awkwardness who had somehow contrived to break the stems of roses he brought to his sister), a dozen or so uniformed policemen, half of them women, detectives in plain clothes, Billy Ewing from Golden Square, and Martin Burr, who clapped Pagan's shoulder as if to say it was a job well done. And so it was, but Burr was never expansive in his appreciations. A professional did what was expected of him, a professional needed no special thanks. Later, there would be reports and interviews, but not for the moment.

Pagan, tired, trying not to yawn, was thanked by the gushing parents and the grandmother who planted a perfumed kiss on his lips. All he wanted was to drift away, go back to his flat, sleep for days. It was a lonely prospect and he was apprehensive about the possibility of bad dreams, a missile rising into the launch position, the sight of a small aeroplane burning in a Cuban field – but it was time to slow down his private clock.

He watched the happy crowd inside the lounge, the smilingly tearful family, Steffie's mother with her white insomniac face lit like a bright lightbulb, Mr Brough in a check suit with a camel hair waistcoat, Steffie herself clinging quietly to her mother.

And yet Pagan felt weird. Displaced. Out of sorts. A feeling that had nothing to do with his fatigue. There was something not quite right about this whole gathering.

He walked to a drinks machine, pressed in a coin, heard a can of Coca-Cola come hurtling down the chute. He popped it, sipped the stuff, longed for a dram of the Auchentoshan to spike it up, and wondered what it was that left him so chilled, that sense of missing something. And then he knew what it was even before Billy Ewing – hushed, confidential, looking like a bookie's clerk – grabbed him by the elbow and took him aside. They stepped out of the lounge and into the grubby dawn, where Billy blew his nose with distinctive flair, a trombonist of the sinuses.

'It's Foxie,' Billy Ewing said.

Of course, Pagan thought. That was it. Foxie wasn't here. Good old Foxie hadn't shown up. He gazed at Billy Ewing and waited for more, but the Scotsman hadn't much to add.

'He hasn't come back yet, Frank. Off he went to Glasgow, called in with one message, and that was the last we heard from him.'

'You've tried to contact him?'

'Oh, aye – last night I talked with Glasgow Central myself.'

'And?'

Billy Ewing shrugged. 'And nothing. No trace. He borrowed a car belonging to Glasgow CID – and it hasn't been returned.'

'Do you have a copy of his last message?' Pagan asked.

'Back at the office.'

'We'll go in your car, Billy,' Pagan said.

'Whatever you say.'

They went in Ewing's Ford through Central London, through streets springing to daily, prosaic life, and by the time they reached Golden Square, Frank Pagan's sleepiness had evaporated, replaced by a general sense of uneasiness.

The message was already two days old and as Pagan fingered the flimsy piece of paper he had the unsettling feeling, given perhaps only to mediums and soothsayers, that Foxie's silence indicated a serious condition.

'Mibbe he's following up on something,' Ewing suggested. 'Mibbe he's on to something hot.'

'And he couldn't find change for a telephone call, Billy?'

Ewing, baffled, shrugged. He knew as well as Pagan that Foxworth was a diligent man who paid conscientious attention to detail. Pagan went inside his office and sat for a time on the sofa. He shut his eyes, rubbed them, worried about Foxie.

He looked up at Billy Ewing. 'Get me on the next available flight to Glasgow, Billy. And get me a gun.'

'Do you want some company, Frank? I know the territory, after all.'

Pagan shook his head, stood up, felt an immense pressure in his chest. He didn't want company, talkative or otherwise. He would follow Foxworth's trail alone. He borrowed Ewing's pistol, a Smith and Wesson, and Billy drove him from Golden Square out along the motorway to Heathrow.

On the way Billy Ewing mentioned the result of his inquiries into Harry Hurt and Sheridan Perry. Pagan could barely recall having made the request; it seemed such a long time ago. Rich pair of buggers, Frank, was how Billy Ewing phrased it. 'But wealth, as my old Grannie used to phrase it, is no guarantee of immortality.'

'Meaning?'

'Harry Hurt was assassinated in Washington, and Sheridan Perry has disappeared.'

'Somehow I'm not surprised,' Pagan said.

Billy Ewing sighed. 'There's a lot of dying going on, Frank.'

Scotland

The flight to Glasgow was uneventful. It was just after eight a.m. when Pagan arrived and took a taxi to the city centre. Morning sunlight in the city, an unexpected state of affairs, and lovely, the breeze off the River Clyde bracing, the clouds rushing across a clear blue sky. In the heart of Glasgow Pagan went at once to the offices of the Executive Motor Car Company in West Nile Street. This was the new Glasgow – gone was a certain tired, washed-out drabness, a weariness of the soul that had given the city the appearance of some Baltic capital. Uplifted, scrubbed, renewed, it was as if the city had overcome an inferiority complex after many years of arduous, expensive therapy.

Pagan found the Executive Motor Car Company located over a philately shop. He climbed the stairs. Halfway up, winded, he paused. A telephone rang somewhere above him, a kettle whistled. This was the way Foxworth had come, these were the stairs he must have climbed. Pagan reached the landing where a lovely young woman stood in a doorway, holding in one hand a mug of hot tea.

'You don't look terrific,' she said. 'Are you feeling sick? Can I get you anything?'

Pagan smiled, shook his head, showed his ID, asked about Foxie. The woman said her name was Miss Wilkie and, yes, she remembered Foxworth, he had been very charming, very much a gentleman of the kind one rarely saw these days – and she blushed, Pagan noticed.

Miss Wilkie frowned, as if she had become suddenly concerned about Foxworth's fate. 'Has something happened to him?'

'I'm not sure,' Pagan replied. 'Where was he going when he left here?'

'I gave him very specific directions, Mr Pagan, to a house in Ayrshire. In fact, I kept a copy of the map our driver made for him. It's a bit rough, but easy to follow.' She paused. She had small, trim hands that gleamed because they had recently been rubbed with skin lotion. 'He hasn't come back yet, is that it?'

Pagan nodded. 'That's it exactly.'

'He asked about some men – let me think a minute. They had names that began with the letter C. One was called Chap, Chap something or other.'

'Chapotin?'

'I believe you're right,' said Miss Wilkie. 'The other man was named Caporelli. Both these men used our limousines to visit the country house in which Mr Foxworth showed such interest.'

Pagan felt a very small pulse in his dry throat. He tried to imagine Foxie's excitement when he uncovered the information that both Chapotin and Enrico Caporelli had visited the same house. That link, that complex knot tying together Caporelli and Chapotin, the same knot that brought both Rosabal and Gunther Ruhr into its ornate folds and twists.

'He might have been in an accident,' Miss Wilkie said in a kindly, hesitant way. 'Some of the roads are bad. Then there are cliffs . . .' She left this line of thought alone, and smiled, and there was bravery in the expression. 'You'll find him, you'll see. People always turn up.'

But in what condition? Pagan wondered. He took the copy of the map, studied it, felt dizzy. He asked about renting a car and Miss Wilkie said she could oblige very easily. A few forms to complete, that was all. Pagan filled in the requisite paperwork, thanked Miss Wilkie, shook her hand, went down into West Nile Street. The city seemed unduly loud to him suddenly, the clatter of buses, clogged streets. He found a small coffee shop near Royal Exchange Square and went inside, drank two cups of strong Kenyan quickly, then returned to Executive Motor Cars Limited to pick up his hired car, a Fiat Uno.

Out of the city and on his way south; easy enough on paper, but his sense of direction was skewed and he went in circles for an hour before finding the route that would take him into Ayrshire, presumably the same route Foxworth had taken before. Pagan drove carefully; sleep kept coming in now, dark wave after dark wave. He studied Miss Wilkie's map now and then, and, noticing the sparkling greenery of the countryside through which he drove, wished he were a tourist and this some casual jaunt directly into the heart of beauty.

He stopped in Ayr, stretched his legs near the harbour, breathed the sea air into his lungs, watched gulls squabble like spectators in search of a sport. Perhaps Foxie had come this way too; pursuing a ghost, Pagan thought. He half-expected to see Foxie by the side of the road, his automobile broken down and young Foxie resting indolently upon a grassy bank while awaiting the arrival of a mechanic. But Pagan saw no Foxworths and no broken-down cars. He drove south out of Ayr and almost at once the countryside became forlorn – lovely, yes, but in a different way, more starkly melancholic, with ancient, white-washed stone cottages and old farmhouses erected in quiet isolation, and here and there a TV antenna to bring another world, an incongruous one, into old parlours. Pagan continued to drive south.

He parked in a place overlooking the sea, examined the map again. He saw Ballantrae on his rough map, and out of that village led a narrow track, and there – an inked rectangle, underlined – was presumably the house. It was unnamed, a simple inky square on copy paper. Had Foxworth gone there? Had he found it? If so, why hadn't he called Golden Square to say so?

Pagan's head throbbed as much from anxiety as pain; dread created a stress all its own. He drove again, thinking that Foxie could take care of himself, he was a grown man, a good cop, he knew how to handle situations: *so why all this damned worry?*

The town of Girvan, sunlight on deep grey water, seabirds, a miniature fairground, tarpaulined for the dead season, near the sea. Pagan was blinded by bright sun rippling on the tide. And then Girvan was behind him and he was headed for the village of Ballantrae, remembering that Robert Louis Stevenson had once written a novel entitled *The Master of Ballantrae*, but Pagan had never read it, never read a word of Stevenson; how remiss of him, he thought now. Foxie, who had gone to an expensive school, had probably read the lot.

The track outside Ballantrae was narrow. Birds flew from hedgerows – bright starlings, thrushes, plain little sparrows, and once a plump plover that flew toward Pagan's windshield as if intent on bringing to a swift conclusion some avian depression. The hedges that rose on either side prevented any kind of view of what lay beyond, and Pagan wondered if Foxie had come this way and felt the same sensation of isolation, almost an eeriness that the forceful sun could not dispel.

Foxie: where the hell are you?

What did you find in this place?

The track grew worse; the hedgerows eclipsed the low morning sun. Pagan felt the Fiat bump and shudder, but it was nothing compared to the ride in Bengochea's chopper. He slowed where the hedges thinned, seeing flat meadowlands vanish toward stands of trees, an empty landscape with neither animals nor people. Only a solitary hawk, casting a squat shadow, suggested motion. He ought to have reached the house some time ago, but then he understood that this roughly drawn map bore no resemblance to actual scale.

When he finally saw the house it surprised him. It rose in sunlight and shadow as though it were a deformed sandstone dream, grand circular towers and narrow windows, a pretension here in a landscape without airs of grandeur. He stopped the Fiat, got out, peered through the hedgerow at the edifice, then pushed his way through – branches springing at him with unexpected harshness – and stepped into a swampy meadow littered with yellow wild flowers.

The house glowed red in morning sunlight. In crannies, in abysses of brickwork, between turrets, shadows were wine-coloured and warm. Pagan walked across the sponge-like grass toward the mansion, then paused when he reached a copse of trees. Somebody had been working there – a wheelbarrow was propped alongside a tree, a spade stuck in the soil, there was the soft scent of good earth newly turned over. A sizeable trench had been dug in the ground. Pagan stepped between the trees, paused, looked off in the direction of the house, which was a half mile away.

A car was parked in the drive, a Jaguar, he thought, but sunlight obscured the lines of the vehicle; there was also a jeep just behind it. Nobody moved, though; the house showed no sign of life. Had it not been for the presence of spade and wheelbarrow and the clammy black perfume of newly shovelled earth, he might have thought the estate abandoned. He took a few steps forward between the overhanging branches of the trees, and loose leaves, disturbed by his passage, drifted to the ground around him. Earth made soft by recent rains sucked at his shoes.

Bloody hell, he was tired. He leaned against a trunk, listened to the lazy buzz of a bee nearby, a lark impossibly high in the sky. There was a narcotic conspiracy here, something to lull a man towards sleep.

The sound of a footfall made him open his eyes and turn around. The twin-barrelled shotgun, large and vicious, was held by a short man with centre-parted hair and the relic of a hare-lip that had been removed surgically years before. A feeble moustache had been grown over the scar.

Pagan reached inside his pocket for his identification, but the man gestured with the shotgun. Frank Pagan stood very still. The man, whose voice had a nasal edge, poked the barrel closer to Pagan and said, 'Another bloody snoop.'

Pagan finally fished out his wallet, but the man was unimpressed and didn't even look. *Another bloody snoop*: had Foxie been the first one?

'I'm looking for somebody,' Pagan said.

'Are you indeed?' the man said.

'A colleague of mine.'

'A colleague, is it?' The man raised one thin eyebrow. For some reason he didn't immediately understand, Pagan's attention was drawn to the spade propped against the tree, the mound of earth inside the wheelbarrow. These simple perceptions, rustic and yet sinister, shook him and he didn't know why; but now the sunlit day seemed bleached, as if colour had drained out of it.

'The man's name was Foxworth. Detective Foxworth.'

'Is that a fact?' asked the short man.

'From Scotland Yard.'

The man was still unimpressed.

'Could you lower your gun?' Pagan asked. 'You make me nervous.'

The shotgun stayed where it was, level with Pagan's heart. The man glanced through the trees toward the house. Pagan turned, saw three figures coming across the landscape, perhaps a half-mile distant and small. There was an instant familiarity about two of them; after a moment Pagan recognised the man who walked in front as Foxworth. The red hair, made almost blood-coloured by sun, was unmistakable.

Pagan's relief at the sight of Foxworth alive and breathing was immense but brief; immediately behind Foxie was a man who carried a shotgun trained on his spine.

At the rear, moving with brisk steps, hands clasped behind his back in the manner of a laird walking his terrain, was the third man. Pagan had one of those odd moments in which inversions take place – the sky tilts, the sun darkens, the heart is suddenly stilled, and perceptions are tunnelled as if through reversed binoculars.

A mistake, Pagan thought.

It had to be.

A resemblance, nothing more.

But as the three figures came closer Pagan saw Freddie Kinnaird sweep a lock of hair from his forehead in that characteristic gesture he had. There was a smile on the famous face, but cold, very cold.

No mistake.

Pagan couldn't swallow. Astonishment and a brutal, burning anger denied him that simple reflex. He thought of all the information to which Kinnaird had been privy. Everything that passed across Martin Burr's desk eventually reached Freddie. He thought of how Freddie Kinnaird had known of Gunther Ruhr's route through Shepherd's Bush, of how Freddie must have passed that juicy item along the line to Rosabal, who had arranged the drastic rescue of Gunther and rented the country hideout. At every turn, every angle, nothing of substance had been withheld from Sir Frederick Kinnaird. And he must have shared everything with his associates who had come to this house in the secret depths of the Scottish countryside – Chapotin and Caporelli, perhaps the late Herr Kluger and the two Americans as well, a tight little gang of old pals.

Pagan raised his face to the sun. He was hot in his raincoat. Freddie Kinnaird approached, stopped some yards away. Pagan glanced at Foxie, who had the slightly red-eyed look of a man who has been held captive for days in a dark room and now sunlight astounds him.

'Well, well, well,' Kinnaird said with a certain cheerfulness. 'Frank Pagan himself.'

Pagan said nothing. He had the unbearable urge to reach for Kinnaird and grab him and crush that smug face until nothing recognisable was left of it. But how could he move with a shotgun shoved into his back?

'We had that whole damned island sewn up,' Kinnaird said and grabbed air in his hand and made a fist, as if what he held there were locks of invisible hair. 'We had it all. Why did you have to stick your nose in?'

Pagan gazed upward again. The lark he'd seen before was imposed against the sun, like an inscrutable punctuation mark in the sky. 'It's my job to stick my nose in, Freddie. You know that.' There was an ugly note in Pagan's voice, which came close to breaking. Control yourself, Frank. It wasn't easy. The depths of his own loathing astonished him.

Kinnaird appeared to be elsewhere, concentrating on some inner lyric of his own. He had in his eye a very small, sharp light that suggested some quiet, well-bred form of craziness. 'You helped balls up the whole damned thing.'

'I think you overestimate me, Fred. I'd dearly love to take the credit for fucking your scheme up, but it wouldn't be fair. All I did was get a young girl out of Cuba. That was my job. I wanted to bring Ruhr back to stand trial, also part of my job. I lost that one. I did the best I could with what I had. But I'm not personally responsible for screwing up your plans for Cuba, Fred. I didn't kill Rosabal. Blame Magdalena Torrente. Blame Rosabal himself for choosing the wrong woman to fuck up over. Blame any damn thing you like. All I did was my job.'

'I rather think you're hiding your light under a bushel, Pagan. After all, you managed to save Magdalena Torrente's life in Miami.'

Pagan shouldn't have been surprised by Kinnaird's knowledge of the murder attempt, because it was plain that very little had escaped Freddie. He'd obviously learned from the Commissioner that Pagan was going to be in Miami with Magdalena Torrente. That simple. But somehow Pagan was surprised anyway, although he wasn't going to give Freddie the satisfaction of showing it.

Kinnaird, who looked all at once like a large, sulking boy, said, 'If you hadn't saved her, she'd never have gone to Cuba. And if she hadn't gone there – '

'If she hadn't gone there, Rosabal might have fired his missile.'

'Nonsense. There was never any question of firing it.'

'That's not the way I saw it.'

'Then your observations are very wrong,' Kinnaird said impatiently. 'Rafael wouldn't have fired the bloody thing. It was a prop, a piece of scenery. What the devil does it matter now anyhow? Castro is still in charge of Cuba – did you see that as part of your job, Pagan? To help keep him in power?'

'I didn't help keep anybody in power. I don't give a shit who runs Cuba, Freddie. Castro or some other old geezer – it doesn't make any bloody difference to me in the long run. They're all the same when you get right down to it.'

'What a dreadfully narrow view of the world stage,' Kinnaird said. His expression was that of a man who finds some foul morsel of very old food between his teeth.

Pagan shrugged. Of course it was a narrow view; he'd never found a broad perspective conducive to his sense of right and wrong. If your view was too wide you encountered too many ambiguities. If you sat around pondering all the issues, and trying to understand all the sides, you froze eventually into inactivity. So he always tried to keep it simple, tightly focused. He didn't know how to do his job any other way.

Kinnaird looked down into the hole in the ground, nudged a pebble with his foot, watched it drop inside the trench.

A grave, Pagan thought. Of course. Foxie's grave. Make it a double. A chill went through him.

He said, 'Here's what I wonder, Fred. How is it that your friends and associates keep getting themselves killed off? How does that come about? If I was a cynical kind of fellow – and I'm not, as anybody will tell you – I'd say you developed some pretty bloody selfish ideas. I'd say you did a hatchet job on your chums. What was it? Afraid there wasn't going to be enough Cuban pie to go around? Needed more than your share, Fred?'

'We all need a little more than our share at times,' Kinnaird said. He folded his arms across his chest. He reminded Pagan of a squire in a magazine ad, a handsome tweedy figure advocating the merits of a certain Scotch, something expensive.

'But now there's no pie, Fred,' Pagan said. 'The cupboard is bare and there's no damned pie at all! Pardon this malicious smirk you see on my features, but I find that hilarious.'

Foxie laughed at Pagan's remark. It was a nervous little sound, but Pagan welcomed it; it established an audience, it gave him a sense of support. He stared at Kinnaird – Sir Freddie, darling of his party, beloved by the electorate, man with a Great Future, tomorrow's England, tomorrow's Europe, Freddie, slavishly devoted to wealth and position and seemingly equipped with a vampire's appetite for blood. Dear Freddie. Dear, crazy Freddie.

Pagan went on, 'I'm not saying you did the hatchet job on your own, Fred. I'm not saying you personally pulled any triggers. You don't have the guts for that. You had some help along the way. Maybe you had other associates, maybe you saw a way of slicing the pie up in thicker pieces. I don't suppose I'll ever get an answer to how it was all supposed to work.'

'Certainly not from me, Pagan. I owe you absolutely nothing. No explanations. No details. Nothing.'

Pagan looked down at the hole in the ground. 'You think you can fit us both in there, Fred?'

'I don't see why not.'

'Bit tight,' Foxie remarked. A brave little comment, a flippancy that almost worked, but Foxie's anxious eyes revealed his fear.

'I really don't think it's going to cause either of you any discomfort,' Kinnaird said. 'Actually, it's all rather convenient for me. Two for the price of one.'

Pagan sniffed the air deeply, like a man doing something he enjoys for the very last time. The smell of earth in his nostrils was the stench of death; simple, unaffected, plain old death. He glanced at the man who held the shotgun at Foxie's back. He was a bulky character with thin white hair flattened across his large skull. The other gunman, the one with the moustache that covered the scar, stood about three feet behind Pagan. It was one of those situations in which there could only be one outcome. You could try to stammer and stall, you could put up this objection and that, and play for time, but finally the result would be the same – a double-decker grave.

Pagan moved his feet very slightly; he was practically standing on the lip of the trench. Less distance to fall when the time came, he thought. He looked down inside the grave; saw a black stag beetle pick its way laboriously through its ruined territory, then he raised his face back to Kinnaird.

Stall. Kill time.

Pagan put one hand to his chest, which had begun during the last few minutes to ache. Ghose's stitches were perhaps coming undone again. What did that matter? He was about to be administered the ultimate painkiller anyway. He stared across the grave at Foxie, whose expression was one of discouragement, as if he'd just frantically searched through his own box of tricks and found no way of pulling a rabbit, at the last possible moment, out of a hat.

Stall.

'As a matter of curiosity, Fred, how do you propose to get away with our murders?' Pagan asked. A desperate question, a last bleat.

Kinnaird clasped his hands behind his back in a pontifical manner that Pagan despised because it suggested superiority and power; Freddie Kinnaird must have thought he was invincible. 'You forget I'm the Home Secretary, old chap. I'll take an active interest in your disappearance. I'll stage-manage the investigation, if I need to.'

'Martin Burr's going to go after this one very hard. He's a tenacious bastard. He'll find his way here. After all, Foxie did. And so did I. It's not exactly a cold trail, *old chap.*'

'But you never came here, Pagan. Nor did your young friend. Nobody saw you. Your car will be found on some side street in Glasgow. You and your associate will simply become mysteries that start on page one and then find their way to page five, and after that oblivion and amnesia and God rest your souls, etcetera.'

'Burr can be persistent,' Pagan said.

'Then I'll fire him,' Kinnaird remarked.

'You've really got it covered, Freddie.' There was that anger inside him again, rising in his throat with the persistence of a gas. What wouldn't he have given to have Kinnaird alone in a locked room for sixty seconds? It was useless to feel such a sense of violence when there was nothing you could do to vent it. But it wouldn't leave him.

'Farewell.' Kinnaird turned away, then stopped, looked round again. 'I'd stay for the finale, but some things simply do not attract me on an aesthetic level.'

'One last question, Freddie. How do you sleep? How the hell do you manage to sleep?'

Kinnaird said nothing. He moved between the trees.

Pagan called out, 'You ever have bad dreams, Kinnaird? Do you have bad dreams about Shepherd's Bush? Does that ever cross your bloody mind?'

Kinnaird stopped, looked round. 'I never dream.'

Then Kinnaird kept going. Pagan, who heard the faraway song of the lark again, felt the shotgun against his spine. He clenched his hands at his side in useless anger. The sun, unseasonably hot, beat at his face; he raised a hand, wiped sweat from his eyelids, blinked across the trench at Foxworth, who looked haggard and resigned.

'This isn't how I imagined an ending,' Pagan said. He felt the pressure of the shotgun and heard the gunman say *Move your arse, Jack,* in his harsh nasal way. He was being forced back to the edge of the grave.

'Nor me,' Foxworth said. 'In my pyjamas. Middle of the night. Heart attack in the arms of some gorgeous thing. I always thought that was the way to go. Bit of bliss for the big ending.'

'I don't think I expected to die in Scotland either,' Pagan said.

'Do you think it's unhallowed ground, Frank?'

Banter on the steps of the guillotine. A quip or two for the executioners. Gallows humour.

The man with the white hair pushed Foxie toward the trench too. Pagan and Foxie faced one another across the hole. There was a moment of intense silence suddenly, as if nothing flapped or flew, sung or buzzed. Pagan saw Freddie Kinnaird still walking between the trees, perhaps now three or four hundred feet from the killing place and stepping briskly, hurrying away from the distasteful scene he had himself arranged. Strangely Kinnaird made no sound either, no crackle of leaves underfoot, no whisper of clothing against tree trunks or low branches. The whole world had become mute.

Pagan stood at the very edge of the trench. He held his breath, thought about the gun in his coat pocket, imagined trying to turn, trying to wrestle the shotgun from the man who held it, but he had nothing going for him, no advantage, no chance to surprise, because the shotgun was pressed to his spine and if he made even one aggressive gesture it would go off immediately.

Out of time, Frank.

He looked down into the bleak cavity, then raised his face in the direction of Freddie Kinnaird.

The man in the black raincoat who stepped unexpectedly from the trees shot Freddie Kinnaird through the skull with a pistol.

It was done swiftly, with professional economy, one bullet that shattered Kinnaird's head and demolished half of his face. Freddie Kinnaird went down on his knees, then pitched forward, and the gunman – the same killer Frank Pagan had last seen shooting Caporelli in his Paris apartment, and who clearly had no interest in anything other than the task he'd just accomplished with such ease – disappeared through the trees like a man accustomed to sudden vanishing acts.

It was a diversion, shocking in its abruptness, and Pagan seized the unattended moment with all the passion of a survivor; he brought one clenched hand up and back, swinging the fist in a tight, powerful arc that ended when his knuckles made noisy thudding contact with the forehead of the hare-lipped man, who gasped and moaned and lowered his shotgun involuntarily. Something was broken in the man's face – the upper part of the nose, the ridge of bone above the eyes. Pagan, whose hand felt weirdly numb, wasn't sure what. The man bled profusely through the nostrils and made a choking sound. Pagan raised a foot, kicked at the shotgun, struck the barrel, but didn't force the gun out of the man's hands. The man stepped back, the contours of his face filled with flowing blood, his flop of a moustache turned scarlet. Pagan whipped the Smith and Wesson out of his pocket and fired it directly into the man's chest even as the other gunman, who had been standing behind Foxie, pulled the trigger of his shotgun despite the fact that Foxworth, alert as only a frightened man can be, had brought his shoulder into contact with his guard, knocking him just slightly off-balance.

The sound of the shotgun was so deafeningly loud that it rolled through Pagan's head like a thunderstorm. He fired his gun once at the white-haired man who took the bullet in the eye – but then Pagan was slipping, tumbling, earth crumbling under the soles of his shoes, and he was going down inside the very grave he'd tried to avoid, a weird view of the world, all sky and branch seen through eyes made hail-blind by pellets of damp soil. He spat earth from his mouth, wiped it from his eyes, rose, clawed the sides of the trench, hauled himself up to a standing position.

Foxworth was looking down at him. He extended a hand towards Pagan, who grabbed it, and pulled himself out of the hole. Breathing heavily, badly, he shook clinging earth from his overcoat and hair, but it was everywhere – in his ears, his mouth, his shoes, fragments of the grave.

For a time Pagan said nothing. He surveyed the trees, the quiet landscape, the house in the distance. He looked at the two men who, only seconds before, had been potential executioners. The white-haired one was dead and had fallen under a spray of dark green fern so that his face, thankfully, was concealed from view. The other sat slumped against the trunk of a tree, holding both hands over his chest and groaning in pain.

'He'll need an ambulance,' Pagan said. 'We can call from the house.'

Pagan, followed by Foxworth, walked to the place where Kinnaird lay. Ants, having scouted an abundant source of unexpected protein, were already filing in an unruly manner over the ruined side of Freddie's face. A fat horsefly crawled across Freddie's hair. Pagan spat a crumb of black earth out from between his teeth.

Foxie said, 'I was never more glad to see you, Frank. I'd been stuck in the cellar of that bloody house for God knows how long. Our guards here were waiting for Kinnaird to turn up and make some kind of decision pertaining to my fate. When he finally showed up he didn't waste time deciding what to do with me. I'll say that for Freddie. He wasn't the vacillating sort.'

Pagan smiled by way of acknowledging Foxie's remarks, but it wasn't much of an expression. He had no energy left to him. It seemed to him that he stood outside of himself, that he had left his own body and was floating like some weird wind-lifted speck toward the sun, a strange sensation. But the pain in his chest brought him back to earth.

'New tenants are already moving in, I see.' Foxworth nodded down at the armies of ants. 'I only hope they find Freddie edible. Who killed him anyway?'

'It's a long story. We'll talk about it later.' Pagan's voice was dry, cracked, almost gone. He walked away from the corpse of Kinnaird. Followed by Foxie, he went down through the meadow toward the big red house. He paused once, looked up at the sun; in the distance, the smallest flash of silver, was a tiny aircraft that could be heard droning, then it was gone and the sky, too blue for this season and this country, was empty again. Inevitably he thought of Magdalena, but it was one of those thoughts that opened and closed like a certain kind of ghostly flower.

Epilogue

Several days after the death of Frederick Kinnaird, the Lider Maximo spoke in the Plaza de la Revolución in Havana. His speech started at two in the afternoon. If the past was any guide, he would not finish until six, perhaps six-thirty, and his audience would by then be numbed and hungry. The day was breezy and warm; flags busily flapped around the Plaza.

The crowd was estimated at three hundred thousand people, many of them bussed in from rural areas. Usually there were some who surreptitiously listened to tiny transistor radios relaying football games or pop music from the USA. But not today. Today there was an atmosphere of tension and uncertainty. Throughout the crowd plainclothes members of security forces mingled, took notes, eavesdropped, dragged away for interrogation anyone who struck them as odd. Security was more tight than anybody could remember – even veterans of these affairs, some of whom had listened to the Lider Maximo for thirty years and knew all the man's nuances and could tell from experience when he was lying or when – the less frequent occurrence – he was telling the truth. There were metal detectors around the Plaza, and certain people were being searched, and scores were being herded inside police vehicles.

Nothing was normal now. Nothing predictable. During the last seven days there had been arrests on an unprecedented scale throughout Cuba. There had been 'disappearances'. The Armed Forces had been purged by Raul Castro himself, who had hurried back from Angola with the indecent speed of an executioner anxious to use his newly sharpened axe. Everybody had at least one story to tell about a neighbour taken away, a son missing, or a daughter, a nephew, a cousin.

Estela Rosabal, who pushed her way through the warm crowd toward the platform because she needed to be as close to the Lider Maximo as possible, had more stories to tell than most. At first she'd been advised that Rafael had been taken prisoner; then two days later that he'd committed suicide. The next day she received a phone call from the Ministry of the Interior telling her that he was alive and well after all and she would be taken to see him. An hour or so later, when she was beginning to allow herself some limited optimism, the coffin was delivered to her apartment by men who said nothing and who wouldn't look at her. They simply dragged it inside the living-room and left it there, lidded, loosely bolted, a long cheap pine box she couldn't bring herself to open.

She had experienced nothing so cruel in her life as that. *He's alive, he's dead, he's alive, he's dead again.* They had known all along. They had played a malicious game with her because she was the traitor's wife. Then they had interrogated her in a hot windowless room for almost twenty hours about her role in her husband's treachery. Seemingly convinced she was innocent, they had released her. But she wasn't fooled. They would come for her again. They would find 'evidence'. They always did.

Now she pushed herself between a pair of young lovers who stood hip to hip, then past an old man with thick eye-glasses and one sleeve of his jacket hanging empty, then a bunch of fat women who smelled of fried food and beer.

The Lider Maximo rose on the platform to speak. His voice, carried by a sophisticated sound system, floated out beyond the Plaza itself and into adjoining streets. Television cameras relayed the event through the whole of Cuba, despite power failures, officially attributed to recent rebel activity, in the provinces of Holguin and Santiago.

The speech began quietly. The Lider Maximo's face was bloated behind the greying beard. His gaberdine fatigues were brand new and stiff; he wasn't altogether comfortable in them. Observers noticed that his movements were somewhat erratic, as if his coordination had been affected by something. Age, many people thought in their secret hearts; he was too old, too rigid, too inflexible, he had to step aside. But who was going to say so to his face?

He gazed across the crowd and the fluttering flags. Chopping the air with one hand for emphasis, he spoke of an evil plot instigated by the imperialist government of the United States to overthrow him and replace him with a puppet regime, at whose head was to be the late Minister of Finance, Rafael Rosabal, assisted by General Capablanca, now arrested (actually dead in a cell even as Castro spoke, hanged by bedsheets from a ceiling beam, an official suicide), and a number of misguided officers in the Armed Forces. These men would have a fair trial because that was the Cuban way, the socialist way.

Agents of the Defence of the Revolution moved through the crowd and acted as cheerleaders, whipping up enthusiasm with their menacing manners. Estela Rosabal had come to a stop where the crowd was jammed together so tightly it created a solid wall of flesh and bone. She couldn't get through. The Lider Maximo's voice boomed in the air all around her, but she wasn't paying any attention. She heard both her husband and father mentioned in a hateful way, but it was background noise, no more. Her father's fate was probably the same as Rafael's anyhow, and how much more grief did she have? Frustrated by the mass of people, she moved in another direction, where eventually she found a way forward between a group of slick young men in fresh white *guayaberas* and blue jeans. They made appreciative noises as she pushed among them, and one laid a hand on her thigh, but she slipped away without looking back. She was lost again in the density of the crowd, surrounded by strangers, and all the while the voice went on and on, now droning, now rising to an hysterical pitch.

Up on the platform the Lider Maximo, his head filled with the approving roar of the audience, closed his eyes a moment; sweat slid from his brow into his eyelids and he wiped it aside. He drifted away, remembering other times, other speeches, when he had stood in this very spot and addressed his people, when La Revolución had been young and glamorous, when he had been filled with vigour and the kind of self-confidence that belongs only to youthful believers.

He spoke of how he had been poisoned by his trusted doctor, Zayas, whose task it was to weaken the Lider Maximo, to confuse him with tranquillisers and tiny doses of a slow-acting poison. That way he could be manipulated and made to believe anything he was told.

There were gasps from the crowd.

But the Lider Maximo was strong the way the Revolution was strong! The Lider Maximo survived the way the Revolution survived!

The crowd cheered again and again.

The Lider Maximo pointed to his bloated face as if by way of proof. His very appearance was the result of Zayas' infamous medications!

Now he condemned treacherous civilians, those who would see the Revolution dismantled, who would see the course of Cuban history altered. Nothing can stop the course of history, he said. Nothing could prevent the destiny of the Cuban people, which was socialism and freedom.

A drunk in the crowd whispered to Estela Rosabal: *Sure, but will we have the freedom to leave socialism?* And he winked at her, but she hardly noticed, because she was still trying to get closer to the platform, pushing, pushing, squeezing between two crones who looked half-dead, wrinkled, their flaccid breasts hanging loose behind cheap floral print dresses. She thought of Rafael's child in her womb. The baby should have been her priority, but somehow it wasn't, not any longer. It lay inside her, a tiny, unformed stranger whose meaning was lost to her. So many things had become lost to her lately.

The Lider Maximo continued to use his hand as a cleaver, a gesture of emphasis. He stared upward into the mid-afternoon sun which was pleasantly warm against his face. He wished he could sit down, and not stand the way he always did, but to sit was a weakness. He had to remain upright; he had to look down from the platform across the multitudes. It was important to maintain the image of standing in a high place.

He spoke about ungrateful civilians who worked against the Revolution. They were scum, murderous scum, with their secret printing-presses, and their illegal radios, and their hidden caches of American rifles. But they would be rooted out and destroyed. *And here his mind strayed again and he remembered how Batista had made similar speeches about La Revolución more than thirty years ago, and how the dictator had sent his armies into the Sierra Maestra to kill the rebels. There was a world of difference, of course, between himself and the evil Batista, who had been an American mannequin: immoral, indecent, corrupt.*

He praised the bravery of loyal Cuban troops who had rounded up treacherous officers and their men swiftly. He praised the officers and men of the reservists who had brought a dangerous situation under control and had captured illegal weapons in the hands of those who misguidedly called themselves rebels and freedom-fighters.

Estela Rosabal didn't think she could get any closer. Strained, sweating, she had come within a hundred and fifty feet of the platform. Behind ropes stood armed guards and security agents with black glasses and all kinds of uniformed men. She fanned the listless air with her hand. She could hardly breathe; the weight of the crowd pressed down on her ribs. Her eyes watered. A streak of mascara slithered down one cheek.

She thought about the coffin again even though she had resolved never to do so. She remembered sitting in her living-room and looking at the thing hour after hour, remembered the sun rising and falling and the shadows thickening, remembered her hands clasped upon her stomach – and the smell that had begun to emerge from the coffin and fill the room, something she couldn't name, didn't want to identify, that awful charred smell like nothing in her experience. And she had thought about the barbarism in the world, a cruelty beyond her understanding, and how it numbed her.

She fumbled with her handbag, which was jammed against her side because of the pressure of people around her. How was she ever going to open it? She suddenly wanted to scream in sheer frustration. What could she accomplish here? Nothing. Nothing. She should go back. Go home. She had been so scared avoiding the metal detectors and now her nerve was going to collapse entirely.

She wouldn't let it. She would be strong.

The Lider Maximo had become quiet, surveying the crowd; the shadow of the tall obelisk known as the José Marti monument fell across the Plaza. It rose some four hundred feet in the air, a monument to a famous independence fighter, the Lider Maximo's hero. Its shape was faintly reminiscent of a rocket. The Lider Maximo gripped the edge of his lectern with both hands. He was assailed by a dizzy sensation. He was thinking of the nuclear weapon destroyed outside Santiago.

Something about the notion of a missile on the island had created pleasing echoes inside him . . .

He coughed into his hand. He talked quietly now, and his hands were still. He talked about the weapon that had been brought to Cuba by imperialists and traitors, and assembled in a field outside Santiago, and made ready to fly. To discredit the Revolution! he roared. To make us appear like warmongers! But it was destroyed by the quick actions of the Cuban Air Force. He was allowed to bend the facts and shape them as he saw fit because nobody contradicted his view of reality, they merely adapted to it.

The Lider Maximo's mind wandered back to the missile again because it reminded him of those glorious days when Cuba stood at the centre of the world, when Kennedy and Khrushchev almost went to war, when the Lider Maximo commanded international respect, when he was a hero and did not have to curry favour with anyone or beg . . .

He struggled to focus his attention on the crowds again. Why did he keep drifting? Why was it so hard to concentrate during his speeches these days? Now he leaned forward, speaking rapidly, spitting as he spoke in denunciation of those enemies of peace who had brought such a monstrous device to Cuba. The crowd, aroused, prodded like animals in a vast holding-pen, cheered louder than ever.

Estela Rosabal felt she was trapped inside the noise, like an atom surrounded by other reverberating atoms. She was overpowered by the sounds of so many people. The well-dressed man alongside her, eyes glazed from alcohol, had a tiny flag he waved now and again. She stared at him, looked away, glanced up towards the platform at the face of the Lider Maximo, that face with which she'd been familiar from the very day of her birth – posters, photographs, history textbooks, newspapers. He was everywhere always. He was the great endless noise that surrounded and overwhelmed her. He was the noise of Cuba.

He was a monster. But he wasn't immortal.

The Lider Maximo thought: *he hadn't had so much attention in years, every journalist in the world wanted to talk to him about the nuclear weapon, he had almost forgotten how good such power felt . . . and all because of one stolen missile.*

He raised his hands, shaking both fists at the sky. This was his response to the cheers of the crowd and suddenly it was almost like the old days, a dialogue between the Lider Maximo and the people who loved him, back and forth, give and take. He didn't see the agents milling through the swarms, didn't see the prompters and persuaders and those who coaxed and menaced the appropriate responses from people who had lived for a whole generation on promises, promises, promises.

How hard would it be to steal a missile? he wondered. *How much planning had gone into it? How long had it taken the conspirators to grab the weapon? It was an idle line of harmless speculation, of course. But interesting just the same . . .*

The Lider Maximo swayed very slightly. The breeze grew in strength, the flags shook, plastic bunting creaked. Somebody set off a firecracker and was immediately dragged away by security agents. The Lider Maximo hadn't heard the noise, didn't see the scuffle in the crowd.

If there was a nuclear missile on Cuba what would the consequences be? Respect? Prestige? Would Cuba then have a strong voice to which others in the hemisphere would be obliged to listen? And how would the Yanquis react? Would they risk invasion? Would they retaliate with force? Not if the missile was pointed, for the sake of argument, at Miami Beach . . . No, they would talk and bargain, they would want to sit down and negotiate the removal of such a missile, because that was their way, all capitalist politicians loved to deal, and something very favourable could come out of it all – say, the removal of the missile in exchange for the return to the Cuban people of the Guantanamo US naval base, which was Cuban soil after all . . .

The Lider Maximo thumped the lectern with the flat of his hand. Cuba, he told the masses, will not be a pawn in anybody's game. He spoke of courage and bravery and loyalty with all the confidence of a man comfortable in a world of abstract nouns. The sun set over the Plaza and the Marti monument and the breeze died and the flags no longer stirred.

Estela Rosabal managed to get her handbag open. She found what she wanted inside, exactly where she'd placed it under a packet of tissues. How ordinary the gun seemed to her, surrounded as it was by lipsticks and a make-up compact, a bottle of eyeliner and coins. Everything was ordinary now, and yet oddly heightened, as if the commonplace contained more secrets than she'd ever realised. The smoothness of a lipstick tube, the fibre of the suit worn by the man standing beside her, the colours of his small flag – everything was sharp suddenly, and richly textured.

She managed to get her fist round the gun.

She looked up at the Lider Maximo, who was silent again.

He was thinking.

He was thinking he knew a wonderful site for such a weapon. A site whose irony amused him. The missile would be placed east of the Peninsula de Zapata, and Playa Giron, where on April 17th, 1961, the last invasion force to make an effort to land on Cuba had provoked the great Cuban victory the Yanquis called The Bay of Pigs – it was the perfect place, and fitting, and comical in its own bleak way . . .

An old flame burned in him, an old taste, barely familiar but delectable still, filled his mouth. He stared out across the crowd, which was quieter now, but he didn't see it as a group of individuals. In the shadows each person had receded, diminished, shedding his or her particular characteristics: one great amorphous mass, controllable, manageable.

Such a weapon would never be fired, of course. It would be a useful negotiating strategy, a device to back up firm diplomacy, and it would give Cuba entry into the nuclear club, where by rights it belonged . . .

Then he wondered where could he acquire such a weapon and who could he get to steal one, if he made such a radical decision. And from where would it be stolen? Fascinating questions.

But pure speculation.

He turned his face in the general direction of Havana Bay, and considered that stretch of water separating Cuba from its natural enemy. Over there, he thought. Over there was a whole arsenal of missiles, each doomed to be scrapped under the terms of a misconceived treaty between the Yanquis and the Soviets.

Perhaps.

Then he faced the crowd again. He didn't see the lovely black-haired woman who stood beyond the barrier where the guards were massed.

Estela Rosabal took the gun from her purse. She drew it up slowly from her hip, her arm jammed against that of the man with the tiny flag. And then she could bring the hand up no further unless the man moved. The pressure was intolerable. She tried to make herself smaller, slimmer, tried to create space for the pistol.

She breathed deeply, drew her ribcage in, released the pinned arm. The man, who suddenly realised what the stranger beside him held in her hand, called out in alarm. Estela pointed the pistol at the platform, directly at the head of the Lider Maximo. The guards, who had been trained to that level of readiness which is almost paranoid, reacted at once. They rushed at her fiercely. She saw their massive shadows eclipse the sky as she was knocked over. And then she was being punched in the, face and kicked in the stomach and the gun fell from her hand. It was funny how little she felt, how little pain from the boots and the nightsticks, as if she no longer had the capacity for it. Brutality could no longer touch or surprise her. She was dragged roughly along concrete. She saw, through swollen, half-shut eyes, the TV cameramen and press photographers who ignored her. She saw the receding face of the Lider Maximo, so lost in his own speculations that he paid no attention to the skirmish, handled so efficiently that it would never be mentioned in any newspaper, never seen on any TV screen.

Another firework was lit, a rocket this time, which flew from the rooftop of a nearby building in a burst of orange smoke and went sailing past the Marti monument as it died. Estela, thrown inside a van without windows, noticed how the firework's rich plumage exploded almost cheerfully in the sky before the door slammed shut and everything became black and smelled of sweat and urine and fear.

The Lider Maximo, who in recent years had come to look for signs and omens as deliriously thirsty men seek oases, saw the firework too, and he smiled for the first time that day.

A rocket, he thought. *How appropriate.*

In the eight or nine days since Sir Frederick Kinnaird's cremation and quiet funeral service, after the newspapermen and columnists and stringers had cobbled together a story out of alleged facts that were frequently no more than the kind of half-truths various government agencies in the United Kingdom and the United States saw fit to provide; days after Frank Pagan, weary of meetings with the Commissioner and interviews with surly men from security agencies he'd never before heard of, took a dreary train down to rainy Brighton for a few quiet nights at an off-season hotel; days after Castro had spoken to the people of Cuba about a capitalist plot against him; after Steffie Brough and her family, harried by newshounds, had gone into seclusion, and Allen Falk had entered hospital for the treatment of a hitherto inactive ulcer, a tiny bespectacled lawyer from Hamburg, Wilhelm Schiller, surfaced in the offices of a German tabloid in Frankfurt with an offer to sell the diaries and papers of his late client, Gunther Ruhr.

Schiller, an unassuming man with a gentle manner, had been advised years before by his client to make certain matters public in the event of the client's untimely death. And since such a circumstance had come, alas, to pass, Schiller was simply following Ruhr's instructions. The sensitive material, which filled eight stout cardboard boxes and covered many years of Ruhr's life and business dealings, would certainly have ruined various influential figures around the world who had used Ruhr's services.

But it never arrived at the editorial offices of the newspaper with whom Schiller had negotiated. Instead it vanished from the safe-deposit box in the Zurich bank where the lawyer had himself placed it.

Horrified bank officials denied any kind of wrongdoing; they were discreet men whose business thrived on privacy and security. The disappearance of Ruhr's papers scandalised them – officially at least. In reality, they had been obliged to turn the documents over to the Swiss government, which had been intensely pressured by its German counterpart. Two officials were dismissed by the bank for malfeasance, a scapegoat gesture. They were later quietly reinstated in different locations.

Herr Schiller, outraged by the loss, promised to give an interview on German television in the course of which he would reveal at least some of the contents of Ruhr's papers. That way, he would discharge a portion of his obligation to his late client; at the same time he intended to raise certain suspicions concerning the fate of the documents. He had guessed that no ordinary thief was behind their disappearance. Only governments – with instruments of legal blackmail at their disposal – had the power to force Swiss bankers to open safe-deposit boxes.

But the interview did not take place; some hours before it was scheduled Herr Schiller was found dead in his room at the Frankfurterhof, an apparent victim of a heart attack. The death certificate was signed by two physicians, both of whom, as coincidence would have it, had begun vacations in remote places beyond the reach of telephones.

The day after Schiller's death, a group of men and women gathered in the private conference room of an expensive hotel in St Helier on the Channel Islands. These people, accompanied by aides and lawyers, represented the British Prime Minister, the President of the United States, the West German Chancellor, the President of France, the Prime Ministers of Italy and Japan, and assorted princes and potentates from the countries of the Middle East.

The subject of their meeting was the disposal of Gunther Ruhr's purloined records. An early perusal of the documents, undertaken with haste by an international panel of six lawyers, indicated that Ruhr had set down, in encyclopedic detail, the dates and places of his terrorist acts, the sums of money that had exchanged hands in return for his services, and the names of those who had employed him. It was the kind of record guaranteed to bring Ruhr a form of immortality, although that hadn't been its principal purpose.

Ruhr, scrupulous and smart, had kept his records diligently. It soon became clear to his readers, his team of auditors, that the late terrorist often knew more about his employers than they could ever have supposed. He investigated the men who hired him. He made careful inquiries. He was no casual extremist. He took extraordinary care. Sometimes he succeeded in penetrating the secrecy surrounding those who bought his services: sometimes he managed to go beyond the names of the lesser figures to the larger ones. Intermediaries gave way to principals, minor players to major ones. Men of high positions in government and financial circles who thought they had hired Gunther Ruhr from a safe distance, who believed themselves anonymous, had their names inscribed in his records.

There were photostats of bank drafts, copies of money orders, numbers of bank accounts on small Caribbean islands; Ruhr's manic eye for detail was evident at every turn. Nothing much had escaped him.

It was an enormously damaging set of documents, in some instances shocking in its revelations. In what became known unofficially as the St Helier Accord, it was decided, within a matter of hours and hardly any debate, that the documents, to be kept from the press at all costs, would be divided among the parties with direct interests – the record of Ruhr's involvement with Basque separatists, for example, would go directly to the Spanish government to deal with as it saw fit; the names of his employers in Japan who had him destroy a resort hotel would be handed immediately to Japanese officials. And so on.

Six hours after it assembled, the conference ended.

Two days later, Martin Burr travelled down to Brighton and walked with Frank Pagan along the promenade on a rainy night. They passed the disheartening ruin of the West Pier, which, in the English Channel mist, had the appearance of a ghost ship. In another age it had been graceful, an elegant edifice that had stubbornly withstood the demands of the sea. Neglected now, it was nothing more than a reminder to Martin Burr of a world that had become bored by the graceful – one that responded only to the quick and the crass. It was a world in which you could find crumpets inside frozen-food compartments and exquisite teas in mass-produced teabags.

'You're looking more like your usual self,' Burr said. 'I'm glad to see that.'

Frank Pagan didn't mention the new course of antibiotics he'd just begun, or the ugly infection Ghose had discovered in the chest wound. These things were tedious inconveniences; they could be kept to oneself. He looked out at the Channel. The mist was magnificently damp and mysterious, crawling up over the pebbled beach. He put a hand in the pocket of his overcoat and fingered the bottle of painkillers there; the wound in his chest, agitated by infection, pierced him sharply. He tried to ignore it.

Burr tapped the promenade rail with his cane and listened a moment to the quiet drumming sound he'd set up. 'I have teams of people going through Kinnaird's records – which are copious and complicated as befitted a man with a great deal to conceal.'

'I imagine,' Pagan said. He was genuinely interested on one level, that of policeman; but the recuperating tourist in him felt removed from Burr's world. He'd go back into that world eventually, and he'd become immersed in it as he always did, but for the present he wanted to be nothing more than a man casually watching the secretive mist on a moist night in Brighton.

Burr said, 'Kinnaird's phone calls are rather intriguing. Several were placed to an apartment in Acapulco, which turns out to have been the property of Rafael Rosabal. Kinnaird and Rosabal. Fine bedfellows.'

Pagan saw a light out there in the folds of the Channel, a small passing ship perhaps. Then it was gone. He turned to look at Martin Burr. Dampness adhered to the Commissioner's eyepatch, reflecting the lamps along the promenade.

Burr stopped tapping his cane. 'Freddie made phone calls to all the members of his little group. Caporelli, the others. Cocky sod, though. Didn't even bother to take the trouble to make these calls from some public phone. He made them either from his house in Scotland or his apartment in The Albany. I daresay he thought he was above the law. Can't get over the gall of the fellow.' Burr shook his head for a while; from his point of view the nefarious activities of Kinnaird and his associates were beyond any reasonable man's comprehension as was Kinnaird's sense of impunity.

Pagan turned away from the misty sea. He thought how Freddie and Rosabal must have decided to eliminate the others. Then Rosabal, who elevated avarice to chilly new heights had taken it on step further and ordered the elimination of Freddie. They were charmers. Real princes.

Burr drew his cashmere scarf up around his neck and shivered slightly. 'What a bloody mosaic,' he said. 'And it doesn't end with Freddie's unprincipled dealings either. I've just seen some of Gunther Ruhr's papers.'

Pagan, intrigued now, had heard about these notorious papers and the waves of utter terror they had set in motion through government circles in various countries.

Burr said, 'In his documents, Ruhr claims he was first approached by Rosabal more than three years ago. Then about twelve months ago in Mexico City he was given the green light. Steal the missile, he was told. Deliver it to Honduras, where an invasion force was waiting with tanks and fighter-planes. Amazing assortment of equipment from all over the place.'

Steal the missile, Pagan thought. Just like that. He looked back out into the Channel, which smelled of winter, dead things. The night was as melancholic as his mood, which he hadn't been able to shake for days. He reflected on the coup Magdalena had talked about, the democratic underground in which she'd had such faith, the uprising, but she'd never mentioned an invasion force. Maybe that was something else Rosabal had concealed from her. There were so many unanswerable questions. What had Burr called it? *A bloody mosaic*. Ambitions, lies, rapacity, warped patriotism, all the grubby little ingredients of the big picture, which was elusive still, and would perhaps remain so for a long time.

Burr lowered his voice, as if the dark might be filled with eavesdroppers. 'One hears the most appalling rumours of mass arrests, tortures, executions all over Cuba.'

Pagan shivered. Cold air rose up from the Channel. He wondered about Estela Rosabal and what had become of her as a consequence of her husband's ambitions. *Executions*, Burr had said. Was that her fate? Had she been propped before a firing-squad and gunned down? He recalled, with a clarity that saddened him, the way she'd looked when he'd seen her in Havana; the ruined innocence of beauty. Had Rosabal in all his life ever touched anything without destroying it?

Pagan was quiet for a moment. He heard the tide whisper coldly over stones. Then, as if to himself, he said, 'I keep seeing that bloody missile. And I keep wondering if Rosabal intended to fire it. I can't get the damned thing out of my mind.'

Martin Burr shrugged. 'If he did, what was his target?'

Pagan had no answer. He looked back into the mist, which seemed to him just then as inscrutable as Rosabal's intention. He imagined the missile on the truck, the way it changed angle, the eerie sense of disaster he'd experienced. And then he remembered Magdalena's doomed little plane and he wasn't sure if the missile had ever moved at all, or if it was something he'd created out of his own awful tiredness, an hallucination, a fanciful perception.

Burr said, 'I rather thought Castro's speech might have shed some light on that question.'

'People like Castro aren't in the business of shedding light. They prefer darkness.'

'Perhaps,' said Burr.

Frank Pagan heard the mournful sound of a ship's fog horn, like the cry of something lost in the night. He turned from the Channel, glanced at the forlorn relic of the West Pier. *Magdalena's doomed little plane*, he thought. Lately he'd had the most unbearable dreams of her. There was always the small plane burning – not quickly, as it had happened in reality, but in a very slow way. Then the dream made that awful upward shift into nightmare when her face appeared in the yellow-red pyre of the cockpit and turned very slightly, sightlessly, mouth twisted open and lifeless, toward the trees under which he stood, and he saw an agonising look in her dark eyes before she was consumed. A horror, repeating itself three or four times during the last ten days.

He always woke with a sense of deep sorrow and depressing loss, as if there were an important word he couldn't quite remember, or a disturbed sensation he couldn't name. Whatever it was, it felt like something burrowing far inside him, something it would take time to destroy.

The fire that coursed suddenly through his chest made him double over against the promenade rail.

'Are you all right, Frank?' Burr asked.

Pagan took out the bottle of painkillers uncapped it. He tipped one into the palm of his shaking hand. He stared at the pill. Did he need this? Would it really reach the place where the pain hurt most and kill it? He let the pill slip from his hand, then tossed the bottle through the air and watched the capsules vanish in the direction of the darkened beach below. They would fall among the pebbles where they'd lie concealed until the tide drew them back into the Channel and they disintegrated in brine.

'I'm fine, Commissioner,' was all he said.